*The Complete Fairy Tales and Stories*

HANS CHRISTIAN ANDERSEN

❊◈❊

# The Complete Fairy Tales and Stories

❊◈❊

Translated from the Danish by
Erik Christian Haugaard

FOREWORD BY VIRGINIA HAVILAND

Doubleday & Company, Inc., Garden City, New York, 1974

ISBN: 0-385-01901-7 Trade
      0-385-05867-5 Prebound
Library of Congress Catalog Card Number 73–83583

*My gift to the world*

—Hans Christian Andersen

*This translation is dedicated to the memory of*
*Ruth Hill Viguers,*
*who knew that the leather outlasts the gilding.*

# *Acknowledgments*

One day in September 1967, I translated a very short Andersen tale, which she did not know, for Ruth Hill Viguers; and then the whole idea of a new Andersen translation came into being. A few months later Peter Hyun took the initiative and set out to make the possibility into a project. Virginia Haviland, Harriet Quimby, Paul Heins, and George Woods were so kind as to lend their good names on an application for a grant to the Chapelbrook Foundation; the response of this foundation was generous and immediate and, thanks to them, the two years that this work has been in progress has not been a time of need. When the translation was nearing completion, Dr. Bo Gronbech told me many interesting and important facts about Hans Christian Andersen. Valborg Lauritzen typed the enormous manuscript; and for her ability, good nature, and patience in trying to make out the many corrections, I am, indeed, grateful. The Jubilee Fund of the Danish National Bank kindly provided a small grant so I could pay my faithful typist. To Sharon Steinhoff I owe my thanks for many an hour's necessary but tedious labor. Most of all, I am indebted to my wife, without whose assistance and help the translation would not have been done at all.

Erik Christian Haugaard
Veksebo, Denmark
September 1972

# Contents

*(handwritten annotations: 1835; 1836; 1837; 1838; 1839; 1838?; went to Greece (1840-41); 1841; 1842; (1829 ... —) (1836 nov))*

Contents                                               xv

# Foreword

In the passage of inherited literature down the years, it has been recognized that changes in language have justified recurrent new looks at the great old tales—as often, it has been said, as in each generation. The judgment can apply to the translation of literary tales as well as to the translation or retelling of the traditional.

This new translation comes from a bilingual Danish author who was educated in Denmark and the United States. (He wrote in English the five novels which have won distinction in the field of children's literature.) With his particular background—he was, he says, related to one of the families who supported Andersen—the new project was a carrying into reality of a particular dream; he had the urge and the ability to take a fresh look at Andersen's writing in its original form.

Haugaard recognizes the rightness of Andersen's own colloquial, simple words, which early Victorian editors too often altered to ornate, even archaic expressions. He understands Andersen's expressed intent: "I wanted the style to be such that the reader felt the presence of the storyteller; therefore the spoken language had to be used." Haugaard as a young man working among the rural folk of Denmark heard the vernacular. Following the text and the order of the stories in the Danish edition of 1874 which Andersen edited, he has made changes to bring the text closer to the original. His INCHELINA (5)—for "Thumbelina"—stems from a recognition of *Tommelise*'s derivation from *tomme* meaning "inch," not from *tommeltot* meaning "thumb": ". . . *entomme lang, og defor Kaldtes hun Tommelise"* becomes ". . . an inch long, therefore she was called Inchelina." Another change, for a more accurate interpretation, substitutes THE MAGIC GALOSHES (10) for "The Galoshes of Fortune," the commonly known title, which the translator perceives to be inaccurate in projecting the idea that the galoshes themselves were magic.

In the total, chronological sequence, including the lesser known tales of adult interest, is to be found the wealth of revelatory autobiographical matter which brings Andersen to life—a more accurate picture, as Haugaard knows, than the best scholar can offer. To apprehend Andersen's feelings about writing and criticism and about his gift of poetry one may read THE MUSE OF THE TWENTIETH CENTURY (109), THE PIXY AND THE GROCER (65), "THE WILL-O'-THE-WISPS ARE IN TOWN," SAID THE BOG WITCH (114) AND THE PIXY AND THE GARDENER'S WIFE (124). In A QUESTION OF IMAGINATION (139) one finds his humorous musings on imagination: "There was once a young man who was studying to be an author, and he wanted to be one before Easter. . . . [He complained]: 'Everything in the world has been written up; no wonder I can't find anything to write down.'"

Haugaard has said that "Andersen was what Andersen wrote"; he sees him as a poet-critic whom we in our time have a need to know. Andersen's satire and unsparing contempt are viewed through poetic Danish eyes, for Haugaard also is a poet. Clear to those eyes are Andersen's satire and unsparing contempt expressed through the clever literary devices of animating objects like the famous darning needle and humanizing such lowly creatures as the dung beetle. Familiar is the country background of bottomless moors, storks, ancient Roskilde, and a belief in bog witches.

This volume is for those who would study Andersen as the creator of a new kind of wonder tale and contributor to an international literature, a storyteller to be understood from more than acquaintance with the beloved tales so often shared with children. Some of the lesser known tales appeared first in England or in the United States. Seventeen were procured by editor Horace E. Scudder, who saw their importance for his *Riverside Magazine,* published in Boston for children, 1867–70. Eleven had their first printing there. (Scudder, we know, learned Danish at the time so that he could

satisfy himself that he was securing good translations for his sub-
scribers.) This new work, in its fresh and authentic transmission, and
with Andersen's notes accompanying the translation, is offered as a
contribution to the history of a literature that belongs to every age.

Virginia Haviland
Library of Congress, Washington, D.C.

# Introduction

After having worked for more than two years on the translation of Andersen's fairy tales, I have come to be on intimate terms with him. It has been said that intimacy breeds contempt; and I am sure it does for those who search for idols. But I think one can love a person for his faults as well as his virtues. Man is made from clay and clay is fragile. But maybe it is its frailty that makes us look with double wonder at an ancient Greek vase: it is so delicate, so brittle, and yet it has survived.

Andersen lived seventy-five years; and I believe his fairy tales will live forever. He had innumerable weaknesses, which I shall not recount, for most of them all men possess; but he had that great courage that poets must have; and that made it possible for him to be totally aware of his own faults and virtues. A poet's laboratory is himself, and Andersen made use of those traits for which he would have been laughed at or censored, as well as those that might earn him applause.

He had an enormous pride, a faith in his own talent, and a belief in his own particular genius; and this brought him into conflict with the intellectuals of his time. What his critics did not understand was that his pride was also the guardian of his talent. He was a very careful writer. Many of his stories were rewritten many times. It was of great concern to him that his tales should be able to be read aloud as if they were being told.

The fairy tale speaks to all of us; that is its particular charm. The beggar and the prince pause in the market place to hear the story-teller; and for the moment they are merely men, subject to the passions that rule us all. Again and again, in his notes and his autobiography, Andersen refers to the stories he had heard as a child. It is a strange irony that our all-embracing modern forms of communication have killed the storyteller, and may end by making us all mute.

These stories that Andersen heard as a child were all very simple tales, and their characters were probably more archetypes than they were individuals. They were not meant to surprise—let alone shock—the listener. Indeed, their attraction lay in the fact that they were familiar. The mean, the petty, the evil, the good, and the kind were so in the manner that one was used to; it was the plot itself that held one's interest. We of the twentieth century, who are so used to plotless novels with heroes so infinitely complex that, after having read the book, it is easier for us to describe the characters' nervous systems than to tell what the story was about, hardly ever come into contact with this early form of literature. Yet these stories, stripped as they are of the fashionable and the modish, give us—at least for a moment—that peace which is necessary for survival. Man must live in his own time—he has no choice—but for the sake of his sanity he must sometimes escape its tyranny—if only to be able to recognize it. *Once upon a time* denies time and thus curtails its power over us.

*Once upon a time* is a definite point in the infinite. It exists somewhere but has no particular date, which is a feat that is hardly explainable—and yet, maybe it is. We have divided time into precise periods. "Was *once upon a time* in the Iron Age, the Bronze Age, or the thirteenth century? we ask, for we are enlightened. But the peasant who heard a fairy tale in the market place and retold it to his family when he came home had no such conceptions. Time, for him, stretched from the creation till that moment which can best be described as *now*. And though he knew that raiment and customs changed, he did not believe they had very much influence on people. He knew the Bible well, yet it did not disturb him to see the Virgin portrayed as if she were a rich Florentine lady. Were not Saul and David like the kings he knew? Was Eve much different from his own wife? *Once upon a time* was not magic or poetic, as it is to us. But then, the twentieth century has produced no fairy tales.

Andersen was the last great teller of fairy tales. We may create tales of imagination and fantasy, but they are not fairy tales. The fairy tale and the folk tale take place in the real world, no matter how exotic and strange their backgrounds may be. Witches, trolls, or mermaids may appear; but they are not figments of anyone's imagination; they are as real as the princess or the peasant. We who are manacled by a belief in progress and theories of natural behavior find it hard to understand this. We prefer to escape into fantasy, into worlds that are safe because they never have existed and never will.

"Once upon a time there was a boy who was so very, very poor that all he owned was the suit of clothes that he was wearing; and that was too small for him. . . ." That could have been the opening of a fairy tale or a description of Hans Christian Andersen setting out from his native Odense to seek his fortune in Copenhagen. Did he see witches, fairy godmothers, and trolls? He did indeed, as certainly as Odysseus heard the Siren sing. Like the heroes of the fairy tales, Andersen went out into the wide world, with a good deal of naïveté, curiosity, and lust for life as ballast. He sought the princess and half the kingdom. Nothing less would do, for he was a real poet. And he did win, if not the princess and half the kingdom, then something even better: fame in half if not the whole world. Did it make him happy? I think it did, for it meant that his suffering had not been in vain. Out of his personal grief and unhappiness, beauty had been born. Yet it was not Andersen but we who gained most from this struggle. The artists, musicians, and poets are the richest of all human beings, for they can leave a legacy that will last as long as men breathe.

Andersen adopted the most ancient literary forms—the fairy tale and the folk tale—and changed them into something that was his own. He was not a collector of folklore, a reteller of what had already been told, as were the brothers Grimm, whom he admired very much.

What often happens to great authors happened to Andersen as well. The enormous success of some of his fairy tales cast a shadow on the rest of his stories and they have been overlooked. How many people have ever heard of THE SHADOW, a brilliant Kafkaesque tale, or ANNE LISBETH, an unsentimental naturalistic story about a girl who abandons her illegitimate child? Andersen felt that each of his works should dictate its own style; and he was constantly experimenting. His very last story, AUNTIE TOOTHACHE, is strangely modern, a psychological fantasy, so different from the literature of the age to which he belonged. The hope that some of Andersen's lesser known stories might now receive the attention they deserve was one of the greatest inducements for starting out on this huge task, and it was an encouragement throughout the work.

A translator is a servant of what he is translating; it is, after all, reduced to sentences and even single words, whose double he has to find. He must try not only to translate the sense but the spirit as well. This is his art, this is what he should and will be judged by. He must be faithful to the original and yet produce a fluent, readable version in another language. But these demands of fluency and readability must not be excuses for changing the author's literary style. Andersen's prose in Danish is not smooth, it is choppy and abrupt; and that is part of his charm. I hope that I have "translated" this as well.

The translator must not let his own personal opinions, or those of his times, influence him. Unfortunately, many of the early translators of Hans Christian Andersen were Victorians, and they had a tendency to make a kiss on the mouth, in translation, land on the cheek. Passion had to be ethereal rather than sensual; and it was so easy and desirable, considering the audience of the time, to change sentiment into sentimentality. I shall not judge these early translators too harshly; for I, too, have been tempted to cut a little here and there to please my audience.

As far as I have been able, I have been faithful to the original text, even when I knew that certain ideas might offend people of my own times, or might—which is far worse—appear ridiculous in their eyes. I have tried to be loyal to only one person, Hans Christian Andersen; and I hope most fervently that I have succeeded.

E.C.H.

## The Tinderbox

A soldier came marching down the road: Left . . . right! Left . . . right! He had a pack on his back and a sword at his side. He had been in the war and he was on his way home. Along the road he met a witch. She was a disgusting sight, with a lower lip that hung all the way down to her chest.

"Good evening, young soldier," she said. "What a handsome sword you have and what a big knapsack. I can see that you are a real soldier! I shall give you all the money that you want."

"Thank you, old witch," he said.

"Do you see that big tree?" asked the witch, and pointed to the one they were standing next to. "The trunk is hollow. You climb up to the top of the tree, crawl into the hole, and slide deep down inside it. I'll tie a rope around your waist, so I can pull you up again when you call me."

"What am I supposed to do down in the tree?" asked the soldier.

"Get money!" answered the witch and laughed. "Now listen to me. When you get down to the very bottom, you'll be in a great passage-way where you'll be able to see because there are over a hundred lamps burning. You'll find three doors; and you can open them all because the keys are in the locks. Go into the first one; and there on a chest, in the middle of the room, you'll see a dog with eyes as big as teacups. Don't let that worry you. You will have my blue checkered apron; just spread it out on the floor, put the dog down on top of it, and it won't do you any harm. Open the chest and take as many coins as you wish, they are all copper. If it's silver you're after, then go into the next room. There you'll find a dog with eyes as big as millstones; but don't let that worry you, put him on the apron and take the money. If you'd rather have gold, you can have that too; it's in the third room. Wait till you see that dog, he's got eyes as big as the Round Tower in Copenhagen; but don't let that worry you. Put him down on my apron and he won't hurt you; then you can take as much gold as you wish."

"That doesn't sound bad!" said the soldier. "But what am I to do for you, old witch? I can't help thinking that you must want something too."

"No," replied the witch. "I don't want one single coin. Just bring me the old tinderbox that my grandmother forgot the last time she was down there."

"I'm ready, tie the rope around my waist!" ordered the soldier.

"There you are, and here is my blue checkered apron," said the witch.

The soldier climbed the tree, let himself fall into the hole, and found that he was in the passageway, where more than a hundred lights burned.

He opened the first door. Oh! There sat the dog with eyes as big as teacups glaring at him.

"You are a handsome fellow!" he exclaimed as he put the dog down on the witch's apron. He filled his pockets with copper coins, closed the chest, and put the dog back on top of it.

He went into the second room. Aha! There sat the dog with eyes as big as millstones. "Don't keep looking at me like that," said the soldier good-naturedly. "It isn't polite and you'll spoil your eyes." He put the dog down on the witch's apron and opened the chest. When he saw all the silver coins, he emptied the copper out of his pockets and filled both them and his knapsack with silver.

Now he entered the third room. Wow! That dog was big enough to frighten anyone, even a soldier. His eyes were as large as the Round Tower in Copenhagen and they turned around like wheels.

"Good evening," said the soldier politely, taking off his cap, for such a dog he had never seen before. For a while he just stood looking at it; but finally he said to himself, "Enough of this!" Then he put the dog down on the witch's apron and opened up the chest.

"God preserve me!" he cried. There was so much gold that there

was enough to buy the whole city of Copenhagen; and all the gingerbread men, rocking horses, riding whips, and tin soldiers in the
whole world.

Quickly the soldier threw away all the silver coins that he had in
his pockets and knapsack and put gold in them instead; he even
filled his boots and his cap with money. He put the dog back on the
chest, closed the door behind him, and called up through the hollow
tree.

"Pull me up, you old witch!"

"Have you got the tinderbox?" she called back.

"Right you are, I have forgotten it," he replied honestly, and went
back to get it. The witch hoisted him up and again he stood on the
road; but now his pockets, knapsack, cap, and boots were filled with
gold and he felt quite differently.

"Why do you want the tinderbox?" he asked.

"Mind your own business," answered the witch crossly. "You have
got your money, just give me the tinderbox."

"Blah! Blah!" said the soldier. "Tell me what you are going to use
it for, right now; or I'll draw my sword and cut off your head."

"No!" replied the witch firmly; but that was a mistake, for the
soldier chopped her head off. She lay there dead. The soldier put all
his gold in her apron, tied it up into a bundle, and threw it over his
shoulder. The tinderbox he dropped into his pocket; and off to
town he went.

The town was nice, and the soldier went to the nicest inn, where he
asked to be put up in the finest room and ordered all the things he
liked to eat best for his supper, because now he had so much money
that he was rich.

The servant who polished his boots thought it was very odd that a
man so wealthy should have such worn-out boots. But the soldier
hadn't had time to buy anything yet; the next day he bought boots
and clothes that fitted his purse. And the soldier became a refined
gentleman. People were eager to tell him all about their town and
their king, and what a lovely princess his daughter was.

"I would like to see her," said the soldier.

"But no one sees her," explained the townfolk. "She lives in a
copper castle, surrounded by walls, and towers, and a moat. The king
doesn't dare allow anyone to visit her because it has been foretold

that she will marry a simple soldier, and the king doesn't want that to happen."

"If only I could see her," thought the soldier, though it was unthinkable.

The soldier lived merrily, went to the theater, kept a carriage so he could drive in the king's park, and gave lots of money to the poor. He remembered well what it felt like not to have a penny in his purse.

He was rich and well dressed. He had many friends; and they all said that he was kind and a real cavalier; and such things he liked to hear. But since he used money every day and never received any, he soon had only two copper coins left.

He had to move out of the beautiful room downstairs, up to a tiny one in the garret, where he not only polished his boots himself but also mended them with a large needle. None of his friends came to see him, for they said there were too many stairs to climb.

It was a very dark evening and he could not even buy a candle. Suddenly he remembered that he had seen the stub of a candle in the tinderbox that he had brought up from the bottom of the hollow tree. He found the tinderbox and took out the candle. He struck the flint. There was a spark, and in through the door came the dog with eyes as big as teacups.

"What does my master command?" asked the dog.

"What's this all about?" exclaimed the soldier. "That certainly was an interesting tinderbox. Can I have whatever I want? Bring me some money," he ordered. In less time than it takes to say thank you, the dog was gone and back with a big sack of copper coins in his mouth.

Now the soldier understood why the witch had thought the tinderbox so valuable. If he struck it once, the dog appeared who sat on the chest full of copper coins; if he struck it twice, then the dog came who guarded the silver money; and if he struck it three times, then came the one who had the gold.

The soldier moved downstairs again, wore fine clothes again, and had fine friends, for now they all remembered him and cared for him as they had before.

One night, when he was sitting alone after his friends had gone, he thought, "It is a pity that no one can see that beautiful princess. What is the good of her beauty if she must always remain behind the high walls and towers of a copper castle? Will I never see her? . . . Where is my tinderbox?"

He made the sparks fly and the dog with eyes as big as teacups came. "I know it's very late at night," he said, "but I would so like to see the beautiful princess, if only for a minute."

Away went the dog; and faster than thought he returned with the sleeping princess on his back. She was so lovely that anyone would have known that she was a real princess. The soldier could not help kissing her, for he was a true soldier.

The dog brought the princess back to her copper castle; but in the morning while she was having tea with her father and mother, the king and queen, she told them that she had had a very strange dream that night. A large dog had come and carried her away to a soldier who kissed her.

"That's a nice story," said the queen, but she didn't mean it.

The next night one of the older ladies in waiting was sent to watch over the princess while she slept, and find out whether it had only been a dream, and not something worse.

The soldier longed to see the princess so much that he couldn't bear it, so at night he sent the dog to fetch her. The dog ran as fast as he could, but the lady in waiting had her boots on and she kept up with him all the way. When she saw which house he had entered, she took out a piece of chalk and made a big white cross on the door.

"Now we'll be able to find it in the morning," she thought, and went home to get some sleep.

When the dog returned the princess to the castle, he noticed the cross on the door of the house where his master lived; so he took a piece of white chalk and put crosses on all the doors of all the houses in the whole town. It was a very clever thing to do, for now the lady in waiting would never know which was the right door.

The next morning the king and queen, the older lady in waiting, and all the royal officers went out into town to find the house where the princess had been.

"Here it is!" exclaimed the king, when he saw the first door with a cross on it.

"No, my sweet husband, it is here," said his wife, who had seen the second door with a cross on it.

"Here's one!"

"There's one!"

Everyone shouted at once, for it didn't matter where anyone

looked: there he would find a door with a cross on it; and so they all gave up.

Now the queen was so clever, she could do more than ride in a golden carriage. She took out her golden scissors and cut out a large piece of silk and sewed it into a pretty little bag. This she filled with the fine grain of buckwheat, and tied the bag around the princess' waist. When this was done, she cut a little hole in the bag just big enough for the little grains of buckwheat to fall out, one at a time, and show the way to the house where the princess was taken by the dog.

During the night the dog came to fetch the princess and carry her on his back to the soldier, who loved her so much that now he had only one desire, and that was to be a prince so that he could marry her.

The dog neither saw nor felt the grains of buckwheat that made a little trail all the way from the copper castle to the soldier's room at the inn. In the morning the king and queen had no difficulty in finding where the princess had been, and the soldier was thrown into jail.

There he sat in the dark with nothing to do; and what made matters worse was that everyone said, "Tomorrow you are going to be hanged!"

That was not amusing to hear. If only he had had his tinderbox, but he had forgotten it in his room. When the sun rose, he watched the people, through the bars of his window, as they hurried toward the gates of the city, for the hanging was to take place outside the walls. He heard the drums and the royal soldiers marching. Everyone was running. He saw a shoemaker's apprentice, who had not bothered to take off his leather apron and was wearing slippers. The boy lifted his legs so high, it looked as though he were galloping. One of his slippers flew off and landed near the window of the soldier's cell.

"Hey!" shouted the soldier. "Listen, shoemaker, wait a minute, nothing much will happen before I get there. But if you will run to the inn and get the tinderbox I left in my room, you can earn four copper coins. But you'd better use your legs or it will be too late."

The shoemaker's apprentice, who didn't have one copper coin, was eager to earn four; and he ran to get the tinderbox as fast as he could; and gave it to the soldier.

And now you shall hear what happened after that!

Outside the gates of the town, a gallows had been built; around it stood the royal soldiers and many hundreds of thousands of people. The king and the queen sat on their lovely throne, and across from them sat the judge and the royal council.

The soldier was standing on the platform, but as the noose was put around his neck, he declared that it was an ancient custom to grant a condemned man his last innocent wish. The only thing he wanted was to be allowed to smoke a pipe of tobacco.

The king couldn't refuse; and the soldier took out his tinderbox and struck it: once, twice, three times! Instantly, the three dogs were before him: the one with eyes as big as teacups, the one with eyes as big as millstones, and the one with eyes as big as the Round Tower in Copenhagen.

"Help me! I don't want to be hanged!" cried the soldier.

The dogs ran toward the judge and the royal council. They took one man by the leg and another by the nose, and threw them up in the air, so high that when they hit the earth again they broke into little pieces.

"Not me!" screamed the king; but the biggest dog took both the king and the queen and sent them flying up as high as all the others had been.

The royal guards got frightened; and the people began to shout: "Little soldier, you shall be our king and marry the princess!"

The soldier rode in the king's golden carriage; and the three dogs danced in front of it and barked: "Hurrah!"

The little boys whistled and the royal guards presented arms. The princess came out of her copper castle and became queen, which she liked very much. The wedding feast lasted a week; and the three dogs sat at the table and made eyes at everyone.

## Little Claus and Big Claus

Once upon a time there lived in a village two men who had the same name; they were both called Claus. But one of them owned four horses, while the other had only one; so to tell them apart the richer man was called Big Claus and the poorer one Little Claus. Now let's hear what happened to the two of them because that's a real story!

Six days a week Little Claus had to work for Big Claus and loan him his horse; and in return Big Claus had to let Little Claus borrow his four horses on Sunday. One day a week Little Claus felt as if all the horses belonged to him, and he would crack his whip in the air and shout orders to them merrily.

One morning when the sun was shining brightly and the villagers, all dressed up in their Sunday best, with their prayer books under their arms, were passing his field, Little Claus cracked his whip in the air, whistled, and called out very loudly, "Gee up, all my horses!"

"You may not say that!" exclaimed Big Claus. "Only one of the horses is yours."

But Little Claus forgot very quickly what Big Claus had said, and the next time someone went by and nodded kindly in his direction, he shouted, "Gee up, all my horses!"

Big Claus turned around and shouted! "I beg you for the last time not to call all those horses yours because if you do it once more I'll take the mallet that I use to drive in the stake for tethering my four horses and hit your one horse so hard that it will drop dead on the spot."

"I promise never to say it again," said Little Claus meekly. But the words were hardly out of his mouth when still another group of churchgoers stopped to watch him plow. They smiled and said good morning in a very friendly way. "What a fine figure I must cut, driving five horses," he thought; and without realizing what he was doing, he cracked the whip and cried, "Gee up, all my horses!"

"I'll give your horse gee up!" screamed Big Claus in a rage; and he took his tethering mallet and hit Little Claus's only horse so hard on the forehead that it fell down quite dead.

"Poor me!" cried Little Claus. "Now I don't have any horse at all!" And he sat down and wept. But as there was nothing else to do he flayed the horse and hung the hide up to dry. When the wind had done its work, Little Claus put the hide in a sack and set off for town to sell it in the market place.

It was a long way and the road led through a forest. The weather turned bad and among the dark shadows Little Claus lost his way. He turned first in one direction and then in another. Finally he did find his way again; but by then it was late afternoon and too late to reach town before nightfall.

Not far from the road he saw a farmhouse. The shutters were closed but above them there shone tiny streams of light. "There I may ask for shelter for the night," Little Claus thought, and made his way to the front door and knocked.

The farmer's wife answered the door, but when she heard what he wanted she shook her head. "You'll have to go away," she ordered. "My husband isn't home and I cannot allow a stranger to come in."

"Then I'll have to sleep outside," said Little Claus. The farmer's wife shut the door without another word; and Little Claus looked about him. Near the house was a haystack, and between that and the dwelling there was a shed with a flat thatched roof.

"I'll stretch out on that," Little Claus mumbled, looking at the roof. "It will make a fine bed and I doubt that the stork will fly down and bite me." The latter was said in jest because there was a stork's nest on the roof of the farmhouse.

Little Claus climbed up on the roof of the shack; and while he was twisting and turning to make himself comfortable, he realized that from where he lay he could see right into the kitchen of the farmhouse because, at the top, the shutters did not close tightly.

A fine white linen cloth covered the large table and on it were not only a roast and wine but a platter of fish as well. On one side of the table sat the farmer's wife and on the other the deacon; and while she filled his glass with wine, he filled himself with fish because that was his favorite food.

"If only I had been invited too!" Little Claus sighed, and pushed himself as near to the window as he could without touching the shutters. There was a cake on the table too; this was better than a party, it was a feast!

He heard someone galloping on the road; he turned and saw the rider: it was the farmer coming home.

Now this farmer was known for two things: one, that he was a good fellow, and the other, that he suffered from a strange disease; he couldn't bear the sight of a deacon. One glance and he went into a rage. And that, of course, was the reason why the deacon had come visiting on a day when the farmer wasn't at home; and that too was why the farmer's wife had made the most delicious food she could for her guest.

When they heard the farmer riding up to the door of his house, both the farmer's wife and the deacon were terrified; and she told him to climb into a large empty chest that stood in the corner. The poor man, trembling with fear, obeyed her. Then the woman hid all the food and the wine in the oven, for she knew that if her husband saw all the delicacies he was certain to ask her why she had made them.

"Ow!" groaned Little Claus when he saw the last of the food disappear into the bread oven.

"Is there someone up there?" the farmer called, and when he saw Little Claus lying on the roof of the shed he told him to come down. "What were you doing up there?"

Little Claus explained how he had lost his way in the forest and asked the farmer to be allowed to spend the night in his house.

"You are most welcome," said the farmer, who was the kindest of men, as long as there was no deacon in sight. "But first let's have a bite to eat."

The farmer's wife greeted them both very politely, set the table, and served them a large bowl of porridge. The farmer, who was very hungry, ate with relish; but Little Claus kept thinking of all the delicious food in the oven and couldn't swallow a spoonful.

At his feet under the table lay the sack with the horse hide in it. He stepped on the sack and the horse hide squeaked. "Shhhhhhhh!" whispered Little Claus to the sack; but at the same time he pressed his foot down on it even harder and it squeaked even louder.

"What have you got in the bag?" asked the farmer.

"Oh, it's only a wizard," Little Claus replied. "He was telling me that there's no reason for us to eat porridge when he has just conjured both fish and meat for us, and even a cake. Look in the oven."

"What!" exclaimed the farmer; and he ran to the oven and opened it. There he saw all the good food that his wife had made for the deacon; and she—not daring to tell him the truth—silently served the roast, the fish, and the cake.

After he had taken a few mouthfuls, Little Claus stepped on the sack again so that the hide squeaked.

"What is the wizard saying now?" asked the farmer eagerly.

"He says that he has conjured three bottles of wine for us and that you will find them in the corner next to the oven."

The farmer's poor wife brought out the wine, which she had hidden, and poured it for Little Claus and her husband, who made so many toasts to each other's health that they were soon very merry. Then the farmer began to think about Little Claus's sack and what a wonderful thing it must be to have a wizard.

"Do you think he could conjure the Devil?" the farmer asked. "For now that I have the courage I wouldn't mind seeing what he looks like."

"Why not?" replied Little Claus. "My wizard will do anything I tell him to. . . . Won't you?" he added, stepping on the sack so that it squeaked. Turning to the farmer, Little Claus smiled. "Can't you hear that he said yes? But the Devil has such an ugly face that he's not worth looking at."

"I'm not afraid," said the farmer, and hiccupped. "How terrible can he look?"

"He looks just like a deacon!"

"Pooh!" returned the farmer. "That's worse than I thought! I must confess that I cannot stand the sight of a deacon; but now that I know that it is only the Devil I will be looking at, maybe I can bear it.

But don't let him come too near me and let's get it over with before I lose my courage."

"I'll tell my wizard," said Little Claus and stepped on the hide; then he cocked his head as if he were listening to someone.

"What is he saying?" asked the farmer, who could only hear the hide squeak.

"He says that if we go over to the chest in the corner and open it up we shall see the Devil sitting inside. But we must be careful when we lift the lid, not to lift it too high, so the Devil can escape."

"Then you must hold onto the lid while I lift it," whispered the farmer to Little Claus as he tiptoed to the chest in which the deacon was hiding. This poor fellow had heard every word that Little Claus and the farmer had said and was quaking with fear.

The farmer opened the chest no more than an inch or two and peeped inside. "Ah!" he screamed and jumped up, letting the lid fall back into place. "I saw him! He looked exactly like our deacon! It was a dreadful sight!"

After such an experience you need a drink; and Little Claus and the farmer had many, for they drank late into the night.

"You must sell me that wizard," the farmer finally said. "Ask whatever you want for it. . . . I'll give you a bushel basket full of money, if that's what you'd like."

"I wouldn't think of it," replied Little Claus. "You have seen for yourself all the marvelous things that wizard can do."

"But I want it with all my heart," begged the farmer; and he kept on pleading with Little Claus until he agreed at last.

"I cannot forget that you gave me a night's lodging," Little Claus said. "Take my wizard, but remember to fill the bushel basket to the very top."

"I shall! I shall!" exclaimed the farmer. "But you must take the chest along too. I won't have it in my house. Who knows but that the Devil isn't still inside it?"

And that's how it happened that Little Claus gave the farmer a sack with a horse hide in it and in return was given not only a bushel full of money and a chest but a wheelbarrow to carry them away.

"Good-by!" called Little Claus, and off he went.

On the other side of the forest there was a deep river with a current that flowed so swiftly that you could not swim against it. But the river had to be crossed and so a bridge had been built. When Little Claus reached the middle of that bridge, he said very loudly—so the deacon, who was still inside the chest, could hear him—"What's the point of dragging this chest any farther? It's so heavy, you'd think it was filled with stones. I'm all worn out. I know what I'll do, I'll dump the chest into the stream and if the current carries it home to me, all well and good; and if not, it doesn't matter." Then he took hold of the chest and pushed it, as if he were about to lift it out of the wheelbarrow and let it fall into the water.

"No, stop it!" cried the deacon from inside the chest. "Let me out! Please, let me out!"

"Oh!" shouted Little Claus as if he were frightened. "The Devil is still in there. I'd better throw the chest right into the river and drown him."

"No! No!" screamed the deacon. "I'll give you a bushel of money if you'll let me out!"

"That's a different tune," said Little Claus, and opened the chest. The deacon climbed out and shoved the chest into the river. Together Little Claus and the deacon went to the deacon's home, where he gave Little Claus the bushel of coins that he had promised him. Now Little Claus had a whole wheelbarrow full of money.

"That wasn't bad payment for my old horse," he said to himself as he dumped all the coins out on the floor of his own living room. "What a big pile it is! It will annoy Big Claus to find out how rich I have become, all because of my horse. I won't tell him but let him find out for himself."

A few minutes later a boy banged on Big Claus's door and asked him if he could borrow his grain measure for Little Claus.

"I wonder what he is going to use that for," thought Big Claus; and in order to find out he dabbed a bit of tar in the bottom of the measuring pail, which was quite clever of him because when it was returned he found a silver coin stuck to the spot.

"Where did that come from?" shouted Big Claus, and ran as fast as he could to Little Claus's house. When he saw Little Claus in the midst of his riches, he shouted even louder, "Where did you get all that money from?"

"Oh, that was for my horse hide, I sold it last night."

"You were certainly well paid!" said Big Claus; and hurried home where he took an ax and killed all four of his horses; then he flayed them and set off for town with their hides.

"Hides for sale! Hides for sale! Who wants to buy hides?" Big Claus shouted from street to street.

All the shoemakers and tanners came out of their workshops to ask him the price of his wares.

"A bushel full of coins for each hide," he replied.

"You must be mad!" they all shouted at once. "Do you think we count money by the bushel?"

"Hides for sale! Hides for sale!" Big Claus repeated. And every time that someone asked him the price he said again, "A bushel full of coins."

"Are you trying to make fools of us?" the shoemakers and the tanners shouted. And while the crowd continued to gather around them, the tanners took their leather aprons and the shoemakers their straps and began to beat Big Claus.

"Hides . . ." screamed one of the tanners. "We'll see to it that your hide spits red!"

"Out of town with him!" they shouted. And certainly Big Claus did his best to get out of town as fast as he could; never in his whole life had he gotten such a beating.

"Little Claus is going to pay for this!" he decided when he got home. "He is going to pay with his life."

But while Big Claus was in town, something unfortunate had occurred: Little Claus's grandmother had died. And although she had been a very mean and scolding hag, who had never been kind to Little Claus, he felt very sad. Thinking that it might bring her back to life, he put his old grandmother in his own warm bed and decided to let her stay there all night, even though this meant that he would have to sleep in a chair.

It was not the first time that Little Claus had tried sleeping in a chair, but he could not sleep anyway; so he was wide awake when Big Claus came and tiptoed across the room to the bed in which he thought Little Claus was sleeping.

With an ax Big Claus hit the old grandmother on top of the head as hard as he could. "That's what you get for making a fool out of me," he explained. "And now you won't be able to do it again," he added and went home.

"What a wicked man!" thought Little Claus. "If my grandmother hadn't already been dead, he would have killed her."

Very early the next morning he dressed his grandmother in her

Sunday best; then he borrowed a horse from his neighbor and harnessed it to his cart. On the small seat in the back of the cart, he put
the old woman in a sitting position with bundles on either side of her,
so she wouldn't fall out of the cart while he was driving. He went
through the forest and just as the sun was rising he reached an inn.
"I'd better stop to get something to keep me alive," he said.

It was a large inn, and the innkeeper was very rich. He was also
very kind, but he had a ferocious temper, as if he had nothing inside
him but pepper and tobacco.

"Good morning," he said to Little Claus. "You're dressed very
finely for so early in the morning."

"I'm driving to town with my grandmother," he replied. "She's sitting out in the cart because I couldn't persuade her to come in here
with me. I wonder if you would be so kind as to take a glass of mead
out to her; but speak a little loudly because she is a bit hard of hearing."

"No sooner said than done," answered the innkeeper; and he
poured a large glass of mead which he carried out to the dead
woman.

"Here is a glass of mead, which your son ordered for you," said the
innkeeper loudly but politely; but the dead woman sat perfectly still
and said not a word.

"Can't you hear me?" he shouted. "Here is mead from your son!"

He shouted the same words again as loud as he could, and still the
old woman sat staring straight ahead. The more he shouted, the mad-
der the innkeeper got, until finally he lost his temper and threw the
mead, glass and all, right into the woman's face. With the mead dripping down her nose, she fell over backward, for Little Claus had not
tied her to the seat.

"What have you done?" shouted Little Claus as he flung open the
door of the inn. "Why, you have killed my grandmother!" he cried,
grabbing the innkeeper by the shirt. "Look at the wound she has on
her head!"

"Oh, what a calamity!" the innkeeper exclaimed, and wrung his
hands. "It is all because of that temper of mine! Sweet, good Little
Claus, I will give you a bushel full of money and bury your grandmother as if she were my own, as long as you'll keep quiet about what
really happened, because if you don't they'll chop my head off; and
that's so nasty."

And that was how Little Claus got another bushel full of coins; and the innkeeper, true to his word, buried the old woman as well as he would have had she been his own grandmother.

As soon as he got home Little Claus sent his boy to borrow Big Claus's grain measure.

"What, haven't I killed him?" Big Claus exclaimed. "I must find out what's happened. I'll take the measure over there myself."

When he arrived at Little Claus's and saw all the money, his eyes grew wide with wonder and greed. "Where did you get all that from?" he demanded.

"It was my grandmother and not me that you killed, and now I have sold her body for a bushel full of money."

"You were certainly well paid," said Big Claus, and hurried home. When he got there he took an ax and killed his old grandmother; then he dumped the poor old woman's body in his carriage and drove into town. He went at once to the apothecary and asked if he wanted to buy a corpse.

"Who is it and where did you get it from?" the apothecary inquired.

"Oh, it is my grandmother, and I have killed her so I could sell her body for a bushel of money," Big Claus said.

"God save us!" cried the apothecary. "You don't know what you're saying. . . . If you talk like that you'll lose your head." And the apothecary lectured him, telling him how wicked a crime murder was and that it was committed only by the most evil of men, who deserved the severest punishment. Big Claus was terrified and leaped into his carriage. He set off in the direction of his home, wildly whipping his horses. But no one tried to stop him, for everyone believed that he had gone mad.

"I'll make you pay for this!" Big Claus cried as soon as he was well out of town. "Little Claus is going to pay for this," he repeated when he got home. Then he took a large sack and went to see Little Claus.

"So you fooled me again!" he shouted. "First I killed my horses and then my grandmother; and it's all your fault. But you have fooled me for the last time!" Grabbing Little Claus around the waist, he shoved him into the sack. As he flung the sack over his shoulder he said loudly, "And now I am going to drown you!"

It was quite far to the river, and as he walked the sack with Little Claus in it seemed to grow heavier and heavier. The road went past the church, and Big Claus heard the organ being played and the congregation singing. "It would be nice to hear a hymn or two before I go on," he thought. "Everybody's in church and Little Claus can't get out of the sack." So Big Claus put down the sack near the entrance and went into the church.

"Poor me! Poor me!" sighed Little Claus. He twisted and turned but he could not loosen the cord that had been tied around the opening of the sack.

At that moment an old herdsman happened to pass. He had snow-white hair and walked with a long crook. In front of him he drove a large herd of cows and bulls. One of the bulls bumped into the sack and Little Claus was turned over.

"Poor me! Poor me!" cried Little Claus. "I am so young and am already bound for heaven."

"Think of poor me; I am an old man," said the herdsman, "and am not allowed to enter it."

"Open up the sack!" shouted Little Claus. "You get inside it, instead of me, and then you will get to heaven right away!"

"Nothing could be better," said the old man. He untied the sack and Little Claus crawled out at once.

"Take good care of my cattle," the herdsman begged as he climbed into the sack. Little Claus promised that he would and tied the sack securely. Then he went on his way, driving the herd before him.

A little later Big Claus came out of the church and lifted the sack onto his back. He was surprised how much lighter it was now, for the old man weighed only half as much as Little Claus.

"How easy it is to carry now; it did do me good to hear a hymn!" he thought.

Big Claus went directly down to the river that was both deep and wide and dumped the sack into the water, shouting after it: "You have made a fool of me for the last time!" For of course he believed that Little Claus was still inside the sack that was disappearing into the river.

On his way home he met Little Claus with all his cattle at the crossroads.

"What!" exclaimed Big Claus. "Haven't I drowned you?"

"Oh yes," answered Little Claus, "You threw me in the river about half an hour ago."

"But where did you get that huge herd of cattle?" Big Claus demanded.

"They are river cattle," replied Little Claus. "I'll tell you everything that happened to me. But, by the way, first I want to thank you for drowning me. For now I shall never have anything to worry about again, I am really rich. . . . Believe me, I was frightened when you threw me over the bridge. The wind whistled in my ears as I fell into the cold water. I sank straight to the bottom; but I didn't hurt myself because I landed on the softest, most beautiful green grass you can imagine. Then the sack was opened by the loveliest maiden. She was all dressed in white except for the green wreath in her wet hair. Taking my hand, she asked, 'Aren't you Little Claus?' When I nodded she said, 'Here are some cattle for you and six miles up the road there is an even bigger herd waiting for you.' Then I realized that to the water people the streams and rivers were as roads are to us. They use them to travel on. Far from their homes under the oceans, they follow the streams and the rivers until they finally become too shallow and come to an end. There are the most beautiful flowers growing down there and the finest, freshest grass; the fish swimming around above your head remind you of the birds flying in the air. The people are as nice as they can be; and the cattle fat and friendly."

"Then tell me why you came up here on land again?" asked Big Claus. "I never would have left a place as wonderful as that."

"Well," said Little Claus, "that is just because I am smart. I told you that the water maiden said that another herd of cattle would be waiting for me six miles up the road. By 'road,' she meant the river; and I am eager to see my cattle. You know how the river twists and turns while the road up here on land is straight; so I thought that if I used the road instead of the river I would get there much faster and save myself at least two miles of walking."

"Oh, you are a lucky man!" exclaimed Big Claus. "Do you think that if I were thrown into the river I would be given cattle too?"

"I don't know why not," replied Little Claus. "But I cannot carry you, as you did me, you're too heavy. But if you'll find a sack and climb into it yourself I'll be glad to go to the bridge with you and push you into the water."

"Thank you very much," said Big Claus. "But if I don't get a herd of cattle when I get down there I'll beat you as you have never been beaten before."

"Oh no! How can you think of being so mean!" whimpered Little Claus as they made their way to the river.

It was a hot day and when the cattle spied the water they started running toward it, for they were very thirsty. "See how eager they are to get to the river," remarked Little Claus. "They are longing for their home under the water."

"Never mind them!" shouted Big Claus. "Or I'll give you a beating right here and now." He grabbed a sack that was lying on one of the bulls' backs and climbed up on the bridge. "Get a rock and put it in with me, I'm afraid that I might float."

"Don't worry about that," said Little Claus. But he found a big stone anyway and rolled it into the sack next to Big Claus before he tied the opening as tightly as he could. Then he pushed the sack off the bridge.

Splash! Plop! Down went Big Claus into the river and straight to the bottom he went.

"I am afraid that he will have trouble finding his cattle," said Little Claus, and drove his own herd home.

## The Princess and the Pea

Once upon a time there was a prince who wanted to marry a princess, but she would have to be a real one. He traveled around the whole world looking for her; but every time he met a princess there was always something amiss. There were plenty of princesses but not one of them was quite to his taste. Something was always the matter: they just weren't real princesses. So he returned home very sad and sorry, for he had set his heart on marrying a real princess.

One evening a storm broke over the kingdom. The lightning flashed, the thunder roared, and the rain came down in bucketfuls. In the midst of this horrible storm, someone knocked on the city gate; and the king himself went down to open it.

On the other side of the gate stood a princess. But goodness, how wet she was! Water ran down her hair and her clothes in streams. It flowed in through the heels of her shoes and out through the toes. But she said that she was a real princess.

"We'll find that out quickly enough," thought the old queen, but she didn't say a word out loud. She hurried to the guest room and took all the bedclothes off the bed; then on the bare bedstead she put a pea. On top of the pea she put twenty mattresses; and on top of the mattresses, twenty eiderdown quilts. That was the bed on which the princess had to sleep.

In the morning, when someone asked her how she had slept, she replied, "Oh, just wretchedly! I didn't close my eyes once, the whole night through. God knows what was in that bed; but it was something hard, and I am black and blue all over."

Now they knew that she was a real princess, since she had felt the pea that was lying on the bedstead through twenty mattresses and twenty eiderdown quilts. Only a real princess could be so sensitive!

The prince married her. The pea was exhibited in the royal museum; and you can go there and see it, if it hasn't been stolen.

Now that was a real story!

## Little Ida's Flowers

"What a pity, all my flowers are dead!" said little Ida. "Last night they were so beautiful, and now all their leaves have withered. Why does that happen?" she asked the student who had come visiting.

The young man was sitting on the sofa. Ida was very fond of him because he knew the most marvelous stories, and with a pair of scissors could cut out of paper the most wonderful pictures: flowers, hearts, little dancing ladies, and castles with doors that could open. He was a happy young man and fond of children.

"Why do my flowers look so sad today?" she asked again, and showed the student her bouquet of dying flowers.

He looked at them a moment before he said, "I know what is wrong with them, they have been dancing all night and that is why they look so tired and hang their heads."

"But flowers can't dance," said little Ida.

"Sure they can," replied the student. "When darkness comes and we go to bed and sleep, then the flowers jump about gaily enough. Nearly every night they hold a grand ball."

"Are children allowed to come to the ball too?" asked little Ida, who was eager to know how flowers brought up their children.

"Oh yes, both the little daisies and the lilies of the valley are allowed to come," smiled the student.

"Where do the most beautiful of the flowers dance?"

"You have been in the park near the king's summer castle, the one that has the splendid garden. You've been there to feed the swans. Remember how they swim toward you when you throw bread crumbs? That's where the grand ball is held; and very grand it is."

"I was there yesterday with my mother," little Ida said, and looked pensive. "But there wasn't a leaf on any of the trees, and not a flower anywhere. There were a lot this summer. Where are they now?"

"As soon as the king and all his courtiers move into town, then the flowers move up to the castle. There they live a merry life; I wish you could see it. The two most beautiful roses sit on the throne; they are the king and queen. The big red tiger lilies are lords in waiting; they stand behind the throne and bow. Then in come all the most beautiful flowers and the grand ball begins. The blue violets are midshipmen. They dance with the hyacinths and the crocuses, and call them Miss. The tulips and the big yellow lilies are the old ladies, they see to it that everyone behaves and dances in time to the music."

"But," interrupted little Ida, "are the flowers allowed to dance in the king's castle?"

"No one knows they are there," continued the student. "Sometimes the old night watchman, who is supposed to take care of the castle when the king is away, does walk through it. He carries a great bunch of keys, one for every door in the castle; and as soon as the flowers hear the rattle of the keys they hide. The old night watchman can smell them but he has never seen them."

"Oh, how wonderful!" little Ida clapped her hands. "Wouldn't I see the flowers either if I were there?"

"I think you could," said the student. "Next time you are in the park, look in through the windows of the castle and you will probably see them. I was out there today, I saw a long yellow daffodil, she was lying stretched out on a sofa. She was a lady in waiting."

"What about the flowers in the botanical garden; are they allowed to attend the ball too? And how do they get out there? It is a very long way from where they live to the castle."

"Oh sure, they can come!" exclaimed the student. "When flowers want to, they can fly. You have seen butterflies. Don't they look like yellow, red, and white flowers? That is exactly what they were once. They are flowers who have jumped off their stems and have learned to fly with their petals; and when they first get a taste for it, they never return to their stems, and their little petals become real wings.

"There's no way of knowing whether the flowers from the botanical garden know about what goes on in the castle. The next time you are there, you can whisper to one of the flowers that there will be a grand ball that night in the castle, and see what happens. Flowers can't keep a secret, so that flower will tell it to the others; and when night comes, they will all fly to the castle. That will certainly surprise the professor who is in charge of the garden. The next day when he takes his morning walk, there won't be a single flower left in the whole botanical garden; and I am sure he will write a paper about it."

"But how will the flower I tell it to talk to the others? I am sure that I have never seen a flower speak," said little Ida.

"They mime. It's a regular pantomime. You have seen how, when the wind blows, all the flowers shake their heads and rustle their leaves; what they are saying to each other is just as plain as what we say with our tongues is to us."

"Does the professor understand what they are saying?" asked little Ida.

"Sure he does. One morning when he came into the garden he saw a large nettle rustle its leaves at a carnation. It was saying, 'You are so beautiful that I love you.' But that kind of talk the professor doesn't like, so he hit the nettle across the fingers—that is, its leaves. But the nettle burned him, and since then the professor has never dared touch a nettle."

"That is very funny!" little Ida laughed.

"I don't think that it's the least bit funny," said the old chancellor, who had just come into the room and had overheard the last part of the conversation; but he never found anything funny. "Such fantastic ideas are nonsense; they are harmful to a child and boring for grownups."

The old chancellor did not like the student, especially when he found him cutting pictures out of paper with a pair of scissors. The student had just finished cutting a hanged man holding a heart; he'd been condemned for stealing hearts. Now the young man had started on another. It was the picture of a witch who was riding on a broom and was carrying her husband on the end of her nose.

Little Ida thought that everything the student did was amusing; and she thought a great deal about what he had said about her flowers. "My flowers are tired from dancing," she thought, and carried her bouquet over to the little table on which her playthings were. She had a whole drawer full of toys too, and even a doll that lay in its own bed.

The doll's name was Sophie. Little Ida picked her up and explained, "Please, be a good doll and sleep in the drawer tonight. The flowers are sick and have to sleep in your bed, so they can get well."

The doll didn't answer; she was angry because someone else was to sleep in her bed.

Little Ida put the flowers in the bed and pulled the covers up around them. She promised them that if they would be good and lie still she would make them a cup of tea. "You will be well enough to be up and around tomorow morning," she added. Then she drew the curtains around the bed so the sun wouldn't shine in their eyes.

All that evening she could not think about anything but what the student had told her. When her bedtime came, she ran over to the window and pulled aside the drapes to look at her mother's plants, which were sitting in flowerpots on the window sill. She whispered to both the tulips and the hyacinths, "I know where you are going tonight." The flowers acted as though they hadn't heard her. They moved neither a petal nor a leaf; but little Ida believed what she had been told.

When she got into bed, little Ida lay awake thinking about how beautiful it must have been when all the flowers danced in the royal castle. "I wonder if my flowers have really been there," she muttered; and then she fell asleep.

Late at night she woke; she had dreamed about the flowers and the student, who the chancellor had said was filling her head with nonsense. It was very quiet in the bedroom. On the table beside her parents' bed, the night light burned.

"I wonder if my flowers are still lying in Sophie's bed," she whispered. "Oh, God, how I would love to know!"

She sat up in bed and looked toward the door. It was ajar; in the next room were her flowers and all her playthings. She listened; someone was playing the piano softly and more beautifully than she had ever heard it played before.

"Now all the flowers are dancing. Oh, God, how I would love to see it," she whispered. But she didn't dare get up, for she was afraid she would wake her father and mother.

"If only the flowers would come in here," she thought. But the flowers didn't come, and the music kept on playing.

Finally she climbed out of bed, tiptoed over to the door, and looked into the living room.

There was no night light burning in there, but she could see anyway, for the moon shone in through the windows onto the floor. It was so bright that it was almost as light as day. All the tulips and the hyacinths stood in two long rows on the floor; on the window sill stood only their empty flowerpots. The flowers danced so gracefully, holding onto each other's leaves. They formed chains and swung each other around, just as children do when they dance.

A big yellow lily sat at the piano and played. Little Ida remembered that she had seen it in the garden that summer. The student had said, "Why, it looks like Miss Line!" Everybody had laughed at him then; but now little Ida thought that the slender yellow flower really did look like Miss Line; and behaved just as she did when she played. There the flower was, turning its yellow face from side to side and nodding in time to the music.

None of the flowers noticed little Ida. Suddenly a big blue crocus jumped up on the table where her playthings were, went right over to the doll's bed, and drew the curtains. There lay the sick flowers. But they didn't seem sick any more. They leaped out of bed. They wanted to dance too. The little porcelain man, whose chin was chipped, bowed to the flowers. They jumped down onto the floor; and what a good time they had!

Now in Denmark at Shrovetide little children are given a bunch of birch and beech branches tied together with ribbons, and fastened to their twigs are paper flowers, little toys, and candies. It is an old custom for the children to whip their parents out of bed with these switches on Shrove Monday. The switches are pretty and most of the children keep them. Little Ida's had been lying on the table among her other toys. Bump! Down they jumped with their ribbons flying; they thought they were flowers. A handsome little wax doll, with a broad-brimmed hat just like the one the chancellor wore, was tied to the top of the longest branch.

The switches danced the mazurka, for they were stronger than the flowers and could stamp their feet. All at once the wax doll began to grow. It became taller and bigger and started screaming at the paper flowers: "What a lot of nonsense to tell a child! What a lot of nonsense!"

Now the wax doll looked exactly like the chancellor; for he, too, wore a broad-brimmed hat and had a yellow complexion and a sour expression. The ribbons started to hit the wax doll across the legs, and he had to pull himself together till he was only a little wax doll again.

It was all so funny that little Ida could not help laughing. The switches kept on dancing, and the chancellor had to dance too—when he was as big and tall as a man and when he was only a little wax doll. He was given no rest, until the flowers begged the switches to stop; the flowers who had lain in the doll's bed felt especially sorry for the little wax doll.

As soon as the switches stopped dancing there came a knocking from the drawer where the doll Sophie lay. The little porcelain man went carefully to the edge of the table, leaned over the side of it, and pulled the drawer open as much as he could—which wasn't very much. Sophie stuck out her head. "I see there is a ball. Why hasn't anyone told me about it?"

"Would you like to dance with me?" asked the porcelain man.

"Pooh! You are chipped," said Sophie, and sat down on the edge of the drawer, with her back to the poor little porcelain man. She thought that one of the flowers would come and ask her to dance, but none of them did. The porcelain man danced by himself and he didn't dance badly at all.

Since none of the flowers seemed to notice her, Sophie jumped down upon the floor. She landed with a crash and all the flowers came running over to ask her whether she had hurt herself; the flowers who had lain in her bed were especially considerate.

But Sophie hadn't hurt herself. Little Ida's flowers thanked her for having been allowed to sleep in her bed, and they told her that they loved her; then they took her out to the middle of the floor, where there was a great splash of moonlight, and danced with her. All of the other flowers made a circle around them, and Sophie was so happy that she told the flowers they could keep her bed, even though she didn't like sleeping in the drawer.

"Thank you," the flowers replied. "It is most kind of you, but our life is short. Tomorrow we shall be dead. Tell little Ida to bury us out in the garden where the canary is buried; and next year we shall come to life again and be even more beautiful than we are now."

"You mustn't die!" cried the doll, and kissed the flowers.

At that moment the door of the dining room opened and the most beautiful flowers came dancing in. Little Ida could not imagine where they had come from, unless they were the flowers from the park near the king's castle.

First entered two roses who wore gold crowns. They were the king and the queen. Behind them came the carnations and the lilies, bowing and waving to the other flowers.

There was music. Big poppies and peonies blew on the pods of sweet peas with such vigor that their faces were red. The bluebells tingled. It was a funny orchestra both to watch and to listen to. At last came all the other flowers, dancing: violets, daisies, and lilies of the valley; as they finished their dance, they kissed each other. It was lovely to see.

The flowers said good night to each other, and little Ida climbed back into her little bed and dreamed about everything she had seen.

The next morning when she woke, she ran right over to the doll's bed to see if the flowers were still there. There they were, but now they were all shriveled and dead. Her doll Sophie was in the drawer; she looked awfully sleepy.

"Can you remember what you are supposed to tell me?" little Ida asked. Sophie didn't say a word.

"You are not a good doll," scolded little Ida. "Remember how all the flowers danced with you!" Then she took a paper box that had a lovely picture of a bird on its lid and laid the flowers in it.

"That will be your honorable coffin," she said. "And when my cousins come from Norway, then we'll have a funeral and bury you, so you can come again next summer and be more beautiful than you are now."

The cousins from Norway were two strong boys. Their names were Jonas and Adolph. Their father had given them each a bow and some arrows; and these they had brought along to show little Ida.

She told them about the poor flowers that had died and allowed them to attend the funeral. It was almost a procession. First came the boys with their bows slung over their shoulders, then little Ida, carrying the pretty little paper box. In the corner of the garden they dug a little grave. Ida kissed the flowers before she buried them. Jonas and Adolph shot an arrow above the grave, for they didn't have a gun or a cannon.

## Inchelina

Once upon a time there was a woman whose only desire was to have a tiny little child. Now she had no idea where she could get one; so she went to an old witch and asked her: "Please, could you tell me where I could get a tiny little child? I would so love to have one."

"That is not so difficult," said the witch. "Here is a grain of barley; it is not the kind that grows in the farmer's fields or that you can feed to the chickens. Plant it in a flowerpot and watch what happens."

"Thank you," said the woman. She handed the witch twelve pennies, and she went home to plant the grain of barley. No sooner was it in the earth than it started to sprout. A beautiful big flower grew up; it looked like a tulip that was just about to bloom.

"What a lovely flower," said the woman, and kissed the red and yellow petals that were closed so tightly. With a snap they opened and one could see that it was a real tulip. In the center of the flower on the green stigma sat a tiny little girl. She was so beautiful and so delicate, and exactly one inch long. "I will call her Inchelina," thought the woman.

The lacquered shell of a walnut became Inchelina's cradle, the blue petals of violets her mattress, and a rose petal her cover. Here she slept at night; in the daytime she played on the table by the window. The woman had put a bowl of water there with a garland of flowers around it. In this tiny "lake" there floated a tulip petal, on which Inchelina could row from one side of the plate to the other, using two white horsehairs as oars; it was an exquisite sight. And

Inchelina could sing, as no one has ever sung before—so clearly and delicately.

One night as she lay sleeping in her beautiful little bed a toad came into the room through a broken windowpane. The toad was big and wet and ugly; she jumped down upon the table where Inchelina was sleeping under her red rose petal.

"She would make a lovely wife for my son," said the toad; and grabbing the walnut shell in which Inchelina slept, she leaped through the broken window and down into the garden.

On the banks of a broad stream, just where it was muddiest, lived the toad with her son. He had taken after his mother and was very ugly. "Croak . . . Croak . . . Croak!" was all he said when he saw the beautiful little girl in the walnut shell.

"Don't talk so loud or you will wake her," scolded the mother. "She could run away and we wouldn't be able to catch her, for she is as light as the down of a swan. I will put her on a water-lily leaf, it will be just like an island to her. In the meantime, we shall get your apartment, down in the mud, ready for your marriage."

Out in the stream grew many water lilies, and all of their leaves looked as if they were floating in the water. The biggest of them was the farthest from shore; on that one the old toad put Inchelina's little bed.

When the poor little girl woke in the morning and saw where she was—on a green leaf with water all around her—she began to cry bitterly. There was no way of getting to shore at all.

The old toad was very busy down in her mud house, decorating the walls with reeds and yellow flowers that grew near the shore. She meant to do her best for her new daughter-in-law. After she had finished, she and her ugly son swam out to the water-lily leaf to fetch Inchelina's bed. It was to be put in the bridal chamber. The old toad curtsied and that is not easy to do while you are swimming; then she said, "Here is my son. He is to be your husband; you two will live happily down in the mud."

"Croak! . . . Croak!" was all the son said. Then they took the bed and swam away with it. Poor Inchelina sat on the green leaf and wept and wept, for she did not want to live with the ugly toad and have her hideous son as a husband. The little fishes that were swimming about in the water had heard what the old toad said; they stuck their heads out of the water to take a look at the tiny girl. When they saw how beautiful she was, it hurt them to think that she should have to marry the ugly toad and live in the mud. They decided that they would not let it happen, and gathered around the green stalk that held the leaf anchored to the bottom of the stream. They all nibbled on the stem, and soon the leaf was free. It drifted down the stream, bearing Inchelina far away from the ugly toad.

As Inchelina sailed by, the little birds on the shore saw her and sang, "What a lovely little girl." Farther and farther sailed the leaf with its little passenger, taking her on a journey to foreign lands.

For a long time a lovely white butterfly flew around her, then landed on the leaf. It had taken a fancy to Inchelina. The tiny girl laughed, for she was so happy to have escaped the toad; and the stream was so beautiful, golden in the sunshine. She took the little silk ribbon which she wore around her waist and tied one end of it to the butterfly and the other to the water-lily leaf. Now the leaf raced down the stream—and so did Inchelina, for she was standing on it.

At that moment a big May bug flew by; when it spied Inchelina, it swooped down and with its claws grabbed the poor girl around her tiny waist and flew up into a tree with her. The leaf floated on down the stream, and the butterfly had to follow it.

Oh God, little Inchelina was terrified as the May bug flew away with her, but stronger than her fear was her grief for the poor little white butterfly that she had chained to the leaf with her ribbon. If he did not get loose, he would starve to death.

The May bug didn't care what happened to the butterfly. He placed Inchelina on the biggest leaf on the tree. He gave her honey from the flowers to eat, and told her that she was the loveliest thing he had ever seen, even though she didn't look like a May bug. Soon all the other May bugs that lived in the tree came visiting. Two young lady May bugs—they were still unmarried—wiggled their antennae and said: "She has only two legs, how wretched. No antennae and a thin waist, how disgusting! She looks like a human being: how ugly!"

All the other female May bugs agreed with them. The May bug who had caught Inchelina still thought her lovely; but when all the others kept insisting that she was ugly, he soon was convinced of it too. Now he didn't want her any longer, and put her down on a daisy at the foot of the tree and told her she could go wherever she wanted to, for all he cared. Poor Inchelina cried; she thought it terrible to be so ugly that even a May bug would not want her, and that in spite of her being more beautiful than you can imagine, more lovely than the petal of the most beautiful rose.

All summer long poor Inchelina lived all alone in the forest. She wove a hammock out of grass and hung it underneath a dock leaf so that it would not rain on her while she slept. She ate the honey in the flowers and drank the dew that was on their leaves every morning.

Summer and autumn passed. But then came winter: the long, cold winter. All the birds that had sung so beautifully flew away. The flowers withered, the trees lost their leaves; and the dock leaf that had protected her rolled itself up and became a shriveled yellow stalk. She was so terribly cold. Her clothes were in shreds; and she was so thin and delicate.

Poor Inchelina, she was bound to freeze to death. It started to snow and each snowflake that fell on her was like a whole shovelful of snow would be to us, because we are so big, and she was only one inch tall.

She wrapped herself in a wizened leaf, but it gave no warmth and she shivered from the cold.

Not far from the forest was a big field where grain had grown; only a few dry stubbles still rose from the frozen ground, pointing up to the heavens. To Inchelina these straws were like a forest. Trembling, she wandered through them and came to the entrance of a field mouse's house. It was only a little hole in the ground. But deep down below the mouse lived in warmth and comfort, with a full larder and a nice kitchen. Like a beggar child, Inchelina stood outside the door and begged for a single grain of barley. It was several days since she had last eaten.

"Poor little wretch," said the field mouse, for she had a kind heart. "Come down into my warm living room and dine with me."

The field mouse liked Inchelina. "You can stay the winter," she said. "But you must keep the room tidy and tell me a story every day, for I like a good story." Inchelina did what the kind old mouse demanded, and she lived quite happily.

"Soon we shall have a visitor," said the mouse one day. "Once a week my neighbor comes. He lives even more comfortably than I do. He has a drawing room, and wears the most exquisite black fur coat. If only he would marry you, then you would be well provided for. He can't see you, for he is blind, so you will have to tell him the very best of your stories."

But Inchelina did not want to marry the mouse's neighbor, for he was a mole. The next day he came visiting, dressed in his black velvet fur coat. The field mouse had said that he was both rich and wise. His house was twenty times as big as the mouse's; and learned he was, too; but he did not like the sun and the beautiful flowers, he said they were "abominable," for he had never seen them. Inchelina had to sing for him; and when she sang *"Frère Jacques, dormez vous?"* he fell in love with her because of her beautiful voice; but he didn't show it, for he was sober-minded and never made a spectacle of himself.

He had recently dug a passage from his own house to theirs, and he invited Inchelina and the field mouse to use it as often as they pleased. He told them not to be afraid of the dead bird in the corridor. It had died only a few days before. It was still whole and had all its feathers. By chance it had been buried in his passageway.

The mole took a piece of dry rotten wood in his mouth; it shone as brightly as fire in the darkness; then he led the way down through the long corridor. When they came to the place where the dead bird lay, the mole made a hole with his broad nose, up through the earth, so that light could come through. Almost blocking the passageway was a dead swallow, with its beautiful wings pressed close to its body, its feet almost hidden by feathers, and its head nestled under a wing. The poor bird undoubtedly had frozen to death. Inchelina felt a great sadness; she had loved all the birds that twittered and sang for her that summer. The mole kicked the bird with one of his short legs and said, "Now it has stopped chirping. What a misfortune it is to be born a bird. Thank God, none of my children will be born birds! All they can do is chirp, and then die of starvation when winter comes."

"Yes, that's what all sensible people think," said the field mouse. "What does all that chirping lead to? Starvation and cold when winter comes. But I suppose they think it is romantic."

Inchelina didn't say anything, but when the mouse and mole had their backs turned, she leaned down and kissed the closed eye of the swallow. "Maybe that was one of the birds that sang so beautifully for me this summer," she thought. "How much joy you gave me, beautiful little bird."

The mole closed the hole through which the daylight had entered and then escorted the ladies home. That night Inchelina could not sleep; she rose and wove as large a blanket as she could, out of hay.

She carried it down in the dark passage and covered the little bird with it. In the field mouse's living room she had found bits of cotton; she tucked them under the swallow wherever she could, to protect it from the cold earth.

"Good-by, beautiful bird," she said. "Good-by, and thank you for the songs you sang for me when it was summer and all the trees were green and the sun warmed us."

She put her head on the bird's breast; then she jumped up! Something was ticking inside: it was the bird's heart, for the swallow was not really dead, and now the warmth had revived it.

In the fall all the swallows fly to the warm countries. If one tarries too long and is caught by the first frost, he lies down on the ground as if he were dead, and the cold snow covers him.

Inchelina shook with fear. The swallow was huge to a girl so tiny that she only measured an inch. But she gathered her courage and pressed the blanket closer to the bird's body. She even went to fetch the little mint leaf that she herself used as a cover and put it over the bird's head.

The next night she sneaked down to the passageway again; the bird was better although still very weak. He opened his eyes just long enough to see Inchelina standing in the dark with a little piece of dry rotten wood in her hand, as a lamp.

"Thank you, you sweet little child," said the sick swallow, "I feel so much better. I am not cold now. Soon I shall be strong again and can fly out into the sunshine."

"Oh no," she said. "It is cold and snowing outside now and you would freeze. Stay down here in your warm bed, I will nurse you."

She brought the swallow water on a leaf. After he had drunk it, he told her his story. He had torn his wing on a rosebush, and therefore could not fly as swiftly as the other swallows, so he had stayed behind when the others left; then one morning he had fainted from cold. That was all he could remember. He did not know how he came to be in the mole's passageway.

The bird stayed all winter. Inchelina took good care of him, grew very fond of him, and breathed not a word about him to either the mole or the field mouse, for she knew that they didn't like the poor swallow.

As soon as spring came and the warmth of the sun could be felt through the earth, the swallow said good-by to Inchelina, who opened the hole that the mole had made. The sun shone down so pleasantly. The swallow asked her if she did not want to come along with him; she could sit on his back and he would fly with her out into the great forest. But Inchelina knew that the field mouse would be sad and lonely if she left.

"I cannot," she said.

The bird thanked her once more. "Farewell. . . . Farewell, lovely girl," he sang, and flew out into the sunshine.

Inchelina's eyes filled with tears as she watched the swallow fly away, for she cared so much for the bird.

"Tweet . . . tweet," he sang, and disappeared in the forest.

Poor Inchelina was miserable. Soon the grain would be so tall that the field would be in shade, and she would no longer be able to enjoy the warm sunshine.

"This summer you must spend getting your trousseau ready," said the field mouse, for the sober mole in the velvet coat had proposed to her. "You must have both woolens and linen to wear and to use in housekeeping when you become Mrs. Mole."

Inchelina had to spin by hand and the field mouse hired four spiders to weave both night and day. Every evening the mole came visiting, but all he talked about was how nice it would be when the summer was over. He didn't like the way the sun baked the earth; it made it so hard to dig in. As soon as autumn came they would get married. But Inchelina was not happy; she thought the mole was dull and she did not love him. Every day, at sunrise and at sunset, she tiptoed to the entrance of the field mouse's house, so that when the wind blew and parted the grain, she could see the blue sky above her. She thought of how light and beautiful it was out there, and she longed for her friend the swallow but he never came back. "He is probably far away in the wonderful green forest!" she thought.

Autumn came and Inchelina's trousseau was finished.

"In four weeks we shall hold your wedding," said the field mouse.

Inchelina cried and said she did not want to marry the boring old mole.

"Fiddlesticks!" squeaked the field mouse. "Don't be stubborn or I will bite you with my white teeth. You are getting an excellent husband; he has a velvet coat so fine that the queen does not have one that is better. He has both a larder and kitchen, you ought to thank God for giving you such a good husband."

The day of the wedding came; the mole had already arrived. Inchelina grieved. Now she would never see the warm sun again. The mole lived far down under the ground, for he didn't like the sun. While she lived with the field mouse, she at least had been allowed to walk as far as the entrance of the little house and look at the sun.

"Farewell. . . . Farewell, you beautiful sun!" Inchelina lifted her hands up toward the sky and then took a few steps out upon the field. The harvest was over and only the stubbles were left. She saw a little red flower. Embracing it, she said: "Farewell! And give my love to the swallow if you ever see him."

"Tweet . . . Tweet . . ." something said in the air above her.

She looked up. It was the little swallow. As soon as he saw Inchelina he chirped with joy. And she told the bird how she had to marry the awful mole, and live forever down under the ground, and never see the sun again. The very telling of her future brought tears to her eyes.

"Now comes the cold winter," said the swallow, "and I fly far away to the warm countries. Why don't you come with me? You can sit on my back; tie yourself on so you won't fall off and we will fly far away from the ugly mole and his dismal house; across the great mountains, to the countries where the sun shines more beautiful than here and the loveliest flowers grow and it is always summer. Fly with me, Inchelina. You saved my life when I lay freezing in the cold cellar of the earth."

"Yes, I will come," cried Inchelina, and climbed up on the bird's back. She tied herself with a ribbon to one of his feathers, and the swallow flew high up into the air, above the forests and lakes and over the high mountains that are always snow-covered. Inchelina froze in the cold air, but she crawled underneath the warm feathers of the bird and only stuck her little head out to see all the beauty below her.

They came to the warm countries. And it was true what the swallow had said: the sun shone more brightly and the sky seemed twice as high. Along the fences grew the loveliest green and blue grapes. From the trees in the forests hung oranges and lemons. Along the roads the most beautiful children ran, chasing many-colored butterflies. The swallow flew even farther south, and the landscape beneath them became more and more beautiful.

Near a forest, on the shores of a lake, stood the ruins of an ancient temple; ivy wound itself around the white pillars. On top of these were many swallows' nests and one of them belonged to the little swallow that was carrying Inchelina.

"This is my house," he said. "Now choose for yourself one of the beautiful flowers down below and I will set you down on it, it will make a lovely home for you."

"How wonderful!" exclaimed Inchelina, and clapped her hands. Among the broken white marble pillars grew tall, lovely white flowers. The swallow sat her down on the leaves of one of them; and to Inchelina's astonishment, she saw a little man sitting in the center of the flower. He was white and almost transparent, as if he were made of glass. On his head he wore a golden crown. On his back were a pair of wings. He was no taller than Inchelina. In every one of the flowers there lived such a tiny angel; and this one was the king of them all.

"How handsome he is!" whispered Inchelina to the swallow.

The tiny little king was terrified of the bird, who was several times larger than he was. But when he saw Inchelina he forgot his fear. She was the loveliest creature he had ever seen; and so he took the crown off his own head and put it on hers. Then he asked her what her name was and whether she wanted to be queen of the flowers.

Now here was a better husband than old mother toad's ugly son or the mole with the velvet coat. Inchelina said yes; and from every flower came a lovely little angel to pay homage to their queen. How lovely and delicate they all were; and they brought her gifts, and the best of these was a pair of wings, so she would be able to fly, as they all did, from flower to flower.

It was a day of happiness. And the swallow, from his nest in the temple, sang for them as well as he could. But in his heart he was ever so sad, for he, too, loved Inchelina and had hoped never to be parted from her.

"You shall not be called Inchelina any longer," said the king. "It is an ugly name. From now on we shall call you Maja."

"Farewell! Farewell!" called the little swallow. He flew back to the north, away from the warm countries. He came to Denmark; and there he has his nest, above the window of a man who can tell fairy tales.

"Tweet . . . tweet," sang the swallow. And the man heard it and wrote down the whole story.

## The Naughty Boy

Once upon a time an old poet—a really nice and kind old poet—was sitting cozily by his potbelly stove toasting apples. Outside a storm was raging and the rain was coming down by the bucket.

"Anyone caught out tonight won't have a dry stitch on," remarked the poet, and sighed.

"Open the door! I am wet and freezing!" cried a little child, and banged on the poet's door, while the wind made all the windows rattle.

"Poor little fellow!" exclaimed the poet, and hurried to open the door. There stood a little boy; he was stark naked and the water was streaming down his golden hair. He was so cold that he was trembling all over; and had he not been let in, he certainly would have died that night out in the awful storm.

"You poor little boy." The poet took him by the hand. "Come in and sit down by the stove and get dry. I'll give you wine and toasted apples. You are a beautiful child!"

And that he was. His eyes shone like two stars, and even though his golden hair was wet, it curled most becomingly. He looked like an angel as he stood there pale and shivering. In his hands he had a bow and some arrows, which were much the worse for having been out in the rain, for all the colors on the pretty arrows had run into each other.

The old poet sat down next to the stove with the child in his lap. He dried his hair and warmed his hands in his own; then he gave

him a toasted apple and a glass of mulled wine. The boy soon re-
covered. The color returned to his cheeks. He jumped down from
the poet's knees and began to dance around his chair.

"You are a lively child," said the old poet, and smiled. "What is
your name?"

"I am called Cupid," answered the boy. "Don't you know me?
There are my bow and arrows. I am good at shooting. Look, the
moon has come out; the weather is fine now."

"But I am afraid your bow and arrows are spoiled," the poet said.

"That is too bad!" The boy picked up the bow and glanced at it.
"Now that it's dry it looks all right," he argued. "Look, the string is
taut. No harm has come to it." Cupid slipped an arrow into the bow
and bent it. He took aim and the arrow pierced the old man's heart!
"There, you can see for yourself, my bow is fine," the naughty, ungrateful boy said laughingly to the poor old poet who had taken him
into his warm living room and given him mulled wine and the very
best of his toasted apples.

The old poet lay on the floor, weeping. He had really been hit,
right in the heart. "Oh . . . oh . . ." he moaned. "The mischievous
child! I am going to tell all the other boys and girls to beware of
Cupid and never to play with him, so he cannot do them any harm."

All the boys and girls who were warned by the old poet did their
best to be on the alert against Cupid; but he fooled them anyway,
because he is very cunning.

When a student is returning from a lecture at the university, Cupid
runs along beside him, wearing a black robe and with a book under
his arm. The student cannot recognize him; he mistakes him for another student and takes his arm; then Cupid shoots an arrow into his
heart. The girls are not safe from him, even in church when they are
being confirmed. In the theater, he sits astride the chandelier and nobody notices him up there among the burning candles, but they feel it
when he shoots his arrows at them.

He runs about in the royal parks and on the embankment where
your parents love to go for a walk. He has hit their hearts with his
arrows once, too. Ask them, and see what they say.

Cupid is a rascal! Don't ever have anything to do with him! Imagine, he once shot your poor old grandmother, right through the heart;
it's so long ago that it no longer hurts, but she hasn't forgotten it.
Pooh! That mischievous Cupid! Now you know what he is like and
what a naughty boy he is.

## The Traveling Companion

Poor Johannes was miserable; his father was ill and there was no hope of his recovering. It was late in the evening; they were alone together. The lamp on the table was burning low.

"You have been a good son," whispered the father. "I am sure that God will help you and protect you." The dying man looked kindly and earnestly at his son, then he breathed very deeply and died.

He looked as if he were asleep. Johannes wept, for now he was alone in the world. He had neither father nor mother, or brothers and sisters. He kneeled down and kissed his father's hand. Many a tear ran down his cheeks before he finally fell asleep with his head resting against the hard board of the bedstead.

He dreamed a strange dream, in which the sun and the moon curtsied before him. He saw his father, too, alive and well. He heard him laugh as he always did whenever something amused him. A lovely girl, with long beautiful hair and a gold crown on her head, took his hand in hers; and his father said to him, "This is your bride: the most beautiful girl in the world." Then he woke, the dream was over. His father was dead. There lay his cold body. He was all alone, poor Johannes!

Next week his father was buried. Johannes walked behind the coffin. He could no longer see his father, whom he loved so much. He heard the earth fall on the coffin lid. He peered down into the grave. He could see the corner of the burial chest; another shovelful of earth and that, too, was out of sight. At that moment Johannes felt that his heart would break from sorrow. A psalm was sung and it sounded so beautiful that he burst out crying, and the tears relieved his grief. The sunlight played on the leaves of the trees; it was as if the sun wanted to say, "Do not be sad, Johannes! Can't you see how beautiful the blue sky is? Your father is up there and he is begging God to help, so that all may go well for you."

"I will try always to be good," thought Johannes. "Then I, too, will go to heaven when I die and see my father again. I will have so much to tell him, and he will teach me about all the beautiful things in heaven, as he taught me about all that is beautiful here on earth. Oh, how wonderful it will be!" For a moment, as the words became a picture in Johannes' mind, he smiled though tears ran down his face.

The little birds in the chestnut tree sang, "Tweet . . . Tweet . . ." They were happy even though they were attending a funeral; or maybe they were happy because they knew that the dead man now had wings more beautiful than theirs, for he had been good while he lived on earth. Johannes saw how the little birds flew from the branches of the tree far out into the world, and he wanted to fly with them. But first he must carve a wooden cross to put on his father's grave.

In the evening when he was finished, he returned to the churchyard and found the grave covered with sand and decorated with flowers. The people of the village had wanted to show that they, too, loved his father and felt sorrow at his death.

Early the next morning Johannes packed his few belongings into a small bundle and put his inheritance of fifty silver marks in a purse which he hid under his belt. Now he was ready to go out into the world, but first he went to his father's grave to pray and say good-by. "I shall always be good, Father," he promised, "so that you may, without shame, bid God to protect me."

As he walked across the fields, leaving the village behind him, the flowers nodded as the wind blew over them and said, "Welcome, Johannes! Welcome to our green world, is it not beautiful?" But Johannes could not hear them; he turned to look once more at the old church where he had been baptized and where every Sunday he had attended service with his father and sung hymns. High up in one of the little windows of the tower he saw the church pixy with his red woolen hat. The pixy was shading his eyes with his hand, the sun was shining right in his face. Johannes waved good-by to him and the pixy took off his hat and swung it over his head; then he put his hand on his heart and blew kisses toward Johannes, to show that he wished him good luck and a happy journey.

Johannes thought about all the beautiful things he would see in the big marvelous world as he walked on, farther and farther away from all that he knew. Soon he no longer recognized the countryside. He passed through villages and towns he had never seen before, and all the people he met were strangers.

The first night he slept in a haystack and thought it was as fine a bed as anyone could have, that a king could not have offered him one more comfortable. The fields, the little river, the haystack, and the blue heaven above him. What a lovely bedchamber! The green grass dotted with red and white flowers was a carpet; the hedge of wild roses and the elderberry bushes were better than bouquets of flowers in vases; and the river, with its clear water, was his washing basin. The reeds that grew along its edge nodded to say both good morning and good night to him, and the moon was an excellent night lamp that couldn't set fire to the curtains. Here Johannes could sleep peacefully and he did, and only woke after the sun had risen and all the little birds started singing, "Good morning! Good morning! Aren't you up yet?"

The bells rang from the church tower; it was Sunday. The people were going to church and Johannes went too; he sang a hymn and listened to the minister preach. Everything was just as it was in the church where he had been baptized and attended service with his father.

In the churchyard there were many graves where the grass grew high, for there was no one to tend them. Johannes thought of his own father's grave which soon would look like these, now that he was not there to weed and plant flowers on it. He pulled up some of the grass and straightened the wooden crosses that had fallen; then he took the wreaths that the wind had blown from the graves and put them back where he thought they belonged, hoping that some stranger would do the same for his father's grave.

Outside the church stood a beggar. Johannes gave him a silver coin and then walked on, happy and content, out into the wide, wide world.

Toward evening a storm began to gather. Johannes looked for

shelter but the landscape was bare and uninhabited; finally, when night had already fallen, he saw a little church on a hill. The door to the church was ajar; here he would seek shelter until the storm was over.

"I will just sit in a corner," he thought. "I am tired and need some rest." He sat down, folded his hands, and said his prayers; then he feel asleep and dreamed, while the storm broke and lightning flashed and the thunder roared.

When he woke it was past midnight, the storm was over, and the moolight shone through the windows into the church. Near the altar stood a coffin; it was open and in it lay a dead man who was to be buried the next day. Johannes was not afraid, for he had a good conscience, and he knew that the dead cannot do anyone any harm. It is living, evil human beings one has to fear. Two such worthless men were now standing before the open coffin. They wanted to harm the dead man; they were preparing to take him out of his coffin and throw him out of the church. Poor dead man!

"What arc you doing?" cried Johannes. "It is sinful to disturb the dead. Let the poor man sleep in Jesus' name!"

"Nonsense!" screamed one of the wicked men. "He has cheated us. He owed us money, which he couldn't pay back, and now he has died, on top of it, and we shan't ever see a penny of our money again. But we shall have our revenge. We shall throw him in front of the church door and there he can lie like a dog."

"I have only fifty marks," said Johannes, "it is my inheritance from my father. I will give it to you if you will promise me to let the dead man lie in peace. I can get along without money, I am strong and God will help me."

"Yes," sneered the wicked men, "if you will pay his debts, we shan't harm him." They took Johannes' money and, laughing at his goodness, went on their way. Johannes put the dead man back into his coffin, folded the cold hands, and then as happily as ever entered the dark forest just beyond the church.

The moonlight shone down through the leaves of the trees and Johannes saw the little elves playing, for they did not mind his coming. They knew he was a good and innocent human being; only from evil and dishonest people do the elves hide. Some of them were no bigger than Johannes' finger. Their long yellow hair was held in place by golden combs. Two by two, they would swing on the drops of dew that clung to the leaves and the tops of the high grass. Sometimes the dewdrops would roll down in among the grass and how the elves would laugh. Oh, it was a joy to watch them! They sang all the songs that Johannes had learned when he was a child. Colorful spiders, with silver crowns on their heads, spun palaces and bridges from bush to bush, which caught the dew and looked like glass in the moonlight. The elves played the whole night through; only when the sun rose did they climb back into their flowers. Then the wind grabbed their bridges and palaces and carried them high into the air as flying spider webs.

Johannes had just come out of the forest when he heard someone call behind him, "Wait, where are you going?"

"Out into the wide world," answered Johannes. "I am a poor fellow who has neither father nor mother, but I am sure that God will help me."

"I want to go out in the wide world too," said the stranger. "Let's be traveling companions."

"That's a good idea," agreed Johannes, and so they went on together.

It took no time for them to become fond of each other, for they were both good and kind. Johannes soon realized that the stranger was much wiser than he; he seemed to be able to talk about everything and to have been everywhere. There was hardly anything that existed that he did not know something about.

The sun was high in the sky when they stopped to rest under a large tree. There they ate their lunch. Just as they were finishing, an old woman came hobbling along. Her back was bent and she had a crutch under one arm. Strapped to her back was a bundle of firewood, which she had gathered in the forest; and in her apron, which she had tied together to make a little sack, there were three bunches of birch switches. Suddenly she slipped and fell. She screamed, for she had broken her leg. The poor woman!

Johannes suggested that they carry her to her home, but the stranger opened his knapsack and took out a little jar. In this there was a salve which he said could cure her leg, make it whole and well again, so that she could walk home by herself, as if her leg had never been broken. As payment he wanted the three bunches of birch switches she carried in her apron.

"You want to be well paid," said the old woman, and nodded very strangely. She did not want to give up her switches, yet it was not pleasant to lie there on the road with a broken leg, so she gave the switches to the stranger. As soon as he had rubbed a little salve on her leg she was up and walking better than she had before. It was an unusual salve, not the kind that you can buy at the pharmacy.

"What will you do with the switches?" asked Johannes.

"Oh, I just took a fancy to them because I am a strange fellow, I suppose," said the wayfarer, and they walked on in silence.

"Look at those heavy, dark clouds," remarked Johannes, pointing to the horizon. "We are in for a storm."

"No," laughed his companion, "they are not clouds, they are mountains. Beautiful high mountains which one can climb right up into the sky, where the air is always fresh. They are marvelous, believe me. Tomorrow we shall reach that far out in the wide world."

But the mountains were farther away than they thought; it was the next evening before they came to the foothills. Here started the great black forests that covered most of the mountainsides. There were boulders as large as whole villages. It would not be easy to cross these mountains; therefore Johannes' traveling companion suggested that they stay at an inn for the night to be fresh for the morning's climb.

In the public room of the inn a crowd had gathered; a traveling puppet theater was just about to give a performance. The spectators sat in rows facing the little stage. In the first row was a fat old butcher. He had taken the best seat and next to him sat his dog, a ferocious-looking bulldog.

The comedy began. It was a very nice play with a king and a queen in it. They sat on a throne and had golden crowns on their heads. The queen had a long dress that trailed behind her; it was expensive but she could afford it. Wooden dolls with handlebar mustaches and glass eyes stood at the doors, opening and closing them in order to air the room. It was a lovely comedy with nothing tragic about it at all; but just as the queen was crossing the stage the bulldog—God knows what the dog was thinking; his master, in any case, was not holding onto him—jumped right up on the stage and grabbed the queen by her waist with his great jaws. Crunch! Crack! It was a tragedy after all!

The poor man who owned the puppet theater and had played all the parts was beside himself with misery. The queen was the most beautiful of all his dolls and now the bulldog had beheaded her. When all the rest of the audience had gone, Johannes' traveling companion said that he would repair the doll. He took out his little jar and put some salve on the doll. It was the same salve that had helped the poor woman when she broke her leg. As soon as the salve had been smeared on the doll she was whole again, but that was not all! The doll could now move her little limbs by herself. She needed no strings to make her walk. The puppeteer was delighted; now he didn't have to pull her strings any more. The queen could dance by herself and that was more than any of the other dolls could do.

When night came and everyone at the inn had gone to bed, deep and sorrowful sighs were heard. The lamenting kept on, and finally they all got up to see what was the matter. The sighing came from the theater. The puppeteer opened the box that was also the small stage. All the wooden dolls were lying in a great heap. There were the king and his followers, and it was they who were sighing so mournfully. They stared with their glass eyes out into the darkness; they wanted to be rubbed with the magic salve so they, too, would be able to move and dance like the queen.

The queen kneeled down and held out her golden crown, while she spoke: "Please take this in return for putting some salve on my husband and his courtiers."

The puppeteer, who owned the theater and all the dolls, felt so sad that he cried, and promised the wayfarer that he would give him all the money he received the following night if only he would smear a little salve on four or five of the other dolls. Johannes' friend said he cared not for money; what he wanted was the old sword that the theater director had hanging from his belt. As soon as it was given to him, he rubbed a little salve on six of the dolls. They started instantly to dance so prettily that all the real people, who had been standing about watching them, began to dance too. The coachman danced with the cook, and the waiters with the maids. The poker tried to dance with the little brass shovel that stood by the fireplace; but they didn't dance far: they fell with a clatter after they had taken their first step. It was an exciting night!

The next day Johannes and his friend left the inn and started to climb the mountains. Upward they went through the dark forest of fir trees, until the church steeples in the valley looked like little red berries amidst all the greenery below them. They could see far and wide;

before them were views of dozens of places where they had not been. Johannes had never seen so much of the beautiful world all at once. The sun shone down from a cloudless blue sky. From the valleys they heard the sound of the hunters' horns; the melody was so beautiful that tears came into his eyes and he could not help saying out loud: "Oh, God, I could kiss you for your kindness to us all, for having given us such a beautiful world to live in!"

His companion had also folded his hands and was looking out over the forest and the towns. All at once they heard a strange but pleasant sound above them; they looked up. There was a great white swan and the beautiful bird was singing as they had never heard a bird sing before. But its voice grew weaker and weaker; and finally it bent its head toward its body and fell to the ground, right at their feet. There the lovely bird lay, dead.

"What wonderful wings!" cried the wayfarer. "A pair of wings as white and large as those must be worth a lot. I shall have them! It is fortunate I have a sword." With a single stroke he cut off both of the dead swan's wings, and now they were his.

They traveled mile after mile, and yet they still were in the mountains. At last they came to a large town. More than a hundred towers shone as if they were made of silver, while the sunlight played upon them. In the middle of the town there was a great marble castle with a roof of gold, and that was where the king lived.

Johannes and his friend stopped at an inn outside the walls because they wanted to wash and change their clothes before entering the city. The innkeeper told them that the king was a very kind and friendly man who never did anyone any harm; but what a daughter he had! Oh, God preserve us, she was a horrible princess! Oh, she was beautiful enough. There was no one lovelier to look at; but what good was that when she was as cruel and wicked as any witch, and had already caused the death of many a fine prince? She had proclaimed that anyone could propose to her—prince or beggar alike. She didn't care who her suitor was; all he had to do to win her hand and become king when her father died was to answer correctly three questions that she asked him; but if he failed, then he must have his head chopped off or be hanged—that's how heartless the beautiful princess was.

Her poor old father was very sad indeed, but he could do nothing about it, for once, long ago, he had promised her never to interfere in the manner she chose a husband. Every prince who had come to woo the princess had failed to guess the correct answers to her questions and had been either beheaded or hanged; but there was not one who had not been warned beforehand, and he need not have proposed. Still the old king was so upset and sorry about all the suffering that once a year he spent a whole day on his knees and ordered his whole army to do the same. They prayed that the princess would become good, but she didn't. The old ladies who drank schnapps colored it black to show that they were in mourning, and that was the most they could do.

"What a horrible princess," said Johannes. "She should be switched, that is what she deserves. If I were the old king, I would beat her until I drew blood."

Just at that moment they heard the people outside shouting, "Hurrah!" The princess was riding by. She was so beautiful that anyone who looked at her forgot how wicked she was; and that's why everyone was now shouting, "Hurrah!" Twelve lovely maidens in white silk dresses, with golden tulips in their hands, riding on jet-black horses, were with her. The princess herself rode a milk-white horse; its bridle was set with rubies and diamonds. Her dress was of the purest gold, and the whip she carried in her hand looked like a sunbeam. The golden crown on her head was like the stars of heaven, and her cape was made out of thousands of butterfly wings; and yet she was far more beautiful than all her clothes.

When Johannes saw her, his face became as red as blood dripping from a wound and he could not utter a word. The princess looked like the girl with a golden crown that he had dreamed about the night his father died. She was so beautiful, and he already loved her so much, that he could not believe that she was an evil witch who ordered men to be beheaded or hanged, because they could not guess the answers to the questions she asked them.

"Anyone can propose to her, even a poor man like me. I will go to the castle, for nothing can stop me from going," Johannes announced.

Everyone begged him not to go, for they all agreed that he would fare no better than the others who had tried; even his traveling companion advised him against it, but Johannes was not to be dissuaded. He brushed his clothes, polished his shoes, and combed his yellow hair; then he went alone into the town and straight up to the castle.

"Come in!" called the old king when Johannes came knocking.

Johannes opened the door to the castle, and the old king, wearing a dressing gown and embroidered slippers, welcomed him. The king had his golden crown on his head, his scepter in one hand, and the golden apple of state in the other. "Wait a moment," he said, while he tucked the apple under his arm so that he could shake hands with Johannes. But as soon as he heard that it was another suitor who had come, he started to cry so bitterly that both the apple and the scepter fell on the floor, and he had to dry his eyes with his dressing gown. Poor old king!

"Don't do it!" he begged. "You will be no more fortunate than any of the others. Come and see!" And he led Johannes into the princess' private garden. Ugh! It was a horrible sight! In every tree were hanging the bodies of three or four princes who had proposed marriage to the princess but had not been able to answer the three questions she asked. When the wind blew, their skeletons rattled and made such a racket that they frightened all the birds, so that none ever flew into the garden. The vines wound themselves around human bones, and grinning skulls filled the flowerpots instead of flowers. Wasn't that a fine garden for a princess!

"Look around you," said the king. "You will end up like all the others. So please, please don't propose to my daughter; it really makes me very unhappy, I am very sensitive on that point."

Johannes kissed the old king's hand and said that he was sure everything would be all right, for he was very much in love with the lovely princess.

At that moment the princess came riding into the castle yard followed by all her ladies in waiting. The king and Johannes went out to greet her. How beautiful she was as she gave Johannes her hand. Now he was even more in love than he had been before; surely, she could not be a cruel and wicked witch. They all went up into the great hall and there the page boys served cookies and jam. But the old king was so sad that he didn't eat anything; besides, he thought the cookies were too hard.

It was decided that Johannes was to come to the castle the next morning and there in front of the judges and the king's council answer the question the princess would ask. If he could answer it, then he would have to come back and answer two more questions on the two following days, but no one as yet had ever answered the princess' first question, so the day she asked it had been the last of their lives.

Johannes was not worried or frightened about what was going to happen. He was happily dreaming about the beautiful princess. He was confident that God would help him, though he didn't know exactly how; nor did he give it much thought as he skipped through the streets on his way back to the inn, where his friend was waiting for him.

Johannes could not stop talking about how beautiful the princess was and how kindly she had received him. He longed for the next day when he would see her again and try his luck at guessing the answer to her question.

His friend shook his head; he was not happy. "I am very fond of you," he said. "We could have remained together a long time yet, and now I have to lose you. Poor, dear Johannes, I feel like crying but shan't do it. It would spoil our last evening together, so let us be happy. Let's be gay; tomorrow when you are gone there will be time for my tears."

The whole town had heard that the princess had a new suitor, and they all went into mourning. The theater was closed, and the little old ladies who sold candy put black crepe around their chocolate pigs. The king and all the priests went to church and prayed on their knees. Everyone was miserable, for no one believed that poor Johannes would fare better than all the other suitors had.

Late in the evening the wayfarer ordered a bowl of punch and said to Johannes that now they ought to drink to the health of the princess. When Johannes had drunk his second glass, he was so tired that he no longer could keep his eyes open and fell asleep. His friend lifted him gently from the chair and laid him on the bed.

When the darkest hour of the night had almost come, Johannes' friend tied the swan's wings on his back and stuck into his pocket the largest bunch of switches that he had got from the old lady for curing her leg. He opened the window and flew out over the town to the royal castle, where he landed on the balcony of the princess and hid in a corner next to her window.

The clock in the tower struck the quarter before the hour; it would soon be midnight. The whole town was still. Suddenly the princess' window opened and out she flew, her white cape trailing behind her; on her back were a pair of large black wings. The wayfarer made himself invisible so that no one could see him. Behind the princess he flew, whipping her so hard that he drew blood. She was flying toward the big black mountain beyond the city. The wind took hold of her cape and spread it out like the sail of a ship, and the moon shone through it.

"Oh, how it is hailing! How it is hailing!" moaned the princess every time the switches hit her back.

Finally, when she reached the mountain, she knocked on it as if it were a door. The mountain rumbled like thunder and opened itself so the princess could enter. Right behind her was Johannes' friend, though she could not see him, for he was invisible.

They were walking through a long, high corridor. The walls were lighted curiously by the glow of red spiders who ran up and down like little flames. Now they were in a great hall built of silver and gold. Along the walls was a row of blue and red flowers, as large as sunflowers; but one could not pick them, for their stems were snakes and their faces were the fire shooting out of the snakes' mouths. The ceilings were studded with glowworms and sky-blue bats whose thin, fragile wings beat constantly. What a strange sight! In the middle of the hall stood a throne, which rested on the skeletons of four horses; their bridles were made of red spiders. The seat of the throne itself was milk-white glass, and the pillows were little black mice who were biting each other's tails. Above it was a canopy made of pink spider webs, decorated with little green flies that shone like precious stones. On the throne sat an old troll with a crown on his ugly head and a scepter in his hand. He kissed the princess on the forehead and invited her to sit down beside him on the throne.

Now the music began. Big black grasshoppers played on mouth organs. Owls beat themselves on their stomachs: they were the drums. It was a funny concert. Small black trolls with jack-o'-lanterns in their hats were dancing. No one could see the wayfarer, who was standing behind the throne watching and listening to everything. The courtiers entered; they were very elegant and distinguished. But anyone who looked at them carefully could see what they really were: cabbage heads attached to broomsticks, which the troll had made alive by witchcraft, and then dressed in beautifully embroidered robes. But they were of no importance: courtiers are only for show.

After the dancing had gone on for a while, the princess told the troll about her new suitor and asked him what question she should ask him the next morning.

"Listen," said the troll, "ask him to guess what you are thinking about, and then think about something very commonplace, because he will never guess that. Just think of your shoes. Then have his head cut off, but don't forget to bring me his eyes tomorrow night, I love to eat them."

The princess curtsied most humbly and said that she wouldn't forget the eyes. Then the troll commanded the mountain to open itself again and the princess started her flight back to the castle. Johannes' friend was flying right behind her, and he beat her so severely with his switches that she moaned loudly about the terrible hailstorm and was glad when she finally reached the window of her bedchamber. The wayfarer flew back to the inn, where Johannes was still sleeping. He took off his wings and went to bed, for he had a right to be tired.

Very early the next morning, when Johannes awoke, his friend told him that he had had a strange dream. He had dreamed about the princess and her shoes. "So when the princess asks you what she is thinking about, do remember to say, her shoes," he said. Of course, that was what he had heard the troll tell the princess that she should be thinking about; but the wayfarer did not tell Johannes about his visit to the mountain.

"Well, I can just as well say one thing as the other," said Johannes, "and maybe you have dreamed the true answer, for I am sure that God wants to help me. Still, I think we should say good-by to each other, for if I guess wrong I shall never see you again."

They kissed and Johannes went into the town and straight up to the castle. The big hall was filled with people; all the judges sat in easy chairs and had eiderdown pillows on which to rest their heads, for they had grave matters to think about. The king paced the floor with a white handkerchief in his hands and constantly dried his eyes. The princess entered; she was even more beautiful than she had been the day before. She greeted everyone graciously and kindly, and took Johannes' hand in hers and said: "Good morning, dear friend."

Now Johannes had to guess what she was thinking about. She looked ever so kindly toward him, but when she heard the word "shoes," her face grew as white as chalk and her body shook. She couldn't hide that Johannes had given the right answer.

Glory be, how happy the old king was! He turned a somersault, and the people clapped both for him and for Johannes, who had guessed the answer to the first question.

Johannes' friend was pleased when he heard how well everything had gone. But Johannes folded his hands and thanked God, for he was certain that it was He who had helped him and would probably help him with the other questions. The following morning he would have to answer the second one.

The second evening passed just like the first. As soon as Johannes slept, his traveling companion tied the swan's wings on his back and followed the princess. But he now brought along two of the bundles of switches and beat her even harder. Again no one saw him and he heard everything that was said. This time the princess was to think about her gloves. Early the next morning he told Johannes that he had dreamed that the princess would think of her gloves.

When Johannes guessed correctly the whole court turned somersaults, as they had seen the king do the day before. But the princess had to lie down on her divan and wouldn't speak to anyone.

Now everything depended on what Johannes said the next morning. If he guessed right the third time, she would have to marry him and he would inherit the kingdom when her father died; but if he didn't he would lose his life and the troll would eat his pretty eyes.

That evening Johannes went to bed early, said his prayers, and slept peacefully; while the wayfarer tied the swan's wings on his back, stuck his sword in his belt, and taking all three bundles of switches with him, flew to the castle.

It was pitch-dark. There was such a storm that the tiles were blown off the roofs, and the trees in the princess' garden, in which the skeletons hung, swayed as reeds do in the wind. Every minute the lightning flashed, and the thunder roared continually, as if it were one great thunderclap that lasted the whole night through.

The window opened, the princess flew out. Her face was as white as death, but she laughed at the storm, which was not wild enough for her taste. Her white cape whirled around her like a great sail. Johannes' friend beat her so hard with the three bundles of birch branches that blood dripped down on the earth far below and the princess could hardly fly.

At last she reached the mountain. "It is hailing! What a storm!" she said to the troll. "I have never been out in weather like that before."

"Yes, you can get too much of a good thing," said the troll.

Now the princess told him that Johannes had guessed what she had been thinking a second time. "If he guesses right again tomorrow, then he will have won. I shall never visit this mountain again and never be able to do any more magic. Oh, it is so sad!"

"He will not be able to guess your thoughts tomorrow, not unless he is a greater wizard than I am! I shall think of something that he has never seen. Now let us be merry!" The troll took the princess by the hand and they danced among the little trolls and the jack-o'-lanterns. On the walls the glowing red spiders ran up and down like tiny tongues of fire. The owls beat the drums. The crickets sang. The black grasshoppers blew on their mouth organs. It was a grand ball!

They danced until it was very late and the princess had to return or she would be missed at the castle. The troll said he would follow her home: that would give them a little more time together.

As they flew through the storm, Johannes' friend wore out his three bundles of switches on their backs. Never before had the troll experienced such a hailstorm. Outside the castle he said good-by to the princess and whispered to her, "Think of my head."

The wayfarer had heard what the troll said. Just as the princess had disappeared into her bedchamber and the troll turned to fly home, he grabbed him by his long black beard and with one stroke of his sword cut off the troll's head. He threw the body into the lake for the fishes to eat, but the ugly head he wrapped in his silk handkerchief and took it with him to the inn; then he went to bed and to sleep.

The next morning he gave the handkerchief to Johannes but told him that he must not untie it before the princess had asked him to guess what she was thinking about.

The big hall in the castle was so crowded with people that they stood as close together as radishes do when they have been bound in bunches by a farmer. The judges and the king's council were sitting in their easy chairs, resting their heads on eiderdown pillows. The king had put on brand-new robes and had had his crown and his scepter polished, which made them look very nice. But the princess was very pale and dressed in black; she looked as if she were attending a funeral.

"What am I thinking about?" she asked.

Johannes untied the handkerchief. He was shocked and frightened when he saw the horrible head of the troll. All the people shuddered, for it was a terrifying sight, but the princess sat as still as a stone statue and did not utter a word. At last she rose. Without looking at anyone or at anything, without turning to the right or the left, she sighed deeply, gave Johannes her hand, and said: "Now you are my master. Tonight we shall be married."

"That's what I like to hear!" shouted the king. "That's the way it ought to be!"

Everyone shouted, "Hurrah!" The royal guards marched down the streets with a band in front of them. The church bells rang; the old ladies who sold the candy took the black crepe off their chocolate pigs. Three oxen, stuffed with ducks and chickens, were roasted on the town square for everyone to eat. The fountains splashed the finest wine; and if you bought two pennies' worth of pretzels, then the baker gave you six muffins with raisins as part of the bargain.

When evening came, the whole town was illuminated; the soldiers fired their cannons, and little boys shot off firecrackers. In the castle all the most elegant people in the country were gathered; they ate and drank and toasted each other and all the young people danced; one could hear the young girls singing far away:

> "So many a fair maiden
> Calls for a dance so gay.
> The air with music is laden.
> Beautiful maiden, turn about,
> Stamp your feet, and whirl,
> Until your shoes are worn out.

But the princess was still a witch and didn't love Johannes at all. The wayfarer had not forgotten this, so he gave Johannes three feathers from the swan's wings and a little bottle filled with liquid, and said to him: "Tonight, next to the marriage bed place a large tub of water and throw these feathers and empty this liquid into it. When the princess starts to get into bed, push her into the tub and duck her three times under the water; then she will no longer be a witch and will love you dearly."

Johannes took his friend's advice. When he shoved the princess underneath the water the first time, she screamed and changed into a black swan with fiery eyes, who wiggled and strained in his grasp. The second time she was plunged into the water, she became a white swan with a black ring around her neck. Johannes prayed to God as he pushed her under the third time; and instantly she changed into the most beautiful princess. She was even lovelier than before; and she thanked him, with tears in her eyes, for having broken the evil spell.

The next day the king came visiting; so did the court and half of the people of the town. They all wanted to pay their respects to the bridal couple. Last of all came Johannes' traveling companion. He had a knapsack on his back and a walking stick in his hand. Johannes kissed him and begged him not to leave. "All my good fortune is your doing!" he cried.

But his friend shook his head; then he spoke softly and gently. "No, my time on earth is over. I have paid my debt. Do you remember the dead man whom the evil men wanted to harm? You gave everything you owned so that he could rest in his coffin. I am the dead man." With these words he disappeared.

The wedding celebration lasted a month. Johannes and the princess loved each other ever so much. The old king lived for many years and enjoyed having his grandchildren sit on his knee and play with his scepter, while Johannes ruled the whole kingdom.

## The Little Mermaid

Far, far from land, where the waters are as blue as the petals of the cornflower and as clear as glass, there, where no anchor can reach the bottom, live the mer-people. So deep is this part of the sea that you would have to pile many church towers on top of each other before one of them emerged above the surface.

Now you must not think that at the bottom of the sea there is only white sand. No, here grow the strangest plants and trees; their stems and leaves are so subtle that the slightest current in the water makes them move, as if they were alive. Big and small fishes flit in and out among their branches, just as the birds do up on earth. At the very deepest place, the mer-king has built his castle. Its walls are made of coral and its long pointed windows of amber. The roof is oyster shells that are continually opening and closing. It looks very beautiful, for in each shell lies a pearl, so lustrous that it would be fit for a queen's crown.

The mer-king had been a widower for many years; his mother kept house for him. She was a very intelligent woman but a little too proud of her rank: she wore twelve oysters on her tail; the nobility were only allowed six. Otherwise, she was a most praiseworthy woman, and she took excellent care of her grandchildren, the little princesses. They were six lovely mermaids; the youngest was the most beautiful. Her complexion was as fine as the petal of a rose and her eyes as blue as the deepest lake but, just like everyone else down there, she had no feet; her body ended in a fishtail.

The mermaids were allowed to play all day in the great hall of the castle, where flowers grew on the walls. The big amber windows were kept open and the fishes swam in and out, just as the swallows up on earth fly in through our windows if they are open. But unlike the birds of the air, the fishes were not frightened, they swam right up to the little princesses and ate out of their hands and let themselves be petted.

Around the castle was a great park where there grew fiery-red and deep-blue trees. Their fruits shone as though they were the purest gold, their flowers were like flames, and their branches and leaves were ever in motion. The earth was the finest sand, not white but blue, the color of burning sulphur. There was a blue tinge to everything, down on the bottom of the sea. You could almost believe that you were suspended in mid-air and had the blue sky both above and below you. When the sea was calm, the sun appeared like a crimson flower, from which all light flowed.

Each little princess had her own garden, where she could plant the flowers she liked. One of them had shaped her flower bed so it resembled a whale; and another, as a mermaid. The youngest had planted red flowers in hers: she wanted it to look like the sun; it was round and the crimson flowers did glow as though they were so many little suns. She was a strange little child: quiet and thoughtful. Her sisters' gardens were filled with all sorts of things that they had collected from shipwrecks, but she had only a marble statue of a boy in hers. It had been cut out of stone that was almost transparently clear and had sunk to the bottom of the sea when the ship that had carried it was lost. Close to the statue she had planted a pink tree; it looked like a weeping willow. The tree was taller than the sculpture. Its long soft branches bent toward the sand; it looked as if the top of the tree and its root wanted to kiss each other.

The princesses liked nothing better than to listen to their old grandmother tell about the world above. She had to recount countless times all she knew about ships, towns, human beings, and the animals that lived up on land. The youngest of the mermaids thought it particularly wonderful that the flowers up there had fragrance, for that they did not have on the bottom of the sea. She also liked to hear about the green forest, where the fishes that swam among the branches could sing most beautifully. Grandmother called the birds "fishes"; otherwise, her little grandchildren would not have understood her, since they had never seen a bird.

"But when you are fifteen, then you will be allowed to swim to the surface," she promised. "Then you can climb up on a rock and sit and watch the big ships sail by. If you dare, you can swim close enough to the shore to see the towns and the forest."

The following year, the oldest of the princesses would be fifteen. From one sister to the next, there was a difference in age of about a year, which meant that the youngest would have to wait more than five whole years before she would be allowed to swim up from the bottom of the sea and take a look at us. But each promised the others that she would return after her first day above, and tell about the things she had seen and describe what she thought was loveliest of all. For the old grandmother could not satisfy their curiosity.

None of the sisters longed so much to see the world above as the youngest, the one who had to wait the longest before she could leave her home. Many a night this quiet, thoughtful little mermaid would stand by the open window, looking up through the dark blue waters where the fishes swam. She could see the moon and the stars; they looked paler but larger down here under the sea. Sometimes a great shadow passed by like a cloud and then she knew that it was either a whale or a ship, with its crew and passengers, that was sailing high above her. None on board could have imagined that a little beautiful mermaid stood in the depths below them and stretched her little white hands up toward the keel of their ship.

The oldest of the sisters had her fifteenth birthday and swam up to the surface of the sea. When she returned she had hundreds of things to tell. But of everything that had happened to her, the loveliest experience by far, she claimed, had been to lie on a sandbank, when the sea was calm and the moon was out, and look at a great city. The lights from the windows and streets had shone like hundreds of stars; and she had been able to hear the rumbling of the carriages and the voices of human beings and, best of all, the sound of music. She had seen all the church towers and steeples and heard their bells ring. And just because she would never be able to enter the city, she longed to be able to do that more than anything else.

How carefully her youngest sister listened to every word and remembered everything that she had been told. When, late in the evening, the little mermaid would stand dreaming by the window and look up through the blue water, then she imagined that she could see the city and hear the bells of the churches ringing.

The next year the second of the sisters was allowed to swim away from home. Her little head had emerged above the water just at the moment when the sun was setting. This sight had been so beautiful that she could hardly describe it. The whole heaven had been covered in gold and the clouds that had sailed above her had been purple and crimson. A flight of wild swans, like a white veil just above the water, had flown by. She had swum toward the sun, but it had set, taking the colors of the clouds, sea, and sky with it.

The third of the sisters, who came of age the following year, was the most daring among them. She had swum way up a broad river! There she had seen green hills covered with vineyards, castles, and farms that peeped out through the great forests. She had heard the birds sing and the sun had been so hot that she had had to swim under the water, some of the time, just to cool off. In a little bay, she had come upon some naked children who were playing and splashing in the water. She had wanted to join them, but when they saw her they got frightened and ran away. A little black animal had come: it was a dog. But she had never seen one before. It had barked so loudly and fiercely that she became terrified and swam right back to the sea. What she never would forget as long as she lived were the beautiful forest, the green hills, and the sweet little children who had been able to swim even though they had no fishtails as she had.

The fourth of the sisters was timid. She stayed far away from shore, out in the middle of the ocean. But that was the most beautiful place of all, she asserted. You could see ever so far and the sky above was like a clear glass bell. The ships she had seen had been so far away that they had looked no bigger than gulls. But the little dolphins had turned somersaults for her and the great whales had sprayed water high up into the air, so that it looked as though there were more than a hundred fountains.

The fifth sister's birthday was in the winter and, therefore, she saw something none of her sisters had seen. The ocean had been green, and huge icebergs had been floating on it. Each of them had been as lovely as a pearl and yet larger than the church towers that human beings built. They had the most fantastic shapes and their surface glittered like diamonds. She had climbed up on the largest one of them all; the wind had played with her long hair, and all the ships had fearfully kept away. Toward evening a storm had begun to blow; dark clouds had gathered and bolts of lightning had flashed while the thunder rolled. The waves had lifted the iceberg high up on their shoulders, and the lightning had colored the ice red. The ships had taken down their sails; and on board, fear and terror had reigned. But the mermaid had just sat on her iceberg and watched the bolts of lightning zigzag across the sky.

The first time that any of the sisters had been allowed to swim to the surface, each had been delighted with her freedom and all she had seen. But now that they were grownups and could swim anywhere they wished, they lost interest in wandering far away; after a month or two the world above lost its attraction. When they were away, they longed for their home, declaring it the most beautiful place of all and the only spot where one really felt at home.

Still, many evenings the five sisters would take each other's hands and rise up through the waters. They had voices far lovelier than any human being. When a storm began to rage and a ship was in danger of being wrecked, then the five sisters would swim in front of it and sing about how beautiful it was down at the bottom of the sea. They begged the sailors not to be frightened but to come down to them. The men could not understand the mermaids' songs; they thought it was the wind that was singing. Besides, they would never see the beauty of the world below them, for if a ship sinks the seamen drown, and when they arrive at the mer-king's castle they are dead.

On such evenings, while her sisters swam, hand in hand, up through the water, the youngest princess had to stay below. She would look sadly up after them and feel like crying; but mermaids can't weep and that makes their suffering even deeper and greater.

"Oh, if only I were fifteen," she would sigh. "I know that I shall love the world above, and the human beings who live up there!"

At last she, too, was fifteen!

"Now you are off our hands," said the old dowager queen. "Let me dress you, just as I dressed your sisters." She put a wreath of white lilies around her hair; each of the petals of every flower was half a pearl. She let eight oysters clip themselves onto the little mermaid's tail, so that everyone could see that she was a princess.

"It hurts," said the little mermaid.

"One has to suffer for position," said her old grandmother. The little mermaid would gladly have exchanged her heavy pearl wreath for one of the red flowers from her garden (she thought they suited her much better) but she didn't dare.

"Farewell," she said and rose, light as a bubble, up through the water.

The sun had just set when she lifted her head above the surface. The clouds still had the color of roses and in the horizon was a fine line of gold; in the pale pink sky the first star of evening sparkled, clearly and beautifully. The air was warm and the sea was calm. She saw a three-masted ship; only one of its sails was unfurled, and it hung motionless in the still air. Up on the yards the sailors sat, looking down upon the deck from which music could be heard. As the evening grew darker, hundreds of little colored lamps were hung from the rigging; they looked like the flags of all the nations of the world. The little mermaid swam close to a porthole and the swells lifted her gently so that she could look in through it. The great cabin was filled with gaily dressed people; the handsomest among them was a young prince with large, dark eyes. He looked no older than sixteen, and that was, in truth, his age; that very day was his birthday. All the festivities were for him. The sailors danced on the deck, and as the young prince came up to watch them, a hundred rockets flew into the sky.

The night became as bright as day and the little mermaid got so frightened that she ducked down under the water. But she soon stuck her head up again; and then it looked as if all the stars of the heavens were falling down on top of her. She had never seen fireworks before. Pinwheels turned; rockets shot into the air, and their lights reflected in the dark mirror of the sea. The deck of the ship was so illuminated that every rope could clearly be seen. Oh, how handsome the young prince was! He laughed and smiled and shook hands with everyone, while music was played in the still night.

It grew late, but the little mermaid could not turn her eyes away from the ship and the handsome prince. The colored lamps were put out. No more rockets shot into the air and no more cannons were fired. From the depth of the ocean came a rumbling noise. The little mermaid let the waves be her rocking horse, and they lifted her so that she could look in through the porthole. The ship started to sail faster and faster, as one sail after another was unfurled. Now the waves grew in size and black clouds could be seen on the horizon and far away lightning flashed.

A storm was brewing. The sailors took down the sails. The great ship tossed and rolled in the huge waves that rose as though they were mountains that wanted to bury the ship and break its proud mast. But the ship, like a swan, rode on top of the waves and let them lift her high into the sky. The little mermaid thought it was very amusing to watch the ship sailing so fast, but the sailors didn't. The ship creaked and groaned; the great planks seemed to bulge as the waves hit them. Suddenly the mast snapped as if it were a reed. It tumbled into the water. The ship heeled over, and the sea broke over it.

Only now did the little mermaid understand that the ship was in danger. She had to be careful herself and keep away from the spars and broken pieces of timber that were being flung by the waves. For a moment it grew so dark that she could see nothing, then a bolt of lightning illuminated the sinking ship. She looked for the young prince among the terrified men on board who were trying to save themselves, but not until that very moment, when the ship finally sank, did she see him.

At first, she thought joyfully, "Now he will come down to me!" But then she remembered that man could not live in the sea and the young prince would be dead when he came to her father's castle.

"He must not die," she thought, and dived in among the wreckage, forgetting the danger that she herself was in, for any one of the great beams that were floating in the turbulent sea could have crushed her.

She found him! He was too tired to swim any farther; he had no more strength in his arms and legs to fight the storm-whipped waves. He closed his eyes, waiting for death, and he would have drowned, had the little mermaid not saved him. She held his head above water and let the waves carry them where they would.

By morning the storm was over. Of the wrecked ship not a splinter was to be found. The sun rose, glowing red, and its rays gave color to the young prince's cheeks but his eyes remained closed. The little mermaid kissed his forehead and stroked his wet hair. She thought that he looked like the statue in her garden. She kissed him again and wished passionately that he would live.

In the far distance she saw land; the mountains rose blue in the morning air. The snow on their peaks was as glittering white as swan's feathers. At the shore there was a green forest, and in its midst lay a cloister or a church, the little mermaid did not know which. Lemon and orange trees grew in the garden, and by the entrance gate stood a tall palm tree. There was a little bay nearby, where the water was calm and deep. The mermaid swam with her prince toward the beach. She laid him in the fine white sand, taking care to place his head in the warm sunshine far from the water.

In the big white buildings bells were ringing and a group of young girls was coming out to walk in the garden. The little mermaid swam out to some rocks and hid behind them. She covered her head with seaweed so that she could not be seen and then peeped toward land, to see who would find the poor prince.

Soon one of the young girls discovered him. At first she seemed frightened, and she called the others. A lot of people came. The prince opened his eyes and smiled up at those who stood around him —not out at the sea, where the little mermaid was hiding. But then he could not possibly have known that she was there and that it was she who had saved him. The little mermaid felt so terribly sad; the prince was carried into the big white building, and the little mermaid dived sorrowfully down into the sea and swam home to her father's castle.

She had always been quiet and thoughtful. Now she grew even more silent. Her sisters asked her what she had seen on her first visit up above, but she did not answer.

Many mornings and evenings she would swim back to the place where she had last seen the prince. She watched the fruits in the orchard ripen and be picked, and saw the snow on the high mountains melt, but she never saw the prince. She would return from each of these visits a little sadder. She would seek comfort by embracing the statue in her garden, which looked like the prince. She no longer tended her flowers, and they grew into a wilderness, covering the paths and weaving their long stalks and leaves into the branches of the trees, so that it became quite dark down in her garden.

At last she could bear her sorrow no longer and told one of her sisters about it; and almost at once the others knew as well. But no one else was told; that is, except for a couple of other mermaids, but they didn't tell it to anyone except their nearest and dearest friends. It was one of these friends who knew who the prince was. She, too, had seen the birthday party on the ship, and she could tell where he came from and where his kingdom was.

"Come, little sister," the other princesses called, and with their arms around each other's shoulders they swam.

All in a row they rose to the surface when they came to the shore where the prince's castle stood. It was built of glazed yellow stones and had many flights of marble stairs leading up to it. The steps of one of them went all the way down to the sea. Golden domes rose above the roofs, and pillars bore an arcade that went all the way around the palace. Between the pillars stood marble statues; they looked almost as if they were alive. Through the clear glass of the tall windows, one could look into the most beautiful chambers and halls, where silken curtains and tapestries hung on the walls; and there were large paintings that were a real pleasure to look at. In the largest hall was a fountain. The water shot high up toward the glass cupola in the roof, through which the sunbeams fell on the water and the beautiful flowers that grew in the basin of the fountain.

Now that she knew where the prince lived, the little mermaid spent many evenings and nights looking at the splendid palace. She swam nearer to the land than any of her sisters had ever dared. There was a marble balcony that cast its shadow across a narrow canal, and beneath it she hid and watched the young prince, who thought that he was all alone in the moonlight.

Many an evening she saw the prince sail with his musicians in his beautiful boat. She peeped from behind the tall reeds; and if someone noticed her silver-white veil, they probably thought that they had only seen a swan stretching its wings.

Many a night she heard the fishermen talking to each other and telling about how kind and good the prince was; and she was so glad that she had saved his life when she had found him, half dead, drifting on the waves. She remembered how his head had rested on her chest and with what passion she had kissed him. But he knew nothing about his rescue; he could not even dream about her.

More and more she grew to love human beings and wished that she could leave the sea and live among them. It seemed to her that their world was far larger than hers; on ships, they could sail across the oceans and they could climb the mountains high up above the clouds. Their countries seemed ever so large, covered with fields and forests; she knew that they stretched much farther than she could see. There was so much that she wanted to know; there were many questions that her sisters could not answer. Therefore she asked her old grandmother, since she knew much about the "higher world," as she called the lands above the sea.

"If men are not so unlucky as to drown," asked the little mermaid, "then do they live forever? Don't they die as we do, down here in the sea?"

"Yes, they do," answered her grandmother. "Men must also die and their life span is shorter than ours. We can live until we are three hundred years old; but when we die, we become the foam on the ocean. We cannot even bury our loved ones. We do not have immortal souls. When we die, we shall never rise again. We are like the green reeds: once they are cut they will never be green again. But men have souls that live eternally, even after their bodies have become dust. They rise high up into the clear sky where the stars are. As we rise up through the water to look at the world of man, they rise up to the unknown, the beautiful world, that we shall never see."

"Why do I not have an immortal soul!" sighed the little mermaid unhappily. "I would give all my three hundred years of life for only one day as a human being if, afterward, I should be allowed to live in the heavenly world."

"You shouldn't think about things like that," said her old grandmother. "We live far happier down here than man does up there."

"I am going to die, become foam on the ocean, and never hear the music of the waves or see the flowers and the burning red sun. Can't I do anything to win an immortal soul?"

"No," said the old merwoman. "Only if a man should fall so much in love with you that you were dearer to him than his mother and father; and he cared so much for you that all his thoughts were of his love for you; and he let a priest take his right hand and put it in yours, while he promised to be eternally true to you, then his soul would flow into your body and you would be able to partake of human happiness. He can give you a soul and yet keep his own. But it will never happen. For that which we consider beautiful down here in the ocean, your fishtail, they find ugly up above, on earth. They have no sense; up there, you have to have two clumsy props, which they call legs, in order to be called beautiful."

The little mermaid sighed and glanced sadly down at her fishtail.

"Let us be happy," said her old grandmother. "We can swim and jump through the waves for three hundred years, that is time enough. Tonight we are going to give a court ball in the castle."

Such a splendor did not exist up above on the earth. The walls and the ceilings of the great hall were made of clear glass; four hundred giant green and pink oyster shells stood in rows along the walls. Blue flames rose from them and not only lighted the hall but also illuminated the sea outside. Numberless fishes—both big and small—swam close to the glass walls; some of them had purple scales, others seemed to be of silver and gold. Through the great hall flowed a swiftly moving current, and on that the mermen and mermaids danced, while they sang their own beautiful songs. Such lovely voices are never heard up on earth; and the little mermaid sang most beautifully of them all. The others clapped their hands when she had finished, and for a moment she felt happy, knowing that she had the most beautiful voice both on earth and in the sea.

But soon she started thinking again of the world above. She could not forget the handsome prince, and mourned because she did not have an immortal soul like his. She sneaked out of her father's palace, away from the ball, from the gaiety, down into her little garden.

From afar the sound of music, of horns being played, came down to her through the water; and she thought: "Now he is sailing up there, the prince whom I love more than I love my father and mother: he who is ever in my thoughts and in whose hands I would gladly place all my hope of happiness. I would dare to do anything to win him and an immortal soul! While my sisters are dancing in the palace, I will go to the sea witch, though I have always feared her, and ask her to help me."

The little mermaid swam toward the turbulent maelstrom; beyond it the sea witch lived. In this part of the great ocean the little mermaid had never been before; here no flowers or seaweeds grew, only the gray naked sea bed stretched toward the center of the maelstrom, that great whirlpool where the water, as if it had been set in motion by gigantic mill wheels, twisted and turned: grinding, tearing, and sucking anything that came within its reach down into its depths. Through this turbulence the little mermaid had to swim, for beyond it lay the bubbling mud flats that the sea witch called her bog and that had to be crossed to come to the place where she lived.

The sea witch's house was in the midst of the strangest forest. The bushes and trees were gigantic polyps that were half plant and half animal. They looked like snakes with hundreds of heads, but they grew out of the ground. Their branches were long slimy arms, and they had fingers as supple as worms; every limb was in constant motion from the root to the utmost point. Everything they could reach they grasped, and never let go of it again. With dread the little mermaid stood at the entrance to the forest; her heart was beating with fear, she almost turned back. But then she remembered her prince and the soul she wanted to gain and her courage returned.

She braided her long hair and bound it around her head, so the polyps could not catch her by it. She held her arms folded tightly across her breast and then she flew through the water as fast as the swiftest fish. The ugly polyps stretched out their arms and their fingers tried to grasp her. She noticed that every one of them was holding, as tightly as iron bands, onto something it had caught. Drowned human beings peeped out as white skeletons among the polyps' arms. There were sea chests, rudders of ships, skeletons of land animals; and then she saw a poor little mermaid who had been caught and strangled; and this sight was to her the most horrible.

At last she came to a great, slimy, open place in the middle of the forest. Big fat eels played in the mud, showing their ugly yellow stomachs. Here the witch had built her house out of the bones of drowned sailors, and there she sat letting a big ugly toad eat out of her mouth, as human beings sometimes let a canary eat sugar candy out of theirs. The ugly eels she called her little chickens, and held them close to her spongy chest.

"I know what you want," she cackled. "And it is stupid of you. But you shall have your wish, for it will bring you misery, little princess. You want to get rid of your fishtail, and instead have two stumps to walk on as human beings have, so that the prince will fall in love with you; and you will gain both him and an immortal soul." The witch laughed so loudly and evilly that the toad and eels she had had on her lap jumped down into the mud.

"You came at the right time," she said. "Tomorrow I could not have helped you; you would have had to wait a year. I will mix you a potion. Drink it tomorrow morning before the sun rises, while you are sitting on the beach. Your tail will divide and shrink, until it becomes what human beings call 'pretty legs.' It will hurt; it will feel as if a sword were going through your body. All who see you will say that you are the most beautiful human child they have ever seen. You will walk more gracefully than any dancer; but every time your foot touches the ground it will feel as though you were walking on knives so sharp that your blood must flow. If you are willing to suffer all this, then I can help you."

"I will," whispered the little mermaid, and thought of her prince and how she would win an immortal soul.

"But remember," screeched the witch, "that once you have a human body you can never become a mermaid again. Never again shall you swim through the waters with your sisters to your father's castle. If you cannot make the prince fall so much in love with you that he forgets both his father and mother, because his every thought concerns only you, and he orders the priest to take his right hand and place it in yours, so that you become man and wife; then, the first morning after he has married another, your heart will break and you will become foam on the ocean."

"I still want to try," said the little mermaid, and her face was as white as a corpse.

"But you will have to pay me, too," grinned the witch. "And I want no small payment. You have the most beautiful voice of all those who live in the ocean. I suppose you have thought of using that to charm your prince; but that voice you will have to give to me. I want the most precious thing you have to pay for my potion. It contains my own blood, so that it can be as sharp as a double-edged sword."

"But if you take my voice," said the little mermaid, "what will I have left?"

"Your beautiful body," said the witch. "Your graceful walk and your lovely eyes. Speak with them and you will be able to capture a human heart. Have you lost your courage? Stick out your little tongue, and let me cut it off in payment, and you shall have the potion."

"Let it happen," whispered the little mermaid.

The witch took out a caldron in which to make the magic potion. "Cleanliness is a virtue," she said. And before she put the pot over the fire, she scrubbed it with eels, which she had made into a whisk.

She cut her chest and let her blood drip into the vessel. The steam that rose became strange figures that were terrifying to see. Every minute, the witch put something different into the caldron. When the brew reached a rolling boil, it sounded as though a crocodile were crying. At last the potion was finished. It looked as clear and pure as water.

"Here it is," said the witch, and cut out the little mermaid's tongue. Now she was mute, she could neither speak nor sing.

"If any of the polyps should try to grab you, on your way back through my forest," said the witch, "you need only spill one drop of the potion on it and its arms and fingers will splinter into a thousand pieces."

But the little mermaid didn't have to do that. Fearfully, the polyps drew away when they saw what she was carrying in her hands; the potion sparkled as though it were a star. Safely, she returned through the forest, the bog, and the maelstrom.

She could see her father's palace. The lights were extinguished in the great hall. Everyone was asleep; and yet she did not dare to seek out her sisters; now that she was mute and was going away from them forever. She felt as if her heart would break with sorrow. She sneaked down into the garden and picked a flower from each of her sisters' gardens; then she threw a thousand finger kisses toward the palace and swam upward through the deep blue sea.

The sun had not yet risen when she reached the prince's castle and sat down on the lowest step of the great marble stairs. The moon was still shining clearly. The little mermaid drank the potion and it felt as if a sword were piercing her little body. She fainted and lay as though she were dead.

When the sun's rays touched the sea she woke and felt a burning pain; but the young prince stood in front of her and looked at her with his coal-black eyes. She looked downward and saw then that she no longer had a fishtail but the most beautiful, little, slender legs that any girl could wish for. She was naked; and therefore she took her long hair and covered herself with it.

The prince asked her who she was and how she had got there. She looked gently and yet ever so sadly up at him with her deep blue eyes, for she could not speak. He took her by the hand and led her up to his castle. And just as the witch had warned, every step felt as though she were walking on sharp knives. But she suffered it gladly. Gracefully as a bubble rising in the water, she walked beside the prince; and everyone who saw her wondered how she could walk so lightly.

In the castle, she was clad in royal clothes of silk and muslin. She was the most beautiful of all, but she was mute and could neither sing nor speak. Beautiful slave girls, clad in silken clothes embroidered with gold, sang for the prince and his royal parents. One sang more beautifully than the rest, and the prince clapped his hands and smiled to her; then the little mermaid was filled with sorrow, for she knew that she had once sung far more beautifully. And she thought, "Oh, if he only knew that to be with him I have given away my voice for all eternity."

Now the slave girls danced, gracefully they moved to the beautiful music. Suddenly the little mermaid lifted her hands and rose on the tips of her toes. She floated more than danced across the floor. No one had ever seen anyone dance as she did. Her every movement revealed her loveliness and her eyes spoke far more eloquently than the slave's song.

Everyone was delighted, especially the prince. He called her his little foundling. She danced again and again, even though each time her little foot touched the floor she felt as if she had stepped on a knife. The prince declared that she should never leave him, and she was given permission to sleep in front of his door on a velvet pillow.

The prince had men's clothes made for her, so that she could accompany him when he went horseback riding. Through the sweet-smelling forest they rode, where green branches touched their shoulders and little birds sang among the leaves. Together they climbed the high mountains and her feet bled so much that others noticed it; but she smiled and followed her prince up ever higher until they could see the clouds sail below them, like flocks of birds migrating to foreign lands.

At night in the castle, while the others slept, she would walk down the broad marble stairs to the sea and cool her poor burning feet in the cold water. Then she would think of her sisters, down in the deep sea.

One night they came; arm in arm they rose above the surface of the water, singing ever so sadly. She waved to them, and they recognized her, and they told her how much sorrow she had brought them. After that they visited her every night; and once she saw, far out to sea, her old grandmother. It had been years since she had stuck her head up into the air; and there, too, was her father the mer-king with his crown on his head. They stretched their hands toward her but did not dare come as near to the land as her sisters.

Day by day the prince grew fonder and fonder of her; but he loved her as he would have loved a good child, and had no thought of making her his queen. And she had to become his wife or she would never have an immortal soul, but on the morning after his marriage would become foam on the great ocean.

"Don't you love me more than you do all others?" was the message in the little mermaid's eyes when the prince kissed her lovely forehead.

"Yes, you are the dearest to me," said the prince, "for you have the kindest heart of them all. You are devoted to me and you look like a young girl I once saw, and will probably never see again. I was in a shipwreck. The waves carried me ashore, where a holy temple lay. Many young girls were in service there; one of them, the youngest of them all, found me on the beach and saved my life. I saw her only twice, but she is the only one I can love in this world; and you look like her. You almost make her picture disappear from my soul. She belongs to the holy temple and, therefore, good fortune has sent you to me instead, and we shall never part."

"Oh, he does not know that it was I who saved his life," thought the little mermaid. "I carried him across the sea to the forest where the temple stood. I hid behind the rocks and watched over him until he was found. I saw that beautiful girl whom he loves more than me!" And the little mermaid sighed deeply, for cry she couldn't. "He has said that the girl belongs to the holy temple and will never come out into the world, and they will never meet again. But I am with him and see him every day. I will take care of him, love him, and devote my life to him."

Everyone said that the young prince was to be married; he was to have the neighboring king's daughter, a beautiful princess. A magnificent ship was built and made ready. It was announced that the prince was traveling to see the neighboring kingdom, but that no one believed. "It is not the country but the princess he is to inspect," they all agreed.

The little mermaid shook her head and smiled; she knew what the prince thought, and they didn't.

"I must go," he had told her, "I must look at the beautiful princess, my parents demand it. But they won't force me to carry her home as my bride. I can't love her. She does not look like the girl from the temple as you do. If I ever marry, I shall most likely choose you, my little foundling with the eloquent eyes." And he kissed her on her red lips and played with her long hair, and let his head rest so near her heart that it dreamed of human happiness and an immortal soul.

"Are you afraid of the ocean, my little silent child?" asked the prince as they stood on the deck of the splendid ship that was to sail them to the neighboring kingdom. He told the little mermaid how the sea can be still or stormy, and about the fishes that live in it, and what the divers had seen underneath the water. She smiled as he talked, for who knew better than she about the world on the bottom of the ocean?

In the moonlit night, when everyone slept but the sailor at the rudder and the lookout in the bow, she sat on the bulwark and looked down into the clear water. She thought she saw her father's palace; and on the top of its tower her old grandmother was standing with her silver crown on her head, looking up through the currents of the sea, toward the keel of the ship. Her sisters came; they looked at her so sorrowfully and wrung their white hands in despair; she waved to them and smiled. She wanted them to know that she was happy, but just at that moment the little cabin boy came and her sisters dived down under the water; he saw nothing but some white foam on the ocean.

The next morning the ship sailed into the harbor of the great town that belonged to the neighboring king. All the church bells were ringing, and from the tall towers trumpets blew, while the soldiers stood at attention, with banners flying and bayonets on their rifles.

Every day another banquet was held, and balls and parties followed one after the other. But the princess attended none of them, for she did not live in the palace; she was being educated in the holy temple, where she was to learn all the royal virtues. But at last she came.

The little mermaid wanted ever so much to see her; and when she finally did, she had to admit that a more beautiful girl she had never seen before. Her skin was so delicate and fine, and beneath her long dark lashes smiled a pair of faithful, dark blue eyes.

"It is you!" exclaimed the prince. "You are the one who saved me, when I lay half dead on the beach!" And he embraced his blushing bride.

"Oh, now I am too happy," he said to the little mermaid. "That which I never dared hope has now happened! You will share my joy, for I know that you love me more than any of the others do."

The little mermaid kissed his hand; she felt as if her heart were breaking. His wedding morning would bring her death and she would be changed into foam of the ocean.

All the churchbells rang and heralds rode through the streets and announced the wedding to the people. On all the altars costly silver lamps burned with fragrant oils. The priests swung censers with burning incense in them, while the prince and the princess gave each other their hands, and the bishop blessed them. The little mermaid, dressed in silk and gold, held the train of the bride's dress, but her ears did not hear the music, nor did her eyes see the holy ceremony, for this night would bring her death, and she was thinking of all she had lost in this world.

The bride and bridegroom embarked upon the prince's ship; cannons saluted and banners flew. On the main deck, a tent of gold and scarlet cloth had been raised; there on the softest of pillows the bridal couple would sleep.

The sails were unfurled, and they swelled in the wind and the ship glided across the transparent sea.

When it darkened and evening came, colored lamps were lit and the sailors danced on the deck. The little mermaid could not help remembering the first time she had emerged above the waves, when she had seen the almost identical sight. She whirled in the dance, glided as the swallow does in the air when it is pursued. Everyone cheered and applauded her. Never had she danced so beautifully; the sharp knives cut her feet, but she did not feel it, for the pain in her heart was far greater. She knew that this was the last evening that she would see him for whose sake she had given away her lovely voice and left her home and her family; and he would never know of her sacrifice. It was the last night that she would breathe the same air as he, or look out over the deep sea and up into the star-blue heaven. A dreamless, eternal night awaited her, for she had no soul and had not been able to win one.

Until midnight all was gaiety aboard the ship, and the mermaid danced and laughed with the thought of death in her heart. Then the prince kissed his bride and she fondled his long black hair and, arm in arm, they walked into their splendorous tent, to sleep.

The ship grew quiet. Only the sailor at the helm and the little mermaid were awake. She stood with her white arms resting on the railing and looked toward the east. She searched the horizon for the pink of dawn; she knew that the first sunbeams would kill her.

Out of the sea rose her sisters, but the wind could no longer play with their long beautiful hair, for their heads had been shorn.

"We have given our hair to the sea witch, so that she would help you and you would not have to die this night. Here is a knife that the witch has given us. Look how sharp it is! Before the sun rises, you must plunge it into the heart of the prince; when his warm blood sprays on your feet, they will turn into a fishtail and you will be a mermaid again. You will be able to live your three hundred years down in the sea with us, before you die and become foam on the ocean. Hurry! He or you must die before the sun rises. Our grandmother mourns; she, too, has no hair; hers has fallen out from grief. Kill the prince and come back to us! Hurry! See, there is a pink haze on the horizon. Soon the sun will rise and you will die."

The little mermaid heard the sound of her sisters' deep and strange sighing before they disappeared beneath the waves.

She pulled aside the crimson cloth of the tent and saw the beautiful bride sleeping peacefully, with her head resting on the prince's chest. The little mermaid bent down and kissed his handsome forehead. She turned and looked at the sky; more and more, it was turning red. She glanced at the sharp knife; and once more she looked down at the prince. He moved a little in his sleep and whispered the name of his bride. Only she was in his thoughts, in his dreams! The little mermaid's hand trembled as it squeezed the handle of the knife, then she threw the weapon out into the sea. The waves turned red where it fell, as if drops of blood were seeping up through the water.

Again she looked at the prince; her eyes were already glazed in death. She threw herself into the sea and felt her body changing into foam.

The sun rose out of the sea, its rays felt warm and soft on the deathly cold foam. But the little mermaid did not feel death, she saw the sun, and up above her floated hundreds of airy, transparent forms. She could see right through them, see the sails of the ship and the blood-red clouds. Their voices were melodious, so spiritual and tender that no human ear could hear them, just as their forms were so fragile and fine that no human eye could see them. So light were they that they glided through the air, though they had no wings. The little mermaid looked down and saw that she had an ethereal body like theirs.

"Where am I?" she asked; and her voice sounded like theirs—so lovely and so melodious that no human music could reproduce it.

"We are the daughters of the air," they answered. "Mermaids have no immortal soul and can never have one, unless they can obtain the love of a human being. Their chance of obtaining eternal life depends upon others. We, daughters of the air, have not received an eternal soul either; but we can win one by good deeds. We fly to the warm countries, where the heavy air of the plague rests, and blow cool winds to spread it. We carry the smell of flowers that refresh and heal the sick. If for three hundred years we earnestly try to do what is good, we obtain an immortal soul and can take part in the eternal happiness of man. You, little mermaid, have tried with all your heart to do the same. You have suffered and borne your suffering bravely; and that is why you are now among us, the spirits of the air. Do your good deeds and in three hundred years an immortal soul will be yours."

The little mermaid lifted her arms up toward God's sun, and for the first time she felt a tear.

She heard noise coming from the ship. She saw the prince and the princess searching for her. Sadly they looked at the sea, as if they knew that she had thrown herself into the waves. Without being seen, she kissed the bride's forehead and smiled at the prince; then she rose together with the other children of the air, up into a pink cloud that was sailing by.

"In three hundred years I shall rise like this into God's kingdom," she said.

"You may be able to go there before that," whispered one of the others to her. "Invisibly, we fly through the homes of human beings. They can't see us, so they don't know when we are there; but if we find a good child, who makes his parents happy and deserves their love, we smile and God takes a year away from the time of our trial. But if there is a naughty and mean child in the house we come to, we cry; and for every tear we shed, God adds a day to the three hundred years we already must serve."

## The Emperor's New Clothes

Many, many years ago there was an emperor who was so terribly fond of beautiful new clothes that he spent all his money on his attire. He did not care about his soldiers, or attending the theater, or even going for a drive in the park, unless it was to show off his new clothes. He had an outfit for every hour of the day. And just as we say, "The king is in his council chamber," his subjects used to say, "The emperor is in his clothes closet."

In the large town where the emperor's palace was, life was gay and happy; and every day new visitors arrived. One day two swindlers came. They told everybody that they were weavers and that they could weave the most marvelous cloth. Not only were the colors and the patterns of their material extraordinarly beautiful, but the cloth had the strange quality of being invisible to anyone who was unfit for his office or unforgivably stupid.

"This is truly marvelous," thought the emperor. "Now if I had robes cut from that material, I should know which of my councilors was unfit for his office, and I would be able to pick out my clever subjects myself. They must weave some material for me!" And he gave the swindlers a lot of money so they could start working at once.

They set up a loom and acted as if they were weaving, but the loom was empty. The fine silk and gold threads they demanded from the emperor they never used, but hid them in their own knapsacks. Late into the night they would sit before their empty loom, pretending to weave.

"I would like to know how they are getting along," thought the emperor; but his heart beat strangely when he remembered that those who were stupid or unfit for their office would not be able to see the material. Not that he was really worried that this would happen to him. Still, it might be better to send someone else the first time and see how he fared. Everybody in town had heard about the cloth's magic quality and most of them could hardly wait to find out how stupid or unworthy their neighbors were.

"I shall send my faithful prime minister over to see how the weavers are getting along," thought the emperor. "He will know how to judge the material, for he is both clever and fit for his office, if any man is."

The good-natured old man stepped into the room where the weavers were working and saw the empty loom. He closed his eyes, and opened them again. "God preserve me!" he thought. "I cannot see a thing!" But he didn't say it out loud.

The swindlers asked him to step a little closer to the loom so that he could admire the intricate patterns and marvelous colors of the material they were weaving. They both pointed to the empty loom, and the poor old prime minister opened his eyes as wide as he could; but it didn't help, he still couldn't see anything.

"Am I stupid?" he thought. "I can't believe it, but if it is so, it is best no one finds out about it. But maybe I am not fit for my office. No, that is worse, I'd better not admit that I can't see what they are weaving."

"Tell us what you think of it," demanded one of the swindlers.

"It is beautiful. It is very lovely," mumbled the old prime minister, adjusting his glasses. "What patterns! What colors! I shall tell the emperor that it pleases me ever so much."

"That is a compliment," both the weavers said; and now they described the patterns and told which shades of color they had used. The prime minister listened attentively, so that he could repeat their words to the emperor; and that is exactly what he did.

The two swindlers demanded more money, and more silk and gold thread. They said they had to use it for their weaving, but their loom remained as empty as ever.

Soon the emperor sent another of his trusted councilors to see how the work was progressing. He looked and looked just as the prime minister had, but since there was nothing to be seen, he didn't see anything.

"Isn't it a marvelous piece of material?" asked one of the swindlers; and they both began to describe the beauty of their cloth again.

"I am not stupid," thought the emperor's councilor. "I must be unfit for my office. That is strange; but I'd better not admit it to anyone." And he started to praise the material, which he could not see, for the loveliness of its patterns and colors.

"I think it is the most charming piece of material I have ever seen," declared the councilor to the emperor.

Everyone in town was talking about the marvelous cloth that the swindlers were weaving.

At last the emperor himself decided to see it before it was removed from the loom. Attended by the most important people in the empire, among them the prime minister and the councilor who had been there before, the emperor entered the room where the weavers were weaving furiously on their empty loom.

"Isn't it *magnifique?*" asked the prime minister.

"Your Majesty, look at the colors and the patterns," said the councilor.

And the two old gentlemen pointed to the empty loom, believing that all the rest of the company could see the cloth.

"What!" thought the emperor. "I can't see a thing! Why, this is a disaster! Am I stupid? Am I unfit to be emperor? Oh, it is too horrible!" Aloud he said, "It is very lovely. It has my approval," while he nodded his head and looked at the empty loom.

All the councilors, ministers, and men of great importance who had come with him stared and stared; but they saw no more than the emperor had seen, and they said the same thing that he had said, "It is lovely." And they advised him to have clothes cut and sewn, so that he could wear them in the procession at the next great celebration.

"It is magnificent! Beautiful! Excellent!" All of their mouths agreed, though none of their eyes had seen anything. The two swindlers were decorated and given the title "Royal Knight of the Loom."

The night before the procession, the two swindlers didn't sleep at all. They had sixteen candles lighting up the room where they worked. Everyone could see how busy they were, getting the emperor's new clothes finished. They pretended to take the cloth from the loom; they cut the air with their big scissors, and sewed with needles without thread. At last they announced: "The emperor's clothes are ready!"

Together with his courtiers, the emperor came. The swindlers lifted their arms as if they were holding something in their hands, and said, "These are the trousers. This is the robe, and here is the train. They are all as light as if they were made of spider webs! It will be as if Your Majesty had almost nothing on, but that is their special virtue."

"Oh yes," breathed all the courtiers; but they saw nothing, for there was nothing to be seen.

"Will Your Imperial Majesty be so gracious as to take off your clothes?" asked the swindlers. "Over there by the big mirror, we shall help you put your new ones on."

The emperor did as he was told; and the swindlers acted as if they were dressing him in the clothes they should have made. Finally they tied around his waist the long train which two of his most noble courtiers were to carry.

The emperor stood in front of the mirror admiring the clothes he couldn't see.

"Oh, how they suit you! A perfect fit!" everyone exclaimed. "What colors! What patterns! The new clothes are magnificent!"

"The crimson canopy, under which Your Imperial Majesty is to walk, is waiting outside," said the imperial master of court ceremony.

"Well, I am dressed. Aren't my clothes becoming?" The emperor turned around once more in front of the mirror, pretending to study his finery.

The two gentlemen of the imperial bedchamber fumbled on the floor, trying to find the train which they were supposed to carry. They didn't dare admit that they didn't see anything, so they pretended to pick up the train and held their hands as if they were carrying it.

The emperor walked in the procession under his crimson canopy. And all the people of the town, who had lined the streets or were looking down from the windows, said that the emperor's clothes were beautiful. "What a magnificent robe! And the train! How well the emperor's clothes suit him!"

None of them were willing to admit that they hadn't seen a thing; for if anyone did, then he was either stupid or unfit for the job he held. Never before had the emperor's clothes been such a success.

"But he doesn't have anything on!" cried a little child.

"Listen to the innocent one," said the proud father. And the people whispered among each other and repeated what the child had said.

"He doesn't have anything on. There's a little child who says that he has nothing on."

"He has nothing on!" shouted all the people at last.

The emperor shivered, for he was certain that they were right; but he thought, "I must bear it until the procession is over." And he walked even more proudly, and the two gentlemen of the imperial bedchamber went on carrying the train that wasn't there.

# The Magic Galoshes

### PART ONE: THE BEGINNING

In one of the houses on East Street, near the King's New Square, which is in the very center of Copenhagen, a big party was being held. It was one of those parties you have to have once in a while, to which you invite everyone who has invited you to a party; then the slate is clean and you can be invited out again. Half of the guests were already playing cards; the other half were sitting in the parlor, waiting for the hostess to entertain them. The conversation lagged, until someone mentioned the Middle Ages; and someone else remarked that he thought that that earlier era was better than our own. Then Councilman Knap held forth ardently on his favorite theory that olden times were far superior to the present. He quite convinced his hostess; and they both agreed to disagree with Oersted's evaluation, to be found in the almanac, which asserts that on the whole modern times are the best. The councilman said that he thought the reign of King Hans was the period in which life had been pleasantest and happiest.

While that discussion is going on, let us go out into the entrance hall, where the wraps, coats, walking canes, umbrellas, and galoshes have been deposited. Here sat two women: one was young, the other old. At first sight you might believe that they were personal maids who had accompanied their mistresses—some ancient dowager or withered old maid—to the party. But on closer examination this thought was dismissed; they were, in any case, not ordinary servants. Their hands were too delicate, they carried themselves too royally, and their clothes were of a strange, if not daring, fashion. They were fairies. The younger one was only a lady's maid to the lady in waiting of the Fairy of Happiness; and she distributed only lesser blessings. The older one looked very serious and was the Fairy of Sorrow herself; she always delivers her gifts personally to make sure you receive them.

They were telling each other what they had done during that day. The fairy who was only a servant of the lady in waiting to the Fairy of Happiness had very little to tell. She had saved a hat from being drenched; she had obtained a greeting—a slight inclining of the head: a nod—for an honest and decent man from a very elegant nonentity, and small things of that nature. "But I'll let you in on a secret," she added. "Today is my birthday and as a present I have been given the honor of giving humanity a very special pair of galoshes. They are magic galoshes and anyone who has them on is transported instantly to the time in history or the place in the world that he desires to be. And so, at last, some people will have a chance to be happy on earth!"

"Do you believe that?" asked Sorrow. "People will be even more unhappy than they were before and will bless that moment when they get rid of the galoshes."

"Don't be silly," said the younger fairy. "I'll leave the galoshes here by the door; somebody will take them by mistake and obtain happiness!"

So ended the fairies' conversation.


PART TWO: WHAT HAPPENED TO THE COUNCILMAN

It was late and Councilman Knap, who was getting ready to go home, was so engrossed in thinking about the times of King Hans that he put on the magic galoshes instead of his own. As he stepped out onto East Street, he was back in the time of King Hans, which meant that he put his foot down in half a foot of slush and mud because in King Hans's times there was no such thing as a sidewalk.

"It's terribly muddy!" he muttered. "Where is the sidewalk? And what happened to the street lamp?"

The moon had not risen high enough to shed any light on the street; the air was dense and heavy. Everything seemed to be shrouded in darkness. At the corner of the street, below the picture of the Virgin, burned a tiny oil lamp. Its light was so dim that the councilman did not notice it until he was standing right underneath the painting of the Mother and Child.

"I'll bet this is an art gallery," he thought. "And they've forgotten to take down their sign."

Two men, dressed as men did in the time of King Hans, walked past him.

"I wonder why they were wearing those clothes? I'll bet they're coming from a masquerade."

Suddenly he heard pipes and drums. Flares lighted up the street. The councilman stopped to look at the strange procession. First there was a group of drummers, who beat their instruments with great force; they were followed by some soldiers carrying torches and armed with crossbows; finally a man, obviously of great importance and belonging to the church, went by. The councilman was so surprised by the sight that he asked a passer-by who the dignitary was.

"He is the Bishop of Zealand," was the answer.

"My God, what has happened to the bishop?" sighed the councilman, shaking his head. "No," he thought. "That couldn't have been the bishop." And, still in a quandary, he walked the full length of East Street and across High Bridge Square; but he could not find the bridge to the Castle Square. In the darkness he could make out the banks of a stream, where he came upon two young men who were lying in a boat.

"Would you like to be rowed over to the island, sir?" one of them asked.

"Over to the island!" exclaimed the councilman, who still did not realize that he had taken a journey backward in time. "I want to go to Christian's Harbor, I live on Little Beech Road."

Amazed, the two young men just stared at him.

"Just tell me where the bridge is," demanded the councilman. "It is disgraceful that none of the lamps is lighted; and there is mud everywhere, as if one were walking in a swamp."

The more he and the ferrymen talked, the less comprehensible they were to each other.

"I can't understand your dialect," he said finally, and turned his back on them.

But where was the bridge? And where was the railing that followed the edge of the stream, to prevent people from falling into it? "It's a scandal that such conditions are allowed." And he had never been as disgusted with his own times as he was now.

"I'll go to the King's New Square where I can get a cab, otherwise I'll never get home."

When he reached the end of East Street, the moon came out. "What is that strange structure?" he muttered to himself when he saw the old eastern gates of the city. He spied a little door and opened it, and expected to be in the King's New Square, but he found himself on a meadow. A channel cut across it; a few bushes were growing; and there were the sheds used for storage by the sea captains from Holland; the whole area was then called the Dutch Meadows.

"Either I have walked into a mirage or I am drunk," whimpered the poor councilman. "Oh, what is this all about? Where am I?"

Convinced that he was very ill, he turned back. When he again stood on East Street, the moonlight had made it possible for him to notice that most of the buildings were half-timbered houses with thatched roofs.

"I am not well," he sighed. "Even though I have had only one glass of punch, it didn't agree with me. It was wrong of them to serve baked salmon and punch, they don't go together. I think I shall return and tell my hostess. They would want to know how wretchedly I feel. . . . But it might be embarrassing; they may have gone to bed already."

He searched for the house where he had attended the party, but he couldn't find it. "Oh, this is horrible! I can't even recognize East Street. Where are all the shops? The houses look as bad as those in the provinces. I am ill. I must not be proud, I need help. This is the house where I dined, I think. . . . It doesn't look the same. But there's a light on. Someone is up. I am terribly sick, I'll have to go in."

The door was ajar and he pushed it open. It was an inn, a tavern of the times. There were several people there: a sea captain, a couple of tradesmen or artisans, and two scholars. They were drinking beer and looking thoughtfully into their tankards. Since they were deep in a discussion, they paid no attention whatever to the new arrival.

"I am sorry to disturb you," began Councilman Knap to the inn-keeper's wife, "but I am not feeling well. Could I trouble you to call a droshky? I have to go to Christian's Harbor and there must still be some cabs at the King's New Square . . ."

The woman stared at him, shook her head, and then spoke to him in German. The councilman thought she could only understand German and therefore repeated his request in that tongue. This, together with his strange dress, convinced the innkeeper's wife that he was a foreigner. She realized, too, that he was ill and she brought him a glass of water. It had been drawn from the well in her garden and was very brackish.

The councilman buried his head in his hands, sighed, and tried to understand what could have happened. He felt that he must say something, and noticing a large sheet of paper lying on a table nearby, he asked, "Is that this evening's newspaper?"

The innkeeper's wife did not understand what he meant; but she handed him the sheet of paper. It was a woodcut of a vision in the sky above the city of Cologne. On seeing such an old print, the council-man got very excited.

"This is very valuable! Where have you found it? It is rare and very interesting! What's written below the woodcut is nonsense, of course. Today we know that what they saw in the sky was the northern lights; and they are probably caused by electricity."

Two of the men who sat near him heard what the councilman had said. One of them rose from his seat, politely doffed his hat, and said in a very serious tone, "You must be a very learned man."

"Oh no!" protested Councilman Knap. "I know just a little about a lot of things, as one is expected to."

"*Modestia* is one of the highest virtues," exclaimed the other man. "Though I must comment: *mihi secus videtur,* to what you have said. But I should be only too glad to suspend my *judicium.*"

"May I be so bold as to ask whom I have the pleasure of speaking to?" asked the councilman.

"I hold a *baccalaureus* in the Holy Writ," he replied.

The councilman thought that the man fitted his title. He was convinced that he was talking to an old schoolmaster from darkest Jutland, where one still could encounter such eccentrics.

"Here is not *locus docendi,*" continued the old man. "But still I beg you to speak, for I am sure you are well read in ancient literature."

"Of course," the councilman replied, "I like to read the classics, but I like to read modern authors as well. But not these new novels about everyday people; there are so many of them already."

"Everyday people?"

"I mean the new naturalistic novels about the poor; they are filled with such romantic ideas," the councilman explained.

"Oh yes!" the scholar smiled. "They are very well done. The king prefers the romances about Sir Iffven and Sir Gaudian, knights of King Arthur of the Round Table."

"I don't know which novel you are referring to, was it written by Heiberg?" asked the councilman, who was talking of the most popular Danish author of the middle of the nineteenth century.

"No, not Heiberg," the man replied, much surprised. "It was put out by Godfred von Gehmen."

"Von Gehmen, so that's the author, he has a very old name; that's what the first printer in Denmark was called."

"Yes, he is our first and foremost printer of books," agreed the scholar.

The conversation continued quite pleasantly for a while. One of the tradesmen talked about the plague that had harassed Copenhagen a few years before—by which he meant in 1484. The councilman nodded; he thought the man was talking about the cholera epidemic that had taken place when he was a young man. The conversation then turned to the activities of the English privateers, who in 1490 had captured the ships in the very harbor of Copenhagen; and since the councilman believed that the War of 1801 was being discussed, he agreed wholeheartedly when the English were condemned.

But then matters got worse; every few minutes he exchanged an undertaker's smile with one of the other guests. The councilman thought the scholar very ignorant; and that man found him too fantastic and daring. Sometimes they just sat staring at each other in wonder; then the *baccalaureus* would break into Latin, thinking that the councilman understood that language more easily; but it was to no avail.

"How goes it with you, good man?" the innkeeper's wife tugged the councilman's sleeve in order to attract his attention; and the poor man—who while he was talking had forgotten what had happened to him—all at once recalled all his misery.

"Oh, my God! Where am I?" he wailed, and almost fainted.

"We want claret, mead, and Bremer beer!" shouted one of the customers. And you"—he pointed at the councilman—"are going to drink with us."

Two girls, one of them wearing a bonnet of two different colors, curtsied and served them.

The councilman shivered, as if he were freezing. "What is this all about? What is happening to me?" he whimpered. But he had to drink and so he did; and he emptied his tankard as often as the other customers.

One of the tradesmen accused the councilman of being drunk. The councilman said that he did not doubt that he was, and begged the other man to get him a cab so he could go home.

"A what?" the man demanded.

"A cab . . . I want to hire a cab, a droshky."

"He's a Muscovite!" someone shouted angrily.

Never before had Councilman Knap been in such vulgar company. He decided that his country must have returned to heathenism. "This is the most horrible moment of my life," he mumbled. And it was then that he got the idea of escaping by diving under the table and crawling toward the door. But just as he was nearing the portal his newly found friends discovered him and decided that he must not escape. They grabbed him by the legs; and luckily for him, they pulled off the galoshes, and that was the end of the magic.

Councilman Knap was lying on the sidewalk. The street lamp was burning brightly above him. The house before him was familiar. He was back on the East Street he knew. Not far from him sat a night watchman, who was sleeping.

"My God, I must have lain here in the street and dreamed it all. Yes, this is East Street. How horribly that one glass of punch upset me."

A few minutes later he was sitting in a cab, on his way to his home in Christian's Harbor. He thought of the misery and the terror he had just experienced; and he praised with all his heart the reality of

his own time, which despite all its faults was superior to the age he
had just been in. And that was very sensible of the councilman.

## PART THREE: THE ADVENTURES OF THE NIGHT WATCHMAN

"Look, there are an old pair of galoshes," said the night watchman.
"They must belong to the lieutenant. They are lying right outside his
front door."

The night watchman would gladly have rung the bell and delivered
the galoshes to their owner, but it was late and he was afraid of waking everyone in the house.

"Such overshoes must keep your feet warm. I wonder what it feels
like to have them on?" he remarked as he pulled the galoshes over
his shoes. "How soft the leather is." They fitted him perfectly.

"Life is strange," the night watchman philosophized, while he
looked up at the lieutenant's windows, where a light was still burning.
"He could be in his comfortable bed, sleeping; but he isn't, he's
pacing the floor. He is a happy man. He has neither wife nor
children, and every evening he is invited to another party. I wish I
were the lieutenant, then I should be happy."

No sooner had he said his desire aloud than the galoshes fulfilled
it. The night watchman entered the body and the soul of the lieutenant. He was standing in his room and in his hand he had a sheet of
pink paper, on which had been written a poem. The lieutenant had
composed it himself.

And who has not, at some time or other, felt like writing poetry?
You have a thought. You write it down, and there is a poem. This
one was called: "I Wish I Were Rich!"

> "I wish I were rich"—Oh, this I swore
> Before my first long pants I wore.
> "I wish I were rich" I cried in despair,
> For then an officer's uniform I would wear.
> The silver spurs, the sword I gained,
> But money, alas, I never obtained.
>
> One evening when I was young and gay
> A tiny girl kissed me in childish play.
> I was rich in fairy tales and clever,

> Though, in money, as poor as ever.
> She cared only for these tales so old
> And then I was wealthy, though not in gold.
>
> "I wish I were rich," without hope I moan,
> The little girl into a woman has grown.
> A maiden so perfect, so clever and good,
> If she my heart's fairy tale understood,
> If she that loved me once, loves me still!
> Oh, God! poverty breaks the strongest will.
>
> I wish I were rich in solace and peace
> And the pain of hope had long ago ceased.
> You, whom I love, shed over this poem no tears.
> Read it, as the old read verses from youthful years.
> No, better it were if these words of despair
> Were writ not on paper but in the night air.

Such are the verses one writes when one is in love; and a sensible man does not have them printed. A lieutenant, love, and poverty: that is an eternal triangle, a broken cupid's arrow. That was the way the lieutenant felt too. He leaned against the windowpane and sighed.

"The poor night watchman, down in the street, is far happier than I am. He has a home, a wife, and children who are sad when he is sad and rejoice when he is gay. Oh, he is far happier than I am. I wish I were he!"

At that very moment the night watchman became the night watchman again; since the galoshes had made him a lieutenant, they could return him to being himself. "That was a terrible dream," he mumbled. "I was the lieutenant, but that was no blessing. I missed my wife and my little ones." He shook his head; the dream stayed with him. A shooting star flew across the heavens.

"There it fell," the night watchman, who was still wearing the magic galoshes, said to himself. "I really wouldn't mind being able to see such things a little closer; especially the moon, for that has a good size and wouldn't slip through your fingers. The student whose clothes my wife washes claims that, when we die, our spirits go visiting the stars. That's not true, I'm sure. But it would be fun to be able to see the moon. I wish my soul would leap up there; then, as far as I am concerned, my body could stay right here on this step."

There are certain wishes that are best left unsaid, especially if you are wearing magic galoshes. Listen to what happened to the poor night watchman.

We have all traveled by steam: either by train or across the sea on a steamer. But the speed of steam is a snail's pace compared to the speed of light. It flies nineteen million times quicker than the fastest race horse; and electricity is even faster than light. Death is an electric shock administered to our hearts; and with the wings of electricity our souls leave our bodies. It takes the light of the sun eight minutes and some seconds to travel more than a hundred million miles. But with the speed of electricity it takes the soul even less time to accomplish the same journey. The space between planets is for the soul no greater than the distance between our own home and that of a friend's, even when the latter is very close by. Unfortunately, the electric shock to the heart deprives us of our bodies; unless, like the night watchman, one is lucky enough to be wearing magic galoshes.

Within seconds, the night watchman had traveled more than two hundred thousand miles and landed on the moon. The moon is made of much lighter material than the earth. It is as soft as new-fallen snow. He found himself overlooking one of the many mountain craters that you can see in Dr. Mälder's *Great Atlas of the Moon*. I'm sure you know of it. A good mile down, inside the dead volcano, there was a city. It looked like the whites of eggs poured into a glass of water. Transparent towers, cupolas, and sail-shaped balconies swayed in the thin atmosphere. Our own earth floated like a fiery red globe far above him.

The town was inhabited by very strange-looking creatures, and all of them were, I suppose, what you would call human. One could hardly expect that the night watchman would be able to understand their language, but he could.

Without any difficulty at all, he followed their discussion about our earth and whether it was possible for people to live on it. They concluded that the atmosphere was too heavy to allow for any highly developed, thinking creature like a moonian to survive there. They agreed that only on the moon could be found the conditions necessary for life; and therefore, moonians were the first human beings.

But let's return to East Street and see what happened to the body of the night watchman. Lifeless, he sat on the stairs; his spiked mace had fallen out of his hands, and his eyes were fixed on the moon, as if they were trying to watch his honest soul walking about up there.

"What is the time, night watchman?" asked a passer-by. When he got no answer, he flicked the good night watchman's nose; and the body lost its balance and lay dead on the sidewalk.

The man who had touched the night watchman was terrified. He looked at the night watchman again: he was dead and dead he remained! It was reported and discussed, and the body taken to the hospital.

Now think what a strange situation it would have been if the soul had suddenly come back to East Street looking for its body and had not found it. Probably it would have gone first to the police station; then to the Lost and Found Office to look among the ownerless objects; and finally, to the hospital. But it's comforting to know that the soul is more cunning when it's on its own and doesn't have a body to weigh it down.

As you know, the body was taken to the hospital and put into the bathroom to be washed. But first, of course, it had to be undressed; and the very first article of clothing that was removed were the galoshes. And the soul had to return; straight down from the moon it came and the night watchman came back to life at once. He declared that this had been the worst night in his life and he wouldn't go through another like it, not even for two marks; but now it was over and done with.

The night watchman left the hospital the same day; but the galoshes stayed behind.

PART FOUR: THE TRAPPED HEAD AND A MOST UNUSUAL TRIP

Everyone who lives in Copenhagen knows what the entrance to Frederiks Hospital looks like; but since it is possible that this story will be read as well by people who don't live there we had better describe it.

All around the hospital there's a high fence of heavy iron bars and a gate that is locked at night. They say that very thin medical students have been able to squeeze themselves in and out between the bars, when they were supposed to be on duty. The part of the body which they always found most difficult to get through was the head.

In this—as in many other uncomfortable situations in this world—the ones with the smallest heads were the luckiest. Enough, that will have to do as the introduction.

One night, one of the medical students, whose head could best be described—if we are speaking only physically—as fat, was on duty. It was also raining in torrents outside. But neither of these facts seemed to deter him; he had something to do in town which would only take about a quarter of an hour, and he didn't want to have to explain to the gatekeeper the nature of his errand. He decided to try to squeeze through two of the bars in the fence.

He noticed the galoshes that the night watchman had left behind. "Lucky they're here, I can use them in this rotten weather," he thought, and put them on. "Now all I have to do is squeeze through those bars.

"If only my head were through," he mumbled aloud. And immediately his big round head glided through the bars. Naturally, it was the galoshes that had accomplished this for him. But now, there he was, with his body on one side and his head on the other.

He took a deep breath and tried to squeeze his body through. "I'm too fat!" he cried as he continued to push. "I thought my head would be the most difficult to get through."

Now he tried to pull his head back between the bars, but that was impossible. He could move his neck but that was all. The magic galoshes had placed him in a very difficult position. Unfortunately, he never thought of wishing out loud that his body and his head were both on the same side of the fence; he just pushed and pulled and yanked.

The rain was pouring down and the street was empty. He was too far away to be heard by the gatekeeper, no matter how loudly he shouted. He would have to stay right where he was until morning; then a blacksmith would be called to saw through one of the iron bars. But that would take time. All the boys, in their blue uniforms, from the school across the street would come to watch the blacksmith at his work, and so would half the neighborhood and all the passers-by. And there he would be like a prisoner in the stocks with the street filled with people laughing at him. He felt the blood rush to his head just thinking about it.

"It will drive me mad," he muttered. "I can feel myself going insane. Oh, how I wish my head were free and it were all over and done with."

It was a pity he hadn't said that right away. As soon as his thoughts became words, his head was free. He ran into the hospital as quickly as he could. He was very disturbed by the scare the magic galoshes had given him.

The night passed and so did the next day, without anyone coming to the hospital to claim the galoshes.

There was a performance that evening in a little theater in Canon Street. There was not an empty seat in the theater. Among the recitations there was a new poem. We must hear it:

Grandmother's Glasses
My grandmother's head is cleverly turned;
Two hundred years ago she would have been burned.
She knows every joy and every sorrow
That will happen to people tomorrow.
She knows the future, what next year will bring,
For whom funeral bells will toll or wedding bells ring.
What is my future? Denmark's? or art?
With such secrets my grandmother will not part.
I plagued her; first she was silent, then she got mad.
With downcast eyes I tried to look sorry and sad.
I am her favorite, her sweet little darling,
And so I became happy, as in springtime the starling.
For Grandmother handed me her glasses and said,
"I grant you your wish. Put these on your head.
Then go where people are gathered, to one of these places
Where you do not see one but a thousand faces.
Then look through my glasses and you will be able
To read their futures, like cards on the table."
With joy I ran, feeling bold and free.
But where should I go, where would most people be?
To an amusement park? No, I might catch cold.
To a church? No, there gather only the very old.
To Main Street? Everyone walks there in such a haste.
To the theater? Yes, there people have time to waste.
So here I am, your futures to read and tell.
I will draw truth, like water from a well.
Permit me to put on Grandmother's glasses
And we shall know the future as time passes.
Your silence as agreement I take
And into cards I you now make.

At this point the actor who was reciting put on an old pair of spectacles, then he continued:

It is true! How amazing! It makes me smile.
I wish you could see it, too, for a while.
There are no kings, but of knaves aplenty,
In spades and clubs I count more than twenty.
The little Queen of Spades, she has her part;
To the Jack of Diamonds, she has lost her heart.
Her passion is great. Oh, I must look away.
No wonder the Jack looks so happy and gay.
I see money inherited and spent in waste.
I see dark strangers arriving in haste.
Oh, it is all to me quite clear,
But other questions are to be answered here.
What will happen to Denmark next year?
I see it! Oh, my goodness! Oh dear!
If I tell, no newspaper will be sold, I fear.
It is better to wait the news to hear.
The theater, what is its future, its fate?
Silence! I seek the director's friendship, not his hate.
As for my own future, which is nearest to my heart,
I see it clearly, but will not with that secret part.
Do you want me the happiest of all here to find?
It would be easy, but would it be kind?
Do you want me to tell which one will live the longest?
Oh, that kind of news will weaken the strongest.
Should I tell this, or that? With doubt I am filled,
I wish no hope in my neighbor killed.
Maybe it is best that I no one's fortune tell
And leave each to his own heaven or hell,
And show my respect to God and to man
By not trying to do what no one can.

The actor had recited the poem very well and there was enthusiastic applause. Among the audience sat the young student, whom we know from the hospital. He had completely forgotten his misadventure of the night before. As no one had come to claim the galoshes and the weather had not changed, the student was wearing them.

He liked the poem very much, and he thought the idea interesting.

He wouldn't mind having such a pair of glasses; but he had no particular desire to see the future through them. What would interest him was to be able to see into other people's hearts. "The future you'll find out about soon enough anyway," he thought. "But what goes on in another man's soul, never. Now take the people who are sitting in the first row; if one could climb into their hearts, as if each one were a different store . . . oh, how my eyes would go shopping! Inside that lady over there"—he bent forward and glanced at a very well-dressed woman—"I'd find a fashion show. . . . The woman next to her has an empty store, in need of being cleaned. . . . Others would sell solider things, there'd be more than one hardware store, I am sure." The student sighed. "I know one little store I'd love to visit; but the owner of that store has already hired a salesman and he's the only bad thing in the whole store. Some owners will stand in their doorways, and, bowing politely, invite one to step in. Oh, how I wish I could!"

That was enough for the galoshes. The student became at once invisible and was sent on the most unusual journey that anyone has ever taken: a trip through the hearts of all the people in the front row of a theater.

The first was the heart of a lady; and the student thought he had entered an orthopedic institute, as the place where doctors remove and straighten bones is called. He was in a room filled with plaster casts of crooked backs, deformed limbs, misshapen bodies. Here the lady preserved all the faults of her friends. She had personally cast them and kept them as a museum, which she visited every day.

He got out as quickly as he could and entered the next person. He seemed to be in a great cathedral; innocent white doves flew above the altar. He would have liked to stay and fall on his knees to worship there, but he had to travel on. Yet even so short a visit had done him good. He could still hear the tones from the organ; he felt as if he were a better person, and not so undeserving to enter the next temple.

This was a garret where a poor, ill mother lay in bed; but God's glorious sun shone in through the windows, and beautiful roses grew in boxes on the roof. Two bluebirds sang in childish joy, while the sick mother blessed her daughter.

Now he was crawling on his hands and knees through a butcher shop. Everywhere there was meat and more meat. He was in the heart of a very rich and highly respected man whose name was well known to all. Then he climbed into the heart of this prominent man's wife. It was an old pigeon coop that was about to fall apart. Her husband's portrait was a weather vane, which was connected to the doors of the coop in such a way that, when he turned, the doors opened or closed.

Now he was in a cabinet of mirrors like the one in Rosenborg Castle. But here the mirrors all greatly enlarged the objects they reflected. On the floor, sitting as still as the Dalai Lama, was this person's tiny personality marveling at its own greatness.

He had entered a sewing box. The place was filled with sharp needles. "I'll bet that this is the heart of an old maid I have gotten into," he thought. But he was wrong. It was the heart of a young officer who had already been decorated several times. He was called a man of esprit!

Very confused, the student tumbled out of the hearts that he had wished to visit. He could not collect his thoughts, and decided that his too lively imagination was playing tricks on him.

"Oh, my God," he sighed. "I think I must have a disposition for madness. Isn't it hot in here? I feel so flushed!" Then he recalled all that had happened to him the night before, how his head had been caught between the iron bars of the fence. "That's where it happened," he muttered. "You have to catch things like that at the outset. What I need is a Russian steam bath. I wish I were lying on the highest shelf in the hot room, right now."

There he was on the top shelf of the steam bath with all his clothes on, including the galoshes. Drops of water dripped from the ceiling down on his face.

"Ow!" he shouted, and jumped down from the shelf and ran to the showers.

An attendant screamed: what was a fully dressed man doing in a steam bath?

The student was quick-witted enough to whisper, "It's a bet." But the first thing he did, when he got back home and into his own room, was to plaster a Spanish fly on his back, in the hope that it would draw out the madness.

The next morning he had a bloody back; and that was all he had got out of wearing the magic galoshes.

PART FIVE: THE COPYIST'S METAMORPHOSIS

The night watchman—have you forgotten him?—well, he had not forgotten the galoshes that he had found in the street. He went back to the hospital for them; and when neither the lieutenant nor anyone else in the neighborhood would claim them, he took them to the police station.

"Why, they look just like mine," said one of the copyists who worked there. He put the galoshes down next to his own. "Not even a shoemaker could tell them apart."

"Excuse me . . ." A policeman had entered; he had some papers that he wanted the copyist to make duplicates of. The two men talked for a while. When the policeman left and the copyist looked down once more at the two pairs of galoshes he didn't know which were his. Was it the pair on the right or the one on the left?

"It must be the ones that are wet," he thought. But that was wrong, for the wet pair were the magic galoshes. But why shouldn't someone who works for the police be allowed to make a mistake? The scrivener put them on and stuck the papers he had just been given in his pocket. He had decided to do the rest of his work at home.

It was Sunday morning, and when he stepped outside the weather was so lovely that he changed his mind and set out for Frederiksberg. A walk would do him good. No one was more conscientious or hardworking than he was, and he deserved a little outing: didn't he spend almost all his time behind a desk?

As he walked along, he thought of nothing at all; and therefore the galoshes had no opportunity to show their magic power.

In a park, along a shaded path, he met a friend, a young poet, who told him that on the following day he was going abroad.

"So you're off again," remarked the coypist. "You poets are so happy and free. You can fly wherever you want to; the rest of us have a chain around our ankles."

"True," the poet replied. "But the other end of that chain is fastened to a breadbox. You don't have to worry about tomorrow; and when you grow old you'll have a pension."

"But you lead a better life," said the copyist. "Both of us use the pen, but I only copy unimportant trivialities, while you write poetry and are complimented by the whole world. That must be a pleasure."

The poet shook his head and so did the copyist. They parted, each with his own opinion intact.

"Poets are a queer lot," thought the scrivener. "I wouldn't mind being one. I am sure I shouldn't write such whining verse as most of them do. This is a day for a poet. The spring air is clear; the clouds look newly washed; and there is the smell of greenness everywhere. I haven't felt like this for many years."

He had become a poet already. It wasn't very noticeable; but the idea that poets are different from other human beings is very foolish. There are many people who are more poetic and more sensitive than some of our best poets. What makes the poet unique is that he has a spiritual memory. He can retain his thoughts and his feelings until he has clarified them in words; and this other people cannot do. This was the gift that had now been given to the copyist. But change needs a period of transition, and this was what the copyist had just gone through.

"How lovely the air smells," mumbled the poet. "It reminds me of the smell of violets in my Aunt Lone's apartment. . . . Strange, I haven't thought of her for years. She was a very kind old maid who lived behind the Stock Exchange. No matter how cold the winter was, she always had something—a flower or a branch that was in bloom or just about to sprout—standing in a vase. In midwinter, I have seen violets in her home.

"I remember how I used to put a copper coin on her stove; and then when it was hot, take if off and put it up against the window where it would melt a hole in the ice on the frozen glass pane. Through that peephole I saw the world in a strange perspective! Down by the canals stood the icebound ships, deserted except for the screeching crows.

"When the first breeze of spring began to blow, everything changed. The port was filled with activity. People bustled about, and then they would sing and shout, 'Hurrah!' as the ice was sawn into pieces and the ships were made ready for their journeys to foreign lands.

"And I have sat behind a desk in the police station making out other people's passports, but never my own. That is my fate." He sighed deeply and stood still. "I have never felt like this before. It must be the spring air. I am uneasy and happy at the same time."

From his pocket he took out a sheaf of papers. "These dry pages will give me something else to think about," he said and held them up, so that he could read.

*MOTHER SIGBRITH, a tragedy in five acts.* That was what was written on the first sheet and it was in his own handwriting. "What's this all about? How can I have written a tragedy?" He started to leaf through the pages.

*THE INTRIGUES ON THE RAMPARTS OF THE CITY, a comedy.* "Where did these plays come from? Somebody must have stuck them in my pocket," he reasoned. "Why, there's a letter, too." It was a note from the director of a theater. His plays had been rejected and not very politely.

"Oh . . . Hum . . ." grumbled the copyist, who was now a playwright, and sat down on a bench.

His imagination was so alive; and he felt so tenderly toward the world. Without thinking, he bent down and picked a flower. It was only a little daisy that had been growing in the grass, yet it was able to explain to him, in one minute, what it would have taken a botanist long hours to tell. The little flower related the myth of its birth, told of the power of the sun: how it forced its petals to unfurl and give off their lovely scent. This made the poet think of how our lives, too, were a struggle and that it was this that aroused so many of the feelings we have. Sunlight and air, the flower explained, were her suitors, but sunlight was her favorite; and she obeyed it and always held her head up toward it. When it disappeared and night came, she closed her petals and slept in the air's embrace.

"The sunlight makes me beautiful," said the daisy.

"But it is the air that gives you breath, so you can live," whispered the poet.

Nearby a boy was splashing the water in a ditch with a big stick; and green branches were being sprayed with muddy water. The copyist began to think of how each drop of water contained millions of tiny, invisible animals, which were so small, in comparison to himself, that their journey into the air, from the ditch to the bush, must have felt to them as he would feel if he were cast high above the clouds.

The copyist smiled at his own thoughts, and how he seemed to have changed. "I must be asleep and dreaming. How curious it is that I can be in a dream and yet feel so natural. I hope I shall be able to remember all that's happened when I wake up. Now I feel so alive and see everything so clearly. . . . Tomorrow it will all seem like nonsense, I know. All the clever and beautiful things we dream about are like subterranean gold; when brought out into the light of day, they are merely stones. . . . Alas!"

Sadly, the copyist was looking at a little bird that sang as it jumped from branch to branch. "That bird is better off than I am. It is happier. To fly! That is the greatest art. Lucky is he who was born with wings. I wish I were a little lark."

No sooner had he uttered the wish than the sleeves of his jacket became wings; his clothers, feathers; and the magic galoshes, claws. The copyist, feeling the transformation, laughed. "I have never had a dream as foolish as this before." He flew up into a tree and started to sing. But there was no poetry in his song. The magic galoshes were thorough; and like everyone else who does things thoroughly, the galoshes could only do one thing at a time. When the copyist wanted to be a poet, he became one; but when he decided that he would rather be a small bird, then he lost his poetic nature.

"This is a fine state of affairs," he peeped. "In the daytime I work in the police station, copying the most unimaginative reports; and at night I fly as a lark, out here in the Frederiksberg Gardens. One could write a comedy about that."

He flew down on the grass and turned his head in all directions before picking up a piece of straw that, considering his size, appeared as large as a North African palm tree.

Suddenly everything was black as night around him. Some huge thing had enveloped him. It was a boy's cap, which an urchin had thrown over him. A hand creeped in under the hat and grabbed the bird around the back, pressing the wings tightly to its little body.

The lark peeped loudly, "You horrible, naughty little boy. I am a copyist in the Central Police Station!" To the child, it only sounded like the ordinary peeping of a bird. He hit its bill and walked off with it.

Along one of the shady paths he met two upper-class boys coming from school. That is, they were upper class by birth; but as far as their character and intelligence were concerned they belonged to the lowest class. For eight pennies they bought the lark from the poor boy; and that's how the copyist was brought back into the city, to stay in an apartment on the Street of the Goths.

"It's a good thing I'm dreaming, or else I'd be very angry," twittered the copyist. "First I was a poet and now I am a lark. It must have been my poetic nature that transformed me into a bird. It's not so much fun to be a bird, especially when you fall into the hands of boys. I wonder how this will end."

The living room was very expensively furnished. The boys were greeted by a fat woman, who was laughing. But she was not amused by the sight of the lark. "A common little bird," she said. But she would let the boys keep it for today, and pointed to an empty cage that stood near the window.

"It's Polly's birthday," she said in a false, mockingly childish voice, "and the little bird of the field has come to pay its respects."

The parrot didn't say a single word; it swung back and forth very gracefully. But a pretty little canary, who only last summer had been brought from its warm, fragrant native country to cold Denmark, began to sing.

"Crybaby!" said the lady, and threw a white cloth over its cage.

"Peep," cried the canary. "What a terrible snowstorm." It sighed and then was silent.

The cage of the lark—or, as the lady called him, the little common bird—had been put between the canary's and the parrot's.

The only words of human speech that Polly had mastered were: "Let us be human!" This often sounded very comical; but everything else it said was as impossible for human beings to understand as the canary's song. The copyist, however, was now a lark and understood his companions perfectly.

"I flew beneath the palms and flowering almond trees," sang the canary. "I flew with my brothers and sisters above beautiful flowers, and across a sea that was clear as glass; and the seaweed waved to us. I have seen many parrots, too; and they told us many very long and amusing stories."

"They were wild birds," commented the parrot. "They didn't have any education or culture. Let us be human!" it screeched.

"Why don't you laugh when I say that? The lady and her guests always laugh, why shouldn't you? It's a great fault to lack a sense of humor. Let us be human!"

"Don't you remember the lovely girls who danced in the tent that was pitched beneath the flowering trees? Don't you remember the sweet fruits with their succulent juice, and the herbs that grew all over the hillside?"

"Oh yes," yawned the parrot. "But I like it much better here. I get good food and am properly taken care of. I am clever, what more need I ask for? Let us be human! . . . You have a poetic soul, as it is called; but I am educated and witty. You may be a genius, but you are too high-strung. You are always trying to reach higher notes, that is why you are covered up. No one would dare to do that to me. I was so expensive, and I am witty, witty, witty. Let us be human!"

"You—little, gray, Danish bird," began the canary. "You are a prisoner too. I think it is cold now, out in your forest; but, at least, there you are free. They have forgotten to close the door to your cage; and one of the top windows over there is open; fly, little bird, fly!"

In a second the copyist was out of his cage. Just then the cat, with its green, shining eyes, came sneaking into the room through the half-open door and tried to catch the lark. The canary flew around in its cage. Polly flapped her wings and screeched, "Let us be human!"

In mortal fear, the copyist flew toward the open window and escaped. He flew above the roofs of the houses and the streets until he was tired and needed to rest. One of the houses seemed more snug, more cozy, somehow friendlier than the others. A window was open and he flew into his own room, where he perched on the table.

"Let us be human," he said. He hadn't meant anything by it, he was only repeating what Polly had said; but he was immediately transformed into his old shape again.

"God preserve me!" he muttered, climbing down from the table. "How did I ever get up here? I must have walked in my sleep. What a strange dream I had; it was all a lot of nonsense!"


PART SIX: HOW THE GALOSHES BROUGHT LUCK

The next morning a young theological student who had rooms on the same floor knocked on the copyist's door.

"May I borrow your galoshes?" he asked. "I should like to smoke my pipe down in the garden, but the grass is still wet from dew."

The copyist, who was still in bed, told the young man to take his galoshes, which he did. After he had put them on he went down into the garden. It was very small and had only a plum and a pear tree; but tiny as it was, it was a marvel, here in the middle of the city.

The student walked back and forth on the little path. It was only six o'clock in the morning. From far away he could hear the sound of the horn that is blown as the stagecoach departs.

"Oh, to travel!" he exclaimed. "Nothing in the world would be so wonderful as to be able to travel. It is my greatest wish! The only cure for my restless wanderlust. But I would like to travel far away: to Switzerland or Italy or—"

The galoshes were very prompt in granting wishes, which was fortunate for both him and us, for he might have ended up too far away. As it was, he was journeying through Switzerland. He was in a stagecoach with eight other passengers. He sat squeezed in the middle. He had a headache and a kink in his neck. All his blood seemed to have gone to his legs; in any case, his feet were swollen and his boots pinched.

He slipped back and forth between the waking and the dozing state. In his right-hand pocket he had some letters of credit; in his left, a passport; and on a string around his neck hung a leather purse which contained a few louis d'or. Every time he fell asleep, he dreamed that one of his valuables had been lost; then he would wake with a start and move his hand in a triangle: from left to right and to center, to make sure that everything was there. The umbrellas, canes, and hats hanging from the net above his head made it difficult for him to see out of the window. And when he finally did get a view of the magnificent Swiss mountains, which are so tremendously impressive, he thought exactly what an acquaintance of ours did, who was a poet and wrote his thoughts down in verse, though he hasn't allowed it to be published yet:

> It is so very lovely here.
> I can see Mount Blanc, my dear.
> Oh, this is the land of milk and honey,
> If only I had some more money.

Grand, somber, and dark was the landscape now. The peaks of the mountains were hidden by clouds; and the pine forests looked as scraggy as heather. Now it was beginning to snow and the wind blew; it was very cold.

"Oh!" shivered the student. "I wish I were on the other side of the Alps. There it is already summer; and I would have cashed my letters of credit. The fear that they might not be honored quite spoils my journey. I can't enjoy Switzerland, I wish I were in Italy!"

Instantly, he was there, traveling between Florence and Rome. Trasimeno Lake, reflecting the rays of the setting sun, shone like gold. The mountains surrounding it were dark blue. Here where Hannibal defeated Flaminius grapevines peacefully intertwined their slender fingers. Underneath a laurel tree was a group of beautiful, half-naked children, who were herding black swine. If this scene had been painted on a canvas, everyone would have shouted: "Oh, beautiful Italy!"

Inside the stagecoach, however, neither the student of theology nor any of his companions felt such enthusiasm. The vehicle was filled with mosquitoes and stinging flies. The sprays of myrtle which the passengers waved back and forth to protect themselves were of no avail; the flies stung anyway. No one escaped; every face was swollen and bloody from insect bites. The poor horses looked like carrion flesh. The flies sat on them in mounds, and it helped little that the driver stopped often to scrape them off.

The sun finally set, and the evening air was icy cold. It was very uncomfortable. The mountains and the clouds turned a remarkable green; everything stood out so clearly, almost brilliantly in the light of evening.—Yes, you must go to Italy and see it for yourself; it is impossible to describe it: a hopeless task.—The travelers would have agreed; but they were hungry, tired, and more interested in finding a night's lodging than looking at the beauty of nature.

The road passed through olive orchards. The trees looked like the gnarled willow trees in Denmark. Finally the stagecoach stopped in front of a lonely inn. Half a dozen crippled beggars were waiting outside the entrance. The most respectable of them looked like "Hunger's oldest son, who had reached maturity." All the others were either blind, lame, or had hands without fingers. They were, in truth, "wretchedness dressed in rags."

"*Eccellenza, miserabili,*" they wailed loudly and held out their maimed and deformed limbs for inspection.

The innkeeper's wife came out to receive her guests. She was barefoot, her hair was unkempt, and her blouse was filthy. The doors were fastened with rope and string. Half the tiles on the floor were missing; and bats flew about above them, just below the high ceilings. It stank foully.

"I wish she would set the table out in the stable instead," one of the travelers said. "Then at least we would know where the stink came from."

The windows were opened so that fresh air might enter; but even quicker than the air were the mutilated arms of the beggars and the sound of their whimpering: *"Miserabili. . . . Eccellenza, miserabili. . . ."* The walls were decorated with inscriptions, and half of them had nothing pleasant to say about *bella Italia.*

At last the food arrived: boiled water with a little pepper and rancid oil in it; it was called soup. The same oil had been used in the salad. The main dish was fried cockscomb and rotten eggs. The wine must have been drawn from the vinegar barrel.

During the night, all the baggage was piled up in front of the door as a barricade; and one of the travelers was to remain awake while the others slept. The first one to stand guard was the student of theology. Pooh! The smell in the room was nauseating, and the heat! From outside came the sound of the *miserabili* moaning in their sleep; and inside the mosquitoes hummed, as they flew about in search of their next victim.

"Traveling would be fine if we only didn't have a body," sighed the student. "If one's spirit were free to go by itself. No matter where I am, there is always something that presses against my heart: something I need or want to be rid of. I want something better than moments like this. . . . Something better. . . . The best: but where is it and how do you get it? I know what I really want: the final goal, where I am sure all happiness lies!"

As soon as these words were spoken, he was back in his own room. The long white curtains were drawn. In the middle of the room was a black coffin; and in it lay the body of the student, sleeping death's sleep. His soul had gone on the journey he had desired for it, while his body was still. *"Call no man happy before he is in his grave."* This story strengthens Solon's words.

Every dead body is an immortal sphinx. It answers no questions and neither did the body of the student of theology, despite his having asked the questions himself, only a few days before, in a poem:

> Death, your silence fills with dread my heart;
> Your footprints are the graves and tombs of men.
> When my Jacob's ladder of thought falls apart,
> Shall I only arise as grass in death's garden, then?
> The greatest suffering, unseen we bear,
> He was alone, even to the last.
> Life's injustice our hearts outwear,
> Kind is the earth on the coffin cast.

Two figures were in the room: Sorrow herself, and the lady's maid to the lady in waiting of the Fairy of Happiness. They were both looking down at the dead body of the student.

"There, you see," began the Fairy of Sorrow. "How much happiness did your magic galoshes bring humanity?"

The servant of Happiness replied, while she nodded toward the coffin, "At least they brought him who is sleeping there eternal peace."

"Oh no!" Sorrow argued. "He chose to leave life behind him, he was not called! He did not have the strength within his soul to accomplish that which even he himself had set as his goal. I shall do him a favor."

Sorrow pulled the galoshes off the student's feet, and the sleep of death was over; and the resurrected young man rose. Sorrow disappeared, and so did the galoshes; Sorrow thought they belonged to her.

## The Daisy

Now I will tell you a story!

There once was a country house with a beautiful garden and a white fence around it. On the other side of the fence were a ditch and a road; on the bank above them there grew among the grass a daisy. The sun shone as pleasantly on the little wild flower as it did on the richly colorful, cultivated flowers in the garden, and the daisy grew taller by the hour. One morning it burst into bloom: the petals were white, and in the center of the flower was a yellow button that looked like a little sun. The flower did not realize that no one could see her among the tall grass, nor that she was merely a poor despised wild flower. No, she was content; turning her face toward the warm sun, she looked straight up into it while listening to the song of the lark.

The little daisy was as happy as if the day were a high holiday and not just a common Monday. All the children were in school, sitting at their desks, learning something; and the daisy sat on its stalk and learned something too. It discovered how warm the sun feels and how pleasant life can be; and it decided that the lark's song was the most beautiful in the whole world, because its melody expressed exactly how she felt. The daisy looked humbly up at the happy bird, which not only could fly but could sing as well. She felt neither envious nor sad because she had not been given such gifts. "I can hear and I can see," she thought. "The sun shines upon me and the wind kisses me; I was born quite rich."

In the garden on the other side of the fence many very elegant flowers grew. The less fragrance they had, the prouder they carried themselves. The peonies puffed themselves up; they wanted to be bigger than the roses, though it is not size that counts. The tulips had the most beautiful colors, but they were well aware of it themselves, and stood up straight so that they could not be overlooked. Not one of them noticed the little daisy outside the fence, but she noticed them all and thought, "How rich and lovely they are. I am sure the bird who sings so beautifully will come and visit them. Thank God I grow so near them that I will be able to see it all."

Just at that moment the lark flew down to the ground, but not among the peonies or the tulips; no, it landed in the grass right beside the daisy. That poor flower felt so honored and got so flustered that it didn't know what to think.

The little bird danced around the daisy and sang, "How soft is the grass. And how sweet is this little flower, with gold in its heart, wearing a silver dress." The yellow center of the daisy did (the lark thought) look like gold and its white petals did shine like silver.

The happiness the little daisy felt cannot be described. The bird kissed her with his beak, sang for her; and then flew away, up into the blue summer sky. It took the daisy more than a quarter of an hour to feel like herself again. Shyly she looked into the garden; the flowers in there must have seen the honor paid to her. She felt ever so happy. But the tulips stood just as stiffly as they had before, only their faces were a little redder, for they were annoyed. The peonies were even more thickheaded, and it is a good thing that they couldn't talk or the little daisy would have been told a thing or two. But the little wild flower sensed their ill humor and it hurt her. Just then a maid came out into the garden with a sharp knife in her hand. She walked right over to the tulips and picked them one after another.

"Oh dear," the daisy sighed and thought, "How terrible, now life is all over for them." The maid walked into the house with the flowers; and the daisy was happy that she grew on the other side of the fence in the grass and was only a poor little wild flower. When night came she folded her petals and fell asleep to dream about the bird and the warm sun.

The next day when the flower joyfully unfurled herself and stretched her petals like little white arms out into the fresh morning air, she heard the bird's song again. But this time its voice was mournful and its song sad. The lark had good reason for its sorrow; it had been caught and now sat near the open window in a cage. He sang of the joy he had felt when he had flown high up in the sky, about the green fields of grain and the strength of his wings when he had been free. Oh, the poor bird was very unhappy in its little cage!

The little daisy wanted to help him but how was she to do it? It was a difficult problem and the little flower pondered so long over it that she forgot the beauty that surrounded her and how lovely her own white petals were. She could only think about the poor caged bird, whom she could not help.

Two little boys came out of the garden; one of them had a sharp knife in his hand. It was just like the one the maid had used to cut the tulips. The boys stopped in front of the daisy, and she understood what they intended to do.

"Here, we can cut a piece of turf for the lark," said the boy with the knife, and began marking out a square in the grass in the midst of which the daisy grew. He cut deep into the earth, for he wanted the grass to keep its roots.

"Tear the flower off," said the other boy, and the daisy shook with fear, for to be "torn off" was the same as to die; and she wanted so badly to be put in the cage with the bird.

"No, let it be," replied the boy with the knife. "It will look nice." And the daisy was allowed to stay in the grass turf that was placed in the bottom of the cage.

The poor bird was still bewailing its lost freedom, and beat its wings against the iron grating. The little daisy could not speak, she could not say the words of comfort that she wanted to.

The morning passed and it was noon. "There is no water," moaned the imprisoned lark. "They have all gone away and forgotten to give me even a few drops of water to drink. My throat is dry and burning! It feels as if there were ice and fire inside me; and the air seems so heavy. I will die, and never again feel the warm sunshine or see the greenness: all the beauty that God has made."

The little bird buried his bill in the grass because it was cooler there; then it saw the little daisy, nodded, and kissed her. "You must wither and die in here, too, poor little flower! You and this little square of green grass have been given to me in exchange for the whole world I had when I was free. So every blade of grass must now be a tree, and each of your petals a sweet-smelling flower. Oh, the only story you can tell me is the tale of what I have lost."

"If only I could comfort him," thought the daisy; but she couldn't even move her leaves. But the sweet smell that came from the flower was much stronger than daisies usually have, and the lark noticed it, and though he tore in pain at the grass, he did not touch the flower.

Evening came and still no one brought the poor bird any water. It spread out its wings, its little body trembled; then it turned its head toward the flower and said one last peep before its heart burst from longing and want. The daisy could not fold her petals that night as she had the night before. Sorrowfully, she bent her sick little head toward the earth.

The next morning the boys came. When they saw that the bird was dead they cried bitterly. They dug a little grave and lined it with leaves. They put the lark's body in a handsome red box. Oh, the poor little bird was royally buried. When it had been alive and could sing, it had been put in a cage, where it suffered from thirst because no one remembered to give it any water; but now neither splendor nor tears were lacking.

The turf of grass with the daisy in it was thrown out on the dusty road. No one gave a thought to the little flower who had felt most deeply for the lark and had tried so hard to console it.

## The Steadfast Tin Soldier

Once there were five and twenty tin soldiers. They were all brothers because they had been made from the same old tin spoon. With their rifles sticking up over their shoulders, they stood at attention, looking straight ahead, in their handsome red and blue uniforms.

"Tin soldiers!" were the first words they heard in this world; and they had been shouted happily by a little boy who was clapping his hands because he had received them as a birthday gift. He took them immediately out of the box they had come in and set them on the table. They were all exactly alike except one, who was different from the others because he was missing a leg. He had been the last one to be cast and there had not been enough tin. But he stood as firm and steadfast on his one leg as the others did on their two. He is the hero of our story.

Of all the many toys on the table, the one you noticed first was a pasteboard castle. It was a little replica of a real castle, and through its windows you could see right into its handsomely painted halls. In front of the castle was a little lake surrounded by trees; in it swans swam and looked at their own reflections because the lake was a glass mirror. It was all very lovely; but the most charming part of the castle was its mistress. She was a little paper doll and she was standing in the entrance dressed like a ballerina. She had a skirt of white muslin and a blue ribbon draped over her shoulder, which was fastened with a spangle that was almost as large as her face. The little lady had her arms stretched out, as if she were going to embrace someone. She stood on one leg, and at that on her toes, for she was a ballet dancer; the other, she held up behind her, in such a way that it disappeared under her skirt; and therefore the soldier thought that she was one-legged like himself.

"She would be a perfect wife for me," he thought. "But I am afraid she is above me. She has a castle and I have only a box that I must share with twenty-four soldiers; that wouldn't do for her. Still, I would like to make her acquaintance." And the soldier lay down full length behind a snuffbox; from there he could look at the young lady, who was able to stand on the toes of only one leg without losing her balance.

Later in the evening, when it was the children's bedtime, all the other tin soldiers were put back in the box. When the house was quiet and everyone had gone to bed, the toys began to play. They played house, and hide-and-seek, and held a ball. The four and twenty tin soldiers rattled inside their box; they wanted to play too, but they couldn't get the lid open. The nutcracker turned somersaults, and the slate pencil wrote on the blackboard. They made so much noise that the canary woke up and recited his opinion of them all in verse. The only ones who didn't move were the ballerina and the soldier. She stood as steadfast on the toes of her one leg as the soldier did on his. His eyes never left her, not even for a moment did he blink or turn away.

The clock struck twelve. Pop! The lid of the snuffbox opened and out jumped a troll. It was a jack-in-the-box.

"Tin soldier," screamed the little black troll, "keep your eyes to yourself."

The tin soldier acted as if he hadn't heard the remark.

"You wait till tomorrow!" threatened the troll, and disappeared back into its box.

The next morning when the children were up and dressed, the little boy put the one-legged soldier on the window sill. It's hard to tell whether it was the troll or just the wind that caused the window to open suddenly and the soldier to fall out of it. He dropped down three stories to the street and his bayonet stuck in the earth between two cobblestones.

The boy and the maid came down to look for him and, though they almost stepped on him, they didn't see him. If only the tin soldier had shouted, "Here I am!" they would have found him; but he thought it improper to shout when in uniform.

It began to rain; first one drop fell and then another and soon it was pouring. When the shower was over two urchins came by. "Look," said one of them, "there is a tin soldier. He will do as a sailor."

The boys made a boat out of a newspaper, put the tin soldier on board, and let it sail in the gutter. Away it went, for it had rained so hard that the gutter was a raging torrent. The boys ran along on the sidewalk, clapping their hands. The boat dipped and turned in the waves. The tin soldier trembled and quaked inside himself; but outside, he stood as steadfast as ever, shouldering his gun and looking straight ahead.

Now the gutter was covered by a board. It was as dark as it had been inside the box, but there he had had four and twenty comrades. "I wonder how it will all end," thought the soldier. "I am sure it's all the troll's doing. If only the ballerina were here, then I wouldn't care if it were twice as dark as pitch."

A big water rat that lived in the gutter came up behind the boat and shouted, "Have you got a passport? Give me your passport!"

The tin soldier didn't answer but held more firmly onto his rifle. The current became stronger, and the boat gathered speed. The rat swam after him; it was so angry that it gnashed its teeth. "Stop him! Stop him!" the rat shouted to two pieces of straw and a little twig. "Stop him! He hasn't got a passport and he won't pay duty!"

The current ran swifter and swifter. The tin soldier could see light ahead; he was coming out of the tunnel. But at the same moment he heard a strange roaring sound. It was frightening enough to make the bravest man cringe. At the end of the tunnel the gutter emptied into one of the canals of the harbor. If you can imagine it, it would be the same as for a human being to be thrown down a great waterfall into the sea.

There was no hope of stopping the boat. The poor tin soldier stood as steady as ever, he did not flinch. The boat spun around four times and became filled to the brim with water. It was doomed, the paper began to fall apart; the tin soldier was standing in water up to his neck. He thought of the ballerina, whom he would never see again, and two lines from a poem ran through his mind.

> Fare thee well, my warrior bold,
> Death comes so swift and cold.

The paper fell apart and the tin soldier would have sunk down into the mud at the bottom of the canal had not a greedy fish swallowed him just at that moment.

Here it was even darker than it had been in the sewer; the fish's stomach was terribly narrow, but the soldier lay there as steadfast as he had stood in the boat,without letting go of his rifle.

The fish darted and dashed in the wildest manner; then suddenly it was still. A while later, a ray of light appeared and someone said, "Why, there is a tin soldier." The fish had been caught, taken to the market, and sold. The kitchen maid had found the soldier when she opened the fish up with a big knife, in order to clean it. With her thumb and her index finger she picked the tin soldier up by the waist and carried him into the living room, so that everyone could admire the strange traveler who had journeyed inside the belly of a fish. But the tin soldier was not proud of his adventures.

How strange the world is! He was back in the same room that he had left in the morning; and he had been put down on the table among the toys he knew. There stood the cardboard castle and the little ballerina. She was still standing on one leg, the other she had lifted high into the air. She was as steadfast as he was. It touched the soldier's heart and he almost cried tin tears—and would have, had it not been so undignified. He looked at her and she at him, but never a word passed between them.

Suddenly one of the little boys grabbed the soldier, opened the stove, and threw him in. The child couldn't explain why he had done it; there's no question but that the jack-in-the-box had had something to do with it.

The tin soldier stood illuminated by the flames that leaped around him. He did not know whether the great heat he felt was caused by his love or the fire. The colors of his uniform had disappeared, and he could not tell whether it was from sorrow or his trip through the water. He looked at the ballerina, and she looked at him. He could feel that he was melting; but he held on as steadfastly as ever to his gun and kept his gaze on the little ballerina in front of the castle.

The door of the room was opened, a breeze caught the little dancer and like a sylph she flew right into the stove. She flared up and was gone. The soldier melted. The next day when the maid emptied the stove, she found a little tin heart, which was all that was left of him. Among the ashes lay the metal spangle from the ballerina's dress; it had been burned as black as coal.

## The Wild Swans

Far, far away where the swallows are when we have winter, there lived a king who had eleven sons and one daughter, Elisa. The eleven brothers were all princes; and when they went to school, each wore a star on his chest and a sword at his side. They wrote with diamond pencils on golden tablets, and read aloud so beautifully that everyone knew at once that they were of royal blood. Their sister Elisa sat on a little stool made of mirrors and had a picture book that had cost half the kingdom. How well those children lived; but it did not last.

Their father, who was king of the whole country, married an evil queen, and that boded no good for the poor children. They found this out the first day she came. The whole castle was decorated in honor of the great event, and the children decided to play house. Instead of the cakes and baked apples they usually were given for this game—and which were so easy to provide—the queen handed them a teacup full of sand and said that they should pretend it was something else.

A week later little Elisa was sent to live with some poor peasants; and the evil queen made the king believe such dreadful things about the princes that soon he did not care for them any more.

"Fly away, out into the world with you and fend for yourselves! Fly as voiceless birds!" cursed the queen; but their fate was not as terrible as she would have liked it to be, for her power had its limits. They became eleven beautiful, wild swans. With a strange cry, they flew out of the castle window and over the park and the forest.

It was very early in the morning when they flew over the farm where Elisa lived. She was still asleep in her little bed. They circled low above the roof of the farmhouse, turning and twisting their necks, to catch a glimpse of their sister, while their great wings beat the air. But no one was awake, and no one heard or saw them. At last they had to fly away, high up into the clouds, toward the great dark forest that stretched all the way to the ocean.

Poor little Elisa sat on the floor playing with a leaf. She had no toys, so she had made a hole in the leaf and was looking up at the sun through it. She felt as though she were looking into the bright eyes of her brothers; and when the warm sunbeams touched her cheeks, she thought of all the kisses they had given her.

The days passed, one after another, and they all were alike. The wind blew through the rosebush and whispered, "Who can be more lovely than you are?"

The roses shook their heads and replied: "Elisa!"

On Sundays the old woman at the farm would set her chair outside and sit reading her psalmbook. The wind would turn the leaves and whisper, "Who can be more saintly than you?"

The psalmbook would answer as truthfully as the roses had: "Elisa!"

When Elisa turned fifteen she was brought back to the castle. As soon as the evil queen saw how beautiful the girl was, envy and hate filled her evil heart. She would gladly have transformed Elisa into a swan at first sight; but the king had asked to see his daughter, and the queen did not dare to disobey him.

Early the next morning, before Elisa was awake, the queen went into the marble bathroom, where the floors were covered with costly carpets and the softest pillows lay on the benches that lined the walls. She had three toads with her. She kissed the first and said, "Sit on Elisa's head that she may become as lazy as you are." Kissing the second toad, she ordered, "Touch Elisa's forehead that she may become as ugly as you are, so her father will not recognize her." Then she kissed the third toad. "Rest next to Elisa's heart, that her soul may become as evil as yours and give her pain."

She dropped the toads into the clear water and, instantly, it had a greenish tinge. She sent for Elisa, undressed her, and told her to step into the bath. As she slipped into the water, the first toad leaped onto Elisa's head, the second touched her forehead, and the third snuggled as close to her heart as it could. But Elisa did not seem to notice them.

When Elisa rose from the bath, there floating on the water were three red poppies. If the toads had not been made poisonous by the kiss of the wicked queen, they would have turned into roses; but they had become flowers when they touched Elisa. She was so good and so innocent that evil magic could not harm her.

When the wicked queen realized this, she took the juice from walnut shells and rubbed Elisa's body till it was streaked black and brown; then she smeared an awful-smelling salve on the girl's face and filtered ashes and dust through her hair. Now it was impossible for anyone to recognize the lovely princess.

Her father got frightened when he saw her, and said, "She is not my daughter." Only the watchdog and the swallows recognized her; but they were only animals and nobody paid any attention to them.

Elisa wept bitterly and thought of her eleven brothers who had disappeared. In despair, she slipped out of the castle. She walked all day across fields and swamps until she came to the great forest. She did not know where she was going; she only knew that she was deeply unhappy and she longed more than ever to see her brothers again. She thought that they had been forced out into the world as she had; and now she would try to find them.

As soon as she entered the forest, night fell. She had come far away from any road or path. She lay down on the soft moss to sleep. She said her prayers and leaned her head against the stump of a tree. The night was silent, warm, and still. Around her shone so many glowworms that, when she touched the branch of a bush, the little insects fell to the ground like shooting stars.

That night she dreamed about her brothers. Again they were children writing on their golden tablets with diamond pens; and once more she looked at the lovely picture book that had cost half the kingdom. But on their tablets her brothers were not only doing their sums, they wrote of all the great deeds they had performed. The pictures in the book became alive: the birds sang, and the men and women walked right out of the book to talk to Elisa. Every time she was about to turn a leaf, they quickly jumped back onto the page, so as not to get in the wrong picture.

When she awoke, the sun was already high in the heavens; but she couldn't see it, for the forest was so dense that the branches of the tall trees locked out the sky. But the sun rays shone through the leaves and made a shimmering golden haze. The smell of greenness was all around her, and the birds were so tame that they almost seemed willing to perch on her shoulder. She heard the splashing of water; and she found a little brook, and followed it till it led her to a lovely little pool that was so clear, she could see the sand bottom in a glance. It was surrounded by bushes; but at one spot the deer, when they came down to drink, had made a hole. Here Elisa kneeled down.

Had the branches and their leaves not been swayed gently by the wind, she would have believed that they had been painted on the water, so perfectly were they mirrored. Those upon which the sun shone glistened, and those in the shade were a dark green.

Then Elisa saw her own face and was frightened: it was so dirty and ugly. She dipped her hand into the water and rubbed her eyes, her cheeks, and her forehead till she could see her own fresh skin again. She undressed and bathed in the clear pool, and a more beautiful princess than she, could not have been found in the whole world.

When she had dressed, braided her long hair, and drunk from the brook with her cupped hand, she wandered farther and farther into the forest without knowing where she was going. She thought about her brothers and trusted that God would not leave her. There ahead of her was a wild apple tree. Hadn't God let it grow there so that the hungry could eat? Its branches were bent almost to the ground under the weight of the fruit. Here Elisa rested and had her midday meal; before she walked on, she found sticks and propped up the heavily laden branches of the apple tree.

The forest grew darker and darker. It was so still that she could hear her own footsteps: the sound of every little stick and leaf crumbling under her foot. No birds were to be seen or heard, no sunbeams penetrated the foliage. The trees grew so close together that when she looked ahead she felt as if she were imprisoned in a stockade. Oh, here she was more alone than she had ever thought one could be!

Night came and not a single glowworm shone in the darkness. When she lay down to sleep she was hopelessly sad; but then the branches above her seemed to be drawn aside like a curtain, and she saw God looking down at her, with angels peeping over His shoulders and out from under His arms. And in the morning when she awoke, she did not know whether she had really seen God or it had merely been a dream.

Elisa met an old woman who was carrying a basket full of berries on her arm, and she offered the girl some berries. Elisa thanked her and then asked if she had seen eleven princes riding through the forest.

"No," the old woman replied. "But I have seen eleven swans with golden crowns on their heads, swimming in a stream not far from here."

She said she would show Elisa the way and led her to a cliff. Below it a little river twisted and turned its way through the forest. It seemed to be flowing in a tunnel, for the trees that grew on either side stretched their leafy branches toward each other and then intertwined. Where the branches were not long enough to span the stream, the trunks had pulled up part of their roots, in order to lean farther out over the water so the branches could meet.

Elisa said good-by to the old woman and followed the stream until its water ran out into the sea.

Before her lay the beautiful ocean. There was not a sail to be seen nor any boat along the shore. She could not go any farther. How would she ever be able to find her brothers? She looked down. The shore was covered with pebbles: all the little stones were round; they had been made so by the sea. Iron, glass, stones, everything that lay at her feet had been ground into its present shape by water that was softer than her own delicate hand. "The waves roll on untiringly, and grind and polish the hardest stone. I must learn to be as untiring as they. Thank you for the lesson you have taught me, waves; and I am sure that one day you will carry me to my dear brothers."

Among the dried-out seaweed on the beach she found eleven swans' feathers. She picked them up; to each of them clung a drop of water, whether it was dew or a tear she did not know.

Although she was alone, Elisa did not feel lonely for she could watch the ever changing scene before her. The sea transforms itself more in an hour than a lake does in a year. When the clouds above it are dark, then the sea becomes as black as they are; and yet it will put on a dress of white if the wind should suddenly come and whip the waves. In the evening when the winds sleep and the clouds have turned pink, the sea will appear like the petal of a giant rose. Blue, white, green, red: the sea contains all colors; and even when it is calm, standing at the shore's edge, you will notice that it is moving like the breast of a sleeping child.

When the sun began to slide down behind the sea, Elisa saw eleven wild swans, with golden crowns on their heads, flying toward the beach. Like a white ribbon being pulled across the sky, they flew one after the other. Elisa hid behind some bushes. The swans landed nearby, still flapping their great white wings.

At the moment when the sun finally sank below the horizon, the swans turned into eleven handsome princes, Elisa's brothers. She shrieked with joy when she saw them. Although they had grown up since she had seen them last, she recognized them immediately and ran out from her hiding place to throw herself in their arms. They were as happy to see her as she was to see them. They laughed and cried, as they told each other of the evil deeds of their wicked stepmother.

"We must fly as wild swans as long as the sun is in the sky," explained the oldest brother. "Only when night has come do we regain our human shape; that is why we must never be in flight at sunset, for should we be up among the clouds, like any other human beings, we would fall and be killed. We do not live here, but in a country on the other side of the ocean. The sea is vast. It is far, far away; and there is no island where we can rest during our long journey. But midway in the ocean, a solitary rock rises above the waves. It is so tiny that we can just stand on it; and when the waves break against it, the water splashes up over us. Yet we thank God for that ragged rock, for if it were not there we should never be able to visit again the country where we were born. As it is, we only dare attempt the flight during the longest days of the year. We stay here eleven summer days and then we must return. Only for such a short time can we fly over the great forest and see our father's castle, and circle above the church where our mother is buried. It is as if every tree, every bush, in our native land were part of us. The wild horses gallop across the plains today as they did yesterday when we were children, and the gypsies still sing the songs we know. That is why we must come back —if only once a year. And now we have found you, our little sister. But we can only stay here two more days; then we must fly across the ocean to that fair land where we live now. How shall we be able to take you along? We have neither ship nor boat!"

"What can I do to break the spell that the queen has cast?" asked Elisa.

They talked almost the whole night through; only for a while did they doze. Elisa was awakened by the sound of wings beating the air. Her brothers had turned into swans again. They flew in circles above her and then disappeared over the forest. But her youngest brother had stayed behind. He rested his white head in her lap, and she stroked his strong white wings. Just before sunset, the others returned; and when twilight came, they were princes once more.

"Tomorrow we must begin the flight back to our new homeland," said the oldest brother. "We dare not stay longer; but how can we leave you behind, Elisa? It will be a whole year before we can return. My arms when I am a man are strong enough to carry you through the forest; wouldn't the wings of all of us be strong enough to carry you over the sea when we are swans?"

"I'll go with you!" exclaimed Elisa.

They worked all night, weaving a net of reeds and willow branches. Just before sunrise, Elisa lay down upon it; and she was so tired that she fell asleep. When the sun rose, and the princes changed into swans again, they picked up the net with their bills and flew up into the clouds with their sleeping sister. The burning rays of the sun fell on her face, so one of the swans flew above her, to shade her with his great wings.

They were far out over the ocean when Elisa awoke. So strange did it feel to be carried through the air that at first she thought she was dreaming. Some berries and roots lay beside her. Her youngest brother had collected this provision for her journey, and it was he who now flew above her and shaded her from the sun.

The whole day they flew as swiftly as arrows through the air; yet their flight would have been even faster had they not been carrying Elisa. Soon the sun would begin to set. Dark clouds on the horizon warned of a coming storm. Elisa looked down; there was only the endless ocean; she saw no lonely rock. It seemed to her that the wings were beating harder now. She would be the cause of her brothers' deaths. When the sun set, they would turn into men again; then they would fall into the sea and be drowned. She prayed to God, but still there was no rocky islet to be seen. Black clouds filled the sky; soon the breath of the storm would be upon them. The waves seemed as heavy as lead, and in the clouds lightning flashed.

The rim of the sun touched the sea. Elisa trembled with fear. Suddenly the swans dove down so fast that she thought that they were falling; but then they spread out their wings again.

Half of the sun had disappeared when Elisa saw the little rock. Looking down from the air, she thought that it looked more like a seal who had raised his head above the water. Just as the sun vanished they landed on the rock; and when the last of its light, like a piece of paper set aflame, flared up and then was gone, her brothers stood around her arm in arm.

The island was so tiny that they had to stand holding onto each other all night. The lightning made the sky bright and the thunder roared. They held each other's hands and sang a psalm, which comforted them and gave them courage.

At dawn the storm was over and the air was fresh and clear. The swans flew away from the rock, carrying Elisa. The sea was still turbulent. The white surf looked like millions of swans swimming on a raging green ocean. When the sun was high in the sky, Elisa saw a strange landscape. There was a mountain range covered with ice and snow. Halfway down the mountainsides was a huge palace, miles long, made of arcades, one on top of the other. And below that was a forest of gently waving palm trees, in which there were flowers with faces as large as millstones. She asked if that were the country where they lived, and the swans shook their heads. What she was seeing was a fata morgana: a mirage, an ever changing castle in the air to which no human being could gain admittance. As Elisa stared at it, the mountains, the castle, and the forest disappeared. It melted together and now there were twenty proud churches, every one alike, with high towers and tall windows. She thought she heard their organs playing, but it was the sound of the sea beating far below. The churches, in turn, changed into ships with towering sails. She was just above them; but when she looked down, she saw only fog driven by wind over the waves. The world of the sea and the air is always changing, ever in motion.

At last she saw the shores of the real country that was their destination. The mountains, which were covered with forests of cedar, were blue in the afternoon light; and she could see castles and towns. Before the sun had set, the swans alighted in front of a cave; its walls were covered with vines and plants that had intertwined and looked like tapestries.

"Tomorrow you must tell us what you have dreamed," said her youngest brother, showing her the part of the cave that was to be her bedchamber.

"May I dream how I can break the spell that the wicked queen cast," she said fervently; and that thought absorbed her so completely that she prayed to God and begged Him to help her; and while she was falling asleep she kept on praying.

Elisa felt as though she were flying into the fata morgana, the castle in the air; and a fairy came to welcome her who was young and beautiful, and yet somehow resembled the old woman whom Elisa had met in the forest and who had told her about the eleven swans with golden crowns on their heads.

"Your brothers can escape their fate," began the fairy, "if you have enough courage and endurance. The waves of the ocean are softer than your hands, yet they can form and shape hard stones; but they cannot feel the pain that your fingers will feel. They have no hearts and therefore they do not know fear: the suffering that you must endure. Look at the nettle that I hold in my hand! Around the cave where you are sleeping grow many of them; only those nettles or the ones to be found in churchyards may you use. You must pick them, even though they blister and burn your hands; then you must stamp on them with your bare feet until they become like flax. And from that you must twine thread with which to knit eleven shirts with long sleeves. If you cast one of these shirts over each of the eleven swans, the spell will be broken. But remember, from the moment you start your work until it is finished, you must be silent and never speak to anyone—even if it takes you years, you must be mute! If you speak one word, that word will send a knife into the hearts of your brothers. Their lives depend on your tongue: remember!"

The fairy touched Elisa's hand with the nettle. It felt like fire and she woke. It was bright daylight. Near her lay a nettle like the one she had seen in her sleep. She fell on her knees and said a prayer of thanks; then she walked outside to begin her work.

Her delicate hands picked the horrible nettles, and it felt as if her hands were burning and big blisters rose on her arms and hands. But she did not mind the pain if she could save her brothers. She broke every nettle and stamped on it with her bare feet until it became as fine as flax and could be twined into green thread.

When the sun set, her brothers came. At first they feared that some spell had been cast upon their sister by their evil stepmother, for Elisa was silent and would not answer their questions. But when they saw her hands covered with blisters, they understood the work she was doing was for their sake. The youngest of her brothers cried and his tears fell on her hands; the pain ceased and the burning blisters disappeared.

That night she could not sleep; she worked the whole night through. She felt that she could not rest until her brothers were free. The following day she was alone, but time passed more swiftly. By sunset the first of the nettle shirts was finished.

The next day she heard the sound of hunters' horns coming from the mountains. They came nearer and nearer and soon she could hear dogs barking. Frightened, she bound the nettles she had collected into a bundle with the thread she had already twined and the finished shirt; then she fled into the cave and sat down on the nettle heap.

Out of the thicket sprang a large dog; then came another and another. Barking, they ran back and forth in front of the entrance to the cave. Within a few minutes the hunters followed. The handsomest among them was the king of the country. He entered the cave and found Elisa. Never before had he seen a girl lovelier than she.

"Why are you hiding here, beautiful child?" he asked. Elisa shook her head. She dared not speak because her brothers' lives depended upon her silence. She hid her hands behind her back so that the king might not see how she suffered.

"You cannot stay here," he said. "Follow me, and if you are as good as you are beautiful, then you shall be clad in velvet and silk, wear a golden crown on your head, and call the loveliest of my castles your home."

He lifted her up on his horse. Elisa cried and wrung her hands. The king would not set her down again. "I only want to make you happy," he said. "Someday you will thank me for what I have done." Then he spurred his horse and galloped away with Elisa. The other hunters followed him.

By evening they reached the royal city with its many churches and palaces. The king led her into his castle with its lofty halls, where the waters of the fountains splashed into marble basins, and where the ceilings and the walls were beautifully painted. But none of this did Elisa notice, for she was crying so sorrowfully, so bitterly.

Silently but good-naturedly, she let the maids dress her in regal gowns, braid her hair with pearls, and pull long gloves over her blistered hands. When she entered the great hall, dressed so magnificently, she was so beautiful that the whole court bowed and curtsied. The king declared that she was to be his queen. Only the archbishop shook his head and whispered that he believed the little forest girl to be a witch who had cast a spell over the king.

The king did not listen to him. He ordered the musicians to play and the feast to begin. Dancing girls danced for Elisa; and the king showed her the fragrant gardens and the grand halls of his castle. But neither her lips nor her eyes smiled. Sorrow had printed its eternal mark on her face. Finally the king showed her a little chamber, near where she would soon sleep. Its walls and floor were covered by costly green carpets. It looked like the cave where she had been with her brothers. In a corner lay the green thread which she had spun from the nettles, and from the ceiling hung the one shirt that she had already knitted. One of the hunters had taken it all along as a curiosity.

"Here you can dream yourself back to your former home," remarked the king. "Here is the work you used to do; it will amuse you amid present splendor to think of the past."

A sweet smiled played for a moment on Elisa's lips when she saw what was nearest and dearest to her heart restored to her. The color returned to her cheeks. She thought of her brothers, and she kissed the king's hand. He pressed her to his breast and ordered that all the church bells be rung and their wedding proclaimed. The silent girl from the woods was to become the queen.

The archbishop whispered evil words in the king's ear, but they did not penetrate his heart. The marriage ceremony was held, and the archbishop himself had to crown the queen. He pressed the golden band down on her head so hard that it hurt. But she did not feel the pain, for sorrow's band squeezed her heart and made her suffer far more.

She must not speak a word or her brothers would die. But her eyes spoke silently of the love she felt for the king, who did everything he could to please her. Every day she loved him more. If only she could tell him of her anguish. But mute she must be until her task was finished. At night while the king slept, she would leave their bed and go to the chamber with the green carpets, and make the nettle shirts for her brothers. But when she had finished the sixth shirt she had no more green thread with which to knit.

She knew that in the churchyard grew the nettles that she needed. She had to pick them herself. But how was she to go there without anyone seeing her?

"What is the pain in my hands compared to the pain I feel in my heart?" she thought. "I must attempt it and God will help me."

As if it were an evil deed she was about to perform, she sneaked fearfully out of the castle late at night. She crossed the royal park and made her way through the empty streets to the churchyard. The moon was out; and on one of the large tombstones she saw a group of lamias sitting. They are those dreadful monsters with the bodies of snakes and the breasts and heads of women. They dig up the graves of those who have just died, to eat the flesh of the corpses. Elisa had to walk past them. She said her prayers, and though they kept their terrible gaze upon her, they did her no harm. She picked her nettles and returned to the castle.

Only one person had seen her: the archbishop, for he was awake when everyone else was sleeping. Now he thought that what he had said was proven true: the queen was a witch who had cast her spell on the king and all his subjects.

When next the king came to confession, the archbishop told him what he had seen and what he feared. He spoke his condemning words so harshly that the carved sculptures of the saints shook their heads as though they were saying: "It is not true. Elisa is innocent!"

But that was not the way the archbishop interpreted it; he said that the saints were shaking their heads because of their horror at her sins.

Two tears rolled down the king's cheeks, and with a heavy heart he returned to the castle. That night he only pretended to sleep and, when Elisa rose, he followed her. Every night she went on with her work; and every night the king watched her disappear into the little chamber.

The face of the king grew dark and troubled. Elisa noticed it, though she did not know its cause; and this new sorrow was added to her fear for her brothers' fate. On her royal velvet dress fell salt tears, and they looked like diamonds on the purple material, making it even more splendid. And all the women of the court wished that they were queens and could wear such magnificent clothes.

Soon Elisa's work would be over. She had only to knit one more shirt; but she had no more nettles from which to twine thread. Once more, for the last time, she would have to go to the churchyard. She shook with fear when she thought of walking alone past the horrible lamias, but she gathered courage when she thought of her brothers and her own faith in God.

Elisa went; and secretly the king and the archbishop followed her. They saw her disappear through the gates of the churchyard. The same terrifying lamias were there, and they were sitting near the place where the nettles grew. The king saw her walk toward them, and he turned away as his heart filled with repulsion, for he thought that Elisa, his queen—who that very night had rested in his arms—had come to seek the company of these monsters.

"Let the people judge her," said he. And the people judged her guilty and condemned her to the stake.

She was taken from the great halls of the castle and thrown into a dungeon, where the wind whistled through the grating that barred the window. Instead of a bed with silken sheets and velvet pillows, they gave her the nettles she had picked as a pillow and the shirts she had knitted as a cover. They could have given her no greater gift. She prayed to God and started work on the last of the shirts. Outside in the streets, the urchins sang songs that mocked and scorned her, while no one said a word of comfort to her.

Just before sunset, she heard the sound of swan's wings beating before her window. It was her youngest brother who had found her. She wept for happiness, even though she knew that this might be the last night of her life. Her work was almost done and her brothers were near her.

The archbishop had promised the king that he would be with Elisa during the last hours of her life. But when he came, she shook her head and pointed toward the door, to tell him to go. Her work must be finished that night or all her suffering, all her tears, all her pain would be in vain. The archbishop spoke some unkind words to her and left.

Poor Elisa, who knew that she was innocent but could not say a word to prove it, set to work knitting the last shirt. Mice ran across the floor and fetched the nettles for her; they wanted to help. And the thrush sang outside the iron bars of the window, as gaily as it could, so that she would not lose her courage.

One hour before sunrise, her brothers came to the castle and demanded to see the king. But they were refused, for it was still night and the guards did not dare wake the king. Elisa's brothers begged and threatened; they made so much noise that the captain of the guard came and, finally, the king himself. But at that moment the sun rose; the brothers were gone but high above the royal castle flew eleven white swans.

A stream of people rushed through the gates of the city. Everyone wanted to see the witch being burned. An old worn-out mare drew the cart in which Elisa sat. She was clad in sackcloth; her hair hung loose and framed her beautiful face, which was deadly pale. Her lips moved; she was mumbling a prayer while she knitted the last shirt. The other ten lay at her feet. Even on the way to her death she did not cease working. The mob that lined the road jeered and mocked her.

"Look at the witch, she is mumbling her spells!" they screamed. "See what she has in her hands! It is no hymnbook; it is witchcraft! Get it away from her and tear it into a thousand pieces!"

And the rabble tried to stop the cart and tear Elisa's knitting out of her hands. But at that moment eleven white swans flew down and perched on the railing of the cart; they beat the air with their strong wings. The people drew back in fear.

"It is a sign from heaven that she is innocent," some of them whispered; but not one of them dared say it aloud.

The executioner took her hand to lead her to the stake, but she freed herself from him, grabbed the eleven shirts, and cast them over the swans. There stood eleven princes, handsome and fair. But the youngest of them had a swan's wing instead of an arm, for Elisa had not been able to finish one of the sleeves of the last shirt.

"Now I dare speak!" she cried. "I am innocent!"

The people, knowing that a miracle had taken place, kneeled down before her as they would have for a saint. But Elisa, worn out by fear, worry, and pain, fainted lifelessly into the arms of one of her brothers.

"Yes, she is innocent!" cried the oldest brother; and he addressed himself to the king and told of all that had happened to himself, his brothers, and their sister Elisa. While he spoke a fragrance of millions of roses spread from the wood that had been piled high around the stake. Every stick, every log had taken root and set forth vines. They were a hedge of the loveliest red roses, and on the very top bloomed a single white rose. It shone like a star. The king plucked it and placed it on Elisa's breast. She woke; happiness and peace were within her.

The church bells in the city started to peal, though no bell ringers pulled their ropes, and great flocks of birds flew in the sky. No one has ever seen a gayer procession than the one that now made its way to the royal castle.

## The Garden of Eden

Once there lived a prince who had a library far greater than anyone else has ever had, either before him or since. All his books were very beautiful; and in them he could read about and see portrayed in pictures, everything that had ever happened in the whole world. There was no country, no people whom he could not learn about; but where the garden of Eden lay was not mentioned in any of his books. This made the prince very sad, for it was paradise that interested him most.

His grandmother had told him, when he was still a little boy just starting school, that in the garden of Eden all the flowers were cakes. On each of them was written, in the finest of sugar: history, geography, addition, subtraction, or the multiplication tables; and all children had to do was to eat the right cakes and they knew their lessons at once. The more cakes they ate, the better educated they became. Then, he had believed his grandmother's story; but as he grew up and became wiser, he understood that the beauty of paradise was far greater and more difficult to conceive.

"Oh, why did Eve pluck the apple and why did Adam eat the forbidden fruit? If I had been Adam, man would never have fallen and sin would not have conquered the world." This he had said to his grandmother when he was a little boy. Now, at seventeen, he felt no differently; and thoughts about the garden of Eden still filled his mind.

His favorite diversion was to take solitary walks in the woods. One day when he had ventured farther than usual a storm overtook him. Though it was not yet evening, the day grew as dark as night and the rain came down in torrents. Soon he lost his way. He slipped in the wet grass and stumbled over the rocks. The poor prince was wet to the skin. Exhausted, he climbed up the side of the cliff, pressing his body against the water-drenched moss. He was about to give up when he heard a strange whistling noise near him; then he came upon a cavern in the cliff wall. Inside the cave was a fire so great that a whole deer could be roasted over it; and that was exactly what was being done. A woman who was so big and strong that she looked like a man, who had put on skirts, was turning a spit on which was a buck, antlers and all.

She put another log on the fire; then she turned and called to the prince, "Come in! Sit down by the fire and dry your clothes."

"It's drafty in here," the prince said. He was shivering as he sat down on the floor near the fire.

"It's going to be a lot draftier when my sons come home," said the woman. "You are in the cave of the winds. The four winds of the world are my sons, do you understand?"

"Where are they now?" asked the prince, who had understood her well enough.

"If a question is stupid, how can one give a clever answer?" grumbled the woman. "My sons are out on their own, playing ball with the clouds, somewhere up there." She pointed upward and toward the entrance to the cave.

"I see," nodded the prince. "You speak more roughly than the women I am used to talking to."

"Well, they are not mothers of sons like mine." The woman grinned. "I have to be tough to keep my sons in tow. But I can take care of them, however stiff-necked they are. See those four leather bags hanging on the wall? They are just as afraid of them as you were of the switch in the corner. I am stronger than they are, and if they don't behave, then I pick any one of them up and put him in a bag, and there he can stay until I let him out again. There is one of them coming now."

It was the north wind. He was clad in bearskin with a sealskin cap pulled down over his ears. He brought hail and snow in with him; and icicles were hanging from his beard.

"You'd better not go near the fire just yet," said the prince, "or you will get frostbite on your hands and your face."

"Frostbite!" laughed the north wind as loud as he could. "Why, frost and coldness are what I love. How has such a little weakling as you found your way to the cave of the winds?"

"He is my guest," said the old woman, "and if you are not satisfied with that explanation, then I will put you in your bag. You know that I mean what I say."

That quieted the north wind down, and he began to tell about where he had been and what he had seen during the month that he had been away.

"I have just come from the Arctic Ocean," he began. "I have been visiting the Barents Sea with Russian whalers. I sat sleeping on their tiller when they rounded the North Cape. Fulmars flew around my legs. They are strange birds. They flap their wings once or twice and then hold them out straight, gliding along at a good speed."

"Don't be so long-winded," interrupted his mother. "What was it like on the Barents Sea?"

"Oh, it was beautiful. Flat as a dance floor. The snow was melting and the moss was green. Skeletons of walrus and polar bears lay among the sharp stones. They looked like the limbs of giants and were covered with green mold. One would think that the sun had never shone on them. I blew the fog away so that I could see a little better. Someone had built a shed from the wreckage of stranded ships, with walrus skin stretched over it; it had turned strange green and red colors. A polar bear sat on the roof and growled. I went down to the beach and had a look at the birds' nests there. They were filled with little naked offspring who were screaming with their bills open. I blew down into them; that taught them to keep their mouths shut. Down at the water's edge lay the walruses, looking like giant maggots with pigs' heads and teeth more than a yard long."

"You describe it well," admitted his mother. "My mouth waters, hearing about it."

"The Russians began to hunt the walruses. They thrust their harpoons into the animals, and the blood spouted like geysers high up in the air and spattered the white ice red. It made me think of playing a little game myself. I blew, and brought my own ships, the great icebergs, down to squeeze their boats. You should have heard them whimper and whine; but I whistled higher than they did. I held their ships in my vise of ice; they got so frightened that they started to unload the dead walruses and everything else they had aboard onto the ice. Then I sent them a snowstorm and let them drift south, for a taste of salt water. They will never return to the Barents Sea."

"Then you have done evil," said his mother.

"What good I do, I will let others tell about," said the north wind and grinned. "But there is my brother, the west wind. I like him better than the others, there is a smell of the salt sea about him and he brings some blessed coldness with him."

"Is that the gentle zephyr?" asked the prince.

"It is the zephyr, all right," said the old woman, "but he is not so gentle any more. When he was young he was a sweet-looking boy, but that is all gone now."

The west wind looked like a savage. He wore a helmet on his head. In his hand he held a big club that he had cut from a tree in one of the great mahogany forests of America.

"Where are you coming from?" asked his mother.

"From the great primeval forest," he answered, "where thorny liana stretches itself from tree to tree, where the water snake lives and man has never set foot."

"And what did you do there?"

"I looked at the deep river that fell from the cliffs down into the valley, sounding like thunder, and made a spray great enough to bear a rainbow. I saw a buffalo swim in the river; the currents caught it and carried it, among a flock of ducks, down toward the waterfall. When they came to the rapids, the ducks flew up; but the buffalo couldn't fly, it had to follow the water down the turbulent falls. Oh, I liked that sight so much that I blew a storm great enough to fell trees that have stood a thousand years and break them into kindling."

"Is that all you have done?" asked the old woman.

"I have turned somersaults on the savannah, patted wild horses, and blown down a coconut or two. I have a couple of stories I could tell; but it is best not to tell everything one knows. That you know well enough, old thing." He kissed his mother so that she almost fell over backward. Oh, he was a wild boy!

The south wind arrived; he wore a turban and a Bedouin's cape. "It's cold in here," he said, and threw more wood on the fire. "You can tell that the north wind came home first."

"It is so hot in here that you could fry polar bears," grumbled the north wind.

"You are a polar bear yourself," retorted the south wind angrily.

"Do you want to be put in the bag?" asked the old woman, and sounded as if she meant it. "Sit down, and tell us about the places you have been."

"In Africa, Mother," began the south wind, crestfallen. "I have been hunting lions with the Hottentots in the land of the Kaffirs; the great plains were olive green; here the antelopes danced, and I ran races with the ostriches, and won every time. I visited the desert, its yellow sand looked like the ocean's floor. There I met a caravan; they had just slaughtered the last of their camels, to get a little to drink. The sun burned down upon them from above, and the hot sand fried them. The great borderless desert stretched all around them. Then I played with the fine dry sand, I whirled it up in pillars, toward the sky. Oh, that was a dance. You should have seen the face of the merchant; he pulled his caftan up over his head to protect himself and then threw himself down in front of me, as if I were Allah, his God. I buried them all in a pyramid of sand. Next time I come I shall blow it away and let their bones be bleached by the sun, so that other travelers can see that which is hard to believe in the loneliness of the desert: the fact other men have been there before them."

"You have only been evil," scolded his mother; "into the bag you go." She grabbed the south wind around his waist, bent him in half, and stuffed him into one of the leather bags. But the south wind wouldn't keep still and the bag jumped all over the floor; then his mother took it and, using it as a pillow, she sat down upon the bag and he had to lie quietly.

"You have got lively sons," said the prince.

"They are plucky enough; but I can manage them," answered the mother. "Here comes my fourth son."

It was the east wind; he was dressed as a Chinese.

"Oh, that is where you have been," said the mother, and nodded. "I thought you had been in the garden of Eden."

"No, that is where I fly tomorrow," replied the east wind. "Tomorrow it is exactly a hundred years since I was there last. Now I am coming from China. I have danced around the porcelain tower so swiftly that all the little bells rang. Down in the streets the state officials were getting a beating. I didn't count how many bamboo canes were worn out on their backs. All the officers from the first to the ninth grades were being punished. Every time they were hit, they screamed: 'Thank you, thank you, our father protector!' But they didn't mean a word of it, and I rang the bells of the tower, and sang: 'Tsing, tsang, tsu!' "

"You are getting a little too frisky," laughed his mother. "I am glad you are visiting paradise tomorrow; it always improves your manners. Remember to drink from the spring of wisdom, and to bring a bottle full of the water back to your mother."

"I certainly will," said the east wind, "but why have you put my brother from the south in his bag? Let him out. I want him to tell me all about the bird phoenix. The princess in the garden of Eden asks to hear about that bird whenever I visit her. Please let him out, and I shall give you two pocketfuls of tea. I picked it myself and it is fresh and green."

"In appreciation of the tea and because you are my favorite, I will let him out." The old woman untied the bag and the south wind climbed out; he looked embarrassed because the prince had seen his punishment.

"I have a palm leaf." The south wind carefully avoided looking at the prince while he spoke. "You can give it to the princess. On it, the bird phoenix has carefully written, with his bill, his whole life story, all that happened to him during the hundred years he lived. She can read it herself. I saw the bird phoenix set fire to its own nest, as if it were the wife of a Hindu. The dry branches crackled and the smoke had a strange fragrance. At last the bird itself burned with a clear flame and became ashes; and the egg lay red hot among the embers. The shell cracked with a bang like a cannon shot, and the young bird flew up. Now he is king of all the other birds; and the only phoenix in the whole world. He has bitten a mark in the palm leaf; that is his way of sending a greeting to the princess."

"No more talk, let us eat," said the mother of the winds, and started to carve the deer. The prince sat down next to the east wind and they were soon fast friends.

"Tell me," begged the prince, "who is this princess that you are all talking about, and where lies the garden of Eden?"

"Ah! Ha!" laughed the east wind. "Would you like to come along tomorrow? You must remember that no man has been there since Adam and Eve were thrown out. I assume you know about them from the Bible."

"Certainly," said the prince gravely.

"Well, when they were banished, the garden of Eden sank down underground, but it kept its beauty, its warmth and mild air. The queen of the fairies lives there, and there lies the Island of Bliss, where death can never come. If you will climb up on my back to-morrow, then I shall take you there. That is enough talking for to-night, I am tired."

Soon they all fell asleep. It was still early in the morning when the prince awoke, but to his surprise, he found himself flying high up among the clouds. The east wind was carrying him and had a good grasp on him so that he wouldn't fall. They were up so high that the earth below him with its forests and fields looked like a colored map.

"Good morning," said the east wind. "You could have slept a little longer yet. There is not much to look at, all the land below us is flat. But if you want to count the churches you can; they look like chalk marks on the green board down there." It was the fields and meadows the east wind referred to as the "green board."

"It wasn't very polite of me not to say good-by to your mother and your brothers."

"Never mind, a man who is asleep is excused!" grumbled the east wind, and flew even faster. As they passed over the treetops, all the leaves and branches rustled. When they crossed the sea, the waves grew white and the big ships curtsied deeply like swans.

When evening came, they flew in darkness over a great city. The thousands of lights burning below reminded the prince of the sparks that fly from a piece of paper when it has been set on fire. It was so lovely that the prince clapped his hands. But the east wind scolded him and said that he could make better use of his hands by holding on, or he might end up hanging from a church spire.

With grace the great eagles fly over the black forests, but the east wind flies more gracefully. Swift is the horse of the Cossacks, but the east wind is swifter.

"There are the Himalayas," said the east wind. "It is the highest mountain range in Asia; soon we shall be in the garden of Eden."

The wind turned in a southeasterly direction, and soon the prince could smell the fragrance of spices and flowers. Figs and pomegranates grew wild as did a vine that bore both red and blue grapes. Here they rested for a while and stretched themselves out in the soft grass. The flowers nodded to the wind as if they were saying, "Welcome back."

"Are we not in the garden of Eden?" asked the prince.

"Not yet," answered the wind, "but it won't be long now before we are there. Can you see the cave up on the side of that cliff? The grapevines almost hide it. We have to fly through it. Wrap your cape tightly around you. Here the sun is burning hot, but in there it is as cold as ice. The birds that fly past the opening of the cave have one wing in the warm summer and the other in the coldest of winters."

"So this is the gate of paradise," thought the prince as he wrapped himself in his cape. In they went, and cold it was; but the distance was short. The east wind spread out his wings, and they burned like fire, lighting the caves through which they flew. There were great blocks of stones, wet from the water endlessly dropping. They had the strangest shapes; some looked like organ pipes and others like banners. Sometimes the room was so large that the ceiling was lost in darkness; other times, the passages were so narrow that they had to crawl on all fours to get through them. The prince thought they looked like burial chambers.

"Are we taking Death's road to paradise?" he asked.

The east wind did not answer. He pointed toward a radiantly blue light ahead of them. The rocks gave way to a mist, which finally looked like a white cloud in the moonlight. It was no longer cold. The air was mild and fresh like mountain air, and yet filled with the fragrance of the roses that grew in the valley.

Below them was a river; its water was as transparent as air. Gold and silver fish swam in it; and so did scarlet eels. Each time they twisted their bodies, blue sparks flew and illuminated the water. The leaves of the water lilies were all the colors of the rainbow, and the flower itself was a flame that drew its substance from the water, as oil lamps draw theirs from oil. A marble bridge carved as intricately as if it had been ivory led to the Island of Bliss, where the garden of Eden lay.

The east wind carried the prince in his arms, across the river to the island, and set him down among the flowers. The leaves and the petals of the flowers sang to him all the songs he had heard as a child, but their voices were far more beautiful than human voices.

The prince could not recognize any of the trees. Were they palm trees or giant water plants? Certainly, he had never before seen any trees so succulent and tall. Long garlands of wonderful vines, like the ones that decorate old holy books and twist themselves around the gilded first letter on their pages, hung between the trees. Around him he saw the strangest mixtures of animals and plants. In the grass stood some peacocks with their great colorful tail feathers spread out. He drew nearer and touched them. They were not animals but giant burdock leaves as splendid as peacocks' tails. Lions and tigers jumped about among the bushes, tame as kittens. Doves as white as pearls beat their wings so near the lions that they touched their manes. Shy antelopes, with dark eyes as deep as pools, nodded their heads as if they, too, wanted to join the game.

There was the fairy, the princess of the garden of Eden. Her clothes were brighter than the sun, and her face as happy as a mother's when she looks at her sleeping child. She was young and beautiful; a train of lovely girls, each with a star in her hair, followed her.

The east wind gave her the palm leaf, the gift from the bird phoenix, and her eyes sparkled with joy. She took the prince by the hand and led him into her castle. The walls had the same transparency that you see when you hold a tulip petal up toward the sun and look through it. The ceiling was a shining flower and the longer you looked at it, the more magnificent it became.

The prince stepped over to one of the windows, looked out through it; and there he saw the tree of knowledge, the snake, and Adam and Eve. Surprised, he turned to the fairy and asked, "Have they not been banished?"

She smiled and explained to him that what he saw were pictures burned into the glass by Time itself. They were not like any painting he had seen, for they were alive: the leaves of the trees moved and the people portrayed in them came and went as in a mirror. He stood before another window and there he saw Jacob's ladder stretching far up into heaven, and he saw the angels, with their great wings, flying around it. Everything that had ever happened still lived inside these glass paintings. Such curious and wonderful works of art only Time could create.

The fairy smiled at his amazement and led the prince into another great hall in the castle, where the walls were transparent paintings of millions and millions of happy faces: all of them laughing and singing; and their laughter merged with the songs into one melodious hymn to happiness. The faces nearest the ceiling were as tiny as rosebuds, or the point you can make with a sharpened pencil on paper. In the middle of the hall grew a large tree and golden apples the color of oranges hid among its greenery. It was the tree of knowledge, the tree of good and evil, whose fruits Eve had picked and Adam eaten. From its leaves fell red dewdrops, as though the tree shed tears of blood.

"Come down into my little boat," bade the fairy. "It rocks as though it were floating on the swelling waters, and that is a most delightful feeling; but it never moves, though all the countries of the world will pass by for us to look at."

And they did; first the prince saw the snow-clad mountains of the Alps, with their black forests of fir trees and lace collars of clouds. He heard the melancholy sound of the hunters' horns and the herdsmen yodeling. The scene around them changed; banana palms bent their long leaves down toward them and coal-black swans swam near them; beyond the beach the most fantastic flowers bloomed. They were in the Dutch East Indies, the fifth continent. They heard the priests of the savages chant and saw them dance their wild dances. The islands and their blue mountains disappeared, and in their place rose the great pyramids of Egypt, the endless desert, the sphinx and ancient ruins of temples half buried beneath yellow sand. At last, northern lights burned above them, nature's fireworks, far more splendid than any man could construct. The prince was ever so happy; but then, he had seen a great deal more than I have described.

"Can I stay here forever?" he whispered.

"That depends upon yourself," answered the fairy. "If you do not let that which is forbidden tempt you, as Adam did, then you can live here forever."

"I won't touch the apples of the tree of knowledge," said the prince hastily. "There are so many other fruits as lovely as they."

"Examine your own heart, and if there is courage enough in it, then stay. But if you find doubt and weakness there, then ask the east wind to take you with him. He is leaving now and he will not be back for a hundred years. The years here pass like hours, but even a hundred hours are long enough for both temptation and sin. Every evening I shall leave you; and as I go I shall cry out to you to follow me. I shall wave my hand to beckon you to come. But do not obey me. Every step you take toward me will make it more difficult for you to turn back. If you follow me, you will enter the hall where the tree of knowledge grows; underneath its sweet-smelling branches I sleep. As you bend over me I shall smile, but if you kiss my mouth, then Eden's garden will sink down farther into the earth and will forever be lost for you. The cruel wind of the desert will enfold you and cold rain drip from your hair; and sorrow and care will be your lot."

"I will stay," said the prince.

The east wind kissed him on his forehead and said, "Be strong! And I shall see you again when a hundred years have passed. Farewell, farewell!" The east wind spread out his great wings that shone like the lightning of summer or the northern lights of winter.

"Farewell, farewell!" shouted all the flowers and the bushes; and the birds of the air followed him as far as the gate of the garden.

"Now begins our dance," whispered the fairy. "When it is over and the sun begins to set, I shall cry out, begging you to follow me. But do not do it. Every night for a hundred years this will happen; but each time you refuse me makes it easier for you to do it the next time, until at last it will give you no pain. This is the first night and I have warned you."

The fairy led him into a chamber made of white, transparent lilies; their yellow stamens were little golden harps and from them came the most delightful music. The loveliest young maidens, light and slender, danced around him; their gauzelike clothes, like mist, half concealed their beautiful bodies. They sang while they danced a hymn to life: to their own eternal life in paradise.

The sun was setting; the heavens became like gold and the lilies turned the color of roses. The maidens handed the prince a cup of wine; he drank it and felt even more intensely happy than he had before. The back wall of the chamber disappeared and he looked into the great hall where the tree of knowledge grew. Its beauty blinded him. The song coming from the countless faces on the wall sounded like his mother's voice singing to him: "My child, my dearest child."

The fairy waved to him, beckoned to him, and cried lovingly, "Follow me, follow me." He forgot all his promises and ran toward her, on this his very first evening in the garden of Eden. The fragrance of all the strange spices of the world that came from the garden grew stronger, and the music of the harps even more beautiful. In the hall of the tree, it seemed to him that all the millions of happy faces nodded yes, and sang, "One must know and experience everything; man is the master of the world." The dewdrops falling from the leaves of the tree of good and evil no longer looked like tears but like red shining stars.

"Follow me, follow me," whispered a voice, and for each step the prince took, his cheeks grew redder and his blood pulsed even faster through his veins.

"I must," he breathed, "it is no sin to follow beauty and happiness. I just want to see where she sleeps, I shall not kiss her. Nothing is lost unless I do that, and I shall not. I am strong, I am not weak!"

The fairy threw off her beautiful robes and disappeared in among the branches.

"I have not sinned yet," muttered the prince, "and I shall not do it." But he pulled the branches apart to look. There she lay sleeping, as beautiful as only the fairy in the garden of Eden can be. She smiled in her sleep; he bent over her and saw a tear hanging from her long eyelashes.

"Are you crying because of me?" he whispered. "Do not cry, fairest, most beautiful woman! Now I understand the happiness of paradise. It flows with my blood through my veins into my brain, my thoughts. I feel the strength of the angels' eternal life within my mortal body. Let everlasting night come, the riches of one moment like this is enough for me." He kissed away her tear, he kissed her eyes, and his mouth touched hers.

A fearful clap of thunder was heard, deeper, more frightening than any ever heard before. The fairy vanished and the garden of Eden sank into the earth: deep, deep down. The prince saw it disappear into the dark night like a far distant star. He felt a deathly coldness touch his limbs; his eyes closed, and he fell down as though he were dead.

The sharp lashes of the wind whipped his face and the cold rain drenched him, then he awoke. "What have I done?" he sighed. "I have sinned as Adam did. Sinned and caused paradise to sink deeper into the earth." He opened his eyes and saw a star blinking far away, sparkling as the garden of Eden had when it disappeared. It was the morning star.

He rose. He was in the forest near the cave of the winds; their mother was sitting on a tree stump. She looked at him with anger and disgust.

"Already the first evening," she scolded. "I thought so. If you were my boy, then I would put you in a bag."

"That is exactly what will happen to him," said Death, who was standing in the shadow of one of the big trees. He was a strong old man with a scythe in his hands and large black wings on his back.

"In a coffin I shall put him, but not now. Let him first wander about on earth, atoning for his sins, becoming good if he can. Then I shall come, when he least expects it, and put him in a black coffin. I shall carry him on my head to the stars, for there, too, blooms the garden of Eden; and if he has learned to be kind and good, then he shall live there forever. But if his heart and thoughts are filled with sin, then he shall sink in his coffin deeper into the earth than the garden of Eden sank. Only once every thousand years shall I come to fetch him, to find out whether he must be sent even deeper into the earth or be taken to the bright and sparkling star."

## The Flying Trunk

Once there was a merchant who was so rich that he could easily have
paved a whole street with silver coins and still have had enough left
over to pave a little alley as well. But he didn't do anything so foolish,
he made better use of his money than that. He didn't give out a
copper coin without getting a silver one in return; that's how good a
merchant he was, but he couldn't live forever.

His son inherited all his money, and he was better at spending
than at saving it. Every night he attended a party or a masquerade.
He made kites out of bank notes; and when he went to the beach,
he didn't skim stones; no, he skimmed gold coins. In that way, the
money was soon gone, and finally he had nothing but four pennies, a
pair of worn-out slippers, and an old dressing gown. He lost all his
friends; they didn't like to be seen with a person so curiously dressed.
But one of them was kind enough to give him an old trunk and say
to him, "Pack and get out." That was all very well, but he had
nothing to pack, so he sat down inside the trunk himself.

It was a strange trunk; if you pressed on the lock, then it could fly.
That is what the merchant's son did, and away it carried him. Up
through the chimney, up above the clouds and far, far away. The
trunk creaked and groaned; its passenger was afraid that the bottom
would fall out, for then he would have a nasty fall. But it didn't, the
trunk flew him directly to the land of the Turks and landed.

The merchant's son hid the trunk beneath some leaves in a forest and started to walk into town. No one took any notice of him, for in Turkey everyone wears a dressing gown and slippers.

He met a nurse carrying a babe in her arms. "Hey, you Turkish nurse," he said, "what kind of a castle is that one, right outside the city, with windows placed so high up the walls that no one but a giant could look through them?"

"That is where the princess lives," replied the nurse. "It has been prophesied that a lover will cause her great suffering and sorrow, that is why no one can visit her unless the king and the queen are present."

"Thank you," said the merchant's son. He ran back into the forest where he had hidden the trunk, climbed into it, and flew up to the roof of the palace; then he climbed through a window, in to the princess.

She was sleeping on a sofa and looked so beautiful that the merchant's son had to kiss her. She woke up and was terrified at the sight of the strange man, but he told her that he was the God of the Turks and that he had come flying through the air to visit her. That story didn't displease her.

They sat next to each other on the settee and he told her stories. He made up one about her eyes being the loveliest dark forest pools in which thoughts swam like mermaids. He told her that her forehead was a snow mountain filled with grand halls, whose walls were covered with beautiful paintings. And he told her about the storks that bring such sweet little children. Oh, they were delightful stories; then he proposed and she said yes.

"Come back on Saturday," she said, "then the king and queen come for afternoon tea. They will be proud that I am going to marry the God of the Turks. But make sure, sir, that you have some good fairy tales to tell them. My mother likes noble and moral stories, and my father lively ones that can make him laugh."

"Stories are the only wedding gift I shall bring," said the merchant's son, and smiled most pleasingly. Before they parted, the princess gave him a sword with a whole lot of gold coins attached to the hilt; and these he was in need of.

The merchant's son flew away and bought himself a new dressing gown. When he returned to the forest he started to compose the fairy tale that he would tell on Saturday. And that wasn't so easy. But finally he was finished and Saturday came.

The king, the queen, and the whole court were having tea with the princess. They greeted him most kindly.

"Now you must tell us a fairy tale," said the queen, "and I want it to be both profound and instructive."

"But at same time funny," added the king.

"I will try," said the merchant's son.

Here is his story; if you listen carefully, you will understand it: "Once upon a time there were some sulphur matches who were extremely proud because they came of such good family. Their family tree, of which each of them was a tiny splinter, had been the largest pine tree in the forest. The matches lay on a shelf between a tinderbox and an old iron pot; and to them they told the story of their childhood and youth:

"'Then we lived high, so to speak. We were served diamond tea every morning and evening; it is called dew. Whenever the sun was out it shone upon us, and all the little birds had to tell us stories. We knew that we were rich, for we could afford to wear our green clothes all year round, whereas the poor beeches and oaks had to stand quite naked in the winter and freeze. Then the woodcutter came, it was a revolution! The whole family was split. The trunk of our family tree got a job as the mainmast on a full-rigged ship; he can sail around the whole world if he feels like it. We are not sure what happened to the branches, but we got the job of lighting fires for the mean and base multitudes; that is how such noble and aristocratic things as we are ended up in the kitchen.'

"'My life has been quite different,' said the iron pot that stood on the shelf beside the matches. 'From my very birth I have been scrubbed and set over the fire to boil. I have lost count of how many times that has happened. I do the solid, the most important work here, and should be counted first among you all. My only diversion is to stand properly cleaned on the shelf and engage in a dignified conversation with my friends. We are all proper stay-at-homes here, except for the water bucket, which does run down to the well every so often, and the market basket. She brings us news from the town, but as far as I am concerned it is all disagreeable. All she can talk about are the people and the government. Why, the other day an old earthen pot got so frightened that it fell down and broke in pieces. The market basket is a liberal!'

"'You talk too much!' grumbled the tinderbox. 'Let us have a pleasant evening.' And the steel struck the flint so that sparks flew.

"'Yes, let us discuss who is the most important person here,' suggested the matches.

"'I don't like to talk about myself,' said an earthenware pot. 'Let's tell stories instead. I will begin with an everyday story, the kind that could have happened to any of us. I think that kind of story is the most amusing: *"By the Baltic Sea where the Danish beeches mirror their—"'*

"'That is a beautiful beginning,' exclaimed the plates. 'We are sure we will love that story.'

"'There I spent my youth in a quiet home,' continued the earthenware pot. 'The furniture was polished each week, the floors washed every second day, and the curtains were washed and ironed every fortnight.'

"'How interestingly you describe it,' interrupted the feather duster. 'One can hear that a woman is talking, there is an air of cleanliness about it all.'

"'How true, how true!' said the water bucket, and jumped, out of pure joy, several inches into the air.

"The earthenware pot told its story; and both the middle and the end were just as interesting as the beginning had been.

"All the plates clattered in unison as applause; and the feather duster took some parsley and made it into a garland with which to crown the pot. She knew it would irritate the others; besides, she thought, 'If I honor her today, she will honor me tomorrow.'

"'We will dance,' said the big black pair of tongs; and so they did! Goodness, how they could stretch their legs. The cover on the old chair, over in the corner, split right down the middle just trying to follow them with his eyes. 'Where are our laurel leaves?' demanded the tongs when they had finished; and they were crowned with a garland too.

"'Vulgar rabble,' thought the matches; but they didn't say it out loud.

"The samovar was going to sing; but it had caught cold—at least so it claimed, but it wasn't true. She was too proud; she would only sing in the dining room, when the master and mistress were present.

"Over on the window sill was an old pen that the maid used to write with. There was nothing special about it except that it had been dipped a little too deeply in the inkwell. The pen thought that this was a distinction and was proud of it. 'If the samovar won't sing,' remarked the pen, 'we shouldn't beg it to. Outside the window hangs a bird cage with a nightingale in it; why not let him sing? True, his voice is untrained and he is quite uneducated; but his song has a pleasing naïve simplicity about it.'

"'I object. I think it is most improper,' complained the teakettle, who was a half sister of the samovar. 'Why should we listen to a foreign bird? Is that patriotic? Let the market basket judge between us.'

"'I am annoyed and irritated,' shouted the market basket. 'It is most aggravating; what a way to spend an evening! Let's put everything back in its right place, then I'll rule the roost, as I ought to. And you'll see what a difference that will make.'

"'Let's make noise! Let's make noise!' screamed all the others.

"At that moment the door opened and the maid entered. Instantly, they stood still and kept quiet, every one of them. But even the smallest earthenware pot thought to herself, 'I am really the most important person here in the kitchen and, if I had wanted to, I could have made it into a most amusing evening.'

"The maid took a match, struck it, and lighted the fire. 'Now everyone can see,' thought the match, 'that we are the true aristocrats here. What a flame we make. What glorious light!' And that was the end of the match, it burned out."

"That was a lovely fairy tale," said the queen. "I feel just as if I had been in the kitchen with the matches. You shall have our daughter."

"Certainly," said the king. "We will hold the wedding on Monday," and he patted the merchant's son on the back, for now he was part of the family.

On Sunday evening the whole town was illuminated in honor of the impending marriage. Buns and pretzels were given away to everyone; and the street urchins whistled through their fingers. It was a moving sight.

"I'd better add to the festivities," thought the merchant's son. He went out and bought all the fireworks he could, put them in the trunk, and flew up in the air.

Ah! how high he flew and the fireworks sputtered, glittered, and banged. Such a spectacle no one had seen before. All the Turks jumped a foot up into the air and lost their slippers. Now they knew it was the God of the Turks who would be marrying their princess.

When the merchant's son had returned in his trunk to the forest, he decided to go back into town in order to hear what everyone was saying about his performance—and it's quite understandable that he should want to.

And the things that people said! Everyone had seen something different, but they all agreed that it was marvelous.

"I saw the God himself," said one man. "He had eyes like stars and a beard like the foaming ocean."

"He flew wearing a cloak of fire," said another, "and the prettiest cherubs were peeping out from under its folds."

It was all very pleasing to hear; and tomorrow was his wedding day!

He hurried back to the forest to sleep the night away in his trunk. But where was it?

It had burned to ashes. A little spark from one of the fireworks had ignited it; and that was the end of the trunk, and the merchant's son too! Now he could not fly to his bride.

She waited for him on the roof all day. She is still waiting for him, while he is wandering around the world, telling fairy tales; but they are not so lighthearted as the one he told about the sulphur matches.

## 16

## The Storks

On the roof of the last house at the edge of the town, storks had built their home. The mother stork was sitting in the nest. Her four little ones stuck their heads up and peeped out over the edge. Their bills were still black, for they were so young that they had not yet turned red. A few feet away on the ridge of the roof stood their father, as rigidly as a soldier on guard. He was standing on one leg, as still as a wooden statue.

"It looks very distinguished to have a sentry at the nest," he thought. "No one knows that it is my own family; people passing by will believe that I am here on duty. It looks most noble." So he stayed where he was without blinking an eyelid.

Some children were playing down in the street. They looked up at the storks, and the boldest boy among them began singing the old nursery rhyme about the storks. Soon the other joined him:

> "Stork, stork, with legs so long,
> And wings so broad and strong,
> Fly home to your wife and your nest.
> The four young ones you love best:
> The first shall be hanged from the gallow,
> The second shall be dipped in tallow,
> The third shall be plucked and burned,
> The fourth upside down shall be turned."

"Listen to what the boys are singing," said the young storks. "They say we are going to be hanged and burned."

"Don't listen to them," advised their mother. "What one does not hear cannot hurt one."

But the little boys kept singing and pointing their fingers at the storks. Only one of them—his name was Peter—said it was a shame to make fun of the birds, and he wouldn't join the others in their naughty game.

The mother tried to comfort her young ones. "Don't pay any attention to them," she said. "Look how calmly your father is standing guard on one leg."

"We are still afraid," squeaked the young storks, and hid beneath their mother.

The next day the children were playing in the street again, and when they saw the storks they began to sing the song once more:

> "The first shall be hanged from the gallow,
> The second shall be dipped in tallow,
> The third shall be plucked and burned,
> The fourth upside down shall be turned."

"Are we really to be hanged and burned?" asked the young storks again.

"Nonsense!" said their mother. "You are going to learn to fly, then we will visit the meadow and the lake. The frogs will give us a concert, Croak . . . Croak! Afterward we eat them, it is a marvelous amusement!"

"What happens after that?" asked her young ones.

"Then comes the harvest maneuvers, when all the storks in the whole district gather together. It is of great importance to be able to fly well then, for if you can't the general kills you. He sticks his bill right into your heart. So pay attention and learn your lessons."

"So we are going to be killed after all," exclaimed the young storks. "Listen, the boys are singing that song again."

"Listen to me and not to those bad boys," grumbled their mother. "After the great maneuvers, we fly to the hot countries. They are far from here. We have to fly over forests and mountains. We travel to Egypt, where they have triangular stone houses so high that their tops reach the clouds; they are called pyramids. They are so ancient that no stork can remember when they were built. Near them flows a river with muddy banks; one walks in mud and eats frogs all day."

"Oh," sighed her young ones.

"Yes," continued their mother, "one does nothing else but eat all day. While we are living in comfort, it is so cold up here that there is not a green leaf left, and all the clouds freeze to pieces and fall down as little white flakes."

"Do the naughty children freeze to pieces too?" asked the young storks.

"Not quite, but almost. They have to stay inside, in little dark rooms, while you are free to fly about among the flowers in the warm sunshine."

Time passed and the young storks were old enough to stand up in the nest and look about them. Their father came every day with frogs, little snakes, and other goodies that he found. He was fond of his children and did his best to amuse them. He twisted his long neck and made noise with his bill and told them stories about the swamp.

"Now I will have to teach you to fly," said their mother one day, and commanded all four of them up on the ridge of the roof. There they stood, and none too steadily; they used their wings to balance themselves, but they almost fell down.

"Now look at me," commanded their mother. "This is the way you must hold your head, and this the way to keep your legs. One . . . two, one . . . two. You flap your wings; they will bring you ahead in this world."

The mother stork flew in a little circle around the house and landed again. The young ones made some clumsy hops and one of them almost fell off the roof.

"I don't want to learn to fly," said the one that had almost fallen, and climbed back into the nest. "I don't care about the warm countries."

"Do you want to freeze to death when winter comes? Shall I call the boys, so that they can come and hang or burn you?"

"Oh no," said the little stork, and jumped out on the roof again.

By the third day of their training they could really fly. One of them thought that he could sit down in the air as in the nest; but then he fell and learned that to stay in the air you have to use your wings. The boys down in the street were still singing their stupid song.

"Shouldn't we fly down and prick out their eyes?" suggested one of the young storks.

"No nonsense here!" called the mother. "Listen to me, that is more important than anything else. One . . . two . . . three. First we circle to the left around the chimney, then we turn and fly the opposite way around. . . . That was fine! You have been so good that to-morrow I am going to take you all down to the swamp. You will meet some other distinguished families of storks there. Now make sure you behave yourselves better than all the other children there. Re-member to hold your heads high and walk straight. It not only looks fine but makes the others respect you."

"But aren't we to avenge ourselves on the naughty children?" asked the young storks.

"Let them scream as loudly as they wish. You will fly high above the clouds, see the pyramids, while they will stay and freeze here, where there is not a green leaf anywhere or a sweet apple for them to eat."

"We want our revenge anyway," the young ones whispered, though not so loud that their mother could hear them.

The child who had started singing the song and mocked the storks most was only six years old and small for his age at that. But the young storks thought he was a hundred, for he was much bigger than their father and mother. They had no real idea of the difference be-tween children and grownups, and all their hate and wish for revenge were directed toward this particular little boy. He had started it and was the worst child, as far as they were concerned. As the storks grew their anger against the children grew too; and at last their mother had to promise them that they would have their vengeance, but she wanted them to wait until one of the days just before they left.

"I have to see first how you get along on the great harvest ma-neuver. If your flying is too poor, then the general will put his bill right through you and pierce your heart, and then, after all, the boys will be proven right and you can't blame them."

"We will do our best," said the young storks, and they did. They trained every day, and soon flew so well in formation that it was a pleasure to watch them.

The harvest began and all the storks gathered in preparation for the long flight down to Africa. It was a grand maneuver; in great flocks, they flew over the forests and the towns, and the general observed each one's flight closely. The young storks in this story did particularly well; they were given the grade: A plus frogs and snakes! That was the best grade one could get, and they were allowed to eat the frogs and snakes and that they quickly did.

"Now is the time for our revenge," they demanded.

"Yes," said their mother. "I have thought about it and now I know how it shall be done. There is a pond where all the little children lie until the stork comes and gets them for delivery to their parents. There they lie dreaming far more pleasantly than they ever will later in their lives. All parents love and desire such little sweet babes and all children want a little sister or little brother. Now we will fly to that pond and bring all the good children who didn't sing the ugly song a little brother or sister; but the bad ones shan't ever get any."

"But the one who started it all, that ugly, horrible little boy," screamed all the young storks, "what shall we do to him?"

"In the pond there is a dead child," said the mother. "He has dreamed himself to death. We will bring that baby to the boy and he will cry because we have brought him a dead little brother. But in all your anger, have you forgotten the good little boy who shamed the others when they made fun of you? Him we will bring both a brother and a sister; and since his name is Peter, you shall all be called Peter."

All that the mother said came true, and the storks in Denmark are still called Peter, even to this day.

## 17

## The Bronze Pig

In the town of Florence, not far from the Piazza del Granduca, there is a little street—I believe that it is called Porta Rossa—and there across from a small market place, where vegetables are sold, stands a fountain cast in the shape of a pig. Clear, fresh water spouts from its snout, which shines as brightly as bronze can, while the rest of the body is green with age. The snout is polished daily by school-boys and beggars who rest their hands upon it, while leaning over to drink. It is a lovely sight to see the beautifully made animal embraced by a thirsty half-naked boy, who almost kisses its ancient snout with his fresh, young mouth.

Anyone who visits Florence can find the fountain; and if he can't, he need only ask the first beggar he meets, and he will show him the way to the bronze pig.

It was late on a winter evening. The tops of the hills that surround the city were covered with snow. But it was not dark, for the moon was out; and the moon in Italy gives as much light as the sun does on a northern winter day.—No, I would even say that it gives more, for here the air is so clear, it seems to reflect the moon's light; it is not cold and gray as the air in the north, which like a leaden lid seems to be pressing you down into the cold, wet earth, as if you were already buried and lying in your coffin.

In the ducal gardens, where thousands of flowers bloom in winter, a ragged little boy had sat all day under a large pine tree. He was the very picture of Italy: laughing, beautiful, and suffering. He was hungry and thirsty; and though he had held out his little hand all day, no one had dropped anything into it. Night fell, and the watch man who came to close the gardens drove him away. On a bridge over the Arno, the boy stood for a long time, staring into the water and dreaming, as he watched the reflections of the many stars, the beautiful marble bridge called Santa Trinita, and himself, shimmering in the river.

He walked back to the fountain, and, putting his arms around the bronze pig's neck, he drank water from its shining spout. Nearby he found some lettuce leaves and a few chestnuts, and they were his dinner. It was cold and the streets were deserted. He was alone. He climbed up on the pig's back and, leaning his curly head forward so that it rested on the pig's head, he fell asleep.

It was midnight. The metal animal beneath him moved and said very distinctly, "Little boy, hold on tight, for I am going to run!"

And it did run; and thus began the strangest ride that anyone has ever taken. The pig went first to the Piazza del Granduca. The bronze horse, on which the duke was mounted, neighed loudly when it saw them. All the colored coats of arms of the old town hall shone brilliantly; Michelangelo's David swung his sling. Every statue was alive. The metal figures around Perseus were much too alive; and the Sabine women screamed that horrible cry of fear before death, and it echoed throughout the beautiful square.

In the arcade of the Palazzo degli Uffizi where the nobles of Florence gathered for their masquerades, the bronze pig stopped.

"Hold tight," the bronze pig warned, "for now we are going up the stairs." The little boy did not answer; half joyfully, half fearfully, he clutched the neck of the pig.

They entered the long gallery. The boy knew it well, he had been there before: the walls were covered with paintings and here were the loveliest statues. But now the gallery was more brilliantly lighted than during the day; and every painting seemed more colorful, every bust and figure more beautiful. But the most magnificent moment— and that one the boy never would forget—was when the door to one of the smaller rooms opened. Here was the sculpture of a naked woman: beauty as only nature, marble, and the greatest of all artists can create it. She moved her lovely limbs, and the dolphins at her feet arched their backs and leaped about. Immortality was the message that could be read in her eyes. This sculpture is known to the world as the Medici Venus. On either side of her stood a marble statue, each proving that man's spirit and art can give life, can create it from lifeless stone. One of the figures was of a man grinding his sword; the other showed two gladiators wrestling: for beauty's sake the weapon was sharpened and the men fought.

The boy was almost blinded by the radiance of the colors of paintings on the walls. There was Titian's Venus, the mortal woman whom the artist had loved, stretching herself out on her soft couch. She tossed her head, her naked breasts heaved; her curly hair fell on her naked shoulders, and her dark eyes revealed the passion of the blood that flowed in her veins.

Although every work of art was intensely alive, they did not dare to leave their frames or their pedestals. Maybe it was the golden halos of the Madonna, Jesus, and John the Baptist that made them all stay in their places, for the holy paintings were no longer works of art, they were the holy person they portrayed.

What beauty! What loveliness! The little boy saw it all, for the bronze pig walked slowly through every room of the palace.

One magnificent work of art superseded the other. But one painting appealed especially to the boy, because there were children in it. He had seen it once before in the daylight. It was the painting of *Jesus Descending into the Underworld;* and many hasten by it without a glance, not realizing that it contains a whole world of poetry. The painter, a Florentine, Agnolo Bronzino, had not chosen to portray the suffering of the dead but the expectation in their faces at the sight of Our Lord. Two of the children are embracing; one little boy stretches his hand out toward another child, at the same time he points to himself, as if he were saying: "I am going to paradise." Some of the older people in the painting look uncertain. Filled as they are with doubt and hope, they beg humbly, while the children, in their innocence, demand.

The boy looked at that painting longer than he did at any of the others, and the bronze pig patiently stood still in front of it.

Someone sighed. Did the sound come from the painting or the bronze pig? The boy lifted his hands toward the children in the painting; but just at that moment the pig turned and ran through the galleries.

"Thank you and God bless you!" whispered the boy as the pig

went bumpity . . . bumpity . . . down the stairs with him on his back.

"Thank yourself and God bless you!" replied the metal animal. "I have helped you and you have helped me, for only when an innocent child sits on my back, do I become alive and have the strength to run as I have tonight. Yes, I can even let the light from the lamp beneath the Blessed Virgin shine upon me. It is only into the church that I am not allowed to go; but with you on my back I can peep through the door. But don't try to get down, for if you do, then I shall be dead, as I am in the daylight, when you see me in the Via Porta Rossa."

"I will stay with you," the child promised; and away they ran, through the streets of the town, till they came to the Church of Santa Croce.

The portals of the church opened by themselves. All the candles on the great altar were lit, and the light shone all the way out to the deserted square, where stood the bronze pig with a boy mounted on his back.

Above a tomb, along the left aisle, a thousand stars formed a halo. A coat of arms decorated the simple monument: on a blue background was a ladder that glowed as if it were on fire. It was the tomb of Galileo and the coat of arms could be the emblem of art itself, for the way of the artist is up a ladder of fire to the sky. Every true prophet of the spirit ascends toward heaven like Elijah!

Down the right aisle, all the marble figures on the richly decorated sarcophagi had come alive. Dante with laurel leaves on his head, Michelangelo, Machiavelli, Alfieri: here they were, side by side, the glory of Italy! The Church of Santa Croce is not as large as Florence's cathedral, but it is much more beautiful.

The marble clothes of the statues seemed to move, while the great men's heads appeared to have turned so that they could look out into the night. From the altar came the sweet voices of the white-clad choir boys, who swung censers, from which the strong smell of incense pervaded the air, even as far as the square.

The boy stretched his arms toward the light of the altar, and the bronze pig turned and ran so fast that the child had to hold on with all his strength not to fall off. The boy heard the wind whistling in his ears, then he heard a loud bang as the big doors of the church closed. He lost consciousness. He felt cold; then he opened his eyes, he was awake.

It was morning. He was sitting—almost falling off—the bronze pig, which stood as immobile as ever in the Via Porta Rossa.

Fearfully, the boy thought of the woman whom he called his mother. She had sent him out yesterday to beg, but no one had given him any money, not so much as the tiniest copper coin. He was hungry. Once more he embraced the bronze pig and drank water from its snout. He kissed it and made his way home through the dirty streets.

He lived in one of the narrowest lanes in the city; it was just broad enough for a loaded donkey to pass. An iron-studded door stood ajar; he slipped past it and began to climb a stone staircase that had a worn-out rope for a banister. The walls were filthy. He came to the courtyard; above there was a gallery all the way around the building. On its railings, clothes that were no more than rags had been hung out to dry. In the center of the yard there was a well, and from it heavy wires were strung to each of the apartments, so that water could be drawn without the inconvenience of having to carry it from below; and the pails danced in the air, spilling water down into the courtyard.

The boy went up another, even narrower, stone staircase. Two Russian sailors who were coming from their night's bacchanal were rushing down the stairs, laughing, and they almost bumped into the child. A woman who was neither young nor old, with beautiful black hair, stood on the landing at the top of the stairs.

"How much did you get?" she asked the boy.

"Don't be angry!" he begged. "I didn't get anything; nothing at all!" The boy grabbed the hem of her skirt as if he were, in humility, about to kiss it.

They stepped inside, into the garret that was their home. Its misery I shall not describe. Only one thing needs to be mentioned: there was an earthenware pot filled with smoldering charcoal, and the woman put her hands around it in order to warm them.

She poked the child with her elbow and screamed, "Where is the money? I know you have money!"

The boy started to weep. She kicked out at him with her foot, and he wailed louder. "Keep still, you sniveling little thing, or I'll bash your head in!" She swung the earthenware pot in the air as if she were about to carry out her threat. Screaming, the child threw himself down on the floor.

Another woman came rushing into the room. She, too, was carrying a dish containing burning charcoal. "Felicita, what are you doing to the child?" she cried.

"He's my child, and I can murder him if I want to," the woman answered. "And I can kill you too, Gianina!" And she flung her clay pot toward the intruder; and Gianina lifted hers in order to ward off the danger; and the two dishes met in mid-air, breaking in pieces and spreading burning charcoal all over the tiny room.

But the child had escaped. He ran down the stairs, across the courtyard, and out of the house. He ran as fast as he could, and he kept on running until he could hardly breathe. He had reached the Church of Santa Croce. He entered the church whose portals had opened for him the night before and he kneeled down in front of one of the tombs; it was Michelangelo's. Still crying, he prayed. The only one, among all those who had come to attend mass, to notice him was an elderly man. He glanced at the child and then walked on.

The little boy felt weak from hunger. He climbed into the niche between the monument and the wall and fell asleep. He was awakened by someone tugging at his sleeve. It was the man who had been in the church earlier in the day.

"Are you ill?" the man demanded. "Where do you live?" He went on asking questions. The boy answered him; and finally the man took him by the hand and led him to his home.

It was a small house in one of the side streets. The man was a glovemaker; and his wife was sitting sewing gloves when they entered. A little white poodle, whose curly coat was cut so closely that its pink skin could be seen, hopped up on a table and sprang up on the boy, barking all the while.

"The two innocent souls recognize each other," said the woman, and patted the dog.

The boy was given something to eat and allowed to stay for the night. The next day the glovemaker, Papa Giuseppi as he was called, would talk with his mother. The boy was given a bed to sleep on which was no more than a bench; but to the child who was used to sleeping on a stone floor, it seemed royal luxury. That night he dreamed about the bronze pig and the paintings he had seen.

When Papa Giuseppi left the house the next morning, the little boy was not happy. He was afraid that he would be taken back to his mother, and he cried and kissed the little dog. The glovemaker's wife smiled and nodded to them both.

When Papa Giuseppi came home, he talked with his wife for a long time alone. When they were finished, she patted the child on the head and said kindly, "He is a sweet little boy. He can be as good a glovemaker as you are. Look at his fingers, how long and thin they are. I am sure Our Lady has meant for him to be a glovemaker."

The boy stayed in their home and the glovemaker's wife taught him how to sew. He was given plenty to eat, and he slept comfortably in his little bed. Soon his boyish spirit returned and he began to tease Bellissima, the little dog. This the glovemaker's wife did not like. She was angry; she shook her finger at him and scolded him.

The child was sorry for what he had done. Thoughtful and repentant, he sat in his tiny room, which was also used for drying skins. There were bars on the window to prevent thieves from entering it. That night he could not sleep. Suddenly he heard a noise outside the window. *Clappidy . . . Clap . . .* The boy felt certain that it was the bronze pig who had come to comfort him. He jumped out of bed and ran to the window. He saw only the empty alley.

"Help the *signore* to carry his paints," the woman said to the boy the following morning. The *signore* was their neighbor, a young painter. He was having difficulty carrying both a large canvas and his box of paints.

The boy took the paint box, and together they went to the gallery: the same one the boy had visited with the bronze pig. The child recognized many of the beautiful marble statues and the paintings. There was the lovely statue of Venus; and he saw again the pictures of Jesus, the Holy Mother, and John the Baptist.

The painter stopped in front of the painting of *Jesus Descending into the Underworld* by Bronzino, in which the children smile so sweetly in their certainty that soon they will be in heaven. The little boy smiled too, for this was his heaven.

"Now you can go home," said the painter, when he noticed that the boy was still there, after he had finished setting up his easel.

"May I not watch you paint, sir?" the boy asked as courteously as he could. "I would so like to know how it is done."

"I am not going to paint now, I am only going to draw," explained the artist. In his hand he had a black crayon; how swiftly it moved across the white surface! With his eye he measured the figures in the painting, and soon the outline of Christ appeared.

"Don't stand there gaping. Go home," ordered the painter irritably.

The boy wandered back to the house of the glover, sat down at the table, and started to sew gloves. But his mind was still on the paintings he had seen, and he pricked his fingers and sewed badly that day. But he did not tease Bellissima.

That evening he noticed that the street door was open and he tiptoed outside. It was a chilly but beautiful starry night. Slowly he walked toward the Via Porta Rossa to see the bronze pig.

He bent down, kissed the pig on its shiny snout, and then mounted its back. "Blessed animal," he whispered in its ear, "I have longed for you. Tonight we shall ride again."

But the bronze pig was motionless, the clear, fresh water flowing from its mouth. Suddenly the boy felt something tugging at his pants leg. It was Bellissima, the naked little dog—even in this light he could see its pink skin beneath its short cropped hair. The dog barked, as if it were saying, "Look, I have followed you. Why are you sitting up there?"

A goblin could not have frightened the boy more than the dog did. Bellissima out in the street at night, without his little sheepskin coat on! The dog was never allowed out in the winter without the coat that had been made especially for him. It was tied at the neck with a red ribbon, and it had little belts that were buckled under its stomach. The little dog looked like a little lamb when it went out walking with its mistress, the glovemaker's wife. How the boy feared her anger when she found out that her darling was not at home!

His wish to ride again with the bronze pig was gone, though he kissed the metal animal as he slid off its back. He picked up the dog who was so cold, it was shivering. And the boy ran, with Bellissima in his arms, as fast as he could toward the glover's house.

"Where are you running?" shouted a policeman. Bellissima began to bark. "Have you stolen this dog?" demanded the policeman, taking the animal from him.

"Oh, give it back to me!" wailed the boy.

"If it's really yours—and you haven't just stolen it—then you can tell them at home that they can get it back by coming to the police station." And the policeman told the frightened child on which street the police station was to be found, and walked away with Bellissima in his arms.

How miserable the poor little boy was! He didn't know whether he should go to the glovemaker's and tell what had happened, or jump in the Arno. "She will kill me," he thought. "But I don't mind dying for them. I will go up to heaven to the Blessed Virgin and Jesus." Having made his decision, he walked home to tell all and be killed.

The door was locked and he could not reach the knocker. The street was empty. He found a stone and banged on the door with it.

"Who's there?" shouted a voice from inside.

"It's me!" screamed the little boy. "Bellissima is gone! Open up the door and kill me!"

They were shocked, especially the glovemaker's wife. Her glance went at once to the peg where the little dog's sheepskin coat was still hanging.

"Bellissima at the police station!" she screamed. "You evil child! How could you have taken him out in such cold weather? The poor dog will freeze to death! That little gentle creature in the hands of such ruffians as the police!"

The glovemaker rushed out of the house to go to the police station and retrieve the dog. His wife kept on screaming, and the boy kept on crying. They made such a lot of noise that all the people in the house were awakened and came down to see what was happening, including the painter.

The artist took the boy on his lap; and slowly the child told him the whole story of the bronze pig and his visit to the Galleria degli Uffizi. The painter shook his head in wonder; it was a strange story. He comforted the boy and tried to calm the glovemaker's wife, but that was impossible. Not until her husband had returned with the little dog did she stop lamenting and wailing. Though when she had examined Bellissima and realized that he didn't seem any the worse for having associated with the police, she did cheer up.

The painter patted the boy on the head and gave him some drawings as a gift. They were marvelous drawings! Some of them were caricatures and very funny, but the picture that the boy loved most was the one of the bronze pig. Only a few lines on a piece of paper and there it was, and even the house behind the fountain was there too.

"If you can draw and paint," thought the child, "then you can call the whole world your own."

The next day, as soon as he had finished his work he took a pencil stub and tried to copy the sketch of the bronze pig on the back of one of the artist's drawings. He succeeded! Well, he almost did—true, one of the legs was a little too long and another was too thin; but still, the pig was there on paper. Joyfully, the boy tried again the following day. It was not easy to make the pencil draw lines as straight as he wanted them to be. But the second pig was better than the first; and the third one, anyone could have recognized.

Although his drawing improved, his glove sewing did not; and when he was sent on errands it took him longer and longer to return, for the bronze pig had taught him that all pictures can be drawn; and Florence is one enormous picture book, for anyone who cares to turn the pages. On the Piazza Santa Trinita there stands a slender column with a statue of Justice on top of it; the goddess is blindfolded and has a pair of scales in her hands. Soon she not only stood on a column, but also on a sheet of paper, for the boy had drawn her.

The folio of the glovemaker's little appentice was growing; but until now he had only drawn dead, immobile objects. One day Bellissima was romping gaily about him.

"Sit still," he said to the dog, "and I shall make a lovely picture of you for my collection."

But Bellissima would neither sit nor stand still. If the boy wanted to draw it, there was nothing else for him to do but tie the animal. The child tied the dog both by the tail and by the neck, which the animal didn't like in the least. It barked and tried to jump; and at last the *signora* came.

"You unchristian boy!" she cried. "Oh, the poor animal!" And she kicked the child. "You ungrateful wretch!" she screamed while she picked up the half-strangled little dog and kissed it. Then she dragged the weeping child out of her home.

At that very moment the painter came down the stairs; and this is the turning point of the story.

In Florence, in 1834, there was an exhibition at the Academy of Art. Two paintings that hung next to each other attracted special attention. The smaller one portrayed a little boy who was sketching a closely cropped little white poodle; the dog had not wanted to stand still and the artist had tethered it with strings around both his neck and his tail. The painting was strangely alive, and there was a loveliness about it that revealed the artist's talent. It was told that the painter was born in Florence and had been found in the streets by an elderly glovemaker who had taken the child in. He had taught himself how to draw. A famous painter had discovered the boy's ability, on the very day that the glover's wife had thrown him out of her house for having tied up her darling poodle, so that he could use him as a model.

The glovemaker's little apprentice had become a great artist; this was proven by the other painting as well. It was a picture of a boy, so poor that his clothes were rags, sleeping on the back of the bronze pig in the Via Porta Rossa. Everyone who saw the painting knew the street and the fountain. The child's arm was resting on the pig's head. The little lamp on the wall under the image of the Blessed Virgin cast its light on the child's pale, beautiful face. It was a marvelous painting, framed in gold. On the very top of the frame was a laurel wreath; among the green leaves there was a band of black crepe, and a long black ribbon hung down the side of the painting.

Only a few days before, the young painter had died!

## 18

## The Pact of Friendship

Let us leave the familiar Danish coast and visit the strange shores of Greece, where the sea is as blue as a cornflower in our northern fields. See the lemon trees, how their branches heavy with yellow, yellow fruit bend toward the earth. Around the marble pillars, thistles are growing and hide the pictures cut in the white stone. Here is a shepherd, beside him is his dog. We sit down nearby; and he begins to tell us about an ancient custom, the friendship pact, in which he himself has taken part:

The walls of our house were made of mud; yet our entrance was framed by two marble pillars. They had been found near where our house was built. The roof almost touched the ground. It was black and ugly, although it had been made from flowering oleander and fresh laurel branches, brought from the other side of the mountains. The plot of land around our house was narrow; behind it rose the black, bare, stone sides of the mountains. Their tops were often covered by clouds that looked like living white figures. Never have I heard a bird sing there, nor did the men of my district ever dance to the tune of the bagpipes. From ancient times it has been considered a holy place. The name itself is sacred: Delphi.

The dark, somber mountains are covered with snow until late spring. The highest, on whose pinnacle the evening sun shines longest, is called Parnassus. The waters of the brook that flows past our house come from up there. It was once holy, but now mules muddy it with their feet; yet it flows so swiftly that soon it is clear again. Oh, I recall it all: the holy, lonely stillness!

In the middle of our hut was the fire; here, when the glowing ashes were piled high, bread was baked. In winter, when there was so much snow that our house was almost hidden, my mother seemed happiest. Then she would take my head into both her hands, kiss my forehead, and sing the songs that she dared not sing in summer; for the Turks were our masters and they did not allow us to sing such songs:

> "On the Mountain of Olympus, among the low fir trees,
>      stood an old stag;
> His eyes were heavy with tears: red, green, and
>      pale blue were their colors.
> A young deer came by and asked: 'Why are you
>      shedding red, green, and pale blue tears?'
> 'The Turks have come to our village, they have
>      brought wild dogs for the hunt.'
> 'I will chase them out upon the islands,' said
>      the young deer,
> But before night had come, the deer was slain;
> And before night was over, the old stag had been
>      hunted down and killed."

As my mother finished her sad song, her eyes grew moist and she had to turn away in order to hide the tears that clung to her long eyelashes.

I clenched my fists and said, "We will kill the Turks." My mother turned our black bread in the ashes and sang again the last lines of the song:

> "But before night had come, the deer was slain;
> And before night was over, the stag had been hunted
>      down and killed."

My father had been away for many days. When I saw him coming I ran to meet him. I hoped that he would be bringing me some shiny shells from the Bay of Lepanto, or maybe even a sharp knife. But he brought us a little naked girl. He had carried her inside his sheepskin coat. She lay in a bag of lambskin, and when she was taken out of it and put into my mother's lap, all that she was wearing were the three silver coins that were braided in her hair.

My father told us that the Turks had killed her parents. He himself had been wounded, and his coat was stiff from his own blood that had frozen to ice. My mother bandaged the wound; it was deep and ugly. That night I had strange dreams.

The little girl was to be brought up as my sister. She was beautiful; her eyes were as kind and as beautiful as my mother's. Anastasia was my little sister's name. Her father had taken a vow of friendship with mine. It was an ancient custom to which we still adhere. Those youths who decide to take an oath of brotherhood choose among the girls of the village the one whom they consider the most virtuous and the most beautiful; and she is the witness: the priestess who confirms their pact of friendship.

Now the little girl had become my sister. She sat on my lap, and I picked flowers for her and brought her feathers that I had found on the mountainside. Together we drank of the waters from Parnassus; and we slept next to each other under the laurel-leaf roof of our hut.

Many long winters we listened to my mother's song about the red, green, and pale blue tears, without understanding that it was the sorrow of our people that was mirrored in these tears.

One day three Frenchmen came. They were dressed so differently from us. They had beds and tents on their pack horses. Twenty Turkish soldiers, all armed with swords and guns, escorted them, for they were friends of the pasha, and had a letter from him to tell us who they were and that we were to be hospitable to them. They had only come to look at our barren, black mountains, to climb to the top of Parnassus, up among the clouds and snow. Our little hut was too small for them all; besides, the smoke from our fire made their eyes smart, as it drifted toward the door. They set up camp on the narrow patch of ground around our house and built their fires, over which they roasted lambs and birds. They drank sweet wine, which they offered to the Turkish soldiers, but they didn't dare touch it.

When they left I followed them part of the way. I carried Anastasia on my back in a bag made from goatskins. One of the Frenchmen asked me to stand, leaning against a cliff, and he would make a sketch of us. In the drawing we looked almost alive, and as though we were only one person. When I saw it I could not help thinking that it was true, we were one, for Anastasia was never out of my sight or out of my mind; even at night, if I dreamed, she was in my dreams.

Two nights later there were other people in our hut. They were armed with guns and knives. They were Albanians—"brave people," my mother said. They did not stay long. One of them took my sister Anastasia on his knee; when they were gone she had only two, not three, silver coins in her braids. They put tobacco in strips of paper and smoked it. They discussed in which direction they should go and the oldest of them said: "If I spit up in the air, the spit will fall in my face; and if I spit downward it will fall in my beard."

But finally they had to make up their minds. They left and my father went with them, to show them the way. A little while later we heard shots.

Soldiers came into our hut. They said that we had hidden robbers and that my father had joined their band, so now we would have to leave our home and follow the soldiers.

We passed the place where the battle had been. I saw the corpses of the robbers and the dead body of my father. All I can remember is crying and crying, and then waking up in prison. But the cell was neither smaller nor more barren than the room in our hut. We were given onions and resined wine, and that, too, was not much different from the fare we were used to.

I do not remember how long we were imprisoned, but many days and weeks must have passed. We were set free on Easter Day. My mother was sick. For her sake, we had to walk very slowly; it took us a long time to walk to the coast. When we arrived at the Bay of Lepanto we entered a church.

The holy pictures glistened, for they were on a background of gold. There were pictures of angels, though none of them seemed to me more beautiful than our Anastasia. In the middle of the church stood a coffin filled with roses. The roses were the symbol of Our Lord Jesus, my mother said. The priest declared: "Christ has risen!" And everybody kissed one another. We were all given a lighted candle, even little Anastasia had one. Someone played the bagpipes and the men made their way from the church dancing, hand in hand, while the women of the village roasted the Easter lambs over great fires. We were invited to eat and sat down by the fire.

A boy a few years older than myself kissed me and said: "Christ has risen!" And that was how we two met: Aphtanides and I.

My mother was clever at weaving fishnets and we stayed several months near the sea. I learned to love the water that tasted of salt and reminded me of the stag's tears, for the beautiful sea is sometimes red, other times green, only to turn pale blue at midday.

Aphtanides was a good sailor; he knew how to steer a boat. As silently as the clouds sail in the sky, we would glide through the waters. Anastasia and I would sit in the bottom of the boat. At sunset the mountains were dark blue. One chain seemed to look over the shoulder of another, farthest away stood Mount Parnassus with its snow-covered peaks; blood-red in the evening sun, it towered over all the others. Its peak looked as if it were made of melting iron. The luminous red glow seemed to come from inside the mountain, for it shone long after the sun had set. Only the wings of the sea gulls disturbed the mirror of the sea. Anastasia was sitting next to me. I leaned back. The first stars of evening had come, shining like the candles under the holy pictures in church. They were the same stars that had looked down on me when I sat outside our hut in Delphi. I closed my eyes. Everything was as peaceful, and I dreamed myself back there.

There was a splash! The boat rocked, I screamed! Anastasia had fallen into the sea. Aphtanides was already in the water. He handed my little sister up to me before she had even swallowed a mouthful of water.

We took off her clothes and wrung them out. Aphtanides did the same with his. We stayed out until their clothes were dry, so that no one else ever knew how close to death my little sister had come, and what a part Aphtanides had played in saving her life.

Summer came. The sun baked down upon the earth, scorching it. I thought of the cool mountains and the brook near our house. My mother, too, longed for home. One evening we started the long walk back.

How silent and still it was! The thyme grew tall, and though the sun had dried its leaves, it still had a sweet smell. We did not pass a hut or see a shepherd. Everything was so motionless, so quiet, that the faraway heavens seemed more alive than the earth. I counted the shooting stars. I don't know whether the blue air lighted itself or was lit by starlight, but we could plainly see the outlines of the mountains. . . . My mother made a fire and roasted onions for us to eat. Anastasia and I lay down to sleep without fear of the monstrous Smidraki—from whose mouths, it is said, come burning fire—or the wolves who live in the mountains. For my mother sat close to us, and my little sister and I were still young enough not to be afraid of the world when she was near.

Finally we reached our old home. It was a ruin. It would have to be rebuilt. A couple of women helped my mother, and within a few days the walls stood again and a new roof of oleander covered them. Out of skin and bark my mother wove nets for covering wine bottles; I tended the priest's little herd of goats. Anastasia and the little turtles were my playmates.

One day Aphtanides came to visit us. He said that he had missed us very much, and he stayed two whole days. A month later he returned. This time to say good-by. He was to become a sailor and was leaving on a ship bound for Patras and Corfu. He had brought a big fish, which he gave to my mother. He could tell so many stories, not only about the fishermen who lived in the Bay of Lepanto but also about the heroes and kings who once ruled Greece, as now the Turks do.

When does the bud on the rosebush open itself: what day, what week or what hour? One does not notice, but suddenly it is there and one realizes how beautiful the flower is. Thus it was with Anastasia: one day I noticed that she was a lovely full-grown girl. Years had gone by. The wolfskins that covered my mother's and Anastasia's bed had come from animals that I had shot.

One evening toward sunset Aphtanides came. He was thin as a reed, strong, and browned by the sun. He kissed us all and told us about his life as a seaman and the places he had seen: the fortress of Malta and the pyramids of Egypt. He spoke well and his stories were like the legends the priest could tell. I felt a great respect and admiration for him.

"How much you have seen and experienced," I said. "And how well you tell about it."

"But you have told me about something that I think is the most beautiful of all," replied Aphtanides. "I can't forget it. I mean the old custom of having a pact of friendship. Let us be brothers, as your father and Anastasia's were. Anastasia, our sister, shall be our witness, for a more beautiful or virtuous girl there is not in all of Greece."

Anastasia blushed and her cheeks turned the color of a rose petal. My mother kissed Aphtanides.

It is an hour's walk from our hut to the church. There the soil is richer and tall trees cast their shade. In front of the altar a little lamp is always burning.

I wore my best clothes. My red blouse fitted me tightly around my waist. Silver was woven into the tassel of my fez. In my belt were stuck not only a knife but a pistol as well. Aphtanides wore the blue uniform of a Greek sailor; on a silver chain around his neck he wore a medallion of the Holy Virgin. His scarf was as costly as only the richest men wear. Everyone could see that we were dressed for no ordinary occasion. We walked into the little church. The evening sun shone through the door, and the many-colored pictures and the silver lamp reflected its light.

We kneeled down on the step in front of the altar. Anastasia stood before us. She was wearing a long white dress that hung loosely over her beautiful young body. A collar made of coins, both ancient and new ones, covered her neck and breast. Her black hair had been set up in a single coil and was held in place by a little cap of gold coins, found in the ancient temples. More beautiful jewels than these, no Greek girl can wear.

Her face was radiant. Her eyes were like two stars. Silently, all three of us prayed. When we were finished, she asked: "Will you be friends in life and death?"

"Yes," we answered.

"Will you remember that, whatever happens, your brother is part of you? That your secret is his and his happiness yours? Devotion, sacrifice, perseverance must your soul bear for his sake, and his for yours."

"Yes," we said again; and Anastasia took our hands and joined them together, then she kissed each of us on the forehead; and together we said our prayers once more.

The priest, who had been standing behind the altar, now came forward and blessed all three of us. As we stood up, I saw my mother at the door of the church; she was crying.

How happy were the days that followed, in our little hut near the waters of Delphi. The evening before Aphtanides was to depart we were sitting outside, on the edge of the cliff, deep in thought; his arm was around my shoulders and mine around his. We talked about Greece, the plight of our poor country, and discussed whom we could trust.

No thought did we hide from each other and therefore I grabbed his hand and said, "One thing you must know—until now I have told no one but God—that in my soul is a love greater than even my love for my mother and for you."

Aphtanides' face and neck turned red and he asked, "Whom do you love?"

"I love Anastasia," I whispered. His hand trembled in mine. His face turned as pale as a corpse. I understood—how clear it all was! I bent down and kissed his forehead. "I have never told her," I said. "Maybe she does not love me. But, Brother mine, remember that I have been with her every day; she has grown up not only in our house but in my soul as well."

"She shall be yours," he said. "I cannot lie to you, and I won't. I admit that I love her too. Tomorrow I am leaving for more than two years; before I return you will be married. I have some money. It is yours. No! You shall have it: you must!"

Slowly we walked back toward the hut. Night had come, and Anastasia met us at the doorstep; she was holding a lamp in her hand.

My mother was not at home. Anastasia looked strangely sad as she spoke to Aphtanides. "Tomorrow you leave us," she said. "How unhappy I shall be!"

"You will miss me?" In Aphtanides' words lay a sadness beyond sorrow, a pain as great as my own.

I said nothing but he took her hand in his and said, "My brother here loves you, do you love him? His silence speaks loudly of his love."

Anastasia shivered and burst into tears. I saw only her and thought only of her. I threw my arms around her and said again and again: "I love you!"

She kissed me and her arms embraced my neck. The lamp fell from her hand and the room was as dark as the heart of my poor brother Aphtanides.

At sunrise he rose, kissed us all good-by, and left. His money he had given to my mother to keep for us. A few days later Anastasia became my wife.

## 19

## A Rose from Homer's Grave

In all the songs of the Orient there is an echo of the nightingale's love for the rose. Through the silent, starlit night the little winged creature sings his serenade to the fragrant flower.

Not far from Smyrna, under some tall plane trees, the merchants let their heavily laden camels rest. The weary animals stretch their long necks proudly as they tread clumsily on the sacred ground. Here I saw a rose hedge in full bloom. Wild doves flew among the branches high above; in the sunlight their wings shone like mother-of-pearl.

One of the roses on the hedge was much more beautiful than any of the others; and to this one the nightingale sang of the joy and the pain of its love. The rose was silent, not even a drop of dew as a tear of pity clung to its petals. It bowed its head in the same direction as the branch, toward some large stones.

"Here rests the greatest singer the world has ever known," said the rose. "My fragrance shall scent the air over his grave; and when the wind tears me apart, then my petals shall fall on it. The poet who composed the *Iliad* became earth in the earth from which I have sprung. I am a rose from the grave of Homer. How can I who am so sacred bloom only for a poor nightingale?"

The nightingale sang himself to death.

A caravan came with its heavily laden camels and its black slaves. The son of one of the camel drivers buried the little singer in the great Homer's grave. The rose trembled in the wind.

When evening came the flower closed its petals and slept. It dreamed that one beautiful day, when the sun was shining brightly, a group of Frenchmen came to do homage at Homer's grave. Among them there was a young man from the north, from a country of fog and northern lights. He picked the flower and pressed it between the pages of a book; in that way, he carried it home with him to his native land on another continent. The rose withered of sorrow in the book, which was opened every once in a while to be shown to guests. "Here is a rose from Homer's grave," the young man would say.

After that dream the flower woke and shivered in the morning breeze. One drop of dew fell from it onto the grave of Homer and the nightingale. The sun rose, and the flower bloomed more beautifully than ever before. Noon came, the hot noon of Asia. The rose heard footsteps. Strangers were coming: the Frenchmen whom the rose had dreamed about, and with them was the poet from the north. He picked the rose, kissed the fresh, living flower, and carried it home with him to the land of fog and northern lights.

Like a mummy, the corpse of the flower rests between the pages of the young poet's copy of the *Iliad*. As in a dream, it hears him open the book and say, "Here is a rose from Homer's grave."

## 20

## *The Sandman*

In all the world there is no one who knows so many stories as the sandman, and he knows how to tell them, too.

When it is evening and children are sitting around a table or in a corner on a stool, then he comes sneaking up the stairs; he walks on his stocking feet and makes no noise. Quietly he opens the door and slips into the room and throws a little sand into the eyes of the children; then they find it difficult to keep them open. He stands behind them and blows softly down their necks; and their heads seem, oh, so heavy! But it doesn't hurt, for the sandman loves children. He just wants them to get into bed and lie there quietly, so that he can tell them stories.

When the children have fallen asleep, the sandman sits on their beds. He wears very strange clothes; his suit is made out of silk, but it is quite impossible to tell what color it is, for it changes all the time. One moment it is green, the next it's red, and then it may turn blue. Under each arm he has an umbrella: one of them is all covered with pictures, and that he puts on the headboards of the beds of good children, so that they will dream wonderful stories all the night through. The other umbrella has no pictures at all; that is the one bad children get. They toss and turn all night; and when they wake in the morning, they haven't dreamed anything at all.

Now I want to tell you the stories that the sandman told a little boy named Hjalmar during one week. There are seven stories, for there are seven days in a week.

MONDAY

"Now look," said the sandman that evening after he had gotten Hjalmar into bed, "I think I'll fix up your room a little."

At once all the potted plants grew into huge trees that reached all the way to the ceiling. They stretched their limbs across it, and up and down the walls. The room became the loveliest green arbor. On all the branches flowers bloomed; every one of them was more beautiful and fragrant than a rose; and if you ate them, they tasted sweeter than jam. There were fruits on the trees that shone like gold, and buns bursting with raisins. Oh, it was quite marvelous! But amidst all this splendor, someone was unhappy. The sound of sighing and whimpering came from the table drawer where Hjalmar kept his schoolbooks.

"Now what is the matter?" said the sandman as he opened the drawer.

It was the slate that was sighing; Hjalmar had done his sums on it, and added everything up wrong. The slate pencil, which hung from a piece of string at the corner of the slate, was jumping about in agony as a little dog does on a leash. It wanted to help but it couldn't. Hjalmar's exercise book was sobbing too; it was heartrending to hear. On the top of each page were printed the most exquisite letters, models for the student to copy. Hjalmar had tried, but his letters did not resemble the printed ones: they didn't stand up straight, but more or less dragged themselves along the lines; they looked as if they were fainting or having fits.

"Stand up straight!" screamed the printed letters. "Look at us!"

"Oh, we would love to," sighed Hjalmar's letters. "But we can't, we are not feeling well."

"You should have cod-liver oil," said the sandman.

That helped; the letters that Hjalmar had written got so frightened that they immediately straightened themselves.

"I see there won't be any time for stories tonight; I'd better drill them!" said the sandman as he looked severely at the poor letters. They, in turn, blushed; and all the A's appeared really ashamed.

"Left . . . right . . . left . . . right," he commanded. And the letters obeyed him as if they were soldiers. Soon they stood as straight and handsome as their printed brothers. But the next morning, when Hjalmar peeped at them, they looked just as wretched as they had the day before.

As soon as Hjalmar had got into bed the sandman touched all the furniture in the room with his magic wand; and they began to talk. They all talked about themselves except for the spittoon; it stood silently in its corner, it was so disgusted by the vanity and egocentricity of all the others, who only thought about themselves and never—not even for a moment—of poor creatures like himself, who had to stand in a corner and be spit at.

On the wall above the chest of drawers hung a painting of a landscape, with trees, flowers, and a meadow. In the background there were several castles; it was a very pretty painting, framed in gold. The sandman touched the painting and everything within it became alive. The birds began to sing and the branches of the trees swayed in the wind. The clouds sailed in the sky, casting their shadows upon the grass in the meadow.

The sandman lifted the sleeping Hjalmar out of his bed and held him up to the picture. The boy took a step, and there he was, inside the painting. The sun was shining through the leaves of the trees. He ran down to the river; there was a little sailing ship moored to the bank. It was painted red and white. The sails shone like silver; and six swans, with golden crowns on their heads, drew it through the water. Hjalmar sailed past the forest and the trees told him stories about robbers, witches, the little elves that lived in flowers, and the tales that they—the trees—had heard from the butterflies.

The most wonderful fish, with silver and gold scales, swam around the boat; they jumped out of the water into the air and then fell with a splash back down into the river. Birds of all colors and sizes flew above him. All the animals, even the mosquitoes and flying beetles, wanted to get near Hjalmar; and each one had a little story to tell him.

It was a real voyage. At one moment Hjalmar was sailing through a dense, dark forest, and the next, through a beautiful garden filled with sunlight and flowers. He sailed past marble castles, and on their balconies stood the loveliest princesses; and the strangest part of it was that they looked exactly like the girls he played with every day. The princesses were holding sugar pigs that were better than the ones you could buy in the market place. The girls offered to share them with Hjalmar. When he took hold of an end of a pig, it broke off and he always received the larger piece and the princess the smaller one. In front of every castle a little prince with a golden sword stood guard; and when Hjalmar sailed by, they ordered it to rain tin soldiers and raisins—for they were real princes.

Sometimes he seemed to be sailing through the halls of great mansions, and at other times, right through fantastic towns. He visited the one where the nursemaid lived, who had taken care of him when he was a baby. Hjalmar loved her dearly. There she stood on the square waving to him and singing a little verse about him, which she had composed herself:

> "Oh, my little boy, how I do miss
> The sight of your sweet face,
> The little mouth that I did kiss,
> Your trusting, innocent gaze.
> I shared your laughter, your mirth;
> And yet we had to part.
> May God bless you on this earth,
> And keep pure your loving heart."

And all the birds joined her song. The flowers danced and the trees nodded, as if they, too, had been told stories by the sandman.

### WEDNESDAY

It was pouring outside. Hjalmar could hear the rain beating on the roof, even though he was sleeping. The sandman opened the window. The street had become a lake and right below Hjalmar's window a great ship was moored.

"Come for a sail, Hjalmar," said the sandman. "This ship will take you far away; and yet, when you wake up tomorrow, you will be back in your bed."

Hjalmar stood up and got dressed in his Sunday suit. Once he was on the deck of the ship, it was no longer raining, the sun was shining.

A wind gently filled the sails. The ship tacked around the church and through the streets. Soon it was out on the ocean. As far as the eye could see stretched the wild sea. Hjalmar saw a flock of storks; they were on their way to the hot countries. One of the storks flew low and far behind the others. They had been flying for days, and this stork was ever so tired. Its great wings beat slower and slower, as it came nearer and nearer to the surface of the sea. It tried to gain height but it couldn't; then it collided with the sail of the ship, falling with a loud bump, down on the deck.

The cabin boy picked it up and put it in the little hen coop amidships. There it stood looking very bedraggled and sad among the hens, ducks, and turkeys.

"What a creature!" cackled all the hens.

The turkey cock rustled his feathers and made himself look twice as big as he was; then he spoke to the stork, asking him who he was and where he came from.

The ducks nudged each other and said, "Quack . . . quack!"

The stork told them about the hot countries, about Egypt with its pyramids, and the ostrich that can run across the desert sands faster than a horse.

The ducks didn't understand a word he said and, therefore, remarked to each other, "Let us agree that he is stupid."

"Certainly he is stupid," gobbled the turkey cock, making so much noise that the stork stopped talking. He just stood in a corner of the coop and thought about Africa.

"What beautiful long thin legs," gobbled the turkey. "What do they cost a yard?"

"Quack quack quack!" laughed all the ducks, while the stork pretended that he hadn't heard the insult.

"You ought to join in the merriment," said the turkey, "for it was very witty indeed. Or do you find it too low a joke? I mean for someone like you who has such high legs? Gobble! Gobble!" laughed the turkey. "You have no sense of humor. The rest of us have both wit and intellect; we are most interesting!"

The turkey gobbled and the ducks quacked, for they found themselves ever so amusing.

Hjalmar walked over to the hen coop, opened the door, and let the stork out. Now that it was rested, the stork could fly again. It nodded to Hjalmar as though it were saying thank you; and then it spread its great wings and flew south toward Egypt.

The hens clucked; the ducks quacked; and the turkey cock got all red in the face.

"Tomorrow we are going to cook soup of you," said Hjalmar, and then he woke up. He was back in his little bed. That certainly had been a strange journey the sandman had taken him out on.

THURSDAY

"Now!" began the sandman. "Don't be afraid, here is a little mouse." And he held a little sweet furry animal up to Hjalmar. "It has come to invite you to a wedding; two of the little mice who live beneath the floor of your mother's larder have decided to marry. They have a beautiful apartment down there."

"But how will I get down through the mousehole?" asked Hjalmar.

"Let me see," said the sandman thoughtfully. "I will have to make you smaller." He touched Hjalmar with his magic wand. Instantly the boy began to grow smaller, until finally he wasn't larger than your forefinger. "Now you can borrow the tin soldier's uniform; it is always nice to wear a uniform when you are invited out."

"I will," said Hjalmar; and in a moment he had the uniform on and looked like the nicest little tin soldier.

"Please, sir, would you be so kind as to sit down in your mother's thimble? That will be your carriage and I will be your horse," said the little female mouse.

"Am I to be pulled by a girl? Won't it be too hard work?" asked Hjalmar politely; but he was already on his way to the mouse wedding. They were driving in a long corridor that was just wide enough for the mouse and her guest to pass through. It wasn't dark at all. Little pieces of dry rotten wood illuminated the way.

"Doesn't it smell lovely here?" asked the mouse. "The hall has been greased with lard, and that of the best quality."

Now they entered the chamber where the wedding was to take place. To the right stood all the female mice; they were whispering to each other and making faces. To the left stood the male mice; they were stroking their whiskers but didn't say much. In the middle of the room were the bridal couple; they sat on a cheese rind and kissed each

other all the time, which was permissible in public, for they were engaged and soon would be married.

More and more guests arrived. The room was soon so crowded that
the smaller mice had to stay in the corners or they would have been
trampled to death. It didn't help that the bridal couple were now
standing in the doorway and nearly blocking it. The room had been
greased with lard, just like the corridor: that was the wedding feast,
which the guests could munch on whenever they wished. As dessert a
pea was served; in it, a member of the family had bitten the bridal
couple's initials. It was most extraordinary!

All the mice declared that it had been a marvelous wedding and
that the conversation had been extremely intelligent.

When it was over, the little female mouse drove Hjalmar back. It
had certainly been a distinguished feast he had been invited to attend.
But he had had to make himself small and put on a tin soldier's
uniform.

FRIDAY

"There are so many grownups who plague me to come and visit
them," said the sandman, "especially those who have a bad conscience. 'Oh, kind sandman,' they beg, 'please come. We can't sleep;
our eyes won't close. We have to lie awake all night and look at our
bad deeds. They sit like little trolls at the end of our beds and throw
boiling water on us to keep us awake. Won't you come and tell them
to go away so that we can sleep?' And then they sigh so deeply and
say, 'We will pay you for it. Just come and say good night to us, sweet
sandman. We have put the money on the window sill.' But that kind
of favor you can't buy for money," explained the sandman.

"What is going to happen tonight?" asked Hjalmar.

"Would you like to go to another wedding?" laughed the sandman.
"It will be a little different from the one you went to last night. Your
sister's doll—the one that is dressed as a man and whom you all call
Herman—wants to marry the doll named Bertha. It is Bertha's birthday today and she's expecting a lot of presents."

"Oh, I know all about that." Hjalmar sounded bored. "My sister is
always making birthday parties or holding weddings for her dolls, es-

pecially when they need new clothes. I think she has done it a hundred times."

"But tonight is the hundred and first time, and that is an anniversary that doesn't take place often. When that is over, everything is over. Come take a look!"

Hjalmar glanced toward the table where his playthings were. There was light in the window of the little paper dollhouse; and outside it stood all his tin soldiers and presented arms. The bridal couple sat on the floor. They were leaning their backs against the leg of the table and looking pensively at each other—and that was not so strange; after all, they were getting married.

The sandman had put on Hjalmar's grandmother's skirt and was busy performing the marriage ceremony. As soon as it was over all the furniture sang this beautiful song, which the pencil had written especially for the occasion; he didn't care whether the words made sense so long as they rhymed.

> Wedding one hundred and one
> Has only just begun.
> He is proud as a pin,
> She is made of skin.
> Hurrah for pin, hurrah for skin
> Whose married life does now begin!

Then it was time to give presents, but the two dolls had declared they didn't want anything eatable, they were going to live on love.

"Should we go to the country or travel abroad for our honeymoon?" asked the groom.

This was a weighty problem; and therefore both the swallow, who had traveled widely, and the old hen from the farmyard, who had hatched five broods of chickens, were asked to give their opinions. The swallow told all about the countries of the south, where grapes hung in clusters on the vines and the air was mild and warm. He described the mountains and their strange and beautiful colors, so different from those one can see in the north.

"Ah, but they don't have any kale!" clucked the hen. "I spent one summer out in the country, I had my little chickens with me. We vacationed in a gravel pit. Sand is so delightful to scratch and scrape in. And we were allowed to visit the part of the garden where the kale grew. It had a lovely green color; I am sure that nothing has a more beautiful color."

"But one kale plant looks just like all the others," said the swallow, "and besides, the weather is always so bad here."

"We are used to that," replied the hen.

"But it is always cold, I am freezing," shivered the swallow.

"That is good for the kale," cackled the hen. "Besides, sometimes the weather is hot here too. I remember a summer four years ago; it lasted almost five weeks. It was so hot you could hardly breathe. Besides in foreign lands they have all sorts of creepy poisonous things, and bandits. I think that people who don't love their native land are ungrateful scoundrels who shouldn't be allowed to live here." And the hen began to cry, though she continued to talk. "I have traveled myself once, twelve miles in a wooden crate. Believe me, traveling is no pleasure."

"I think the hen is a very sensible woman," said the doll called Bertha. "I don't like to travel in mountains myself. What is it but up one side and down the other? No, let us move out to a gravel pit and go for walks among the kale stalks."

And that was what they decided to do.

### SATURDAY

"Are you going to tell me a story?" asked Hjalmar as soon as he had gotten into bed.

"No, tonight I haven't got time for one," said the sandman, and opened his most beautiful umbrella over Hjalmar's bed. "But you can look at this. It is all Chinese."

Suddenly the umbrella looked like a Chinese bowl. Inside it there was a whole world: blue trees and blue bridges, with little Chinese men and women standing on them and nodding their heads at Hjalmar.

"Today I have to see to it that the whole world is properly cleaned, for tomorrow is Sunday, you know. I have to go to the church towers to find out whether the church elves have remembered to polish the bells, so they won't sound false. Then I have to go out into the fields and inspect them, to make sure that the wind has dusted all the flowers and trees. But the most important work is to take down all the stars and polish them. I put them in my apron; but first I have to number all the holes so that I can put them back in the right place again. If I don't, some of them might not fit correctly; then they might slip out and there would be too many shooting stars, falling down one after the other."

"Now look here, Mr. Sandman," said the old portrait of Hjalmar's great-grandfather, which hung on the wall opposite Hjalmar's bed. "I am the boy's great-grandfather, and I am pleased that you tell Hjalmar stories, but you must not confuse the child. One cannot take down stars and polish them; the stars are planets like our earth; and that is exactly what is so exciting about them."

"Thank you, thank you, old Great-grandfather," said the sandman; but he didn't look the least bit grateful. "You are the head of the family, the great head, the grand head. But I am a great deal older than you are; I am a heathen. The Romans and the Greeks worshiped me and called me the God of Dreams. I have visited the grandest palaces and am still a welcome guest anywhere. I know how to please both children and grownups. But why don't you tell a story?" With these words the sandman left, taking his umbrella with him.

"These days, one is not even allowed to express an opinion," grumbled Great-grandfather's portrait. And then Hjalmar woke up.

SUNDAY

"Good evening," said the sandman.

Hjalmar nodded his head as a greeting, then jumped out of bed, ran over to Great-grandfather's portrait and turned his face to the wall so he couldn't interrupt as he had done yesterday.

"Now tell me the story about the five peas in the pod, the tale of the cock that crowed too loud, and the one about the darning needle that was so proud that she thought she was a sewing needle," demanded Hjalmar.

"That was a lot," said the sandman. "You know, you can get too much of a good thing. Besides, I like to show you things rather than tell you stories. I think I will let you see my brother; he is also called the sandman, but he only visits you once and then he carries you away on his horse. He tells you a story, but he only knows two. One is the loveliest story ever told, so beautiful that you cannot imagine it; the

other is so ugly and terrifying that it, too, is indescribable." The sandman lifted little Hjalmar up so that he could see out the window. "There
rides my brother, the other sandman who is called Death. He is not
really as frightening or horrible as he is portrayed in books. He is not
a skeleton. That is just the silver embroidery on his uniform. Being in
the cavalry, he rides a horse. Look at his lovely velvet cape fluttering
in the wind behind him as he gallops by."

And Hjalmar saw how Death rode and dismounted to take away
the people who had died; some were old, but others were young.
Some he placed in front of him and others behind him. He asked everyone the same question: "How is your report card?"

And all of them replied: "Oh, it is fine!" But he was not satisfied
with their answers, he had to look himself. Everyone who had good
marks he put in front of him, and to them he told the loveliest story in
the world; but those who had bad marks he put behind him, and they
were told a terrible story. They cried and wanted to jump down from
the horse but they couldn't.

"I think Death is a nice sandman," said Hjalmar. "I am not afraid
of him."

"Oh, there is no reason to be," smiled the sandman. "Just make certain that you have a good report card."

"Now that is what I call a very instructive story," mumbled Great-
grandfather's picture. "You see, it helps to complain and express
one's opinion." Now he was satisfied.

Now you have heard the story of the sandman. You can ask him to
tell you stories, himself, when he comes tonight.

## 21

## The Rose Elf

In the middle of the garden grew a rosebush; it was filled with flowers, and in the most beautiful of them all lived an elf. He was so small that he could not be seen by the human eye. Within every petal of the rose he had a bedchamber. He was wonderfully well proportioned and as lovely as any child. From his shoulders to his heels stretched his beautiful wings. Oh, what fragrant air there was where he slept; and how clear and transparent were the walls, for they were the delicate pink petals of a rose.

All day the little elf flew about in the warm sunshine. He visited all the flowers in the garden, rode on the backs of butterflies, and just for fun he counted how many steps long all the roads and paths on a linden leaf were. What he called roads and paths we call the veins of the leaf; but he was so tiny that they seemed to him like endless roads. The sun set before he was finished, for he had started the work too late.

It was chilly. The dew was falling, and the evening breeze began to blow. The elf hurried home as fast as he could but the rose had already closed itself for the night. He couldn't get in. He flew around the bush but not one of the flowers was open. The poor little elf became frightened. He had spent every night of his life sleeping sweetly within the petal of a rose. Never before had he been out in the dark. "Oh, this will be my death!" he muttered.

At the end of the garden there was an arbor whose latticework was covered with honeysuckle. The flowers looked like painted trumpets; and inside one of these, the elf hoped he would be able to sleep.

He flew toward the shaded nook but someone was there: two human beings, a beautiful young woman and a handsome young man. They sat close to each other on the little bench and wished never to be separated, for they loved each other, even more than the best little child loves his father and mother.

"We must part," the young man said, and sighed. "Your brother frowns on our love and that is why he is sending me away. I am going on a business trip far, far away, across the mountains. Farewell, my sweet bride! For my bride you are!"

They kissed and the young girl wept. She picked a rose for him, but before she handed it to the young man, she kissed it so passionately that the flower opened. The elf flew into the rose and leaned his head up against one of the fragrant, soft walls: at last, he had got inside! Through the petals of the rose he could hear the two young people saying good-by to each other. The young man pinned the rose on his chest. Oh, how his heart beat! The little elf couldn't sleep for all the noise.

As the young man walked through the dark forest he took the rose in his hand. Again and again he kissed it, so fervently that he almost crushed the elf to death. He could feel how the young man's lips burned; and the rose opened itself as if it were midday.

Another man was also afoot in the forest that night: the young girl's evil brother. In his hand he had a long sharp knife. While the young man kissed his rose, the evil man stabbed him to death. He cut off his head; and then buried both head and body in the soft earth under a linden tree.

"Now he is gone and soon he will be forgotten," thought the evil man. "He was supposed to go on a long journey across the mountains. On such a trip one can easily lose one's life, and that is what will have happened to him. He will never return and my sister will never dare ask me why."

He covered the newly dug earth with leaves and twigs and walked home through the dark night. But he was not as alone as he thought he was, for the little elf was with him. He was inside a rolled-up, withered linden leaf that had fallen into the evil man's hair, while he made the grave. Afterward the murderer had put his hat on again; and in the darkness the poor little elf shook both with fear and with anger, thinking of the ugly deed he had witnessed.

At sunrise the evil man returned to his house. He took his hat off and went into his sister's bedchamber. The beautiful young girl was still asleep, dreaming about the young man she loved, who she thought had started on his long journey across the mountains. Her evil brother bent over her and laughed: the laughter of a devil. The leaf fell from his hair without his noticing it. He tiptoed out of his sister's room and went to his own, to sleep.

The little elf rushed out of the leaf and into the sleeping girl's ear. He told her of the evil deed he had seen. To the girl it was like a dream. He described how her brother had murdered the young man she loved and buried him under a flowering linden tree; then he explained where in the forest the linden tree was. Finally he remarked, "You will find on your bed a wizened linden leaf and then you will know that this is not a dream."

The girl woke and there was the leaf! Oh, how she cried! How many salt tears she shed. And there was no one to comfort her, no one she could tell of her misery. The window was open; the elf could have flown out to his rose in the garden; but he could not bear to leave the girl all alone. On the window sill was a plant, and there on a flower he spent the rest of the day.

Several times the evil brother came. He joked and laughed boisterously. The poor girl did not dare show her sorrow.

As soon as night came, she sneaked out of the house and went to the forest to find the linden tree. Beneath it she dug up the corpse of the young man she loved. She cried and lamented and prayed to God that she, too, soon would die.

She would have liked to take his body back to have it properly buried, but that was impossible. She held the head in her hands and kissed the cold, pale lips; then she shook the earth out of his beautiful hair.

"This shall be mine forever," she said. She covered the dead body; and walked home, carrying her lover's head and the branch of a jasmine bush that grew near the linden tree.

As soon as she returned, she buried the head of the young man in the largest flowerpot she could find, and planted the jasmine branch above it.

"Farewell," whispered the little elf. He could no longer bear to see the girl's sorrow and flew out into the garden to find his rose. Only a few petals clung to the green hip; the flower bloomed no more.

"Soon all that is beautiful will fade and disappear," sighed the elf. But he did find one rose that still had fragrant petals in which he could live.

Every morning he flew to the poor girl's window. He always found her standing by the flowerpot crying, her tears falling on the branch from the jasmine bush; and as the poor girl grew paler and paler, the jasmine branch grew greener. New leaves unfolded and soon white flower buds appeared. The girl kissed them. Her brother chided her and said she must be crazy or stupid to stand like that, crying before a plant. He did not know whose bright eyes and red lips had become dust beneath the lovely jasmine.

One day the young girl rested her head on the window sill next to the flowerpot and fell asleep. The elf found her slumbering and crawled into her ear to tell her about the evenings in the arbor, when the sweet-smelling roses were in bloom. And while she dreamed, her life ebbed out. She died and went to heaven where she was reunited with the young man whom she loved.

The jasmine flowers, like great white bells, opened and spread their sweet fragrance throughout the room; that was their way of crying for the dead.

When the evil brother saw the beautiful flowering bush he took it into his own bedchamber, as if it were his inheritance. It was so pleasant to look at and smelled so nicely. The little elf followed him and then flew from flower to flower to tell everyone of the evil brother's deed and the poor girl's suffering—for in every flower grew a soul that could understand.

"We know all about it," said the flowers. "We know everything! Haven't we grown from the eyes and lips of the dead man? We know all! We know all!"

The little elf could not understand how the flowers could be so calm. He flew out to the bees, who were collecting honey, and told them the story. They, in turn, told it to their queen; and she declared that they would murder the guilty man on the following morning.

But that night—the very first after the girl's death—while the brother slept, the flowers of the jasmine bush opened. The invisible souls of the flowers, every one carrying a poisoned spear, gathered around his ears and told him stories that gave him terrible dreams.

When he screamed in fear, they stuck the deadly points of their spears into his tongue.

"Now we have revenged the dead," they cried, and flew back into their flowers.

In the morning when the window of the bedchamber was opened, the rose elf and the bees, led by the queen, flew into the room to kill the brother. But he was already dead. People were standing around his bed. "The strong smell of the jasmine killed him," one of the men said.

Now the elf understood the flowers' vengeance, and told the queen bee about it. She and all the other bees swarmed about the jasmine bush. The people tried to shoo them out. Finally a man picked up the plant and was going to carry it outside. One of the bees stung his hand. The flowerpot fell to the floor and broke.

All the people looked in horror at the white skull that was loosened from the black earth. Now they knew that the dead man had been a murderer.

The queen bee hummed a song about the flowers' revenge and about the little elf that may live within even the tiniest leaf and can expose and avenge evil.

## 22

*The Swineherd*

There once was a poor prince. He had a kingdom and, though it wasn't very big, it was large enough to marry on, and married he wanted to be.

Now it was rather bold of him to say to the emperor's daughter: "Do you want me?" But he was a young man of spirit who was quite famous, and there were at least a hundred princesses who would have said thank you very much to his proposal. But the emperor's daughter didn't. Let me tell you the story.

On the grave of the prince's father there grew a rose tree. It was a beautiful tree that only flowered every fifth year; and then it bore only one rose. That rose had such a sweet fragrance that anyone who smelled it forgot immediately all his sorrow and troubles. The prince also owned a nightingale which sang as though all the melodies ever composed were in its throat—so beautiful was its song. The prince decided to send the rose and the nightingale to the emperor's daughter, and had two little silver chests made to put them in.

The emperor ordered the gifts to be carried into the grand assembly room where the princess was playing house with her ladies in waiting. That was their favorite game and they never played any other. When the princess saw the pretty little silver chests she clapped her hands and jumped for joy.

"Oh, I hope one of them contains a pretty little kitten," she said; but when she opened the chest, she found a rose.

"It is very prettily made," said one of the ladies in waiting.

"It is more than pretty; it is nice," remarked the emperor. Then the princess touched the rose and she almost wept with disappointment.

"Oh, Papa," she shrieked. "It is not glass, it's real!"

"Oh, oh!" shrieked all the ladies in waiting. "How revolting! It is real!"

"Let's see what is in the other chest first, before we get angry," admonished the emperor. There was the nightingale, who sang so beautifully that it was difficult to find anything wrong with it.

"*Superbe! Charmant!*" said the ladies in waiting. They all spoke French, one worse than the other.

"That bird reminds me of the late empress' music box," said an old courtier. "It has the same tone, the same sense of rhythm."

"You are right," said the emperor, and cried like a baby.

"I would like to know if that is real too," demanded the princess.

"Oh yes, it is a real bird," said one of the pages who had brought the gifts.

"In that case we will let the bird fly away," said the princess; and she sent a messenger to say that she would not even permit the prince to come inside her father's kingdom.

But the prince was not easily discouraged. He smeared his face with both black and brown shoe polish, put a cap on his head, then he walked up to the emperor's castle and knocked.

"Good morning, Emperor," said the young man, for it was the emperor himself who had opened the door. "Can I get a job in the castle?"

"Oh, there are so many people who want to work here," answered the emperor, and shook his head. "But I do need someone to tend the pigs, we have such an awful lot of them."

And so the prince was hired as the emperor's swineherd. There was a tiny, dirty room next to the pigpen, and that was where he was expected to live.

The young man spent the rest of the day making a very pretty little pot. By evening it was finished. The pot had little bells all around it, and when it boiled, they played, ever so sweetly:

Ach, du lieber Augustin,
Alles ist weg, weg, weg.

But the strangest and most wonderful thing about the pot was that, if you held your finger in the steam above it, then you could smell what was cooking on any stove in town. Now there was something a little different from the rose.

The princess was out walking with her ladies in waiting, and when she heard the musical pot she stopped immediately. She listened and smiled, for "Ach, du lieber Augustin" she knew. She could play the melody herself on the piano with one finger.

"It is a song I know!" she exclaimed. "That swineherd must be cultured. Please go in and ask him what the instrument costs."

One of the ladies in waiting was ordered to run over to the pigpen, but she put wooden shoes on first.

"What do you want for the pot?" she asked.

"Ten kisses from the princess," said the swineherd.

"God save us!" cried the lady in waiting.

"I won't settle for less," said the swineherd.

"Well, what did he want?" asked the princess.

"I can't say it," blushed the lady in waiting.

"Then you can whisper it," said the princess; and the lady in waiting whispered.

"He is very naughty," said the princess, and walked on. But she had gone only a few steps when she heard the little bells play again, and they sounded even sweeter to her than they had before.

> Ach, du lieber Augustin,
> Alles ist weg, weg, weg.

"Listen," she said, "ask him if he will be satisfied with ten kisses from one of my ladies in waiting."

"No, thank you!" replied the swineherd to that proposal. "Ten kisses from the princess or I keep my pot."

"This is most embarrassing," declared the princess. "You will all have to stand around me so no one can see it."

And the ladies in waiting formed a circle and held out their skirts so no one could peep. The swineherd got his kisses and the princess the pot.

Oh, what a grand time they had! All day and all evening they made the little pot boil. There wasn't a stove in the whole town that had anything cooking on it that they didn't know about. They knew what was served for dinner on every table: both the count's and the cowherd's. The ladies in waiting were so delighted that they clapped their little hands.

"We know who is going to have soup and pancakes and who is eating porridge and rib roast! Oh, it is most interesting."

"Very!" said the imperial housekeeper.

"Keep your mouth shut. Remember, I am the princess," said the emperor's daughter.

And all the ladies in waiting and the imperial housekeeper said: "God preserve us, we won't say a word."

The swineherd—that is to say, the prince whom everyone thought was a swineherd—did not like to waste his time, so he constructed a rattle which was so ingenious that, when you swung it around, it played all the waltzes, polkas, and dance melodies ever composed since the creation of the world.

"It is superb!" exclaimed the princess as she was walking past the pigsty. "I have never heard a more exquisite composition. Do go in and ask what he wants for the instrument, but I won't kiss him!"

"He wants a hundred kisses from the princess," said the lady in waiting who had been sent to speak to the swineherd.

"He must be mad," declared the princess. She walked on a few steps and then she stood still. "One ought to encourage art," she said. "I am the emperor's daughter. Tell him he can have ten kisses from me just as he got yesterday. The rest he can get from my ladies in waiting."

"But we don't want to kiss him," they all cried.

"Stuff and nonsense!" replied the princess, for she was angry. "If I can kiss him, you can too. Besides, what do you think I give you room and board for?"

And one of the ladies in waiting went to talk with the swineherd. "One hundred kisses from the princess or I keep the rattle," was the message she came back with.

"Then gather around me!" commanded the princess. The ladies in waiting took their positions and the kissing began.

"I wonder what is going on down there by the pigsty," said the emperor, who was standing out on the balcony. He rubbed his eyes and put his glasses on. "It is the ladies in waiting. What devilment are they up to? I'd better go down and see." Then he pulled up the backs of his slippers, for they were really only a comfortable old pair of shoes with broken backs. Oh, how he ran! But as soon as he came near the pigsty he walked on tiptoe.

The ladies in waiting were so busy counting kisses—to make sure that the bargain was justly carried out and that the swineherd did not get one kiss too many or one too few—that they didn't hear or see the emperor, who was standing on tiptoe outside the circle.

"What's going on here?" he shouted. When he saw the kissing he took off one of his slippers and started hitting the ladies in waiting on the tops of their heads, just as the swineherd was getting his eighty-sixth kiss.

"*Heraus!* Get out!" he screamed, for he was really angry; and both the swineherd and the princess were thrown out of his empire.

There they stood: the princess was crying, the swineherd was grumbling, and the rain was streaming down.

"Oh, poor me!" wailed the princess. "If only I had married the prince. Oh, I am so unhappy!"

The swineherd stepped behind a tree, rubbed all the black and brown shoe polish off his face, and put on his splendid royal robes. He looked so impressive that the princess curtsied when she saw him.

"I have come to despise you," said the prince. "You did not want an honest prince. You did not appreciate the rose or the nightingale, but you could kiss a swineherd for the sake of a toy. Farewell!"

The prince entered his own kingdom and locked the door behind him; and there the princess could stand and sing:

"Ach, du lieber Augustin,
Alles ist weg, weg, weg."

For, indeed, everything was "all gone"!

## 23

## The Buckwheat

It happens often after a thunderstorm that the buckwheat fields appear all black, as if they had been burned. If you ask the farmer, he will say that the buckwheat has been singed by lightning, but he doesn't know why. Let me tell you what I heard from a sparrow, who had the story from an old willow tree. This willow tree grew right next to a buckwheat field, and it's still there if you want to see it. It's a large, dignified tree; but it's ancient and has a knobby bark. It's split down the middle and in the crevice grass and blackberries grow. The trunk leans a little to one side and the branches hang down toward the earth like long green hair.

All around it are fields of grain: rye, barley, and oats. How lovely oats are! The kernels, when they are ripe, look like so many canary birds sitting on a branch. It stands so gloriously as harvest time approaches, for the heavier the oats become, the more humbly they bend their heads toward the ground.

But on the field nearest the old willow tree grew buckwheat; and buckwheat do not bow their heads but hold them high. They always stand stiff and proud.

"We are as fruitful as any of the others," said the buckwheat. "And we are more beautiful, besides. Our flowers are as lovely as the apple tree's. It is a delight to look at us. You, old willow tree, do you know of anything more beautiful than we are?"

The old willow tree nodded its head vigorously, as if it were saying, "Yes, I certainly do!"

The buckwheat were so indignant that they stood even straighter. "You stupid tree! You are so old that you have grass growing in your stomach."

The weather turned nasty. A storm was brewing and all the flowers of the fields folded their leaves and bent their delicate heads, while the wind tore past them; but the buckwheat proudly tossed their heads.

"Bend your heads as we do," called the flowers.

"I don't need to," replied the buckwheat.

"Bend, bend," screamed the other grains. "In a minute the storm's angel, with its great wings that stretch from the clouds down to the earth, will be here! And he will cut you in two if you do not ask him to be merciful!"

"I will not bow and bend," shouted the buckwheat.

"Close your flowers and fold your leaves," warned the old willow tree. "And do not look at the bolts of lightning that appear when the clouds burst; even man does not dare do that, for through the lightning you can see right into God's heaven and that sight makes men blind. Think what would happen to us if we, who are so much less than man—we who are merely humble plants—should dare to do such a thing."

"Much less?" scowled the buckwheat. "Now I am going to look right into God's heaven!" And it did, confidently and proudly, while the whole sky was aflame with lightning.

When the bad weather was over the grain and the flowers, refreshed by the rain, raised their heads in the still, clear air; but the buckwheat had been singed black; they were dead and useless, not fit for the reaper but only for the plow.

The old willow tree swayed her branches gently in the breeze. Drops of water fell from its leaves, and the little sparrows asked, "Why are you crying? The weather is so glorious now. See how the sun shines and the clouds sail by above us. Can't you smell the sweet fragrance of the flowers and the bushes? Why are you weeping, old willow tree?"

The old tree told the sparrow about the buckwheat's pride, presumption, and its punishment—for punishment always follows presumption.

Now I have told you the story, as the sparrow told it to me, one evening when I asked him to tell me a fairy tale.

## 24

## The Angel

"When a good child dies, an angel comes down from heaven and takes the dead child in his arms; then the angel spreads out his wings and flies with the child to visit all the places that the little one has loved. They pick a whole armful of flowers and bring them to God; in heaven, these flowers will bloom even more beautifully than they have on earth. God presses all the flowers to His heart; but the one that is dearest to Him, He gives a kiss, and then that flower can sing and join in the hosanna."

This was what one of God's angels was telling to a dead child whom he was carrying up to heaven. The child heard it as though in a dream, while the angel flew with him above all the places where he had played and been happy. At last they came to a garden filled with the most beautiful flowers.

"Which ones shall we take along and plant up in heaven?" asked the angel.

There was a tall rosebush whose stem some evil hand had broken, so that all the branches, with their half-open buds that had already begun to wither, lay limp all around it.

"Oh, the poor bush!" cried the child. "Take it along that it may flower again up with God."

The angel kissed the child for the choice he had made and took the rosebush. They picked other flowers. Some were the most elegant in the garden; but they took some wild pansies and violets too.

"Now we have enough flowers," said the child, and the angel nodded. Now they could fly up to God, but the angel tarried.

Night came, and the town grew still. The angel flew with the child above the narrow streets where the poor lived. The day before had been moving day, and the lanes were filled with old straw, broken pots and plates, rags and garbage. It was a sorry sight.

The angel pointed to a broken earthenware pot; near it lay a dried-out wild flower, to whose roots a clump of soil still clung. It had been thrown out in the street together with the other trash.

"That flower we shall take along," said the angel. "And I shall tell you its story while we fly." The angel picked up the dead wild flower and they flew on their way.

"Down in that narrow street," the angel began, "there lived in a cellar a little poor boy who had been ill from birth and had spent his life in bed. When he was 'well,' he would walk around the room, leaning on two crutches. In the middle of the summer, when the sun was so high in the sky that its rays fell into the little courtyard, a chair would be placed by the door of the cellar, and there the boy would enjoy the warm sunshine. The child had to hold up his hands in front of his face, for his eyes were used to the twilight of the cellar. His hands were white and thin, and beneath the transparent skin one could see the blood pulsing through his veins. After such a day his parents would say: 'Today he has been outside.'

"He knew about the greenness of the forest in spring because the neighbor's children would bring him the first green branch of the beech tree. The sick boy would hold it over his head and pretend that he was out in the woods, where the sun shone and the birds sang. One day one of the children brought him a bouquet of wild flowers. Among them was one flower that still had roots. This was planted in an earthenware pot and placed next to the bed. It grew. Each year it had new shoots and new flowers unfolded. The wild flower became the sick child's garden: his treasure on this earth. He watered it and took care of it, making sure that it always stood where the bit of light that came through the tiny cellar window would fall upon it. The flower became part of his world, not only when he was awake but when he dreamed as well. It bloomed for him alone: to give pleasure to his eyes and send sweet fragrance for him to enjoy. When God called him, the boy turned in death toward the flower.

"He has been with God a year now. A whole year the flower stood in the window forgotten; then it was all dried out, so it was thrown out in the street with the other garbage. We shall take the poor dead flower along in our bouquet, for it has spread more happiness than the grandest flower in any royal garden."

"But how do you know all this?" asked the child whom the angel was carrying up to heaven.

"How do I know?" the angel said, and smiled. "I was myself that sick little boy who could not walk without crutches. Oh, I recognize my flower again!"

The child opened his eyes as widely as he could and looked into the happy face of the angel. Just at that moment they flew into heaven, where all sorrows cease. God embraced the dead child, pressed him to His heart; and he grew wings and flew away, hand in hand, with the angel who had brought him into heaven. God pressed all the flowers that they had given Him to His heart; but the dead wild flower He kissed and it gained a voice and could sing with the angels that flew around God, in ever widening circles out into infinity. All sang with equal bliss and fervor: those who had died when old and those who had come as children, and the little wild flower that had been thrown out among the trash in the dark and narrow lane.

## 25

## The Nightingale

In China, as you know, the emperor is Chinese, and so are his court and all his people. This story happened a long, long time ago; and that is just the reason why you should hear it now, before it is forgotten. The emperor's palace was the most beautiful in the whole world. It was made of porcelain and had been most costly to build. It was so fragile that you had to be careful not to touch anything and that can be difficult. The gardens were filled with the loveliest flowers; the most beautiful of them had little silver bells that tinkled so you wouldn't pass by without noticing them.

Everything in the emperor's garden was most cunningly arranged. The gardens were so large that even the head gardener did not know exactly how big they were. If you kept walking you finally came to the most beautiful forest, with tall trees that mirrored themselves in deep lakes. The forest stretched all the way to the sea, which was blue and so deep that even large boats could sail so close to the shore that they were shaded by the trees. Here lived a nightingale who sang so sweetly that even the fisherman, who came every night to set his nets, would stop to rest when he heard it, and say: "Blessed God, how beautifully it sings!" But he couldn't listen too long, for he had work to do, and soon he would forget the bird. Yet the next night when he heard it again, he would repeat what he had said the night before: "Blessed God, how beautifully it sings!"

From all over the world travelers came to the emperor's city to admire his palace and gardens; but when they heard the nightingale sing, they all declared that it was the loveliest of all. When they returned to their own countries, they would write long and learned books about the city, the palace, and the garden; but they didn't forget the nightingale. No, that was always mentioned in the very first chapter. Those who could write poetry wrote long odes about the nightingale who lived in the forest, on the shores of the deep blue sea.

These books were read the whole world over; and finally one was also sent to the emperor. He sat down in his golden chair and started to read it. Every once in a while he would nod his head because it pleased him to read how his own city and his own palace and gardens were praised; but then he came to the sentence: "But the song of the nightingale is the loveliest of all."

"What!" said the emperor. "The nightingale? I don't know it, I have never heard of it; and yet it lives not only in my empire but in my very garden. That is the sort of thing one can only find out by reading books."

He called his chief courtier, who was so very noble that if anyone of a rank lower than his own, either talked to him, or dared ask him a question, he only answered, "P." And that didn't mean anything at all.

"There is a strange and famous bird called the nightingale," began the emperor. "It is thought to be the most marvelous thing in my empire. Why have I never heard of it?"

"I have never heard of it," answered the courtier. "It has never been presented at court."

"I want it to come this evening and sing for me," demanded the emperor. "The whole world knows of it but I do not."

"I have never heard it mentioned before," said the courtier, and bowed. "But I shall search for it and find it."

But that was more easily said than done. The courtier ran all through the palace, up the stairs and down the stairs, and through the long corridors, but none of the people whom he asked had ever heard of the nightingale. He returned to the emperor and declared that the whole story was nothing but a fable, invented by those people who had written the books. "Your Imperial Majesty should not believe everything that is written. A discovery is one thing and artistic imagination something quite different; it is fiction."

"The book I have just read," replied the emperor, "was sent to me by the great Emperor of Japan; and therefore, every word in it must be the truth. I want to hear the nightingale! And that tonight! If it does not come, then the whole court shall have their stomachs thumped, and that right after they have eaten."

"*Tsing-pe!*" said the courtier. He ran again up and down the stairs and through the corridors; and half the court ran with him, because they didn't want their stomachs thumped. Everywhere they asked about the nightingale that the whole world knew about, and yet no one at court had heard of.

At last they came to the kitchen, where a poor little girl worked, scrubbing the pots and pans. "Oh, I know the nightingale," she said, "I know it well, it sings so beautifully. Every evening I am allowed to bring some leftovers to my poor sick mother who lives down by the sea. Now it is far away, and as I return I often rest in the forest and listen to the nightingale. I get tears in my eyes from it, as though my mother were kissing me."

"Little kitchenmaid," said the courtier, "I will arrange for a permanent position in the kitchen for you, and permission to see the emperor eat, if you will take us to the nightingale; it is summoned to court tonight."

Half the court went to the forest to find the nightingale. As they were walking along a cow began to bellow.

"Oh!" shouted all the courtiers. "There it is. What a marvelously powerful voice the little animal has; we have heard it before."

"That is only a cow," said the little kitchenmaid. "We are still far from where the nightingale lives."

They passed a little pond; the frogs were croaking.

"Lovely," sighed the Chinese imperial dean. "I can hear her, she sounds like little church bells ringing."

"No, that is only the frogs," said the little kitchenmaid, "but any time now we may hear it."

Just then the nightingale began singing.

"There it is!" said the little girl. "Listen. Listen. It is up there on that branch." And she pointed to a little gray bird sitting amid the greenery.

"Is that possible?" exclaimed the chief courtier. "I had not imagined it would look like that. It looks so common! I think it has lost its color from shyness and out of embarrassment at seeing so many noble people at one time."

"Little nightingale," called the kitchenmaid, "our emperor wants you to sing for him."

"With pleasure," replied the nightingale, and sang as lovely as he could.

"It sounds like little glass bells," sighed the chief courtier. "Look at its little throat, how it throbs. It is strange that we have never heard of it before; it will be a great success at court."

"Shall I sing another song for the emperor?" asked the nightingale, who thought that the emperor was there.

"Most excellent little nightingale," began the chief courtier, "I have the pleasure to invite you to attend the court tonight, where His Imperial Majesty, the Emperor of China, wishes you to enchant him with your most charming art."

"It sounds best in the green woods," said the nightingale; but when he heard that the emperor insisted, he followed them readily back to the palace.

There every room had been polished and thousands of little golden lamps reflected themselves in the shiny porcelain walls and floors. In the corridors stood all the most beautiful flowers, the ones with silver bells on them; and there was such a draft from all the servants running in and out, and opening and closing doors, that all the bells were tinkling and you couldn't hear what anyone said.

In the grand banquet hall, where the emperor's throne stood, a little golden perch had been hung for the nightingale to sit on. The whole court was there and the little kitchenmaid, who now had the title of Imperial Kitchenmaid, was allowed to stand behind one of the doors and listen. Everyone was dressed in their finest clothes and they all were looking at the little gray bird, toward which the emperor nodded very kindly.

The nightingale's song was so sweet that tears came into the emperor's eyes; and when they ran down his cheeks, the little nightingale sang even more beautifully than it had before. His song spoke to one's heart, and the emperor was so pleased that he ordered his golden slipper to be hung around the little bird's neck. There was no higher honor. But the nightingale thanked him and said that he had been honored enough already.

"I have seen tears in the eyes of an emperor, and that is a great enough treasure for me. There is a strange power in an emperor's

tears and God knows that is reward enough." Then he sang yet another song.

"That was the most charming and elegant song we have ever
heard," said all the ladies of the court. And from that time onward
they filled their mouths with water, so they could make a clucking
noise, whenever anyone spoke to them, because they thought that
then they sounded like the nightingale. Even the chambermaids and
the lackeys were satisfied; and that really meant something, for servants are the most difficult to please. Yes, the nightingale was a success.

He was to have his own cage at court, and permission to take a
walk twice a day and once during the night. Twelve servants were to
accompany him; each held on tightly to a silk ribbon that was attached to the poor bird's legs. There wasn't any pleasure in such an
outing.

The whole town talked about the marvelous bird. Whenever two
people met in the street they would sigh; one would say, "night,"
and the other, "gale"; and then they would understand each other
perfectly. Twelve delicatessen shop owners named their children
"Nightingale," but not one of them could sing.

One day a package arrived for the emperor; on it was written:
"Nightingale."

"It is probably another book about our famous bird," said the
emperor. But he was wrong; it was a mechanical nightingale. It
lay in a little box and was supposed to look like the real one, though
it was made of silver and gold and studded with sapphires, diamonds,
and rubies. When you wound it up, it could sing one of the songs the
real nightingale sang; and while it performed its little silver tail would
go up and down. Around its neck hung a ribbon on which was written: "The Emperor of Japan's nightingale is inferior to the Emperor
of China's."

"It is beautiful!" exclaimed the whole court. And the messenger
who had brought it had the title of Supreme Imperial Nightingale
Deliverer bestowed upon him at once.

"They ought to sing together, it will be a duet," said everyone,
and they did. But that didn't work out well at all; for the real bird
sang in his own manner and the mechanical one had a cylinder inside
its chest instead of a heart. "It is not its fault," said the imperial
music master. "It keeps perfect time, it belongs to my school of

music." Then the mechanical nightingale had to sing solo. Everyone agreed that its song was just as beautiful as the real nightingale's; and besides, the artificial bird was much pleasanter to look at, with its sapphires, rubies, and diamonds that glittered like bracelets and brooches.

The mechanical nightingale sang its song thirty-three times and did not grow tired. The court would have liked to hear it the thirty-fourth time, but the emperor thought that the real nightingale ought to sing now. But where was it? Nobody had noticed that he had flown out through an open window, to his beloved green forest.

"What is the meaning of this!" said the emperor angrily, and the whole court blamed the nightingale and called him an ungrateful creature.

"But the best bird remains," they said, and the mechanical bird sang its song once more. It was the same song, for it knew no other; but it was very intricate, so the courtiers didn't know it by heart yet. The imperial music master praised the bird and declared that it was better than the real nightingale, not only on the outside where the diamonds were, but also inside.

"Your Imperial Majesty and gentlemen: you understand that the real nightingale cannot be depended upon. One never knows what he will sing; whereas, in the mechanical bird, everything is determined. There is one song and no other! One can explain everything. We can open it up to examine and appreciate how human thought has fashioned the wheels and the cylinder, and put them where they are, to turn just as they should."

"Precisely what I was thinking!" said the whole court in a chorus. And the imperial music master was given permission to show the new nightingale to the people on the following Sunday.

The emperor thought that they, too, should hear the bird. They did and they were as delighted as if they had gotten drunk on too much tea. It was all very Chinese. They pointed with their licking fingers toward heaven, nodded, and said: "Oh!"

But the poor fisherman, who had heard the real nightingale, mumbled, "It sounds beautiful and like the bird's song, but something is missing, though I don't know what it is."

The real nightingale was banished from the empire.

The mechanical bird was given a silk pillow to rest upon, close to the emperor's bed; and all the presents it had received were piled around it. Among them were both gold and precious stones. Its title was Supreme Imperial Night-table Singer and its rank was Number One to the Left.—The emperor thought the left side was more distinguished because that is the side where the heart is, even in an emperor.

The imperial music master wrote a work in twenty-five volumes about the mechanical nightingale. It was not only long and learned but filled with the most difficult Chinese words, so everyone bought it and said they had read and understood it, for otherwise they would have been considered stupid and had to have their stomachs poked.

A whole year went by. The emperor, the court, and all the Chinese in China knew every note of the supreme imperial night-table singer's song by heart; but that was the very reason why they liked it so much: they could sing it themselves, and they did. The street urchins sang: "Zi-zi-zizzi, cluck-cluck-cluck-cluck." And so did the emperor. Oh, it was delightful!

But one evening, when the bird was singing its very best and the emperor was lying in bed listening to it, something said: "Clang," inside it. It was broken! All the wheels whirred around and then the bird was still.

The emperor jumped out of bed and called his physician but he couldn't do anything, so the imperial watchmaker was fetched. With great difficulty he repaired the bird, but he declared that the cylinders were worn and new ones could not be fitted. The bird would have to be spared; it could not be played so often.

It was a catastrophe. Only once a year was the mechanical bird allowed to sing, and then it had difficulty finishing its song. But the imperial music master made a speech wherein he explained, using the most difficult words, that the bird was as good as ever; and then it was.

Five years passed and a great misfortune happened. Although everyone loved the old emperor, he had fallen ill; and they all agreed that he would not get well again. It was said that a new emperor had already been chosen; and when people in the street asked the chief courtier how the emperor was, he would shake his head and say: "P."

Pale and cold, the emperor lay in his golden bed. The whole court believed him to be already dead and they were busy visiting and paying their respects to the new emperor. The lackeys were all out in the street gossiping, and the chambermaids were drinking coffee. All the floors in the whole palace were covered with black carpets so that no one's steps would disturb the dying emperor; and that's why it was as quiet as quiet could be in the whole palace.

But the emperor was not dead yet. Pale and motionless he lay in his great golden bed; the long velvet drapes were drawn, and the golden tassels moved slowly in the wind, for one of the windows was open. The moon shone down upon the emperor, and its light reflected in the diamonds of the mechanical bird.

The emperor could hardly breathe; he felt as though someone were sitting on his chest. He opened his eyes. Death was sitting there. He was wearing the emperor's golden crown and held his gold saber in one hand and his imperial banner in the other. From the folds of the curtains that hung around his bed, strange faces looked down at the emperor. Some of them were frighteningly ugly, and others mild and kind. They were the evil and good deeds that the emperor had done. Now, while Death was sitting on his heart, they were looking down at him.

"Do you remember?" whispered first one and then another. And they told him things that made the cold sweat of fear appear on his forehead.

"No, no, I don't remember! It is not true!" shouted the emperor. "Music, music, play the great Chinese gong," he begged, "so that I will not be able to hear what they are saying."

But the faces kept talking and Death, like a real Chinese, nodded his head to every word that was said.

"Little golden nightingale, sing!" demanded the emperor. "I have given you gold and precious jewels and with my own hands have I hung my golden slipper around your neck. Sing! Please sing!"

But the mechanical nightingale stood as still as ever, for there was no one to wind it up; and then, it couldn't sing.

Death kept staring at the emperor out of the empty sockets in his skull; and the palace was still, so terrifyingly still.

All at once the most beautiful song broke the silence. It was the nightingale, who had heard of the emperor's illness and torment. He sat on a branch outside his window and sang to bring him comfort and hope. As he sang, the faces in the folds of the curtains faded and the blood pulsed with greater force through the emperor's weak body. Death himself listened and said, "Please, little nightingale, sing on!"

"Will you give me the golden saber? Will you give me the imperial banner? Will you give me the golden crown?"

Death gave each of his trophies for a song; and then the nightingale sang about the quiet churchyard, where white roses grow, where fragrant elderberry trees are, and where the grass is green from the tears of those who come to mourn. Death longed so much for his garden that he flew out of the window, like a white cold mist.

"Thank you, thank you," whispered the emperor, "you heavenly little bird, I remember you. You have I banished from my empire and yet you came to sing for me; and when you sang the evil phantoms that taunted me disappeared, and Death himself left my heart. How shall I reward you?"

"You have rewarded me already," said the nightingale. "I shall never forget that, the first time I sang for you, you gave me the tears from your eyes; and to a poet's heart, those are jewels. But sleep so you can become well and strong; I shall sing for you."

The little gray bird sang; and the emperor slept, so blessedly, so peacefully.

The sun was shining in through the window when he woke; he did not feel ill any more. None of his servants had come, for they thought that he was already dead; but the nightingale was still there and he was singing.

"You must come always," declared the emperor. "I shall only ask you to sing when you want to. And the mechanical bird I shall break in a thousand pieces."

"Don't do that," replied the nightingale. "The mechanical bird sang as well as it could, keep it. I can't build my nest in the palace; let me come to visit you when I want to, and I shall sit on the branch outside your window and sing for you. And my song shall make you happy and make you thoughtful. I shall sing not only of those who are happy but also of those who suffer. I shall sing of the good and of the evil that happen around you, and yet are hidden from you. For a little songbird flies far. I visit the poor fishermen's cottages and the peasant's hut, far away from your palace and your court. I love your heart more than your crown, and yet I feel that the crown has a fragrance of something holy about it. I will come! I will sing for you! Only one thing must you promise me."

"I will promise you anything," said the emperor, who had dressed himself in his imperial clothes and was holding his golden saber and pressing it against his heart.

"I beg of you never tell anyone that you have a little bird that tells you everything, for then you will fare even better." And with those words the nightingale flew away.

The servants entered the room to look at their dead master. There they stood gaping when the emperor said: "Good morning."

## 26

## The Sweethearts

A top and a ball were lying in a drawer among a lot of other toys. One day the top said to the ball, "Shouldn't we become engaged? After all, we are lying right next to each other in the drawer." But the ball, who was made of morocco leather, thought of herself as a very refined young lady and would not even answer a question like that.

The next day the little boy, whose toys they all were, painted the top red and yellow and hammered a brass nail in the middle of it. It looked marvelous when it spun.

"Look at me now!" called the top to the ball. "What do you say, wouldn't we make a fine pair? You can jump and I can dance! How happy we would be together."

"That's what you think," replied the ball. "Are you aware that my mother and father were a pair of morocco slippers, and that I have a cork inside me?"

"But I am of mahogany," boasted the top. "The mayor made me, himself, on a lathe he has in his cellar. It gave him great pleasure."

"How do I know that what you're saying is true?" asked the ball.

"May I never be whipped into a spin again if I am lying," answered the top.

"You speak well for yourself," admitted the ball. "But I have to refuse because I am almost engaged to a swallow. Every time I jump up into the air, he puts his head out of the nest and asks, 'Will you? Will you?' Even though I haven't said yes, I have thought it; and that's almost the same as being engaged. But I promise that I shall never forget you."

"A lot of difference that will make," growled the top. And that was the end of their conversation.

The next day the ball was taken out of the drawer, and the top watched as she was thrown so high up into the sky that she looked like a bird and finally all but disappeared. Every time she hit the ground she bounced up again quite high; and the top could not make up his mind whether she jumped up like that because she wanted to get another glimpse of the swallow, or just because she had cork inside her.

The ninth time the ball went up into the air, it did not return. The boy searched for it everywhere but it was gone.

"I know what's happened to her," said the top, "she's up in the swallow's nest and is getting married to the swallow."

The more the top thought about the ball, the more in love with her he was. And because he couldn't have her, he wanted her all the more. The strangest part of it was that she had preferred another. The top spun and whirled; round and round he went; and all the time he was thinking of the ball. And in his imagination she grew prettier and prettier. Years passed and finally she became an old love.

The top was not young any more; but then one day he was painted all over with gold paint. Now he was a golden top; and he spun and leaped up into the air. . . . Oh, that was something! But then it sprang too high and was gone! Everyone looked for it everywhere, even in the cellar, but it was not to be found. Where was it?

It had jumped into the garbage bin. There all kinds of things were lying: gravel, a cabbage stalk, dirt, dust, and a lot of leaves that had fallen down from the gutter under the roof.

"This is a fine place to be!" thought the top. "I wonder how long my gilding will last here. What a lot of riffraff!" The top glanced at the cabbage stalk and then at a funny round thing that looked like a rotten apple. But it wasn't an apple; it was the old ball who had lain for years in the gutter, where the water had oozed through it.

"Thank God! At last someone of one's own kind has come, someone I need not be ashamed to talk to," said the ball, and looked at the golden top. "I was made from morocco leather by the hand of a fine young lady, and have a cork inside me. Although, I admit, it's hard to see it now. I was just about to marry a swallow when I fell into the gutter under the roof. There I have lain and oozed for five years; that's a long time for a young girl."

The top didn't say anything. He was thinking of his old sweetheart; and the more he heard, the more certain he was that it was she.

At the moment a maid came to throw something away. "Hurrah! There's the golden top!" she cried.

The golden top was brought back to the living room, where he was honored and respected. There no one ever talked about the ball, and the top never mentioned his old love again. You get over it when your beloved has lain in a gutter and oozed for five years. You never recognize her when you meet her in the garbage bin.

## 27

## The Ugly Duckling

It was so beautiful out in the country. It was summer. The oats were still green, but the wheat was turning yellow. Down in the meadow the grass had been cut and made into haystacks; and there the storks walked on their long red legs talking Egyptian, because that was the language they had been taught by their mothers. The fields were enclosed by woods, and hidden among them were little lakes and pools. Yes, it certainly was lovely out there in the country!

The old castle, with its deep moat surrounding it, lay bathed in sunshine. Between the heavy walls and the edge of the moat there was a narrow strip of land covered by a whole forest of burdock plants. Their leaves were large and some of the stalks were so tall that a child could stand upright under them and imagine that he was in the middle of the wild and lonesome woods. Here a duck had built her nest. While she sat waiting for the eggs to hatch, she felt a little sorry for herself because it was taking so long and hardly anybody came to visit her. The other ducks preferred swimming in the moat to sitting under a dock leaf and gossiping.

Finally the eggs began to crack. "Peep . . . Peep," they said one after another. The egg yolks had become alive and were sticking out their heads.

"Quack . . . Quack . . ." said their mother. "Look around you." And the ducklings did; they glanced at the green world about them, and that was what their mother wanted them to do, for green was good for their eyes.

"How big the world is!" piped the little ones, for they had much more space to move around in now than they had had inside the egg.

"Do you think that this is the whole world?" quacked their mother. "The world is much larger than this. It stretches as far as the minister's wheat fields, though I have not been there. . . . Are you all here?" The duck got up and turned around to look at her nest. "Oh no, the biggest egg hasn't hatched yet; and I'm so tired of sitting here! I wonder how long it will take?" she wailed, and sat down again.

"What's new?" asked an old duck who had come visiting.

"One of the eggs is taking so long," complained the mother duck. "It won't crack. But take a look at the others. They are the sweetest little ducklings you have ever seen; and every one of them looks exactly like their father. That scoundrel hasn't come to visit me once."

"Let me look at the egg that won't hatch," demanded the old duck. "I am sure that it's a turkey egg! I was fooled that way once. You can't imagine what it's like. Turkeys are afraid of the water. I couldn't get them to go into it. I quacked and I nipped them, but nothing helped. Let me see that egg! . . . Yes, it's a turkey egg. Just let it lie there. You go and teach your young ones how to swim, that's my advice."

"I have sat on it so long that I guess I can sit a little longer, at least until they get the hay in," replied the mother duck.

"Suit yourself," said the older duck, and went on.

At last the big egg cracked too. "Peep . . . Peep," said the young one, and tumbled out. He was big and very ugly.

The mother duck looked at him. "He's awfully big for his age," she said. "He doesn't look like any of the others. I wonder if he could be a turkey? Well, we shall soon see. Into the water he will go, even if I have to kick him to make him do it."

The next day the weather was gloriously beautiful. The sun shone on the forest of burdock plants. The mother duck took her whole brood to the moat. "Quack . . . Quack . . ." she ordered.

One after another, the little ducklings plunged into the water. For a moment their heads disappeared, but then they popped up again and the little ones floated like so many corks. Their legs knew what to do without being told. All of the new brood swam very nicely, even the ugly one.

"He is no turkey," mumbled the mother. "Look how beautifully he uses his legs and how straight he holds his neck. He is my own child and, when you look closely at him, he's quite handsome. . . . Quack! Quack! Follow me and I'll take you to the henyard and introduce you to everyone. But stay close to me, so that no one steps on you, and look out for the cat."

They heard an awful noise when they arrived at the henyard. Two families of ducks had got into a fight over the head of an eel. Neither of them got it, for it was swiped by the cat.

"That is the way of the world," said the mother duck, and licked her bill. She would have liked to have the eel's head herself. "Walk nicely," she admonished them. "And remember to bow to the old duck over there. She has Spanish blood in her veins and is the most aristocratic fowl here. That is why she is so fat and has a red rag tied around one of her legs. That is the highest mark of distinction a duck can be given. It means so much that she will never be done away with; and all the other fowl and the human beings know who she is. Quack! Quack! . . . Don't walk, waddle like well-brought-up ducklings. Keep your legs far apart, just as your mother and father have always done. Bow your heads and say, 'Quack!'" And that was what the little ducklings did.

Other ducks gathered about them and said loudly, "What do we want that gang here for? Aren't there enough of us already? Pooh! Look how ugly one of them is! He's the last straw!" And one of the ducks flew over and bit the ugly duckling on the neck.

"Leave him alone!" shouted the mother. "He hasn't done anyone any harm."

"He's big and he doesn't look like everybody else!" replied the duck who had bitten him. "And that's reason enough to beat him."

"Very good-looking children you have," remarked the duck with the red rag around one of her legs. "All of them are beautiful except one. He didn't turn out very well. I wish you could make him over again."

"That's not possible, Your Grace," answered the mother duck. "He may not be handsome, but he has a good character and swims as well as the others, if not a little better. Perhaps he will grow handsomer as he grows older and becomes a bit smaller. He was in the egg too long, and that is why he doesn't have the right shape." She smoothed his neck for a moment and then added, "Besides, he's a drake; and it doesn't matter so much what he looks like. He is strong and I am sure he will be able to take care of himself."

"Well, the others are nice," said the old duck. "Make yourself at home, and if you should find an eel's head, you may bring it to me."

And they were "at home."

The poor little duckling, who had been the last to hatch and was so ugly, was bitten and pushed and made fun of both by the hens and by the other ducks. The turkey cock (who had been born with spurs on, and therefore thought he was an emperor) rustled his feathers as if he were a full-rigged ship under sail, and strutted up to the duckling. He gobbled so loudly at him that his own face got all red.

The poor little duckling did not know where to turn. How he grieved over his own ugliness, and how sad he was! The poor creature was mocked and laughed at by the whole henyard.

That was the first day; and each day that followed was worse than the one before. The poor duckling was chased and mistreated by everyone, even his own sisters and brothers, who quacked again and again, "If only the cat would get you, you ugly thing!"

Even his mother said, "I wish you were far away." The other ducks bit him and the hens pecked at him. The little girl who came to feed the fowls kicked him.

At last the duckling ran away. It flew over the tops of the bushes, frightening all the little birds so that they flew up into the air. "They, too, think I am ugly," thought the duckling, and closed his eyes—but he kept on running.

Finally he came to a great swamp where wild ducks lived; and here he stayed for the night, for he was too tired to go any farther.

In the morning he was discovered by the wild ducks. They looked at him and one of them asked, "What kind of bird are you?"

The ugly duckling bowed in all directions, for he was trying to be as polite as he knew how.

"You are ugly," said the wild ducks, "but that is no concern of ours, as long as you don't try to marry into our family."

The poor duckling wasn't thinking of marriage. All he wanted was to be allowed to swim among the reeds and drink a little water when he was thirsty.

He spent two days in the swamp; then two wild geese came—or rather, two wild ganders, for they were males. They had been hatched not long ago; therefore they were both frank and bold.

"Listen, comrade," they said. "You are so ugly that we like you. Do you want to migrate with us? Not far from here there is a marsh where some beautiful wild geese live. They are all lovely maidens, and you are so ugly that you may seek your fortune among them. Come along."

"Bang! Bang!" Two shots were heard and both the ganders fell down dead among the reeds, and the water turned red from their blood.

"Bang! Bang!" Again came the sound of shots, and a flock of wild geese flew up.

The whole swamp was surrounded by hunters; from every direction came the awful noise. Some of the hunters had hidden behind bushes or among the reeds but others, screened from sight by the leaves, sat on the long, low branches of the trees that stretched out over the swamp. The blue smoke from the guns lay like a fog over the water and among the trees. Dogs came splashing through the marsh, and they bent and broke the reeds.

The poor little duckling was terrified. He was about to tuck his head under his wing, in order to hide, when he saw a big dog peering at him through the reeds. The dog's tongue hung out of its mouth and its eyes glistened evilly. It bared its teeth. Splash! It turned away without touching the duckling.

"Oh, thank God!" he sighed. "I am so ugly that even the dog doesn't want to bite me."

The little duckling lay as still as he could while the shots whistled through the reeds. Not until the middle of the afternoon did the shooting stop; but the poor little duckling was still so frightened that he waited several hours longer before taking his head out from under his wing. Then he ran as quickly as he could out of the swamp. Across the fields and the meadows he went, but a wind had come up and he found it hard to make his way against it.

Toward evening he came upon a poor little hut. It was so wretchedly crooked that it looked as if it couldn't make up its mind which way to fall and that was why it was still standing. The wind was blowing so hard that the poor little duckling had to sit down in order not to be blown away. Suddenly he noticed that the door was off its hinges, making a crack; and he squeezed himself through it and was inside.

An old woman lived in the hut with her cat and her hen. The cat was called Sonny and could both arch his back and purr. Oh yes, it could also make sparks if you rubbed its fur the wrong way. The hen

had very short legs and that was why she was called Cluck Lowlegs.
But she was good at laying eggs, and the old woman loved her as if
she were her own child.

In the morning the hen and the cat discovered the duckling. The
cat meowed and the hen clucked.

"What is going on?" asked the old woman, and looked around.
She couldn't see very well, and when she found the duckling she
thought it was a fat, full-grown duck. "What a fine catch!" she exclaimed. "Now we shall have duck eggs, unless it's a drake. We'll give
it a try."

So the duckling was allowed to stay for three weeks on probation,
but he laid no eggs. The cat was the master of the house and the hen
the mistress. They always referred to themselves as "we and the
world," for they thought that they were half the world—and the better half at that. The duckling thought that he should be allowed to
have a different opinion, but the hen did not agree.

"Can you lay eggs?" she demanded.

"No," answered the duckling.

"Then keep your mouth shut."

And the cat asked, "Can you arch your back? Can you purr? Can
you make sparks?"

"No."

"Well, in that case, you have no right to have an opinion when
sensible people are talking."

The duckling was sitting in a corner and was in a bad mood. Suddenly he recalled how lovely it could be outside in the fresh air when
the sun shone: a great longing to be floating in the water came over
the duckling, and he could not help talking about it.

"What is the matter with you?" asked the hen as soon as she had
heard what he had to say. "You have nothing to do, that's why you
get ideas like that. Lay eggs or purr, and such notions will disappear."

"You have no idea how delightful it is to float in the water, and to
dive down to the bottom of a lake and get your head wet," said the
duckling.

"Yes, that certainly does sound amusing," said the hen. "You must
have gone mad. Ask the cat—he is the most intelligent being I know
—ask him whether he likes to swim or dive down to the bottom of a
lake. Don't take my word for anything. . . . Ask the old woman,

who is the cleverest person in the world; ask her whether she likes to float and to get her head all wet."

"You don't understand me!" wailed the duckling.

"And if I don't understand you, who will? I hope you don't think that you are wiser than the cat or the old woman—not to mention myself. Don't give yourself airs! Thank your Creator for all He has done for you. Aren't you sitting in a warm room among intelligent people whom you could learn something from? While you, yourself, do nothing but say a lot of nonsense and aren't the least bit amusing! Believe me, that's the truth, and I am only telling it to you for your own good. That's how you recognize a true friend: it's someone who is willing to tell you the truth, no matter how unpleasant it is. Now get to work: lay some eggs, or learn to purr and arch your back."

"I think I'll go out into the wide world," replied the duckling.

"Go right ahead!" said the hen.

And the duckling left. He found a lake where he could float in the water and dive to the bottom. There were other ducks, but they ignored him because he was so ugly.

Autumn came and the leaves turned yellow and brown, then they fell from the trees. The wind caught them and made them dance. The clouds were heavy with hail and snow. A raven sat on a fence and screeched, "Ach! Ach!" because it was so cold. When just thinking of how cold it was is enough to make one shiver, what a terrible time the duckling must have had.

One evening just as the sun was setting gloriously, a flock of beautiful birds came out from among the rushes. Their feathers were so white that they glistened; and they had long, graceful necks. They were swans. They made a very loud cry, then they spread their powerful wings. They were flying south to a warmer climate, where the lakes were not frozen in the winter. Higher and higher they circled. The ugly duckling turned round and round in the water like a wheel and stretched his neck up toward the sky; he felt a strange longing. He screeched so piercingly that he frightened himself.

Oh, he would never forget those beautiful birds, those happy birds. When they were out of sight the duckling dove down under the water to the bottom of the lake; and when he came up again he was beside himself. He did not know the name of those birds or where they were going, and yet he felt that he loved them as he had never loved any other creatures. He did not envy them. It did not even occur to him to wish that he were so handsome himself. He would have been happy if the other ducks had let him stay in the henyard: that poor, ugly bird!

The weather grew colder and colder. The duckling had to swim round and round in the water, to keep just a little space for himself that wasn't frozen. Each night his hole became smaller and smaller. On all sides of him the ice creaked and groaned. The little duckling had to keep his feet constantly in motion so that the last bit of open water wouldn't become ice. At last he was too tired to swim any more. He sat still. The ice closed in around him and he was frozen fast.

Early the next morning a farmer saw him and with his clogs broke the ice to free the duckling. The man put the bird under his arm and took it home to his wife, who brought the duckling back to life.

The children wanted to play with him. But the duckling was afraid that they were going to hurt him, so he flapped his wings and flew right into the milk pail. From there he flew into a big bowl of butter and then into a barrel of flour. What a sight he was!

The farmer's wife yelled and chased him with a poker. The children laughed and almost fell on top of each other, trying to catch him; and how they screamed! Luckily for the duckling, the door was open. He got out of the house and found a hiding place beneath some bushes, in the newly fallen snow; and there he lay so still, as though there were hardly any life left in him.

It would be too horrible to tell of all the hardship and suffering the duckling experienced that long winter. It is enough to know that he did survive. When again the sun shone warmly and the larks began to sing, the duckling was lying among the reeds in the swamp. Spring had come!

He spread out his wings to fly. How strong and powerful they were! Before he knew it, he was far from the swamp and flying above a beautiful garden. The apple trees were blooming and the lilac bushes stretched their flower-covered branches over the water of a winding canal. Everything was so beautiful: so fresh and green. Out of a forest of rushes came three swans. They ruffled their feathers and floated so lightly on the water. The ugly duckling recognized the birds and felt again that strange sadness come over him.

"I shall fly over to them, those royal birds! And they can hack me to death because I, who am so ugly, dare to approach them! What difference does it make? It is better to be killed by them than to be bitten by the other ducks, and pecked by the hens, and kicked by the girl who tends the henyard; or to suffer through the winter."

And he lighted on the water and swam toward the magnificent swans. When they saw him they ruffled their feathers and started to swim in his direction. They were coming to meet him.

"Kill me," whispered the poor creature, and bent his head humbly while he waited for death. But what was that he saw in the water? It was his own reflection; and he was no longer an awkward, clumsy, gray bird, so ungainly and so ugly. He was a swan!

It does not matter that one has been born in the henyard as long as one has lain in a swan's egg.

He was thankful that he had known so much want, and gone through so much suffering, for it made him appreciate his present happiness and the loveliness of everything about him all the more. The swans made a circle around him and caressed him with their beaks.

Some children came out into the garden. They had brought bread with them to feed the swans. The youngest child shouted, "Look, there's a new one!" All the children joyfully clapped their hands, and they ran to tell their parents.

Cake and bread were cast on the water for the swans. Everyone agreed that the new swan was the most beautiful of them all. The older swans bowed toward him.

He felt so shy that he hid his head beneath his wing. He was too happy, but not proud, for a kind heart can never be proud. He thought of the time when he had been mocked and persecuted. And now everyone said that he was the most beautiful of the most beautiful birds. And the lilac bushes stretched their branches right down to the water for him. The sun shone so warm and brightly. He ruffled his feathers and raised his slender neck, while out of the joy in his heart, he thought, "Such happiness I did not dream of when I was the ugly duckling."

## 28

## The Pine Tree

Out in the forest grew a very nice-looking little pine tree. It had plenty of space around it, so that it got both fresh air and all the sunshine it could want. Near it grew some larger pine and other evergreen trees; but the little pine was so busy growing that it took no notice of them, or of the children who came to the forest to pick wild strawberries and raspberries, not even when they sat down near it and said so loudly that anyone could have heard them: "Goodness, what a beautiful little tree!" No, the tree heard nothing, for it was not listening.

The following year it was a little taller and had a new ring of branches; and the next year it had one more. That is the way you can tell the age of a pine tree—by the rings of branches it has.

"Oh, how I wish I were as big as the big trees," moaned the little pine tree. "Then I could spread my branches out, and with my top, I could see far out into the wide world! The birds would come and nest in me; and when the wind blew, then I would bend and sway as elegantly as the other trees."

The warm sunshine gave it no pleasure, nor did the songs of the little birds or the sight of the red clouds that drifted across the sky at sunset.

Winter came. The snow lay white and sparkling. Rabbits came running, and jumped over the little pine tree. "Oh, how mortifying!" it cried every time. But two years passed before the little tree had grown so tall that the rabbits could no longer jump over it but had to run around it instead.

"To grow, to grow," thought the pine tree, "to become tall and old; there's nothing in the world so marvelous!"

In the autumn the woodcutter came to chop down some of the older trees. He came every year and the young tree, now that it was growing up, shook inside itself when the tall, mighty trees fell with a thunderous crash to the ground. Their branches were shorn and there they lay: naked, thin, and long. One could hardly recognize them. They were loaded onto a horse-drawn wagon and carried out of the forest.

Where were they being taken? What would happen to them?

In spring, when the swallows and the storks returned, the young pine put the question to them: "Do any of you know where the trees go and what happens to them?"

The swallows didn't know, but the storks looked thoughtful for a moment. Then one of them said, "I think I know. I have met many tall ships on my way to Egypt. The ships have lofty masts and they smell of pine, so I'm sure they must be pine. I tell you, they stood proudly."

"If only I were old enough to become a mast and sail across the ocean," said the pine tree. "Tell me about the ocean. What does it look like?"

"It's too big for me to try to tell about it," replied the stork, and walked away.

"Be glad that you are young," whispered the sun's rays. "Enjoy your strength and the pleasure of being alive."

The wind kissed the young tree and the dew shed tears over it; but the pine tree noticed neither.

Just before Christmas, some of the trees that were cut down weren't any older or taller than the one who was so dissatisfied. These trees did not have their branches shorn; but they were loaded onto wagons and driven out of the forest just as the other, larger trees had been.

"Where are they going?" asked the pine tree. "None of them was any taller than I am; and I saw one that was at least a foot shorter. Why were they allowed to keep their branches? And where were they going?"

"We know! We know! We know!" chirped the sparrows. "We have been in the town and looked through the windows. We know where they are. They have come to glory. They have been given the greatest honor a tree could wish for. They have been planted right in the middle of the warm living rooms of people's houses. They are decorated with silver and gold tinsel. There are apples and toys and heart-shaped cookies and hundreds of candles on their branches."

The pine tree was so excited that its boughs trembled. "And what else happened to them?"

"We don't know," chirped the sparrows. "We've told you everything we saw."

"Have I been created to become like that?" thought the tree jubilantly. "Will that glory be mine? Why, that is much better than sailing across the oceans. Oh, how I long for it to happen! I wish it soon would be Christmas again. I am as tall and as good looking as the trees that were chosen last year. I wish I were on the wagon already. I wish I were in the warm room being decorated. I wonder what will happen after that? Something even better, even grander will happen, why else should they put gold and silver on me? But what will it be? How I long for it to happen! How I suffer from anticipation. I can hardly understand myself. . . . Oh, how difficult it is to be me!"

"Be happy with us," said the wind and the sunshine. "Be glad that you are young; enjoy your youth and your freedom, here in nature."

But the tree was not happy. It grew and grew; and now it was dark green both in winter and summer, and people who passed by often remarked, "What a lovely tree!"

Then one Christmas, it was the first tree to be cut down. It felt the ax sever it from its roots; and it fell with a sigh to the ground. A feeling of pain, of helplessness, came over it, and never for a moment did it think of the glory that was to come. It only felt the sadness of leaving the place where it had grown. It knew that it would never see again the little bushes and flowers that had grown around it, or hear the songs of the little birds that had sat on its branches. No, parting was no pleasure.

The tree didn't recover before it was being unloaded in town and heard someone say, "What a beautiful tree! We shall have that one and no other."

Two servants in livery carried the tree up to a magnificent hall. Portraits were hanging on the walls, and next to the big tile stove stood two Chinese vases with lions on their lids. There were rocking chairs, and sofas covered with silk; and on a table lay picture books and toys worth more than a hundred times a hundred crowns—so at least the children claimed. The tree was planted in a bucket filled with sand, but nobody could see that it was an old one, for it was covered by a green cloth and stood on a many-colored rug.

The tree shook with expectation. What was about to happen? The servants and the young ladies of the family started to decorate it. On the branches they hung little colored nets that were filled with sweets; and golden apples and walnuts were tied to the tree so that they looked as if they were growing there. A hundred little red, blue, and white candles were fastened on the branches; and among them, on the green needles, sat little dolls that looked exactly like human beings. At last, on the very top of the tree was placed a golden star. It was magnificent, unbelievably magnificent!

"Tonight . . . tonight," everyone said. "Tonight it will be glorious!"

"Oh," thought the tree, "why doesn't night come! The candles will be lit—I wonder what will happen then! Will the other trees come from the forest and look at me? Will the sparrows peep in through the windows? Will I grow roots and stand here both summer and winter?"

The poor tree had a bark-ache from anticipation, which for a tree is as annoying as headache is to a human being.

Finally evening did come, and the candles were lit. Oh, how beautiful it looked. The poor tree trembled with emotion. In fact, it shook so much that one of its branches caught on fire, which smarted and hurt.

"God preserve us!" cried the ladies, and put out the fire.

Now the poor tree didn't even dare tremble; it was horrible! There it stood, rigid and still, and fearing every moment that it might lose some of its decorations. How bewildering everything was! The big doors opened and the children came running in. They were so wild, especially the older ones, they looked as if they wanted to overturn the tree. The little children were so overawed by the tree that they just stood and stared silently. But that didn't last long; soon they were making as much noise as the older ones. The grownups came last; but they had seen the sight many times before. Soon they all were dancing and singing around the tree; then the presents, which had been hung on the tree, were given out.

"What are they doing?" thought the tree. "What is going to happen now?"

The candles burned down and were extinguished, and the children were allowed to plunder the tree. They grabbed the little nets with sweets in them and pulled at the candied fruit and the nuts. They were so rough that they almost broke off the branches; and they would certainly have upset the tree, had it not been for the string with which its top was attached to the ceiling.

Now the children danced and played, and no one but the old nurse paid any attention to the tree; she kept walking around and around it, looking among the branches to see if she could find an apple or a fig which the youngsters might have overlooked.

"A story! A story!" screamed all the children, and pushed a fat man toward the Christmas tree.

He sat down beneath it, for, as he said, he liked sitting among the "greenery," and it wouldn't harm the tree to hear a story. "But I shall tell only one," he declared. "You can choose between 'Willowy, Wollowy' and 'How Humpty-dumpty Fell Down the Stairs but Won the Princess Anyway.'"

"'Willowy Wollowy'!" screamed several of the children.

"'Humpty-dumpty'!" screamed the others; and the room was filled with their shouting.

"Isn't there something that I am supposed to do?" thought the tree, not knowing that it had already done everything that it was supposed to do.

The man told the story of "How Humpty-dumpty Fell Down the Stairs but Won the Princess Anyway." When he had finished all the children screamed that they wanted more, for they hoped to be able to persuade him to tell the story of "Willowy, Wollowy" too; but they couldn't. They had to be satisfied with the story about Humpty-dumpty.

The pine tree stood still, deep in its own thoughts. The birds out in the forest had never told a story like that. "No, that's the way of the world," it said to itself. "Humpty-dumpty falls down the stairs but he wins the princess anyway." The tree believed that the story it had heard was true because the man who had told it looked so trustworthy. "Yes, who knows?" it whispered to itself. "Maybe I, too, will fall down the stairs and win the princess." And the tree looked forward to the next day, when it would again be decorated with lights and hung with toys.

"Tomorrow," it thought, "tomorrow I shan't tremble as I did today. I shall really enjoy myself, and hear the story of Humpty-dumpty again; and maybe the one about 'Willowy, Wollowy' too." All night long the tree silently thought of the glory that was to come on the following day.

The next morning the servants came.

"Now it all starts all over again," thought the tree.

But it didn't. The servants dragged the tree up two flights of stairs into the attic, where they threw it in a dark corner which the daylight never reached.

"What is the meaning of this?" the tree asked itself. "Why have I been put here? What will happen now?"

The tree leaned itself up against the wall and thought and thought. It had plenty of time for thinking, because days and nights went by without anyone coming into the attic to disturb it. When finally someone did come, it was only to put some old boxes up there. The tree was hidden in the corner and quite forgotten.

"Now it is winter outside," thought the tree. "The earth is so hard and covered with snow that they cannot plant me. They are sheltering me here till spring. How considerate man is! I just wish it weren't so dark and so terribly lonely! There isn't even a rabbit here. It was so nice out in the forest when the ground was covered with snow and the rabbits darted about. Though I didn't like it when I was very small and they could jump over me. But here it is so quiet and I am terribly lonely."

"Twick . . . twick," said a little mouse, and nipped its way out of the wall.

"Twick . . . twick . . ." And another, even smaller mouse appeared.

The two little mice sniffed at the tree and then climbed up among the branches.

"It is cold," remarked the mice. "But otherwise it is a quite nice attic. Don't you think so, old pine tree?"

"I am not old," protested the pine tree. "There are lots of trees in the forest much older than I am."

"Where do you come from?" asked one of the little mice. Those little creatures were very curious and they asked the tree one question after another. "What do you know? What can you tell us? Tell us about the most beautiful place in the world. Have you been there? . . . Have you ever been in the larder, by the way? In the larder where there are cheeses lying on shelves, hams hanging from the ceiling, and where you can dance on tallow candles; and where you can come in thin and go out fat?"

"I don't know of any such place," replied the tree. "But I know the forest where the sun shines and the birds sing." And the pine tree told them of its youth in the woods.

The little mice listened quietly, for they had never heard of such a place; and when the tree was finished they said, "Think how much you have seen! How happy you must have been!"

"Happy?" repeated the pine tree, and thought about what it had told the little mice. "Yes, I suppose I had a quite good time," it confessed. Then the tree told about Christmas Eve and how it had been decorated with candles and sweets.

"Oh," sighed the mice, "how fortunate you have been, old pine tree."

"I am not old!" protested the tree. "I have come this very winter from the forest. I am in my prime. I just appear a little stunted because I have been cut down."

"You tell about everything so marvelously," exclaimed the little mice; and the next night they brought along four of their friends.

The pine tree again told the story of its youth in the forest and what had happened to it on Christmas Eve; and the more it told, the more clearly it could remember everything.

"Yes, they were good times; and they can come again. They will come again! Humpty-dumpty fell down the stairs but he won the princess anyway." And the pine tree remembered a little birch tree that had grown nearby it in the forest, for to the pine tree the little birch was a real princess.

"Who was Humpty-dumpty?" asked the little mice.

The pine tree told them the fairy tale it had heard. It could remember every word of it. The little mice were so pleased that they climbed to the very top of the tree to show their appreciation. The next night more mice came; and on Sunday two rats arrived. But they criticized the story and said it wasn't amusing at all. This made the poor little mice sad, for now they thought less of the story too.

"Don't you know any other stories?" asked one of the rats.

"No, I only know that one," admitted the pine tree. "I heard it on the happiest night of my life; but then I didn't know that it was the happiest night."

"It is a particularly uninteresting story. Don't you know any about bacon or candle stumps? No stories that take place in a larder?"

"No," the tree answered.

"Well, in that case you're not worth listening to," said the rats, and left.

The mice stayed away too; and the pine tree sighed in its loneliness. "It was nice when the quick little animals came visiting and listened to what I had to tell. But now that is over too. I must remember to be happy when I am taken out again," the tree muttered. "I wonder when that will be."

Finally, one morning it happened. The servants came up to the attic and started moving boxes about; they were cleaning up. When they found the tree in the corner they handled it roughly and threw it about. At last a young man carried it down the many flights of stairs out into the yard.

"Now life begins again," it thought. There was fresh air and it felt the sun's rays. Everything was happening so fast, and it was so excited at being outside, that the tree looked at the world about it but not at itself. The yard was bordered by a garden where all the bushes and trees were in flower. The roses covered the little fence and smelled so sweetly. The linden tree was in bloom. The swallows flew about singing, "Tweet, tweet. . . . My lover has come." But they didn't mean the pine tree.

"Now I am going to live!" shouted the tree joyously, and spread out its branches. But all its needles were yellow and dead. It was thrown into a corner of the yard where the nettles prospered. The golden star from Christmas Eve was still on its top and the sun reflected in it.

Playing in the yard were two of the children who had danced around the tree on Christmas Eve and had loved it so much then. The younger child now ran over and tore the golden star from the tree.

"Look what I found on this horrid old Christmas tree," he said. He was wearing boots and he kicked the tree's branches so that many of them broke.

The pine tree saw all the greenness about it; then it looked at itself and wished it had been left in the dark corner of the attic. It remembered its youth in the forest, the glory of Christmas Eve, and the little mice who had listened so contentedly to the story about Humpty-dumpty.

"Gone! Gone!" sighed the poor tree. "If I only could have been happy while I had a chance to be. Now it is all over and gone! Everything!"

One of the servants came and cut the tree up for kindling. It became a little pile of wood. The cook used it to light the kitchen range. It flared up instantly and the tree sighed so deeply that it sounded like a shot. The children who were playing in the yard heard it, and they ran in and sat down in front of the stove.

"Bang! Bang!" they cried.

Every time the tree sighed, it thought of a summer day in the forest, or a winter night when the stars are brightest, and it remembered Christmas Eve and Humpty-dumpty: the only fairy tale it had ever heard and knew how to tell. Then it became ashes.

The children returned to the yard to play. The little boy had fastened the golden star to his chest. The star the pine tree had worn on the happiest evening of its life. But that was a long time ago; now the pine tree is no more, just as this story is over; for all stories —no matter how long they are—must eventually come to an end.

## 29

## The Snow Queen

### a fairy tale told in seven stories

THE FIRST STORY, WHICH CONCERNS ITSELF WITH A BROKEN
MIRROR AND WHAT HAPPENED TO ITS FRAGMENTS

All right, we will start the story; when we come to the end we shall
know more than we do now.

Once upon a time there was a troll, the most evil troll of them all;
he was called the devil. One day he was particularly pleased with
himself, for he had invented a mirror which had the strange power
of being able to make anything good or beautiful that it reflected
appear horrid; and all that was evil and worthless seem attractive
and worth while. The most beautiful landscape looked like spinach;
and the kindest and most honorable people looked repulsive or
ridiculous. They might appear standing on their heads, without any
stomachs; and their faces would always be so distorted that you
couldn't recognize them. A little freckle would spread itself out till it
covered half a nose or a whole cheek.

"It is a very amusing mirror," said the devil. But the most amusing
part of it all was that if a good or a kind thought passed through anyone's mind the most horrible grin would appear on the face in the
mirror.

It was so entertaining that the devil himself laughed out loud. All
the little trolls who went to troll school, where the devil was head-
master, said that a miracle had taken place. Now for the first time
one could see what humanity and the world really looked like—at

least, so they thought. They ran all over with the mirror, until there wasn't a country or a person in the whole world that had not been reflected and distorted in it.

At last they decided to fly up to heaven to poke fun of the angels and God Himself. All together they carried the mirror, and flew up higher and higher. The nearer they came to heaven, the harder the mirror laughed, so that the trolls could hardly hold onto it; still, they flew higher and higher: upward toward God and the angels, then the mirror shook so violently from laughter that they lost their grasp; it fell and broke into hundreds of millions of billions and some odd pieces. It was then that it really caused trouble, much more than it ever had before. Some of the splinters were as tiny as grains of sand and just as light, so that they were spread by the winds all over the world. When a sliver like that entered someone's eye it stayed there; and the person, forever after, would see the world distorted, and only be able to see the faults, and not the virtues, of everyone around him, since even the tiniest fragment contained all the evil qualities of the whole mirror. If a splinter should enter someone's heart—oh, that was the most terrible of all!—that heart would turn to ice.

Some of the pieces of the mirror were so large that windowpanes could be made of them, although through such a window it was no pleasure to contemplate your friends. Some of the medium-sized pieces became spectacles—but just think of what would happen when you put on such a pair of glasses in order to see better and be able to judge more fairly. That made the devil laugh so hard that it tickled in his stomach, which he found very pleasant.

Some of the tiniest bits of the mirror were still flying about in the air. And now you shall hear about them.

### THE SECOND STORY, WHICH IS ABOUT A LITTLE BOY AND A LITTLE GIRL

In a big city, where there live so many people and are so many houses that not every family can have a garden of its own and so must learn to be satisfied with a potted plant, there once lived a poor little girl and a poor little boy who had a garden a little bit larger than a flowerpot. They weren't brother and sister but loved each other as much as if they had been. Their parents lived right across from each other; each family had a little apartment in the garret, but the houses were built so close together that the roofs almost touched. Between the two gutters that hung from the eaves and collected the water when it rained, there was only a very narrow space, and the two families could visit each other by climbing from one gable window to the other.

In front of the windows each family had a wooden box filled with earth, where herbs and other useful plants grew; but in each box there was also a little rose tree. The parents got the idea that, instead of setting the boxes parallel to their windows, they could set them across, so they reached from one window to the other. In that manner, the two gables were connected by a little garden. The peas climbed over the sides and hung down; and the little rose trees grew as tall as the windows and joined together, so that they looked like a green triumphal arch. The sides of the boxes were quite high and since the children could be relied upon not to try to climb over them, they were allowed to take their little wooden stools outside and sit under the rose trees; and there it was pleasant to play.

In winter that was not possible; then the windows were tightly closed and sometimes they would be covered by ice. Then the little children would heat copper coins on the stove and press them against the glass until the roundest of holes would melt in the ice; through each of these peeped the loveliest little eye: one belonged to a little boy and the other to a little girl. His name was Kai and hers was Gerda. In summer they had to take only a few steps to be together; but in the winter they had to run down and up so many stairs and across a yard covered by snowdrifts.

"The white bees are swarming," said the old Grandmother.

"Do they have a queen too?" asked Kai, for he knew that real bees have such a ruler.

"Yes, they have," said the old woman. "She always flies right in the center of the swarm, where the most snowflakes are. She is the biggest of them all, but she never lies down to rest as the other snowflakes do. No, when the wind dies she returns to the black clouds. Many a winter night she flies through the streets of the town and looks in through the windows; then they become covered by ice flowers."

"Yes, I've seen that!" said first one child and then the other; and now they knew that what the Grandmother said was true.

"Could the Snow Queen come inside, right into our room?" asked the little girl.

"Let her come," said Kai." I will put her right on top of the stove and then she will melt."

The Grandmother patted his head and told them another story. But that night, as Kai was getting undressed, he climbed up on the chair by the window and looked out through his peephole. It was snowing gently; one of the flakes fell on the edge of the wooden box and stayed there; other snowflakes followed and they grew until they took the shape of a woman. Her clothes looked like the whitest gauze. It was made of millions of little star-shaped snowflakes. She was beautiful but all made of ice: cold, blindingly glittering ice; and yet she was alive, for her eyes stared at Kai like two stars, but neither rest nor peace was to be found in her gaze. She nodded toward the window and beckoned. The little boy got so frightened that he jumped down from the chair; and at that moment a shadow crossed the window as if a big bird had flown by.

The next day there was frost; but by noon the weather changed and it thawed. Soon it was spring again and the world grew green; the swallows returned to build their nests and the windows were opened. The little children sat in their boxes, above the eaves and high above all the other stories of the houses.

The roses bloomed particularly marvelously that summer. The little girl had learned a psalm in which roses were mentioned in one of the verses; her own roses reminded her of it, and so she sang, and the boy joined her:

"In the valley where the roses be
There the child Jesus you will see."

The two little children held each other's hands, kissed the flowers, and looked up into the blessed sunshine. Oh, these were lovely summer days, and it was ever so pleasant to sit under the little rose trees that never seemed to stop flowering.

One afternoon as Kai and Gerda sat looking at a picture book with animals and flowers in it—it was exactly five o'clock, for the bells in the church tower had just struck the hour—Kai said, "Ouch, ouch! Something pricked my heart!" And then again, "Ouch, something sharp is in my eye."

The little girl put her arms around his neck and looked into his eyes but there was nothing to be seen. Still, it hurt and little Gerda cried out of sympathy.

"I think it is gone now," said Kai. But he was wrong, two of the splinters from the devil's mirror had hit him: one had entered his heart and the other one of his eyes. You remember the mirror, it was that horrible invention of the devil which made everything good and decent look small and ridiculous, and everything evil and foul appear grand and worth while. Poor Kai, soon his heart would turn to ice and his eyes would see nothing but faults in everything. But the pain, that would disappear.

"Why are you crying?" he demanded. "You look ugly when you cry. There is nothing the matter with me. Look!" he shouted. "That rose up there has been gnawed by a worm; and look at that one, it is all crooked. They are ugly roses, as ugly as the boxes they grew in." Then he kicked the sides of the box and tore off the two roses.

"What are you doing, Kai?" cried the little girl, and when Kai saw how frightened she was, he tore off yet another flower; and then climbed through the window into his parents' apartment, leaving Gerda to sit out there all alone.

Later, when she came inside with the picture book, he told her that picture books were for babies. And when the Grandmother told stories he would argue with her or—which was much worse—stand behind her chair with a pair of glasses on his nose and imitate her most cruelly. He did it so accurately that people laughed. Soon he learned to mimic everyone in the whole street. He had a good eye for their little peculiarities and knew how to copy them.

Everyone said, "That boy has his head screwed on right!" But it was the splinters of glass that were in his eyes and his heart that made him behave that way; that, too, was why he teased little Gerda all the time—she who loved him with all her heart.

He did not play as he used to; now his games were more grown up. One winter day when snow was falling he brought a magnifying glass and looked at the snowflakes that were falling on his blue coat.

"Look through the glass, Gerda," he said to his little playmate; and she did. Through the magnifying glass each snowflake appeared like a flower or ten-pointed star. They were, indeed, beautiful to see.

"Aren't they marvelous?" asked Kai. "And each of them is quite perfect; they are much nicer than real flowers. They are all faultless as long as they don't melt."

A little bit later he came by, with his sled on his back, and wearing his hat and woolen gloves. He screamed into Gerda's ear as loud as he could, "I have been allowed to go down to the big square and play with the other boys!" And away he went.

Now down in the snow-covered square the most daring of the boys would tie their sleds behind the farmers' wagons. It was good fun and they would get a good ride. While they were playing, a big white sled drove into the square; the driver was clad in a white fur coat and a white fur hat. The sled circled the square twice and Kai managed to attach his little sled onto the back of the big one. He wanted to hitch a ride.

Away he went; the sled turned the corner and was out of the square. It began to go faster and faster, and Kai wanted to untie his sled, but every time he was about to do it, the driver of the big white sled turned and nodded so kindly to him that he didn't. It was as if they knew each other. Soon they were past the city gate; and the snow was falling so heavily that Kai could not see anything. He untied the rope but it made no difference, his little sled moved on as if it were tied to the big one by magic. They traveled along with the speed of the wind. Kai cried out in fear but no one heard him. The snow flew around him as he flew forward. Every so often his little sled would leap across a ditch and Kai had to hold on, in order not to fall off. He wanted to say his prayers, but all he could remember were his multiplication tables.

The snowflakes grew bigger and bigger until they looked like white hens that were running alongside him. At last the big sled stopped and its driver stood up and turned around to look at Kai. The fur hat and the coat were made of snow; the driver was a woman: how tall and straight she stood! She was the Snow Queen.

"We have driven a goodish way," she said, "but you look cold. Come, creep inside my bearskin coat."

Kai got up from his own sled and walked over to the big one, where he sat down next to the Snow Queen. She put her fur coat around him, and it felt as if he lay down in a deep snowdrift.

"Are you still cold?" she asked, and kissed his forehead. Her kiss was colder than ice. It went right to his heart, which was already half made of ice. He felt as though he were about to die, but it hurt only for a minute, then it was over. Now he seemed stronger and he no longer felt how cold the air was.

"My sled, my sled, don't forget it!" he cried. And one of the white hens put it on her back and flew behind them. The Snow Queen kissed Kai once more, and then all memory of Gerda, the Grandmother, and his home disappeared.

"I shan't give you any more kisses," she said, "or I might kiss you to death."

Kai looked at the Snow Queen; he could not imagine that anyone could have a wiser or a more beautiful face; and she no longer seemed to be made of ice, as she had when he first saw her outside his window, the time she had beckoned to him. In his eyes she now seemed utterly perfect, nor did he feel any fear. He told her that he knew his multiplication tables, could figure in fractions, and knew the area in square miles of every country in Europe, and what its population was.

The Snow Queen smiled, and somehow Kai felt that he did not know enough. He looked out into the great void of the night, for by now they were flying high up in the clouds, above the earth. The storm swept on and sang its old, eternal songs. Above oceans, forests, and lakes they flew; and the cold winter wind whipped the landscape below them. Kai heard the cry of the wolves and the hoarse voice of the crows. The moon came out, and into its large and clear disk Kai stared all through the long winter night. When daytime came he fell asleep at the feet of the Snow Queen.

### THE THIRD STORY: THE FLOWER GARDEN OF THE OLD WOMAN WHO KNEW MAGIC

But how did little Gerda feel when Kai did not return? She asked everyone where he had gone and none could answer. The boys who had been in the square could only tell that they had seen him tie his little sled to the back of a big white sled that had driven out of the city gate.

No one knew where he had gone and little Gerda cried long and bitterly. As time passed people began to say that he must have died; probably he had drowned in the deep, dark river that ran close to the city. It was a long and dismal winter.

Finally spring came with warm sunshine.

"Kai is dead and gone!" sighed little Gerda.

"I don't believe that," said the sunbeams.

"No, he is dead and gone," she repeated, and asked the swallows if that were not true.

"We don't believe it either," they answered; and at last little Gerda was convinced that Kai was not dead.

"I will put on my new red shoes, the ones Kai has never seen," she said one day. "And then I will go down to the river and ask it a few questions."

It was very early in the morning; she kissed the old Grandmother, who was still asleep, put on her new red shoes, and walked out through the city gate and down to the river.

"Is it true that you have taken my playmate? I will give you my new red shoes if you will give him back to me."

She thought that the little waves nodded strangely; so she took her treasure, her new red shoes, and threw them out into the river. They struck the water not far from shore, and the little waves carried them back to her. It was as if the river did not want her little shoes since it had not taken Kai. This little Gerda did not realize, she thought that she just hadn't thrown them far enough out; therefore, she climbed into a rowboat that lay among the reeds, stood up in its stern, and threw the shoes out over the water again. The boat had not been moored and, by stepping into the stern, she loosened the bow from the sand and the rowboat started to drift. Although she noticed it at once and turned around, prepared to leap up onto the bank, the boat was already several feet away from shore and she didn't dare jump.

The boat floated faster and faster downstream with the current. Poor Gerda was so frightened that she just sat down and cried. No one heard her except the sparrows and they could not carry her to shore. But they flew alongside the boat, twittering: "We are here! We are here!" to comfort her.

The boat drifted down the river. Gerda sat perfectly still; she was in her stocking feet; the shoes followed the boat but they were far behind. The landscape was beautiful on both sides of the river. Beyond the banks, which were covered with flowers, there were meadows with cows and sheep grazing upon them; but there was not a human being to be seen anywhere.

"Maybe the river will carry me to where Kai is," thought Gerda.

And that thought was a great comfort and she felt much happier. For hours she sat looking at the green shores; then the boat drifted past a cherry orchard; in the middle of it stood a strange little house with blue and green windows and a straw roof. Before the doors two wooden soldiers kept guard and presented arms when a boat glided by on the river.

Little Gerda, thinking that they were alive, waved and called; but naturally they did not answer. The current of the river carried the boat to the shore, and Gerda started to shout for help as loudly as she could. An old lady came out of the house; she had on a big broad-brimmed hat with the loveliest paintings of flowers on it.

"Poor little child!" she cried when she saw Gerda. "How did you get out there on the river, all alone, and sail so far out into the wide world?" The old lady waded out till she could catch hold of the boat with her shepherd's crook and drew it into shore. Then she lifted Gerda out of the boat. The poor child was happy to be on dry land once again, but she was a little afraid of the old lady.

"Tell me who you are and how you have gotten into such a predicament," the old woman asked.

Gerda told her everything and the old lady shook her head. When Gerda asked whether she had seen little Kai, all the old lady could say was that he hadn't gone by her house but that he probably would arrive there sooner or later. She told little Gerda not to be so sad but to come and eat some of her cherries and look at her flowers. They were prettier than any picture book, and every one of them could tell a story. The old lady took Gerda by the hand, opened the door to her little house, and led her inside.

The windows were placed high up, and the colored glass gave a strange light to the room. On the table stood a bowl filled with the most delicious cherries, and Gerda ate as many of them as she could. While she ate, the old woman combed Gerda's hair with a gold comb and her hair curled prettily around her little rosebud face.

"I have longed so much for a little girl like you," said the old woman. "You just wait and see what good friends we shall become."

While her hair was being combed, Gerda began to forget her playmate Kai more and more. The old lady knew witchcraft; but she was not an evil witch, she just liked to do a little magic for her own pleasure. She wanted little Gerda to stay with her very much; that was why she went with her shepherd's crook out into the garden and pointed it at all the rosebushes. Immediately, the sweet flowering bushes sank down into the earth and disappeared. One could not even see where they had been. Now she need not fear that when little Gerda saw the roses she would think of Kai and run away.

Then she took Gerda out into the garden and showed it to her. Oh, what a beautiful place it was! All the flowers imaginable were there; and all of them in full bloom, although they belonged to different seasons. Certainly no picture book could be as beautiful as they were. Gerda almost jumped for joy, and she played among them all day until the sun set behind the tall cherry trees. Then she was given the loveliest of beds with a red quilt stuffed with dried violets to cover herself; and there she slept, dreaming sweeter dreams than even a queen on her wedding night.

The next day she played in the warm sunshine with the flowers again; and in this manner many days went by. Gerda, at last, knew every flower in the garden, and though there were so many different kinds, there seemed to be one missing, but she did not know which it was.

One day as she was sitting looking at the old lady's grand hat, with its painted flowers, she saw among them a rose. The old woman had forgotten the one in her hat when she got rid of all the roses—that happens if you are absent-minded.

"What!" exclaimed Gerda. "Are there no roses in the garden?" She ran about the garden, looking and searching, but nowhere did she find a rosebush. She felt so sad that she wept and her tears fell on the very plot of earth where a rose tree had grown. Through the earth, moistened by her tears, the tree shot upward again, blooming just as beautifully as when the old woman had made it vanish. Gerda kissed the flowers and thought of the roses at home and of little Kai.

"I have stayed here much too long," she cried. "I must find little Kai. Do you know where he is?" she asked the roses. "Do you think that he is dead?"

"No, he is not dead," answered the roses. "We have been down under the earth, where the dead are, and Kai was not there."

"Thank you," said little Gerda. She asked the other flowers if they knew where Kai was.

Every flower stood in the warm sunshine and dreamed its own

fairy tale; and that it was willing to tell, but none of them knew anything about Kai.

What story did the tiger lily tell her? Here it is:

"Can you hear the drum: boom . . . boom! It has only two beats:
boom . . . boom. Listen to the woman's song of lament; hear the
priest chant. The Hindu wife is standing on the funeral pyre, dressed
in a long red gown. Soon the flames will devour her and her husband's
body. She is thinking of someone who is standing among the mourners; his eyes burn even hotter than the flames that lick her feet, his
flaming eyes did burn her heart with greater heat than those flames
which soon will turn her body into ashes. Can the fire of a funeral
pyre extinguish the flame that burns within the heart?"

"That story I don't understand," said little Gerda.

"Well, it is my fairy tale," answered the tiger lily.

Next Gerda asked the honeysuckle; and this is what it said:

"High up above the narrow mountain road the old castle clings to
the steep mountainside. Its ancient walls are covered by green ivy; the
vines spread over the balcony where a beautiful young girl stands. No
unplucked rose is fresher than she, no apple blossom, plucked and
carried by the spring wind, is lighter or dances more daintily than
she. Hear how her silk dress rustles. Will he not come soon?"

"Is that Kai you mean?" asked little Gerda.

"I tell only my own story, my own dream," answered the honeysuckle.

Now it was the little daisy's turn:

"Between two trees a swing has been hung. Two sweet little girls,
with dresses as white as snow and from whose hats green ribbons
hang, lazily swing back and forth. Their brother, who is older than
they are, is standing up behind them on the swing. He has his arms
around the ropes so that he will not fall. In one hand he has a little
bowl; in the other, a clay pipe. He is blowing soap bubbles. The
swing glides, and the bubbles with their ever changing colors fly
through the air. The last bubble clings to the pipe, then the breeze
takes it. A little black dog, which belongs to the children, stands on
its hind legs barking at the bubble and it breaks. Such is my song: a
swing and a world of foam."

"Your tale may be beautiful but you tell it so sadly, and you didn't
mention Kai at all," complained little Gerda. "I think I will ask the
hyacinth."

"There were three beautiful sisters; they were so fine and delicate that they were almost transparent. One had on a red dress; the second, a blue; and the third, a white one. They danced, hand in hand, down by the lake; but they were not elves, they were real human children. The air smelled so sweet that the girls wandered into the forest. The sweet fragrance grew stronger. Three coffins appeared; and in them lay the three beautiful sisters. They sailed across the lake, and glowworms flew through the air like little candles. Were the dancing girls asleep or were they dead? The smell of the flowers said they were corpses, the bells at vespers ring for the dead."

"Oh, you make me feel so sad," said little Gerda. "And the fragrance from your flowers is so strong that it makes me think of the poor dead girls. Is Kai dead too? The roses, who have been down under the earth, said that he wasn't."

"Ding! dong!" rang the little hyacinth bells. "We are not tolling for Kai, we do not know him. We are singing our own little song, the only one we know."

Gerda approached a little buttercup that shone so prettily between its green leaves.

"You little sun, tell me, do you know where my playmate is?" she asked.

The buttercup's little shining face looked so trustfully back at her, but it too had only its own song to sing and it was not about Kai.

"Into a little narrow yard," began the buttercup, "God's warm sun was shining; it was the first spring day of the year. The sunbeams reflected against the white walls of the neighbor's house; nearby the first little yellow flower had unfolded itself. It was golden in the sunlight; the old grandmother brought her chair outside to sit in the warm sun. Her grandchild, the poor little servant maid, had come home for a short visit. She kissed her grandmother. There was gold in that kiss: the gold of the heart. Gold in the mouth, gold on the ground, and gold in the blessed sunrise. Now that was my little story," said the buttercup.

"Oh, the poor Grandmother," sighed little Gerda. "She must be longing for me and grieving, as she did when little Kai disappeared. But I will soon go back home and bring little Kai with me. There is no point in asking any of the other flowers, each one only sings its own song."

She tied her long dress up so that she could run fast, and away she went. The narcissus hit her leg smartly when she jumped over it and Gerda stopped. "What, do you know something?" she asked, and bent down toward the flower.

"I can see myself, I can see myself," cried the narcissus. "High up in the garret lives the little ballerina; she stands on tiptoe and kicks at the world, for it is but a mirage. She pours a little water from the kettle on a piece of cloth; it is her corset that she is washing, for cleanliness is next to godliness. Her white dress is hanging in the corner; it has also been washed in the teakettle, then it was hung out on the roof to dry. Now she puts it on, and around her neck she ties a saffron-colored kerchief; it makes the dress seem even whiter. She lifts one leg high in the air. She is bending her stem. I can see myself! I can see myself!"

"I don't care either to see you or to hear about you," said Gerda angrily. "Your story is a silly story," and with those words she ran to the other end of the garden.

The door in the wall was closed; she turned the old rusty handle and it sprang open. Out went little Gerda, in her bare feet, out into the wide world. Three times she turned to look back but no one seemed to have noticed her flight.

At last she could not run any farther, and she sat down on a big stone to rest. She looked at the landscape; summer was long since over, it was late fall. Back in the old lady's garden, you could not notice the change in seasons, for it was always summer and the flowers of every season were in bloom.

"Goodness me, how much time I have wasted," sighed Gerda. "It is already autumn, I do not dare rest any longer," and she got up and walked on. Her little feet hurt and she was tired. The leaves of the willow tree were all yellow, the water from the cold, fall mist dripped from it, as its leaves fell one by one. Only the blackthorn bush bore fruits now, and they are bitter. Oh, how somber and gray seemed the wide world.

THE FOURTH STORY, IN WHICH APPEAR A PRINCE AND A PRINCESS

More and more often did Gerda have to rest. The ground was now covered with snow. A big crow landed near her; the bird sat there a long time, wriggling its head and looking at her. "Caw . . . Caw!" he remarked, which in crow language means "Good day." He was kind, and asked the girl why she was out all alone in the lonely winter world.

The word "alone" Gerda understood only too well; and she told the crow her story and asked him if he had seen little Kai.

The crow nodded most thoughtfully and said, "Maybe, maybe!"

"Oh, he is alive!" screamed little Gerda, and almost squeezed the poor bird to death, while she kissed him.

"Be sensible, be sensible," protested the crow. "It may be little Kai I have seen; but if it is, then I am afraid he has forgotten you for the sake of the princess."

"Does he live with a princess?" asked little Gerda.

"Yes, he does," answered the crow, "but are you sure you don't understand crow language? I much prefer speaking it."

"No, I have never learned it; but the Grandmother knows it, I wish now that she had taught it to me."

"Never mind, it can't be helped," said the crow. "I shall do my best, which is a lot more than most people do," and the crow told Gerda all that he knew:

"Now in this kingdom, where we are at present, there lives a princess who is immensely clever; she has read all the newspapers in the whole world and forgotten what was written in them, and that is the part that proves how intelligent she is. A few weeks ago, while she was sitting on the throne—and that, people say, is not such an amusing place to sit—she happened to hum a song which has as its chorus the line 'Why shouldn't I get married?'

"'Why not, indeed?' thought the princess. 'But if I am to get married it must be to a man who can speak up for himself.' She didn't want anyone who just stood about looking distinguished, for such a fellow is boring. She called all her ladies in waiting and told them of her intention. They clapped their hands, and one of them said, 'Oh, how delightful. I had such an idea myself just the other day.' . . . Believe me, everything I tell you is true," declared the crow. "My fiancée is tame, she has the run of the castle and it is from her I got the story." His fiancée was, naturally, another crow, for birds of a feather flock together.

"The newspapers were printed with a border of hearts and the princess' name on the front page. Inside there was a royal proclamation: any good-looking man, regardless of birth, could come to the castle and speak with the princess, and the one who seemed most at home there and spoke the best, she would marry.

"Believe me," said the crow, and shook his head, "as sure as I am sitting here, that proclamation got people out of their houses. They came thick and fast, you have never seen such a crowd. But neither the first nor the second day did the princess find anyone who pleased her. They could all speak well enough as long as they were standing in the street; but as soon as they had entered the castle gates and saw the royal guards, in their silver uniforms, the young men lost their tongues. They didn't get them back, either, when they had to climb the marble stairs, lined with lackeys dressed in gold; or when they finally arrived in the grand hall with the great chandeliers and had to stand in front of the throne on which the princess sat. All they could do was repeat whatever she said; and that she didn't want to hear once more. One should think every one of them had had his tummy filled with snuff or had fallen into a trance. But as soon as they were down in the streets again they got their tongues back, and all they could do was talk.

"There was a queue, so long that it stretched from beyond the city gate all the way up to the castle. I flew into town to have a look at it. Most of the men got both hungry and thirsty while they waited; the princess didn't even offer them a glass of lukewarm water. Some of the more clever ones had brought sandwiches, but they didn't offer any to their neighbors, for they thought: 'Let him look hungry and the princess won't take him.'"

"But Kai! What about Kai?" asked Gerda. "Did he stand in the queue too?"

"Don't be impatient. We are coming to him. Now the third day a little fellow arrived, he didn't have a carriage nor did he come on horseback. No, he came walking straight up to the castle. He was poorly dressed but had bright shining eyes like yours, and the most beautiful long hair."

"That is Kai!" shouted little Gerda, and clapped her hands in joy.

"He had a little knapsack on his back," continued the crow.

"It wasn't a knapsack," interrupted Gerda. "It was his sled."

"Sled or knapsack, it doesn't matter much," said the crow. "I didn't look too closely at him. But this I know from my fiancée: when he entered the castle and saw the royal guards and all the lackeys, they didn't make him the least bit fainthearted. He nodded kindly to them and said, 'It must be boring to spend your life waiting on the stairs, I think I will go inside.' The big hall with its lighted candelabra, its servants carrying golden bowls, while courtiers stood around dressed in their very best, was impressive enough to take away the courage of even the bravest—and, on top of all that, the young man's boots squeaked something wicked—but he did not seem to notice either the elegant hall or his noisy boots."

"It must be Kai," said Gerda. "His boots were new and I know they squeaked, I have heard them myself."

"Well, squeak they did," said the crow. "But he walked right up to the princess, who was sitting on a pearl as big as a spinning wheel. Behind her stood all her ladies in waiting with their maids and their maids' maids; and all the gentlemen of the court with their servants and their servants' servants, each of whom, in turn, kept a boy. And the servant's servant's boy, who stood next to the door, always wore slippers and was so proud that one hardly dared look at him!"

"It must have been horrible!" Little Gerda shook her head. "But Kai got the princess anyway?"

"If I hadn't been a crow, I would have taken her and that even though I am engaged. My fiancée tells me that he talks as well as I do when I talk crow language. He said that he hadn't come to propose marriage but only to find out whether she was as clever as everybody said she was. He was satisfied that what he heard was true; and the princess was satisfied with him."

"I am sure it was Kai, for he is so clever, he can figure in fractions. Won't you take me to the castle?"

"That is easier said than done," said the crow, and looked thoughtfully at Gerda. "I will talk to my fiancée about it, she might know how we can do it. For I can tell you, it is not easy for a poor little girl like you to get into the castle."

"But I will get in!" protested Gerda. "As soon as Kai hears that I am here he will come and fetch me himself."

"Wait here by the big stone," commanded the crow, wriggled his head, and flew away.

The crow didn't return before dusk. "Caw! Caw!" he said, and alighted on the stone. "I bring you greetings from my fiancée, she sends you this little piece of bread. She took it in the kitchen where there is bread enough, and you must be hungry. It is quite impossible for you to enter the castle. You have bare feet; the guards in their silver uniforms and the lackeys in their golden ones won't allow it. But don't weep, we will get you in anyway. My fiancée knows where the key is kept to the back stairs, and they lead right up to the royal bedchamber."

They entered the royal garden and watched the lights in the castle being extinguished, one by one. At last the crow led her to a little door in the rear of the castle that was half open. Little Gerda's heart beat both with fear and with longing, she felt as though she were doing something wrong; and yet all she wanted to do was to see whether it was little Kai who had won the princess. She was sure it must be he.

In her mind she saw his lively, clever eyes, his long hair; he was smiling as he did when they sat under the little rose trees at home. He would be happy to see her, and she would tell him of the long journey she had made for his sake. She would tell him, too, how sad everyone had become because he had gone, and how they all had missed him. She felt so happy and so fearful.

They had reached the stairs; a little lamp burned on a chest. In the middle of the floor stood a tame crow, twisting its head about and looking at her quizzically. Gerda curtsied as the Grandmother had taught her to do.

"My fiancé has told me so many nice things about you. He has narrated your *vita* as it is called, I have found the story most touching! Will you take the lamp and I shall walk ahead and show the way."

"I think someone is coming," whispered Gerda. There was a whirling, rushing sound; and on the wall were strange shadows of horses with flying manes, dogs and falcons, servants and hunters.

"Oh, they are only dreams," said the crow. "They have come to fetch their royal masters. That is only lucky for us; the easier it will be for you to have a good look at them while they are sleeping. But remember, when you gain honor and position, to be grateful and not forget those who helped you get it."

"That is no way to talk," grumbled the crow from the woods.

Now they entered the first of the great halls. The walls were covered with pink satin and decorated with artificial flowers. The shadows of the dreams reappeared, but they flew past so quickly that Gerda did not even get a chance to see whether Kai was mounted on one of the horses. Each hall they passed through was more magnificent than the one before it. At last they came to the royal bedchamber. The ceiling looked like the top of a large palm tree with glass leaves; from the center of it eight ropes of pure gold hung down, attached to them were the two little beds that the royal couple slept in. Each bed was shaped like a lily; in the white lily slept the princess, and in the red lily the young man who had won her. Gerda peeped into it and saw a head of long brown hair. "It is Kai!" she shouted in her joy. The dreams returned as fast as the wind and the young boy awoke.

He wasn't little Kai!

It was only the long brown hair they had in common, although he was young and handsome too. From the white lily bed the princess raised her head and asked what the commotion was about. Poor Gerda started to cry; and then between sobs, she told her story and explained how the crows had helped her.

"You poor thing!" said the prince. The princess said the same, and they did not scold the crows, on the contrary they praised them; although they warned them not to do it again. Still, they were to have a reward.

"Would you rather be free," asked the princess "or receive permanent positions as royal court crows, with permission to eat all leftovers?"

Both the crows curtsied and said they preferred permanent positions. After all, they had to think of their old age. "To be secure is better than to fly," they said.

The prince got out of his bed and let Gerda sleep in it; he could hardly do more. She folded her little hands and thought, "How good all animals and human beings are." Then she closed her eyes and slept. The dreams returned and this time they looked like little angels; and one of them was drawing a sled behind her; and on it sat little Kai; and he nodded to Gerda. But that was only a dream and it was gone as soon as she awoke.

In the morning Gerda was dressed from head to toe in silk and velvet; and the little prince and princess begged her to stay with them. But she asked only for a little carriage and a horse and some boots, so that she could continue on her journey out in the wide world to find Kai.

She was given not only new boots but a muff as well, and good warm clothes. When she was ready to leave, a fine carriage of the purest gold drove up in front of the castle. The coat of arms of the princess was on the door, and not only was there a coachman to drive her, but a servant stood on the back of the carriage and two little soldiers rode in front. The prince and the princess themselves helped her into the carriage and wished her luck. Her friend, the crow from the woods, drove with her the first couple of miles. They sat beside each other, for the crow got sick if he had to ride sitting backward. The other crow stood at the gate and flapped her wings; she had had a headache since she had been given a permanent position, and besides, she had overeaten. The carriage was lined with candy, and on the seat across from Gerda was a basket of fruit.

"Good-by, good-by!" shouted the little prince and princess; and Gerda wept, for she had grown fond of them, and the crow wept too. When they had driven a little way the crow said good-by, and that was even harder to bear. He flew up into a tall tree and sat there waving with his black wings until he could no longer see the carriage that glistened as though it were made of sunlight.

### THE FIFTH STORY, WHICH IS ABOUT THE ROBBER GIRL

They were driving through a great dark forest, and the golden carriage shone like a flame right in the robbers' eyes, and they couldn't bear it.

"Gold! Gold!" they screamed as they came rushing out of the woods. They grabbed hold of the horses and killed the coachman, the servant, and the soldiers; then they dragged little Gerda out of the carriage.

"She is lovely and fat, I bet she has been fed on nuts," said an old robber woman; she had a beard and eyebrows so big and bushy that they almost hid her eyes. "She will taste as good as a lamb," and the robber woman took a long shining knife from her belt; it was horrible to look at.

"Ouch!" screamed the old hag, for just at that moment she had been bitten in the ear by her own little daughter, whom she carried on her back. The child was such a wild and naughty creature that it was a marvel. "Ouch!" the woman cried again, and missed her chance to kill Gerda.

"The girl is to play with me!" declared the little robber girl. "But she is to give me her muff and her dress and sleep in my bed with me." And just to make certain that her mother had understood her, she bit her again as hard as she could.

The robber woman turned and jumped into the air from the pain; and all the robbers laughed and said, "Look how she dances with her brat."

"I want to drive in the carriage," cried the little robber girl, and she was allowed to, for she was terribly spoiled. She and Gerda sat inside the carriage while it was being driven along little paths that brought it deeper and deeper into the forest. The little robber girl was as tall as Gerda but much stronger, and her skin had been tanned by the sun. Her eyes were almost black and looked sad. She put her arms around Gerda and said, "I won't allow them to kill you, so long as you don't make me angry. You must be a princess?"

"No, I am not," answered Gerda, and then she told her whole story and how much she loved little Kai.

The robber girl looked very seriously at her, nodded her head, and said: "I won't allow them to kill you even if I do get angry at you, I will do it myself." Then she dried Gerda's eyes and put her own hands inside the warm soft muff.

At last the carriage stopped; they had come to the robber castle. The walls were cracked and the windows were broken. Crows and ravens flew in and out of the big holes in the tower. Big dogs ran about in the courtyard; they looked ferocious enough to be able to eat human beings; they sprang up in the air but they didn't bark, that wasn't allowed.

In the middle of the great hall a fire burned. The smoke drifted up among the blackened rafters; how it ever got out was its own business. A big copper kettle filled with soup hung over the fire, and next to it, on spits, hares and rabbits were being roasted.

"You are going to sleep with me, over here among all my little pet animals," said the little robber girl, and dragged Gerda over to a corner of the hall, where there lay some straw and some blankets. Above them, on poles, sat about a hundred doves; they were asleep, but a couple opened their eyes and turned their heads when the little girls came.

"They are all mine," said the girl, and grabbed one of them by its legs. The dove flapped its wings. "Kiss it," demanded the robber girl, and shoved the frightened bird right up into Gerda's face.

"Up there are two wood pigeons," the robber girl explained as she pointed to a recess in the wall, high above them, that had been turned into a cage by a few wooden bars. "They would fly away if they could, but they can't."

"Here is my old sweetheart, bah!" She took hold of the antlers of a reindeer that stood tied near her bed and gave them a hard pull. "One has got to hold onto him too, or he would leap away. Every evening I tickle his throat with my sharp knife, that frightens him." The little girl pulled a knife out from a crack in the wall and let its sharp point glide around the reindeer's neck; the animal backed as far away as it could, in terror. That made the little robber girl laugh; and she pulled Gerda down into her bed.

"Do you sleep with your knife?" asked Gerda, frightened.

"I always sleep with the knife," answered the little robber girl. "One never knows what might happen. But tell me again the story of little Kai and why you have gone out into the wide world." Gerda told her story once more, and the wood pigeons, up in their cage, cooed; the doves were all asleep. The little robber girl put one of her arms around Gerda—in her other hand, she kept her knife—and fell asleep. She snored loudly.

Poor Gerda didn't dare close her eyes; she didn't know whether she was going to live or die. The robbers all sat around the fire and sang while they drank. The little girl's mother was so drunk that she turned a somersault. Oh, it was a pretty sight for a little girl to see!

Suddenly one of the wood pigeons cooed, "We have seen little Kai. A white hen carried his sled. He sat in the Snow Queen's sled when she flew low over the forest. We had just come out of our eggs and she breathed on us; all the other young ones died. We, alone, survived. Coo! Coo!"

"What is it you are saying?" cried Gerda. "Where was the Snow Queen going? Do you know?"

"I suppose she went to Lapland, where there always are snow and ice, but ask the reindeer that stands tied by your bed."

"Oh yes, ice and snow are always there; it is a blessed place," sighed the reindeer. "There one can jump and run about freely in the great, glittering valleys. The Snow Queen keeps a summer tent there, but her castle is far to the north, near the pole, on an island called Spitsbergen."

"Oh, Kai, little Kai!" mumbled Gerda.

"Lie still," commanded the robber girl, "or I will slit open your stomach!"

In the morning Gerda told her what she had heard from the wood pigeons. The little robber girl looked quite solemn, then nodded her head and said, "I am sure it is he, I am sure." Then she turned to the reindeer and asked him if he knew where Lapland was.

"Who should know that better than I?" answered the poor animal. "There I was born, there I have run across the great snow fields." And his eyes gleamed, recollecting what he had lost.

"Listen," whispered the little robber girl to Gerda. "All the men are gone. Only Mama is here and she won't leave; but in a little while she will take a drink from the big bottle and then she will take a nap. And then . . . I will help you!"

She jumped out of bed, ran over and threw her arms around her mother, pulled her beard, and said, "Oh, my own sweet billy goat, good morning!"

The mother tweaked her daughter's nose, so that it turned both red and blue, but it was all done out of love.

When the mother had drunk from the big bottle, she lay down for her midmorning nap; then the robber girl spoke to the reindeer: "I would have loved to tickle your throat for many a day yet, for you look so funny when I do it. But never mind, I will let you loose so that you can run back to Lapland; but you are to take the little girl with you and bring her to the Snow Queen's palace where her playmate is. I know you have heard everything she said, for you are always eavesdropping."

The reindeer leaped into the air out of pure joy. The robber's daughter lifted Gerda up on the animal's back and tied her on so she wouldn't fall off; and she even gave her a little pillow to sit on. "I don't really care about your boots, you need them," she said. "It is cold where you are going. But the muff I am keeping, for it is so soft and nice. But you shan't freeze, I will give you my mother's great big mittens; they will keep you warm all the way up to your elbows. Here, put them on! Now your hands look as ugly as my mother's."

Gerda cried from happiness and relief.

"I don't like all your tears," scolded the little robber girl. "You should look happy now. Here are two loaves of bread and a ham, so you won't go hungry," she said as she tied the bread and the ham on the back of the reindeer; then she opened the door and called all the big dogs in. She cut the rope that tethered the reindeer and said in parting, "Run along, but take good care of the little girl!"

Gerda waved good-by with her great big mittens, and away they went, through the forest and across the great plains, as fast as they could. They heard the wolves howl and the ravens cry; and suddenly the sky was all filled with light.

"There are the old northern lights," said the reindeer. "Look how they shine!"

Still they went on both day and night: farther and farther north.

The bread was eaten and the ham was eaten; and then they were in Lapland.

### THE SIXTH STORY: THE LAPP WOMAN AND THE FINNISH WOMAN

They stopped before a little cottage; it was a wretched little hovel: the roof went all the way down to the ground and the door was so low that you had to creep through it on all fours. The only person at home was an old Lapp woman who was busy frying some fish over an oil lamp. The reindeer told her Gerda's story; but first he had told his own, because he thought that was more interesting. Poor Gerda was so cold that she couldn't even talk.

"Oh, you poor things!" said the Lapp woman. "You have far to go yet. It is more than a hundred miles from here to the camp of the Snow Queen. She amuses herself by shooting fireworks off every night. I shall give you an introduction to the Finnish woman who lives up there. She knows more about it all than I do and will be able to help you. Paper I have none of, so I will write on a dried codfish."

When little Gerda had eaten and was warm again, the Lapp woman wrote a few words on a dried codfish and told Gerda not to lose it. Then she tied her on the reindeer's back again and away they ran.

Whish . . . Whish . . . it said up in the sky as the northern lights flickered and flared; they were the Snow Queen's fireworks. At last they came to the Finnish woman's house; they had to knock on the chimney, for the door was so small that they couldn't find it.

Goodness me, it was hot inside! The Finnish woman walked around almost naked. She pulled off both Gerda's boots and her mittens so that the heat would not be unbearable for her. The reindeer got a piece of ice to put on its head. Then the Finnish woman read what was written on the codfish; she read it three times and then she knew it by heart. The fish she put in the pot that was boiling over the fire. It could be eaten, and she never wasted anything. The reindeer told first of his own adventures and then of Gerda's. The Finnish woman squinted her intelligent eyes but didn't utter a word.

"You are so clever," said the reindeer finally. "I know you can tie all the winds of the world into four knots on a single thread. If the sailor loosens the first knot he gets a fair wind; if he loosens the second a strong breeze; but if he loosens the third and the fourth knots, then there's such a storm that the trees in the forest are torn up by the roots. Won't you give this little girl a magic drink so that she gains the strength of twelve men and can conquer the Snow Queen?"

"The strength of twelve men," laughed the Finnish woman. "Yes, I should think that would be enough." Then she walked over to a shelf and took down a roll of skin which she spread out on the table. Strange words were written there, and the Finnish woman read and studied till the perspiration ran down her forehead.

The reindeer begged her again to help little Gerda; and Gerda looked up at her with eyes filled with tears. The Finnish woman winked, then drew the reindeer into a corner, where she whispered to him while she gave him another piece of ice for his head.

"Little Kai is in the Snow Queen's palace and is quite satisfied with being there; he thinks it is the best place in the whole world. This is because he has gotten a sliver of glass in his heart and two grains of the same in his eyes. As long as they are there he will never be human again, and the Snow Queen will keep her power over him."

"But can't you give Gerda some kind of power so that she can take out the glass?" asked the reindeer.

"I can't give her any more power than she already has! Don't you understand how great it is? Don't you see how men and animals must serve her; how else could she have come so far, walking on her bare feet? But she must never learn of her power; it is in her heart, for she is a sweet and innocent child. If she herself cannot get into the Snow Queen's palace and free Kai from the glass splinters in his eyes and his heart, how can we help her? Two miles from here begin the gardens of the Snow Queen. Carry Gerda there and set her down by the bush with the red berries, then come right back here and don't stand about gossiping." The Finnish woman lifted Gerda back on the reindeer's back, and he ran as fast as he could.

"I don't have my boots on, and I forgot the mittens," cried Gerda when she felt the cold making her naked feet smart. But the reindeer did not dare return. He ran on until he came to the bush with the red berries. There he put Gerda down and kissed her on her mouth; two tears ran down his animal cheeks; then he leaped and ran back to the Finnish woman as fast as he could.

There stood poor Gerda, barefooted and without mittens on, in the intense arctic cold. She entered the Snow Queen's garden and ran as fast as she could in the direction of the palace. A whole regiment of snowflakes advanced against her. They had not fallen from the sky, for that was cloudless and illuminated by northern lights. The snow-flakes flew just above the snow-covered earth; and as they came nearer they grew in size. Gerda remembered how they had looked when seen through a magnifying glass, but these were even bigger and horrible to look at. They were the Snow Queen's guard. And what strange creatures they were! Some of them looked like ugly little porcupines, others like bunches of snakes all twisted together, and some like little bears with bristly fur. All of the snowflakes were brilliantly white and terribly alive.

Little Gerda stopped and said her prayers. It was so cold that she could see her own breath; it came like a fine white smoke from her mouth, then it became more and more solid and formed itself into little angels that grew as soon as they touched the ground; all of them had helmets on their heads and shields and spears in their hands. When Gerda had finished saying her prayers a whole legion of little angels stood around her. They threw their spears at the snow monsters, and they splintered into hundreds of pieces. Little Gerda walked on unafraid, and the angels caressed her little feet and hands so she did not feel the cold.

But now we must hear what happened to little Kai. He was not thinking of Gerda—and even if he had been, he could not have im-agined that she could be standing right outside the palace.

### THE SEVENTH STORY: WHAT HAPPENED IN THE SNOW QUEEN'S PALACE AND AFTERWARD

The walls of the palace were made of snow, and the windows and doors of the sharp winds; it contained more than a hundred halls, the largest several miles long. All were lighted by the sharp glare of the northern lights; they were huge, empty, and terrifyingly cold. Here no one had ever gathered for a bit of innocent fun; not even a dance for polar bears, where they might have walked on their hind legs in the manner of man and the wind could have produced the music. No one had ever been invited in for a little game of cards, with something good to eat and a bit of not too malicious gossip; nor had there ever been a tea party for young white lady foxes. No, empty, vast, and cold was the Snow Queen's palace.

The northern lights burned so precisely that you could tell to the very second when they would be at their highest and their lowest points. In the middle of that enormous snow hall was a frozen lake. It had cracked into thousands of pieces and every one of them was shaped exactly like all the others. In the middle of the lake was the throne of the Snow Queen. Here she sat when she was at home. She called the lake the Mirror of Reason, and declared that it was the finest and only mirror in the world.

Little Kai was blue—indeed, almost black—from the cold; but he did not feel it, for the Snow Queen had kissed all feeling of coldness out of him, and his heart had almost turned into a lump of ice. He sat arranging and rearranging pieces of ice into patterns. He called this the Game of Reason; and because of the splinters in his eyes, he thought that what he was doing was of great importance, although it was no different from playing with wooden blocks, which he had done when he could hardly talk.

He wanted to put the pieces of ice together in such a way that they formed a certain word, but he could not remember exactly what that word was. The word that he could not remember was "eternity." The Snow Queen had told him that if he could place the pieces of ice so that they spelled that word, then he would be his own master and she would give him the whole world and a new pair of skates; but, however much he tried, he couldn't do it.

"I am going to the warm countries," the Snow Queen had announced that morning. "I want to look into the boiling black pots." By "black pots," she meant the volcanoes, Vesuvius and Etna. "I will chalk their peaks a bit. It will do them good to be refreshed; ice is pleasant as a dessert after oranges and lemons."

The Snow Queen flew away and Kai was left alone in the endless hall. He sat pondering his patterns of ice, thinking and thinking; he sat so still one might have believed that he was frozen to death.

Little Gerda entered the castle. The winds began to whip her face, and could have cut it, but she said her prayers and they lay down to sleep. She came into the vast, empty, cold hall; then she saw Kai!

She recognized him right away, and ran up to him and threw her arms around him, while she exclaimed jubilantly: "Kai, sweet little Kai. At last I have found you."

But Kai sat still and stiff and cold; then little Gerda cried and her tears fell on Kai's breast. The warmth penetrated to his heart and melted both the ice and the glass splinter in it. He looked at her and she sang the psalm they had once sung together:

> Our roses bloom and fade away,
> Our infant Lord abides alway.
> May we be blessed his face to see
> And ever little children be.

Kai burst into tears and wept so much that the grains of glass in his eyes were washed away. Now he remembered her and shouted joyfully: "Gerda! Sweet little Gerda, where have you been so long? And where have I been?" Kai looked about him. "How cold it is, how empty, and how huge!" And he held onto Gerda, who was so happy that she was both laughing and crying at the same time. It was so blessed, so happy a moment that even the pieces of ice felt it and started to dance; and when they grew tired they lay down and formed exactly that word for which the Snow Queen had promised Kai the whole world and a new pair of skates.

Gerda kissed him on his cheeks and the color came back to them. She kissed his eyes and they became like hers. She kissed his hands and feet, and the blue color left them and the blood pulsed again through his veins. He was well and healthy. Now the Snow Queen could return, it did not matter, for his right to his freedom was written in brilliant pieces of ice.

They took each other by the hand and walked out of the great palace. They talked of the Grandmother, and the roses that bloomed on the roof at home. The winds were still; and as they walked, the sun broke through the clouds. When they reached the bush with the red berries the reindeer was waiting there for them. He had brought another young reindeer with him and her udder was bursting with milk. The two children drank from it and the reindeer kissed them. Then they rode on the backs of the reindeer to the home of the Finnish woman, where they got warm, were given a good meal and instructions for the homeward journey.

They visited the Lapp woman. She had sewn warm clothes for them and was getting her sled ready.

The two reindeer accompanied them to the border of Lapland. There the green grass started to break through the snow and they could not use the sled any longer. They said good-by to the reindeer and to the Lapp woman. Soon they heard the twitter of the first birds of spring and in the woods the trees were budding.

They met a young girl wearing a red hat and riding a magnificent horse. Gerda recognized the animal, for it was one of the horses that had drawn her golden carriage. The girl had two pistols stuck in her belt; she was the little robber girl, who had got tired of staying at home and now was on her way out into the wide world. She recognized Gerda immediately and the two of them were so happy to see each other.

"You are a fine one," she said to Kai, "running about as you did. I wonder if you are worth going to the end of the world for?" Gerda touched her cheek and asked her if she knew what had happened to the prince and the princess. "They have gone traveling in foreign lands," answered the robber girl.

"And what about the crow?"

"The crow is dead," said the girl. "His tame fiancée has become a widow, she wears a black wool thread around her leg. She thinks mourning becomes her, but it is all nonsense. But tell me what happened to you and how you managed to find him!"

And both Gerda and Kai told her everything that had happened to them.

"Well, the end was as good as the beginning," said the robber girl, and took each of them by the hand and promised that if she ever came through the town where they lived she would come and visit them. Then she rode away out into the world; and Kai and Gerda walked hand in hand homeward.

It was really spring. In the ditches the little wild flowers bloomed. The churchbells were ringing. Now they recognized the towers; they were approaching their own city and the home they had left behind.

Soon they were walking up the worn steps of the staircase to the old Grandmother's apartment. Nothing inside it had changed. The clock said: "Tick-tack . . ." and the wheels moved. But as they stepped through the doorway they realized that they had grown: they were no longer children.

The roses were blooming in the wooden boxes and the window was open. There were the little stools they used to sit on. Still holding each other's hands, they sat down, and all memory of the Snow Queen's palace and its hollow splendor disappeared. The Grandmother sat in the warm sunshine, reading aloud from her Bible: *"Whosoever shall not receive the Kingdom of Heaven as a little child shall not enter therein."*

Kai and Gerda looked into each other's eyes and now they understood the words from the psalm.

> Our roses bloom and fade away,
> Our infant Lord abides alway.
> May we be blessed his face to see
> And ever little children be.

There they sat, the two of them, grownups; and yet in their hearts children, and it was summer: a warm glorious summer day!

## 30

## Mother Elderberry

Once upon a time there was a little boy who had caught cold. He had got his feet wet, and no one could imagine how, for the weather had been dry for days. His mother undressed him and put him to bed; then she took out the teapot to make elderberry tea, for that is such a good remedy for colds. Just at that moment the pleasant old man who had his lodgings on the top floor entered. He lived completely alone, for he had neither wife nor children of his own, but he was very fond of other people's children and knew how to tell the most amusing fairy tales and stories.

"Now drink your tea like a good boy," said the mother, "and maybe you will be told a story."

"If I only knew one that he hasn't heard already," said the old man, and nodded kindly. "But tell me, how did the little fellow get his feet wet?"

"Where, indeed!" The mother shook her head. "That is a mystery."

"Are you going to tell me a story?" asked the boy.

"Maybe, if you can tell me exactly how deep the ditch is that runs along the lane next to your school; I would rather like to know that."

"In the deepest place, the water is halfway up to the top of my boots," answered the boy.

"That solves the mystery of the wet feet," said the old gentleman. "Now I should tell you a story, but I can't remember any that you haven't heard."

"You can make one up. Mother says that anything you touch becomes a fairy tale."

"No, that kind of story or fairy tale is not worth much; it is not like the real ones who come knocking on my forehead and say: 'Here I am, let me in.'"

"Won't one come knocking soon?" asked the boy. And his mother laughed as she put the elderberries in the teapot and poured boiling water on them.

"Please tell me a story! Please!" begged the boy.

"A fairy tale only comes when it wants to, for fairy tales and stories are so highborn that they won't obey anyone, not even kings . . . Stop!" he cried suddenly, and held up his forefinger. "There it is! Be careful. It is in the teapot."

The boy looked at the teapot. Slowly the lid lifted; up out of the top of the pot came fresh elderberry branches and from them hung clusters of white flowers. Now they were coming out of the spout as well. They grew and grew until they became a full-grown elderberry tree whose limbs crossed his bed and pushed aside the curtains. It was a grand tree! And how beautifully it smelled!

In the middle of the tree sat an old woman. She wore a dress that was as green as the elder leaves and had a pattern of white elder flowers. It was hard to tell whether her dress was made of cloth or out of real flowers and leaves. The old woman smiled kindly down at the boy.

"What is her name?" the lad asked.

"The Greeks and the Romans thought she was a wood nymph and called her dryad. Down in the 'new cottages'—which aren't very new, being three hundred years old—the old sailors who live there call her Mother Elderberry," the old man explained. "Now keep an eye on her. I shall tell you a story, while you look at the beautiful elder tree.

"It takes place in the 'new cottages.' Down in one of those tiny, narrow yards that the old sailors call their gardens, there grew a lovely elder tree, just like the one you are looking at. One sunny afternoon an old couple were sitting in its shade. He was an old, retired sailor, and she was a very old woman, who was his wife. They were so old that they had great-grandchildren and soon would celebrate their fiftieth wedding anniversary. But, alas! they could not remember the date. Mother Elderberry sat up in her tree looking very pleased with herself. 'I know which day it is,' she said.

"The old couple hadn't heard her. They were talking about the old times, when they had been young.

"'Can you remember,' began the old seaman, 'when we were children and played in this very yard, how we used to stick twigs in the earth and make believe we were making a garden?'

"'Yes, I remember,' said his wife. 'We watered them and one of them was an elder branch and it struck roots and began to grow. And now it is such a big tree that we two old souls can sit in its shade.'

"'Yes,' agreed the old sailor. 'Over there in the corner of the yard there used to stand an old tub, filled with water; that was the ocean my ships sailed on. I had carved them myself with my own knife. But it didn't take long before I walked the deck of a real ship, did it?'

"'No, but first we went to school,' the old woman smiled. 'And then we were confirmed and we both cried in church that day. In the afternoon we walked hand in hand up to the top of the Round Tower and looked out over the world. Later, we trudged all the way out to the Royal Gardens in Frederiksberg; there we saw the king and queen being rowed in their beautiful boat through the canals of the park.'

"'Rougher voyages than that were to be my lot. Remember how long I was to be away; it was not months but years.'

"'And I cried.' Again the old woman smiled. 'I thought for sure that you were dead and I would never see you again. I thought you were drowned and were lying deep down, under the dark waves. Many a night I got out of my warm bed to look at the weather vane to see if the wind had changed; it changed often enough but still you didn't come home. I remember one day—oh, what terrible weather we had; it was pouring!—I had heard the garbage wagon rumbling down the street and I came running down from the kitchen with the garbage pail. I was a servant then. I stood for a moment in the open door to look at the rain, and the mailman came and gave me a letter. It was from you. I tore it open and read it right through. I was so happy that I both laughed and cried. You wrote that you were in the warm countries where coffee grows.—How lovely it must be there!—You described it all so well that I feel as if I had been there. . . . There I stood with the garbage pail in my hand, while the rain streamed down, when all at once I felt an arm around my waist—'

" 'Yes, and you gave that poor fellow such a box on the ears that it could be heard all the way down the street.'

" 'How could I have known it was you! You had come home as fast as your letter. Oh, how handsome you were, and that you are still! You had a long yellow silk handkerchief sticking out of your pocket and a shiny hat on your head. You looked so fine. But what a day it was, the street looked like a river.'

" 'And then we got married,' laughed the old man. 'Do you remember? Then came the children: first the boy, then Marie, Niels, Peter, and Hans Christian.'

" 'And they all turned out so well. They are liked and respected by everyone.'

" 'And their children, in turn, have got little ones now,' said the old sailor, and nodded. 'We have great-grandchildren who have spirit. You know, I think it was about this time of the year that we got married.'

" 'Yes, this very day is your golden wedding day,' said Mother Elderberry, and put her head between the old man and his wife. They thought she was a neighbor who had stuck her head in over the fence.

"They looked at each other; and each reached out for the other's hand. A few minutes later their children and grandchildren came to congratulate them, for they knew that it was the old couple's fiftieth wedding anniversary and had been there earlier that day; but the old couple had forgotten their visit, while they could recall everything that had happened half of a century ago.

"The scent of the elder flowers was heavy; the sun was just setting, and its glow gave the old man and his wife red cheeks. Their youngest grandchild danced around them happily. 'Tonight we are going to have a feast and eat roast potatoes.' That was his favorite food.

"Old Mother Elderberry nodded and shouted, 'Hurrah!' with everyone else."

"But that was no fairy tale," complained the little boy.

"That is your opinion," said the kind old man who had told the story. "Let us ask Mother Elderberry."

"The child is right, it was no fairy tale," said Mother Elderberry. "But now it comes, for out of reality are our tales of imagination fashioned. If this were not true, then my elder tree could not have grown out of the teapot."

Mother Elderberry lifted the boy in her arms and pressed him to her breast. The flowering branches of the elder tree enfolded them. Now they were in an arbor and it was flying through the air with them inside it. It was a most delightful feeling. All at once Mother Elderberry changed into a young girl. She still had on her green dress with the pattern of white elder flowers, but there was a live flower pinned to her breast and around her curly golden hair there was a wreath of elder flowers. She and the boy kissed each other; and then they were one in age and desires.

Hand in hand, they left the arbor. On the green lawn lay his father's cane, tethered to a stick; for, to the children the cane was a horse. And when they mounted it to gallop around the garden, it had both a head and a flowing black mane.

"Now we shall ride for miles and miles!" shouted the boy. "We shall ride all the way to the castle we visited last year."

They rode round and round the garden. The little girl, who we know was none other than Mother Elderberry, said to the boy, "Now we are out in the country. Look, that's a farmer's house. See that wall with the big lump, protruding from the wall, like a giant egg, that's the oven for baking bread. In the shade of the elder tree nearby, you can see a flock of hens scratching the earth for worms. Look at the cock. See how he swaggers! . . . Now we are passing the church. It is built on a hill; near it are two ancient oak trees; one of them is wizened. . . . Now we are at the blacksmith's shop. The red fire glows. The man is naked to the waist. See his muscles as he lifts his hammer. . . . The sparks are flying all about him. . . . Away we go to the castle!"

Everything the little girl, who was riding behind him on the stick, described, the little boy saw; and yet they had only ridden around the lawn. Later they played on the gravel path and made a little garden of their own, and the girl took the elder flowers from the wreath in her hair and planted them. They grew just as the branch had, which the old seaman and his wife had planted; and they walked, hand in hand, just as the old people had done when they were children. But they didn't climb up the Round Tower or go out to the Royal Gardens of Frederiksberg. No, the little girl put her arm around the boy's waist and away they flew all around Denmark.

Spring changed into summer; soon it was harvest; and then the white winter came. A thousand pictures were mirrored in the little boy's eyes and heart, while the little girl repeated: "This you shall never forget!"

During their flight the sweet scent of elder flowers was all about them. The boy smelled only faintly the perfume of the roses and the fragrance of the fresh beech branches, for the elder flower bloomed in the girl's heart, and the boy never strayed from her.

"How beautiful spring is here!" she said; and they were standing in the midst of the tender green beech forest. At their feet grew the woodruff like a green carpet; and the fragile anemones, with their pale pink petals, were everywhere.

"Oh, I wish it were always spring!" exclaimed the little boy.

"How beautiful summer is here!" she said. Now they were flying past an old castle. Its red brick walls reflected in the water of the moat, where white swans made ripples in the mirror-like surface. The great white birds were looking at the long cool avenue of trees. The wind made waves in the field of grain as if it were a sea. In the ditches along the roads, yellow and red flowers bloomed; and the stone hedges were covered with wild hops and flowering bindweed. In the evening the pale moon rose. Down in the meadow the scent of newly cut hay filled the air. "This you will never forget."

"How beautiful autumn is here!" said the little girl; and the sky suddenly seemed twice as high and twice as blue. The woods had turned yellow, brown, and red, and they heard the barking of the hunting dogs. Flocks of screeching birds flew above the blackberry-covered stones of the Viking graves. The sea had turned almost black, and the sails appeared whiter against the dark color of the water. Down in the barn old women and young girls and children were busy picking the hops, dumping them into large vats. The young people sang the songs of the day, but the old women told stories of trolls and gnomes. What could be pleasanter?

"How beautiful winter is here!" said the little girl; and the trees were decked in hoarfrost and looked like a coral forest. Snow crunched under the children's boots and sounded as if they were wearing new shoes. At night shooting stars fell from the dark heavens. Christmas trees were lit and gifts exchanged. Someone was playing the violin; there was dancing in the farmer's living room, and from the kitchen came platters full of apple fritters that were refilled as soon as they were eaten. Then even the poorest child could say: "It is lovely in winter!"

Yes, it was truly beautiful. The little girl showed him the whole country of Denmark; and everywhere they went there was the smell of elder flowers; and there flew the flag with a white cross on the red background, the same one that flew from the mast of the ship on which the old sailor had sailed.

The boy became a young man. Now he was ready to journey out into the wide world: far, far away to the warm countries, where coffee grows. When they parted the little girl took the elder flower from her bosom and gave it to him. He put it between two of the pages of his hymnbook, and far from home, when he took down the book, it would always open to the pages where the elder flower was. The more he gazed at the dry, pressed flower, the more alive and fresh it became. He smelled the perfume of the Danish forest, and among the green branches he saw the face of the little girl peeking out at him and whispering: "Oh, it is beautiful here in spring, in summer, in autumn, and in winter." And his mind would paint a hundred pictures of all that he had seen.

Many years went by, the young man became an old man who sat underneath the elder tree with his wife. They held each other's hands, as the great-grandfather and great-grandmother from the "new cottages" had. They talked of bygone times and how it soon would be their golden anniversary.

The little girl with the big blue eyes and the wreath of elder blossoms in her hair sat up in the tree and nodded kindly down at them. "Today is your golden wedding day," she declared, and took two elderberry flowers from her wreath and kissed them. First they shone like silver and then like gold; she put one on each of the old couple's heads and they became golden crowns. The old man and the old woman sat like a king and queen under the fragrant elder tree. The old man told his wife the story of Mother Elderberry as it had been told to him when he was a little boy. And they both realized that much of the story could have been about themselves, and that was the part they liked best.

"Well," said the little girl in the tree, "some people call me Mother Elderberry; others call me the dryad; but my real name is memory. I sit in the tree that grows and grows; I can remember everything and therefore I can tell stories. Now let me see, do you still have your flower?"

The old man opened his hymnbook and there lay the elder flower, as fresh as if it had just been put there. Memory nodded and the setting sun shone on the heads of the two old people who were wearing golden crowns. They closed their eyes and then . . . Well, then the fairy tale is over.

The little boy lay in his bed; he didn't quite know whether he had dreamed the last part of the story or whether it had been told to him. The teapot stood on the table, but no elder tree was growing out of it. And the old man who had told him the story was about to go out through the door; it closed, and he was gone.

"Mother, it was wonderful," said the little boy. "I have been in the warm countries."

"I will believe that," laughed his mother. "If one drinks two big cups of elder tea, it is no wonder!" Then she tucked the blankets around him so he wouldn't be cold. "I think you fell asleep while we were arguing about whether the story was a proper fairy tale or not."

"And where is Mother Elderberry?" asked the boy.

"She is in the teapot," answered the mother, "and there she can stay."

## 31

## The Darning Needle

Once upon a time there was a darning needle who was so refined that she was convinced she was a sewing needle.

"Be careful! Watch what you are holding!" she shouted to the fingers who had picked her up. "I am so fine and thin that if I fall on the floor you will never be able to find me again."

"Don't overdo it," snarled the fingers, and squeezed her around the waist.

"Look, I am traveling with a retinue," said the needle. She was referring to the thread that trailed behind her but wasn't knotted. The fingers steered the needle toward the cook's slippers; the leather had split and had to be sewn.

"This is vulgar work," complained the darning needle. "I can't get through it. I shall break! I shall break!" And then she broke. "Didn't I tell you I was too fine?" she whined.

Had it been up to the fingers, then the darning needle would have been thrown away; but they had to mind the cook, so they dipped the needle in hot sealing wax and stuck it into the cook's blouse.

"Now I have become a brooch," exclaimed the darning needle. "I have always felt that I was born to be something better. When you are something, you always become something." Then she laughed inside herself; for you cannot see from the outside when a needle is laughing. There she sat as proudly as if she were looking out at the world from a seat in a golden carriage.

"May I take the liberty of asking you whether you are made of gold?" The darning needle was talking to her neighbor, a pin. "You look very handsome, and you have a head, even though it is small. Take my advice and let it grow a little bigger; not everyone can be so fortunate as to be dipped in sealing wax." The darning needle drew herself up a little too proudly; for she fell out of the blouse and down into the sink, at exactly the moment when the cook was rinsing it out.

"Here we go, traveling!" exclaimed the darning needle. "I hope I won't get lost." But she did get lost.

"I am too fine for this world," she remarked when she finally came to rest at the bottom of a gutter. "But I know who I am and where I come from, and that is always something." And the darning needle kept her back straight and remained cheerful.

All sorts of garbage were floating by above her: twigs, straw, pieces of newspaper. "Look how they sail on," mumbled the needle. "They have no idea what is sticking up right beneath them; and I can stick! Look at that old twig; it does not think about anything else in the whole world but twigs, because it is one. There goes a straw. . . . Look how it turns first one way and then the other. . . . Don't think so much of yourself, or you may get hurt on the curbstone. . . . There comes a newspaper; everything written in it is already forgotten, and yet it spreads itself out as if it were of great importance. . . . I sit patiently and wait. I know who I am and that I shall never change."

One day something shiny came to rest near the needle. It was a glass splinter from a broken bottle, but the darning needle thought it was a diamond. Since it glittered so nicely, she decided to converse with it. She introduced herself as a brooch. "I presume you are a diamond," she said. And the glass splinter hastily agreed that he was "something of that nature." Each of them believed that the other was valuable, and so they began to discuss how proud and haughty the rest of the world was.

"I have lived in a box belonging to a young lady," began the darning needle. "She was a cook, and she had five fingers on each hand. There never existed creatures so conceited as those fingers; and yet they were only there to take me out of the box and put me back."

"Did they shine?" asked the glass splinter.

"Shine!" sneered the needle. "Oh, they were haughty. They were five brothers: all born fingers; and they stood in a row next to each other, in spite of there being so much difference in their sizes. The one who resembled the others the least was the thumb. He was short and fat and had only one joint in his back, so he could only bend once. He always kept to himself, and said that if he were ever chopped off a man's hand that man could not become a soldier. The other four fingers stuck together. The first one was always pointing at everything, and if the cook wanted to find out whether a sauce was too sour or too sweet, that finger was stuck into the dish or the pot; and it guided the pen when she wrote. The next finger was the tallest and he looked down on the others. The third one wore a gold ring around his stomach; and the fourth one never did anything, and that's what he was proud of. They bragged and boasted day and night! That was all they could do well. And I dived into the sink."

"And here we sit and glitter," said the glass splinter. At that moment the water in the gutter suddenly rose and went over its sides, taking the glass splinter with it.

"Well, he got his advancement," said the darning needle. "I was left behind, but I am too refined to complain. That, too, is a form of pride but it is respectable." And the needle kept her back straight and went on thinking.

"I am almost convinced that a sun ray must have given birth to me. When I think of it, the sun is always searching for me underneath the water; but I am so fine that my own mother cannot find me. If I had my old eye—the one that was broken off—I think I would cry. No, I wouldn't anyway, crying is so vulgar."

One day some street urchins were rummaging in the gutter. They found nails, coins, and the like. They made themselves filthy and they enjoyed doing it.

"Ow!" cried one of the boys. The needle had pricked him. "What kind of a fellow are you?"

"Fellow! I am a lady!" protested the darning needle. The sealing wax had long since worn off and she was black; but black things look thinner, so she thought that now she was even finer than before.

"Here comes an eggshell!" shouted another boy, and stuck the pin into it.

"How well it becomes a black needle to stand before a white sail! Everyone can see me. I hope I shan't get seasick and throw up, that is so undignified.

"There is no remedy against seasickness better than an iron stomach, and the awareness of being just a bit above the common herd. I feel much better. The more refined one is, the more one can bear."

"Crash!" said the eggshell. A wagon wheel had rolled over it.

"Ow!" cried the darning needle. "Something is pressing against me. I think I am going to be seasick after all. I fear I will break!"

But it didn't break, even though a loaded wagon drove over it. There it lay, lengthwise in the gutter; and there we'll leave it.

## 32

## The Bell

In the narrow streets of the city, at dusk, just as the sun was setting and painting the clouds above the chimney pots a fiery red, people would sometimes hear a strange sound like the knell of a great churchbell. Only for a moment could it be heard, then the noise of the city—the rumbling of the carts and the shouting of the peddlers—would drown it out. "It is the vesper bell, calling folk to evening prayers; the sun must be setting," was the usual explanation.

To those who lived on the outskirts of the town, where the houses were farther away from each other and had gardens around them—some places were even separated by a field—the sunset was much more beautiful and the sound of the bell much louder. It seemed to come from a church in the depth of a fragrant forest, and it made the people who heard it feel quite solemn as they looked toward the darkening woods.

As time passed people began to ask each other whether there wasn't a church in the woods. And it was not far from that thought to the next: "The bell sounds so beautiful, why don't we go out and try to find it?"

Now the rich people got into their carriages and the poor people walked; but to all of them the road to the forest seemed very long. When they finally reached some weeping willows that grew on the edge of the woods they sat down under the trees to rest; and, looking up into the branches, believed that they were sitting in the middle of the forest. One of the bakers from town pitched a tent there and sold cakes. Business was good, and soon there were two bakers. The second one to arrive hung above his tent a bell, which was tarred on the outside to protect it from the rain, but it had no tongue.

When the people came back to town they said that their outing had been very romantic; and that word is not as tepid as a teaparty. Three persons claimed to have penetrated the forest and come out on the other side. They had heard a bell, but they said that the sound seemed to come not from the woods but from the town. One of them had written a sonnet about the bell, in which he compared its sound to that of a mother's voice when she speaks to her lovely, beloved child; the last line declared that no melody could be sweeter than that bell's song.

At last the emperor heard about it, and he promised that whoever found out where the sound came from would be given the title of "Bell Ringer of the World"; and that even if he discovered that it wasn't a bell that made it.

Now many people went out in search of the bell; they did it for the title and for the wages that went with it. But only one returned with an answer: an explanation of a sort. He had been no farther in the forest than the rest—and that hadn't been very far—but he claimed that the bell-like sound came from a great owl who was sitting inside a hollow tree. It was the bird of wisdom and it was incessantly knocking its head against the trunk; but whether the ringing was caused by the bird's head or the tree trunk he had not yet decided. The emperor bestowed upon him the title of "Bell Ringer of the World," and every year he published a paper on the subject, without anyone becoming any wiser.

One Sunday in May, when the children who had reached the age of fourteen were confirmed, the minister preached so movingly that all the young people present had tears in their eyes. It was a solemn occasion; after all, it was expected that they should become grownups; and that as soon as the ceremony was over, their child-souls would enter the bodies of reasonable adults. It was a beautiful day, and after the service all the children who had been confirmed walked, in a flock, to the forest. The sound of the unknown bell was particularly strong that day; and all of them had a great desire to go and search for it. That is, all of them except three: One girl had to hurry home for the final fitting of her new dress, which had been especially sewn for a ball she was to attend that night. The dress and the ball had been her real reasons for being confirmed. Another was a poor boy who had had to borrow both shoes and suit from the son of his parents' landlord; and they were to be delivered back as soon as the ceremony was over. The third was a boy who declared that he never went anywhere without his parents' permission. He had always been a good boy and would continue to be one even after he was confirmed; that is nothing to poke fun at—but all the other children did.

So three of them stayed behind but all the rest went on. The sun was shining, the birds were singing, and the young people who had just been confirmed were singing too. They walked hand in hand, for they hadn't become anything in the world yet, and they could afford to be friendly.

Soon two of the smallest became tired and turned back toward the town; and a couple of girls sat down in a meadow to braid wreaths of wild flowers; so they were four fewer. When the rest of the group reached the weeping willow trees, where the baker's tent was pitched, most of them said, "Well, here we are; you can see that the bell doesn't really exist. It is just something one imagines."

But from deeper in the woods came the sound of the bell: sweet and solemn; and five of the children decided to go on, just a little farther. It was not easy to make one's way through the forest; the trees grew close together, blackberry brambles and other thorny bushes were everywhere. But it was beautiful; the sun rays played and they heard the nightingale sing. It was glorious, but it was no place for girls; their dresses would be torn.

They came to great boulders covered with different kinds of moss. They heard the gurgling of a spring: "Gluck, gluck."

"I wonder if that isn't the bell," said one of the five, and lay down on the ground in order to hear the bubbling of the water better. "I think I ought to investigate this some more," he added, and let the other four go on without him.

They came to a house made of branches and bark. A huge wild apple tree towered above it and roses grew in such abundance up its walls that they covered the roof of the little cottage. On one of the ramblers hung a little silver bell. Was that the bell that they had heard? All but one of the boys agreed that it was. He claimed that this bell was too small and delicate to be heard so far away; besides, it did not produce the kind of music that could touch a man's heart. "No," he said. "It is an entirely different bell that we heard before."

But the youth who had spoken was a king's son, and one of his comrades remarked, "Oh, his kind always wants to think themselves cleverer than the rest of us."

They let him go on alone. When the cottage and his friends were lost from sight, the great loneliness of the forest engulfed the prince. He could still hear the little bell, which had pleased his friends, tingle merrily; and from farther away—borne on the wind's back—came the sound of the people at the baker's tent singing as they drank their tea. But the knell of the great bell of the forest grew stronger and stronger; then it seemed to be accompanied by an organ; he thought the sound of it came from the left where the heart is.

Leaves rustled, twigs snapped; someone else was making his way through the woods. The prince turned; in front of him stood another boy. He had wooden shoes on his feet, and the sleeves of his tunic were too short because he had outgrown it. He was the youth who had had to return the clothes he had worn at confirmation, as soon as the ceremony was over. The landlord's son had got his finery back, and the poor lad had put on his own old clothes, stuck his feet into his clogs, and set off in search of the great bell whose deep clang had called on him so powerfully that he had had to follow it.

"Let us go on together," proposed the prince. But the poor boy looked down at his wooden shoes and pulled at the sleeves of his tunic to make them a little longer. His poverty made him shy, and he excused himself by saying that he feared he could not walk as fast as the prince. Besides, he thought that the bell was to be found on the other side of the forest; on the right, where everything that was great and marvelous is.

"Then I suppose we shall not meet again," said the prince, and nodded to the poor boy, who walked into the densest part of the forest, where brambles and thorns would tear his worn-out clothes to shreds and scratch his face, legs, and hands till blood streamed down them. The prince did not escape being scratched, but the sun did shine on the path he took, and we shall follow him, for he was a good and courageous boy.

"I will find the bell," he declared, "if I have to go to the end of the world to do it."

On the limbs of a tree sat ugly monkeys; they grinned and screamed to each other: "Throw something at him! Throw something at him. He is a royal child!"

But the prince did not even notice them; he walked on deeper and deeper into the forest. Here grew the strangest flowers: lilies shaped like white stars, with blood-red stamens; tulips as blue as the sky; and apple trees, whose fruit looked like soap bubbles.—How such a tree would have glittered in the sunlight!—He passed green meadows where deer played in the grass underneath solitary oak trees. In every crack and crevice of their trunks grew grass and moss.

There were many lakes in which white swans swam; he could hear the beating of their great wings. He lingered and listened. More than once he wondered whether the knell might not come from somewhere deep inside one of the lakes; but then, when he strained his ears, he understood that the sound came from far away, from the very depth of the forest.

The sun was setting and the sky turned red as fire. The forest became so still that the prince sank down on his knees and said, "I shall never find what I seek! The sun is setting; soon the night will come—the dark, dark night. . . . But maybe I can still get another glimpse of the sun, see it once more before it disappears, by climbing that cliff over there, which is higher than the tallest trees."

His hands grabbed the brambles that grew among the wet stones, and he pulled himself upward. So eager was he to reach the top of the cliff that he noticed neither the slimy snakes nor the toads who barked like dogs.

Just before the sun set he reached the summit. Oh, what splendor! Below him stretched the ocean, that great sea that was flinging its long waves toward the shore. Like a shining red altar the sun stood where sea and sky met. All nature became one in the golden sunset: the song of the forest and the song of the sea blended and his heart seemed to be part of their harmony. All nature was a great cathedral: the flowers and the grass were the mosaic floors, the tall trees and swaying clouds were its pillars and heaven itself was the dome. High above the red color was disappearing for the sun had set. The millions of stars were lighted: the millions of little diamond lamps. The prince spread out his arms toward it all: the forest, the ocean, and the sky. But just at that moment, from the right side of the cliff came the poor boy with his ragged tunic and his wooden shoes. He had arrived there almost as quickly by going his own way.

The two boys ran to meet each other. There they stood, hand in hand, in the midst of nature's and poetry's great cathedral; and far above the great invisible holy bell was heard in loud hosanna.

## 33

## Grandmother

Grandmother is terribly old. She has white, white hair and her face
is filled with wrinkles; yet her eyes sparkle like two stars and are even
more beautiful, for when you look in them, they are so gentle and
filled with love. She wears a long dress with flowers printed on it. It is
made of silk and rustles when she walks; and she can tell so many
stories. Grandmother knows more than Father and Mother do, that is
certain, because she has lived much longer. Grandmother's hymnbook
has a silver clasp to close it, and she reads in it often. Between two of
the pages of the book lies a rose; it is pressed and dry and not nearly
as pretty to look at as the roses that stand in a vase on the table in her
room. Yet Grandmother smiles more kindly toward it than toward the
fresh roses; and sometimes the sight of it will bring tears into her eyes.

Why do you think that Grandmother looks with such fondness at
the pressed rose in the old book? Do you know why? Every time that
a tear falls from Grandmother's eyes down upon the wizened rose, it
regains its color and freshness and the whole room is filled with its
fragrance. The walls of her room disappear as the morning mist and,
instead, she is in the middle of a forest and the sun is shining down
through the green leaves. Grandmother has become a girl again, with
yellow hair and red cheeks: lovely and young, like a flowering rose.
But her eyes, her gentle loving eyes, they are the same, they are still
Grandmother's. Beside her sits a young and handsome man; he plucks
the rose and hands it to her and she smiles. No, that smile is not
Grandmother's.—Oh, but it is! He is gone. Many thoughts, many

persons pass by in the green forest, but at last they all disappear as the young man did. The rose is back in the hymnbook and Grandmother is again an old woman, sitting looking at the withered rose in the book.

Now Grandmother is dead. She sat in her easy chair and had just finished telling a long, long story. "That is the end of it," she said. "Now I think I am tired, let me sleep a little." She leaned back in the chair, closed her eyes, and breathed ever so softly. The room grew quieter and quieter; her face looked so peaceful, so happy, as though the sun were shining on it. Then they said that she had died.

She was put into a black coffin; there she lay wrapped in white linen. She looked beautiful even though her eyes were closed. All the wrinkles were gone, and on her lips was a smile. She looked so dignified with her silver-white hair, and not frightening at all. She was our sweet, good grandmother. The hymnbook was put under her head, as she had wanted it to be, and in the old book lay the rose. Then Grandmother was buried.

On her grave, close to the wall of the churchyard, was planted a rose tree; and every year it bloomed, and the nightingale sat on its branches and sang. From inside the church came the sound of the organ, playing the hymns that were printed in the book, upon which the dead woman's head rested. The moon shone down upon the grave; but the dead are not there. Any child could come, even at midnight, and pluck a rose from the tree. The dead know more than we living do; they know our fear of ghosts and, being kinder than we are, they would never come to frighten us. There is earth inside as well as above the coffin. The hymnbook and the rose, which was the keeper of so many memories, have become dust. But up on the earth new roses bloom and there the nightingale sings; and inside the church the organ plays. And there are those who remember old Grandmother with the sweet, eternally young eyes. Eyes cannot die! And ours shall see her once again, young and beautiful as she was the first time that she kissed the fresh, newly plucked rose that now is dust in the grave.

## 34

## The Hill of the Elves

Some lizards were darting in and out of the cracks and crevices of an old oak tree. All of them could speak lizard language, so they understood each other.

"Have you heard all the rumbling and grumbling inside the old hill where the elves live?" asked one of the lizards. "I haven't been able to sleep a wink these last two nights. I might as well have had a toothache."

"Oh yes, something is going on up there, for sure," began another lizard. "Last night they put the hill on four red pillars and let it stand like that until it was almost time for the cock to crow. They certainly gave their home a good airing. The elfin maidens have to learn a new dance in which they stamp their feet. There is no doubt about it, something is up."

"I have talked with an acquaintance of mine, an earthworm," declared a third lizard. "I met him as he was coming out of the hill, where he has been digging for the last two days. He has heard a good deal.—The poor creature can't see but he's a master at both hearing and feeling.—The elves are expecting very important guests. The earthworm wouldn't tell me who they were, but that's probably because he didn't know. The will-o'-the-wisps have all been hired to make a torchlight procession, as it's called. All the gold and silver in the whole hill—and there's enough of it—is to be polished and set out in the moonlight."

"Who can the visitors be?" cried all the lizards. "What is going to happen? Listen to the humming! Listen to the buzzing!"

Just at that moment the hill of the elves opened and an old elfin lady came tripping out. She had the same hollow back that all elves have, and she was very respectably dressed. She was the elfin king's housekeeper, and distantly related to him; that was why she wore an amber heart on her forehead. Goodness, how she could run. Away she went down to the marsh where the night raven lived.

"You are invited to the Mount of the Elves this very night," she said. "But you will have to do us the favor of delivering the invitations. Since you have no home of your own and cannot return our hospitality, you will have to make yourself useful instead. We are expecting distinguished guests, trolls of the greatest importance, and the elfin king wants to impress them."

"Whom am I to invite?" asked the night raven.

"Well, to the grand ball, anyone can come," began the old elfin lady. "Even human beings are invited; that is, those who have some small talent akin to ours: such as being able to talk in their sleep. But the party tonight is to be more select; only those of the highest rank are to attend. I argued with the elfin king about the guest list, for in my opinion neither ghosts nor spooks should be on it. . . . The old merman and his daughters, the mermaids, must be the first ones you invite. They don't like to be where it's dry, so tell them that they can count on having a wet stone each to sit on, if not something better. Remember to say that that's a promise; and I don't think they'll refuse. After that call on all the older trolls of the highest rank who have tails, the river spirit, and the gnomes. Then there are the graveyard sow, the Hell horse, and the three-legged church monster; it wouldn't do to forget them. They belong to the clergy; but that is their profession, so I shan't hold it against them. Besides, we are all related, and they visit us regularly."

"Caw!" said the night raven, and flew away to deliver the invitations.

The elfin maidens were already dancing on top of the hill. Over their shoulders were long shawls woven from mist and moonlight. They looked very pretty, if you like that sort of thing.

The great hall in the middle of the mount had certainly been done up. The floors had been washed in moonlight, and all the walls had been waxed with witches' grease till they shone like tulip petals.

Out in the kitchen frogs were being roasted on spits, and snakes stuffed with children's fingers were baking. The salads were made of toadstool seeds, garnished with moist snouts of mice; and for dressing there was hemlock juice. Saltpeter wine that had been aged in tombs and beer from the bog-witch brewery had been poured into decanters. Altogether a festive—though a bit conservative—menu. Rusty nails and bits of colored glass from a church window were the desserts.

The old elfin king's crown had been polished with powder ground from slate pencils. For this purpose only pencils that have belonged to especially studious boys may be used; and those are hard to find. In the bedchambers the newly washed curtains were being made to stick to the walls with the help of snakes' spit. Everywhere, everybody was busy. There were bustle and commotion throughout the hill.

"Now I'll burn some horsehair and swine bristles, and then I shall have done my share," remarked the old elfin lady who was the elfin king's housekeeper.

"Dear . . . dear Father," pestered the youngest of the elfin king's daughters, "won't you tell us who the distinguished guests are?"

"Well, I suppose I have to," began the king. "Two of you had better be prepared to get married because two of you are going to get married. The old troll king of Norway is coming. Dovre—his castle—is made of granite, and it is large and so high that on the roof of the great hall there is always snow. He has a gold mine, too; and that is nothing to sneeze at, even though some people do. He is bringing his sons along, and they are thinking of getting married. The old troll is a real Norwegian: honest, full of life, and straightforward. I have known him a long, long time. We became friends at his wedding. He had come to Denmark for a wife. She was the daughter of the king of the chalk cliffs of Möen; but she's been dead a long time now.

"How I look forward to seeing the old fellow again. I have been told that his sons are a spoiled couple of cubs: cocky and bad-mannered. But who knows, such talk may all be slander. Time will rub the nonsense off them, anyway. Let me see you show them how they ought to behave."

"When are they coming?" asked his oldest daughter.

"That depends upon the wind and the weather," sighed the king. "They are traveling by ship. I wanted them to journey through Sweden, but the old troll is conservative. He doesn't keep up with the changing times, which in my opinion is very wrong of him."

At that moment two will-o'-the-wisps came running into the hall. One ran faster than the other and that was why he came first.

"They are coming! They are coming!" they both shouted.

"Hand me my crown and I shall go out and stand in the moonlight," said the king of the elves and, followed by the elfin maidens, he went to meet the guests.

His daughters lifted their shawls and curtsied all the way to the ground.

There he was: the troll king from Dovre! His crown was made of ice and polished pine cones. He was wearing a bearskin coat and heavy boots. His sons, on the other hand, were lightly dressed: their collars were open and they weren't wearing suspenders. They were two big strapping fellows.

"Is this a hill?" laughed the younger one. "In Norway we would call it a hole in the ground."

"Don't be silly," said the old troll king. "Holes go inward and hills go upward. Don't you have eyes in your head?"

The thing that surprised the two young men most was that they could understand the language; and they said so.

"Don't make fools of yourselves," scolded their father, "or everybody will think that you were born yesterday and put on the stove to dry overnight."

They entered the great hall where all the guests were gathered; they had arrived so fast you would think that the wind had blown them there. The old merman and his daughters were sitting in tubs full of water and feeling right at home. Except for the sons of the troll king, everyone exhibited his or her best table manners, while the two young men put their feet on the table. But they thought that anything they did was becoming.

"Take your feet out of the dishes!" bellowed the old troll king.

His sons obeyed him, but not right away. They tickled their dinner partners—two young elfin maidens—with pine cones that they had brought in their pockets from Norway. In the middle of the dinner they took off their boots to make themselves more comfortable and handed them to the elfin maidens to take care of.

But the old troll king was a different sort than his sons. He de-

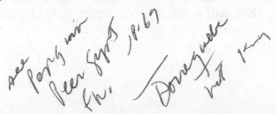

scribed so well the proud mountains of Norway, the rivers and streams that leaped down the cliffs, white and bubbling, and sounded like both a thunderclap and an organ playing, when they plunged into the valleys far below. He told about the salmon that could leap up the swiftest waterfall, while the river nymphs played on their golden harps. He made them imagine a still winter night, when you can hear the sound of sleigh bells and see the young people skate, carrying burning torches, across the glasslike surface of the lakes, when the ice is so transparent that the skaters can watch the fish fleeing, in terror, below them. Yes, he knew how to tell a story well; it seemed to all the other guests that they could hear the buzz of the great sawmills and the singing of the young men and women as they danced the halling dance.

"Hurrah!" the troll king suddenly cried; and in the midst of his storytelling kissed the old elfin lady so that it could be heard throughout the hall. "That was a brotherly kiss," he explained, in spite of their not being related at all.

Now the young elfin maidens danced. First the simple dances and then the new one in which they stamped their feet. The final one was the most difficult and was called "Stepping Outside the Dance." How they twirled and twisted. One could hardly make out which were legs and where were arms, or which end was up and which was down. The poor Hell horse got so dizzy watching it that he began to feel sick and had to leave the table.

"Whoa!" shouted the old troll king. "They have got legs, and they can dance; but what else can they do?"

"Judge for yourself," said the elfin king, and called his youngest daughter to him. She was as fair as moonlight and the most delicate of the sisters.

She stuck a white wand in her mouth and vanished—that was her accomplishment.

The old troll king said that this was not the kind of talent he would want his wife to have, and he was sure that his sons agreed with him.

The second sister could walk beside herself, so that she looked as if she had a shadow; something that neither elves nor trolls possess.

The third sister's talent lay in an entirely different direction. She had been apprenticed to the bog witch and knew both how to brew beer and how to garnish elder stumps with glowworms.

"She will make a good housewife," said the troll king, and winked at her. He would have drunk a toast in her honor but he thought he had drunk enough already.

Now came the fourth sister. She had a golden harp. When she struck the first string, they all lifted their left legs—for trolls and elves are left-legged—and when she struck the second string they all had to do exactly what she commanded.

"She is a dangerous woman," said the troll king. His two sons sneaked out of the hall; they were bored.

"And what can the next one do?" asked the troll.

"I have learned to love Norway," she said softly. "And I will only marry a Norwegian."

But the youngest of the elfin king's daughters whispered to the old troll king, "She says that because she once heard a Norwegian verse in which it was prophesied that, when the world went under, the mountains of Norway would stand as a tombstone over it; and she is terribly afraid of dying."

"Ha-ha!" laughed the old troll king. "And you let the cat out of the bag. . . . And what can the seventh and last of them do?"

"The sixth comes before the seventh," said the elfin king, who knew how to count.

The sixth daughter was so shy that she did not want to step forward. "I can only tell people the truth," she finally whispered, "and that no one likes to hear, so I am busy sewing on my shroud."

Now came the seventh; and she was the last of the sisters. What could she do? She could tell fairy tales, as many as anyone wanted to hear.

"Here are my five fingers, tell me a fairy tale for each of them," demanded the troll king.

The elfin maiden took his hand in hers and began. The king of the trolls laughed so hard that he almost split his sides. When she came to the finger that was encircled by a gold ring—it looked as if it knew that there was an engagement in the air—the troll cried, "Hold onto what you have got! My hand is yours. You I shall marry myself!"

But the elfin maiden protested that she still had two stories to tell: one for the ring finger and one for the little finger, which would be short.

"They can wait," said the king of the trolls. "We can hear them next winter. And you shall tell us about the pine trees, the birches, the crinkling frost, and about the gifts that the river nymphs bring;

for we do so love a well-told tale in Norway, and no one there knows how to tell them. We shall sit in my granite hall that is lighted by pine pitch torches and drink mead out of golden horns that once belonged to Viking kings. The river nymph has given me a couple of them. The echo—he is a tall, thin fellow—will come and sing for us. He knows all the songs that the milkmaids sing when they drive their herds into the meadows. Oh, we'll have a good time! The salmon will leap and knock on our granite walls, but we won't let him in. Oh, believe me! Norway is a dear old place! . . . But where are my sons?"

Where were his sons? They were racing about on the field blowing out the poor will-o'-the-wisps, who had been peacefully assembling for the torchlight parade.

"What do you mean by running about like this?" scolded their father. "I have chosen a mother for you. Now you can find wives for yourselves among your aunts."

But the boys said they would rather drink toasts and make speeches, for they had no desire to get married. So they made speeches and they toasted each other, and when they were finished they turned their glasses upside down so that everyone could see that they were empty. Then they took off their shirts and lay down on the table to sleep, for, as they said, they didn't "stand on ceremony."

The old troll king danced with his young bride and exchanged boots with her, for that is more refined than exchanging rings.

"Now the cock crows!" shouted the old elfin lady who was the housekeeper and kept an eye on everything. "We have to close the shutters or the sun will burn us all."

And the hill of the elves closed. But outside the lizards were running up and down the old oak tree.

"Oh, I did like that old Norwegian troll king," said one of the lizards.

"I liked his sons best," said the earthworm, but the wretched little creature couldn't see.

## The Red Shoes

Once there was a little girl who was pretty and delicate but very poor. In the summer she had to go barefoot and in the winter she had to wear wooden shoes that rubbed against her poor little ankles and made them red and sore.

In the same village there lived an old widow whose husband had been a shoemaker; and she sat sewing a pair of shoes from scraps of red material. She did her very best, but the shoes looked a bit clumsy, though they were sewn with kindness. They were meant for the poor little girl, whose name was Karen.

Now on that very day that her mother was to be buried, Karen was given the red shoes. Though they weren't the proper color for mourning, she had no others, so she put them on. Raggedly dressed, barelegged, with red shoes on her feet, she walked behind the pauper's coffin.

A big old-fashioned carriage drove by; in it sat an old lady. She noticed the little girl and felt so sorry for her that she went at once to the minister and spoke to him. "Let me have that little girl, and I shall be good to her and bring her up."

Karen thought it was because of her new red shoes that the old lady had taken a fancy to her. But the old lady declared that the shoes looked frightful and had them thrown into the stove and burned. Karen was dressed in nice clean clothes and taught to read and to sew. Everyone agreed that she was a very pretty child; but the mirror said, "You are more than pretty, you are beautiful."

It happened that the queen was making a journey throughout the country, and she had her daughter, the little princess, with her. Everywhere people streamed to see them. When they arrived at a castle near Karen's village, the little girl followed the crowd out there. Looking out of one of the great windows of the castle was the little princess. So that people could see her, she was standing on a little stool. She had no crown on her head but she wore a very pretty white dress and the loveliest red shoes, made from morocco. They were certainly much prettier than the ones the old shoemaker's widow had made for Karen. But even they had been red shoes, and to Karen nothing else in the world was so desirable.

Karen became old enough to be confirmed. She was to have a new dress and new shoes for this solemn occasion. The old lady took her to the finest shoemaker in the nearby town and he measured her little foot. Glass cabinets filled with the most elegant shoes and boots covered the walls of his shop. But the old lady's eyesight was so poor that she didn't get much out of looking at the display. Karen did; between two pairs of boots stood a pair of red shoes just like the ones the princess had worn. Oh, how beautiful they were! The shoemaker said that they had been made for the daughter of a count but that they hadn't fit her.

"I think they are patent leather," remarked the old lady. "They shine."

"Yes, they shine!" sighed Karen as she tried them on. They fit the child and the old woman bought them. Had she known that they were red, she wouldn't have because it was not proper to wear red shoes when you were being confirmed. But her eyesight was failing—poor woman!—and she had not seen the color.

Everyone in the church looked at Karen's feet, as she walked toward the altar. On the walls of the church hung paintings of the former ministers and their wives who were buried there; they were portrayed wearing black with white ruffs around their necks. Karen felt that even they were staring at her red shoes.

When the old bishop laid his hands on her head and spoke of the solemn promise she was about to make—of her covenant with God to be a good Christian—her mind was not on his words. The ritual music was played on the organ; the old cantor sang, and the sweet voices of the children could be heard, but Karen was thinking of her red shoes.

By afternoon, everyone had told the old lady about the color of Karen's shoes. She was very angry and scolded the girl, telling her how improper it was to have worn red shoes in church, and that she must remember always to wear black ones, even if she had to put on an old pair.

Next Sunday Karen was to attend communion. She looked at her black shoes and she looked at her red shoes; then she looked at her red shoes once more and put them on.

The sun was shining, it was a beautiful day. The old lady and Karen took the path across the fields and their shoes got a bit dirty.

At the entrance to the church stood an old invalid soldier leaning on a crutch. He had a marvelously long beard that was red with touches of white in it. He bowed low toward the old lady and asked her permission to wipe the dust off her feet. Karen put her little foot forward too.

"What pretty little dancing shoes!" said the soldier and, tapping them on the soles, he added, "Remember to stay on her feet for the dance."

The old lady gave the soldier a penny, and she and Karen entered the church.

Again everyone looked at Karen's feet, even the people in the paintings on the wall. When she knelt in front of the altar and the golden cup was lifted to her lips, she thought only of the red shoes and saw them reflected in the wine. She did not join in the singing of the psalm and she forgot to say the Lord's Prayer.

The coachman had come with the carriage to drive them home from church. The old lady climbed in and Karen was about to follow her when the old soldier, who was standing nearby, remarked, "Look at those pretty dancing shoes."

His words made her take a few dancing steps. Once she had begun, her feet would not stop. It was as if the shoes had taken command of them. She danced around the corner of the church; her will was not her own.

The coachman jumped off the carriage and ran after her. When he finally caught up with her, he grabbed her and lifted her up from the ground, but her feet kept on dancing in the air, even after he managed to get her into the carriage. The poor old woman was kicked nastily while she and the coachman took Karen's shoes off her feet, so she could stop dancing.

When they got home, the red shoes were put away in a closet, but Karen could not help sneaking in to look at them.

The old lady was very ill. The doctors had come and said that she would not live much longer. She needed careful nursing and constant care, and who else but Karen ought to give it to her? In the town there was to be a great ball and Karen had been invited to go. She looked at the old lady, who was going to die anyway, and then she glanced at her red shoes. To glance was no sin. Then she put them on; that too did no great harm. But she went to the ball!

She danced! But when she wanted to dance to the left, the shoes danced to the right; and when she wanted to dance up the ballroom floor, the shoes danced right down the stairs and out into the street. Dance she did, out through the city gates and into the dark forest.

Something shone through the trees. She thought it was the moon because it had a face. But it was not; it was the old soldier with the red beard. He nodded to her and exclaimed, "Look what beautiful dancing shoes!"

Terrified, she tried to pull off her shoes. She tore her stockings but the shoes stayed on. They had grown fast to her feet. Dance she did! And dance she must! Over the fields and meadows, in the rain and sunshine, by night and by day. But it was more horrible and frightening at night when the world was dark.

She danced through the gates of the churchyard; but the dead did not dance with her, they had better things to do. She wanted to sit down on the pauper's grave, where the bitter herbs grew, but for her there was no rest. The church door was open and she danced toward it, but an angel, dressed in white, who had on his back great wings that reached almost to the ground, barred her entrance.

His face was stern and grave, and in his hand he held a broad, shining sword.

"You shall dance," he said, "dance in your red shoes until you become pale and thin. Dance till the skin on your face turns yellow and clings to your bones as if you were a skeleton. Dance you shall from door to door, and when you pass a house where proud and vain children live, there you shall knock on the door so that they will see you and fear your fate. Dance, you shall dance. . . . Dance!"

"Mercy!" screamed Karen, but heard not what the angel answered, for her red shoes carried her away, down through the churchyard, over the meadows, along the highways, through the lanes: always dancing.

One morning she danced past a house that she knew well. From inside she heard psalms being sung. The door opened and a coffin decked with flowers was carried out. The old lady who had been so kind to her was dead. Now she felt that she was forsaken by all of mankind and cursed by God's angel.

Dance she must, and dance she did. The shoes carried her across fields and meadows, through nettles and briars that tore her feet so they bled.

One morning she danced across the lonely heath until she came to a solitary cottage. Here, she knew, the executioner lived. With her fingers she tapped on his window.

"Come out! Come out!" she called. "I cannot come inside, for I must dance."

The executioner opened his door and came outside. When he saw Karen he said, "Do you know who I am? I am the one who cuts off the heads of evil men; and I can feel my ax beginning to quiver now."

"Do not cut off my head," begged Karen, "for then I should not be able to repent. But cut off my feet!"

She confessed her sins and the executioner cut off her feet, and the red shoes danced away with them into the dark forest. The executioner carved a pair of wooden feet for her and made her a pair of crutches. He taught her the psalm that a penitent sings. She kissed the hand that had guided the ax and went on her way.

"Now I have suffered enough because of those red shoes," thought Karen. "I shall go to church now and be among other people."

But when she walked up to the door of the church, the red shoes danced in front of her, and in horror she fled.

All during that week she felt sad and cried many a bitter tear. When Sunday came she thought, "Now I have suffered and struggled long enough. I am just as good as many of those who are sitting and praying in church right now, and who dare to throw their heads back with pride." This reasoning gave her courage, but she came no farther than the gate of the churchyard. There were the shoes dancing in front of her. In terror she fled, but this time she really repented in the depth of her heart.

She went to the minister's house and begged to be given work. She said that she did not care about wages but only wanted a roof over her head and enough to eat. The minister's wife hired the poor cripple because she felt sorry for her. Karen was grateful that she had been given a place to live and she worked hard. In the evening when the minister read from the Bible, she sat and listened thoughtfully. The children were fond of her and she played with them, but when they talked of finery and being beautiful like a princess, she would sadly shake her head.

When Sunday came, everyone in the household got ready for church, and they asked her to go with them. Poor Karen's eyes filled with tears. She sighed and glanced toward her crutches.

When the others had gone, she went into her little room that was so small that a bed and a chair were all it could hold. She sat down and began to read from her psalmbook. The wind carried the music from the church organ down to her, and she lifted her tear-stained face and whispered, "Oh, God, help me!"

Suddenly the sunlight seemed doubly bright and an angel of God stood before her. He was the same angel who with his sword had barred her entrance to the church, but now he held a rose branch covered with flowers. With this he touched the low ceiling of the room and it rose high into the air and, where he had touched it, a golden star shone. He touched the walls and they widened.

Karen saw the organ. She saw the old paintings of the ministers and their wives; and there were the congregation holding their psalmbooks in front of them and singing. The church had come to the poor girl in her little narrow chamber; or maybe she had come to the church. Now she sat among the others, and when they finished singing the psalm they looked up and saw her.

Someone whispered to her: "It is good that you came, Karen."

"This is His mercy," she replied.

The great organ played and the voices of the children in the choir mingled sweetly with it. The clear, warm sunshine streamed through the window. The sunshine filled Karen's heart till it so swelled with peace and happiness that it broke. Her soul flew on a sunbeam up to God; and up there no one asked her about the red shoes.

## 36

## The Jumping Competition

The flea, the grasshopper, and the jumping jack decided to hold a competition to see which of them could jump the highest. They invited the whole world, and anyone else who wanted to come, to look at it. Each of them felt sure that he would become the champion.

"I will give my daughter to the one who jumps the highest," declared the king. "Honor is too paltry a reward."

The flea was the first to introduce himself. He had excellent manners; but then he had the blood of young maidens in him and was accustomed to human society, and that had left its mark on him.

Then came the grasshopper. He was stout but not without grace and dressed in a green uniform, which he had acquired at birth. He said he was of ancient family and that his ancestors came from Egypt. He claimed that he was so highly esteemed in this country that he had been brought directly from the fields and given a card house. It was three stories high and all made of picture cards. It had both doors and windows.

"I sing so well," he boasted, "that sixteen native crickets, who have been cheeping since birth—but never have been honored with a card house—grew so thin from envy, when they heard me sing, that they almost disappeared."

Both the flea and the grasshopper gave a full account of their merits. Each of them thought it only fitting that he should marry a princess.

Now came the jumping jack. He was made from the wishbone of

a goose, two rubber bands, some sealing wax, and a little stick that was mahogany. He didn't say a word, which made the whole court certain that he was a genius. The royal dog sniffed at him and said that he came of good family. The old councilor, who had received three decorations as a reward for keeping his mouth shut, declared that the jumping jack was endowed with the gift of prophecy. One could tell from looking at its back whether we would have a mild winter or not; and that was more than one could tell from the back of the fellow who wrote the almanac.

The old king merely said, "I don't talk much, but I have my own opinion about everything."

The competition began. The flea jumped so high that one could not see him; and then everyone said he hadn't jumped at all, which was most unfair! The grasshopper only jumped half as high as the flea but landed right in the face of the king and that did not please His Majesty, who said it was repulsive.

Now it was the jumping jack's turn; he sat so still and appeared so pensive that everyone decided that he wouldn't jump at all.

"I hope he hasn't got sick," said the royal hound, and sniffed at him; but just at that moment he jumped. It was a little, slanted jump, but high enough so that he landed in the lap of the princess, who was sitting on a golden stool.

"The highest jump is into my daughter's lap," declared the king. "The jumping jack has shown both intelligence and taste; she shall marry him." And the jumping jack got the princess.

"I jumped highest," said the flea. "But it is of no importance; she can keep him: wishbone, rubber bands, sealing wax, mahogany stick, and all! I don't care! I know I jumped the highest, but in this world it's only appearance that counts."

The flea enlisted in a foreign army and it was rumored that he was killed in battle.

The grasshopper sat down in the ditch and thought about the injustice of the world. "It's appearance that counts! It's appearance that counts!" he said. And then he sang his own sad song. It's from him that we have the story, which, even though it has been printed, may still be a lie.

## 37

# The Shepherdess and the Chimney Sweep

Have you ever seen a really old cabinet, the kind whose wood is dark from age and that doesn't have a spot on it that isn't carved, so that it looks like a mass of vines and twirls? Once there stood in a parlor just such an heirloom that had been in the family for four generations. From the bottom to the top there were roses and tulips; everywhere there were curlicues, and little deer heads with numerous antlers peered out from among them. But the most amazing figure was in the center panel. It was a man with a long beard, who had little horns sticking out of his forehead and the legs of a goat. He had a grin on his face—for you could hardly call it a smile. He looked so funny that the children who lived in the house gave him a name. They called him Mr. Goat-legged Commanding-General-Private-War-Sergeant because it was so difficult to say, even for a grownup; and they knew of no one—either living or carved—who could boast of such a fine title.

From his cabinet he was always looking straight across the room at a little table that stood beneath a mirror, for on the table was the loveliest little porcelain shepherdess. She had her skirt pinned up with a red rose; on her feet were golden shoes, on her head she had a golden hat, and in her hand was a shepherd's crook. Oh, she was beautiful! Next to her stood a little chimney sweep, and he was black as coal, except for his face, which was as pink and white as hers. Somehow this seemed wrong; he ought to have had at least a dab of soot on his nose or his cheek. But he was of porcelain too, and his profession was make-believe; he might just as well have been a prince. There he stood with his ladder in his hands looking as delicate as the shepherdess. They had been standing close together, for that was the way they had always been placed; and so they thought it was natural that they be engaged. They had much in common: both were young, both were made from the same clay, both were breakable.

Near them on the table there was another figure; he was three times as big as either of them. He was a Chinese mandarin and he knew how to nod. He was of porcelain too, and insisted that he was the shepherdess' grandfather. Although he couldn't really prove that he was related to her at all, he behaved as if he had as much right over her as her parents and demanded that she obey him. Now Mr. Goat-legged Commanding-General-Private-War-Sergeant had asked for the shepherdess' hand in marriage, and the Chinese mandarin had nodded.

"You will have a husband who I am almost certain is made of mahogany," said the old mandarin. "You will be called Mrs. Goat-legged Commanding-General-Private-War-Sergeant. He has a whole cabinetful of silverware, plus all that he has hidden in the secret compartments."

"I don't want to live in a dark closet!" wailed the shepherdess. "They say that he has eleven porcelain wives in there already."

"Then you shall be number twelve!" declared the Chinese mandarin. "And tonight! As soon as the cabinet creaks, there shall be a wedding, my dear, and that is as certain as it is that I am Chinese!" And he nodded his head back and forth until he fell asleep.

The little shepherdess cried and cried; then she looked up at her beloved, the chimney sweep. "I beg you to go with me out into the world, for we cannot stay here," she sobbed.

"I will do anything that you ask," he replied. "Let's go at once. I must be able to earn a living at my profession."

"If only we were down on the floor already," she said anxiously. "I won't feel safe before we are out in the wide world."

The chimney sweep did his best to console her. He showed her where she should set her little feet along the carved edges of the table and on the leaves of the gilded vines that wound themselves around its legs. He made use of his ladder and soon they had reached the floor. But then they looked up at the cabinet, where there was an uproar. All the carved deer were shaking their antlers in fury; and

Mr. Goat-legged Commanding-General-Private-War-Sergeant was jumping up and down. "They're eloping! They're eloping!" he cried as loud as he could over to the Chinese mandarin.

A drawer in the wall, just a little above the floor, was luckily open and the frightened lovers jumped inside it. Here lay three or four incomplete decks of cards and a little puppet theater. The puppets were performing a play. In the front row of the audience sat all the queens: hearts, diamonds, spades, and clubs, fanning themselves with their tulips; behind them sat the knaves and looked both above and below the ladies in the front row, just to show that they had heads at both ends, exactly as they always do in a deck of cards. The play was about two lovers who weren't allowed to be together and reminded the poor shepherdess so much of her own situation that she wept and wept.

"I can't bear it!" she said. "We must get out of here."

By the time they were back down on the floor again, the old Chinese mandarin was awake. He was nodding his head and rocking back and forth with his whole body, which was rounded at the bottom, for he had no legs.

"Here comes the old mandarin!" screamed the little shepherdess, and fell down on her porcelain knees because she was so upset.

"I have an idea," said the chimney sweep. "We could climb down into the potpourri jar, over there in the corner. There we shall be among roses and lavender and we can throw salt in the eyes of anyone who comes."

"It won't do!" cried the shepherdess. "The potpourri jar and the mandarin were once engaged. It's a long time ago but a certain amount of affection always remains for the lovers of one's youth. . . . No, we have no choice, we must go out into the wide world."

"But do you realize what that means?" asked the chimney sweep. "Have you thought about how wide the world is and that we can never come back?"

"I have!" she said determinedly.

The chimney sweep looked steadfastly into her eyes. "The only way I know how to get out is through the chimney. Have you the courage to climb into the belly of the stove and up through the flue into the chimney? From there on, it's upward, ever upward, where no one can reach us, till we come to the opening; and then we shall be out in the wide world."

He led her over to the stove and opened the door. "Oh, how dark it looks," she said. But she followed him into the belly of the stove and crawled with him up the flue, though it was pitch-dark.

"Now we are in the chimney. Look up and you will see a star!"

It was true, there was a star shining through the darkness, as if it wished to guide them on their way. They climbed, they crawled; it was a terrible journey: up, up they went. The chimney sweep hoisted and held onto the shepherdess, showing her where to put her little porcelain feet. Finally they reached the top of the chimney and sat down on the edge of it. They were exhausted and they had every right to be.

The star-filled sky was above them and all the roofs of the city were below them. They could see far and wide, out into the world. The poor little shepherdess had never imagined that the wide world would be so big. She leaned her head on the chimney sweep's shoulder and cried so hard that the gold in her waistband began to chip.

"It's far too much!" she sobbed. "I cannot bear it! The world is much too big. I wish I were back on the table beneath the mirror. I shall never be happy again until I am! I followed you out into the wide world; now you must take me home, if you care for me at all."

The chimney sweep tried to reason with her. He talked about the Chinese mandarin and Mr. Goat-legged Commanding-General-Private-War-Sergeant; but that just made her cry all the more. Finally she kissed him, and then he could only obey her.

And they climbed back down the chimney with great difficulty, crawled through the flue, and entered the belly of the stove; there they peeped out through the door to see what was going on in the parlor.

Not a sound came from the room. In the middle of the floor lay the old Chinese mandarin. He had fallen off the table when he tried to follow them. Now he was in three pieces and his head had rolled over in a corner. Mr. Goat-legged Commanding-General-Private-War-Sergeant stood where he always had been, deep in thought.

"How horrible!" exclaimed the little shepherdess. "Old Grandfather is broken and it's all our fault! I shan't live through it!"

"He can be glued," said the chimney sweep. "He can be put together again. . . . Don't carry on so! . . . All he needs is to be glued and have a rivet put in his neck, and he'll be able to say as many nasty things as he ever did."

"Do you think so?" she asked. They climbed up onto the table and stood where they had before.

"Well, this is as far as we got!" the chimney sweep said. "We could have saved ourselves a whole lot of trouble."

"Do you think it will be expensive to have Grandfather put together again?" asked the shepherdess. "Oh, how I wish it were already done!"

And Grandfather was glued and a rivet was put in his neck; and then he was as good as new, except for one thing: he couldn't nod any more.

"You seem to think so much more highly of yourself since you have been broken," said Mr. Goat-legged Commanding-General-Private-War-Sergeant. "I can't understand why anyone should be proud of being glued. Am I to have her or not?"

The chimney sweep and the little shepherdess looked pitifully at the Chinese mandarin; they were so terrified that he would nod. But he couldn't nod; and he didn't want to admit to a stranger that he had a rivet in his neck and would never be able to nod again. So the two young porcelain lovers stayed together. They blessed the rivet in Grandfather's neck and loved each other until they broke.

## Holger the Dane

In Denmark there lies an old castle. It is called Kronborg; foreigners
know it as Elsinore. It is built right on the edge of the Sound, that
narrow strait between Denmark and Sweden. Hundreds of ships sail
through it: Russian, English, and Prussian; and every one fires a sa-
lute as it sails by the old castle. From Elsinore a cannon answers,
"Boom!" And that, in the language of cannons in peacetime, means,
"Good day and thank you!"

In the winter no ships can sail there, for then ice covers the Sound
all the way over to Sweden. You can walk or even drive to the opposite shore, where the blue and yellow flag of Sweden flies. The Danish
and the Swedish people meet and say, "Good day and thank you," to
each other; not with cannons but with a handclasp. They go shopping
in each other's towns, for foreign food tastes best.

The old castle dominates the scene and deep down in its cellar, in a
dark room where no one ever comes, sits Holger the Dane. He is clad
in iron, his head is resting in his hands. He is sleeping and dreaming,
his long beard hangs down over the marble table. In his dreams he
sees everything that is happening in all of Denmark; and once a year,
on Christmas Eve, God sends an angel down to reassure him that
what he has dreamed is true and that Denmark is not in danger,
therefore he can sleep on. Should Denmark ever be in danger, then he
will rise, grab his sword, and fight so that all the world will hear it.

This legend about Holger the Dane an old grandfather was telling his little grandson; and the little boy believed every word of it, for he knew that his grandfather never lied.

The old man, who was a wood carver, was making the figurehead for a new ship, which would have the name of *Holger the Dane*. It was a tall wooden statue that stood proudly, with a long beard; in one hand he held a sword, while the other leaned on a shield, on which the coat of arms was yet to be carved.

Grandfather told stories about Danish men and women who had performed mighty deeds; and his little grandson thought that soon he would know as much as Holger the Dane had ever dreamed. When the boy was put to bed that night he dreamed that he had grown a large white beard.

His grandfather worked late, for he had only one thing left to do, and that was to finish the shield with the coat of arms of Denmark on it.

The statue was finished, his work was done. He looked at it and thought about all the tales he had told his grandson, the stories he himself, "In my time, Holger the Dane will never wake, but it might his glasses off, and polished them, then put them back on and said to himself, "In my time, Holger the Dane will never wake, but it might happen during the lifetime of the boy sleeping over there." He looked again at his work and the more he looked at the statue the better he liked it. It had not yet been painted; but in the old man's mind it took on color; the suit of armor shone and was steel-blue, the hearts in the coat of arms were scarlet, and the lions had golden crowns on their heads.

"No country in the world has a finer coat of arms than ours," he said. "The lions for strength and the hearts to symbolize gentleness and love." As he looked at the first of the lions he thought of King Canute, who had conquered England; as he looked at the second one, he remembered Valdemar, who had freed Denmark and taught the Hanseatic towns to fear us; the third lion was Margaret, the queen who had united Denmark, Sweden, and Norway. The old man looked at the red hearts and they seemed as red as burning flames, they moved and danced, and his thoughts followed them.

The first of the flames took him to a dark prison; there sat a woman. She was Eleanora Ulfeldt, daughter of King Christian IV; the flame jumped to her chest and became one with her heart, the most noble of all Danish women.

"Yes, that is true; she is one of the hearts in the shield of Denmark," mumbled old Grandfather.

The next flame took him out on the sea. Cannons were firing. A great naval battle was being fought. The flame was a decoration on Hvitfeldt's bedraggled uniform as he stood on the deck of a burning ship until it exploded, in order to save the Danish fleet.

The third flame led him to Greenland, to the poverty-stricken hovels where Hans Egede preached the message of love.

Quicker than the fourth flame could fly, Grandfather's thoughts flew. In a poor peasant's hut King Frederik VI stood; he wrote his name with chalk on the beam in the living room. Here in a poor man's house his heart became one with Denmark's. The wood carver dried a tear from the corner of his eye, for King Frederik had reigned during his own lifetime: the king with the silver hair and the honest, pale blue eyes. At that moment his son's wife came to call him to the table to have a bite to eat.

"It is a beautiful sculpture you have made, Grandfather," she said. "Holger the Dane and the coat of arms of Denmark. It seems to me I have seen his face before; who is he?"

"No, you cannot ever have met him," said the old man, "but I have once. From memory, I have tried to reconstruct his features. It was during the Battle of Copenhagen, when we suddenly learned that we were Danes. I was serving aboard the frigate *Denmark;* our ship was part of Steen Bille's fleet. There was a man beside me; it was as if the bullets were afraid of him. While he fought he sang all sorts of old songs; his valor was unbelievable. I recall his face well, although where he came from—or, for that matter, where he went when the battle was over—no one knows. I have often thought that he was Holger the Dane and that he had swum out to the ship from Elsinore to help us when we were in peril; since I believe that, the features on the sculpture are his."

The wooden figure cast a giant shadow on the wall and the ceiling of the room; the shadow moved as if it belonged to a real person, but that was because the tallow candle was flickering.

The girl kissed her father-in-law, took his hand, and the two of them went over to the table where his son already was seated. The wood carver sat in the big chair at the head of the table and during the meal he talked about the coat of arms of Denmark, in which love, mildness, and strength were mixed. He emphasized that there were other forms of strength that the one symbolized by the sword. He pointed to his bookcase where there were many old books and among them the works of Holberg. They had often been taken down and read, for his comedies are, indeed, amusing and all his characters seem to be people one knows.

"He was good at carving too," said Grandfather. "Holberg tried to file the rough edges off his fellow men, but that is difficult!" Grandfather laughed and nodded toward the almanac that hung on the wall and had a picture of the Round Tower on it. That was where Tycho Brahe had had his observatory. "Now Tycho Brahe was another one who used his strength, not to chop other people's flesh and bones to pieces, but to cut a road through the stars. And Thorvaldsen, whose father was a simple wood carver like myself; he can carve in marble so the whole world takes notice. Yes, Holger the Dane appears not only dressed in armor; and strength can be shown in other ways than with the sword. Let us drink a toast to Bertel Thorvaldsen."

But the little boy who was sleeping in the bed thought that it all had been meant quite literally. He saw in his dreams the Sound and Elsinore Castle with old Holger the Dane sitting down in the dark cellar, where he dreamed about everything that happened in all of Denmark, even about the conversation that we have listened to in the wood carver's house. Holger mumbled in his sleep, while he nodded his head: "Yes, do not forget me, Danes. Remember me! I will come when you are in need."

It was a sunny day, the wind carried the sound of the hunters' horn from Sweden across the Sound. The ships sailed by and greeted the castle, "Boom! boom!" And from Elsinore the answer came: "Boom, boom." But that won't wake Holger the Dane; after all, it only means "Good day and thank you." There must be a different kind of shooting before he wakes, but if that should come, do not worry, he will open his eyes.

## 39

## The Little Match Girl

It was dreadfully cold, snowing, and turning dark. It was the last evening of the year, New Year's Eve. In this cold and darkness walked a little girl. She was poor and both her head and feet were bare. Oh, she had had a pair of slippers when she left home; but they had been too big for her—in truth, they had belonged to her mother. The little one had lost them while hurrying across the street to get out of the way of two carriages that had been driving along awfully fast. One of the slippers she could not find, and the other had been snatched by a boy who, laughingly, shouted that he would use it as a cradle when he had a child of his own.

Now the little girl walked barefoot through the streets. Her feet were swollen and red from the cold. She was carrying a little bundle of matches in her hand and had more in her apron pocket. No one had bought any all day, or given her so much as a penny. Cold and hungry, she walked through the city; cowed by life, the poor thing!

The snowflakes fell on her long yellow hair that curled so prettily at the neck, but to such things she never gave a thought. From every window of every house, light shone, and one could smell the geese roasting all the way out in the street. It was, after all, New Year's Eve; and this she did think about.

In a little recess between two houses she sat down and tucked her feet under her. But now she was even colder. She didn't dare go home because she had sold no matches and was frightened that her father might beat her. Besides, her home was almost as cold as the street.

She lived in an attic, right under a tile roof. The wind whistled through it, even though they had tried to close the worst of the holes and cracks with straw and old rags.

Her little hands were numb from cold. If only she dared strike a match, she could warm them a little. She took one and struck it against the brick wall of the house; it lighted! Oh, how warm it was and how clearly it burned like a little candle. She held her hand around it. How strange! It seemed that the match had become a big iron stove with brass fixtures. Oh, how blessedly warm it was! She stretched out her legs so that they, too, could get warm, but at that moment the stove disappeared and she was sitting alone with a burned-out match in her hand.

She struck another match. Its flame illuminated the wall and it became as transparent as a veil: she could see right into the house. She saw the table spread with a damask cloth and set with the finest porcelain. In the center, on a dish, lay a roasted goose stuffed with apples and prunes! But what was even more wonderful: the goose—although a fork and knife were stuck in its back—had jumped off the table and was waddling toward her. The little girl stretched out her arms and the match burned out. Her hands touched the cold, solid walls of the house.

She lit a third match. The flame flared up and she was sitting under a Christmas tree that was much larger and more beautifully decorated than the one she had seen through the glass doors at the rich merchant's on Christmas Eve. Thousands of candles burned on its green branches, and colorful pictures like the ones you can see in store windows were looking down at her. She smiled up at them; but then the match burned itself out, and the candles of the Christmas tree became the stars in the sky. A shooting star drew a line of fire across the dark heavens.

"Someone is dying," whispered the little girl. Her grandmother, who was dead, was the only person who had ever loved or been kind to the child; and she had told her that a shooting star was the soul of a human being traveling to God.

She struck yet another match against the wall and in its blaze she saw her grandmother, so sweet, so blessedly kind.

"Grandmother!" shouted the little one. "Take me with you! I know you will disappear when the match goes out, just like the warm stove, the goose, and the beautiful Christmas tree." Quickly, she lighted all the matches she had left in her hand, so that her grandmother could not leave. And the matches burned with such a clear, strong flame that the night became as light as day. Never had her grandmother looked so beautiful. She lifted the little girl in her arms and flew with her to where there is neither cold nor hunger nor fear: up to God.

In the cold morning the little girl was found. Her cheeks were red and she was smiling. She was dead. She had frozen to death on the last evening of the old year. The sun on New Year's Day shone down on the little corpse; her lap was filled with burned-out matches.

"She had been trying to warm herself," people said. And no one knew the sweet visions she had seen, or in what glory she and her grandmother had passed into a truly new year.

## 40

## From the Ramparts of the Citadel

It is autumn; we are standing on the ramparts of the citadel, looking out over the sea at the many ships in the Sound and beyond it to the coast of Sweden, which rises high and clear in the light of the evening sun. On the other side of the ramparts we see tall trees below us; they are shedding their leaves. They shield some gloomy-looking houses with high wooden fences around them. There sentries are walking back and forth. Inside the hovels it is dark and miserable; but even more wretched are the cells behind the barred holes in the walls. Here are kept the most dangerous criminals.

A ray from the setting sun penetrates the naked cell, for the sun shines upon the evil as well as upon the good. The prisoner looks with hatred upon the sunbeam that is too weak to give off any warmth. A little bird flies down and perches upon the iron bars of the grating. Birds do sing for the evil man as well as for the good. It sings only a short little song but does not fly away; instead it preens itself, flutters its wings, and finally picks one little feather off. The prisoner in his chains looks at it, and his face, so filled with hate, for a moment changes its expression. A thought, a feeling has passed through him without his being aware why or how. And this feeling is kin to the sunbeam, to the violets that in springtime bloom outside the prison and whose fragrance penetrates its walls. From far away a hunter's horn is heard, so full of life is the music. The bird flies away from the prison bars and the sun rays disappear. Now the cell is as dark as the prisoner's heart and yet the sun has shone into both and the bird has sung there.

Play on, so gay is the hunter's tune. The evening is warm and the sea is as calm as a mirror.

## 41

## From a Window in Vartov

Right next to the green embankment that surrounds Copenhagen and once was part of its defenses stands a large building with many windows; in each is a potted plant. Poverty has stamped its mark both on the outside and the inside of the building; this is Vartov, a home for the aged poor.

An old maid is leaning out of the window; she picks a dead leaf from the balsam plant that stands on the window sill, and looks out at the children who are playing on the embankment.

What is she thinking about? She is reliving the drama of a life.

How happily the poor children are playing. They have healthy red cheeks and shiny eyes but are wearing neither stockings nor shoes. They are dancing on the green grass, at the very place where, according to an old legend, a child was offered. In ancient times, when the first embankment was being built here, for the defense of the city, the ramparts sank as fast as they were constructed. An innocent child was lured with flowers, cakes, and toys into an open tomb; and while the little one ate and played, he was sealed in. From then on the ramparts stood on solid ground and the embankment was soon covered by grass. The little children playing there now do not know the legend; if they did they would be able to hear the little child crying from under the ground, and the dew in the morning would seem to them like tears. They do not even know the story of the King of Denmark who rode on that very embankment when the enemy had surrounded the city and swore that he would die in his nest. It was the dead of winter when the enemy attacked, and the foreign soldiers put white shirts over their uniforms. The men and women of the city poured boiling water down over them, as they crawled over the snow-covered ramparts.

Gaily do the children of the poor play.

Play, little girl, play, the years will pass: the blessed years. Soon you will be fourteen and confirmed; then you will walk, hand in hand, with the other little girls, here on the green embankment. Your white dress will have cost your mother more than she can spare; and that even though it will be made out of an old dress she has bought cheaply. You will be given a red shawl which, like your other clothes, will be too big. It will hang almost to the ground. But then people can see that it is a proper grown-up shawl. You will be thinking about your pretty dress and about God, and what happened in church. It is lovely to walk here on the ramparts. The years will pass with many unhappy days to darken even a youthful heart.

At last you will have a friend; you will meet a young man. Together you now walk on the embankment in the green grass. It is early in the year; the violets are not blooming yet, but down at Rosenborg, the royal castle, you stop to admire a young tree that already has large buds. Yes, every year the trees have new, fresh leaves; but that is not true of the human heart. Through the hearts of men, more dark clouds drift than the sky of the north will ever know.

Poor young girl, your bridegroom's bridal chamber was a coffin and you became an old maid. From your little room in Vartov with the green balsam plant on the window sill, you look out at the playing children and imagine that you see your own story repeated.

This was the life story that the old maid relived as she looked at the sun-filled ramparts where the red-cheeked, barefoot children shouted with joy, like all the other little birds of the heavens.

## 42

# The Old Street Lamp

Have you ever heard the story of the old street lamp? It is not really very amusing, but one can bear to hear it once, anyway.

There was once a respectable old street lamp who had performed his duties faithfully and well for many years; but now had been declared to be too old-fashioned. This was the last evening that it would hang from the lamppost and illuminate the street; and he felt like a ballerina who was dancing for the last time and knew that tomorrow she would be a has-been. The lamp was very frightened of the coming day, for he had been told that he would be inspected by the six and thirty men of the town council. They were to decide whether the lamp was fit for further service and, if so, what kind. They might suggest that he be hung over one of the lesser bridges, or be sold to a factory, or condemned altogether, which meant that he would be melted down. Then he would be made into something else, of course; but what worried him was that he did not know whether he would then be able to recall that he had been a street lamp.

No matter what happened to him, one thing was certain: tomorrow he would be separated from the night watchman and his wife, and that was a tragedy, for he considered them to be his family. He had been hung on his lamppost the very year that the man became a night watchman. His wife had been young and snobbish. She would look at the street lamp at night but she wouldn't so much as glance at it in daylight. During recent years, however, when all three of them—the night watchman, his wife, and the street lamp—had grown old, the wife had taken care of the lamp: polished it and filled it with oil. The old couple were an honest pair who had never cheated the lamp out of a single drop of oil.

This was to be the last night that the old lamp would shine down upon the pavement. Tomorrow it would be taken to a room in the town hall. These two facts made the lamp feel so sad that he flickered. Other thoughts came: memories of all he had seen. He had cast his light upon many a curious sight and had seen more than all the six and thirty men of the town council put together. But the old lamp would never have expressed such a thought out loud, for he had the greatest respect for the authorities.

It is always pleasant for the old to reminisce, and each time the lamp remembered something different, the flame inside him seemed to grow brighter. "They will remember me as I remember them," thought the lamp. "Many years ago there was a young man who stood right under me and opened a letter. It had been written on pink stationery and the handwriting was a woman's. He read it twice; then he kissed it. His eyes when he looked up at me said, 'I am the happiest of all men.' He had received a love letter from the girl he loved; and only he and I knew it.

"I remember another pair of eyes.—How strangely one's thoughts can jump!—There had been a funeral. Someone who had lived in this street had died: a young, rich woman. The hearse had been drawn by four black horses and the coffin had been covered with flowers. The mourners had walked behind it carrying torches, which had outshone my light. But when the procession had passed and I thought the street was deserted once more, I suddenly noticed someone standing right under me and weeping. I shall never forget those sorrow-filled eyes that stared right into me." Such were the thoughts—the memories—of the old street lamp as it shone for the last time. A sentry who is to be relieved of his duty is allowed to exchange at least a few words with the man who will take his place. But the lamp did not even know who his successor would be, so he would not be able to give him a bit of advice about the wind, and tell him from which corner it usually blew; or the moon, and explain how it shone upon the sidewalk.

Down in the gutter there were three who were ready to take over the job of lighting up the street as soon as it became vacant; and thinking that the lamp could appoint his own successor, they presented themselves to him. The first was a rotten herring head, which can shine in the dark, as you know. It pointed out that his appointment would mean a great saving in oil. The second was an old piece of dry rotten wood. It can also glow and that a lot brighter than an old codfish, as it said itself. Besides, it was the last piece of a tree that had been the pride of a whole forest. The third was a glowworm. The old street lamp could not imagine where it could have come from, but there it was shining like the others. The herring head and the piece of old, dry, rotten wood claimed that the worm did not glow all the time but only when it had fits, which ought to disqualify it.

The old lamp tried to explain to them that none of them had sufficient light to become a street lamp. But none of the three would believe that; and when they were told that the lamp could not, in any case, appoint his own successor, they all declared that this was good news, for—as they all agreed—the old lamp was too senile to make such an important decision.

Just then the wind came around the corner and whistled through the cowl of the lamp. "What's this I hear about your leaving us tomorrow? Will this be the last evening that I shall find you here? Well, let me give you a farewell present, since we must part. I shall blow your brain clean of all cobwebs, so that you will not only be able to remember everything you have ever heard or seen, but you will be able to see clearly anything that is told or read aloud in your presence, as well."

"What a marvelous gift!" said the old lamp. "If only I am not melted down."

"It hasn't happened yet," replied the wind. "And now I'll blow on your memory. If you can get a few more presents like mine, your retirement and old age will be a pleasure."

"But what if I am melted down?" sighed the lamp. "Can you ensure my memory then too?"

"Be reasonable, old lamp," said the wind, and blew with all its might. Just then the moon came out from behind a cloud. "What will you give the old lamp?" asked the wind.

"Me? I will give him nothing," said the moon. "I am on the decline; besides, the lamp has never shone for me, though I have shone for him." And the moon hid behind the clouds because it hated anyone who made demands on it.

A drop of water fell upon the cowl. It announced that it had been sent by the gray clouds above and that it brought a valuable gift.

"Now that I am inside of you, you can rust into dust in one night—any night that you choose, even tonight."

The lamp thought that a very poor present and the wind agreed with him. "Hasn't anyone anything better to offer . . . anything better to offer?" screeched the wind as loudly as it could.

A shooting star fell from the sky, making an arch of fire.

"What was that?" shouted the herring head. "I think a star fell right down into the old lamp! Well, if the office is being sought by those of such high rank, the rest of us might as well go home." And that was what all three of them did.

The old lamp shone more brightly than it ever had before. "That was a lovely gift!" exclaimed the lamp. "The brilliant stars above, whom I have always admired and who shine so much more clearly than I have ever done—even though I have striven, throughout my whole life, to do just that—have sent down to me—poor, dim street lamp that I am—a most wonderful gift! They have given me the power to make those whom I love see clearly anything that I can remember or imagine. What a marvelous present! For that happiness that cannot be shared with others is only half as valuable as the one that can."

"A very respectable and decent sentiment, old lamp," said the wind. "I am afraid, though, that they forgot to tell you that you need to have a lighted wax candle inside you in order for anything to happen. Without the burning candle, nobody will ever see anything. The stars probably didn't think about telling you because they think that anything that shines down here has at least one wax candle inside it. But now I am tired. I think I'll rest." And the wind was gone.

The next day . . . Oh, we might as well skip the next day and jump to the next evening, when we find the lamp lying in an easy chair. But where? In the home of the old night watchman. He had petitioned the six and thirty men of the town council to reward his long and faithful service by giving him the old street lamp. Although they laughed, it had been good-naturedly, and the old man had been allowed to take the lamp home with him. Now the lamp lay in the easy chair next to the stove and looked twice as big as it had when it hung from the lamppost.

The old couple, who were having supper, looked fondly toward it. They would have given the lamp a seat at the table had there been a point to it. The room where they lived was in a cellar, two feet under the ground, which had to be entered through a stone-paved corridor. Around the door there was weather stripping, and the room was warm. It was also clean, neat, and cozy. Curtains concealed the bed and covered the two tiny windows. On the window ledges stood two strange-looking flowerpots which their neighbor, who was a sailor, had brought home from the Indies—whether it was the East or the West Indies, the old people didn't know. They were two ceramic elephants whose backs had holes in them that could be filled with earth. In one there grew leeks, and that was the old couple's vegetable garden. In the other a geranium bloomed, and that was their flower garden. On the wall hung a large colored print of *The Congress of Vienna.* In this picture, all the kings and emperors of Europe were portrayed, and you could see them all in one glance. In the corner an old grandfather clock ticked away. It was always fast but, as the old man said, that was better than if it had been slow.

While the old couple were eating dinner, the lamp lay in the easy chair—as we have already been told—near the old stove. The lamp felt a bit as if his world had been turned upside down. But as soon as the old man began reminiscing, talking about all the things that he and the lamp had experienced together—in rain and shine, during the clear summer nights and the long cold winter ones—the lamp realized how pleasant it was to be sitting by a warm stove in the cellar. The lamp remembered everything as vividly as if it had just happened. The wind had really done a good job of refreshing its memory.

The old people were very hard-working; they never wasted a moment. Sunday afternoon, the old watchman would take down a book and read aloud. He preferred travel books, especially ones about Africa. He liked to read about the great tropical forests where the elephants roamed. His wife would glance up at the window ledges where the two clay elephants were and say, "I can almost see it all."

How much the old street lamp wished he had a lighted candle inside him! Then the old people would be able to see it all just as he envisioned it. He saw the tall trees growing so close together that their branches intertwined; the naked natives riding on horses; and herds of elephants tramping through the underbrush, crushing reeds and breaking saplings with their great broad feet.

"What is the good of my gift if they have no wax candles?" sighed the street lamp. "They cannot afford them; they are too poor to own anything but tallow candles or oil."

But one day a whole handful of wax candle stumps arrived in the cellar. The old couple used the larger ones for light, but it never occurred to them to put one in the old street lamp. With the smaller pieces of candle the woman waxed her thread for sewing.

"Here I sit, possessing a rare gift," complained the lamp. "I have a whole world within me, and I cannot share it with the old couple. They don't know that I could decorate these whitewashed walls with the most splendid tapestries. They could see the richest forest. . . . They could see anything they desired; but alas! they do not know it."

The lamp had been polished and cleaned and now stood in a corner where all the visitors could see it. Most of them thought it was a piece of old rubbish, but the night watchman and his wife truly loved the lamp.

It was the night watchman's birthday. The old woman stood before the lamp and said with a smile, "I think that you ought to be illuminated in his honor."

Hopefully, the lamp thought, "A light has dawned on them. Now they will give me a wax candle."

The old woman filled the lamp once more with oil and he burned all evening. And now he felt certain that the gift the stars had given him—the best present he had ever received—would remain a useless, hidden treasure during the rest of his life.

That night he dreamed—and anyone who possesses a talent as great as the lamp's really can dream—that the old couple had died and that he had been sent to the foundry to be melted down. He was just as frightened as he had been on the day that the six and thirty men had inspected him. But even though he had the ability to rust and disappear into dust, he didn't make use of it. When he had been melted down, the iron was used to make the most beautiful candlestick, which was cast in the shape of an angel holding a bouquet of flowers. In the center, among the flowers, there was a hole for a wax candle. The candlestick was placed on a green writing desk that stood in a very cozy room, which was filled with books and had many paintings hanging on the walls. It was the room of a poet. All that the poet thought, imagined, and wrote down seemed to exist within the room. The dark solemn woods, the sunlit meadows where the stork strode, even the deck of a ship sailing on the billowy sea.

"What a gift I have!" said the old lamp. "I could almost wish to be melted down. No! Not as long as the old couple are alive. They love me for myself. I am like a child to them; they have given me oil and polished me. They honor me as much as they do *The Congress of Vienna* and that picture is highborn."

From then on, the old street lamp seemed to have acquired within him the peace that he deserved; he was, after all, a very respectable old street lamp.

## 43

## The Neighbors

There was such a commotion in the duck pond that you would think some great event was taking place. It wasn't; there is no accounting for ducks, you never know what they will do next. All the ducks who had been peacefully swimming or standing on their heads in the water—that is a trick that ducks know how to do—suddenly, all at the same time, swam toward land and ran away. In the mud on the shore you could see the imprint of their feet. One moment before, the pond had been like a mirror. In it you had been able to see every tree, every bush that grew along its banks, and in the background had been the gable of an old cottage with a swallow's nest under the eaves, but clearest of all had been the rose tree whose branches hung out over the water. It had looked like a painting, but on its head, of course. Now all was in motion, all the colors were mixed, and the picture had disappeared. Two duck feathers that had fallen from a fleeing drake were sailing on the surface; they turned about as if the wind were blowing, but it wasn't, so they soon lay still and the pond turned into a mirror again. Again the upside-down picture appeared: the gable of the cottage with its swallow's nest and the rose tree. Every flowering rose was beautiful, but they didn't know it themselves, for no one had told them about it. The sun shone among their leaves that were so fragrant, and every rose felt as we do when we are having the pleasantest daydreams.

"How lovely it is to be alive," said one of the roses. "I wish I could kiss the sun, because it is so beautiful. The roses down in the water I

would like to kiss too; they look exactly like us. And the sweet little
birds in the nest. They are beginning to chirp, though they have no
feathers like their mother and father yet. Both the nest in the water
and the one above us on the gable are our good neighbors. . . . Oh,
how lovely it is to be alive!"

The little birds in the nest—both the ones above and those below
in the water, who were merely a reflection—were sparrows and so
were their father and mother. They had found the empty swallow's
nest and made themselves at home in it.

"Are those ducklings swimming about?" asked the little sparrows
when they saw the two duck feathers that were floating on the pond.

"Be sensible when you ask questions," snapped the mother. "Can't
you see they are feathers, just like the ones I wear? You, too, will
grow feathers; but ours are of a better quality than ducks'! I wish we
had them up here in the nest though, they would be handy on a cold
night. I wonder what frightened the ducks so? Probably something in
the water. But it could also have been me; that last peep I said was
awfully loud. Those fatheaded roses ought to be able to tell us, but
they don't know anything; nor do they ever do anything, all day long,
but look at themselves in the mirror and smell. . . . I am bored
with our neighbors."

"Listen to the sweet little birds," said the roses. "I think they are
beginning to sing. They haven't caught the tune yet; but they will. It
must be nice to be musical. It's lovely to have such happy neighbors."

Just then two horses came galloping down to the pond to drink.
A farmer's boy was riding on one of them. He had taken off his
clothes and was quite naked except for a broad-brimmed black hat on
his head. He was whistling as if he, too, were a bird; and he rode
right out to the deepest part of the pond. When he passed the rose tree
he broke off a flower and stuck it in his hat. As he rode away the
other roses wondered where she was going, but none of them could
guess.

"I would like to travel out into the world too," said the roses to
each other, "but it is pleasant here at home. In the daytime the sun
shines warmly down on us, and at night it shines even more beautifully through the holes in the sky." It was the stars that the roses
thought were holes in the sky; they did not know any better.

"It is amusing to have us around the house," said the mother sparrow. "A swallow's nest brings luck, people say; and therefore they

are happy to have us. But a rose tree growing so close to the wall makes it damp. But they will probably cut it down; and then they could sow a little grain there. Roses are only something to look at, smell, or at best to stick in your hat. Every year they fall off, so my mother told me. The farmer's wife preserves them with salt and then they are called something in French, which I cannot pronounce nor would I care to if I could; sometimes they are put in the fireplace to make a room smell nicely. That is their life, they are just something for the eyes and nose. And now you know all there is to know about them."

In the evening when the mosquitoes were dancing above the waters of the pond, the nightingale came. He sang for the roses and his song was about the warm sunshine and how that which is beautiful never can die. But the roses thought that the nightingale sang about himself and that was not so strange. They did not think for a moment that the serenade was for them, but that did not make them appreciate it less. They wondered if all the little sparrows up in the nest might not turn out to be nightingales.

"We understood the whole song," said the little sparrows, "except for one word: 'beauty'! What does that mean?"

"Nothing!" said their mother. "It is merely appearance. . . . Up at the castle where the doves have their own house—there birds are fed peas and grain every afternoon; I sometimes dine with them, and I will take you up there as soon as you can fly, for it is important to be seen in good company: tell me who your friends are and I will tell you who you are.—Well, up at the castle, as I was about to say, they have two birds; each has a green tail and a crest on its head; the tails can be spread out like a big wheel; and then, it has so many bright colors that it hurts your eyes. They are peacocks, and they are called _beautiful_. But if you plucked them a bit, then they would look no different from the rest of us. I would pluck their feathers off if they weren't so big."

In the cottage lived a young couple who were very fond of each other. They were content, hard-working, and kept the cottage clean and cozy—everything about them was pleasant. Sunday morning the young wife picked a bouquet of roses and put them in a water glass, which she placed on the large chest in which their winter clothes were packed.

"Now I know that it's Sunday," laughed her husband, and kissed her. Later in the day he read to her from the Book of Psalms, and the two of them sat hand in hand, while the warm sun shone in through the windows.

"It is a bore to look at," declared the mother sparrow, and flew away.

Next Sunday the same thing happened, for every summer Sunday the young woman plucked roses, though there never seemed to be fewer flowers on the tree afterward, nor was it less beautiful. For the young sparrows, however, this Sunday was different. They had feathers and wanted to follow their mother when she left the nest.

"You stay here!" she ordered; and then she flew away.

All at once, she was no longer flying, no matter how much she moved her wings. Unluckily, she had been caught in a bird snare of horsehair that some boys had suspended from the branch of a tree. The horsehair tightened around her legs; it felt as if it would cut her left leg off. It was very painful, and the poor sparrow beat wildly with her wings. The boys came running out of their hiding place, and one of them took hold of the bird and squeezed it.

"It is only a sparrow," he said with disappointment to the others. But they did not let her go.

Every time the sparrow peeped, one of the boys hit it across its bill. When they arrived at the farmyard where one of them lived, there was a traveling hawker there. He knew the art of making soap: both the ordinary kinds and the ones used for shaving. He was a merry old man who still liked playing tricks as much as boys did. When he saw the sparrow and heard that the children didn't care for it, he said: "Shall we make it beautiful?"

The mother sparrow shuddered when she heard that word. The old man took some powder for the making of bronze gilt, which he kept in his box of colors and paints. He sent the boys into the farmhouse for an egg, of which he took only the white and smeared it on the bird, so that the gilt would stick to the poor creature's feathers. From the red lining of his own old coat, the soapmaker cut a cock's comb and stuck it on the sparrow's head.

"Now let us see the golden bird fly," he said, and let the poor bird free.

Terrified, the sparrow flew up into the clear sunshine. Goodness! How brightly it shone. The other sparrows and even an old crow, who was no fledgling, got so frightened at the sight that they fled, but not very far. Soon they were following the poor sparrow to see what would happen.

"Where do you come from? Where do you come from?" screamed the crow.

"Wait for us! Wait for us!" chirped the other sparrows.

But the poor mother sparrow would not wait; in terror, she was flying home to her nest. The gilding made it hard for her to fly and she sank closer and closer toward the earth. More and more birds were following her, both big ones and small ones; some of them flew up to her and pecked her with their bills and all of them screamed, "Look at her! Look at her!"

"Look at her! Look at her!" screamed her own little ones when the poor mother sparrow came near her nest. "It is a peacock chick! Look at her colors! They hurt our eyes just as Mother said they would. It is the *beautiful!*"

And the little sparrows pecked with their beaks at their own mother and prevented her from taking refuge in her own nest. She was so frightened that she could not even utter a peep to tell them who she was. The other birds pecked at her now too. Soon most of her feathers were gone and, bleeding, she fell down into the rose tree.

"Poor little bird," said the roses. "We will hide you. Lean your head against us."

The sparrow spread out her wings once more and then closed them tight against her body; and died among her neighbors, the roses.

"Peep . . . peep," said the little sparrows in the nest. "Where is our mother? I wonder if this is a way of telling us that we can take care of ourselves. Well, she has left us the house; but which one of us is to keep it, to live in, when every one of us has a family?"

"I can't have the rest of you here when I take myself a wife and have children," said the smallest of them.

"I will have more wives and children than you will ever get," said the second one.

"But I am the oldest," said the third. The argument soon became a fight; they flapped their wings and pecked each other with their little beaks until three of them had fallen out of the nest. There they lay on the ground, as angry as could be, with their heads drawn in among their feathers, so that they looked as though they had no necks at all, and they blinked constantly, which was their way of looking sulky.

They could fly a little; and after they had practiced a bit, they decided that when they met out in the world they would say, "Peep," and then scratch the earth three times with their left legs, so that they could recognize each other.

The sparrow who had won the fight spread himself out in the nest; after all, he was the owner of property now, though that honor did not last long. That very night the house burned. The flames shot out from underneath the thatch roof and soon the whole house was engulfed in fire. The swallow's nest with the little sparrow in it burned to ashes, but the young people got out safely.

When the sun rose, after the mild summer night, all that was left of the cottage were a few charred beams leaning up against the chimney, who, being alone, was now his own master. The ruins were still smoking, but the rose tree had not been hurt. It stood as green and flowered as beautifully, and mirrored itself, as ever, in the still pond.

"How beautiful that rose tree is, in front of the house that burned down," exclaimed a young man. "That is a beautiful picture." And he took out his sketchbook, for he was a painter. He drew the charred beams, the naked chimney, and the smoke that rose from the ashes. In the foreground of the picture stood the rose tree in full bloom. It looked beautiful; but after all, it was the one who had inspired the painter.

Later in the day, two of the sparrows that had been born there came flying by. "Where is the nest?" they peeped. "Where is the house? Peep! . . . Everything has burned down and even our strong brother has burned; that is his punishment for wanting the nest. Only the roses escaped; look at their red cheeks, they are not mourning for their neighbors. We won't talk to them. In our opinion this place is ugly!" And they flew away.

One warm fall afternoon, when the sun was shining as though it were summer and the courtyard of the castle had been newly raked, the doves were walking about, pecking at the ground, in front of the big granite steps that led to the entrance of the castle.

"Form groups! Form groups!" the pigeon mothers were continually admonishing their young ones. They believed they looked more beautiful that way.

"What are the little gray ones called, that are always running about among us?" asked a young dove.

"Small gray ones?" said an older pigeon with red and green speckled eyes. "Why, they are sparrows, harmless little things. We have a reputation for piety, that is why we don't chase them away. But they know their station and they scrape so prettily with their little legs."

Three little sparrows were standing nearby and they did scratch the ground three times with their left legs and say, "Peep!" Then they knew they were from the same nest.

"A very good place to eat," remarked one of them.

The doves walked in circles around each other, throwing out their chests. Every one of them had an opinion of all the others; and not one was pleasant to hear.

"Look at her! How greedily she eats! She will get sick from all those peas."

"Coo! She is losing her feathers; she will be bald soon! Coo! Coo!"

They glanced at each other with eyes red with rage, while they shouted to their young ones: "Form groups! Form groups!"

"Look at those little gray things! Coo!" they cried with contempt. Such was the pigeon talk then, and such it will be a thousand years hence.

The sparrows ate and listened, they even tried forming groups; but the result was not decorative. When they had eaten their fill, they flew in a flock far enough away not to be heard by the doves and there they expressed their opinion of them. Then they flew up on the garden wall and looked out over it. The broad glass french doors of one of the rooms stood open. One of the sparrows flew down and landed right on the doorstep. He had overeaten and that gave him courage. "Peep," he said. "Look how bold I am!"

"Peep!" replied the second sparrow. "I dare do that too, and a little more." And with those words he flew a few feet inside the castle.

The room was empty, and therefore the third sparrow flew in even farther, while it chirped, "All the way or it doesn't count!"

"What a funny place the nest of a human being is. But what is that over there? Look at it!"

There was the flowering rose tree, the ruins of the house with the chimney still standing, and charred beams leaning against it. How had that got into the castle hall?

All three of them wanted to fly up to it, but the first one who did hit the wall, for it was only a painting, which the painter had made from the little sketch he had drawn. It was a lovely work of art.

"Peep," said the sparrows. "It is nothing! It only appears to be something. It is what they call the *beautiful,* whatever that means; we don't understand it!" And with those words the three sparrows flew out of the room, for they heard someone coming.

Days and years passed. The doves cooed, and the sparrows lived on the fat of the land in summer and froze through the winter. They had all become engaged or married or whatever such relationships are called between sparrows. Children they had, and each couple claimed that theirs were the prettiest, the cleverest little sparrows in the whole world. Whenever the three from the same nest met, they recognized each other by scratching three times with their left legs and saying, "Peep!" By now the oldest sparrow was so old that she no longer had a mate, nest, or children; and therefore she decided to move to a city to find out what that was like, so she flew to Copenhagen.

In Copenhagen there was a large castle too, and near it was a building with frescoed walls. It was in a pleasant area where there was a canal and one could see sloops laden with apples and earthenware pots. The old sparrow looked in through the windows of the strange house; and she thought she was looking down into a tulip every time, for each room was painted a different lovely color, and in the center stood some white figures. They were of marble—that is, some of them were; others were of plaster, but a sparrow cannot see the difference. On top of the building was the Goddess of Victory driving a chariot to which horses were harnessed; it was in bronze. The sparrow had landed on the Museum of Thorvaldsen, the great Danish sculptor.

"How it shines, how it shines!" chirped the sparrow. "I presume that it must be the *beautiful!* Well, it is bigger than a peacock at least." The sparrow still remembered what her mother had told her about the nature of beauty. She flew down into the courtyard of the museum; here the outside walls of the building were decorated with paintings of palm trees. In the center of the yard grew a rose tree. Its branches hung down over a grave. There three sparrows were pecking at the ground trying to find a crumb; she flew over to them.

"Peep!" she said, and scratched the ground three times with her left leg. She did this out of habit; she was not really expecting to meet any of her family again; it would be mere chance if one did, and not very likely.

"Peep!" replied the other sparrows, and they scratched the ground just as she had done.

"Wonderful to see you again!" they all said to each other. Two of the sparrows were her brothers and the third was a young niece. "It is a grand place to meet! Peep! I think this must be the *beautiful;* there is not much to eat here. Peep!"

People came out of the side door of the museum, where they had been admiring the statues. Their faces still shining from what they had seen, they looked down at the grave of the sculptor who had created it. Some of the people bent down to pick one of the rose petals that had fallen on the grave, to take home as a memento. Many of the visitors came from far away: from France, Germany, and England.

A beautiful young woman plucked a rose and pinned it to her blouse. The sparrows, who had been watching everything that went on, decided that the whole house had been built for the sake of the roses. They thought that so much respect was rather overdoing it, but since the human beings seemed to care so much for roses, the sparrows didn't voice their opinion.

"Peep . . . Peep," they said, and even swept the grave with their little tails, while they glanced, with one eye, up at the rose tree.

They hadn't looked at it long before they decided that it was their old neighbor; and they were right. The painter who had drawn the sketch of the ruined cottage and the rose tree in full bloom had got permission to dig the rose tree up, because he thought it was so beautiful, and have it planted on Thorvaldsen's grave. And here it grew, with its fragrant red flowers, the personification of beauty.

"Have you got a permanent appointment?" asked the sparrows. And the roses nodded, for they recognized their little gray neighbors and were happy to see them again.

"How lovely it is to be alive and to be in flower! How lovely it is to see kind faces around you and have your old friends come to visit you! Every day here is like a high holy day."

"Peep!" said the sparrows. "Here are our old neighbors. We remember them from the time when they grew by the village pond. They have come far. See how they are honored now. But it is all chance, not merit. What is so marvelous in a red blotch? We can't see it. But there is a dead leaf, we can see that."

One of the sparrows flew up and pecked at the withered leaf until it fell off; and the rose tree was even greener and lovelier than it had been before. It bloomed on the grave of the artist, and its beauty and fragrance mingled in men's memory with his immortal name.

## 44

## Little Tuck

This is a story about a little boy named Tuck. His real name was Carl, but when he was very tiny he had pronounced it "Tuck" and the name had stuck. Such things are always nice to know.

Now Tuck had to take care of his sister Gustava, who was much younger than he was, and study his lessons at the same time. These are two jobs that are not easily combined. The poor boy was singing little rhymes to his sister, who was sitting in his lap, and trying to read his geography book at the same time. The book lay open on the table beside him. He was supposed to learn where all the towns of Zealand were, and everything else that was important about them. The only one that he knew anything about at all was Copenhagen.

At last his mother came home and took little Gustava from him. But now it was almost dark and they could not afford to light a candle just so he could study. Little Tuck sat by the window, trying to read in the fading light.

"There is the old washerwoman from the alley," said his mother, who was looking out of the window. "She can hardly walk and yet she must carry water all the way from the pump in the square. Be a good boy, Tuck, and go and carry it for her."

Little Tuck ran at once to help the old woman. When he got home it was dark; there was no point in even asking for a candle, for it was Tuck's bedtime. His bed was a bench in the living room; and there he lay trying to recall everything the teacher had said about the cities and towns of Zealand. He had put the geography book

under his pillow, for someone had told him that this could help him
learn his lessons—though that kind of advice one shouldn't put much
faith in.

He was thinking as hard as he could, when suddenly it felt as
though someone were kissing him gently on his eyes and then on his
mouth. He felt as if he were awake and asleep, both at the same time.
There was the old washerwoman looking down at him kindly. "It
would be a sin and a shame," she said, "if you did not know your
lesson tomorrow in school because you helped me. Now I shall help
you and the Lord will help us both."

The book under his pillow began to move about as if it were alive;
and then a hen crawled out of it.

"Cluck! Cluck!" said the hen. "I come from the town of Køge!
Cluck! Cluck!" And the hen told him the number of inhabitants the
town had and all about the battle that had been fought there, though
she added that it wasn't worth talking about.

"Bang! Bang! Bang!" A parrot made out of wood fell from the
sky and landed in little Tuck's bed. It was the popinjay from the fair-
grounds of Praestø; the one that the good citizens shot at when they
held their famous marksmanship competition. The popinjay claimed
that he had as many nails in his body as the town of Praestø had
inhabitants; and that he was very proud of. "Thorvaldsen lived right
outside me, and my location is superb," the popinjay remarked as if
he were the town itself.

All at once little Tuck was no longer in bed; he was riding along
on a handsome horse; sitting behind him was a knight who was
holding onto him so he wouldn't fall. Away they galloped. The gaily
colored plumes on the knight's helmet streamed in the wind; they
were riding through the forest toward Vordingborg. Here, in his
royal castle, King Valdemar was holding court. The town was filled
with people; banners flew from the high towers; and in the great
hall musicians were playing; and the king, his courtiers, and the
ladies of the court were dancing. Without warning, the sun began
to rise; the night was over and the towers of the castle disappeared
one after the other, until only one remained standing. The town was
no longer a city but had shrunk to being a large hamlet, poor and
wretched. Some school children, with books under their arms, were
passing in one of the streets. "Two thousand inhabitants," they re-

marked. But they were bragging; the formerly so important royal city was even smaller than that.

Little Tuck was back in bed: half dreaming, half awake. Someone was approaching his bed.

"Little Tuck, little Tuck," cried a voice. It was a sailor boy who looked young enough to be a cadet or a cabin boy; but he was neither. "I bring you greetings from Korsør. It is a new town, a town that is growing! The mail coach from Copenhagen stops here, and steamships are moored in our harbor. Once people thought that Korsør was a horrid, vulgar place, but that was only prejudice. Listen to what Korsør says about itself: 'I am surrounded by green forests and blue sea. Inside my walls a poet was born, who is amusing to read— which is more than most poets are. I thought of sending a ship around the world. I didn't, but I could have if I had wanted to. My city gate is covered with roses, which smell so sweetly. . . .'"

Little Tuck thought he saw the roses; but then the colors blended and the roses were gone. Green, forest-clad banks rose above a blue fjord. The tall spires of an old cathedral stretched upward toward the sky. On one of the sloping hills, water splashed in broad streams; they came from a spring, and near it sat an old man with long white hair and a golden crown on his head. It was old King Hroar. In olden times the town was called "Hroar's spring"; today the Danes call it Roskilde (*kilde* is the Danish word for "spring"). In the cathedral, all the kings and queens of Denmark are buried. Little Tuck seemed to be able to see them all as they walked hand in hand, with golden crowns on their heads, into the cathedral; and he could hear the organ playing, mixed with the sound of the water rushing from the spring. "Don't forget that here the Estates assemble!" called King Hroar.

Suddenly the cathedral was gone; as if someone had turned the pages of a picture book, a woman now stood before him. She looked like a gardener's helper. Indeed, that's what she must have been, for she was busy weeding the town square of Sorø, where grass grows between the cobblestones. She had draped her gray linen apron over her head. It must have just rained, for she was all wet. "In Sorø it always rains," she commented. She knew stories about both King Valdemar and Bishop Absalon, and could recite long, amusing passages from Holberg's plays. But then, without warning, she hunched her shoulders, her head began to bob, and she looked like a frog.

"One has to dress according to the weather. . . . Croak! Croak! . . . It is as wet and as peaceful as the grave in this town. Croak! Croak. . . . That is, except when the boys from the academy are here reciting Greek, Latin, and Hebrew. . . . Croak! Croak!" And the old woman who was a frog—or the frog who was an old woman —kept making the same sound: "Croak! Croak!" The monotone made Tuck sleep even more deeply.

But still dreams came to him. His little sister Gustava, with her big blue eyes and long, curly, yellow hair, had grown up; and even though neither of them had wings, they were both able to fly. Hand in hand, Tuck and Gustava flew above the fields and green forests of Zealand.

"Listen to the cock crowing, little Tuck," she said. "See the hens fly up from Køge. You shall have a henyard so big, so huge, that you will never know hunger or want. When you aim at the popinjay, you shall hit the mark and become a rich and happy man. Your house shall rise as proudly as King Valdemar's castle once did in Vordingborg; and in your garden there will stand marble sculptures like those of Thorvaldsen near Praestø. Your name will be praised around the world, just as far as the ship from Korsør could have sailed. 'Remember the assembling of the Estates, Little Tuck,' says King Hroar, for there you shall give wise and good counsel. Finally, you will become old and die; then you shall sleep peacefully. . . ."

"As though I were lying in Sorø," said little Tuck, and woke up. It was a lovely morning and all his dreams were immediately forgotten—and that was just as well, for it is not good for us to know the future.

Tuck jumped out of bed and quickly took his geography book out from underneath his pillow and began to study.

The old washerwoman stuck her head in through the door and nodded kindly to him. "Thank you for the help yesterday, little Tuck. May the Lord bless you and make your best dreams come true."

Little Tuck didn't remember what he had dreamed; but Our Lord did.

## 45

## The Shadow

On the shores of the Mediterranean the sun really knows how to shine. It is so powerful that it tans the people a mahogany brown; and the young scholar who came from the north, where all the people are as white as bakers' apprentices, soon learned to regard his old friend with suspicion. In the south one stays inside during most of the day with the doors and shutters closed. The houses look as if everyone was asleep or no one was at home. The young foreigner felt as if he were in prison, and his shadow rolled itself up until it was smaller than it had ever been before. But as soon as the sun set and a candle lighted the room, out came the shadow again. It was truly a pleasure to watch it grow; up the wall it would stretch itself until its head almost reached the ceiling.

"The stars seem so much brighter here," thought the scholar, and he walked out onto his balcony where he stretched himself just as his shadow had done. And on all the balconies throughout the city people came out to enjoy the cool evening. Had the town appeared dead and deserted at noon, certainly now it was alive! People were flocking into the streets. The tailors and the shoemakers moved their workbenches outside; the women came with their straight-backed chairs to sit and gossip. Donkeys heavily laden with wares tripped along like little maids. Children were everywhere. They laughed, played, and sometimes cried as children will do, for children can run so fast that they are not certain whether it is a tragedy or a comedy they are enacting. And the lights! Thousands of lamps burned like so many falling stars. A funeral procession, led by little choir boys in black and white, passed with mournful but not sad-looking people following the black-draped horse and wagon. The church bells were ringing. "This is life!" thought the young foreigner, and he tried to take it all in.

Only the house directly across from his own was as quiet now as it had been at midday. The street was very narrow and the opposite balcony was only a few yards away. Often he stood and stared at it, but no one ever came out. Yet there were flowers there and they seemed to be flourishing, which meant that they were cared for or else the sun would long since have withered them. "Yes," he concluded, "they must be watered by someone." Besides, the shutters were opened, and while he never saw any light, he sometimes heard music. The scholar thought this music "exquisite," but that may be only because all young northerners think everything "exquisite" the first time they are in the south.

He asked his landlord if he knew who lived across the street, but the old man replied that he did not and, in fact, had never seen anyone enter or leave. As for the music, he could hardly express how terrible he thought it. "It's as if someone were practicing," he said. "The same piece, over and over and over again! And it's never played all the way through! It's unbearable!"

One night the young foreigner, who slept with his balcony door open, awakened with a start. A breeze had lifted his drapes so that he caught a glimpse of the opposite balcony. The flowers were ablaze with the most beautiful colors and in their midst stood a lovely maiden. For an instant the scholar closed his eyes to make sure that he had had them open. In a single leap he was standing in front of the drapes. Cautiously, he parted them; but the girl had vanished, the light had disappeared, and the flowers looked as they always did. The door, however, had been left open, and from far inside he could hear music; its gentle strains seemed to cast a spell over him, for never before had he taken such delight in his own thoughts. How does one get into that apartment? he wondered; and he perused the street below. There was no private entrance whatever, only a group of small shops; surely one could not enter a home through a store.

The next evening the scholar was sitting as usual on his balcony. From his room the lamp burned brightly, and since his shadow was very shy of light, it had stretched itself until it reached the opposite balcony. When the young man moved, his shadow moved. "I believe my shadow is the only living thing over there," he muttered. "See how it has sat down among the flowers. The balcony door is ajar. Now if my shadow were clever, it would go inside and take a look around; then it would come back and tell me what it had seen. Yes, you ought to earn your keep," he said jokingly. "Now go inside. Did you hear me? Go!" And he nodded to his shadow and his shadow nodded back at him. "Yes, go! But remember to come back again." There the scholar's conversation with his shadow ended. The young man rose, and the shadow on the opposite balcony rose; the young man turned around and the shadow also turned around; but then there happened something that no one saw. The shadow went through the half-open door of the other balcony, while the scholar went into his own room and closed the drapes behind him.

The next morning on his way to the café where he had his breakfast and read the newspapers, the scholar discovered that he had no shadow. "So it really went away last night!" he marveled. More than anything else, the young man was embarrassed; people were certain to notice, and might demand that he explain or, worse than that, might make up explanations of their own. He returned at once to his room and there he remained for the rest of the day. That evening he walked out onto his balcony for a bit of fresh air. The light streamed from behind him as it had on the evening before. He sat down, stood up, stretched himself; still there was no shadow, and though it was doubtful that anyone could see him, he hurried inside again almost immediately

But in the warm countries everything grows much faster than it does in the north, and less than a week had passed before a shadow began to sprout from the scholar's feet. "The old one must have left its roots behind, what a pleasant surprise!" he thought happily. Within a month he walked the streets unconcerned; his shadow, though a little small, was quite respectable. During the long trip, for the scholar was going home, it continued to grow until even a very big man, which the scholar was not, would not have complained about its size.

Settled once more in his own country, the scholar wrote books about all that is true and beautiful and good. The days became years. The scholar was now a philosopher; and the years became many.

One evening when he was sitting alone in his room there was a very gentle knock at the door.

"Come in," he called. But no one came, so the philosopher opened the door himself. Before him stood the thinnest man that he had ever seen but, judging from his clothes, a person of some importance. "Whom do I have the honor of addressing?" the philosopher asked.

"I thought as much," replied the stranger. "You don't recognize me, now that I have a body of my own and clothes to boot. You never would have believed that you would meet your old shadow again. Things have gone well for me since we parted. If need be, I can buy my freedom!" The shadow jiggled its purse, which was filled with gold pieces, and touched the heavy gold chain that it wore around its neck. On all of its fingers were diamond rings, and every one was genuine.

"I must be dreaming!" exclaimed the philosopher. "What is happening?"

"Well, it isn't something that happens every day," said the shadow, "but then, you're not an ordinary person. Nobody knows that better than I do, didn't I walk in your first footsteps? . . . As soon as you found that I could stand alone in the world, you let me go. The results are obvious. Without bragging, I can say few could have done better. . . . Of late, a longing has come over me to talk with you before you die—you must die, you know. Besides, I wanted to see this country again, only a rogue does not love his native land. . . . I know that you have a new shadow. If I owe you or it anything, you will be so kind as to tell me."

"Is it really you?" cried the philosopher. "It's so incredible! I wouldn't have believed that one's shadow could come back to one as a human being!"

"Tell me how much I owe you," insisted the shadow. "I hate to be in debt."

"How can you talk like that?" replied the philosopher. "What debt could there be to pay? Be as free as you wish! I am only happy to see you again. And I rejoice in your good luck. Sit down, old friend," he invited most cordially. "Tell me how all this came about, and what you saw that night in the house across the street."

"Yes, I will tell you about it," agreed the shadow, and sat down. "But first you must promise me that you will never tell anyone that

I once was your shadow. I've been thinking of becoming engaged; after all, I am quite rich enough to support a large family."

"Don't give it another moment's thought," the philosopher said. "I will never tell anyone who you really are. Here is my hand on it. A man is no better than his word."

"And a word is a shadow," remarked the shadow, because it could not speak otherwise.

It was really amazing, how human the shadow appeared. It was dressed completely in black, but everything was of the finest quality from its patent leather boots to its hat of the softest felt. The gold chain and the rings have already been described, but one's eye fell upon them so often that one cannot help mentioning them again. Yes, the shadow was well dressed, and clothes make the man.

"Now I shall begin," announced the shadow, and it stamped its boots as hard as it could on the philosopher's new shadow, which was curled up like a poodle at the feet of the man. Perhaps it did this because it hoped to attach the philosopher's shadow to itself, or maybe just because it was arrogant; but the new shadow did not appear ruffled. It lay perfectly still and listened, for it too wanted to know how one could be free and become one's own master.

"Do you know who lived in the house across the street?" asked the shadow. "That's the best of all, it was Poetry! I was there for three weeks, and that is just as edifying as having lived three thousand years and read everything that's ever been composed or written. This I say, and what I say is true! I have seen all and I know all!"

"Poetry!" cried the philosopher. "Yes . . . yes. She is often a hermit in the big cities. I saw her myself once, but only for a short moment and my eyes were drowsy from sleep. She was standing on the balcony and it was as if the northern lights were shining around her. . . . Go on, go on! There you were on the balcony; then you walked through the doorway and . . . and . . ."

"I was in the entrance hall. That's what you sat looking at all the time, the vestibule. There was no lamp in there, and that's why from the outside the apartment appeared dark. But there was a door. It opened onto another room, which opened onto another, which opened onto another. There was a long row of rooms and anterooms before one reached the innermost where Poetry lived. And these were ablaze with more than enough light to kill a shadow, so I never saw the maiden up close. I was cautious and patient, and that is the same as being virtuous."

"Come, come," commanded the philosopher curtly. "Tell me what you saw."

"Everything! And I'll tell you about it, but first . . . It has nothing whatever to do with pride, but out of respect to my accomplishments, not to speak of my social position, I wish you wouldn't address me so familiarly."

"Forgive me!" exclaimed the philosopher. "It is an old habit, and they are the hardest to get rid of. But you are quite right, and I'll try to remember. . . . Please do continue, for I am immensely interested."

"Everything! I have seen all, and I know all!"

"I beg you to tell me about the innermost room where Poetry dwelled. Was it like the beech forest in spring? Was it like the interior of a great cathedral? Or was it like the heavens when one stands on a mountaintop?"

"Everything was there!" replied the shadow. "Of course, I never went all the way in. The twilight of the vestibule suited me better, and from there I had an excellent view. I saw everything and I know all. I was at the court of Poetry, in the entrance hall."

"But what did you see?" urged the philosopher. "Did Thor and Odin walk those halls? Did Achilles and Hector fight their battles again? Or did innocent children play there and tell of their dreams?"

"I am telling you that I was there. And you understand, I saw everything that there was to see. You could not have stayed there and remained a human being, but it made a human being of me! I quickly came to understand my innermost nature, that part of me which from birth can claim kinship to Poetry. When I lived with you, I didn't even think about such things. You'll remember that I was always larger at sunrise and at sunset, and that I was more noticeable in the moonlight than you were. Still, I had no understanding of my nature; that did not come until I was in the vestibule, and then I became a human being.

"I was fully mature when I came out; by then you had already left the south. Being human made me ashamed to go around as I was; I needed boots, clothes, and all the other trimmings that make a man what he is. So there was nothing else for me to do but hide. . . . I wouldn't say this to anyone but you, and you mustn't mention it in any of your books. . . . I hid under the skirts of the woman who sold gingerbread men in the market. Luckily, she never found out how much her petticoats concealed. I came out only in the evening; then I would walk around in the moonlight, stretching myself up the walls to get the kinks out of my back. Up and down the streets I went, peeping through the windows of the attics as well as the drawing rooms. And I saw what no one ever sees, what no one ever should see! It's really a horrible world, and I wouldn't be human if it weren't so desirable. I saw things that ought to be unthinkable; and these were not only done by husbands and wives, but by parents and the sweet, innocent children! I saw," said the shadow, "I saw everything that man must not know, but what he most ardently wishes to know—his neighbor's evil! If I had written a newspaper, everyone would have read it; but instead I wrote directly to the persons themselves, and I wreaked havoc in every city that I came to. People feared me so much and were so fond of me! The universities gave me honorary degrees, the tailors gave me clothes, and the women said that I was handsome. In a word, each donated what he could, and so I became the man that I am. . . . But it is getting late, and I must say good-by. Here is my card. I live on the sunnier side of the street and am always home when it rains."

"How strange!" remarked the philosopher after the shadow had left.

The years and the days passed, and the shadow came again. "How are things going?" it asked.

"Oh," replied the philosopher, "I have been writing about all that is true and beautiful and good, but no one cares to hear about anything like that, and I am terribly disappointed because those are the things that are dear to me."

"Well, they aren't to me," said the shadow. "I've been concentrating on gaining weight, and that there's some point in. You don't understand the world, that's what's the matter with you. You ought to travel. I am going on a trip this summer, would you like to join me? If you would like to travel as my shadow it would be a pleasure to have you along. I'll pay for your trip!"

"You go too far!" retorted the philosopher.

"It all depends how you look at it. The trip will do you good and, traveling as my shadow, you'll have all your expenses paid by me."

"Monstrous!" shouted the philosopher.

"But that's the way of the world, and it isn't going to change," said the shadow, and left.

Matters did not improve for the philosopher; on the contrary, sorrow and misery had attached themselves to his coattails. For the most part, whenever he spoke of the true and the beautiful and the good, it was like setting roses before a cow. Finally he became seriously ill. "You look like a shadow of your former self," people would say, and when he heard these words a shiver went down his spine.

"You ought to go to a health resort," suggested the shadow when it came to visit him again. "There's no other alternative. I will take you along for old time's sake. I'll pay the expenses, and you'll talk and try to amuse me along the journey. I'm going to a spa, myself, because my beard won't grow. That's a disease too, you know, because beards are a necessity. If you're sensible, you'll accept. We'll travel as friends."

And so they traveled, the shadow as master and the master as shadow, for whether they were being driven in a coach, riding horseback, or simply walking, they were always side by side and the shadow kept itself a little in the fore or in the rear, according to the direction of the sun. It knew how to create the impression that it was the superior. The philosopher, however, was not aware of any of this. He had a kind heart, which did not even have a guest room reserved for envy. The journey was not yet over when the philosopher suggested to the shadow, "Now that we're traveling companions—and when you consider the fact that we've grown up together, shouldn't we call each other by first names? It makes for a much pleasanter atmosphere."

"There's something in what you say," began the shadow, who now was the real master. "You have spoken frankly, and what you have said was well meant; therefore, I ought to be honest with you. As a philosopher, you know how strange nature can be. Some people cannot bear to have a rough piece of material next to their bodies, and others can't hear a nail scratching on glass without it upsetting their nervous systems. Well, I would have the same feeling if you were to call me by my first name. I would have the feeling that I was being pressed to the ground, as if my relationship to you had never changed. You understand it's merely a feeling, it has nothing whatever to do with pride. But I could call you by your first name and satisfy half of your request."

From then on, the shadow always spoke and referred to the philosopher by his first name. "He goes too far," thought the man. "He's hardly civil to me." But when one is poor, one does more thinking than speaking.

At last they arrived at the famous resort where people came from all over the world to be cured. Among the guests was a beautiful princess who suffered from seeing too clearly, which is a very painful disease. She noticed at once that one of the new arrivals was very different from everyone else. He had come to make his beard grow, she was told. "But that's not the real reason," she muttered to herself. And to satisfy her curiosity, she went right up and spoke to the stranger, for the daughter of a king need not stand on ceremony with anyone.

"Your trouble is that you cannot cast a shadow," the princess announced.

"Your Royal Highness is getting well!" exclaimed the shadow. "I know that you suffered from seeing too clearly, but you must be getting over it. You show signs of perfect health. . . . I grant you that it is a very unusual one, but I do have a shadow. Other people have just ordinary shadows, but I despise the ordinary. You know how one dresses one's servants so that their livery is finer than one's own clothes; well, I let my shadow pretend that he is human. As you can see, I have even bought him a shadow. It was very expensive, but I am fond of doing the original."

"What!" thought the princess. "Have I really been cured? This is the finest spa there is. How fortunate I am to be born in the time when these marvelous waters were discovered. . . . But just because I am well is no reason to leave. I'm enjoying myself here. That stranger interests me, I hope his beard won't grow too quickly."

That night there was a grand ball that everyone attended, and the shadow danced with the princess. The princess was light on her toes, but the shadow was even lighter; such a graceful partner she had never had before. They discovered that he had once visited her country while she was abroad. There, too, the shadow had peeped through all of the windows, those that faced the street and those that did not. He had seen both this and that; and he knew how to tell about some of what he had seen and how to hint at the rest, which was even more impressive. The princess was astounded. She had never spoken to anyone who was so worldly wise, and out of respect for what he knew, she danced with him again.

The next time they danced together the princess fell in love. The shadow noticed the sudden change with relief. "She's finally been cured of seeing too clearly," he thought.

The princess would have confessed her feelings immediately if she hadn't been so prudent. She thought of her realm and of the people she ruled. "He knows well the ways of the world, that's a good sign," she commented silently. "He dances well, that is also a virtue. But is he really educated, for that is very important? I'd better test him." Then she began to ask the shadow questions so difficult that she herself did not know the answers.

An expression of confusion came over the shadow's face. "You cannot answer!" exclaimed the princess.

"I learned the answers to questions like that in childhood," said the shadow. "I believe that even my shadow, who is sitting over there by the door, could respond correctly."

"Your shadow! That really would be remarkable!"

"I can't say for certain," continued the shadow. "I just wouldn't be surprised if he could. After all, he's never done anything but follow me around and listen to what I say. Yes," he cried in a sudden burst of enthusiasm, "I believe he will be able to answer you! . . . But, Your Royal Highness, if you will allow me to make a suggestion. My shadow is so proud of being thought to be human, if Your Royal Highness wishes to create the right atmosphere, so that the shadow will be able to do his best, please treat him as if he were a man."

"I'd prefer it that way," said the king's daughter, and she joined the philosopher, who was alongside the door. She questioned him about the sun and the moon, and about the human race, both inside and out; and he answered every query both cleverly and politely.

"What must the man be worth, if his shadow is so wise!" thought the princess. "It would be a blessing for my people if I chose him for my husband. I shall do it!"

The shadow was very amenable. It agreed without hesitation that their plans must not be revealed until the princess had returned home. "I will not even tell my shadow," he said, while he thought how admirably the world had been created.

Not long after they came to the land which the princess ruled whenever she was there.

"My good friend," the shadow began to the philosopher. "Now that I am as happy and as powerful as anyone can hope to be, I'd like to share my good fortune with you. You may live with me always, here in the castle; you may drive with me in the royal coach; and you will be paid one hundred thousand gold pieces a year. In return, all I ask is that you let everyone call you a shadow; that you never admit to anyone that you have ever been a human being; and that once a year, when I sit on the balcony so that the people can pay me homage, you lie at my feet as a shadow should. . . . I might as well tell you that I am marrying the princess, and the wedding is tonight."

"No, this cannot happen!" cried the philosopher. "I don't want to do it, and I won't! You are a fraud! I will tell everything! You've fooled both the people and the princess; but now I will tell them that I am a human being and that you are only my shadow, who's been masquerading as a man!"

"No one will believe you," warned the shadow. "Now be reasonable or I'll call the guard."

"I intend to ask for an audience with the princess," replied the philosopher.

"But I will speak with her first," said the shadow, "and you will be imprisoned."

The shadow's threat very quickly became a reality, for the royal sentry knew whom the princess had chosen to be her husband.

"You are shivering," remarked the princess as soon as he entered her chambers. "You must not get sick this evening, not for the wedding!"

"I've just had the most horrible experience that one can have," replied the shadow. "Imagine! . . . Oh, how fragile a shadow's brain must be! . . . Imagine, my shadow has gone mad. He believes he is a man. And that I . . . that I am his shadow!"

"How dreadful!" she exclaimed. "He isn't running around loose, I hope."

"No, no, he's not," he said softly. "I am so afraid he will never get well."

"Poor shadow," continued the princess. "He must be suffering terribly. It would really be kinder to free him from that particle of life he has. Yes, the more I think about it, the more convinced I am that it's necessary for him to be done away with. . . . Quietly, of course."

"It seems so cruel," said the shadow, "when I think of how loyal a servant it was," and a sound resembling a sigh escaped from the shadow's lips.

"How noble you are!" exclaimed the princess.

That night the whole city was brilliantly lighted. The cannons were shot off. Bum! Bum! Bum! The soldiers presented arms. Oh, what a wedding it was! The shadow and the princess came out onto the balcony, and the people screamed, "Hurrah!"

The philosopher heard nothing of all of this, for they had already taken his life.

## 46

## The Old House

Once upon a time there stood in a street a very old house; it was nearly three hundred years old. You could tell what year it had been built by reading the date cut into one of the beams; all around it tulips and curling hop vines had been carved. Right above the entrance a whole verse had been inscribed, and above each window appeared a grinning face. The second story protruded out over the first. The lead gutters, which hung under the roof, were shaped like dragons, with the monster's head at either end. The water was supposed to spout out of their mouths, but it didn't; the gutter was filled with holes and the water ran out of the dragons' stomachs.

All the other houses in the street were new and well kept, their walls were straight and smooth, and they had large windows. It was quite reasonable that they should feel themselves superior to the old house. Had they been able to speak they probably would have said: "How long are we to tolerate that old ruin? Bow windows are out fashion and, besides, they obstruct our view. It must believe itself to be a castle, judging from the size of the steps leading up to the entrance, and that iron railing makes one think of funerals; not to speak of the brass knobs. It's embarrassing!"

Right across from the old house stood a new house; it was of the same opinion as all the other houses in the street. But behind one of its windows sat a little boy, a little red-cheeked child with bright, shining eyes who preferred the old house, and that both in the daytime when the sun shone and at night in the moonlight. When he looked at the walls of the old house, with its cracks and bare spots where the mortar had fallen off, then he could imagine how the street once had looked: in olden times, when all the houses had had broad steps leading up to their doors, and bay windows, and gables with tall pointed roofs. He could see the soldiers marching through the streets armed with halberds. Oh, he found the old house worth looking at and dreaming about.

Its owner was an old man who wore the strangest old-fashioned pants, a coat with brass buttons, and a wig that you could see was a wig. Every morning an old servant arrived to clean and run errands for the old gentleman; otherwise, he was all alone. Sometimes he came to the window and looked out into the street; then the little boy nodded to him and the old man nodded back. In this manner they became acquainted; no, more than that, they were friends, although they had never spoken to each other.

The little boy heard his parents say, "Our neighbor, across the street, must be terribly lonely."

Next Sunday the boy made a little package and, when he saw the servant going by in the street, he hurried down and gave it to him. "Would you please give this to your master?" he asked. "I have two tin soldiers, and I would like your master to have one of them, for I have heard that he is so terribly lonely."

The old servant smiled and nodded and took the little package, with the tin soldier inside it, to his master. Later that day a message arrived, inviting the boy to come and visit the old man. The child's parents gave their permission; and thus he finally entered the old house.

The brass knobs on the iron railing seemed to shine so brightly that one might believe that they had been newly polished in honor of the boy's visit. The little carved trumpeters in the oak doorway seemed to be blowing especially hard on their instruments, for their cheeks were all puffed up. It was a fanfare! "Tra . . . tra . . . trattalala! The boy is coming! Tra . . . tra . . . trattalala!" The door was opened and he stood in the hall. All the walls were covered with paintings portraying ladies in long silk gowns and knights in armor. The boy thought that he could hear the silk gowns rustle and the armor clang. Then there were the stairs; first they went up a goodish way, and then down a little bit, and ended in a balcony. It was wooden and a bit rickety, grass and weeds grew out of every crack, making it look more like a garden than a balcony. Antique flowerpots with human faces and donkey ears stood ranged in a row; the plants grew to suit themselves. One of them was filled with carnations that spread out over the rim in all directions; that is, the green leaves and the stems, the flowers hadn't come yet. One could almost hear the plant saying: "The breeze has caressed me and the sun has kissed me and promised me a flower next Sunday, a little flower next Sunday."

The old servant led the boy into a chamber where the walls did not have paper on them; no, they were covered with leather, which had gilded flowers stamped upon it.

> "Gilding fades all too fast.
> Leather, that is meant to last,"

said the walls.

In the room were high-backed armchairs with carvings all over them. "Sit down, sit down!" they cried. And when you sat down in them they mumbled. "Ugh, how it cracks inside me! I think I got rheumatism like the old cabinet. Ugh, how it creaks and cracks."

At last the little boy entered the room with the bow windows. Here the old master of the house greeted him. "Thank you for the tin soldier, my little friend," said he. "And thank you for coming."

"Thanks, thanks," said all the furniture, although it sounded a little more like: "Crack . . . Crack." There were so many chairs, tables, and cabinets in the room that they stood in each other's way, for they all wanted to see the little boy at once.

In the center of one of the walls hung a picture of a beautiful young girl. She was laughing and dressed in clothes from a bygone time. She did not say "thank you" or "crack" as the furniture had, but she looked down so kindly at the little boy that he could not help asking, "Where did you get her?"

"From the pawnbroker's," replied the old gentleman. "His shop is filled with pictures that no one cares about any more. The people they portray have been dead so long that no one remembers them. But though she has been dead and gone for fifty years, I knew her once."

Under the portrait hung a bouquet of faded flowers, carefully preserved behind glass. They looked old enough to have been picked half a century ago. The pendulum of the grandfather clock swung back and forth, and the hands moved slowly around, telling everything in the room that time was passing and that they were getting older; but that did not disturb the furniture.

"My parents say that you are terribly lonely," said the little boy.

"Oh," the old man smiled, "that is not altogether true. Old thoughts, old dreams, old memories come and visit me and now you are here. I am not unhappy."

Then from a shelf he took down a book that was filled with wonderful pictures. There were processions in which there were golden carriages, knights, and kings who looked like the ones in a deck of cards; and then came the citizens carrying the banners of their trades: the tailors' emblem was a pair of scissors held by a lion; the shoemakers had an eagle with two heads above their banner—for, as you know, shoemakers do everything in pairs. What a picture book that was!

The old man left for a moment to fetch some comfits, apples, and nuts; it was certainly nice to be visiting in the old house.

"But I can't stand it here!" wailed the tin soldier, who was standing on the lid of a chest. "It is so lonely and sad here; once you have lived with a family one cannot get accustomed to being alone. I can't stand it! The days are ever so long and the evenings feel even longer. It is not the same here as in your home, where your parents talked so pleasantly and you sweet children made such a lot of lovely noise. No, that poor old man really is lonely. Do you think anybody ever gives him a kiss? Or looks kindly at him? Here there is no Christmas tree ever, or gifts! The only thing he will ever get will be a funeral! . . . I can't stand it!"

"You mustn't take it so to heart," said the little boy. "I think it is very nice here. All the old thoughts and dreams come to visit, so he said."

"I see none of them and I don't want to either," screamed the tin soldier. "I can't stand it!"

"You will have to," said the little boy just as the old man returned with the comfits, apples, and nuts; and at the sight of them the boy forgot all about the soldier.

Happy and content, the little boy returned home. Days and weeks went by. The boy nodded to the old man from his window, and from the funny bow window of the old house the greeting was returned. Finally the little boy was asked to come visiting again.

The carved trumpeters blew, "Tra . . . tra . . . tratralala. . . .

The boy is here! . . . Tra tra!" The knights in armor clanged with their swords and the silk gowns of the ladies rustled, the leather on the wall said its little verse, and the old chairs that had rheumatism creaked. Nothing had changed, for in the old house every day and hour were exactly alike.

"I can't stand it!" screamed the tin soldier as soon as he saw the boy. "I have wept tin tears! It is much too mournful and sad here. Please, let me go to the wars and lose my arms and legs, that at least will be a change. I can't stand it, for I know what it is like to have old thoughts and old memories come visiting. Mine have been here and that is not amusing. Why, I almost jumped right off the lid of the chest. I saw all of you and my own home as plainly as if I had been there. It was Sunday morning and all you children were standing around the big table singing hymns, as you always do on Sunday. Your parents were nearby, looking solemn. Suddenly the door opened and little Maria, who is only two years old, entered. She always dances whenever she hears music, and she tried to dance to the tune you were singing, but hymns are not made for dancing they are too slow. She stood first on one leg and flung her head forward, and then on the other and flung her head forward, but it didn't work out. You looked grave, all of you, but I found it too difficult not to laugh—at least inside myself. I laughed so hard that I fell off the table and hit my head so hard that I got a lump on it. I know it was wrong of me to laugh and the lump was punishment for it. That is what the old man meant by old thoughts and memories: everything that has ever happened to you comes back inside you. . . . Tell me, do you still sing your hymns on Sunday? Tell me something about little Maria and about my comrade, the other tin soldier. He must be happy. Oh, I can't stand it!"

"I have given you away," said the little boy. "You will have to stay, can't you understand that?"

The old man brought him a drawer in which lay many wonderful things. There were old playing cards with gilded edges, a little silver piggy bank, and a fish with a wiggly tail. Other drawers were opened and all the curiosities were looked at and examined. Finally the old man opened the harpsichord; on the inside of the lid was a painting of a landscape. The instrument was out of tune but the old man played on it anyway, and hummed a melody.

"Ah yes, she used to sing that," he sighed, and looked up toward the painting he had bought from the pawnbroker and his eyes shone like a young man's.

"I am going to the wars! I am going to the wars!" screamed the tin soldier as loudly as he could, and fell off the chest.

"What could have happened to him?" said the old man. Together he and the boy were searching for the little soldier on the floor. "Never mind, I will find him later," said the old man, but he never did. There were so many cracks in the floor and the tin soldier had fallen right down through one of them; there he lay buried alive.

The day passed and the little boy returned home. Many weeks went by, winter had come. All the windows were frozen over. The little boy had to breathe on the glass until he could thaw a little hole so that he could see out. Across the street the old house looked quite deserted; the snow lay in drifts on the steps. They had not been swept; one would think no one was at home. And no one was. The kind old man had died.

That evening a hearse drew up in front of the old house and a coffin was carried down the steps. The old man was not to be buried in the town cemetery but somewhere out in the country, where he had been born. The hearse drove away. No one followed it, for all his friends and family had died long ago. The little boy kissed his fingers and threw a kiss after the hearse as it disappeared down the street.

A few days afterward an auction was held; the furniture in the old house was sold. The boy watched from the window. He saw the knights in armor and the ladies with their silken gowns being carried out of the house. The old high-backed chairs, the funny flowerpots with faces and donkey ears were bought by strangers. Only the portrait of the lady found no buyer; it was returned to the pawnbroker. There it hung; no one remembered her and no one cared for the old picture.

Next spring the house itself was torn down. "It was a monstrosity," said the people as they went by. One could see right into the room with the leather-covered walls; the leather was torn and hung flapping like banners in the wind. The grass and weeds on the balcony clung tenaciously to the broken beams. But at last all was cleared away.

"That was good," said the neighboring houses.

A new house was built, with straight walls and big windows but not quite where the old house had stood; it was a little farther back from the street. On the site of the old house a little garden was planted, and up the walls of the houses on either side grew vines. A fine iron fence with a gate enclosed it, and people would stop in the street to look in, for it was most attractive. The sparrows would sit in the vines and talk and talk as sparrows do, but not about the old house, for they were too young to remember it.

Years went by and the little boy had become a grown man, a good and clever man of whom his parents could be justly proud. He had just got married and had moved into the new house. His young wife was planting a little wild flower in the front garden. He was watching her with a smile. Just as she finished, and was patting the earth around the little plant, she pricked her little hand. Something sharp was sticking out of the soft earth. What could it be?

It was—imagine it!—the tin soldier! The one that had fallen off the chest and down through a crack in the flooring. It had survived the wrecking of the old house, falling hither and thither as beams and floors disappeared, until at last it had been buried in the earth and there it had lain for many years.

The young woman cleaned the soldier off with a green leaf and then with her own handkerchief. It had perfume on it and smelled so delicious that the soldier felt as though he were awakening from a deep sleep.

"Let me have a look at him," said the young man; then he laughed and shook his head. "I don't believe it can be him, but he reminds me of a tin soldier that I once had." Then he told his wife about the old house and its old master and about the tin soldier that he had sent over to keep the old man company, when he had been a boy, because he had known that the old man was so terribly alone.

He told the story so well that his young wife's eyes filled with tears as she heard about the old house and the old man. "It could be the same soldier," she said. "I will keep it so that I shall not forget the story you have told me. But you must show me the old man's grave."

"I do not know where it is," her husband replied. "No one does; all those who knew him were dead. You must remember that I was a very small boy then."

"How terribly lonesome he must have been," sighed the young woman.

"Yes, terribly lonesome," echoed the tin soldier. "But it is truly good to find that one is not forgotten."

"Good," screamed something nearby in a so weak a voice that only the tin soldier heard it. It was a little piece of leather from the walls of the old house. The gilding had gone long ago, and it looked like a little clod of wet earth. But it still had an opinion, and it expressed it.

> "Gilding fades all too fast,
> But leather, that is meant to last."

But the tin soldier did not believe that.

## 47

## A Drop of Water

Surely you know what a magnifying glass is. It looks like one of the round glasses in a pair of spectacles; but it is much stronger, and can make things appear a hundred times larger than they are. If you look at a drop of water from a pond through it, a thousand tiny animals appear that you cannot see with the naked eye; but they are there and they are real. They look like a plate of live shrimps jumping and crowding each other. They are all so ferocious that they tear each other's arms and legs off, without seeming to care. I suppose that is their way of life, and they are happy and content with it.

Now there once was an old man whom everybody called Wiggle-waggle, because that happened to be his name. He always made the best of things; and when he couldn't, he used magic.

One day when he looked through his magnifying glass at a drop of ditch water he was shocked at what he saw. How those creatures wiggled and waggled: hopping, jumping, pulling, pushing, and eating each other up—yes, they were cannibals.

"It is a revolting sight!" exclaimed old Wiggle-waggle. "Can't one do anything to make them live in peace, and each mind his own business?" He thought and thought, and when he couldn't find an answer, he decided to use magic.

"I'll give them a bit of color; then they will be easier to study," he decided. He let a drop of something that looked like red wine fall into the ditch water—but it wasn't red wine, it was witch's blood of the very finest type, the one that costs two shillings a drop. All the little creatures immediately turned pink. Now they looked like a whole town of naked savages.

"What have you got there?" asked an old troll who had come visiting. He had no name, which among trolls is distinguished.

"If you can guess what it is," replied Wiggle-waggle, "then I will make you a present of it. But it isn't easy, unless you know it."

The troll who had no name looked through the magnifying glass. What he saw looked like a city with all the inhabitants running around naked. It was a disgusting sight, but even more disgusting to see was the way people behaved. They kicked and cuffed each other; they beat and bit and shoved; those who were on the bottom strove to get to the top, and those on the top struggled to be on the bottom.

"Look, his leg is longer than mine! I will bite it off! Away with you!"

"Look, he has a lump behind his ear. It is small but it embarrasses him and gives him pain. We will really make him suffer!" And they pushed and pulled him; and finally they ate him up, all because he had had a little lump behind his ear.

One little creature sat still, all by herself in a corner, like a modest, sensitive little maiden. She wanted peace and quiet. But she was dragged out of her corner, mistreated, and finally she was eaten up.

"It is most instructive and amusing," said the troll.

"But what do you think it is?" asked Wiggle-waggle. "Have you figured it out?"

"That is easy," answered the troll. "It's Copenhagen or some other big city, they are all alike."

"It's ditch water," said Wiggle-waggle.

## 48

## The Happy Family

The largest leaves here in Denmark are the burdock leaves. If a little girl holds one in front of her tummy, then it will serve as an apron. If it should rain, one can use one as an umbrella; it is big enough. The burdock plant never grows alone; it is fond of company. Where you find one you will find more, and sometimes a whole forest of them. They look beautiful; and all this beauty is snail food. Those large white snails that the aristocrats and other grand people used to make into fricassee in the old times, and exclaim enthusiastically about how delicious they were—"What a flavor!" they used to cry—well, those white snails live on burdock leaves. And, as a matter of fact, it was for their sake that the burdock was originally planted.

Now there once was an old manor house where no one ate the snails; the custom had died there long ago, as had most of the snails; but the burdock, it thrived. They spread out all over the paths, and some of the lawns, for burdocks are not easy to get rid of. A good part of the park was a jungle of burdock leaves; and if a solitary plum or apple tree had not survived, no one would ever have believed that there once had been a garden there. In the very center of this forest lived the last survivors of the white snails. They were a couple and very, very old.

Exactly how old they were they didn't know, but they could remember that once their family had been numerous, and that their ancestors had come from some foreign land. That the burdock forest had been planted for their sake they knew too; and that they were proud of it.

They had never been outside, but they knew vaguely that there was a world outside; it was called the manor house. There snails were cooked until they turned black and then they were served on a silver dish. What happened afterward was not clear to them. They didn't have any idea either what it was like to be "cooked" or "served on a silver dish." But that the whole ceremony was extremely elegant and distinguished they had no doubt. Neither the toad, nor the dung beetle, nor the earthworm—all of whom had been asked—could tell them anything about it, since none of their family had ever been "cooked" or served on a "silver dish."

The old white snails knew that they were the most distinguished beings in the whole world, that the forest of burdocks had been planted for their sake, and that the manor house stood merely so that they someday could be brought there, to be cooked and put on a silver dish.

They lived a lonely yet happy life; as they had no children of their own, they had adopted an ordinary garden snail. They had brought him up carefully, as though he were their own; their only disappointment had been that he wouldn't grow. However, the mother snail was always imagining that he was becoming fatter—in spite of his being just an ordinary snail—and she would beg her husband, who hadn't noticed it, to just feel their son's house. This the father snail would do, and then he would agree with her.

One day the rain was pouring down!

"Listen to how it is drumming on the burdock leaves," said the father snail.

"It is raining through," cried his wife. "Look how the water is running down the stalks. Everything will be soaked down here. But we have our houses and even the little one has his. Certainly, we were created superior to all other creatures in the world. We are the true aristocrats, born with houses on our backs, and with a whole forest of burdock leaves especially sprouting and growing for our sake. I wonder how far our forest stretches and what is beyond it?"

"Nothing," replied her husband. "There can be no better place than this, and what is beyond does not interest me."

"Oh, I am not sure of that," argued his wife. "I wouldn't mind being taken up to the manor house to be boiled and served on a silver plate. All our ancestors have been; I am sure it is something very special, to have that happen to one."

"I believe it possible that the manor house has fallen apart and become a ruin," said the father snail. "Or possibly the burdocks have grown so large around it that the people inside it can't get out. But all that is of no importance! You are always fretting. I am afraid our son takes after you, he is so restless. For the last three days he has been crawling up that stalk there, it gives me a headache just to look at him."

"Don't scold him!" said the mother snail. "He keeps a dignified pace, I am sure he will be a credit to us. After all, what have we old people to live for but our children? Have you thought about where we are going to find a wife for him? I wonder if anywhere in this forest there lives anyone of our own kind."

"Black slugs there are enough of; but they are not real snails, they have no houses of their own. Although they are common they think a lot of themselves. But we could ask the ants, they are always running about as if they had something important to do; they may have come across a snail that would make a wife for our little son."

"Oh yes! We know of the sweetest one," said the ants. "But it may be difficult to arrange; you see, she is a queen."

"That is of no importance," said the old snails. "Does she have a house of her own?"

"She has a castle," replied the ants proudly. "The loveliest ant castle with seven hundred corridors."

"Thank you," said the snail mother but she didn't mean it. "Our son is not going to live in an anthill. If you have nothing better to suggest, then we will ask the mosquitoes, they fly about everywhere."

"We have found a wife for him," buzzed the mosquitoes. "About a hundred yards from here there lives, on a gooseberry bush, a little snail. She has a house of her own; she lives all alone and is old enough to get married."

"I think she should come to him," said the father snail. "It is more fitting, since she only has a gooseberry bush; whereas, our son has a whole burdock forest."

The mosquitoes flew to make the proposal; it took her a whole week to come; but that only proved that she was a proper snail.

A wedding was held. Six glowworms shone as brightly as they could, but otherwise the affair passed off very quietly, for the old folks could not endure riotous merriment. The mother of the bridegroom made the speech, for her husband was much too overcome by emotion to say a word. The young people were given the burdock forest as their inheritance; and both of the old snails declared that it was the best place in the whole world. The old snail mother promised them that if they lived a decent and upright life, and multiplied, then they and their children would be taken to the manor house to be cooked and served on a silver dish.

After the speech, the two old snails crept inside their houses and slept; and that so deeply that they never came out again.

The young couple reigned over the burdock forest and had a very, very large family. But none of them was ever boiled or served on a silver dish, which made them believe that the manor house had fallen into ruin and that all the human beings in the world had died. Since no one ever contradicted them, it was true enough. The rain drummed down on the burdock leaves to make music for them, and the sun shone on the forest for their sake; and every little snail in the whole family was very, very happy.

## The Story of a Mother

A mother sat by the bedside of her little child; she was very sorrowful, for she feared that her little one was dying. The face of the child was pale and his little eyes were closed; he breathed softly and gently; every once in a while he would gasp for breath and it sounded as if he were sighing; then his mother would look even more grief-stricken.

Someone knocked at the door and an old man entered. He was poorly dressed and had a big horse blanket wrapped around him to keep himself warm. It was winter and bitterly cold outside. The earth was covered with snow and ice, and the wind blew hard enough to make one's face smart.

The old man was shivering from cold, and when the mother saw that her child had fallen asleep, she walked over to the stove to warm a little beer for the old man. He sat down beside the cradle and rocked it, and the mother took a chair and sat down near him. She looked at her sick child. The baby took a deep breath and raised one of his little hands.

"I will be allowed to keep him, won't I? Our Lord wouldn't take him from me!"

The old man nodded so curiously, it could as easily have meant yes as no. It was Death himself who had come into her room. The mother looked down at the folds of her skirt, and tears ran down her face. Her head was so heavy—she had not slept for three days and three nights —for a moment her eyes closed.

She woke with a start, trembling from the cold. "What happened?"

she cried, and looked about her. The old man was gone and her little boy was gone; he had taken the child with him. In the corner, the hands of the grandfather clock whirled around, Boom! The heavy weights hit the floor and the clock stood still.

The mother ran out of the house and into the darkness, calling her son's name.

There sat a woman dressed all in black. "Death has been in your house," said the strange woman. "I saw him hurrying off with your child. He runs swifter than the wind, and what he takes he never brings back."

"Tell me which way he went," pleaded the mother. "Just tell me that and I shall catch up with him."

"I know which way he went," the woman in the black dress answered. "And I shall point it out to you as soon as you have sung all the lullabies that you sang to your baby. I have heard them before, and I am very fond of them. I am Night, and I have watched the tears running down your cheeks while you sang them."

"I shall sing them all, every one of them," said the mother. "But not now! I must catch up with Death and get my child back."

But Night sat silently and the mother wrung her hands in despair. She sang all the songs that she had sung to her boy, while she wept more tears than there were verses. Then Night said to her, "Go to the right when you come to the dark pine forest; that was the road I saw Death take with your child."

Deep inside the woods two roads met, and the mother did not know which to take. At the crossroad grew a bush full of thorns; it stood naked in the winter cold, and its branches were covered by ice.

"Have you seen Death go by with my little child?" the mother asked.

"Yes," answered the rosebush, "but I will not tell you which way he went unless you warm me with your heart. I am freezing to death! I will turn into ice!"

The mother pressed the bush to her breast in order to warm it, and the thorns pierced her, so that drops of blood fell. But the rosebush shot new leaves and flowers bloomed in the cold winter night, so warm was the heart of the grieving mother; and the rosebush told her which of the roads to take.

She came to a large lake, and there was no boat for her to sail across it. The water had not frozen to ice yet, and the lake was too deep for her to wade across. Yet she had to get to the other side if she were to see her child again. She lay down at the edge of the lake and tried to drink it dry; this no human being could do, but the mother in her sorrow hoped that a miracle would happen.

"No, that will never work," said the lake. "Let us two come to an agreement instead; I like to collect pearls, and your eyes are the clearest that I have ever seen. If you will cry them out, and give them to me, then I shall carry you over to the place where Death has his greenhouse. It is filled with plants and trees; each of them is a human life, and Death tends them."

"I will give anything to be with my child," said the weeping mother, and wept even harder; and her eyes sank to the bottom of the waters and became two precious pearls.

The lake lifted her and swung her across to the other side, where the strangest house stood. It was miles wide and miles long and looked more like a mountain covered with forest and filled with caves than a house. But the poor mother couldn't see it, for she had cried her eyes out.

"Where shall I find Death? He has taken my child away with him," she called.

"He hasn't come back yet," explained an old woman who guarded Death's great greenhouse while he was away. "How have you found your way here and who helped you?"

"God has helped me, for He is merciful, and you will help me too, won't you? Where is my child?"

"I don't know your child," said the woman, "and you cannot see to find it. So many flowers and trees have withered tonight. Soon death will come and transplant them. You know, of course, that every human being has his life-tree or life-flower. The trees and flowers here look like trees and flowers anywhere else; the only difference is that they have heartbeats. Even an infant's heart has a particular beat. Try to find your child's. But what will you give me if I tell you what to do when you have found it?"

"I have nothing to give," said the grieving mother, "but I will walk to the end of the world for you."

"There is nothing you could fetch for me there," said the old woman, "but you can give me your long black hair. I think you know, yourself, how beautiful it is and I like it! You can have my white hair in exchange; it is better than nothing."

"Is that all you want!" she exclaimed. "That I will give up gladly." And she gave away her long black hair and received the old woman's snow-white hair in return.

Together they walked into Death's greenhouse where the flowers and trees grew next to each other in the strangest manner. There were lovely hyacinths under glass bells and big healthy peonies. In basins, waterplants grew; some of them looked fresh and healthy, others were sickly: water snakes had wound themselves around them and the black crayfish pinched their stems and roots. There were palm trees, oak and plane trees, and parsley and flowering thyme as well. Every flower or tree had a name, for each was a human life. They were people who were still alive: one in China, another in Greenland, all over the world. There were big trees in small pots; they looked cowed and subdued, while their roots were about to burst the crockery. There were also dull little flowers growing in rich soil, surrounded by moss and most carefully tended. The poor mother went from one to another of the tiniest plants and listened to the heartbeats inside them, and among millions she knew her own child's.

"This is his!" she cried, and stretched out her hands protectively toward a little blue crocus whose flower hung sickly to one side.

"Do not touch the flower!" said the old woman. "But stay where you are. When Death comes—and I am expecting him any minute—prevent him from pulling it up. Threaten him, say that you will pull up some of the other flowers if he touches your little crocus. That will frighten him, for he has to answer to Our Lord for every one of them; and none may be pulled up before God has given His permission."

An ice-cold wind blew through the room and the blind mother knew that Death had come.

"How did you find your way here?" demanded Death. "And how did you travel faster than I can?"

"I am a mother," she replied.

And Death reached out toward the delicate flower, but she protected it by covering the little crocus with her hands, without touching a single leaf.

Death blew on her hands; and his breath was colder than the coldest wind and her hands fell to her sides.

"Against me you can do nothing!" said Death.

"But Our Lord can," she replied.

"I am only doing His bidding," Death said. "I am His gardener. I uproot His flowers and trees and plant them again in the garden of paradise, in the unknown land. How they grow there and what that land is like I do not dare tell you."

"Give me back my child!" cried the mother, and wept and prayed. All at once she grabbed the two flowers nearest her, one in each hand, and screamed at Death, "I will tear up all your flowers, for I don't know what else to do!"

"Don't touch them!" said Death. "You say that you are so unhappy, and yet now you will make another mother as unhappy as you are."

"Another mother," the poor woman whispered, and let go of both flowers.

"Here are your eyes," said Death. "I fished them up from the bottom of the lake; they shone so brightly. I didn't know they were yours, but here, take them back; you will be able to see even more clearly now than you could before. Look down into the well over there, and I shall whisper the names of the two plants that you were about to pull up. You shall see their future, their whole lives, so that you will understand what you were about to destroy."

The mother looked down into the well; and the first life she saw was a blessed one for the world, bringing happiness and joy. The second life was all sorrow, distress, and wretched misery.

"Both are the will of God," said Death.

"Which is the flower of sorrow and misery, and which is the blessed one?" she asked.

"That I shall not tell you," Death replied. "But this much you shall know: one of the flowers was your own child's; it was his fate that you saw, his future."

In terror the poor woman cried, "Which one was my child? Tell me! He is innocent! Save my child from such suffering! Carry him away with you, carry him up to God! Forget my tears! Forget my prayers! Forget everything that I have said and done!"

"I do not understand you," said Death. "Do you want your child back, or shall I carry him into that land which you do not know?"

The mother wrung her hands in despair and fell on her knees and prayed: "Oh, God, do not listen to me when my prayers are against

Your will, for that is always for the best. Do not listen to me! Do not listen to me!"

She bowed her head into her lap while Death carried her child into the unknown land.

## 50

## The Collar

Once upon a time there was a fine gentleman whose only worldly possessions were a bootjack, a comb, and a loose collar; but that was such a fine one that it would have enhanced the best shirt in the world; and this story is about the collar. He was old enough to begin thinking about marriage when, by chance, he found himself being washed in the same tub as a lady's garter.

"Ah," sighed the collar. "Never have I met anyone so soft and dainty, with so slender and lovely a figure. May I ask your name?"

"I won't tell you," snapped the garter.

"Where exactly do you . . . belong?" asked the collar.

The garter, who was by nature shy, found the question indiscreet and didn't answer.

"I think you must be a kind of waistband," continued the collar. "Something that is worn on the inside. I see that you are both useful and decorative, Miss . . . Miss . . ."

"Please don't talk to me!" said the garter. "I have given you neither cause nor permission to do so."

"Your beauty is cause enough and gives its own permission," replied the collar, who thought himself not only gallant but also witty.

"Don't come near me!" screamed the garter. "There is something . . . something masculine about you."

"I am a gentleman. I own both a bootjack and a comb," boasted the collar, but he was lying: the comb and bootjack belonged to his master.

"Don't come near me!" moaned the garter. "I am not used to such treatment."

"Prude!" snapped the collar. Just at that moment he was taken out of the tub; then he was starched and hung over a chair out in the sunshine. A little bit later he was taken in and put on an ironing board.

"Madam," began the collar as soon as he saw the warm iron, "I assume that you are a widow. The very sight of you makes me warm, and all my wrinkles disappear. Be careful not to burn a hole in me. . . . Please, will you marry me?"

"Rag!" snarled the iron as it passed proudly over the collar, imagining that it was a steam engine drawing a whole string of railway cars behind it. "Rag!" repeated the iron on its return journey.

The collar was found to be just a little frayed on the edges and the maid took a pair of scissors to cut off the few loose threads.

"Oh!" exclaimed the collar when he saw the scissors. "You must be a prima ballerina. What leg movement! Never have I seen anything so elegant; no human being could surpass you!"

"I know that," said the scissors.

"You deserve to be a countess!" declared the collar. "All I have is a bootjack, a comb, and a gentleman to wait upon me; I wish I were a count!"

"Is he proposing?" snarled the scissors; she was angry, so she really cut the collar and then it was spoiled.

"I suppose I'd better propose to the comb!" thought the collar, and said, "How pretty your teeth look, miss, and you have not lost one of them. Tell me, have you never thought of marriage?"

"Didn't you know," said the comb, and blushed, "that I am engaged to the bootjack?"

"Engaged indeed!" sneered the collar. Now that there was no one to propose to, he had decided to become a cynic.

Time passed and finally the collar ended in the rag pile of the paper mill. There was a big rag party, and the fine linen stayed in one bunch and the coarse in another, as is the custom in this world. All the rags liked to talk and had a lot to tell, but the collar talked more than anyone else because he so loved to brag.

"I have had so many sweethearts! Women couldn't leave me alone! But then, I was a gentleman and so well starched. I had both a comb and a bootjack though I never used either of them. You should have seen me then, when I was buttoned and lying on my side. I shall never forget my first fiancée. She was a waistband: so soft, so refined and beautiful, I was the cause of her death; she drowned herself in a washtub for my sake. Then there was the widow, she was red hot with passion but I abandoned her. My wound, which you can still see, was given me by a prima ballerina; she was infatuated and fierce. My own comb loved me. She lost all of her teeth because of it—I believe she cried them out. Oh yes, I have lived! And I have a great deal on my conscience. But what troubles me most is to think of the garter—I mean the waistband—and her unhappy end in the washtub. I deserve to be made into paper, that will atone for it."

All the rags were made into paper, but the collar became the particular piece of paper that this story is printed on. This was his punishment for having bragged so much and told so many lies. The collar's fate is worth remembering. How can you be sure that you won't end in the rag pile, be made into paper, and have your whole life's story—even the most intimate and secret parts—printed on you; and then, like the rag, have to run around the world telling everyone about it?

## 51

## The Flax

The flax was blooming. It had the most beautiful blue flowers; their petals were as soft as the wings of a moth and even more delicate. The sun shone on the flax, and the rain clouds watered it, which is just as pleasant to the flax and just as good for it as it is for a child to be washed by his mother and given a kiss. Both flax and children thrive on such treatment.

"People say that this year's crop will be the best for many a year," said the flax. "They say that we are taller than our parents were, and that fine linen can be woven from our stalks. Oh, how happy I am! None can be happier than I am. I am well and strong and I know I shall become something. The sunshine's kisses make me cheerful, the rain refreshes me. I am the most fortunate of all plants."

"Take it easy," mumbled the old fence. "You don't know the world as I do. I am filled with knots and that is as good as having a memory." Then the old wooden fence creaked a doleful song:

> "Crack and break,
> Snap and bend,
> A song must end."

"No, no!" shouted the flax. "The sun will shine tomorrow as well, and the dew will fall. I can hear myself growing, I can feel every flower. I am happy!"

But one day the farmer and the hired hands came and pulled the flax up, roots and all; and that hurt! Then it was thrown into a tub filled with water, as if they meant to drown it. And when the poor flax was finally taken out, it was only to be toasted over a fire. It was most terrifying.

"One cannot always be fortunate," sighed the flax. "Suffering is a form of experience, and one can learn from it."

But the suffering, the pains and aches grew worse. The flax was beaten and bruised, hacked and hackled, and then finally put on the spinning wheel. That was almost the worst of all: around and around it went, getting dizzier and dizzier, till it was not able to think at all.

"I was happy once," moaned the flax amid all the tortures. "One must learn to appreciate the happy childhood and youth one has had, and be happy! Happy! . . . Oh!"

The flax had now been spun; and the farmer's wife set the loom and wove a lovely large piece of linen out of it.

"Oh, this is truly marvelous! I never imagined that this could happen to me," said the flax. "I am always fortunate! The fence was just talking nonsense with its

> "Crack and break,
> Snap and bend,
> A song must end."

"A song is never over. I think mine is just beginning now. I have suffered but I have also been rewarded for my suffering. I am most fortunate. . . . I am strong yet soft, white and ever so long. This is much superior to being merely an herb, even a flowering one. Then I wasn't taken care of as I am now, I only got water to drink if it rained. Now the maid turns me over each morning so the sun can bleach me on both sides; and she sprinkles me with water when I get too dry. The minister's wife has declared that I am the finest piece of linen in the whole county. I cannot become any happier."

Now the linen was ready to be cut and sewn. Again it hurt; the scissors cut and the needle pricked, it was no pleasure! Well, what did it become? Something that all of us have use for but we never mention: twelve pairs of them.

"Now I have become something," thought the linen. "Now I know what I was meant for. It is a blessing to be useful in this world; it is a true pleasure. Out of one we have become twelve, all alike, a whole dozen. Again how fortunate I am!"

Years went by; and even the strongest linen can't last forever.

"Sooner or later the end must come," said each of the twelve pieces of linen. "I would like to have lasted just a little bit longer, but one must not make impossible demands."

The linen, that now had become rags, was torn into tiny pieces, and now it thought that all was over, for it was chopped and hacked and finally boiled. It hardly was aware, itself, of all that it went through, and then it became fine white paper!

"Now that was a surprise . . . a most happy surprise," exclaimed the paper. "Why, now I am whiter and more elegant than I was before! This is too marvelous, I wonder what is going to be written on me?"

A very excellent story was written on the paper, and everyone who heard it or read it became both better and cleverer because of it. They were a real blessing: the words that had been written down on that paper.

"That is more than I ever dreamed possible when I was a little blue flower in the fields. How could I imagine then that I would ever become the messenger of happiness and knowledge to human beings? I can't even understand it now. But it is so, even though God knows I have done little to deserve it; I have only lived. Yet each time that I have thought, 'Now the song is over,' it hasn't been. It has merely started all over again: finer, better, more beautiful than before. I wonder if I shall travel now, be sent all over the world so that everyone can read me? I think it is very probable. For every flower that I used to have, I now have a thought that is equally beautiful. I am the most fortunate, the happiest thing in the whole world."

But the paper was never sent on any journey, except a very short one, down to the printers. Every word written on the paper was set in type and then printed; hundreds of books were made and in each of them you could read exactly the same words as had been written down on the paper. This, after all, was much more sensible. Many more people could read it, while the poor paper would have worn itself out before it had got halfway around the world.

"Yes, I agree," thought the paper, which now had become a manuscript. "It is far more sensible, I never thought about it. I will stay home like an old grandfather who is respected and honored, and the books will run about and do the work. After all, I am the original, it was on me that the words first were written. The ink flew from the pen down on me and penetrated me. I am most happy, most fortunate."

Once the book was printed, the manuscript was put away on a shelf. "It is good to rest after such an achievement," said the paper. "It is well to contemplate what one is and what one has inside one. It is as if I only realize now what is written on me. I am getting to know myself and that is half the way to wisdom. I wonder what will happen to me now? Something even better I am sure, even more wonderful."

One day the manuscript was taken from its shelf to be burned, for the printer was not allowed to sell it to the grocer so that he could use it to wrap his wares in. It made quite a pile next to the fireplace. All the children in the house were there, they wanted to watch, see it flare up high and then slowly die until only a few embers, a few sparks, hopped out of the gray ashes, like school children hurrying home; then, when it was all over, a single last spark would fly past and that was the schoolteacher running after the children.

All the paper was thrown into the fire. *Whish!* the flames shot up, high up into the chimney. Never had the flax been as tall as it was now and never had it shone so brightly—not even when it had been white linen. All the black written letters became for a moment—as thought and words were burned—fiery red.

"Now I will become one with the sun," said a thousand voices within the flame that shot up high above the chimney stack. Lighter even than the flames, too tiny to be seen, flew the little beings. There were as many as there once had been flowers on the flax. As the paper became black ashes, they ran across it, and their footsteps were those last sparks that the children said were "school children going home." The last spark flared; it was the schoolmaster running after his pupils. The children clapped their hands and chanted:

> "Crack and break,
> Snap and bend.
> A song must end."

But the little invisible ones did not agree, they said: "No, the song never ends. That is the most wonderful part of it. We know it and that is why we are the happiest of all."

But the children didn't hear them, nor would they have understood if they had. And that is just as well, for children shouldn't know everything.

## 52

## The Bird Phoenix

In the garden of Eden, near the tree of knowledge, grew a rosebush, and here when the first rose bloomed a bird was hatched, whose flight was as swift as light, and whose colored feathers were as beautiful as its song was sweet.

But when Eve picked an apple from the tree and she and Adam were banished from the garden by an angel with a sword of flames, a spark from it fell into the bird's nest and set it on fire. The bird died in the flames, but from one of the eggs, red hot from the heat, flew a new bird, the one and only bird Phoenix. Legends tell us that it nests in Arabia, and that every century it sets fire to its own nest and dies; but from the glowing egg a new bird Phoenix flies out into the world.

Swift as light does it fly; beautiful are its colored feathers and lovely its song. When a mother sits by the cradle of her child, the bird rests on the pillow and its bright feathers make a halo around the child's head. It flies through the rooms of the poor, to shed some sunlight there and leave the fragrance of violets.

The bird Phoenix is not alone Arabia's bird. No, it can be seen flying across the snow-covered plain of Lapland, where the northern lights burn. It hops between the little flowers that bloom even during Greenland's short summer. Into the copper mines of Fahlun and the coal mines of England it flies too; in the shape of a moth, it is there when miners sing their songs and hymns. It has sailed on a lotus leaf down the holy waters of the Ganges River and the Hindu girl's eyes brighten when she sees it.

The bird Peoenix! Don't you know it? The bird of paradise, the holy bird of song. On the Thespian cart, it sat in the shape of a chattering raven and flapped its wings covered with filth. The harps of the Icelandic bards it struck disguised as a swan. On Shakespeare's shoulder it sat as one of Odin's ravens and whispered in his ears, "Immortality." Through the halls of Wartburg it flew when songs were sung.

The bird Phoenix! Don't you know it? He sang the *Marseillaise* for you and you kissed the bright feather that fell from his wing. He came in the glorious colors of paradise; but maybe you turned away to look at the sparrows instead.

The bird of paradise, reborn each century, created in flames to perish in flames, your picture hangs in the hall of the rich and the mighty, while you yourself fly lonely in the wilderness. A legend only, the bird Phoenix of Arabia.

In the garden of Eden, in paradise, you were born under the tree of knowledge while the first rose of the world bloomed. God kissed you and gave you your right name—Poetry.

## 53

## A Story

In the garden all the apple trees were blooming; they had been in such hurry to flower that they didn't have a green leaf yet. In the yard the little ducklings were waddling around; and in a corner sat the cat and licked his paws. The fields of grain were green and everywhere the sound of birds singing could be heard. Judging from their jubilant song, the day must have been a high holiday; and this was not altogether wrong, for it was Sunday. The bells in the church tower peeled and happy people dressed in their best clothes were on their way to church. The whole scene was one of joy and gaiety, and truly, on a spring day as beautiful as that day was, one could say, "How good and kind God is to man!"

But inside the church the minister stood in the pulpit preaching loudly and angrily about the impious and ungrateful behavior of men. He said that God would punish them: all men who had been evil would burn forever in the flames of hell. Their suffering would never end, eternal fires would roast them.

It was horrible to listen to; and he spoke so well, so convincingly. He described hell as a stinking cave where all the putrid waste of man was gathered; there no breezes blew to spread, even for a moment, the misty steam of sulphur. Endless, bottomless was the pit and the condemned sank slowly down through this mire in eternal silence. It was terrible to hear, but what made it worse was that the minister spoke from his heart; the whole congregation was frightened and horrified, although outside the birds were still singing as happily as before, and the sun was shining. Each of the little flowers was preaching a sermon and every one was different from the minister's; they said: "God is good and kind toward us all."

Later that evening, just before bedtime, the minister noticed that his wife looked very sad; she was sitting in a chair, staring thoughtfully down at her hands.

"What ails you?" he asked.

"What ails me?" repeated his wife, and smiled forlornly. "I cannot understand your sermon, that is what is the matter with me. No matter how much I add and subtract I do not get the same sum as you do. You said that evil men—the sinners—would burn in hell eternally; how terribly, terribly long that is. I am only a poor sinful human being and yet I could not bear to think that even the worst sinner in the whole world should burn eternally. How then do you think that God could bear it—He that is infinitely good and knows how we are tempted by evil, both from inside ourselves and from the world? I cannot imagine it, even though you have told me that it is true."

It was fall; the leaves had fallen from the trees. The minister sat by a dying woman's bed; she was his wife.

"If anyone deserved God's grace it is you, and peacefully you shall sleep in your grave," he mumbled. The woman died and he closed her eyes and folded her hands as though in prayer. Then he sang a psalm and prayed.

She was carried to her grave, and two tears ran down the cheeks of the earnest rector. His home was silent and still, there was no sunshine there, for she whom he loved had died.

It was the middle of the night; a whiff of cold air blew across the minister's face and woke him. It was as if the room were filled with moonshine, but the moon was not yet up. A specter stood by his bed, the ghost of his wife. She looked so sorrowfully at him, the minister felt that she wanted to ask him something.

He sat up in bed and stretched his arms out toward her. "Have you not found peace in your grave? Do you suffer? You, the most pious, the best of all women?"

The specter bent her head to answer, yes, and placed her hand upon her breast.

"Can I help you to obtain peace?" whispered the minister.

"Yes," answered his poor wife.

"But how?"

"Get me a hair, just one hair, from the head of a sinner who is to burn eternally in hell," pleaded the ghost.

"Yes, so easy it must be to release you from your pain, you who were so good," exclaimed the minister.

"Then follow me," commanded the ghost. "For it has been granted you that you can fly as swiftly as your thoughts, to wherever you desire to go. I shall accompany you, but before the cock crows you must have found one man who is by God condemned to the eternal fires."

Quickly, carried by thought, they were in the big city. On the walls of the houses, written in fiery letters, were the deadly sins: pride, miserliness, gluttony, the whole seven-colored rainbow of man's mortal sins.

"In there, yes, in there. Oh, if I were only sure," mumbled the minister as they stood outside the great portals of a rich man's house. Broad stairs led up to a great ballroom and the sound of dance music could be heard all the way down in the street. A servant in livery, carrying a cane with a gold knob on its end, barred the entrance to those who were not invited.

"Our ball is as elegant as the king's," he said as he looked at the mob that had gathered outside, and on his face contempt and arrogance were plainly written.

"Pride," whispered the ghost, "look at him!"

"Him!" The rector shook his head. "He is only a fool, a clown, he will not be punished in the eternal fires."

"Only a fool!" His words echoed through the house of pride, and the title fitted everyone there.

They flew through the bare rooms of the miser, where an old man lay, freezing and hungry on a rickety bed. So miserable, and yet his thoughts clung to his gold. They saw him rise and throw off his threadbare covering. With feverish, trembling hands he removed a stone in the wall, and from the hole there he took out a stocking filled with gold coins—that was its hiding place. His cold hands shook as he counted and recounted every coin.

"He is sick! It is insanity, hopeless, meaningless insanity. What fears, what evil dreams must he not experience?"

They fled and soon they stood in the large cell of a prison, where the criminals slept, side by side, on their plank beds. Like a wild animal, one of them screamed in his sleep, then he awoke and with his elbow tried to wake his neighbor.

The other man only turned while he mumbled angrily, "Shut up, you ox, and sleep! You wake me every night."

"Every night," repeated the man who had screamed. "Yes, every night I hear it howl and it comes to try to strangle me. My evil temper has led me to do wrong, and twice before have I been inside these walls. But have I not been punished! One crime, though, I have never confessed. It happened on the day when I was released from prison last. As I came past my master's house, I remembered an old insult and anger boiled within me. I took a match and struck it against the wall and set the thatched roof on fire. The house burned, for the fire had a temper like mine. I helped save the furniture and got the horses out. No living thing, man or beast, lost their lives, except for some pigeons and the old dog who was chained, I forgot him. One could hear him howling amid the flames. That howling cur I still hear every time I want to sleep; and if I finally close my eyes, then the dog comes, big and furry, and lies down upon my chest until I suffocate. . . . Listen to me! You who sleep all night while I only rest for minutes, listen!" In fury, the man threw himself upon his comrade, who had turned his back on him, and hit his face as hard as he could.

"Angry Lars has gone mad again!" shouted the other criminals as they jumped out of bed and threw themselves upon the furious man. They wrestled with him and forced his head down between his legs, and in that position they tied him up. His eyes were bloodshot and he could hardly breathe.

"You will kill him!" shouted the minister. "Poor unfortunate!" And he stretched out his arm to protect the poor sinner who suffered so.

As the night passed they flew through the halls of the rich and hovels of the poor. Envy, greed, lust: all the mortal sins they saw, and an angel read out both the men's crimes and what could be said in their defense. Often that was not much, but God, who can read our hearts and knows all, He knows too of all the evil that tempts us both from within and without. He is all mercy, all love.

The minister's hand shook; he did not dare raise it to tear a hair from the head of a sinner. He cried and tears are the waters of grace and love, and they shall put out hell's fires.

Then the cock crowed!

"Have pity, God," the minister begged, "and give her peace in her grave that I could not bring her."

"Oh, but you have," said the ghost of his wife. "For it was your hard words, your dark and severe human judgment over God and His creation, that made me come tonight. Learn to know your fellow men, for even in the most evil of them there is a godly part, which will at last become victorious and quench the fires of hell."

Someone pressed a kiss on the minister's mouth; he opened his eyes. The sun was shining into the room. There stood his wife alive and smiling at him; she had just awakened him from a dream that God had sent him.

## 54

## The Silent Album

The highway passed through a forest; in the midst of it lay a lonely
farm. The road divided the farmyard in two. The sun was shining
and all the windows were open; the place seemed very much alive.
But in the garden under a little bower of lilac trees stood an open
coffin. There were no mourners; no one stood near it shedding tears.

The dead man's face was covered with a piece of white linen and his
head rested on a big book. It was an album or, more correctly, a
herbarium, for on each of the thick gray pages of the book a different flower or plant had been pressed. Each one of them must have
been a chapter in the man's life, for it had been his wish that this
album with the dried and withered plants should be buried with him.

"Who was he?" we asked; we were travelers passing through, and
filled with curiosity.

"He was the old student from Uppsala," explained an old man who
worked on the farm. "They say that once he was respected, knew how
to speak foreign languages and write verses. But then something went
wrong, and he drank both his talent and his health away. He was
sent down here to the farm; someone paid for his keep. He was as
good and kind as a child, except when dark moods came over him.
Then he would run away into the forest like a hunted deer. We
caught him every time and brought him back. Then when we got
him into the house we would give him his album to look at, as
you give a child a picture book. He could sit all day quietly looking
at it. Sometimes tears would run down his cheeks. God knows what

he saw when he looked at those dead plants. He asked that the book be put in the coffin with him; now he has it as a pillow. In a little while the carpenter will come and nail down the lid and he, poor fellow, can sleep sweetly in his grave."

The old man lifted the linen. The dead man's face looked peacefully up at us. The sunlight played on his brow. A swallow dove down over the coffin and turned in the air, just above our heads.

How strange it is! I think we have all had the experience of reading old letters that we have received in our youth. A lost world is regained for a moment; all the expectations and all the disappointments are experienced once more. And where are all the people now who meant so much to us then? For us, they are dead, even though they are still alive, for we have forgotten them. We no longer give them a thought, though they once were so close to us that we shared our happiness and our sorrow with them.

The dried oak leaf on the gray page: had that been picked the year he graduated from school? Had it been given to him by a friend when they pledged eternal friendship? Where does that friend live now? The leaf is still there, but the friendship is gone, forgotten! Here is a plant that must have been grown in a hothouse; it is too delicate for the climate of the north. Had it been plucked in a castle garden? Had he received it from the hand of a young noblewoman? The white water lily on the next page I am sure he picked himself and watered with many a salt tear. Here is a nettle, why had he picked that? What could it have reminded him of? A lily of the valley, that flower grows in the loneliest spots. On the next page a leaf from a honeysuckle. Had it been plucked from one of the potted plants that cover the window sills of an inn? On the last page is a single blade of grass, why that?

The fragrant lilac branches, heavy with flowers, shade the dead man's coffin. The swallow flies by again. It darts through the bower singing: "Tweet . . . tweet."

Here comes the carpenter, with hammer and nails; he will close the coffin. Inside lies the dead man, his head resting on the book that is now forever silent. Gone—forgotten!

## 55

## The Old Gravestone

In one of the smaller towns in Denmark, one evening in August, the whole family was gathered in the living room of the home of one of the wealthier citizens. The weather outside was still summer-mild, but the evenings had begun to grow darker; the lamp had been lighted and the curtains drawn, so only the flowers on the window sill enjoyed the moonlight. The conversation was about an old stone that lay out in the yard. The children liked to play upon it, and the maids, when the sun shone, put the newly polished copper pots and pans out to dry on it. It had once been a gravestone.

"Yes," said the husband, "I believe it comes from the old cloister church. When it was torn down, everything was sold: the pulpit and gravestones—the whole lot. My father bought some of them and had them broken up to use as filling in the road; that old stone was left over and it has been lying in the yard ever since."

"You can see that it has been a gravestone," said one of the older children. "You can still make out an hourglass and part of an angel. But the names of the dead are almost gone. When the stones have been washed by the rain you can see the name Preben and the letter S. A little further down is carved the name Martha."

"Goodness me, it must be old Preben Svane's and his wife Martha's gravestone," exclaimed an old, old man who was old enough to be grandfather to anyone in the room. "Yes, they were among the last to be buried in the churchyard of the old cloister. They were a fine old couple, I remember them, I was a boy then. Everybody knew them and everybody liked them. They were the oldest couple in the town! People said that they were rich and had more than one barrel filled with gold in the cellar. They were always simply dressed, in homespun cloth, but their linen was clean and shiny white. They were a nice old couple, Preben and Martha. I remember them sitting on the little bench that stood at the top of the stone staircase that led to the entrance of their house. A big linden tree grew nearby and its branches shaded the old people. They would smile and nod so kindly to you that you could not help but feel happier because of it. They were marvelously kind to the poor, helped them with both food and clothes. They were true Christians in their charity, and very sensible, too.

"The wife died first. I remember that day well, I was a little boy and my father had taken me along to visit old Preben. The old man was crying like a little child.—The body of his wife was still lying in the bedroom—he talked about how lonely he would be now, and how good and kind his wife had been. Then he told us how they had met and fallen in love with each other so very many years ago. As I have already said, I was only a little boy then, but it moved me strangely to hear the old man and watch how his cheeks grew rosy and his eyes lively as he talked about his engagement, and the innocent little tricks he had played, just so that they could meet each other. When he talked about his wedding day, one could almost believe from looking at him that he was back in that time of happiness and hope. While in the little room nearby lay his wife; she was dead, and he was a very old man. Well, that is life. Then I was a child and now I am old, as old as Preben Svane was. Time never stops and only change is constant.

"I remember his wife's funeral; old Preben walked behind the coffin. A few years before they had had their gravestone made, then their names had been cut into the stone, everything but the dates of death. That evening the stone was put on the grave, and the following year another date was inscribed and old Preben was laid to rest underneath it. The riches, those barrels of gold that people had talked so much about—well, they were never found. Some nephews and nieces who lived in another town inherited what there was. Their house under the linden tree with the stone stairs and the little bench was torn down by order of the town council because it was so dilapidated, it could be dangerous. The old cloister church had the same fate, and when the churchyard finally was closed and no longer was called holy ground, then all the gravestones were sold to anyone who cared to buy them. Most of them were used to pave roads. Chance saved Martha's and Preben's gravestone and made it a place where pots and pans are put out to dry and children play. I think the new road goes right over the old people's grave. No one remembers them any more." The old man shook his head sadly. "They are forgotten, just as everything else will be forgotten."

The conversation in the room turned to other subjects, but the youngest child, a boy with big, thoughtful eyes, climbed up on a chair and looked through the window down into the yard. The moonlight fell on the stone; he had never thought about it before as anything but a flat stone. Now it seemed to him like a page from a story book. All that the child had heard about Preben and wife seemed to be inside the stone. He looked down at it once more and then up at the full moon. The night was clear and the moon was the face of a God shining down upon the earth.

"Yes, everything will be forgotten," someone in the room said.

Just at that moment an angel kissed the boy's head and whispered to him: "Keep this little seed, keep it until it has become ripe. For you, my child, shall rewrite the faded inscription on the old gravestone so that, golden and clear, it will be able to be read by coming generations. The old couple shall again walk down the streets of the town, smiling with fresh rosy cheeks; they shall sit on their little bench nodding to everyone, rich or poor, who passes by. The seed planted in your soul this night shall grow and produce poetry. For all that is truly good and all that is truly beautiful on this earth is not forgotten, it lives in songs and legends."

## 56

## There Is a Difference

It was in the month of May; the wind was still a bit cool, but all the trees and bushes agreed that spring had finally come. The fields and meadows were filled with flowers; and in the hedge, along the road, stood a small apple tree and proclaimed that spring was truly here. One of its branches—but only one—was flowering. Its pinkish-white buds had almost opened. The branch knew very well how beautiful it looked and therefore it was not surprised when the carriage from the castle stopped near it.

The young countess declared that the branch of the apple tree was the very image of spring and very lovely. The branch was broken off the tree and given to the countess. She held it carefully in her hands, shading it under her parasol, all the way back to the castle. There it was carried through long corridors and pretty rooms into the great hall. The tall windows were open and the white muslin curtains swayed gently in the breeze. The hall was filled with flowers that stood in crystal vases. One of the vases looked as if it had been cut out of new-fallen snow; into that the apple branch was put together with some beech branches with pale green leaves; it was a joy to look at them.

The apple branch grew proud and that was very human of it!

There were lots of people coming and going through the hall and, according to their rank, they spoke and commented upon the beauty of the flowers. Some did not dare say anything at all and others spoke a little too much and too long. It did not take long for the apple branch to understand that there was a difference between people as there was between plants.

"Some are born to be beautiful, others to be useful, and some we could very well do without," said the apple branch confidently.

The vase was standing by the open window, and therefore the apple branch had all the opportunity it could wish for to see and contemplate the other trees and plants in the garden. There were both rich and poor plants, and some that were much too poor.

"The poor neglected herbs!" said the apple branch. "What a difference is made between myself and them! How wretched they must feel, knowing how low their position is—that is, if they can feel, as we higher plants can. But there must be a difference, or everybody would be equal."

The apple branch glanced with most pity down at the flowers in the ditches and the fields. There was one flower that the branch felt particularly sorry for, a most common little plant that seemed to grow everywhere. It was much too ordinary ever to be taken inside and put in a vase. Why, it even grew between the cobblestones. It was the dandelion; and in Denmark it is called by that ugly name, "the devil's milk pail."

"Poor despised little plant," moaned the apple branch. "It is not your fault that you are what you are, that you are so wretchedly common and have been given such a dreadful nickname. But there must be a difference among plants as among men."

"'Difference!'" mocked the sun rays, and kissed both the blossoms of the apple branch and the little yellow dandelion flowers in fields. They did not distinguish between the rich flowers and the poor ones.

The apple branch had never thought of God's love for everything living on this earth. It had never even considered the possibility that much of the good and beautiful could be hidden, but because of that it was not necessarily forgotten, and least of all by God. In this, too, the branch was quite human.

The sun rays knew better. "You do not see very clearly or very far," they said. "What plant is it you feel so sorry for?"

"The dandelion, the one they call the devil's milk pail," answered the apple branch. "No one ever picks it to make a bouquet. People step on it. There are too many dandelions. When they go to seed, they fly with the wind, like tufts of wool, and get into people's clothes.

They are just weeds! I suppose there have to be weeds, but I am very grateful that I was not born one of them."

A group of children came across the field; the smallest among them were so tiny that they could not walk, and they were carried by the older ones. In the middle of the field the little ones were put down on the grass to play. They laughed and tumbled and picked the yellow dandelion flowers, kissing them sweetly and innocently. The older children made golden chains out of the flowers and decorated themselves with them. First they made chains to put on their heads like crowns; then longer ones to hang around the neck, and finally, belts. They looked very lovely. Two of the older children had carefully picked a dandelion that had turned to seed; the fine down that would carry seeds out into the world was all there. The dandelions looked like two little airy summer snowballs. The children held them close to their mouths and then they blew as hard as they could. Now if they could blow off all the seeds in one puff, then they would get new clothes that year, so their grandmother had told them. The despised flower was really a prophet.

"There!" said the sun rays. "Do you now see their beauty, their power?"

"Only children care for them," replied the apple branch.

An old woman came out in the field where the children were playing. She dug up the dandelions by the roots with a handleless knife. Some of these roots she would cook, to make what was called a "poor man's coffee." The others she would sell to the apothecary, for the dandelion root is used in medicine.

"But beauty is even more important," argued the apple branch. "Only the most select are allowed into the kingdom of beauty. There is a difference among plants, as there is among men."

The sun rays talked about God's love for the world He had created and for all living things, and how everyone is equal, seen through the eyes of eternity.

"Well, that is your opinion," retorted the apple branch.

Some people entered the hall. Among them was the young countess who had put the apple branch in the crystal vase, where it stood so beautifully with the sunlight falling on it. She was carrying something very gingerly in her hands. Whatever it was, you could not see it, for she had constructed a cone of green leaves around it to protect it from the wind and drafts. She carried it much more carefully than she had carried the beautiful apple branch. Gently she removed the big leaves. She was holding a dandelion flower that had gone to seed, a "devil's milk pail." She had picked it and carried it so carefully so that not one of the seeds would be lost; they were all there, making a perfect crown of white mist. She admired its beautiful form, its airy clearness, its complex pattern, created as it was so that each seed—every down—was free to follow the wind.

"Look how beautifully God has made it," she said. "I want to paint it standing next to the apple branch. That everyone admits is beautiful, but the little, common flower God has given a lovely form too. They are different, but they are both children of beauty."

The sun rays kissed the dandelion flower and they kissed the apple branch, causing its flowers to blush a little.

## 57

## The World's Most Beautiful Rose

There once was a mighty queen in whose garden grew the most beautiful flowers. Every season there were some in bloom, and they had been collected in all the countries of the world. But roses she loved above all flowers, and in her garden were many kinds, from the wild hedge rose with green leaves that smell like apples to the loveliest rose of Provence. Roses grew up the walls of the castle, twined themselves around the marble columns, and even entered the halls and corridors of the castle, where their ramblers crept across the ceilings and filled the rooms with the fragrance of their flowers.

But inside the castle sorrow lived, for the queen was dying. The wisest of all the doctors who were attending her said, "There is only one remedy that can save her. Bring her the world's most beautiful rose, the one that symbolizes the highest and purest love, and when her eyes see that flower, then she will not die."

The young and the old brought their roses—the most beautiful ones that grew in their gardens—but it was not such a flower that could cure the queen. From love's garden the rose must be brought, but which flower would be the symbol of the highest and purest love?

The poets sang of the world's most beautiful rose, and each mentioned a different one. Word was sent to all, regardless of rank and class, whose hearts did beat for love.

"No one has as yet mentioned the right flower," said the wise man. "No one has pointed to that place where it grows, in all its glory and beauty. It is not the rose from Romeo's and Juliet's tomb or Valborg's grave, though those roses will always bloom and shed their fragrance in stories and poetry. Nor is it the rose that blooms on Winkelried's blood-covered lance. From the hero's blood, shed in defense of his native land, the reddest rose springs; and it is said that such a death is sweet, but it is not the most beautiful rose in the world. The magical wonderful rose, which can only be grown under constant care, through days and years and sleepless nights: the rose of science, it is not either."

"I know where it blooms," exclaimed a happy mother who, carrying her babe, had entered the queen's bedchamber. "I know where the world's most beautiful rose is to be found, the rose of the highest and purest love. It blooms on the cheeks of my child, when he wakes from his sleep and laughs up at me, with all his love."

"Yes, in truth, that rose is lovely, but there are those even more beautiful," said the wise man.

"Yes, far more beautiful," said one of the ladies in waiting. "I have seen it, and a more exalted, sacred rose than that does not exist. It is as pale as the petals of a tea rose and I have seen it on our queen's cheeks when, without her golden crown, she walked, carrying her sick child in her arms, back and forth across the room one whole long night. She kissed her babe and prayed to God as only a mother prays in her agony."

"Yes, wonderful and holy is the white rose of sorrow, but that is not the one."

"No, the world's most beautiful rose I saw before the altar of Our Lord," a pious old priest said. "I saw it shine on an angel's face. Among a group of young girls who had come to take communion, there was one who looked with such simple and innocent a love up toward her God that on her face bloomed the rose of the highest and purest love."

"Blessed is that rose too," said the wise man. "But none of you has yet mentioned the world's most beautiful rose."

At that moment into the room stepped a little boy, the queen's son. His eyes were filled with tears and he was carrying a big book with silver clasps and bound in vellum. The book was open.

"Mother!" said the little one. "Listen to what I have read." And the child sat down by his mother's bedside and read about Him who suffered death on the Cross in order to save humanity. "Greater love there cannot be."

The queen's pale cheeks took on a pinkish shade, and her eyes became big and clear, as from the pages of the book grew the world's most beautiful rose, the one that grew from Christ's blood on the Cross.

"I see it," she said. "'And those who have seen that rose, the most beautiful in the world, shall never die.'"

## 58

## *The Year's Story*

It was one of the last days in January; there was a horrible snow-storm. The wind was whirling the snow through the streets and lanes of the town. The windows of the houses were so covered with snow that you could not see through them, and from the roofs little avalanches fell down into the streets. People could hardly walk against the wind; and if they had it behind them, it was almost worse, for then they had to run. When two people met they held onto each other in order not to fall. All the carriages and horses were covered with snow, it looked as if they had been powdered; and the servants who stood on the backs of the carriages bent their knees, in order not to be so tall that their faces got whipped by the wind. The pedestrians walked as close to the carriages as they could, to get a bit of protection from the wind; they could easily keep up with them, for the vehicles could not drive very fast. When the storm finally died down, a narrow path was shoveled along the sidewalks. Every time two people met, they paused, for the path was too narrow for them to pass each other. Which one was to be polite and step into the snowbank, that was the question. Uusally neither of them was willing to get his feet wet in order that the other man could keep his dry. Silently, they faced each other, until by some unspoken agreement both of them would sacrifice one foot by putting it into the deep snow.

Toward evening the wind disappeared completely; the heavens looked as if they had been swept, and the stars shone as if they had been newly minted. Some of them had a blue tinge to them. And it froze. In the morning the snow had formed a crust strong enough to bear the weight of a sparrow. There were enough of them; they hopped around on the snow and on the shoveled path, but they couldn't find much to eat, and all of them froze.

"Peep!" said one sparrow to another. "So that is what they call the New Year! Why, it is worse than the old one; we might as well have kept it. I am very dissatisfied and I have good reasons for being so."

"Yes, all the human beings were lighting firecrackers to celebrate the New Year," piped a particularly cold little sparrow. "They were so happy to get rid of the Old Year that I expected that the weather would get warm. But what happened! It is colder now than ever. I think the calendar is not working."

"You are so right," said a third sparrow. He was old and had a tuft of white on top of his head. "It is their own invention, the calendar; they believe that everything obeys it. But they are wrong. I go by nature's calendar and, according to that, the New Year starts when Spring comes."

"But when does Spring come?" asked all the other sparrows.

"Spring comes when the stork comes back. But he is not very dependable. Here in the city he never shows himself, he prefers the country. Let us fly out there and wait for him; Spring is always a little closer out there."

"That is all very well," said a little sparrow that had been peeping all the time without really saying anything. "But in the city one has certain conveniences that I am afraid I shall miss in the country. The family who live in a house near here have hung little wooden boxes on the walls for us to nest in. My husband and I have made our home in one, and there we have brought up our children. I know the family have done it in order to have the pleasure of seeing us fly about; I am sure they wouldn't have done it otherwise. They throw bread crumbs out, too. It amuses them and gives us a living. We feel we are being taken care of. That is why my husband and I will stay here; not that we are satisfied, mind you, we certainly are not! But we will stay."

"And we shall fly out to the country and see if Spring isn't coming soon," said the others; and away they flew.

It certainly was colder out in the country than it had been in the city; at least, a couple of degrees. The wind was as sharp as a knife when it blew across the snow-covered fields. The farmer, driving in his sleigh, would slap his hands on his back to keep them warm, and that even though he had woolen mittens on. The whip lay in his lap and his lean horses ran so fast that steam rose from their sweaty flanks.

The sparrows jumped about in the sleigh track and froze. "Tweet . . . Peep!" they said. "When does Spring come? Why does it take so long?"

"So long, so long." The words seemed to echo across the fields. Where did the voice come from? Were the words spoken by that strange old man who was sitting in the middle of the big snowdrift over there? A long white beard, he had, and frosty silver hair; he was dressed in a white cloak like the ones the peasants used to wear. His cheeks were pale but his eyes were clear.

"Who is that old fellow?" asked the sparrows.

"I know who he is," answered an old raven who was sitting on a fence post. Since we are all small birds in the eyes of God—and the raven knew it—he condescended to answer the sparrows' question. "I know the old man! It is Winter: the old fellow from last year. He didn't die on the first of January, just because the calendar said so. No, he is the guardian of the little prince, Spring. He is the governor. Oh, it is so cold! You little birds must be freezing."

"That is what I said," piped the smallest of the sparrows. "That calendar is only a human invention. It doesn't fit nature. They should have let us figure it out, we are more delicately created."

A week went by and then another. The forest was black and the little lake was frozen. It looked as if it were not water but lead. The clouds were not real clouds but more like frozen bits of fog hanging over the landscape. The crows flew in flocks but did not scream. It was as if the world slept. Suddenly a ray of sunlight fell upon the ice of the frozen lake and the surface looked like melting tin. The snow on the fields and the hills looked a little different; it didn't sparkle any more. But the white figure, the old man, still sat on top of the snow-dirft and looked toward the south. He did not seem to be aware that the blanket of snow that covered the ground was slowly melting and seeping into the earth. A little patch of green appeared and here all the sparrows gathered.

"Tweet . . . Peep! Spring is coming!" they shouted.

"Spring, Spring!" The word traveled across the fields and meadows, through the black-brownish woods, where the moss that grew on the tree trunks already was green. From the south, flying through the air, came the first two storks of the year. On the back of each rode a little child: a girl and a boy. They kissed the earth and, wherever they walked, snowdrops bloomed in the snow. Hand in hand, they went over to old man Winter, greeted him and embraced him; at that moment they were all three hidden in a heavy fog. It spread and covered the whole landscape: everything! Then the wind began to blow; first weakly, making the fog dance like a curtain, then more strongly, until it had swept the fog and mist away. Warmly the sun shone. Winter, the old man, had gone; the children of Spring now sat on the throne of the year.

"That is what I call a proper New Year," said the sparrows. "Now we will have our rights back and compensation for all we have suffered this winter."

Wherever the two children went, green buds appeared on the bushes and trees. The grass in the meadows grew taller and taller. The little girl carried flowers in her apron, and these she threw all about her as she walked; but no matter how many she cast, her little apron was full as ever. In her eagerness she shook her apron over the apple trees, so that they were filled with flowers long before they had green leaves; they looked almost as if they had been covered by snow.

She clapped her hands and the boy clapped his, and birds came, no one knew from where, and they all sang and twittered: "Spring has come!"

It was lovely to watch! Many an old granny came outside in the sunshine; how nice and warm it was. Down in the meadow all the yellow flowers bloomed just as they had when she was a girl. "The world is young again," she thought; and said, "What a blessed day it is!"

The woods were still a brownish green, and every branch was covered with buds. But down among the roots the fragrant woodruff grew, and violets and tender anemones. Each blade of grass was filled with power. Oh yes, the earth was covered by the most elegant carpet, and on it sat Spring's young couple and held hands. They sang and laughed; and grew and grew.

A mild rain fell, but the young ones did not notice it, for who can distinguish between raindrops and the tears of happiness? The bride and the bridegroom kissed each other; and at the moment the buds on the trees burst, and when the sun rose all the woods were green.

Hand in hand, Spring's children walked beneath the new green roof of the forest, where the fleeting shadows caused shadings in the greenness. Each leaf had a maiden's innocence. The river and the brooks sang as their clear water rushed across stones, coloring the gravel. All nature seemed to shout of its own eternity, and the cuckoo and the lark sang. It was a beautiful spring, only the willow tree was cautious; it was wearing woolen mittens on its flowers.

Days passed and weeks passed; great waves of heat came rolling from the south and turned the wheat yellow. In the little lakes in the woods, the big leaves of the northern lotus spread themselves out over the still waters; and the fishes would swim underneath them, enjoying their shade. Ripe, juicy, almost black cherries hung from the trees and all the rosebushes were blooming. The sun baked the cottage walls. There on the south side, on a bench, sat Summer. She was a beautiful woman; maybe even lovelier than she had been, when last we saw her, as the young bride of Spring. She is looking toward the horizon where black clouds are building a mountain range all the way up to the sun. Like a petrified black-blue ocean, the clouds swallow up the sky. In the forest, not a bird is singing. Nature is silent. No breezes blow, everything is still, locked in expectancy. But along roads and paths everyone is hurrying, and that whether they are walking, riding, or driving in a carriage. They have one thought, all of them, and that is to seek shelter.

Suddenly a great light bursts forth, blinding and sharper than the sun's. Then again darkness, followed by the noise of a great thunderclap. The rain pours down. Light and darkness, silence and thunder alternate. In the marshes the young reeds, with their brown featherlike tops, sway and roll like waves on an ocean. The branches of the trees are hidden behind sheets of water, and the grain on the field lies prostrate flat on the ground. It looks as though it could never raise itself up again.

But as suddenly as the thunderstorm came it is gone. A few single drops of rain fall, and then the sun breaks through the clouds. To every straw and leaf pearly drops of water cling. Again the birds are singing, and in the pools in the woods the fishes are leaping, while mosquitoes fly in swarms above the water. On a boulder on the beach sits Summer. He is a powerful man; his arms and legs are muscular. His hair is wet from the shower. He stretches himself; he and all the nature around him seem rejuvenated by the bath. Summer is strength and fertility, the crowning of hopes.

Sweet was the fragrance of the field of flowering clover. The bees flew across it; in the center lay some stones. In Viking times it had been a holy place. Blackberry brambles now covered the altar stone. Here the queen bee and her court built a castle of wax and filled it with honey. Only Summer and his wife saw it; and truly, it was for their sake that the offering was laid on the altar stone.

When the sun set, the evening sky shone more golden than any church cupola, and from the pale darkness of the summer night the moon looked down.

Weeks went by, and days. The farmers began to harvest, and their sharp scythes glistened in the sunlight as they reaped the grain. The branches of the apple trees bent toward the ground, heavy with red and yellow fruit. The hops smelled sweetly. Under the hazelnut bushes, filled with nuts, rested a man and a woman: Summer and his grave and beautiful wife.

"What richness," she sighed, "a blessed homely wealth, and yet I long for something else, I do not know what it is. Rest? Peace? No, it is neither, and more than both, that I wish for! Look, they are plowing again. Man always wants more; he is never satisfied. The storks are flying in flocks now, following the plowman. The bird from Egypt that carried us through the air. Do you remember when we, as children, came here to the north? We brought sunshine and flowers and the green woods. The wind is turning them yellow and brown now, like southern trees; but here they do not bear golden fruits."

"You shall see them," said Summer. "Be happy!" And he spread out his arms toward the woods, and its leaves turned red and golden. The fruit of the wild rose shone red on its brambles and the elderberries hung like black grapes from the trees. The wild chestnuts fell out of their blackish-green shells; and deep in the forest the violets flowered once again.

The queen of the year grew more and more silent and thoughtful. "The evening air is cold," she said, and her cheeks grew pale. "The night mist is damp! I long for the land of my childhood."

She watched the storks fly south, following each one with her eyes until it disappeared. She looked up at the empty nest; a cornflower grew in one of them, as though the nest were there for its protection; then the sparrows came visiting.

"The noble owners have left," they mocked as they searched the nest for something eatable. "I guess they couldn't take a bit of wind; it was too much for them, and so they left. Well, a pleasant journey is all I can wish them. Tweet!"

The leaves turned more and more yellow, and soon the tree would stand naked again. The harvest was over and the fall storms had begun. On a bed of yellow leaves lay the queen of the year; she looked toward the twinkling stars; the sun had set. Her husband stood near her. The wind rustled the leaves and she was gone. A butterfly, the last of the year, flew through the cold air.

From the sea drifted the wet and cold autumn fogs; the long nights of winter had begun. The king of the year stood with snow-white hair, and the first snow of the year covered the fields. The church bell rang the joyous message of Christmas.

"The bells are ringing to celebrate the birth of the New Year," said the king of the year. "Soon they will come, the new king and queen, and I shall be allowed to rest, as she does now. Rest and find peace in the stars."

Out in the forest, among the pine and spruce trees, walked the Christmas angel; she consecrated those trees that were to take part in the feast.

"May you bring happiness and joy," said the king of the Old Year. The last few weeks had made an ancient man of him; his hair was no longer white but silver, like the frost. "Soon I shall rest. The new rulers are now receiving their scepter and their crown."

"But still the power is yours, not theirs," said the angel of Christmas. "You must rule, not rest. Let the snow lay like a warm blanket over the young grain. Learn to bear the burden it is to rule, while others are praised and honored; and yet you are still master. Learn to be forgotten while you live! The hour of your freedom will come when Spring comes."

"And when does Spring come?" asked Winter.

"When the first storks arrive," answered the angel.

With silver hair and snow-white beard, Winter sat and waited; old but not decrepit, strong as the winter storms and the all-powerful ice. He sat on his snowbank and looked toward the south, as Winter had done the year before.

The ice on lakes and fjords groaned and the snow creaked when you walked on it. The children were skating. The ravens and crows looked very decorative on the white background. Everything was still, not a wind stirred. Winter clenched his hands, and the thickness of the ice grew by inches, every night.

The sparrows came flying out from town and asked, "Who is that old man over there?"

And the raven who sat on the fence post—it was either the same as last year or his son—answered, "It is Winter. The old fellow is not dead as the calendar says. He is the guardian for the New Year, for Spring, who will soon be here."

"When does Spring come?" asked the sparrows. "Then we will get a decent government, the last one was no good!"

Deep in thought, Winter nodded toward the naked, leafless forest, where every branch, every trunk, showed its graceful forms. An ice-cold mist covered all. Winter, the master of the world, was dreaming of his youth, his manhood. When the sun rose, the forest was clad in ice, the white frost decked each branch, each twig. It was Winter's dream of Summer. The sunlight melted the ice, and it fell from the branches, down onto the snow.

"When is Spring coming?" asked the sparrows.

"Spring, Spring!" came the echo from the drifts of snow; and the sun grew warmer and warmer.

The snow was melting and the birds sang, "Spring is coming!"

The storks flew high in the air: the first of the year. On their backs rode two lovely children; the birds landed on a field. The children kissed the earth and embraced old man Winter, and like a mist he disappeared. The year's story had ended!

"It is all very true," said the sparrows. "And it is a pretty story, but that's not what the calendar says, and that is what counts in his world."

## 59

## On the Last Day

The most sacred of all the days of our life is the day we die. It is holy, it is the great day of change, of transformation. Have you ever seriously thought about the hour that is certain to come and will be your last hour on earth?

There once was a man. He was "strong in the faith," as they say. He was a warrior for God and His Word, a zealous servant of a zealous God. Death was now standing by his bed. Solemnly Death looked at him and said: "The hour has come for you to follow me." And he touched the man's feet with his ice-cold hand and they turned cold. He touched his forehead, then his chest; the man's heart ceased to beat and his soul followed the angel of Death.

But in the few seconds that passed between Death's fingers touching his feet and his chest, the dying man experienced everything that life had given him. Like a great wave of the ocean, it engulfed him. He felt as you do when you stand on a mountaintop and can see the whole valley below you; or as on a starlit night, when with one glance you can take in the whole universe.

At such a moment the sinner trembles with fear. He has no one to lean on and he sinks into the void. The pious man leans on God and says with the innocence of a child: "Thy will be done."

But this dying man had not a child's faith, he had a man's. He did not shiver as a sinner would have, for he knew that he had been faithful. His life had been guided by the strictest religious doctrines. He knew that millions of people walked the broad highway of sin that leads to the everlasting doom, and he would willingly have punished their bodies with fire and sword, as he knew their souls were destined to suffer eternally. His road was toward heaven, where the grace that had been promised him would open the great doors.

As his soul followed the angel of Death, he looked back for a moment at his own dead clay, this strange, now already foreign shell of his ego. They flew and they walked. They were in a gigantic hall or a forest, it was as if nature had been pruned, cut, formalized in squares and rows as in a French garden. Here a masquerade seemed to be taking place.

"This is humanity!" said the angel of Death.

They were wearing costumes. Not all the rich and mighty were dressed in silk and gold, nor were all the poor in ragged clothes. It was a strange masquerade. All the people partaking in it seemed to be hiding something under their clothes; everyone seemed to have something he felt ashamed of, but which the others wanted revealed, so they could see it. They tore at one another's clothes, while at the same time everyone tried to protect his own secret. Every once in a while, peeping out from under a cloak or a robe would be the grinning head of an ape or a goat, or the slimy body of a snake or a fish.

That was the animal, the beast we all carry within us, which grows and becomes part of our bodies and wants to come out and be seen. And though everyone held his clothes about him as tightly as he could, the others tried to pull them aside, screaming and pointing. "Look! Look at her! Look at him!" Each revealed the other's misery.

"And what kind of animal lives within me?" asked the dead man. The angel of Death pointed to a proud man who stood apart from the others. Above his head was a many-colored halo, but near the heart of the man the animal's feet protruded! Peacock's feet, and the halo was the bird's tail.

As they proceeded on their journey the trees grew taller. In them sat strange birds that cried with human voices, "You, Death's companion, do you remember us?" They were the evil thoughts, the evil desires he had had on earth.

For a moment the soul shivered in fear, for he did recognize the voices, his evil thoughts, the desires that now came to bear witness against him.

"In our flesh, in our evil nature, no goodness lives," said the soul. "But my thoughts never became deeds! The world never saw their evil fruits!" He walked on in haste to escape the large black birds, but they circled about him in flocks, screaming so loudly that the whole world could hear them. He ran like a wounded deer, but now the ground seemed covered with sharp flint stones which cut and hurt his feet.

"Where do these sharp stones that lie like dead leaves on the earth come from?"

"Each one is a thoughtless word that you have uttered and which hurt your neighbor's heart far more than they now hurt your feet."

"I never thought about that," admitted the soul of the dead man.

"Judge not and you shall not be judged!" The words rang through the heavens.

"We have all sinned," whispered the soul, but then he said with a more forceful voice: "But I have kept the law and lived according to the gospels. I did try, I am not like the others."

At last they arrived at the gate of heaven; the angel who guarded it asked: "Who are you? Tell me the creed you believed in and what deeds you have done."

"I have kept all the commandments. I have humbled myself in the eyes of the world. I have hated evil and those men who were evil. Those who walked the broad highway of sin I have pursued with fire and sword and would do so today if I could."

"You are one of the followers of Mohammed?" asked the angel.

"No! Never!" shouted the soul.

"He that lives by the sword shall perish by the sword, the Son of God has said. It cannot be he you worship. Are you one of the Children of Israel who believes as Moses did: 'An eye for an eye and a tooth for a tooth?' A son of Israel whose jealous God cares only for His people?"

"I am a Christian."

"That I would not have guessed either from your faith or from your deeds. Christ teaches redemption, love, and mercy."

"Mercy, mercy!" The words rang through the eternal never ending heavens, and the doors opened for the soul to enter.

But the light that came from inside was so sharp, so penetrating, that the soul drew back and did not dare enter. The music was so soft, so sweet, so touching, that no human tongue could describe it. The soul bowed down lower and lower as the godly wisdom entered him;

and at last he felt what he had never felt before: the burden of his own arrogance, hardness, and sin. Now he finally understood.

"What good I did in the world I did because I could not do otherwise, but the evil—that I chose to do myself."

The soul was blinded by the heavenly light; weak and faint, it fell, it was not yet wise enough to enter the kingdom of heaven. He remembered his own belief in God's justice and righteousness and did not dare to beg for mercy.

At that moment he received God's grace, His unexpected mercy.

God's heaven was everywhere in the endless space, God's love filled everything.

"Holy, glorious, loving, and eternal is the human soul," said a voice and the angels sang the message.

Every one of us will on the last day and hour of life here on earth draw back in fear and humility from the glory and splendor of heaven. We will fall; but His grace will support us and our souls will fly in new orbits, nearer and nearer the eternal light, His mercy will give us the strength to understand the final, godly, eternal wisdom.

## 60

## It Is Perfectly True!

"It is a monstrous story!" said a hen. She lived in a part of the town far away from where the event had taken place. "It is a horrible story and it has happened in a henhouse. I am glad that I am not sleeping alone on the perch tonight. I would not dare close my eyes!"

And then she told the story. The other hens were so shocked that their feathers stood up, and the rooster's comb fell down. It is perfectly true!

But we will start at the beginning and that took place in another corner of the town in a henhouse. The sun had just set and all the hens had flown up on their roost. Among them was a white-feathered hen with stumpy legs; she laid an egg every day and was very respectable. Now as she sat down on her perch she picked at her feathers a bit, and one little feather fell out.

"There it went," she said. "The more I pick myself, the more beautiful I will become." This was said for fun, for she was a cheerful soul, though otherwise—as I have already said—very respectable. It was dark on the perch; the hens sat roosting side by side, but the hen that sat nearest to the one who had lost a feather wasn't asleep. She had heard what had been said and she hadn't; and that is a very wise thing to do if you want to live in peace with your neighbors. But still she could not help telling the hen next to her what she had heard.

"Did you hear what was said? I won't mention names, but there is a hen among us who is going to pluck her feathers off just to look more attractive. If I were a rooster I would despise her!"

Right above the henhouse lived an owl family; and they have sharp ears. They heard every word that the hen had said and the mother owl rolled her eyes and beat her wings. "Don't listen, but I suppose you couldn't help but hear it. I heard it with my own ears and one has to hear a lot before they fall off. There is one of the hens in the henhouse that has so forgotten all decency and propriety that she is sitting on the perch and picking off all her feathers, while the rooster is looking at her."

*"Prenez garde aux enfants!"* said the father owl. "It is not fit for the children to hear!"

"But I will tell our neighbor about it," said the mother. "She is such a courteous owl. I hold her in the highest esteem." And away she flew.

"Tu-whit! Tu-whoo!" both the owls hooted, and so loudly that the pigeons could not help hearing it. "Have you heard, have you heard! Tu-whoo! There is a hen that has plucked all her feathers off for the rooster's sake. She will freeze to death, if she hasn't already, tu-whoo!"

"Where? Where?" cooed the pigeons.

"In the neighboring yard! I have almost seen it with my own eyes. It is a most indecent story, but it is perfectly true."

"True, true, every word," cooed the pigeons, and repeated the story in their own henhouse. "There is a hen—some say that there are two—that have plucked all their feathers off in order to look different and in that way gain the attention of the rooster. They have played a dangerous game, for one can catch a cold that way and die of fever; and they are dead, both of them!"

"Wake up! Wake up!" crowed the cock, and flew up on the fence. Sleep was still in his eyes, but he crowed anyway. "Three hens have died of unrequited love for a rooster! They have plucked all their feathers off. It is a nasty story. I won't keep it, pass it on!"

"Pass it on, pass it on," piped the bats. And the hens clucked and the roosters crowed: "Pass it on, pass it on." And in this manner the story went from henhouse to henhouse until it arrived back at the very place where it had started.

"There are five hens, so it is said, that have all plucked their feathers off to prove which one of them had become thinnest because of unhappy love for the rooster. Then they pecked each other until blood flowed and they all fell down dead! It's a shame for their families and a great loss to their owner."

The hen who had lost the first little feather naturally did not recognize the story; and as she was a decent and respectable hen, she said, "I despise those hens! But there are more of that kind! Such things must not be kept secret! I will do whatever I can to have it printed in the newspaper, then the whole country will hear about it. And that is what those hens and their families deserve."

And it was published in the newspaper and it is perfectly true that one little feather can become five hens!

## 61

## The Swans' Nest

Between the Baltic and the North Sea lies an old swans' nest called Denmark. In that have been and will be hatched swans whose fame will never die.

In ancient times one flock of swans flew across the Alps down to the green plains of the land of eternal May, where it is pleasant to live. That flock of swans were called Lombards.

Another flock flew to Byzantium. Shiny white were their feathers and faithful their eyes; around the emperor's throne they gathered and their great wings were like shields that guarded and protected him. They were given the name of Varangians.

From France came screams of terror and fear. Bloodthirsty swans with fiery wings had come from the north and the people prayed: "Free us, O Lord, from the wild Normans."

On the green fields of England, by the open sea, stood the trebly crowned Danish swan, holding his golden scepter out over the country.

The heathens on the coast of Pomerania fell on their knees when the Danish swans came, sword in hand, carrying the flag of the cross.

"That was all in ancient, bygone times!" you may object.

But also in an age not so distant from our own has a swan flown from the nest, and as it flew through the air it illuminated it and the light spread over all countries. It was as if the beat of its wings caused a mist to disperse, and all the stars in the sky became clearer and more visible to our eyes, as if the heavens had come closer to our earth. That swan was Tycho Brahe.

"That, too, is long ago!" I hear you say. "What about now in our times?" We have seen swans, too, fly with powerful wings high up in the sky. One touched, with his wings, the golden harp, and the music resounded through the north. The stark mountains of Norway rose high in the light from an ancient sun. The gods of the north and the heroes and heroines from the Viking age again walked in the deep green forest.

One swan beat with its wing on the marble cliff so hard that it broke, and the beauty locked in the stone became visible to all.

Another swan tied threads of thoughts from land to land, so that words with the speed of light could travel from country to country.

God still loves the swans' nest that lies between the Baltic and the North Sea. Let giant birds of prey gather to destroy it; it shall survive. Even the little cygnets, with their downless chests, will make a ring around the nest and defend it with their bills and claws, as we have seen them do in our times.

Many centuries will pass and swans will fly from the nest, and be seen and heard around the world, before that time shall come when truthfully it can be said: "That was the last song, the last swan from the swans' nest."

## 62

## A Happy Disposition

From my father I have inherited a happy disposition, a cheerful soul. And who was my father? Well, it is really not of any great importance; but he was lively, chubby, round, and plump, both inside and out. He personified the very opposite of his profession. And what was his profession? If one told that in the very beginning of a story, I am afraid that the reader would go no further; he would put the book aside saying, "That is much too depressing to read about." Yet my father was not an executioner. No, on the contrary, his profession often let him assume a position ahead of the very best society. This elevated post was his by right, he had to be in front of bishops and princes. . . . He was the driver of a hearse!

Well, now it has been said! But this I can guarantee, that anyone who saw my father in his black cloak and three-cornered hat, sitting high up on a death stagecoach, would not have been reminded of sorrow and the grave. For my father's face was round and smiling like the sun. It was a face that said without opening its mouth, "Don't worry, everything is all right, everything is for the best."

It is from him I have my happy disposition and the habit of visiting the churchyard on my afternoon walk. Such a place is not really depressing if you have a happy disposition and a cheerful soul. I also read the Copenhagen *News* just as he did.

I am not so young any more, I have neither wife nor children or library; but I do subscribe to the Copenhagen *News*. It is sufficient for me as it was for my father. It is useful and contains all the news of real importance, such as, who is preaching in which church on Sunday and who is preaching in which new book on weekdays. It is filled with ads if you happen to need a new house, a servant, new clothes, or food for your larder. It tells you who is having a sale and who has been sold, who is holding a charity ball and who was charitable enough to dance at it. It is also filled with the kind of sweet verses that do not offend anyone. Then there are the personal ads: marriages and engagements. Yes, one can live very happily reading the Copenhagen *News;* and one would even lie more comfortably in one's grave if one's coffin were lined with it. It is softer than wood shavings.

Yes, the Copenhagen *News* and the churchyard have always been the most edifying places for my mind to wander. They have been the bathing establishments of my soul, so to speak, and have kept me ever in good humor.

Now anybody can let his mind wander through the Copenhagen *News,* but please accompany me on a stroll through the churchyard. Let us choose a day when the sun is shining and trees and bushes are green. Each gravestone is like a book on a library shelf. You can only read the title, which usually tells everything and nothing about the book. But I know the stories, I know them from my father or learned them myself. I have written them down in my "grave book." Here all the secrets of the graves are revealed; it is a useful and amusing book.

Here we are in the churchyard. Behind that little iron fence is the grave of a very unhappy man. There used to be a rosebush near his tombstone, but it died. The ivy that covers it now does not properly belong there but to the grave next to it. When he was alive he was, as the world calls it, well off. But he was a very unhappy man, and why? Because he took everything too seriously, especially art. If he went to the theater, could he enjoy the performance of a fine play with his whole heart and soul? No, he would find that the lighting was not quite right: the moon was a bit too bright. The stage designer had placed a palm tree in a scene taking place in Denmark or a beech tree in one from Norway. But do these things really matter? After all, a play is just amusement. Why worry about it? But he did, he could not help it. The audience applauded either too much or too little. "The wood is wet, it won't catch fire," he would say; and turn around to watch the other spectators. Then he would notice that they laughed at the wrong places, at something they shouldn't have laughed at, and that irritated him. He was a very unhappy person and now he rests in his grave.

Here is buried a man who was both happy and fortunate. He came from a very good family, and in that he was fortunate, for otherwise nothing would ever have come of him. But everything in this world is so wisely arranged that it cannot help but put one in a good humor. He was, so to speak, "embroidered both in front and in back" and placed in the parlor. In the same manner that a valuable bellrope decorated with pearls is hung there. Behind the showy bellrope there is real rope, which you cannot see but which rings the bell. He had a big strong rope behind him that, unseen and unheard, did good service; and is, as a matter of fact, still doing it, behind another embroidered bellrope. Yes, everything is so wisely arranged that it is easy to be cheerful.

Here rests a man . . . This story is really too sad. . . . He lived sixty-seven years and during all that time had only one ambition, to say something witty. He finally thought of something that in his own opinion was witty and that made him so happy that he died of a stroke. He died from happiness because he had thought of something witty to say, and the irony of it was that no one ever heard it. I am sure he cannot even rest in his grave; after all, it might be a lunchtime joke; and according to popular belief, the dead can only rise around midnight. Imagine him telling it then; nobody would laugh and he would return to his silent tomb. Oh, it is a very unhappy grave.

Next to him lies a woman who was so miserly while she lived that she used to go out in her back yard at night and meow like a cat, so that her neighbors would think that she kept a pet. That is how tight she was!

And here rests an old maid of good family. She never attended a party without performing; she used to sing, *"Mi manca la voce!"* and that was the only time she ever told the truth.

Here is buried a maiden of a different nature! Whenever love's canary bird twittered, she put the fingers of common sense in her ears. She wanted to get married but she never did. That is what one might call an everyday story. It could have been told more brutally, but let the dead sleep in peace.

Under this large tombstone lies a widow; she had the gall of an owl instead of a heart. She used to search out the failings of friends and acquaintances with the pains of a reformer visiting a slum.

This is what is called a family plot; even in death they keep as close as they did in life. If the whole world and the newspapers said that a certain thing had happened in a certain way, and then their youngest child came from a school and said, "I have heard a different story," they would agree with him, for he was part of the family. If their cock crowed in the middle of the night, then they would declare that it was morning, even though all the clocks and night watchmen of the city said it was midnight.

The great Goethe ends his *Faust* with the sentence: "Can be continued." Our little walk in the cemetery can be continued too. I come here often! If one of my friends or enemies makes life a little too hard for me, then I go out to the cemetery and find a nice unused plot and there I "bury" him or her. There they can lie peacefully and harmlessly until I resurrect them as new and better human beings. The story of their lives I write down in my grave book—seen from my point of view, naturally. This is what everyone else should do. Instead of being annoyed when someone harms you, you should bury him immediately and then write his obituary.

Keep cheerful, read the Copenhagen *News,* that paper which people are allowed to write themselves, as long as the journalists hold the pen. And remember to visit the cemeteries.

When my own time comes, and my life has to be bound in a tombstone, write this inscription on it:

A HAPPY DISPOSITION!

That was my story.

## 63

## Grief

This is a story in two parts; the first is not really necessary but it provides background and that is always useful.

We were visiting friends who lived in a manor house out in the country and it so happened that my host was called away for a few days. A woman came from a nearby town; she had her lap dog along, which she carried under her arm. She had come in order to ask my host to buy stock in her tannery and she had all her papers with her. I advised her to put them in an envelope and write on the outside my friend's name and his titles: War Commissary General, Knight of the Danish Flag, etc.

The woman grabbed the pen, began, and then stopped. She asked me to repeat what I had said a little more slowly. I did and she started to write once more; but in the middle of the word "Commissary" she sighed and said, "I am only a woman!"

Her lap dog, which she had put down on the floor, began to growl. He had been taken along for his health and his amusement, and so he thought he wasn't supposed to be put down on the floor. He was fat and flat-nosed.

"He doesn't bite," said his mistress. "He hasn't got a tooth left in his mouth. He is like a member of the family: faithful but bad-tempered; and that's my grandchildren's fault. They like to play 'getting married' and the dog has to be a bridesmaid, and that tires him out, the poor old thing!"

She left and took her little dog under her arm and went home. That was the first part of the story, the one that could have been skipped.

The lap dog died; that is the second part.

It was about a week later. We had come to the town and had taken a room in an inn. Our windows faced the back of the building and we had a view of the yard; it was divided in two by a fence. In one half hides had been hung to dry, both tanned and untanned ones; it was a tannery and belonged to a widow, the woman we had met at the manor house. Her lap dog had died that very morning and was being buried in the yard. The widow's grandchildren—that is, the tannery owner's widow, not the lap dog's, for the dog had never been married —were busy patting the earth smooth on top of the grave. It was a beautiful grave, in which it must have been a pleasure to lie.

It was fenced in by broken flowerpots and covered with sand; as a tombstone there stood a beer bottle with its neck upward; it was not meant symbolically.

The children danced around the grave, and the oldest of the boys, an enterprising young lad of seven, suggested that they should exhibit the grave to anyone in the street who would care to see it. The entrance fee should be one button, for that was something that every boy who wore suspenders owned; and he could even pay for a girl without losing his trousers. The proposal was carried unanimously.

All the children in the street and in the alley behind the yard came and paid their buttons. Many a boy that day had to wear one suspender instead of two, but at least he had seen the little dog's grave and that was worth it.

Outside the gate of the tannery yard stood a litle girl. Although she was dressed in rags she was lovely; she had the most beautiful curly hair, and eyes so clear and blue that it was a pleasure to look at them. She didn't utter a word nor did she cry; but every time the gate was opened she peeked in. She didn't own a button and therefore she stood dejected outside the gate all afternoon, until the last of the children had left. Then she burst out crying and, hiding her eyes in her little sunburned hands, she sat down upon the ground. She alone, of all the children in the street, had not seen the little lap dog's grave! Now that was grief, a sorrow as sharp as a grownup's can be!

We saw it from above; and the little girl's sorrow—like many of our own—was laughable when seen from above. That is the story and if you haven't understood it, then you can buy stock in the widow's tannery.

## 64

## Everything in Its Right Place

More than a hundred years ago there stood, near a forest, a manor house that had a moat around it, which made it look almost like a castle. In the moat reeds and bulrushes grew. To enter the farm you had to cross a bridge, and there, beside it, was an old willow tree that spread its branches out over the water.

From the road not far away came the sound of hunting horns and the trampling of horses' hoofs. The girl who was tending the geese tried to hurry them over the bridge before the hunters came. But they were galloping so fast that she had to jump onto one of the big rocks next to the bridge in order not to be run down herself. She was no more than a child; finely built, with a blessedly sweet expression on her face, and two unusually clear eyes; but this the master of the manor house did not notice. As he galloped over the bridge, with the shaft of his riding whip he poked the girl's chest so that she lost her balance.

"Everything in its right place!" he shouted. "Down in the mud you go!" And he laughed, for he thought that a wonderful joke; and so did his companions. They all laughed and shouted, and the hunting dogs barked. Just as it says in the nursery rhyme: *"The rich bird came blustering . . ."* But only God knows how rich he really was.

The poor girl had caught hold of one of the willow branches as she fell, and it saved her from landing in the mud. As soon as the hunting party and their dogs were out of sight she tried to pull herself up by the branch. But it broke off and she would have fallen into the moat had not a strong hand grabbed her and held her up. A peddler who had been watching the scene had come to her rescue.

"Everything in its right place," he said jokingly, repeating her master's words, and pulled her up on the bank. Then he took the branch and held it up to the limb from which it had broken off. "Not everything can be put back in its right place," he said, smiling. He stuck the branch into the soft earth. "Grow if you can. And may there be cut from you a whistle that can play a tune your master will have to dance to." What he meant was that he hoped that haughty master and his friends would one day get a good whipping.

The peddler went up to the manor house; he did not go into the great hall but into the servants' quarters. There he showed his wares: good woolen stockings and other knitted goods. While the servants bargained, they could hear above them their masters shouting, screaming, and singing: that was what they were best at. Laughter and the barking of dogs mixed with the sound of glasses breaking. It was a great party! There were wine and old beer in glasses and tankards. Their dogs ate from the table. One of the guests kissed his favorite dog; but first he wiped its snout with its own long, curly ears. The peddler was called up to the hall with his wares; they wanted to make fun of him. Wine had gone to their heads and pushed their brains out. They filled one of the peddler's stockings with beer and ordered him to drink—but he had to be quick about it. Oh yes, it was really very, very funny. Later that night they played cards: horses, cows, and even farms changed hands.

"Everthing in its right place," said the peddler as soon as he was well away from "Sodom and Gomorrah," as he called the manor house. "And my right place is the open road. Up there in the hall, I certainly felt out of place." The girl who tended the geese waved to him as he walked away.

Days went by and weeks went by. The broken willow branch, which the peddler had stuck down into the bank of the moat, did not die; fresh shoots appeared and the girl knew that it had taken root. It pleased her, for she felt that now she had a tree all her own.

Yes, the willow branch was prospering, but that was the only thing that thrived on the estate. Drink and gambling are two rollers that are not easy to balance on.

Six years passed, and the master of the manor had to leave his fine estate; he was a poor man. The new owner had once been a peddler.

Honesty and thrift had brought him far. He was the same man who had been made to drink beer from a stocking; now he was the master of the house. From that time on, card playing was never allowed.

"When the Devil saw the Bible he sneered. Then he invented a deck of cards and called them his Bible, but they are not good reading," he declared.

The new owner took a wife and whom do you think it was? The girl who had tended the geese and had always been good-natured, kind, and gentle. In her new clothes she looked as beautiful as any young lady born to wealth and position. How did all this come about? Well, that is too long a story to tell in times as busy as ours, but it did happen; besides, the more important part of the story comes later.

Everything on the old manor prospered; the master ran the farm and his wife the house. It was truly a blessed time. Wealth brought more wealth. The old house was painted and restored, inside and out. The moat was cleaned and an orchard planted. The floors in the hall were scoured until they were white, and there during the long winter evenings the mistress sat with her maids spinning. Every Sunday evening the master, who held the title of privy councilor, read aloud from the Bible. They grew old and their children—and they had quite a few of them—grew up. They were all given a good education; although, as is true in most families, they were not equally intelligent.

The willow branch had become a tall lovely tree, which had never been shaped as such trees usually are in Denmark. "It is our family tree, remember to honor and protect it," said the old people to all their children, also the ones who were not so intelligent.

A hundred years went by.

Now we are in our times; the moat has become a swamp and the old manor house is no more. Some stonework reveals where once the old bridge was, and here a wonderful old willow tree still stands. The old "family tree" is a fine example of how beautiful a willow tree can be if it is allowed to grow freely, without being pruned.

True, a storm has twisted the tree, but it remained standing; and there's also a cleft in the trunk, from the root all the way up. In all its cracks, crevices, and the cleft, the wind has deposited dirt and soil; and flowers and grass now grow there. At the top, where the boughs go each its own way, there's a hanging garden of wild flowers and raspberry bushes. Even a little rowan tree has taken root and stands, straight and slender, up against the old willow tree. When the wind blows the green algae down to the other end of the swamp, then the tree mirrors itself in the dark waters. Across the fields there's a little path that leads past it.

The new farm buildings stand on a high hill, and from there the view is beautiful. It's a grand house with big windows that are so polished that one can hardly see the glass. A broad flight of stairs leads up to the front door. There are lovely roses, and the lawns are so green that one might think that each blade of grass was inspected morning and evening. On the walls of the lofty rooms valuable paintings hang. Handsome chairs and sofas, upholstered in silk and leather, are in every corner. Some of the chairs have legs carved to resemble lion's claws, so that they look as if they could get up and walk by themselves. On the marble tops of the tables lie books bound in morocco, with gilt edges. . . . Yes, a rich family must own this house: distinguished people; and they are, for the father is a baron.

This family, too, felt that "everything should be in its right place." And all the paintings that once held honorable places in the old manor houses were now hung along the servants' corridors. They were junk, especially the portraits of the man in a pink robe, wearing a wig, and the one of a woman with powdered hair, holding a rose in her hands. Both figures were encircled by a wreath of willow branches. There were so many holes in the canvases because the sons of the baron had used them for targets when they were playing with their bows and arrows. They were the portraits of the privy councilor and his wife, from whom the family descended.

"But they are not really part of the family," declared one of the young boys. "He was once a peddler and she a barefooted girl tending geese. The weren't at all like our mama and papa."

They were poor paintings and if "Everything in its right place" is your motto, then they belonged in the servants' quarters, even if they were the great-grandparents of the master of the house.

One day the parson's son, who had been hired as private tutor, took the baron's sons and their older sister for a walk. They went down toward the swamp where the old willow tree grew. The young girl, who had been confirmed that spring, was picking a bouquet of wild flowers. She did it with taste and, since every flower was put in its right place, it looked beautiful. She listened with pleasure to the young man, who was talking about the power of nature and drawing portraits, in words, of great men and women from history. She had been blessed with a sweet and healthy nature. Her soul and thoughts were noble; she had a heart that welcomed everything that God had created.

They stopped by the old willow tree and the youngest boy demanded that their teacher make him a willow flute. The young man broke off a branch.

"Please don't!" exclaimed the young baroness, but it was too late. "It is our famous old tree," she said, and smiled. "I love it so! They all laugh at me for it, but I don't care. You know, there is a story about that tree. . . ."

Now she told the story that we have already heard, about the poor little girl tending the geese and the peddler who met here, and how they became the ancestors of a noble family.

"The old couple refused a title," said the young daughter of the baron. "They had a motto, 'Everything in its right place,' and they felt that nobility bought by money would not bring them in their right place. It was their son, my grandfather, who became the first baron. He is supposed to have been very learned and was always being invited to the royal court. He is the one my family thinks most highly of. But I don't know . . . I think there's something so cozy about the old couple that makes me love them. I look back on their times with a kind of longing. I can see them: the old man, like an old patriarch, reading from the Bible, while my great-grandmother sits with her maids, who are sewing and spinning."

"Yes, they must have been wonderful people and very sensible," agreed the young tutor, and very soon they were deep in a discussion about nobility and the bourgeoisie. And if one had not known better, one would have believed that parson's son did not belong to the middle class, so warmly did he speak of the aristocracy.

"It is good fortune to belong to a family that has distinguished itself," he began, "for that is a spur that drives one forward to further excellence. It is a blessing to have a name that opens all doors to one. Nobility ennobles. It is a golden coin stamped with its value.

"I know it is the fashion of the day—and many a poet dances to that tune—to say that everything aristocratic is stupid and bad. They claim that only among the poor—and the lower you decend the better—does true gold glitter. But that is not my opinion; I think it is wrong, absolutely false reasoning. Among the highest classes one can often observe the most elevated traits. My mother can tell of many examples; here is one, though I know many more. Once when my mother was visiting one of the most distinguished homes in Copenhagen—I believe my grandmother had been the nurse to the noble mistress—she was standing in the hall conversing with the old aristocratic gentleman who was the master of the house, when he spied through the window an old beggar woman who had come for her weekly alms. He noticed how difficult it was for her to walk. 'Poor old thing,' he said, and ran down the stairs himself to give her the few shillings. His Excellency is over seventy. Oh, it was a deed of no importance but, like the widow's mite, it came from the heart. It is toward things like that our poets should point, for they atone and redeem. But where nobility has gone to a man's head and he behaves like an Arabian horse that rears and kicks, just because his blood is pure and he has a pedigree, there nobility has degenerated. When noblemen sniff the air in a room because a plain citizen has been there and say, 'It smells of the street,' why then Thespis should exhibit them to the just ridicule of satire."

That was the parson's son's speech; it was a bit long but in the meantime the whistle had been finished.

There was a big party at the manor house. People had come from the neighborhood and from Copenhagen. Some ladies were dressed with taste and others without. The big hall was filled with people. The local ministers stood humbly in a little group by themselves; they looked as though they were attending a funeral but they weren't, they were being entertained! Or they were going to be, for it hadn't really started yet.

Since there was going to be a concert, the little son of the baron had taken his willow flute along, but he couldn't get a tone out of it, and neither had his papa been able to when he tried, so the willow flute was declared a failure.

The music and the singing were of the kind that give greater pleasure to the performers than to the audience. But on the whole it was enjoyable.

"But you are a virtuoso, I hear," exclaimed a young cavalier who was his parents' darling. "You not only can play the flute, you carve them yourself. You are the genius who commands—the one who is seated on the right side—God preserve us! But I follow the fashion, one has to. Please, will you not charm us all by performing on this little instrument?" With these words he handed the little willow flute to the young tutor, while announcing loudly that the young man now would play a little piece for solo flute.

That he was to be made the butt of a joke was easy to see, and the young tutor refused to play. But now the rest of the company entreated him and finally he put the little willow flute to his mouth and blew.

It was a strange flute! The tone that came from it sounded like the whistle of a steam engine, but it was even louder and could be heard all throughout the farm, in the forest, and for miles around. At the same time a storm broke and the wind roared: "Everything in its place!"

Papa, the baron, was blown right down into the little cottage where the man who tended the cows lived, and that fellow was carried right up into—no, not into the grand hall of the manor house, that was not "his place"; he flew up among the most important of the servants: the ones who wore silk stockings. They were dumfounded at seeing a person of such low quality daring to sit down among them.

In the grand hall the young baroness flew up to the head of the table, because that was her place, and the young tutor got a seat right beside her. They looked like a bride and groom. An old count, who belonged to one of the oldest families in the country, remained seated where he was, for the whistle was just—and that it is important to be. The witty young cavalier who was the cause of it all, the one who was his parents' darling, flew headfirst right down into the henhouse and he was not the only one who ended up there.

The whistle, as I have said, could be heard for miles and it caused strange things to happen. A wealthy merchant who always drove with four horses in front of his carriage was blown right out of it, together with his family, and none of them was even allowed to stand on the back of the carriage as a footman. Two rich peasants who had grown too big for their breeches were blown into a muddy ditch.

That willow flute certainly was dangerous; luckily it cracked this first time that it was played upon. Back into the young man's pocket it went, "everything in its right place."

The next morning nobody talked about what had happened and everything was back in its old order, except for the portraits of the peddler and his wife: they had blown up on the wall in the grand hall. An art expert who saw them declared that they had been painted by a master; they were repaired and given the very best place on the wall to hang. After all, the baron had not known they were valuable, how could he have? "Everything in its right place," and eventually everything is put in its right place. Eternity is long, a lot longer than this story.

## The Pixy and the Grocer

There once was a proper student; he lived in a garret and didn't own a thing. There once was a proper grocer; he lived on the first floor and owned the whole house. Now the pixy stayed with the grocer, for there on Christmas Eve he was given a whole bowlful of porridge with a lump of butter in it. That the grocer could afford, therefore the pixy lived in his store, and from that a moral can be drawn.

One evening the student came knocking on the grocer's back door. He needed a candle and a piece of cheese for his supper; and he was, as usual, his own errand boy. He was given his wares and paid for them. The grocer wished him good evening and the grocer's wife gave him a friendly nod, though she was a woman who could do more than nod her head: she could talk anyone's ear off. The student nodded back and would have gone, had he not started reading what was written on the paper that the cheese had been wrapped in. It was a page torn from an old book of poetry that deserved a better fate than to be used as wrapping paper.

"Most of the pages of that book are still here," said the grocer. "I gave an old woman some coffee beans for it; you can have the rest for eight pennies."

"Thank you," replied the student. "Let me have what is left of the book instead of the cheese, I can eat plain bread for supper. It would be a pity if all of it were torn to pieces. You are a splendid person, a practical man, but you have no more idea of what poetry is than that old barrel over there."

Now that was not a very nice thing to say, especially about the barrel. But both the grocer and the student laughed; it had been said in fun. It annoyed the pixy though. He had overheard the remark and thought it was an insult to the grocer, who owned the whole house and sold the very best quality butter.

Night fell; the store was closed and everyone had gone to sleep except the student and the pixy. He sneaked into the grocer's bedroom. The grocer's wife was sleeping with her mouth open and the pixy stole her sharp tongue: she didn't use it while she slept. Everything in the whole house that he put the tongue on was given the power of speech. Each of them could express its feelings and formulate its thoughts just as well as the grocer's wife could. But since there was only one tongue, they could only speak one at a time, which was a blessing, I am sure, or they all would have talked at once.

The first thing that was allowed to borrow the tongue was the barrel; it was filled with old newspapers. "Is it really true," asked the pixy, "that you don't know what poetry is?"

"Certainly I know what poetry is," said the barrel. "It's something printed on the back page of a newspaper that people cut out sometimes. I think that I have more poetry inside me than the student has. And what am I compared to the grocer, just a poor old barrel."

Then the pixy put the tongue on the coffee grinder and there it certainly wagged. He also put it on the tub of butter and the cash drawer just to hear their opinions. They agreed unanimously with the barrel, and the opinion of the majority must be respected.

"I will fix that student!" muttered the pixy, and sneaked up the back stairs to the garret where the young man lived. The student was still up, a light was burning in his room. The pixy looked through the keyhole. The young man was sitting reading the old book he had bought for eight pennies.

How bright the room seemed! It was as if a ray of light came from the book, a luminous tree whose branches spread out across the ceiling. There leaves were fresh and green and on each branch flowers bloomed and fruit hung. The flowers were faces of young maidens, some with radiant dark eyes and others with clear blue ones. The fruits were sparkling stars. All the while the most beautiful music could be heard.

Such splendor the little pixy had never seen or even thought possible. He stood on his toes and looked and looked until the light was put out. Even when the student had blown out his candle and gone to bed, the pixy tarried. He could still hear the music, a song so soft and comforting; a lovely lullaby for the student, who was falling asleep.

"But that was fantastic!" mumbled the pixy. "That I had not expected! I think I will move in with the student!" Then he thought—and he thought very sensibly—"But the student does not have any porridge." And he sighed.

Down the stairs he went, down to the grocer. And that was lucky, for the barrel had almost worn out the grocer's wife's tongue. It had lectured, giving all the opinions that were written in the old newspapers inside it. When the pixy came it had just begun to repeat them. He took the tongue and gave it back to its owner. But from that time on the whole store, from the cash drawer to the firewood that lay by the stove, all had the same opinions as the barrel, whom they so honored and respected that when the grocer, in the evening, would read aloud the theater column to his wife, they thought that the barrel had written it.

But the pixy no longer stayed downstairs in the evening to listen to the grocer and his wife. No, as soon as the student had lit his candle, it was as if the light from the garret were an anchor cable that drew him up. He had to go and peek through the keyhole. He experienced greatness. He saw what we see when God, disguised as the storm, walks across the turbulent ocean. He cried without knowing why he cried, but found that in those tears happiness was hidden. "How wonderful it must be," he thought, "to sit under the magic tree together with the student." But that was not possible; he had to be satisfied with looking through the keyhole.

The autumn winds blew; the cold air whistled through the loft and down the corridor where the little pixy was standing, his eyes glued to the keyhole of the student's door. It was cold, wretchedly cold; but the pixy did not feel it before the student had put out his light and the sound of the music that came from the garret had ceased. But then he froze! He hurried down into his own little warm corner that was so cozy and comfortable.

At Christmas when the porridge with the lump of butter in it was served, the pixy acknowledged no other master than the grocer.

One night the pixy was awakened by a terrible noise. People were banging on the shutters of the store, the whole street was as light as day from a fire. Everyone wanted to know whose house was burning. Was it his own or the neighbor's? It was terrible! The grocer's wife got so disconcerted that she took off her gold earrings and put them in her pocket, in order to save something.

The grocer hurriedly collected his bonds and the maid her silk shawl: that was her luxury, the one she could afford. All the people wanted to save what was dearest to them, and so did the pixy. He ran up the stairs and into the student's room. The young man was standing calmly at the window looking at the fire in the house across the street. The little pixy grabbed the book that was lying on the table, put it into his red cap, and ran. He had saved the most valuable thing in the house.

He climbed out on the roof and up on the chimney stack; there, illuminated by the burning house, he sat holding his treasure tightly with both his hands.

Now he finally understood his heart's desire, where his loyalty belonged! But when the fire in the house across the street had been put out, then he thought about it again. "I will share myself between them," he said, "for I cannot leave the grocer altogether. I must stay there for the sake of the porridge."

That was quite human! After all, we, too, go to the grocer for the porridge's sake.

## 66

## The Millennium

They will come on wings of steam, the young citizens of America will
fly through the air, across the great ocean, to visit old Europe. They
will come to see the monuments of bygone ages, the ruins of the
great cities, just as we today visit Southeast Asia to stare at the crumbling glories of the past.

Thousands of years hence, they will come.

The Thames, the Danube, and the Rhine will still be flowing;
Mount Blanc will stand with its snow-covered peak. The northern
lights will be shining above the Scandinavian countries, though generations upon generations will have become dust. Many of those men,
who to us seem so mighty, will be as nameless as the Vikings who rest
in their grave chambers inside the hills, on top of which the farmers
today like to place a bench, so that they can watch the wind make
waves in the flat fields of grain.

"To Europe!" cry the young Americans. "To the land of our
forefathers! To the wonders of an earlier civilization. To beautiful
Europe!"

The airships will be crowded, for it is much faster to fly than to sail.
The passengers will have already made their hotel reservations by
telegraphing ahead. The first European coast to come into view will
be Ireland's, but the passengers will still be sleeping; they will have
given orders not to be awakened before the airship is over England.
The airship will land in Shakespeare's country, as the more cultured

of the passengers call it—others call England the "land of the machine" or the "land of politics."

A whole day will these busy travelers give to England and Scotland; then they will be off via the tunnel under the Channel to France: the country of Charlemagne and Napoleon. The learned among them will discuss the Classicist and Romantic movements that so interested the Frenchmen of the distant past. Molière's name will be mentioned. Heroes, scientists, and poets whom we have never heard of—they have yet to be born in that crater of Europe, Paris!—will be on the lips of these young people.

Then the airship will fly over that country from which Columbus sailed and where Cortes was born: Spain, the home of Calderón, who composed his dramas in perfect verse. Beautiful dark-eyed women will still inhabit its fertile dales; one will hear the names of *el Cid* and the Alhambra in the old songs that people will still be singing.

Through the air, across the sea to Italy, where the Eternal City of Rome once was. It will be gone; the Campagna will be a desert. Only one wall of St. Peter's will still be standing, and there will be doubt as to its authenticity.

To Greece, to sleep one night in a luxury hotel on the top of Mount Olympus, so one will be able to say that one has been there; and then onward to the Bosporus, to rest for a few hours on the site of Byzantium. They will watch poor fishermen repairing their nets, while they listen to tales about Turkish harems of an all but forgotten age.

They will fly above ruins of great cities along the Danube, which in our times are still unknown. They will land to look at impressive monuments—accomplishments that lie in the future, but which will be admired as achievements of the fruitful past.

They will come to Germany, which once was crisscrossed by railroads and canals: the land where Luther spoke, Goethe sang, and Mozart once held the scepter of music. When they speak of science and the arts, they will mention other names that we do not know. One day will be the time they allot to Germany and one for all of Scandinavia: for the fatherlands of Oersted and Linnaeus, and for Norway, the young country of old heroes. Iceland will be visited on the homeward journey; the geyser will spout no longer, and the volcano Hekla will have died; but the cliff-bound island will stand in the turbulent sea as a memorial tablet to the sagas.

"There's so much to see in Europe," the young Americans will say. "And we have seen it all in a week, just as the famous guidebook promised we could." Then they will discuss the author of the book which they all will have read: *Europe Seen in Seven Days.*

## 67

## Under the Willow Tree

The countryside around Køge is very barren. True, the town is situated on the coast, and the seaside is always lovely, but it can be much prettier than it is there. The city is surrounded by flat fields and it is far to the nearest forest. And yet, if it is the place that you call home, you will find something beautiful about it: something that you will long for when, later on in life, you see places that are truly beautiful.

On the outskirts of Køge there is a little stream that ebbs out in the sands of a beach, and along its banks it is quite lovely, especially in summer. Knud and Johanna thought this place was as beautiful as any place could be. They were two children who lived next door to each other and whose gardens went right down to the stream. Both of the families were very poor, but there was an elderberry tree in one of the gardens and a willow tree in the other. The children had only to crawl under the hedge to be together. Sometimes they played under the elderberry tree but more often under the willow, even though this grew on the bank of the stream. Our Lord looks after all small creatures; otherwise, very few of them would survive. Besides, the children were careful, especially the boy, who was so frightened of the water that even in summer he never waded in the sea as all the other children did. He had had to bear a lot of teasing about it, until little Johanna had a dream that she was out sailing in a boat, on Køge Bay, and Knud walked out to meet her—first the water went up to his throat and then over his head, but he walked on. From then on, whenever the children teased him, he would refer to Johanna's dream as proof of his courage. He was very proud of it; but he went no nearer the water.

The parents of the children often visited each other, and the children played together all the time, either in the gardens or out in the road. Along the sides of the road many willow trees grew, but they were stunted, for they had not been planted there to be looked at but for the sake of their branches, from which fences and baskets could be woven. The willow tree in the garden was allowed to grow as it wanted to, and under its widespread branches the children passed many happy hours.

On market day the great square in the center of Køge became a little city of tents. Here silk ribbons, boots, and many other kinds of wares were sold. There were always big crowds of people and usually there was rain. Every peasant for twenty miles around came to Køge. The smell of the damp woolen clothing blended with the delicious odor of gingerbread. There was a booth where gingerbread alone was sold, and the best part of it was that the man who owned it stayed with Knud's parents whenever he was in town, so the boy was always given a piece of gingerbread which he shared with Johanna. There was another wonderful thing about the gingerbread baker, he knew how to tell stories. He could make them up about almost everything, even his own gingerbread figures.

One evening he told a tale about a gingerbread man and a gingerbread woman that made such a deep impression on the two children that they never forgot it; so maybe it is a good idea that we hear it too, especially since it is short.

"Once there lay on the counter of my booth two gingerbread figures. One of them was a man with a hat on his head, the other a girl, who had no hat but did have a dab of gold for hair. Their faces were on the front of their heads just as human beings' faces are; and they, too, shouldn't be judged by how they look from behind. The man had a bitter almond on the left side of his chest and that was his heart. The gingerbread girl was just plain gingerbread. They were displayed on the counter as samples. And as the days went by they fell in love, but neither of them spoke of their love, and if you don't do that, nothing will ever come of it.

" 'He is a man, it is only proper that he should speak first,' thought the gingerbread girl, though she was dying to know whether her love was returned.

"His thoughts were more ferocious: men's usually are. He dreamed that he was an urchin who had fourpence, so he could buy the little gingerbread girl and eat her up.

"For weeks they lay on the counter and became more and more dried out. The gingerbread girl's ideas became more refined, more womanly. 'It is enough to have lain on the same counter with him,' she thought, and then she broke in two at the waist.

"'If she had known of my love, she might have lasted longer,' thought the gingerbread man.

"That was their story and here they are, both of them," said the baker. "Theirs was an unhappy fate and proves that silent love leads to unhappiness. . . . Now look at them!" And he gave the gingerbread man to Johanna and the two pieces of the gingerbread girl to Knud, but the children were so touched by the story that they couldn't eat the cakes.

The next day the children went to the churchyard. Its walls were so overgrown with ivy that they looked as if the red bricks were covered by a green carpet. Here among the greenery Knud and Johanna leaned the gingerbread man and the gingerbread woman up against the wall and told the other children the story of silent love and what a waste of time it was—the love, that is, not the story, for the children found that very amusing. They were all so absorbed in the tale that they didn't notice that a bigger boy had stolen one of the gingerbread figures. It was the maiden and out of meanness he ate her all up. The children wept when they realized what had happened; and then they ate the gingerbread man—probably so that the poor fellow would not suffer from being alone in the world. They never forgot the story.

The two children were always together either under the elderberry tree or under the willow. Johanna had a voice that was as clear as a silver bell, and she would sing the loveliest songs. Knud had no voice at all, but he knew the words of all the songs by heart—and that is always something. The people of Køge, even the rich grocer's wife, would stop when they passed the gardens, to listen to Johanna sing. "That little brat has a beautiful voice," they would say.

Those were beautiful, happy days but they did not last. Little Johanna's mother died and her father decided to move to Copenhagen. The neighbors had tears in their eyes when they parted, and the two children wept aloud. The grown-ups promised to write to each other at least once a year.

Shortly afterward Knud was apprenticed to a shoemaker—such a big boy could not spend all his time playing. In the autumn he was confirmed in the church in Køge. How Knud would have liked to go to Copenhagen on that solemn day, to see Johanna. He had never been in the capital, though the distance was not more than twenty miles. On a clear day you can see the towers of Copenhagen across the bay; and the morning he was confirmed, Knud saw the golden cross on the top of the steeple of the Church of Our Lady.

How often he thought of Johanna! But did she remember him?

At Christmas a letter arrived from Johanna's father. All had turned out well for him and he had married again; but Johanna had had even greater good luck. Her lovely voice had won her a position in the theater. She sang in the kind of play in which there was music and she already earned quite a bit of money. That was why she was sending her "dear neighbors in Køge a silver mark, to buy wine for Christmas Eve and to toast my health—" that she had written herself; and she added: "My very best regards to Knud!"

They all wept. Everything was so wonderful and their tears came from happiness. Not a day passed without Knud thinking of Johanna, now that he could read in her letter that she thought of him.

The nearer the time came for his apprenticeship to end, the more certain he was that he loved Johanna and that one day she would become his wife.

He would think of Johanna; a smile would play on his lips and he would pull the leather even tighter to the last. Once he stuck the big needle right into his thumb; but it did not matter, he was so happy in his dreams. He was not going to be silent as the two gingerbread figures had been; from that story he had learned a lot.

Finally his apprenticeship was over and he packed his knapsack. He was going to Copenhagen for the first time in his life. He had already got a position there with a shoemaker. How surprised Johanna would be when she saw him. She was now seventeen and he was nineteen.

He had thought of buying a gold ring for her in Køge but had decided that he could probably buy a much more beautiful one in Copenhagen. He said good-by to his parents, took his knapsack on his back, and set out. It was a rainy and windy autumn day; he was wet to the skin by the time he had walked the twenty miles to the big city and found the home of the shoemaker he was to work for.

The very first Sunday he went to the address that had appeared on Johanna's father's letter. He had put on his new suit and was wearing the hat he had bought in Køge. He looked well in it; it was his first hat, until then he had always worn a cap.

He found the house. They lived on the top floor, and it almost made him dizzy to walk up so many flights of stairs. "How strangely people live in the huge lonesome city," he thought, "all on top of each other."

Johanna's father greeted him kindly; his new wife, whom Knud had not met before, shook his hand and offered him coffee. Their apartment was neat and well furnished.

"Johanna will be so pleased to see you," said the father. "You have grown up to be a nice-looking young man. I will call her. She is a girl that a father can be proud of; she has gone far. And with God's help she will go even further. She has her own room and she pays me rent."

Her father knocked on her door as if he were a stranger to his own daughter. They stepped inside. Oh, what a beautiful room she had! Knud felt certain that there was not a room so elegant in all of Køge. The queen could not have a better one. The floor was covered by a rug, and the curtains were so long that they almost reached the floor. There was a little upholstered chair covered with velvet, several pictures on the walls, and a mirror as big as a door. Knud noticed it all and yet he saw only Johanna! She looked quite different from what he had expected; she was much more beautiful than he had imagined she would be. There was not a girl in Køge as lovely as she, or as refined. For a moment she stared at him strangely as if she didn't know him, but then she came running over to him. Knud thought that she was going to kiss him. But she didn't, though she was happy to see him.

She had tears in her eyes when she looked at the friend from her childhood. And she asked so many questions: about Knud's parents and everyone else in Køge, including the elderberry tree and the willow tree. She called them "mother elderberry" and "father willow," and talked about them as if they were human beings. And why shouldn't she? After all, they were as human as the two gingerbread cakes. Of those she talked too; about their silent love and how they lay on the counter beside each other, not daring to speak of it.

She laughed so warmly, so kindly. "No, she hasn't changed,"

thought Knud. His cheeks blushed and his heart beat so strangely. Knud also sensed that it was for her sake that he was invited to stay all evening.

They had tea. Later she read aloud from a book, and Knud felt that every word she read was about him and his love for her. When she sang a little song for them, the song became more than a song, it was a little story that came from her heart. The tears ran down his cheeks; he could not stop them and to speak was impossible. He thought that he had behaved very stupidly, but when he left she shook his hand warmly and said: "You have a kind heart, Knud. Always stay as you are."

After such a marvelous experience it was difficult to sleep, and Knud did not close his eyes all night. When he said good-by, Johanna's father had remarked, "Now don't let the whole winter pass before you visit us again." Knud thought that this was as good as an invitation and decided to go back on the following Sunday.

In the meantime, every day when he was finished working for his master—and this could be quite late, for they also worked by lamplight—he would walk through the street on which Johanna lived. Beneath her window he would stop and look up. Once he saw her shadow against the curtains and that was a very pleasant evening. The shoemaker's wife complained that he was always running about at night, but his master laughed and said, "Knud is a young man."

"On Sunday I will see her again," thought Knud. "Then I will tell her how she has always been in my thoughts. I will ask her to be my little wife! True, I am only a poor shoemaker, but I will work hard and one day I shall have my own shop. Yes, that is what I will say. Love must have a voice, the silent kind is of no use; that I learned from the gingerbread cakes."

Sunday came and Knud along with it; but unfortunately Johanna and her family were all going out that day. Johanna took his hand in a most friendly way and asked him if he had ever been to the theater. "I will send you a ticket," she said. "Next Wednesday I will be singing. My father knows where your master lives."

That certainly was thoughtful of her. At noon on Wednesday an envelope with a ticket had arrived for him, but there was no note or letter with it. In the evening Knud went for the first time in his life to the theater; and what did he see? He saw Johanna, so beautiful, so lovely. In the play she got married to a stranger; but then, it was only a play,

not real life, or Johanna would not have sent him a ticket to come and
see it. Knud knew that well enough, so he didn't mind. Everybody
clapped and shouted, and so did Knud. He screamed, "Hurrah," as
loud as he could.

Even the king, who attended the performance, smiled most kindly
down at Johanna; one could see he was pleased. Knud felt himself terribly small among such splendid company, but he loved his Johanna
ever so much and felt sure that she cared for him too. A man must say
the first words; that was what the little gingerbread girl had thought,
and that story Knud had not forgotten.

Next Sunday Knud set off to visit Johanna. He felt as solemn as if he
were going to church to receive the sacraments. Johanna was home
alone, nothing could have been luckier.

"I am glad you have come," she said. "I nearly sent Father off to
fetch you, but I felt sure that you would come. Next Friday I will be
leaving Copenhagen. I am going to France. I must, for only there can
I learn to be a great singer."

Knud felt as though the whole room were turning around him and
that, within him, his heart were breaking, but he did not cry. Even
though no tears could be seen in his eyes, it was obvious that he was
very sad.

Johanna saw it right away, and she almost cried. "Oh, you poor,
faithful, honest soul!" she exclaimed, and her words loosened Knud's
tongue. He told her how much he loved her and how much he wanted
her to be his wife.

Johanna, who had been holding his hand in hers, let go of it and
turned as pale as death. Then she said, seriously, almost mournfully,
"Don't make yourself and me unhappy, Knud. I will always be your
good sister whom you can trust. But I can never be more." She
stroked his moist forehead with her soft hands. "God gives us
strength when we ask it of Him."

At that moment her stepmother came into the room.

"Knud is beside himself because I am leaving," said Johanna to her
stepmother, and then patted him on the back. "Now be a man," she
said smilingly, as if they had only been talking about her journey.
"Child," she added, "you will have to be kind and sensible as you
were when we were children and sat under the willow tree."

Knud's world broke into pieces and one piece was lost forever. He
felt that his thoughts were like loose threads that the wind could play

with. He stayed even though he was not sure whether he had been invited to. But Johanna's father and his wife treated him kindly, and Johanna poured the tea as she had the last time he had been there. She sang, too, but her voice did not sound as sweet; yet it was beautiful enough to break one's heart. When they parted, Knud did not offer her his hand but she took it anyway. "Will you not give your sister your hand when you say good-by? My dear old playmate!" She smiled while tears ran down her cheeks. "Sister," she repeated. That word brought no comfort to Knud; thus they parted.

She sailed to France. Knud stayed in Copenhagen and walked its muddy streets. The young shoemakers asked him what he was brooding about and invited him to come along with them. "To amuse yourself is almost a duty when you are young," one of them explained.

He went with them to a dance. There were many pretty girls, but none as lovely as Johanna. In the midst of all the gaiety, where he had expected to forget her, he remembered her most clearly. "God gives us strength when we ask it of Him," she had said. Knud folded his hands as if he were going to kneel down and pray right there, with the dancing couples all about him, and the violins playing. He was shocked! What had he done? How could he have taken Johanna with him to such a place? For she was with him; didn't he carry her in his heart?

He rushed out into the street and did not stop running till he stood once more before the house where she had lived. The house was dark; everything was dark and lonesome. The world went its way and Knud went his.

Winter came and the Sound froze; it was a real ice winter and all of nature seemed dead and buried.

Finally spring came. The ice thawed and ships from foreign countries came to the harbor of Copenhagen once again. Knud longed to go away, far away, out into the wide world, but not to France.

He packed his knapsack and set out. He wandered along the roads of Germany without purpose or peace. He walked from one city to the next, too restless to remain in any one of them. Only when he reached Nuremberg, far to the south, did his feet begin to drag, so that he felt that he had the power to make himself stay put.

It was a strange city that looked as though it had been cut out of an old-fashioned picture book. Each street went its own way, not one of them was straight; and the houses did not necessarily follow them.

Some of the houses jutted out and filled half the sidewalk, and not two of them looked alike. Some had bay windows and little towers, others had gables and carved cornices. Around the crooked roofs ran copper gutters shaped like dragons or strangely elongated dogs.

Here, on the main square, Knud stood one morning with his knapsack on his back. He was looking at one of the old fountains whose waters fell down over marvelous bronze figures depicting scenes from the Bible and history. A pretty servingmaid had come to fetch water; she gave him a rose from the handful of flowers she was carrying. This, Knud decided, was a good omen.

He could hear the music of an organ. He was reminded of home, of the church in Køge. The church here was very large; it was a cathedral. Knud entered. The sunlight shone through the stained-glass windows and between the tall, slender columns. He felt the holiness of the place and for the first time his soul was at peace.

He sought and found a good master; he stayed in Nuremberg and learned the language.

The old moat and defenses around the town had been made into gardens, but the city wall, with its sturdy towers, was still intact. There was a wooden gallery along the outside of the walls where ropemakers twisted their long cords into strong rope. In the cracks and crevices of the old stonemasonry, elderberry trees had taken root; their branches spread out over the low cottages built at the base of the walls. Here the master for whom Knud worked lived; and he had a little garret room in his master's house. The elderberry branches shaded the window of the attic in which Knud slept. He lived there one summer and the following winter, but when spring arrived he could not remain. The smell of the flowering elderberry was too much for him. It reminded him of Køge, of his home. He felt that he was back in the garden of his childhood. Knud found another master and moved farther inside the city where there were no elderberry trees.

His new master lived near one of the old bridges, across from a water mill. The houses were built at the water's edge and they all had rickety old balconies that hung out over the river. Here were no elderberry trees, not even a single flower could grow; but there was an old willow tree. It clung to the house, holding onto it so that the raging waters could not uproot it and tear it away. Its branches hung down over the river just as the willow tree's at home had over the little stream.

He had moved from "mother elderberry" to "father willow." Especially at night in the moonlight the willow tree would make him yearn for home. At last he could not stand it any longer. And why? Ask the flowering elderberry tree, ask the willow. He bade his master good-by and left Nuremberg to travel farther south.

He never talked to anyone about Johanna; he kept his sorrow locked within himself. But he often thought about the story of the two gingerbread figures and how the man had had a bitter almond on his left side. Now he felt he knew its bitter taste. Johanna, who was always gentle and smiling, was like the girl, gingerbread all the way through. The straps of his knapsack cut his shoulders and neck, he felt that he had difficulty breathing; he readjusted them but it did not help. The world was not whole around him, he carried half of it inside him, and that he could do nothing about.

It was not before he reached the great mountains that the dimensions of the world grew real and his thoughts turned outward, not inward to torture himself.

The sight of the Alps brought tears to his eyes. He thought they looked like the folded wings of the world. What would happen if the world spread its wings, with their great feathers of black forests, waterfalls, clouds, and snow fields? "On doomsday it will happen and the earth will fly toward God and break like a soap bubble! Oh, I wish doomsday would come!" he sighed.

The countryside he passed through seemed to him like an enormous orchard.

The young girls, sitting on the little wooden balconies of the houses doing lacework, would nod to the wanderer. The snow on the tall mountains glowed like embers in the light from the setting sun. The green lakes, surrounded by dark pine trees, reminded him of the color of the sea at home in Køge, but the sadness that he felt was more filled with sweetness than with pain.

Where the Rhine like a gigantic wave rushed forth and its waters were crushed and transformed into mist where rainbows play, he thought of the water mill near Køge. There, too, the water roared and was crushed into foam. He would have liked to stay in the little town by the Rhine but there were too many elderberries and willows growing there. So he set out across the great mountains. He walked through narrow passes, along roads that clung to the steep mountainside like swallows' nests. Far below him were clouds which hid the waterfalls that he could hear roaring in the abyss.

Amidst the eternal snow he walked and the summer sun warmed his back. He said farewell to the north and came to the country where chestnut trees spread their crowns between fields of corn and vineyards. The mountains were a wall between himself and his memories, and that was a blessing.

He came to the great city of Milan. There he found a German shoemaker who would hire him. The master and his wife were a kind, elderly couple who soon grew fond of the young journeyman, who, though he was so silent, worked so hard. It was as if God had finally given Knud peace, taken the burden from his heart.

His greatest pleasure was to climb to the top of Milan Cathedral, which seemed to him to have been shaped out of the white snow of his own country. He stood among the spires and arches, with sculptures peeping out at him at every turn. Above him was the blue sky and below him the city and the great plains of Lombardy. Looking toward the north, he could see the snow-covered Alps, and at the sight of them he would recall Køge and its church with ivy-covered walls. But he no longer thought of it with longing. He had decided that here, beyond the great mountains, his grave would be.

It was now three years since he had left Denmark and one whole year since he had come to Milan. One evening his employer, the old German shoemaker, invited him to the opera. What a fantastic theater it was, with its seven balconies, gold leafing, and silk curtains. Every seat was occupied by an elegantly dressed lady or gentleman; they looked as though they were at a ball. The women carried little bouquets of flowers in their hands. So many lamps burned that the huge room was as light as if the sun itself had been the chandelier. The orchestra began to play. It was much larger than the one in the theater in Copenhagen, but that evening Johanna had sung, while here . . .

It was magic! The curtain rose and there stood Johanna clad in gold and silk, with a crown on her head! She sang as beautifully as only one of God's angels can and then she stepped to the front of the stage and smiled—as only Johanna could smile—down at Knud.

Poor Knud grabbed his master's hand and screamed as loudly as he could, "Johanna!" But his cry was drowned in the music.

The old shoemaker nodded and said, "Yes, her name is Johanna," and then he took the program and pointed to the spot where her full name stood.

It was no dream! The audience applauded and shouted her name and the ladies threw their flowers up on the stage. Endless curtain calls were demanded. When she left the opera house the crowd unharnessed the horses of her carriage and drew it in triumph through the city. Knud helped to pull it, and he was the happiest among that happy group. When they came to the brilliantly lit villa where she lived, Knud stood by the door of her carriage. It opened and she stepped out. The light from the many lamps illuminated her dear face. She smiled and thanked them all. She was deeply touched. Knud looked straight into her face and she looked straight into his, but she did not recognize him.

A gentleman wearing a decoration on his chest offered her his arm. She took it. "They are engaged," he heard people behind whisper.

Knud walked straight home and packed his knapsack. Now he wanted to return to the elderberry tree and to the willow tree. Yes, under the willow tree one could dream a whole life in one short hour.

Everyone begged him to stay, but they could not keep him from leaving. They told him that the first snow had already fallen in the mountains. But he only said that he would walk in the wheel tracks of a carriage and cut himself a good stout cane.

He walked toward the mountains. He climbed up and came down on the other side. Weak and tired, he stumbled toward the north.

The stars came out; it was night, no house or town was near. Far down below him, in the valley, stars were shining—it was the lamps in the houses but to Knud it appeared as if there were two heavens: one above him and one below. He felt that he was ill. More and more stars appeared below him. Finally he realized that it was a little village, and he gathered the last of his strength and walked toward it.

He stayed a few days in a little inn. Down here in the valley the snow had already melted and the roads were muddy. One morning someone played a Danish melody on a barrel organ. His restless longing for home returned.

Knud set out again. He walked so fast, as if he feared that if he did not get home soon he would find everyone there dead. To no one had he spoken of his grief, the greatest sorrow that a man can experience. Such misery you cannot tell to the world, for it does not amuse or entertain anyone, even your friends. And poor Knud had no friends. A foreigner in a foreign land, he wandered homeward toward the north.

He had received only one letter from his parents and that had been more than a year ago. In it they had written, "You are not really Danish like we are. We love our country but you love only foreign lands." His parents felt they had a right to write like that because they knew him, because they were his father and mother.

It was evening. He was walking along a broad highway; it began to freeze. The landscape had become more and more flat, there were fields and meadows. At the side of the road stood a big willow tree. Everything looked so homely, so Danish. He sat down under the willow tree. He was terribly tired; his head fell down on his chest and he closed his eyes. He felt that the branches of the tree engulfed him, embraced him. The tree became an old man, "father willow" himself; and he lifted Knud up in his arms and carried his tired son home to the bleak beach of Køge, to the garden of his childhood.

Yes, it was the willow tree from Køge, it had gone out into the world to find him, and now "father willow" had found him and brought him back to the little garden by the stream. And there stood Johanna, dressed in all the beautiful clothes she had had on when last he saw her, and with the golden crown on her head. She shouted to him, "Welcome!"

Beside her stood two strange figures; they looked larger and more human than they had when he was a child. They were the gingerbread man and the gingerbread girl.

"Thank you," they said to Knud. "You have taught us always to speak up and say what one feels, or else nothing will come of it. We have, and now we are engaged."

Then the gingerbread couple walked ahead of them through the town of Køge, and they looked very decent and proper even from behind. They walked right up to the church, and Knud and Johanna followed them; they, too, were walking hand in hand. The church looked as it always had, with green ivy covering its walls. The big doors of the church opened, the organ was playing.

At the entrance the gingerbread couple stepped aside and said, "The bridal couple must go first." Knud and Johanna walked up to the altar and kneeled down. Ice-cold tears ran from Johanna's eyes. It was his great love that was thawing the ice around her heart; the tears fell on his burning cheeks and woke him.

There he sat under a willow tree in a foreign land on a cold winter evening, while the winds whipped hail into his face.

"That was the loveliest moment of my life," he mumbled. "And it was only a dream. God, let me dream it once more!" He closed his eyes. He slept, and he dreamed.

In the early morning it began to snow, and the wind made a snow-drift that covered his legs and his feet while he slept. At church time the peasants found the journeyman; he had frozen to death under-neath the willow tree.

*Five Peas from the Same Pod*

There once were five peas in a pod; they were green and the pod was green, and so they believed that the whole world was green, and that was quite right. Now the peas grew and the pod grew, and each little pea adjusted itself to its accommodations; they sat five in a row, one right next to the other. The sun shone on the pod and the rain washed it. It was warm and cozy inside, light in the daytime and dark at night, just as it is supposed to be. As the peas grew bigger they also reasoned better and thought much more; after all, they had to do something to pass the time away.

"I wonder if we shall sit here forever," said one of them. "I am afraid that I shall grow hard from sitting so long. I have a notion that there is something outside, I can feel it!"

Weeks passed and the peas turned yellow and the pod turned yellow. "The world is turning yellow," they all five said; and that was not an unreasonable thing for them to say.

Suddenly they felt the pod being torn off the plants. They had fallen into the hands of a human being. The pod was stuck down into a pocket where a lot of other pods lay. "Soon they will open up for us," said the peas, and that's what they were waiting for.

"I wonder which one of us will go farthest," said the smallest of the peas. "I am sure something will happen soon."

"Come what will!" said the largest.

"Crack!" The pod was opened; and all five peas rolled out into the sunshine. They were in a little boy's hand. He inspected them and said that they were perfect ammunition for a peashooter. One he shot off right away.

"Now I fly out into the wide world. Catch me if you can!" the pea shouted, and away it went.

"I shall fly right up into the sun, for that is a fitting pod for me!" shouted the second.

"Oh! We shall sleep wherever we end up," said the next two peas. "Rolling is as good as flying." They had fallen out of the boy's hand and were rolling along on the floor; but they were picked up and put in the peashooter anyway. "We will get the farthest," they shouted as they flew.

"Come what will!" said the last of the peas as it soared high into the air. It hit an old rotten board underneath the garret window. The board was filled with cracks; in them earth had collected and moss grew. The pea landed in one of the crevices, the moss closed around it, and it lay hidden but not forgotten by Our Lord.

"Come what will!" it repeated.

In the little garret room lived a very poor woman who did heavy work. She cleaned and polished stoves or chopped wood; she was willing to do anything she could. Strength she had, and hard-working she was; and poor as a church mouse she remained. Living with her was her daughter, who had been lying in bed ill for more than a year. The little girl was thin and delicate; it was as if she could neither live nor die.

"She will soon be going up to her sister," the woman would say. "I had two children once and God saw how difficult it was for me to provide for them; therefore He decided to share the work with me and took one. I would like to keep the other one, but God probably thinks it was a shame to separate them, and now she will be going up to her sister."

But the little sick girl stayed on; patiently, she lay in her bed all alone, while her mother went out to earn money for their keep.

It was spring. Early one morning the sun shone brightly in through the little window and across the floor. The little girl happened to notice something on the other side of the lowest windowpane. She called to her mother, who was just about to leave. "Mother, what's that bit of green? There in the lower pane, it moves in the breeze."

Her mother walked over to the window and opened it. "My!" she said. "It is a little pea. I wonder how that has got up here? Look, it already has green leaves. It will be a little garden for you to look at."

She moved the girl's bed closer to the window so that she could watch the little plant and then she left.

"I think I am getting well, Mother," said the little girl that evening. "The sun has shone so warmly down upon me all day. The little pea has been growing. I think I will soon be out in the sunshine too."

"If only that would happen," said the mother, but she did not believe that it would. Yet she did tie the plant to a stick which she had fastened to the board, so the wind could not break the little pea plant; then she ran a string from the top of the window down to the bottom, giving it something to cling to as it grew. And it certainly did grow; you could see the difference from one day to the next.

"I think it is going to flower," said the woman one morning, and now she, too, began to hope and believe that her little sick girl would get well. She had been aware that the child spoke more lively, and the last few mornings she had sat up in bed by herself in order to see her little garden that consisted of one solitary pea plant.

A week went by and the sick girl was up for the first time; she sat for a whole hour in a chair. The window was opened. Outside in the warm sunshine grew the little pea plant; the flower had opened its red and white petals. The little girl bent down and kissed its fine leaves. That day was a very special day for her, like a birthday.

"God Himself planted that pea and made it thrive for your sake, to give you back your health, my sweet little girl, and to give me joy and hope," the mother said, and smiled toward the flower as though it were an angel sent from God.

But the other peas, what happened to them? The one who had shouted, "Catch me who can," was swallowed by a pigeon. There it lay in the bird's gizzard, like Jonah in the whale. The two lazy peas had not fared any better, they had become pigeon food too. But that is after all a useful and respectable end for a pea. The fourth one, the one that wanted to fly right up to the sun, fell down into a gutter and there it lay for weeks and days in the stagnant water. It grew fat and soggy.

"I am getting nice and plump," it said. "I will get so fat that I burst and that is more than any pea has ever done. I certainly am the most remarkable of the five peas that were in the pod."

And the gutter agreed!

The girl stood at the garret window; her eyes were bright and the color of health was in her cheeks. She folded her hands above the pea flower and thanked God for it.

"I'll stick to my own pea!" said the gutter.

## 69

## A Leaf from Heaven

High, high up in the sky where the air is thin, an angel was flying; he carried in his hands a flower from paradise. As he bent his head to kiss the flower, one little leaf fell from it down to earth. It landed in the middle of a forest. As it sank down upon the soft earth it put forth roots and started to grow amid all the other greenery.

"That is a funny shoot, I wonder where it comes from," said the other plants; but none of them would claim it as a relation, not even the nettle or the thistle.

"It is probably a garden flower!" they mocked, and laughed. They thought that they had made a proper fool of it by calling it that. But the plant grew and grew and spread its long runners far and wide.

"Where do you think you are going?" asked the thistle that stood tall and proud with a thorn on every leaf. "You're doing your running backward. Upward, that is the right direction to grow. Do you think we are going to lift you up and carry you?"

Winter came and the world grew white. The snow covering the plant that had come from heaven, glittered and shone as though there were sunlight beneath it. When spring arrived the plant bloomed and its flowers were more beautiful than any of the others in the whole forest.

A professor of botany came; he was an expert and he had papers to prove it. He looked at the plant, picked a leaf and chewed on it, then declared that the plant was not in any botany book. He said it was impossible to determine which family of plants it belonged to.

"It is a subspecies," he said. "I don't recognize it, it is not recorded or classified."

"Not recorded, not classified!" shouted the thistles and nettles.

The tall trees that grew nearby heard every word; they could see that the plant did not belong to their family, but they did not say anything either for or against the plant—which is the safest thing to do if you are stupid.

A young girl, sweet and innocent, came walking through the forest. She was so poor that all she owned in this world was a Bible, but from its pages God spoke to her: "If anyone wishes to do you harm, remember the story of Joseph and how God turned the evil done against him into a blessing." She remembered, too, the words of our Saviour —He Who was most pure and virtuous, Whom men had mocked and nailed to a Cross; He Who from that Cross prayed: "Father, forgive them, for they know not what they do."

She stopped to look at the strange plant. Its green leaves gave off a fragrant smell—sweet and refreshing. Many-colored flowers bloomed on every branch, and in the strong sunlight they appeared like a display of fireworks. With awe she looked at the heavenly beauty; she took hold of one of the branches to look at the flowers more closely and smell the sweet odor. She would have liked to pick one of the flowers but felt that it would have been a pity, for, once picked, it would die. She took only one solitary green leaf which she placed between the pages of her Bible. There it would lie forever as green as on the day she had picked it, for it could not wither.

It was hidden among the pages of the Bible, and the Bible itself was soon to be hidden in the dark earth. The young girl had died, and the Bible was put under her head as a pillow in her coffin. On her sweet face was the solemn expression of death, as if the mortal clay wanted to prove that now she was with her Maker.

Out in the forest the wonderful plant flourished. Soon it was almost as big as a tree. All the migratory birds showed it great respect and would bow in front of it, especially the stork and the swallows.

"Foreign nonsense!" said the thistle and the nettles. "We who are born here never behave like that."

And the black slugs that lived in the forest spat on the big plant.

A swineherd came to gather food for his pigs. He tore up nettles, thistles, and the wonderful plant from heaven, roots and all. "It might as well be of some use," he said.

The king of the country was suffering from melancholy. He was so very sad that even working did not help. Serious and profound books were read aloud to him, and humorous and light ones, but neither did any good. Then a letter came from one of the wisest men in the world, whom the king had asked to help him. In it he declared that there existed a remedy certain to cure the king of his affliction.

"And it grows within His Majesty's own kingdom. It is a plant that has come down to earth from heaven; its leaves are shaped like this . . . and its flowers like that. . . . It is easy to recognize." Here followed a drawing of the plant. "It is green both winter and summer. Pluck one leaf from it each evening and lay it on the king's forehead before he goes to sleep. His melancholy will disappear. Sweet dreams will come to him during the night, which will refresh him and give him strength for the coming day."

All the doctors and the professor of botany knew immediately which plant was meant. They all went out into the forest to look for it. —But where was the plant?

"I guess I tore it up with the nettles," said the swineherd. "It has long ago been eaten. It isn't my fault, I didn't know any better."

"You didn't know any better!" screamed all the doctors and the professor of botany. "Ignorance, ignorance. Oh, how profound it can be!" They lamented; and the swineherd took the words to his heart, for they were meant for him alone.

Not one leaf from the plant could be found. The one that lay in the young girl's casket none of them knew about.

The unhappy king himself, in despair, made an expedition to the forest to see the place where the plant had grown. "This spot is holy," he declared.

A golden fence was erected around the plot of earth where the heavenly plant had grown, and a sentry was posted to guard it both day and night.

The professor of botany wrote a paper about the marvelous plant, and for that he was gilded just like the fence. This pleased him greatly, and the gilding suited both him and his family. And this is the happiest part of this story, for the plant was gone and the king was still depressed and melancholy—"But he has always been that way," said the sentry.

## 70

## She Was No Good

The mayor was standing by the open window; he was in shirt sleeves and his face was even more ruddy than usual, for he had just shaved —a job he preferred doing himself and which he did well, although there was a tiny nick on his chin that he had covered with a bit of paper.

"Hey, you, little boy!" he called.

The little boy was none other than the washerwoman's son, who, as he was passing, had noticed the mayor and had politely taken off his cap. It was the kind that had a fold in its peak, so it could be readily stuffed into a pocket. His clothes were clean though covered with patches, and on his feet he wore a pair of clumsy clogs. There he stood before the open window as respectfully as if the mayor were the king himself.

"You are a good boy," said the mayor. "You are a polite little boy. Your mother is washing down at the river, and that is where you are heading for. You are carrying something in your pocket. Your mother is in a bad way! How much do you have in the bottle?"

"Half a pint," whispered the frightened boy.

"And this morning she drank the same amount," continued the man.

"No, that was yesterday," answered the boy.

"Two halves make a whole. She is no good! It is a pity what happens to people of that class. Tell your mother that she ought to be ashamed of herself! And don't you ever become a drunkard, but I suppose you won't be able to avoid it. . . . Poor child. Well, run along!"

The boy left. He kept his cap in his hand, and the wind played with his yellow hair, so that long tufts of it stood straight up. He walked across the street and down an alley to the river. There stood his mother, in water up to her knees, rinsing some clothes she had just washed. The river flowed rapidly, for the lock by the water mill had been opened. It was hard work just keeping the sheets from being carried away by the current.

"I am about to sail away," said the mother, and laughed. "I am glad that you have come. I need a little something to help me. I have stood here in the water for six hours, and it is cold. You have brought me something?"

The boy took the bottle from his pocket and gave it to his mother, who put it to her lips and drank.

"Oh! That was good. How it warms one! Why, it is just as good as a hot meal and a lot cheaper. Take a swallow, my boy. You look pale, I am afraid that you are freezing, too, in those thin clothes, now that it is fall. Huh! How cold the water has become. I hope I won't get sick. But why should I? Give me back the bottle; now it's my turn to have another drink. You can take another one, too, but only a drop. Don't let it become a habit. My poor little child!"

The woman climbed up on the bank and stood next to her son; water was streaming from her skirts and from the rush mat that had been tied around her waist. "I work my fingers to the bone," she said. "But that doesn't matter, as long as you get a good start in life."

At that moment another woman appeared. She was older and walked with a limp; somehow her skin seemed as threadbare as her clothes. A large spit curl hung down over her forehead. It was meant to hide a missing eye but only made one more aware of the defect. "Crippled Maren with the curl" was the name her neighbors had given her, and she was a friend of the washerwoman. "Poor creature," she began at once. "Always standing in the cold water, always slaving away. If anyone needs a drop to keep them warm, then it's you; and to think some people grudge you a drink."

Maren repeated to the washerwoman everything the mayor had said. She had heard it all and it had made her angry. "How dare he say such things to a boy about his own mother. He begrudges you a drop of liquor, but when he throws a party, why, they drink wine by the case. Many of his guests get a drop too much, but no one calls them drunkards. They are good, and you are no good!"

"Did he really talk like that to you?" she asked, turning to her son, while her lips trembled. "Did he say that you had a mother that was no good? Well, maybe he's right. But he should never have said it to a child, though it's not the first time that that family has been the cause of my suffering."

"That's right!" Maren exclaimed. "You used to work in the mayor's house when his parents were still alive. But that's such a long time ago. We've eaten a ton of salt since then; no wonder we are so thirsty." Maren laughed. "They are having a big dinner party there now, though they wish they weren't. . . . But it is too late to do anything about it now . . . The guests were invited long ago and the food was all made. But the mayor got a letter an hour before saying that his younger brother had died in Copenhagen. The gardener told me all about it."

"Dead!" said the washerwoman, and turned pale.

"Oh my!" exclaimed Maren. "One would think he was your brother. I suppose you knew him well when you were a servant there."

"So he is dead! There never lived a kinder person. It is not often that God receives such a blessed, such a good person." Tears started to run down the washerwoman's cheeks. "Oh, my God! I feel so dizzy! Everything is turning about. I shouldn't have emptied the bottle. It was too much. I feel terribly ill." The woman tottered over to a fence and leaned against it.

"Goodness me, you do look sick." Maren looked unhappily at her friend. "But I am sure it will pass! . . . No, I am afraid you are really ill, I'd better take you home."

"But the clothes!" wailed the washerwoman.

"I will wash them later. You take my arm. The boy can stay and watch the clothes until I come back."

The washerwoman could hardly walk. "I have been standing in the cold water too long. I have had nothing to eat since this morning. I think I have a fever. Dear Jesus, help me! Help me to get home! Oh, my poor child!" And she wept.

Slowly, the two women made their way up through the alley. The boy, left alone to guard the clothes at the riverbank, cried too.

Just as the women, leaning on each other, were passing the mayor's house, the washerwoman fell. A crowd gathered around her, while Maren went into the house for help.

The mayor and his guests were looking out of the window. "She has had one too many again," he explained. "She is no good. It is a pity for her son. I feel sorry for him; his mother is no good."

The washerwoman was carried to the hovel where she lived and put to bed. Maren warmed a bowlful of beer with sugar and butter—for of all the medicines she knew, this one was the best. Then she went back to the river to rinse the clothes. She meant well, but she didn't do a very good job. In fact, all she did was pull the wet clothes out of the water, wring them out, and put them in a box.

Later that evening Maren sat at the bedside of the washerwoman. The cook at the mayor's house had given Maren a large slice of ham and some fried potatoes for the sick woman, but the washerwoman couldn't eat anything, so Maren and the boy ate the food, which the washerwoman declared smelled so good, she was sure that the aroma, alone, must be nourishing.

The boy slept in the same bed as his mother. He stretched himself out at her feet, widthwise across the bed. An old rug, which had been patched with blue and white strips of cloth, was his blanket.

The washerwoman began to feel a little better. The warm beer and the smell of the food had done her some good. "Thank you, you good, kind soul," she said to Maren. "Is the boy asleep?" she whispered. "If he is, I'll tell you the story."

Maren nodded.

The washerwoman lifted her head so she could see the child. "Yes, he's sleeping already. Look how sweet he looks with his eyes closed. He does not know how I have suffered; and may God spare him from ever knowing such suffering. . . . I was a maid in the old judge's house, where his son the mayor now lives; and while I was there his youngest son came home: 'the student,' as they called him. I was young then, wild and full of life; but I was a good girl—and that I would say even if it were God who asked me. The student was gay and happy: a blessed young man. There was not a bad drop of blood in his veins. A more honest, more honorable, more upright person has never walked God's green earth. He was the son of the judge and I was only the maid, but we loved each other in the most respectable way. For a kiss is not a sin between two people who really care for each other.

"He told his mother about it; she was his God here on earth. She was good, clever, and kind. . . . He went away; but before he left he put a gold ring on my finger. When he had been gone a few days, my mistress said she wished to talk with me. She spoke gravely yet gently, as God Himself would have spoken. She explained about the wide gap between his upbringing and education and my own.

"'Now he sees your beauty, but beauty fades,' she said. 'You do not understand the things that he does. In the world of the mind, of the intellect, you are not equal; and that is a real tragedy. I respect the poor, and know that in heaven many a poor man will be seated nearer to God than many rich men will be. But here on earth, a carriage has to follow the tracks in the road or it will turn over; and you two would overturn! I know that there is an artisan, Erik Glovemaker, who has asked for your hand. He is a widower but has no children and is doing very well. Why don't you think it over?'

"Every word that she said was like a knife piercing my heart. The worst of it was that I knew that what she said was true; and it was that that crushed me. I kissed her hand and I cried bitter tears, but not as many as I wept when I returned to my own room. The Lord knows how I struggled and suffered all through that long, terrible night. The next day was Sunday; I took holy communion in the hope that God would give me light. It was like an act of providence; as I was leaving the church, I met Erik Glovemaker. All my doubt was gone, we suited each other; we came from the same station in life, we had been brought up alike. He was even quite wealthy. I walked straight up to him and took his hand. 'Am I still in your thoughts?' I asked.

"'Yes. . . . Forever and always,' he replied.

"'Would you want to marry a girl who honors and respects you but does not love you, though that may come in time?'

"'It will, I am sure,' he said. And we shook hands.

"Around my neck on a string I had carried the ring the student had given me. It lay next to my bare breast for I never dared wear it where anyone might see it. Only at night did I put it on my finger. When I came home that day, I kissed the ring until my lips bled; and then gave it to my mistress and told her that on the following Sunday the minister would announce from the pulpit banns for Erik Glovemaker and me.

"My mistress threw her arms around me and kissed me. She did not say that I was no good then. But maybe I was a better person when I was younger, before I had been tried by misfortune. We were married, and for the first few years all went well. Erik had a journeyman and an apprentice working for him and I had you, Maren, to help me."

"And you were the best mistress one could have!" said Maren. "I shall never forget how gentle and kind both you and your husband were."

"Yes, those were the good years, when you were with us. . . . We had no children yet. . . . I never saw the student again. . . . No, that is not true, I did see him once but he did not see me. He had come home for his mother's funeral. I saw him standing by her grave; his face was so white and grief-stricken because of his sorrow over his mother's death. After his father died he never came back here; he was always traveling in foreign countries. He never married, that much I know. I think he became a lawyer. . . . I am sure he did not remember me, and if he had seen me he would not have recognized me. I have grown so ugly. And that, too, is probably for the best."

She talked about the difficult years, when one misfortune followed another. She and her husband had had five hundred silver marks and had bought an old house in the street for two hundred. This they had meant to tear down in order to build a new one. The mason and the carpenter had estimated that the new house would cost a thousand marks to build. Someone in Copenhagen had readily offered to loan Erik Glovemaker the sum, but the captain who was to bring the money was lost at sea and so were the thousand marks.

"It was then that that sweet child"—the washerwoman nodded toward the foot of the bed—"who is sleeping so soundly, was born. Right after that his father fell ill. I had to dress and undress him for nearly a whole year; he was too weak to do it himself. We sank deeper and deeper into debt. Finally we had nothing left, not even any clothes; then I lost my husband. . . . All the work I could get was drudgery; but I have toiled and struggled and fought for my boy's sake. I have scrubbed floors and washed clothes. My lot will never change, that is God's will. But soon He will call me up to Him, and then He will have to take care of my child." With those words, she fell asleep.

In the morning she felt better and mistakenly thought herself well enough to work. She had no sooner stepped into the cold water than she felt faint and began to tremble. She turned around, back toward the shore; and she fell. Her head lay on the bank, but her feet were in the river; her wooden clogs—stuffed with straw for warmth—went sailing away with the current. She was found by Maren, who had come to bring her a mug of coffee.

A message had come from the mayor that the washerwoman was to come to his office, he had something to tell her. It was too late. A barber had been called to bleed her, but the washerwoman was already dead.

"She has drunk herself to death," declared the mayor.

The letter that brought the news of the death of the mayor's brother had also contained his will. In it was written that six hundred silver crowns were to be paid to the glovemaker's widow, "who once worked in my parents' house." She and her child were to have the money in appropriate portions, according to their needs.

"There was once some nonsense between my brother and her. It's a good thing that she's out of the way," the mayor said. "Now the boy will get all of the money. I'll find a good family who will take him in. He will make a fine artisan."

The mayor called the boy to him and promised him that he would take care of him. He also explained to the child how lucky he was that his mother was dead, for she had been no good.

The washerwoman was brought to the churchyard, where she was buried in the corner set aside for the poor. With the boy standing beside her, Maren planted a rosebush on her grave.

"My sweet mother," the child said with the tears running down his cheeks. "Is it really true that she was no good?"

"Oh, she was good!" said Maren. "I knew her for many years and was with her the last night of her life. And I say that she was good; and God in His heaven will say the same; let the world go on saying that she was no good."

## 71

## The Last Pearl

It was a well-to-do home, a happy home. Everyone was jubilant: master, mistress, friends, and servants. That very day an heir had been born, and mother and son were fine.

The lamp in the cozy bedchamber was shaded. Heavy silk curtains were drawn in front of the windows. The carpets on the floor were thick and soft like moss. Everything in the room seemed to be slumbering. The night nurse was asleep, too; which did no great harm, for everything in that home breathed security. The guardian spirit of the house stood by the bed; the child was asleep next to the mother. Around the little boy a circle of stars appeared; they were the pearls from fortune's necklace. The good fairies had come and given gifts to the newly born. Health, wealth, love, and happiness: everything that man could wish for here on earth.

"Every gift has been brought and accepted," said the guardian spirit.

"No," said a voice close by. It was the child's own guardian angel speaking. "One fairy has not brought her gift yet, but she will bring it sooner or later, though years may go by before she comes. The last of the pearls is missing."

"Missing? Nothing must be missing here! If it is true, then let us go to the mighty fairy and ask her for her gift."

"Be patient, she will come. Her pearl is necessary for the necklace to be strung."

"Where does she live? Where is her home? Tell it to me and I will go and fetch the pearl."

"If you wish," said the child's guardian angel, "then I shall lead you to her. She has no permanent home but is forever traveling. She visits the king in his castle and the poor in their hovels. No house exists that she passes by without entering at least once. To all she brings her gift. This little swaddled child will meet her too. You think that time is long but that is no reason to waste it. Well and good, let us seek her."

Hand in hand, the two spirits flew to seek the fairy in the place where she, for the moment, made her home.

It was a big house with long corridors and empty rooms. Everything was strangely still and quiet, the windows were open, letting in the raw, damp air. Silently, the long white curtains moved in the breeze.

In the middle of a large room stood a coffin and in it lay the body of a woman. She was neither young nor old but in that period of life which people sometimes call the best. Freshly plucked roses covered her body; among the flowers her folded hands could be seen. Her noble face, transfigured by death, looked expectantly up toward God.

By the coffin stood a man and a whole flock of children; the youngest of them the father carried in his arms. This was their leave-taking. The father bent down and kissed his wife's hand. Now that hand that had been so strong, so loving, was like the withered leaf.

Tears fell from their eyes, but not a word was spoken, no sound broke that stillness, which contained a world of pain. Weeping, they left.

One candle burned in the room. Its flames wavered in the wind, was almost put out, and then shot up clearly and brightly again. Strangers came; they closed the coffin and hammered the lid down with nails. The sound of the hammering echoed through the corridors and rooms of the house and beat upon the bleeding hearts.

"Where have you led me?" asked the guardian spirit. "Here lives no fairy whose pearl would be one of life's most valuable gifts."

"In this holy hour, she lives here," said the child's guardian angel, and pointed to a corner of the room. There in the chair where the mother used to sit, surrounded by flowers and pictures, where she—the good fairy of her own household—used to smile to her children, husband, and friends, in that spot which once had been the center, the very heart of the household, now sat a stranger, a woman dressed in long black clothes. It was Sorrow; now she reigned, she had become their mother. A tear dropped from her eyes down into her lap and became a pearl; it sparkled with all the colors of the rainbow and the angel caught it.

"The seven-colored pearl of sorrow must be in the necklace too. It makes the other pearls shine stronger, more beautifully. In it is locked the flow of the rainbow, the arch that connects the earth with heaven. Everyone we love and who dies makes another friend in heaven for us to long for. In the dark nights here on earth, we look toward the stars, toward the consummation, the fulfillment. Look, contemplate the pearl of sorrow, for it contains the wings of Psyche, which shall carry us away from here."

## 72

# The Two Maidens

Do you know what a rammer looks like? It is a tool that workmen use when they pave a street with cobblestones. In Denmark it is called a "maiden"; and therefore, it is appropriate to use the feminine gender when describing it.

She is made of a solid piece of wood, broad at the base and reinforced with heavy iron bands. Her top is slender and from it protrude two arms. These the workman holds when he uses the "maiden" to stamp the cobblestones into place.

Now in a tool shed, among shovels, measuring rods, and wheelbarrows, stood two such rammers or "maidens." They had heard that it had been decided that they were no longer to be named "maidens" but were to be called stampers instead. This was considered a great innovation for the Danish language, a technical one that every layer of cobblestones approved of.

Among human beings there exist a group called "emancipated women." To this category belong headmistresses of schools, midwives, dancers who can stand professionally on one leg, milliners, and nurses. The two "maidens" from the tool shed decided to join this society; after all, they were employed by the Ministry of Works. They did not want to lose their ancient and honorable title, and just be called stampers.

"Maiden is a human name, a stamper is a thing; and we will not allow ourselves to be called things, it is an insult."

"My fiancé may break off our engagement when he hears of it," said the youngest of them. She was engaged to a pile driver, which is a machine that drives piles far down into the ground. It does the heavy work and the rammers, or "maidens," that which is more refined. "He has learned to love me as a 'maiden.' How do I know if he will feel the same way toward me when I am a stamper? I won't allow them to change my name."

"I would rather have my arms broken than permit it," wailed the older of them.

The wheelbarrow was of a different opinion, and the wheelbarrow was not a nobody in that society. He considered himself a quarter of carriage, because he had one wheel. "The name 'maiden' is rather ordinary or common, whereas the word 'stamper' signifies that one is related to a signet, which stamps too; for example, the royal seal stamps. If I were you, I would gladly give up the name 'maiden.'"

"Never! I am too old for that," shouted the older of the rammers.

"I think you are all unaware of something called European Standards," said an honest old measuring rod, who had been retired because it was inaccurate. "One has to know one's limitations and submit to time and necessity. If a law has been passed that 'maidens' are to be called 'stampers,' then they must be called it. Everything has only its measured time here on earth, even a name."

"If I have to change mine," said the younger of the two rammers, "then I would prefer something feminine like 'miss.'"

"I would prefer being chopped into firewood," asserted the older of them, who, in truth, was an old maid.

They all went to work. The two "maidens" were driven in a wheelbarrow, which was a respectable way to travel; but they were called stampers.

"Maid!" they said every time they hit a cobblestone. "Maid!" They would have pronounced their names in full, but they were too angry and bit it off short. Among themselves they always used the name "maiden." They talked well of the "good old times," when things were called by their proper names. Maidens they remained, both of them, for the pile driver broke his engagement to the younger of them. He did not want an affair with a "stamper."

## 73

## The Uttermost Parts of the Sea

Two ships had been sent up to the far north to discover what was land and what was sea; and to find out whether there was a passage through the Arctic Ocean. Through fog and ice they had sailed, ever steering north; now winter had come, and soon they would see the sun for the last time that year, and for months there would be only night. The ships lay surrounded by ice, and the frozen sea was covered by snow. Nearby, out of snow, houses had been made, in the shape of beehives. Some were as large as Viking graves, others were so small that only three or four men could lie outstretched in them.

But though the sun had disappeared, it was not dark, for the northern lights were a permanent fireworks display in the dark sky. The snow glittered and reflected their light, day and night were dusk. The Eskimos came; strange men dressed in skins, with sleds piled high with furs. Now the floors of the snow huts got fur carpets, and the sailors slept warmly underneath their ice cupolas.

Outside the temperatures dropped far below anything we can ever experience, even in the coldest winter. At home it was only late fall, and the seamen recalled how the sunbeams looked when they played upon October's yellow and brown leaves. Their watches told them that night had come.

In one of the smaller snow huts, two of the sailors had already lain down to sleep. The younger of them had been given a treasure by his grandmother; it was the Bible. From his childhood, he re-

membered so many of its stories and the psalms of David. Every day
he read from it and these words from the songs brought him comfort:
*"If I take the wings of the morning, and dwell in the uttermost parts
of the sea. Even there shall thy hand lead me, and thy right hand
shall hold me."*

His faith in the truth of these words made sleep come as soon as he
had closed his eyes. He dreamed that his soul was awake while his
body rested. He felt as if he were listening to well-known songs and
melodies that breathed summer's warmth. The snow cupola above
him became even whiter; it was the giant wing of an angel whose
gentle face he could look up into. From the pages of the Bible, as
from the cup of the lily, the angel rose; he spread out his arms and
the walls of the snow hut disappeared like a mist. The green fields
and hills, the autumn-brown forest of his home were there instead;
and the sun was shining, it was a lovely fall day. The stork nest was
empty but apples still hung on the wild apple trees. The captured
starling whistled in its little cage, which hung outside the window of
the little farmhouse that was his home. The starling whistled in
the manner that he had taught it to, and his grandmother was feeding
it, just as he used to. The blacksmith's daughter stood by the well
drawing the water, and she was as beautiful as ever. She nodded to
Grandmother, who waved back with a letter in her hand. It had come
that morning from the cold lands high up north where her grandchild was. They laughed and cried while they read it; and he, lying
under the ice and snow—by the grace of the dream and the angel's
wings—was also at home with them, and he laughed and cried too.
They read the letter aloud, even the words from the psalm: *"In the
uttermost parts of the sea . . . thy right hand shall hold me."* The
words rang like a beautiful hymn and the angel folded his wings. The
dream was over, it was dark again in the snow hut; but the Bible lay
next to him and hope and faith were in his heart. God was there,
and, therefore, so was his home, *"in the uttermost parts of the sea"!*

## 74

## The Piggy Bank

The children's room was filled with toys; on top of the cabinet stood a piggy bank. It was a fat clay pig with a slit in back that had been enlarged with a knife, so that silver crowns could slide through it. Two of those heavy coins had made that journey, besides innumerable pennies. The piggy bank was so filled that it didn't rattle when you shook it; and higher no piggy bank can rise. He stood on top of the cabinet and looked down upon everything in the room; he knew he could buy it all with the money he had in his stomach, and that was a very comfortable feeling.

Everything else in the room knew it, too, though they didn't talk about it. One of the drawers in the chest was open; in it lay a doll. She was old and had once broken her neck, but it had been repaired. Now she sat up and suggested, "Let us play human beings, it is amusing." At once everything started to jump about. The paintings on the wall turned around, in order to show that they had backs as well as fronts. That irritated the doll, who thought they had done it just to be contrary.

It was the middle of the night, but the moon was shining in through the window, giving free illumination. All the toys were invited to join the game, even the old baby carriage, though it didn't really belong. "Everyone has his own good points," it said. "We can't all be aristocrats; some have to work for a living."

The piggy bank was the only one that had received a written invitation; the others feared that he was so far above them that he couldn't hear a spoken one, even if they shouted. He didn't answer. If he were going to watch the game, then he would only do it from his own home. He felt that everyone should comply with his wishes, even when he hadn't expressed them; and everyone did.

The little doll theater was erected in such a place that the piggy bank could watch the performance. They would start the evening by giving a play; later on there would be tea and intelligent conversation. But the rocking horse began talking immediately about the breeding and the breaking of horses; and the baby carriage talked about railroads and steam engines; they were always so professional. The clock on the wall talked politics; it declared that it knew the time, but the other toys said it was slow. The walking cane just stood about admiring its own silver knob, and the two embroidered pillows on the sofa, who were pretty but stupid, giggled.

Finally the play could begin. Everyone had been told that they could applaud or make any noise they wished, such as banging, rumpling, or whistling. The riding whip said it would "crack" for the young people in the play but not for the old: they were so boring.

"I will bang away for anyone," said the firecracker.

The spittoon stood humbly in the corner and mumbled, "One has to be somewhere."

The play was terrible but the acting was marvelous. All the players played in the center of the stage, to make sure their performances were seen.

The doll who once had broken her neck almost lost her head, she was so moved. The piggy bank was touched too, but in his own way; he thought of doing "something" for one of them, such as leaving him a small sum in his will.

All enjoyed themselves so much that they decided to skip the tea and just have the "intelligent conversation." They all felt "just like human beings," and that was not meant satirically. All of them thought their own opinions cleverer than their neighbors', and they all wondered what the piggy bank was thinking about. He was thinking very seriously about wills and funerals: long, slow-moving thoughts. But death and funerals have a habit of coming before one wishes them to come. . . .

"Crash!" Down fell the piggy bank and broke into hundreds of pieces, while the money rolled all over the floor. One of the silver crowns rolled all the way to the door; it wanted to get out into the world and it did, and so did the pennies. The broken pieces of the piggy bank were thrown in the trash can. It wasn't the kind of funeral he had expected.

The next day a new piggy bank stood on the cabinet. He looked just like the other one; and he too couldn't rattle but that was because he was empty. He had just started his career; and with those words we will end our story.

## 75

## Ib and Little Christina

There is a river in Denmark called the River of the Gods, the Gudenaa; and not far from its shores, as it flows through the forest of Silkeborg, rises a ridge, on the west side of which was situated a small farm—in fact, it is still there. Even when the rye and barley stand high in the fields, you can see the sandy soil beneath the grain; and the harvest is always meager. This story takes place some years ago; and the farmer who tilled it then had three sheep, a pig, and two oxen. He could have kept a couple of horses but he felt as most farmers in that area did: "Horses eat up their profits themselves." Jeppe was the farmer's name. He farmed in the summer and carved wooden shoes in the winter. He was a skillful carver; but he had a younger helper who was even better than he was, and understood how to make clogs so that they were strong; and yet not heavy and shapeless. They also made other household wares which fetched a good price. Although Jeppe and his family were not rich, no one in that district would have called them poor.

Little Ib was seven years old. He was an only child, and he liked to sit by his father and watch him carve. The boy whittled sticks and sometimes he cut his fingers. One day he did manage to carve two little objects that looked like a pair of tiny wooden shoes. These he wanted to give to Christina, the daughter of the bargeman, who lived in a cottage on the heath. The little girl was very beautiful, and so delicate that she did not look at all like a bargeman's daughter. Had she had clothes to match the loveliness that God had given her, then no one would have guessed that she had been born in a poor cottage on the lonely heath. Her father was a widower who made his living by transporting lumber from the woods down to the locks at Silkeborg. Sometimes he would even sail as far as Randers with his barge. As there was no one at home to take care of little Christina—she was a year younger than Ib—she was always with her father, except on his journeys to Randers. Then her father would bring her to Jeppe's house to stay.

Ib and little Christina never fought, neither when they played nor at table. They would play in the sand, pretend they were making a little garden, or just tumble about. One day they ventured as far as the top of the ridge beyond which was the forest. They found the nest of a snipe with eggs in it; that had been a very exciting adventure.

Ib had never been on the heath, nor had he ever sailed with a barge down the river and through the lakes. But one day Christina's father invited him on a trip, and his parents gave their consent. The evening before they were to set out, the bargeman came to fetch him, and he spent the night in the little cottage on the heath.

Early the next morning the children were sitting on top of the woodpile, in the barge, eating bread and raspberries. Christina's father and his helper were poling the barge down the river; they were following the current, so they sailed along at a good speed. One after another they sailed through the lakes. Every time they entered one, Ib was sure that the river had ended, for bulrushes, reeds, and trees seemed to enclose the lake; but finally a narrow opening would appear that they could sail through. Sometimes the trees leaning out over the narrow river would almost hinder their passing, but always the barge sailed on. Some of the oak trees had naked branches that had lost all their bark and looked as if they had rolled up their sleeves to show their withered old arms. Many of the old alder trees had loosened themselves from the banks and now stood like little islets in the river. White and yellow water lilies floated amid their big green leaves. It certainly was a lovely trip. At last they came to the locks where eels were caught and shipped as far away as Copenhagen. The water rushed over the lock and fell as a waterfall on the other side; and that was something for Ib and little Christina to look at.

At that time no factory or town had been built there yet; there was only the old farm on which not many people lived. The water rushing over the lock and the cry of the wild ducks were the only sounds to be heard. The lumber was loaded onto a bigger barge; and Christina's father bought a little newly slaughtered pig and some eels. Then they were ready for the homeward journey. The pig and the eels were put into a basket. Now they had the current against them, but not the wind; so they hoisted a sail and that was as good as having two horses pull the barge.

When they reached the part of the forest where the bargeman's helper lived, they moored the barge at the bank. Christina's father told the children to stay on board and not to touch anything, while he accompanied his young helper to his home. The bargeman said that he would be back very soon.

The children obeyed him at first, but not for long. They had to peep into the basket that contained the eels and the pig. They took the little pig out; and when they both tried to hold it at once, it fell overboard; and the little dead animal floated away with the current.

It was a terrible calamity! Ib leaped to the shore and soon Christina followed him. "Take me with you!" she cried. They ran in among the trees; and within a few minutes the barge and the river disappeared from their view. Christina fell and began to cry, but Ib calmed her.

"The house is right over there. Come along," he said; but the house was not "right over there," and soon the two children were lost. They walked on and on; the dried leaves rustled and dead branches broke with cracking sound as they stepped on them.

Someone was shouting far away. The children stopped to listen, but then they heard the hoarse frightening cry of an eagle; and they ran. A little while later they came upon a blueberry patch covered with the most delicious large, ripe berries. They were so tempting that they had to sit down and eat them. Their cheeks and lips were stained deep blue. Again they heard someone shouting.

"We will get spanked because of the pig," observed little Christina.

"Let us go home to my parents," said Ib, who was certain that Christina was right. "It is not far from here." The children walked on and finally they came to a road, but it did not lead home. It began to grow dark, and they were very frightened. The terrible stillness of the forest was broken by the terrifying hooting of owls and the cries of other birds that they did not know. Christina cried and Ib cried. They wept for an hour or more before they both lay down under some bushes and fell asleep.

The sun was already high in the sky when they awoke, but they were very cold. They could see the sun shining on top of a nearby hill. Up there they would be able to get warm, and Ib hoped that he would be able to see his home. But they were in another part of the forest, far away from the little farm. When they climbed the hill they found a little pool, and where the sun's rays fell on the water, they could see the fishes swimming. Such a sight they had never seen before. A few minutes later they found some hazelnut bushes and their fears were forgotten. They cracked the nuts and ate them. Although they were far from ripe, they already had little kernels. Then something terribly frightening happened!

A tall woman stepped out from behind the bushes. Her face was brown and her hair was black. She carried a bundle on her back and a big strong cane in her hands; she was a gypsy. At first the children could not understand what she said. She took three nuts out of her apron pocket and told them that they were "wishing nuts," and that each of them contained something marvelous.

Ib looked at the woman for a long time; her expression seemed kind. He asked her if he could have her "wishing nuts," and she gave them to him. Then she picked a whole pocketful of nuts from the bushes for herself.

The two children stared wide-eyed at the "wishing nuts."

"Is there a carriage and horses in one of them?" asked Ib.

"In that one there is a golden carriage with golden horses," answered the woman, and pointed to one of the nuts in the boy's hand.

"Give it to me then," begged little Christina; and Ib gave it to her.

"Is there a pretty little necklace like the one Christina is wearing in this one?" demanded Ib.

"There are ten necklaces," said the woman, "and dresses, stockings, and hats."

"Then I want that one too," shouted little Christina, and Ib gave it to her. The third nut was a little black one. "That one you can keep," said Christina. "It is a pretty one, too."

"And what is in that?" asked Ib.

"What is best for you," said the gypsy.

Ib kept the nut. The gypsy woman said that she would show them the way home; but she led them astray, sending them in the opposite direction from the one they should have gone. But one cannot accuse her of trying to steal the children, and she might have acted in good faith.

In the middle of the forest they met Chris the forester. He knew Ib and he took the children home. Both the bargeman and Ib's parents had been so upset that the children were forgiven, though they deserved a spanking, not only for having let the pig fall in the water but also for running away.

That evening after Christina and her father had returned to their home on the heath, Ib took out the nut that contained what was "best for him." He placed it between the door and its casing and cracked it by closing the door. There was no kernel in it, just some black dirt; it was worm-eaten.

"I thought so!" Ib was not surprised. "How could there be room in a little nut for what was 'best'? Christina will get no carriage or dresses out of her nuts either," Ib muttered.

Winter came; and the years passed by. Finally Ib was old enough to be confirmed. Every Sunday that spring he walked the many miles to the church to receive religious instruction. One day the bargeman came by. He had news to tell: little Christina was old enough to earn her own keep and he had found her a good position in the family of a wealthy innkeeper near Herning. She was to help in the house and they would see to it that she was confirmed.

Ib and little Christina said good-by to each other. "The little sweethearts," they were called. Christina showed Ib the two little "wishing nuts" he had given her, and which he had received from the gypsy that day in the forest; and she told him that the little pair of wooden shoes that he had cut for her were in the bottom of the chest in which she had packed her clothes. Then they parted.

Ib was confirmed but continued living at home, for his father had died and he had to help his mother. He had become as good a carver of wooden shoes as his father had been; and in the summer he took good care of their little farm. Not often did they hear from Christina, but the news that they did get was always good. She wrote to her father about her confirmation and the letter was filled with descriptions of the new clothes she had received from her mistress.

The next spring, on a particularly beautiful day, someone knocked on the door of the little farm. It was the bargeman and Christina; she had been offered a ride in a carriage as far as Tem and back. This had been an opportunity to come home for a visit. Beautiful she was and her clothes were as elegant as any lady's. Ib, who was wearing his work clothes, could hardly utter a word. He took her hand and held it tightly, but his tongue was all tied up in knots. Christina's wasn't: she talked and talked, there was so much to tell, and she kissed Ib boldly on the mouth.

"Don't you know me any more?" she asked.

All he could manage to reply, even though they were alone together, was: "You have become a fine lady and I am so . . . so coarse! But oh, Christina, how I have thought about you and of the time when we were children together!"

Arm in arm, they walked up to the top of the ridge; from there they could see the river and as far as the heath, where Christina's father lived. Ib did not say a word; but as they were returning—and Ib was to go to his home and Christina to her father's—Ib realized how very much he wanted Christina to be his wife. Hadn't they been called "sweethearts" since they were little children? Now he knew that he had always expected that one day they would marry; and he felt as though they were engaged though neither of them had ever spoken a word about it.

Christina could only stay a few hours because she had to be in Tem early the following morning, when the carriage departed that would take her back to the inn at Herning.

Ib and the bargeman accompanied her to Tem. It was a lovely night; the moon was full. All the way, Ib held Christina's hand, and when they finally arrived at their destination he did not want to let go of it. He had great difficulty saying what anyone could have read in his eyes. He spoke only a few words but every one of them came from his heart. "If you have not become used to finer things than I can give you, and if you will be satisfied with living in my mother's house with me as your husband, then I think the two of us should become man and wife. . . . But I will not hurry you."

"Yes, let us wait a little while, Ib," replied Christina, and pressed his hand; then he kissed her on the mouth. "I trust you, Ib," she said. "And I think that I love you! But I would like to have time to think about it."

They parted and Ib told the bargeman that he and Christina were as good as engaged. Christina's father was pleased and not surprised. Although he spent the night at Ib's home, they did not talk any more about it.

A year went by. Two letters had passed between Ib and Christina, and both of them had been signed: "Yours unto death." Then one day the bargeman arrived; he had greetings from Christina. That was easy enough to say. What followed was more difficult and he took his time saying it. Everything went well for Christina; more than well, but then she was a good girl. The innkeeper's son had been home on a visit, he had a good job in an office in Copenhagen. He had taken a liking to Christina and she to him. His parents were not against them marrying, but Christina felt that she had given Ib her word; and therefore she was going to say no. "Even though such a marriage would be fortunate for a poor girl like herself," concluded the barge-man.

At first, Ib did not say a word, but his face turned as white as a newly washed sheet. He shook his head and then mumbled, "I would not wish Christina to say no to good fortune for my sake."

"Write her a few words about it," urged the bargeman.

Ib wrote, but every time he had written a sentence he crossed it out again. All the words seemed wrong to him. Many pages he tore up, but by morning the letter to little Christina was finished. Here it is:

> I have read the letter that you wrote to your father. In it you say that everything goes well for you and that you have an opportunity for bettering yourself. Ask your own heart, Christina! If you want to marry me, then remember that I am poor. Do not consider me or my feelings, but only yourself. You are not bound to me; should you feel that you have given me your "promise," then I release you from it. May all the happiness in the world be yours, Christina. God may console my heart.
>
> Ever your devoted friend,<br>Ib

The letter was sent and Christina received it.

A few months later, the banns were read in the little church on the heath and in the big church in Copenhagen. The bridegroom was too busy with his affairs to be able to travel to Jutland. Christina journeyed with her future mother-in-law to the capital, where the young people were to live. Christina had arranged to meet her father in the little village of Funder, which was on the main highway to the south; there they said good-by to each other.

Every once in a while someone would speak about Christina when

Ib was present; but Ib himself never mentioned her. He had become so silent, so pensive. He often thought about the nuts that the gypsy woman had given them. Now Christina had got her carriage and all the dresses she could wish for, over across the water in the king's city, Copenhagen. The "wishing nuts" had proven themselves. His nut had been filled with black earth, and the gypsy had said that that was best for him. Now he understood what she had meant: the dark grave was best for him.

Years went by; not many, but to Ib they seemed long. The old innkeeper and his wife died and their son inherited their wealth: several thousand silver crowns. Now certainly Christina could have her golden carriage and even more dresses than she ever could wear.

Then two years passed during which not even the bargeman received any letters from Christina. Finally one came; it was not a happy one. Poor Christina, neither she nor her husband had been able to handle the sudden richness; it had not been a blessing, for they had not earned it themselves.

The heather bloomed and withered; and many a snowstorm swept across the heath and up over the ridge that protected Ib's little farmhouse. Spring came and Ib was plowing his meager fields. Suddenly he felt the plow shake as if it had hit a stone. Something black, shaped like a wood shaving, stuck up from the earth. Ib picked it up; it was metal and, where the plowshare had cut into it, it shone. It was a heavy arm ring of gold from heathen times.

The Viking grave had long ago been leveled. Now its treasure had been found. Ib showed it to the minister, who admired it and told him to take it to the district commissioner.

The official sent a report to Copenhagen and advised Ib to deliver the golden arm ring to the museum himself. "You have found in the earth the finest treasure, the best that could be found," he said.

"The best!" thought Ib. "The best for me, and found in the earth. The gypsy woman was right, my wishing nut, too, has proven true."

Ib sailed from Aarhus to the capital; and since he had never sailed before except with the bargeman up and down the river Gudenaa, it felt like an ocean journey.

In Copenhagen he received the gold value of the arm ring: six hundred silver crowns! Now Ib—who knew so well the forest and the heath—took a walk along the endless streets, lined with stone buildings, of the city.

The evening before he was to sail back, he lost his way, when he was out walking, and ended in one of the poorest quarters of the city, called Christian's Harbor. It was late and the street was deserted. He noticed a little child coming out of one of the most dilapidated of the houses, and he asked her for directions. The little girl looked up at him; she was crying, and said nothing. He asked her what was the matter; and she answered, but he could not understand her.

They were standing under a street lamp. Ib looked down at the child; the light was shining in her face. How strange! He saw with wonder that she looked exactly as Christina had, when she was a child.

He followed the little girl into a miserable house and up the worn, rickety stairs to the garret. They entered a little room right under the roof. The air was foul and it was dark. Ib struck a match. Over in a corner stood a bed; in it lay a woman: the little girl's mother.

"Can I help you?" asked Ib. "This little girl found me down in the street but I am a stranger to the city, myself. Can I call the neighbors?" He stepped closer to the bed and looked down at the woman: it was Christina!

At home, he had not heard her name mentioned in years, because everyone knew that Ib did not like to be reminded of her. Besides, all the rumors had been unpleasant. It was said that the inherited money had made her husband lose his common sense. He had given up his good position and they had traveled in foreign countries. When they returned, they had lived high and got into debt, rather than curtail the luxuriousness of their way of life. It was the old story of the cart going down the hill so fast that it finally overturned. The many merry friends who had dined at their table when wealth decked it now felt no pity. They said he deserved his fate, he had acted like a madman. One morning the body of Christina's husband had been found in a canal near the harbor.

Christina had been pregnant then; her child conceived in wealth was born in poverty. The baby had only lived a few weeks. Now Christina lay ill to death in a garret room more naked and bare than the one she had known as a child on the heath. And now, when she had known luxury, she could not bear her poverty, her wretchedness. The little girl, who had brought Ib to her, was her daughter, her older and only living child. Her name, too, was Christina.

"I am afraid that I am dying," she mumbled. "What will happen to my child? Where in the world can she find a home?"

Ib lit another match and found a stump of candle; its little flame lighted up the dismal chamber.

Ib looked at the little girl and was again reminded of Christina as she had looked as a child. For her sake he would take the little girl, bring her up, and be kind to her. The dying woman looked up at him; the pupils of her eyes grew larger and larger. Did she recognize him? Ib never knew, for she never spoke again.

We are back in the forest near the River of the Gods as it is called, not far from the heath. It is fall, the western storms have started. The wind is blowing the leaves off the trees. In the bargeman's hut strangers are living. Inside the little farmhouse, so snugly protected from the wind by the ridge, the stove is burning. It is as warm and comfortable as if it were summer; sunshine is here, the kind that shines from a child's eyes. Though it is October, the lark still sings in the little girl's laughter. Here lives gaiety and winter is far away. Little Christina is sitting on Ib's knee; he is both father and mother to her. Her real parents have disappeared, as dreams do to a grownup. The little farmhouse is cozy and neat. The girl's mother sleeps in the churchyard for the poor in Copenhagen.

They say that Ib has a tidy sum put away, gold from the earth; he is rich and he has his little Christina.

## 76

## Clod Hans

## An old tale retold

Far out in the country there was an ancient manor house. The squire who lived in it had two sons. Both of them were so clever that they could answer more questions than anyone would care to ask them. They decided to propose to the princess; this they dared do because the princess had officially proclaimed that she would marry the man in her kingdom who spoke most wittily.

They had only a week to prepare themselves, but that was enough, for they were well educated and that is an advantage. One of them knew by heart the Latin dictionary and the town newspaper for the last three years, and that backward as well as forward. The other one had memorized all the guild laws and regulations, even the ones that most guild masters had never heard about. He felt that this enabled him to discourse on politics; besides that, he could embroider suspenders, for he was artistic.

"I will win the princess!" said both of them.

Their father gave them each a horse; the son who knew the dictionary and the newspapers by heart was given a black one; the embroiderer and expert on guild laws, one as white as milk. Now they greased their jaws with cod liver oil in order to be able to speak even faster than usually; and then they were ready to depart. All the servants were lined up to wave good-by. Just as the two brothers were mounting their horses, their younger brother came running out of the house. I haven't mentioned him before because no one thought anything of him, and he wasn't really considered part of the family.

He was not a scholar like the other two, and that is why they called him Clod Hans.

"You are all dressed up, where are you going?" shouted Clod Hans.

"To the king's castle, to win the princess by our wit. Haven't you heard what the drums have announced and the herald proclaimed?" one of them asked; and the other brother told Hans of the princess' decision to marry the man who could speak most wittily.

"Goodness me! I am going too!" declared Clod Hans while his brothers laughed and rode off.

"Father, let me have a horse!" he shouted. "I have just decided to get married. If she takes me, well and good. If she doesn't, then I will take her."

"Nonsense!" said the father. "I will not give you a horse; you can't speak well; you have no wit. You're not even presentable!"

"Well, if I can't have a horse," laughed Clod Hans, "then I will take the billy goat; that is mine and I can ride it." Up he jumped on the billy goat, dug his heels into its sides, and away he rode. The goat ran as fast as it could and Clod Hans sang and shouted as loud as he could: "Here am I, here am I!"

His two brothers did not say a word to each other. They were too busy getting witty ideas. They rode so sedately you might think they were attending a funeral.

"Hello! Hello!" shouted Hans as soon as he caught up with them. "Here am I! And look what I found in the middle of the road!" He held up a dead crow for them to look at.

"Clod!" they said. "And what are you going to do with that?"

"Give it to the princess!"

"You do just that!" they laughed, and rode on a little bit faster, for they didn't want to be seen in company with their brother.

"Hello, hello, here I am again. Look what I have found! It is not every day that one stumbles across such a treasure!"

The two brothers turned around in their saddles to see what their little brother had now. "Clod!" they said. "It is only an old wooden shoe and broken at that. Are you going to give that to the princess too?"

"I certainly will!" declared Hans, while his brothers laughed and spurred their horses.

"Hello, hello! Here am I!" screamed Clod Hans a little while later. "It is too marvelous, just look!"

"What have you found now?" asked the brothers.

"Oh!" sighed Hans. "Can you imagine how pleased the princess will be?"

"Ugh!" exclaimed his brothers. "Why, it is only mud from a ditch."

"Yes, that is exactly what it is," agreed Hans, "but of the very best quality, the kind that slips right through your fingers. I have filled my pockets with it."

This time the brothers did not laugh, they just rode as fast as they could and arrived at the city gate a whole hour before Clod Hans. Everyone who had come to propose to the princess was given a number and had to line up in a row. They stood so close together that they couldn't move their arms; and that was fortunate, for otherwise they would have torn each other's eyes out, just because one had got there ahead of the other.

All the other citizens of the town crowded around the castle and tried to look through the windows; they wanted to watch the princess receiving her suitors. But as each of them entered the royal hall, he seemed to lose his tongue, for all of them could only stammer and mutter.

"No good!" said the princess every time. "Out!"

The first of the brothers entered, the one who knew the Latin dictionary and the newspapers by heart; but he had forgotten every word of them while he stood in the row with the other suitors. The floor creaked as he walked across it, and the ceiling of the room was an enormous mirror that reflected everything upside down. At one of the windows stood three scribes and an alderman, who wrote down all that was said, so that it could be printed in the newspaper, which would be sold in the streets that very afternoon for twopence. And if that was not frightening enough, the heat would have made anyone uncomfortable; the stoves had red-hot potbellies.

"It is hot in here!" said the unhappy suitor.

"That is because my father is roasting roosters today," said the princess.

"Bah!" That wasn't what he had expected and there he stood with his mouth open. He wanted to say something witty, but he couldn't.

"No good!" said the princess. "Out!"

And outside he had to go. Now came the second brother.

"It is terribly hot," he said.

"Yes, we are roasting roosters," said the princess.

"What did—What?" mumbled the poor man; and all the scribes wrote: "What did—what?"

"No good!" said the princess. "Out!"

Now came Clod Hans. He rode on his billy goat right into the royal hall. "Goodness me, it is hot in here," he said.

"That is because I am roasting roosters today," said the princess.

"That is fine," said Clod Hans, "maybe I can get my crow fried as well."

"That might be possible," laughed the princess. "But do you have anything to fry it in? All our pots and pans are in use."

"Sure, I have," said Clod Hans, and held up the old wooden shoe. "Here is a pot to put it in," and he dropped the crow into the broken shoe.

"Why, it is enough for a meal," said the princess, "but where are you going to get the gravy?"

"I've got pockets full of it! So much that I have some to spare." And Clod Hans showed her the mud.

"That is what I like!" exclaimed the princess. "Somebody who can speak up for himself. I will marry you! But do you know that every word we have said has been written down and will be printed in the newspaper? At one of the windows stand three scribes and an old alderman, and he is the worst, because he does not understand a word of what anyone says." The princess said this to frighten Clod Hans, and the scribes neighed like horses and shook their pens, so blots of ink sprayed onto the floor.

"Well, if the alderman is the most important, then he deserves the best!" shouted Clod Hans, and took all the mud out of his pockets and threw it in the old man's face.

"That was nobly done!" laughed the princess. "I couldn't have done it, but I am sure I will learn how!"

Clod Hans married the princess and became king. He sat on a throne with a crown on his head. I got the story straight out of the alderman's newspaper and that cannot be trusted.

## 77

## The Thorny Path

There is an old fairy tale named "The Thorny Path." It describes the road of trial and tribulation that a true hero must wander before he receives his reward: honor, glory, and fame. Many of us heard the tale when we were children; and when we hear it again or recall it, as adults, we cannot help reflecting on our own anonymous path of thorns, on our own trials and tribulations. The fairy tale and reality are not far apart, but the fairy tale is in harmony: earthly and time-bound. Reality has harmony too, but it can only be found in the boundless time of eternity.

The history of the world is a magic lantern show on the dark background of times past; it shows us the great men, the true benefactors of mankind, walking their thorny path.

From all ages, from all countries, are these pictures gathered; each lasts but a moment and yet tells of the struggle of a long life, of its defeats and victories. Let us look for a moment at a few men and women in this endless procession of martyrs, which will never end before the earth does.

We are in an amphitheater, the actors are performing Aristophanes' *The Clouds*. Waves of ridicule, of sarcasm, make the audience roar with laughter. The play is mocking the spirit and person of Athens' strangest man—the one who was the shield of the people against the tyrants, the one who on the battlefield saved Alcibiades and Xenophon—Socrates, whose spirit soared higher than the gods of antiquity. He is in the audience himself. Now he stands up so that the laughing

Athenians can compare the real man with the caricature shown on the stage, and judge for themselves how much they resemble each other. He stands among them and yet so far above them.

The green, succulent, poisonous leaf of the hemlock should symbolize Athens, not the olive leaf.

Seven towns fought and quarreled over the honor of being Homer's birthplace; that is, long after he was dead. Watch him while he was alive: in the streets of these cities he walks, reciting his verses for bread. The fear for tomorrow has made his hair gray. The greatest seer of them all is blind and lonely; the thorns have torn the mantle of the poet king into rags.

His songs live still and with them live the gods and the heroes of antiquity.

Picture upon picture follow one another like waves; some are from times just passed, others from ages which the sun has long since set upon. Different in time and place and yet all part of the same thorny path, that road where the thistle does not bloom before it decorates a tomb.

A train of camels, loaded with treasures, moves beneath the palms. They have been sent by the ruler of the country as a gift to the poet whose songs have delighted his people and who is the glory of his country, the one whom envy and lies had driven into exile. The caravan draws near a small city, the town where he found refuge. Just then the body of a poor man is being carried through the city gate, the train of camels stop. The dead man is he whom the caravan has come for; now they have found him: Firdausi. For him the path of thorns has ended.

A Negro sits on the marble stairs of a palace in the capital of Portugal; the dark-skinned man mumbles pleading words to passers-by. He is Camoëns' faithful slave. Without him and the coins that were flung to him, the beggar, Portugal's greatest poet would have died of hunger. Now a costly tomb covers Camoëns' grave.

Yet another picture: Behind the bars of a cell stands a man; his face is deadly pale, his beard is long and dirty. "I have made the greatest discovery in centuries!" he shouts. "More than twenty years you have kept me locked up here!"

"Who is he?" you ask.

"A madman," answers his keeper in the asylum. "He is insane, he believes that there is power locked within steam—"

Salomon de Caus, the discoverer of the power of steam, was not understood but imprisoned in a lunatic asylum where he died.

Here is Columbus, whom every street urchin made fun of. He discovered the New World and the bells sounded jubilantly when he returned; but the bells of envy were struck, too, and their tones are deeper and more powerful than those of joy. The man who discovered a world, who lifted the golden continent from the seas and gave it to his king, was rewarded with iron chains. He wanted these prison chains to be put in his coffin when he died, as proof of how the world and his times had appreciated him.

Picture after picture appears; the thorny road has been well traveled.

In pitch-darkness sits he who had measured the height of the mountains on the moon, whose spirit had traveled far out into space among planets and stars. The great one who understood Nature's order and spirit, and could feel that the world beneath him moved. Galilei, blind and deaf, in his old age, sits transfixed on the thorn of suffering. Weak and powerless in his debasement, with hardly the strength left to move that foot with which he once—when truth was blotted out—stamped the earth and said, "It still moves."

Here stands a woman with a child's nature, enthusiasm, and faith. She carries a banner in her hand; she is leading an army. She saved her country and brought it victory. The shouts of joy had hardly faded away before the stake was lit. Jeanne d'Arc, the witch, was burned. Yes, even a later century spat on the while lily; Voltaire, that satyr of wit, sang about *"La pucelle."*

At Viborg the nobles are burning the king's laws. The flames shoot up, reflecting the times, the laws, and the man who made them. They cast a halo around the head of the prisoner in the dark prison tower. Gray-haired, bent, and old, he sits by the stone table which he has walked around so long that his thumb has made a groove in it. He was once ruler of three kingdoms: the people's monarch, friend of farmers and merchants, King Christian II. His character was harsh and severe, but so were the times. Besides, his enemies wrote his biography. Twenty-seven years he spent in prison; we should not forget that when we remember the blood he spilled.

A ship is sailing from Denmark, the man standing before the mast looks toward the island of Hveen for the last time. Tycho Brahe, who lifted Denmark's name high up among the stars—and who received as reward only insults and injury—is sailing into exile in foreign lands. "The heavens are everywhere, and I need nothing else," were his words. Denmark's most famous son is leaving, sailing to another country to be honored.

Now we are in America, near one of the great rivers. Along its shores, crowds have gathered; they have come to watch a ship that can sail against the wind. Robert Fulton is the name of its inventor. The ship starts its voyage, but soon it stops. The crowd laughs and jeers. Fulton's own father is among those who whistle and scream. "Pride! Foolishness! Serves you right. You're mad!" they cry to the young man.

A small nail lost in the machinery has stopped it; now the nail breaks and the great paddle wheels turn again, the ship is sailing! Steam has conjured with time and distance, transformed hours into minutes, and brought the continents nearer to each other.

Humanity! Can you understand the bliss of such a moment, when your spirit, your art, knows its mission? The moment when all the pain endured along the thorny path—even that self-inflicted—becomes knowledge, truth, power, clearness, and health? The disharmony becomes harmony, and this revelation that God grants one man, he, in turn, gives to all of humanity.

The thorny path becomes a halo around the world; and fortunate are those who have been chosen to travel it. They are the builders of the bridge between man and God.

On giant wings flies the spirit of history through time, casting its brilliant picture against a background dark as night. The story of the thorny path does not end as a fairy tale in bliss and happiness here on earth, it reaches out into space and into eternity.

## 78

## The Servant

Among the pupils of the School for the Poor there was a Jewish girl;
she was always attentive and well-behaved; she was, indeed, the nicest
of all the children. But during one hour of the day she wasn't supposed to pay attention, for it was a Christian school and the teacher
was required to instruct in religion. Then she would be told to take
out her geography book or do her arithmetic; but a few examples of
arithmetic took no time at all and the geography lesson was always
short. For the remainder of the hour she would have an open book in
front of her, but she did not read it. She was listening to the teacher
more attentively than any of the other children.

"Read your book," he would say gently but seriously.

She would glance up at him with her dark, glistening eyes; and if
he asked her any questions about what he had read aloud, she replied
better than the other pupils. She had heard, understood, and remembered the whole lesson.

Her father was a very kind and poor man. He had let his daughter
attend school on one condition: that she not be taught anything about
Christianity. At first the teacher had thought of sending her out to
play during the hour of religious instruction, but he feared that this
would make the other children envious. "Then they might begin to
think about certain things," he reasoned. "And that might create an
atmosphere. . . ." So she was allowed to remain, although this was
no solution.

Finally the teacher went to visit her father. "If your daughter is to continue in school, then she must become a Christian," he began, and then he tried to explain. "I see in her eyes such longing; it's as if her very soul sought Christ's teaching. It's unbearable to watch."

The poor father said sadly, "There is nothing to be done. I know very little about Judaism, but my wife was different. She kept alive the faith of our fathers, and on her deathbed she made me promise that our daughter would never be converted to Christianity. I gave my word and God was my witness." So the little Jewish girl no longer attended the Christian school.

Years later in one of the more modest homes in a small town in Jutland, there was a poor servant of the Jewish faith. Her name was Sara. Her hair was as black as ebony, and her eyes shone with the brilliance and luster of a daughter of the Orient. Her glance still possessed that same pensive, searching expression it had had when she attended the school.

Every Sunday the sound of the organ and the singing of the congregation could be heard in the house across the street from the church where the Jewish girl faithfully did her work.

*"Remember the Sabbath to keep it holy,"* was the law she should obey; but her Sabbath was an ordinary working day for the Christians, and she could only keep it holy in her heart. Often she had asked herself whether it was enough; and she had not been fully convinced that it was, until one day it occurred to her that, to God, hours and days could not possibly have the same meaning as they do to us. From then on she listened peacefully to the playing of the organ and the singing of the psalms that came each Sunday morning from the church; and it seemed to her that also where she stood, in the kitchen next to the sink, it was holy.

Sara read the Old Testament, which was her people's property and treasure; and only that, for she had been present when her father and the schoolteacher had the conversation that resulted in her being taken out of school. And it had made a deep impression on her, to know of the vow her father had made to her dying mother that she must not abandon the faith of her ancestors.

One evening while she sat in her usual corner of the parlor, which the light of the lamps hardly reached, the master of the house took down an old book and began to read aloud. It was not a religious book, so Sara thought there was no reason not to listen. The story had taken place a long time ago. It was about a Hungarian who had been captured by a Turk: a pasha of such cruelty that he had ordered that the poor knight be treated as a beast of burden; and like a horse or a mule, the Hungarian had been hitched in front of a plow and driven forward with curses and the lash of a whip.

The nobleman's wife sold all her jewelry, mortgaged their castle and their ancestral lands, and with the help of generous friends, finally succeeded in collecting the incredible sum that the pasha had demanded as ransom. Thus, a sick and suffering creature was freed from slavery and inhuman mistreatment. He had been home only a short time when the usual cry was heard again: the Christians were being threatened by their enemies. Weak as he was, the knight put on his armor and demanded to be lifted upon his war horse. To the pleading of his wife he replied, "But I cannot rest when there is no peace in my soul." And as he spoke the color appeared in his cheeks, his former strength came back. This time he returned from the campaign victorious. Such are the accidents of fate that the very pasha who had so mercilessly debased him became his captive. The knight had been home only a few hours when he approached his prisoner.

"Tell me," the knight said, "what do you expect will happen to you now?"

"I know!" cried the Turk. "Vengeance!"

"Yes," the knight replied, "Christian revenge. Christ taught us to forgive our enemies and love our neighbors as ourselves. Our God is merciful! Go in peace back to your home and loved ones. In the future, be gentle and kind to those who are suffering."

The prisoner burst into tears. "How could I have known! How could I have guessed that, after the horrible way I treated you, anything but the most unbearable misery awaited me? I have taken poison, a deadly poison, against which there is no antidote; in a few hours it will kill me. But before I die, tell me of that teaching that has so much love and mercy, for it has the strength of God. I must die, but let me become a Christian first!" And his wish was granted.

It was a legend, a story; everyone had listened attentively and appreciated it, but none of them as much as Sara, the Jewish girl, the servant who sat in the corner. For her it had become alive, and large tears appeared in her bright, dark eyes. There she sat with the same childish faith that she had had when she listened to the New Testament in school. Down her cheeks the tears flowed.

"My child must never be a Christian!" had been her mother's dying wish. And Sara's very being resounded with the words: "Honor your father and mother!"

"I am not a Christian," she cried. "Didn't the neighbor's son call me Jew, with his voice filled with scorn, when I was standing before the open portal of the church, looking at the lights of the altar and listening to the singing of the congregation? From my schooldays until this moment Christianity has had a power over me; it is like the sun; even though I close my eyes, it shines in my heart. But I shall not betray you, Mother. I shall not break that vow my father gave you. I will not read the Christians' Bible. I have my father's God to live by."

The years passed. The master of the house died. The family was badly off. They could not afford a servant, but Sara stayed. She helped them, now that they needed her. It was she who held the family together. She worked at night to earn enough money to buy food for them. None of the relatives offered to help, even though the wife grew weaker day by day, and for months had not been able to leave her bed. Sara sat by her bed, took care of her, and worked. Gentle and kind Sara was a blessing to that poor family.

One night the widow begged Sara to read from the Bible. "Read a little for me; the night is long and I need to hear God's words."

Sara bowed her head, folded her hands over the Bible, and read aloud for the sick woman. Tears appeared in Sara's eyes, but her sight was clearer and her soul was clearer.

"Mother, your child has not been baptized. Among the Christians, she is known as a Jew. That promise which was made to you on earth has been kept. But to keep God's word is greater: *'He will be with us in death!* . . . *He visits the earth and makes of it a desert, and turns it into a fruitful place.* . . .' I understand! Although I don't know where my understanding comes from! It is Christ's work!"

When she said the holy name she trembled. She felt a shock go through her body, and she fell forward; now she was weaker than the invalid she had been reading to.

"Poor Sara," people said. "She overworked herself, taking care of others."

She was brought to the charity ward and there she died. From there she was buried.

She was not buried in hallowed ground, for that was not the place for a Jewish girl. No, outside the churchyard, next to the wall, was her grave.

And when God's sunshine shone on the Christian graves, it also shone on the grave of the Jewish girl, outside. And the singing from the Christian churchyard reached her grave; also out there could the words be heard: *"The resurrection will come! In the name of Christ!"* He who had said to his disciples: *"John has baptized with water; but you shall be baptized with the Holy Ghost!"*

## 79

## The Bottle

In a crooked alley, among other ill-repaired houses, stood one that was particularly narrow and tall. It was a half-timbered house, and many of the beams were rotten. Only very poor people lived there. Outside the garret window hung a bird cage; it was as decrepit as the house, and its inhabitant did not even have a proper bath: the neck of a broken bottle, corked and hung upside down, had to suffice. The old maid who lived in the garret was standing by the open window, enjoying the warm sunshine. She had just fed the little linnet, and the songbird was hopping back and forth in the cage, singing merrily.

"Yes, you may sing," said the bottleneck. It didn't really speak, for bottlenecks can't talk, but it thought all this inside itself, as we all do sometimes. "Yes, you can sing. You are healthy and well, not an invalid like me. You don't know what it's like to lose your whole lower parts and be left with only a neck and mouth; and then, on top of it, to have a cork stuffed into you. Then you wouldn't sing so loud! But it is good that someone is happy. I have nothing to sing about, and I can't sing. But I have lived an exciting life! I remember when the tanner took me along on a picnic and his daughter got engaged. I was a whole and proper bottle then. Goodness me, it seems just like yesterday. . . . Oh yes, I have experienced a lot. I was created in fire and heat, have sailed across the ocean, lain in the dark earth, and been higher up in the sky than most people. Now I am perched above the street in the sunshine; yes, my story bears repeating. But I am not going to tell it out loud, because I can't."

But the bottleneck could reminisce and it did. The bird sang, and the passers-by down in the alley thought about their own problems or didn't think at all, while the bottleneck reflected upon its life.

It remembered the great oven in the factory, where it had been blown into life. As soon as it had been formed, while it was still burning hot, it had been able to look into the burning red oven. It had felt a desire to jump back into it and be melted down again, but as it cooled that fancy had disappeared. The bottle had stood in a row together with all his sisters and brothers; there had been a whole regiment of them. They had all come from the same oven, but some had been blown into champagne bottles and others into beer bottles, and that makes a difference. Although later on, after they have come out into the world and the beer or the champagne has been drunk, then a beer bottle can be refilled with the costly wine from Vesuvius, Lachryma Christi, and the champagne bottle with boot blacking. But birth still counts and that you can tell from the shape. Nobility remains nobility, even when it contains only boot blacking.

All the bottles were put into cases, and so was the bottle that this story is about. It never occurred to him then that he would end as a useless bottleneck, and then have to work his way up to becoming a bird's bath—for that is better than being nothing at all.

He saw daylight again when the cases of bottles were unpacked in the wine merchant's cellar. Now he was rinsed for the first time, that was a strange experience; then he was put on a shelf. There he lay empty and without a cork, he felt awkward; something was missing but he did not know quite what it was. Then the bottle was filled with wine, corked, and sealed. A label was pasted on it which said, "very fine quality." The bottle felt as though he had passed an examination and received the highest grade. The wine was young and the bottle was young; and the young tend to be lyrical. All sorts of songs about things, that the bottle couldn't possibly know a thing about, seemed to be humming inside him. He saw clearly the green sunlit mountains, where the grapes had grown, as well as the maidens and young men who had kissed each other while they picked the fruit. Oh yes, it is lovely to live! The bottle was filled with passion and love, just as young poets are before they know much about either.

One morning the bottle was sold. The tanner's apprentice had been sent down to buy a flask of the "very best wine." It was put into the picnic basket together with ham, cheese, sausage, the best-quality butter, and the finest bread. It was the tanner's daughter who packed the basket. She was young and lovely, with a smile in her brown eyes and laughter on her lips. Her hands were soft and white, but the skin on her neck was even whiter. She was one of the most beautiful girls in the town and not yet engaged.

She had the picnic basket basket on her lap, while they drove out into the forest. The bottle peeped out through the snowy white tablecloth that covered the basket; his cork was covered by red sealing wax. He could look right into the face of the young girl and he saw, too, the young seaman who was sitting beside her. They had been friends since childhood. He was the son of a portrait painter. He had just received his mate's license and was to sail the following day on a long voyage to foreign lands. While preparing the basket for the picnic they had talked about the voyage; and there had been no joy or laughter to be seen in the young girl's face.

When they arrived in the forest the young couple went for a walk alone, and what did they talk about? Well, the bottle never knew, for he had stayed in the picnic basket. A very long time seemed to pass before he was taken out. But when it finally happened, something very pleasant seemed to have taken place. Everyone was smiling and laughing, the tanner's daughter too. She didn't say much, but two red roses were blooming on her cheeks.

The tanner took out his corkscrew and grabbed the bottle! It was a strange experience to be opened for the first time. The bottleneck had never forgotten that solemn moment when the cork was drawn and the wine streamed into the glasses.

"To the engaged couple!" toasted the tanner. They all emptied their glasses, and the young mate kissed his bride-to-be.

"Happiness and contentment!" exclaimed the old couple to the young.

The glasses were filled once more. "A happy homecoming and a wedding, a year from now!" shouted the young man. When they had drunk this toast, he grasped the now empty bottle. "You have been part of the happiest day of my life, you shall serve no one after that!"

The young mate threw the bottle high into the air. The tanner's daughter followed it with her eyes; she could not know then that she would see the very same bottle fly through the air once more during her life. The bottle landed in a little pond in the woods. The bottleneck remembered it all very clearly; he could even recall what he had thought when he lay in the water! "I gave them wine, and they gave me swamp water in return, but they meant well." The poor bottle could no longer see the picnic party, but heard them laughing and singing. Finally two little peasant boys came by, looked in among the reeds, noticed the bottle, picked it up; and now he had an owner again.

In the house in the woods, the oldest son had been home the day before; he was a seaman and was about to set out on a long voyage. His mother was making a package of one thing and another that she thought might be useful on so long a journey. His father would take it to the ship and give it to the lad together with his parents' blessings. A little bottle of homemade liquor had already been filled; but when the boys entered with the larger and stronger bottle, the woman decided to put the liquor in that one instead. It was brewed from herbs and was especially good for the stomach. So the bottle was filled once more, this time not with red wine but with bitter medicine, and that was of the "very best" quality too.

Lying between a sausage and a cheese, it was delivered to Peter Jensen, who was the older brother of the two boys who had found the bottle. Now the ship's mate was the very young man who had just become engaged to the tanner's daughter. He did not see the bottle; and if he had, he would not have recognized it, or imagined that the very bottle that had contained the wine with which he had toasted to a happy homecoming could be on board his ship.

True, the bottle was no longer filled with wine, but what it contained was just as desirable to Peter Jensen and his friends. They called Peter the "apothecary," for it was he who doled out the medicine that cured stomach-aches so pleasantly. Yes, that was a good period in the bottle's life; but at last it was empty.

It had stood forgotten in a corner a long time; then the terrible tragedy occurred. Whether it happened on the journey out or on the return voyage was never clear to the bottle, since he had not gone ashore. The ship was caught in the midst of a storm; great heavy black waves broke over the railing and lifted and tossed the vessel; the mast broke; and a plank in the hull was pressed loose. The water poured in so fast that it was useless to try to pump it out. It was a dark night. In the last few minutes before the ship sank, the young mate wrote on a piece of paper, "In Jesus' name, we are lost." Then he added the name of the ship, his own name, and that of his sweetheart.

He put the sheet of paper into an empty bottle he had found, corked it, and threw it into the raging sea. He did not know that he had once before held that bottle in his hands, on the day of his engagement.

The ship sank, the crew was lost, but the bottle floated like a gull on the waves. Now that he had a sad love letter inside him, he had a heart. The bottle watched the sun rise and set, thought that the red disk was like the opening of the oven in which he had been born; he longed to float right into it. Days of calm were followed by a storm. The bottle was not broken against a cliff-bound shore, nor was it swallowed by a shark.

For years it drifted, following the currents of the ocean toward the north and then toward the south. He was his own master, but that, too, can become tiresome in the long run.

The note, the last farewell from a bridegroom to his bride, would only bring pain if ever it were held by the hand it had been meant for. Where were they now, those little white hands that had spread the tablecloth on the green moss the day of the picnic? Where was the tanner's daughter? Where was the country where it had happened? The bottle didn't know, he just drifted with the waves and the wind. Although he was thoroughly tired of it; after all, that wasn't what he was meant for. He had no choice in the matter, but finally he floated to shore. It was a foreign country, the bottle didn't understand a word of what was said; and that was most irritating. You miss so much when you don't understand the language.

The bottle was picked up, opened, and the note was taken out to be read. But the finder did not understand what was written on it; he turned the note both upside down and right side up, but he could not read it. He realized that the bottle had been thrown overboard and that the note was a message from a ship, but what it said remained a mystery to him. The note was put back in the bottle and the bottle put away in a closet.

Every time there were visitors the note was shown in the hope that someone could read it, but no one who came ever could. The note that had been written with pencil was made less and less legible by the many hands that held it. Finally the letters could no longer be seen and the bottle was put up in the attic. Spider webs and dust covered him, while he dreamed about the past: the good old days when he had been filled with wine and had been taken on a picnic. Even the days on the ocean seemed pleasant now; the years when he had floated on the sea and had had a secret inside him: a letter, a sigh of farewell.

It remained in the attic twenty years and would have stayed there even longer had not the owner decided to enlarge his house. The whole roof was torn down. The bottle was brought out and the story of how it was found told once more. The bottle did not understand what was being said, for you don't learn a language by standing twenty years in an attic. "If only they had allowed me to stay in the closet downstairs, then I would probably have learned it," thought the bottle.

Once more he was washed and rinsed—and he certainly needed it. The bottle was so clean and transparent that he felt young in his old age; but the note had been lost in the process.

Now the bottle was filled up with seeds: what kind they were the bottle didn't know. Again he was corked, and then wrapped in paper so tightly that not a bit of light came through. He could see neither the sun nor the moon; and the bottle felt that this was a great shame, for what is the point of traveling if you don't see anything? But travel it did; and it arrived safely at its destination and was unpacked.

"They certainly have been careful"—the bottle heard someone say —"but I suppose it has broken anyway." But the bottle was whole, and he understood every word that was said. They spoke his own language, the first one he had heard when he came red hot out of the melting pot: the language that had been spoken at the wine merchant's, at the picnic, and on the ship—his native tongue, the one he understood! The bottle had come home! Oh, what a lovely welcome sound! The bottle nearly jumped for pure joy out of the hands that had picked him up. He hardly felt the cork being drawn and the seeds being shaken out, so happy was he!

He was put down in a cellar, again to be hidden and forgotten by the world. But it's good to be home even when one has to stay in the cellar. The bottle did not even count the years and days he stayed there. Finally somebody came and removed all the bottles, himself included.

The garden outside the house had been decorated. Colored lamps hung from all the trees and bushes; they looked like shining tulips. It was a lovely evening, perfectly still, and the sky was filled with stars. There was a new moon, a tiny sliver of silver surrounding a pale disk; it was a beautiful sight for those who look at beauty.

The paths at the edges of the garden were illuminated too—at least, enough so you could find your way. In the spaces between the bushes of the hedge, bottles with candles in them had been placed. Here, too, stood the bottle that was fated to end as a birdbath. He found the whole affair marvelously to his taste; here he stood, among the greenery, attending a party; he could hear laughter and music and all the sounds of gaiety. True, it came mostly from another part of the garden, where the colored lamps were hung. He had been placed in the more lonesome area; but that gave the bottle more time for reflection. He felt that he stood there not only for amusement and beauty but also because he was useful. Such a combination is superior and can make one forget the twenty years one has spent in the attic—and that sort of thing it is best to forget.

A young couple came walking by, arm in arm, just as the other young couple, on the day of the picnic, had: the tanner's daughter and the mate from the ship. The bottle felt that he was reliving something that had happened once before. Among the guests were some who had not been really invited but were allowed to come and look at the festivities. One of these was an old maid; she had no kin but she had friends. She was having exactly the same thoughts as the bottle; she was also recalling an afternoon spent in the woods, and a young couple walking arm in arm. She had been half of that sight and those had been the happiest moments of her life, and they are not forgotten, regardless of how old one becomes. She did not recognize the bottle nor he her.

That is the way of the world, we can pass each other unnoticed until we are introduced to each other again. And those two were to meet once more, now that they lived in the same town.

From the garden, the bottle was taken to the wine merchant, rinsed, and then once more filled with wine. It was sold to a balloonist, who, on the following Sunday, was to ascend into the sky in a balloon. A great crowd of people gathered to see the event and the regimental band played. The bottle saw all the preparations for the air voyage from a basket, where he lay together with a rabbit who was to be dropped down with a parachute on. The poor bunny, who knew its fate, looked anything but happy. The balloon grew and grew and finally rose from the ground when it couldn't grow any fatter; then the ropes that held it down were cut and it slowly ascended into the sky, carrying the basket with the balloonist, the bottle, and the frightened rabbit up into the air. The crowd below cheered and screamed: "Hurrah!"

"It is a strange feeling," thought the bottle. "It is another way of sailing but, at least, up here you can't run aground."

Many thousands of people were watching the balloon and the old maid in the garret was looking at it too. She was standing at her window, where the bird cage with the little songbird hung; at that time it did not have a glass birdbath but only a cracked cup that had lost its handle. On the window sill was a myrtle bush; the flowerpot had been moved a little out of the way so that the woman could lean out of the window and get a better view of the balloon.

She could see everything clearly: how the balloonist threw the rabbit out and its tiny parachute unfolded.

Now he was taking the bottle and uncorking it. He drank a toast to all the spectators. But he did not put the bottle back; instead he cast it high into the air. The old maid saw that too, but she did not know that this was the very bottle she had seen fly once before: in the springtime of her life, on that happy day in the green forest.

The bottle had hardly the time to think half a thought, not to talk of a whole one. The high point of his life had come and so unexpectedly! Far below him were the towers and roofs of the city; the people looked so tiny.

The bottle decended with quite a different speed than the rabbit had. The bottle performed somersaults as he fell; he had been half filled with wine, but soon that was gone. He felt so young, so joyful and gay. What a journey! The sun reflected in him and every person below was following him with their eyes.

The balloon was soon out of sight and so was the bottle; it fell on a roof and splintered. It hit with such force that all the little pieces danced and jumped, and did not rest before they had fallen all the way down into a yard. The neck of the bottle was whole; it looked as if it had been cut from the rest of the bottle with a diamond.

"It would do as a birdbath," said the man who found it. He lived in a cellar. But since he had neither cage nor bird, he thought it a little expensive to buy them just because he had an old bottleneck that could be used as a birdbath. He remembered the old maid who lived up under the roof, she might find it useful.

A cork was put in the bottleneck, and it was hung upside down in the cage of the little bird that sang so beautifully. Now it was filled with fresh water instead of wine; and what used to be "up" was "down," but that is the sort of change that sometimes does happen in this world.

"Yes, you can sing," sighed the bottleneck, who had had so many adventures. The bird and the old maid knew only of the most recent one when he had been up in a balloon.

Now the bottle had become a birdbath; he could hear the rumble of the traffic down in the street and the voice of the mistress talking to an old friend. They were not talking about the bottleneck but about the myrtle bush in the window.

"There is no reason for you to spend two crowns on a bridal bouquet for your daughter," the old maid was saying. "I will cut you a beautiful one from my bush. You remember the myrtle bush you gave me the day after I had become engaged? Well, the little bush over in the window is a cutting from that one. You hoped that I would cut my bridal bouquet from it, but that day never came. Those eyes are closed that should have shone for me and been the happiness of my life. On the bottom of the sea he sleeps now, my beloved. The bush you gave me became old, but I became even older. When it was just about to die, I cut a branch from it and planted it. Look how it has thrived; finally, it will attend a wedding: your daughter's."

There were tears in the old woman's eyes as she talked about the young man who had loved her when she was young. She recalled his toast and the first kiss he had given her; but that she did not tell about, for she was truly an old maid. No matter how much she thought about the past, it never occurred to her that just outside the window, in the bird cage, hung a witness to those times: the neck of the very bottle that had contained the wine with which her engagement had been celebrated. The bottleneck did not recognize her either, nor did he listen to what she was saying, but that was mostly because the bottleneck never thought about anyone but himself.

## 80

## The Philosopher's Stone

You remember the story about Holger the Dane? I don't want to tell it to you; I am only asking to find out whether you remember how Holger won great India, which stretches east as far as the end of the world, where grows a tree called the Tree of the Sun. As Christian Pedersen says—you don't know who Christian Pedersen is? Well, that doesn't matter, it is of no importance whether you know him or not. Holger the Dane made the priest Jon ruler over all of Indialand. You have never heard of priest Jon? Well, never mind, he is not really important either; he is not in the story at all. What I want to tell you about is the Tree of the Sun, that stands in Indialand, which stretches east to the end of the world. Once anyone would have understood immediately what I was talking about; but that was before one was taught geography in the manner that we are now—and that, too, is of no importance.

The Tree of the Sun was magnificent; I have never seen it and neither will you. Its crown was the size of a whole forest and was miles and miles around. Its limbs were so gigantic that their crooked shapes were like dales and hills; they were covered with moss as soft as velvet, in which the most beautiful flowers grew. Every branch and twig that protruded from the main boughs was a tree, and each was different from all the others: one was a palm tree, another a beech tree, a third a plane tree; all the kinds of trees in the whole world were there. The sun was always shining on it, for truly it was the Tree of the Sun. Birds from all corners of the world visited it. They came from the forests of America, the rose gardens of Denmark, and the jungles of Africa, where elephants and lions believe that they are the rulers. Birds from both the poles came; and naturally, the swallows and the storks were there as well. Not only birds lived in the Tree of the Sun; deer, antelope, squirrels, and thousands of other animals made their home there.

The crown of the tree was like a fragrant garden, and in the very center of it, where the great limbs were high hills, there was a crystal palace; and from its towers you could see all the countries of the world. The towers were shaped like lilies. Their huge stems were hollow and you could climb them because there were staircases inside. Every leaf was a balcony; you could step out on it and admire the view. And in the tallest flower was a round hall that had no other roof than the blue sky with its sun and stars. The lower chambers of the castle were magnificent, too, though in a different manner. On their polished walls the whole world was mirrored, and you could see what was happening everywhere. You did not have to read a newspaper, which was lucky because there wasn't any. The pictures on the walls were alive and moving; they showed everything that was taking place, no matter where it was happening; all one had to have were the time and the desire to look. But too much is too much, even for the wisest of men; and it was he who lived in that castle: the wisest of all mankind. His name was so difficult to pronounce that you wouldn't be able to say it, so there's no point in my mentioning it: it is of no importance.

He knew everything that a man can hope to know while on earth. He knew about every invention that had already been made and all those that ever would be; but no more than that, for everything has its limits. He was twice as wise as old King Solomon, who was known for his wisdom. He understood the powers of nature and ruled over them; Death himself had to bring him a list of those who were to die. One thought, however, disquieted the mighty ruler of the castle in the Tree of the Sun, and this was that King Solomon had died. In his fate, he saw his own; and although he had raised himself even higher than Solomon had above the rest of humanity, through knowledge and wisdom, he would someday die too; and so would his children. Like leaves on the trees, they would wizen, fall to earth, and become dust. The generations of man were like leaves, he thought: new leaves always unfolded to take the place of the old, but those that withered never lived again; they became fertilizer for other plants.

What happened to the human being after the angel of death visited him? What did it mean, to die? The body disintegrated, but the soul —yes, what was the soul? What happened to it? Where did it go?

Religion, man's solace, said: "To an everlasting life." But how was the transition possible? Where and how did the soul live? The pious answered: "We are going to heaven above."

"Above," repeated the wisest of men, and looked toward the sun and the stars. But he knew that the world was a globe; and above and below depended upon where you stood on it. He knew, too, that if he climbed the highest mountain on earth, then the "clear blue sky," which we see, would appear black below him. The sun would be a glowing ball without its rays, and the earth itself seem to be in a shroud of orange mist. Limited is the power of our sight and so much knowledge is denied our souls. How little we know, even the wisest of us. How few of the questions that most concern us can we find answers to.

In a small chamber of the castle lay the greatest treasure on earth, the Book of Truth. Everyone may read it, but only a short section at a time. For many eyes the letters quiver and move so much on the page that they cannot make out the words. In some places the print is so faded that the pages appear blank. The wiser one is, the more one can read. And the wisest of all men, who lived in the middle of the Tree of the Sun, could read more than anyone else. He knew how to collect the light of the sun, of stars, and of the hidden powers of the spirit and make them illuminate the pages, so that even the most difficult parts became easy to read. But the chapter titled, "Life after Death," remained a perfect blank, even to him. This made the wisest of men very sad. He speculated and speculated as to how he could find, here on earth, a light strong enough to bring forth the letters, so that he could read what was written in the Book of Truth on that subject.

Just like the wise King Solomon, he understood the language of the animals, but that did not help in this matter. He found herbs and metals, medicines that could cure sickness, remove death for a while; but in none did he find anything that could destroy death itself. In everything and everywhere did he search for a light that could make it possible for him to read the chapter about "Life after Death."

But he did not find it; the Book of Truth lay open in front of him with its blank page. The Bible of Christianity promises in words of consolation an everlasting life, but he was not satisfied with that. He wanted to read it in his own book and he couldn't.

He had five children: four sons, brought up as only the wisest father could do it, and one daughter. She was beautiful, gentle, and clever, but blind. This affliction did not seem to trouble her; her father and her brothers were her eyes and her own pure nature the judge of everything she heard.

The sons had never been farther away from the castle than the great branches reached. The sister had not even been that far; they were happy being children in the land of childhood, in the fragrant magic world of the Tree of the Sun. Like all other children, they loved to be told stories, and their father told them many tales and strange things, which ordinary children might not have understood; but they were as wise as the most mature people among us are. He helped them to understand the living, moving pictures on the wall of the castle, which showed the ways of men and the events that were happening in the whole world.

Many times his young sons expressed a wish to take part in the struggles they were seeing on the walls and to perform great deeds of valor. Then their father would sigh and say: "The ways of the world are bitter and filled with grief. What you see is not reality, for you watch it from the safe world of childhood and that makes all the difference." He spoke to them about beauty, goodness, and truth: the three concepts that kept the world from falling apart; and how the pressure that the world inflicted on goodness, beauty, and truth transformed them into a precious stone that was far more beautiful than any diamond. This gem was, in truth, the philosopher's stone. Their father explained that, just as you became more certain of God's existence by studying nature, so by studying man did you become assured that this jewel called the philosopher's stone, existed too. He could not tell any more about it, for he knew no more. Now this would have been very difficult for other children to understand, but these children could; and we may hope that, later on, others will understand it as well.

The children asked their father to tell them what beauty, goodness, and truth were and he did. He told them, too, how God had created the first human being out of clay and then had kissed His creation five times: five kisses of fire, five kisses from the heart. These kisses from God gave us our five senses; with them and through them we understand, feel, and protect beauty, goodness, and truth. The five senses are our sensitivity both outward toward the world and inward into our souls; they are the root and the flower of the human plant.

The children thought and thought about what their father had told them; indeed, it was never out of their minds. One night the oldest brother had a marvelous dream, and the strangest part of it was that his three brothers dreamed the same dream. Each of them had dreamed that he had journeyed out into the world, found the philosopher's stone, and returned bearing it as a living flame on his forehead. Each one had come home riding on his horse, over the velvet boughs of the Tree of the Sun to his father's castle, just as the sun was rising. The light that shone from the jewel had clearly illuminated the pages of the Book of Truth, so that they could read what was written there about life beyond the grave. Their sister had not had the dream; she had no thought of going out into the wide world, her world was her father's house.

"I will ride out into the wide world," declared the wise man's oldest son. "That is a journey I must make. I want to take part in the affairs of men. Goodness and truth shall I serve, and they will guard beauty. Much will be different once I am part of the world." Yes, these were courageous words: the kind that are easy to say in front of the fireplace in your father's house, before you have been in a storm or felt the bramble's thorns.

The four brothers had five senses just as everyone else has, and they were excellent in all of them, but each brother had especially developed one of his senses. The oldest brother had a sense of sight that was far stronger than is usual. He could see the past as well as the present. He could see all the countries of the world at once, and under the earth, where its treasures are hidden. He could see into other human beings as if their chests were windows, so he knew more than the rest of us, who have to be satisfied with being able to guess what a blush on the cheek or a tear in the eye means. The deer and the antelope accompanied him as far as the western border; from there he followed the flight of the wild swans toward the northwest; and soon he was far away from his father's realm that stretched east to the end of the world.

How wide he opened his eyes! There was a lot to look at. And it is very different to see things with your own eyes than to look at them in pictures, regardless of how marvelous the pictures are, and the ones he had seen in his father's castle had been excellent. So surprised was he when he saw the trash, the cheap tinsel that mankind considered beautiful, that his eyes almost popped out of his head; but he held onto them, for he needed his eyes for the deeds he wanted to do.

Wholeheartedly and steadfastly he went to work for the cause of beauty, truth, and goodness. But all too often he saw ugliness receive the praise that should have been given to beauty. The good was hardly noticed, while mediocrity was applauded instead of being criticized. People looked at a man's name, not at his deeds; his appearance and not his character; his position and not how he fulfilled it. But that is the way of the world and it cannot be different.

"There is work enough for me," he said, and began at once. He sought truth; but when he found it, the Devil—the Father of all Lies —was there too. The Devil would have liked to put out the seer's eyes, but he thought that too crude. The Devil prefers to do things in a refined way. He let the young man look at truth and beauty, and goodness as well; but while he was looking at them, the Devil blew motes into his eyes: one into each of them. Then he blew on the motes until they became beams, and his sight was no more. The seer was blind! There he stood in the middle of the wide world, not trusting it and not trusting himself; and once you have given up both the world and yourself, then it is all over.

"Over," sang the wild swans that flew across the ocean toward the east.

"Over," chirped the swallows on their way toward the Tree of the Sun; and the tidings they brought were not good.

"The seer did not succeed," said the second brother. "Maybe he who hears will fare better." The second brother had developed his sense of hearing so much that he could hear the grass grow.

He said good-by to his father, his two brothers, and his sister, mounted his horse, and rode away filled with the very best intentions. The swallows followed him, and he followed the swans, and soon he was far from home, out in the wide world.

But one can get too much of a good thing, and that the second brother found only too true. For he heard not only the grass grow, but every human heartbeat, both in joy and in sorrow. The world was like a watchmaker's shop and all the watches were going tick-tock and the great clocks were striking ding-dong. It was more than anyone could bear! He kept listening as long as he could, but at last all the noise and din were too much for him. Street urchins screamed and shouted. Some of them were sixty years old, for it is not age but behavior that makes a guttersnipe, though they were really more amusing than annoying. He heard gossip whistling through all the streets and alleys, and lies shouting that they were the masters of the world. The bells on the fool's cap claimed that they were church bells. Oh, it was all too much for the young man!

He put his fingers into both his ears but that didn't help. He could still hear the singer who sang out of tune, the clamor of evil, the voices of slander and pompous chatter, the stubborn shouting of worthless ideas till they were recited in a chorus like thunder. Everywhere there was sound: marching, crying, clattering, screeching, wailing, banging. It was too frightening, too horrible! Deeper and deeper he dug his fingers into his ears; and finally the eardrums burst. Now he could hear nothing at all. Beauty, truth, and goodness were silenced too. His hearing, which was the bridge for his thoughts, was gone. He grew silent and suspicious and trusted no one, not even himself. That was a great misfortune. He would never find the philosopher's stone and take it back to his father's castle. He abandoned his search and he abandoned himself; and the second was worse than the first. The birds that flew east to the Tree of the Sun brought the message. He wrote no letter, for there was no mail service.

"Now it is my turn," said the third brother. "I have a nose for the work." That was not the most elegant way to express oneself, but that was the manner in which he usually spoke, and one had to take him as he was. He had a cheerful disposition and he was a poet, a real one who could say in verse what couldn't be said in prose. He perceived many things long before other people could.

"I can smell a rat," he would boast; and in truth, it was sense of smell that he had especially developed. This made him an expert on beauty, he felt. "Some love the smell of apples, others the odor in a stable," he said. "Each region of smell in beauty's realm has its adherents. Some feel most at home in the smoke-filled atmosphere of cheap cafés, where tallow candles smoke rather than burn, and the odor of stale beer mixes with the stink from cheap tobacco. Others like the pungent perfume of the jasmine flowers, or they rub their bodies with oil of cloves and that smell is not easy to get rid of. Some seek the clean air of the seashore and others climb the mountains to be able to look down upon the trivial life below!" This he said before he had left his father's house; one would think he already knew the world of man, but he didn't. It was the poetical part of him that had spoken: the gift of imagination that God had given him while he lay in his cradle.

He bade good-by to his father's house in the Tree of the Sun. He did not ride away on a horse; no, he mounted an ostrich, for that could run faster. But as soon as he saw the wild swans he picked out the strongest among them and rode on that instead, for he liked a change. He flew across the ocean to foreign lands, where great forests surrounded deep lakes, and there were huge mountains and proud cities. Wherever he flew, the sun broke forth from behind dark clouds. Every flower, every bush smelled more fragrant, as if they wanted to do their very best, while such a friend and protector of odors was near them. Yes, even an ill-tended rose hedge, that was half dead, unfolded new leaves and bloomed. Its single flower was particularly lovely, even the black slug saw the beauty of the little rose.

"I will put my mark on it," the slug said. "I will spit on it, for more I cannot do for anyone."

"That is the fate of beauty in this world," said the poet. He composed a little song about it, and he sang it himself; but no one listened to it. So he gave the town crier two silver coins and a peacock feather as payment; and he shouted the song, accompanied by his drum, through all the streets and squares. Then people listened and said that they understood it—it was so profound. Now the poet composed other songs about beauty, goodness, and truth. They were listened to in the cafés, where the tallow candles smoked; and they were heard in the fragrant meadow, the forest, and on the boundless sea. It seemed he would be more successful than his two other brothers.

This did not please the Devil. He came at once, bringing with him large portions of incense. There were all kinds: royal and ecclesiastical, and the very strongest that the Devil distills, which is brewed from honor, glory, and fame. It is potent enough to make even an angel dizzy, not to speak of a poet. The Devil knows how to catch everyone; and the youngest brother was caught with incense. He couldn't get enough of it and soon he had forgotten his quest and his home as well as himself; he went up in smoke, the smoke of incense.

When the little birds heard it they became ever so sorrowful; they mourned so deeply that they did not sing for three whole days. The slug became even blacker than he was before, but that was because he was envious, not because he mourned.

"It was I that gave him the idea," he claimed, "they should have burned incense for me. I inspired his famous song for drums about the ways of the world. It was I who spat on the rose; and I háve witnesses to prove it."

But back in Indialand, which stretches east to the end of the world, they heard no news. All the little birds had mourned for three days and not sung a note. They had felt their sorrow so intensely that by the time the three days were over they had forgotten what it was they had been mourning over; that happens in this world.

"Maybe I'd better go out into the world and get lost too," said the fourth brother. He had a sense of humor, although he wasn't a poet, which was a good enough reason for his feeling happy. The two younger brothers had brought gaiety and laughter to the castle, and now they both would be gone.

Sight and hearing have always been considered the most important of the senses, the ones it is a virtue to develop. The others are considered lesser; but that was not the opinion of the fourth brother. He had developed his taste, in the widest sense of the word, and he thought that taste was the real governor of everything. It ruled over not only what went through the mouth but what went into the soul as well. He stuck a finger into every pot and pan, and every barrel and bottle, to taste what was in them; but that was the coarser part of his duties. To him every human being was a pot in which a dinner was cooking and every country in the world a kitchen—in a spiritual sense, of course. Now this he considered the finer duty of taste and he was eager to try it.

"Maybe I will have more luck than my brothers," he said. "But what means of transportation should I choose? Is the balloon invented?" he asked his father, who knew about all the inventions that had been made or were ever going to be made; but he was told that no one had thought of a balloon yet; nor had steamships or railways been invented.

"I will take a balloon anyway," he declared. "My father knows how to make one; and I will learn how to steer it as I fly. Everyone who sees me will think that he is seeing a mirage. As soon as I get to my destination I will burn the balloon; therefore, I'd better have a few of those future inventions called sulphur matches, too."

He received all he had asked for, and away he flew. The birds followed him farther than they had his brothers; they wanted to see how that flight would end. Other birds joined them. They, too, were curious; they thought the balloon was a new kind of bird. He certainly had company. The air was black with birds; they looked like a cloud, a locust swarm from Egypt. Soon he was far out in the wide world.

"The east wind is certainly a true friend and a great help to me," he said.

"You mean the east and the west," said the winds. "If we both hadn't helped you, you couldn't have sailed northwest."

He didn't hear what the winds said; and it really doesn't matter whether he did or not for our story. The birds got tired of following him. When the flock was largest, two of the birds had declared that too much was being made of the balloonist; he would get a swollen head from it.

"It is nothing to follow, after all it is only air, we find it degrading," one said to the other.

They stayed behind; and so did all the other birds. "A balloon is nothing," they all agreed.

Finally the balloon descended above a big city. The balloonist searched for the highest place in the town; it was a tall church spire. There he sat down so that he could observe what was going on; the balloon flew away, which was not according to plan. What happened to it I don't know—and it doesn't matter; after all, it hadn't been invented yet.

He sat on the very top of the spire all alone; the birds were tired of him and he of them. Out of all of the city's chimneys came smoke and smell.

"They are altars raised for your sake," said the wind, who wanted to pay him a compliment.

The fourth brother looked down in the street below him and watched the passers-by: one was proud of his money; the next of his keys, though they opened nothing; a third of his clothes, though moths would eat them; a fourth of his body, though worms would eat that.

"Vanity! I think I will have to stir this soup a little and taste it," he said. "But not right away; I will stay here for a while. The wind blows so nicely on my back; it is very enjoyable. I think I will stay as long as it comes from the same direction. I need a little peace in order to think. 'It is best to sleep late in the morning if one has a hard day's work ahead,' say the lazy. Laziness is the root of all evil, but there is no evil in me or in my family. That's what I say and the world agrees with me. I will stay as long as that wind blows, it is just to my taste."

The fourth brother, the one who had developed taste, stayed right where he was. He was sitting on top of the weather vane, and when it turned, he turned with it, so the wind always blew on his back. We will leave him there, he can sit there forever and taste.

But the castle in the center of the Tree of the Sun seemed empty now that all the brothers had gone, one after the other.

"I am afraid that they have fared badly," said their father. "They will never bring back the brilliant stone. It will never be found. They are gone! They are dead!" He bent over the Book of Truth and stared at the page on which he should have been able to read about the life after death, but he could see nothing.

His blind daughter was his only consolation, his only joy, and she loved him dearly. For his happiness' sake she wished that the jewel would be found and brought home to the castle. She longed for her brothers, and thought sadly about where they could be and whether they were still alive. She wished fervently that she would dream about them; but even in her dreams she never saw them. Finally one night she dreamed that she heard their voices; they called to her from the wide world. She had had to follow them. She was far, far away and at the same time in her father's house, as is possible in dreams. She did not meet her brothers, but she felt something in her hand. It burned like fire but did not pain her; it was the philosopher's stone, the gem that her father desired so much, and she took it to him.

When she woke she thought that she still held the jewel in her hand, but it was a spindle from her spinning wheel. Through the night she had spun a thread finer than that which spiders make. It was so thin that the human eye could not see it, and yet because it had been moistened by her tears it was as strong as the anchor tow of a ship.

She rose from her bed. She felt that the dream had to be realized. It was still night and her father was sleeping. She kissed his hand and, taking the spindle, she fastened one end of the thread to her father's house—for otherwise, being blind, she would not be able to find her way back—and set out into the wide world. She trusted that the thread would guide her home. From the Tree of the Sun she picked four leaves. These she would give to the wind that it might take one to each of her brothers as a greeting if she did not meet them.

How would she fare, this poor blind child? She had the invisible thread and she had one quality that her brothers had not had, which would serve her well: devotion. It gave her eyes on each of her fingers and made it possible for her to hear with her heart.

Out into the strange, turbulent world she walked; and wherever she went, the sun would shine so she could feel its warmth and a rainbow would span from the dark clouds to the clear blue sky. She heard the birds sing and smelled the orange groves and apple orchards so intensely that she could almost taste the fruits. She heard soft and lovely music, sweet songs of joy, but also discordant screams. It was a strange duet; the verses were at war with each other; it was humanity's thoughts and judgments she was listening to.

> "Life is a dungeon dark and deep,
> A night in which we weep."

Then another voice sang:

> "Life is the rose on the vine
> And every day the sun does shine."

Then a more bitter voice was heard:

> "Man's life in self-interest is spent,
> That truth is evident."

But still another voice argued:

> "Love's river winds its way,
> Changing November into May."

Then a whining voice mocked,

> "Everything is small and mean
> And truth on lies will lean."

A moment later another sang,

> "Truth and goodness are strong.
> Right always outlives wrong."

Then many voices in a great chorus sang,

> "Make fun of all, sneer and attack,
> Bark with the dogs in the pack."

This was not answered by the world but by a voice that came from the blind girl's heart.

> "Trust yourself and trust your God,
> And let His will be done. Amen."

Wherever the girl came, among young or old, women or men, her devotion brought forth truth, goodness, and beauty. She brought a ray of light—a ray of hope—into the artist's workshop, the salons of the rich, and even into the dismal factories where great wheels clattered and turned. She was like the drop of dew that falls on a thirsting plant.

That was more than the Devil could allow. He has more brains than ten thousand men. He found a way to put a stop to it. He took the bubbles that form in the rotten waters of a swamp and caused the sevenfold echoes of lies to pass over them in order to make them stronger. Then he made a powder of false obituaries, verses of homage for which the poets had been paid, and sermons for which the preacher expected to be paid. This he dissolved and cooked in tears that envy had shed; at last he sprinkled a little powder from a vain old maid's cheek into it. Out of this brew he constructed a girl who in appearance and movement was a perfect copy of the blind girl, whom humanity had given the name "The Angel of Devotion." The Devil had begun his game, for the world did not know which of the two girls was the true one. And how should humanity know? After all, they looked alike.

The poor blind girl repeated to herself the words she had sung before:

> "Trust yourself and trust your God,
> And let His will be done. Amen."

Then she gave the four leaves that she had plucked from the Tree of the Sun to the winds that they might deliver them to her brothers. She felt certain that they would receive them, just as she had been sure that jewel that was more precious than all others would be found and brought to her father's house.

"My father's house." The girl said the words out loud. "Yes, here on earth the gem is to be found, here is its hiding place. I am bringing back something more than my mere certainty of its existence: I feel within my closed hand the glow of the jewel. I can feel it pulse and swell. Every little grain of truth that the wind carried have I caught and kept. I have let them absorb the odor of beauty—and I took the sound of the human heart beating for the good, and added that. It is nothing but dust; but from these grains the jewel is formed. Look, my hand is filled with it!"

With the speed of thought she had returned to father's house following the invisible thread. Now she held out her hand to him.

The evil one brewed a storm and whipped the Tree of the Sun; the doors to the castle sprang open and the wings of the wind rushed through the chambers.

"It will blow away!" shouted the father, and grabbed his daughter's hand.

"No," she shouted back at him. "It cannot be blown away, for I feel that its warmth and power have entered my soul."

The shining dust was blown from her hand. Like a flame, it flew across the page of the Book of Truth on which one could read about the eternal life. The page was no longer blank. One word in illuminated letters was written there, one single word:

## FAITH!

The four brothers had returned; they had felt a longing for their home when the leaves from the tree fell on their chests, and they had obeyed it. The birds, the deer, and antelope, yes, all the animals of the forest had come to join in their gladness. And why shouldn't they, when they were allowed to?

As you have often seen when a single ray of light shines through a keyhole into a dark room, a shiny column of dust appears. Much more splendid than this—even more colorful than the rainbow— glittered and sparkled the word "FAITH" on the page, made as it was from grains of truth mixed with beauty and goodness. It shone more powerfully than the column of fire did that night when Moses and the people of Israel left for the Land of Canaan. From the word "FAITH" begins the bridge of hope that leads to the All-loving, to eternity.

## 81

## How to Cook Soup upon a Sausage Pin

In all countries there are old sayings that everyone knows, even the school children, and it is hard to understand that the rest of the world does not know them too. Such a familiar expression in Danish is "to cook soup upon a sausage pin." It means to make a lot out of nothing; gossips and journalists are experts at preparing this dish. But what is a sausage pin? It is a small wooden peg used for closing the sausage skin after the meat has been stuffed into it; you can imagine how strong a soup one could cook on that. Well, that was the introduction; it contained information and that is always useful. Now I can begin the story.

"It was a delightful dinner last night!" exclaimed an old female mouse to an acquaintance, who had not been invited to the party. "I was seated number twenty-one from the right of the old mouse king, and that is a respectable place. Shall I tell you what we ate? It was a very well-composed dinner. Moldy bread, pork crackling, tallow candles, and sausages; and everyone was served everything twice; it was as good as getting two meals. The atmosphere was most congenial, everyone spoke the most charming nonsense just as they would have at home. Everything was eaten; the only things left were the sausage pins. And that is the reason why we talked about them and the saying 'to cook soup upon a sausage pin.' Everybody had heard the expression but no one had ever tasted the soup or knew how it was made. We drank a toast to its inventor; he deserved to be made director of a poorhouse! Now wasn't that witty? The old mouse king

stood up and made a promise that he would marry the young mouse
who could make the best-tasting soup cooked upon a sausage pin.
She would become his queen; and he gave the female mice a year
and a day to find out how it was done."

"That is fair enough!" said the second mouse. "But tell me, how
do you make it?"

"Yes, how does one cook soup upon a sausage pin? That is what
everybody asked, both the young and the old. They all wanted to be
queen; but no one knew how and few wanted to trouble themselves
by going out into the wide world to find out, and that seemed necessary. It is not so easy to leave one's family—the old familiar nooks
and corners where one might stumble over a cheese rind or smell pork
crackling—to go out in the world and risk starvation—or an even
worse fate: to be eaten alive by a cat!"

It was probably thoughts like these that kept most of the young
female mice from leaving their homes in order to find the recipe.
But four young and very poor mice declared that they would try
their luck; they would each go to one of the corners of the world and
see whom fortune smiled upon. They were each given a sausage pin
so that they wouldn't forget why they were traveling; they could use
them as walking canes.

It was in the beginning of May when they left; and a year later on
the first of May they were back. But only three of them; the fourth
one did not arrive, though the day of trial and decision had come!

"Why must there always be sadness mixed with joy?" said the
mouse king, while he sent out invitations to all the mice within
miles. They were to meet in the royal kitchen, for that was the most
appropriate place to hold the contest. The three mice who had been
out traveling were lined up in a row; where the fourth should have
stood was placed a sausage pin with black crepe around it. No one
dared say anything before the three mice had spoken and the king
had given his judgment. Now we shall hear what happened!

WHAT THE FIRST LITTLE MOUSE HAD HEARD AND LEARNED
ON HER JOURNEY:

"When I started on my journey out into the wide world," began
the little mouse, "I thought, as most young mice do, that I knew just

about everything there is to know; but in that I was mistaken; it takes years and days to grow wise. I found a ship that was sailing north and sailed on it, for I had heard that a cook on board a boat has to learn to make much out of nothing. But the pantry was filled with bacon and barrels full of salt pork. We lived well; and it was no place to learn how to cook soup upon a sausage pin. We sailed many days and nights. The ship rolled and tossed, and the place was too damp for my taste. When we arrived at our destination I disembarked; that was far up north!

"It is strange to come from one's own nook, sail on a ship that is also a kind of nook, and then come out into the wide world. The ship had become a little like home; and once I left it I realized that I was more than a hundred miles away in a foreign country! Great forests stretched farther than the eye could see, all of them were pine and birch; they smelled so fresh and strong, I found it very unpleasant. The wild flowers had such a spicy odor that they made me sneeze. I was thinking of sausages all the time. The water in the lakes looked clear enough at the shore, but when you looked at them from a distance they were black as ink. There was something white floating on the surface; at first I thought it was foam, but I found out that it was swans. I saw them fly and walk, too. When you have seen a swan walk, then you know that it is a cousin of a goose: it waddles; there is no way of hiding the family that one belongs to. I stayed with my own kind, the field mice; they were, however, ignorant of finer culinary art, and that, after all, was the purpose of my journey. That it was possible to cook soup upon a sausage pin was to them such an absurd idea that soon the whole forest knew about it. They all deemed it impossible; and at that moment I would never have guessed that that very night I was to learn how it is done.

"It was midsummer, that was why the forest smelled so strong and the flowers so spicy, and the lakes where the swans swam looked so black. At the edge of the forest near a little cluster of houses, a pole as tall as the mast of a ship had been raised. On its very top hung a wreath and colored ribbons: it was a maypole. Young people were dancing around it and singing, while the violins played. Oh, it was a gay sight, as the sun set; and later on, too, as the moon rose, but I didn't join them; after all, a little mouse does not belong at a dance. I sat in the soft moss and held onto my sausage pin.

"The moonlight fell especially on a spot beneath a big tree where the moss was particularly soft and delicate—if I dared I would say that it was as exquisite as the mouse king's fur! It was green and healthy for the eyes to look at. Suddenly a band of little creatures came; they were so small that they only reached my knees. They looked like human beings, but their proportions made them far lovelier. The called themselves elves. Their clothes were made from the petals of flowers, embroidered with the wings of flies and mosquitoes, which looked very fetching indeed. They appeared to be looking for something; I couldn't make out what it was.

"Two of them came over to me; the most distinguished of them pointed at my sausage pin and said, 'This is exactly what we need! It has been cut to the right size.' The more he looked at my walking cane, the happier he became.

" 'You may borrow it but not keep it,' said I.

" 'Not keep it,' repeated all the little creatures who now had gathered around my pin. I let go of it and they carried it over to the spot where the moss was so particularly soft; and there in the center they raised the sausage pin. They wanted a maypole too; and I must admit, the pin was just the right size for them. Then they decorated it and that was a sight!

"Tiny little spiders spun golden threads all around it; and on these veils and banners were hung; they were so white that they hurt one's eyes to look upon. They had been bleached in moonlight. Colors gathered from butterflies' wings were sprinkled on the white linen; and then the banners and veils looked like flowers and glittered like diamonds. I could hardly recognize my old sausage pin. Such a maypole as it became you could not match in the whole world. Not until now did the main party of the elves arrive. They had no clothes on at all, because among elves that is considered most elegant. I was invited to attend the party, but at a distance, because I was too big.

"Now began the music! It was as if a thousand glass bells were being struck. At first I thought that swans were singing; then I believed that I recognized the voices of the thrush and the cuckoo. 'All the forest is singing,' I thought. I seemed to hear children's voices and birds' songs and glass bells all merging in the most beautiful melodies. And all that lovely music came from the elves' maypole, which was nothing but my sausage pin! I couldn't believe that so much could be made out of a wooden peg, but I suppose that everything depends not upon the material but upon whose hands form it. I was so touched that I cried for joy as only a little mouse can.

"The night was all too short, but that far north it isn't very long at that time of the year. As day broke, there came a breeze; ripples appeared upon the surface of the lake, and all the banners and veils disappeared into the air, as did the bridges and balconies the spiders had strung from leaf to leaf in the trees. Six elves brought the sausage pin back and asked me if I had any wish that they could grant me. I begged them to tell me how one cooked soup on a sausage pin.

" 'How we do it you have already seen,' laughed their leader. 'I am sure even you did not recognize your old sausage pin.'

" 'But that was not cooking soup,' I said, and explained why I had set out on my travels and what I was expected to find out. 'What use is it to our king, or to our great kingdom, that I have seen this wonderful sight? I can't shake it out of the pin while I declare: "Here comes the soup!" Though I suppose it would do as a dish for the mind after one's stomach was filled.'

"The elf dipped his finger in a blue violet and said to me, 'Watch, now I will stroke your walking cane, and when you have returned to the mouse king's palace, then touch the warm, royal chest of the king with the cane and immediately violets will be growing all the way up the stick; and that even if it is the middle of the winter. That is a gift worth bringing home and I will give you something more. . . .' "

But before the little mouse told what else the elf had given her, she touched the chest of the king and immediately the loveliest bouquet of flowers sprang forth. It smelled so strongly that the mouse king ordered the mice who stood nearest the fire to put their tails into it so that the smell of singeing hair could clear the air. The odor of violets was not a favorite; everyone found it nauseating.

"Yes," said the little mouse, "that, I believe, is what is called the first course." She turned; the sausage pin and the flowers were gone and she stood with the bare stick in her hand. Now she lifted it as if it were a conductor's baton.

" 'Violets are for sight, smell, and feeling,' said the elf to me, 'but I will give you something, too, to please hearing and taste.' "

Now the little mouse swung her baton and the music began—not the kind she had heard in the forest when the elves held their ball; no, it was the kind fit for a kitchen. What a lot of noise! It was as though the wind suddenly were whirling down the chimney and through all the stovepipes. Pots and kettles boiled over. The big frying pan clattered as if it were going to jump down on the floor; then suddenly all was silent and you could hear the little teakettle's solitary song. It sounded so strange; it had neither a beginning nor an end. Then the pots and pans began again; they did not care for harmony but sang each its own song. The little mouse swung her baton more and more wildly. Again the pots boiled over and the wind shot down the chimney. Ugh! it was a frightening racket; and at last the little mouse got so scared herself that she dropped the baton: her sausage pin.

"That was strong soup," said the old mouse king. "Are you going to serve it now?"

"That was all," declared the little mouse, and curtsied.

"Was that all?" said the mouse king. "Well, let us hear what the next one has to tell us."

### WHAT THE SECOND LITTLE MOUSE HAD TO TELL

"I was born in the royal library," began the second mouse. "Neither my family nor I had ever had the pleasure of being in a dining room, not to speak of a larder. Not before I had traveled did I see a kitchen like the one we are gathered in. Frankly, we starved in the library; but we did acquire knowledge. The rumor reached us about the royal reward that had been promised the one who could cook soup upon a sausage pin. My old grandmother drew forth a manuscript wherein it was written—she couldn't read herself, but had heard it once read aloud—that poets could cook soup upon a sausage pin. Now she asked me if I was a poet. I told her no, whereupon she told me to become one.

" 'But how does one do that?' I asked, for that seemed to me as difficult as cooking soup. But my grandmother, who had listened to a lot of books being read out loud, said that three ingredients were necessary, namely: intelligence, fantasy, and feeling! If I could manage to get those things inside me, then I would be a poet, and the problem of the sausage pin would be easily solved.

"I walked west, out into the wide world, to become a poet.

"I knew that intelligence was the most important, the other two parts were not nearly as respected. Therefore I set out to acquire intelligence first; but where was it to be found? Go to the ant to become wise, an old king of the Jews had once said. This I knew from the library, so I went straight for the nearest anthill and hid near it, in order to become wise.

"They are a very respectable nation, the ants; they are pure intelligence. Everything in their world is solved as though it were an arithmetic problem; it is all figured out. To work and lay eggs, they say, is living: both in your own time and in the future; and that is what they do. They are divided into the clean ants and the dirty. All ranks are numbered: the queen ant is number one, and her opinions are the only ones that count, for she has swallowed all the wisdom there is.

"Now that was very important for me to know. She said so much that was so clever that I found it stupid. She said that the top of her anthill was the highest point in the world; it was built right next to an old oak tree, and that the oak tree was much higher than the anthill could not be disputed; so the ants never talked about the tree. One day one of the ants, having lost its way, climbed up the trunk of the tree. It didn't get to the top but just a bit of the way up. When it returned home to the hill, it told everyone of the discovery it had made: that there existed in the world outside something much taller than their hill. The ants found this an insult to them, to their nation, and to society. The ant who had made the discovery was condemned to wear a muzzle and to spend the rest of its life in solitary confinement. A short time later, another ant made the same journey and came to the same conclusion. He, too, spoke about his discovery but in a learned and vague manner. Since he was a very respectable ant and belonged to the faction called 'clean,' the other ants believed him. When he died an eggshell was put up as a monument to him, for all the ants agreed that they respected science.

"I noticed," continued the little mouse, "that the ants carried their eggs on their backs. One of them lost hers and in spite of her strenuous efforts could not get them up on her back again. . . . Two other female ants came running over to help her. They pushed and they shoved until they were almost about to lose their own eggs in the process; but then they stopped trying to assist the other poor ant, for they believe that one has to think of oneself first. The queen ant said they showed both heart and brain: 'These are the two attributes that place us first among respectable creatures! But intelligence must be the master, it is far more important, and I have more brains than any other ant.' She stood up on her two hind legs, you couldn't mistake any of the lesser ants for her, and I ate her.

" 'Go to the ant and become wise.' Now I had swallowed the queen.

"I walked over to the oak tree. It was very ancient; it had a massive trunk and a great spreading crown. I knew from my time in the library that within each tree lives a woman called a dryad; she is born with the tree and dies when it does. When this oak girl saw me she screamed, for she was as afraid of mice as all women are. But in truth she had more reason to be; after all, I could have gnawed the tree in two, and then she would have died. But I spoke to her in a friendly and warm manner to put her at her ease, and she allowed me to climb right up on her fine little hand. I told her why I had gone out into the wide world and she promised me that that very evening she would help me to obtain another of the treasures I was searching for. She told me that Fantasy was a very dear friend of hers and that he often came to rest under the boughs of the tree. She told me that he was as beautiful as the God of Love and that he called her 'his dryad.'

" 'This great rugged, craggy, beautiful old oak tree is just to his taste, with its roots deep down under the ground and its crown high up in the sky. This oak has experienced drifts of cold snow, sharp and bitter winds, and the sweet sunshine: to know them all is a blessing.' Yes, that is the way the dryad talked.

" 'The birds in my branches sing about foreign lands, on one of my dead limbs a stork has built its nest; it looks nice and I like to hear about the land of the pyramids,' the dryad explained. 'Fantasy likes all this too, but it is not enough for him, I have to tell him tales of life in the woods as well; about my own childhood when I was a little sapling—so small that the nettles grew taller than I—and all that I have experienced since them. Hide over there among the woodruff, and when Fantasy comes I shall tear a little feather from his wings. You can have it; no poet has ever had a better one.'

"Fantasy came and the dryad tore a little feather from one of his wings and I caught it," said the little female mouse. "I put it in water to soften it a bit, for it was very difficult to digest; but I finally managed to get it down. It is not so easy to become a poet by the way of the stomach, one has to swallow an awful lot. But now I had both intelligence and fantasy; and the third ingredient necessary for a poet, I knew, could be found in the library. I had heard a critic of much importance say that novels exist to free humanity from superfluous tears; in other words, they are a kind of sponge that absorbs feelings. I recalled a couple of these books, and they had always looked very appetizing to me; they had been read so often and were so filled with greasy fingerprints that I felt sure they had a wealth of feeling within them.

"I hurried home to the library and ate almost a whole novel that very first day. I only ate the soft part, which is the most important; the crust or the binding, as it is called, I didn't touch. When I had digested two novels I could already feel things moving inside me. I ate a little of a third and then I had become a poet—that is what I said to myself and everybody agreed with me.—I had headaches, stomach-aches, and . . . I can hardly list all the aches I had.

"I began to think of all the stories that one could make up about a sausage pin. My thoughts were full of pins—the queen ant must have had an extraordinary brain. I thought of the man who became invisible when he put a white pin in his mouth; and the pin people used to pin their hopes with; and the pins and needles that people stood on; not to speak of the length of the pin needed to pin one down. All my thoughts became pins. And for every pin a story could be told, for I am a poet and I have worked hard to become one. I can serve you a pin, a story each day of the week, that is my soup!"

"Let us hear the third mouse," said the mouse king.

"Pip, pip," someone said at the kitchen door. That was the fourth mouse: the one they had all believed to be dead. She came running in so fast that she overturned the sausage pin with the black crepe around it. She had been running both day and night, and even though she had been able to ride on a freight train for part of the way, she had almost come too late. She pushed her way through the crowd until she stood before the king. She looked awfully rumpled. She had lost her sausage pin but not her tongue. She began to talk at once. She must have thought that everyone had just been waiting to hear her, and that nothing in the world was as important as what she had to say. She took them all by surprise and gave no one time to object while she talked. This is what she had to say.

### WHAT THE FOURTH MOUSE, WHO SPOKE BEFORE THE
### THIRD MOUSE, HAD TO RECOUNT

"I set out for the big city immediately," she began. "The name of it I don't recall; I have such difficulty remembering names. I had traveled by rail and was taken from the station, among some confiscated goods, to the courthouse. There I happened to overhear a prison warden who was talking about his prisoners. He was especially talking about one of them; this prisoner had said some rash words that had been printed and commented upon all over the city. 'It is all soup upon a sausage pin,' said the warden, 'but that soup may cost him his head.'

"This naturally made me very interested in that prisoner and I managed to get into his cell, for behind every locked door there is usually a mousehole. He looked very pale. He had a long beard and two shining eyes. The lamp smoked but the walls and the ceiling were used to it, they couldn't have got any blacker than they were. The prisoner scratched pictures and verses on the wall, white on black. I did not read them. I think he was lonely; I was a welcome guest. He tempted me with little pieces of bread and whistled softly to make me come nearer. He was so happy to see me that I gained confidence and we became friends. He shared his bread and water with me and gave me sausage and cheese to eat.

"I lived well but it was especially the company that kept me there. He let me run up and down his arms, even inside his sleeve. I climbed into his beard and he called me his little friend; I grew very fond of him and he of me. I forgot my errand out in the wide world; I forgot my sausage pin. It fell into a crack in the floor and is lying there still. I wanted to stay where I was, for, if I left, the poor prisoner would have no one, and that is too little to possess in this world.

"I stayed but he didn't! He talked ever so sorrowfully to me that last night we were together, and gave me a double ration of bread and cheese; then he threw me a finger kiss and was gone. I never saw him again. I do not know his story.

"'Soup on a sausage pin,' the warden had said, and I moved in with him; but I should never have trusted him. He took me in his hands but only to put me in a cage, in a treadmill. You can run and run in that as long as you want to; you will still stay in the same place. The only thing that happens is that you make a fool of yourself.

"But the warden's little grandchild was a sweet little girl with golden curly hair, happy eyes, and a mouth made for laughing. 'Poor little mouse,' she said, while she looked into my ugly cage; then she pulled out the iron pin and let me go. I jumped down upon the window sill, and from there out on the roof and down in the gutter. I was free, free! That was my only thought, not the purpose of my journey.

"It was dark, the middle of the night; I had found shelter in an old tower where there lived a watchman and an owl. I didn't trust either of them, least of all the owl. It looks like a cat and has one great fault: it eats mice. But one can make a mistake, and I had, for the owl was a very respectable old bird, terribly well educated; she knew more than the night watchman and almost as much as I.

"The little owlets made a fuss over everything. 'Don't make soup on a sausage stick,' their mother would say, and that was just about the strongest reprimand she ever gave them, for she loved her young ones dearly. I felt so confident, so trusting toward her, that I said aloud, 'Pip,' from where I was hiding. My faith in her made her very pleased and she assured me that she would protect and keep all other animals from harming me; she wouldn't eat me before winter, when it was hard to find food.

"She was very intelligent and wise. She proved to me that the night watchman could not hoot unless he used the horn that hung from his shoulder. 'He thinks so much of himself. He believes that he is as wise as an owl. They are supposed to be so great, and they are so little. Soup on a sausage stick!'

"I asked her then for the recipe and she explained to me. 'Soup on a sausage stick is a phrase human beings have constructed; it can be interpreted in many ways, and every person thinks his own is the best. But the truth of the matter is that it is nothing.'

" 'It is nothing!' I repeated, and then the truth dawned on me. The truth is often unpleasant, yet nothing is above it, and to this the owl agreed. I thought long about it; finally I decided that when I brought back the truth with me, then I was bringing more than soup on a sausage pin. I hurried in order to get home in time." She took a deep breath and then announced: "The mice are an enlightened nation, and the king of the mice is above everyone else. He will make me his queen, for truth's sake!"

"But your truth is a lie," shouted the little mouse who had not been allowed to speak yet. "I can cook the soup and I will do it!"

HOW THE SOUP WAS COOKED

"I have not traveled," declared the fourth mouse. "I have stayed in our country and that, I think, was the most sensible thing to do. One does not have to make a journey, everything can be got here

just as well. I stayed at home! I have not learned anything from supernatural beings, or eaten my way to being a poet, or held conversations
with owls. What I know I have taught myself! Now put the pot on the
fire and fill it with water, all the way up to the brim. Make the fire
burn well, for I want the water to be really boiling, then throw in the
sausage pin. Now will Your Majesty be so kind as to stick his tail
down in the soup and stir it? The longer Your Majesty does it the
stronger the soup will be. No more is needed, no other ingredients,
it needs only to be stirred."

"Couldn't someone else do it as well?" asked the mouse king.

"No!" said the little female mouse." That kind of power can only be
found in a royal tail."

The water in the pot was boiling furiously. The mouse king stood
as close to it as he dared, then he stuck out his tail, in the same manner
as mice do when they take the cream off the top of the milk with their
tails. But here was no cream to lick afterward, only steam from the
boiling water. Quickly, he jumped away!

"Yes, naturally, that must be the way it is made. You are to be my
queen!" he declared. "But I think we will wait to make the soup
until our golden wedding. Then the poor in my country will have
something to look forward to."

The wedding was held, but some of the mice said—not at the
castle but when they came home later—that that could not be called
cooking soup upon a sausage pin, it was more like cooking soup upon
a mouse tail.

They found a few of the other things that had been said quite
clever; but most of it could have been said somewhat differently and
better.

"Now I would have explained it this way or that way. . . ." That
was the critique; it is always clever; and it comes last.

The story went around the world; people's reactions to it were
divided, but the story remained whole. And that is the most important in great things as well as in small—in cooking soup upon a
sausage pin. Just remember, don't expect to be thanked for it.

## 82

## The Pepperman's Nightcap

In Copenhagen there is a street with a strange name; it is called Hyskenstræde. Why does it have that name and what does it mean? It was originally German but the Danes have changed it to fit their own tongue. *Häuschen* means "little houses" in German, and once, several hundred years ago, that was, indeed, the right name for the street. The houses were really nothing more than large wooden sheds; they looked a little bit like the booths you see in the market place. They had windows, but not with glass in them. No, they were either very tiny and made of horn, or just small and covered by a pig's bladder, for glass was terribly expensive then. It all happened so long ago that even your great-grandfather's great-grandfather would have referred to it as "olden times."

In those days the rich merchants of Bremen and Lübeck had much of their trade in Copenhagen. They did not come up here themselves but sent their agents; and it was they who lived on the street of the small houses, where they sold beer and spices. The German beer was better than the Danish; and there were so many kinds: Bremer, Prysing, and Emser; yes, and Braunschweiger Mumme; and then there were all the different spices: saffron, anise, ginger, and pepper. The greatest trade was, naturally, in pepper; and that is why these emissaries of the merchants of Bremen and Lübeck were called peppermen. The merchants, thinking only of what was good for their own purses, demanded that their agents promise not to marry while abroad. For once a man has taken a wife and settled down with a family, one cannot be assured of his loyalty.

Some of the German peppermen spent most of their lives in foreign countries. They became odd, lonely old men who cooked their own food, darned and repaired their own clothes, and tended their own lonely fires. Cut off by their different customs and habits from the rest of the people, they were left to themselves. In Denmark to this day a bachelor—an unmarried, middle-aged man—is called a pepperman. All of this I have told you so that you will be able to understand my story.

The pepperman was an object of ridicule. In the streets people would shout after him, telling him that he ought to put on his nightcap, pull it down over his eyes, and go to bed!

> "Chop, chop firewood.
> Woe, woe to the pepperman
> With a nightcap on his head,
> He snuffs out his candle and goes to bed."

Yes, that is what they used to sing. They made fun of the pepperman and his nightcap, and that was because they did not know him or the nightcap. Oh, that nightcap! That was a curse that no one should wish upon himself! Why? Listen, and I will tell you why.

In the street of the little houses, in olden times, there were no cobblestones and the passers-by were always stepping into muddy holes. It looked like a country road with too much traffic on it—nor was it broad. The booths were built close together, and the street was so narrow that in summer it was often covered by stretching a canvas awning from the roofs on one side of the street to those opposite them. Then it would smell even more strongly of pepper, saffron, and ginger. The agents standing behind the counters were, on the whole, not young men; nor did they wear wigs, tight-fitting pants, and the long dress coats with silver buttons that our great-grandfather's great-grandfather wore, as we know from paintings.

The peppermen could never afford to have themselves painted, they were much too poor for that. Though it certainly would have been nice, now, to have a picture of one of them as he looked when he stood behind his counter or went to church on Sunday. Then he wore a broad-brimmed hat with a high crown—the younger peppermen sometimes put feathers in their hats. The woolen shirt was almost hidden by a large linen collar; the pepperman's jacket was tight-fitting, and he had a wide cape over his shoulders. His pants were long and hung all the way down to his broad, square-toed shoes —for he never wore any stockings. Stuck in his belt were a spoon and a knife; and the knife was there not only to eat with; it was often necessary for men to defend themselves in those times.

In just this manner one of the older peppermen, Anton, dressed, except that he never wore the broad-brimmed hat with a crown, but only a cap with a nightcap underneath it. Anton had two nightcaps; they were exactly alike, and one of them was always on his head. He would have been a wonderful model for a painter. He was thin as a stick, his face was filled with wrinkles, and his hands were long and thin. His eyebrows were bushy and gray, and the one above his left eye was heavier than the other; this did not make him more handsome but certainly easier to recognize. It was said that he came from Bremen, but that was not true; Bremen was the home of his master. He was from Thuringia, from a town called Eisenach not far from Wartburg. Anton seldom talked about his home, and that made him think about it all the more.

The old peppermen had little to do with each other. Each lived by himself in his own booth. When they closed their stalls early in the evening, the street was deserted.

From the little tiny windows of the second story, where the peppermen lived, a faint glow could be seen. Inside each one, a man would be sitting on his bed with his German hymnbook on his lap singing a psalm before he went to bed; or he might be darning, or straightening up his booth for the morning. It was not an enviable life. To be a stranger in a strange country is a bitter lot. One is never noticed unless one gets in someone's way, and then one is cursed.

On a rainy winter night the street looked gloomy and forbidding. There were no street lamps; the only light came from the little lamp in front of the picture of the Virgin painted on the wall at the corner. From the other end of the street, the melancholy sound of the water splashing against the oak timbering of the wharf could be heard.

Such lonely evenings were very long. One could not polish the metal pans of the scales or find things to unpack and arrange every evening. Then one had to find something else to do; and old Anton would repair his clothes or mend his shoes until he was tired enough to sleep. When he got into bed he would pull his nightcap a little further down over his eyes. But soon he would lift it again to make sure that he had blown out the tallow candle properly; he would press with his finger around the wick to be certain that it wasn't smoldering; then he would lean back, pull the nightcap down again, and turn onto his side. But he could not sleep; now it was the little brazier down in the shop he was worrying about. Were all the embers dead, and had they been properly covered with ashes? One little spark could do great damage!

He got out of bed and made his way down the ladder, for one could not call anything as rickety as they were stairs. There wasn't an ember left in the brazier, it was cold. He could go back to bed; but as often as not he would not get more than halfway up the ladder, when a doubt about whether he had secured the door with the iron bar, and locked the shutters, would make him climb down again. He was so cold that his teeth chattered even after he finally had got back into bed. It is often then that coldness is worst, just before it leaves.

Anton pulled the covers up and his nightcap down, and thought no more about his daily difficulties and his trade. But the thoughts that came to him now weren't pleasant either, for when the curtains of old memories are filled with pins, then you stick yourself on them. Ouch! you scream as the blood drips where the pins pricked, and it hurts so much that tears come into your eyes.

Anton cried often. Hot tears fell like pearls on his covers. If he dried his eyes with his nightcap, the tears would disappear but not the spring from which they had sprung; that would be there still, for it lay in his heart. The pictures from the past did not come in the order they had happened. Those that were the saddest came more often; but, strangely enough, it was the memory of happy moments that cast the longest and most painful shadow.

"The Danish beech forest is lovely," people would say, but far lovelier to Anton was the forest near Wartburg. In his eyes the old oak trees that grew near the castles in his homeland were grander and more dignified than any oak tree here. The apple trees smelled stronger there than they did in Denmark, where everything was flat and no green creepers covered granite cliffs. He saw it all and still felt it within his heart.

A tear fell. He saw so clearly, so vividly, two children playing to- gether: a boy and a little girl. The boy had red cheeks, blond curly hair, and two honest blue eyes. The boy was himself—Anton. The little girl had brown eyes and black hair; she looked brave and spirited; she was the mayor's daughter Molly. They were playing with an apple. They shook it and heard the seeds rattle inside it, then they cut it in two and shared it; they divided the seeds as well and ate them all but one, which the girl had decided ought to be planted.

"Then you shall see what will happen, you won't believe it! But a whole apple tree can grow from it, though not right away."

The seed was planted in a pot. The two children were equally eager; the boy dug a hole with his fingers in the soil, and the girl dropped the seed into it. They both filled up the hole and smoothed down the earth.

"You mustn't look tomorrow to see whether it has taken root," said the girl. "I did that to my flowers twice, I wanted to see if they were growing. I didn't know any better then, and the flowers died."

The flowerpot stayed at Anton's all winter. He looked at it every morning, but there was nothing to be seen, only the black earth. Spring came, and the sun began to give warmth. Something happened: two little green leaves peeped up through the soil.

"There are Molly and I!" said Anton. "They are beautiful, they are marvelous!"

Soon a third leaf appeared. What could that mean? More leaves unfurled themselves. Day by day, week by week, the plant grew until it was a tiny apple tree. All of this was mirrored in one tear, which dried and disappeared, but could spring forth again from old Anton's heart.

Near Eisenach is a chain of craggy mountains. One of them—to its shame, it is rather rounded—has neither trees nor bushes growing on it. It is called the mountain of Venus, and a goddess from heathen times lives inside it. The local people call her Frau Holle.

Every child in Eisenach can tell you the legend of how she enticed the noble knight Tannhäuser, the minnesinger from Wartburg, inside her mountain.

Little Molly and Anton often walked as far as the foot of that mountain, and once Molly asked, "Do you dare knock on the stone and say: 'Frau Holle, Frau Holle, open up, Tannhäuser has come!'"

Anton didn't dare but Molly did. True, she only said the words "Frau Holle, Frau Holle," loudly; the rest she mumbled so softly that

Anton could not even hear her, and he felt certain that she hadn't mentioned Tannhäuser's name.

But brave and bold she was. Sometimes when she was playing with other girls and Anton would come, and all the other girls would try to kiss him, just because they knew he didn't like it and would hit out at them, Molly would declare proudly: "I'm not afraid to kiss him." And she would throw her arms around his neck. It pleased her vanity and Anton did not object nor did he think much about it, though Molly was beautiful and full of spirit. Frau Holle, who lived in the mountain, was supposed to be beautiful too, but her beauty was evil. The most beautiful of all was the Blessed Elisabeth. She was the patron saint of Anton's country. How many places had not her good deeds sanctified? And how many legends were told about her! A painting of the pious princess hung in the church above a silver lamp. But Molly didn't look at all like her.

The apple tree that the two children had planted grew, year by year. Finally it was so big that it had to be planted in the garden, where the air was fresh, where the dew fell and the sun shone so warmly. It lived through the winter and when the next spring came it blossomed; in the fall there hung two apples on it, one for Molly and one for Anton—less could not have been expected.

The tree flourished and Molly grew: fresh and lovely as an apple blossom she was; but Anton was not to look much longer at this flower. The only thing constant is change! Molly's father moved away from his old home and Molly went with him. Today in the age of steam, the journey to her new home would have taken no more than a few hours, but then it seemed like a great distance. From Eisenach one traveled east for a full day and a night till one reached the border of Thuringia. Molly's new home was in a town called Weimar.

Molly wept and Anton wept, and all their tears shed then became one tear on an old man's cheek so many years later. But then there had been one ray of happiness in all the sorrow: Molly has said that she cared more for him than all the splendor of Weimar.

Three years passed and in all that time Anton received only two letters: one the freightman had carried, the other a traveler brought. The distance between the two towns was long. They were separated by a poor, winding road that passed through many towns and villages.

Often Molly and Anton had heard the story of Tristan and Isolde, and Anton had imagined that the story was about him and Molly.

Though the name Tristan did not fit Anton, for it means "he who is born to sorrow," and that Anton did not believe he was. Nor did Anton ever think that Molly would forget him, as Tristan had suspected of Isolde. But Isolde had not forgotten her Tristan; that had been something he imagined. When they were dead and buried on opposite sides of the churchyard, the linden trees—one on each of their graves—grew so tall that their branches could meet and flower together above the high roof of the church. That part of the legend had seemed to Anton so beautiful and yet so melancholy. Nothing as sorrowful as that could happen to him and Molly. Whenever he thought of the legend, Anton would whistle a song of the minnesinger, Walther von der Vogelweide:

"Under the linden tree, by the heath . . ."

He liked especially the lines:

"By the forest, in the quiet dale,
    Tandaradai!
    Sang the nightingale."

It was his favorite song and he sang it that moonlit night while he was riding along the sunken road to Weimar to see Molly. He wanted to come unexpected and unexpected he arrived.

He was bade welcome and his glass filled up with wine. Everyone was polite and pleasant. He was introduced to distinguished people. He was given a cheerful chamber with a good bed to sleep in. Yet none of it was as he had dreamed it would be. He could not understand what was the matter with himself or the people around him—but we can!

Sometimes you can live in a home, among a family, belonging and yet not belonging. You know the others, you talk with them, but you talk as you would to other passengers in a stagecoach; and you know them as you would know fellow travelers. They annoy you, and you wish that you had reached your destination and were no longer in the coach; or you wish that the person sitting next to you had got off at the last stop. Such were the feelings that Anton had.

"I wish to be honest, " Molly finally said to him. "Therefore, I want to tell it to you myself. Many things have changed since we were children together. Our souls as well as our bodies are not the same. Old habits and dreams have not the same power over our hearts as they once had, Anton! I do not want to make you my enemy. Soon I will be living so far away from here. I have only the kindest memories of you, but I do not love you as I have learned now that a woman can love a man. I have never loved you in that way, you will have to accept that, Anton! Good-by!"

Anton bade her good-by, but not a tear came into his eyes; he felt that he was no longer Molly's friend, he was her enemy. An iron bar, whether it is heated red hot or cools below zero, will smart the lips in the same way if you kiss it; and Anton kissed equally hard in love and hate.

His journey back to Eisenach did not take even a day, but his horse would never be able to be ridden again. "Of what importance is a horse?" he said. "I am ruined and that is worse. I shall destroy everything that reminds me of Molly: Frau Holle! Frau Venus, you heathen woman! I shall tear the apple tree up by the root and break all its branches; they shall never be allowed to bloom again!"

But the apple tree was not destroyed, it was Anton whom fever and sickness almost destroyed. What could cure him? Only the bitterest medicine, the one that can make both the sick soul and body tremble; and he tasted it. Anton's father lost all his money, he was no longer a rich merchant's son. Now came the days of trial, when suffering and poverty knocked on his door. One misfortune followed another. Like great waves on an ocean, they broke over the once so wealthy house. His father was crushed by his losses, he became ill, lamed by adversity; and Anton had to become the head of the family. Now there was no time to be angry at Molly, he had to decide what was to be done; and finally, when all was lost, he had to go out into the wide world to seek work for his daily bread.

He went to Bremen, but there his trials were not over. Sorrow and distress had marked him for their own, and this can make your soul grow either hard or soft—often all too soft. How strange and different were now the world and the people in it from what he had known in his childhood. "The minnesingers' songs were nothing but idle chatter!" he sometimes mumbled, but at other moments the echo of their songs calmed him.

"God's will be done," he thought. "It was fortunate that Molly did not love me. For what kind of a life could I have given her now, when fortune has turned its back on me? She refused me while I was still rich, and that was God's grace toward both her and me. If everything else had to happen, then that was for the best. It was not her fault that she did not love me, but I chose to hate her."

Years passed, Anton's father died, and strangers lived in his old home. Yet he was to see it once more. His master, the rich merchant, sent him on a business trip, and he passed through Eisenach. The old fortress of Wartburg stood unchanged high up on the cliffs, and the old oak trees spread their branches over the craggy rocks, just as they had when he was a child. The mountain of Venus, gray and barren, rose up from the valley. Now Anton would gladly have called, "Frau Holle, Frau Holle, open up your mountain!" for then, at least, he could have stayed in his native land.

The thought frightened Anton: it was sinful and he crossed himself. Just at that moment a little bird sang in a bush nearby and he remembered the old song:

> "By the forest, in the quiet dale,
> Tandaradai!
> Sang the nightingale."

There was so much here that reminded him of his childhood and youth. His parents' house had not changed, but the garden was different. A road now passed through a corner of it, and the old apple tree—the one he had not destroyed though he had wanted to—stood no longer in the garden but on the other side of the new road. Still, the sun shone on it and the dew fell on its leaves in the morning, and its branches bore so much fruit in autumn that they bent toward the earth.

"It thrives," he said. "It is luckier than I."

But one of the big branches had been broken off, probably in play; the tree stood by a public road.

"People steal its flowers and its fruits without ever saying thank you," thought Anton. "They break its branches in play, for it no longer belongs in the garden. The tree's story began so full of beauty, but how will it end? Alone, forgotten, standing by the side of the road, where there is no protection from wind and weather; and no hands to prune it or take care of it. It won't die yet, but as the years pass the flowers will be fewer and the apples smaller, until its story is over."

This Anton thought as he sat underneath the tree and these same thoughts he had often many, many years later in the lonely room of the wooden shed on the street of the little houses, in Copenhagen. Here his master, the merchant in Bremen, had sent him to sell wares, on the condition that he never married.

"Marry, ha-ha," laughed Anton bitterly.

The winter came early that year. There was a great snowstorm in November. Everyone who was not forced to go out stayed inside. That was the reason that none of Anton's neighbors noticed that he had not opened his store for two days.

The days were dark and gray. Inside the little store that did not have proper glass windows, twilight became as black as pitch. Anton had not left his bed for the last two days; he did not have the strength to get up. It was as if the evil weather outside had entered his weak old limbs. Forsaken lay the old pepperman; he was so feeble that he could hardly reach for the jug of water he had put beside his bed. This was not sickness, he had no fever; it was old age that had enfeebled him. In the eternal night of the little hut he lay. A spider spun a web from the dying man to the wall; it would do as mourning crepe.

Time moved slowly, in empty drowsiness. He felt no pain and had no more tears to shed. No longer did he think of Molly. He felt that the world and he had parted company. All its sounds and activities were no longer his. For a while he felt thirst and hunger, but since no one came to help that passed too. He thought of the Blessed Elisabeth, the saint of his homeland and his childhood. While she lived here on earth, this noble lady, a princess of Thuringia, had visited the poor and the sick in their hovels. He recounted her blessed deeds: how she had talked of hope to those who suffered, how she had washed and cleaned the sores of the sick, and brought food to those who starved. Her deeds had made her husband angry, and he had forbidden her to leave the castle. An old legend tells that once, when she was on her way with a basket filled with food and wine to some poor starving family, her husband stopped her and demanded to know what was in her basket. She became so frightened that she lied and said, "Only some roses I have picked in the garden." Her husband tore off the linen cloth that hid the food and wine, but God had performed a miracle to save the pious woman. He had transformed the bread and wine into roses.

The more old Anton thought about the saint, the more real she became to him, until at last he thought he saw her standing at the end of his bed. He took off his nightcap to show his respect, and she smiled kindly as she looked down at him. The whole room seemed filled with roses but the fragrance was not that of roses but of apple blossoms. Above him he saw the flowering branches of a big apple tree, and he knew that it was the very tree that had grown from the seed that he and Molly had planted.

The petals from the blossoms fell on his forehead and on his parched lips, and they felt like wine and quenched his thirst. They fell on his breast and he breathed like a child, so confidently and freely.

"Now I shall sleep," he whispered. "The sleep will do me good. Tomorrow I shall be well again and be able to get up. I am glad to have seen once more the tree that we planted with love." And he slept.

The next day was the third one that the booth hadn't been opened. The snow had stopped falling and the wind had died down. One of Anton's neighbors came to see what had happened and he found Anton dead, still holding the nightcap in his hand. That wasn't the nightcap he was buried in. The clean one was taken out of his drawer and put on his head when he was laid in his coffin.

Where were all the tears he had cried? Where were those pearls? They were in the nightcap, for real pearls are not destroyed in the washtub. They stayed in the pepperman's nightcap together with his old dreams and his long, sad thoughts. Don't wish that cap on your head: it would make you sweat and your pulse would beat faster. It would bring dreams that would be too real. One man tried it, and that fifty years after the old pepperman had died. It was the mayor of Copenhagen, who had a wife and twelve children and plenty of money; but that night he dreamed about unhappy love, bankruptcy, and starvation!

"Huh! That nightcap is too warm!" he shouted, and tore it off his head; and a few pearls fell out of it and rolled down on the floor. "It must be my rheumatism," said the mayor. "I see sparks in front of my eyes."

Those pearls were the tears shed by old Anton from Eisenach, more than fifty years before, but the mayor didn't know that.

Those who have worn the nightcap since have had the same nightmares. They became Anton and had to relive his story in their dreams. And that is why I will repeat the advice I gave in the beginning of the story: don't ever wish to wear the pepperman's nightcap.

✳✧✳

## 83

## "Something"

"I want to become something!" declared the oldest of five brothers. "I want to do something useful in this world. It does not matter whether I reach a high position, so long as the work that I have done has been done well. I want to make bricks—the world can't get along without them—and then I can say I have done something!"

"But much too little," said the second brother. "The work you want to do is nothing; it is unskilled, the kind of work a machine could do just as well. No, it is better to become a mason, that's what I shall become. That is a trade. Masons have their own guild and are honorable citizens of the town; they have their own banner and a guildhall where they meet. Maybe I can become a master mason and have other masons work for me; and my wife will be able to wear a silk dress on weekdays."

"That is nothing!" declared the third brother. "You will belong to the lower middle class at best. There are many classes in our society and most of them are above a master mason's. You will still belong to what is called the 'common people.' No, I want to become something better than that! I want to be a builder, construct houses; be concerned about art and beauty, and belong to the intellectuals. I know I have to start from the bottom. I might as well face it: I have to learn carpentry first, and that means I shall have to be an apprentice, wear a cap on my head instead of a silk hat, and run errands for the journeymen—and they are not polite. But I will just make believe that I am taking part in a masquerade, for you gain freedom by wearing a mask. Then when I have finished my apprenticeship I shall forget those simple fellows and their insults. I shall attend the academy and learn to draw, and then I shall become an architect. And that, I know, is something! I can become respectable and be entitled to be called 'Sir.' I shall build houses like our fathers did, solid and sturdy buildings. That is something!"

"If that is something, then I don't care for it!" said the fourth brother. "I don't want to sail in the wake of other ships, copy what others have already made. I want to be a genius! I want to be cleverer than all the rest of you put together! I will invent a new style, make buildings that fit our climate. I shall use new materials, give expression to our national spirit and the new age! On the very top of my largest building I shall put an extra story, just to prove my own genius."

"But what if neither the style nor the materials are any good?" asked the fifth brother. "That wouldn't do, would it? As for the national spirit, that is affectation. A new age! Bah! What does that mean? Progress is as often as not a runaway horse, just like youth. I see that none of you will ever become something, even though you all think you will. But you can do whatever you want to, it is no concern of mine. I shan't copy you. I want to stand apart. I will contemplate and criticize what you do. There is always something wrong with anything man makes. I shall point it out so all can see it. That is something!"

He did exactly what he had said he would do, and everyone said about the fifth brother: "He is really something. He has got a good head on his shoulders and can make something into nothing." It was especially the latter that made him "something."

That was a very short story; and yet it will never end before the world does.

But what happened to the five brothers? After all, what we have heard wasn't everything. Well, listen and I will tell you more, it is almost a fairy tale.

The oldest brother made bricks and every finished brick brought him a little copper coin. It wasn't worth much, but if you added them up they became a silver coin, and if you knock on the door of the butcher, the baker, or the tailor with such a coin, then their doors open right away. As a matter of fact, there is hardly a door in the whole world that a silver coin can't open; it is the very best key. The bricks gave him what we call a living and that is not so poor a reward; some of them were cracked or had split in two, but even the broken bricks could be used.

There was a poor woman called Mother Margrethe—"Mother" was the title that poor people used to give to old women of whom they were fond. Well, Mother Margrethe wanted to build a house for herself down at the shore, on the dike. She got all the broken bricks free from the oldest brother, who had a kind heart, even though he never rose above being a brickmaker. The poor woman built her house herself. Narrow it was, the window was crooked, the door was low, and the thatch on the roof could have been laid better; but still it was a house; and it kept out wind and weather, even when the storms came and the waves broke against the dike, sending showers of salt water up over the house. When the brickmaker died, it was still standing.

The second brother—the one who became a mason—knew his craft well. As soon as he had finished his apprenticeship he packed his knapsack and set out to see how life was led in foreign lands. When he returned, he set himself up as a master mason and built a whole street full of houses; then all the houses, in turn, built a small house for him. But how can houses build a house? If you ask them, they won't answer; so ask instead the people in any town and they will tell you how it is done. It was a small house with an earthen floor, but when the master mason swung his bride in a dance across it, it got polished. Every stone in the wall seemed to the mason and his wife as pretty as a flower, and they thought that whitewash was as beautiful as the finest wallpaper. It was a lovely little house and a happy couple who lived there. The banner of the guild hung outside, and on their wedding day the apprentices and journeymen had shouted, "Hurrah!" Yes, that was something. Finally he died; and that was something too.

Now we come to the architect, the third brother—the one who first had to be a carpenter's apprentice, wear a cap, and run errands. He graduated from the academy and became a master builder. Now the houses on the street that had built a small house for the brother who had become a mason built a big one, the largest in the street, for the architect; and not only that, but the street itself bore his name. That was something and he had become something. He had a title both in front and behind his name; his children were called "children of good family" and when he died his widow became "a widow of good family." That is something! His name can still be read on the street sign and that, too, is something!

Then there was the fourth brother, the genius, who wanted to build something new and different, with an extra story. Well, it fell down; and so did he, and broke his neck. But he got a splendid funeral, with both guild banners and music in the funeral procession, and flowers on the coffin, as well as in the newspaper. Three funeral sermons were held over him, one longer than the other, and that would have made him happy, for he loved to be talked about. He got a monument on his grave; it was only one story, but still it was something.

Now four of the brothers had died, the only surviving one was the critic. He had the last word, and that was very important to him. He had a good head on his shoulders, as everybody said; but at last he too died and was on his way to heaven.

Now people always enter heaven in pairs, that is the custom. And that's how the fifth brother happened to be standing before the heavenly gate with another soul, who hoped to be able to enter paradise. And who should that be but old Mother Margrethe, who had built her little house down on the dike.

"I suppose it is for the sake of the contrast that this poor miserable soul and I have to wait here together," thought the critic. "Who are you? Poor thing, do you want to enter too?" he asked.

The old lady curtsied as well as she knew how. She thought that St. Peter himself was speaking to her. "I am just a poor old woman without any family: old Margrethe from the house down by the dike."

"Hm, and what have you accomplished down there?"

"Accomplished? Nothing, I guess," answered old Mother Margrethe, "nothing that can open this portal for me. It will only be because of God's grace if I am allowed in."

"And why did you have to leave the world?" asked the critic just to make conversation; he was bored with waiting.

"Exactly why I don't know," answered the old woman. "I have been ill for the last two years; and I guess the cold and the frost killed me, while I lay outside, after I had climbed out of my bed. It was a hard winter this year; but now I don't feel any pains at all. You remember, sir, the two bitterly cold days we had. Not a wind moved and the sea froze as far as you could see. Everyone from town came down to look at it, and they skated on the ice. I think they danced, too, for I could hear music. They were selling beer out there. I could hear all the rumpus right up in my room, where I lay in my bed. It was toward evening; the full moon was out, but it was kind of pale and weak yet. My bed stood right by the window and I could look down on the beach and out on the ice. Suddenly I noticed that out where the sky and the sea met there was a strange white cloud. I was lying there watching it and I noticed that a little black point in the center of it kept growing bigger and bigger. And I knew what that meant.

"I have lived a long time and experienced much, but it is not often you see such a cloud. I knew what it meant and it filled me with horror. Twice before in my life had I seen the same sign in the sky. I knew that it forewarned a storm, and that the spring tide would be coming. It would catch all the poor people out there on the ice by surprise, in the midst of their gaiety and drinking. The young and the old, it looked like the whole town were out there. How could they be warned? I think none of them knew what that white cloud with the black center meant even if they had seen it. I was so frightened that some of my strength came back to me. I got to the window and managed to open it, and then I could do no more. I could see all the people on the ice. Some of them had gone out far. The booth that sold beer had little flags around it and all the children were screaming and shouting, and the young men and girls were singing. It was a gay scene, but behind them rose the white cloud with the black spot looking like a big bag inside it.

"I shouted as loud as I could; but no one heard me, they were too far away. Soon the storm would come, the ice would break, and everyone out there would drown; not one of them would be saved. They could not hear me, and I had not the strength to walk even as far as the beach. How could I manage to get them to shore? Then God gave me the idea that I could set fire to the straw in my bed; it was better that my poor house should burn than that all those people should die. I lit a candle and set the straw on fire. A great red flame shot up and I managed to get outside the house, but then I fell. The flame followed me out the door and caught hold of the thatch. The people out on the ice saw it and they all came running to help me, for they thought that I might be inside the burning house. Not one of them stayed behind. I heard them running, and I heard the storm coming, too; it made such a great stir in the air. Then came the terrible sound of the ice breaking: it was like great cannons shooting.

The spring tide lifted the ice and broke it into splinters. But everyone had got ashore. People were running up on the dike, where I lay amid the sparks from the fire. They were safe, but I think the fright and the cold must have been too much for me. And here I am at the gate of heaven. They say that it also opens for the wretched, like me. And now I don't have a house any more; not that that would help me gain admittance here."

Just at that moment the gates of heaven opened and an angel came out to lead the poor old woman inside. A straw from her bed, the one she had set fire to in order to save the people out on the ice, fell from her skirt. It was immediately changed into the purest gold; and the golden straw grew and became the prettiest piece of art work.

"Look at what the poor woman brought," said the angel to the critic. "What have you brought? I know you never have accomplished anything, you have never even made a brick. If you only could go back and fetch one, and then bring it as a gift. Oh, I know it would be badly made, but if you had done the best you could, it would at least be something. But you can't return and I can't do anything for you!"

The poor old woman, Margrethe from the little house on the dike, pleaded for him. "His brother gave me all his broken bricks so that I could build my house. Those broken pieces meant an awful lot to me then. Can't they count now as one whole brick, for his sake? It would be a merciful act and this is the home of mercy."

"Your brother, the one whom you deemed the poorest among you," said the angel, "he whose honest work you considered low, gives you now a beggar's coin. You shall not be turned away, you shall be allowed to stand here outside and think about your life down on earth. But enter you cannot before you have done one good deed—at least something!"

"I could have expressed that better," thought the critic, but he didn't say it out loud and that was already something.

## 84

# The Old Oak Tree's Last Dream

## A Christmas Story

On the outskirts of the forest, on a bank above the beach, grew an old oak tree. It was three hundred and sixty-five years old, but to the tree those years did not seem longer than as many days and nights would to a human being. We are awake during the day and sleep at night, and it is then we have our dreams. But the oak tree is awake three seasons of the year and only sleeps during the fourth. It is only in the winter that it rests; that is its night after that long day that is called spring, summer, and autumn.

Many a warm day the mayflies danced around its leaves and branches, soared on their fragile wings to the very crown of the tree. Ever happy were the little insects and, when they grew tired, they rested on a broad green oak leaf. Then the tree could not help saying, "Poor little you, one day is your whole life. How short, how sad is your fate!"

"Sad," the mayfly always replied. "What do you mean by that? Everthing is so beautiful, so warm, and so lovely; and I am so happy."

"But only one day and then all is over."

"Over," said the mayfly. "What is over? Are you over too?"

"No, I live many thousands of your days, and my days are so long that they last almost a year, which is so long that you cannot even figure it out."

"I do not understand you. You live thousands of my days, but I have thousands of moments to be happy in. Do you think that all the beauty in the world will die when you do?"

"No," answered the tree. "That will last much longer than even I can imagine."

"Well there, you see, we live equally long; it is just our ways of figuring that are different."

And the little mayfly flew away again, up into the air, and rejoiced that it had been given such lovely fine wings. The air was filled with the scent of flowering clover from the fields, wild roses from the hedges, elder trees, honeysuckle, woodruff, primroses, and wild mint. The fragrance was so strong that the mayfly felt quite drunk from it. The day was long and beautiful, so filled with happiness, so full of joy. When finally the sun did set, the little fly felt tired from all it had experienced so intensely. The wings were no longer strong enough to carry it. Ever so gently it sank down among the soft grass, nodding its head as if it were saying yes. It slept so peacefully, so happily, and that was death.

"Poor little mayfly," said the oak tree, "its life was much too short."

Every summer the mayflies repeated their dance and the oak held the same conversation with them. Generations upon generations of mayflies died, and yet each new insect born was just as happy, just as carefree, as all those that had gone before it. The oak tree was awake through its spring morning, its summer noon, and its fall evening. It felt that soon it was time to sleep; the oak tree's night, winter, was coming.

Already the storms were singing: "Good night, good night! We pluck your leaves. See, there one fell. We pluck, we pluck! We sing you to sleep. We undress you and shake your old branches; they creak but it does them good. Sleep now, sleep, it is your three hundred and sixty-fifth night, which means you are young yet. Sleep. From the clouds snow is falling, it is a warm blanket around your feet. Sleep and dream sweet dreams!"

The oak tree stood nude with its bare branches against the sky, ready to sleep through its long night, ready to dream many a dream just as human beings do.

It, too, had been tiny once: an acorn had been its cradle. By human reckoning it was now in the fourth century of its life. It was the biggest tree in the forest, and its crown rose up high above the others. Sailors used it as a landmark to navigate by, and the wood pigeons built their nests in it. In the fall the migrating birds would rest among its bronze leaves before they flew south. But now in the winter its branches were naked, and only crows and jackdaws used them; they sat there discussing hard times and complaining about how difficult it was to find food, now that winter was here.

It was at the holy Christmastime that the oak tree dreamed the most beautiful dream it had ever dreamed. We shall hear it:

The tree felt that something holy, something solemn and yet joyful, was happening. From every direction it heard church bells ringing. In its dream, it was not winter but the loveliest warm summer day. The branches in its great crown spread themselves out green and fresh, the sun rays played upon its leaves, and the air was filled with the fragrance of flowering trees and bushes. Colorful butterflies played hide-and-seek and the mayflies danced as if the whole world had been created just for their enjoyment. Everything the tree had seen and experienced through its long life passed by in an endless parade. It saw knights with their ladies; they were riding out to hunt, with feathers in their caps and falcons on their hands. And the tree heard the dogs bark and the sound of the hunters' horns. Then strange soldiers camped beneath its branches; they pitched their tents and made fires. The sun reflected in their shining weapons; they ate and drank and sang as if they had conquered time as well as the country. Two shy lovers came and cut their names in its bark; they were the first to do it but others would follow. Once an aeolian harp had been hung in the oak's branches by a happy youth. That had happened so many years ago, yet it hung there again in the dream; and the wind blew through it and made music. The wood pigeons cooed, and the cuckoo called out once for each year that the oak tree had left of its life; but the cuckoo is not to be trusted.

The tree felt as if a great wave of strength, of life, were passing through it. From its tiniest root, deep down in the ground, to its topmost little twigs, it experienced an awareness of life and warmth. It felt its strength increase, it was growing taller and taller. Its great crown was now enormous. As it grew, its feeling of happiness became more and more intense, and it had such a great longing for the sun that it wanted to grow right up into that golden warm sphere.

In its dream, the tree had grown so tall that its top branches were above the clouds; flocks of birds were flying below them; even the swans could not fly above its crown.

Every leaf had become an eye that could see. All the stars were out, even though it was day, and they looked so clear, so bright, and shone as brilliantly as the eyes of children or of the lovers who met beneath the old oak tree.

What a wonderful moment, so full of joy! Yet in the midst of all its happiness the tree felt a longing for other trees and the bushes that grew far below it. It wished that they, too—as well as the little flowers and herbs—could lift themselves high up in the sky as it was doing, and experience its joy. The great oak tree wanted to share its godlike ecstasy. It felt that unless everyone took part in this great dream of happiness it would not be complete. This wish ran through it from root to leaves and was as strong as a human being's desires.

The crown of the tree swayed as its branches turned to look downward. It smelled the odor of woodruff and the stronger fragrance of violets and honeysuckle, and thought that it could hear the cuckoo call.

The top branches of the other trees of the forest now peeped through the clouds; they, too, were growing, lifting themselves up to the sky, toward the sun. Bushes and flowers followed; some of them had freed themselves from the earth and were flying. The birch, like a bolt of white lightning, passed the old oak. The whole forest was flying up toward the sky, even the brown reeds from the swamp were coming. The birds had followed the plants. On a blade of grass sat a grasshopper and played with his wings on his hind legs. Beetles and bees and all the other insects had come, and all of them shared the old oak tree's joyous ecstasy.

"But where are the little blue flowers from the pond?" shouted the oak tree. "And the red harebell and the little primrose?" The old oak did not want anyone to be forgotten.

"We are here, we are here!" sang voices all around it.

"But the woodruff from last summer and all the lilies of the valley from the summer before that, where are they? I remember the year when the wild apples bloomed so beautifully. Oh, so much beauty do I recall through all the years of my life! If it only were all alive now and could be with us!"

"We are, we are," came cries from somewhere higher up; they must have flown there earlier.

"That is the most marvelous of all," rejoiced the old oak tree. "Everything that I have known is here. Nothing has been forgotten, not the tiniest flower or the smallest bird. How is such joy possible? Where is such happiness conceivable?"

"In heaven it is possible," sang the voices.

And the tree felt its roots loosen their grasp on the earth.

"Yes, that is best!" the oak cried. "Now no bands hold me down. I can fly up into the everlasting light, the eternal glory! And all that I held dear is with me. None has been forgotten, all are here with me, all!"

That was the oak tree's dream; and while it was dreaming a great storm blew across the sea and the land. The waves rushed toward the shore and were crushed on the beach, and the wind tore at the old oak tree's branches. Just at the moment when it dreamed that its roots gave way, in its flight toward heaven, it was torn from the ground by the wind and fell. Its three hundred and sixty-five years of life were now as a day is for the mayfly.

Christmas morning the sea had calmed and the storm was over. The church bells were gaily ringing, and above each house, even the smallest and poorest cottages, a blue ribbon of smoke rose from the chimney, like the smoke at a Druid feast of thanksgiving. The sea grew calmer and calmer, and on board the big ships, which the night before had been so hard pressed by the storm, the sailors hoisted gay colorful flags in the rigging to celebrate the holy day.

"The big tree is gone! The old oak tree we used as a landmark!" the sailors shouted, amazed. "It fell in the storm. What shall we use now? There is none that can replace it."

That was the old oak tree's funeral sermon; it was short but well meant. The tree itself lay stretched out on the snow-covered beach. From the ship came the sound of the sailors singing a carol about the joyful season, when Christ was born to save mankind and give us eternal life. The sailors were singing of the same dream, the beautiful dream that the old oak tree had dreamed Christmas Eve: the last night of its life.

## 85

## The Talisman

There once were a prince and a princess who had just gotten married. They were so very happy that they had only one worry: the thought that they might not always be as happy as they were now. Therefore, they wanted a talisman that could protect them against discontent in their marriage. They had heard of a wise hermit who lived out in the forest, of whom it was said that he had remedies for all the griefs of this world. The prince and the princess went to seek his advice and told him about what troubled their hearts.

The wise man listened to them and said, "Travel through all the countries of the world and, when you meet a couple who are truly contented in their married life, ask them to give you a small piece of the linen that they are wearing next to their bodies. Once you have that, keep it always with you. A little piece of such linen is, indeed, a very powerful charm!"

The prince and the princess set out on their journey. They had not ridden far when they heard of a knight who was supposed to be most happily married. They rode up to his castle and asked him and his noble wife if it were true, as it had been rumored, that they were perfectly content in their marriage.

"Yes," answered the knight, "it is true, except for one thing. We have no children." Here the talisman was not to be found, so the young royal couple continued their journey.

They came to a large city where lived an honorable citizen of whom it was said that he had lived a long life in perfect union with his wife. To his home they made their way to ask the couple if their marriage was as happy as everyone said it was.

"Yes, it is!" answered the good man. "My wife and I have lived in perfect harmony; if only we had not had so many children, for they have caused us so much trouble and grief." Here, too, they need not ask for any talisman.

And the prince and princess traveled on, asking everywhere if anyone knew a couple whose marriage had brought them only joy, but nowhere were they told of any.

One day as they were riding through a meadow they saw a shepherd sitting and playing on his flute. Just at that moment his wife, carrying an infant in her arms, with a little boy beside her, came walking out to her husband. As soon as the shepherd spied his wife he jumped up and ran to meet her. He greeted her and took the babe from her arms and fondled and kissed it. The shepherd's dog had come too; it jumped for joy around the boy and licked his hand. The wife put down a pot that she had brought with her and said, "Come, my husband, and eat." The shepherd was hungry but the first bite he gave the baby, and the second he shared between his son and the dog.

All this the prince and princess heard and saw. They dismounted, walked up to the little family, and asked: "You seem to us to be what we would call a happily married couple, aren't you?"

"Yes, truly we are happy," answered the shepherd. "I think no prince or princess could be happier than we are."

"Then listen to me," said the prince. "Be so kind as to give us a tiny piece of the linen you are wearing under your clothes. You shall be well paid for it."

The shepherd and his wife blushed and looked embarrassed. Finally he said, "God knows that we would gladly give you not only a tiny piece of our linen but our shirts and shifts as well, if we only had any, but we don't."

The prince and princess had to travel on without the talisman they sought. Finally they grew tired of this endless journey and set their course for home. As their road went through the forest and past the wise hermit's cottage, they stopped to tell him how poorly he had advised them.

The wise man smiled and said, "Has your journey really been in vain? Have you not returned enriched from your experiences?"

"Yes," admitted the prince, "I have learned that contentment is the rarest blessing on this earth."

"And I have learned," said the princess, "that for contentment all that is needed is to be content!"

The prince took the princess' hand in his, and with expressions of the deepest love they looked at each other.

The wise man blessed them and said, "In your hearts you have found the true talisman. Guard it carefully, and the evil spirit of discontent will never—no matter how long you live—have any power over you."

## 86

## The Bog King's Daughter

The storks tell their young ones many stories and fairy tales. All of them take place in the swamps and bogs where storks like to live. They usually choose stories that fit the ages of their children. The smallest are satisfied if their parents say: "Muddle, duddle . . . cribble crabble"; that is plot and morality enough for their taste. But the older ones are not so easily satisfied; they demand something with a deeper meaning or at least a story about their own family. The storks know two stories that are very ancient and very long: one of them is the story of Moses, who was set sailing out upon the waters of the Nile by his mother and was found by a princess. He was carefully brought up and well educated and became a great man. Where he is buried no one knows. That story every child has heard. The other tale is not well known, possibly because it is a bit provincial. It is a fairy tale that has been told by stork mothers for a thousand years; each one of them has told it a little better than her mother, and we shall tell it best of all.

The first storks who told it had experienced it themselves, they had been part of it. They had their summer residence on top of the roof of the wooden house of a Viking chieftain who lived near the great bog in the north of Jutland, which is called Vendsyssel. If one were to describe it learnedly—as it is described in a Danish geography book —then one must explain that once this was an ocean bed, but the waters departed and the land rose. Today the bog is very large, but once it was even larger; there were miles and miles of swamp, marshland, and stretches of peat. There were no trees worth talking about, and over the bog hovered, almost always, a dense fog. At the turn of the eighteenth century there were still wolves there; and it was even wilder a thousand years ago. Yet the landscape was the same; the reeds were no taller, and they had the same feathery flowers and slender leaves. The birch tree's bark was as white as it is now, and its branches with their fine green leaves hung toward the earth as gracefully. The animal life, too, has not changed. The flies, then, were as troublesome as they are now; and the storks wore the same black and white livery with red stockings. But the human beings were dressed differently, though their fate was the same, if they stepped out upon the surface of the great bog: a thousand years ago—as today—they would slowly sink into the muddy ooze down to the bog king. That was the name given to the ruler of the great bog. Some called him the swamp king, but we prefer the bog king and the storks agree with us, for that is what they called him. Very little is known about his rule, which may be just as well.

Near the bog, on the shores of the fjord, a Viking chief had built a big house. It has a stone cellar, three floors and a tower, constructed of logs. On top of the roof a pair of storks had built their nest. The mother stork, who was brooding, was convinced that every one of her eggs would hatch.

One evening the father stork was away from the nest longer than usual, and when he finally returned he looked upset and unhappy. "I have something horrible to tell you," he said.

"Don't!" exclaimed his wife. "Remember I am brooding. If you upset me, it might harm the eggs!"

"You must know what has happened!" insisted the male stork. "She has come, the daughter of our landlord in Egypt, and now she has disappeared!"

"The girl who is related to the fairies? Tell me, tell me! Don't keep me in suspense, that is not good for me when I am sitting on eggs!"

"You know, my dear, that she believed the doctors who said that the water lilies, here in the north, would cure her father. She has flown up here. She was wearing a swanskin and came together with the two other princesses who fly up here every year to bathe—they believe the waters make them regain their youth. The young princess was here and now she is gone!"

"You are so long-winded, get to the point!" complained his wife. "The eggs may catch cold; I can't stand being kept in suspense."

"You know I keep an eye on everything," the male stork continued. "Last night I was down in the reeds, where the mud is solid enough for me to stand, and I saw three swans. There was something about their flight that said: 'Look out, they are not swans, they are something else wearing swanskins.' You know as well as I, how one can feel that a thing just isn't right."

"Yes, yes!" His wife was getting very impatient. "Tell me about the princess and never mind the swanskins, they bore me!"

"You know that right in the center of the bog there is a lake—you can see part of it from here if you stand up. Near the reeds at the shore, there lay the trunk of an old alder tree, and the three swans landed on it. They flapped their wings and looked around. Then one of them cast off her swanskin and I recognized her. She was the princess from the palace in Egypt. She had nothing to cover herself with but her long black hair. She asked the other two to guard her swanskin, while she dived down into the water to pluck the flower that she thought she had spied underneath the water. The other two swans flew up, taking the princess' swanskin with them in their bills. I wondered what they wanted to do with it; and I am sure the princess would have liked to ask the same question. We were answered soon enough.

"'Dive down into the dark water!' cried the swans. 'Never again shall you see Egypt, you shall stay here in the wild bog forever!' Then, with their beaks, they tore her swanskin into hundreds of pieces. The feathers flew around them; it looked like a snowstorm. Then the two evil princesses flew away."

"It is horrible!" exclaimed the mother stork. "I can't bear hearing stories like that. I am sure it is not good for me. . . . But tell me what happened afterward, please tell me!"

"The princess cried and her tears fell on the trunk of the old alder tree. It began to move! It wasn't an alder tree, it was the bog king himself! The one who lives in the bog and rules it. I saw the tree trunk turn in the water, and then it no longer looked like a tree trunk. Its long branches were not branches but arms! The poor girl got frightened. She tried to jump up onto the shore, but she was too heavy to stand in the muddy bog. At that place the ooze can't even bear me. She sank down into the bog and at the same moment the bog king disappeared. I think he pulled her down. Some big black bubbles rose to the surface, burst, and were gone. Now she is buried in the bog and she will never return to Egypt and bring her father the flower. You couldn't have borne seeing it, I am sure!"

"I don't think you should even have told me about it now; it may spoil the eggs! The princess will take care of herself, I am sure; there is always someone who is ready to help her kind. Now if it had been you or I who had been sucked down into the mud, then everything would have been over."

"Still, I will keep an eye on the place," said the male stork, and he did.

A long time passed; then one day a green stalk shot up through the water. When it reached the surface a leaf unfolded, and in the center of it was a bud. The leaf grew bigger and bigger, and so did the bud. One morning when the stork flew above it he saw that the bud was opening in the warm sunshine. In the flower lay a little girl, a beautiful child; she looked so much like the princess from Egypt that the stork thought it might be she, grown smaller. But on second thought he found it more reasonable that the child was her daughter with the bog king, and that was why she was lying in a water lily.

"She can't stay there," thought the stork. "There is no room in my nest, we are already crowded. But the Viking chief's wife has no child, and I know she wants one badly. I have heard her sighing. Since they claim that I bring children I might as well do it for once. I will give it to our landlady; it will make her happy."

The stork took the little girl in his bill and flew up to the house. There he pecked a hole in the window—that was easy, for it was only covered by a pig's bladder. He lay the baby beside the sleeping woman, then he flew back up to his wife to tell her all about it. The children were allowed to listen; after all, they were almost grown up.

"You see, the princess isn't dead, she must have sent the little girl up with the water lily. And I found a home for her."

"I told you all the time that, if she couldn't take care of herself, then someone else would take care of her," said the mother stork. "But you should think a little more about your own faimly and less about others. It will soon be time to leave; my wings are itching. The cuckoo and the nightingale have already left, and the quails are saying that the wind will soon blow just right for flying south. I am sure our children will do well on the maneuver; I know them, I am their mother.".

The Viking chieftain's wife was ever so happy when she awoke and found the little girl. She kissed and fondled the little baby, but the child did not seem to like it, she kicked and screamed and cried. Finally she fell asleep and no child has ever looked lovelier than she did then. The Viking woman felt so happy and lighthearted that she was sure that her husband and his men would be home soon: they would come just as unexpectedly as the child had. She got busy putting the house in order. She ordered the slaves to polish the old shields that hung on the walls and told her maid to bring out the tapestries that had pictures of their gods woven in them: of Odin, Thor, and Freya. Skins were placed on the wooden benches and dry firewood on the great central fireplace, so that it could be lit as soon as the voyagers returned. The mistress worked along with the others; by evening she was very tired, and she slept well throughout the night.

Just before the sun rose she awoke. The child was gone! She got terribly frightened and jumped out of bed to look for it. She lit a bit of kindling and then she saw at the foot of her bed not the child but a big ugly frog. She felt sick at the sight of it and grabbed a large piece of firewood to kill it. But the toad looked up at her with such infinitely sad eyes that she couldn't. She looked around the room. The frog gave a pathetic little croak, and the woman shivered at the sound. Then she ran and opened up the shutters. Just at that moment the sun rose. Its first rays came in through the opening and fell on the bed, where the big frog was sitting. Its broad mouth became small; its ugly limbs straightened and took on the lovely shape of her little child. The ugly frog was gone.

"What has happened!" she cried. "I must have had an evil dream. There is my lovely fairy child!" She picked up the little girl, kissed her, and pressed her to her heart. But the baby acted more like an angry kitten; she scratched and bit.

The Viking chief did not return that day or the next. He was on his way home but had the wind against him. It blew toward the south for the storks' sake. Fair winds for one are foul for another.

The next night the Viking woman realized how things were with her little child; she was bewitched. By day she was as beautiful as a fairy but her character was wild and evil; at night she was an ugly frog with sad sorrowful eyes and sat whimpering quietly. These transformations in the girl, whom the stork had brought, were caused by the two natures within her. In the daytime she had the shape and appearance of her lovely mother but the soul of her father. At night her kinship with the bog king could be seen in her body, but then she had the sweet character and heart of her mother.

The chieftain's wife was frightened and sorrowful: who could break such a curse? Yet she loved the unfortunate creature that fate had brought to her. She was determined not to tell her husband about the child being bewitched, for she feared that he would set her out in the wilderness to be eaten by wolves, as this was the Viking custom with babies that were deformed. She vowed—poor woman—that her husband would never see the child except by day.

One morning the sound of the wings of storks could be heard. They were resting after the big maneuver and were now ready for the flight south. There were more than two hundred of them.

"Everybody ready!" was the command. "Children and wives stay with your husbands!"

"I feel so light," said one of the stork children. "It creeps and crawls inside me right down into my legs, as if I were filled with living frogs. How wonderful it is to travel!"

"Keep in your places," admonished their mother and father, "and don't talk too much, it is bad for the breathing."

And away they flew!

Right at that moment a horn was blown. The Vikings had landed. Their ships were loaded with rich booty. They had come from the coasts of Gaul, where the people—just as they did in England—prayed: "Free us from the wild Norsemen."

A great celebration took place in the Viking hall near the great bog. A vat of mead was carried in and the great fire was lit. Horses were butchered, and the warm horse blood was sprayed on the new slaves, in honor of Odin: a heathen baptism. The smoke drifted from the fire up to the roof, soot dripped from the great beams; but no one took any notice.

The house was filled with guests and everyone received a costly present. All old disagreements and broken promises were forgotten. They drank and they ate, and they threw the gnawed bones in each other's faces—that was considered amusing. The poet of the time, who was called a *skjald,* was a warrior too; he had been on the voyage, so he knew what he was composing verses about. He sang ballads about their adventures, recalling every battle each Viking had fought in. His verses always ended with the same words! "Richness vanishes and friends die, as one must die oneself; only the fame of greatness never dies." Then they would all bang with their knives or hit their shields with their gnawed bones, so the noise could be heard far away.

The chieftain's wife sat on the women's bench, dressed in a silken gown; she wore gold bracelets and an amber necklace. The *skjald* did not forget to mention her in his verses; he sang about the golden treasure she had brought her rich and famous husband. In truth, the chieftain was pleased with his child, whom he had only seen while the sun was in the sky. She was beautiful, and as for her temper, he liked it. "She will become a valkyrie, who will fight as well as any man and not be frightened by the sound of a sword as it cleaves the air," he said proudly.

The vat of mead was empty and another one was carried into the hall. Oh yes, these were people who could drink. The Vikings had a proverb: "Cattle know when it is best to stop grazing, but a fool never realizes the size of his own stomach." Although all of them knew these words, they seemed to have forgotten them. Just as they did not remember another proverb from that time: "A good friend becomes a bore if he stays too long in another man's house." For weeks the guests stayed, for the sake of the meat and the mead.

Once more that year the Vikings went on a raid, but only across the waters to England. The Viking woman was again alone with her little girl. By now she loved more deeply the sighing frog with the sad lovely eyes than the beautiful girl who bit and tore at her.

The raw and cold autumn fog, which, although it has no mouth, gnaws the leaves of the trees, now covered the landscape. The first snowflakes had followed each other down from the clouds. Winter was not far away. The sparrows had moved into the storks' nest and were criticizing endlessly the departed owners. But where were the father and mother stork and all their children?

They were in Egypt, where the sun in winter shines as warmly as it does in Denmark in the summer. Tamarisks and acacias were in bloom there, and above the temple dome shone Mohammed's moon. On the tops of the tall, slender towers many stork couples sat resting from their long journey. Whole flocks of them had built their nests in the ruins of the other temples; those once busy places that were forgotten now. The date palms lift their leaves high up in the air like gigantic parasols. The whitish-gray pyramids look as if they had been drawn on the clear air of the desert. There the ostrich demonstrates that, although it cannot fly, it at least can run; and the lion, with its sad and knowing eyes, contemplates the marble sphinx that stands half buried in the sand. The waters of the Nile were low and the muddy river bed was alive with frogs. For a stork that was the most pleasant sight of all. The young ones, who had not been in Egypt before, thought it was all an optical illusion, so marvelous was it.

"No, it is real, and that is the way it always is here in our winter residence!" said the stork mother.

"Aren't we going any farther?" asked the young ones. "Aren't we going to see even more?"

"There isn't much more to see," answered their mother. "The part that is fertile is a little too wild. The trees grow too close together in the jungle, and among their branches are thorny vines; only the elephants with their thick skins and broad feet can make their way through there. The snakes are too big to eat and the lizards too agile to catch. And if you go in the other direction, toward the desert, you will get sand in your eyes, and that is not pleasant. No, it is best to stay here, where there are plenty of frogs and grasshoppers. I will stay here, and so will you!"

And they stayed. The old ones had a nest on top of a minaret; there they rested, while they smoothed down their feathers and polished their bills on their long red legs. They would lift their heads and nod gravely toward other storks, as they looked out over the landscape with their brown eyes that seemed to shine with intelligence. The young female storks would wander about in the swamp, making friends and eating a frog for every third step they took. Often they would walk around with a little snake dangling in their bills; they thought it looked attractive, and besides, it tasted good. The young males fought with each other; they would flap their wings and fight such duels with their beaks that sometimes blood would flow.

After a while they all got engaged, which was only natural; then they built nests of their own, and argued and fought some more. In the hot countries everyone has a hot temper, but it was all very entertaining. The older storks, found it amusing to watch; they thought anything their own offspring did most marvelous and unique. Every day the sun shone, and every day there was enough to eat; the only thing left to do was to enjoy oneself.

But inside the great castle life was not amusing at all. The great powerful ruler of the country lay as still as a mummy on his couch in the great hall of the castle. The walls were all covered with murals; it looked as if he were lying in the center of an enormous tulip. Servants and relations flocked around him. He wasn't dead, but he wasn't alive either. The water lily from the north that could have saved him would never be found. His young and beautiful daughter who had flown in a swanskin over the ocean and the great mountains, far to the north, to fetch it would never return. "She is dead and gone," said the two princesses who had accompanied her on the journey. Listen to the pretty story they told:

"We were flying, all three of us, high up in the air when a hunter saw us; he shot an arrow and it hit our friend. She sank down toward a little lake, while she sang her good-by: her swan song. By the shore of the lake, under a birch tree, we buried her! We took revenge. We tied burning tinder under the wings of the swallow that lived underneath the hunter's roof. It flew home to its nest and set fire to his house. The hunter died in the fire and the flames could be seen as far as the birch tree under which the princess rests, where she has become dust in the dust. She will never come back to Egypt."

Then they cried, both of them; and the father stork, who heard it all, clattered with his bill, he was so angry.

"Lies and more lies," he said. "I felt like running my beak right through them!"

"And breaking it!" replied his wife. "You would be a sight then! Think a little more about yourself and your family. What is outside it shouldn't concern you."

"I will fly over to the great dome and listen tomorrow, when all the wise men assemble to discuss the king's illness. Maybe they will get a little nearer to the truth."

The learned and the wise gathered, and talked and talked; but the stork couldn't understand their chatter. It did not help the sick man either, or his daughter who was lost in the great bog. We could listen a little to what was said; one has to hear an awful lot of that kind of talk before one dies. But since this is a story and we are free to travel in time as well as space, let's hear about the first assembly of the wise and learn what happened when the king became ill, a year before. We ought to know at least as much as the stork could understand.

"Love breeds life, and the highest form of love breeds the highest form of life. Only through love can our sick king be brought back to life." This had been said at the first assembly, and the learned and the wise had all agreed that it was true.

"It is a beautiful thought," the stork had explained as soon as he came home to the nest.

"I don't quite understand it," his wife had said, "and I don't believe the fault is mine. It is unclear! But it doesn't matter, I have enough to think about already."

The learned and the wise had then gone on to discuss the different forms of love: the one between lovers, and the one that parents feel for their children, besides the more complicated forms, such as the one between light and the plants—how the sun rays kiss the black earth, making the seeds sprout. That part of the discussion was so learned and so filled with long and difficult words that the stork could understand almost none of it, let alone be able to repeat it when he got home. He became very morose, half closed his eyes, and stood on one leg for a whole day. Excessive learning is very hard to bear.

But one thing he did know, for he had heard it said often enough, both by the courtiers and the ordinary people—and they had talked from their hearts: it was a disaster to the whole country that the king was sick, and it would be a great blessing to the people if he got well.

"But where grows the flower that can give him back his health?" That was the question everyone had asked last year. They had studied old learned books, the stars, the weather, and the clouds, and used every possible detour to get at the truth. The wise and the learned— as we know—had agreed upon the maxim, "Love breeds life, life to our father." They repeated it over and over again and wrote it down as a prescription: "Love breeds life." But how the prescription was to be filled, that no one knew. At last they had agreed that the princess, who loved her father so much, must be the one to find the answer. And the wise men even decided how she was to go about it. At night, when the new moon had disappeared from the sky, she was to go out in the desert to the marble sphinx. There she should cast away the sand from the half-buried door at its base and walk through the long corridors that led to the center of one of the great pyramids. Here lay buried one of the great kings from ancient times. The princess was to enter this chamber of death and splendor, and lean her head against the decorated casing that contained the mummy. The dead king would then reveal to her how her father could be saved.

She had done what had been demanded of her, and in a dream she had learned that in the wild bog in the north—the place had been very accurately described—there grew a lotus flower that would bring back her father's health. She was to dive into the black water and pick the first flower that touched her breast.

This had all happened a year and a day before, and that was why the princess had flown in a swanskin from Egypt north to Denmark. The storks knew all about this; and now we know it, which makes the whole story easier to understand. We know, too, that the bog king took her down to his castle and that everyone in Egypt thought she was lost forever—that is, everyone but the wisest of all the wise; he was of the same opinion as the mother stork: "The princess will take care of herself."

"I think I will steal the swanskins from the two evil princesses," proposed the father stork, "then they won't be able to fly north and do more harm. I will hide the swanskins up there until there will be a use for them."

"What do you mean by up there?" asked his wife.

"In our nest up by the bog, in Denmark. Our children can help me carry them. Should they be too heavy, then we can find a hiding place along the way and carry them the rest of the way next year. One swanskin is enough for the princess, but you know how it is when you travel in the north, you can never have clothes enough along."

"Nobody is going to thank you for it," grumbled his wife. "But you are the master; no one listens to me except when I am laying eggs."

In the Viking hall by the great bog, the young girl had been given a name. She was called Helga. A name too soft to fit her character. Years passed; each spring the storks traveled north and each fall they returned to Egypt. Helga grew, became a big girl, and then a maiden sixteen summers old. Beautiful was the shell, but the kernel was hard and cruel; she was wilder and more ferocious than most people in those grim and brutal times.

She found pleasure in seeing the red blood of the horses that were offered to Odin stain her white hands. And once, in a fit of temper, she had bitten the head off a black cock that was to be offered to Thor. To her father she said—and she meant it—"Should your enemies come and tear the roof off the hall while you slept, I should not wake you. I would not warn you, for my cheeks are still burning from the time, years ago, when you slapped my face."

But the Viking chieftain did not believe her; his daughter's beauty blinded him to all her faults. He did not know how Helga's soul and body changed when night fell. When she rode, she sat on the horse as if she and the animal were one; and if sometimes the horse got into a fight with another horse, she stayed on its back, laughing while the animals kicked and bit each other. When the Vikings returned from a raid, she would throw herself into the waters of the fjord and swim out to the boat to greet them. From her beautiful long hair she cut strands and with them she made bowstrings.

"Self-made is well made," she would say, and laugh.

Her foster mother—the Viking woman—according to the times and habits of the country, was a strong-willed and capable woman; but toward her daughter she was soft and frightened, for she knew the curse that rested on the poor child.

To make her mother miserable—as if she enjoyed seeing the poor woman's terror—Helga would throw herself over the side of the well when her mother was nearby. The wretched woman would watch while, froglike, she swam in the freezing well water; then, more agilely than a cat, she would climb the steep stone sides of the well and rush into the hall, while her clothes were still dripping wet, so that she dampened the fresh leaves that had been strewn on the floor.

But at twilight, just before the sun set, Helga changed; she became quiet and thoughtful. Then she was obedient and would listen to what was said to her. She would draw close to her mother and, when the sun went down and her appearance and nature were transformed, she would sit still and sorrowful in her frog shape. Her body was much larger than any frog's, and therefore she was all the uglier; she looked like a horrible dwarf with a frog's head and webbed hands and feet. Her eyes alone were lovely with their infinite sadness. Of voice she had none. All she could manage was a hollow croak that sounded like a child sobbing in its dreams. Then her foster mother would take her on her lap and, disregarding her ugly body, she would look into her sad eyes and say, "I could almost wish that you always would be my silent frog child, for you are far more frightening to look at when your outside is beautiful and your inside ugly."

And the poor woman wrote magic runic letters on birch bark and put them on her frog child to break the spell, but none of them worked.

"One wouldn't think she had ever been so small that she could lie in a water lily," said the father stork. "She is a real woman now and the image of her mother, the Egyptian princess. We have never seen her again. And you, my dear, and the Egyptian wise man were wrong, she couldn't take care of herself. Through all these years, ever since she disappeared, I have flown back and forth across the bog but I have seen no sign of her. Once, when I came up here a few days before you and the young ones, in order to repair the nest and put things in order, I flew all night—as if I were an owl or a bat —above the place where she disappeared, but I didn't see a thing. The swanskins that it took us three years to bring up here will never be used. Now they have lain on the bottom of the nest these many years; and if this log house burns down, they will be lost."

"And so will our good nest!" said his wife angrily. "You are less concerned about that than those toys made of feathers, and that precious bog princess of yours. Why don't you dive down and stay with her! You are neither a good father nor a good husband; that I said the very first time that I laid eggs. We will be lucky if that Viking hussy doesn't send an arrow through our own children. She is a madwoman and doesn't know what she is doing. But she ought to remember that we are of an ancient family and have lived here a lot longer than she has. We pay our taxes—and that is only right—one feather, one egg, and a young one, every year. When she is around, then I stay in the nest. Don't think that I fly down in the yard as I used to, and still do in Egypt, where I am friends with almost everyone and even take a look into the pots and pans. No, here I stay at home, and grow more and more irritated over that wench and over you, too! You should have let her stay in the water lily, then we would have been rid of her."

"You are more respectable than your speech shows," said her husband. "I know you even better than you know yourself."

He made a little jump, beat the air twice with his wings, and sailed upward on the breeze. When he had risen, he again flapped his wings as he turned and made a circle. The sunlight shone upon his white feathers; his long neck and bill were stretched straight forward, it was a lovely sight.

"He is the handsomest of the lot of them," said his wife, "but that I will never tell him."

The Vikings returned from their raids abroad early that autumn. Among the prisoners was a Christian priest, one of those who were enemies of Odin and Thor. This new religion, which had already won so many converts in the south, was often discussed among the warriors, as well as among the women of the house. A man called the holy Ansgarius was preaching it, no farther away than Hedeby near Slien. Even Helga had heard about Christ, who for love of humanity gave up his life. But it had gone in one ear and out the other. The word "love" did not seem to have any meaning to her, except at night when, in the wretched shape of a frog, she sat silently in a tiny locked room. But her foster mother had been deeply moved when she listened to the legends told about this strange man who was the Son of God.

The Vikings, who had been abroad, described the great temples built of costly stones for this God whose message was love. Once they had brought back with them two big vessels made of gold; they were richly decorated and had smelled of strange spices. They were censers, which the Christian priests swung in front of their altars, where blood never flowed, although bread and wine were changed into the blood of Him who had sacrificed Himself for the sake of generations yet unborn.

Down into the deep stone cellar of the house the young Christian was carried. His hands and feet were bound. He was handsome. "As handsome as the God Balder," the chieftain's wife claimed.

His plight did not move Helga. She suggested that his legs should be pierced, a rope pulled through them and tied to the tail of a bull. "Then let the dogs loose, and the bull will run as fast it can across the meadows toward the heath, dragging him behind it. That would be an amusing sight and it would be fun to follow on horseback!" she suggested.

Such a horrible death the Vikings would not make him suffer, but because he had offended the gods, he would be offered to them. In the little copse where the stone altar to Odin stood, he was to be killed; and this would be the first time a human being had been sacrificed there.

Young Helga begged to have the privilege of spraying the warm blood on the statues to the gods. She sharpened her knife and when a dog—of which there were so many around the house—ran by her she stuck her knife into it and said with a laugh, "That was to test it."

With horror her mother looked at the evil girl. When night came, and Helga's body and soul changed, then she spoke to her of her sorrow and misery. The ugly frog with the troll-like body stood in front of her and looked up at her with sad eyes and seemed to understand what she was saying.

"Never, even to my husband, have I admitted how doubly you have made me suffer," said the Viking chieftain's wife. "I have more pity for you than I even knew I had. Great is a mother's love; but you, you have never felt love for anything. Your heart is made from the black cold mud of the bog! Why did you ever come to my house!"

The pathetic creature shook, it was as if the words had touched the invisible cord that connects soul and body; great tears formed in its eyes.

"But dark times will come for you," her foster mother continued, "and they will be hard for me too. Better would it have been if you had been set out as a babe on the heath and the cold night air had lulled you to sleep." The woman cried bitterly, then she rose and walked to her bed, which stood on the other side of the leather curtain that divided the room. She was angry and in despair.

The miserable frog sat forlorn in its corner. Every once in a while a sound like a stifled sigh was heard; full of pain was this muffled cry that came from the heart of the poor creature. She seemed to be listening as if she were waiting for someone; then she waddled over to the door and with great difficulty she removed the bar that locked it. Her webbed hand grabbed the tallow lamp, then she drew the iron bar that closed the trap door that led to the cellar. Noiselessly she descended the stairs. In a corner of the underground room she found the helpless prisoner sleeping. She touched him with her cold and slimy hand. He awoke and, seeing the horrible creature in front of him, he shivered with fright, for he thought that she was an evil spirit. The frog took a knife and cut the ropes that bound the man, then she waved her hand to make him understand that he was to follow her.

He mumbled all the holy names that he could remember and crossed himself, but still the creature in front of him stood unchanged. Then he quoted a line from the psalms: "'Blessed is he that considereth the poor, the Lord will deliver him in time of trouble.' . . . Who are you? Why have you, who are so filled with mercy, the shape of an animal?"

The frog beckoned and led the priest through a corridor out into the stable. She pointed to a horse; he led it outside and swung himself onto its back. With surprising agility, the big frog mounted the animal too; she sat in front of the priest and held onto the horse's mane. The priest understood that his strange companion wanted to guide him, and followed the directions that the frog indicated by a nod or a movement with its webbed hands. Soon they were out on the heath, far away from the Vikings' hall.

The priest felt that the grace and mercy of Our Lord manifested themselves through the strange creature who had saved him. He prayed and sang a hymn. The frog trembled. Was it the prayer that touched the monster's soul? Or did she shiver because it soon would be morning? What did she feel? Suddenly the frog straightened itself and grabbed the bridle to stop the horse; she wanted to dismount. But the priest would not let go of his strange companion. He held onto it while he sang another hymn, hoping that this might break the magic spell that the poor creature so obviously was suffering under.

The horse galloped on. The horizon turned pink, and soon the first ray of the sun broke through the low clouds of morning. With it came the transformation of soul and body: the frog with the sad eyes became the beautiful girl with the evil heart. The priest was horrified when he realized that he held not a giant frog but a beautiful girl in his arms. He jumped down from the horse; he was convinced that the powers of evil were playing some terrible trick upon him. Helga dismounted as quickly as he had and, drawing the knife that hung from her belt, she attacked the shocked and confused young priest.

"Let the blade of my knife reach you," she screamed. "Let it draw blood! You look pale, slave! Beardless fool!"

The two of them wrestled, but it was as if unseen powers gave the young priest strength. The roots of an old tree that grew on the bank of the tiny stream helped him, for Helga's feet got caught in one of them and she fell. The priest dipped his hand in the clear water and, spraying it on her forehead and chest, he bade the unclean spirit leave her and baptized her in the name of Our Lord Jesus Christ. But the water of baptism only has strength when those it falls upon have faith.

Yet had she not the faith herself, it was that very attribute in the young priest that gave him power over her. His strength fascinated her, and she let her arms fall to her sides and stopped fighting with him. To her he seemed a mighty magician: pale and amazed, she looked at this man who knew so many enchantments and charms. To her, his prayers and psalms sounded like magic and the sign of the Cross looked like witchcraft. Had the young man swung a knife or a sharp ax in front of her face, she would not have blinked; but, when he drew with his finger the sign of the Cross on her forehead, she shuddered and closed her eyes. There she sat like a tame bird, with her head bowed.

He spoke to her gently about that deed of love she had performed herself when, in her frog shape, she had come and cut the ropes that held him and led him back to freedom and to life. She was still bound by bands far stronger than those a knife could cut. But also she could gain her freedom and learn to love the eternal light of God. He would take her to Hedeby, the town where the holy Ansgarius lived and worked. He would be able to break the spell.

Although she was willing to ride in front of him, he would not allow her to. "You must sit behind me on the horse, for your magic beauty comes from the Evil One, I fear it!" said the young priest, paused and then added: "But the victory was mine, in Christ!"

He fell on his knees and prayed most piously. The whole forest became a holy church; the birds sang as if they belonged to the congregation, and the wild mint smelled so fragrantly that one could believe it was trying its best to pretend that it was incense. The young priest said aloud the words from the Gospel: " 'To give light to them that sit in the darkness and in the shadow of death, to guide our feet into the way of peace.' "

Then he preached about the nature of God and His love for all; and while he spoke the horse stood still as if it, too, were listening.

Patiently, Helga let the young priest help her up on the animal's back and there she sat like a sleepwalker. The young man tied two twigs together in the form of a cross and, holding the sign before him, they rode deeper and deeper into the forest. The trees grew close together, the road became narrower and narrower; soon it was hardly a path. Sharp brambles grew everywhere and scratched the travelers as they forced their way through them. They followed a stream that soon became a swamp and they had difficulty finding their way around it.

The young priest talked while they rode. His words were not without power, for his faith in the mild God of love, Whom he followed, was great, and he was earnest in his wish to save this young girl's soul. Drops of water will hollow out the hardest stone and the surf of the ocean will wear down the sharpest reefs. Now the dew of God's grace was wearing down the hardness in Helga's soul. She did not know it, any more than the seed in the earth knows that the warm sun and the rain are bringing forth its green sprouts and its flower.

As the mother's lullaby enters the baby's mind and the child can repeat the sounds without understanding their meaning, so did the young priest's words enter Helga's soul.

The forest gave way to open country but not for long; the green woods soon closed around them again. Just before sunset they met a band of robbers.

"Where have you stolen that beautiful maid!" one of them cried as he grabbed the bridle, while the others forced the riders down from their horse.

They were many and the priest had no other weapon than the knife he had taken from Helga. He defended himself well with it; one of the robbers flung an ax at him but he sprang aside and the ax made a deep wound in the neck of the horse. The blood spouted out of the gash and the animal fell to the ground. Then Helga, who had seemed to be in a trance, suddenly awoke and threw herself upon the dying beast. The young priest stood in front of her to protect her, but one of the robbers swung his heavy iron hammer and hit the young man's head so hard that his skull was split. Blood and brain spattered all around him as he fell to the ground, dead.

The robbers grabbed Helga's white arms, but just at that moment the sun set; the last ray of its light disappeared and she changed into an ugly frog. A whitish-green mouth covered her whole face, her arms became thin and slimy, her fine hands became broad with webs between the fingers. The robbers let go of her in horror; there she stood as an ugly monster in their midst. True to her frog nature, she jumped high above the robbers' heads and disappeared in the greenery. The robbers thought that what they had seen was the secret magic of the evil demigod Loke, and they hurried away.

The full moon had risen in the sky when Helga in her pitiful frog shape climbed out of the thicket. She stopped by the bodies of the priest and the dead horse and looked down at them with eyes in which there almost were tears. She made the same sobbing sound a child makes just before starting to cry, and threw herself down over one and then the other of the still bodies. She carried water from a nearby stream and sprayed it on them in the hope of reviving them. But dead they were and dead they would remain. The thought that the wild animals of the woods would eat them was too horrible to bear. She began to dig in the earth, but she had no spade, only a stick: a thick branch of a tree. The webs between her fingers burst and bled.

Soon she realized that she would never be able to dig a hole deep enough. She washed the blood from the dead priest's face and covered it with fresh leaves; then she took the biggest branches she could find and piled them over the bodies of the man and the horse. She knew that even this would not keep the wolves or foxes away, and therefore she looked for the biggest stones that she could carry, and placed them on top of the branches. When the mound was finished she stuffed moss between the stones, and only then did she believe that the grave would be undisturbed.

It had taken her the whole night to finish her work. Now the sun rose, and in its first rays Helga stood as beautiful as ever, but her fine hands were bleeding and for the first time tears ran down her blushing, youthful cheeks.

Now the two natures within her fought. She trembled as if she had had a fever. She looked about with fear and wonder in her eyes. She appeared like a person that had just awakened from a nightmare. She rushed over to a birch tree and held onto it to support herself; then suddenly she climbed up the tree agilely as a squirrel. There in the top of the tree she remained all day sitting perfectly motionless.

All around her reigned the stillness of the forest—thus it is often described, although if one listens carefully and looks closely enough, nature is never still. Two butterflies flew in circles around each other: were they fighting or playing? At the foot of the tree in which the frightened Helga sat were some anthills, and hundreds of tiny creatures moved unceasingly in and out of their homes. In the air danced clouds of little flies and mosquitoes, and big dragonflies flew about on their golden wings. Earthworms crawled out of the wet ground, and moles emptied the earth from their burrows, making little hills. But no one saw little Helga or paid any attention to her, except for a couple of magpies. They landed on the branch on which Helga was sitting. She did not move and the birds, as filled with curiosity as only magpies can be, hopped a little closer to her. The girl blinked and that was enough to frighten the birds. They flew away no wiser than they had come.

When the sun was near setting, Helga felt herself beginning to transform and she slid down the trunk of the tree. When the sun disappeared beneath the horizon, she stood as an ugly frog once more, her webbed hands still torn from the work of the night before. But her eyes had changed, they were not a frog's but the lovely eyes of a young girl, the mirror of a human soul.

Near the grave lay the cross that the young priest had made, the last work of his own hands. Helga picked it up and planted it among the stones that covered the dead priest and the horse. The act brought back the memory of the day before, and she burst into tears. In grief, she decided to make a border of crosses around the graves to decorate them. As she drew the crosses the webs between her fingers fell off: like a torn glove, they lay in the dust. She walked down to the stream and washed; with wonder she looked at her fine white hands. She made the sign of the Cross in the air in the direction of the grave. Her broad frog mouth quivered; her tongue tried to form a word, and that name she had heard so often on that ride through the forest came from her lips. Clearly and distinctly she spoke: "Jesus Christ."

The frog skin fell from her body and there she stood in all her youthful, girlish beauty. But her head was bent; she was tired and she lay down on the moss by the stream and slept.

Toward midnight she awoke. In front of her stood the dead horse; little flames played in the wound on its neck and its eyes glowed. Close by the horse stood the young priest. "More beautiful than Balder," would the Viking woman have said, if she had seen him. Like the horse, he was strangely luminous.

He looked at Helga with eyes so sad and serious and yet so gentle, she felt that she was being judged justly and that there was no corner of her heart that he did not see. With that sharpness of memory that the souls will have on the Day of Judgment, Helga remembered her

life. Every kindness performed toward her, every loving word spoken
to her, became terribly real. She understood that it was love that had
fought and been victorious in the struggle within her, between her
soul and the mire from the bog. She realized that she had followed a
will greater than her own and that she herself had not been the maker
of her own fate. She had been guided and led. She bent her head
humbly in front of Him who can see into the most secret compart-
ment of our hearts. And in that moment she felt a flame that purified her, the flame of the Holy Ghost.

"You, daughter of the bog," said the ghost of the priest, "of earth
were you made and from the earth you shall be resurrected. The sunbeam within you shall return to its Maker, not to the sun but to God.
No soul is doomed, but earthly life can be long and the flight into
eternity can seem endless. I come from the land of the dead, where
the radiant mountains are, and where all perfection lives. You, too,
shall one day travel through the dark valleys to that land. I cannot
lead you to Hedeby and a Christian baptism now, for you have a duty
to perform back in the bog. You must return and break the shield of
water that covers and hides the living root from which you grew."

He lifted her up on the horse and gave her a golden censer to
hold like the ones she had seen in the Vikings' hall. A strong, sweet
fragrance came from it. The wound in the young priest's head shone
like a jewel as he picked up the cross and, holding it high, mounted
the horse. The horse galloped but not along the paths—no, they flew
through the air, high above the forest. Far down below them, Helga
could see the mounds where Viking chiefs had been buried mounted
on their horses. Now they rose, these giant specters of man and horse,
and stood on top of their grave-hills. In the moonlight the golden
bands around their foreheads shone, while their capes fluttered in the
wind. The monstrous lind-worm that guards buried treasure stuck its
ugly head out of its cave and looked about. Tiny dwarfs ran back and
forth carrying lanterns; they looked like sparks from the ashes of
burned paper.

Above the heath, the forest, the lakes, and streams they flew, toward
the great bog. They circled it and the priest held high the cross, and
in the moonlight the two sticks looked like gold. He chanted the mass,
and when he sang a hymn, Helga sang too, like a child copying her
mother. She swung the censer, and the fragrance of incense spread
across the bog and became so strong that the reeds in the swamp shot

forth blossoms, and from the muddy depth water lilies sprouted and grew. Everything alive responded, and the dark waters of the bog became covered by a colorful tapestry of water lilies. In the center of it lay a sleeping woman, young and beautiful. Helga thought that she was seeing her own reflection in the water; but it was the bog king's wife, the princess from Egypt.

The dead priest ordered that the sleeping woman be lifted up on the horse, but the burden was too great, the body of the horse was now like a shroud in the wind. The priest made the sign of the Cross and the phantom horse gained strength enough to carry all three of them onto the shore.

Just as they reached solid ground the cock crowed. The priest and the horse became a mist that was borne away by the wind. Helga and her mother stood facing each other, alone.

"Is this my own image I see, reflected in the deep waters?" asked the mother.

"Is that myself I see mirrored in the lake's shiny shield?" exclaimed the daughter.

The two drew near to each other and embraced. The mother understood who it was she held in her arms. "My daughter, the flower of my heart! The lotus of the deep waters," she said, and cried. Her tears were like a baptism of love for Helga.

"In a swanskin I came here and I shed it by the dark lake," the mother explained. "Then I sank down into the deep mire of the bog and it closed around me like a dark wall. Something drew me down, ever downward. I felt a pressure on my eyes, as if sleep were closing them. And I did sleep, I dreamed. I was back in Egypt in the stone chamber of the pyramid. In front of me stood the trunk of the alder tree that had frightened me so, when I stood on the shores of this lake. I looked closely at the cracks and clefts in its bark, and they gained color and became the hieroglyphic writing on a casket such as mummies are laid in. As I stared at it, it opened and out stepped the ancient king: a mummy, black as pitch, glittering like the black slugs that creep in the forest. Whether it was the bog king or the mummy from the pyramids, I did not know. He flung his arms around me, and I felt that now I would die. But life did not desert me. I felt a warmth in my chest. The bog king was gone and a little bird was singing and flapping its wings. It flew from my chest up toward the dark ceiling: a long green string connected the bird to me. I heard its

song and understood its message: 'Freedom! Sunshine!' A longing for
the father of things! I thought of my own father, far away in the sun-
drenched land of Egypt. I loosened the string and freed the bird, let
it fly home to my father. A deep, heavy sleep came over me and I
dreamed no more, until a fragrance and chanting voices woke me
and drew me up from the dark."

The green string from the mother's heart to the bird's wing, where
was it now? Thrown away among other useless things. Only the stork
had seen it. It was the green stalk that had shot up through the
water to form the flower that had made a cradle for the child who
now stood beside her mother.

While they stood there embracing, the stork saw them and flew in
circles above them. Then he flew back to the nest to get the swanskins
he had kept there so faithfully. He threw one to each of the women.
The feathery skins covered them, and they rose from the ground as
two white swans.

"Now we can talk together," said the stork, flying beside them.
"True, we have not the same shaped bills, but we will understand
each other. It was lucky that you came this morning. If you had
waited a day longer we would have been gone. My wife and I and the
young ones will be going south today. . . . Yes, look at me, I am an
old friend of yours from the Nile. So is my wife. Her heart is softer
than her bill; she was always of the opinion that the princess would
take care of herself. My children and I have carried the swanskins up
here. . . . Oh, it makes me happy to see you! It is so lucky that we
are still here. As soon as the sun is high in the sky we will be gone. We
are not flying alone, there is a whole party of storks going. We will
fly ahead and you can follow, then you won't lose your way; but don't
worry, my youngsters and I will keep an eye on you."

"The lotus flower that I was to bring will fly beside me," said the
Egyptian princess. "The flower of my heart I bring and the riddle
has been solved. Homeward! Homeward!"

But Helga insisted that she could not leave before she had bade
good-by to her foster mother, the Viking chieftain's wife. She remembered every kind word, every tear her foster mother had shed
because of her; and at that moment she loved her more than she
loved her real mother.

"Yes," said the stork. "Let us fly to the Vikings' hall. There
my wife and children are waiting. They will open their eyes wide and

clatter their bills when they see you. Not that my wife is one for idle clatter; she talks in short sentences, but she means every word she says. I will make a clatter so they know we are coming."

And the stork clattered loudly with his long bill, and away they flew to the Viking hall.

There everybody was still asleep. Helga's foster mother had lain awake until late, worrying about what could have happened to her daughter who had disappeared together with the Christian priest three days before. She realized that Helga must have helped him to escape, for it was her horse that was missing in the stable. What strange powers had been the cause of this? The Viking woman had pondered long about it. She had heard that Christ had performed miracles for those who followed him. These thoughts stayed with her in her sleep and became real in her dreams. She dreamed that she was awake, sitting up in her bed; outside the world was dark and a horrible storm was brewing. Now the winds gathered, she could hear the surf breaking on the beaches; the great Midgard-worm which encircles the earth was racked by convulsions. The days of the old gods were over, their night had come: Ragnarok, the last battle of the gods, was being fought. The end of the world was near; now the gods would die. The horns blew, and over the rainbow rode the gods, clad in armor, on their way to fight their last battle. In front of them flew the valkyries and behind them walked the Viking chiefs, whom fame had brought to Odin's hall. The northern lights glittered as they illuminated the sky and yet darkness was victorious. It was a fearful sight.

Close to the frightened woman sat little Helga in her frog shape; she also seemed filled with fear, she drew closer to her foster mother. And the Viking woman dreamed that she took the frog on her lap and held it close; in spite of its horrible shape she pressed it with love to her heart. Outside the hall the sound of a furious battle could be heard. The arrows flew like hailstones. The time had come when the earth and the heavens would burst and the stars fall from the sky. All would be destroyed in the great fire, but from its ashes a new earth and heaven would rise. She knew it would come, and that grain would grow where now the waves of the salt sea rolled over the desolate sand. Balder, the gentle loving God, would be released from the Kingdom of the Shadows and rise into the heavens. He came! In her dream the Viking woman saw him, and she recognized him. Balder the God was the Christian priest.

"Jesus Christ!" she cried to him, and kissed the frog-child on her lap. At that moment the frog disappeared and Helga stood before her, as beautiful as ever; but kind and gentle as she had never been before. Helga kissed the hands of her foster mother and thanked her for all the love and care that she had given her. She blessed her for the thoughts that she had sown in her heart, which now bore fruit. The Viking woman said aloud, once more, the name of the "New God," as people called him in the north: "Jesus Christ." Helga became a great swan. She spread out her wings and flew away and the beat of her wings woke the sleeping woman.

As she opened her eyes, she heard still the sound of the feathered blows from her dream. She knew that now was the time that the storks flew south. She rose from her bed and walked outside to see them fly and wish them farewell. The air was filled with storks, flying in great circles; but in the yard by the well, where Helga had frightened her so often with her wild tricks, stood two swans. They looked at her and the dream was still real within her; she recalled how she had seen Helga change into a swan. Then she remembered the face of the young priest as she had seen it in her dream, and she felt a sudden joy that she could not explain.

The swans flapped their big wings and bent their slender necks as if they were greeting her. The Viking woman spread out her arms toward them and smiled, though tears ran from her eyes.

At that moment the last of the storks flew up. The whole sky resounded with the noise of their wings beating and the clatter of their bills.

"We won't wait for the swans," declared the mother stork. "If they want to come along it has to be now. We can't wait any longer. I think it is very cozy to fly together in a family. The way the finches fly, males and females separately, is, in my eyes, indecent! And I don't like the way the swans flap their wings. What formation do they fly in?"

"Everyone flies in his own manner," said her husband patiently. "The swans fly in a slanted line, the cranes in a triangle, and the plover in a winding line, like a snake."

"Don't mention the word 'snake' while we are in the air," admonished his wife. "It will awaken desires in the young ones that can't be satisfied!"

"Are those the high mountains that I have heard about?" asked Helga, who was flying in her swanskin.

"They are thunder clouds drifting by underneath us," answered the mother.

"What are those tall white clouds ahead?" Helga asked a little while later.

"They are the tops of the great mountains where the snow never melts," said her mother; and they flew over the Alps and across the blue Mediterranean.

"Africa, Egypt!" Jubilantly the daughter of the Nile said the words as she, in the feathered dress of a swan, saw below her the yellow-white sandy coast of her home. The storks, too, flew faster when they saw it.

"I can smell the mud of the Nile and the frogs!" said the mother stork to her young ones who were seeing Egypt for the first time. "It tickles my stomach! Oh! You'll see how good everything is going to taste! You will meet the marabou, cranes, and the ibis. They all belong to our family, but they are not nearly as handsome or beautiful as we are. They believe that they are something, especially the ibis, who has been spoiled by the Egyptians. They make a mummy out of him when he dies, and stuff him full of spices, so he won't smell. I prefer stuffing myself with live frogs, and so will you, my children. Better a full stomach while one is alive than a lot of glory after one is dead. That is my opinion and I am always right!"

"Now the stork has come," the servants said in the palace by the Nile.

On a couch covered by leopard skins their royal master lay, neither dead nor alive, waiting, hoping for the lotus flower from the north that would bring his health back to him. Into the great hall flew two white swans; they had come with the storks. They cast off their shiny feathers and there stood instead two beautiful women, as alike as two drops of dew. They bent over the withered shape of the old man on the couch, and as Helga touched her grandfather, blood flowed to his cheeks, his eyes gained luster again, and his lifeless limbs moved. He stood up, well and rejuvenated, and embraced his daughter and his grandchild, like a man happily greeting the dawn after a long dark dream.

There was great joy in the palace and in the storks' nest, too; but in the latter it was mostly over the food: the place was swarming with frogs. While the learned and wise men quickly wrote down the story of the two princesses and the flower of health, which was such a blessing for the royal house and the whole country, the two storks told the story in their own way to their family and friends. But not before everyone had eaten their fill; after all, that was more important than listening to stories.

"Now you must become something," whispered the mother stork to her husband. "You deserve a reward!"

"What should I become?" said her husband. "And what have I really done? It was nothing!"

"You have done more than anyone else. Without you and our youngsters, the princesses would never have seen Egypt again. I am sure you will become something! I think they will give you a doctor's degree, and our children will inherit it, as will their children in turn. You already look like a doctor of philosophy—in my eyes!"

The learned and wise men developed the fundamental idea and moral that ran through the story: "Love breeds life!" It could be explained in several ways: "The warm sunlight was the Egyptian princess and she entered the darkness of the bog; in the meeting between light and dark—the latter being the bog king—the flower sprang . . ."

"I can't remember it word for word," said the father stork, who had been listening from the top of the roof to the learned and wise men discuss the matter, and now was telling about it at home in his nest. "Everything that was said was very complicated and so intelligent that they all were decorated immediately by the king. Even the cook got a medal, but I think that was because of the soup."

"And what did you get?" asked his wife. "Don't tell me they have forgotten the most important person of all, namely, you? The learned ones have only clattered their bills. But maybe they will remember you later?"

When night fell and the peace of sleep reigned over the house there was one who was still awake. It was not the stork who stood guard on one leg at his nest, for he was sleeping soundly. No, it was Helga who was not asleep; she was standing on the balcony of her room, looking up at the stars. They seemed so much clearer and brighter here than in the north, and yet they were the same. She thought about her foster mother, the Viking woman, who lived near the great bog. She remembered her sweet, gentle eyes and the tears they had shed over the wretched frog-child who had now become a princess and was standing in the warm night by the waters of the Nile and dreaming. She thought about how full of love that woman's heart must have been, for her to be able to feel affection for a creature so miserable that when she wore a human shape she was an evil beast, and when she became an animal was ugly to look at and repulsive to touch. A bright star reminded her of how the wound in the dead priest's head had glittered when they rode through the night. She thought of the words he had spoken on their first ride together, how he had talked of the origin of love and its greatest expression, which is the love of all living things.

So much had been given her, so much had she won, so much had she accomplished. Helga's thoughts dwelled both day and night upon this great sum of her good fortune. She was like a child who quickly turns from the giver to the gift. She felt certain that even greater happiness would come, gifts even more splendid than the ones she had already received. Was she not fortune's child for whom miracles had been performed? One day these feelings of exuberance became so overwhelming that she forgot the giver completely. The arrogance of youth possessed her, and her eyes sparkled with a wild courage. Suddenly she heard a great noise from the courtyard below her. She saw two ostriches running in circles around each other. She had never seen this animal before, this great bird, so plump and heavy with its short wings that looked as though they had been clipped. She wondered whether some misfortune might have happened to it and asked someone why it looked like that. And she heard, for the first time, the old Egyptian legend about the ostrich.

Once he had been a very beautiful bird with big strong wings. One evening the other big birds of the forest had said to him: "Brother, should we not tomorrow—if God wills—fly down to the river to bathe and drink?"

And the ostrich had answered, "Yes, I will it!"

Next morning they flew high up in the sky toward the sun, which is the eye of God. Higher and higher they went. The ostrich flew faster and higher than all the others. Arrogantly he flew toward the light, trusting his own strength and not the Superior Being who had given it to him. He would not say "if God wills." The chastising angel drew the veil from the fiery sun and the hot flames burned the wings of the ostrich. The wretched bird sank down to the earth. Never again would his wings carry him high up in the air. He and his kind were condemned to stay forever on the ground. Frightened, the ostrich runs in meaningless circles to remind us human beings to say, as we set out on a journey: "If God wills."

Helga bent her head thoughtfully; then she looked down at the running bird. She sensed its fear and foolish joy in seeing its own shadow cast on the sunlit white wall. In her mind—in her soul— grave, serious thoughts struck root. A life so rich, so happy, had been won, what would the future bring? The best—"if God wills."

In the early spring, when the storks got ready to fly north, Helga took a golden ring and scratched her name in it. She beckoned to the stork and he came. She asked the stork to take it to her foster mother, that the Viking woman might know that the child she had cared for was still alive and well, and had not forgotten her.

"It is uncomfortable," said the stork who was wearing the ring around his neck, "but gold and honor one does not throw in the ditch. Now they will know, up there in the north, that the stork brings good luck."

"You lay gold and I lay eggs," said his wife, "but see if we get any thanks for it. I think it is humiliating!"

"But one has one's good conscience, my dear!" answered her husband.

"You can't hang that around your neck," replied his wife. "And no one has ever grown fat on it."

And away they flew!

The little nightingale that sang among the tamarisk bushes would soon be leaving for the north too. Near the wild bog, Helga had often heard it sing. She would send a message with it; the language of the birds she knew because she had once flown in a swanskin. She had kept in practice by talking to the storks and the swallows. The nightingale would surely understand her. She asked him to fly to the place in the forest in Jutland where the grave of branches and stones was, and there to sing a song and ask the other little birds to do the same.

And the nightingale flew; and so did time!

At harvest the eagle, from the top of a pyramid, saw a caravan of richly loaded camels traveling across the desert. Magnificently clad soldiers, on white Arabian horses, with pink soft muzzles and nostrils, and long manes and tails, guarded it. Important guests were coming. A royal prince from Arabia, who was as handsome as princes ought to be, was making his way to the royal palace.

The stork nests were empty, for the owners had not returned yet, but they were expected. And by chance and good fortune, they did arrive later that day. It was a day of festivity and joy. A wedding was to take place, and Helga was the bride. Clad in silk and jewels, she sat at the head of the table with her bridegroom, the young prince of Arabia. On one side of them sat Helga's mother, and on the other her grandfather.

Helga was not looking at her bridegroom's brown handsome face, nor did she notice his passionate glances. She was looking through the big window out at the night sky where the bright stars sparkled in the heavens.

Suddenly the air was filled with the sound of the beating of storks' wings. Although the old stork couple were tired from their long flight and certainly deserved to rest, they flew first to the balcony of Helga's room and perched there on the railing. They had already heard about the feast and knew in whose honor it was being held. They had also been told, as soon as they entered the country, that they had been depicted in a mural that told the story of Helga's life.

"That was very thoughtful of them," said the male stork.

"I don't think it was so much," disagreed his wife. "They could hardly have done less."

Helga rose from the table and went to her balcony. She knew the storks would be there. Affectionately, she stroked their backs, and the old storks bent their necks. Their young children, who had come with them, felt themselves greatly honored.

Helga looked again up at the clear, star-filled sky. She saw a figure floating near her. It was the dead young priest. He had also wanted to see her on this her wedding day; he had come from paradise.

"The splendor, the glory, is far greater than anything found on this earth," he said.

Helga pleaded so sweetly and so fervently—as she never before had begged for anything—to be allowed to look into paradise—if only for a moment, to see the face of God.

The young priest lifted her up into the glory which cannot be described, to see that which cannot be imagined. And she herself felt transformed so that the splendor which she saw before her was also within her.

"Now we must return," said the young priest.

"Just one more glance," begged Helga. "One short minute more."

"We must return to the earth, all the guests are leaving," he warned.

"One last glance, the very last!"

Helga was back on the balcony, but all the lights had been put out. The great hall was empty and the storks were gone. Where was her bridegroom? In three short minutes, everything had disappeared.

Frightened, Helga walked through the great hall into the smaller room next to it. There she found some strange foreign soldiers sleeping. She opened another door, which should have led to her own room, but now it led out into the garden. The sun was just rising. Three minutes and a whole night was gone!

She saw some storks and called to them in their own language. A male stork looked at her and came nearer.

"You speak our language," he said, "but who are you and where do you come from?"

"It is me, it is Helga! Don't you know me? We spoke together three minutes ago up on the balcony."

"You are mistaken," said the stork. "It must have been something you dreamed."

"No! No!" protested Helga, and reminded him of the Viking hall near the great bog, and how he had brought her the swanskins.

The stork blinked with its eyes. "That is an old, old story. It happened so long ago that my great-great-great-grandmother was alive then. It is true that such a princess once lived here in Egypt, but she disappeared on her wedding night and never returned. It happened hundreds of years ago. You can read the story on the monument in the garden. There are pictures of swans and storks, and on top stands a statue of the princess herself." Finally Helga understood what had happened and she fell on her knees.

The sun was ascending in the sky and its strong rays fell on the kneeling girl; and just as the rays of the sun in time past had changed the ugly frog into the beautiful princess, so did they now change Helga into one single beautiful ray of light, that shot upward to God.

Her body disappeared, became dust; and where she had knelt lay a withered lotus flower.

"That was a new ending to an old story," said the male stork. "I hadn't expected it, but I rather liked it."

"I wonder what the children will think of it?" asked his wife.

"Yes, that is most important," agreed her husband.

## 87

## The Winners

The winner of the annual prize was to be announced; as a matter of fact, there were two prizes: a big one and a little one. They were awarded to those who ran the fastest, not in a single race, but for general, all-year-round running.

"I won the first prize," declared the hare. "And it is only just; after all, I have both family and friends on the committee. But that the snail should be given the second prize, I think, is an insult."

"No!" argued the fence post, who had witnessed the awards being presented. "One has to consider diligence, industry, and perseverance as well; several very sensible people have said that and I agree with them. It took the snail half a year to get across the threshold, and he broke his hipbone in the rush. He has lived for and thought about nothing else but his running and this race. Besides, he ran with his house on his back, which is very praiseworthy. That is why he was given second prize."

"They might have thought of me," interrupted the swallow. "No one is faster than I, and that both in forward flight and in turns. If there is someone, I have never seen him, and I have traveled far and wide."

"Yes, that is what is the matter with you," answered the fence post. "Always traveling, always ready to leave your country. You are not a patriot, you can't be considered."

"What if I stayed in the swamp all winter?" asked the swallow. "If I slept half the year, would I qualify then?"

"Get a signed certificate from the bog witch that you have slept half the year in your native land, and I promise you that you will be eligible next year."

"I really think I deserved first prize, not second," mumbled the snail. "Everyone knows that the hare only runs because he is such a coward. He is afraid of his own shadow! But I have made running into my occupation, my life's work! And I have become an invalid in its service. If anyone should have won first prize, it should have been me! But I don't make a fuss, I despise people who do."

And the snail spat.

"I can explain and defend the choosing of the winners—my votes, in any case, were justly cast," said the old pole that the surveyor had dug down to mark the boundary between two farms; the pole had been a member of the committee. "I believe in order, regularity, and calculation. Seven times before have I had the honor of being a member of the committee that has awarded the prizes, but this is the first time that it has been done according to my system. Each time I have looked for something solid, a certain fixed point to start from; therefore I have always begun with the beginning of the alphabet for the first prize, and from the end for the second prize. Now you will notice that the eighth letter after *A* is *H,* and that is why I voted for the *hare* for the first prize. Now the eighth letter, counting from the end of the alphabet, is *S* and that is why I voted that the *snail* should receive the second prize. Next time, *I* ought to be given the first prize and *R* the second. There must always be order in everything, one has to know where one stands!"

"I would have voted for myself if I hadn't been on the committee," said the mule, who had been one of the judges. "Mere speed is not the only consideration; how much one can pull is of importance too. But I didn't let that influence my judgment, nor did I pay any particular attention to how cleverly the hare behaves in flight, how he jumps first to one side, then to the other in order to fool his pursuer. No, I was particularly concerned about another point, which should not be passed over lightly: beauty! It was this I took into consideration. I saw the hare's lovely long ears, they were a pleasure to look at! They reminded me of my own when I was young; and therefore I cast my vote for the hare!"

"Hush," said the fly, "I don't want to make a speech, I just want to say something. I have run faster than many a hare. The other day I broke the hind leg of one of them. I was sitting on the front of the engine that pulls the train. I often travel by rail, it is the best place I know of to contemplate one's own speed. A young hare was running in front, I am sure it wasn't aware that I was there. In the end, it either had to get off the track or be run over. It didn't make it, my engine drove over its leg. I was there. The hare stayed behind and I rushed on. If that is not called winning a race, I would like to know what is. But I don't need any prize."

"I think," began the wild rose, but it didn't say anything out loud, for that was against its nature, although in this case it would have been a good thing if it had. "I think the sunbeam should have received the first prize, and the second too. In no time at all it flies the long way from the sun down to us and yet arrives with strength enough left to waken all of nature. It has a beauty within it that makes us roses blush and gives us our scent. The honorable committee seem not to have noticed the sunbeam at all. If I were a sunbeam I would give them all a sunstroke; but that would only make them mad, and mad they are already. I shan't mention it," thought the wild rose. "Peace in the forest! How lovely it is to bloom, to spread one's fragrance, please those that love one, and to live in legend and song. The sunbeam will survive us all."

"What was the first prize?" asked the earthworm who, having overslept, had just arrived.

"Free admittance to a cabbage garden," answered the mule. "I was the one that suggested the prize. Since the hare was to win it, I—as a rational member of the committee—decided it might as well be something useful. Now the hare is provided for. The snail got permission to sit on a stone fence and bask in the sunshine, besides being given the first permanent appointment as a judge for all future races. It is always a good thing to have an expert on the committee. I must say that I am expecting great things in the future, since we have had such a promising start."

## 88

## The Bell Deep

"Ding, dong! Ding, dong!"

The ringing comes from the bell deep in Odense River.

What river is that?

Don't you know? Well, all the children in the town of Odense do. They may not be able to tell you where it comes from—its source, that is too far away—but the part from the lock, past the gardens and down to the water mill, where the wooden bridges are, all the children have explored.

Little yellow water lilies grow in the water—the ones that are called "river buttons." Along the shore there are reeds with feather-like tufts and sturdy, big, black bulrushes. Where the river passes through the "monk's meadow" and the field on which linen used to be laid out to bleach, the bank of the river is lined with willow trees; they are so old and crooked that they lean far out over the water. Nearer the town there are gardens on both sides of the river. No two of these are alike. Some of the plots are all but covered with flowers and have pretty little bowers that look like big dollhouses. Other gardens are more practical, and here cabbages grow in straight lines like soldiers on parade. Some places the river is so deep, an oar can't reach the bottom. The deepest place is near where the cloister used to be; here the old man of the river lives. During the day when the sun rays shine down through the water, he sleeps. But at night, especially when the moon is full, he sometimes shows himself. He is ancient. Grandmother says that she heard about him from her grandmother. He is a very lonesome old man and has no one to talk to except an old church bell. The bell once hung in the tower of St. Alban's Church, and of that building not a trace is left today.

"Ding dong! Ding, dong!" pealed the bell one evening when the church and the tower were still standing. Just as the sun set and the bell was at the highest point in its swing, it tore itself loose and flew out of the tower and through the air. In the light from the setting sun it looked fiery red.

"Ding dong! Ding, dong! I am going to bed," tolled the bell, and disappeared in the river at its very deepest point. And that is how that place got its name: the bell deep. But the bell was mistaken about one thing, it wasn't going to get much sleep down there. The old man of the river likes to ring the bell. Sometimes he rings it so loudly that it can be heard through the water, up on the shore. Some people say that this is a warning that someone is about to die, but that is not true. It rings in order to tell the river man stories; since the bell came, he is not so alone any more.

What kind of stories can the old bell tell? It is terribly old. It existed long before Grandmother's grandmother was born, although it is a child compared to the old man of the river, for he is as ancient as the river itself. He is a quite funny old man. His pants are made of eelskins, his jacket of fish scales, and it is buttoned with the little yellow water lilies. His hair is filled with reeds and his long beard with duckweed, which is not really very attractive.

It would take more than a year to tell all of the stories the bell knows. Some of them are short, others are long, and the bell tells them as it likes—often it repeats itself. All the stories are about earlier times: the dark and cruel ages.

"There used to be a monk who often climbed up in the tower of the church. He was young and handsome, but also more pensive than the other monks. He would look across the river—which was broader then—toward the cloister on the other side. He used to come in the evening just as the nuns were lighting the candles in their cells; he knew which one was hers. He had known 'her' well once.

"And when he thought about those days, his heart would beat like a bell: Ding, dong!"

Yes, this was the manner in which the bell used to talk.

"I remember the bishop's fool, he used to sit right under me while I was pealing. He didn't seem to worry, although I might have hit him, and if I had, I would have crushed his skull. He would play with two little sticks and sing or maybe, one should say, shout:

"'Here I can sing loudly what I do not dare to whisper below. I can sing about all that is hidden behind lock and key, where it is cold and wet and the rats eat the living. No one knows it. No one hears it! Not even now, for the bells are tolling so loud! Ding! Dong!'

"Oh yes, he was mad, that fool!"

Here is another story: "There was a king called Knud. The monks and the bishops bowed to him, but when he taxed the peasants of Jutland too heavily and spoke ill of them, they took weapons in hand and drove him out. They hunted him down as though he were a stag. He fled to the church and locked its doors. Outside a great mob gathered—I heard all about it, for the crows, the ravens, and the jackdaws were so frightened from the noise of the screaming and the shouting that they sought refuge with me, up in the bell tower. Although the jackdaw was frightened, it was as nosy as ever, and it flew down to look through the church windows. King Knud lay in front of the altar praying, and his two brothers, Erik and Benedict, stood near him with their drawn swords, ready to defend him. But the king's servant, Blake, had betrayed his master, and the crowd outside knew where the king was. Soon stones flew through the windows; the king and his men were killed. There were screams and cries of birds and men, and I shouted too. I sang and I rang. Ding, dong! Ding, dong!

"A church bell is hung up high so it can see far and wide. The birds visit it and the bell understands their language. But the bell's best friend is the wind who knows everything. For the wind and the air are brothers, and all that is living the air surrounds; it can even come inside our lungs. No word is spoken, no sigh is made, without the air having heard it. The wind tells what the air knows, and the church bells understand and ring it out for the whole world to know: Ding, dong! Ding, dong!

"But I heard too much, I learned too much, and my knowledge became too great, too heavy a weight to carry. The beam that I was fastened to broke, and I flew out into the air and fell down into the Odense River, into the deep hole where the river man lives. He is terribly lonesome; and so I tell him all the stories I know: Ding, dong! Ding, dong!"

This is the story Grandmother heard when she listened to the sound coming from the bell deep in Odense River.

But the schoolteacher does not agree with her. He says, "There is no bell down in the river, and even if there was, it couldn't ring under water. And there is no old man of the river, either, that is only an old wives' tale!" The schoolteacher also claims that, when the church bells peal so merrily, it is not the bells as much as the air that rings, for without the air the sound would not carry. But that is what Grandmother said the bell had told her; and if Grandmother and the schoolteacher agree, then I am sure that it is true. Be careful, be cautious, take good care of yourself. That is the motto of both of them.

The air knows everything! It is around us and inside us. It tells about our deeds and thoughts; its song can be heard farther than the pealing of the bell in Odense River—the one that is living with the old river man. The air delivers its message far up in the heavens. It exists eternally, or at least till the bells of paradise will ring: "Ding, dong! Ding, dong!"

## 89

## The Evil King

### A legend

There once lived an evil and arrogant king whose ambition was to conquer all the countries of the world and make every man alive fear his name. With sword and fire he scourged the world; his soldiers tramped down the grain and set fire to the farms. Even the apple trees in the gardens did not escape. They stood black and leafless, and their fruits hung roasted on the branches. Many a poor mother, carrying her naked babe in her arms, would try to hide behind the crumbling, soot-smeared walls that had once been her home. If the soldiers found her and her child, then they would laugh like fiends: evil spirits from hell itself could not have behaved worse. But the king found that everything was going just as he wanted it to. Day by day his power increased and his name became more fearful to all. Luck seemed to smile on whatever he did. The plunder from the conquered towns, their gold and treasures, he had brought to his own capital, and soon it was rich beyond belief. Now he built beautiful palaces, churches, and arcades, and everyone who saw them exclaimed, "Oh, what a great king!" None gave a thought to the suffering he had caused the world, none heard the sighs and cries of lament that came from the ruins of the towns he had destroyed.

The king looked at his golden treasures and at his palaces and he thought as the man in the crowd did: "What a great king!" But he also thought, "I must have even more, more! No power must be mentioned as equal to mine!" And the king made wars upon all his neighbors and he conquered them all. When the king drove through the streets of his city, the vanquished kings were bound to his carriage with golden chains. In the evening, when he dined, they had to lie like dogs at his and his courtiers' feet, and they would throw them scraps from their table.

The king had statues of himself placed on all the squares of the cities and in the royal castles. He wanted them in the churches too, up at the altar, but the priests refused, saying, "King, you are great, but God is greater, we do not dare!"

"Well," said the evil king, "then I must conquer God too."

In foolish arrogance he had an artificial ship built with which he could sail through the air. It was as colorful as a peacock's tail and seemed to contain a thousand eyes. But every eye was the muzzle of a gun. The king himself sat in the middle of the ship and when he pressed a button a thousand bullets would fly and the guns would then reload themselves. A hundred strong eagles were harnessed to the ship and he flew up toward the sun. The earth was below him. At first, with its forests and mountains, it looked like a plowed field, where the grass peeped up through the overturned turf. Later, as he flew higher, it appeared like a flat map; until, at last, it was hidden by clouds and mist.

The eagles flew higher and higher. At last God sent one of his countless angels, and the evil king fired a thousand bullets at him. Like hailstones hitting the earth, the bullets sprang in all directions when they touched the angel's shining wings. One, only one, drop of blood dripped from the white feathers of his wings. That drop fell on the ship of the evil king. It burned itself into it and it was as heavy as a thousand hundredweights of lead. The ship fell down toward the earth so fast that the strong wings of the eagles were broken. The wind rushed past the king's head, and the great clouds around him, which had been formed by the smoke from the burning cities he had destroyed, took on the strangest menacing shapes. One was like a gigantic crab reaching out its great pincers toward him, and another looked like a dragon. When at last his ship came to rest in the top of some trees, he lay half dead among the ruins.

"I will conquer God!" he screamed. "I have sworn to do it and I shall!"

For seven years he set all his workmen to building ships that could fly through the air; and he ordered his blacksmith to form thunderbolts of the strongest steel, with which he planned to destroy the fortress of God's heaven. Then, from all the countries he ruled, he gathered an army greater than any seen before. When they stood in formation, shoulder to shoulder, they covered many square miles.

They all embarked in the marvelously constructed airships; and the king himself was ready to enter his, when God let a swarm of mosquitoes loose. Like a little cloud, they flew around the king and stung his face and hands. In fury, he drew his sword and slashed the air but harmed not a single insect. He ordered that costly blankets be brought and that he be wrapped in them, so that no mosquito could reach him. His command was obeyed, but one mosquito had hidden in the innermost blanket; it crept into the king's ear and stung him there. The sting burned like fire and the poison entered his brain. He threw off the blankets and tore his clothes in rage from the pain. Naked and screaming, he danced in front of his brutish soldiers. They laughed and mocked the mad king who would conquer God and was himself vanquished by one tiny mosquito.

## 90

## What the Wind Told About Valdemar Daae and His Daughters

When the wind runs across the fields, then the grass ripples like water and the fields of grain form waves like the sea. That is the dance of the wind. But try to listen to it when it sings. Its songs sound differently according to where you hear them, whether you are in a forest or listening when the wind makes its way through cracks and crevices in a wall. Look up and watch how the wind is chasing the clouds, as if they were a flock of sheep. Listen as it howls through the open gates; it thinks it is the night watchman blowing a horn. Now it is coming down the chimney; the fire in the fireplace burns higher and sparks fly. The light from the flames illuminates the whole room for a minute. It is so nice and warm and cozy in here, just right for listening. Let the wind tell us what story it wants to, it knows so many more tales and stories than we do. "Whoo . . . whoo . . . All will pass. . . . Whoo . . . whoo!" that is the chorus of all its songs.

"On the shores of the Great Belt lies an old castle with red brick walls," began the wind. "I know every stone in the building. Most of them had been used before in Marsk Stig's castle, but that was torn down by order of the king. Its great walls were destroyed but the bricks were saved; they could become new walls in another place. They were used to build Borreby Castle and that is still standing.

"I have seen and known all the noble gentlemen and ladies who have lived there; all the different families who have claimed it as theirs. But I will tell only about one of them: Valdemar Daae and his daughters.

"He was proud, Valdemar Daae, royal blood flowed in his veins. He knew how to do more than hunt deer and empty a tankard of beer. He could take care of himself, as he said.

"His wife's clothes were embroidered with gold. She walked proudly and stiffly across the polished tile floors of the castle. Tapestries hung on the walls and the furniture was carved and inlaid with rosewood. Much silver and gold had she brought to her husband's house. In the cellar was German beer and in the stable stood handsome black horses. Oh, everything was fine and rich in Borreby Castle, while it lasted. Three children they had, three young noble maidens: Ida, Johanne, and Anna Dorthea. I remember their names still.

"They were rich, they were noble. They had been born and had grown up in splendor and magnificence. Whoo . . . who . . . All will pass! Whoo . . . whoo!" sang the wind, and then continued its story:

"In most of the castles in olden times, the noble mistress herself would sit with her maids in the great hall and spin; but not here at Borreby. Her hands would do no harder work than touching the strings of the lute; and the melodies she played and the songs she sang were more often foreign than Danish. Guests came every day: noble friends from far and wide. The noise from the feasting and drinking was so loud that I could not drown it. Here were arrogance and willfulness: masters who recognized no master.

"It was the evening of the first of May. I had come from the west, where I had seen a ship being wrecked by the waves on the coast of Jutland. I had danced across the heath and the forests of Fyn. I crossed the Great Belt, blowing hard and whipping the waves. When I came to the coast of Zealand I was tired and lay down to rest in the oak forest near Borreby Castle.

"The young men from the district had come to gather wood for a bonfire. They selected the driest branches and twigs they could find and took them back to the village. I followed them as quietly and softly as a cat. It was the custom there that each of the young men selected a stick; and when the fire was ablaze, they all put their sticks in the flames to see whose would catch fire first. The lucky one would be called the 'prince of spring,' and he could select among the girls his 'spring lamb,' who would be his partner in the dance. As the flames grew, the young men and maidens of the village sang and made a ring around the bonfire. I was lying so still," continued the wind, "that no one knew I was there. Quietly, I breathed a little on one of the branches and the flames flared up. The young man whom I had selected laughed. I had chosen the one I found the handsomest. Now he was the May prince and could select his lamb among the blushing girls. Oh, here were happiness and gaiety, much greater than in the rich castle of Borreby.

"With six horses in front of their golden carriage the noble lady of Borreby and her daughters, three lovely flowers—the rose, the lily, and the pale hyacinth—came driving by. The mother herself was a tulip, showy but without fragrance. She did not nod or greet the young people, some of whom had stopped dancing in order to curtsy and bow. Maybe her stalk was so fragile, it would have broken if she had tried.

"The rose, the lily, and the pale hyacinth; I saw them and thought: 'Whose lambs will they be? Will their May princes be knights or maybe real princes?' Whoo . . . whoo . . . All will pass. . . . Whoo . . . whoo!

"That night I rose and blew upon the highborn lady of Borreby. She took to her bed and she never rose again. Death came to her as it comes to all human beings, that story is not new. Valdemar Daae stood by her bedside. Sadly and thoughtfully he looked at his dead wife. 'The proud trees can be bent but they cannot be broken,' he thought. The daughters wept. Everyone in the castle had moist eyes that day, but the Lady Daae had passed hence, as all will pass. Whoo . . . whoo! All will pass," said the wind.

"Often I returned to Borreby and sang in the great oak forest, where the fish hawk, the blue ravens, the wood pigeons, and the rare black storks nest. It was in early summer—when the birds were still nesting or had young ones that could not yet fly—that the sound of the ax was heard. How the birds screamed in anger and fury; but that did not help, the forest was to be cut down. Valdemar Daae had decided to build a ship, a costly vessel with three decks. He felt certain that the king would purchase it, and Valdemar was in need of money. That was the reason why the ancient oaks were being felled, that had been the landmark of the sailors, the home of the birds. Terrified, the blue raven flew up as its nest, with young ones in it, was destroyed. The fish hawk circled above its wrecked nest with its crushed eggs. How they all screamed in fear and anger. I understood them. Only the crows seemed not to care and mocked the others.

"In the middle of the forest stood Valdemar Daae with his three daughters. They laughed at the cries of the birds; only the youngest of them, Anna Dorthea, felt pity. When the workmen wanted to cut down a half-dead oak tree on whose naked branches the black stork had built its nest, Anna Dorthea begged with tearful eyes that the tree be spared for the sake of the little fledglings that were sticking their heads up above the brim of the nest. That tree was allowed to stand because of the black stork, but that did not help the other birds.

"All that year the noise of hammers, saws, and axes was heard; a ship was being built. The master builder who had designed the ship had a common name and a noble soul. His face, his eyes spoke of intelligence; and Valdemar Daae liked to listen to the young man and so did his daughter Ida. She was the oldest of the three, she was fifteen. While the young man built a ship for her father, he built a castle of dreams in the air for himself and Ida to live in, as man and wife. Married they could have been if his castle had been built of stones and its moat and apple orchards had been real. But despite his cleverness he was only a poor bird, and the sparrow fares ill in the company of hawks. Whoo, whoo! I flew away and so did he. Little Ida got over it, because she had to."

"In the stable the black horses neighed. They were worth looking at, and someone looked. The admiral, who had been sent by the king to inspect the ship and decide whether the king should buy it and, if so, at what price, looked at the horses and praised them loudly. I heard him," said the wind. "I followed the high and mighty gentlemen into the stable and blew little bits of golden straw where they walked. Valdemar Daae wanted gold and the admiral wanted the black horses, that was the reason he praised them so highly. But Valdemar Daae did not, or would not, understand the hints, and so the king did not buy his ship. It stood down on the beach, under a roofing of planks looking like a Noah's ark that had never been launched. Whoo! whoo! All will pass. . . . Whoo! Whoo!

"In the winter when the fields were covered with snow and drifting ice floes filled the Great Belt, I sometimes packed the ice so far up on the shore that it almost reached Valdemar Daae's ship. Great flocks of ravens and crows, one blacker than the other, were perched on this bare, lonesome, dead ship that lay on the beach. With their hoarse cries they told about the forest that was no more, of the nests that had been destroyed, of the old birds that had been made homeless, and the young who had died. For what? For a ship that would never sail.

"I whirled the snow high up over it as though it were foam breaking against the hull. I let it hear what I had to say: the voice of the storm. I did my best to teach it a bit of seamanship. Whoo! . . . All will pass.

"The winter passed and the summer passed, as all seasons and years do pass. I pass, too, and yet I stay. . . . Whoo . . . whoo! . . . The daughters were still young. Little Ida was a rose, as beautiful to look at as when the shipbuilder saw her. Often I would play with her long brown hair when she stood under the apple trees in the garden, so lost in thought that she did not notice that I filled her long loose hair with apple blossoms. She would be watching the sun set and the golden sky behind the dark trees and bushes of the park.

"Her sister Johanne was more like a lily: shining and with a back as straight as her mother's had been. Her stem, too, was brittle. She liked to walk in the gallery where the paintings of her ancestors hung. The ladies had been painted dressed in silk and velvet. Their hair was braided and on their heads were little black caps embroidered with pearls. Beautiful they were, all of them. Their husbands were portrayed, with swords at their sides, wearing armor and capes lined with squirrel skin. Where would Johanne's picture one day hang? Who would be her noble husband, and what would he look like? Johanne thought about it and even talked about it to herself; I heard her when I whistled through the long gallery.

"Anna Dorthea, the pale hyacinth, was still only fourteen years old, but quiet and thoughtful. Her big, water-blue eyes looked pensively out at the world, but on her lips was a sweet childlike smile; I could not have blown that away, nor did I want to.

"I met her often in the garden, when she was searching for herbs and flowers that she knew her father could use in distilling strange medicines and potions. Valdemar Daae was arrogant and proud, but he was also clever, and knew more than most men. People mentioned that when they discussed why he kept a fire in his chamber, even in midsummer. The door to his room was locked, and sometimes no one saw him for several days at a time. When he finally did come out, he told no one of what he had been doing in such secrecy behind the barred door. The powers of nature are best studied in solitude. Soon he expected to solve its mystery and win what was best of all, gold!

"That is why the smoke rose from his chimney and strange vapors rose from the caldrons. I know all about it," said the wind, "for I was there. I blew down the chimney and sang: 'Whoo . . . Let it pass. . . . Whoo! Smoke, embers, and ashes, you will burn yourself up. Whoo . . . Let it pass. . . . Whoo!' But Valdemar Daae would not let it pass.

"Where were the black horses? Where were all the gold and silver plates, the cows, the grain? All had been melted down in the caldron, and yet he found no gold.

"The stables were empty, the lofts bare, and no longer were the cellars filled with wine and beer. Less servants and more mice; a windowpane broke and was never replaced; and I no longer had to trouble myself with finding cracks through which to enter," said the wind. "When the chimney smokes the table will soon be set, but not at Borreby; here the smoke pleased only one appetite: Valdemar Daae's for gold.

"I blew through the gates and made a noise like the night watchman's horn, but there was no longer any night watchman. I turned the weather vane on the tower; it was rusty and squeaked like a guard sleeping on duty, but there was no guard. Rats and mice there were aplenty; poverty set the table, and poverty sat in the larder and in the clothes closet as well. Hinges broke and doors sat askew, everywhere cracks appeared. I know," said the wind, "for I entered them all.

"In smoke and ashes, in sorrowful sleepless nights, the hair and beard of Valdemar Daae grew gray and his skin yellow; but his eyes searched as greedily as before for gold.

"I blew smoke and ashes in his face; and blew through the broken windows right into his daughters' bedrooms. In their closets were rags that once had been riches, for even the finest dress can be outworn. The song they heard now had not been sung to them when they were in their cradles. Their noble life had become a miserable life; and I, the wind, was the only one that sang in the castle. One winter day I snowed them in; great drifts I piled against the castle walls. They say that snow makes it warmer. But they had nothing to burn; their forest had been cut down and where should they get wood from? It was fine frosty weather, and I danced and jumped across walls and gables, through windows and doors. They all lay abed, freezing, the three poor noble ladies and their father, who tried to keep warm under his fur blanket. Whoo . . . Nothing to eat, and not a log for the fire. Whoo! That was a noble life. Whoooo . . . All will pass. . . . Whooooo!

"Valdemar Daae could not, and would not, give up. 'After winter, spring must come,' he said. 'After lean times come the fat, but they take their time coming. Soon I must pay my debts. I have no time left, I must find gold before Easter!'

"I heard him mumble all this and, as he looked at the spider's web, he smiled and said, 'Oh, you busy little spinner, I can learn from you! If I tear your web, you start another right away, and finish it; and if that is torn, you are not disheartened but begin again. One must not lose faith but do things over and over, if one must; and then the reward is sure to come!'

"It was Easter morning, the church bells rang, and the sun was playing in the sky. Feverishly, Valdemar Daae had worked: boiled, distilled, and mixed the strangest potions; he had not slept for many a night. I heard him sigh like a tormented soul and I heard him pray. The candles had long ago burned down and he had not noticed it. I blew on the coals and they glowed and their light turned his pale white face red. He squinted his eyes, then he opened them up wide— so wide that I was afraid they might fall out.

"Something shone and glittered in the glass beaker. He lifted it up high with trembling hands and then shouted loudly: 'Gold! gold!' He swayed as if he were going to faint. If I had blown on him I am sure he would have fallen," said the wind. "But I didn't, I blew on the smoldering coals and followed him out through the door and into the chamber where his daughters lay abed, still freezing. His clothes were filled with ashes, as were his unkempt hair and beard. He straightened himself and held up, triumphantly, the fragile glass beaker. 'I have won, I have won! Gold!' he screamed. And the sunlight played on the sparkling residue in the bottom of the glass; his hand shook and the alchemist's glass fell on the floor and broke into a thousand pieces. The last of his bubbles had burst! Whooo . . . whooo . . . All will pass! . . . Whooo! And I did pass out of the alchemist's house, out to the free and open fields.

"It was late in the year when the days in the north are short and the fogs, like a wet dishrag, wipe the landscape. That is a good time for house cleaning. I blew the clouds out of the sky and the rotten branches and twigs off the trees; it is the kind of work that has to be done every once in a while. Borreby Castle was also being swept, but in another manner. Valdemar Daae's enemy, Ove Ramel, had bought the mortgages and now he owned the castle and everything that was in it. I beat on the cracked windows like drumsticks on a drum, and I banged the latchless doors and whirled myself through cracks and crevices. I would teach Master Ove how pleasant it was to live in Borreby. Ida and Anna Dorthea wept, but Johanne was pale and bit her thumb so hard that it bled. But neither weeping nor biting one's thumb was of any help. Master Ove Ramel said that Master Daae could stay as long as he lived in the castle, but he got no thanks for this offer. I listened and heard it all! And I saw proud Valdemar Daae toss his head in scorn as he refused. I gathered strength and hit the old elm tree in the yard so hard that its biggest branch broke off; and that though there wasn't a bit of rot in it. It fell right in front of the entrance and lay there like a big broom ready to do the sweeping. And Borreby Castle was swept. Oh yes! I saw it all!

"It was a hard day, a long day; but Valdemar Daae was stiff-necked; he could be neither bent nor broken! They owned nothing now but the clothes on their backs and a new glass beaker in which the alchemist had carefully gathered every bit that could be scraped from the floor of what had been spilled there on that Easter Day when he thought he had found gold. Valdemar Daae carried the beaker under his cloak, next to his breast. In his other hand he had a staff, as he walked with his daughters out of Borreby Castle, never to return. I blew cold air on his burning cheeks, I patted his white hair and long beard and sang loudly so that they could hear it. Whooo, whooo! . . . All will pass. . . . Whoo, whooo!

"Ida and Anna Dorthea walked beside him; Johanne lingered a moment in the gateway, turned and looked back; but that did not help, luck and good fortune would never turn to come back to them. She glanced at the red bricks of the castle wall. Once they had been part of Marsk Stig's castle; that mighty man the king had broken; and his daughters, too, had been left to fend for themselves. Did Johanne at that moment recall the lines from the folk song about Marsk Stig's daughters?

> "The older took the younger by the hand
> And out in the wide world they walked!"

"But Johanne and her sisters were not two; they were three—or four, if you counted their father. Along the same road that they so often had driven on in their carriage, they walked now like beggars. At Smidstrup Fields stood a humble peasant cottage. This they had rented for ten marks silver a year and that was to be their 'castle.' Empty was every room and bare their larder. The crows and the jackdaws followed them screaming and mocking them, 'Craw! craw! Now your nest is gone. Craw! Craw!' They remembered when Valdemar Daae had cut down the oaks of Borreby and made so many birds homeless.

"Whether in their misery they could have understood the crows, I do not know. I whistled past their ears so that they need not listen to what the foolish birds were screaming.

"They moved into the little house, whose walls were made from mud, not stones. I flew away across the fields and through the naked forest, to the open sea. I wanted to visit foreign lands. Whooo . . . whooo . . . All will pass. . . . Whoo . . . whoo! That truth the years can't change . . . whoo!"

How did Valdemar Daae fare and what happened to his daughters? The wind will tell us.

"I saw Anna Dorthea, the pale hyacinth, for the last time about fifty years after they had left the castle. She was an old woman then, bent and broken, yet she remembered everything that had happened.

"On the edge of the great heath, near the town of Viborg in Jutland, a new and splendid house had been built as residence for the archdeacon. It was made of red bricks and had corbie gables. The smoke poured from the kitchen chimney, telling what a good table was kept here. The archdeacon's wife was sitting before the bay window together with her daughters. They were looking out over the hawthorn trees toward the yellow heath. What were they looking for? They were watching the storks hover over their nest, which they had built on the roof of the ruins of a cottage. The straw roof was overgrown with moss and had several big holes in it; the part that gave the best protection against the weather was the one that the stork's nest covered, for the nest was in fine condition, the storks saw to that.

"It was the kind of hut that it was safer to look at than to touch. I had to be gentle when I was near it," declared the wind. "The house was considered an eyesore by everyone, and the archdeacon would have had it torn down if it hadn't been for the storks. Because of those birds and their nest it was allowed to stand; and the wretched old woman who lived in it could stay. She owed her home to the Egyptian bird. Maybe it was a kind of justice, because she once had begged that the nest of the wild black stork in Borreby forest should be spared. Yes, it was she, the pale hyacinth from the aristocratic garden. She remembered all that had happened. Poor Anna Dorthea. She sighed, for human beings can sigh as I do when I blow gently through the reeds that grow around the lake.

" 'Oh!' whispered Anna Dorthea. 'No bells rang when you died, Valdemar Daae. No poor school children sang while they carried the former master of Borreby to his grave! . . . Oh, oh, all things must end; misery and sorrow also pass. My sister Ida married a serf. My father took that hard: his daughter married to an unfree man, a slave who had to obey his master. Father is dead and so is Ida, both rest now under the earth. Oh yes, oh yes. But for me, poor wretched thing, everything is not yet over. Oh, Christ, you who are so rich, give me peace. Let me die.'

"That was Anna Dorthea's prayer as she lay sick and old on her bed in the little hut that was allowed to stand for the sake of the stork's nest.

"The bravest of the sisters I took care of myself," declared the wind. "She got her clothes cut to fit her nature and took hire on board a ship. Tight-lipped she was and sour, although willing enough to do her work. But she couldn't climb the rigging. I blew her overboard, before anyone found out she was woman. I think I did well.

"It was on Easter morning that Valdemar Daae thought he had discovered the secret of making gold, and it was on Easter morning that Anna Dorthea died. I heard her singing the last hymn she was ever to sing. There was no windowpane or window in her hut, just a hole in the wall. The sun rose and filled that hole like a great lump of gold. What splendor and brilliance! Her eyes grew blind and her heart stopped just at that moment. But that they would have done even if it had been a cloudy day and the sun had not shone on her.

"The stork had given her a roof over her head until she died, and I sang at her grave. I had sung at her father's grave, too; I know where both the graves are and that is more than anyone else does. A new age, a time of change, has come. Old roads are overgrown with weeds and new ones cross old graves. Soon the steam engine, with its endless row of cars, will rush ahead over tombs and graves of people whose names are forgotten. Whoo! All will pass. . . . Whoo!

"That is the story of Valdemar Daae and his daughters. Let others tell it better if they can!" said the wind, turned, and was gone.

## 91

## The Girl Who Stepped on Bread

I suppose you have heard about the girl who stepped on the bread in order not to get her shoes dirty, and how badly she fared. The story has been both written down and printed.

She was a poor child, but proud and arrogant; she had what is commonly called a bad character. When she was very little it had given her pleasure to tear the wings off flies, so they forever after would have to crawl. If she caught a dung beetle, she would stick a pin through its body; then place a tiny piece of paper where the poor creature's legs could grab hold of it; and watch the insect twist and turn the paper, round and round, in the vain hope that, with its help, it could pull itself free of the pin.

"Look, the dung beetle is reading," little Inger—that was her name —would scream and laugh. "Look, it is turning over the page."

She did not improve as she grew up; in fact, she became worse. She was pretty, and that was probably her misfortune; otherwise, the world would have treated her rougher.

"A strong brine is needed to scrub that head," her own mother said about her. "You stepped on my apron when you were small, I am afraid you will step on my heart when you grow older."

And she did!

A job was found for her as a maid in a house out in the country. The family she worked for was very distinguished and wealthy. Both her master and mistress treated her kindly, more as if she were their daughter than their servant. Pretty she was and prettily was she dressed, and prouder and prouder she became.

After she had been in service for a year her mistress said to her, "You should go and visit your parents, little Inger."

She went, but it was because she wanted to show off her fine dresses. When she came to the entrance of her village, near the little pond where the young men and girls were gossiping, she saw her mother sitting on a stone. The woman was resting, for she had been in the forest gathering wood, and a whole bundle of faggots lay beside her.

Inger was ashamed that she—who was so finely dressed—should have a mother who wore rags and had to collect sticks for her fire. The girl turned around and walked away, with irritation but no regret.

Half a year passed and her mistress said again, "You should go home for the day and visit your old parents. Here is a big loaf of white bread you can take along. I am sure they will be very happy to see you."

Inger dressed in her very best clothes and put on her new shoes. She lifted her skirt a little as she walked and was very careful where she trod, so that she would not dirty or spoil her finery. That one must not hold against her; but when the path became muddy, and finally a big puddle blocked her way, she threw the bread into it rather than get her shoes wet. As she stepped on the bread, it sank deeper and deeper into the mud, carrying her with it, until she disappeared. At last, all that could be seen were a few dark bubbles on the surface of the puddle.

This is the manner in which the story is most often told. But what happened to the girl? Where did she disappear to? She came down to the bog witch! The bog witch is an aunt of the elves, on their father's side. The elves everyone knows. Poems have been written about them and they have been painted, too. But about the bog witch most people don't know very much.

When the mist lies over the swamps and bogs, one says, "Look, the bog witch is brewing!" It was into this very brewery that Inger sank, and that is not a place where it is pleasant to stay. A cesspool is a splendidly light and airy room in comparison to the bog witch's brewery. The smell that comes from every one of the vats is so horrible that a human being would faint if he got even a whiff of it. The vats stand so close together that there is hardly room to walk between them, and if you do find a little space to squeeze through, then it is all filled with toads and slimy snakes. This is the place that Inger came to. The snakes and toads felt so cold against her body that she shivered and shook. But not for long. Inger felt her body grow stiffer and stiffer, until at last she was as rigid as a statue. The bread still stuck to her foot, there was no getting rid of it.

The bog witch was at home that day; the brewery was being inspected by the Devil's great-grandmother. She is an ancient and very venomous old lady who never wastes her time. When she leaves home, she always takes some needlework with her. That day she was embroidering lies and crocheting thoughtless words that she had picked up as they fell. Everything she does is harmful and destructive. She knows how to sew, embroider, and crochet well, that old great-grandmother!

She looked at Inger, and then took out her glasses and looked at her a second time. "That girl has talent!" she declared. "I would like to have her as a souvenir of my visit. She is worthy of a pedestal in the entrance hall of my great-grandson's palace."

The bog witch gave Inger to the Devil's great-grandmother. And that is the way she went to hell. Most people go straight down there, but if you are as talented as Inger, then you can get there via a detour.

The Devil's entrance hall was an endless corridor that made you dizzy if you looked down it. Inger was not the only one to decorate this grand hall; the place was crowded with figures all waiting for the door of mercy to open for them, and they had long to wait. Around their feet, big fat spiders spun webs that felt like fetters and were as strong as copper chains, and they would last at least a thousand years. Every one of these immovable statues had souls within them that were as restless as their bodies were rigid and stiff. The miser knew that he had forgotten the key to his money box in its lock and he could do nothing about it. Oh, it would take me much too long to explain and describe all the torments and tortures that they went through. Inger felt how horrible it was to stand there as a statue, her foot locked to the bread.

"That is what one gets for trying to keep one's feet clean," she said to herself. "Look how they are all staring at me!" That was true, they were all looking at the latest arrival, and their evil desires were mirrored in their eyes and spoken without sound by their horrible lips. It was a monstrous sight!

"I, at least, am a pleasure to look at," thought little Inger. "I have a pretty face and pretty clothes on." She moved her eyes; her neck was too stiff to turn. Goodness me, how dirty she was! She had forgotten all the filth and slime she had been through in the bog witch's brewery. All her clothes were so covered with mire that she looked as if she were dressed in mud. A snake had got into her hair and hung down her neck. And from the folds of her dress big toads looked up at her and barked like Pekinese dogs. It was all very unpleasant. But she comforted herself with the thought that the others didn't look any better than she did.

But far worse than all this was the terrible hunger she felt. She couldn't bend down and break off a piece of the bread she was stepping on. Her back was stiff and her arms and legs were stiff, her whole body was like a stone statue; only her eyes could move. They could turn all the way around, so that she looked inside herself and that, too, was an unpleasant sight. Then the flies came; they climbed all over her face, stepped back and forth across her eyes. She blinked to scare them away, but they couldn't fly; their wings had been torn off. That was painful too, but the hunger was worse. Inger felt as if her stomach had eaten itself. She became more and more empty inside, horribly empty.

"If this is going to last long, then I won't endure it!" she said to herself. But it didn't stop, it kept on; and she had to endure it.

A tear fell on her head, rolled down her face and chest, and landed on the bread; and many more tears followed. Who was weeping because of little Inger? She had a mother up on earth, it was she who was weeping. Those tears that mothers shed in sorrow over their bad children always reach the children, but they do not help them, they only make their pain and misery greater. Oh, that terrible hunger did not cease. If only she could reach the bread she was stepping on. She felt as if everything inside her had eaten itself up, and she was a hollow shell in which echoed everything that was said about her up on earth. She could hear it all, and none of it was pleasant, every word was hard and condemning. Her mother wept over her, but she also said: "Pride goes before a fall! That was your misfortune, Inger! How you have grieved your poor mother!"

Everyone up on earth—her mother, too—knew about the sin she

had committed, how she had stepped on the bread and disappeared into the mire. A shepherd had seen it happen, and he had told everyone about it.

"You have made me so miserable, Inger!" sighed her mother. "But that is what I expected would happen."

"I wish I had never been born," thought Inger. "That would have been much better. But it doesn't help now that my mother cries."

She heard her master and mistress, who had been like parents to her, talking. "She was a sinful child," they said. "She did not appreciate God's gifts but stepped on them; it will not be easy for her to find grace."

"They should have been stricter," thought Inger, "and shaken the nonsense out of me."

She heard that a song had been made up about her, "The haughty girl who stepped on the bread to keep her pretty shoes dry." It was very popular, everyone in the country sang it.

"Imagine that, one has to have it thrown in one's face so often, and suffer so much for such a little sin," thought Inger. "The others should also be punished for their sins. Then there would be a lot to punish! Uh! How I suffer!"

And her soul became as hard as or even harder than her shell. "How can one improve in such company as there is down here?" she thought. "But I don't want to be good! Look how they stare!" And her soul was filled with hatred against all other human beings. "Now they have something to talk about up there. Oh, how I suffer!"

Every time that her story was told to some little child, Inger could hear it; and she never heard a kind word about herself, for children judge harshly. They would call her the "ungodly Inger" and say that she was disgusting, and even declare that they were glad that she was punished.

But one day, as hunger and anger were tearing at her insides, she heard her story being told to a sweet, innocent little girl, and the child burst out crying. She wept for the haughty, finery-loving Inger. "But won't she ever come up to earth again?" she asked.

And the grownup who had told her the story said, "No, she will never come up on earth again."

"But if she said she was sorry and she would never do it again?"

"But she won't say she is sorry," answered the grownup.

"I wish she would," cried the little girl. "I would give my dollhouse, if she only could come back up on earth again. I think it must be so terrible for poor Inger."

Those words did reach Inger's heart and, for a moment, relieved her suffering. For this was the first time someone had said "poor Inger" and not added something about her sin. A little innocent child had cried for her sake and begged that she should be saved. She felt strange and would have liked to cry herself, but she could not weep, and that, too, was a torment.

As the years passed she heard little from the earth above her; she was talked about less and less. Down in hell's entrance hall nothing ever changed. But one day she did hear a sigh and someone saying, "Inger! Inger! How you have made me suffer, but I thought you would." That was her mother, she was dying.

Sometimes she heard her name mentioned by her old master and mistress; but they spoke kindly, especially her mistress. "I wonder if I will ever see you again, Inger! After all, one cannot be certain where one will go."

But Inger was pretty certain that her kind old mistress would not end where she herself was.

Time passed: long and bitter years. When Inger, finally, again heard her name, she seemed to see above her, in the darkness of the endless hall, two bright stars shining; they were two kind eyes up on earth that now were closing. So many years had gone by that the little child who once had wept so bitterly because of "poor Inger" now was an old woman whom God had called up to Him. At that last moment when all her memories and thoughts of a long life passed through her mind, she remembered, too, that as a little child she had cried bitterly when she heard the story of Inger. In the moment before death, that which had happened so long ago was re-experienced so vividly by the old woman that she said aloud, "Oh, my Lord, have I not, like Inger, often stepped on Your gifts, and not even been aware that I have done it? Have I not, too, felt pride within me, and yet You have not deserted me. Do not leave me now!"

As the old woman's eyes closed, the eyes of her soul opened for all that before had been hidden. Since Inger had been in her thoughts as she died, she now could see her in all her misery. At that sight, she burst into tears just as she had done as a child; in paradise she stood weeping because of Inger. Her tears and prayers echoed in the shell of the girl who stood as a statue in the Devil's entrance hall. Inger's tortured soul was overwhelmed by this unexpected love from above: one of God's angels was crying for her. Why had this been granted her? Her tortured soul thought back upon its life on earth and remembered every deed it had done. The soul trembled and wept the tears that Inger had never shed. The girl understood that her folly had been her own; and in this moment of realization she thought, "Never can I be saved!"

No sooner had she had this thought than a light far stronger than that of a sunbeam shone from heaven down upon her. Far faster than the sun rays melt the snowman, or the snowflake disappears when it lands on a child's warm mouth, did the statue of Inger melt and vanish. Where it had stood, a little bird flew up toward the world above.

Fear-ridden and full of shame, the bird hid in the darkest place it could find, a hole in an old crumbling wall. Its little body shivered. The bird was afraid of every living thing. It could not even chirp, for it was voiceless. It sat in the dark for a long time before it dared peek out and see the glory around it—for the world is, indeed, gloriously beautiful.

It was night; the moon was sailing in the sky and the air was fresh and mild. The bird could smell the fragrance of the trees and bushes. It glanced at its own feather dress and realized how lovely it was; everything in nature had been created with loving care. The bird would have liked to be able to express her thoughts in song; gladly would she have lifted her voice as the nightingale or the cuckoo does in spring, but she couldn't. But God, who hears the silent worm's hymn of praise, heard and understood hers, as He had David's when they only existed in the poet's heart and had not yet become words and melody.

Through days and weeks these soundless songs grew within the little bird; although they could not be expressed in words or music, they could be asserted in deeds.

Autumn passed and winter came, and the blessed Christmas feast drew near. The farmers hung a sheaf of oats on a pole in the yard so that the birds of the air should not go hungry on this day of Our Saviour's birth.

When the sun rose Christmas morning, it shone on the sheaf of oats and all the twittering little birds that flew around it. At that moment the little lonesome bird that did not dare go near the others, but hid so much of the time in the little hole she had found in the old wall, uttered a single "Peep." A thought, an idea, had come to her! She flew from her hiding place, and her weak little peep was a whole song of joy. On earth she was just another sparrow but up in heaven they knew who the bird was.

The winter was hard and harsh. The lakes were covered with ice, and the animals in the forest and the birds knew lean times; it was difficult to find food. The little bird flew along the highway. In the tracks made by the sleds she sometimes found a few grains of oats. At the places where the travelers had rested, she would sometimes find little pieces of bread and crumbs. She ate very little herself but called the other starving sparrows, so that they could eat. In town, she looked for the yards where a kind hand had thrown bread and grain for the hungry birds, and when she found such a place she would eat only a few grains and give all the rest away.

Through the winter, the little bird had collected and given away so many crumbs that they weighed as much as the bread that Inger had stepped on, in order not to dirty her shoes. As the last little tiny piece of bread was found and given away, the wings of the little bird grew larger and their color changed from gray to white.

"Look! There's a sea gull flying out over the lake," said the children as they followed the flight of the white bird that dived down toward the water and then swung itself up high into the sky. The white wings glittered in the sunshine and then it was gone. "It has flown right into the sun," the children said.

## 92

## The Watchman of the Tower

"Everything in the world goes up and down, and I can't get any farther up than I am right now," said the watchman of the tower, whose name was Ole. "Up and down, we all have to try it, and most of us end up as the watchman of a tower, who sees the world and everything in it from above."

That was the way my friend Ole, the watchman of the tower, spoke. He was an amusing, talkative fellow, who seemed to poke fun at most things and yet was serious at heart. They say that he came of good family and that his father had been a city alderman, or could have been one if he had wanted to. Ole had studied, and been an assistant teacher in some school that a deacon kept. He was supposed to get room and board, plus his clothes washed and his boots polished. It was the latter that caused the trouble. Ole was still young and liked to cut a figure, if not in the town, then at least on the street where he lived. He insisted that his shoes were to be polished with proper English blacking, but the deacon said lard would do just as well. They had an argument in the course of which they accused each other of miserliness and vanity. The blacking blackened their friendship and they parted.

What Ole had asked from the deacon he also demanded of the world: English blacking, and all he ever got was lard! This had made him turn into a hermit; and the only place a hermitage could be found in a large city, which also provided a living, was in a church tower. He ascended into the sky and smoked his pipe all alone, while from his lofty post—as a hired watchman—he looked out over the city.

He looked above and he looked below; and he read books and he thought and thought. He liked to talk about all that he had seen and not seen, and he loved to discuss what he had read in books and in himself while on his lonely duty. I often lent him books—good books —and a man can be judged by the company he keeps. He didn't like English governess novels, or their French cousins: they were brewed on the rose branch, without the flower; and on drafts from doors their author never had entered. He liked biographies and books of natural history. I visited him at least once a year, usually just after New Year, for he always has something interesting to say about that event.

I shall tell you what he said on two of my visits and try to do it in his own words, as well as I remember them:

## THE FIRST VISIT

Among the books that I had lent Ole last was one about cobblestones. These are the stones that nature has worn round and smooth, and they are often used for paving streets. This book had interested Ole especially.

"They certainly are old Methuselahs, those cobblestones," he began. "Here I have walked on them without ever having given them a thought. On the beaches and in the fields one sees them by the thousands. When one walks along a cobblestoned street, one is walking on our primeval history. From now on, every single cobblestone has my respect! Thank you for lending me the book, it has made me discard many old notions and has given me a different outlook upon the world. I am eager to read more books of that kind. The greatest of all romances is the story of our earth. Too bad that the first volumes are written in a language we have not yet learned. Only after one has read the stones, the layers of earth as they were formed through periods of climatic changes, do the living characters in the romance step forth. Mr. Adam and Mrs. Eve do not appear before the sixth volume. Many readers will find that a little too late, but I don't care. Of all of the romances it is the most marvelous, and we are all in it. We crawl and creep and yet stay in the same place while the great ball rotates, without splashing the oceans all over us. The crust we walk on keeps it all together, and it is so strong we don't fall through it. It is the history of millions of years of constant advancement. Thank you again for that book! Those cobblestones could tell a story if they were able to.

"It is wonderful, every once in a while, to become nothing—a zero—especially for someone placed as loftily as I am. It is amusing to think that everyone, even those who have their boots polished with English blacking, are merely ants with a minute of life in their little bodies. True, there are ranks in the anthill, and some wear ribbons and have titles, but ants they are. One feels oneself so small and unimportant compared to these cobblestones, with their millions of years of history behind them. I read the book New Year's Eve and found it so fascinating that I forgot to watch 'the wild crowd rushing to Amager,' as I usually do. I don't suppose you know about that?

"But you do know about the witches and how they fly to the mountain in Germany called Brocken, on Midsummer night, and there keep a witches' Sabbath. Well, we have a local affair that is something like it. I call it 'the wild crowd rushing to Amager.' It takes place New Year's Eve and all the bad poets and poetesses, journalists, and artists of notoriety and no talent participate. They fly through the air on their pens and brushes out to Amager. It is not so far away, only ten miles or so. They would never have made it to Brocken; a journalist's pen is no witch's broom. I watch them every New Year's Eve, and I could mention most of them by name but I won't, they are dangerous people to cross. They don't like the general public to find out about their ride.

"I have a sort of niece, who sells fish in the market place and claims to have a job on the side, supplying three of our most respectable newspapers with fresh curses, maledictions, oaths, and generally abusive words and phrases. She was invited to the feast and, since she keeps no pen of her own and can't ride, she was carried out there. Half of what she says is lies, but if half of it is true, then it is much too much! When they all were gathered out on Amager, they started their feast with a song; they had each written one, and naturally, everyone sang his own song, for that was the best. But that didn't matter so much, for they all were sung to the same tune. Then they gathered in groups, according to their interests: those who lived on gossip in one group, those who wrote under pseudonyms in another—that, by the way, is lard trying to pass itself off as English blacking.

"The executioner and his boy were there. The boy was tougher than the master. They stood in the group of literary critics. They were dressed either as schoolteachers or as garbage collectors, and were busy giving everything grades.

"In the midst of all this gaiety, an enormous toadstool shot up from the earth and made a roof over the whole gathering. It was created from everything they had written or painted during the preceding year. Great sparks flew from it; they were the thoughts and ideas that had been borrowed. Now they were flying back to their owners; it looked like a fireworks display. After that they played hide-and-seek. But since none of them wanted to hide, though they all had good reason to, and everyone wanted to be found, that was not a success. The lesser poets played 'I love you'; but they couldn't remember the rules, and nobody paid attention to them. The witty made puns and laughed at them themselves. It was all very merry, my niece claimed. She told me a good deal more, all very funny and very malicious. But I think that one should be a good human being and not criticize others. But as you can well imagine, since I know about the feast, I usually do take a look New Year's Eve to see who has been invited. If I miss one in 'the wild crowd rushing to Amager' one year, then I can be sure that six new ones have joined it. But this year I forgot to watch them, I was so busy reading about the cobblestones and following them on their journey.

"I saw them loosening themselves way up north, and drifting with the ice south, million of years before Noah built his ark. I saw them sink to the bottom of the sea and then reappear. There they were, sticking up out of the water, saying: 'I am going to be Zealand one day.' Types of birds that disappeared long ago nested among them; and wild chieftains of savage tribes whom we have never heard of built their thrones of them. Not until quite recently, when the ax, for the first time, bit some runic letters into the stones, do we reach historical times, leaving all those millions of years that make me feel like a zero totally unaccounted for."

Luckily, just at that moment four shooting stars lighted up the heavens and that turned Ole's thoughts in a different direction. "You know what a shooting star is? Well, the wise men don't know either, really. I have my own idea about them. How often, in the secrecy of their hearts, do people give thanks and bless those who have done something good and beautiful? These silent thanks do not fall forgotten to earth; I think the sun rays catch them and carry them to the person for whom they were meant. Now if lots of people, perhaps even a whole nation, experience such feelings of gratitude, then they fall as a shooting star on their benefactor's grave. I find it very amusing, when I watch the shooting stars, especially on New Year's Eve, to speculate as to whom each tribute is meant for. I saw one falling in the southwestern corner of the sky; it was particularly bright, I think a good deal of gratitude had gone into producing it. Whom could it be for? I felt sure that it had fallen on the banks by Flensborg fjord, where the graves of Schleppegrel, Laessoe, and their comrades are. One fell not too far away, in the middle of Zealand. I am sure it landed in Sorö: a bouquet for Holberg's coffin, a thanks from the many who have enjoyed his wonderful comedies.

"It is an awesome thought, but at the same time a happy one, to know that shooting stars may fall on our graves. There won't be any falling on mine, I know that; there won't even be a sun ray giving thanks. That is because there is nothing to be thankful for. I will never receive English blacking," sighed Ole. "Lard is my fate!"

### THE SECOND VISIT

It was on a New Year's Day that I visited Ole last. He talked about all the toasts that had been made from the "old drop" to the "new drop." He referred to the years as "drops," and I suppose that, when you live in a tower so far above it all, each year may seem like a drop in the ocean. He made a whole speech about glasses, and there was a lot of sense in it. Here it is:

"When the bells on New Year's Eve strike twelve, people rise and, glass in hand, toast the New Year. One begins the year with a glass in one's hand, a fine beginning for a drunkard. Now some start the year asleep in bed; that is a good start, too, for a lazy person. Both sleep and glasses will play their part in the year that comes. Do you know what can be found in a glass?" asked Ole. "Health, happiness, and joy! But it can also contain harm and bitter misery. As one counts the glasses, of course, one has to take into account what's in them and who is drinking them.

"The first glass contains health. It has a healing power, an herb, within it. Pick it and it will grow.

"Take the second glass. In that is hidden a little bird that sings an innocent song, and man listens to it and agrees: life is beautiful! Let us not be downhearted, but live!

"The third glass contains a little winged child, half angel, half pixy. He does not tease maliciously but is filled with fun. He climbs into our ears and whispers amusing thoughts and warms our hearts so that we feel young and gay and become witty and amusing, even according to the judgment of our friends at the party.

"The fourth glass has only an exclamation point in it, or maybe a question mark. This is the point which sense and intelligence never go beyond.

"After you have drunk the fifth glass, then you either weep over yourself or you become sentimental. Prince Carnival jumps from the glass and draws you into a dance, and you forget your own dignity; that is, if you ever had any. You forget more than you should, more than it is good for you to forget. All is song, music, and noise. The masked ones whirl you along; the Devil's daughters in silk dresses, with their long hair and their beautiful legs, join the dance. And you, can you tear yourself away?

"In the sixth glass sits the Devil himself; he is a little well-dressed man, most charming and pleasant. He understands you and agrees with everything you say. He even brings a lamp to light your way— not to your home, but to his. There is an old legend about a saint who was ordered to experience one of the seven deadly sins. He decided that drunkenness was the least of them. But as soon as he got drunk, then he committed the other six sins. In the sixth glass the Devil and man mix blood; in that thrives everything evil within us, and it grows like the grain of mustard in the Bible until it becomes a tree so large that it shades our whole world. Then we are fit for nothing but to be melted down again.

"That is the story of the glasses," said Ole, the watchman of the tower. "It can be told both with English blacking and with lard. I have used both."

## 93

## Anne Lisbeth

Anne Lisbeth was like milk and blood: young, gay, and lovely to look at. Her eyes were bright and her teeth shiny white. She stepped lightly in the dance; she was thoughtless and frivolous. And what did all this beauty and lightheartedness gain her?

"That disgusting little brat!" True, he was no beauty. An unwanted child can be got rid of, and this one was given to the ditch digger's wife to take care of, for she asked the smallest payment. Then Anne Lisbeth moved up to the count's castle; there she sat dressed in her Sunday best every day of the week. Not a wind was allowed to blow on her, nor was an angry word ever spoken to her, because that might harm her! She was the wet nurse of the infant count; he had been born at the same time as her own child. Oh, how she loved this noble little baby! He was as delicate as a prince and as handsome as an angel!

Her own child? Well, he was down in the ditch digger's hut, where the tempers boiled more often than the pots, and hard words stood on the menu every day. Often no one was home. The little boy cried, but unheard tears can't touch anyone. He would cry himself to sleep; and sleep is marvelous, for while you are asleep you can't feel either hunger or thirst. As time passes the weeds shoot up, as people say; and Anne Lisbeth's boy did grow, though he was always smaller than the other boys his age. He belonged in the ditch digger's family; after all, they had been paid to take him in. Anne Lisbeth was rid of him; she moved to the city and married well.

In her home it was always nice and warm, and should she walk outside, then she had both hat and coat to put on. She never went to the ditch digger's hut, it was much too far away. Besides, the boy was theirs. He had too hearty an appetite, they claimed, so they set him to work to earn his keep. He could take care of the neighbor's cow and see to it that it didn't stray into the wheat fields.

The watchdog of the castle stood outside in the sunshine and barked at anyone who came by, but if it rained it had a doghouse that was warm and dry. Anne Lisbeth's boy sat in the ditch when the sun shone and whittled a stick. One spring day he found three wild strawberry plants. He was sure they would have berries and the thought made him happy, but the flowers fell off and no strawberries came. If it rained he had to stay where he was, for he was tending the cow; he was wet to the skin and he had to wait for the wind to dry him. Whenever he came to the farm, the servant girls and the other hired hands played tricks on him and hit him.

"You are ugly, disgusting!" they cried. He was used to hearing those words.

Well, what happened to Anne Lisbeth's boy? What do you suppose? What does happen to those whose lot is never to be loved?

Since the land had no use for him, he took to the sea. He sailed on a broken-down old tub, stood at the tiller while the captain drank. Dirty and disgusting he looked, always cold and always hungry; one would think he had never got enough to eat: and that was true, he hadn't.

It was late in the year. The weather was raw and cold, the wind cut right through his clothes. It was blowing hard and they had only one sail up. It was a rotten little sloop, with only two men as crew. To be more accurate, only one and a half: the skipper and his boy. The clouds had made twilight of the day, but now it was growing really dark and bitterly cold it was. The skipper poured himself a drink to get some warmth inside him. The glass he drank from was old; its foot had been broken off, and the skipper had made a new one of a piece of wood that was painted blue. If one drink helped, then two ought to help twice as much, thought the skipper, and poured himself another. The ditch digger's boy, as he was called—though in the church register it was written that he was Anne Lisbeth's—held onto the tiller with hands that were dirty from pitch and filth. He was ugly, his hair stuck out in all directions, and he was cowed and had squinty eyes.

The wind blew from the stern, the sail filled out. The wind caught it fully and the old ship raced ahead. The top of a wave broke over the railing and drenched the boy. The wind was raw and wet. Something happened! What was it? What burst?

The boat lurched and turned broadside on to the waves. With a loud crack, the mast broke, and sail and rigging came falling down. The boy at the tiller screamed: "Jesus Christ save me!"

The boat had hit a rock and now it sank like an old shoe in the village pond. It went down with mice and men, as the saying goes. There were plenty of mice on board, but of men only one and a half: the skipper and the ditch digger's boy. No one saw it happen, except the screaming gulls and the fishes; and they didn't see it, really, for they fled as the water roared in through the hole in the hull. The boat sank in about ten feet of water, just deep enough to hide both ship and crew. Gone and forgotten they were. Only the glass with the blue-painted wooden foot remained afloat; it drifted toward shore and was finally broken in the surf. It had done good service and it had been loved, which was more than Anne Lisbeth's boy ever had been. Only in heaven are there no souls that can say, "I have never been loved."

Anne Lisbeth had lived for many years in the town and was used to being spoken to respectfully. She liked to boast about the time when she had lived in a castle, driven in a carriage, and conversed with baronesses and countesses. She would fall into ecstasy about her little count, who had looked like an angel and who had loved her as much as she had loved him. He had kissed her and put his arms about her neck. Why, he was all her joy, and half her life!

Now he was almost a grownup: fourteen years old and as clever and learned as anyone and handsomer than everyone. Of this she was certain, although she had not seen him since she had carried him in her arms; it was, after all, quite far to the castle, almost a journey.

"But I must go there soon," said Anne Lisbeth. "I must see my joy once more, my sweet little count. I am sure he longs for me too, and still cares for me and remembers the time when he put his little angelic arms around my neck and whispered, 'Anne Lis.' Oh! that sounded as lovely as a violin. Yes, I must go and visit him!"

She drove with a freight wagon as far as the village near the castle; the rest of the way she had to walk.

The castle looked as large and impressive as it had the first time she had seen it. The park around it had not changed either; but all the servants were strangers, not one of them remembered an "Anne Lisbeth." They did not seem to appreciate her importance, but surely the countess would tell them who she was—and so would her own little count, whom she was at long last to see.

Anne Lisbeth had to wait a long time—and time is always long when you have to wait. Just before dinner she was called in to the countess, who spoke very kindly to her. She would be able to see her little sweet boy after dinner; she would be called in again then.

How tall and thin he had become, but he had the same eyes and the same angelic mouth. He looked at her but didn't say a word. Maybe he had not recognized her. He turned as if he were going to leave, and Anne Lisbeth grabbed his hand and pressed it to her mouth.

"That is enough," he said, and left the room.—He whom all her loving thoughts had dwelled upon; he whom she had loved above all else; he who had been all her earthly pride.

Anne Lisbeth walked back along the road toward the village. She was so unhappy. He had acted toward her as though she were a stranger. He had not given her a thought or said a kind word, although she once had carried him in her arms through long nights; and since that time, not one day had passed without her thinking about him.

A big black raven landed on the road in front of her and screeched again and again. "My God!" she cried. "What bird of ill omen are you?"

She was passing the ditch digger's house, and his wife was standing in the doorway. Anne Lisbeth stopped to talk to her.

"You have done well," said the ditch digger's wife. "You look healthy and plump. One can see you have prospered."

"Oh yes, I can't complain," answered Anne Lisbeth.

"The boat went down. Both Lars the skipper and the boy drowned. Well, that was the end of it. I had hoped that the boy might help me in my old age with a few coppers. He won't cost you any more money, Anne Lisbeth."

"Are they drowned!" exclaimed Anne Lisbeth, and then they talked no more about it.

Anne Lisbeth was still feeling miserable because her little count whom she loved so much had not even talked to her. It had cost her money to take that journey and what had she gained from it? Not much, but that she was not going to tell the ditch digger's wife. After all, she did not want her to think that Anne Lisbeth was not welcome in the castle any more. At that moment the raven screeched again.

"You black monster!" shouted Anne Lisbeth. "Why are you trying to scare me?"

She had brought some coffee and chicory with her; it was an act of kindness to give them to the ditch digger's wife so that she could make some coffee. While the ditch digger's wife was in the kitchen, Anne Lisbeth sat down in a chair and fell asleep.

She had a strange dream in which appeared a person she had never seen in a dream before. She dreamed about her son: the child who had starved and frozen in this very hut, and now lay at the bottom of the sea—only God knows where. She dreamed that she was sitting right where she was and that the ditch digger's wife had gone out to make coffee—even in her dream she could smell it brewing. Suddenly a boy, as beautiful as the young count, stood in the door of the hut and said to her: "Now the end of the world is coming, hold onto me, for in spite of everything you are my mother. You have an angel in heaven to guard you, hold onto me!"

He grabbed her by the sleeve, and at that moment she heard a great noise; and Anne Lisbeth guessed that that was the end of the world. The angel lifted her up, but something heavy held onto her shoulders and her legs. It felt as though a hundred women had grabbed hold of her and they were shouting: "If you are to be saved we have a right to be saved too. Hang on! Hang on!"

And they did hold onto her, and that was too much for Anne Lisbeth's sleeve. "Ritch," it said, and was torn to pieces; and she fell back down on the ground. So real and so frightening was the dream that she woke and almost fell off the chair. Afterward she felt so dizzy and confused that she couldn't remember exactly what it was she had dreamed, only that it had been unpleasant.

The coffee was served and drunk. The two women talked and then it was time for Anne Lisbeth to leave. She walked to the nearest village, where she was to meet the freightman and drive in his wagon back to the town where she lived. Unfortunately his wagon had broken and he would not be able to leave before the following evening. Anne Lisbeth speculated upon the cost of a night's lodging at the inn and then decided that, if she did not walk along the road but followed the beach instead, she would save many a mile and could be home by morning.

The sun had set, but the church bells seemed still to be ringing— no, it wasn't bells, it was the big frogs down in the lake that were croaking. But at last they grew silent too. And now the whole world was still, not a bird was heard; they had gone to sleep, and the owl, who is usually up at this time, was not home. So still was the mirror of the sea that not even the tiniest ripples lapped on the shore. The only sound that Anne Lisbeth heard was that of her own footsteps in the sand. No splash from leaping fish broke the silence, everything under the water, both living and dead, was mute.

Anne Lisbeth did not think about anything while she walked, but that did not mean that no thoughts were in her mind. They lie asleep within our heads and never leave us, old thoughts that we have had before, as well as new ones that we have still to encounter.

"Virtue is its own reward," so it is written; and it is also written, "The wages of sin is death." So much has been written, so much has been said, and one does not remember it all. So it was with Anne Lisbeth, but one can be made to remember!

Within our hearts are all virtues and vices—in yours and in mine! They lie there like grains, so small that they are invisible; then, from outside a sun ray or an evil hand touches them. You turn a corner, whether to the right or to the left may be of supreme importance. And the little seed grows till it suddenly bursts and enters your blood. From then on it directs where you will go. When you are walking along drowsily, such fearful thoughts do not come to your mind, but that does not mean that they are not there.

Anne Lisbeth was tired. She felt as if she were about to doze, but her thoughts were aroused. From one midsummer to the next, our hearts have a whole year to account for: How many sinful thoughts have we had? How many words have we spoken against God, our neighbors, and our own conscience? But we forget, we do not think about them, and neither did Anne Lisbeth. She had not broken any laws of the land; she knew that others considered her a decent, upright woman.

As she walked along the beach she saw something lying in the sand. What was it? She stopped. It was a man's hat that the waves had thrown up on land. She wondered when and from what ship it had fallen overboard. She took a few steps toward it. But what was that lying over there? She got very frightened, but there was nothing to be frightened of. What had scared her was merely a large stone covered by broken reeds and seaweed. It looked like the body of a human being, but it was only a stone and some seaweed. Yet her fear stayed with her as she walked on; and now so many thoughts came to her. She remembered all the old tales and superstitions she had heard, when she was a child, about the ghosts of those who had drowned. How these specters attacked the lonesome wanderer and demanded that they carry them to the churchyard and bury them there.

"Hang on, hang on!" the ghosts had cried in the stories she had heard. And as Anne Lisbeth repeated these words to herself, she suddenly remembered the dream she had had in the ditch digger's cottage. So real did it become to her that again she felt the weight of the other mothers clinging to her, while they screamed: "Hang on! Hang on!"

And she remembered how the world had come to an end, and how the sleeves of her blouse had ripped, so that her child, who on the Day of Judgment had tried to save her, could no longer hold onto her. Her own child, the one she had borne but never loved, and had never even given a thought to. Now that child rested on the bottom of the sea, and his ghost could come and demand of her, "Bury me in Christian soil. Hang on! Hang on!"

As these thoughts passed through her mind, fear bit her heels and she hurried on. Dread like a cold hand squeezed her heart so that it hurt. She looked out over the sea. A mist came rolling in; it obscured and changed the shapes of bushes and trees. She looked up at the moon. It appeared as a pale, pale disk. Her body felt heavy, as if she were carrying a great weight. "Hang on! hang on!" the words echoed in her mind.

Again she turned to look at the moon, and now its white face seemed very close to her and the fog hung like a winding sheet from her shoulders. "Hang on, hang on, bring me to my grave!" She expected to hear those words any moment.

There was a sound! What was it? It could not be frogs or the cry of a raven or a crow. A hollow voice said, "Bury me, bury me." She had heard it plainly. It was the voice of her child, the one who now rested on the bottom of the sea. He would never find peace until he was carried to the churchyard and there buried in hallowed ground. She would dig his grave. She walked in the direction where she thought a church stood, and now it seemed to her that her body felt lighter, that the burden was gone.

Hurriedly she turned and walked instead toward her home, but then the weight returned. "Hang on, hang on!" The cry sounded again like the deep voice of some monstrous frog or frightened bird.

"Bury me, bury me."

The fog was cold and wet, and her face and hands were cold and damp from fear. The world outside was pressing on her and she herself had become an empty void in which thoughts she had never had before were free to fly.

In the north, in one warm spring night, the whole beech forest can put forth leaves, and when the sun rises it stands in all its tender green glory. In one second within us, when our conscience awakes, all the evil, all the sins committed throughout a lifetime, can unfold before us. At this moment no excuses, no mitigating circumstances, help; our deeds bear witness against us and our thoughts are formed into words that shout the truth to the world. We are horrified at what we see, at the evil that has been inside us, which we have not even tried to destroy—the harm we have done in arrogance and thoughtlessness. Inside our hearts are all virtues and all vices; but vices thrive in the poorest soil.

What we have said in words, Anne Lisbeth felt, and her feelings so overpowered her that she fell to the ground and crawled on all fours like an animal.

"Bury me, bury me," whispered the voice, and gladly would she have buried herself, if that would have meant the end of all memories.

It was her day of reckoning, and it brought her only fear and dread. All the superstitions she knew mixed as heat and icy coldness with her blood, and tales she had not remembered for years came back to her. As soundlessly as the clouds that pass by the pale moon, a specter rushed by her. Four dark horses with fire coming from their nostrils drew a carriage in which sat the evil count who, more than a hundred years before, had lived and ruled in this district. Now at midnight he drove from the churchyard to his castle and back again. He was not pale as ghosts usually are described. No, his face was as black as burned-out coals. He nodded to Anne Lisbeth and waved.

"Hang on, hang on!" he shouted. "Then you can again drive in a count's carriage and forget your own child!"

She ran and at last she reached the churchyard. The black crosses on the graves and the black ravens that lived in the church tower became one. All the crosses became ravens that cried and screamed at her. She remembered that unnatural mothers are called "raven mothers," for that bird is known, to its shame, for not taking good care of its young. Would she become a black bird when she died: a raven?

She threw herself down on the ground and with her fingers dug in the hard earth until blood ran from her nails. And all the time she heard the voice saying, "Bury me, bury me!" She feared that the cock would crow and the eastern sky grow red before she had finished her work; and then all would be lost.

The cock crowed and the sun rose. The grave was but half finished! A cold hand caressed her face and a voice sighed, "Only half a grave." It was the spirit of her son, who now had to return to the bottom of the sea. Anne Lisbeth sank to the ground and all thoughts and feelings left her.

It was almost noon when she awoke. Two young men had found her. She was not lying in the churchyard but on the beach. In front of her was the big hole she had dug. She had cut her hands on a broken glass, the stem of which had been forced down into a little square piece of wood that was painted blue.

Anne Lisbeth was sick. Her conscience had dealt the cards of superstition, and she had read them. She now believed that she had only half a soul; the ghost of her son had taken the other half with him, down to the bottom of the sea. She would not be able to enter heaven unless she could get back that part of her soul that lay beneath the deep waters of the ocean.

Anne Lisbeth was brought home, but she was no longer the woman she had been. Her thoughts were like threads, all tangled up in knots; only one idea was clear to her: that she must find again the ghost of her child, carry him to the churchyard, and bury him there, so that she could win back her soul.

Many a night she was missed at home, but they knew where they could find her: down on the beach, waiting for the ghost of her son to come. A year went by and then one night she disappeared, and this time they could not find her; all day they searched in vain.

Toward evening the bell ringer who had come to ring the bells for vespers saw her. In front of the altar lay Anne Lisbeth. She had been there since morning. She had no strength left but the light in her eyes was one of joy. The last of the sun's rays fell on her face and gave it the pink color of health. The sun rays were reflected in the brass clasps of the old Bible that lay upon the altar. It had been opened upon the page of the prophet Joel, where it is written: "Rend your heart and not your garments, and turn unto the Lord your God." This, they said, was quite by chance, as so much is in this world.

In Anne Lisbeth's sun-filled face one could see that she had found peace. She whispered that she was well, that she was not afraid any more. The ghost had come at last. Her son had been with her and said: "You dug only a half a grave for me, but for a whole year and a day you have buried me in your heart, and that is the right place for a mother to keep her child." Then he had given her back the half of her soul that he had taken with him and led her up here to the church.

"Now I am in God's house," she said, "and here one is blessed."

When the sun finally went down, Anne Lisbeth's soul went up to where fear is unknown and all struggles cease. And Anne Lisbeth had striven.

## 94

## Children's Prattle

At the merchant's they were having a children's party; all the children who were attending it had parents who were either rich or distinguished. The merchant himself was wealthy and not without learning. He had graduated from the university. His father had insisted upon it. That decent and honest gentleman had started out in life as a cattle dealer; he had made money and his son had understood how to turn it into a fortune. The younger man had both intelligence and a kind heart, but people did not mention these attributes as often as they did his great wealth.

People of distinction gathered in his house. Some had noble blood, others noble spirits; and a few had both, and a number had neither. But now there was a children's party, and children have a habit of saying what they think.

There was a very beautiful little girl who was terribly proud; the servants had kissed that pride into her, for her parents were really very sensible people. Her father was a Knight of the Royal Bedchamber and that, the little girl knew, was something extraordinarily important. "I am a chamber child," she declared, although she could just as easily have been a "cellar child," for, after all, we can't choose our parents. She explained to the other children that she was "wellborn" and that if one was not wellborn, then one couldn't become anything. It didn't matter how hard one studied, it was being properly "born" that counted.

"And as for those whose names end in *sen,* there is no hope for them. Nothing can ever become of them," she explained. "One has to put one's hands on one's waist and keep these common people with their *sen, sen* names at elbow's length." And to illustrate what she meant, she put her pretty little hands on her waist so that her elbows stuck out sharply. She looked very charming.

But the merchant's daughter got angry. Her father's name was Madsen, and that name, she knew, ended with a *sen;* therefore she said as proudly as she could: "My father can buy a hundred silver marks' worth of candy and throw it in the street, so all the poor children can scramble for it. Can your father do that?"

"But my father," announced the newspaper editor's daughter, "can put your father, and yours too, and all the fathers in the whole town, in the newspaper. And that is why everybody is frightened of him, so my mother says. It is my father who rules the newspaper." And she held her head high as if she were a proper princess with a father who ruled a kingdom.

Behind the door, which stood ajar, was a poor little boy; he was looking in through the crack. The little lad was much too poor to be permitted to go to the party. He had been turning the spit for the cook, and as a reward he had been allowed to stand behind the door and watch the other children play; and he had been pleased to have such a chance.

"If only I were one of them," he had thought while he listened to everything that was being said; much of it was really not too pleasant for him to hear. His parents never had so much as a copper to spare and could not even afford to buy a newspaper, let alone write in it. The worst of it all was that his father's name ended in *sen.* Nothing could ever become of him! It was very sad. But born he had been, and since he had never heard otherwise he must have been wellborn, too, of that he felt certain.

Now that was that evening.

Years went by, and the years made the children into grownups.

In the center of Copenhagen a palace had been built and it was filled with splendid treasures that everyone wanted to see. People came from far and wide to look at them. Now to which of the children whom we have described did this palace belong? That ought to be an easy question to answer, but it isn't. It belonged to the poor boy, the one who had stood behind the door. Something had become of him: he was a great sculptor, and the palace was a museum for his works. It had not really mattered that his name ended with *sen: Thorvaldsen,* whose marble statues stand in St. Peter's in Rome.

What happened to the other children: the offspring of good family, wealth, and intellectual arrogance?—None of them could point a finger at any of the others; they had all been equally silly.—They had become decent and kind human beings, for they were, in truth, not evil. What they had thought and said then had only been children's prattle.

## 95

## A String of Pearls

The railroad here in Denmark stretches only from Copenhagen across Zealand to Korsør. It is a string on which pearls are strung. Of such pearls Europe has many; the costliest are Paris, London, Vienna, Naples . . . Yet many a person does not consider these great cities the most beautiful pearls, but instead points to some little, humble, unknown town, for that to him is home, there live those whom he holds dear. He may even talk about a farm, or a little house surrounded by green hedges, which can hardly be noticed from the window as the train rushes by.

How many pearls are there on the string from Copenhagen to Korsør? Let us consider six of them: six that most people know and have noticed. Old memories and poetry itself give them an added luster, so that we can remember them.

Near the hill on which stands the castle of Frederik VI, protected by the great trees of the forest called Sondermarken, lies one of the pearls: a house that was affectionately called "the Philemon and Baucis cottage." Here lived Rahbek and his wife Kamma, and under their hospitable roof, for a whole generation, all the poets and artists of busy Copenhagen gathered; it was truly a refuge for the spirit and the spirited. And now? Please do not say, "Oh, how it all is changed!" No, it is still a home for the spirit, for the mind. It is now a greenhouse for sick plants, for the bud that has not the strength within it to unfold but still contains the germ for the leaves and seeds. The sun shines into a home where the spirit and the mind are protected, and reflects down into a depth that we cannot reach. The home of the feeble-minded, created out of human love, is a holy place, a greenhouse for the sickly plants that will someday be replanted in God's garden. Those whose spirit is the weakest are now gathered here where once the strongest, most creative minds met. Oh, it is not unfitting, for still the mind and the soul are the concern of those who live in the "Philemon and Baucis cottage."

The town of royal tombs—Hroar's spring—the old Roskilde, now lies before us. The slender spires of the cathedral point to the sky above the low houses and mirror themselves in the fjord. We shall visit one grave—one pearl. Not that of the mighty Queen Margrethe who united Denmark, Norway, and Sweden. No, we shall visit a grave behind the white wall of the churchyard; we can see it from the train as we fly by. A simple stone stands there and beneath it rests a king of the organ, he who renewed the Danish romance and through melody made old legends part of us. Roskilde is the town of royal tombs, a pearl in which we shall seek only a simple grave: the stone on which is carved a lyre and the name *Weyse*.

Now the train goes by Sigersted near Ringsted. The water in the stream is low. Where Hagbarth's boat once landed, there are now fields of grain. Who does not know the story of Hagbarth and Signe? How he was hanged and she was burned to death, the story of passionate love.

"Beautiful Sorø garlanded by forests," the little cloister town, has now a peephole out to the great world. Eagerly and youthfully, it looks from the old academy, across the lake, to the new "road of the world," where the dragon of a new age snorts and lets off clouds of white steam as it draws its wagons through the forest. Sorø, you are literature's pearl, for the dust of Holberg rests here. Like a giant white swan, your academy, your house of learning, stands near the forest lake. Not far from the walls is a humble cottage, and to this our eyes are drawn. It shines like a little white flower in the green moss. Here hymns were written which were sung far and wide; peasants and workingmen learned from the words spoken here about their own past and history. As the green forest and the song birds belong together, so do the names Sorø and Ingemann.

The town of Slagelse, what is reflected in this pearl? Antvorskov Cloister has long been torn down. Its splendid hall exists no more; even the lesser parts, which stood abandoned so long, are gone. Yet one sign from ancient times is still there, and when it crumbles it is always renewed. It is the wooden cross that stands on the hill outside the city, which sanctifies the place to which the Blessed Anders was carried, according to the legend, in one night from Jerusalem.

Korsør. Here Baggesen was born, the master of words and wit. The ramparts of the abandoned fortress are the last witness of your childhood home. At sunset the shadow they cast points toward the spot where the house stood that you were born in. From these embankments you looked out over the Great Belt when you were a child, and "watched the moon glide down behind the island." You sang of it, with immortal words, as later you described the great mountains of Switzerland: you who traveled into the world's labyrinth to find that:

> Nowhere are the roses so red,
> And nowhere are the thorns so tiny,
> And nowhere are the pillows so soft
> As those our childish innocence rested on.

You, the great poet of moods and feelings, we shall weave you a wreath of woodruff and throw it into the sea, and let the waves carry it to the banks of the fjord of Kiel, where your dust rests. A greeting to you from your birthplace, Korsør, where the pearl string ends.

II

"Yes, truly from Copenhagen to Korsør is a string of pearls," said Grandmother, who had been listening to what had just been read aloud. "To me it was already such a precious string more than forty years ago. Then we did not have steam engines. In 1815, when I was just twenty—and that is a lovely age, though now that I am in my sixties I recognize that old age, too, has its blessings.

"When I was young, a trip to Copenhagen was a rare and difficult journey. The town of towns, we thought it was. It had been twenty years since my parents last visited it, and now they were to go there again and I was to go along. We had talked about making this journey for years, and at last we were going! I felt as if my life were beginning all over again; and in a way, it was.

"Dresses had to be sewn, clothes repaired and packed, before we finally were ready. All our friends came to say good-by. It was no small trip we were setting out on. In the early morning we left Odense, in my parents' Holstein coach. Acquaintances nodded from every window, until we had passed through the city gate. The weather was lovely. The birds were singing and everything was so gay that one forgot how far it was to Nyborg. We arrived toward evening. The mail coach had not come yet, and the sloop on which we were to sail could not leave before it came. We went on board.

"Before us lay the sea, the Great Belt. As far as our eyes could see, there was only water. The night was still and the sea was calm. We lay down fully dressed and slept. In the early morning I climbed up on deck. Fog covered the whole world and I could see nothing. I heard a cock crow, and realized that the sun had risen. A church bell rang and I wondered where we were. The fog lifted and we were still just outside of Nyborg. Later, a breeze began to blow, but it was against us, and we had to tack all the way across. Not before eleven at night were we lucky enough to reach Korsør. It had taken us twenty-two hours to sail fifteen miles.

"It was lovely to get ashore, but the night was dark and the street lamps were burning low and gave little light. Everything looked so strange to me, for I had never been in any town but Odense.

" 'Here Baggesen was born,' said my father.

"When I heard these words, the old town with its tiny houses suddenly seemed much larger and not so dark. We were all happy to have solid ground under our feet again. I could not sleep that night, I was much too excited about all that had happened since we had left our home.

"The next morning we rose early. We had a bad piece of road to travel to get to Slagelse; the hills were steep and the highway was filled with holes—and they said that beyond Slagelse the road was in no better condition. We wanted to reach the little inn called the Crayfish House early enough so that we could walk into Sorø and visit 'Miller's Emil,' as we called him. . . . Yes, that was your grandfather and my blessed husband, the dean. But at that time he was only a young student in Sorø.

"We arrived at the Crayfish House in the early part of the afternoon. It was a fashionable place then, the best inn we stayed at during the whole journey—and the surroundings were beautiful and are so still, that you must admit. Madame Plambek was the name of the innkeeper's wife, and she was a wonderful housekeeper, everything was scoured and scrubbed. On the wall hung Baggesen's letter to her, in glass and framed; that was something worth looking at and I found it most interesting.

"We walked to Sorø and there we met Emil. Believe me, he was happy to see us and we to see him. He was so kind and considerate. He showed us the church where Absalon and Holberg were buried. We saw the old inscriptions that the monks had made. We sailed across the lake. It was the most beautiful evening that I can remember. Is there any place in the whole world better suited for writing poetry than the peaceful beauty of nature around Sorø? In moonlight, we walked along the 'philosophers' path,' back to the Crayfish House, where we had supper. Emil stayed and ate with us. My parents thought that he had grown much cleverer and handsomer since they had seen him last. He promised us that in five days he, too, would be in Copenhagen. He would be staying with his family there and would be seeing us. Those hours in Sorø and at the Crayfish House are the most precious pearls of my life.

"We left early the next morning, for we had a long journey in front of us before we reached Roskilde. We wanted to get there in time to see the church, and my father had an old friend in the town whom he wanted to spend the evening with. Everything went according to our plans, and we spent the night in Roskilde.

"The next morning we drove on. We did not arrive in Copenhagen before noon, for the road was in terrible condition from all the traffic.

"It had taken us three days to travel from Korsør to Copenhagen; now you can do it in as many hours. The pearls have not become any more precious, but the string is new and marvelous. My parents and I stayed for three weeks in Copenhagen, and Emil and I were together for eighteen days. When we returned to Fyn and our home in Odense, Emil journeyed all the way to Korsør with us, and there we became engaged, just before we parted. So now you can understand why I, too, call the distance between Copenhagen and Korsør a string of pearls.

"Emil became minister at the church in the town of Assens, and we were married. We often talked about our journey to Copenhagen and how we would like to do it all over again. But then your mother arrived, and she had brothers and a sister; and there was so much to do that we never found time for that. Your grandfather was appointed dean and everything went very well for us, but our trip to Copenhagen we never got. Still, there was pleasure in talking about it. Now I have grown too old to travel by railroad. But I am pleased that it is there; it is a blessing! For now all my children and grandchildren can come much faster and oftener to visit me. Odense is not much farther away from Copenhagen than it was from Nyborg in my childhood. You can almost travel to Italy in the time it took us to get to Copenhagen. Yes, that is something! But I stay where I am and let the others travel; let them come to me.

"You shouldn't smile like that, just because I sit so still in my chair. I have a greater journey ahead of me than yours. And I shall travel swifter than the railroads. When God wills, I shall journey up to Grandfather. And when you have done your duty down here and enjoyed this blessed earth of ours, then you will come up to us and we shall talk about our lives down on earth, and I shall still say as I do now: 'From Copenhagen to Korsør, yes, that is a string of pearls.'"

## 96

## The Pen and the Inkwell

It was once remarked by someone who was looking at the inkwell on an author's desk: "Isn't it strange, all that can come out of an inkwell? I wonder what will come from it next? Oh, it is a wonder!"

"That it is," agreed the inkwell. "It is very hard to understand. And that has always been my opinion." The inkwell was talking to the pen and everything else that happened to be on the desk. "It is, indeed, strange and wonderful what can come out of me! Why, I would call it almost unbelievable! Sometimes I don't even know myself what will come next—what will happen when human beings dip into me. One drop of me is enough to cover half a page of paper, and what cannot be written on that! I am someone quite extraordinary. From me springs all poetry; descriptions of people who have never lived, and yet are more alive than those who walk around on two legs; the deepest feelings; the greatest wit; and the loveliest word paintings of nature. How can all that be inside me—I who do not even know nature —but nonetheless it is! All of these gallant knights on their magnificent horses and all the beautiful young girls who live in books have, in fact, been born in me. Yes, I cannot even understand it myself."

"There you spoke the truth!" said the quill pen. "You do not understand because you cannot think; if you could, you would realize that you contain merely liquid. You exist so that I can express upon paper the thoughts that are within me, so that I can write them down. It is the pen that writes! This no man doubts, and I can assure you that most human beings have a great deal more insight into poetry than an old inkwell."

"You have not had much experience yet," said the inkwell. "You are young in the service, though already half used up, I am afraid. Do you really believe that you are the poet? You are only a servant, and I have had many of them before you arrived. Both English steel pens and those who can claim geese as their family. I have known all kinds of pens. I cannot even count the number that have been in my service; and more will come, I am sure. He wears them out, the human being who does the manual labor, he who writes down what is inside me. I wonder what he will lift out of me next."

"Ink tub!" sneered the pen.

Later in the evening the poet came home. He had attended a concert where he had heard an excellent violinist play. He was still very excited about what he had heard. The musician had enticed such marvelous sounds out of his instrument. At one moment it sounded like drops of water falling from the trees, one pearly drop after another; and the next, like a storm riding through a pine forest. The poet had thought he had heard his own heart weeping, so captured had he been by the music. It was not only the strings that had sung but the whole instrument, wood and all. And all the while it had looked so easy: the bow had danced so lightly across the strings. One was almost convinced that anyone could have done it, so effortless had the performance appeared. The violin sang by itself and the bow moved by itself; the two were one. One almost forgot their master: the musician who played upon them and gave to these two dead objects a soul. But the poet had not forgotten him; he pondered over it and wrote down his thoughts.

"How absurd it would seem if the bow and the violin should be proud and haughty about their accomplishments. Yet we, human beings, often are; the poets, the artists, the scientists, and even the generals often boast in vain pride. Yet they are all but instruments that God plays upon. To Him alone belongs all honor. We have nothing to pride ourselves upon!"

Later the poet wrote a parable and called it "The Genius and His Instrument."

"Well, madam, that put you in your place," said the pen to the inkwell when the two of them again were alone. "I suppose you heard him read aloud what I had written down?"

"You wrote what I ordered you to write," retorted the inkwell. "It was especially your silly arrogance and pride that made me think of it, I am sure. But I suppose you can't even understand when you are being made fun of! That whole thing was meant for you and it came from the very depth of me. Don't you think I can recognize my own sarcasm?"

"Ink skirt!" screamed the pen.

"Scribble pin!" shouted the inkwell.

Each of them thought his own repartee the cleverer, and there is nothing so satisfying as the feeling that one has had the last word. It makes for pleasant slumber, and both the inkwell and the pen went to sleep. But the poet was not asleep; like tones from a violin, thoughts upon thoughts came to him. They fell like pearls and rode through the forest as the storm; he felt the cry of his own heart and the spark of the Eternal Master.

To Him alone belongs the honor and the glory!

## 97

## *The Dead Child*

The house was in mourning, and sorrow lived in every heart. The youngest child in the family, a four-year-old boy, had died. The parents' pride and hope, their only son. They had two daughters. One of them was to be confirmed that year; they were kind and good girls, both of them. But the child one loses is always closest to one's heart, and this child had been the youngest, and their only son. It was a time of trial. The two young sisters mourned, as young hearts do; they were especially moved by the sorrow of their parents. The father walked as if he were bent by sorrow, but their mother was completely beside herself with grief.

Night and day she had sat beside the bed of her sick child, she had lifted him in her arms, carried him, and nursed him. The child had become an inseparable part of her; and now she could not believe that he was dead and had to be placed in a coffin and hidden in a grave.

How could God take her child from her? But it had happened; and when she could no longer say that it was not so, then in her grief and distress she cried: "God does not know about it. His servants are heartless and do what pleases them. They do not listen to a mother's prayers."

Her pain was so great that she let go of God; and dark thoughts came, thoughts about eternal death—that all was over when our bodies became dust in the dust. With such thoughts, she could hold onto nothing, and she fell into the deepest despair.

She could no longer cry. She paid no attention to her daughters, nor did she notice the tears in her husband's eyes. All her thoughts were with her dead child. She tried to remember everything he had done, every childish, innocent word he had uttered.

The day of the funeral came. The night before she had not slept, except for an hour in the early morning when tiredness had overwhelmed her. During that time the coffin was moved to the most distant room in the house and the lid was nailed down.

When she woke she wanted to see her child again, but her husband, with tears in his eyes, said, "We have closed the coffin, we had to."

"If God is hard and cruel toward me, why should I expect better treatment from you?" she said, sobbing.

The coffin was carried to its grave. The mother, who could find consolation nowhere, sat with her daughters but she did not see them. Her thoughts were homeless, she had abandoned herself to her grief; she was floundering now in a dark ocean, like a ship that has lost its rudder. Thus passed the day of the funeral, and the days that followed were as uniformly filled with suffering. With eyes red from weeping, her family looked at her. They tried to console her but she did not hear them; and maybe they could not find the right words, for they were grieving too.

She and sleep had parted company, although he could have been her best friend, for she needed rest to strengthen her body and give peace to her soul. Her husband persuaded her that she must lie down; and she did. She was not asleep; she only pretended to be by lying very still. Her husband, who was listening to her breathing, was convinced that she had finally fallen asleep. He closed his own eyes and soon slept deeply. He did not hear his wife rise and dress herself. Silently, she let herself out of the house and hurried to that place which her thoughts did not leave, neither day nor night: her son's grave. She saw no one on her way along the path that crossed the meadows to the churchyard; and no one saw her.

The sky was clear and all the stars were out; it was in the beginning of September and the air was warm. The little grave of her child was still covered with flowers; their perfume smelled strongly in the still night. She sat down and bent her head, as if she hoped to be able to see down through the earth to her little boy.

Everything about him was still alive to her. She remembered his smile, the expression of love for her in his face. How could anyone forget how eloquently his little face had spoken as he lay on his sick-bed? She remembered how she had bent down over him and taken his hand when he was so weak he could not move it. As she had sat by his bed, she now sat by his grave, but here she could weep freely and her tears fell on his grave.

"Do you want to go down to your child?" asked a voice near her. It sounded so deep and clear, as if her own heart had spoken to her. She turned her head and saw standing beside her a man dressed in a long black cloak with a hood that hid his face. As he looked down at her, she caught a glimpse of his features. He looked austere and yet inspired confidence rather than fear, and his eyes sparkled like a young man's.

"Down to my child," she repeated, and her words sounded like a desperate prayer.

"Do you dare follow me?" asked the man. "I am Death!"

She nodded and suddenly all the stars seemed to shine with the power and glory of the full moon. She noticed the splendor of the flowers that covered the grave, as the earth grew soft under her and she sank slowly down into it. Death covered her with his cape and it was night, and dark as death. She sank deeper than the gravedigger's spade ever will reach; the churchyard became a roof over her head.

Death's cape fell away from her and she was standing in a great hall. Although it was twilight all about her, the place was more comforting than frightening.

There was her child! She pressed him to her heart. He smiled and laughed and looked even more beautiful than he had when he was alive. She shouted for joy but was aware at the same moment that no sound came from her lips. From far away beautiful and strange music reached her ears; it seemed to come nearer and nearer, only to recede again. It came from somewhere beyond the great curtain, black as night, that divided the hall from the land of eternity.

"My sweet mother, my own mother!" she heard her little boy say. Oh, it was his voice, the voice she loved. Kiss followed kiss, in one unending joy.

The little boy pointed toward the curtain and said: "It is not as beautiful up on earth as it is here. Look, Mother! Do you see them all? Such is heavenly bliss."

The mother looked in the direction her son was pointing, but she saw nothing except the curtain dark as night. Her eyes belonged still to the earth, and she could not see what he saw. She heard the music and the singing that came from beyond, but she could not understand the words that were sung.

"I can fly now, Mother," said the child, "fly together with all the other happy children, right up to God. I would like to so much, but your tears hold me back. When you weep I cannot leave you, and I want to. Please let me go, may I? After all, it is but so short a time, and then you will be with me."

"No, stay, stay!" cried the mother. "Only a little while longer. Let me look at you just once more, and kiss you and hold you in my arms!"

And she held onto the child and she kissed him. Mournfully her name was called by someone up above. Who could it be?

"Do you hear?" asked the child. "It is Father who is calling you."

Then she heard deep sobs, like those children make when they have cried too long.

"Hear my sisters," said the boy. "You have forgotten them!"

Suddenly she remembered all that she had left behind. She saw shades fly by her, through the hall of death, and thought that she recognized some of them. What if one of those shades should prove to be her husband or her daughters! No, she could still hear their sighs and their weeping. She had forgotten them for the sake of her dead child.

"Now all the bells of heaven ring," said the little boy. "Mother, the sun is rising!"

A blinding light engulfed her, the child was gone, and she rose upward. She felt bitterly cold and lifted her head to see where she was. She was in the churchyard; she had been lying on the grave of her dead child. But in her dream God had guided her and taught her to understand. She fell on her knees and prayed, "Forgive me, Lord, that I would keep a soul from its flight toward you, and forgive me for forgetting my duties toward the living."

In these words her heart found peace. The sun rose; a bird sang above her head and she heard it. The bells of the church rang for morning prayers. She felt the holiness of everything around her, and that sacred holiness was in her heart as well. She knew again her God and her duties. Longingly she ran toward her home. She bent over her sleeping husband and woke him with a kiss; and they talked, words that came from their hearts. And she was strong and yet at the same time gentle, as a wife should be. Her strength she found in the belief that God's will is always for the best.

Her husband asked her, "Where did you get the strength to comfort others?"

She kissed him and she kissed her children. "From God," she said, "and from my dead child in his grave."

## 98

## The Cock and the Weathercock

There were two cocks on the farm, one on the roof and one on the manure heap. They were vain and proud, both of them. But which one had the greater right to be? Tell us your opinion—it won't make any difference, we will stick to our own anyway.

The henyard was divided from the manure heap by a wooden fence and in the manure grew a cucumber; it knew that it was a vegetable and it was proud of being one.

"That is something one is by birth," the cucumber mumbled to herself. "We can't all be born cucumbers; there must be other species as well. Hens and ducks and the other animals on the farm had to be created too. The cock I look up to; he is always sitting on the fence crowing. He is of a great deal more importance than the weathercock, who is placed a little too high up and can't even say, 'Peep,' not to speak of crowing. He has no hens or chickens of his own, and when he sweats, it is green. He never thinks about anyone but himself. Now the cock on the farm, he is something else! When he struts about, it is a dance, a ballet. When he crows, it is music! Wherever he goes, people know how important a trumpeter is! If he came in here and ate me up, leaves and stalk and all, I would call it a blessed death. My body would become his!" said the cucumber.

Toward night there was a horrible storm. The hens, the chickens, and the cock sought shelter. The wooden fence fell, which made a frightening noise. Several tiles flew off the roof, but the weathercock stayed where he was, he did not even turn. He couldn't, which was really strange since he was quite new and had been cast recently. But he was the kind that was born old; steady and sober-minded from birth. He resembled in no way the fluttering birds of the air, the swallows or the sparrows; as a matter of fact, he despised them. "Small birds, common and ordinary," he called them. As for shape and coloring, he found the pigeons more to his taste; their feathers shone like mother-of-pearl, they could almost pass for weathercocks. But he declared that they were fat and stupid and never thought about anything except filling their stomachs. They were uninteresting company. Most of the migrating birds had visited the weathercock and told him fantastic stories about foreign lands, where there were eagles and great birds of prey. The tales had been amusing and interesting the first time he heard them, but the birds always repeated themselves and that the weathercock found tedious. They were tiresome, and life was boring. There was no one worth associating with, everything was flat and dull!

"The world is no good!" he declared. "Twaddle and nonsense: all of it!"

The weathercock was oversophisticated. The cucumber would have found him very interesting and attractive, but she didn't know him, so she admired the cock from the henyard; and now that the fence had blown down, he came visiting.

"What did you all think of that cock's crow?" he asked the hens and the chickens—he was referring to the storm. "I found it a bit raw, it lacked elegance."

Then he stepped up on the manure pile with the determined step of a hussar—he was wearing spurs. All the hens and chickens followed him.

"Vegetable," he said to the cucumber; and in that one word she found such breeding and refinement that she did not even notice that the cock pecked at her and ate her up.

"A blessed death!"

The hens gathered around and the chickens came too, for where one ran the others followed. They clucked and they peeped and they all looked at the cock and admired him, for he was one of their own kind.

"Cock-a-doodle-doo," he crowed. "All the chickens become hens in the henyards of the world, if and when I say so!"

The hens and the chickens clucked and peeped in agreement, all of them. Then the cock crowed some news to the world: "A cock can lay eggs! And do you know what is in such an egg? In it lies a basilisk! No one dares or can stand to look at such a monster. Human beings know it and now you know it too. Now you understand what I am capable of! What a fantastic creature I am!"

The cock flapped his wings, raised his red cockscomb, and crowed once more. All the hens and chickens were a little scared, and very thrilled that someone they knew so well should be such an incredibly important creature. They clucked and peeped so loud that the weathercock could hear them.

And he did; but he pretended that he hadn't, and didn't move. "Nonsense, all of it!" he said to himself. "Henyard roosters cannot lay eggs; and I can't be bothered to lay one. If I wanted to, I am sure I could, but the world is not worthy of an egg. Everything is tiresome, life is a bore! I can't even be bothered to sit here any longer!"

And at that moment the weathercock broke and fell down into the yard. It didn't hit the rooster and kill it. "Though that was its intention," declared all the hens.

Here is the moral of the story: "It is better to boast and crow than to be blasé and break."

## 99

## "Lovely"

The sculptor Hans Alfred, you know him, I am sure. We all know him. He received the gold medal when he graduated from the Art Academy, then he traveled to Italy and came home again. That was when he was young. Oh, he is still young, although he is at least ten years older now than he was then.

After his return he visited one of the smaller towns on Zealand. Everybody knew who he was and in his honor a party was given by one of the richer families of the town. Everyone who was anybody, or owned anything, was invited. It was an important event and the whole town knew about it without the town crier having mentioned it. Outside the house stood a group of apprentices and children—and a few of their parents, too—staring up at the curtained windows through which a festive glare shone. One might think that the night watchmen were having a party, so many people were there in the street. The spectators felt that they at least got a whiff of the amusements going on inside. And truly it was a grand party; after all, Mr. Alfred the sculptor was there.

He liked to talk, to tell about his travels, and everyone listened to him with pleasure and some with more than that. An elderly widow, whose husband had been a civil servant, was particularly impressed by the young man. Like a sponge she soaked up everything he said and asked for more. She was most naïve and unbelievably ignorant: a female Caspar Hauser.

"I wouldn't mind seeing Rome," she said. "It must be a pretty town. Why, everyone in the whole world visits it. Now describe Rome for us. What do you see when you enter the city gate?"

"It is not so easy to describe," said the young sculptor. "There is a great square and in the center of it stands an obelisk that is four thousand years old."

"An organist!" exclaimed the widow. She had never heard of an obelisk before.

Some of the other guests smiled, and others were about to laugh— the young man among them. But he didn't, for just at that moment he noticed two eyes, as blue as the sea, staring at him. They belonged to the daughter of the widow; and if one has such a daughter, it does not matter that one is a bit naïve and talkative. Mama was a gushing fountain of questions, her daughter was the fountain's beautiful nymph. She was lovely! There was something for a sculptor to look at and admire, he need not talk with her. And the young lady hardly ever opened her mouth.

"Has the Pope a big family?" asked Mama.

The young man answered as if the question had been just incorrectly phrased. "No, the Pope does not come from a large family."

"That is not what I mean!" said the old lady. "Does he have a wife and children?"

"The Pope does not dare marry," said the young man.

"I don't like that!" was the widow's verdict.

She could have spoken more cleverly and asked more intelligent questions, but if she had, would her daughter have leaned so close to her and looked at her with such a gentle and sweet smile?

Mr. Alfred spoke about the splendid colors of Italy, the pale blue mountains and the deep blue Mediterranean Sea. "Only in the color of the eyes of our women here in the north," he declared, "is that blueness surpassed." It was meant as allusion to the young lady's eyes, but she acted as if she had not understood it; and that, too, the sculptor found "lovely."

"Italy," sighed some of the guests.

"To travel," whispered others. "Lovely, lovely."

"When I win the fifty thousand silver marks in the lottery," exclaimed Mama, "then my daughter and I will travel. We will take you, Mr. Alfred, along as a guide. We will go abroad, the three of us. And we will take a few of our old friends along too." And then she nodded so gaily to everyone around her that each had a right to believe that she meant him.

"Yes, we will go to Italy. But not in any of the places where there are bandits. No, we will stick to Rome and the big highways where one is safe."

Her daughter sighed. Oh, how much can be expressed in a sigh, and how much can one imagine is being expressed in a sigh! The young sculptor found profound depth of feeling in it. The two lovely blue eyes hid within them all the treasures of the heart and spirit. Riches far greater than all the wealth of Rome. When he left the party he was lost; he had fallen in love with the young lady.

The widow's house was the place where you most often found Mr. Alfred. Everyone realized that it couldn't be because of Mama that he came, although she was the one who talked to him, so it had to be because of her daughter. She was called Kala. Her name was really Karen Malene, and by adding the two names together and subtracting a few letters, her pet name, Kala, had been invented. Lovely she was, though a bit lazy, some people said, for she never got up very early.

"She is used to that from childhood," explained her mother. "She has always been a Venus child and they tire easily. She sleeps a little late but that keeps her eyes bright."

What power there was in those eyes! Those sea-blue eyes! Still waters run deep. The young man felt their power. After all, he had run aground in those still waters. He talked and explained, and Mama asked the questions with the same ease as she had on their first meeting.

It was a pleasure to hear Mr. Alfred talk. He described Naples and told about the walks he had taken up to Vesuvius, and showed them pictures, in color, of the volcano erupting. Mama had never heard of a volcano before, nor ever imagined that such a thing could exist.

"God preserve us!" she said. "A mountain that spouts fire! Isn't it dangerous?"

"Whole towns have been buried by it," explained the young man, "Pompeii and Herculaneum."

"Oh, the poor wretched people! Did you see it happen?"

"No, but I will draw you a picture of one little eruption that I did see."

He took his sketch block and pencil and started to draw. Mama, who had just been looking at the very colorful pictures he had shown her, looked with surprise at the pale pencil drawing.

"But why is what's shooting up from it white?" she exclaimed.

At that moment Mr. Alfred's respect for Mama reached an all-time low. But soon, with the help of Kala, he understood that Mama just did not have much sense of color. And after all, what did that matter, when she had the best, the most beautiful thing in the whole world? She had Kala.

And Kala and Alfred became engaged, and that was not surprising. An announcement of the engagement was printed in the local newspaper, and Mama bought thirty copies of it so that she could send one to each of her friends. The young couple were very happy and so was Mama. She felt that now she was related to Thorvaldsen, the most famous Danish sculptor.

"After all, you are his successor," she said.

And for once Mr. Alfred thought she had said something clever. Kala did not say anything at all, but her eyes were bright, and she smiled so prettily, and the movements of her body were so graceful and lovely. Oh yes, lovely she was: lovely it cannot be repeated too often.

Alfred made two busts: one of his future mother-in-law and one of Kala. They were his models and they watched him form the soft clay with his hands.

"Is it for our sake that you do the simple work yourself?" asked the widow. "You might have hired someone to throw the clay together, then your hands wouldn't get dirty."

"It is necessary that I form it myself from the very beginning," said Alfred.

"I am sure that is very gallant of you," said Mama; and Kala pressed his clay-covered hand.

While he worked he explained to them his theory of why creation gave expression to the wonder of nature. Living matter, he said, was more important than dead, plants were above minerals, animals above plants, and man above animals. Spirit and beauty could be seen in form, and the sculptor revealed the human form in its perfection.

Kala was silent, although she seemed to sway a little in time with his thoughts and ideas. His future mother-in-law confessed openly:

"It is difficult to follow you! My thoughts walk a little slower, but I am holding my own and I am sure I will catch up."

The loveliness of Kala bound the young sculptor, it touched and fascinated him; it captured him. It was not only the single parts but all of Kala that was lovely. Her body, her glance, her mouth, even the movement of her fingers. That was Mr. Alfred's judgment; and he was a sculptor. He understood that sort of thing. He talked only about her, he thought only about her, the two of them had become one! In this manner silent Kala became talkative too, for Mr. Alfred talked enough for two, if not three.

That was the engagement, then came the wedding. There were bridemaids and gifts. Both were mentioned in the speech to the bridal couple.

Mama had put a bust of Thorvaldsen at the end of the table and draped her husband's old dressing gown around it. She wanted the famous sculptor to be among the guests; it was her own idea. Several songs had been written for the occasion, and innumerable toasts were drunk. It was a delightful wedding with a lovely bridal couple.

"Pygmalion got his Galatea," so ran one of the lines in one of the songs written for the occasion.

"That is mythology!" declared Mama-in-law.

The day after the wedding the young couple left for Copenhagen; there they were going to build their nest. Mama-in-law followed. She was to attend to the coarse part, she said. She was to run the household, Kala was just to sit in the doll's house.

Everything was new, bright, and lovely! There they sat, the three of them. And how did Mr. Alfred sit? Well, to explain it, one might use an old proverb: he sat as a bishop does in a goose's nest.

The magic of form had charmed him, he had looked at the beautiful decoration of the box without bothering to find out what was inside it. And that is a misfortune, a great misfortune in a marriage. When the gluing comes apart and the gilding wears off the casing, then one regrets the bargain. When you are out at a grand party, it is a horrible sensation to be aware that you have lost two of your suspender buttons and you can't depend upon your belt because you have forgotten to put one on. But what is even worse at such a party is to be aware that both your wife and your mother-in-law say one stupidity after another, while you are not certain that you can think up witty replies to counteract their foolishness.

Often the young couple would sit, hand in hand, and he would talk; she would only say a word every now and then, and they were always the same. The same little notes from the bell, the same melodies. Her girl friend Sophie, when she came for a visit, provided a breath of fresh air, spiritually speaking.

Sophie was not beautiful. She was not misshapen, her figure was a little "crooked," as Kala claimed. But this "crookedness" was not so great that it could be observed by anyone except Sophie's girl friends. She was a sensible and intelligent girl who was completely unaware that she might become dangerous in such company. She was a bit of fresh air in the dollhouse, as I have said; and they needed it, this they were all aware of. A change of air was needed, so the young couple and Mama-in-law set off for Italy.

"Thank God that we are home again," said both Mama and daughter when they returned the following year together with Mr. Alfred.

"It is not amusing to travel!" insisted Mama-in-law. "It is really very boring! Excuse me for being so frank. But I was bored a good deal of the time, even though I had my children along. And it is expensive! It is terribly expensive to travel. Then there are all the galleries and museums you have to visit. One is always running about. You have to see everything so you can answer all the questions people are going to ask when you get home. And what's the result? Everyone tells you that you missed the most beautiful one of all. I got tired of looking at those eternal madonnas; why, you ended up looking like one yourself."

"And the food one has to eat!" interrupted Kala.

"One can't get a decent bowl of soup," agreed Mama. "Foreigners don't know how to cook food!"

Kala was fatigued by the journey. She couldn't get over it, and that was the worst of it. Sophie came to help in the house; and she was a help.

"I have to admit it," said Mama-in-law. "Sophie knows how to run a house and she understands all that art business. She is what one might call educated beyond her position and fortune. And besides all that, she is really a very decent human being and very loyal." The latter was proven when Kala lay sick and grew daily weaker.

Where the casing is all, it must survive or all is over. The casing did not last: Kala died.

"She was lovely," said Mama. "More beautiful than all those

Greeks and Romans; they were always missing their heads or arms. Beauty has to be whole, and Kala was whole!"

Alfred wept and Mama wept, and both of them dressed in black. Black was very becoming on Mama; therefore she wore it longer than Alfred. She mourned and soon had another cause for grief! Her son-in-law married again. He took Sophie, the girl who was a bit "crooked."

"He went from one extreme to another!" said his former mother-in-law. "From the loveliest to the ugliest. He has forgotten my Kala! There is no loyalty in men. My husband was different! But then he died before me."

"Pygmalion got his Galatea," said Alfred. "That is a quote from a song that was written for my first wedding. And it was true, I had fallen in love with a beautiful statue, and it became alive in my arms. But that kindred soul whom heaven sends us—one of the angels, who can sympathize with us, understand our thoughts, and when we are downhearted lift us up—I have not won until now. You, Sophie! Not so beautiful, not so glorious, but pretty enough, lovelier than one deserves. You came and taught the sculptor that his works are only clay, dust; only an impression of the hidden kernel inside one, the kernel that one should seek. Poor Kala, our life together was merely a journey. If we meet up there, where all the souls meet in eternal sympathy, we will be almost strangers."

"That was not very kind to say," admonished Sophie. "It wasn't very Christian. Up there where no one is to marry and all the souls meet in sympathy, as you phrased it, up there where all unfold themselves fully, her soul may ring with a sweeter and purer tone than mine. And you! You will say again, as you did when you first saw her and fell in love, 'Lovely, lovely!'"

## 100

## A Story from the Dunes

This is a story from the dunes of Jutland, but it begins far from there, in Spain. The sea connects these two distant places. Imagine yourself in Spain. It is warm and beautiful; here the scarlet pomegranate flowers bloom amid dark green laurel trees. From the mountains a cool, refreshing breeze descends into the valley, where orange trees grow; it passes through the town and enters the Moorish palaces with their golden cupolas and colorfully painted walls.

Children are walking in procession in the street; with wax candles in their hands they are following golden, embroidered banners. High above them is the great arch of clear sky with its countless stars. The sound of singing and of castanets can be heard. The young girls and boys are dancing under the flowering acacia trees. On the carved marble step sits a beggar. He is quenching his thirst with a watermelon. He has slept his life away. And truly, this world is like a dream, and all it asks is that you abandon yourself to it. That was exactly what the young married couple did. They were the children of fortune and had been given by God all that one can desire: health, a happy disposition, wealth, and worldly honor.

"We are as happy as anyone can possibly be," they said, both of them, and they meant it from the bottom of their hearts. There was one joy that they had not yet tasted and that they would not experience before God had sent them a child, a son whose body and soul would mirror their own.

That happy child would be greeted with shouts of joy and be

brought up with the greatest care and love. He would be given all that wealth and a famous name can give.

Like one everlasting feast did the days glide by for this young couple.

"Life is given to us by the grace of love. How incredible it is!" exclaimed the young wife. "That gift, the result of our happiness, shall live and grow, and that through all eternity. It is beyond my comprehension."

"But maybe that is human presumption," said her husband. "Is it not pride that makes us believe that we shall live eternally? Become like God! That was what the snake promised Eve, and he was the master of lies."

"Do you doubt that there is a life after this?" asked the young woman, and for the first time a shadow crossed her sun-filled world.

"Our religion and the priests promise it," he answered. "But when I feel so overpoweringly my own happiness and good fortune, I cannot help but wonder if it is not presumption to ask for more—for eternal happiness. Has not so much been given us that we ought to be satisfied?"

"Yes, we have received much," replied his wife. "But what about the thousands for whom life has been a harsh and cruel trial? How many are destined to know only poverty, infamy, sickness, and misfortune. The blessings of life are too unequally divided. If there is no life after this one, then God would not be just."

"The beggar may experience pleasures as great as a king's," smiled the young man. "And what about the poor donkey whose life is work, hunger, and beatings until it dies; do you think it knows and understands its own wretched lot? And if it does, can it not claim that it has been unjustly treated and demand another life as a more enviable creature?"

"Christ has said that in his mansion there are many rooms," replied the young wife. "The kingdom of heaven is as unending as God's love is. The animals, too, are His creation and I do not think that any life is ever lost; they, too, will receive the bliss, the happiness, that they need."

"I need nothing more than this world, it is enough," said her husband, and put his arms around his loving wife.

They sat on the open balcony. He lit a cigarillo. The cool evening air was filled with the perfume of orange blossoms and carnations.

From the street came music and the sound of castanets; above in the sky a thousand stars sparkled. His young wife looked at him, and her eyes were filled with love, love as eternal as life.

"A moment like this," he said, "is well worth being born for! To feel and appreciate it, and then, to disappear!" He smiled and his wife shook her finger at him, admonishing him playfully. The cloud that had passed between them was gone, they were happy.

Everything seemed to yield in order that this young couple should advance in honor and glory. There were changes, but only physical ones—in place, not in pleasure. The young man had been appointed by his king as ambassador to the imperial court of Russia. The position was one of honor, and by birth and education he had the right to it. Wealth he had, too, and his marriage had made him even richer. His wife was the daughter of a very wealthy respected merchant. One of the largest of his father-in-law's ships was bound for Stockholm; orders were given that it should sail the young couple to St. Petersburg.

The cabin for the young couple was royally furnished. Everything was soft and lovely; the pillows were covered with silk and there were thick carpets on the floor.

There is a Danish folk song called "The Son of the King of England." This tells of a prince who sailed on a magnificent ship whose anchor was inlaid with gold and whose ropes were made of silk. The ship that sailed from Spain might have reminded a Dane of that song. Here were the same splendor and the same dream as they embarked:

God, let all of us our happiness find.

The wind blew them quickly away from the Spanish coast; they had only a brief parting glance of their home. Soon they would reach the goal of their journey. The voyage should not take much more than two weeks, but they were becalmed. The ocean was as motionless as glass and, like a mirror, it reflected the stars of the heavens. Every evening there was a party in the luxurious cabin.

Still, they wished the wind would blow, especially in the right direction. But every time the calm finally was broken the wind was always against them. Two months went by before the wind blew fair from the southwest. By then they were midway between Scotland

and Jutland. The wind gathered force and blew a storm, just as in the old song about "The Son of the King of England":

> From dark clouds blew the wind,
> No shelter could they find.
> They let go their anchors in despair.
> Toward Denmark blew the raging air.

The story we are telling took place many years ago, when Christian VII had sat but a short time on the Danish throne. Much of the countryside has changed since then; lakes and peat bogs have become fruitful meadows, and parts of the great moors of Jutland are under the plow. In the shelter of the houses, apple trees and roses grow, but they are small and crooked, for the west wind is a hard master. If one visits the west coast of Jutland, it is still easy to dream oneself back to times long before the reign of Christian VII. The great brown moorland has not changed, and it stretches for miles and miles. The grave mounds of the Viking chieftains can be seen from afar, and the sandy roads are hardly more than wheel tracks winding their way along. As one approaches the sea, the little streams and brooks broaden to form marshland, and by the time they empty themselves in the fjord they are almost rivers. At the shore rise the dunes, like a miniature mountain range; facing the sea there are clay cliffs, which the ocean year by year eats, taking giant mouthfuls each time there is a storm and changing the contours of the coast. There the scenery looks the same today as it did years ago when the two young children of fortune sailed on their splendid ship.

It was one of the last days in September: a sunny warm Sunday. Along the fjord of Nissum one could hear the church bells ringing. In this area all the churches are built of granite. Each one stands like a cliff; the sea can break against them and yet they will survive. Most of them have no tower, and the bells hang from an oaken crossbeam of a structure that stands beside the church, but looks like a gallows.

The service was over and the congregation were coming out of the church; the churchyard was barren then as it is today, not a bush or tree grew there. No flowers are laid on the graves. Little tiny mounds show where the dead are buried; and rough, stiff, wind-blown grass covers all the graves. A few of them have little markers; these are always the same: a piece of wood shaped like a coffin, with a name cut into it.

The wood has been gathered in that "forest" that grows on the west coast: the raging sea. There can be found beams and planks already cut and planed, and the sea supplies both firewood and building materials for the poor fishermen. That morning a woman was standing deep in thought in front of such a wooden grave marker. It was a child's grave. The western wind and salt air had already disintegrated the wood so much you could hardly read the name that had been cut into it. Her husband came up to her; they did not speak to each other, but he took her hand and together they walked across the moorland toward the dunes.

"That was a good sermon," said the man. "Yes, if one did not have God, then one would be alone and have nothing at all."

"Yes," agreed his wife. "He gives us joy and He gives us sorrows and that is His right!—Tomorrow our little boy would have been five, if we had been allowed to keep him."

"Mourning won't bring him back," said her husband. "After all, he has escaped so much. He is where we have to pray to be allowed to go."

They walked on in silence. It was an old conversation, the kind that never ends. Their house was among the dunes. Suddenly from the top of a sandy hill, where no lyme grass grew, smoke appeared to rise. It was a puff of wind that was whirling the fine sand up into the air. Another gust of wind came; a little stronger than the first, it made the codfish, which were hung up to dry, bang against the walls of the cottage. Then everything was calm again. The sun was baking down.

The couple disappeared into the house, to change from their Sunday clothes to weekday ones. Then they hurried across the dunes, which looked like gigantic waves. The sharp, blue-green blades of the lyme grass gave a little color to the white landscape. When they arrived at the beach they found some of their neighbors already there; together they pulled the boats farther up on the sand. Now the wind had really begun to blow. It was cold and, as they made their way back across the dunes, sand and tiny stones were blown into their faces. Out at sea the waves had white tops, and the wind blew the spray from the surf far inland.

Toward evening the storm gathered force. It sounded as if a whole army of desperate spirits were moaning and groaning up in the sky; so loudly did they sing that it drowned out the noise of the surf breaking. The sand beat like rain upon the windowpanes of the little cottage, and every once in a while an especially violent gust of wind shook the walls, as if the wind thought it were master here on land as well as on the sea. Outside everything was dark; toward midnight the moon would be up.

The sky was cloudless, but the storm blew worse than ever out over the dark sea. The fisherman and his wife had long ago gone to bed, but they had not closed their eyes. It was no weather to sleep in.

Someone knocked on the window. The door was opened, and a voice shouted: "There is a big ship aground on the outermost of the sandbanks."

Both man and wife jumped out of bed and put on their clothes.

The moon had come out so that one would have been able to see a little, if only one could have kept one's eyes open, but the wind whipped sand into them. So furiously was the wind blowing that when they came to the top of dunes they could not stand up but had to crawl on all fours. Here the foam from the surf flew like swan's-down through the air. The sea looked like one mass of boiling turbulence; one had to have keen sight to be able to make out the wreckage. A beautiful two-masted ship she had been.

Just as the fisherman and his wife joined the others, who were gathered as near to the water as they dared to go, a giant wave lifted the ship across the first sandbank; there were three in all. Now she stood solidly on the ground. It was impossible even to think of rescue. The sea was much too rough; wave after wave broke over the ship. Those on shore thought they could hear the people on board screaming in terror, in fear of death. Now that the ship was closer they could watch the useless efforts of the doomed crew as they ran back and forth in senseless activity. A great wave broke over the ship and took along a mast and the bowsprit. Another lifted the stern up high; at that moment two figures could be seen hurling themselves into the sea. They disappeared.

A huge wave rolled up toward the dunes, broke, and retreated, leaving a body on the sand. It was a woman, or the corpse of one. Some of the fishermen's wives dragged her up on the dry sand. They turned her over; she seemed to be still alive. She was carried up to the fisherman's cottage.

"So beautiful and delicate," one of the women muttered. "She must be some highborn lady."

They put her to bed. Here were no linen sheets, only a woolen blanket, but that was good and warm. She opened her eyes, but a fever had hold of her mind and her body; she did not seem to remember what had happened or understand where she was. But maybe that was just as well, for that which was dearest in life to her rested at the bottom of the sea. Only she had not had the same fate as the people in the song, who had sailed with "The Son of the King of England":

> The proud ship into small pieces split.
> How could one look without pity on it?

Wreckage drifted up on the shore, but she was the only survivor. The wind kept on howling and screaming as it ran up the coast of Jutland. The woman slept for a little while, but then she cried out in pain. She opened her lovely eyes and spoke a few words, but in a strange language that no one could understand.

She had suffered and fought, not only for her own life but for that of the child within her. The infant was born, that child who should have slept in a beautiful cradle, on embroidered sheets, in a house of wealth. That boy, whose birth should have been a cause of great joy and whose life would have been one of plenty, was now to live in a poor fisherman's cottage, and not even receive a kiss from his own mother, because God had decided that thus it should be.

The wife of the fisherman laid the child next to the woman who had borne it, next to her heart, but it no longer beat. She was dead. That child who should have been suckled by fortune and wealth the sea had thrown out into the world, to try poverty and know the lot of misery.

Again one is reminded of a verse from the old folk song.

> A tear ran down the young prince's cheek.
> By Christ, I fear that death us will seek,
> For we will be wrecked on Bovbjerg!
> If only there Master Bugge lived and reigned
> We need not fear that our blood be drained.

The ship had been wrecked a little south of Nissum Fjord, on a beach that once, long ago, Master Bugge had called his own. But that period of history when those who were shipwrecked had to fear not only the waves but the people who lived as robbers on the west coast as well, had long since passed. Now the shipwrecked sailor would meet help and charity whichever stretch of the coast of Jutland misfortune threw him up upon. The dying mother and the newborn child would have been kindly treated no matter where the wind had blown them. Though no place would the child have been more welcome than in the cottage where the wife still mourned the death of her own little child, who on that very day would have been five years old, "if God had permitted him to live."

No one knew who the strange foreign woman was or from which land she had come. The wreckage did not solve the mystery.

No letter came to the house of the rich merchant in Spain; no message told of the young couple's fate. They had not arrived at their destination; heavy storms had raged in the area for weeks. Finally, a month later, word was brought: "The ship was totally destroyed, all on board lost their lives."

But in the fisherman's cottage among the dunes there was a little boy again. Where God supplies food for two, a third mouth will find something to eat. Near the ocean there are always fish. The infant was named Jurgen.

"I think he is Jewish," said some. "He looks so dark."

"He could just as well be an Italian or a Spaniard," said the minister.

To the fisherman's wife it did not matter which of the three peoples her son had belonged to. He was hers now and had been baptized in her own church. The boy thrived. His noble blood gained warmth and strength from the dried fish and potatoes of the poor. The Danish language as it is spoken on the west coast of Jutland became his native tongue. The pomegranate seed from Spain had become a lyme-grass plant on the dunes that face the North Sea. These things can and do happen to people. To this, his new home, the roots of his life—long as the years—would cling. He would experience hunger and cold, the want and need of the poor, but he would also have his part of their joys.

One's childhood has its periods of happiness which shine with a special light that lasts a lifetime. Jurgen loved to play and he had a whole beach miles wide filled with toys. A great mosaic of colorful stones: some as red as coral, others as yellow as amber, and still others as white and round as birds' eggs; they were every shade of color, and all worn smooth by the ocean. Even the dried skeletons of fishes, the seaweed with its strange forms were things to play with.

The boy was clever, there was no doubt about that. Rich gifts lay dormant in him. He could remember all the songs and stories he heard, and he could make pretty pictures of ships out of shells and small stones that looked nice enough to hang on a wall. His foster mother said that he could carve a stick into any shape that he chose. He could sing, too; he had a lovely voice and learned a melody as soon as he had heard it. There were many strings in that little chest that might have been plucked so they could have been heard all over the world, had he not been born in a poor fisherman's cottage on the west coast of Denmark.

One day a ship was stranded and a box of rare flower bulbs drifted to shore. Some of them the fishermen cooked, others lay rotting in the sand. None of them was ever allowed to fulfill its mission in life. The beauty, the gay colors within them, were never given a chance to bloom. Would Jurgen fare better? The bulbs were soon destroyed; he had years of trial before him.

Neither Jurgen nor anyone else who lived on the coast ever thought that their days were monotonous and alike. There was always something to do, something to look at. The ocean itself was like a big book, and each day a new leaf was turned. Storms, dead calm, breeze, or swells from a storm far away: on no two days was the sea ever alike. Every stranding was a high point that children never forgot; but also the Sunday service was festive. What Jurgen liked best of all were visits from his foster mother's uncle. He had a small farm near Bovbjerg but lived mainly from catching and selling eels. He came in a red-painted wagon with a chest on top of it that looked like a coffin; this had blue and white tulips painted on it, and in it he kept his eels. Two steers pulled this strange vehicle, and Jurgen was allowed to ride in it.

The eelman was a clever fellow and a merry guest. He always brought a little barrel of schnapps with him and gave everyone a drink. If there weren't glasses enough, then coffee cups would do. Even when Jurgen was still a little boy he was given a few drops in his mother's thimble. "It helps you to hold onto the fat, slimy eels," his uncle explained. Then he would always tell the same story and, if people laughed at it, he would repeat it. This is something that most very talkative people have a habit of doing. Since Jurgen, throughout his youth and early manhood, often used expressions from this story, we will have to suffer through hearing it:

"There were some eels living in a stream. One day all of the mother eel's daughters asked for permission to swim upstream. 'Don't go too far, or the wicked eelman will catch you, every one,' their mother warned. But the eels swam as far as they pleased; and of the eight who had set out, only three came home. 'We had just stepped outside the door,' the three wailed, 'when the wicked eel catcher came and killed our five sisters.' 'They will come back,' said the mother eel. 'No,' cried the sisters, 'for the evil eelman skinned them, cut them in pieces, and fried them.' 'They will come back!' repeated their mother. 'But he ate them,' the little eels wept. 'They will come back,' the mother eel insisted. 'But he drank a schnapps when he finished eating them,' the sisters said. 'Oh . . . oh . . . then they will never come back!' wept their mother, 'for a schnapps buries an eel.'

"And that is why," said the eel merchant, "one always has to drink a schnapps when one eats an eel."

This particular silly story became important in Jurgen's life. It was a family joke and that is not always appreciated by strangers. He, too, begged to be allowed outside the door, to swim a little up the stream. He wanted to sail on a ship, but his mother answered as the mother eel had: "Out in the world there are many wicked people who might hunt my little eel."

But he did go on a short journey to the world outside the dunes. Four whole days, a magic time, in which the happiest hours of his childhood were concentrated. All the beauty of Jutland, all the happiness of his home, seemed revealed and symbolized in that short time. He was going to attend a party. True, it was a wake, a funeral, but that was a kind of party too.

A wealthy member of the family had died, a farmer whose farm lay to the east, "and two points north," from their home, as his father described it. His parents had been invited to the funeral, and they decided to take Jurgen along.

From the dunes they walked across the moor and the peat bogs until they came to the green meadows near Skaerum Stream. Here the mother eel lived with her daughters, those that the wicked eel hunter caught and cut into pieces. But often man does not treat his fellow men much kindlier.

Master Bugge, the knight mentioned in the old song, had finally been killed by evil men. But Master Bugge himself, who in the song is described as good, what kind of a man had he been? Jurgen and his parents were standing on the very spot where his castle had once stood, near the point where Skaerum Stream runs out into the fjord of Nissum. According to one legend, he had wanted to kill the man who had constructed his castle. As the master builder was leaving, after the heavy walls and the proud tower were finished, Master Bugge had called one of his servants to him and told him to ride after the master builder. "Before you catch up with him," instructed Master Bugge, "call out as loud as you can, 'The tower leans! The tower leans!' If he turns around to look, then kill him and take the money I have paid him and bring it back to me. But if he does not look back, then let him go in peace."

The servant did as he was told. But the master builder had not turned around. He had only said, "The tower is straight; it does not lean. But one day a man who wears a blue cape will come from the west and he will make the tower lean." And it happened, a hundred years later, during a terrible storm, the North Sea broke in over the land and destroyed the castle and the tower fell. Predbjoern Gyldenstjerne owned the castle then, and he built a new castle on higher ground, above the meadows. That one is still standing; it is called Norre Vosborg.

During the long winter evenings Jurgen had often heard about the places he was seeing now. His foster parents had told him about the castle with its double moat, trees and bushes, its ramparts overgrown with ferns. What Jurgen found most beautiful of all were the tall linden trees that reached up to the roof of the castle and filled the air with the sweetest fragrance. In the northwestern part of the garden there was a tree that seemed to be covered by snow. It was a flowering elderberry, the first that Jurgen had ever seen. The memory of this and the linden trees, the child's soul kept for the sake of the old man he would one day become.

The journey continued a little more comfortably; they met some other people who had been invited to the funeral and they were offered a ride. True, all three of them had to sit in the back of a wagon on a little wooden chest, but they thought it was better than having to walk. Here began the great heath, the immense moor that stretches over most of central Jutland. The road was bumpy and filled with holes; the steer that pulled the wagon went none too fast. When they spied some green grass they stopped and grazed.

The sun shone warmly down upon them, and the air was clear. They could see far. Out toward the horizon a column of smoke rose. It twirled and danced in the still air.

"It is Loke driving his sheep," said someone. The remark was made for Jurgen's sake. And truly, the boy felt that he was driving right into a fairy-tale country, and yet it was real.

Like a costly carpet stretching in all directions lay the heath. The juniper bushes and scrub oaks made green bouquets amid the blooming heather. The place seemed so inviting for a boy to run across, but the grownups warned Jurgen about the vipers. They also talked about the many wolves that once had lived there; the district was still called "wolves' castle." The old man who was driving told stories from his father's youth, which had been long before the last of the wolves were killed. The horses and the wolves used to fight. His father had come out one morning and found a horse still stamping on the dead body of a wolf, but one of the horse's front legs had been chewed to the bone.

Far too short was the road across the heath; and far too soon, thought Jurgen, did they arrive at the house of mourning. There were guests everywhere: both inside the farmhouse and in the fields. Wagons, carriages, and carts crowded the yard. Oxen and horses grazed together, sharing the meager grass there was. Behind the farm there were some great sandy dunes like the ones by the sea. How had they come here, fifteen miles inland? The wind had moved them here; there was also a legend about that.

Psalms were sung and some tears shed, but only by a few old people; otherwise everything was most amusing. There was plenty of food and drink; lovely fat eels were fried every day, and properly "buried" in schnapps as the eelman had said they should be. Here indeed his advice was followed.

Jurgen was inside, Jurgen was outside, Jurgen was everywhere. By the third day he felt as at home here on the heath as on the dunes by the sea. The heath was richer. Among the heather grew crowberries and blueberries, big and sweet to eat. Jurgen's feet were blue from their juice.

Viking graves were spread out over the heath, little hills with big stones on top of them. And columns of smoke danced in the air. They came from fires on the heather; during the night you could see their red glow.

On the fourth day the funeral feast was over and they had to leave the inland dunes for the dunes by the sea.

"Ours are the real dunes," declared Jurgen's foster father. "These serve no purpose."

And they talked about how it had happened that there were dunes here, so far inland. The explanation was very logical. Long, long ago down on the beach a body had been found; the fishermen had carried it up to the churchyard and given it a Christian burial. But that very day the wind began to blow and the sand to drift in clouds inland, the sea thundered against the dunes, there was a storm. One man in the district, who was wiser than the rest, suggested that they open the grave to see whether the man they had buried was sucking his thumb, for, if he was, then he was not a human being but a merman, and a merman belonged to the sea and it would try to get him back! The grave was opened and there the buried man lay sucking his thumb. Quickly he was put on an oxcart and driven across the moors as fast as if the oxen had been stung by gadflies. He was thrown into the sea and then the storm was over. But the inland dunes are still there. All this Jurgen heard and later remembered from the happiest days of his childhood, the four days when he had attended a funeral.

It had been lovely to see a different countryside and meet new people. But he was to travel much farther than that. He was not yet fourteen, still a child, when he persuaded his foster parents to let him go to sea. He was to discover what the world is like, try its storms and rough weather, and learn what it means to be everyone's servant and have to bend to the will of brutal and evil men. He was a cabin boy! Half starved, beaten, and mistreated. His noble Spanish blood rebelled; inside he boiled with rage; hard words and curses came to his lips but not across them. He was like the eel: flayed, cut to pieces, and put in the frying pan.

"I will come back," a voice said within him. The ship sailed for Spain, the country of his parents, and he was even to see the town where they had lived in wealth and bliss. But he knew nothing about them, and his rich family knew even less about him.

The wretched cabin boy was not even allowed to go ashore except on the last day they lay in the harbor, and that was only because he was needed to carry food and vegetables from the market place to the ship.

There stood Jurgen, dressed in rags that looked as if they had been washed in a ditch and dried in a chimney. This was the first time that the boy from the dunes had seen a real city. How tall the houses were, how narrow the streets, and so filled with people. Everyone pushed and shoved. It was a maelstrom of human beings. There were peasants, monks, soldiers, and just ordinary citizens of the town, and how noisy it was! People screamed and shouted; bells rang —not only in the churches but on the harnesses of the donkeys and mules as well. Someone was singing and someone else was hammering, for the artisans used the sidewalks as their working place. It was terribly hot and the air was heavy. Jurgen felt as though he had been put right into a baker's oven, and one filled with insects, at that. Flies and bees and dung beetles flew everywhere.

Jurgen had no idea where he was or in which direction he was walking. He looked up. He was standing before a cathedral. He could see into the cool, dark interior, and he smelled the odor of incense. Even the poorest beggars seemed to dare walk in there. The sailor who had taken Jurgen along as a donkey, to carry what was bought, was making his way into the cathedral. Jurgen entered the holy place; he stared at the colorful paintings on the golden background. On an altar, among flowers and candles, stood a statue of the Virgin with the little child Jesus in her arms. The priests, wearing their ceremonial clothes, sang mass, and choir boys in long robes swung silver censers. The glory, the magnificence of what he saw overwhelmed Jurgen; the church, the faith of his parents, touched a chord within his soul and his eyes filled with tears.

From the cathedral they went on to the market place and he was given some baskets of vegetables to take back to the ship. They were heavy and the road back was long; on the way he rested outside a palace, with marble pillars, broad staircases, and statues. He leaned his burdens against its wall, but a uniformed lackey threatened him with a silver-tipped cane. Jurgen got up and went on—he who was the heir, the grandchild of the house; but neither Jurgen nor the servant knew that.

He returned to the ship, there to receive more beatings, more hard words and curses, and too little sleep and too much work. But then he had tried that, too. It is said that it is good for one to suffer in one's youth. This may be, but only if manhood and old age have better things to offer.

The voyage was over, the ship was back in Denmark, lying in Ringkøbing Harbor. Jurgen packed his clothes and walked back to his home on the dunes. His foster mother had died while he was away.

A hard and cruel winter followed. Snowstorms raged across the land. One could hardly stand upright outside. How strangely the rain, wind, and sun are distributed in this world. Such icy coldness here in the north, and in Spain too much of the burning sunshine. Yet on a clear frosty winter day, when Jurgen saw flocks of swans fly across Nissum Fjord toward Norre Vosborg, he felt that here one breathed more freely; and after all, summer did come here too. He remembered how the landscape had looked when the heather bloomed and the blueberries were ripe; he recalled the time he had seen the tall linden trees and the flowering elderberry at Norre Vosborg. And he thought, "Next summer I will go there again."

Spring came and the fishing began. Jurgen helped his foster father. The boy had grown a lot during the last year. He did his work well, he was a lively lad, and he could swim better than anyone else. Often when he played in the sea the older men would warn him to be careful of the mackerel, for it was said that if a swimmer met a school of mackerel they would drag him down into the water, drown him, and eat him. But that was not to be Jurgen's fate.

In a neighboring house on the dunes lived a boy named Morton. He and Jurgen had become friends. They hired themselves out on the same ship; both of them sailed to Norway, and afterward for a voyage to Holland as well. Never had a hard word passed between them, but troubles can arise even between the best of friends, especially if one of them has a temper. It is easy to make a gesture one does not mean, and that is what Jurgen did one day. The two of them had got into an argument while they sat on the cabin roof eating out of the same earthenware dish. Jurgen had an open jackknife in his hand that he had been using to eat with; now he lifted it as if he were going to attack his friend. Jurgen's face was pale as death and there was fury in his eyes.

"Oh, are you one of those who will use a knife," was all Morton said.

No sooner were the words spoken than Jurgen lowered his hand with the knife in it. He ate his food in silence, then he went back to his work. When his duties were over he walked up to Morton and said, "Hit me in the face! I deserve it! I have a pot inside me that sometimes boils over."

"Forget it," said Morton, and after that they were better friends than they had been before. Yes, when they returned to Jutland and told about all that had happened to them, they even mentioned this incident. "Jurgen can boil over," said Morton, "but he is a good and honest pot anyway."

They were both young and strong, but Jurgen was the more agile of the two.

In Norway the farmers, in summer, take their cattle up into the mountains, and young boys and girls, who tend the animals for their parents, live up there in little houses. On the west coast of Jutland the fishermen, in early spring, also live in huts. By the sea, they construct tiny hovels out of driftwood, peat, and heather and stay in them during the weeks when the fishing is best. Each of the men has what is called a "bait girl"; her job is to put the bait on the hooks, make food, and bring a mug of warm beer down to the beach when the men return, wet and cold, from fishing. Since they also carried the catch up to the huts and cleaned the fish, the "bait girls" had lots of work to do.

Jurgen, his father, and a couple of other fishermen and their bait girls lived in one hut; Morton slept in another nearby.

Among the girls there was one called Else, whom Jurgen had known from early childhood. They were good friends and had the same opinions about many things, but in appearance they were opposites. He was brown-skinned, and she was white, had yellow hair, and eyes as blue as the sea in summer.

One day as they were walking along the beach, hand in hand, she said to him, "Jurgen, there is something I want to tell you. Let me be your bait girl, for you are like a brother to me. Morton and I are sweethearts but don't tell anyone else about it."

To Jurgen it felt as if the sand were moving beneath his feet, but he said not a word. Finally he nodded, which was the same as saying yes—no more needed to be said.

Suddenly he hated Morton; and the longer he thought and brooded over it, the more certain he felt that Morton had stolen Else away from him, though, in truth, before she told him that she loved Morton, he had never thought that he was in love with her. But now he was convinced that he had lost what was dearest to him: Else.

If the weather is rough when the fishermen return, it is exciting to see the boats pass the sandbanks. One of the men stands in the bow of the ship, while the others all sit with their oars in hand, prepared to row. Just before they reach the first sandbank, they hold the boat still in the water. The man facing the sea is waiting for the biggest wave; when he sees it, he gives a sign, and the rest of the men row with all their might, and the boat rides the wave across the sandbank. Sometimes the wave lifts the boat so high that you can see the keel. Once across, the boat slips down and is hidden by the great wave so completely that an onlooker might fear that it was lost. A moment later, like a sea monster, it climbs a new wave, the oars moving as if they were weird, thin little legs. The other two sandbanks are crossed in the same manner. At last, as the keel touches the sand of the beach the fishermen leap out of the boat and push it, with the help of the waves, as far up on shore as they can.

A wrong judgment, a moment's hesitation, and the boat does not ride across the bar but is thrown by the wave down upon it, instead; and then all is lost.

"Then everything would be over for me and for Morton as well," thought Jurgen. They were returning from fishing. His foster father was sick, he was running a fever. Just as they drew near the first of the three sandbanks that they had to cross, Jurgen jumped into the bow of the ship and said, "Let me get us across!" He looked out over the sea and cast a glance, too, at Morton's face; his friend sat at his oar with the other men, ready to row as hard as he could when Jurgen gave the order.

A big wave was on its way. Jurgen looked at his foster father's white suffering face and gave the order just at the right moment, and the boat shot over the sandbank and was safe. But the evil thought he had had remained in his mind and poisoned his blood. Every little thread of bitterness that he could recall from the very beginning of their friendship he saved, but there were not enough of them to twine a rope, so he tried to forget about it. But that Morton had "spoiled his life" he was convinced, and that was enough reason for hating him. A few of the other fishermen noticed Jurgen's ill will, but Morton didn't, he was as usual, very helpful and very talkative—annoyingly so.

Jurgens' foster father was put to bed, and a week later it became his deathbed. Jurgen inherited the cottage on the dunes; it was not much, but still it was something and, at least, more than Morton owned.

"Now you won't have to hire yourself out to strangers but can stay here with us," said one of the older fishermen.

Jurgen had not even thought about that possibility; he had been thinking about seeing a little more of the world. The eel catcher had an uncle up in the north of Jutland. He was not only a fisherman but a merchant and owned a small schooner. Everyone said that he was such a good and honest old man that it was a pleasure to be in his service. That Skagen was as far away from his home as it is possible to get and still stay in Jutland, did not make it less attractive to Jurgen. He wanted to leave right away, for in two weeks Morton and Else were to be married.

One of the older fishermen tried to stop Jurgen. "Why go away now, when you have a house of your own? After all, that might make Else change her mind."

Jurgen did not answer; he merely mumbled something that could not be understood. To his surprise, later that day the old man came to his home. Else was with him. She said little, but what she said could not be misunderstood.

"You have a house, and that must be reckoned!"

"Now or on the Day of Reckoning?" Jurgen exclaimed.

Great waves rise and break on the ocean, but sometimes even greater waves exist within the human heart. Many thoughts passed through Jurgen's mind and, like the waves on the ocean, some were big and some were small. At last he asked Else, "If Morton had a house as good as mine, whom would you marry then?"

"Morton will never get a house of his own," she replied.

"But imagine that he has," insisted Jurgen.

"Then I would take Morton, for it is he I love. But you can't live on love."

Jurgen thought about it the whole night. Something within him— he did not know himself what it was, only that it was stronger than his love and desire for Else—made him go to Morton the next day. He had carefully thought out every word he was going to say; he offered his friend the house at the lowest possible price, and on the very best and easiest conditions. He explained that he preferred to see a bit of the world. Else kissed Jurgen on the mouth when she heard it, although that was not because she loved him but because she loved Morton.

Jurgen had decided to leave early the next morning. Late in the evening, he suddenly felt a desire to see Morton once more. On his way he met the old fisherman who had warned him against leaving. "Morton must have a duckbill sewn in his pants, the way the girls are crazy about him," he said. That kind of talk did not please Jurgen; he bade the old man good night. As he approached the house where Morton lived he could hear loud voices coming from inside. Morton was not alone. Jurgen could not make up his mind what to do; he did not want to meet Else, and the more he thought about it the less he desired to have Morton thank him once more for what he had done, so he turned around and walked home.

The next morning before sunrise he made a bundle of his belongings, packed some food, and he was ready. He walked along the beach; that was faster than the sandy roads, and shorter, too, for he wanted to visit the eel catcher who lived near Bovbjerg on his way.

There was no wind, the ocean was deep blue and completely still. Spread out on the damp sand were shells: the toys of his childhood. As he walked he heard them crack and crumble under his feet. Suddenly his nose began to bleed. It wasn't anything really, but such things can become important. A couple of drops of blood fell on his sleeve. He washed it off and managed to stop his nosebleed. Later he felt that the slight loss of blood had done him good, he felt happy and lighthearted. A solitary flower bloomed on the beach. He picked it and stuck it in his hat. Free and easy, he would face the world. "I am just going outside the door," he said to himself, remembering the story of the eels. "Beware of the wicked eel catcher, who will flay you and cut you to pieces and fry you," he repeated, and laughed out loud. He felt confident that he would get through his life with his skin on his back, for courage is a good weapon.

The sun was already high in the sky when he came to the narrow channel that connects Nissum Fjord with the sea. Far behind him he saw some men on horseback. They were riding fast, but Jurgen did not give them a thought—they did not concern him.

He had reached the place on the shore of the fjord where there was a ferryman who rowed travelers to the other side. Jurgen waved his arm and called, and a few moments later he was on board the little boat. When they reached the middle of the narrow channel the riders had arrived at the landing. They shouted and screamed and shook their fists. Jurgen could not understand what they wanted, but he did hear them shout: "In the name of the law!" He told the ferryman to turn back, and he himself took one of the oars. No sooner had they touched the shore than the men jumped into the boat, grabbed Jurgen, and tied his hands behind him.

"You are going to pay with your life for the evil deed you have done!" they shouted, and congratulated each other on having caught Jurgen.

What he was accused of was nothing less than murder! Morton had been found with a knife wound in his neck. The old fisherman had told of his meeting with Jurgen late the night before, and the story of how he had threatened Morton once before with a knife everyone knew—he had told it himself. No, there was no doubt in the minds of the people who had captured him: Jurgen was the murderer. But now that they had caught him they were in doubt as to what to do with him. They ought to take him to the jail in Ringkøbing but that was far away. They borrowed the ferryman's boat and rowed across the fjord; the wind was against them and it took them half an hour to reach the point where Skaerum Stream runs into the fjord. From there it was no distance to Norre Vosborg—the castle with its moat and defenses—where one of the men had a brother who worked as an overseer. He suggested that they might get permission to put Jurgen in the dungeon until the young man could be taken to Ringkøbing. It was the same dungeon that the gypsy, Tall Margrethe, had been locked up in before she was executed.

Jurgen tried to persuade his captors of his innocence, but the drops of blood on his sleeve spoke against him. He quickly understood that he would receive no justice here, and, knowing that he was not guilty, he did not try to resist or flee.

They landed exactly at the point where Master Bugge's castle had stood in olden times. Here Jurgen had walked with his foster parents when they were on their way to the funeral of their kin, the four happiest days of his childhood. Now he was led across the meadow to Norre Vosborg; the elderberry tree was flowering and the linden trees smelled just as they had then. It seemed to Jurgen only yesterday that he had been there.

Under the steep flight of stairs that leads to the castle there is a

small door down to a vaulted cellar. It was here that Tall Margrethe
had been imprisoned. She had eaten five children's hearts, for she had
believed that she would be able to fly and make herself invisible if she
could eat seven human hearts.

There was only one slit in the wall. The smell of the linden trees
was not strong enough to enter and freshen the damp and moldy air
of the prison. The only furniture was a wooden bench, but if a good
conscience is the best of pillows, then Jurgen's head could rest easily.

The heavy oak door was closed and barred on the outside. Fears,
especially those that come from superstition, can creep through the
keyholes of castles and fishermen's cottages, and certainly they have
no difficulty entering a dungeon. Jurgen sat in the cellar and thought
about Tall Margrethe and her horrible crimes; her last thoughts
must have filled the room on the night before she was executed.
Jurgen recalled, too, all the stories he had ever heard about the
witchcraft performed in the castle when Squire Svanwedel had lived
here. That was long ago. But today there were still those who said
they had seen the old watchdog, from that time, standing on the
drawbridge at night. The terror of these tales made the stone chamber
doubly dark. The only single ray of sunshine was his memory of the
flowering elderberry and the tall linden trees.

He did not spend many days there. Soon he was taken to Ringkøbing, but the jail there was almost as severe.

Those times were not like our own, the poor were harshly treated.
Peasants' farms, even whole villages, could still disappear and become new estates for hungry noblemen. Under their regime, servants
and coachmen were sometimes advanced to being judges, and they
for the slightest offense could condemn the poor to the loss of their
cottages and a whipping as well. It was far away from the king and
his court, who were influenced by the Enlightenment and were bringing about blessed changes in the rest of the country. In Ringkøbing,
the law was antiquated; and—fortunately for Jurgen—this meant
that it was slow.

He sat in the bitterly cold jail and wondered when it would all be
over. His lot in life had been misery and shame, though he was innocent. He had plenty of time to contemplate his fate. Why had all
this happened to him? This would all be explained in the life after
this, which he knew awaited him. This faith in eternal life had grown
within him in the poor cottage on the dunes and was now beyond

doubt. What his father in the warmth and sunshine of Spain had not been able to believe had become to the son a light of consolation and hope in the cold and darkness: the gift of God's grace, and that is never disappointing.

The spring storms came. The thunder of the surf on the west coast could be heard far inland, especially just after the wind had died. The great swells breaking upon the sands sounded like heavily loaded carts driving along a cobblestone street. Jurgen heard it in his prison cell, and it was a diversion. No melody touched him more than this song of the endless ocean, the rolling sea that carried one to all the corners of the world; and wherever one went, like the snail, one had one's house; in foreign lands the ship was always native ground.

He listened to the deep sound that was like distant thunder, and all his thoughts became memories of things past.

"To be free! To be free! There is nothing better even though your shirt is patched and there are holes in your shoes." Sometimes in anger and hopelessness, he would hit his clenched hands against the walls.

Weeks, months, a whole year passed; then a ruffian called Niels Thief or the Horse Dealer was imprisoned and what really had happened that night came to light. North of Ringkøbing Fjord lived a poor fisherman who unlawfully kept an inn where he served liquor to anyone with a penny in his pocket. There on the afternoon of the day before Jurgen had decided to leave, Morton and Niels Thief met. They drank a few glasses of schnapps together, not enough to make either of them drunk, but enough to make Morton talk more than he should. He talked big; he told Niels that he was getting married and bragged that he was going to buy a farm of his own. When Niels asked him where he had got so much money, Morton had foolishly patted his pocket and boasted: "It's all there where it's supposed to be!"

This stupid display of vanity cost him his life. When he left, Niels followed him and stuck his knife into Morton's neck to steal the money, which did not exist!

How all the threads of what happened that night were finally unwound does not concern us, it is enough to know that Jurgen was set free. But what was he given in compensation for all his suffering, for the long year he had spent in the cold cell of the prison cut off from his fellow men? He was told that he should be pleased that he was found to be innocent; and now was free to go wherever he wanted to. The mayor gave him ten marks as traveling money. Some of the people of the town gave him good food and beer, because they were decent people. Not everyone "flays you, cuts you to pieces, and fries you." But Jurgen's real luck was that the merchant Bronne from Skagen—the man whom he had been on his way to see when he was arrested—was in Ringkøbing. He heard about the whole case and he had a heart that could understand what Jurgen must have experienced. He was determined to show Jurgen that not everyone was evil, that the good and the kind existed as well.

From prison directly to an almost heavenly freedom, to love and friendship; that also Jurgen was to try. No man would offer another man a glass to drain that contained nothing but bitterness. How should God then be able to do it, He who is all goodness?

"Let all that happened be forgotten, bury it!" said merchant Bronne. "Cross out the last year with a thick heavy line. We will throw away the old calendar. In two days we leave for good old Skagen. It is a little out of the way, they say. But I say it is a comfortable chimney corner, with windows open to the whole world."

Oh, that was a journey! To be able to breathe again! To come from the damp air of the prison out into the warm sunshine. The heather was blooming and the shepherd boy sat on the Viking grave and played on his flute, which he had carved out of a sheep's bone. It was so warm that Jurgen saw a mirage, a floating forest and gardens that disappeared as they came near it. As in his childhood, he saw the strange columns of smoke, which the people who live on the heath say is Loke driving his sheep.

They were traveling toward the great fjord that cuts Jutland almost in half. When they had crossed it, they entered the ancient land where the Longobards, the people with the long beards, had come from. In the times of King Snio there had been such a famine here that he had wanted to kill the children and the old. The wealthy and clever woman, Gambaruk, who owned much land, had suggested that instead all the young men and women should leave the country and travel to the south where they might fare better.

This old legend Jurgen knew; and though he had never been in the country that the Longobards had conquered, which now is called Lombardy, he could imagine what it looked like. He had, after all, when he was a boy, been in Spain. He recalled the flowers, the fruits in the market place, the church bells, and the humming and buzzing of the great city he had seen; it had been like a beehive. But of all the places he had been, he thought that the loveliest was his homeland; and to Jurgen that was Denmark.

At last they reached "Vendilskaga," as Skagen was called in the old Norwegian and Icelandic sagas. A landscape made up of dunes and sandy acres, it stretches for miles and miles, till it ends in a peninsula called "the branch," where there is a lighthouse.

The houses and farms are spread out among the dunes, a desert where the wind plays with white sand. There the voices of gulls, terns, and wild swans are heard, sometimes so loud that it hurts your ears. Five miles south of "the branch" lies old Skagen and here merchant Bronne lived. This was to be Jurgen's new home. The house had tarred walls, and each of the little outhouses had an old rowboat turned upside down for a roof. The pigpen was made out of the wreckage from ships, and there were no fences anywhere, for there was nothing to fence in. Fish were suspended on poles to dry in the wind. The beaches were strewn with rotten fish. The nets were hardly in the water before they bulged with herring; tons of fish were dragged ashore. There were so many that fish were often thrown back into the sea or left to rot on the beach.

The merchant's wife and daughter—yes, and his servants too—came out to welcome him when he and Jurgen arrived. It was a jubilant home-coming with no end of handshaking. The daughter had a pretty face and friendly eyes.

The house was large and pleasant. They were served fish: plaice that were fit for the table of a king. And there was wine from the vineyards of Skagen, where the grapes are never pressed but arrive in bottles or in casks.

When mother and daughter heard how much and how unjustly Jurgen had suffered they looked upon him with even more good will and affection. Especially the lovely Miss Clara's eyes shone with compassion. Here in old Skagen, Jurgen had found a place where his heart could heal. How much that heart had experienced; even the bitterness of love, and that either hardens or softens it. Jurgen's heart was still soft, and he was young, so maybe it was just as well that Miss Clara was going to Christianssand in three weeks to spend the winter with her aunt. This had been decided long ago.

The Sunday before her departure, they all attended church and received Holy Communion. The church was large; it had been built some hundred years ago by the Scots and the Dutch. It was a distance from the town. Time had been hard on it. The road was sandy, a tiring walk, but one suffered it gladly to come into God's house and sing a psalm and hear the minister preach. The sand reached the top of the outer side of the wall around the churchyard, but the graves were kept free of sand.

It was the largest church in the northern provinces of Jutland. The Virgin Mary, with a golden crown on her head and the little child Jesus in her arms, looked down most lifelike from the altar. In the choir the Apostles were carved in wood, and along the walls hung portraits of all the mayors and councilors of the town of Skagen. The pulpit too was carved. The sun shining in through the windows reflected on the brass chandeliers that hung from the ceiling. In the nave—as in all the other Danish churches—there hung a model ship.

A sweet childlike feeling of faith overwhelmed Jurgen. He felt as he had when he stood in the cathedral in Spain. But here in Skagen he was conscious that he belonged among the worshipers.

After the service, Holy Communion was celebrated. When he had received the bread and wine, he noticed that he had been kneeling beside Miss Clara. So preoccupied had Jurgen been with the holy act, so much had God filled his mind, that only now did he see the girl. One single tear ran down her cheek. Two days later she left for Norway.

Jurgen helped both on the farm and with the fishing. And there were lots of fish to catch, many more then than nowadays. Schools of mackerel gleamed in the dark night and revealed where they were. The gurnards grunted when they were caught, for fishes are not as silent as they are believed to be. There was more to Jurgen than greeted the eye, too; he kept a secret, but that would one day be told.

Every Sunday when he attended church he looked with fascination at the painting of the Virgin Mary, but his glance would also pause for a moment at that spot where Clara had kneeled and he would remember how kind and sweet she had been to him.

Fall came, with rain and sleet. Everywhere there was water; the sand couldn't manage to absorb it all, one almost needed a rowboat to get around. The storms came and many a ship was wrecked on the deadly sandbanks. There were snowstorms and sandstorms; sometimes the cottages were almost buried by sand, so that the people had to climb out through the chimney; this was not uncommon in that district.

In the merchant's house it was cozy and warm. Wood, gathered on the beach, and heather and peat burned in the stoves. In the evenings Mr. Bronne read aloud from the old chronicles. One of the stories was about Prince Hamlet of Denmark who, returning from England, had landed at Bovbjerg, where he fought a battle. He was buried at Ramme, only ten miles from the eelman's home. That part of the heath was filled with Viking graves. The merchant had seen Hamlet's.

They liked to discuss what had happened long ago and to talk about their "neighbors" on the other side of the North Sea: the English and the Scots. Jurgen sometimes sang "The Son of the King of England." When he came to the line: "'The King's son embraced the maiden so fair,'" then his voice would be softer and his dark, shining eyes would glisten.

They sang and they read. Here indeed was wealth: family life—and down to the least of the animals, everything was well kept, both inside and out. On the shelves were polished tin plates; sausages and hams hung from the ceilings; they were well stocked for winter. On the west coast one can still visit these rich fisherman farmers if one is lucky. Their larders are filled and their rooms cozy with homely comforts. Clever they are, with a sense of humor, and as hospitable as the Arabs in their tents.

Except for the four days of his childhood when he had been a guest at a funeral, Jurgen had never found life so interesting or so pleasant as it was now, and that even though Miss Clara was not there; but she was ever present in Jurgen's thoughts.

In April a ship was to leave for Norway, and Jurgen was to sail on it. He was in fine spirits and he looked healthy and strong. Mother Bronne—as the merchant's wife was called—declared that he was a pleasure to look at.

"And you are too," said her husband. "Jurgen has made both the winter evenings and our mother livelier. Why, you have lost a couple of years this winter, you look younger and more beautiful. True, you were the prettiest girl in Viborg when I married you, and that is saying a lot, for I have always found the girls in that town the prettiest in the country."

Jurgen did not say anything, it was not his place to do so, but he thought of a girl from Skagen, and he sailed up to her. The ship moored in Christianssand. The wind had been fair and the trip had taken only half a day.

One morning merchant Bronne went out to the lighthouse, which is a long walk from old Skagen. The charcoal fire had long ago been put out; the sun was already high in the sky when he climbed up the tower. From there you can see how the narrow peninsula continues as a sand bar for five miles under the sea. Out there, where the sand bar ended, there were several ships. He looked through his binoculars and saw that his own ship, *Karen Bronne,* was among them.

Clara and Jurgen were on board; the lighthouse and the tower of the church of Skagen looked to them like a heron and a swan floating on the blue waters. Clara was standing by the railing. The highest of the dunes had come into view, just above the horizon. If the wind continued to blow from the same direction, then they would be home within an hour. So near were they to all happiness, and so near were they to death and all its terror.

A plank in the hull burst and the ship took in water rapidly. The seamen did what they could; they set all sails and pulled up a flag to signal distress. They were still five miles out. There were fishing boats about but they were too far away. The wind blew toward land and the currents were favorable, too, but it was not enough, the ship sank. Jurgen embraced Clara with his right arm and held her. She looked up into his face, but when he jumped with her into the sea she screamed.

Like "The King's son that embraced the maiden so fair," so in this moment of danger and fear did Jurgen hold onto Clara. How fortunate it was that he was such a good swimmer. He swam with his feet and one hand; with the other he held the young girl up. He used every movement that he knew, and tried to float for a while in order to have enough strength to reach the shore. He heard Clara sigh, felt a convulsion pass through her, and he held onto her even tighter. A single wave broke over them, another lifted them up. The water below them was so clear and deep, he thought he saw a school of mackerel pass beneath him; or was it a leviathan that would swallow them? The clouds cast great shadows across the waters, then the sun broke through and the waves glittered and glimmered. Screaming gulls flew above them, and the wild ducks that drifted lazily on the water flew up when they saw the swimmer. Jurgen grew weaker and weaker. Land was still several hundred feet away, but help was near, a rowboat was coming. Suddenly Jurgen saw, beneath the water, a white shape that seemed to be staring at him. A wave lifted him; the ghostly shape came nearer; he felt something hit him and everything around him became dark.

On the sand bar nearest land, just covered by water, lay a wreck. What Jurgen had seen was a carved figurehead; it was the wooden image of a woman, leaning against the ship's anchor. The wave had lifted Jurgen's head and banged it down upon the sharp blade of the anchor, which reached almost to the surface of the water. It had knocked him unconscious, and he and the girl he carried in his arms began to sink. A new wave lifted them up, and the fishermen grabbed them and hauled them into their boat. Blood was running down Jurgen's face, he looked as if he were dead. But his arm still held onto the girl with such force that it was difficult to tear her out of his grasp. Pale and lifeless, she lay in the bottom of the boat.

They tried everything to bring Clara back to life, but she was dead. Jurgen had swum long bearing a corpse, struggling against the sea to save the dead body of the girl.

Jurgen was still breathing. They carried him to the nearest house; there his wound was bandaged by the local blacksmith, who was clever at it, and always called upon when someone was hurt. Not until the next day did the doctor from Hjørring come.

Jurgen's brain seemed to have been hurt. He raged and screamed, but on the third day he grew quiet and lay still, hardly breathing; his life was hanging by a thread, and the doctor said that, for Jurgen, it would be best if that thread broke. "Let us pray to God to take Jurgen's life, for he will never be a real human being again."

But life held onto Jurgen, the thread did not break, although his mind and memory were gone. That was the most terrifying of all. What was left was a body—a living body that would get well and regain its health.

Jurgen stayed in Mr. Bronne's house.

"He had been maimed because he tried to save our child," said the old man. "Now he is our son."

People called Jurgen either "silly" or "foolish," but neither word really fitted. He was more like a violin whose strings have been so loosened that they no longer can make any sound. Only for moments —seconds—did they seem to tighten themselves; bits of melody, simple in rhythm, a hint, a fragment would be played; then Jurgen would stare again, out into space, empty-eyed. His dark eyes had lost their luster; he seemed to be looking through a cloudy black glass.

"Poor foolish Jurgen," people said.

This was the boy who had been conceived to live a life of wealth and ease, an earthly life so glorious that it was "a presumption to ask for or believe that there was anything beyond it." Were all his talents, all his intelligence wasted then? Only pain, bitter days, and disappointments had life given him; he was the flower bulb that never would flower but rot on the sand, torn as he had been from the rich soil where he should have grown. Could anything made in the image of God have such little value? Can life really be only a game of chance that is played and is over? No! God who is all loving would compensate him for all he had suffered in a life after this one. "'The Lord is good to all: and his tender mercies are over all his works.'" This line from the Psalms of David did the kind wife of merchant Bronne often utter in sincere belief of its truth. She prayed that God would take Jurgen up to Him, so that he could receive God's merciful gift: eternal life.

On the sand-swept churchyard of Skagen church was Clara's grave. Jurgen did not seem to be aware of it. It had not been among the pieces of wreckage from his past that sometimes had reached his mind. Every Sunday he followed the family to church and sat in the pew staring vacantly into space. One day during the singing of the hymns he sighed deeply. He was staring up at the altar, at that place where, more than a year ago, he had knelt beside the young girl. His eyes had regained their luster, he said her name out loud and then turned as pale as death. Tears ran down his cheeks.

He was helped out of the church but, once outside, he seemed not to remember at all what had happened. He mumbled something in his usual meaningless manner. Jurgen had been tried by God, thrown aside by Him.—Our Lord, our Creator, is all-loving. Who can doubt it? Our hearts and our understanding tell us He must be and the Bible confirms it. *And his tender mercies are over all his works.*

In Spain, among the orange and laurel trees, the warm winds caressed the golden Moorish domes and the sound of castanets and singing were heard. There in a garden of his palace sat an ancient man, the richest merchant in the town. Through the streets, children were walking in procession, carrying candles and banners. How much of his richness would he not have given to have a child of his own: his daughter or her child, who perhaps had not been born—and therefore he might never meet him in paradise, in eternity. "Poor child!"

Yes, indeed, poor child! For Jurgen, although he was thirty years old, was a child, wandering aimlessly around old Skagen.

Time passed, though Jurgen hardly understood the passing of the seasons or could count the years. Merchant Bronne and his wife died and were laid to rest in the churchyard of old Skagen. The sand had crept over the walls and now the churchyard itself was covered; only the path up to the church was kept free of sand.

It was early in the spring, the time of storms. Great waves beat upon the beaches and the wind carried the sand from the dunes far inland. Great flocks of birds flew screaming above the storm-whipped sea. From Skagen down to the dunes of Husby, where Jurgen had played as a child, stranded ships were reported.

One afternoon as Jurgen sat alone in the house, it was as if light broke through the darkness of his mind; he felt a restlessness, like the one he had felt in his youth which had driven him to take long walks on the heath or among the dunes.

"Home! Home!" he mumbled. No one heard or saw him as he left the house. The wind whipped sand and small stones into his face; he took the path toward the church. The sand lay in drifts high up against the walls of the building, covering the lower parts of the window. But the path to the church had been shoveled the day before. The door was not locked. Jurgen entered and closed it behind him.

The storm whistled and screamed over Skagen. It was a hurricane, the worst in man's memory! But Jurgen was inside God's house, and as the darkness came to the world outside, light penetrated his soul. The heavy stone that he had felt in his head broke with a crack. He thought he could hear the organ playing, but that was the noise of the surf and the storm. He sat down in a pew, and all the candles in the church were lit. No, there were more candles than ever had burned in Skagen church, it was like the cathedral he had seen in Spain.

The old mayors and councilmen in the paintings became alive; they stepped out of their frames and sat down in the choir. The doors of the church opened and all the dead entered, dressed in their best clothes, while beautiful music played. Among the dead he recognized his foster father and foster mother from the dunes of Husby. They took their seats in the church. Merchant Bronne, his wife, and his daughter came and sat next to Jurgen. Clara took Jurgen's hand in hers and together the two walked up to the altar and kneeled on the spot where they had kneeled together so many years ago. The minister blessed them, joined their hands, and wedded them to a life of love. Then trumpets blew and they sounded like children's voices filled with longing and joy. The music grew louder as though an enormous organ were playing—a hurricane of sounds, lovely to listen to and yet so strong and powerful that it could break the tombstones on the graves.

The model ship that hung in the choir floated down in front of the young couple. It grew and became the ship the son of the King of England had sailed on in the old song. Its sails were made of silk, its yards and masts were made of silver, its anchor of the purest gold, and every rope was twisted of silken thread. Jurgen and Clara, the bride and bridegroom, stepped on board and the whole congregation followed. There was room enough for all. The walls of the church bore blossoms like the elderberry tree and the air was filled with the fragrance of the linden trees. The ship lifted itself and sailed up into the air, into eternity. The candles of the church became the stars of the sky and the wind sang the old hymn: "No life shall be forever lost."

These were the last words Jurgen uttered. Finally the thread that held his eternal soul did break. In the dark church lay a dead body. Outside the storm was still raging.

The next morning was Sunday. The tempest was not over. With difficulty the minister and the congregation managed to make their way to the church. They found it so deeply buried in sand that the door was completely hidden. The minister read a short prayer and declared that God had closed the door of this His house, and that they would have to build Him a new one. Then they sang a hymn and walked back to their homes.

They searched for Jurgen everywhere: among the dunes as well as in the town. Finally they decided that he must have walked down to the beach during the storm, and one of the waves had taken him out to sea.

His body lies buried in a great sarcophagus, a church. God had, with the storm, cast earth on his coffin, buried it in a heavy layer of sand, and there it still lies. The great arches and vaults are completely covered; only the tower, like a giant tombstone, juts out of the sand. It can be seen miles away, and visitors come to pluck the wild roses that bloom there. No king ever received a greater tomb. No one disturbs the dead man, and no one until now knew that Jurgen was buried there. The storm told me the story, sang it to me among the dunes.

## 101

## The Puppeteer

Among the passengers on the steamer was an elderly man with such a cheerful expression on his face that—unless it lied—he must have been the happiest person in the world. He claimed he was; told me so himself. He was a fellow Dane, a traveling theater director. He carried his whole troupe of actors in a wooden box, for the theater he directed was a puppet theater. He told me that he had been born with a cheerful disposition, but this had been further purified and strengthened by his meeting with a student from the Polytechnic Institute. I did not understand what he meant; but then he explained, and here is his story:

"It happened in Slagelse," he began. "I was giving a performance at the inn on the square. I had a marvelous audience; all the spectators were under fourteen except for a couple of elderly matrons. Then there arrives a man, dressed in black, with a studious look on his face. He takes a seat and watches my performance. The newcomer laughs at the right moments and applauds at the right moments —a most unusual spectator! The play was over at eight. Children should go early to bed, and a good theater director is always concerned about his audience. At nine o'clock the student was to give a lecture, with demonstrations. Now I became a spectator. Most of it was above my head, as they say, but it was interesting to listen to and to watch. I could not help thinking that, if our minds can figure out such complicated matters as the lecture was about, then they ought to be able to last a bit beyond the point when we are put down below the ground.

"The young student only performed some lesser miracles, all of them according to the laws of nature. If he had lived at the time of Moses and the prophets, he would have been one of the wise men; and if he had lived in the Middle Ages, then he would have been burned at the stake. I could hardly sleep all night; and when, at my performance the next night, I saw the student once more among my audience, I was as happy as could be. I have heard a great actor say that when he has to play a lover, then he chooses one woman in the audience and plays the part for her alone. Well, the Polytechnical student was my 'woman,' the one spectator for whom I was performing.

"When the play was over and the puppets had made their curtain calls, the student invited me to share a bottle of wine with him. He talked about my comedy and I about his science, and I think he found the conversation as pleasant as I did, although I held my own a little better, for there was so much in his science that he couldn't explain. For instance, why a bar of iron passing through a spiral with electricity in it became magnetic. It was as if it had gained a spirit or a soul, so to speak; but why? how? and where did it come from? It is much the same with human beings. God drops us through the spiral of our times, and the spirit takes over. Presto! You have a Napoleon or Luther! Or some other important figure.

" 'Our world is filled with miracles,' explained the student. 'We are just so used to seeing them that we don't recognize them as such, because they are everyday occurrences.'

"He talked and explained; and in the end I felt as if the top of my skull had been lifted off. And I admitted to him that I would most enthusiastically have entered the Polytechnical Institute and learned how to examine this world of ours a little closer if it weren't that I was a little too old. This I would do even though I was very happy in my own profession.

" 'Are you happy?' he asked.

" 'Yes,' I answered. 'I am most welcome in every town in the country. True, there is one wish, that every once in while rears its head, like a troll, and can make me a little unhappy. I would like to be a director of a real troupe of actors: real live ones!'

" 'You mean you would like your puppets to become alive, to be real actors?' he said. 'Then you would be completely happy. Do you really believe that?'

"I said that I did; and he said that he didn't. We discussed it at length without agreeing, but we were just as good friends and drank to each other's health. The wine was excellent but I think it was mixed with magic; it must have been, for otherwise the whole story boils down to nothing more than that I was drunk. I am sure I wasn't, I saw very clearly indeed.

"The whole room seemed to be filled with sunshine, and the light came from the face of the student from the Polytechnical Institute. I was reminded of the old tales in which the gods descend into the world and mix with ordinary mortals. I told him this and he smiled; and then I felt certain enough to swear on it that he was a god in disguise—or, at least, related to them.

"And he was! My greatest wish was to be granted, the puppets were to become alive and I was to be the director of a real live troupe. We drank yet another glass of wine; and then he packed all my dolls into their wooden box and strapped it on my back. Then he let me down through a spiral. I can still feel and hear the bump with which I landed.

"There I lay on the floor with the box beside me. Up came the lid and out jumped my whole troupe. The spirit had entered them and every puppet was alive. They were all the most excellent actors, so they said themselves. And I was their director!

"Everything was ready for the first performance, when every member of the troupe insisted that he had to talk to me! The little ballerina just wanted to point out that all the spectators came to see her stand on one leg, and if she fell, then the show fell flat too, and that I'd better remember that. The woman who played an empress suggested that maybe it would be better if we treated her as an empress off stage, otherwise she might get out of practice. The fellow whose only role was to come in with a letter in the second act declared that his part was as important as the hero's. 'After all,' he said, 'it is the artistic whole that makes the play, and so the small and the big parts are equally important.'

"The hero wanted the play changed, he wanted nothing but exit lines because they got the most applause. The first lady wanted the lighting changed; no blue lights, only red; they made her look lovelier. The actors were like flies in a bottle, and I was in the bottle too, for I was the theater director. I got a headache, I could hardly breathe. I was as miserable as a human being could possibly be. I felt that I had been put among a new race of human beings that I had never heard of before. I wished they were all back in my box. I told them straight to their faces that they were nothing but a bunch of puppets! Then they killed me!

"When I woke I was lying in my bed in my room. How I got there I could not imagine. Maybe the student knows, but I don't. The moon was shining in through the window and the box in which I keep the puppets was turned upside down and all the marionettes, big and small, lay spread out all over the floor. I jumped out of bed immediately and threw them all back into the box, some headfirst and others feet first. I had no time to be careful. Then I banged down the lid and sat down upon it.

"Can you imagine the sight? Well, I can still see it in front of me. Somebody should have made a painting of it. 'Now you have to stay where you are,' I commanded loudly, 'and I will never wish you alive again!'

"Now I was utterly and completely happy. As I have said, the Polytechnical student had purified and strengthened me. Out of sheer happiness, I fell asleep sitting on the box. I was still sitting there the next morning—it was actually noon, I had slept marvelously late that day—and I was as gloriously happy as I had been when I fell asleep. I had learned that the only wish I had had in this world had been foolish. I asked about the student but he had disappeared just as a Roman or Greek god would have. Ever since then I have been completely and perfectly happy, the happiest theater director there has ever been. My actors never complain and neither do my public; they have come to enjoy themselves and they do. I can make up my own plays, taking what I like best from others, and no one finds fault with it. Those tragedies that the big theaters now would not dream of performing, but which everybody ran to see and cry over thirty years ago, I rewrite and produce for the children. And the little ones cry just as their mothers and fathers did when they saw them. I play *Johanna Montfaucon* and *Dyveke,* but I shorten them a bit. Very young people don't like the love nonsense to last too long; they like unhappiness but it must be quick. I have traveled all over Denmark, I know everyone and they know me. Now I am trying Sweden. If I have success and earn some money, then I will be for the Nordic Union; otherwise I won't. I have told you all this just because you are my countryman."

And I, as his countryman, now have told his story to everyone, just in order to tell it.

## 102

## The Two Brothers

On one of the Danish islands, where the Viking graves still stand high above the fields of grain and giant beeches grow, there lies a little town with small red-roofed houses. In one of them the strangest things were taking place. Liquids were boiling in glass tubes, being distilled, and in mortars herbs were being crushed into powder. An elderly man was in charge of the work.

"One has to search for the truth," he said, "for in all that is created truth is to be found, and without it nothing can be accomplished."

In the living room sat his wife and his two sons. They were still children but they already had grown-up thoughts. Their mother had talked to them about the importance of right and wrong, and knowing the difference between them. She had spoken about truth, too; she called it "God's face in this world."

The older of the boys was full of fun. He loved to read about nature and science. He found no fairy tale so entertaining as reading about the sun and the stars. How wonderful it would be to become an explorer, or to study how birds fly and from them learn to fly oneself. "Yes, Father and Mother are right," he thought. "The laws of nature are truth, as they were created by God."

The younger brother was quieter; eagerly, he entered the world of his books. When he read how Jacob, by fraud, obtained the birthright of Esau, he clenched his little hand in anger. When he read about tyranny, cruelty, and injustice, tears would come into his eyes.

Justice and truth were ever in his thoughts. One evening he was lying in bed and should have been asleep, but enough light came through the partly closed curtains to allow him to read, and he wanted to finish the story about Solon.

His thoughts lifted him, carried him on a strange journey. His bed became a boat sailing on a great sea, and in his mind he asked himself if he were dreaming. He traveled across the great ocean of time and he heard Solon speak; and though spoken in a foreign tongue, he heard the old Danish proverb: "Upon law shall a country be built."

And the spirit of Human Genius stood in the room of the poor cottage and pressed a kiss on the boy's forehead and said: "May you have strength and honor in the battle that life is. May your life be a flight toward the land of truth."

The older brother was not in bed yet. He stood by the window and looked out at the meadows over which lay a mist. It was not the elves dancing—an old woman had tried to tell him that, but he knew better. The mist was caused by the heat, by the water evaporating from the earth. He saw a falling star and the boy's mind flew from the earth up to the burning meteor. All the stars sparkled and blinked as if they were connected by golden threads to the earth.

"Fly with us," sang the child's heart, and faster than a bird, an arrow, or anything earthly his genius carried him out into space, where the rays of light bind the whole universe together. In the thin atmosphere our earth turned and all the great towns were close together. "But what are near and far when you are borne by the spirit of Human Genius?"

Again the older boy stood by the window; his little brother lay asleep in his bed. Their mother called their names: "Anders and Hans Christian!"

Denmark knows them well and the world knows them: the two Oersted brothers!

## 103

## The Old Church Bell

## Written for the "Schiller Album"

In the district of Germany called Württemberg, where the acacia trees bloom along the roads and the apple and pear trees in autumn are filled with fruit, there lies a small town called Marbach. It is one of the poorest towns in the district, although it is beautifully situated on the banks of the Neckar. This river flows past many towns, castles, and mountains covered with vineyards before it finally becomes part of the Rhine.

It was late in the year. The leaves on the grapevines had turned red. It was raining and a cold wind blew. That is not the time of year most pleasant for the poor; it was dark outside and even darker and more dismal inside the little old houses of the town. One of them had its gable facing the street; its windows were tiny and the whole house gave an impression of poverty, and truly, the family that lived there were poor. But they were kind, hard-working, and God-fearing. A child was just about to be born. The mother lay in pain.

The great deep tone of the church bell was heard, so solemn and yet so comforting; and just at that moment the mother gave birth to her son. She felt terribly happy and the bells seemed to her to be telling of her happiness to the whole town. Two bright little eyes looked at her, and the baby's hair shone as if the sun were shining on it. The boy arrived in this world on a dark November day to the sound of the ringing of bells. His mother and father kissed him and then wrote in their Bible: "The tenth of November, 1759, God has given us a son."

Later they added that he had been baptized "Johan Christoph Frie-dcrich."

Whut bccamc of thc little fellow, the poor boy from the little town of Marbach? When he was born no one could have predicted how far and wide he was to be known, not even the old bell, although it hung up so high and therefore could see so much. But it had been the first to sing for him. One day he would repay that serenade with a lovely song called "The Bell."

The little boy grew and the world grew; at least, so it seemed to him. His parents moved to another town but they still had friends in Marbach. When the boy was six, mother and son went back for a visit. The boy was a lively lad who knew several psalms by heart and could retell the fables of Gellert, which his father had read aloud for him and his younger sister. They knew the story of Our Saviour, too, and had wept when they heard how he died on a Cross.

The town of Marbach had not changed very much. The same little houses with tall gables, small windows, and crooked walls lined the streets. In the churchyard new graves had been dug; and in the grass by the wall stood the old bell: it had fallen down from the church tower and cracked. It would never ring again and a new bell now hung in its place.

Mother and son stood in front of the old bell and the mother told her son how the bell, for several hundred years, had served the citizens of the town. It had rung for baptisms, weddings, and funerals; it had tolled when a fire broke out; in every event of importance—whether of joy, sorrow, or terror—it had played its part. The boy did not forget what his mother told him that day. It was as if the bell were ringing in his chest. His mother recalled how the bell had comforted her when, in fear and pain, she was giving birth to him, and how it had pealed in happiness when he finally was born. The boy looked with affection at the old bell. He bent down and kissed it, there where it stood among nettles and weeds.

The bell was part of the boy's memory. He grew and became a lanky young man with red hair and freckles, and a pair of eyes as clear as the deep waters. But what happened to him? Oh, everything went well for him, enviably so. He had been accepted at the Military Academy. Most of the other young cadets were noblemen. It was an honor and a piece of luck. He wore boots, a silk neckband, and a powdered wig. Learning he got too: "March! Halt! About face!" He had it drilled into him.

The old church bell that stood forgotten, overgrown with weeds and grass, would someday be melted down and what would become of it? Then, that was as impossible to tell as what was to become of the bell inside the young soldier's chest. Its tone was deep; certainly one day it must be heard far out in the world.

Narrower and narrower grew the walls of the academy, and the commands, "March! Halt! About face!" became more and more deafening. Stronger and more forcefully other tunes rang in the young man's chest; he sang his songs for his friends and comrades, and they echoed even outside the borders of his country. But it was not for the sake of poetry he had been given free schooling, a uniform, and his keep. In the practical world, he was destined to be a small wheel in the great clock. When it is so difficult for us to understand ourselves, how then can others understand us, even those who love us? But by great pressure, diamonds are created; here, too, was pressure. Would it in time produce a gem?

A celebration took place in the capital of the state. Thousands of lamps illuminated the town and rockets shot up into the air. We can still read about it, for it was on that very night that the young man, though filled with pain and sorrow, fled from his country. Everything that was dear to him he had to leave behind or he would have drowned in the river of mediocrity.

The old church bell still stood forgotten by the wall of the churchyard. The wind flew above it and could have told the old bell what had happened to the young man at whose birth it had rung. The wind could have told how it blew coldly upon him as he sank to the ground from exhaustion, in a forest of a neighboring state. His only wealth, his only hope for the future, were some pages of a manuscript. The wind could have told, too, how his only friends—artists and poets like himself—would sneak out to the bowling greens to avoid reading them. Oh yes, the wind knew all about the impoverished, pale, young exile who lived at a sordid inn where the innkeeper was a drunkard and every night there was a noisy drinking bout. Here in a garret he wrote, and composed songs about the ideal. These days were dark, but the heart has to learn suffering or it will never be able to sing about it.

The old bell was experiencing dark and dismal days too, but it could not really feel them. It is only the bell within one's chest that can feel the days of trial. What happened further to the young man? And what happened to the old church bell? The bell traveled farther than it was ever heard when it hung, in all its glory, in the bell tower. And the bell in the young man's chest was heard farther than his feet would ever wander or his eyes ever see. It still can be heard across the great oceans, the whole world round.

But let us hear what happened to the church bell first. It was sold as old metal and transported from Marbach all the way to Bayern. There it was to be melted down. When did this happen and how? Well, that the bell can tell itself, if it is capable of it; it is of little importance. The only thing that is certain is that it arrived in the royal capital of Bayern many, many years after it had fallen from the tower and its metal was to be used for a statue, a monument to a great figure who had cast glory on the German people.

Now listen to what else happened. Strange are the ways of this world of ours. In Denmark, on the green islands where the Viking graves are and the beech tree grows, there lived a poor child who, wearing wooden clogs, had carried the lunch basket to his father's work place; the older man was a woodcarver. This poor child had grown up to become the pride of his nation. He carved in marble such beauty that all the world looked with wonder at it. He had been given the honor of forming in clay the figure of this great and distinguished man; the sculpture was then to be cast in bronze. It was to be a likeness of the poor boy whose name his father had written down in the Bible: Johan Christoph Friederich.

The melted bronze was flowing into the form. The old church bell was no more; now it was the chest and head of a statue. The monument was placed on the square in Stuttgart in front of the old castle, where he whom the sculpture portrayed had so often walked: the boy from Marbach; the student at the military academy; the exile; Germany's great, immortal poet, who has sung about the liberator of Switzerland and St. Joan of France.

The day that the monument was to be unveiled was warm and sunny. From all the roofs and towers of the city banners flew. The church bells rang in celebration and joy. A hundred years had passed since the bell in the church tower of Marbach had rung to give comfort to the mother in pain: she who in poverty had borne the child who was to become so rich that he could leave a treasure to the world; he, the great poet of the heart, the immortal singer of all that is great and beautiful, Johan Christoph Friedrich Schiller.

## 104

## The Twelve Passengers

It was freezing cold. The night was clear, the wind was still, and the sky was filled with stars. "Bang! Bang!" That was a firecracker. They were being shot off because it was New Year's Eve and the clock was just striking twelve.

"Trat tra . . . Trat tra!" the coachman's bugle was heard as the stagecoach arrived at the city gate. There were twelve passengers; exactly the number that there was room for: every seat was occupied.

"Hurrah! Hurrah!" In all the houses people were shouting, "Hurrah!" for the New Year. They were standing glass in hand, ready to toast: "Health and prosperity in the New Year!" they said. Or they made other wishes for each other; such as: "May you find a nice wife," or "May you earn lots of money," or "May all this unpleasant nonsense come to an end." This latter, of course, was rather too much to ask.

While everyone was welcoming in the New Year, the stagecoach waited outside the city gate with its passengers.

Who were these strangers? They had their passports and luggage, and in it there were gifts for you and me, for everyone in the whole city. But what did they want and what did they bring?

"Good morning," they said to the sentry at the gate.

"Good morning," he answered; and it was, after all, past midnight. "Your name and profession," the sentry asked the first man who descended from the coach.

"Look in the passport," he grumbled. "I am I!" He was big and gruff. He was wearing a bearskin coat and sled boots. "I am the man a lot of people pin their hopes on. Come around tomorrow and I will tell you what New Year is like. I throw away pennies and silver coins as well; you can scramble for them. And I give grand balls: thirty-one of them, that is all the nights I have to give away. I am a merchant, my ships are all icebound, but it is warm in my office. My name is January; my luggage is filled with unpaid bills."

The next passenger was more amusing. He was a theater director who only played comedies and held masquerades. He traveled with an empty barrel as luggage.

"I live for the pleasure of others and for myself because I have such a short life, only twenty-eight days. Sometimes a collection is made among the family and I am given an extra day, but I don't care one way or the other. Hurrah!"

"Don't shout so loud!" said the soldier on guard.

"Certainly I may!" said the traveler. "I am Prince of the Carnival, though I travel under the name of Februarius."

Now the third of the strangers came out of the coach. He was thin and tall. One would think that he had never got enough to eat. He was always fasting and proud of it. They say that he can tell the weather for the rest of the year, but that is not a profession one can grow fat on. He wore a black suit with a few violets in his buttonhole; they were very small.

"March, March!" screamed the fourth, and pushed him out of the way with a laugh. "March, March, right inside with you. I can smell they are brewing punch in there." But that wasn't true at all. He was just playing an April fool's prank on the thin man. Now this fourth traveler looked like a lively fellow; he did not work hard and kept a lot of holidays. But he was subject to moods.

"With me it is always rain or sunshine," he declared. "I can both laugh and cry at the same time. My suitcase is filled with summer clothes, but it is not wise to put them on. You will have to accept me as I am. When I am dressed up I wear a silk shirt and a woolen muffler."

Now a lady got out of the coach.

"Miss May," she said. She was wearing summer clothes but had overshoes on her feet. Her light green dress was made of silk. She had put anemones in her hair and she smelled so strongly of woodruff that the poor guard sneezed.

"God bless you," she said, and meant it. She was very pretty indeed, and she sang—not in the theaters, but out in the forest, among the fresh green trees. She sang for her own pleasure and not for applause. In her sewing bag she kept a book of poetry.

"Here comes our young mistress!" they cried from inside the stage-coach. Out stepped a young woman, beautiful and proud. She was born to wealth, one could see that. She waited for the longest day of the year to throw a party; she wanted her guests to have time enough to eat all the courses. She could afford to drive in her own carriage, but she had sat in the coach along with the others because she didn't want them to think that she was too proud to join them. As traveling companion she had her younger brother, Julius.

He also was well to do and was wearing a white suit and a Panama hat. He carried so little luggage that it could hardly have been less: a pair of bathing trunks.

Now came Madame August. She was a wholesale dealer in apples and other fruits. She owned farms, too; she looked big and fat and comfortable. She took part in all the work and could carry the beer barrel herself out to her workers at harvest time. "In the sweat of thy brow shalt thou eat thy bread." That is written in the Bible, but afterward one can hold a feast and dance. Yes indeed, she was a straightforward person.

Next a man came out. He was a painter by profession. The trees in the forest were his canvas. He changed their color and made them even more beautiful. Red, yellow, and brown were his favorites. He could whistle like a starling and had decorated his beer mug with a garland of hops; it was very pretty and he had an eye for the pretty. He traveled light, a pot of paint and some brushes were all his baggage.

Now came the farmer; he was concerned about plowing and getting the soil ready for the coming year, though he had time to think of hunting. He carried a gun and a dog ran at his side; he had his hunting bag filled with nuts. Goodness me, he carried a lot of goods with him, among other things, an English plow. He talked incessantly about economics, but one had a hard time hearing what he said, for the next passenger, who had already got out of the coach, had a bad cold and was sniffing and coughing.

He was November! His cold was so bad that he used a sheet as a handkerchief. But he thought he might get rid of it as soon as he had found some lumber to cut, for that was his profession.

Now came the last of the passengers, a little old lady carrying a brazier. She was freezing, but her eyes shone like two stars. In her other hand she had a little potted pine tree. "I will tend it so well that it will grow big enough by Christmas to reach all the way up to the ceiling. Then it shall have lighted candles, apples, and sugar pigs on it. My little brazier gives as much warmth as a stove. I shall take my fairy-tale book out of my pocket and read aloud. And the children will sit perfectly still, while the dolls on the tree come alive, and the little wax angel on the top of the tree will flutter his golden wings and fly down and kiss every person in the room, both grownups and children. Yes, he will kiss the poor children, too, who are standing outside, singing Christmas carols, singing about the star that once shone over Bethlehem."

"The coach is leaving," shouted the guard, "now that the passengers have got out."

"Let the twelve of them enter the city one at a time," said the captain of the guard. "I will keep your passports, they are only good for one month each. When that is over, then I shall write a report on your behavior. Mr. January, you may enter first."

And Mr. January entered.

When the year is over I shall tell you what the twelve passengers brought me and you and all of us. I don't know now, nor do I think they even know themselves—for surely we live in a strange time.

## 105

## The Dung Beetle

The emperor's horse had been awarded golden shoes, one for each hoof. It was such a beautiful animal, with strong legs and a mane that fell like a veil of silk over its neck. Its eyes were sad, and when you looked into them you felt certain that if the horse could speak it would be able to answer more questions than you could ask. On the battlefield it had carried its master through a rain of bullets and a cloud of gun smoke. It was a true war horse, and once when the emperor was surrounded by the enemy, it had bit and kicked their horses and then, when all seemed lost, it had leaped over the carcass of an enemy steed to carry the emperor to safety. The horse had saved his master's golden crown and his life, which was worth a great deal more to the emperor than all the crown jewels. And that was why the blacksmith had been given orders to fasten a golden shoe on each of its hoofs.

The dung beetle climbed to the top of the manure pile to watch. "First the big and then the small," he said. "Not that size is important," he added as he lifted one of his thin legs and stretched it up toward the blacksmith.

"What do you want?" the man asked.

"Golden shoes," replied the dung beetle while balancing on five legs.

"You must be out of your mind to think that you should have golden shoes," the blacksmith exclaimed, and scratched himself behind his right ear.

"Golden shoes!" repeated the dung beetle crossly. "Am I not as good as that big clumsy beast that needs to have a servant to groom it, and even to see to it that it doesn't starve? Do I not belong to the emperor's stable too?"

"But why does the horse deserve golden shoes, have you any idea about that?"

"Idea!" cried the dung beetle. "I have a very good idea of how I deserve to be treated and how I am treated. Now I have been insulted enough; there is nothing left for me to do but go out into the wide world."

"Good riddance," said the smith.

"Brute!" returned the dung beetle, but the blacksmith, who had already returned to his work, did not hear him.

The dung beetle flew from the stable to the flower garden; it was a lovely place that smelled of roses and lavender.

"Isn't it beautiful here?" a ladybug called to him. She had just come for a visit and was busy folding her fragile wings beneath her black-spotted armor. "The flowers smell so sweet that I think I shall stay here forever."

The dung beetle sniffed. "I am used to something better. Why, there isn't even a decent pile of dung here."

The dung beetle sat down to rest in the shadow of a tiger lily. Climbing up the flower's stem was a caterpillar. "The world is beautiful," the caterpillar said. "The sun is very warm and I am getting quite sleepy. When I fall asleep—or die as some call it—I am sure that I shall wake up as a butterfly."

"Butterfly, indeed! Don't give yourself airs. I come from the emperor's stable, and no one there—not even the emperor's horse—has any notions like that. Those who can fly, fly. . . . And those who can crawl, crawl." And then the dung beetle flew away.

"I try not to let things annoy me; but they annoy me anyway," the dung beetle thought as it landed with a thud in the middle of a great lawn, where it lay quietly for a moment before falling asleep.

Goodness, it was raining. It poured! The dung beetle woke with a splash and tried to dig himself down into the earth but he couldn't. The rain had formed little rivers, and the dung beetle swam first on his stomach and then on his back. There was no hope of being able to fly. "I shan't live through it," he muttered, and sighed so deeply that his mouth filled with water. There was nothing to do but lie still where he was, and so he lay still.

When the rain let up for a moment the dung beetle blinked the water out of his eyes and looked about. He saw something white and crawled through the wet grass toward it. It was a piece of linen that had been stretched out on the grass to bleach. "I am used to better but it will have to do," he thought. "Though it's neither as warm nor as comfortable as a heap of dung; but when you travel you have to take things as they come."

And he stayed under the linen a whole day and a whole night; and it rained all the time. Finally, the following morning, the dung beetle stuck his head out from the fold of the linen and, seeing that the sky was gray, he was very annoyed.

Two frogs sat down on the linen. "What glorious weather," said one to the other. "It's so refreshing and this linen is soaking wet; to sit here is almost as pleasant as to swim."

"I would like to know," began the other frog, "if the swallow, who travels a good deal in foreign countries, ever has been in a land that has a better climate than ours. As much rain as you need; and a bit of wind, too—not to talk of the mist and the dew. Why, it is as good as living in a ditch. If you don't love this climate, then you don't love your country."

"Have you ever been in the emperor's stable?" the dung beetle asked. "There the wetness is spicy and warm. I prefer that kind of climate because I am used to it; but when you travel you can't take it along, that's the way things are. . . . Could you tell me if there is a hothouse in this garden, where a person of my rank and sensitivity would feel at home?"

The frogs either couldn't or wouldn't understand him.

"I never ask a question more than once," said the dung beetle after he had repeated his query the third time without getting an answer.

He walked along until he came upon a piece of a broken flowerpot. It shouldn't have been lying there but the gardener hadn't seen it, so it provided a good home for several families of earwigs. Earwigs do not need very much room, only company, especially lady earwigs, who are very motherly. Underneath the piece of pottery there lived several lady earwigs; and each of them thought that her children were the handsomest and most intelligent in the whole world.

"My son is engaged," one of them announced. "That innocent joy of my life . . . His most cherished ambition is to climb into the ear of a minister. He is charmingly childish, and being engaged will keep him from running about, and that is a great comfort to a mother."

"Our son," began another mother earwig, "came straight out of the egg. He is full of life and that is a joy. He is busy sowing his wild oats, and that, too, can make a mother proud. Don't you agree with me, Mr. Dung Beetle?" She had recognized him by his shape.

"You are both right," remarked the dung beetle; and the earwigs invited him to come into their home and make himself comfortable.

"Now you must meet my children," said a third mother earwig.

"And mine!" cried a fourth. "They are so lovable and so amusing, and they only misbehave when they have stomach aches and it's not their fault that you get one so easily at their age."

All the mothers talked and their children talked; and when the little ones weren't talking, they were pulling at the dung beetle's mustache with the little tweezers that each of them had in his tail.

"Always up to something! Aren't they darling?" the mothers said in a chorus, and oozed mother love. But the dung beetle was bored and asked for directions to the nearest hothouse.

"It is far, far away, nearly at the end of the world, on the other side of the ditch," explained one of the lady earwigs. "If one of my children ever should think of traveling so far away I would die. I am sure of it."

"Well, that is where I am going," said the dung beetle, and to show that he was really gallant, he left without saying good-by.

In the ditch he met many relatives: all of them dung beetles. "This is our home," they said. "It is quite comfortable: warm and wet. Please step down into the land of plenty. You must be tired after all your travels."

"I am!" replied the dung beetle. "I have lain a whole day and a whole night on linen. Cleanliness wears you out so. Then I stood under a drafty flowerpot until I got arthritis in my wings. It is a blessing to be with my own kind again."

"Do you come from the hothouse?" one of the older dung beetles asked.

"Higher still. I was born in the emperor's stable with golden shoes on. I am traveling incognito on a secret mission. And no matter how much you coaxed, I wouldn't tell you about it." With these words the dung beetle crept into the mud and made himself comfortable.

Nearby sat three young lady dung beetles. They were tittering because they didn't know what to say.

"They are not engaged, though they are beautiful," remarked their mother. The young ladies tittered again, this time because they were shy.

"Even in the emperor's stable I have never seen anyone more beautiful," agreed the dung beetle, who had traveled far and wide.

"They are young and virtuous. Don't ruin them! Don't speak to them unless you have honorable intentions. But I see you are a gentleman, and therefore I give you my blessings!"

"Hurrah!" cried all the other dung beetles, and congratulated the foreigner on his engagement. First engaged, then married; there was no reason to put it off.

The first day of married life was good, and the second was pleasant enough, but on the third began all the responsibilities of providing food for his wives, and soon there would probably be offspring.

"They took me by surprise," thought the dung beetle. "Now I shall surprise them."

And so he did. He ran away. All day the wives waited, and all night too; then they declared themselves widows. The other dung beetles were angry and called him a ne'er-do-well, because they feared that now they would have to support the deserted wives.

"Just behave as if you were virgins again," said their mother. "Come, you are still my innocent girls. But shame on the tramp who abandoned you."

In the meantime, the dung beetle was sailing across the ditch on a cabbage leaf. It was morning and two human beings who happened to be passing noticed him and picked him up. They turned the dung beetle over and looked at him from all sides, for these two men were scholars.

The younger of the two, who was the most learned, said, "'Allah sees the black scarab in the black stone that is part of the black mountain.' Isn't it written thus in the Koran?" Then he translated the dung beetle's name into Latin and gave a lecture in which he explained its genealogy and history. The older scholar remarked that there was no reason to take the dung beetle home with them, because he already had a much more beautiful scarab in his collection.

The dung beetle's feelings were hurt and he flew right out of the scholar's hand, high up into the sky. Now that his wings were dry he was able to make the long journey to the hothouse in one stretch. Luckily, a window was open and he flew straight in and landed on a pile of manure that had been delivered that morning.

"This is sumptuous," he said as he dug himself down into the dung, where he soon was asleep. He dreamed that the emperor's horse was dead and that he—the dung beetle—had not only been given its four golden shoes but had been promised two more. It was a pleasant dream and when the dung beetle awoke he climbed out of the manure to look about him. How magnificent everything was!

There were slender palm trees, whose green leaves appeared transparent when the sun shone on them; and below the trees were flowers of all colors. Some were red as fire, and some were yellow as amber, and some were as pure white as new-fallen snow. "What a marvelous display!" exclaimed the dung beetle. "And think how delicious it all will taste as soon as it is rotten. It is a glorious larder. I must go visiting and see if I can find any of my family living here. I cannot associate with just anybody. I have my pride, and that I am proud of." Then he crawled on, recalling as he did so, his dream and how the horse had died and was given its gold shoes.

Suddenly a little hand picked him up, and again he was pinched and turned over. The gardener's son and one of his playmates had been exploring in the hothouse and, when they saw the dung beetle, they decided it would be fun to keep it. They wrapped it in a leaf from a grapevine, and the gardener's son stuck it in his pocket.

The dung beetle tried to creep and to crawl, and the boy closed his hand around him and that was most uncomfortable.

The boys ran to the big pond at the other end of the garden. A worn-out wooden shoe with a missing instep became a ship. With a stick for a mast and the dung beetle, who was tied to the stick with a piece of woolen thread, as the captain, the ship was launched.

The pool was large and the dung beetle thought he was adrift on an ocean. He got so frightened that he fell over on his back and there he lay with all his legs pointing up toward the sky.

There were currents in the water and they carried the wooden shoe along. When it got out too far, one of the boys would roll up his trousers—both boys were barefooted—and wade out to bring the shoe nearer the shore. Suddenly, while the shoe was quite far out, almost in the center of the pond, someone called the boys, called them in so stern a voice that they forgot all about the shoe and ran home as

fast as they could. The wooden shoe drifted on and on. The dung
beetle shuddered with fear, for he couldn't fly away, tethered as he
was to the mast.

A fly came to keep him company. "Lovely weather, don't you
agree? I think I'll rest here for a moment in the sun. A very comfortable place you have here."

"Nonsense!" cried the dung beetle. "How can I be comfortable
when I am tied to the mast? You talk like an idiot, so I'm sure you
must be one."

"I'm not tied to anything," said the fly, and flew away.

"Now I know the world," muttered the dung beetle. "It is cruel and
I am the only decent one in it. First they refused to give me golden
shoes, then they made me lie on wet linen and stand for hours in a
draft. Finally, I am tricked into marriage; and when I show my courage by going out into the world to find out what that's like and see how
I will be treated there, I am captured by a human puppy who ties me
to a mast and sets me adrift on a great ocean. And all the while the
emperor's horse runs about with golden shoes on; and that's almost
the most annoying part of it all. In this world you must not ask for
sympathy. My life has been most interesting. . . . But what difference does that make if no one ever hears about it? . . . But does
the world deserve to hear my story? . . . If it did, I would have been
given the golden shoes. Had I got them, it would have brought honor
to the stable. The stable missed its chance, so did the world, for everything is over."

But everything was not over; some young girls who were out rowing on the pond saw the little ship.

"Look, there is a wooden shoe," one of them said.

"Someone has tied a beetle to the mast," said another; and she
leaned over the side of the boat and grabbed the wooden shoe. With
a tiny pair of scissors she carefully cut the woolen thread, so that no
harm came to the dung beetle. When they returned to shore the girl
let him go in the grass. "Crawl or fly, whichever you can, for freedom
is a precious gift," she said.

The dung beetle flew straight in through an open window of a
large building and landed in the long, soft, silken mane of the emperor's horse, who was standing in the stable where they both belonged. He held on tightly to the mane, then he relaxed and began to
think about life.

"Here I am, sitting on the emperor's horse. I am the rider. . . . What am I saying?" The dung beetle was talking out loud. "Now everything is clear to me! And I know it is true! Didn't the blacksmith ask me if I didn't have some idea why the emperor's horse was being shod with golden shoes? Now I understand that it was for my sake that the horse was given golden shoes."

The dung beetle was in the best of humors. "It is traveling that did it!" he thought. "It broadens your horizon and makes everything clear to you."

The sun shone through the window. Its rays fell upon the horse and the dung beetle. "The world is not so bad," remarked the dung beetle. "It all depends on how you look at it." And the world, indeed, was beautiful, when the emperor's horse was awarded golden shoes because the dung beetle was to ride it.

"I must dismount," he thought, "and go and tell the other dung beetles how I have been honored. I will tell them of my wonderful adventures and how I enjoyed traveling abroad. And I'll tell them, too, that I have decided to stay at home until the horse wears out his golden shoes."

## 106

## What Father Does Is Always Right

Now I want to tell you a story that I heard myself when I was a very little boy, and every time that I have thought of it since, it has seemed to me to be more beautiful. For stories are like people: some—though not all—improve with age, and that is a blessing.

Have you ever been in Denmark and seen the countryside? If you have, then you must have seen one of those really old cottages that has a thatched roof that is overgrown with moss and a stork's nest perched on its ridge. The walls are crooked. The windows are small, and only one of them has a hasp and hinges so that it can be opened. The oven for baking bread juts out of the wall like a well-filled stomach. There are a hedge of elderberries and a tiny pond surrounded by willow trees, where a duck and some ducklings swim. In the yard there is an old dog that barks at everyone who goes by.

In such a cottage, far out in the country, there once lived a farmer and his wife. They had little that they could get along without, but they did have something, and that was a horse that had to graze at the edge of the road because they didn't have a paddock. Sometimes the farmer rode on the horse when he went to town; and sometimes his neighbor borrowed it, and that was to the farmer's advantage, for country people believe that one good turn deserves another. But one day the farmer realized that he'd be doing himself a better turn if he sold the horse or traded it for something which he had more use for, though he didn't know what it could be.

"That you'll find out soon enough," said his wife. "You know best,

Father. There's a market in town today. Why don't you ride in on the horse, and there you can sell it or trade it for something else. Whatever you do, I am sure it will be right."

She tied his cravat, which she knew how to do better than anybody else. She made a double bow because that made him look more gallant. She brushed his hat with the palm of her hand, and then she kissed him warmly on the lips. Off he rode on the horse that was to be sold or traded, just as he saw fit; for striking a bargain was something he knew how to do.

The sun was shining and there wasn't a cloud in the sky. The dusty road was filled with folk on their way to market; some in wagons, others on horses, and many on their own poor legs. It was terribly hot and there was not a scrap of shade along the road.

The farmer noticed a man who was leading a cow that was as beautiful as any cow could be; and he thought, "I'll bet that cow gives a lot of good milk." Then he called to the man, "Listen—you with the cow—I'd like to talk with you!" And when the other man turned around, he continued: "I know that a horse is worth more than a cow. But a cow would be more useful to me. Shall we trade?"

"Why not?" said the man.

Now here is where the story should have ended but then it wouldn't have been worth telling. The farmer had done what he had set out to do, and so he should have turned around and gone back home with his new cow. But he thought that, since he had meant to go to the market, it was a pity to miss seeing it.

He walked quickly and the cow walked quickly, and pretty soon they had caught up with a man who was leading a sheep. It was a fine animal with a heavy coat of wool. "A sheep like that I wouldn't mind owning," he thought. "In the winter when it gets too cold you can always take a sheep inside with you. Besides, I don't have enough grazing for a cow, and a sheep is satisfied with what it can find on the side of the road." And the more he looked at the sheep, the better he liked it.

"How would you like to trade your sheep for my cow?" he finally asked. And that bargain was made.

He hadn't gone far with his sheep when he spied a man who was sitting and resting on a big stone. He had good reason for wanting to rest: he was carrying a goose that was bigger than most ganders.

"A fine fat goose!" the farmer cried as he lifted his hat. "How pretty it would look in our pond and then Mother would have someone to give the potato peelings to. How often has she said that we ought to have a goose. And now she can have one! What about trading? I'll give you a sheep for a goose and throw a thank you into the bargain."

"A sheep for my goose?" said the stranger. "Why not? And you can keep your thank you, for I don't like to drive too hard a bargain."

The farmer tucked the goose under his arm and walked on. As he came nearer the town the traffic became greater and greater. All about him were people and animals. There wasn't space for them all on the road; they walked in the gutters and the embankments, and even on the fields. The town's gatekeeper had tethered his hen in his potato patch for fear that she might get frightened by all the confusion and run away. The hen's tail was as finely feathered as a cock's, and as she said, "Cluck! Cluck . . ." she winked. What that meant I cannot tell you, but I do know what the farmer thought: "That hen is as good as the minister's best hen, the one that won the prize at the fair. I wish it were mine. A hen can always find a grain of corn by itself; besides, it can lay eggs. I think I will strike a bargain."

From thought to action is no further than the tongue can travel in a few seconds. The gatekeeper got the goose and the farmer the white hen.

The farmer had done a lot that morning and traveled far. He was thirsty and hungry. The sun was baking hot, as if it had been hired by the innkeeper.

As he was entering the inn, the farmer collided with one of the servants, who was carrying a sack over his shoulder. "What have you got in the sack?" the farmer asked.

"Rotten apples," the other man replied, "and I am on my way to the pigpen with them."

"A whole sackful, what an awful lot that is! I wish Mother could see it. Last year, on our old apple tree next to the woodshed, there was only one single apple. Mother put it in the cupboard and there it lay till it was all dried up and no bigger than a walnut. 'It makes me feel rich just to look at it,' she used to say. Think how she would feel if she had a sackful."

"What will you give me for it?" asked the servant.

"My hen," the farmer replied; and the words were no sooner said than he found he had a sack of rotten apples in his hands instead of a hen.

He went into the taproom, which was crowded with people. There were butchers, farmers, merchants, horse dealers, and even a couple of Englishmen, who were so rich that their pockets were bursting with gold coins. All Englishmen like to gamble, that's a tradition in their country. Now just listen to what happened.

The taproom was next to the kitchen, and the stove that was used for cooking extended right through the kitchen wall into the taproom. Innkeepers are economical and this kind of stove is a great saving in winter. The farmer, without giving it a thought, put his sack of apples down on the stove, and soon they began to simmer and sputter.

"Suss! Suss!" the apples said, and aroused the curiosity of one of the Englishmen.

"What's that?" he asked.

And the farmer told him the whole story of how he had traded his horse for a cow, his cow for a sheep, his sheep for a goose, his goose for a hen, and finally the hen for a sack of rotten apples.

"Your wife will beat you with a rolling pin when you get home. She'll raise the roof," the Englishman commented.

"Beat me?" exclaimed the farmer. "She'll kiss me and say that what Father does is always right."

"I'll make you a wager," said the two Englishmen both at once. "A barrel of gold and a sackful of silver."

"The barrel of gold is enough and, if I lose, I'll fill a barrel with rotten apples and you can have Mother and me for good measure."

"Done! Done!" cried the Englishmen, for betting is in their blood.

They hired the innkeeper's horses and his carriage, and off they went, rotten apples and all. When they came to the farmer's house they drove right up to the door; the old dog barked, and the farmer's wife came out to greet them.

"Good evening, Mother," said the farmer.

"Thank God you arrived home safely," his wife replied.

"Well, I traded the horse."

"Trading is a man's business," she said and, in spite of the strangers, she threw her arms around him.

"I traded it for a cow."

"Thank God for the milk," she exclaimed. "Now we'll have both butter and cheese. That was a good bargain."

"But I traded the cow for a sheep."

"How clever of you," she said happily. "We have just enough grass for a sheep; and sheep's milk is good and the cheese is good, too. I can knit socks and a nightshirt from the wool; and I wouldn't have been able to do anything with cow's hair. A cow just sheds her hair and that's all. What a wise and thoughtful husband you are!"

"But I traded the sheep for a fat goose."

"Oh, my good husband, are we really going to have goose on St. Martin's Eve? You are always thinking of ways to please me. We will tether the goose in the ditch and by November she'll be even fatter."

"I traded the goose for a hen," he said proudly, for now he realized how very well he had done that day.

"That was a good exchange," said the wife. "Hens lay eggs and from eggs come little chicks. Soon we shall have a real henyard and that is something I have always wanted."

"I traded the hen for a sackful of rotten apples."

"Now I must kiss you, my dear husband! While you were away I thought that I should like to make a fine supper for you to eat when you got home; and I decided to make an omelet with chives. I had eggs but no chives. Our neighbor, the schoolmaster, has chives; but, as all the world knows, his wife is a stingy old crow, and when I asked her whether I could borrow some chives, 'Borrow!' she squawked. 'Nothing grows in your garden, not even a rotten apple.' Now I can lend her ten rotten apples, or even a whole sackful, if she wants them. That was the best bargain of all; and now I must give you a kiss." And she kissed him full on the mouth.

"I like that!" cried one of the Englishmen, while the other laughed. "From bad to worse, and they do not even know it! Always happy, always contented. That was worth the money!" And they gave a barrel full of gold coins to the farmer whose wife gave him kisses instead of blows.

Yes, it pays for a wife to admit that her husband is cleverer than she is.

Well, that was that story. I heard it when I was a boy and now you have heard it too; and now you know that what Father does is always right.

## 107

## The Snowman

"It crackles and creaks inside of me. It is so cold that it is a pleasure," said the snowman. "When the wind bites you, then you know you're alive. Look how the burning one gapes and stares." By "the burning one" he meant the sun, which was just about to set. "But she can't make me blink; I'll stare right back at her."

The snowman had two triangular pieces of tile for eyes, and a children's rake for a mouth, which meant that he had teeth. His birth had been greeted by the boys with shouts of joy, to the sound of sleigh bells and the cracking of whips.

The sun set and the moon rose, full and round, beautiful in the blue evening sky.

"There she is again, just in another place. She couldn't stay away." The snowman thought that the sun had returned. "I guess that I have cooled her off. But now she's welcome to stay up there, for it is pleasant with a bit of light, so that I can see. If only I knew how to move and get about, then I would go down to the lake and slide on the ice as the boys do. But I don't know how to run."

"Out! Out! Out!" barked the old watchdog, who was chained to his doghouse. He was hoarse and had been so ever since he had been refused entrance to the house. That was a long time ago now; but when the dog lived inside, it had lain next to the stove. "The sun will teach you to run. I saw what happened to last year's snowman and to the one the year before last. . . . Out! Out! Out! . . . They are all gone."

"What do you mean by that, comrade?" asked the snowman. "How can that round one up there teach me to run?" By "that round one," he meant the moon. "She ran when I looked straight into her eyes. Now she is trying to sneak back from another direction."

"You are ignorant," said the watchdog. "But you have only just been put together. The round one up there is called the moon. The other one is the sun and she will be back tomorrow. She will teach you how to run, right down to the lake. I've got a pain in my left hind leg and that means the weather is about to change."

"I don't understand him," thought the snowman, "but I have a feeling that he was saying something unpleasant. The hot one—the one that was here a moment ago and then went away, the one he called the sun—is no friend of mine. Not that she's done me any harm; it's just a feeling I have."

The weather did change. In the morning there was a heavy fog. During the day it lifted, the wind started to blow, and there was frost. The sun came out and what a beautiful sight it was! The hoarfrost made the forest appear like a coral reef; every tree and bush looked as if it were decked with white flowers. In the summer when they have leaves, you cannot see what intricate and lovely patterns the branches make. But now they looked like lace and were so brilliantly white that they seemed to radiate light. The weeping birch tree swayed in the wind as it did in summer. Oh, it was marvelous to see. As the sun rose higher in the sky its light grew sharper and its rays made everything appear as if it were covered with diamond dust. In the blanket of snow that lay upon the ground were large diamonds, blinking like a thousand small candles, whose light was whiter than snow.

"Isn't it unbelievably beautiful?" said a young girl who was taking a walk in the garden with a young man. "I think it's even lovelier now than it is in summer." And her eyes shone, as if the beauty of the garden were reflected in them.

They stopped near the snowman to admire the forest. "And a handsome fellow like that you won't see in the summer either," remarked the young man, pointing to the snowman.

The girl laughed and curtsied before the snowman, then she took the young man's hand in hers and the two of them danced across the snow, which crunched beneath their feet as if they were walking on grain.

"Who were they?" the snowman asked the dog. "You've been here on the farm longer than I have. Do you know them?"

"Certainly," answered the old dog. "She has patted me and he has given me bones. I would never bite either of them."

"Why do they walk hand in hand? I have never seen boys walk like that."

"They are engaged," the old dog sniffed. "Soon they will be moving into the same doghouse and will share each other's bones."

"Are they as important as you and I?" asked the snowman.

"They belong to the house and are our masters," replied the dog. "You certainly know precious little, even if you were only born yesterday. I wouldn't have believed such ignorance existed if I hadn't heard it with my own ears. But I have both age and knowledge, and from them you acquire wisdom. I know everyone on the farm; and I have known better times, when I didn't have to stand here, chained up and frozen to the bone. . . . Out! Out! Get out!"

"I love to freeze," said the snowman. "Tell me about the time when you were young, but stop rattling your chain like that, it makes me shudder inside."

"Out! Out!" barked the old dog. "I was a puppy once. 'See that lovely little fellow,' they used to say, and I slept on a velvet chair. I lay in the lap of the master of the house and had my paws wiped with embroidered handkerchiefs. They kissed me and called me a sweetheart, and their little doggy-woggy. When I grew too big to lie in a lap they gave me to the housekeeper. She had a room in the cellar.— You can look right into her window from where you are standing.— Down there I was the master. It wasn't as nicely furnished as upstairs, but it was much more comfortable. I had my own pillow to lie on, and the housekeeper gave me just as good food and more of it. Besides, upstairs there were children and they are a plague, always picking you up, squeezing you, and hugging you, and carrying you about as if you had no legs of your own to walk on. . . . Then there was the stove. In winter there is nothing as lovely as a stove. When it was really cold I used to crawl all the way under it. I still dream of being there, though it's a long time since I was there last. . . . Out! Out! Out!"

"Is a stove a thing of beauty?" asked the snowman. "Does it look like me?"

"You're as much alike as day and night. The stove's as black as coal; it has a long black neck with a brass collar around it. The fire's in the bottom. The stove lives on wood, which it eats so fast that it breathes fire out of its mouth. Ah! To lie near it or, better still, underneath it; until you have tried that you have no idea what comfort is. . . . You must be able to see it from where you are. That window, there, just look in."

And the snowman did and he saw the stove: a black, polished metal figure with brass fixtures. The little door at the bottom, through which ashes could be removed, had a window in it; and the snowman could see the light from the fire. A strange feeling of sadness and joy came over him. A feeling he had never experienced before. A feeling that all human beings know, except those who are made of snow.

"Why did you leave her?" The snowman somehow felt certain that the stove was of the female sex. "How could you bear to go away from such a lovely place?"

"I had to," answered the old watchdog. "They threw me out, put a chain around my neck, and here I am. And all I had done was to bite the youngest of the children from upstairs. I was gnawing on a bone and he took it away. A bone for a bone, I thought, and bit him in the leg. But the master and the mistress put all the blame on me. And ever since then I have been chained. The dampness has spoiled my voice. Can't you hear how hoarse I am? . . . Out! Out! Get out! . . . And that is the end of my story."

The snowman, who had stopped listening to the watchdog, was staring with longing through the cellar window into the housekeeper's room, where the stove stood on its four black legs. "She is exactly the same height as I am," he thought.

"It creaks so strangely inside of me," the snowman muttered. "Shall I never be able to go down into the cellar and be in the same room with her? Isn't it an innocent wish, and shouldn't innocent wishes be granted? It is my greatest, my most earnest, my only wish! And it would be a terrible injustice if it were never fulfilled! I shall get in, even if I have to break the window to do it."

"You will never get down into the cellar," the old dog said. "And if you did manage it, then the stove would make sure that you were out in a minute. . . . Out! Out!"

"I am almost out already!" cried the snowman. "I feel as if I were about to break in two."

All day long the snowman gazed through the window. In the evening the housekeeper's room seemed even more inviting. The light from the stove was so soft. It was not like the moonlight or the sunlight. "Only a stove can glow like that," he thought. Every so often, when the top door of the stove was opened to put more wood in, the bright flames would shoot out, and the blaze would reflect through the window and make the snowman blush from the neck up.

"It's more than I can bear!" he exclaimed. "See how beautiful she is when she sticks out her tongue."

The night was long, but not for the snowman, who was daydreaming happily. Besides, it was so cold that everything seemed to tingle.

In the morning the cellar window was frozen; the most beautiful white flowers decorated the glass, which the snowman did not appreciate because they hid the stove from his view. It was so cold that the windows couldn't thaw and the running nose on the water pump in the yard grew an icicle. It was just the kind of weather to put a snowman in the best of moods, but it didn't. Why, it was almost a duty to be content with weather like that; but he wasn't. He was miserable. He was suffering from "stove-yearning."

"That is a very serious disease, especially for a snowman to get." The old watchdog shook his head. "I have suffered from it myself, but I got over it. . . . Out! Out! Get out! . . . I have a feeling that the weather is going to change."

And it did. It became warmer and the snowman became smaller. He didn't say a word, not even one of complaint, and that's a very telling sign.

One morning he fell apart. His head rolled off and something that looked like the handle of a broom stuck up from where he had stood. It was what the boys had used to help hold the snowman together and make him stand upright.

"Now I understand why he longed for the stove," said the old watchdog. "That's the old poker he had inside him. No wonder. Well, now that's over. . . . Out! Out! Out!"

And soon the winter was over, and the little girls sang:

> "Come, anemones, so pure and white,
> Come, pussy willows, so soft and light,
> Come, lark and cuckoo, and sing
> That in February we have spring."

And no one thought about the snowman.

## 108

## In the Duckyard

In the duckyard . . . The hens called it the henyard, for there were hens there too, but this story is about a duck, so we shall call it the duckyard since that is the name the ducks prefer. . . . In the duckyard there once was a duck who came from Portugal. She had laid eggs, been slaughtered, and then eaten; and that was her biography. But all the little ducklings who had crawled out of her eggs had been called Portuguese and that name they were very proud of. When our story takes place there was only one member of the family left, and she was very fat, which is considered beautiful among ducks.

"Cock-a-doodle-doo," cried the cock, who had twelve wives and was very haughty.

"Ugh, how his crowing hurts my ears," the Portuguese said. "I wish he would learn to modulate his voice. But he is beautiful. I won't deny it, even though he isn't a drake. But to be able to modulate your voice is a sign of culture. Now the little songbirds who nest in the linden tree, they know the art. They sing so beautifully. . . . There's something in their songs that touches me indescribably. . . . I call it something Portuguese. If I had such a little songbird I would be a mother to it—kind and loving! It is part of my nature to be loving. It is in my blood: my Portuguese blood."

She had no sooner finished speaking than a little songbird fell, headfirst, from the roof of the house into the duckyard. The cat had caught the poor little fellow, and somehow he had managed to escape but not without a broken wing.

"Isn't that exactly what you would expect from a cat—brutality!" exclaimed the Portuguese. "I know that cat, hasn't he eaten two of my ducklings? That such a creature should be allowed to walk about freely, especially on roofs, is more than I can understand. It would never be allowed in Portugal."

She felt very sorry for the little songbird, and so did all the other ducks, even though they weren't Portuguese. As they stood in a circle around him, they said, "Poor unfortunate creature. We cannot sing, but we appreciate music and are sensitive to art, though we don't talk about it."

"And why not?" said the Portuguese. "Just to show my appreciation, I will do something for the poor little thing, for that is a duty." Then she climbed into the water trough and splashed with her wings.

The water streamed down over the little songbird and he nearly drowned, but he knew he had been drenched out of kindness.

"That was a good deed!" said the Portuguese to the other ducks. "I hope it will be a good example to all of you."

"Pip," said the little songbird. His broken wing made it very difficult for him to shake himself dry. "You have a good heart, madam." He wanted to show his appreciation for the shower, though he hoped he would never get another.

"I have never thought about being good-hearted," the Portuguese began, and spread her wings. "But this I know: I love all my fellow creatures, all except the cat. And to demand that I should love the cat would be quite unreasonable. You can make yourself at home. I am from a foreign land, and you can see it by the beauty of my feathers and my posture. All the other ducks are natives. They don't have my blood. But it hasn't gone to my head. Only this I must say: if anyone here understands you, then it is I."

"She has a *wortugal* stuck in her gizzard," cried one of the ordinary ducklings, who was known to be wittier than all the others.

The other ordinary ducks nudged each other and snickered. "Wortugal . . . Quack . . . Quack . . . Wortugal, Portugal . . . Quack . . . Quack . . ." They all agreed that their companion's joke was one of the funniest they had ever heard "Wortugal, Portugal." But now it was time that they, too, befriended the little songbird.

"We don't waddle around with long and difficult words in our bills, but that doesn't mean that we are not kind or sensitive. We care about

you too, but when we do you a favor we won't shout about it. Kind
acts are best done quietly."

"You have a beautiful voice," one of the older drakes began as he
stepped closer to the songbird. "It must be very gratifying for you to
know how much pleasure you give to others. Not that I understand
art; and that is why I keep my bill shut about it. After all, it is better
to be silent than to say a lot of stupidities, as some people do."

"Don't pester him," the Portuguese ordered. "He needs lots of rest
and proper attention." Turning to the little bird, she suggested,
"Would you like another shower?"

"Oh no. Please let me stay dry," whispered the songbird.

"Water is the best cure for everything. It has never done me any
harm," the Portuguese argued. "Amusing company helps too. Look
who's coming. It's the Chinese hens. They have feathers on their legs,
but they are quite respectable anyway. They have foreign blood in
their veins, but they were born here, and that in my opinion is a virtue."

The Chinese hens came and before them walked the cock. "You
are a songbird," he said politely, and this was very unusual, for he
considered courtesy unmasculine. "You do what you can with the
little voice you have and I appreciate it. But in order really to be
heard one needs a chest," he asserted while he took a deep breath
and held it as long as he could.

"Isn't he sweet?" remarked one of the Chinese hens. The songbird
looked up at her; his feathers were still wet and ruffled from his
shower. "He looks almost as beautiful as a newly hatched Chinese
chick."

The Chinese hens spoke kindly to the songbird—very softly and in
the most educated Chinese. Every word had a *ph* sound. "We belong
to the same race as you do. The ducks, even the Portuguese, are web-
footed. You don't know us yet, but then, who does? Who has taken
the trouble to find out who we are? No one! And yet we are members
of an aristocratic family, born to position above the others. We don't
make a fuss about it. We try to see everyone else's good points and
only talk about their virtues—though this can be difficult when so
few of the creatures here have any. Excluding ourselves and the cock,
there isn't an intelligent fowl in the henhouse, but at least they are all
respectable, that's more than you can say about any of the ducks.
Don't trust that duck with the curled tail, she is false. As for the one

with the green feathers in her wings, she is too talkative. She won't let you get a word in edgewise, and she has never held an opinion worth listening to. The fat one is a gossip, always telling malicious tales. We couldn't talk that way if we wanted to, because it would be against our nature; we say nice things about others or we don't say anything at all. The Portuguese is the only one of the whole lot of them who is the least bit educated, and she is too passionate and talks too much about Portugal."

"Goodness, how those Chinese hens whisper," said one ordinary duck to another ordinary duck. "But what a bore they are, and that's why we've never talked to them."

The drake joined the little group around the songbird. He was a little surprised at all the attention it was receiving, for he thought it was a sparrow. "I can't see the difference," he explained. "They all belong to the artistic crowd and they are all the same size. Since they exist, we shall have to put up with them."

"Don't mind him," the Portuguese whispered to the little songbird. "He is all business and business is all to him. . . . Now I think I had better take a nap. One owes it to oneself to take good care of oneself. I must grow fat, otherwise I shall never be stuffed and roasted, and this, after all, is the purpose of life."

The Portuguese blinked. She was a good duck; she found a good place to lie down, and there she slept soundly. The little songbird plucked at his broken wing, then he nestled as close as he could to his protector. "The duckyard is a pleasant place to be," he thought.

The hens walked about among the ducks only while they were looking for food; now that there was nothing more to be found, they went back to their own part of the yard, led by the Chinese hens.

The witty duckling remarked to the other ducklings that the Portuguese was waddling about in her second "ducklinghood."

"Ducklinghood . . . Ducklinghood!" screamed all the other young ducks. "My, how clever he is. . . ." Then they eagerly repeated his previous joke over and over again: "Wortugal . . . Portugal . . ." they cried until they grew tired and fell asleep.

For a while all was quiet, then a maid came from the kitchen of the farmhouse and emptied a bucketful of garbage into the duckyard. Splash!

At once all the ducks were up and about with their wings spread.

The Portuguese woke too, and as she rose she stepped right on top of the little songbird.

"*Peep,*" he cried. "You are so heavy, madam."

"It was your own fault, weren't you in the way? Don't be so thin-skinned. I am nervous too, but you will never hear me say '*Peep.*'"

"Don't be angry," said the little bird, "the *peep* just escaped me by mistake."

The Portuguese was not listening. She was too busy eating, gobbling down garbage as quickly as she could. In the meantime the songbird composed a song for her, and when she had finished eating and again lay down, he began to sing:

> "Tweet . . . Tweet . . .
> Of your good heart I sing
> And its message bring,
> Tweet . . . Tweet . . .
> To the sky
> Oh, so high.
> Tweet . . . Tweet . . ."

"I always rest after meals," the Portuguese complained. "When you live in a duckyard you must learn to behave like a duck. Now it is time to sleep."

The poor little songbird was amazed and unhappy; he had only meant to please the Portuguese. While she slept he found a grain of wheat and placed it in front of her. But when the duck woke up she was irritable because she had slept badly.

"That's something for a chicken, not for me; and please don't bother me all the time."

"Why are you mad at me, when all I want to do is to make you happy?" the songbird cried.

"Mad!" she exclaimed. "How dare you call me mad? Don't ever make such a mistake again."

"Yesterday," sniffed the little songbird, "yesterday there was only sunshine. Today everything is dark and gray. It makes me so sad."

"Hum. . . . You can't tell time," replied the Portuguese crossly. "The day isn't done yet. Don't stand there with such a long, sad face."

"Please don't look at me like that," the little bird begged. "That's the way those two evil eyes looked at me just before I fell down from the roof into the duckyard."

"Of all the nerve!" screamed the Portuguese. "Imagine anyone comparing me to a cat, to a carnivorous animal! I who haven't a mean bone in my body! I who have taken such good care of you! I'll teach you better manners, I will!" And she bit off the songbird's head and left his body dead and still.

"Now what have I done?" the Portuguese asked herself. "Was I too severe? Well, if he couldn't take that, then he wasn't meant for this world. Didn't I try to be a mother to him? How could I have done otherwise, when I have such a kind heart?"

The neighbor's cock stuck his head over the fence and crowed so that he could be heard in the next county.

"You'll be the death of us all, with your crowing," the Portuguese cried. "The little songbird lost his head because of it, and I almost lost mine."

"He doesn't look like much now," the cock admitted as he glanced at the headless songbird.

"Speak with respect of him," snapped the Portuguese. "His breast was small but he sang with true artistry. And he had that loving nature and tender soul which all animals and so-called human beings ought to have."

All the ducks gathered around the body of the little songbird. Ducks have a passionate nature and their passions are most deeply aroused by envy and pity. And as there was no reason to envy the songbird, they were filled with pity.

They were joined by the Chinese hens. "We shall never see another songbird like him. . . . He was almost Chinese," they said. And then they clucked and cried. And all the other hens clucked and cried. But the ducks had the reddest eyes.

"We have soft hearts," the ducks exclaimed. "No one can deny it."

"It is true," cried the Portuguese. "Ducks are almost as softhearted here as they are in Portugal."

But the drake, who hadn't cried, grunted, "What about something to eat! Is there anything more important than eating? A dead musician more or less doesn't matter. There are plenty more where he came from."

## 109

## The Muse of the Twentieth Century

The muse of the twentieth century we shall never know, but our children may and our grandchildren certainly will. Yet we cannot help wondering what she will look like or what songs she will sing: which string in man's soul she will touch, and to what heights she will raise her age.

What a lot of questions to ask in a time like ours, when poesy is only in the way, a time when we know full well that what our "immortal" poets compose will, in the future, exist, if at all, as scratchings on the walls of prisons, and be of interest only to the curious few.

Poesy ought to take an interest in what is to come; it should be the fuse that starts those struggles, causing both blood and ink to flow.

You think that I am only expressing my own opinion. You want to protest that poetry is not forgotten in our age.

I will grant that there are still people who on a weekday—when they have nothing else to do—feel a need for poetry; and that when this "hunger" makes them uncomfortable in their precious organs, they send a messenger to the bookstore to buy four crowns' worth of the latest poetry: a copy of the volume that has received the most laurel leaves from the critics. That is, if they are not content with the poetry that they get free from the grocer who wraps his wares in printed sheets. The publisher sells these pages very cheaply.

Cheapness is a virtue in an age as busy as ours. We have need of what we have, and that is enough! The poetry of the future and its music are subjects for Don Quixote. To spend time wondering about such things is as fruitful as discussing a trip to the remote planet Uranus. Our time is too valuable and too short for games of fantasy. Shouldn't we decide, once and for all, to talk reasonably about literature? What is poetry? Those notes, those sounds that try to express thought and feeling, and are caused by the movement and vibrations of our nerves. All joy, all happiness, all pain—yes, even our material ambitions—are, the learned tell us, determined by the functioning of our nervous systems. We are merely stringed instruments: all of us!

But who plays upon the strings? Who makes them throb? The spirit, the invisible God's spirit, plucks them; and the other stringed instruments, inspired by His movements and His mood, respond in harmony or in disharmony and discord. So it has always been and so it will always be, even in the next century when men will make great strides forward because they will be conscious of their freedom.

Each century—also each millennium—reflects its greatest in poesy. Born at the end of one epoch, it steps forward to rule the next. In our busy machine age she is already born, she who will be the muse of the coming century. We send her our greetings. Someday she may hear them or read them, as I have already said, scratched on the walls of a prison.

Her cradle is large, stretching as far south as explorers have gone, and as far south as astronomers have pointed their telescopes. But we do not hear the cradle rock; for the sound of it is drowned out by the banging and whirring of the machines from our factories, the locomotive whistles, and the explosions as both real rock cliffs and the spiritual ties that bind us to the past are blown to pieces. She was born in our factories where steam and the machine rule: Master Bloodless and his helpers, who are hard at work both night and day.

She is capable of love and possesses a real woman's heart; full of the flames of the virgin and the fire of passion. Her intelligence shines in all the colors of the spectrum, since thousands of years of dispute have proven that which color is the most beautiful is only a matter of taste. Her strength and her pride are her great swan wings of fantasy. Science constructed them for her and the laws of nature lent them power.

In the muse's veins two very different bloods have mixed. On her father's side she is related to the people. Her soul and thoughts are healthy; the expression of her eyes is earnest and on her mouth a smile plays. Her mother was wellborn, brought up strictly by the academy. As an immigrant's daughter, this noble woman had memories of the golden rococo.

The gifts the muse received at her birth were extravagant. She was given so many of nature's secrets, one might suppose that they were merely sweets to be eaten and forgotten. From the depths of the oceans the diving bell brought her the strangest species. A map of the heavens—that silent ocean with millions of islands, each one a world —was her coverlet.

Her nanny sang to her. She chose verses from the great skald Eivild, from Firdausi, from the minnesingers, and Heine, who sang with the eagerness of a boy from the depth of a truly poetic soul. She recited the *Eddas,* those tales of blood and vengeance that belong to our primeval ancestors. All of *The Thousand and One Nights* were recounted in a quarter of an hour. The muse learned much from her nanny.

The muse of the next century is still a child, although she no longer sleeps in a cradle. She is willful, determined, capricious; for she still does not know in which direction she wants to go. She is still playing in the great kindergarten that has been filled with treasures from the rococo and the distant past. Characters from Greek tragedy and Roman comedy are there, carved in marble to be her dolls. All the folksongs ever sung are there, waiting like dried flowers for the kiss of genius to make them bloom and smell even more sweetly than before. The chords of Beethoven, Gluck, Mozart, and all the other great composers are played for her. On her bookshelves stand many books that in their time were thought to be immortal and now are forgotten. But there is still room for those of our age, of whose immortality the telegraph wires sing, and who are dead before the telegram is delivered.

The muse is very widely read; indeed, she has read too much. But she was born in our age of which so much must be forgotten that she will learn the art of forgetting.

As yet she has not given any thought to her own song: the great work that she will inspire and that will live in the millennium to come alongside the Books of Moses and Bidpai, golden fable of the fox. And while she amuses herself, nations struggle against each other so that the very air reverberates from the din of their battles. Cannons and pens are inscribing runes which perhaps no one will ever understand.

With a Garibaldi hat on her head, she sits reading Shakespeare; she raises her glance from the book and murmurs, "Yes, he will live and be understood when I am grown up." Calderon rests in a sarcophagus constructed from his own works and decorated with words of homage and tribute. Holberg—oh yes, the twentieth-century muse is cosmopolitan, she has also heard of the Danish playwright—has been placed in a volume together with Molière, Plautus, and Aristophanes; but when she takes down the book it is usually to read Molière.

In her search for the meaning of life she is as single-minded as the chamois ransacking the mountains for salt, but she is free of the restless anxiety that plagues the little deer. The peace that reigns in her soul is like that of the Hebraic tale—and not even the hearts of the joyous warriors of Thessaly swelled with such strength, as that of this nomadic tribe who lived on a green plain beneath the clear and starfilled sky.

Is she religious, you ask, is she Christian? She knows the rudiments of philosophy. She broke a baby tooth on the theory of the atom, but another tooth has now grown up in its place. She ate of the apple while she was still in her cradle: she ate and she became wise. And then she thought about immortality and decided that no more beautiful thought had ever been conceived.

When will this new era begin? When shall we see and hear the muse of the next century?

One lovely morning she will arrive. She will come riding on the back of the modern dragon, a locomotive, through tunnels and over bridges. She will come sailing across the great oceans on a dolphin blowing steam out of its nostrils. Or she will come flying on the wings of Montgolfier's bird, *Rock,* gliding toward the earth, toward that spot where first she will make her divinity known.

But where, in which country? Will it be on the continent that Columbus discovered? That land of liberty whose original inhabitants were hunted down like wild animals, where the Africans were turned into beasts of burden, the land from which we hear *The Song of Hiawatha?* Or will it be on the underside of the world: that lump of gold in the southern seas, the land of contrasts, where much is the opposite of what we know, where day is night and swans with black wings sing in forests of mimosa? Or will she stand first on the statue of Memnon, the desert sphinx who still sings at sunrise though we cannot understand her song? Or will she choose the island of coal, where Shakespeare has ruled since Elizabeth's times? Or that country that Tycho Brahe called his own but from which he was banished? Or California, that fairy-tale land where the redwood lifts its head high above any other living thing?

We cannot answer either question: neither where nor when that light, that star in the forehead of the muse, will first be seen, and the flower unfold on whose leaves will be inscribed the twentieth century's conception of all that is beautiful in form, color, and sound.

"What is the new muse's program?" the clever politicians ask a little nervously. "What does she want?"

What they ought to ask is, what she does not intend to do.

She will not perform as a ghost of the past. She does not want to try to create new dramas out of leftovers. She does not intend to patch with poetry, faulty plots and badly thought-out tragedies. She will outdistance us, as the marble amphitheater surpassed the mimer's cart. She will not dissect man's natural speech and paste bits and pieces together so that they sound as artificial as the song of a music box, and fill it with phrases of flattery that the troubadours were forced to compose to please their masters. To her, poetry will not be the aristocrat and prose the peasant; they will be equal in power and importance, and beauty as well.

She will not attempt to chisel out of that gigantic block of Icelandic granite—the *Sagas!*—new versions of old gods. They are dead. The twentieth century will have no sympathy for them and will deny all kinship to them. Nor will the muse be willing to live in hired rooms of the French novel of another age, any more than she will wish to anesthetize her contemporaries with the "true" story of "ordinary" people. She will bring to art and literature the essence of life. Her songs in prose and poetry will be short, clear, and varied. A new alphabet will be developed and the heartbeat of each nation will be a letter; and the muse will love them equally, and from the letters she will form words, and from the words a song that will be the hymn of the future.

And when will she appear? For those who have gone before us and are familiar with eternity, it will be a short while; but for us who are alive now, it will be a long time to come. Soon the Great Wall of China will crumble. The railroads of Europe will reach the closed archives of Asian culture. The two streams of culture will meet and the rapids of the double river will have deeper tones than have ever been heard before. We—the old of our own times—will tremble with fear, and hear in the new music the voice of Ragnarok and the fall of the old gods. But how can we forget that this is the fate of every civilization? On earth every nation and every epoch disappears, leaving only a single picture in a capsule made of words that floats on the surface of the eternal river like a lotus flower. These flowers bear witness that all ages are flesh of our flesh; only the clothing differs. The Hebrew flower is the Old Testament; the Greeks' is the *Iliad* and the *Odyssey*. What will ours be? Ask the twentieth-century muse in the time of Ragnarok, when the new heavens will be formed and their message understood.

All the power of steam, all the present's strength, was only a lever. Master Bloodless and his helpers—whom we in our times believed were rulers—were merely servants, slaves, to decorate the halls and carry the treasures and lay the table for the great feast over which the muse will preside, with the innocence of a child, the earnestness of a young girl, and the confidence and knowledge of a woman. She will lift the marvelous lamp of poesy. She—the new muse!—in whose human heart the flame of godliness will burn.

We hail you, muse of the poesy of the coming century! Our shout of welcome will be heard as the ideas and prayers of the worms are heard when the plow cuts them in two. Yet when a new spring dawns the plow must draw its furrows across the land and cut us worms in pieces, so that crops can grow to feed the coming generations.

All hail the muse of the twentieth century!

## 110

*The Ice Maiden*

CHAPTER ONE: LITTLE RUDY

Let us visit Switzerland. Let us travel a little in that marvelous land of mountains where forests spread themselves up walls of granite. Let us climb the mountains until we come to the great fields of snow; and then descend to the green meadows, where rivers and streams run so swiftly that one would think they were afraid of missing their chance to meet the ocean and disappear. Down in the valleys the sun feels burning hot, but it also makes its strength felt on the mountaintops. There it shines on heavy masses of snow, melting them through the years into huge, shining blocks of ice, into glaciers.

Two such glaciers have been formed beneath the pinnacles of Schreckhorn and Wetterhorn, filling the wide clefts near the little mountain village of Grindelwald. They are strange and awesome, and in the summer travelers come from all over the world to see them. Either the strangers cross the snow-clad mountains or they come from the valleys far below, climbing for many hours. As they ascend, the valley below them seems to descend, and they look back at it as if they were looking down from a balloon. Often the very tops of the mountains are hidden in what looks like a curtain of smoke, while in the valley with its little brown houses the sun is still shining. Its rays make the greenness of the meadows so brilliant as to appear transparent. Water splashes, gurgles, and sputters below; water tinkles and chimes above, and looks like silver bands as it falls down the sides of the cliffs.

On both sides of the road there are log chalets, each with its own potato patch. The potato patch is necessary, for in every little chalet live large families, and even small stomachs can be very hungry.

As soon as a stranger is spied on his way up the mountain, a flock of children will be there to greet him. Little tradesmen they are, selling charmingly carved toy houses that look just like the ones they live in themselves. About twenty years ago there could sometimes be seen among these children a boy who kept a little apart from the others. He appeared so serious and held the plain box containing his wares so tightly that he looked as if he were unwilling to part with them. Although the boy himself could never have guessed it, it was his very lack of eagerness for his task that attracted buyers; and this very young boy with his very solemn expression sold more than the other children.

Farther up the mountain lived the boy's grandfather, and it was he who carved the lovely little houses that the boy sold. In the old man's house there was a whole chest full of the finest wood carvings: nutcrackers, knives, forks, prancing mountain antelopes, and little boxes covered with vine leaves. Everything that could please the eye of a child was there, but little Rudy—for that was the boy's name—looked with greater interest and longing toward the rifle that hung from the rafters, for his grandfather had promised him that it would be his when he grew strong enough to use it.

Though Rudy was still very young he was set to taking care of the goats; and if a goatherd is to be judged by the way he keeps up with his animals, then Rudy was an excellent goatherd, for he could climb even higher than the goats. Up the trees he would go to fetch the birds' nests. He was daring and brave, but he never smiled except when he stood near the great waterfall or heard in the distance the sound of an avalanche. He did not play with the other children and was to be seen among them only when his grandfather sent him down to sell wood carvings. This work was a real chore for Rudy. He preferred climbing in the mountains or sitting at home with his grandfather. The old man told the boy stories of bygone days. He told him about his ancestors, the people of Meiningen.

"They have not always been Swiss," he explained. "In ancient times they migrated from the north, and there are people living up there to whom you are related; they are called Swedes."

Rudy learned much from his grandfather, but he had other teachers as well, and perhaps what they taught him was even more valuable. They were the dog, Ajola, that Rudy had inherited from his father; and the tomcat, whom Rudy loved especially because he had taught him how to be a climber.

"Come up here on the roof," the cat had said to him when he was yet so young that he could not talk himself. Rudy had understood the cat, as all small children understand the languages of hens, ducks, dogs, and cats.

Animals speak to children as plainly as their parents do; and to very young children even Grandfather's cane can talk. It can neigh and become a horse with swift legs and a flying mane. Some children retain this gift longer than others, and then grownups shake their heads and say that they are slow in developing and start remarking about it being time for them to start growing up. Grownups are always talking, but they are not always worth listening to.

"Come up here, up on the roof," were the first words that the cat said to Rudy and he had understood them at once. "Don't be afraid. All that about falling is all the way you look at it; and if you don't imagine what it's like to fall, you won't fall. You only fall if you're afraid of falling. Come follow me, first one paw and then the other, eyes straight ahead. And when you come to a gap, you leap; and hold on with your claws when you get to the other side. That's the way I do it!"

And that's what Rudy did; and he spent many hours with the tomcat on top of the roof or in the uppermost branches of a tree. Later Rudy learned to climb higher than his friend, to the very edges of the cliffs where the cat never came.

"Higher! Higher!" exclaimed the trees and bushes. "Look how we climb, how near the sky we reach! See how we hang on with our roots to the ledges of the cliffs."

Often Rudy would be on the mountaintop before the sun was up there; then he would be given his breakfast drink, that draft that only God can brew, though man knows the recipe. It is made up of the fragrance of mountain herbs mixed with the smell of mint and thyme from the valleys. All that is heavy, the clouds absorb; then the wind drives the clouds across the tops of the pine trees, to comb and card them. The very essence of all these aromas becomes air, fresh and light; and this was Rudy's first drink in the morning.

The daughters of the sun, its rays, kissed his cheeks, and Dizziness, though she stood nearby, waiting, did not dare to touch him. The swallows from his grandfather's houses, where there were never less than seven nests, joined Rudy and his herd of goats. "You and we . . . You and we!" they sang, bringing messages from all the animals back at the house, even from the hens, the only birds to whom little Rudy paid no attention.

Rudy had traveled much for a child of his tender years. Born in the canton of Valais, he had been carried across the mountain range to his grandfather's house, and recently he had gone by foot to visit Staubbach, that mountain which stands in front of its greater sister, who is called "The Maiden," and covers part of its bright white face with a silver veil as the face of an Arabian woman is concealed. During his first trip Rudy had crossed the great glacier near Grindelwald, but that had been a journey of sorrow, for his mother had died, and as his grandfather once explained: "It was on the glacier that Rudy had his child's merriment stolen from him."

When Rudy was a baby his mother had described him in a letter to her father as a baby who laughed more than he cried. "I think his soul has been changed. While he was imprisoned in the cleft all his laughter froze," his grandfather had been heard to say, though as a rule he seldom spoke about this event.

Yet everyone knew the story of Rudy's life. His father had been a postman and, with a dog as his only companion, had carried the mail across the Simplon Pass. That was in the canton of Valais, and there in the valley of the Rhone, Rudy's father's brother still lived and was a well-known hunter and guide.

When Rudy's father died, Rudy's mother decided that she would return with her year-old son to her father's home in the Bernese Oberland, a few hours' walk beyond Grindelwald. One June day she set out for her father's house, carrying her little boy in her arms. She did not travel alone but went with two hunters who were returning to Grindelwald.

They had traveled the greatest part of their journey and had reached the great snow fields on the mountain ridge, from where Rudy's mother could see her father's house and the green mountainside where she had played as a child. The only difficulty left was the crossing of the upper part of the glacier. Newly fallen snow hid a crevasse—not a deep cleft with a raging river at the bottom but a narrow split in the ice that was deeper than a man's height. The young woman, with her babe in her arms, slid, fell, and was gone. She had not screamed or even uttered a sound, but from below them in the glacier her companions heard a baby cry.

More than an hour passed before the hunters were able to return with ropes and a ladder, so that they could climb down into the crevasse. With great difficulty they brought up the two bodies. The baby was still alive, but though they tried, they could not bring the mother back to life.

So it was that the woodcarver who had lost a daughter received a son. But the little boy had changed. No more could it be said of him, as his mother had, that he laughed more than he cried. His visit to the cold, ice world—where the Swiss mountain people believe the souls of the condemned are frozen till Doomsday—had altered him.

Not unlike raging water frozen and crushed into green blocks of glass is the glacier, one gigantic block tipped on top of another. Far below—deep, deep down—flows a raging river of melted snow and ice; its waters twist themselves through the glacier, making deep caves and great caverns, a wonderful palace of ice. This is the home of the Ice Maiden. She, who kills and crushes all living things that come near her, is both a child of the air and a ruler of the mighty rivers. That is why she can reach, swifter than the mountain goat, the highest peaks, where mountain climbers must wearily cut steps in the ice to gain a foothold; and why she can sail on a twig down a great river, or leap from cliff to cliff with her snow-white hair and her blue-green dress, which glistens like water, streaming behind her.

"Mine is the power!" she exclaims. "I crush anything that comes within my grasp and never let it go! A lovely boy was stolen from me. I had kissed him but not so hard that he died from it. Now he is again among human beings. He herds goats in the mountains. Upward, ever upward, he climbs, away from everyone else, but not from me. He is mine and I claim him."

And she called upon Vertigo to obey her. It was too humid for the Ice Maiden down in the meadows where the mint thrives. Vertigo stretched herself and came swimming up the river. Two of Vertigo's sisters had come with her. Their family is a large one. The Ice Maiden chose the one who has power both inside and out of doors to help her.

She is the one who can sit on the top of a flight of stairs or perch herself on the railing of a church tower. She is as agile as a squirrel and can tread air as a swimmer treads water. She tempts her victims to climb too high and then pushes them down into the abyss.

The Ice Maiden and Vertigo are like the polyp that lives in the sea: they grasp anything that comes within their reach; and now Vertigo was ordered to capture Rudy.

"I cannot catch him," Vertigo answered. "I have already tried, but the cat has taught him his own tricks. Besides, that human child has a power of his own, he can push me away. I cannot reach him, even when he hangs from the topmost branches of the tree. If only I could tickle him under the soles of his feet or give him a ducking in the air, but I can't."

"We can do it!" shouted the Ice Maiden. "You and I together."

"No! No!" came the answer, and it sounded like a mountain echo of the tolling of church bells, but it was a song. Other spirits of nature, those that are mild, loving, and good, had joined in a chorus, to have their say. They were the rays of the sun, its daughters, who when night comes retire to the highest mountaintops and there fold their rose-colored wings, which turn a deeper and deeper red as the sun sets.—Man sometimes calls that sight "rose of the evening."—When the sun finally disappears its daughters sleep until their mother again rises above the horizon. The rays of the sun love flowers, butterflies, and human beings, and among the latter, they especially loved little Rudy.

"You will never catch him! You will never catch him!" they said.

"Bigger and stronger men have I caught and carried away!" replied the Ice Maiden.

Then the daughters of the sun sang a song about a wanderer in the mountains and how the whirlwind had robbed him of his cape. "The covering of the man, the wind could take and fly away with, but not the man himself. For man is powerful, more powerful even than we are. His spirit can soar even higher than our mother, the sun. He knows the magic words that make him master of both winds and sea, so that they are his servants and must obey him." Theirs was a lovely song.

Every morning the sun rays shone through the only little window in Rudy's grandfather's house and rested on the sleeping child. The daughters of the sun kissed him, for they hoped to thaw and destroy that kiss of ice which the royal ruler of the glacier, the Ice Maiden, had pressed upon his forehead while he was lying in his dead mother's lap, that time he fell into the crevasse in the glacier and was saved as if by a miracle.

## CHAPTER TWO: JOURNEY TO A NEW HOME

When Rudy was eight years old, his uncle who lived in the Rhone Valley sent for him. Here the boy could get better schooling and, when he was grown, would have more opportunity for earning his living. His grandfather had to admit that this was true, and therefore he let the boy go.

It was the day that Rudy was to depart and there were many to say good-by to besides his grandfather. First of all there was the old dog, Ajola.

"Your father was the postman and I was the post dog," said Ajola. "We have climbed both up and down. I know the people and the dogs on the other side of the mountains. I am not in the habit of speaking, but now, when we shall not have the opportunity of talking with each other much longer, there is something I would like to say. I want to tell you a story. It is one I have given much thought to; I don't understand it and you probably won't either. Not that it matters whether we understand it or not, but it has set me to thinking that everything is not right, either among men or among dogs.

"Once I saw a puppy that was traveling by stagecoach. It had a seat for itself like a regular passenger. Its mistress—whether she was a lady or a maid, I cannot tell—had taken a little bottle of milk along for the dog to suck on. She offered the puppy cake, but it only sniffed at the cake and wouldn't eat it; then the woman ate it herself. I was running along beside the coach. It was spring and the road was filled with mud. I was hungry—hungry as only a dog can be. I saw it, and I have thought about it since, and somehow I do not think it's right. I hope that someday you will be able to drive in your own carriage, little Rudy. They tell me that such things are up to yourself. I am not sure. I have never been able to, no matter how loud I barked."

That was Ajola's speech. Rudy kissed the old dog on the wet tip of his nose, then he picked the cat up in his arms, but cats don't like to be carried.

"You are getting too strong, don't squeeze me. You know that I will never use my claws against you. Go and climb over the mountains; haven't I taught you how to climb? Believe that you can't fall, and you won't." And the cat ran away before Rudy could see the look of sorrow in its eyes.

His grandfather's two hens were running about at Rudy's feet. One of them had lost its tail. It had been shot off by a tourist who had mistaken it for an eagle.

"Rudy is going across the mountains," said one of the hens.

"He is always in a hurry," said the other. "I cannot bear saying good-by, I am too sensitive." And both the hens scurried outside to look for something to eat.

Rudy said good-by to the goats, and their braying sounded melancholy and sad.

Two of the guides from the district who were going across the mountains took Rudy with them. It was a long march for so small a boy, but Rudy was strong and his courage was tireless.

The swallows flew above him during the first part of the journey. "You and we! You and we!" they sang. The road led across the Lütschine River, which emerges as several small streams from the dark caves of the Grindelwald glacier. The only bridge across the raging waters were steppingstones and fallen trees, which had been carried downstream by the river and now were locked among the rocks.

Near a thicket of alders they began to ascend the side of the mountain, then, when it seemed safe, they walked out on the glacier itself. Sometimes they climbed over the great blocks of ice and sometimes they encircled them. Sometimes they crawled and sometimes they walked. Rudy's eyes shone with delight and he strode forward, stepping so hard that his boots with the iron taps on his heels made marks in the ice, leaving a trail behind him.

Black earth, which had been carried and deposited by the water coming from the melted snow higher up the mountains, covered much of the surface of the glacier, but here and there its blue-green glasslike ice shone through. There were little pools among the ice packs that one had to skirt. At one point Rudy and his companions saw a big boulder that was tottering at the edge of an ice sheet suddenly break loose, roll, and fall into a crevasse in the ice. They heard the echo come from the dark tunnels of the glacier as it continued its descent.

Upward, ever upward they went. The glacier seemed to be trying to stretch itself as high as the mountain peaks, a wild frozen river with towers of ice caught between craggy cliffs. Rudy remembered what he had been told about how he and his mother had been down at the bottom of one of the frost-breathing crevasses. But the story was no more real to him than so many other stories that he had been told, and he soon stopped thinking about it. When the men thought that the climb was getting particularly difficult, one of them would stretch out his hand to help Rudy. But the boy was not tired and he ran across the slippery ice like a mountain goat.

Soon they were walking among barren rocks, then they reached low, wind-swept forest; next they came to a green pasture. The landscape was ever changing, always different, except for its sentinels, the great snow-covered peaks, which Rudy—like all the other children of the district—knew by name: "The Maiden," "The Monk," and "Eiger." Rudy had never before been up so high, never before set foot on that sea of snow with its immobile waves that the wind sweeps across, raising only the fine powder of the surface, as it blows foam on a turbulent ocean. Up here the glaciers hold hands—if one may say that of glaciers—each one of them a palace for the Ice Maiden, whose power and pleasure it is to imprison and bury all.

The sun was hot and the snow blinding to look at, as if it had just been sown with blue-white, glittering diamonds. Innumerable insects, bees, and butterflies had been brought up here by the wind and now lay dead on the snow. Around the top of Mount Wetterhorn rested a dark cloud; it looked as if it were a wad of black cotton. Hidden inside it was a foehn wind, which could spread terror if it were let loose.

Rudy never forgot that day's journey, or the scene high up there at dusk, with a view of the road he had yet to travel and the deep ravines made by water rushing down the mountains for so many thousands of years that it made one feel lost just to think about how many there must have been.

On the other side of the ocean of snow an abandoned stone building was their shelter for the night. Here they found charcoal and kindling. The men lighted a fire and sat down before it to smoke and drink hot spiced wine. Rudy was given his share of the wine, and he listened to the men, who were talking of the mysteries and secrets of the Alps. They told of the great snakes that lived in the deep lakes, of the gypsies, of ghosts who carried sleeping travelers through the air to a strange floating city called Venice. Then they began to talk about the strange, wild shepherd who drove his black sheep across the pastures at night. Many, though they had not seen him, had heard the sheep bells and the ghostly bleating of the ram. While the men spoke, Rudy listened with curiosity but not fear—for he was frightened of nothing —and in the distance he thought he did hear a hollow, weird animal cry. It became clearer and clearer. The men grew silent; they had heard it too. They warned Rudy that he must not fall asleep.

It was the foehn wind that was speaking: that tempest that casts itself from the mountain peaks down into the valleys with such force that it can snap full-grown trees as if they were reeds, and move houses as if they were pawns in a chess game.

The storm lasted only an hour, then the men told Rudy that he could close his eyes. The boy was so tired that he fell asleep at their command.

Early the next morning they broke camp. The sun now shone on new fields of ice, new glaciers, and new mountains, whose names Rudy did not know. They had entered the canton of Valais on the other side of the mountains and great snow peaks lay between them and Grindelwald; still they had far to go before Rudy would reach his new home, a long journey through valleys, forests, and meadows. Rudy looked eagerly at everything.

As the travelers approached, people came rushing out of their houses to stare at them. Rudy had never seen such strange-looking folk before. They all seemed to be deformed. They were disgustingly fat; below their pale, sallow faces, their yellow flesh sagged in rolls. Their eyes were vacant and told of their stupidity. They were Cretins. The women seemed even more monstrous than the men.

"Are these the kind of people I will find in my new home?" Rudy thought.

## CHAPTER THREE: RUDY'S UNCLE

Happily, the people who lived in Rudy's uncle's house looked like the kind of human beings whom Rudy was used to seeing. All of them, that is, except one. Here, too, was one of those poor silly creatures whom you find in the canton of Valais, clothed in loneliness and poverty, whose lot it is to spend a few months of each year with different members of the family. Just at the time when Rudy came, it was his uncle's turn to house and feed poor Saperli.

Rudy's uncle was still a mighty hunter, and besides, he was skilled in barrelmaking. His wife was a tiny, lively woman with a birdlike face. She had the eyes of an eagle and a long neck that was covered with fine hair like down.

Everything was new to Rudy: clothes, habits, and even the language; but a child's ear picks things up easily and he soon would learn to understand it. Rudy's uncle seemed rich in comparison to his grandfather. The rooms in the house were large and the walls were covered with polished guns and the horns of chamois that Rudy's uncle had killed. Over the entrance was a picture of the Blessed Mother. Beneath it a little lamp burned and there was a bouquet of rhododendron.

Rudy's uncle was known not only as the best hunter of the chamois in the district but also as the most experienced and trusted guide. In his house Rudy was now to be the favorite, the one whom the grownups spoiled a little. True, he had a rival: an old hunting dog, useless now but honored and petted for all the use he had once been. Everyone remembered and talked about his former feats, and that is why he was treated like a member of the family who was entitled to spend his old age in leisure. Rudy tried to be friendly and pet the dog, but it did not respond to strangers. Rudy did not remain a stranger long; he soon grew roots in house and heart.

"Life is not so bad in the canton of Valais," his uncle said. "We still have the chamois, and that won't die out as the mountain goat did. Things are much better now than they were—though you'll hear a lot of boasting about the 'good old times.' There is a hole in the sack now. There is fresh air in the valleys; we are not as closed in as we used to be. The new bud is always better than the fallen leaf."

Sometimes Rudy's uncle was very talkative. Then he would tell of his childhood, of the time when his own father was in his prime, when the canton of Valais was "closed tight as a sack" that was full of many unpleasant things, among them the poor unfortunate Cretins.

"When the Frenchmen came, they killed many people, but they killed the sickness as well. Oh, the French can fight in more ways than one. They fought the mountains, the rocks were forced to give up; we have a road across the Simplon. I can say to a three-year-old child, 'Go to Italy.' And if he keeps to the road he will get there. . . .

Frenchwomen are good at fighting too." Rudy's uncle laughed and nodded toward his wife, who had been born in France; then he sang a French song and shouted hip-hip-hurrah for Napoleon Bonaparte.

This was the first time that Rudy had heard of France and of the great town on the Rhone River, called Lyon, which his uncle had once visited.

"It won't be long before the boy becomes a good hunter. He has a natural bent for it," Rudy's uncle said more than once, as he taught the boy how to hold a rifle, take aim, and shoot.

During the hunting season he took him up in the mountains and gave him the blood of chamois to drink, for Swiss hunters and guides believe this is an antidote against vertigo. He taught him how to judge when an avalanche would take place—whether it would happen in the morning or the evening—by observing the conditions of the snow and the strength of the sun. He told Rudy to take the chamois as teacher in the art of climbing, to watch how it could leap and land on its feet without sliding. He explained what he should do when there was no foothold on the face of a cliff: how he could hold onto the rock with his elbows or use the muscles of his legs and thighs—even his neck—to prevent himself from falling.

The chamois are clever; they even post guards to tell the flock when a hunter is approaching. The hunter must be cleverer; he must walk against the wind so that the animal cannot pick up his scent. Sometimes Rudy's uncle would fool the chamois by hanging his hat and his tunic on a cane. The chamois, mistaking the clothing for the hunter, would expect an attack from the wrong direction.

One day Rudy and his uncle were out hunting. His uncle had spied a chamois on the side of a mountain. The snow was wet and slippery. The path along the face of the cliff was so narrow that it soon disappeared and became only a thin ledge above a deep abyss, so he lay down and crawled.

Rudy was standing on more solid ground, about a hundred feet below him. Suddenly the boy saw a vulture, the kind that can take a half-grown sheep and fly away with it; it was circling in the air above Rudy's uncle. The boy knew what it intended to do. Any moment it would sweep down on the man and with its wings hurl him into the valley, where it could later feed on his corpse. Rudy's uncle had eye only for the chamois, which could be seen running with its kid. Rudy took aim and was about to shoot the vulture. Just at that moment the chamois leaped up to the ridge of the cliff. Rudy's uncle fired and the antelope was dead. The kid fled; all its life had been spent in training for this moment of flight. The echo from the shot frightened the vulture and it flew away. Rudy's uncle did not know about the danger he had been in until he was told about it later by Rudy.

As they were returning home in high spirits—Rudy's uncle whistling a tune from his childhood—they heard a terrifying but familiar noise coming from not far away. They looked about them and then they looked upward. There above them they saw a part of the snow field being lifted as if it were a linen tablecloth that the wind had caught. It snapped in two, like a gigantic slab of marble breaking. Stones, snow, and ice tumbled down the mountainside. There was a sound like a thunderclap. It was an avalanche! They would not be buried by it, but it would pass much too near them.

"Hold on, Rudy!" his uncle screamed. "Hold on with all your might!"

Rudy threw his arms around the trunk of a tree, while his uncle climbed up into the branches above him. The landslide passed several yards away from them, but the turbulence caused winds of such strength that trunks and branches of trees were broken as if they were dry reeds. Rudy lay pressed to the ground. The tree trunk that he held onto was now a stump, as if it had been sawed in half. The wind had broken off the crown and thrown it a distance away. There among the splintered branches lay his uncle. The man's head was smashed, his face was unrecognizable, although his hand holding onto the branch was still warm. Pale and trembling, Rudy looked at him; this was the first time the boy had become acquainted with fear, the first time he had experienced horror.

Late that night he returned home, bearing the message of death to the house that now belonged to sorrow. His aunt was silent; she did not cry until the following day when her husband's body was carried to the house.

The poor Cretin stayed in bed the whole day, but in the evening he got up and approached Rudy. "Will you write a letter for me? Saperli cannot write, but Saperli can go to the post office."

"Whom do you want to write a letter to?" Rudy asked.

"To our Master Christ," replied the Cretin.

"What are you talking about?"

The half-wit, as they called him, looked with pleading eyes at

Rudy, folded his hands, and said very solemnly and piously but in a gentle voice, "Jesus Christ. Saperli wants to beg him to let Saperli lie dead and not the master of this house."

Rudy took Saperli's hands in his. "Such a letter would never be delivered, and it would not bring him back to us." It was difficult for Rudy to explain to the Cretin why what he was asking was impossible.

"Now you are master of the house," Rudy's aunt said to him. And Rudy became the master.

### CHAPTER FOUR: BABETTE

"Who is the best hunter in the canton of Valais?" The chamois could answer that question. "Watch out for Rudy," they would say.

"Who is the handsomest hunter?"

"Rudy is the handsomest," the girls would reply, but they did not add, "Watch out for Rudy." Not even the strictest mothers said that, for he nodded as pleasantly to them as he did to their daughters.

He was always happy, with a smile on his lips. His cheeks were tanned bronze by the sun, his teeth were white, and his eyes were dark as coal. A handsome lad and only twenty years old. The ice water in the lakes did not seem freezing to him, he swam like a fish. He could hang onto the sheer, granite mountainside as if he were a snail; no one could climb as well as he. His sinews and his muscles were good. How to leap and to jump he had learned first from the cat and later from the chamois.

With Rudy as a guide any traveler was safe, and he could have made a fortune that way. Barrelmaking he had learned from his uncle, but he never thought of making a living that way either. Rudy was a hunter, and to stalk the chamois was his greatest pleasure. Good hunters weren't poor, and everyone in the district agreed that Rudy was a good match, as long as he did not set his eyes on those above him.

"He kissed me while we were dancing," said the schoolmaster's daughter Annette to her dearest friend. But Annette should never have told such a thing to her dearest friend, for a secret like that is as hard to keep as it is to stop sand from running out of a bag with a hole in it. Soon everyone knew that Rudy, in spite of being so honest and good-natured, could steal a kiss while he was dancing—and yet he had never kissed the girl whom he wanted most to kiss.

"Keep an eye on him," said an old hunter. "He has kissed Annette, and since he has started with *A*, he'll kiss through the whole alphabet."

A kiss during a dance was as yet all the gossips could bring to market. He had kissed Annette and yet she was not the flower his heart pined for.

Down at Bex, between two great walnut trees and beside a rushing mountain stream, lived a rich miller. His house was large: three stories high with small towers at each corner, and roofed with shingles that were held fast by strips of lead that reflected the light of both the sun and the moon. The highest of the towers had a weather vane in the form of an apple with a golden arrow piercing it, in honor of William Tell. The mill looked prosperous and decorative, and with a bit of skill one could describe it or sketch it; but the miller's daughter was another matter. In any case, Rudy would have said that you could not possibly draw or tell about such beauty in words. Yet her picture was in his heart, and there her eyes shone with such brilliance that they had set his heart afire. Like all fires, it had broken out suddenly; and the strangest part of it was that the miller's daughter Babette did not even know about it, for she and Rudy had never exchanged a single word.

The miller was rich, and his wealth put Babette a good many notches above a hunter. "But nothing is up so high that it cannot be reached," thought Rudy. "All you have to do is climb, and you never fall unless you believe that you are going to." This was his philosophy and he had learned it at home.

Now it happened that Rudy had business in Bex. In those days it was quite a journey, for the railroad hadn't reached there yet. From the Rhone glacier along the foothills of the Simplon, surrounded by mountains of varying heights, stretches the valley of Valais, and through it runs the mighty Rhone River. The river is master of the valley, and often in spring it swells over its banks to flood the fields and ruin the roads. Between the towns of Sion and St. Maurice the valley turns sharply, and at St. Maurice it becomes so narrow there is only room for the river and the road that connects the two towns.

An ancient tower stands guard on the mountainside and looks out across the bridge to the customs house on the other side of the river.

Here the canton of Valais ends and the canton of Vaud begins. The nearest town is Bex; from there on the valley seems to grow wider with every step, and as it broadens it grows richer and more fertile. It becomes a garden with walnut, chestnut, and tall cypress trees. Here even the pomegranate will ripen, and it is so warm that you might think you were as far south as Italy.

Rudy soon finished his errand at Bex and walked about the town. But he did not even see any of the apprentices from the mill, let alone Babette. Luck, which was usually kind to him, seemed to frown upon him that day.

It was evening. The air was filled with the fragrance of flowering thyme and the blossoms of the linden trees. A blue veil seemed to cover the forest-clad mountains. The world was silent, not with the silence of sleep or death, but rather as if Nature were holding her breath because she was about to be photographed.

Across the valley ran the telegraph lines; the poles could be seen among the trees. Something was leaning against one of them. At a distance you would have mistaken it for a log because it looked so motionless, but it was Rudy. He was as completely still as his surroundings, and he, too, was neither dead nor asleep. As you cannot tell by looking at a telegraph line that the news it is carrying may change the course of a person's life—or even shake the world—so you could not have guessed by looking at Rudy how overwhelming his thoughts were. He was thinking about happiness, life, and the purpose of existence, and he was wondering what would become of his "constant thought": that thought which from now on would never leave him.

His glances rested on a light in the miller's house where Babette lived. Rudy was standing as still as he did when he took aim before shooting a chamois, but at that moment he resembled the antelope itself, which can stand so motionless that it appears to be made of stone, only to leap and vanish if it hears a tiny pebble fall. And this was exactly what Rudy did when, like a falling pebble, a thought came to him.

"Don't give up," he said aloud. "I will visit the mill and say good evening to the miller and good day to Babette. Believe that you can't fall and you won't. After all, Babette has to meet me sooner or later if I am to be her husband."

Rudy laughed. His spirits rose as he made his way to the mill. He knew what he wanted, he wanted Babette.

The path followed the river with its turbulent yellowish water. The willow and linden trees grew along the banks and their branches hung like tresses above the edges of the rapid flowing water. Rudy walked as it says in the nursery rhyme:

> . . . till he came to the miller's house
> Where no one was home
> But a cat and a mouse.

The cat was on the steps that led to the front door. It stretched itself, arched its back, and meowed. But Rudy paid no attention; he went straight up to the door and knocked. "Meow," said the cat again. Had Rudy been still a child, he would have understood that the cat said, "There is no one at home." But now Rudy was a grownup, so he had to ask one of the workers in the mill to learn why the miller's house was empty.

They had gone to Interlaken: *inter lacus,* as Annette's father, the schoolteacher, called it, "among the lakes." There on the following day were to begin the competitions for marksmanship, and people would be there from all the German-speaking cantons to watch them. The contests would last a whole week. Poor Rudy, he had not timed his visit to Bex very well and now there was nothing for him to do but start on the long road home: back over the mountains via St. Maurice and Sion, to his own valley; and that's what he did. But the next morning, by the time the sun had risen, his spirits had risen too.

"Babette is at Interlaken," he thought. "It is far from here, several days' journey, if you follow the road. But not if you go over the mountains, then it's not nearly as far. And that's the way for a hunter to travel, by climbing the mountains. Haven't I done it before? Don't I come from there? Didn't I live there with my grandfather? I will win the competition at Interlaken just as I will win Babette's heart . . . as soon as she gets to know me, that is."

He packed his Sunday suit in a small knapsack, slung his hunting bag across his shoulders, and with his rifle in his hand set out to climb the mountains that separated him from Interlaken. But even this short route was long enough. However, the competition would only begin today, and he had been told that Babette and the miller were staying with relatives at Interlaken for the whole week. Rudy decided to cross the great glacier Gemmi because he wanted to descend the mountains near his old home at Grindelwald.

Healthy and happy, he was a fine sight, if anyone had been there to look at him. As he strode along, the valley disappeared and the horizon broadened. First one and then another of the snow-capped mountains came into view. Rudy knew them all. He walked toward Schreckhorn, which stretched upward into the blue sky like a snow-covered stone finger.

Finally, he had crossed the mountains and the green meadows of his childhood stretched themselves toward him. His soul was as light as the mountain air. The valleys were green and filled with the flowers of spring, and in his heart was the wisdom of youth: One cannot die! One cannot age! Live! Live and enjoy! Be free as a bird. Light as a bird he was, walking and dancing along the path, the swallows singing above him as they had when he was a child: "You and we! You and we!"

Below on the velvet green meadow, he saw the little brown wooden houses and the Lütschine River. He saw the glacier covered with dirty gray snow, and its clear green glass borders, lined with deep crevasses, for he could see both the top and the bottom of the great field of ice. The bells of the village rang to greet him and welcome him home. For a moment the memories of childhood so filled his heart that he forgot Babette.

Again he was walking the road alongside which, as a child, he had stood waiting to sell the little wooden toy houses his grandfather had carved. Up among the pine trees was his grandfather's house, but strangers were living in it. Children came. They wanted him to buy their parents' handicraft. Rudy smiled and one of the children gave him a rhododendron. "The rose of the mountains," he whispered. "It is a good omen." And at that moment Babette came back into his mind.

He crossed the bridge where the two streams meet to become the river Lütschine. The evergreens gave way to the birch and oak and elm, and finally he was walking in the shade of the walnut tree. In the distance he saw flags flying: a white cross on a red background, the national banners of both Switzerland and Denmark. Spread out in front of him lay Interlaken.

Rudy thought it was one of the most beautiful sights he had ever seen, a Swiss town dressed up for Sunday. It was not like any other city. It was not a collection of big stone buildings: stodgy, forbidding, and important. No, it was as if all the small wooden houses from the mountainsides had decided to move down into the green valley and had lined themselves up as they pleased, in not too straight rows along the banks of the clear river.

The houses looked exactly like the ones his grandfather had carved, the ones that had stood in the closet of his childhood home. For a moment Rudy imagined that it was so, that the toy houses had grown up like the old chestnut trees that lined the streets.

Each house had intricately carved woodwork around its windows and balconies; the latter were protected by overhanging roofs from rain and snow. On the loveliest street all the houses were new; they had not been there when Rudy, as a boy, visited Interlaken. They were hotels, every one; each had a flower garden in front of it and the road was macadamized. Here there were buildings only on one side of the street, so as not to hide from view the green meadow with its grazing cows, which wore bells around their necks just as they did in the mountains. The pasture was encircled by mountains. In the middle of the chain towered the snow-capped "Maiden," and it was as if the other mountains had stepped aside to give the onlooker a better view of this shining white mountain that is the most beautifully shaped of all the mountains of Switzerland.

How many elegantly dressed foreigners one saw in the streets, which were already crowded with hunters and farmers from the different cantons. The hunters who were participating in the competition wore ribbons with numbers on them in their hats. The houses and bridges were draped with banners, and on some of them there were verses. There was music—trumpets and horns and barrel organs. There were the screams of children and the shouts of adults as they hailed old friends and new acquaintances. Yet all the while could be heard shooting, one shot after another. The sound of the guns was the most inspiring music to Rudy's ears, and once more he forgot Babette and why he had come to Interlaken.

Rudy joined the men competing at target shooting. Every time he fired, his bullet hit the little dark spot at the center of the shield.

"Who is that very young hunter?" people began to ask each other.

"He talks French as if he came from the canton of Valais," someone remarked. "Yet he can speak German as we do here."

"They say," someone else explained, "that when he was a child he lived near Grindel."

Yes, Rudy was full of life! His hands were strong and steady, his eye sharp, so his bullets always hit their mark. Happiness is the mother of courage, and Rudy was always courageous. He made friends easily and soon was surrounded by a group of admirers wherever he went. Everyone knew who he was and spoke well of him; he had no time to think of Babette.

Suddenly a firm hand grasped his shoulder and a man asked him in French, "Are you from the canton of Valais?"

Rudy turned around and saw a fat man with a cheerful red face: it was the rich miller from Bex. He was so heavy-set that he almost hid his daughter Babette, who was standing on tiptoe behind him to get a better view of the young hunter.

The rich miller had been pleased when he heard that it was a hunter from a French-speaking canton who was winning all the competitions, and he had made up his mind to meet him. Fortune certainly was smiling on Rudy, when what he had set out to seek now sought him.

When you are in a strange place and you meet someone from home, you talk to him as if you had always been friends. Rudy was now a man of importance at Interlaken because of his skill at marksmanship just as the miller was a man of importance in Bex because of his mill and his money. They shook hands as equals, which under other circumstances they might never have done. Babette, too, offered Rudy her hand, and as he took it in his he looked so intently into her eyes that she blushed.

The miller told Rudy about their journey, of the many towns they had passed through, and how they had traveled by steamer, railroad, and stagecoach in order to reach Interlaken.

"I took a shorter route," Rudy said. "I went over the mountains; they aren't so high that you can't climb them."

"If you are willing to risk breaking your neck," replied the miller. "And you may well break yours, if you are as daring as you look."

"You can't fall if you don't believe you can," Rudy said.

The miller's relatives at Interlaken, at whose home he and Babette were staying, invited Rudy to visit them—after all, he came from the same district as their own family. Rudy accepted readily. Luck was with him, as she always is with those who have confidence in themselves and remember the proverb: "God provides the nuts but He does not shell them for us."

Rudy sat at the dinner table as if he were already a member of the family. A toast was made to the best marksman at Interlaken. They all lifted their glasses to Rudy, even Babette; and he made a short speech of thanks.

In the late afternoon they all went out for a walk along the beautiful street where all the hotels were. Here there was so much going on and such a throng that Rudy had to offer Babette his arm.

"I am so happy to have met someone from the canton of Vaud," he declared. "The cantons of Vaud and Valais have always been such good neighbors."

Babette thought that he sounded so sincere that she must hold his hand. Soon they were talking as if they had known each other for ever so long. And Rudy thought that he had never heard anyone speak so charmingly, so sweetly, as she pointed out to him how ridiculously the foreign women dressed and carried themselves.

"You mustn't think I am making fun of them. Foreigners can be honest and very kind. And no one knows that better than I because my godmother is an English lady. She was visiting Bex when I was born."

Babette was wearing a gold pin that her godmother had given her. "She has written to me twice, and I have been expecting her at Interlaken this year. She is supposed to come with her daughters. They are unmarried and quite old—nearly thirty." Babette herself was only eighteen.

She gave her little mouth no rest and everything that she had to say seemed to Rudy of great importance. When his turn came, he told her everything that he could tell. He said that he had been in Bex often and knew her father's mill. He admitted that he had seen her many times, though she probably had not noticed him. Finally he confided the thoughts he had had that night when he went to Bex and was told that Babette and her father had gone to Interlaken. "You were far, far away. But there are two ways to get around a wall, and the shorter is to climb over it."

Yes, he said that and he said other things, too. He told her how much he cared for her and that he had come to Interlaken for her sake, and not to prove his skill as a marksman.

While he talked Babette grew very quiet; his confession was al-most more than she could bear.

As they walked the sun set and the snow-capped "Maiden," framed by the forest-clad mountains, showed herself in all her glory. For a moment everyone stood still and looked at the majestic sight, even Rudy and Babette.

"Nowhere is it as beautiful as here!" said Babette.

"Nowhere!" echoed Rudy, who was looking at Babette. "Tomor-row I must leave," he said a little while later.

"Come and visit us in Bex," she whispered. "I am sure it will please my father."

CHAPTER FIVE: THE WAY HOME

How many things Rudy had to carry on his way home the next day! There were three silver cups, two quite good rifles, and a silver coffee-pot that would come in handy when he settled down. And he was carrying something else that was even more valuable, something that was not a burden and seemed almost to carry him over the high mountains.

The weather was far from pleasant. It was gray, rainy, and raw. Heavy clouds rested on the mountains like veils of grief, obscuring their peaks. From far below, Rudy heard the woodman's ax, and the trees as they rolled down the mountainside looked like toothpicks, though many were tall and stout enough to become the masts of ships. The Lütschine River continuously struck its single chord, and the wind sang its monotonous song as the clouds sailed by overhead.

Just ahead of Rudy a girl suddenly appeared, walking in the same direction as he was, on her way across the mountains. Her eyes seemed to have a strange power. Rudy found himself looking into them; they were clear as glass and fathomlessly deep.

"Have you a sweetheart?" Rudy asked, for those in love can think only of love.

"I have no one!" she exclaimed, and laughed, but something in her voice made him think that she was lying. "Let's not take the longest way," she said. "Here we must go more to the left; it's a shorter way."

"Yes, to the bottom of an ice crevasse," said Rudy. "If you don't know the mountains better than that, you shouldn't play guide."

"Oh, I know the way," she replied. "I have my wits about me. You seem to have left yours down in the valley. Watch out, when you are in the mountains you must think about the Ice Maiden. Men believe that she is no friend of human beings."

"I am not afraid of her," Rudy said with confidence. "She had to let me go when I was child; now that I am a man she will not dare to touch me."

It grew darker. There was a heavy rain that finally turned to snow, a white blinding world.

"Come, take my hand. I will help you climb," the girl offered, and stretched out her hand toward him. Her fingers were cold as ice.

"You help me!" Rudy exclaimed. "I do not need a girl's help to climb."

He walked faster, away from her. The snowstorm swept around him like a blanket. Through the whirling of the wind he could hear a girl's laughter and singing. "She must be a servant of the Ice Maiden," he thought; and he remembered the tales he had heard from the guides on his journey across the mountains when he was a boy.

It almost stopped snowing. He had climbed above the clouds. Still he heard laughter and singing below him, but the voices did not sound human.

When Rudy reached the top of the pass, where the way begins to descend into the Rhone Valley, he saw a patch of clear sky in the direction of Chamonix. Two brilliant stars appeared. He thought of Babette and himself, and of how lucky he had been.

CHAPTER SIX: A VISIT TO THE MILL

"You will bring honor to our family. You will rise above both your father and your uncle," Rudy's aunt said; and her strange eaglelike eyes gleamed, while she moved her long neck more quickly than usual in the peculiar birdlike way she had. "You are fortunate, Rudy. Come, let me kiss you, for you are as good to me as any son could have been."

Although he submitted and let his aunt kiss him, Rudy's expression told that he considered it a duty.

"How handsome you are!" the old woman sighed.

"That's just something you tell yourself," he replied, and laughed; but her words had pleased him.

"I'll repeat it. You are lucky," his aunt said, and smiled.

"There I agree with you!" Rudy exclaimed, for he was thinking of Babette. Never before in his life had he longed for the valley as he did now. "They must have come home by now. They have probably been home two days already. I must go to Bex."

When Rudy arrived in Bex he found the miller at home. He even seemed glad to see him and mentioned that he had regards for him from his family in Interlaken. Babette hardly spoke. She seemed to have become so silent, but her eyes talked and their message was eloquent enough for Rudy.

The miller, who was used to being the center of attention, to having people laugh at his jokes and listen to his stories, took an interest in what Rudy had to say. He enjoyed hearing about the life of a hunter, of the difficulties and dangers that one had to endure to hunt the chamois. It was exciting to listen to Rudy tell how he had to make his way along a narrow ledge, high up where the mountainside was a sheer cliff, and how he sometimes had to make use of the bridges nature furnished to cross many a cleft, bridges made only of ice and snow that might give way beneath his foot at any moment, hurling him to his death far below. Rudy looked bold and his eyes shone as he spoke of hunting the chamois. He told, too, about the animal itself: the chamois, that goatlike antelope that lives in the Alps. He described how clever it could be and how courageous it was. He talked of the foehn wind, of avalanches, of landslides that could bury a whole village. And all the while he was speaking he knew that, the better the miller liked his stories, the fonder he would grow of the storyteller.

The miller appeared to be most interested in hearing about buzzards, falcons, hawks, and eagles. Rudy told him about an eagle's nest. It was not far away in the canton of Valais. It had been built very cleverly, on a tiny ledge underneath an overhanging cliff. In the nest there was a young eagle. Only a few days ago an Englishman had offered Rudy a handful of gold coins for the live eaglet.

"But that's too dangerous even for me," laughed Rudy. "That young eagle is quite safe. It would be madness to try to climb up there and get it."

As the wine flowed freely, tongues were loosened, and the evening seemed very short to Rudy, even though it was after midnight when he walked homeward after his first visit to the mill.

It was a while before the last candle in the miller's house was put out. From a little window in the roof the parlor cat stepped out for a bit of fresh air, and in the gutter beneath the eaves she met the kitchen cat.

"Something new has happened at the mill, do you know what it is?" the parlor cat asked. "Someone is secretly engaged in this house, and Father doesn't know about it yet! Rudy and Babette sat all evening stepping on each other's paws under the table. Twice they stepped on my tail, but I didn't meow for fear of attracting attention."

"I would have," said the kitchen cat.

"What can pass for manners in the kitchen is improper behavior in the parlor. I wonder what the miller is going to say when he hears about the engagement."

Yes, what would the miller say? Rudy wanted to know that too, so before many days had passed he was seated in a stagecoach on his way to Bex. He was filled with confidence as the vehicle rumbled over the Rhone bridge, which separates the canton of Valais from that of Vaud. He was imagining the scene when he would be officially engaged that very evening.

When the coach returned later that evening, Rudy was again on it; this time he was going home. Down at the mill the parlor cat ran all over the house spreading the news.

"You there, kitchen cat. . . . Do you want to know what's happened? . . . The miller knows everything. Rudy came early this evening, and he and Babette stood out in the hall, near the miller's room, and whispered and whispered. I heard everything they said, for I was lying at their feet.

" 'I am going straight in to your father,' Rudy said.

" 'Shall I come with you to bolster your courage?' Babette asked.

" 'I have courage to spare; but come along anyway, because when your father sees you he cannot help but look upon us kindly, whether he wants to or not,' he answered. Then into the miller's room the two of them went.

"Rudy's a clumsy fellow. He stepped on my tail and I meowed as loud as I could, but it was as if they had all lost their ears. But I was first in the room and I jumped up on a chair. It's dangerous to get anywhere near Rudy's feet, for you might get kicked. But I needn't have worried about that because it was the miller who did the kicking. He gave Rudy a good kick right out the door and back up into the mountains. Now he can aim at chamois and not at our Babette."

"But tell me how it happened. What did they say to each other?" demanded the kitchen cat.

"Say? . . . They said everything that you have to say when you are courting: 'I love her and she loves me. . . . When there is milk enough in the pail for one, then it will do for two.'

"But the miller replied, 'You aim too high! Babette is sitting on a whole pile of grain sacks, sacks filled with golden grain! You can't get up there.'

" 'Nothing is so high that you cannot reach it if you want to badly enough,' Rudy said, for he is very bold.

"The miller smiled. 'What about the eagle you told me about the last time you were here? That was too high for you, you admitted that; well, Babette is even higher.'

" 'I will reach them both!' Rudy exclaimed.

" 'All right. I will give Babette to you when you give me the little eagle alive.' Then he laughed till tears streamed down his face. 'But thank you for calling all the same. Come again tomorrow and we'll be sure not to be home. Good-by, Rudy.' Babette said good-by too, but she sounded as miserable as a kitten that cannot find its mother.

" 'Don't cry, Babette,' Rudy consoled her. 'A word is a word, and a man is a man. I will bring back the eaglet.'

"The miller stopped laughing and said, 'I hope you will break your neck, so that we will be spared the sight of you here again.' Now that was a kick, wasn't it?

"Rudy is gone. Babette is crying, and the miller is singing a German song that he learned at Interlaken. I wouldn't have cried. What's the point of it? It doesn't help."

"But it keeps up appearances," said the kitchen cat.

## CHAPTER SEVEN: THE EAGLE'S NEST

Someone was yodeling as he came up the mountain, yodeling as if he did not have a care in the world. It was Rudy on his way to visit his friend Vesimand.

"You must help me. I will get Ragli to join us. There's an eagle's nest on a tiny ledge near the top of the canyon and I must have the eaglet."

"Why don't you try to fetch the dark of the moon instead? It would be easier." Vesimand smiled. "What makes you so happy today?"

"I am thinking of getting married. But seriously, let me tell you what has happened."

Less than an hour later both Vesimand and Ragli knew why Rudy wanted the eaglet. "You are too daring," they said. "It can't be done. You will break your neck."

"You cannot fall if you don't believe you can," Rudy replied.

At midnight they set out, carrying staves, ropes, and ladders. The path led through brushwood and over huge boulders, ever upward in the dark night. Far below they heard the voice of the river and above them the songs of the tiny waterfalls. Clouds heavy with rain sailed by. Finally they reached a crag on the side of a cliff; they could climb no farther. Above them the granite sides of the cleft almost met, leaving only a sliver of the sky visible. The night seemed to grow darker. They sat down on the narrow ledge to wait for morning to come. In the ravine, far below, the water was rushing. Silently and patiently they waited for dawn. First they must shoot the eagle before making any attempt to capture the eaglet. Rudy sat on his haunches, as motionless as the rock he was sitting on. His gaze rested on that part of the bluff that jutted out and hid the tiny ledge on which the eagle had built its nest. His gun was ready. But the three hunters had long to wait.

At last they heard that terrible whizzing sound of the eagle's great wings beating the air. Against the tiny patch of sky between the cliffs of the crevice they could clearly see the shape of the huge bird. Two of the hunters had their rifles trained on the eagle, but only one shot rang out.

For a moment the wings continued to flap, then they stopped and the bird fell slowly downward. So large did the bird seem, so great the span of its wings, that the hunters suddenly feared that there might not be space enough in the narrow canyon for the bird to fall without brushing against them in its descent, so that one or even all of them might be pushed into the abyss. But the bird did not touch them and soon they heard the breaking of branches below them.

Now the hunters had to get busy. Believing that three ladders, when tied together, would reach the eagle's nest, they began tying the top of one to the bottom of another. Resting the lowest ladder on the very edge of the crag, they leaned the ladders up against the side of the cliff. They were not long enough! Above the top rung of the third ladder the granite continued to rise and it was as straight as a man-made wall for several feet before it curved outward, and thereby protected the eagle's nest.

The young hunters decided that there was only one way to reach the nest. They must retrace their steps and find a place where they might ascend to the top of the canyon, and from there lower two ladders and somehow attach them to the other three.

It was only with the greatest difficulty that they managed to carry the ladders up to the highest point of the precipice. They tied them together and slowly lowered them into the abyss. On the lowest rung of the second ladder sat Rudy.

It was an ice-cold morning. The bottom of the canyon far below him was hidden in vapors. Rudy was like a fly sitting on a piece of straw that some bird while nest building had dropped and that had alighted on the rim of a tall factory chimney; the difference being that, should the straw fall, the fly would take flight, but Rudy had no wings, he could only break his neck. The wind blew around him. He heard the voice of the rushing river in the depths below; it carried the water from the melting snow of the glacier that was the palace of the Ice Maiden.

Rudy swung on the ladders as a spider dangles on a single thread, searching for a place to fasten her web. The fourth time that his fingertips touched the ladders that were leaning against the side of the cliff he managed to get a good grasp. With steady hands he bound the two sets of ladders together, then, as his friends slackened their ropes from above, he forced the two new additions to his giant ladder to rest against the granite wall.

The five ladders were like a reed that at any moment might begin to sway, but they appeared to reach up high enough for Rudy to climb from their topmost rung into the eagle's nest. Now came the most dangerous part of the expedition. Rudy must climb as well as a cat, but he knew how, for a cat had been his teacher. The Ice Maiden's servant, Vertigo, reached out her arms like a sea anemone, but Rudy did not feel her touch.

Rudy's ladder was, after all, not long enough; he could reach the nest by stretching his arms upward but he could not see into it. With his hands he explored the outermost layer of branches that had been braided by the eagle to form its nest. Finding a particularly heavy bough that did not give way when he pulled on it, Rudy swung from the ladder to the nest. His head and shoulders were above its rim. A stench of rotten meat greeted him: half-consumed carcasses of chamois, lambs, and birds were strewn everywhere. Vertigo, who had not been able to disturb him before, now gently blew the odious smell into his face, hoping that the fumes would make him dizzy. Down in the waters of the rushing river waited the Ice Maiden with her white-green hair and her deadly eyes which, like the muzzles of a gun, were trained on Rudy. "Now I shall catch you!" she exclaimed.

Near the rim sat the eaglet. Although it could not fly, it was large, almost full grown. Rudy stared intently at the bird. Holding onto the branch with one hand, he cast a noose around the feet of the eaglet with the other. He pulled the string and the bird was captured. He flung the captive over his shoulder; because of the length of the cord, it hung down below Rudy's feet. Now his other hand was free to grasp the rope that held the ladders, until his feet were on the rungs once more.

"Hold on! Don't believe that you can fall and you won't." That was the wisdom that he had taken with him as he scaled the shaking ladders and cleaved to the wall of granite. He had not believed that he could fall, and he hadn't fallen.

Through the canyon the happy sound of yodeling could be heard. Rudy was again standing on solid earth and he had the eaglet with him.

### CHAPTER EIGHT: WHAT THE PARLOR CAT KNEW

"Here is what you asked for," Rudy announced. As he stepped into the miller's house at Bex, he put a large covered basket down on the floor. When he lifted the cloth two savage yellow eyes, rimmed in black, stared wildly at first one thing and then another, as if those eyes burned to attack everything they saw. Its short but strong bill was half open, prepared to bite. Its red neck was covered with down.

"The eaglet!" shouted the miller.

Babette screamed and stepped back, but she did not take her eyes away from Rudy or the bird.

"You do not frighten easily." The miller looked at Rudy and the hunter returned his gaze.

"And you, sir, always keep your word. Each of us has a trait that he likes to be known by."

"Why didn't you break your neck?" the miller asked, but he smiled at the same time.

"Because I held on—and I am still holding on—to Babette."

Now the miller laughed, and Babette knew that this was a good sign. "You haven't got her yet," he said. "But we'd better take the eaglet out of the basket. Look how it stares! Now you must tell me how you captured it."

And Rudy told of his adventure so well that the miller's eyes grew larger and larger. "With your courage and your luck, you can support three wives."

"Thank you, thank you!" Rudy said quickly.

The miller slapped Rudy on the back and again he reminded him, "You haven't got her yet."

"Do you want to hear the latest news from the parlor?" the parlor cat asked the kitchen cat. "Rudy brought the eaglet and exchanged the bird for Babette. They kissed each other while the miller looked on, and that's as good as announcing your engagement. The old man didn't kick this time. He drew in his claws. He let the young couple be alone together while he took his afternoon nap. They sat and purred. They seemed to have so much to say to each other that they won't be finished by Christmas."

And they weren't finished by Christmas. The wind blew and undressed the trees. The snow came to the valleys as well as to the mountains. The Ice Maiden sat in her proud castle which enlarged itself in the winter. The cliffs glistened with ice, and where in summer waterfalls had leaped down the mountainside there now hung elephant-heavy icicles that a man could not encircle with his arms. Snow crystals decorated the branches of the evergreens. The Ice Maiden rode on the wind through the deep valleys. Down at Bex lay a blanket of snow, so she could come there and peek through the windows of the mill and see Rudy, who had never before spent so much time indoors, sitting close to Babette. When summer came, they were to be married; and if their ears were ringing, it was quite understandable because their coming marriage was much discussed among their friends. Finally the sun gained strength, flowers bloomed, but not more beautifully than the happy, laughing Babette, for she was like the spring; and all the birds sang of summer to come and their wedding day.

"How those two can just sit about, hanging onto each other's words, is more than I can understand," said the parlor cat. "I'm bored. . . . Meow."

## CHAPTER NINE: THE ICE MAIDEN

Spring had come. The chestnut and the walnut trees formed garlands of greenness from the bridge at St. Maurice to the Lake of Geneva and all along the Rhone, that river which rushes headlong from its source, deep down underneath the green glacier, where the palace of the Ice Maiden is. From there she rides on the wind up to the fields of everlasting snow, to stretch herself in the sunlight and look down into the valleys where human beings are scurrying about like ants on a sun-brightened boulder.

"Reasonable beings you are called by the sun's children; you are nothing but vermin! One rolling ball of snow and that is the end of you, your houses, and your towns. All of them I can crush!" The Ice Maiden lifted her proud head and gazed with eyes as cold as death far and wide. From one of the valleys came the sound of an explosion, the work of men who were blasting to make way for a new railroad line by cutting tunnels through the mountains.

"They are playing mole, digging passages through the earth, that's why it sounds like small stones cracking. If I made one of my castles move, then you would hear a din greater than thunder."

From one of the valleys smoke appeared, like the feathered plume of a hat, streaming out of the funnel of the engine that drew the train along the newly constructed track: a bending, whistling snake of swiftly moving cars.

"They are playing that they are masters, those reasonable beings, but the power of nature commands them." And the Ice Maiden laughed and sang so it echoed throughout the valleys.

"Avalanche!" exclaimed the people of the valley.

The children of the sun—its golden rays—sang their song about human achievement even louder. Human thought has spanned the oceans, moved the mountains, and filled in the valleys. "The human mind is master of nature," they sang.

At the moment the Ice Maiden was watching a group of travelers make their way across a snow field. They were tied together with a heavy rope so they could help each other if one of them should fall into a crevasse as they walked on the slippery ice.

"Vermin!" screamed the Ice Maiden. "How can you be masters of nature?" And she looked away from them, down into the valley where the train was passing.

"Human thought! There they sit, those thinkers, being carried by nature's power. I can see every one of them. Look at them! One alone sits as proud as a king. The others sit in a clump. Half of them are asleep. When the steam dragon stops they will get off and go their way. These thinkers will go out into the world." Again the Ice Maiden laughed.

"Avalanche!" the people exclaimed in the valley.

"Another avalanche, but it cannot reach us," said two of the passengers of the steam dragon simultaneously, for they were two minds with the same thought, as the saying goes. It was Rudy and Babette; and the miller was with them.

"As baggage," he said. "I had to come along because I am necessary."

"I see the two of them," the Ice Maiden said. "Many chamois have I killed. Millions of rhododendrons have I broken and crushed, not even their roots have I spared. I have obliterated them. Thinkers! The power of reason!" And once more she laughed.

"Another avalanche!" cried the people of the valley.


CHAPTER TEN: THE GODMOTHER


In Montreux—one of the towns that together with Clarens, Vernex, and Crin forms a garland around the northeastern shore of Lake Geneva—Babette's godmother was staying. She had come from England a few weeks before, accompanied by her daughters and a nephew. The miller had already visited them and told them of Babette's engagement. When they had heard the whole story of the romance—how it had begun at Interlaken and how Rudy had captured the eaglet—they were so amused and interested that they insisted that the miller must come again soon, bringing both Babette and Rudy with him.

And so they had come, for Babette to see her godmother and the English lady to see her godchild.

At the little town of Villeneuve, at the end of the lake, the travelers embarked on a small steamer that within half an hour would bring them to Vernex, just below Montreux. They sailed along the coast that the great poets had sung about. Here on the shore of the blue-green lake, under the shade of a walnut tree, Byron had composed his melodious verses about the prisoner of the dismal castle of Chillon. At Clarens where weeping willows mirror themselves in the waters of the lake, Rousseau had walked dreaming of Héloïse.

Where the Rhone River, flowing from beneath the snow-clad mountains of Savoy, runs into the lake, there is a tiny island. From shore it might be mistaken for a small boat, though it is a mass of rocks. About a hundred years ago a lady had had these rocks encircled by a wall, and earth transported from the mainland; then she had planted three acacia trees. Now these trees were full grown and they kept the little island in perpetual shade. Babette thought that the island was lovely, the most beautiful sight she had seen on the whole boat trip, and she wanted to go ashore. "For surely," she declared, "it must be a delight to be there." But the steamer sailed on and landed its passengers where it was supposed to, at Vernex.

Now they had to walk, up the mountain in the direction of Montreux. The mountainside was covered with vineyards, and around each was a white wall. Between the rows of walls, on which the sunshine played, the three of them made their way. The houses stood in the shade of fig trees; and they passed gardens where laurel bushes and cypress trees grew. The pension where Babette's godmother was staying was halfway between the shores of the lake and Montreux.

There they were given a most hearty welcome. Babette's godmother was a tall, pleasant woman with a round smiling face; as a child she must have resembled one of Raphael's angels, for her white hair now curled about an old angel's face. Her daughters were tall and slender and pretty. Their cousin was dressed from top to toe in white. He had gilded sideburns that were so ample that he could have shared them with three other gentlemen and still have had enough for himself. His hair was also golden; and he immediately turned his full attention to Babette.

Richly bound books, musical scores, and drawings were lying on the large table. The doors to the balcony were open, offering a view of the lake, in whose calm, glossy water the mountains of Savoy with their villages, forests, and snow-covered peaks were perfectly reflected, upside down.

Rudy, who was usually so cheerful, confident, and filled with life, felt out of place. He moved about gingerly, as if the polished floors had been strewn with dry peas. Time seemed like a solid rock that would never be worn down. He felt as if he were on a treadmill, and now someone was suggesting that they take a "promenade"!

The others walked so slowly that Rudy had to take one step backward for every two that he took forward, in order not to get ahead of the company. They were going to Chillon, to that crumbling old castle on the rock. There they would look at the whipping post and at the cells of the condemned; at the stone slabs on which the wretched prisoners slept; and at the trap door through which they were flung to meet their deaths on the iron spikes jutting up through the surf. To see all this is called a pleasant amusement. It is a chamber of horrors that was lifted by Byron's song into the world of poetry.

Rudy felt the horror as he leaned against the castle's massive wall. He peered through a narrow window and looked out over the lake. There was the tiny island with its three acacia trees. He wished he were there, away from the chattering people who surrounded him. But Babette was enjoying herself. She had been much amused.

Later that day, when she was alone with Rudy and the miller, she remarked that she thought her godmother's nephew was "perfect."

"Yes, a perfect ass," said Rudy; and this was the first time that he had said something that did not please Babette. The Englishman had given her a book as a souvenir. It was Byron's *Prisoner of Chillon* in a French translation, so she could read it.

"Maybe the book is all right," Rudy said, "but I don't care much for the fellow who gave it to you."

"He looked like a flour sack without any flour in it," said the miller, laughing at his own joke. Rudy joined in the laughter; he thought that the miller had been both witty and precise.

CHAPTER ELEVEN: THE COUSIN

When Rudy came to the mill a few days later he found the Englishman there. Babette was serving him broiled brook trout. The plate was decorated with parsley, which Rudy felt certain that the girl had picked herself in order to make the dish look as it did when it was served in the finer hotels. Why all this to-do? What did the Englishman want? Why was Babette running back and forth like that? It wasn't necessary at all.

Rudy was jealous and this amused Babette. She wanted to know everything about her lover, his weaknesses as well as his strength. She was so young that love was still a game to her. Yet it must not be forgotten that, though she played with Rudy's heart, he was her happiness, the center around which her thoughts played, and the source of all her joy. The more furious he looked, the more laughter there was in her eyes. She would gladly have kissed the Englishman with the blond hair and the gilded sideburns, just to see Rudy show how much he loved her by stamping out of the room in a rage. She was being neither fair nor clever, but Babette was only nineteen years old. She did not give too much thought to what she was doing, and none whatsoever to the impression that she might be creating on the Englishman, who might well misunderstand and decide that she was more pleasure-loving and frivolous than a recently engaged miller's daughter ought to be.

The mill was situated on the road to Bex, in the shadow of the high snow-covered mountains that the local people call the Diablerets. Nearby is a raging mountain stream whose waters are always foaming and filled with bubbles; but this is not the stream that turns the great wheel of the mill. A smaller one that leaps down the cliff as a waterfall, passes through a stone tunnel under the road and from there across the larger stream in a trough, finally falls upon the paddles of the mill wheel. The wooden trough was almost always filled and often the water overflowed, so anyone deciding to use one of its rims as a short cut to the mill would find that he had chosen a very slippery path. And this was exactly what the Englishman had done.

Guided by the light in Babette's window, and dressed all in white as if he were a miller, he attempted to make his way to the garden by balancing himself on the narrow ledge of one of the sides of the trough. But he had never learned how to hold on where there was nothing to hold onto, so he slipped into the trough and almost fell into the larger stream below it.

Wet to the skin, he climbed the linden tree next to Babette's window; then he started to hoot like an owl, as this was the only bird he knew how to imitate. Babette lifted the curtain and peeped out. She saw the figure in white and recognized him; then she grew not only frightened but very angry. She put out the candle and in the darkness let her fingers make certain that the windows were securely locked.

"Let him howl and hoot to his heart's content," she thought; then it suddenly struck her how terrible it would be if Rudy were in the vicinity.

And Rudy was: he was right below her, in the garden. She heard angry words and shouting. They were going to fight! One of them might even be killed. She had to do something!

Babette opened her window and called out Rudy's name. In her confusion and alarm, she begged him to go away. "You must go away!" she cried.

"So I must go away!" he demanded. "Oh, I see, you had another and better appointment! You are shameless, Babette!"

"You are horrible!" she screamed back. "I hate you! Go away! Go away!"

"You have no right to say that to me!" he called up to her. His cheeks were burning and his heart was burning. He turned and walked away.

"When I love you so much, how could you think such things of me!" Babette was very angry, which was fortunate, for if she hadn't been, she would have been very sad and could not have fallen asleep.

CHAPTER TWELVE: THE POWER OF EVIL

When Rudy left Bex on his homeward journey, he set out for the mountains: high up where the air was fresh and cool, where there was snow, and the Ice Maiden reigned. There the tops of the leaf-bearing trees appear no larger than potato plants. Only the evergreen grows and it is stunted. A few rhododendrons bloomed in great patches of snow. A blue gentian was in flower, and with the handle of his rifle Rudy broke its stem.

Far ahead of him, he spied two chamois. His eyes looked toward them eagerly. For the moment new thoughts banished the old. But the mountain antelope were too far away to attempt a shot. Rudy continued climbing higher to where the only vegetation, even in summer, are a few blades of grass growing among the boulders.

There were the two chamois walking serenely as if Rudy were not there; they were making their way toward a great field of snow. Rudy hurried after them. Suddenly the clouds rolled down from the mountain peaks and engulfed him. He took a few steps and then stopped. In front of him was a wall of stone.

It had started to rain. He felt tremendously thirsty, and though his head was burning hot as though he had fever, his body was cold. He reached for his water bottle, only to find that it was empty; he had forgotten to fill it before setting out. Rudy had never been ill before in his life, but now he knew how it felt to be ill. He was tired and his only desire was to lie down and sleep, but everything about him was soaking wet. He tried to pull himself together, but tiny quivering objects danced before his eyes.

All of a sudden he noticed something that he could remember having seen in this place before. It was a small house, built right up against the side of the cliff. In the doorway stood a young girl. At first he thought it was Annette, the schoolmaster's daughter, the one he had kissed at the dance. No, it wasn't Annette; and yet he felt sure that he had seen her before. Maybe it was the girl he had met near Grindel, the night he returned from Interlaken.

"What are you doing here?" he asked.

The girl smiled. "This is my home. I have a flock to herd."

"Where is your flock? There is no grazing here among the rocks and snow."

The girl laughed. "You seem to know the mountains well; but not far below here there is a meadow. That's where my goats are grazing. I tend them well. I have never lost a single creature. What is mine I keep."

"You talk boldly," Rudy said.

Again the girl laughed. "So do you!"

"Have you any milk? I am so dreadfully thirsty."

"I have something better than milk. Some travelers and their guides passed by here yesterday, and they left a half bottle of wine behind. I am sure they'll never return for it and I don't want it. You shall have it. I am sure you have never tasted any better wine," she added while she poured the wine into a wooden bowl.

"It is good," he agreed. "I have never drunk wine that warmed me so quickly. A moment ago I was freezing and now I feel as if I were sitting before a fire." Rudy's eyes gleamed with new life. All his sorrow and troubles were forgotten, and his natural human desires were aroused.

"You are the schoolmaster's daughter. Come, Annette, give me a kiss," he demanded.

"Yes, if you will give me the beautiful ring you are wearing on your finger."

"My engagement ring?"

The girl poured more wine into his bowl. "Yes, that's the one: that ring and no other." She lifted the bowl to his lips and Rudy drank.

A feeling of power and happiness flowed through his veins. The world was his and only now did he understand how to live. All was created for our sake, for us to enjoy. The river of life was a river of pleasure; you need only let the current carry you to know a life of bliss. He glanced at the young girl who was Annette—and yet wasn't. But neither was she the "phantom" girl, as he called the creature he had met near Grindelwald.

The girl before him had a freshness about her like new-fallen snow and, like the rhododendron, she was in bloom; she moved as gracefully as the chamois; and yet, surely, she had been created of Adam's rib and, like Rudy, was a human being.

He threw his arms around her and looked into her marvelous clear eyes for a second. Only for a second! And how is one to describe, to tell in words, what he saw in that fraction of a moment? What was it that overpowered him: a ghost? Or was it a bit of life that exists in death? Had he been lifted upward or had he been plunged into a deep, death-filled world of ice?

He saw the blue-green glass walls and the bottomless chasm that surrounds them. He heard the sound of water dripping like a thousand bells, and each drop appeared like a tiny blue-white flame. The Ice Maiden kissed him, and the eternal coldness penetrated his backbone and touched his forehead. He cried out in pain. Tearing himself from her arms, he stumbled and fell. Night closed his eyes. But a moment later he opened them again. Evil's performance was over.

The girl was gone. The house was gone. Water was dripping down the cliff. He was lying in the snow, shivering with cold. His clothes were drenched and his ring was gone: his engagement ring that Babette had given him. Beside him lay his hunting rifle. He picked it up and pulled the trigger but it did not go off. Nearby in the cleft were heavy clouds that appeared as solid as snow. Inside them Vertigo sat and waited for some powerless prey. There was a noise; it sounded like a boulder falling from the top of the canyon to its bottom, carrying with it everything in its path.

Down at the mill Babette sat crying. She had not seen Rudy for six days. Rudy, who was in the wrong and ought to come and ask for forgiveness, for she loved him with all her heart.

### CHAPTER THIRTEEN: IN THE MILLER'S HOUSE

"What a terrible mess these humans make of their lives," said the parlor cat to the kitchen cat. "The engagement between Babette and Rudy has been broken off. She cries all the time and he has probably forgotten her."

"That's too bad," replied the kitchen cat.

"I agree with you." The parlor cat licked her left front paw. "But I won't spend my time mourning about it. After all, Babette can just as well get engaged to the one with the red sideburns. Though we haven't seen hide nor hair of him since the night he tried to climb up on the roof."

The powers of evil have their own rules; they can play with us and within us. This Rudy had learned while he was high up in the mountains, and he had not stopped wondering about it since. What had happened? Had the apparition been something he imagined because he had a high fever? He had never known fever or any illness before. But he had new insight into himself since the night he had judged Babette so harshly. He remembered how wildly his heart had been made to beat by jealousy; like a foehn wind, jealousy had swept through him. If only he could tell Babette his thoughts. If only he could confess to her his temptation and how it had become a deed. He had lost her ring, and because of that loss she had regained him.

Would she make any confession to him? Every time that Rudy thought of Babette he feared that his heart was about to break. So many memories rushed into his mind. He saw her laughing like a happy child. He remembered all the sweet words she had spoken so innocently, so tenderly; and it was as if a ray of the sun had entered his breast and soon his whole heart was full of the sunshine of Babette.

She would make a confession to him; she must!

Down to the mill Rudy went; and the confession began with a kiss and ended with Rudy admitting that he was the sinner. His error had been that he had doubted Babette's fidelity. Such lack of faith was almost unforgivable! Such mistrust was almost disgusting! And his violent passion might have caused a catastrophe for them both. About that there could be no doubt! And Babette preached a little sermon for him. She enjoyed the task very much, and she did it charmingly. On one point, though, she was in perfect agreement with Rudy: her godmother's nephew was a conceited puppy. She would burn the book he had given her, for she wanted nothing ever to remind her of him.

"Well, it is all over," said the parlor cat. "Rudy has come back. They understand each other and they say that in understanding the greatest happiness is found."

"I heard the rats talking last night," said the kitchen cat, "and they decided nothing could make you as happy as tallow candles, unless it was rancid lard. Who do you think is right: the rats or the lovers?"

"Neither one of them," answered the parlor cat. "If you don't take anybody's word for anything, then you never make a mistake."

The event that would bring Rudy and Babette their greatest happiness was not far off: the most beautiful day in their lives, their wedding day.

The ceremony was not to take place in the church in Bex, or in the miller's parlor. Babette's godmother had requested that they be married in Montreux: the wedding celebration at her pension and the wedding itself in the beautiful little church in the town. The miller, who was the only one who knew what the English lady intended to give her godchild as a wedding present, said that he thought this was the least one could do; it was only a trifling inconvenience which the wedding gift would more than make up for. The day was decided upon, and the miller and the young couple planned to go to Villeneuve the night before, so that they could take the boat to Montreux early the next morning, for the two daughters of Babette's godmother wanted to have time to dress the bride.

"If there is to be no party when they come home, then I don't give a meow for the whole wedding," said the parlor cat.

"Oh, but there is going to be a party! The larder is full. There are ducks and pigeons and a whole deer hanging out there. It makes my mouth water just to think of it all." The kitchen cat licked her chops. "Tomorrow they are leaving."

Yes, tomorrow! And that evening Babette and Rudy would sit on the bench outside the mill for the last time as an engaged couple. There was a red glow above the mountains, the vesper bells began to peal. The sun's rays, the daughters of the sun, were singing: "Everything that happens is always for the best!"

## CHAPTER FOURTEEN: VISIONS IN THE NIGHT

The sun had set. The clouds rolled down into the valleys along the Rhone. The wind blew from the south: an African wind, a foehn wind that tore the clouds to bits and then was gone. In the stillness that followed, the shattered clouds re-formed themselves and floated between the forest-clad mountains and over the swift turbulent river in the most fantastic shapes; they looked like prehistoric animals: giant eagles and great leaping frogs. The clouds seemed to sail on the water rather than float in the air. A fir tree that had been uprooted by the storm was carried by the current. The water made whirling eddies in its wake. Vertigo and her sisters were turning and twisting in the onrushing torrent. The moon casting its light on the snow-covered mountaintops, the dark forests, and the white clouds made everything appear ghostly; nature's spirits were abroad. The mountain folk looking through their windows saw them. In great crowds these phantoms passed in homage before the Ice Maiden. She had come down from her glacier castle; a fir tree was her boat and the waters from the melting ice fields carried her downstream to the lake.

"The wedding guests have come." The message was sent through the air and could be heard in the water.

Visions! Visions can be seen inside as well as out. Babette was having a strange dream.

She was married to Rudy and had been for many years. He was in the mountains hunting chamois, she was at home in their living room; next to her sat the Englishman with the gilded sideburns. He was talking to her. His eyes were tender, his voice was soft. His words seemed to be casting a spell over her. He reached out his hand; she took it and followed him out of the house. They were going downward, ever downward!

Babette felt that her heart was heavy with guilt. She had committed a sin against Rudy, a sin against God. Suddenly she was alone: abandoned. She had to make her way through hawthorn bushes whose thorns ripped her clothes. Her hair was gray. Painfully she turned and looked upward. There on the edge of a cliff stood Rudy. She raised her arms toward him but she did not dare to call his name; nor would it have helped if she had, for what she was seeing was not Rudy but his hat and coat hanging on a cane: a trick the hunters used to fool the chamois.

Babette wept in anguish. "It would have been better had I died on my wedding day—on that day that was the happiest of my life. My Lord . . . my God, it would have been merciful! It would have been a blessing. . . . It would have been best for Rudy and me. No one knows his future." In front of her was an abyss; with infinite pain she threw herself into it. From the depths came a tone of sorrow, as if a string had snapped.

Babette woke; the dream was over and forgotten. Only the memory of having dreamed something terrifying remained. She knew that the Englishman had been in the dream. She had neither seen nor thought about him for months. Would he be in Montreux? Would she have to see him at her wedding? A shadow fell across her delicate face. She wrinkled her brow. But soon she was smiling again and her eyes were bright with happiness. It was a beautiful day. The sun was shining; and tomorrow was Rudy's and her wedding day.

He was already up and waiting for her when she came downstairs. In a little while they would be on their way to Villeneuve. How happy they were. And so was the miller. He smiled and joked; he was a good father and a thoroughly honest man.

"Now we are masters of the house!" said the parlor cat.

### CHAPTER FIFTEEN: THE END

It was still afternoon when the three happy travelers reached Villeneuve. After they had eaten, the miller lighted his pipe and made himself comfortable in an easy chair. Soon he was asleep. The young couple went for a walk, arm in arm, out into the town. They followed the main road; on one side were cliffs covered with greenery, and on the other the deep, blue-green lake. The heavy walls and towers of the gloomy castle of Chillon were reflected in the clear water. They saw the little island with the three acacia trees not far away. It lay like a bouquet on the water.

"It must be beautiful over there." Babette felt again the same wish to visit the little island, and this time it was easy to fulfill. There at the water's edge was a small rowboat. There was no one about, so they could not find out to whom it belonged. They would borrow it anyway. The mooring was easily untied and Rudy knew how to row.

The oars slid through the yielding water like the fins of a fish. Water is so strong and yet so pliant; it has a back that can carry great weights, a mouth that can swallow and smile gently. It can portray perfect serenity and yet it has the most horrifying power to destroy. In the wake of the boat was a track of foam. Within minutes they reached the island, which was only just big enough for two to dance upon.

Rudy whirled Babette into the air three times, and then they sat down on the little bench under the acacia trees to hold hands and look into each other's eyes. The setting sun gave a brilliance to everything about them. The pine forest on the mountainside became lavender, as if it were a field of heather in bloom, and higher up, the naked rocks seemed almost transparent. The clouds appeared to screen a fire, and the lake itself was like the petal of a rose. As the shadows from the valleys crept farther and farther up the sides of the snow-clad mountains they became blue-black, while their peaks were still as red as lava. For a moment the scene was like a picture of the Creation, when the crust of the earth—still burning—rose to form the mountains. Never had Rudy or Babette seen such a sunset. The snow-covered Dent du Midi shone like the full moon when it rises above the horizon.

"There is so much beauty and so much happiness," one said to the other.

Rudy in a burst of passion exclaimed, "The world has no more to give me. An evening like this is a whole life. And this is not the first time that I have felt like this; and then, too, I have thought: 'Were my life to end now, how good a life it would have been!' The world is good. This day is over. But a new one will come, and it will be even more beautiful. How great and good God is, Babette!"

"I am so happy," she said, looking at him.

"The world has no more it can give me," Rudy repeated.

The vesper bells rang from the mountains of Savoy and from the mountains of Switzerland. To the west, framed in gold, were the blue-black Jura Mountains.

"May God give you all that is beautiful, everything that you ask for!" she exclaimed.

"He will!" Rudy replied. "Tomorrow you are mine, all mine: my own little, beautiful wife."

"The boat!" screamed Babette.

The little rowboat had loosened its moorings and was drifting away from the island.

"I'll get it," Rudy said. Hurriedly he took off his jacket and his boots, then he dove into the lake and started swimming.

Cold and deep was the blue-green water. It had come from the melting glaciers. Rudy looked down into it. He saw a shining round object roll, twinkle, and wink, as if it were playing. "It must be my engagement ring," he thought, "the one I lost." The ring grew larger and larger until it was a glittering circle and in the center of it was a glacier.

Deep gorges gaped around him. The dripping water played a carillon, while each drop burned with a blue-white flame; and in a single glance he saw a vision that I must use much space and many words to describe. He saw young hunters and young girls: men and women who had been swallowed by the glacier appeared before him alive; their eyes were wide open and they were smiling. He heard church bells chiming from far below, from towns and villages that had long since been buried. People were kneeling in a great church, and mountain streams played the organ, whose pipes were huge icicles. The Ice Maiden sat on the smooth, transparent floor. She rose to welcome Rudy, then she bent down and kissed his feet. A deathly ice-cold quiver like an electric shock passed through him. Ice and fire! From a single touch you cannot tell the difference.

"Mine! Mine!" The cry came from all about him, and within himself. "I kissed you when you were a child. Kissed your mouth. Now I kiss you on your toe and your heel. Now you are mine!"

Silence. The church bells had stopped ringing. The last tone disappeared in the fading rose color of the clouds.

"You are mine!" came the cry from the depths of the lake. "You are mine!" came the cry from the boundless heights.

It is lovely to fly from love to love, from earth into heaven.

A string snapped. A mournful tone was heard. Death's kiss of ice was victorious against corruption. The prologue was over, now the drama of life could begin; discord was absorbed into harmony.

Do you think it was a tragic story?

Poor Babette! Nothing could have been more terrifying, more horrible, than those hours she spent on the island alone. No one knew where the young couple had gone. The evening grew darker. Desperate, she stood sobbing, while above the Jura Mountains a storm was gathering.

Lightning flashed over the mountains and could be seen in Switzerland and in Savoy, one bolt after another. The thunderclaps came so close to each other that one became part of the next. The lightning was as bright as light from the sun, and for brief moments everything was as light as midday and you could see the individual vines in the vineyard. Then came the darkness and it was doubly dark. The lightning came in ribbons, in zigzags, in balls of fire, making strange patterns in the air as it was drawn by the water of the lake. Lightning came from all sides, and the peals of thunder were made louder by their own echoes. On the shore, people were busily pulling their boats up on land. The rain came and everything that could move searched for shelter.

"Where are Rudy and Babette in this terrible weather?" the miller asked.

Babette was sitting with her hands folded and her head bent. Now she was silent, made mute by sorrow, from the screams and moans she had uttered. Inside her a voice said, "Rudy is in the water: deep down as if he were under a glacier." She recalled what she had been told about his mother's death and his own rescue. How Rudy was thought to have been dead when he was carried out of the crevasse in the glacier. "The Ice Maiden has taken him back," she whispered.

Suddenly there was a flash of lightning as blindingly white as snow when the sun shines upon it. Babette looked about her. The lake seemed to be raising itself; its water looked for a moment like a glacier. And she saw the Ice Maiden, standing majestically in shimmering blue-white. At her feet lay the body of Rudy. "Mine!" she cried. And again there was only darkness and the murmuring waters were black.

"It is too cruel," Babette moaned. "Why should he die, just as our day of happiness had come? God, help me to understand! Make my heart lighter. I do not know Your ways. I grope in darkness. I am too weak. I need Your wisdom."

God did lighten her heart. He sent her a thought, a ray of grace. In that moment she relived the dream she had had the night before. She remembered the words she had spoken and what she had wished for Rudy's sake and her own.

"Woe is me! Was the seed of sin in my heart? Would my dream have been my future, had not the string been snapped for my sake? Oh, how wretched I am!"

In the gloom-filled darkness she sat lamenting. In the deep silence of nature, she thought she heard again Rudy say, "The world has no more it can give me." The words had been shouted in joy and now they were echoed in pain.

A few years have gone by. The lake is smiling and its shores are smiling; the vines are heavy with grapes. The steamship, with its many flags flying, sails by, and the sailing ships, like white butterflies, play on the mirror of the lake. The railroad has come. It goes past Chillon and far up and down the Rhone Valley. At every station are foreigners carrying red leather-bound guidebooks under their arms, and when they sit down in the train they read about what they have already seen. They visit the castle of Chillon and, looking out over the lake, they notice the tiny island with the acacia trees. They look it up in their books. They read about a young betrothed couple who, one spring evening in 1856, rowed out to the island; and how the young man met his death. "It was not until the following morning that people on the shore heard the bride's despairing, fearful screams."

The guidebook does not tell what happened to Babette, of her quiet life that was spent with her father—not in the mill, strangers live there now, but in a pretty house near the new railroad station. Many a night from its upper windows she has looked out over the topmost branches of the chestnut tree to the snow-capped mountains where Rudy once played. Often she has watched the sunset, seen the children of the sun go to sleep in their splendor on the peaks, and heard them repeat the tale of the man from whom the whirlwind had stolen a cap: how the wind could take his covering but not the man himself.

The snow on the mountainside has a rose luster, and so does the heart who believes that "God wills the best for us all." But few are so fortunate as Babette, who had it revealed to her in a dream.

## 111

## The Butterfly

The butterfly wanted a sweetheart, and naturally it had to be a flower. He inspected them. Everyone sat as properly and quietly on her stalk as a young maiden should. The trouble was that there were too many of them to choose from, and the butterfly didn't want to be bothered by anything so fatiguing. He flew over to the camomile flower. She is called by some the French daisy and she knows how to tell the future. Young maidens and boys who are in love ask her questions, and then answer them by tearing off her petals, one at a time. This is the rhyme they usually recite:

"With all her [or his] heart . . .
With only a part . . .
Not lost forever . . .
She'll love me never."

Or something like that. You can ask the camomile flower any questions you want to. When the butterfly came, he did not tear off any of the petals; he kissed them instead, for he was of the opinion that you get furthest with compliments.

"Sweet daisy, dear camomile flower, matron of all the flowers, you who are so clever that you can see the future, answer me: which of the flowers will be my sweetheart? This one or that one? Please tell me so that I can fly directly over to her and propose at once."

The camomile flower did not answer. The butterfly had insulted her by calling her a matron. She was a virgin and hadn't been proposed to yet. The butterfly asked the same question a second time and a third, then he got bored and flew away to go courting on his own.

It was early spring. Snowdrops and crocuses were still in bloom. "How sweet they are," he remarked. "Just confirmed, but they have no personalities." Like so many young men, he preferred older girls. He flew to the anemones but he found them too caustic. The violets were a little too romantic and the tulips a little too gaudy.

Soon the Easter lilies came, but they were a little too bourgeois. The linden blossoms were too small and had too large a family. The apple blossoms were so beautiful that they could be mistaken for roses, but they were here today and gone tomorrow. "Our marriage would be too short," the butterfly muttered.

He was most attracted by one of the sweet peas. She was red and white, pure and delicate; and was one of those rare beauties who also knows what a kitchen looks like. He was just about to propose when he happened to notice a pea pod with the withered flower at its tip. "Who is that?" he asked with alarm.

"That is my sister," replied the sweet pea.

"So that is what she will look like later," thought the butterfly. "How frightening!" And he flew away.

The honeysuckle had climbed over the fence. What a lot of girls there were, and all of them with long faces and yellow skins. The butterfly didn't care for them. But whom did he like? To find out, you must ask him.

Spring passed, summer passed, and then autumn came. Still the butterfly had no wife. The flowers were dressed in their finery, but they had lost their fresh innocence and scent of youth. As the heart grows older it needs scent, odor, perfume to arouse it; and the dahlias and the hollyhocks have none.

The butterfly lighted on a little mint plant with curly leaves. "She has no flowers, but she is a flower from her roots to the tip of her tiny leaves. She smells like a flower. I shall marry her." And the butterfly proposed.

The mint plant stood stiff and silent. At last she replied: "Friendship, but no more! I am old and you are old. We can live for each other, but marriage, no! It would be ridiculous at our age."

And that is how it happened that the butterfly never got married.

He had searched too long for a wife, and now he had to remain a bachelor.

It was late in the autumn. The rains had come and the wind blew down the backs of the willow trees. It was not the weather to be out flying in, especially in summer clothes. But the butterfly was not outside, he was in a room that was kept summer-warm by a stove, where he could keep himself alive.

"But to live is not enough," declared the butterfly. "One must have sunshine, freedom, and a little flower." He flew to the window-pane. There he was seen, admired, and a pin was stuck through him. He was "collected" and that is as much as a human being can do for a butterfly.

"Now I sit on a stalk just like the flowers," he said. "It isn't very comfortable, probably just like being married: you are stuck." And with that he consoled himself.

"Not much of a consolation," said the potted plants who lined the window sill.

"But you cannot trust potted plants," thought the butterfly, "they have associated too much with human beings."

## 112

## Psyche

At dawn, when the very air seems red and pink, a great star shines brightly. It is the star of morning. Its rays fall on the white walls of the city as if it wanted to write upon them all the stories it knows: all that it has seen through the thousands of years that it has been observing our swift-moving world.

Listen! Here is one of its stories: Not long ago—and by "Not long ago" the star means "a few hundred years ago"—its rays followed a young artist who lived in the Papal States, that capital of the world called Rome. Time has changed the city, but not as rapidly as it changes a human being from infancy to old age. The palace of the emperors is now as it was then: a ruin where, among the broken marble columns, fig trees and laurel bushes grew, and even stretched their limbs into the baths that once boasted of having walls inlaid with gold. The Colosseum was also a ruin. Church bells rang and the smell of incense was everywhere. There was always some kind of procession passing through the streets, in which lighted candles and colorful baldachins were carried. The Church was holy and all-powerful; and art was holy and at its height. In Rome lived' the world's greatest painter, Raphael, and that epoch's leading sculptor, Michelangelo. The Pope himself admired these artists and paid visits to their workshops. Yes, artists were esteemed, honored, and even rewarded; but this does not mean that every great talent was recognized.

In a narrow street was an old house that had once been a temple.

Here lived a young artist who was poor and unknown. But he had friends—other artists with the hopes and ideals of youth—who told him that he had great talent and skill and that he was a fool for doubting it. The young artist was never satisfied with his work. Every clay figure that he made he destroyed the following day, so that he never had any finished work; and one must have something to show if one wants to be known and earn a living.

"You are a dreamer," one of his friends said. "That is your misfortune and the cause of it is that you have not lived. You have not tasted life. You ought to take a big healthy swallow and enjoy it. Youth and life must be one! Look at the great Master Raphael, honored by the Pope, admired by the world; but he does not say no to either bread or wine."

"They say he not only eats bread but devours the baker woman, the young and lovely *fornarina,* as well," added Angelo, who was the boldest of the young artists.

His friends who talked a great deal about their ideals were always trying to persuade the young artist to join them in their pleasures: their revelries that some call madness. And he was not disinclined. His blood ran swiftly through his body, his imagination was strong, and he could laugh and talk as wittily as any of his friends. But when he stood in front of one of Raphael's paintings, it seemed as if he caught a glimpse of God; and then what his friends called "Raphael's gay life" disappeared like a morning mist. The masters of antiquity had a similar effect on him. He felt within himself a purity, a sense of piety, a feeling of the power of goodness that made him want to create in marble as these great men had. What he wanted to describe was how his heart sought and sensed infinity, but how was he to do it?

The soft clay took the form his fingers commanded; but the next day, as usual, he destroyed the figure.

One day he was passing one of Rome's more splendid palaces. He paused in front of the entrance. Looking through the frescoed archway, he saw a small garden filled with roses. In the center of it there was a fountain; water splashed into a marble basin, where large white calla lilies, with their glossy green leaves, bloomed in abundance. A young girl was there; she was walking—no, floating, for so light was her step—near the fountain. She was the daughter of the nobleman who owned the palace. The young artist had never seen anyone so beautiful, so delicate, so dainty, so lovely . . . except once:

Raphael's *Psyche;* but that had been a painting hanging on the wall of a palace, while this girl was alive.

And as he went about his poor workshop she remained alive in his mind; and he molded a clay Psyche, which was an image of the young noblewoman. And for the first time he was satisfied with his work. Here at last was something of value: it was the girl.

His friends came and, when they saw it, they were jubilant. They had said he had great talent; they had never doubted it; and now this work would reveal his greatness to the world.

Clay has a fleshlike aliveness but does not last as long as marble; nor has it the whiteness. In marble his Psyche would come to life. He had a block of marble. He had had it for years. In the yard behind his father's house it lay, hidden by broken glass and discarded vegetables: the tops of fennel and the rotten leaves of artichokes had made it dirty; but underneath it was as white as the snow of the mountains.

One day a party of wealthy Romans came to the humble street where the young artist lived. They had left their coach behind in one of the broader streets. They had come to see the young artist's work; but the star does not tell us how they had happened to hear about it.

Who were these distinguished visitors?

Poor young man! Or should we say too happy young man? There before him, in his own workshop, stood the young noblewoman. And when her father said, "But it is you!" the girl smiled; and the artist could not have reproduced her smile in marble—or her glance, which ennobled and crushed him.

"You must make that figure in marble," the rich nobleman remarked. "When it is finished, I shall buy it." His words brought life to the dead clay, to the heavy marble, and to the young artist.

A new era began in the workshop: a time of joy and laughter. The morning star watched the work progress. It was as if the clay itself had been inspired by the visit of the model, as if once having seen those beautiful features it could more readily become them.

"Now I know what life is," rejoiced the young man. "It is love! It is to be able to appreciate loveliness and to delight in beauty. And what my friends call 'life' is nothing but empty vanity, bubbles from fermentation of the dregs, instead of the pure wine, drunk at the altar to consecrate life."

The marble block was raised into place and the tools made ready. The first rough work was done. Measurements were made and marked in the marble and large pieces of it chopped away. Soon the young artist had to use all his craftsmanship and skill to give shape to the stone. The beautiful figure of Psyche appeared. She was so light, she seemed about to take flight. She danced, she smiled, and in her smile was reflected the innocence of the young artist.

The star of the rose-colored dawn knew what affected the young man, why the color of his cheek changed and his eyes brightened; for in creating he used God's gift to reproduce God's work.

"You are a master as the sculptors of ancient Greece were," his friends said. "Soon the whole world will admire your Psyche."

"My Psyche . . ." he repeated. "Yes, she must be mine. My work shall be immortal. I have been given God's grace, and that makes me noble."

He sank down on his knees and wept because of his gratitude to God. But soon both God and his tears were forgotten; instead he thought of his Psyche, who stood before him, looking as if she had been cut out of snow and blushing in the light of the dawn. He was going to see her: the living, breathing girl who stepped so lightly, as if she walked on air, the girl whose innocent words were music.

He went to the palace to report that the marble statue had been finished. He walked through the rose-filled courtyard, where water splashed out of the mouths of the little bronze dolphins into the marble basin, in which calla lilies bloomed. He stepped into the entrance hall, whose walls and ceilings were covered with paintings and over whose doors were painted the family's coat of arms. Servants dressed in livery, holding their heads as proudly as horses do in winter when they wear sleigh bells around their necks, walked to and fro; some were even reclining arrogantly on the carved wooden benches, as if they were the masters of the palace.

He told one of them his errand and was led up a flight of carpet-covered marble stairs, on either side of which there were statues, to a great hall filled with paintings and carpets, which had a mosaic floor. Such splendor made the heart of the young visitor heavy and would have tied his tongue had not his patron treated him so kindly. The nobleman spoke so warmly to him that the young artist soon felt at ease.

When the interview was over, he asked the artist to visit the young signorina as well, for she, too, would like to speak with him.

A servant accompanied him through beautiful banquet halls and galleries until, finally, they came to the chamber of the young girl.

She talked to him and no miserere, no holy chant, had ever touched his heart and lifted his soul as much as her words. He grabbed her hand and kissed it, and he thought it was softer than a rose petal and yet it inflamed him. He was so excited, so aroused, that he hardly knew what he was saying; words gushed out of his mouth and he could no more control their flow than the crater can stop the volcano from vomiting burning lava. He told her how much he loved her.

At first she appeared surprised, then insulted; and finally proud and full of disdain, as if her hand by mistake had touched the damp, clammy skin of a toad. Her cheeks grew red and her lips pale; her eyes were afire and yet as dark as the night.

"Madman!" she exclaimed. "Leave me alone! Go away!" And as she turned her back to him the expression on her beautiful face resembled that of the stone creature whose hair is snakes.

He made his way out of the palace as lifelessly as an object sinks into the sea. Once in the street, he walked like a sleepwalker; but when he reached his workshop he awoke in rage and pain. He grabbed his mallet and lifted it: he was about to destroy the marble statue. Someone grasped his arm; it was Angelo, who until now he had not noticed was there.

"What were you about to do? Have you gone mad?" he shouted. They began to wrestle, but Angelo was the stronger. The young artist gave up and threw himself into a chair.

"What has happened?" Angelo asked kindly. "Pull yourself together and tell me."

But what was there to tell? What could the young artist say? Angelo's questions were answered with silence, and he soon stopped trying to unravel a secret to which he had no threads.

"Your blood will grow thick and stop flowing from all your dreaming! Admit that you are a man. If you live only for your ideals, then life will break you! Drink some wine, get a little drunk, and you will sleep better. Let a beautiful girl be your physician. The girls of the Campagna are as lovely as the princess in the marble castle. Both are daughters of Eve, and in paradise you would not be able to see the difference between them. . . . Come, follow me. Let Angelo be your guide, your angel of life. It shall come to pass that you, too, will grow old; then your body will have collapsed like an abandoned cottage.

The sun will still shine and the world will still be filled with laughter, but you will be like a broken reed, unable to take nourishment. I do not believe what the priests tell of a life beyond the grave. It is a fiction, a fairy tale for children, delightful if you can convince yourself that it's true. I don't want to live through dreams but in reality. Be a man and come with me."

Angelo had come at the right time. A fire was burning in the young artist's blood; his soul seemed to have changed, he wanted to tear himself away from the life he had led, from all his old habits. He wanted to be free from his former self. So that day he followed Angelo.

On the outskirts of Rome was a little restaurant. It was built in the ruins of an ancient bath and was the favorite meeting place for young artists. Big yellow lemons hung among the dark shining foliage that almost hid the ancient red brick walls. The restaurant itself was located in a deep vault that resembled a grotto. A lamp burned in front of a picture of the Madonna and in the great fireplace a fire was burning, over which food was roasted, boiled, and fried. Outside, under the lemon and laurel trees, stood some tables.

The young men were greeted with shouts of joy from their friends. They ate a little but drank a lot, for wine makes you cheerful. They sang and someone began to play on a guitar. It was a *saltarello* and they started to dance. Two Roman girls, who earned their living as models for the artists, joined in the lively dance. They were lovely bacchantes. They had not the figure or the bearing of Psyche: they were not roses but two young, fresh carnations in full bloom.

How hot it was that day, even at sunset. Blood was afire, air was afire, and there was fire in every glance. The air seemed filled with gold and roses; that was the substance of life, gold and roses.

"At last you are among us! Let yourself go, let the currents that are flowing all about you and within yourself carry you."

"Never before have I felt so well and happy," the young artist replied. "You are right: all of you are right! I have been a fool, a dreamer. Man belongs to the world of reality, not to the world of the imagination."

Through the narrow streets the young people walked, playing their guitars and singing. The lovely carnations of the Campagna were with them.

In Angelo's studio, among the half-finished sketches and the glowingly colorful, ornate paintings, their voices grew soft but not less passionate. Everywhere drawings of the daughters of the Campagna could be seen in all their robust loveliness; and yet they were much more beautiful in reality. The six-armed candelabrum burned brightly, casting its light in all directions, and the passion-filled faces of the young people shone as if they were gods.

"Apollo! Jupiter! To your heaven do I want to ascend. Now, at this moment, for the first time, the flower of life is blooming in my heart."

Yes, it bloomed, bent its head, and withered. A strange, horrible smell of corruption blended itself with the odor of roses, it lamed his mind and blinded his sight. The fireworks of sensuality were over and darkness came.

He reached home and sat down on the bed. "Shame!" The word was not only on his tongue, it came from his heart. "Wretch! Leave me alone! Go away!" and he sighed deeply and painfully.

"Leave me alone. Go away!" Those were the words that the living Psyche had said to him. He lay down on the bed; his thoughts became unclear and he fell asleep.

At dawn he awoke. What had happened? Was it all a dream: the visit to the restaurant, the evening and the night with the girls of the Campagna? . . . No, it was real; and now he knew that reality that he had never known before.

Through the purple dawn shone the clear star of morning. Its light fell upon him and upon the marble Psyche. He trembled when he saw the divine innocence of the sculpture. Convinced that his glance sullied it, he threw a cloth over it. For a moment he let his hands glide over the figure, but he could not look at it.

Silently, motionlessly, turned inward—into himself—he sat through the long day. He knew nothing about what was happening outside in the world, and no one knew what took place within him, in his soul.

Days passed and weeks. The nights were the longest. Then one morning the star saw him get out of bed. He was pale and feverish. Walking over to the marble statue, he lifted the cloth and gazed at his work. His face was filled with anguish and pain. Bending under its weight, with great difficulty he carried it out into the garden, where there was an abandoned well. It had long since dried up and was half filled with rubbish and dirt. Into it the young artist threw the marble

Psyche; then he filled up the hole with earth, and spread branches and nettles over the burial place.

"Leave me alone! Go away!" That was the funeral oration.

The star saw everything through the rose-red dawn and mirrored itself in the two tears on the young man's pale cheeks.

Everyone who saw him agreed that he was dying. From the nearby monastery Brother Ignatius arrived. He was both a friend and a physician. He came with the comfort and consolation of religion. He talked of man's sins, of God's grace and forgiveness, and of the peace and happiness to be found within the Church. And his words fell like the rays of the sun on the moist, fermenting earth. A mist rose and in a mist can be seen strange shapes and pictures. From these "islands" floating above him, the young artist saw himself looking down at all mankind. Errors and disappointments had guided his life. Art was only an enchantress who with her magic gave him vain dreams of earthly glory. She could make us all false to ourselves, false to our friends, false to God. The snake was ever whispering: "Taste and you shall be a god."

He felt that now, at last, he had found the road to truth and peace. In the Church God's light shone in all its glory; in the tranquillity of the monk's cell his soul would know eternity.

Brother Ignatius encouraged him and a child of the world became a servant of the Church. The young artist bade the world adieu.

How kindly, how happily his new brothers greeted him, and how like a festival on a high holy day it was when he took his vows. "Here," he thought, "God is our sunlight; it shines from the holy paintings and from the cross." At sunset, he would stand at the open window of his cell and look out over the ancient city with its crumbled temples and gigantic but dead Colosseum. Especially in spring, when there were roses everywhere, the evergreens were fresh, the acacia trees were in bloom, the yellow and red of the lemons and oranges could be seen through the dark foliage, and the palm trees waved their great leaves in the breeze, he felt himself to be more alive and to feel more deeply than he ever had before. The broad, silent Campagna stretched toward the blue, snow-covered mountains. Everything melted into one, everything spoke of peace and beauty: a fairy tale, everything was a dream!

Yes, the world was a dream. Dreams can reign for hours and can be recaptured for hours, but life in a monastery is made up of years: many years, long years.

Unclean, evil thoughts come from inside yourself, he learned. What were these strange flames that seemed to set his body on fire? Where did the evil come from that he wanted no part of, yet that seemed always to be present within him? He punished his body, but the evil did not come from the surface but from deep within him. One part of his soul was supple as a snake and could bend and twist itself around his conscience, so that it became one with it—and thus could come under the cloak of the all-loving, who would console him: the saints who pray for us; the Madonna who prays for us; and Jesus, God's son, who has given his life for us. He asked himself whether it was his childlike innocence or the flightiness of youth—which made everything and nothing seem serious—that had made him seek refuge in God's mercy and grace and had made him feel that he had been elevated, chosen out of so many, to give up the vanity of the world, to become a son of the Church.

One day, many years later, he met his friend Angelo, who recognized him immediately.

"My friend!" he cried. "Are you happy now? You have sinned by throwing away the gift God gave you. Read the parable of the ten pieces of silver. The Master who told it, told the truth. What have you won? What have you sought and what have you gained? Is your life not a life of dreams? Have you not created a religion out of your own head, as all monks do? What if it is only dreams? Only imagination? Only beautiful thoughts?"

"Satan, leave me alone!" shouted the monk, and fled from his friend Angelo.

"That was the devil . . . my personal devil. I have recognized him," said the monk. "Once I gave him a finger and he grabbed my whole hand. . . . No," he sighed. "That is not true. The evil is within myself. It is within Angelo. Yet to him it is no burden. He holds his head high and seems to prosper. And I . . . I search for happiness and comfort in the consolation of religion. But what if it is only consolation? If everything here, as in the world I left behind, is but vain dreams: an illusion that disappears as the beautiful pink color of the sunset, or changes when you come close to it as the blueness of the distant mountains does? Eternity, you are a great ocean of endless stillness. You fill us with curiosity and foreboding; you beckon and call; but if we step out upon your quiet waters we disappear, die, cease to exist. A fraud! Deceit! . . . Leave me alone! Go away!"

Without tears, sunken into himself, he knelt on his hard bed. Why did he kneel? Was it for the stone cross in the wall? No, it was out of habit that his body assumed that position.

The deeper he looked into his soul, the darker it seemed to him. "There is nothing within me, and there is nothing outside me. My life has been wasted." And this thought grew, like snow sliding down the mountainside, until it was an avalanche that crushed him.

"No one do I dare tell about this worm within my heart. This secret is my prisoner; if I told it, I would be its captive."

Faith and doubt wrestled within him. "O Master! Master!" he cried out, in his despair. "Have pity on me and give me faith. I threw Your gift away. Your purpose I ignored. I did not have the strength! You gave me the skill but not the strength! Immortality, the Psyche in my heart— Leave me alone! Go away! Why can you not be buried like the Psyche I once created? That one part of my life, let it remain buried in the grave, never to be resurrected."

The star of dawn shone brightly; someday even that star would cease to be. Only the human soul is immortal. The star's rays fell on the whitewashed walls of the cell, but they wrote no message there of God's greatness and grace, nor of the all-embracing love that lives within the heart of those who truly believe.

"The Psyche within my heart will never die," he thought, and then he asked himself aloud, "Will it be conscious forever? Can that which is beyond understanding happen? Yes! Yes! That which is incomprehensible is my own soul! O God, O Master, it is You and Your whole world that are beyond understanding and let it remain so: a wonder of power and glory and love!"

His eyes brightened and then they grew glazed. The ringing of the church bells was the last sound he heard in this world; the man was dead. They buried him in earth brought from Jerusalem and mixed with the dust of the pious dead.

Years went by; then, as was the custom, his skeleton was dug up and dressed in a monk's frock, while in his hands was placed a rosary. Finally he was put in a niche among other human bones, in the tombs of the monastery. Outside, above him, the sun shone; inside there was the sweet smell of incense; mass was being recited.

Again the years passed, many years. The skeletons fell apart and became merely bones. With the skulls the monks constructed a wall around the church of the monastery, and his skull was among them. There were so many dead. No one knew their names or remembered any of them. Look! In the bright sunshine you could see something moving. What was it? A bright-colored lizard had made his home in that skull, and ran in and out of the holes. That was all the life that now existed in the space where once there had been great thoughts, happy dreams, love of art and all innocent beauty; where tears had fallen, and where hope of immortality had lived.

Centuries later, the morning star shone as before, as brightly as it had for thousands of years. The air had been made red by the up-coming sun: as red as a rose, as red as blood.

Where there once had been a narrow street and the remains of an old temple there now stood a convent. That morning a young nun had died and a grave was being dug in the cloister's garden. A shovel struck stone and something brilliantly white could be seen beneath the dirt. The earth was lifted carefully. First a shoulder appeared, then a woman's head.

That beautiful pink summer morning, a sculpture of Psyche had been unearthed, while a grave was being dug for a nun. Everyone agreed that it was beautiful. "A perfect work of art from that period which was the height of artistic achievement." But whose work was it? Who was the master who had created it? No one knew but the star of dawn, who knew of his earthly struggle, his trial, his weaknesses, his humanity! But all that was dead, had disappeared, turned to dust. But his gain, his profit from his struggle and his search, the glory that proved the godliness within him, his Psyche, will never die. It will live beyond the name of its creator. His spark still shines here on earth and is admired, appreciated, and loved.

The light of the morning star shone on the Psyche and on that happy crowd of people who stood admiring that soul that had been carved in marble.

What belongs to the earth follows the winds and is forgotten; only the stars can remember forever. What belongs to heaven shines in its creator and, when he dies, his Psyche lives still.

## 113

## The Snail and the Rosebush

Around the garden ran a hedge of hazelnuts, beyond it there were fields and meadows, where cows and sheep grazed; but in the center of the garden there was a rosebush in full bloom. Under it lay a snail who was very satisfied with the company he kept: his own.

"Wait till my time comes," he would say, "and see what I shall accomplish. I am not going to be satisfied with merely blossoming into flowers, or bearing nuts, or giving milk as the cows and sheep do."

"Oh, I do expect a lot of you. Won't you tell me when it's going to happen?" asked the rosebush very humbly.

"I must take my time," replied the snail. "Do you think anyone would expect very much of me if I hurried the way you do?"

The following year the snail lay in the same sunny place, under the rosebush. The plant was full of buds and flowers, and there were always fresh roses on it, and each and every one was a tiny bit different from all the others. The snail crept halfway out of his house and stretched his horns upward; then he pulled them back in again.

"Everything looks exactly as it did last year. No change and no advancement. The rosebush is still producing roses; it will never be able to do anything else."

Summer was past and autumn was past. Until the first snow, the rosebush continued to bloom. The weather became raw and cold. The rosebush bent its branches toward the ground and the snail crawled down into the earth.

Another spring came. The rosebush blossomed and the snail stuck its head out of its house. "You are getting old," he said to the rosebush. "It is about time you withered and died. You have given the world everything you could. Whether what you gave was worth anything or not is another question, and I don't have time to think about it. But one thing is certain and that is that you have never developed your inner self, or something more would have become of you. Soon you will be only a wizened stick. What have you got to say for yourself? . . . Aren't you listening? . . . Can you understand what I am saying?"

"You frighten me so." The rosebush trembled. "You have asked me about things I have never thought about."

"I don't think you've ever thought about anything. Have you ever contemplated your own existence? Have you ever asked yourself why you are here? Why you blossom? Why you are what you are, and not something else?"

"No," the rosebush said. "My flowers spring forth out of joy! I cannot stop them from coming. The sun is warm, the air refreshing. I drink the dew and the rain. From the soil and the air I draw my strength. I feel so happy that I have to flower. I cannot do anything else."

"You have lived a very comfortable and a very indolent life," said the snail severely.

"How true! I have never lacked anything. But you have been given much more than I. You are a thinker. You can think deeply and clearly. You are gifted. You will astound the world."

"Astound the world! Not I!" The snail drew in his horns and then stretched them out again. "The world means nothing to me. Why should I care about the world? I have enough within myself. I don't need anything from the outside."

"But isn't it the duty of all of us here on earth to do our best for each other, to give what we can? I know I have only given roses. But you who have received so much, what have you given? What will you give?"

"What have I given! What shall I give!" snarled the snail. "I spit on the whole world. It is not worth anything and means nothing to me. Go on creating your roses, since you cannot stop anyway. Let the bushes go on bearing their nuts, and the cows and the sheep giving their milk. Each of them has their own public; and I have mine in myself. I am going to withdraw from the world; nothing that happens there is any concern of mine." And the snail went into his house and puttied up the entrance.

"It is so sad," said the rosebush. "No matter how much I wanted to, I couldn't withdraw into myself. My branches are always stretching outward, my leaves unfolding, my flowers blooming. My petals fall off and are carried away by the wind. But one of my roses was pressed in a mother's psalmbook, another was pinned on a young girl's breast, and one was kissed by a child to show his joy in being alive. Those are my remembrances: my life."

The rosebush went on blooming innocently, and the snail withdrew from the world, which meant nothing to him, by hibernating in his house.

The years passed. The rosebush had become earth and the snail had become earth; even the rose that had been pressed in the psalmbook was no more. But in the garden rosebushes bloomed and there were snails, who spat and retreated into their houses: the world meant nothing to them.

Should I tell the story from the beginning again? I could but it would be no different.

## 114

## "The Will-o'-the-Wisps Are in Town," Said the Bog Witch

Once there was a man who was well acquainted with fairy tales. They used to come knocking at his door. But lately he had not had any such visitors, and he wondered why the fairy tales didn't come any more. True, he had not thought of the fairy tales during the last few years and had not been expecting them to just come to his door, for outside there was war and inside—in the houses—there were the sorrow and despair that war brings.

Without thinking of the dangers, the stork and the swallow had made their long journey home, only to find their nests destroyed, the houses in the villages burned, and the fences around the fields broken. In the churchyards the enemy horses grazed among the tombstones. These were hard times, dark times, but even periods of unhappiness must end. "Now it is over," he said, but still the fairy tales did not come and knock at his door.

A whole year went by, and he missed them sorely. "Maybe they'll never come again," he thought. He recalled vividly the many forms that they had taken in the past. One had been a lovely young girl with a wreath of flowers in her hair and a birch branch in her hand. She had been as beautiful and fresh as spring itself, with eyes as deep and clear as the little lakes in the forest. Often the fairy tale had been a peddler, who would take his pack from his back and open it right there in the living room; and out would come the loveliest silk ribbons and every one had a verse on it. Best of all had it been when the fairy tale came as a little old woman with silver-white hair, and eyes large with age and filled with knowledge. For she could tell tales from the really ancient times: from the era before the one in which the princesses spun on golden spinning wheels and were guarded by dragons. And she could make the stories seem so alive that you saw spots in front of your eyes and the floor became black with human blood. Oh, she told gruesome tales, dreadful to hear and see, and yet such a pleasure, for they had happened so very long ago.

"I wonder whether she will ever come again," said the man, and looked so intently at the door that he saw black spots in front of his eyes and on the floor. "But maybe it is not blood," he muttered, "maybe it is bits from the mourning bands of the dark days that are only just past."

Suddenly it occurred to him that the fairy tales might be in hiding like the princesses in the old tales: that, like the princesses, they wanted to be found, and when, finally, they were discovered they would be more brilliant and more beautiful than they had ever been before.

"Who knows where a fairy tale can hide? It can be under a piece of straw that has been carelessly dropped at the edge of a well. I must be careful . . . ever so careful. It can be hidden in a withered flower that has been pressed between the leaves of one of the big, heavy books on my bookshelves."

The man walked over to his bookcase and took down the latest book; it was very serious and he thought it would help to clear his mind. There was no flower pressed between any of its leaves, but only a learned discourse concerning the national hero of his country: Holger the Dane. It seems that this very courageous man had never existed but had been invented by a French monk, who wrote a novel that was "translated into and widely printed in the Danish language." So Holger the Dane could never have taken part in any battle, nor was he liable to come to save his native land, if and when the nation were in mortal danger. Danish children could sing of his exploits, and even the grownups could hope it was not only a legend that he would return; but Holger the Dane was no different from William Tell. Both of them were no more than hot air, not worth wasting one's time on, according to the author of this very scholarly book.

"I believe what I believe," said the man, and put the book back. "No path is made where no foot has trod."

He went to the window sill and looked at the plants and flowers.

Maybe the fairy tale had hidden in the red tulip with the golden-edged petals, or in the rose, or in the colorful camellia. But he did not find any fairy tale; only the sunshine playing among the leaves.

"The flowers that bloomed in our days of sorrow were more beautiful than these. But those we cut and made into wreaths to decorate the coffins that were draped in flags. Maybe the fairy tale was buried with the flowers. But would not the flowers have known, and the earth? Yes, even the coffin would have sensed it; and the new flowers as they bloomed—and even each blade of grass—would have told us that fairy tales do not die.

"Maybe it has been here and knocked at my door, but I did not hear it. Then life seemed so hard to bear, and all our thoughts were dark. Spring seemed an intrusion then, and the songs of the birds and the fresh green leaves on the trees, that should have made us happy, instead almost made us angry. Even the old songs that we loved were put aside with all the other things that were so dear to us, because our hearts were too heavy to bear them. Yes, then the fairy tale could have knocked on our doors and it would not have been heard; and no one would have bade it welcome. It probably just knocked and when no one answered it walked away.

"I shall go out and search for it, out in the country, in the forest, by the open sea."

Far away from any city there stood an old castle with red brick walls, corbie gables, and towers, one of which had a banner flying above it. Here the nightingale sits singing on the branch of a beech tree, gazing at the apple blossoms and believing them to be roses. In summer the bees swarm around their queen, singing their own songs. In the autumn storms raid the forest, whip the leaves from the branches, to tell of man's fate. At Christmas, from the open sea, one hears the song of the wild swan, while up at the castle everyone moves closer to the stove and is in a mood to hear the old ballads and sagas.

In the older part of the garden there was an avenue of chestnut trees, and there, attracted by their shade, walked the man who had set out to find a fairy tale. For here the wind had once sung to him the story of "Valdemar Daae and His Daughters." Here, too, a druid, who lived in an old oak tree—she is the mother of all the fairy tales—had told him the tale of the old oak tree's last dream. When his grandmother on his mother's side had been alive, there had been hedges here that had been carefully trimmed; but now there were only ferns and nettles that grew as they pleased and concealed almost all the sculpture. The mosses grew right up into the old stone figures' eyes. For all of that they could see just as well as they always had been able to, but the man who was searching for the fairy tale could not. He could not see the fairy tales any more. Where could they be?

From the tops of the old trees crows by hundreds cried, "Here! Here! Here!"

He left the garden by crossing the bridge over the moat, and entered the little copse of alder trees. Here were the henyard and the duckpond, and the little hexagonal house where the old woman who ruled over this little world lived. She knew exactly how many eggs had been laid and how many chickens had been hatched; but she was not a fairy tale, for she had been both baptized and vaccinated, and lying in the top drawer of her chest, she had certificates to prove it.

Not far from the old woman's house was a hillock covered with red hawthorn and lovely yellow laburnum bushes. Here there was an old tombstone. It had been brought there many years before from the churchyard in the market town, where it had been chiseled to honor the memory of a former member of the town council. There he was surrounded by his wife and five daughters, all wearing ruff collars and with their hands folded. If you look long enough at such a stone it becomes part of your thoughts; then it is as if your mind has entered the stone until both are one, and it will tell you about bygone times. In any case, that was what happened to the man who was looking for the fairy tale.

This particular day, he found a living butterfly resting on the stone head of the councilor. It fluttered its wings and flew a little distance away, as if it meant to show the man what was growing there. He bent down. The butterfly had alighted on a four-leaf clover. Four-leaf clovers bring good luck, and here there was not only one but seven of them.

"Luck comes in crowds," said the man, and picked them all and put them in his pockets. "They say that good luck is like ready cash, but I would have preferred to find a fairy tale," he added with disappointment.

The large red sun went down, and from the meadows vapors rose. The bog witch was brewing something.

It was late in the evening. The man stood alone by the window in his room and looked out over the garden, the fields, the meadows, and beyond them to the seacoast. The moon was almost full and its rays played upon the mist and made the meadow appear like a silver lake, as if the moon wished to prove the old legend true that told how there once had been a lake there. The man thought about the book he had read explaining that William Tell and Holger the Dane were merely folklore. "As the moonlight can make the lake that is no longer there reappear, so can the beliefs of the ordinary people make the legends of old live. Oh yes, Holger the Dane is not dead! And when his country is in mortal danger he will come back!" the man concluded.

There was a noise at the window. Perhaps it was a bird: an owl or a bat; the kind of guests one does not open the window for, no matter how often they knock. Suddenly the window opened by itself and there stood an old woman looking in at him.

"I beg your pardon!" exclaimed the man, very surprised. "Who are you? You must be standing on a ladder because my room is on the second story."

"You have four-leaf clovers in your pocket, seven of them, and one is a six-leaf clover." The old woman sniffed and looked about the room.

"Who are you?" demanded the man.

"I am the bog witch," she replied at last. "The bog witch who brews, that's me. And I am brewing beer right now, but one of the bog children, in a fit of temper, pulled the tap out of the barrel and cast it up here, at the castle, where it hit your window; and now all the beer is running out, which is really to no one's advantage."

"Please," began the man, who was looking for a fairy tale, "could you tell me—"

"Maybe I could," she interrupted, "but now I have something more important to attend to." And she was gone.

Just as the man was about to close the window she was back again.

"Well, that's done," she said. "Half of the beer has run out, and I'll have to brew again tomorrow, if the weather keeps. What did you want to ask me? I've come back again because I always keep my word. Besides, you have seven four-leaf clovers in your pocket, one of which is a six-leaf clover, and that I respect. A six-leaf clover is one of nature's medals. It can be found growing along the side of the road but not by just anyone. What do you want? Don't stand on ceremony, I have to get back to my barrels and my brewing."

The man asked the bog witch whether she had seen a fairy tale.

"By the eternal brewing vat!" said the bog witch, and laughed. "Haven't you known enough fairy tales? I am sure most people have. In our times, we have more important things to think about. Why, even the children don't care about them any more. The little girls would rather have a new dress; and as for the boys, I think they'd prefer a cigar. To listen to fairy tales! You are behind the times! Today we don't listen, we do things!"

"What do you mean?" asked the man. "How can you know so much about the world when you only associate with frogs and will-o'-the-wisps?"

"Yes, you be careful of the will-o'-the-wisps; they've got loose. Come down to the meadow and I'll tell you about it. I haven't the time to stand here any longer. But hurry, while your four-leaf clovers are still fresh and the moon is up." And away she went.

The bell in the tower clock struck twelve. Before the quarter chimes were heard, the man had run through the garden and was approaching the meadow. The fog was gone. The bog witch had finished her brewing.

"What a time it took you," said the bog witch. "Troll beings are faster than human beings. I am glad I was born a troll."

"What can you tell me?" The man was quite out of breath because he had hurried so much. "Is it something about a fairy tale?"

"Can't you talk about anything else?" The bog witch sounded irritated.

"Can you tell me what the poetry of the future will be like?"

"Don't be so high-flown. Come down to earth and maybe I'll answer you," replied the bog witch. "You only think about poetry and the fairy tale—as if she were the madam who ruled the roost. She is probably older than I am though she looks younger. I know her quite well. . . . I was young once myself—and that's not a disease that only children suffer from. I was quite a beautiful elf maiden then. And, like the others, I danced by the light of the moon and listened to the song of the nightingale; and I went for walks in the forest where I sometimes met the fairy tale. She was always running about. She would sleep one night in a tulip and the next in a rose; and then she used to like to dress herself up in the mourning crepe that was draped around the candles in the church."

"You know a lot of lovely things," said the man quite humbly.

"I know as much as you do, anyway," said the bog witch, and wrinkled her nose, which wasn't as pretty as it had been when she was an elf maiden. "Poetry and the fairy tales are cut from the same cloth; and as far as I am concerned, they can go and lie down wherever they please. All their work and all their talk—the same stuff can be brewed both cheaper and faster than they do it. I'll give you some for nothing. I have a chestful of bottled poetry. There you will find the essence of poetry, the very best of it, brewed from both bitter and sweet herbs: all the poetry that a man needs, and he can put a drop or two on his handkerchief for Sundays and holidays."

"How amazing!" exclaimed the man. "You mean you actually have poetry in bottles?"

"More than you could bear to sniff," answered the bog witch. "Have you heard the story about the girl who stepped on a loaf of bread to avoid getting her shoes dirty? I believe someone wrote it down and it has since been printed."

"I am the one who wrote it," said the man.

"Well, in that case you must be familiar with it. Do you remember what happened to the girl, how she sank down into the ground? Well, she landed right in my brewery, on the very day when the Devil's great-grandmother was paying me a visit. 'Give me that creature who's just sunk down here as a memento,' begged the Devil's great-grandmother, 'and I'll put her on a pedestal to remind me of my visit with you.'

"So I gave her the girl and the Devil's great-grandmother in return gave me her portable medicine chest—not that I have any use for it, it's filled with poetry in bottles. Look around! You have your seven four-leaf clovers in your pocket and one of them is a six-leaf clover, so you ought to be able to see it."

There in the middle of the meadow was something that looked like the stump of an alder tree, but it was the cabinet that had belonged to the Devil's great-grandmother. "Anyone in the whole world could come and make use of it, the problem is to be able to find it," said the bog witch.

The cabinet could be opened in front and in back, on all four sides, and at the corners. It was a work of art and yet it resembled an ordinary tree stump. Poets from all over the world, but especially from our own Denmark, were to be found here in imitation. The best of their work had been selected, criticized, improved upon, and finally brought up to date. With great talent—that is the word generally used when one does not want to say "genius"—the Devil's great-grandmother had taken from nature the smell or the taste that seemed most like this or that poet, added a bit of witchcraft to it, and presto! she had poetry in bottles, preserved for eternity.

"Let me have a look inside!" begged the man.

"I have more important things than that to talk with you about," the bog witch insisted.

"But now that we are here," mumbled the man as he opened the chest. "There are bottles of all different sizes," he said excitedly. "What's in this one? . . . And in that?"

"That one is called 'Aroma of May.'" The bog witch stared at the small green bottle. "I haven't tried it, but they say that, if you spill a little on the floor, where it falls a beautiful pond appears, the kind you find in the forest in which water lilies and mint are growing. A drop or two in a notebook, even one from the first grade, and you have a comedy of fragrance strong enough to be produced and long enough to make you fall asleep. I am sure that it is meant as a compliment to me that the label reads: 'Brewed by the Bog Witch.'"

Another bottle was called "Scandal." It looked as if it contained only dirty water, and that was what was in it; but a powder of town gossip, made up of two grains of truth and two barrels of lies, had been added to make it fizz. The mixture had been carefully stirred with a birch branch—not one that had been used on a criminal's back or by a schoolmaster on naughty children, but a branch that had been taken from a broom with which the gutters were swept.

There was also a bottle of devotional poetry, ready to be set to music like the psalms. Every drop in the bottle had been inspired by the portals of hell, and penned with the sweat and blood of penance. Some say that this bottle contains only the gall of doves; but others, who know nothing about zoology, claim that doves are so good and gentle that they don't have any gall.

There stood the bottle of all bottles: the largest of them all, and it took up half the space in the cabinet. It was filled with true-to-life everyday stories. It had been doubly sealed with skin from both the hide and the bladder of a pig, because it lost its flavor so easily. From this bottle, every nation could make its own soup, all depending on how you turned and tipped the bottle. There was old German blood soup with robber dumplings; tasteless English governess soup; a French *potage à la Coque,* made from the legs of cock and sparrows' eggs—in Danish, it is called cancan soup. There was also a soup for those who like high society, with counts and courtiers in the bottom of the plate and a greasy glob of philosophy floating on top. Oh, there was an endless variety in that bottle; but the best soup of all was Copenhagen soup, at least that was what everybody in Denmark said.

Tragedy had been put into champagne bottles because it must begin with a bang. Light comedy was nothing but a bottleful of sand to throw into the eyes of the audience. There were bottles of the more vulgar kind of comedy but they were empty except for the play-bills, on which the titles were in the boldest type: "Do You Dare to Spit in the Machine?" "A Right to the Jaw." "The Sweet Donkey."

The man looked thoughtfully at all the bottles, but the bog witch had no patience with them, she had more important matters to think about.

"You have looked long enough at that junk shop," she said. "Now you know what's to be found there, but what it is really important for you to know I haven't told you yet. The will-o'-the-wisps are in town; and some people, who have more sense in their legs than in their heads, have already fallen into the bog chasing them. This is more important than talking about poetry or fairy tales. Maybe I should keep quiet about it, but something—I don't know what it is, maybe fate—bids me speak. It is stuck in my throat and has to come out: the will-o'-the-wisps are in town! They are on the loose. Beware, all human beings!"

"I don't understand a word you're saying," said the man, who looked as confused as he was.

"Make yourself comfortable. Sit down on the cabinet, but be careful not to fall in and break the bottles; after all, you know what's inside them. I shall tell you all about the great event. It happened only yesterday. It has happened once or twice before in history, but that doesn't make it any less important. There are three hundred and sixty-four days left. . . . You know how many days there are in a year, I suppose."

With that as an introduction the bog witch finally began her tale: "Yesterday a great event took place out in the swamp. A will-o'-the-wisp was born; that is, twelve will-o'-the-wisps were born, for that is the number there is in a litter. And it was a very special event, for these will-o'-the-wisps, if they want to, can change themselves into human beings, and live and rule among you as if they had been born of women. It caused great excitement; and all the will-o'-the-wisps—both the male and the female—were dancing in the fields. There are female will-o'-the-wisps, but there is none in that litter.

"I was sitting on the cabinet, right where you are now, and had all twelve of the little ones in my lap. They were shining like glowworms and had already begun to hop about. They grew by the minute; and within a quarter of an hour they were as big as their father or their uncles. Now it is an old law—a boon granted long ago to the will-o'-the-wisps—that when the moon is in the particular position that it was last night, and the wind is blowing from the particular direction that it did last night; then all of the will-o'-the-wisps born during that hour and that minute can become human beings. For a whole year they have a chance to show what use they can make of their powers. A will-o'-the-wisp can move so quickly that he can travel around the whole world. The only things he needs to be careful of are sea and storm, which could put out his light. They can enter any human being—man or woman—they choose to and imitate his talk and behavior to perfection. If during one year the will-o'-the-wisp can make three hundred and sixty-five people err in a grand, not a small way, leaving the road of truth and decency, then he will be rewarded by being appointed to the greatest position that a will-o'-the-wisp can hope for; namely, to become a runner in front of the Devil's carriage of state. He will be given a bright orange uniform and taught how to breathe fire.

"Now that is something to make any will-o'-the-wisp lick his chops. But there are also dangers for such an ambitious will-o'-the-wisp. If a human being sees through his disguise, he can blow out the light and back into the swamp the will-o'-the-wisp must go. If he gets sick with longing for his family and the bog, his light will flicker and finally go out; and that is the end of him, he can never be relighted. And even if he does manage to remain a whole year among men, he still runs a risk; for if he fails to turn three hundred and sixty-five people from searching for truth and beauty, and doing good, then he must lie forever in a rotten tree and just glow, without being able to move about. And no punishment could be worse for a will-o'-the-wisp because they do so like to gallivant about.

"While they sat in my lap I told them of the honor they could achieve, but also of the risks they would have to run. I warned them that it would be more comfortable and secure to remain in the marsh, instead of running after fame and glory. But they were already imagining themselves dressed in bright orange and breathing fire out of their mouths. Some of the old will-o'-the-wisps said, 'Stay with us.' But there were others who encouraged them.

"'Go and play all the tricks you can on human beings,' they cried. 'Man has drained our swamps and dried up the meadows, what will become of our descendants?'

"'We want to breathe fire! We want to breathe fire!' shouted the newly born will-o'-the-wisps; and there was nothing more to discuss.

"To celebrate the decision there was a minute-long dance; it couldn't have been shorter. The elf maidens joined in the dance, but that was in order not to appear too proud, for in truth they preferred dancing by themselves. Then came the time for the giving of gifts to the twelve will-o'-the-wisps. Down in the swamp we call it playing ducks and drakes because the presents are skimmed across the water like stones.

"Each of the elf maidens gave a will-o'-the-wisp a piece of her veil. 'Take it,' the elf maidens explained, 'for as soon as you have it in your hands, you'll know all the difficult dance steps; you'll be able to do all the swings and turns, exactly when and as you should; and you'll have a bearing that will make you respected in the proudest company.'

"The raven taught every will-o'-the-wisp to say, 'Braaaa . . . Braaaa . . . Braaaaa.' And that is well worth knowing how to say, especially at the right moment.

"The stork and the owl presented their gifts, but they said that they weren't worth mentioning, so I won't tell what they were.

"While these festivities were going on, King Valdemar and his men came riding by. And when the old king, who has been condemned to hunt until Judgment Day, heard of the event he gave away two of his hounds as a gift. These dogs are as swift as the wind and can carry as many as three will-o'-the-wisps at a time on each of their backs.

"Two old nightmares, who earn their living by hauling wares for those who live in the swamp, taught the will-o'-the-wisps the art of slipping through keyholes, which means that every door will be open to them.

"Two witches—but no relations of mine—offered to show the will-o'-the-wisps the way to town. Usually they ride on their own long hair, which they tie into knots to have something hard to sit on; but this time they rode on King Valdemar's dogs and had on their laps the young will-o'-the-wisps, who were setting out on their travels to bewilder and mislead human beings. Whoosh! And away they went!

"Now you know everything that happened last night. The will-o'-the-wisps are in town and they've already started their work. Exactly how or what they are doing I cannot say. But I have had a pain in the big toe of my left foot most of the day and there's always a reason for that."

"What a fairy tale!" exclaimed the man, who had not said a word while the bog witch was talking, but who had felt like interrupting a couple of times.

"No, it is only the beginning of the adventure," the bog witch corrected him. "Do you know what shapes the will-o'-the-wisps have taken or whose bodies they may enter, in order to lead the poor human creatures astray?"

"It is a whole novel about will-o'-the-wisps, and in twelve volumes: one for each will-o'-the-wisp. . . . Or better still, a musical comedy," the man said excitedly.

"Why don't you write it?" the bog witch asked. A moment later she added, "But maybe you shouldn't."

"It is a great deal easier and pleasanter not to." The man sighed. "If I write anything, then I shall be at the mercy of the newspapers, and that is as horrible for an author, as it is for a will-o'-the-wisp to lie in a rotten tree stump and glow, without being able to move or say a word."

"That's for you to decide," said the bog witch. "Let those write who can; and those who can't, they can write too. They need only come to me and I'll let them take anything they want from the cabinet filled with bottled poetry. . . . But as for you, my good man, it seems to me that you have had enough ink on your fingers already. You have reached an age when you ought to be old enough not to chase fairy tales. Have you understood my tale? Do you realize what is going on?"

"I know that the will-o'-the-wisps are in town. You have told me so. I have heard it and, what is more, I have understood what it means," the man replied sadly. "But what do you want me to do? If I start saying that certain honorable men are only will-o'-the-wisps in disguise, I'll be stoned."

"They can wear skirts as well," said the bog witch, looking at him thoughtfully. "They can enter a woman, too. They don't mind going to church, but they prefer to creep inside the minister and hold the sermon. On election day they are busy; they are speaking not for their country's sake but for their own. They become artists, too. But when they have taken over art, then there is no art. . . . I talk on and on. . . . Whatever it was that got stuck in my throat is almost gone now. I have spoken against my own family—for, though distant, the will-o'-the-wisps are cousins of mine—and now I am the savior of humanity! I don't know why I have done it, it is certainly not to get a medal. It's the maddest thing I could do: to tell everything to a poet and now the whole town will know about it."

"But no one will care," said the man. "Not one person will pay any attention to anything I say. They will all believe that I am telling a fairy tale when I say: ' "Beware! The will-o'-the-wisps are in town!" said the bog witch!' "

## 115

## The Windmill

On top of a hill stood a windmill. "It is a proud sight," people said; and the windmill did feel proud.

"Absolutely not! I am not proud," the windmill declared. "I am enlightened: both inside and out. For outside illumination I have the sun and the moon; and inside me there are candles and oil lamps —so, you see, I have every right to call myself enlightened. I am capable of thought and have a beautifully shaped body. Two millstones grind away in my chest, and I have four wings in my head just beneath my hat. Birds have only two wings and they have to carry them on their back. I was born in Holland, and you can see that in my figure. I am a 'Flying Dutchman,' but there's nothing supernatural about me. No, I am modest, normal, and natural.

"Around my stomach runs a gallery, and in my lower parts there's an apartment, where my thoughts live. My strangest thought—the one that rules and gives orders to all the others—I call the miller. He knows what he wants, and both the grain and the flour have to obey him. Yet he has his equal—some even call her his 'better half'—his wife, who is called 'Mother.' The good wife has the heart, but she doesn't flutter about; she, too, knows what she wants and what she is capable of doing. She can be as mild as a summer breeze and as strong as a November storm. She knows how to get her way by coaxing. The wife is the soft part of my soul and the husband the firm. They are two and yet one: that is almost a riddle. They have offspring, little thoughts that can grow. These little ones aren't so easy to control. Just listen to what happened the other day, when I had wisely decided to let the miller and his helper have a look inside me.

"Something was wrong, I could feel it, and it does one good, every so often, to find out exactly what is going on inside one. But while the miller was looking at my wheels, the offspring made an awful rumpus. They shouted and ran all over, which was most unbecoming. You must remember that I stand high up on a hill where everyone can see me. Reputation is also a kind of illumination and it reflects on one's soul. And there were those little ones climbing high up into my hat and singing so loud that it tickled me. Yes, little thoughts can grow, that I am aware of; and outside there are other thoughts that don't belong to me or even to members of my family. For there are no members of my family in the neighborhood; not as far as I can see and I can see very far. But there are the wingless houses without grindstones in their chests, and they have thoughts too. Sometimes their thoughts come to visit mine. Lately, two of them got engaged—whatever that means.

"Things are changing inside me. But that is as it should be, though it is strange. It is as if the miller had changed his other half. She has grown softer and sweeter. Time has blown away what was bitter and has left her younger; and yet she is the same, only milder and gentler.

"Days come and go. We move ever forward to greater happiness and greater understanding. It has been said—and what is even more important, it has been written—that someday I shall be no more and still I shall be. I shall be torn down and resurrected. I shall cease to exist and yet continue to exist. I shall become another windmill and yet remain the same windmill. It is difficult to understand, even for one who is thoroughly enlightened by the sun, the moon, candles, and oil lamps. My old bricks and beams shall be raised from the dust. I only hope that I shall be allowed to keep the same old thoughts: the miller and his wife and the little thoughts. The 'family' as I call them, who are one and yet many, the thought-makers; I wouldn't want to have to get along without them! I'd like myself not to change, too. I'd like to know that I am myself with millstones in my chest, wings on my head, and a gallery around my stomach. Otherwise I wouldn't recognize myself, nor would anyone else recognize me; and no one would say, 'We have a windmill high up on top of the hill, and it's a proud sight, though it isn't by nature proud.'"

All this the windmill said, and a great deal more, for it was very talkative; but I have only written down what was most important. Days came and went, one after another, until the last day became the last: it was the one on which the windmill burned.

The windmill was on fire. Flames leaped higher and higher. They shot out and struck in; they licked the beams and the woodwork and ate them up. The windmill toppled down and was soon only a heap of ashes. The smoke rose from the embers and the wind carried it away.

Nothing happened to the miller and his family, not even the cat was singed; if anything, they profited from the accident. A new windmill was built on the same spot and they moved into it; and the family was as it had been before: one soul with many thoughts and yet only one. The new windmill was a beauty and a great improvement on the old one, though it looked like it and people still called it "a proud sight." It was inside that the advancements had been made; it had been modernized, for, after all, we do progress. The old beams, rotten and worm-eaten, had been turned to ashes and dust and were never resurrected, as the old windmill had believed they would be. It had taken everything too literally, and that was a mistake.

## 116

## The Silver Shilling

"Hurray! Here I go out into the wide world," exclaimed the newly minted silver shilling. It clinked and rolled and out into the world it came.

It passed through the warm, moist hands of children; felt the cold, clammy palm of the miser; and was kept a whole week by a poor old couple before they dared to spend it. Whenever it got into the purse of a young person it was soon out again. As I have said, it was a silver shilling; and it was made of quite pure silver, with only a very little copper in it. Now it happened that after it had traveled about in its native country for a whole year it went for a trip abroad. By chance it was overlooked in the bottom of a purse, and its owner did not even know that he had it along.

"Why, there is a shilling from home," he said when he finally noticed it. "Well, since it's come this far, it might as well do the trip with me as a tourist." The shilling almost jumped for joy. It was dropped back into the purse, which now was filled with foreign coins, but they came and went, while the silver shilling remained: and this, it felt, was an important distinction.

Several weeks went by. The coin had traveled far, without knowing exactly where it was. The other coins explained that they were in France or in Italy, and mentioned the names of towns, but how could the little shilling have any idea what the place looked like? One really cannot see the world from the bottom of a purse.

One morning the shilling noticed that the opening of the purse wasn't completely closed; and so it moved up there in order to get a glance outside.

This it never should have done, for now it would have to pay the penalty for being curious. The shilling slid out of the purse and into its owner's trousers' pocket. That evening, after the purse was put aside for safekeeping, the traveler's clothes were brushed; and the coin fell out of the pocket and down onto the floor. No one heard it and no one saw it.

In the morning the man dressed and traveled on, but without his silver shilling. It was found by someone else, who put it in his purse where there were three other coins, all ready to do service.

"It is lovely to travel," said the shilling, "to see different people and learn their customs."

But at that very moment someone shouted: "That coin is false! It is counterfeit!" And it is at this point that the silver shilling's real adventures began; at least, so the coin itself seemed to think, for it would always start its story here:

"'False! Counterfeit!' A shiver went through me. After all, hadn't I been made at the Royal Mint of almost pure silver? Couldn't I clink as a silver coin ought to? Wasn't my stamp genuine? I felt sure that there must be some mistake. The voice couldn't be talking about me; but it was! I was called false and said to be worth nothing. Then I heard another voice say, 'I'll spend it tonight, when it's dark.' And that was to be my future. I was to be spent in the dark, and discovered and cursed in the daylight. 'Counterfeit! Worthless! I must get rid of it,' were the words that always greeted me."

Every time the coin was picked up, it would tremble and quake, for it knew that it was being passed on dishonestly, as a coin of the realm.

"Oh, poor me!" it lamented. "What good did it do me that I was made of silver, and bore a picture of our king, when he wasn't respected there? In this world you only have the value that the world gives you. How horrible it must be to really be counterfeit, to sneak through life knowing that one deserves no better fate. It must be monstrous, for even though I was innocent, I had a bad conscience. Every time I was taken out of a purse I dreaded the moment when I would be looked at. I knew what would happen. I would be rejected, thrown across the counter, as if I were the personification of deceit.

"Once I was given to a poor working woman as payment after a long day of toil. But she didn't know how to get rid of me. No one would accept me. Oh, I was a disaster for the poor woman.

"'I will have to fool someone,' she said, 'even though it is a sin and a shame, for I am too poor to keep a false coin. I can try to pass it off on the rich baker. It won't hurt him because he can afford it.'

"Now I was to give that poor woman a bad conscience," sighed the shilling. "And I thought to myself, 'Could I really have changed so much with age?'

"And the woman took me to the rich baker, but he knew his currency. I had hardly been put down on his counter before I was flung right back into the poor woman's face. I felt a great sadness come over me. I, who had had such a happy youth, confident of my value and my genuineness, now was the cause of grief to others. I became melancholy, as melancholy as a silver coin can be when it is unwanted. The woman picked me up and took me home with her. 'I won't try to fool anyone with you again,' she said, gazing at me with kindness and generosity. 'I shall drill a hole in you so everyone can see that you are counterfeit. . . . And yet, it suddenly struck me that you might be a lucky coin! Just like that, out of nowhere the thought came to me that you were a lucky coin. I'll make a hole in you anyway, but then I will put a string through it and give you to the neighbor's little girl to wear as a good-luck charm.'

"And that was what she did. It isn't very pleasant to have a hole drilled through you, but you can bear an awful lot when you know that the intentions are good. A string was drawn through me and that's how I became a medal and was hung around a little girl's neck. The child smiled at me and kissed me; and I spent one whole night sleeping on her innocent, warm breast.

"In the morning the girl's mother took me between her thumb and her forefinger and looked at me intently; she had her own ideas about what ought to be done with me. She took a pair of scissors and cut the string.

"'A good-luck charm, let's see how much your luck amounts to.' She put me in vinegar, so that I became green; and then she puttied up my hole and rubbed me so that no one would notice that I had a hole. When it grew dark, she took me to the office of the state lottery, to find out how much luck I would bring.

"How horrible I felt! I had a pain in the middle of myself, as if I were about to break in two. At the state lottery office there would be a whole till full of coins both large and small, and every one of them proud of their faces and inscriptions; and there in front of them all, I knew I would be called counterfeit and thrown back at the woman. But it didn't happen. There were so many people buying tickets that I was thrown unnoticed in among the other coins. Whether or not she ever won anything on that lottery ticket, I cannot tell you. All I know is that the next morning I was discovered and humiliated again. Once more I was put aside and then sent on my way to deceive someone else. And it is unbearable to have to play the fraud when you are honest; and I see no reason to deny that I am honest.

"A year and a day went by. I passed from one hand to another, from one house to another. Always cursed, always unwelcome. No one had any faith in me and finally I had no faith in myself, or in the world. It was a difficult time.

"One day I was given to a tourist. He looked so ignorant and innocent that, naturally, he was cheated. He took me for good currency without a glance but, when he wanted to use me, he heard the hue and cry, 'Counterfeit! Valueless!'

"'I was given it as change,' he said, looking at me carefully. Then he smiled broadly and that was the first time that a face had smiled when it was examining me. 'What are you doing here?' he asked. 'It is a coin from my own country. A good honest silver shilling that has had a hole drilled through it, as if it were counterfeit. That's really funny! I'll take good care of you and see to it that you come home again.'

"Happiness rushed through me when I heard myself being called 'good' and 'honest.' And now I was to go home. Back to my native country again, to that land where everyone knew that I was made of pure silver—almost pure silver, that is—and that the face on my head was that of our king. I would have sparkled with joy if nature had meant for me to sparkle, but only steel can sparkle, not silver.

"I was wrapped in a piece of fine white paper so that I would not have to associate with the other coins and get lost again. I was only brought out on special occasions when my owner met people from his own country, and they spoke well of me and said that I was very interesting. Isn't it funny that you can be called interesting when you haven't said a single word?

"Finally, I was home and my trials and tribulations were over. Life was pleasant again. I was silver and my inscription was authentic. It didn't matter that a hole had been drilled through me to proclaim me as false, because I wasn't and that is all that is important. Don't give up, eventually justice will triumph. That's my philosophy," said the silver shilling.

## 117

## The Bishop of Børglum Cloister and His Kinsmen

We are on the west coast of Jutland, a bit north of the great peat bog. We can hear the waves beating on the beach, but we cannot see the ocean because a long hill of sand stretches between us and the sea. Our horses are weary. It has been hard work pulling the carriage along the sandy road, but we have reached our destination. On top of the hill there are buildings: it is a farm built on the remains of Børglum Cloister; the church is still standing.

It is late in the evening, but it is summer, it is a clear, white night. Standing on the summit of the hill, we can see eastward as far as Alborg Fjord and westward, out over the heath and the meadows, to the dark blue sea.

We pass the outbuildings of the farm and drive through the old portals of the cloister into the courtyard. Like sentinels, the linden trees grow in rows along the walls. Here there is shelter from the west wind, and the trees have become so tall that their branches hide the windows.

We climb the old, worn, circular staircase, and through the long corridors we walk under ancient beams. The voice of the wind sounds strange; one does not know why but its tone is different. When you are afraid or you want to make someone else afraid, you begin to notice things that you have not seen before, and old legends come into your mind. They say that the monks of the cloister, who have long since been dead, still attend mass in the church; they appear like shades and you can hear their singing in the strange sound of the wind. A curious mood comes over us. We think of bygone ages and our thoughts turn backward to become one with the past.

There is a shipwreck on the coast. The Bishop of Børglum's men are already on the beach, and those sailors who survived the merciless sea do not survive the bishop's men. The tongues of the waves lick away the blood from the cloven skulls. All that drifts ashore— both the remains of the ship and its cargo—belong to the bishop, if there are no survivors to lay claim to them. Through the years Børglum Cloister has been well supplied by the sea. In the cellars, alongside the barrels of native beer and mead, stand casks of the finest wines. In the kitchens there is not only game from the Danish forests but hams and sausages from far away; and in the ponds of the cloister gardens swim fat carp. The Bishopric of Børglum is rich; and Olaf Glob, the bishop, is a powerful man, already wealthy in the property of this world, but he still desires more. In his hands he holds the reins of power and everyone must bow and bend to his will.

Not far away, at Thy, his rich kinsman has died. "Kin are worst against kin," as the saying goes. The man who died was rich, and all of the district of Thy that did not belong to the Church had been his. Now the Bishop of Børglum, in the name of the Church, claims the estate. The son of the dead man is not in Denmark; he is studying abroad. It is years since any message has come from him, perhaps he has been laid in his grave and will never return to govern where his widowed mother now rules in his place.

"A woman should obey, not command," says the bishop. He sends a summons to her that she must appear before the assembly. She comes, but she has broken no laws or done any wrong. Her defense is the justice of her cause and her peers have no complaint against her.

Tell us, Bishop of Børglum, what are you so pensive about? What are you writing on that parchment? You smile as you seal it. What message is within that letter, which is closed by the ribbon and seal of the Bishop of Børglum? You give the letter to one of your horsemen; he has far to ride, for he is being sent to Rome, with a message for the Pope.

Summer is over. The leaves have turned yellow and are ready to fall. The storms are coming. It is the season of shipwrecks. Twice winter follows summer before the bishop's servant returns from

Rome. He returns with another letter that is closed by a more important seal than that of the Bishop of Børglum.

The widow has been excommunicated, punished by the Pope for
her willful offense against a pious servant of the Church, the Bishop
of Børglum: "Expelled from the congregation. She and anyone who
follows her are banned; both kith and kin must avoid her as they
would one who had the plague or leprosy."

"Those who will not bend must be broken," says the Bishop of
Børglum.

Only an old servant remains with the widow. No one else dares help
her. She has lost her friends and her family, but she has not lost her
faith in God. Together the two women plow the earth; and the grain
grows, even though the soil has been condemned by both the bishop
and the Pope.

"You child of hell! I shall teach you to obey. With the hand of the
Pope, you shall be summoned to the Ecclesiastical Court, where you
will be judged and punished," threatens the Bishop of Børglum.

The widow still has two oxen, which she harnesses to a cart, and
with her servant she sets out. She will leave Denmark, travel abroad,
where she will be a stranger among strangers. She will hear languages
that she cannot understand and live among people who have customs
and habits she does not know.

The two women travel south, to where the green hills become
high mountains and the grape ripens. Along the way they meet rich
merchants who fear for their wealth when their wagons go through
the dark forests. But the widow's poverty guards her against the
robbers, who prey on other travelers. Two women in an old cart,
drawn by two black oxen, pass safely along the unsafe, narrow roads.

They are in France, and there one morning they meet a dignified-
looking young nobleman. He is richly dressed and followed by twelve
armed servants. He stops to look at the cart and the strange women.
He asks them where they come from, and the widow answers that
they are from Thy in Denmark.

As her lips pronounce the name of her native land, she cannot help
but speak of her sorrow and the injustice that has been done to her.
But God had willed her to tell her story, as He had willed that this
meeting between herself and the young knight, who was her son,
should take place.

The young man gave her his hand, then he embraced her; and the poor mother wept. During all those years she had remained dry-eyed, even though she had bitten her lips till tiny drops of blood appeared on them.

Again it is time for the trees to give up their leaves. The storms come. Ships are wrecked; and casks of wine pass from the beaches to the cellars of the cloister. In the bishop's kitchens the fires glow; meat is being roasted. While the winter wind whips the cloister walls, inside it is warm and comfortable. At table the news is told: "Jens Glob of Thy has returned with his mother. They say he will summon the bishop before the Ecclesiastical Court and the King's Court."

"Fat lot of good that will do him," says the bishop, and smiles. "If my young kinsman is wise, he will forget our quarrel."

Another year passes, again it is autumn. The first frost has come, and the white bees sting your face before they melt. It is bracing weather, say those who have been out of doors. But Jens Glob has been sitting in front of his fire all day. He is deep in thought. To himself he mumbles, "Bishop of Børglum, I shall defeat you! As long as you hide under the cloak of the Pope, the law cannot touch you, but I—Jens Glob of Thy—know how to reach you!"

He writes a letter to his brother-in-law, Olaf Hase of Salling, and bids him come to Hvidberg Church on Christmas Eve, when the Bishop of Børglum is to celebrate mass there. Jens Glob has just heard the news that soon the bishop will go from Børglum into the district of Thy.

The meadows and the peat bogs are frozen and covered with snow. The ice can easily bear the weight of a horse. The bishop and his train of priests, monks, and armed servants take the shortest route, riding through the forest of yellow reeds, where the wind blows so sorrowfully.

"Play on your trumpet!" the bishop orders; and a musician wearing a foxskin cape puts the instrument to his lips. The air is clear as they ride from the heath onto the frozen marshes, south to Hvidberg Church.

Soon the wind plays on its trumpet. It blows a storm and with each puff it gains strength. To visit God's House, through the storm of God's wrath, they travel. God's House stands undisturbed by God's weather that sweeps over the marsh and the meadow and the sea. The Bishop of Børglum and his companions arrive safely. But the journey of Olaf Hase of Salling is not so easy. He is on the other side of the fjord. The wind has whipped the waters into foam in the sound between Salling and Thy.

Jens Glob has summoned Olaf Hase to Thy this Christmas Eve to sit in judgment on the Bishop of Børglum. God's House is to be their courthouse, and the altar the bar. The candles are lit in the great brass candlesticks; and the wind is reading from the Book of Judges. Strange and terrible are the sounds that come from the heath and the marsh and the storm-swept waters that no boat can cross.

Olaf Hase has reached the coast. He decides that he will send his men back with a message to his wife; he will ford the tempest-torn waters alone. But first he says farewell to his men. He sets them free from their oaths to him and gives each the weapon he bears and the horse he rides. "But all of you shall be my witness that if Jens Glob stands alone in Hvidberg Church tonight, no man may say that the fault is mine."

But Olaf Hase's men are loyal, they courageously follow him into the dark, deep waters. Ten are drowned. Only Olaf and two of his younger men reach the other side of the sound. And still they have far to ride.

It is past midnight. Soon the dawn will break on Christmas Day. The wind has stopped blowing. The light from the church shines through the windows onto the snow. Mass has long since been said; the church is still. The melted beeswax from the candles drips onto the stone floors. Now Olaf Hase arrives. Jens Glob meets his kinsman on the porch of Hvidberg Church.

"Merry Christmas! I am reconciled with the Bishop of Børglum."

"If you are reconciled," replies Olaf as he draws his sword, "then neither you nor the bishop shall leave the church alive."

Jens Glob opens the door of the church. "Be not so hasty, dear cousin. See first how I have settled my dispute. I have slain the bishop and his men. He is mute forever, and now neither he nor I shall ever speak again about the injustice done to my mother."

On the altar the flames of the candles glow with a reddish hue, but not as red as the blood upon the floor. The Bishop of Børglum's skull has been cloven in two. He lies among the still bodies of his servants. It is silent, nothing is heard from the church on this holy Christmas night.

On the third day after Christmas the bells toll in Børglum Cloister. Beneath a black baldachin lie the bishop and his men. Black crepe has been wound about the great candelabra. Wearing his cloak of silver sable, clasping his crozier in his powerless hands, rests the dead—formerly so mighty—Bishop of Børglum. There is a smell of incense. The monks are chanting their lament. The winds take up the song of grief, and now it sounds like a judgment, a message of anger and damnation.

Here the wind never dies; it only rests for a while before it begins to sing again. When the storms of the autumn come, its song is of the Bishop of Børglum and his kinsman's revenge. The timid peasant driving his cart along the sandy road any dark winter night hears the singing and he shivers, not alone from the cold. Those sleeping within the old cloister walls, they, too, hear the song of the wind. Something moves along the long corridor on the other side of the bedroom door. This was once the passage to the church; the entrance has long since been walled up. Now fear and imagination open it. Again the candles in the candelabra are lit. Once more the smell of incense fills the church. The monks are singing mass for their dead bishop, whose body lies dressed in sable, with his shepherd's crook— the sign of his power—in his powerless hands. His pale, proud forehead is cloven and the bloody wound shines as red as a flame from hell. They are the sins of this world—of the will and the desire to do evil—that are burning.

Stay in your grave, disappear into the night, into oblivion, Bishop of Børglum! Memories of a time that is past.

The wind blows furiously tonight. It drowns the noise of the surf. There is a storm raging on the sea. It will take its toll in human life. For time does not change the character of the sea. Tonight it is a mouth eager to swallow; tomorrow it will be a clear eye that you can mirror yourself in, just as it was in that earlier age that we have just buried. Now sleep peacefully, if you can.

It is morning. Outside the sun is shining, but the wind is still blowing. A message comes that there has been a shipwreck during the night. Time has changed nothing!

A ship went aground near the tiny fishing village of Lokken, not far away. From the windows of the farmhouse we can see the red-tiled roofs of the cottages, the beach, and the sea. There on a sandy reef is the wrecked ship.

During the night rockets with lines attached to them were fired out to the doomed ship. Within hours, heavy cables connected the ship and the land. Everyone on board was rescued, brought ashore, and given a warm bed.

In the cozy rooms of the manor house, built on the remains of Børglum Cloister, the survivors of the ill-fated ship are welcome. The wealthy farmer can speak the language of their country. Tonight there will be a dance in the old building. Someone will play the piano and the Danish youth will dance with the foreigners. The magic messenger, the telegraph, has brought news of the rescue to the seamen's homes. Tonight there will be a celebration and the sound of merriment inside the long corridor that once led to the church of Børglum Cloister.

Blessed be the new age! Let its sunshine blanch the dark shadows of the past, the sinister stories of those hard, cruel times.

## 118

## In the Children's Room

Father and Mother and all the other children had gone to the theater. Only Anna and her grandfather were at home.

"We want to go to the theater too," announced Grandfather, "and the performance might as well begin at once."

"But we have no theater," sighed little Anna. "And no actors, for my old doll can't act because she is too dirty; and my new doll may not, because I don't want her clothes to get wrinkled."

"You can always find actors as long as you aren't too choosy. Now let's build the theater," Grandfather said, and took down some books from the bookcase. "We stand them up: three on one side and three on the other, in slanting rows; and here, we'll put this old box in the middle as a backdrop. The scene is a living room, as anyone can plainly see. And now for the actors. Let's take a look in this chest here. . . . As soon as we have the characters and know their personalities, the play will write itself. Here is a pipe; it has a bowl but no stem; and here is a glove that has lost its mate. They could be father and daughter."

"But two characters are not enough," complained little Anna. "What about my brother's vest—he has grown too big to wear it— couldn't that be in the play too?"

"It is big enough for a part," agreed Grandfather, examining the vest. "It can be a suitor. Its pockets are empty, how interesting. Empty pockets are often the cause of an unhappy love affair. . . . Look what we have here: a high heeled boot with spurs. He can dance the waltz and the mazurka, for he can both swagger and stamp. He is made for the part of the troublesome suitor whom the heroine doesn't care for. Now tell me what kind of play you would like: a tragedy or the kind of comedy that the whole family can attend?"

"A family play!" cried the little girl. "Both Mother and Father say that those are the best."

"I know at least a hundred of them. Those that are translated from French are the most popular, but that wouldn't quite do for a little girl. We can take the nicest of them, though the stories are almost all alike. Here, I'll put all the plots in a bag and shake it well, and then you pick one. . . . That's right. Here it is: age-old and brand-new. Now for the playbill." Grandfather held up the newspaper and pretended that he was reading it:

*"The Pipe Bowl*
or
*Love's Labors Are Never Lost*
A family play in one act.

List of Characters:  Mr. Pipe Bowl . . . . . . . . . . . . . Father
Miss Glove  . . . . . . . . . . . . . . . Daughter
Mr. Vest  . . . . . . . . . . . . . . . . Sweetheart
Mr. Boot  . . . . . . . . . . . . . . . . A Suitor.

"Now the play can begin. The curtain slowly goes up. . . . True, we have no curtain, but only very narrow-minded people make a fuss about trifles. All the characters are on stage. The first one to speak is the pipe bowl. He is very angry. If there had been any tobacco in him, he would have fumed.

" 'No back talk here. I am master in my own house. I am father of my own daughter. Is no one going to listen to what I say? Von Boot has a shining personality. He is so well polished that you can mirror yourself in him. He is made of morocco and wears spurs. No more talk! He shall have my daughter!'

"Now listen carefully, little Anna," Grandfather warned. "Now the vest is going to speak. He has a silk lining but that hasn't made him smug. He is modest and yet he knows his own value. He has a right to say what he is going to say:

" 'I am spotless and of quality, so I should be taken into consideration. I am lined with genuine silk and have braiding.'

" 'Your spotlessness won't last till the day after the wedding; then you'll have to be washed and your colors aren't fast.' That was the pipe bowl who was speaking; and he goes on, 'Now Von Boot is waterproof and his skin is strong, yet he is finely made. He can creak and his spurs can jingle. He is of the latest fashion.' "

Suddenly little Anna interrupted. "Why don't they speak in verse? Mother says that it's so charming."

"What the public demands the actors must do," replied her grandfather with a smile. "Now watch little Miss Glove and how she stretches her fingers toward Mr. Vest and sings!

> " 'To be without a mate
> That fate I should hate.
> But all the owls can hoot,
> I'll not marry Von Boot.
> I would rather die,
> Or forever in a drawer lie.'

" 'Nonsense!' says the pipe bowl. Now Mr. Vest speaks to Miss Glove:

> " 'Beloved glove, beloved dove,
> My heart beats all for love.
> You shall be mine
> And I'll be thine.
> Love!
> Glove!'

"In the meantime Von Boot begins to stamp on the floor. He is terribly angry. His spurs are jingling."

"Oh, what a wonderful play!" Anna applauded with both her little hands.

"Quiet, please," said her grandfather. "During a play the best applause is silence. You must show that you are well brought up and deserve to sit in the orchestra. Now Miss Glove is going to sing her aria:

> " 'I cannot speak,
> I am so weak.
> Yet I must sing
> Of love's broken wing.'

"Now we come to the intrigue. That is the most important part of the plot and the whole originality of the play depends on it. Mr. Vest steps upstage. Watch him! He is approaching old Mr. Pipe Bowl. There! He took old Pipe Bowl and put him in his pocket. Don't applaud him, that is so plebeian; though he would probably like you to do it. Actors can't get enough applause. Now Mr. Vest speaks directly to the audience.

"'You are in my pocket, my deepest pocket, and you shall never get out again until you have agreed to our marriage. I hold out my right hand to the left-hand glove.'"

"It's awfully exciting!" exclaimed little Anna.

"From inside the pocket of Mr. Vest we hear the voice of Mr. Pipe Bowl:

> "'I am so sick.
> What a terrible trick!
> Here I am in the dark,
> There's no light, not a spark.
> I cannot move about.
> Let me out! Let me out!
> If you set me free,
> I promise to agree
> To your future marriage
> If you let me out of this carriage!'"

"Is that the end already?" asked little Anna, a bit disappointed.

"Oh no," answered Grandfather. "Only for Von Boot; the others have a long play ahead of them still. Now the lovers kneel before Mr. Pipe Bowl, and Miss Glove sings:

> "'Father!'

"And Mr. Vest sings:

> "'Bless your son and daughter!'

"Then Mr. Pipe Bowl gives his blessings and there is a wedding. Everyone joins in the chorus:

> "'The play is over
> The moral taught,
> Please applaud
> As you ought.'

"Now we clap and call everyone out to take a bow; even the furniture, for though they only sang in the chorus, they are made of mahogany."

"Tell me," said little Anna, "was our play just as good as the one the others are seeing in the real theater?"

"Oh, our comedy was much better," replied Grandfather. "It was shorter and inspired. And now I am sure the water for tea must be boiling."

## 119

## The Golden Treasure

Every town that wants to be called a town, and not a village, has a town crier; and every town crier has two drums. One he plays when he makes ordinary announcements, such as, "There's fresh fish for sale in the harbor!" The other is larger and has a deeper tone; and it is only used to call the people together when a fire has broken out or some other calamity has taken place; it is called the fire drum.

The town crier's wife had gone to church to look at the new altarpiece. It was full of angels, some were painted and others were carved. They were all beautiful, both the ones on the canvas, with their painted halos, and those that had been carved out of wood and had gilded halos. Their hair shone as brightly as gold or sunshine. Oh, it was a marvel to see! But as the woman stepped outside she decided that God's sunshine was even more beautiful. It was so red and shone so clearly through the dark trees as it set. It was a blessing to be able thus to see God's face! And as she looked at the sun, the town crier's wife thought of the child that the stork would soon bring her. She was so happy and, staring at the disappearing sun, she wished that her child would be given some of its brightness, or at least come to look like the angels on the new altarpiece.

When the child was born, she held him in her arms and lifted him up toward the town crier, so that he, too, could admire his son. The baby did look like one of the angels on the altarpiece and his hair had the color of the setting sun.

"My golden treasure, my wealth, my sunshine!" said the mother, and kissed the baby on the top of his head. Her words sounded like music, like a song; and the town crier played on his little drum the roll that accompanies glad tidings.

The big drum—the fire drum—had a different opinion. "Believe me and not his mother," said he. "The brat has red hair. . . . Boom! Boom! Booom!" And most of the people in the town agreed with the fire drum.

The baby was taken to church and baptized. There was nothing unusual about his name; he was called Peter. The whole town, including the big drum, called him "the town crier's redheaded son Peter." But his mother kissed him and said, "My golden treasure."

On the clay banks of the sunken road, many children—and grown-ups, too—had scratched their names, in the hope that they would be remembered. "Fame is worth having," said the town crier, and he inscribed his and his son's names among all the others.

The swallows came in the spring. They are great travelers. They have been in Hindustan, where they have seen inscriptions, carved in stone on the cliffs and on the walls of the temples, that tell of the deeds of mighty kings: immortal names written in letters that no one today can read or even pronounce. Such is fame!

The swallows built their nests in the clay banks, which made holes in them. When the rains came and ran down the surface of the banks, they crumbled. And the names were no more.

"But Peter's name stayed for a whole year and a half," the town crier boasted.

"Fool!" thought the fire drum, but he only said, "Boom! Boom! Boom!"

"The town crier's redheaded son Peter" was full of life. He had a beautiful voice, and since he knew how to sing, he sang. His songs were like the songs of the birds of the forest: they had melodies and yet they didn't.

"He is going to sing in the church choir as soon as he is old enough," said his mother. "He will stand right under the gilded angels whom he looks like."

"Carrot top!" the witty citizens of the town called him; and the big drum heard it from the neighbor's wife.

"Don't go home, Peter!" the street urchins called after him. "If you sleep in the attic you will set the house on fire and your father'll have to play the fire drum!"

"Beware of the drumsticks," replied Peter, and he hit one of the boys so hard that he fell, and the others ran away.

The town musician, who directed the local orchestra, was a distinguished man whose father had played for the king. He liked Peter and would talk to him for hour after hour. One day he gave him a violin and began to teach him how to play. The boy's little fingers held the instrument as if they already knew what to do. He would learn to do more than beat on a drum, he would become a real musician.

"But I want to be a soldier," said Peter, for he was still so young that he could think of nothing more marvelous than to wear a uniform, have a sword and a rifle, and march along: "Left . . . right! Left . . . right!"

"Then you will learn to obey the drums. Boom! Boom!" said both of the drums at once.

"He will march up to the top of the ranks and come home a general," said his father. "That is, if there is a war."

"God save us from that," sighed his mother.

"We have nothing worth losing," said the town crier.

"Yes, we have my son," replied his wife.

"Oh, but he will come home a general." The town crier laughed, for his son was still a boy, and he didn't take the conversation seriously.

"He could come home without a leg or an arm." Peter's mother looked at the boy. "No, I want my golden treasure all well and whole."

"Boom! Boom! Boom!" The fire drum spoke. All the fire drums in the whole country rolled. The soldiers marched away and the town crier's son followed them.

"Good-by, carrot top!" the townspeople called.

"My golden treasure," his mother whispered, while his father dreamed that his son would win fame and honor. The town musician thought that the boy ought not to have gone to war, but stayed at home and studied his music: one of the arts of peace.

"Red" was what the soldiers called Peter and he laughed. But when someone called him "Fox" he pressed his lips together, looked straight ahead and pretended that he had not heard the insult.

He was a good boy, usually cheerful and good-natured; "like a water bottle filled with wine," his older companions said.

Many a night it was damp; they slept out in the open. Sometimes it rained and he was wet to the skin, but his spirit was not daunted. He beat the drum: "Rat-a-tat-tat! Form ranks!" Oh yes, he was a born drummer boy.

It was the day of the battle. The sun hadn't risen, but it was morning. The air was damp and cold. A fog covered the landscape: a fog made by the smoke of exploding powder. Shells and bullets flew above their heads, and they saw the patches of deep red blood and the white, white faces of those who fell all around them; and still they marched forward. The little drummer was as yet unhurt, and he smiled at the regimental dog that pranced around him, as if they were playing and the bullets were only toys.

"Forward march" had been the command; and the drummers beat it on their drumheads. That order is not easily reversed—though it can be done and often there are wisdom and good sense in doing it.

"Run!" someone screamed. But the drummer boy kept beating the proper message: "Forward march!" The other soldiers obeyed the roll of the drums. It was a good drumbeat; at a decisive moment it prevented the retreat of an army which later that day was victorious.

Life and limbs were lost in that battle. Shells tore the flesh into bloody pieces. Shells set fire to a haystack where the wounded had dragged themselves to lie unattended for many hours—perhaps for the rest of their lives. Oh, there is no point in thinking about such things; and yet people do, even when they are in a peaceful town, far away from the scene of the battle. The town crier and his wife were thinking about it because their son Peter was a drummer boy.

"All this whimpering sickens me," said the fire drum.

It was the day of the battle. The sun had not risen, but it was morning. The town crier and his wife were sleeping, but they hadn't slept all night. They had been awake talking about their son who was "out there," with only God to protect him. Now the boy's father was dreaming that the war was over and the soldiers were returning. His son came home with a medal on his chest: a silver cross.

The mother was dreaming too. She was in the church looking at the altarpiece; and there among the angels she saw her son. He sang so beautifully, as only an angel can sing. He saw his mother and nodded kindly to her.

"My golden treasure!" she cried out, and woke up. "Now God has taken him," she muttered, and folded her hands. She hid her head in the cotton curtains that hung around the bed and wept. "Where is he resting now? Is his body already in the mass grave that they dig after a battle? Maybe it is in the deep waters of a swamp! No one will ever know where he is buried. No one will ever say a prayer over his grave!" Silently, her lips said the Lord's Prayer; then her head fell back on the pillow and she slept again, for she was very tired.

In dreams and in reality, days fly.

It was evening. A rainbow stretched its arch across the battlefield. It touched the forest and the swamp with its deep, still, dark waters. In folklore it is said that, where a rainbow ends, there is a golden treasure; and one had also been buried here. No one had thought about the little drummer boy but his mother, and that was why she had had this dream.

And days fly, both in dreams and in reality.

Nothing had happened to him, not a strand of his golden hair had been hurt. "Rat-a-tat-tat. He's alive! He's alive!" The drum could have told his mother, and then she could have sung about it, had she seen it or dreamed it.

With cheering and singing and parades, they returned. They had been victorious. The war was over, peace had come. The regimental dog ran ahead of them, making great circles, as if he wanted the distance to be thrice as long as it was.

Weeks went by and took the days with them.

Peter came home! Sunburned as a savage, with clear eyes, and his face shining like the sun, he stepped into his parents' house. His mother threw her arms around him and kissed him on his mouth and his eyes and his red hair. Her boy was back; and though he hadn't any silver cross on his chest as his father had dreamed, he was alive and in good health as his mother hadn't dreamed. Everyone was so happy that they all laughed and cried.

"Are you still here, you old rascal?" Peter said to the old fire drum, and embraced it.

His father played a roll on the big drum. "Boom! Boom! This is as exciting as it is when there's a fire," said the drum. "Fire in the attic! Fire in the heart! The golden treasure! Tummalumalum!"

And what happened after that? You might ask the town musician.

"Peter has outgrown the drum. He will be a greater musician than

I am," said the man whose father had played for the king. "Peter can learn in six months what it has taken me a whole life to learn."

There was something about the boy: he was always so good-natured, so deeply kind. His eyes shone as if they had never seen ugliness. . . . There was no getting away from it, his hair shone too.

"He should dye it," said the neighbor's wife. "The policeman's daughter dyed hers and now she's engaged."

"But her hair turned as green as grass, and now she has to have it done once a week," argued her husband.

"She can afford it," replied his wife. "And so can Peter. He is invited to the best families in town. Why, he teaches the mayor's daughter to play the piano."

Peter played beautifully, and the most beautiful pieces he played came from his heart and hadn't been written down yet. He played through the light summer nights and through the long dark winter ones. "It's more than we can stand," said the neighbors to each other; and the fire drum agreed with them.

The mayor's daughter, Lotte, sat at the piano. Her delicate fingers flew across the keys and what they played echoed in Peter's heart. It beat so fast that it seemed to have too little room in his chest. This happened to him not once but many times. At last, one evening, he grabbed her finger and took her little hand in his and kissed it. He looked into her brown eyes and said . . . No, only God knows what he said; but the rest of us may guess it.

Lotte didn't answer but she blushed right down to her shoulders. At that moment a guest was announced. It was the son of one of the king's councilors. He had a high, smooth forehead that shone as if it were polished; so did the top of his head. Peter stayed and Lotte entertained them both, but her fondest glances she gave to Peter.

When he came home, later that evening, he talked about the wide world and the golden treasure he would win with his violin: fame and immortality!

"Boom . . . Boom-alum . . . Boom!" said the fire drum. "He has gone quite crazy. I think there is a fire in his brain."

The next day, when his mother came home from shopping, she asked, "Have you heard the good news, Peter? The mayor's daughter, Lotte, is engaged to the son of one of the king's councilors. It happened last night."

"No!" exclaimed Peter, and jumped up from his chair. But his mother said yes. She had the news from the barber's wife, whose husband had been told it by the mayor himself.

Peter's face grew white, and he sat down again.

"My God, what's the matter with you?" asked his mother.

"Nothing's the matter! Nothing! Just leave me alone," Peter answered while the tears ran down his face.

"My sweet child, my golden treasure!" And now the mother cried out of sympathy.

"*Lotte ist tot!* . . . Lotte is dead!" the big fire drum hummed inside himself, so that no one could hear him. "And that's the end of that song!"

But it wasn't the end of a song, only of a verse; and there were many more verses to come. Some of them were long and they were golden verses, all about life's golden treasure.

"She gives herself airs; she brags and she boasts," said the neighbor's wife. "She carries his letters about everywhere and shows them to everyone. Her own Peter! Her golden treasure! They have written about him and his violin in the newspapers. Peter sends her money; and she certainly needs it, now that she's a widow."

"He plays before kings and emperors!" the town musician said proudly. "Fame was not my fate. But he is my pupil, and he hasn't forgotten his old teacher."

"His father dreamed that he would come home from the war with a silver cross on his chest. He didn't; but now the king has made him a Knight of the Danish Flag. . . . I suppose it would have been more difficult to win a medal in war," said the mother naïvely. "How proud his father would have been of him."

"Famous!" boomed the fire drum; and everyone in town said the same. "The town crier's redheaded son Peter," whom they had all known when he was a boy wearing clogs on his feet, the child who had been a drummer boy, was famous!

"He played for us before he played for the king," said the mayor's wife. "He was in love with our Lotte. He always had ambitions above his station. Then we thought he was impertinent and ridiculous! My husband laughed when he heard such nonsense. Our Lotte is the wife of the king's councilor!"

There was a golden treasure in the heart and the soul of that boy, born in poverty, that little drummer who had played "Forward march!" and given courage to those who had been about to retreat. The treasure he could share with others sprang from his violin. He could play as if a whole organ were hidden within it; and he could play so tenderly that the listener would hear fairies dancing on a summer night and the thrush singing. It was as though his instrument were a human voice of such purity and beauty that all who heard it felt the ecstasy of art. His name flew from country to country, it spread like fire, the fire of enthusiasm!

"And then he is so handsome," said the young ladies and the older ones. One woman, past seventy, had bought an album in which to "keep the locks of famous men," just so that she could ask for one from the young violinist.

Into the humble house of the town crier stepped the son. He was as elegant as a prince and happier than a king. He took his mother in his arms, and she cried, as you do when you are very happy, then she kissed him. Peter nodded to everything in the room: to the chest, to the closet where the fancy glasses and Sunday teacups were kept, and to the little bed that he had slept in when he was a child. He took down the old fire drum and placed it in the middle of the room.

Speaking to both his mother and the fire drum, he said, "If Father had been here, he would have played a roll on the drum. Now I will have to do it."

He beat the drum so hard that it sounded like a thunderstorm; and the fire drum felt the honor so deeply that its drumhead cracked. "He beats a drum well," it said. "Now he has given me a souvenir. I shouldn't be surprised if his mother burst from joy."

That was the story of the golden treasure, and now you have heard it.

## 120

## How the Storm Changed the Signs

In olden times when Grandfather was a little boy, he wore red trousers, a red jacket, a sash around his waist, and a feather in his cap, for that was the way little boys were dressed when they were dressed up. So many things were different then. There were often parades in the streets, and we hardly ever have parades any more because they are so old-fashioned. But it is fun to hear Grandfather tell about them.

When the Shoemakers' Guild moved their sign from the old guild-hall to the new, that was a day! At the head of the procession was carried a great silk banner with a big boot and a double-headed eagle painted on it. Then came the oldest of the master shoemakers; he had a drawn rapier in his hand, that had a lemon stuck onto its tip. Behind him were the young journeymen, with red and white ribbons tied to their shirts; the youngest of them carried the great silver cup and the chest in which the guild's money was kept. There was music, too, and the best of all the instruments, according to Grandfather, was the "bird." This was a tall staff with a brass half-moon on top of it, and hanging from it were all shapes and kinds of metal bits that dangled and jingled and clanged to make real Turkish music. The "bird" was waved and swung, and the sun reflected so sharply in its gold, silver, and brass that it hurt your eyes to look at it.

In front of the procession, ahead even of the standard-bearer, ran Harlequin. His clothes were made of patches just as quilts sometimes are. His face had been painted black, and from his cap bells rang merrily as they do on a horse that is pulling a sleigh. He danced, leaping through the air, and sometimes he would run in among the spectators and hit them with his wand. There was a loud cracking noise but no one was ever hurt.

People rushed forward and were pushed backward. Little children ran alongside the parade, and sometimes they fell over their own running feet, right into the dirty gutter. Old ladies poked with their elbows and looked as sour as week-old milk. Some people laughed, others talked. There were people everywhere; they stood on every doorstep and in every window, and even on the roofs.

The sky was clear and the sun was bright. . . . Well, not always. Sometimes a shower would come, but that was good for the farmers; and when it really rained and the people got wet to the skin, that was a blessing for the whole country.

Grandfather was so good at telling stories. He had seen so many wonderful things when he was a little boy. That day, when the Shoemakers' Guild had moved into their new guildhall, he had heard the oldest of the journeymen make a speech. He stood on the scaffolding that had been raised in front of the new building to enable the old guild sign to be put up. The speech was in verse and the way the journeyman recited it made it sound as if it had been written by someone else; and it had. Three of the young shoemakers had spent a whole evening composing it, and they had drunk a whole bowl of punch for inspiration. When the speech was over everyone applauded. But when Harlequin jumped up on the scaffolding and mocked the speech, they cheered. The fool was so clever, he made the clever shoemaker appear foolish. Then Harlequin drank beer out of tiny liqueur glasses and, as he finished each one, he threw it out among the crowd. Grandfather had a glass that had been given to him by a mason, who had been lucky enough to catch it. Finally, the new sign was hung and garlands of flowers and greenery were draped over it. It had been a great occasion and everyone had had a good time.

"You never forget a day like that, even if you live to be a hundred," said Grandfather. And Grandfather never did forget it, though he had seen so many other wonderful things. But the funniest story of all was about the big storm and how the wind changed all the signs around.

It was the day that Grandfather's parents moved to Copenhagen. Grandfather was a little boy and this was his first visit to the capital.

At first, seeing so many people in the street, he thought that some guild was moving into a new guildhall and people were waiting for the parade to begin. He looked at the buildings; in front of every one there was a sign. He had never imagined that there could be so many signs. He wondered how many rooms they would have filled, if they had been stacked inside instead of hanging outside.

The tailors' sign had a pair of scissors and all kinds of clothes—from the simplest work clothes to the finest evening dress—painted on it, to show that the tailor could make whatever you needed. There were signs with pictures of butter vats and herrings, and one with a priest's ruff and a coffin. The tobacconist's sign was a picture of the sweetest-looking little boy smoking a cigar, which little boys shouldn't but often do. There were billboards and posters, too, and they had writing as well as pictures on them. You could spend a whole day strolling up and down the street, reading, and still not have read them all. It was a whole education just to go for a walk in the city. You could tell who lived in every house you passed, and what their profession was as well. Every family had a sign of its own. "To know who lives in every house is a great advantage in a big city," Grandfather explained.

The great storm started the very night that Grandfather was to sleep in Copenhagen for the first time. When he told me about it, he didn't have that twinkle in his eye that my mother always says he has, when he is making something up just to amuse us. No, he looked very earnest indeed.

The weather that night was worse than any storm that you have ever read about in the newspapers. No one could remember the wind ever having blown like that before. Tiles from the roofs rained down on the streets, and in the morning every fence in the whole city was lying flat on the ground. Somebody saw an old wheelbarrow running down the street all alone, just to save itself. The din was frightening; up and down every street there were banging, clamoring, and howling. The water in the canals was so frightened, it didn't know where it ought to be, so it leaped up over its sides into the streets. The storm rushed over the rooftops and took most of the chimneys with it. Many a proud church spire had to bow its head and has not been able to raise it since.

Outside the house of the fire chief, a sweet old man who was always the last one to arrive at a fire, stood a sentry box. The storm turned it over and rolled it down the street and then, curiously enough, turned it upright again outside the house of a poor carpenter. He was a humble man who had saved three people from burning to death at the last big fire. But the sentry box didn't care where it stood.

The barber's sign—a great big brass plate that looked just like the smaller one that was put under a customer's chin, so that the soap wouldn't get all over his clothes while he was being shaved—was blown off its hinges and through the air, to land on the window sill of the judge's house. All the neighbors agreed that there was something spiteful about that, for the judge's wife had a tongue as sharp as a razor. She knew more about everyone in town than most people knew about themselves.

The wind carried a sign with a dried codfish on it to the door of a newspaper editor. I think that was a very poor joke. In the first place it's only in Denmark that a codfish is a sign for stupidity; and the storm should know of the great power of the press, which makes an editor king on his own newspaper and in his own opinion.

A weather vane flew across the street to the neighbor's roof; and stood with its head down, as if it were pecking away with the intention of boring holes up there.

A hooper's sign, with the picture of a barrel on it, found itself hanging in front of a corset maker's.

The Menu of the Day that hung in a brass frame in front of the restaurant flew across the square to the theater, which was usually half empty. It was a strange playbill! "Horseradish Soup and Stuffed Cabbage." But that night the theater was full.

The furrier's sign, which is the skin of a red fox, is perfectly honorable as long as it hangs in front of a furrier's house; but that night, the storm wound it around the bell rope of a house in which a young man lived. This particular young man looked like a closed umbrella, attended early service, and was so honorable that his aunt declared that he ought to be an example to other young men.

A sign with the inscription "Academy for Higher Learning" was placed by the wind above a poolroom. In its place there now hung above the academy a sign that read: "Here babies are suckled on bottles." This was more naughty than it was witty; but the guilty party was the storm, and you cannot tell a storm how to behave.

It was a terrible night. In the morning the people found that every sign in the whole city had been changed. It had been done with so much malice and cunning that Grandfather said he couldn't tell me about all the exchanges; but he smiled inwardly when he thought about them, and maybe then there was a twinkle in his eye.

It was very confusing for everyone, but especially for strangers to Copenhagen. If they went according to the signs, they were bound to go wrong. Some people, who had come to the capital to discuss a grave and serious matter with a congregation of elders, found themselves in a boys' school with screaming and shouting pupils all around them; some of whom were even standing on their desks. Some other poor people mistook a church for the theater, and that was a dreadful error!

There has never been a storm like that one since. Grandfather may be the only one alive who can remember it, for it happened when he was a little boy. I doubt that we will ever experience such a storm, but maybe our grandchildren will, so we had better warn them to stay inside while the storm changes all the signs.

## 121

## The Teapot

Once there was a teapot who was very proud. She was proud of being porcelain. She was proud of her spout and she was proud of her broad handle, for they gave her something to boast about both in front and in back. She didn't talk about her lid, which had been broken and then glued together. There is no point in talking about your shortcomings; others willingly do that for you. The cups, the cream pitcher, the sugar bowl—the whole tea service preferred discussing the mended lid to talking about the fine spout and the strong handle. And this the teapot knew.

"I know what they think," she said to herself. "And I know my own faults, too, and admit them; and that I call modesty and humility. We all have faults, and we all have our talents, too. The cups have a handle and the sugar bowl has a lid, but I have both. And one thing more that neither one of them will ever have: a spout. That is what makes me queen of the tea table. The sugar bowl and the cream pitcher are servants of taste, but I am its mistress. I disseminate my blessings among a thirsting humanity. In my interior, fragrant Chinese leaves are mixed with insipid boiling water."

This was the way the teapot had talked when she was still a youngster. One day while she was standing on the tea table, she was lifted by a very refined and delicate hand. Unfortunately, the refined and delicate hand was also careless. The teapot fell to the floor, and both her spout and her handle were broken off.—We shan't talk about the lid, for that has been mentioned enough already.—The teapot had fainted: there she lay with boiling water running out of her. But the worst was yet to come: they laughed at her—the teapot!—not at the careless hand that had dropped her.

"I shall never forget it! Never . . ." she would mutter to herself when she thought about her youth. "They said I was an invalid and put me in a corner of the closet. But I didn't stay there long; the next day I was given to a beggar woman, who had come to ask for leftovers from the table. I was to know poverty, and the thought made me quite speechless. Yet then and there began what I would call a better life. One is one thing and becomes another.

"I was filled up with earth, which for a teapot is the same as being buried. But inside the earth a bulb was placed. I don't know who put it there, but there it was. I am sure it was meant as a subsititute for the Chinese leaves and the boiling water, and to console me for my broken spout and lost handle. The bulb lay in the earth inside me, and it became my heart: my living heart. And I was alive, something I had never been before. Within me were power and strength, and my pulse beat. The bulb sprouted. It was so filled with thoughts and feelings that it almost burst; then it flowered. I could see it. I carried it within me and I forgot myself when I looked at its beauty.

"Oh, that is the greatest blessing, to be able to forget yourself in caring for others. The flower didn't say thank you; I don't think it even noticed me. But everyone admired the flower, and if that made me happy, think of how much happier it must have made the flower.

"One day I heard someone say that the flower was so lovely that it deserved a better flowerpot. They cracked me in two, and that hurt terribly. My plant was placed in a finer flowerpot, and I was thrown out into the yard, and here I lie, an old broken piece of pottery. But I have my memories and they cannot be taken from me."

## 122

## The Songbird of the People

### (A Mood)

It is winter. The ground is covered with snow and looks like the white marble that is hewn out of the mountains. The sky is bright and clear. The wind blows sharply and cuts into your face as if it were a sword made by the elves. The ice-decked trees look like white coral, like flowering almond trees. The air is as fresh as it is in the heights of the Alps. The night is lovely; there are northern lights and innumerable stars in the sky.

A storm is coming! The clouds shake themselves and snowflakes, like the down of the swan, drift across the scene. Soon the open fields and the narrow lanes, the highways and the houses are covered with snow.

We are sitting inside around the stove in the living room, talking of olden times. Now we are listening to a saga that opens on the seacoast, where there was an ancient burial mound. At midnight the ghost of the king who had been interred there would rise from the dead. He would climb to the top of the hill above his own burial chamber and sit there on a great stone, sorrowfully moaning and sighing. His hair, beneath the gold band that was his crown, would flutter in the wind. He was dressed in iron and steel, in the armor that he wore in battle.

One night a ship anchored nearby and its crew came ashore. Among them there was a poet, who approached the ghost and asked, "Why do you suffer so? What are you waiting for?"

The dead man answered: "No one has sung of my deeds; therefore, death has undone them. Poetry did not carry them through the land so that they would be kept alive in human heart. And that is why I cannot find peace, why I cannot rest." Then he told about his adventures and the acts of courage he had performed, which had brought him fame in his own time but were unknown now, because no poet had sung of them.

The bard took his harp and sang of the hero's youthful courage, of his power during the days of his prime, and how great his good deeds had been. The face of the king grew as bright as the edge of a cloud illuminated by the moon. He rose and glanced happily, blissfully upward. His ghostly figure shimmered like a northern light and was gone. Now all there was to be seen on that grassy knoll were the big boulders on which no runic letters had been carved.

When the last chord was struck, a bird flew up; it seemed to have come out of the harp. It was small but it is the most wonderful of all the songbirds. It is the one whose voice has the melodious throb of the thrush and the soulful beat of the human heart, and whose song calls the migrant bird back to his native land. It flies high over the mountains and across the valleys, above the dark forest and the meadows. It is the songbird of the people: the bird that sings the folk songs, and it will never die.

We heard its song while we sat in the warm room, with the snow falling outside and the storm increasing. We hear not only of the tragedies of heroes, but the bird sings softer songs as well: tender love songs, ballads of fidelity and loyalty. They are like fairy tales told in melody and in words. They are like the proverbs of the people, like the magic runic letters that can give life to a dead man's tongue and make him tell us of his home.

In pagan times, during the Age of the Vikings, this songbird built its nest in the harp of the poet. Later, in the Age of Chivalry, when the knights ruled and justice was an iron fist—for might determined right—then when a peasant and a hunting dog were of equal value, where did the songbird hide? The cruel and the petty never gave the bird a thought, but somewhere in the thick-walled castle sat a noblewoman with ink and parchment and wrote down songs and ballads. Across from her sat an old woman who lived in a turf hut; or a peddler, who went from place to place with his wares on his back. While they told their stories, the immortal bird flew about the room and sang, for it will never die, as long as there is a place for it to nest.

It is singing for us now. Outside it is dark and there is a snowstorm. The bird puts its magic runic letters on our tongue, so that we can understand our homeland. God talks to us in our native tongue, in the language of the folk tale and the folk song. Old memories come alive, colors that were faded become bright; the sagas and the ancient songs are a blessed drink that raise our souls and lift our thoughts to make the evening as joyful as Christmas Eve. The snow lies in drifts, the ice creaks and groans, the storm rages; it is master but it is not God.

It is winter. The wind is as sharp as the sword made by the elves. The snow falls for days, for weeks; it has covered the whole city: an evil dream in the winter night. Everything is hidden, buried beneath the snow, except the golden cross on the church steeple. The symbol of our faith rises above the snow into the blue air to reflect the sunlight.

Above the buried city fly the birds of heaven, both the large and the small, and each of them is singing as well as he can. First come a flock of sparrows. They sing of the small incidents, of the things that happen in the streets and the lanes, in the nests and in the houses, where they know what goes on in the garret and on the first floor. "We know everyone in the buried city and everything about them. But none of them knows a thing . . . a thing . . . a thing."

Now come the ravens and the crows. "Dig! Dig!" they screech. "There is something underneath to eat. Dig! Dig! Nothing is more important than to eat! Everybody agrees with us and we agree with everybody. . . . Dig! Dig!"

The wild swans come. Hear the whirring of their wings. They sing of the greatness and the wonder of the things that the minds of the men who are buried under the snow can create.

Death is not there but life. We sense it in sound; it comes to us like the tones from a great church organ. We hear the Valkyrian wings, the song of Ossian, and the music of the elves. They are in harmony and speak directly to our hearts, to give our thoughts hope. It is the songbird of the people that we hear, and God's warm breath begins to blow. The rays of the sun again shine upon the city, the mountain of snow cracks.

Spring has come. The birds have come, and among them are fledglings singing the homely tunes we know so well. Here is the drama of the year: the power of the snowstorm, the dream and hope of the long winter night is redeemed. It is told by the bird who cannot die: the songbird of the people.

## 123

## The Little Green Ones

On the window sill stood a rosebush. Just a week ago it had looked healthy and filled with buds; now it looked sickly, something was the matter with it.

It had soldiers billeted on it, they were eating it up. They were a respectable lot and wore green uniforms. I talked with one of them; he was only three days old and already was a grandfather. Do you know what he said? He talked about himself and the whole army that were quartered on the rosebush, and everything he said was quite true:

"Of all the inhabitants of the earth, we are one of the strangest regiments. In the summer, when the weather is warm, we give birth to our children. As soon as they are born, they get engaged and married. But when the weather turns cold we lay eggs instead. That is for the little ones' sake, to keep them warm. The wisest of all the animals, the ant, whom we hold in esteem, has studied us and evaluated our worth. He doesn't eat us right away, he takes our eggs and carries them to the family anthill. There on the bottom floor, he numbers them and stores them. The ants put our eggs side by side, layer on layer, and in such a way that they always know which egg is ready to hatch. The young ones they put in their stable, then they squeeze us and milk us until we die. It is a great pleasure. They have the nicest name for us: 'The Sweet Little Milk Cows.' All animals with the intelligence of an ant call us by that name; only man calls us something else, and the name he has given us is so great an insult that it is enough to lose one's sweetness, just thinking about it.

Couldn't you write a protest against it? Explain to them how wrong they are, these human beings. They look disdainfully at us, with their glassy eyes, just because we eat a rose leaf, while they themselves eat everything that is alive. Then they call us a contemptible, a disgusting name. I can't even mention it without feeling sick to my stomach. I am not going to say it, at least, not so long as I am dressed in my uniform; and I never take it off.

"I was born on a rose leaf. The whole regiment and I live on that rosebush, but in a way it lives again inside us. After all, we belong to one of the higher orders of animals. Man can't stand the sight of us; he is always trying to kill us with soapy water. Ugh, that is a horrible drink! I can almost smell it now. It is terrible to be washed, when you have been created not to be washed.

"Human beings! You, who are looking at me now, with your soapy-water eyes, consider our place in nature's order, our strange ability to give birth to live children and to lay eggs. Also we were blessed and told to 'be fruitful and multiply.' We are born in a rose and we die in a rose; our whole life is poetry. Don't give us a name that you yourself consider loathsome and ugly. That name . . . No, I won't say it! Call us the milk cow of the ants, or the rose's regiment or just: the little green ones."

And I, the human being, stood and looked at the rosebush and thought about the little green ones, whose name I, too, shan't mention, for I do not want to offend the tenants of a rose: a family so clever that it can both lay eggs and give birth. The soapy water that I was going to wash the rosebush with—for I had come with evil intentions —I shall whip into suds and then blow soap bubbles with it. I shall look at the beautiful bubbles and maybe I shall find a fairy tale hidden in them.

The soap bubble grew bigger and bigger, it was filled with the most radiant colors, and in the bottom of it lay a silver pearl. It rose, flew across the room, hit the door, and burst. The door flew open and there stood an old lady: Dame Fairy Tale, herself.

Now she can tell us the story much better than I can. She will tell us about the . . . No, I won't say any name . . . the story of the "little green ones."

"Plant lice!" exclaimed the old lady. "One ought to call everything by its right name, and if one doesn't dare do it in everyday life, then at least one should do it in a fairy tale."

## 124

## The Pixy and the Gardener's Wife

Pixies you know, but do you know the gardener's wife?

She had read a lot of books and knew many verses by heart. She could even write them herself; only with the rhymes did she have any difficulty—"the gluing together of the verses" as she called it.

She had a talent, both for writing and for conversation. She ought to have been a minister, or at least a minister's wife.

"The earth is lovely in its Sunday dress," she wrote, and "glued" that thought, using rhymes as paste, to a great many other thoughts, until she had composed a ballad that was both long and beautiful.

The schoolteacher, Mr. Kisserup—the name is of no importance whatsoever. He was a nephew of the gardener, and while he was visiting, he heard the poem and claimed that this experience had done him no end of good. "You have both spirit and talent," he said.

"Chatter and twaddle," said the gardener. "Spirit indeed! Don't put her up to any nonsense. A wife is a body—a decent one. She is to tend to her pots and make sure that the porridge doesn't burn."

"If the porridge burns, I take off the burned part with a little wooden spoon; and if you are burned, I take it off with a kiss," said his wife. "One would think you only thought of heads of cabbage and potatoes, but you love your flowers." Then she kissed him. "And flowers are the spirit of the garden."

"Take care of your pots and pans," said he, and walked out into the garden, which was his "pots and pans," and he took good care of it.

The schoolteacher stayed and talked with his aunt. In his own way, he held a whole sermon over her words: "The earth is lovely."

"The earth is beautiful; and it was said that we should subdue it and be its master. One is so by the power of his spirit, another by the power of his body. One man is created in the image of a thoughtful question mark, another like an exclamation point. One becomes a bishop, another merely a schoolteacher. But everything is for the best: the earth is beautiful and always dressed in its Sunday best. It is a very thoughtful poem, madam; filled with feeling and geography."

"You have spirit yourself, Mr. Kisserup!" said the gardener's wife. "A great deal of spirit, I assure you. Why, after a conversation with you, one understands oneself so much better."

And they talked on and on, just as cleverly and intelligently as we have just heard them. Out in the kitchen sat the pixy. You know what he looks like: dressed in gray, with a red woolen cap on his head. He, too, was talking, but no one heard him except the black cat, who was called "cream thief" by the gardener's wife.

The pixy was angry at the mistress of the house because she did not believe that he existed. She had never seen him but, considering all the books she had read, she ought at least to have known about him. A little attention would have been appreciated. But even on Christmas Eve, not a spoonful of porridge was given him; and his ancestors had all got a whole bowlful, and that from women who couldn't even read or write. The porridge had had a lump of butter in the middle and cream around the sides. The cat licked its chops just hearing about it.

"She calls me a notion, a conception, a fancy," grumbled the pixy. "What she means by that is more than I can understand. But that she denies my existence, that I have figured out. And I have figured out one thing more; and that is that she is sitting in there spinning like a cat for the favor of that boy-thrasher called a schoolteacher. I say, as the man in the house does, 'Keep to your pots, woman!' And now I will make them boil over."

And the pixy blew on the fire and the flames rose and the pot boiled over. "Now I am going upstairs and unravel some of the gardener's socks. I will make holes in both the toes and heels, then there will be something for her to mend," laughed the pixy. "If she isn't too busy poetizing to mend her husband's socks."

The cat sneezed but said nothing; it had caught cold even though it always wore a fur coat.

"I have opened the door to the larder," the pixy said to the cat. "There is cream in there as thick as butter. If you won't lick it, I will."

"I will get the blame and the beating, so I might as well lick the cream," replied the cat, stretching herself.

"First the cream, then the scream," grinned the pixy. "I am going up to the schoolmaster's room and hang his suspenders on the mirror and put his socks into the washbasin. Then he will think that the punch he drank was too strong, and that he is dizzy. Last night I was sitting on the wood pile, teasing the watchdog. He jumped for my legs but he couldn't reach them. It didn't matter how high he jumped, I was higher, and that irritated the stupid dog so much that he barked and barked. He made an awful din. The schoolmaster stuck his head out of the window but he didn't see me, even though he had his glasses on; he always sleeps with them on."

"Say meow if the mistress comes," the cat begged. "I am not feeling so well today, I can hardly hear."

"You are dying for something sweet," said the pixy. "Go into the larder and lick the cream—lick your sickness away; but remember to wipe your whiskers. I am going to the parlor, to listen."

And the pixy ran to the door. It was standing ajar. Only the school-master and gardener's wife were in the room. They were talking about what the schoolmaster had so beautifully called, the most important thing to have in the pots and pans of a household: the gift of under-standing.

"Mr. Kisserup"—the gardener's wife blushed—"I will show you something that I have never shown to another earthly being—least of all a man—my poems! Some of them are quite long. I have called them *Poesy of a Danish Goodwife*. I am so fond of the old words."

"One must honor our language," the schoolteacher agreed. "We ought to get rid of all the German words."

"I do!" said the gardener's wife. "I never say *Kleiner* or *Blätterteig*, I say fat cakes and leafy dough." Then she took out of a drawer a little notebook with a green cover, that had two ink spots on it.

"There is a great deal of pathos in this book. I have a strong incli-nation toward the tragic. There is one titled 'Sighs in the Night' and another called 'My Sunset.' The one named, 'When I Married Clem-mensen,' you may skip, it is about my husband, and it is deeply felt. 'The Housewife's Duty,' I think, is the best of them all. They are all tragic, that is the direction in which I am most talented. One of them is humorous; it has some playful thoughts. I sometimes think—you mustn't laugh!—think of becoming a poetess. No one knows my verses but myself, the drawer, and now you, Mr. Kisserup. I love poetry; it comes to me, teases me, conquers and rules me. I have described my feelings in that poem named 'The Little Pixy.' You know the old peasant belief about the house pixy who is always playing tricks around the farmhouse. I have thought that I am such a house and that poetry—the feelings inside me—is the pixy, the spirit that commands. His power and greatness I have described in my poem, 'The Little Pixy.' Please read it aloud to me, so I can hear it—if you can read my writing. But promise—swear to me—that you will never tell my husband or anyone else about it."

The schoolteacher read and the gardener's wife listened. And so did the little pixy, who had just taken up his post by the door, when the schoolteacher read the title: "The Little Pixy."

"Why, it concerns me!" he thought. "What has she written about me? Why, I will steal her eggs and chickens and chase the fat off her calf. You'd better be careful, madam!"

He puckered his lips and listened with his long ears; but as he heard about the pixy's glory and strength and his power over the gardener's wife, his eyes began to gleam with happiness. She had meant it symbolically, but he took it all literally. Around the pixy's mouth spread an expression of nobility. He stood on tiptoe, gaining by this a whole inch in height. He was immensely satisfied with the poem.

"Why, she has spirit and culture. I have done her a great injustice. She has composed a poem to me, it will be printed and read. I won't allow the cat to touch her cream any more. I will drink it myself. One drinks less than two; that is a saving. I will introduce thrift into the household, because I honor and respect that woman."

"He is a regular human being, that pixy," said the cat. "One sweet meow from the mistress—a meow about himself—and he changes his mind. She is clever, madam."

But the gardener's wife wasn't clever; it was the pixy that was human.

If you haven't understood this story, ask someone to explain it to you, but don't ask the gardener's wife, or the pixy.

## Peiter, Peter, and Peer

It is unbelievable how much children in our age know. Why, one hardly knows what they don't know. That the stork has brought them from the well of the millpond and delivered them to their father and mother is such an old story that they don't believe it; and that is too bad, for it is the truth.

But how do the little babies get in the millpond or the well? That is something not everybody knows, yet there are some who do. Have you ever looked at the heavens on a clear night when all the stars are out? Then you will have noticed the shooting stars. They look as if they were falling and then suddenly they disappear. The most learned cannot explain what they don't understand themselves; but if you know, then you can, even if you are not learned. What looks like a little Christmas-tree candle falling from the heavens is the spark of a soul coming from God. It flies down toward the earth. As it comes into our heavy atmosphere, its glow becomes so faint that our eyes can no longer see it. It is so fine and fragile, it is a little child of the heavens, a little angel; but without wings, for it is going to be a human being. Slowly, it glides through the air, and the wind carries it and puts it down inside a flower. It may be a violet, a rose, or a dandelion. There it lies for a while. It is so tiny and airy that a fly—or, in any case, a bee—could fly away with it.

When the insects come to search for honey, the little air-child is in the way; but they don't kick it out, they are too kind for that; no, they carry it to a water-lily leaf and leave it there. The air-children climb down into the water, where they sleep and grow until they have reached the right size. Then, when the stork thinks one of them is big enough, he picks it up and flies with it to a family who want a sweet little child. But whether the children are sweet or not, depends upon what they have drunk while they lay in the millpond; whether they have drunk clear water, or water filled with mud and duckweed, for that makes them very earthy.

The stork never tries to do any matching up, he thinks that the first place is the best. One baby comes to wonderful parents, another to a mother and father so hard and mean that it would have been better to stay in the millpond.

The little ones cannot remember what they have dreamed while they lay under the water lilies and the frogs sang for them, "Croak . . . croak . . . croak!" That, in human language, means: "Come sleep and dream." They have no memory either of which flower they have lain in, though sometimes when they grow up, one of them will say, "I like that flower best." And that is the flower they slept in when they were air-children.

The stork lives to be very old, and he always takes an interest in the children he has brought and how they fare in this world. He can't do anything for them, he can't change their circumstances, for he has his own family to look after. But he doesn't forget them; on the contrary, he thinks about them often.

I know an old stork, a very honest bird, who is very learned. He has delivered a lot of children and knows the story of them all. There isn't a one that doesn't have a bit of duckweed and mud in it. I asked him to tell the biography of just one child, and he gave me three for the one I asked for. They all had the same family name: Peitersen.

Now the family Peitersen was very respectable. The husband was one of the town's two-and-thirty councilors, and that was a great distinction, so he devoted his whole life to being a councilor, and that was what he lived for. Now first the stork brought them a little Peiter; that was the name they gave the child. And the next year he came with another boy, and they called him Peter. And the third year Peer was brought. Peiter, Peter, and Peer—all variations of the same name: Peitersen.

They were three brothers, three shooting stars. Each had lain in a flower and slept beneath the leaf of a water lily in the millpond, and from there they had been brought by the stork to the family Peitersen who lived in the house on the corner; and everyone in town knew whose house it was.

They grew in body and spirit, and all three wanted to be something finer than one of the town's two-and-thirty men.

Peiter said he wanted to be a robber, but that was because he had seen the comedy, *Fra Diavolo,* which had convinced him that a robber's trade was the best in the world. Peter wanted to be a trumpet player. And Peer, that sweet little well-behaved child, so plump and round, whose only fault was that he bit his nails, he wanted to be a "daddy." These were the answers they gave when anyone asked them what they wanted to be when they grew up.

They were sent to school, and one was the head of the class; another in the middle; and the third was the dunce, which doesn't mean that they weren't equally clever and good. Their parents, who had insight, swore that they were. The boys attended their first children's ball, smoked cigars when no one was looking, and generally became cleverer and more and more educated.

Peiter was the most difficult, which is not unusual for a robber. He was, in truth, a very naughty child; but that was caused, according to his mother, by worms. Naughty children always suffer from worms, they have mud in their stomachs. Once his stubbornness and obstinacy brought about the ruin of his mother's new silk dress.

"Don't shake the coffee table, my little lamb," she had said. "You might upset the cream pitcher and splash my new silk dress."

The little "lamb" grabbed the handle of the cream pitcher and poured its contents right down in Mama's lap. The poor woman could not help saying, "My lamb, my little lamb, how could you do such a thing?" That the child had a will of his own she had no doubt. A will of one's own is the same as character; and that to a mother is a sign of great promise.

He could have become a robber but he didn't; he only dressed like one. He wore an old hat and let his hair grow. He was going to be an artist, but he never got any further than dressing like one. More than anything else, he looked like a bedraggled hollyhock. As a matter of fact, he drew all his models so terribly tall that they looked like hollyhocks. It was the flower he loved best of all; the stork said that he had once lain in one.

Peter had lain in a buttercup, and he looked greasy around the corner of his mouth. His skin was so yellow that, if the barber had cut his cheek, I am sure butter would have oozed out instead of blood. He was born to sell butter, and could have had his own shop with a sign about it, except that, deep inside himself, he was a trumpet player. He was the musical member of the Peitersen family, and that single one was noisy enough for them all, said the neighbors. He composed seventeen polkas in one week and then transcribed them into an opera for trumpet and drums. Ugh! Was it lovely!

Peer was white and pink, little and ordinary; he had lain in a daisy. He didn't fight back when the older boys hit him; he was sensible, and the sensible person always gives up. When he was very small he collected slate pencils; later he collected stamps; and finally he was given a little cabinet to keep a zoological collection in. He had a dried fish, three newborn blind rats in alcohol, and a stuffed mole. Peer was a scientist and a naturalist. His parents were very proud of him and Peer was very proud of himself. He preferred a walk in the forest to going to school. Nature attracted him more than education.

Both his brothers were engaged, while Peer was still dedicating his life to completing his collection of the eggs of web-footed birds. He knew a great deal more about animals than he did about human beings. As for the highest feeling, love, he was of the opinion that man was inferior to the animal. He knew that the male nightingale would serenade his wife the whole night through, while she was sitting on the eggs. He—Peer—could never have done that; nor could he, like the stork, have stood on one leg on top of the roof all night, just to guard his wife and family; he couldn't have stood there an hour.

One day, as he was studying a spider and its web, he gave up the idea of marrying altogether. Mr. Spider weaves his nets to catch thoughtless flies, young or old, fat or thin; he exists only to weave nets and support his family. But Mrs. Spider has only one thought in her mind: her husband. She eats him up, out of love. She eats his head, his heart, and his body; only the long thin legs are left dangling in the web, where he used to sit worrying about the family. This is the truth, taken right out of a zoology book. Peer saw it, and thought about it. "To be so adored by one's wife that she eats one up —no human being can love like that, and maybe it's just as well."

Peer decided never to get married and never to give any girl a kiss, for that is the first step toward marriage. But he got a kiss, the kiss none of us escapes, the final kiss of death. When we have lived long enough, the order is given to Death: "Kiss away!" and away we go. A light comes from God, so bright that it blinds us and everything grows dark. The human soul that came as a falling star flies away again, but not to rest in a flower or dream beneath the water-lily leaf. Now its journey is more important; it flies into eternity and what that is like, no one knows. No one has seen that far, not even the stork, however good his eyesight is, and however much he knows.

He didn't know any more about Peer, but a great deal more about Peiter and Peter. I had heard enough about them, and I am sure you have too. I said thank you to the bird. And imagine, for such an ordinary story, the stork wanted payment. He wanted it in kind: three frogs and grass snakes. Will you pay him? I won't! I have neither frogs nor grass snakes on me.

*❖*

## 126

## Hidden but Not Forgotten

There was an old manor house with a moat around it and a drawbridge. The drawbridge was raised as much as it was down, for not every guest who came was welcome. In the upper part of the walls there were holes to shoot through, and to pour boiling water or lead down over the enemy, should they try to cross the moat. Inside, in the hall, the ceilings were high, which was fortunate, for the wet wood, burning in the fireplace, smoked. On the walls hung portraits of knights clad in armor and their noble wives wearing heavy, embroidered dresses. But the noblest and most honorable of them was still alive; she was called Mette Mogens and she was the mistress of the castle.

One night robbers attacked the castle. They killed three of the servants and the watchdog; then they fastened the dog's chain around Mistress Mette's neck, and let her stand outside the doghouse while they sat in the great hall, drinking the wine and good beer from her cellar.

Mistress Mette was chained where the dog had been, but she could not even bark. A young boy who was with the robbers sneaked down to her. Had the others known what he was up to, they would have killed him.

"Mistress Mette Mogens," whispered the boy, "do you remember that, when my father was punished by having to ride the wooden horse, you begged your husband to be merciful? It did not help; he was hard and wanted my father to ride until he became a cripple.

Then you sneaked down as I have sneaked down now, and put two stones under my father's feet so that he could rest. Nobody saw it or acted as if they had seen it—for you were the young, noble mistress. My father has told me about it, and that story I have hidden in my heart, but I have not forgotten it. Now I will loosen you from your chain, Mistress Mette Mogens."

They ran to the stable and saddled two horses and rode through the night to friends for help.

"I have been well paid for the good deed that I did for your father," said Mette Mogens.

"Hidden but not forgotten," said the boy. The robbers were hanged.

Once there was an ancient castle. As a matter of fact, it is still there. It wasn't Mette Mogens' but belonged to another noble family.

We are in our own times. The sun is shining on the tower's golden spire; little forest-clad islands lie like bouquets in the lake near the castle and among them swim white swans; in the garden the roses are blooming. The lady of the manor is herself the fairest rose of them all, blooming in joy: the joy of good deeds, not the ones that are done in the big world but those that are done with the heart, those that are unseen but not unnoticed.

She walks from the castle down to a little cottage where an invalid girl lives. Yesterday the only window in her room faced north; the sun never reached it. She could only see a bit of a field, for her view was cut off by a high hedge. But today there is sunshine, God's warm, wonderful sun is shining in through another window, facing south. The invalid can sit in the warm sunshine and look out over the lake and see the forest beyond it. Her world has become so much larger and so much more beautiful, and that just because of a word from the lady of the manor.

"That word was easily spoken and the deed so small," she said. "But the happiness I received in return was great and blessed."

And that is why she does her good deeds and thinks about the poor in the cottages and of the rich, too; for unhappiness and sorrow are not privileges of the poor. They are often hidden but are not forgotten by God.

There was a large house in the busy city. It contained many fine rooms, but we won't enter them, we will stay in the kitchen. It was comfortably warm and light and airy and spotlessly clean. The copper pots and pans were shiny, the floor varnished, and the table by the sink scrubbed as clean as a carving board. It was one girl's work, and yet she had had time to get as properly dressed as if she were going to church. The bonnet she wore was black. That is a sign of mourning, yet the girl had neither parent nor other relations; and she was not engaged, although she had been once. She was a poor girl and so had been the young man who had loved her.

One day he had come and said, "We have nothing—we two. The rich widow who lives down the street has looked at me kindly. She would make me rich, but you are in my heart. What shall I do?"

"What you believe is best for you," she answered. "But treat her well and kindly, and remember that from now on we can never see each other again."

Some years passed and she met by chance her former fiancé. He looked sick and unhappy, and she could not help asking him how he was.

"I am rich and I have nothing to complain of," he answered. "My wife is both kind and good, but you are still in my heart. I have fought my battle. It will soon be over, and we shall not see each other again before we are with God."

A week later she read in the newspaper that he was dead. That is why the girl's bonnet is black. Her beloved is dead. He died leaving a wife and three stepchildren. The bell sounds cracked, but the bronze is pure.

The color of the bonnet tells of mourning, and the expression in the girl's face tells of it even more plainly. The sorrow is hidden in the heart but it will never be forgotten.

Yes, they were three little stories, three leaves on one stem. Would you like some more leaves of clover? There are many in the book of the heart: hidden but not forgotten.

## 127

## The Janitor's Son

The general lived on the second floor and the janitor in the cellar. There was a great distance between them: all of the ground floor plus the class difference. Still they slept under the same roof and had the same view of the street and the back yard. In the yard there was a little lawn and in the middle of it stood a flowering acacia tree. Sometimes the nurse from the general's household, who was very finely dressed, would sit under the tree with the even more elegantly dressed daughter of the general, little Emilie. The janitor's son would dance for them. He always walked barefoot in the summer. He had brown eyes and dark hair. The little girl would laugh and reach out toward him with her little arms. The general, looking down from the window of his apartment, would nod his head and say, *"Charmant!"* The general's wife, who was so young that she could almost have been his daughter, never looked out the back window. She had given her orders that the janitor's boy might play near her little daughter but that he might not touch her; and the nurse obeyed them.

The sun shone in through the windows on the second floor and through the windows of the cellar. The acacia tree bloomed, lost its flowers, and then next year bloomed again. The tree flourished and the janitor's little son flourished; he looked like a fresh tulip.

The general's little daughter looked delicate and pale, like a pink leaf of an acacia flower. Now she did not sit as often under the tree; she got her fresh air riding with her mother in the general's carriage. But she always nodded to the janitor's son, George. She even kissed her finger and threw him a kiss, until her mother, one day, told her that now she was too grown up for that sort of thing.

One morning when the boy was bringing the general's mail up-stairs—for the postman left all letters and newspapers in the janitor's apartment—he heard a sound coming from the closet on the first landing, as if a little bird had been locked in there. He opened the door and there on the floor, in the middle of a pile of sand—the closet was used for storing the sand that was needed for scrubbing the floor—sat the general's daughter dressed in lace and muslin.

"Don't tell Papa and Mama, they will get angry," she wailed.

"What is the matter, little miss?" asked George.

"It is burning! Everything is burning!" she cried.

George ran to the little girl's room and opened the door. The cur-tains were already ashes and the wooden curtain rods had caught fire. Quickly George pulled them down and called for help. Without him the whole house would have burned down.

The general and his wife cross-examined little Emilie.

"I only took one match!" She was still crying. "It lighted right away, and then the curtains were on fire. I spat on them to put it out; I spat all that I could, but I didn't have spit enough in my mouth, so I went and hid, for I knew Papa and Mama would be terribly angry."

"Spat!" said the general. "What kind of a word is that? Have you ever heard your mother and father say *spat?* You have learned that downstairs."

Still, little George got four copper pennies. He didn't use them at the baker's, he put them in his piggy bank. Soon he had so many pennies that he could buy a paintbox, so that he could color the draw-ings that he made. He had a lot of them; it was as if they came right through his fingers and out of the pencil. The first one he colored he gave to little Emilie.

"*Charmant!*" said the general, and even his wife admitted that one could easily recognize what the boy had meant to portray. "He has genius!" were her words; and the janitor's wife heard them and carried the news down to the cellar.

The general and his wife were people of distinction. They had two coats of arms on their carriage, one for each of their families. The general's wife had hers embroidered on all her clothes, even her nightgowns. Hers was a costly coat of arms; it had been bought by her father for many a shiny gold coin, for he had not had one from birth. And neither had his daughter, she had been born seven years before the coat of arms came into existence. Most people could remember that, although the family couldn't. The general's coat of arms was old and very grand; even alone, it would have been quite a burden to bear. The general's wife did feel her backbone creak a little when she sat straight as a ramrod on her way to a royal ball in a carriage with a coat of arms on either side.

The general was old and gray, but he looked well on a horse and he knew it. Every day he would go for a ride, with a groom trotting a proper distance behind him. When he rode with others, it always seemed as if he were leading a regiment. He had so many medals that it was almost incredible, but that was really not his fault.

When he was young, he had been in the army and had partaken in one of the great harvest maneuvers that were held every year in time of peace. It was from that period he had his anecdote, the only one he had to tell. One of his sergeants had cut off a small group of "enemy" soldiers and taken them prisoners. Among them had been a prince! Now the prince and his fellow prisoners had had to ride behind the general into the town. It had been an unforgettable experience, and whenever the general told the story he always ended it with his own memorable words, as he handed the prince his saber: "Only one of my non-commissioned officers could have taken Your Highness prisoner, I never could have!" To which the prince had answered: "You are peerless!"

The general had never been in a real war; when that plague had swept through the country, he had chosen the road of diplomacy. It had led him through three foreign courts. He spoke French so well that he almost forgot Danish, and he danced well, and he rode well, and the decorations increased and multiplied on his chest; it was quite incomprehensible. The guards presented arms for him and stood at attention when he passed; and so did one of the prettiest girls in the town, and she became his wife. They had the sweetest little daughter. She was like an angel fallen down from heaven to them. And the janitor's son danced for the sweet little thing, as soon as she was old enough to appreciate it, and he gave her all his little colored drawings. She looked at them, played with them, and tore them to pieces. She was so delicate and refined.

"My little rosebud," said the general's wife. "You were born for a prince!"

The prince was already standing outside the door, but they didn't know it. Most people can't see any farther than their own doorstep.

"The other day our son shared his sandwiches with her," boasted the janitor's wife. "They had neither cheese nor meat on them, but she ate them as if they were roast beef. If the general or his wife had seen that meal, there would have been no end of rows, but they didn't."

George had shared his sandwiches with little Emilie, but he would gladly have shared his heart with her if it would have made her happy. He was a good boy, clever and intelligent. He went to evening school at the art academy to learn to draw properly. Little Emilie also advanced on the path of learning; she spoke French with her governess and had a dancing master.

"George is going to be confirmed at Easter," said the janitor's wife.

"We shall have to find him an apprenticeship," his father remarked. "It has got to be a good trade, and his master will have to give him room and board."

"He will have to sleep at home," said the mother. "Not many masters have rooms for their apprentices; and his clothes we have to buy whether he is an apprentice or not. He eats very little and is happy with some boiled potatoes. I think he should stay at home and go his own way. The learning he gets at the academy is free, and the professor says that one day he will be a great comfort to us."

The suit he was going to wear for his confirmation his mother was sewing herself, but the cloth had been cut by a tailor. True, this tailor had no workshop of his own and had to make his living by repairing the threadbare clothes of the poor, but—as the janitor's wife said—if he had had as much good luck as he had talent, he would have been the tailor of the king.

The suit was ready, and the day of the confirmation came. From a godfather George received a big brass pocket watch. It was old and tried, and always ran a little too fast, but that was better than if it had been slow. George had several godfathers, but the giver of the watch was the richest of them. He was an old man who was a clerk in the neighborhood grocery store. It was a costly gift. The general's family also gave George something: a hymnbook bound in morocco. The little girl to whom George had given the drawings had written on the flyleaf herself: "From a favorably disposed patroness." That was what had been dictated by the general's wife, and the general had read it and said, *"Charmant!"*

"It was very considerate of such a distinguished family to give you a gift, George," said his mother, and sent him upstairs in his new suit, with the hymnbook tucked under his arm, to say thank you.

The general's wife was sitting on the sofa with a shawl around her. She had her "grand headache," which always occurred when she was bored. She spoke very kindly to George, wished him well, and added that she hoped he would never have a headache like hers. The general was wearing his dressing gown; he had a tasseled nightcap on his head and Russian red leather boots on his feet. He walked back and forth across the room, deep in his own thoughts; then he stopped in front of George and said: "Little George, now you are a Christian. Be a good and honest man and always respect your superiors. When you yourself are an old man, you will be able to say that the general gave you this advice."

That was one of the longest speeches the general had ever made. He returned to his introspection and looked extremely noble. As for George, what he remembered best from his visit "above his station" was little Miss Emilie. How beautiful she was, how gentle; she did not walk, she floated. If he had drawn her, it would have been inside a soap bubble. There was a fragrance of roses from her yellow curly hair and her clothes. Once he had shared his sandwiches with her; she had eaten them with a good appetite and nodded to him at every second mouthful.

George wondered if she still remembered it. He believed that she did and that was why she had given him the hymnbook.

When the new moon rose for the first time after the New Year, George went out into the garden with a penny, a piece of bread, and the hymnbook. It was an old belief that if you opened the hymnbook at random—at that time and carrying those objects—the psalm you first saw would tell you what the New Year would bring. George's book opened on a hymn of thanks, in praise of Our Lord. Then he thought he might also try one for little Emilie, to find out what her future would be like. Though he was careful and tried to cheat so that the book would not open on one of the funeral hymns, it did! He told himself that it was nothing but superstition and that he didn't believe in it; but it frightened him when the girl got sick, and that the very next day. For a long time afterward the doctor's carriage could be seen in front of the house every morning for at least an hour.

"They won't keep her, she will die!" sighed the janitor's wife. "The Lord knows whom He wants."

But they kept her, she didn't die; and George sent a drawing up to her of the czar's palace, the old Kremlin in Moscow. There it was with all its towers and cupolas that looked like green and golden cucumbers; at least, in George's drawing they did. The sketch amused the little girl so much that during the following week George made several more. All of them were of buildings, for then Emilie could amuse herself by trying to imagine what took place behind the doors and windows.

He drew a Chinese house with sixteen stories, and every one had little bells. A Greek temple with slender pillars and marble steps; and a Norwegian church that had been built of great beams, all carved, and each of whose stories looked as if it had rockers under it like a cradle. The best drawing was one that was called "Little Emilie's Castle." George had designed it himself; this was to be her house. From all the buildings, he had borrowed what he considered the most beautiful: from the Norwegian church, the carved beams; from the Greek temple, its slender pillars; and from the Chinese pagoda, the little bells. The roof had cupolas, green and golden, just as the czar's palace had. It was a real children's castle! Under each of the windows was written what the room inside was used for: "Here little Emilie sleeps." . . . "Here little Emilie dances." . . . "Here little Emilie plays house." It was wonderful to see, and everybody who came looked at it.

*"Charmant!"* said the general.

But the old count—there is a count in the story, too—who was much more distinguished than the general and had his own castle, he said nothing. He listened to what was told about the young artist. He learned that he was the janitor's little son and that he wasn't so little, for he had already been confirmed. The old count looked at the pictures, and silently he formed his own opinion of them.

One terrible gray and wet day was one of the happiest in little George's life. The professor of the academy had called him in. "Now, my friend," he began, "let us have a little talk. God has been kind to you and given you a talent; and maybe even kinder in that He has given you good friends. The count who lives in the house on the cor-

ner of the square has spoken to me about you. I, too, have seen your
pictures, I won't talk too much about them, there is a lot to be corrected in them. You can come to my drawing class twice a week and
you will learn something. I think there is an architect in you, more
than there is a painter. But that time and you yourself will have to
decide. But do go to the count and thank him; and thank God, too,
that He has given you such friends."

The count lived in an old house. It was almost a palace. Around
each window were figures of camels and dromedaries cut in stone.
They had been carved long ago. The old count preferred his own
time; he could appreciate the good things that came out of it, whether
they came from the cellar, the second floor, or the garret.

"I think," said the janitor's wife, "that the higher up a man is on
the ladder, the less he thinks of himself. The old count is straightforward and speaks just as you and I do; and that the general can't.
George was so happy that he could hardly talk sensibly when he came
from visiting the count yesterday; and today I am in the same state,
after having talked to such a great and mighty man. Wasn't it lucky
that we didn't apprentice George in a trade? He has talent."

"Yes, but talent needs help or nothing comes out of it," said the
janitor, who always kept his feet on the ground.

"But he is getting help!" exclaimed the mother. "The count said
it most plainly."

"It all came from the general," said the father. "We ought to
thank him too."

"Oh, it will do no harm," replied the boy's mother, "but I don't
think that there is that much to be grateful for. I will thank God, and
I will thank Him, too, for little Emilie's getting well."

Things went well for Emilie and they went well for George. First
he got the academy's silver medal, and later he got the gold one.

"If we had only apprenticed him, it would have been much better,"
wailed the janitor's wife. "Then we would have kept him at home.
What is he going to do in Rome? I will never live to see him again,
even if he should get home to Denmark, and I don't think he ever
will. Oh, my sweet little boy!"

"But it is his good luck and a great honor," protested the father.

"That is a fine piece of luck. You are not saying what you really
mean. You are feeling just as miserable as I am." George's mother

sniffed; for it was all too true, about both the journey to Rome and the parents' sorrow. But for George, everybody agreed, it was a marvelous good fortune.

George said good-by, on the second floor at the general's as well. He didn't see Emilie's mother, for she had her "grand headache" that day. The general told his one and only anecdote, about what he had said to the prince and what the prince had said to him—"You are peerless!" Then he shook hands with George; the general's hand was weak and slack.

Emilie also shook hands with George and looked a little sad; but of the two George was by far the sadder.

Time passes if you work; as a matter of fact, it passes even if you don't. It is all the same to time what you use it for, but not to you. George used it profitably and did not find it long, except sometimes when he thought of his home. How was everything going, both on the second floor and in the cellar? News of that sort is best carried in a letter, and so much can be written on a little piece of paper. Inside the envelope can be sunshine or dismal dark days. Such were in the letter George received from his mother that told of his father's death. His mother was all alone now. "Emilie has been a comforting angel," his mother wrote. "She comes to visit me." The job as a janitor his mother had been allowed to keep, alone. But only a few months later she, too, was dead.

The general's wife kept a diary. In it she wrote about every party and ball she had attended, and kept a list of all the guests who had visited her. The diary was illustrated with the visiting cards of all the most prominent diplomats and noblemen. She was very proud of her diary. It had grown with time, through periods of "grand head-aches" and of "wonderful evenings," for that is what she called the royal balls. Emilie had attended one for the first time. Her mother had been in pink with black Spanish lace, and she had been dressed all in white—so bright and delicate. Among her yellow tresses were tied green silk ribbons and her hair was crowned with a garland of water lilies. Her eyes were so clear and blue, and her little mouth so red; she looked like a little mermaid, as beautiful as one could imag-ine. Three princes danced with her—that is to say, first one and then another—and her mother did not have a headache for a whole week.

The first ball was not the last, and soon it was all too much for Emilie. She was glad when summer came. The general's family had been invited to spend some time at the castle of the old count. There she could rest and enjoy the fresh country air.

Surrounding the castle was a park that was well worth exploring. Part of it was in the style of earlier times, with hedges like green screens that had peepholes cut in them; box trees and yews that had been trimmed to look like pyramids and stars. In the center there was a grotto covered with sea shells, and here there was a fountain surrounded by stone figures. The flower beds had been planted so that they resembled a fish or a coat of arms; one of them depicted the count's initials, another the initials of one of his ancestors. That was called the French garden. There was another area where the trees grew freely and, therefore, were large and beautiful. The lawns were like carpets and ever so pleasant to walk on. They were well taken care of and had been both cut and rolled; this was the English part of the gardens.

"The old and the new times meet here and complement each other," said the count. "In two years the castle itself will be changed and will become both more comfortable and more beautiful. I will show you the drawings and the architect who made them, for I have invited him to dine with us tonight."

"*Charmant!*" said the general.

"This place is a paradise," said his wife. "Oh, and look, there is a little castle!"

"That," said the count, "is my henhouse. The pigeons are in the tower and the turkeys on the first floor. Below on the ground floor old Else reigns. She has lots of guest rooms. The roosting hens and those with chicks have their own rooms; and so do the ducks, they have a view of the lake."

"*Charmant!*" repeated the general. They all walked over to have a look at the hens' castle.

Old Else greeted them and beside her stood the young architect, George. He and little Emilie met again after so many years—met in the henhouse.

There he stood, handsome enough to bear being looked at carefully. His expression was open yet determined. His face was framed by his black hair; at his mouth there played a smile, which said, "I know you, I know all about you!"

Old Else had taken her wooden clogs off and was standing in her stocking feet, in honor of her highborn guests. The hens clucked and the cock crowed; the ducks just waddled around and said: "Quack . . . quack!" But the delicate pale girl, his childhood friend, the general's daughter—a faint tinge of pink touched her pale cheeks, and they took on the color of a rose petal. Her eyes grew large and her mouth spoke, without saying a word; and that greeting was the best that any young man could hope for from a young lady to whom he was not related and had never danced with. Emilie and the young architect had never been to the same ball.

The count shook George's hand and presented him to the others. "My young friend, Mr. George, is not altogether a stranger."

The general's wife curtsied, and her daughter was just about to give George her hand, but then held back.

"Our little Mr. George," said the general, "an old friend of the family. *Charmant!*"

"You have become an Italian!" exclaimed his wife. "I am sure you speak the language like a native."

"My wife sings in the language, but she cannot speak it," remarked the general.

At dinner, George sat on Emilie's right, the general on her left; and it was he who had escorted her to the table. The general's wife had entered on the arm of the count.

George talked and he talked well. He was the most brilliant and witty member of the party, although the count, when he wanted to be, was very charming. Emilie was silent, but her ears listened and her eyes sparkled.

After dinner they were alone together, out on the veranda, among the flowers. A hedge of roses hid them from the others. George spoke first. "Thank you for your kindness to my mother," he began. "I know that you were with her the night that my father died. Thank you!" He grabbed Emilie's hand and kissed it, which was quite proper considering the occasion. She blushed, pressed his hand, and looked at him with her big blue eyes.

"Your mother's soul was filled with love. She cared so much for you! She let me read your letters to her and from them I know you.

You were so kind to me when I was a child and gave me your drawings."

"Which you tore up," interrupted George.

"No, not all of them. I have the drawing of my castle yet."

"Now I must build it, really," George said, and became quite
breathless.

Inside the castle the general and his wife also talked about the
janitor's son. They said that he had learned to carry himself well
and spoke with both knowledge and education.

"He could become a professor," said the general.

"He has *esprit*," said his wife.

The young architect came often to the count's castle that summer
and, what is more, when he was absent he was missed.

"God has given you so much more than He gave the rest of us
poor human beings," said Emilie. "I hope that you appreciate it."

George was flattered that the young girl admired him, and at such
moments he found her very intelligent.

The general felt more and more uncertain about George being a
"cellar" child. "His mother was a very respectable woman," he often
said, "and that is not a bad epitaph."

Summer passed and winter came; and again they talked about Mr.
George. He had been seen in the highest circles. The general had
met him at a royal ball.

Now the general was giving a ball for little Emilie. Could Mr.
George be invited? "Whom the king invites the general can also invite," said the general, and straightened himself so much that he
appeared a whole inch taller.

Mr. George was invited and he came; and princes and counts
came; and each danced more elegantly than the other. But Emilie
only danced once, her first dance; she stumbled and sprained her
ankle. Not badly, but still you have to be careful; and therefore she
sat the whole evening and watched the others dance. The young
architect stood at her side.

"Are you making her a present of St. Peter's?" asked the general
as he passed and smiled as friendly as could be.

He had the same friendly smile on his face the next day when he
received George. The young man had probably come to thank him

for the invitation, what else could he have come for? But he hadn't come to say thank you; he had come to make a most shocking, fantastic, quite insane proposal. The general could not believe his own ears. It was unthinkable! Mr. George had asked for little Emilie's hand.

"My good man!" The general's face was as red as a boiled lobster. "I don't understand you. What is it you want? What are you saying? . . . I don't know you! What do you mean, coming like this into my house, is it mine or is it not mine?" And with these words the general backed out of the room and went into his bedroom, where he turned the key in the lock. He had left George standing in the middle of the drawing room, and there the young man remained for several moments; then he turned and walked out. In the corridor he met Emilie.

"What did my father say?" she asked, and her voice quivered.

George took her hand. "He didn't answer, he ran away from me. Don't worry, a better moment will come."

There were tears in Emilie's eyes, but fortitude and courage in the young man's. The sun shone in through the windows, and its rays fell upon them and gave them its blessings.

The general sat in his study. He was still boiling; as a matter of fact, he was boiling over. "Madness. . . . Insanity," he muttered.

Not an hour had gone by before he told his wife all about it; and she asked Emilie to come to her room.

"Poor child," she said. "It is an insult to you and an insult to us. I see you have tears in your eyes. I don't blame you for crying, though they are becoming. You look as I did on my wedding day. Cry, Emilie, it helps."

"I will," she said. "If you and Father don't say yes."

"Child!" screamed the general's wife. "You are sick; you have fever, you are delirious! Oh! I am getting my grand headache! What a misfortune has befallen our house! I will die from it! And then, Emilie, you will have no mother." The general's wife had tears in her eyes; she hated to think of her own death.

In the newspaper you could read in the list of appointments that Mr. George had become a professor: Fifth Rank class, Subdivision Number Eight.

"It is a shame that his parents did not live long enough to read this," said the new janitor who now lived in the cellar below the general. They knew that the newly appointed professor had been born and brought up inside their four walls.

"Now he will have to pay rank tax," said the husband.

"Isn't that too much for a child of poor parents?" said the wife.

"Eighteen gold marks a year, that is a lot of money." The janitor looked solemn as he mentioned the great sum the professor would have to pay in tax for his newly won rank at court.

"I don't mean the money, I mean his success, his . . . elevation." The good woman looked concerned. "The money is nothing, he can earn much more and probably will marry a rich girl. My good man, if we had a child, then he should be an architect too, and a professor."

They talked kindly about George in the cellar; and they were talking well about him, too, on the second floor. The old count was visiting.

It was his childhood drawings they were discussing. They had talked about Moscow and then about the Kremlin, and then one of them had recalled the picture George had drawn of it for little Miss Emilie. He had given her so many pictures, but the count had remembered best the one called "Little Emilie's Castle," the one that had titles under every window: "Here little Emilie sleeps." "Here little Emilie plays." . . . "Here little Emilie dances."

"The young professor is a very intelligent man," said the count. "He will become an adviser to the king before he dies. Maybe he will build a castle for the young lady, why not?"

"That was a strange thing to say," commented the general's wife when the count had left. Her husband shook his head and went for a ride, followed by his groom, and looking prouder than ever on his high horse.

It was little Emilie's birthday, and no end of flowers, books, letters, and visiting cards arrived. The general's wife kissed her on her mouth and the general on her forehead, for they were affectionate parents.

Guests arrived, very highborn guests, including two princes from the royal family. They conversed about the latest balls and theater performances, about Danish diplomacy abroad and the state of the country and its government. Then they went on to talk about ability and talent, and soon they were talking about the young professor, the architect.

"He is building an immortal name," someone said.

"I have been told that he is building his way right into one of our first families," remarked another.

Later in the day when they were alone, the general repeated the words. "One of our first families." And then he asked his wife, "Which one did they mean?"

"I know whom they were hinting at," she answered, "but I will not say it, I will not even think it. God wills, but it would surprise me."

"Oh well, let it surprise me too, for I haven't an idea who it could be," said the general, and looked thoughtful.

Powerful is the man whom God has favored; and powerful, too, is he whom the king favors; and George was favored by both. . . . But we mustn't forget Emilie's birthday party.

Her room was filled with flowers from all her friends. On the table lay beautiful gifts, but none from George. He could not send her one, but he would be remembered without it, for everything in the house reminded her of him. Even in the closet on the way up the stairs, where the sand was kept, there bloomed a forget-me-not. It was there that she had hid when she set fire to the curtains, and George had arrived and saved the house from burning. A glance out the window and there was the acacia tree. True, it had no flowers or leaves on it now. Frost covered its bare branches, and through them the moon was shining, making the tree look like coral. Always changing and always constant in its change, it was the tree under which George had shared his sandwiches with her.

Out of a drawer she took the drawing of the castle of the czar, and then the one of her own castle. Remembrances from George; and as she looked at them other memories came. She thought of the night when his mother died, how—unbeknown to her parents—she had sat by her bedside and heard her last words. "A blessing! . . . George." The mother had thought of her son, but now Emilie interpreted the words in her own way. George had not been forgotten on her birthday; he had been there.

The next day there was another birthday, the general's. He had been born the day after his daughter; that is, quite a few years earlier, about four decades. Again presents arrived, and among them was a costly saddle, comfortable and handsome. The only person the general knew who had one like it was a prince.

Who could have given the saddle to him? The general was very excited. A little note had been enclosed. Now had there been written: "Thank you for yesterday . . ." or something like that, the general might have been able to guess who his well-wisher was; but it only said: "From one whom the general does not know."

"Who in the world don't I know?" said the general. "Why, I know everybody!" And through his mind the whole court passed in review. "It is from my wife!" he exclaimed. "She is always flirting, the little coquette."

But she didn't flirt any more; that time had passed.

Again there was a party; it was not at the general's, but at the home of a prince. It was a costume ball, at which masks were also allowed.

The general arrived dressed up as Rubens: Spanish attire, with a lace ruff, rapier, and a firm bearing. His wife was Madame Rubens: a black velvet dress, buttoned up to the neck, with an enormous ruff collar, the size of a millstone; she was terribly hot. Their costumes had been copied from a Dutch painting which the general owned. It was especially the hands in the painting that everyone admired; they resembled those of the general's wife.

Emilie was Psyche, dressed in silk, white muslin, and lace. Light as swan's-down, she floated through the room. She didn't need any wings, but she wore them because she was Psyche.

It was a brilliant and magnificent ball. There were so many candles burning, so much richness and good taste, so much to look at, that no one had time to look at Madame Rubens' beautiful hands.

A man dressed as a black domino, with an acacia flower attached to his hood, danced with Psyche.

"Who is he?" asked the general's wife.

"His Royal Highness," replied the general. "I could recognize him by his handshake."

His wife said that she doubted it, but General Rubens was so certain that he was right that he walked up to the black domino, held up his own hand, and wrote in it, with one of his fingers, His Royal Highness' initials. The domino shook his masked head and looked away; but he said pointedly: "I am one whom the general does not know."

"But then I do know you!" exclaimed General Rubens. "You are the one who gave me the saddle."

The black domino raised his hand. What he meant by that movement was hard to tell. Then he disappeared among some dancers.

"Who is the black domino that you danced with, Emilie?" asked the general's wife.

"I didn't ask his name," answered her daughter.

"You didn't ask who he was because you knew it! It is the professor!" Turning to the old count, the general's wife said: "Your protégé is here. He is dressed as a black domino and has an acacia flower in his hood."

"It is possible," said the count, and smiled. "But one of the princes is wearing the same costume."

"I know him by his handshake," repeated the general. "I am so sure that the prince is the one who gave me the saddle that I dare go right up to him now and invite him to my house."

"Why don't you?" asked the count. "If it is the prince, then he will come."

"And if he is the other one, he won't!" The general looked determined as he approached the black domino, who was conversing with the king. Most respectfully, the general invited the young man to visit him in his home, so that they might learn to know each other better. The general smiled; so little doubt was there in his mind that he was speaking to the prince that he did not lower his voice but spoke loudly enough for everyone to hear him.

The black domino lifted his mask. It was George. "Will the general be so kind as to repeat his invitation?" he asked.

The general drew himself up a whole inch, took two steps backward and one step forward, as if he were going to dance a minuet. He looked so serious and proud that in spite of his delicate features his face did have a general's expression. "I never go back on my word, the professor is invited." He bowed a little stiffly and glanced toward the king, who probably had overheard all that had been said.

Now there was a dinner party at the general's; only the old count and his protégé had been invited.

"My foot is under the table, that is as good a foundation to build on as any," thought George. And the foundation really was laid that evening during that very formal dinner.

George had come; and—as the general had expected—he conversed like someone who belonged to the best society. His stories he told so brilliantly that the general had had to say, *"Charmant!"* sev-

eral times in a row. Later the general's wife had talked freely about
that evening, and had even mentioned it to her most noble and most
intellectual friend at court. This lady in waiting had begged to be invited when next they entertained the professor. There was no way
out of it; he would have to be invited once more. He came and was
again "*charmant!*" And on top of all that, he could play chess.

"He is not really from the cellar," explained the general. "His father was highborn, that sort of thing is not uncommon, and certainly
not the young man's fault."

The professor who was invited to the king's palace could come
from now on to the general's house. But he must not take root; that
was the general's opinion, although no one in the whole town shared
it.

He did take root, and he grew. By the time he became a councilor
of state Emilie was already his wife.

"Life is a tragedy or a comedy," said the general. "In the tragedy
they die; and in the comedy they get each other."

In this story they got each other and three sons besides; but not
right away. The sweet little children rode their hobbyhorses through
the rooms of their grandfather's and grandmother's home. The general rode one too, rode behind the three little sons of the king's
councilor; he was their groom. His wife sat on the sofa and smiled,
even when she had her "grand headache."

George became someone of great importance. He rose even higher
than I have told you; if he hadn't, the story of the janitor's son would
not have been worth telling.

## 128

## Moving Day

In the old times, people used to move once a year; that is, not every-body, or there wouldn't have been carts and horses enough to carry all the furniture, but those who wanted to move. For all the leases signed by people who didn't have houses of their own, but had to rent them, began on the same day in the year. It was printed on the calendar and it was called Moving Day.

Do you remember the night watchman Ole who lived in the tower? I have told you about two of my visits to him; now I will tell about the third one, and it won't be the last. I usually visit him around New Year, but this time it was on Moving Day. All the streets of the town were filled with rubbish: broken pots and rags, not to speak of the straw that the poor people used in their beds instead of mattresses. In this profusion of garbage, I found two little children playing. They were making believe that they were going to sleep in the old straw, and they had a filthy rag for covers. They said that that was having fun, but it was too much for me, and that was why I went up to visit Ole.

"It is Moving Day," he said, a fact I already knew, so I only nodded my head. "All the streets and alleys are garbage pails— marvelous, big trash bins. As for me, a cartload will do. I remember one I saw on a raw, cold, windy day, shortly after Christmas.—It was just the kind of day to catch cold on.—The garbage wagon was filled to the brim with just the sort of things that are dirtying up the city streets today. In the back of the wagon there was a Christmas tree.

It still had some green needles, and gold and silver tinsel hung from its branches. The garbage collector had stuck it on top of the load for everyone to see. It was a sight that made one either cry or laugh, according to one's disposition. It made me think. And I am sure it made some of the inhabitants of the garbage pile think, too; or could have made them think, which is about the same thing. There was a worn lady's glove. What were its thoughts? Would you like to know? The little finger was pointing right at the Christmas tree. 'I am moved by the sight of that tree,' she thought. 'I, too, was once at a feast, when all the candles in the chandeliers were lighted. My whole life was one night at a ball. A handshake and I split; I tore. There my memories end, and I have nothing more to live for.' That is what the glove thought, or could have thought.

"'It is embarrassing to have to ride with that old pine tree,' said some broken pieces of pottery, but they always found everything embarrassing. 'When one has ended up on the garbage wagon, the least one can do is not to show off by wearing tinsel. We know that we have been a great deal more useful in our life than that old green stick.' That was their opinion, and I am sure that it was shared by quite a few others. Still the Christmas tree looked pretty; it was a bit of poetry right in the middle of the trash. And trash and garbage there are too much of in the streets on Moving Day, or on any other day; that is why I like to stay in my tower. From here I can look down without losing my good humor.

"They are all playing let-us-switch-houses, carting and carrying their belongings about. But their pixy moves along with them. The troubles in the household: their griefs, worries, and afflictions, they move from their old apartment to the new; and what is to be gained from the exchange? There was a line in a poem, written a long time ago and printed in the newspaper, that read: 'Think of Death's great moving day.'

"It is serious thought, a sobering thought; I hope it does not upset you that I speak of it. Death, you know, is one of the most trustworthy of all our public officials; and that in spite of all the small jobs he has besides his main one. Have you ever thought about it?

"He drives the stagecoach for our last journey, writes out our passports, and signs our report cards. He is the director of the great savings bank of life. Are you aware that all the deeds we have done throughout our lives have been deposited in an account there? When

Death comes with his great vehicle and we—whether we like it or not—have to board it as passengers and go to the land of eternity, he gives us a report card, which we will use as a passport at the border. For traveling expenses, he withdraws from the savings bank a deed or two that is most typical of our life. It can be something amusing or something horrible.

"No one as yet has missed that ride, although they tell of one— Jerusalem's shoemaker—who had to run behind the omnibus. If Death had allowed him into his coach, he would have been spared the ill treatment he has received from the poets. Look for a moment at the passengers in the coach, use your imagination as eyes. The company is mixed. There they all are, sitting one next to the other: the king and the beggar, the genius and the idiot. Their richness and power have been taken from them, all they have left are their report cards and their traveling expenses, drawn from their account. What kind of deed will Death give us to take along? Maybe one as small as a pea; but from a pea, a vine can grow and flowers bloom.

"The poor scapegoat who sat on his little footstool near the fire and had to bear many an unjust word and unearned beating, maybe he receives his footstool as a symbol with which to pay his traveling expenses. And the footstool becomes a comfortable sedan chair in which he will be carried to the eternal land, where it will change into a throne, bright and beautiful as if it were made of gold, fragrant and flowering as a bower.

"That fellow who was always tippling, drinking the spiced wine of amusement, to forget every wrong that he had done, he will get a wooden cup to sip from on his trip, but the drink in it will be pure and clear. His thoughts will become clearer; all the emotions that are good and honest will be aroused within him. He will look at and understand all that he had not taken the trouble to see or understand before. His punishment will be the gnawing worm that cannot die. On the glass he drank out of during his life was written 'Forgetfulness'; on the glass he now holds is engraved 'Remembrance.'

"Whenever I read a book of history, I cannot help wondering which deed the person I am reading about will receive from Death as traveling money. There was once a French king, I have forgotten his name. One is always forgetting the names of the virtuous; but maybe it will come to me later. This king had reigned during a period of famine and had by his charity saved his people. They, in turn, erected a monument in his honor made out of snow. On it was written: 'More quickly than this will melt did you help us.' I think that Death gave him, because of the monument, one unmeltable snowflake; perhaps it flew over his royal head, like a white butterfly, as he entered the eternal land.

"Then there was Louis XI, I remember his name. The names of the evil persons in history we do not forget. I often think of one of his deeds and then I wish that I could call history a liar. He ordered his chief councilor to be executed; that he had the power to do, whether the man was guilty of anything or not. The councilor's two children—one was eight and the other seven years old—he ordered to witness the execution at so close a range that the father's warm blood sprayed and splashed on his own children. Then the innocent ones were taken to the Bastille and imprisoned in an iron cage and not even given a blanket to cover themselves. Once a week King Louis sent his executioner to the jail to pull out one tooth from each of the children's mouths, so that they should not think it a pleasure to be imprisoned by him. The oldest of them, when he was told of the penalty, said, 'My mother would die of sorrow if she knew how much my little brother is suffering. Pull two of my teeth and let him go free.' A tear fell from the executioner's eye when he heard those words, but the command of the king had to be obeyed, for it was stronger than any tears. Once a week two children's teeth on a silver plate were presented to the king; he had demanded them and he received them. I think Death must have withdrawn two teeth from life's great savings bank and given them to King Louis XI for his traveling expenses to the eternal land. The teeth of two innocent children must have flown in front of him, burning brightly, nipping and pinching him.

"It is a grave journey, the one taken in Death's stagecoach on the great Moving Day. When will it happen?

"Yes, that is a serious thing to think about: any day, any hour, any minute, the stagecoach can arrive. What deed that we have done will Death withdraw from the savings bank and give us to take along? Yes, let us think about that. Your Moving Day is not printed in the calendar, you can't look it up."

## 129

# The Snowdrop

It was winter. The air was cold and the wind was sharp, but indoors it was comfortable and warm, and the flower was indoors. It lay inside its bulb, underneath the snow and earth.

One day it started to rain. The drops of water penetrated the snow and the earth and touched the bulb, bringing a message from the world above. Soon a sun ray found its way down through the snow to the bulb and pricked it.

"Come in," said the flower.

"I cannot," answered the sun ray. "I am not strong enough yet to open your door; but I will be, come summer."

"And when is it summer?" asked the flower, and it repeated its question each time a sun ray touched it. But it was long to summer. Snow still lay on the ground and every night the puddles of water froze.

"Oh, how long it takes, how long," sighed the flower. "It is prickling and tingling inside me. I have to stretch myself, I want to get out, I must! I want to nod good morning to the summer; it is going to be delightful!"

And the flower stretched itself inside the bulb and broke through the thin skin, which the water had softened and the earth and snow had warmed and the sun rays had touched. Out through the earth, under the snow, it came, with a white bud on its green stalk, and its long, narrow, thick leaves that hugged the flower to protect it. The snow was cold but porous; the light came through it and the flower felt that the sun rays were more powerful.

"Welcome, welcome!" they sang; and the flower lifted its head through the snow into the world of light. The sun rays petted it and kissed it so much that it opened. It was as white as the snow with some fine green lines in it. Because of its happiness and because of its humbleness, it bent its head.

"Sweet flower," said the sun rays, "you are fresh and pure, you are the first, you are the only flower. We love you! Your little white bell shall ring that summer has come, that the snow will melt and the cold wind cease to blow. We, the sun rays, shall govern the world and everything will become green, and your little flower shall have company. The lilacs and laburnum will bloom, and last of all the roses. You, little snowdrop, are the first flower, so pure and bright."

It was a great pleasure. The little flower felt as though the air itself sang to it, while the sun rays penetrated its leaves and its stalk. There it stood, so delicate, so fragile, and yet so powerful in all the beauty of its youth. Dressed in its white dress with green ribbons, it praised the coming of summer.

But it was long to summer yet; the clouds obscured the sun and the bitter cold winds blew. "You have come a little too early," they grumbled. "We are still powerful and we will make you feel it. You should have stayed indoors; this is not the time for running about in such finery."

The weather turned bitterly cold. The days that came were so dark that not one sun ray was seen. It was proper weather to freeze to death, for such a little flower. But it had more strength within itself than it had realized. Its faith that the summer, which it longed and cared for, would come had once been confirmed by the warm sun; so there it stood, confident in its white dress amid the white snow, bending its head as the heavy snowflakes fell around it and the cold winds flew above it.

"You are going to break!" screamed the winds. "First you will freeze, then you will wither. Why did you let the sun rays tempt you to bloom? They have tricked you. They have made you a summer fool in winter weather."

"Summer fool," the little snowdrop repeated the words in the cold morning air.

"Summer fool!" shouted some children who had come into the

garden and spied the flower. They gave it the same name as the winds had, which was not so strange, for a snowdrop is called a summer fool in Danish.

"It is so beautiful, so graceful. It is the first flower of the year and the only one in the garden." The children said these words, too; and to the flower they felt as sweet as the sun rays had. She was so happy that she did not even feel that she was being picked.

A little child's hand closed around the flower; it was kissed and carried into the house. There in the warm room the snowdrop was put in a glass of water and that was very refreshing. The flower thought that summer had suddenly come.

The daughter of the family was a very sweet girl; she was fourteen and had just been confirmed. She had a friend, a boy; he, too, had just been confirmed, but he was not living at home, he was in the town studying. "He shall be my summer fool," said the girl, and took the little flower and put it inside a folded paper on which she had written a poem. For in Denmark it is a custom that the young people send the first snowdrops of the year to one another, together with a verse. But the letters are never signed, the receiver has to guess who has sent them.

It was very dark inside the envelope, as dark as it had been inside the bulb. The letter was put in the postbox and started on its journey. The snowdrop wasn't very comfortable. Several times it was squeezed, but everything, even the unpleasant, comes to an end.

The journey was over. The letter was opened and read by a young man. He was pleased. He kissed the flower and put it with the letter, down in the drawer of his writing desk. There were many other letters in the drawer, but only one had a flower in it. It was still the first, the only flower, as the sun rays had called it, and that was pleasant to think about. And the snowdrop was given a long time to think about it, for it lay there all summer and all winter. Only when it again became summer was it taken out. But this time the young man was not happy to see it. He crumpled up the poem and threw it across the room. The flower fell on the floor, and even though it was wizened by now, it was a pity that it should lie on the floor.

Still it was better than to be burned, and that was what happened to the letter. Into the stove went all the letters and the poem. What had happened? She had made a summer fool of him, and found another friend. This sort of thing happens quite often.

The next morning the sun shone through the windows and its rays fell on the little dried, pressed snowdrop; it looked as if it had been painted on the floor. The maid who came to sweep picked it up and put it between two leaves of a book that was lying on the table. Again the snowdrop was among poems, but this time they were printed, and they are more important than those that are written by hand, for they have involved expense.

Years went by. The book stood in the bookcase. Every once in a while it was taken down and read. It was a good book, the poems of Ambrosius Stub, a Danish poet well worth being acquainted with.

The man who was reading the book turned a page and then exclaimed, "Why, there is a snowdrop, a summer fool," and then he said more thoughtfully, "A summer fool. Maybe there is a reason why it should lie in this book. Ambrosius Stub was a summer fool too: a jester, a poet. He, too, came too early, before summer; therefore, the sharp winds whipped him and snow and ice froze him. A winter fool, summer's dupe, a joke of nature, out of season; but yet the first one, the only one of the Danish poets who is still summer-young. Yes, little snowdrop, you fit the book, I think someone has put you there for a reason."

And the snowdrop was put back in the book; and it felt both honored and happy to know that it now was a bookmark in a volume of poems written by a poet who was the first to write about the snowdrop; a poet who, like the flower, had stood in the bitter, winter weather with a dream of summer in his soul: a summer fool. The snowdrop interpreted what she had heard her own way, as we all do.

That was the snowdrop's tale.

## 130

## Auntie

You should have known my mother's sister! She was a lovely person; that is to say, she was not beautiful, but she was sweet and kind and, most important of all, she was so good to tell stories about. She could have been a character in a comedy, and that she wouldn't have minded, for she loved and lived for the theater. Agent Pinjay, whom Auntie called Popinjay, said she was theater-crazy.

"I go to school in the theater," Auntie would declare. "It is the well from which I draw my learning, it has even helped me to recollect what I learned in Sunday school. *Moses* and *Joseph and His Brothers* are both operas, and I have heard them. All that I know about history, geography, and human nature I have learned in the theater. From the French plays I know what life is like in Paris—it is obscene but interesting. Oh, how I cried when I saw *The Family Rigquebourg*. It is all about a poor man who has to drink himself to death so that his wife can marry her young lover. . . . Yes, I have shed many tears during the last fifty years that I have had a season ticket to the Royal Theater."

Auntie knew every play, every backdrop and set, and every actor who was playing or had played on the stage. She only really lived when the theater was open. The summer months, when it was closed, aged her, while a performance that kept on well past midnight was a prolongation of her life. She did not say, as other people did, "Now the newspaper says that the strawberries are here."

She was only interested in the arrival of the autumn. But she would not say something about it soon being fall; no, she would remark: "They have announced the auction of the boxes; soon the theater season will begin."

The value of a house or an apartment she reckoned by its nearness to the theater. It was a great sorrow when she had been forced to move from her apartment in the little lane behind the Royal Theater to a broad street a little farther away. The street was so wide that she could not even see across it to watch what was going on in the houses on the other side.

"My window must be my theater. One can't just sit at home and only be interested in oneself. One must see other human beings! The way I live now, I might as well have moved to the country. If I want to see other human beings I have to go out in the kitchen and sit down on the cupboard, for it is only in back I have neighbors. Now when I had an apartment in the lane I could look straight into the living room of the grocer across from me; and then, I had only three hundred steps to the theater, not three thousand as I have now."

Sometimes Auntie was sick, but never so ill that she could not go to the theater. One day her doctor had prescribed an oatmeal plaster for her feet. She obeyed his order, but she still went to the theater, attending the performance wearing the oatmeal plaster. The death of the great Danish sculptor Thorvaldsen she called a "blessed departure"; he had died in the theater.

Auntie could not believe that there was no theater in heaven, although she admitted that there was no mention of one in the Scriptures. "But what about all the great actors and actresses who have departed from this world?" she argued. "What are they to do but act?"

Auntie had a "direct line" to the theater, as she called it. It came to her parlor for coffee on Sundays. The name of the "direct line" was Mr. Sivertsen. He was an assistant stage manager; it was he who gave the orders for the curtain to be drawn and the sets to be changed. From him, Auntie received a short—and very much to the point—critique of all the plays: "Shakespeare's *Tempest* is a lot of nonsense, with too much stage business, and then, it starts with a storm and water in the first scene." The rolling waves were the responsibility of Mr. Sivertsen. A well-written play, with "no nonsense," was one that kept the same scenery throughout all five acts and did not require any "accessories."

"In earlier times," as Auntie called the period some thirty-odd years before, when she and Mr. Sivertsen had been young—he had already risen to be assistant stage manager and become Auntie's "direct line"—the theater director had allowed a few people to watch the plays from the "attic," above the stage. It was deemed so interesting to see it all from above—so to speak—that it was whispered that both a general and the wife of a king's councilor had seen performances from there. What was most fascinating of all was to see how the actors looked and behaved when the curtain was down. The tickets to these "exclusive seats" could only be obtained from a friend who worked at the theater; even someone as insignificant as an assistant stage manager had the right to a seat or two.

Auntie had been there many times and seen both ballet and opera, for the performances that involved the greatest number of people were the most interesting to watch from the loft. One sat in almost complete darkness; and most of the spectators had brought their dinners with them. Once, three apples and half a sausage fell right down into Ugolino's jail, to the great amusement of the paying public, on the other side of the curtain, since the prisoner, according to the plot, was starving to death. It was the sausage that caused the director of the theater to close the loft to the public.

"But I was there, thirty-seven times," Auntie would declare. "And I am forever grateful to Mr. Sivertsen."

As a matter of fact, it was on the last evening that the loft was open to the public that Auntie had managed to get a ticket for Agent Pinjay. They were playing *Solomon's Judgment*. The agent had not deserved the ticket, for he always made fun of the theater, but Auntie had a kind heart. He went because he wanted to see the theater "turned inside out"—those were his own words.

And he saw *Solomon's Judgment* from the inside and above; and fell asleep. One might suspect that he had come from a dinner where too many toasts had been drunk, for he slept so soundly that he did not even wake up when the performance was over.

When Agent Pinjay at last awoke, it was past midnight. The lights were out and the theater was empty; then, as he himself told the story —though Auntie never believed it—the real play began. It wasn't *Solomon's Judgment* that was performed. No, it was *Judgment Day in the Theater*.

Now listen to the story that Agent Pinjay tried to make Auntie believe, as thank you for her having been kind enough to get him a ticket:

"It was dark up in the loft," began Agent Pinjay. "But then commenced the great magic play, *Judgment Day in the Theater*. The attendants stood by the doors and would not let the spectators in until they had shown their moral and spiritual report cards. Those with bad grades had their hands tied and their mouths muzzled so they couldn't speak or applaud. Anyone who came late, as young people usually do—youth having no respect for time—had to wait until the first act was over."

"What you are saying is all malice and wickedness; and that the good Lord never approves of," interrupted Auntie; but Agent Pinjay did not pay any attention to her.

"Any scenery painter who wanted to get into heaven had to walk up the staircases that he had painted himself, and that no human legs could possibly climb; this was their punishment for having sinned against perspective. The stage managers—and all their assistants—had to return to their proper country or century all the plants and buildings that, through a lifetime in the theater, they had put in the wrong places. And it had to be done before the cock crowed, or the gate of heaven would remain forever closed for them."

Mr. Pinjay had more to tell. He also listed what the actors and the dancers would have to do in order to get into heaven. But he should have worried more about how he himself would reach that destination: the Popinjay! Auntie was furious and declared that he had not deserved the privilege of having been in the loft and that she, at least, would never repeat his words. To this Agent Pinjay replied that he had written the whole affair down but would not have it published until after his death, because he did not want to be flayed alive.

Once Auntie had been in great dread and terror while attending her Temple of Joy. It had been a winter day, one of those days when daylight consists of two hours of gray twilight. It was cold and had been snowing, but they were performing *Herman von Unna,* a one-act opera, plus a grand ballet, with both a prologue and an epilogue. It would last until the small hours of the morning. Auntie just had to go! From the lodger who had rented her spare room she borrowed a pair of sled boots with sheepskin lining, though they were too big for her and reached all the way up to her knees.

But she managed to make her way to the Royal Theater and to her box: second circle on the left. It is the better side; and here, too, the royal family has their box. The scenery is arranged so that it looks more beautiful seen from there.

All at once someone screamed: "Fire!" And smoke poured out of the loft. Panic broke out! Auntie had kept the sled boots on during the performance because they were so nice and warm. And that they were, but they were not meant for running. Auntie was on her way to the door of the box when the terrified person in front of her slammed the door so hard that it locked. She couldn't get out of the door of her own box, nor could she climb into any of the neighboring boxes, for the partitions were too high.

She screamed, but no one heard her. She looked down at the circle of boxes below her; it didn't seem far. In her fear, Auntie felt all the agility of youth returning to her: she would jump down! She got one leg over the balustrade but could not manage to get the other one over. There she sat as if she were riding a horse, with her skirt tucked up under her and her long leg with the sled boot on it hanging in the air. It was a sight! And it was seen and Auntie was saved from a death in flames—which was not so strange, for the theater wasn't burning at all.

It was the most memorable evening in her life, she often remarked; and it was a good thing that she could not have seen herself sitting on the balustrade, for if she had been able to she would have died of shame.

Her "direct line," Mr. Sivertsen, the assistant stage manager, always came to visit her on Sunday. But from one Sunday to the next was a whole week; therefore Auntie, in later years, invited a child from the ballet for "leftovers" on Thursday. The little one was to come and feast on the remains of the dinner. The child was as hungry for food as Auntie was for news of the theater. The child had already played the parts of an elf and a page. Her most difficult role had been the hind end of a lion in *The Magic Flute,* but since she had last performed it, she had grown, and now she had to play the head of the lion, for which she only received three crowns. The rear end was better paid—she had earned five crowns—because she had had to walk bent over, and "there hadn't been any fresh air to breathe."

All this Auntie had found very interesting.

Auntie deserved to live as long as the Royal Theater stood, but few people get what they deserve. She didn't die in her box either, but decently, at home, in her bed. Her last words are worth quoting: "What are they playing tomorrow?" she asked.

She must have left an estate of about five hundred crowns, judging from the interest: twenty crowns a year. This sum was bequeathed for a seat in a box, in the second circle on the left on Saturday night—when the best plays are always performed—and it was to be given to any elderly, unmarried lady without family. The beneficiary's only duty was to think—every Saturday, while she attended the performance—of Auntie, who lay in her grave.

The theater had been Auntie's religion.

## 131

## The Toad

The well was deep, and therefore the rope that held the bucket was long and the winch difficult to turn. Although the water was clear, the sun had never mirrored itself in it; but as far as its rays reached, green plants grew among the stones.

In the well lived a family of toads. They were immigrants and had arrived there—or rather the old mother toad, who was still alive, had arrived there—head over heels. The green frogs, who had been the earliest inhabitants and swam in the water, acknowledged the toads as part of the family and called them guests. The toads, however, had no thought of leaving. They lived in the "dry part" of the well; that is what they called the wet stones.

The mother frog had once been on a journey; she had traveled in the water bucket on its way up. The light had been too much for her, it had hurt her eyes; and happily, she had escaped. With a huge splash she had landed in the well again. She had survived the jump, but her back had ached for three days. She could not tell much about the world above, but that the well was not the whole world both she and her children knew. The old mother toad could have told them something about it, but she never answered any of the questions anyone asked her, which made the frogs tired of talking to her, but not about her.

"Fat and ugly, and ugly and fat, she is," they said. "And her children will be just as ugly as she is."

"It may be true," grumbled the old toad. "But one of them has a precious stone—a gem—in his head; or maybe I have it."

The young frogs heard her and stared at her but, not liking what they saw, they dived back down into the deep water. But the young toads stretched their back legs in pride and kept their heads perfectly still. After a while, when they had got tired of that, they asked their mother what it was they were proud of and what it meant to have a "precious stone" in one's head.

"It is something so valuable, so costly," said their mother, "that I cannot even describe it. One has it for one's own pleasure, and everybody envies one for having it. But don't ask any more questions, for I am not going to answer them."

"I am sure I don't have any precious stone in my head," said the smallest of the toads, who was particularly ugly. "Such splendor is not for me. And if it made everyone envy me, then it wouldn't give me any pleasure. I just wish that I could get up to the top of the well and look out, just once. That must be delightful!"

"You stay where you are," croaked old mother toad. "You know the well, and what is familiar is best. Be careful of the bucket, so you don't get hit by it. And if you should get caught inside it, jump! Though not everyone can be as lucky as I was and make such a great leap without breaking one of my legs or losing my eggs!"

"Croak," said the little toad; and that in human language means, "Oh!"

Still its longing for the green world above did not cease, and the next morning, when the full bucket paused for a moment right near the stone that the little toad was sitting on, he jumped in and lay still at the bottom of the bucket.

"Pooh! What an ugly fellow!" said the young man who had drawn the water. "That is the most repulsive thing I have ever seen." Then he poured the water out on the ground and tried to kick the little toad with his wooden shoes, but the little creature escaped among the nettles.

It looked at the stalks of the nettles and up above at the leaves; they were transparent and the sunlight sifted through them. For the little toad it was the same experience as we have when we come to a great forest and see the sunlight playing on the branches and leaves of very tall trees.

"It is much prettier here than it was in the well! I think I could stay here all my life!" said the little toad, and lay down in the nettle forest. It lay there for an hour, it lay for two. But then it started thinking, "I wonder what is beyond here. Since I have gotten this far, I might as well go on."

He crept out of the nettles and onto a road. The sun baked down upon him and the dry dust of the road powdered his little body white. "This is really dry land, almost too much of a good thing. It makes my back itch," the toad said to himself as he marched across the road. In the ditch on the other side, forget-me-nots and meadowsweet were in bloom; and on the bank of the ditch grew elderberry and hawthorn bushes; bindweed twined itself around their branches.

Here were colors to look at! A little butterfly flew up and the toad thought that it was a flower who had decided to fly out and see the world just as he had—and that was not an altogether stupid thought.

"If only one could fly like that flower," said the little toad. "Croak! Oh, how beautiful it is here!"

The toad stayed for eight days and eight nights in the ditch and didn't eat a thing during all that time. On the ninth day he thought, "I must go on," though how anything could be more beautiful than the ditch was hard for him to imagine, unless it were toads or some frogs. The night before, the wind had blown, and he had heard his cousins' voices.

"It is wonderful to live," he said to himself. "It is wonderful to have come out of the well, to have lain in the the nettle forest and to have crawled across the dusty road, and to have rested in the damp ditch; but I must go on! I must find another toad or at least a frog, one cannot do without company. Nature is not enough!" And right then and there he set out on another journey.

He wandered across a great field until he came to a lake surrounded by a forest of reeds.

"It may be too wet for you here," said the frogs, "but you are welcome. Are you a he or a she? Not that it matters, you are equally welcome whichever you are."

That night he was invited to a concert, a family concert. You know what that kind of affair is like: there's a great deal of enthusiasm with rather feeble voices. There was nothing to eat, but there were free drinks from the lake.

"I think I will move on," said the little toad. He was always seeking something better.

He saw the stars blinking in the sky, the new moon, and he noticed how the sun rose higher and higher in the heavens. "I am still in a well," he thought. "It is just a bigger one. I must try and get up higher. I feel so restless, there is a strange longing within me!"

Later, when the moon grew full and round, the poor animal thought, "I wonder if that is the bucket they will let down into the well. I will jump into it and rise even higher; or maybe the sun is the great bucket? It is so big and shines so brightly. I am sure there is room enough for all of us to get into it. I must watch for an opportunity. I have so many thoughts in my head; it feels as if a flame were burning there. I am sure it shines brighter than any precious stone. That gem I am sure I don't have; and I won't cry about it either. No, I just want to travel upward, upward to greater beauty and glory. I have faith in myself, and yet I am fearful. It is difficult to take the first step, but I must travel on: forward, straight ahead."

And it took the kind of steps that such a little animal could take, and soon it was on the road again. And then it came to a place where human beings lived. There were both a flower and a vegetable garden; the toad rested under a cabbage.

"How many different creatures there are that I have never seen before. How huge and glorious is the world! One should look around in it and not stay in one place. It is so beautifully green here!"

"I should say it is!" said a caterpillar that was sitting on a cabbage leaf. "My leaf is the biggest in the whole garden; half the world is hidden by it: the half I don't care about."

"Cluck! Cluck!" said a couple of hens who were out for a walk among the cabbages. The foremost of them was farsighted. She spied the caterpillar first, and pecked at the cabbage leaf so that the little creature fell. Once on the ground, the caterpillar twisted himself from one side to the other, while the hen looked at it, first with one eye and then with the other, wondering what it hoped to accomplish by its acrobatics. "I don't think it is doing it for pleasure," thought the hen, while she lifted her head, in readiness for pecking it.

The toad was horrified at what he saw, and hopped over toward the hen.

"So it has auxiliary troops!" exclaimed the hen. "What a horrible crawling thing!" And she backed away and let the caterpillar be. "I really don't care about that little green mouthful, it tickles your throat." The other hen was of the same opinion and both of them left.

"I wiggled away from them!" shouted the caterpillar. "It is important to keep one's presence of mind. But the most difficult problem is left. How do I get up on my cabbage leaf again? Where is it?"

The little toad was very happy that its ugliness had saved the caterpillar and offered his sympathy for its being so defenseless.

"What do you mean?" grumbled the caterpillar. "I twisted myself and managed to wiggle away from the hen. It is true that you are pretty horrible to look at, but I saved myself. I owe nothing to anyone. Where is my cabbage leaf? I smell it. Here is the stalk. There is nothing like one's own property! But I must get up a little higher."

"Yes, higher up!" echoed the little toad as he went away. "Higher up, I bet it feels just as I do. Such a frightful experience would put anyone out of humor. We all want to climb higher." And the little toad looked up as high as it could.

On top of the roof of the farmer's house was a stork's nest. The male stork was chattering with his long bill, and his wife was answering him.

Inside the farmhouse lived two young students: one was a poet, the other a scientist. One sang and wrote joyfully about everything God had created that mirrored itself in his heart. He sang about it in brief powerful verses. The other examined the things themselves—yes, even cut them up at times, if he had to. He looked at God's work as a huge mathematical formula; he added and divided, and wanted to understand everything with his mind—and it was an intelligent mind. He talked of nature with both understanding and appreciation. They were good young people, both of them.

"Look, there is a fine example of a toad. I will catch it and keep it as a specimen in alcohol," said the scientist when he saw the little toad.

"You have two already. Let it live in peace," suggested the poet.

"But that one is so wonderfully ugly," said the scientist regretfully.

"If we could be sure it had a precious stone in its head, I would help you cut it up myself," laughed the poet.

"Precious stone?" his friend retorted unbelievingly. "I don't think you know any zoology."

"I think that there is a bit of poetry in the old folklore that the toad, the ugliest of all animals, hides inside its head the most precious of all stones. Think of Æsop and Socrates: didn't each of them have a precious jewel in his unhandsome head?"

The toad did not hear any more of the conversation and it only understood half of it. The two friends walked on, and the toad escaped being preserved in alcohol.

"They also talked of precious stones," mumbled the little toad. "How fortunate for me that I do not possess one or I would have been in trouble."

From the top of the roof came the sound of the male stork clattering; he was giving a lecture to his family, but he kept his glance downward, for he was watching the two young men at the same time. "The human being is the most conceited of all the animals," he said. "Listen to them chattering; they should give their bills a rest. They pride themselves on their ability to speak, their linguistic ability! But if they travel as far as we do in a single day, they cannot comprehend one word that is spoken. They cannot understand each other, while we storks talk the same language all over the world, both in Egypt and in Denmark. As for flying, the human beings can't. When they want to move fast from one place to another, they have to use something called a railroad. It is an invention they will break their necks on. The very thought of it makes a chill run up and down my bill. The world can exist without them. We do not need human beings, all we need are frogs and worms."

"That was a great speech," thought the little toad. "The stork is a very important animal and it lives so high up, I have never seen anyone who lives higher!

"And look how it can swim!" the toad exclaimed out loud as the stork spread its wings and flew away through the air.

The female stayed in the nest and told the young ones about Egypt, about the waters of the great River Nile, and about all the remarkable mud to be found in foreign countries. It was all new and wonderful to the little toad.

"I must travel to Egypt," he said aloud. "I wonder if the stork or one of its young ones would take me. I would serve it faithfully all the rest of my days. Yes, I will get to Egypt, I am sure of it, for I am so happy. In me there is a longing and a desire that is sweet, and so much more valuable than any precious stone."

And that was the precious stone; and this was the toad who had it in his head: the eternal longing and desire for rising ever upward.

That was the jewel! That was the flame that sparkled and shone with joy and desire.

At that moment the stork came. It had spied the little toad in the grass. Its bill did not grab it gently; it squeezed the toad. He was uncomfortable and frightened, yet he felt the wind blowing around him and knew that his course was upward toward Egypt; and therefore his eyes shone with expectation, as though a spark were flying from them.

"Croak!"

The heart stopped; the body was still, the toad was dead. But the spark that had shone in its eyes, what happened to that? The rays of the sun caught it, caught the gem that the little toad had carried in its head. But where did they take it?

Don't ask the scientist that question, ask the poet. He will tell you the answer, as a fable or a fairy tale. The caterpillar will be in his story, and the family of storks as well: The caterpillar changes itself into a beautiful butterfly. The stork flies over mountains and across oceans to distant Africa, and returns by the shortest route to Denmark —to that particular place, to that particular house where his nest is. That, too, is magic and unexplainable, and yet it happens. You may ask the scientist, he has to admit it; and you yourself know it is true, for you have seen it.

But what about the gem in the toad's head?

Seek it in the sun, see if you can find it there!

No, the light is too intense; we do not yet have eyes that can see all the glory God has created. But maybe someday we will have such eyes. That will be the most wonderful fairy tale of all, for we ourselves will be part of it.

## 132

## Godfather's Picture Book

Godfather could tell stories; he knew so many and such long ones. He could cut pictures out of newspapers and could draw them himself. A few weeks before Christmas he would take from his desk a new exercise book and on its clean white pages he would paste pictures that he had cut out of the newspapers and from books; and if he had not found the right pictures to illustrate the story he wanted to tell, then he would draw them himself. When I was a little child I received many such picture books. My favorite one was called: "The Strange Year When Copenhagen Changed from Oil Lamps to Gas Lamps." At least, that was what was written on the first page.

When my parents saw the book my father said, "You must take good care of it." And my mother added, "You must wash your hands before you look at it."

Underneath the title Godfather had written:

> Be not afraid if a page you tear, while you look.
> Other little friends have done it to another book.

Best of all was when Godfather himself showed us the book. He would not only read the verses and anything else that was written on the pages, but he would explain so many things and tell so much that history became a real story.

The picture on the first page had been cut out of the *Flying Post*. It was a sketch of the center of Copenhagen, and both the Round

Tower and the Church of Our Lady were on it. To the left had been pasted a picture of a lamppost and under that was written: "Oil Lamp." On the other side was a picture of a candelabrum and under that was written: "Gas."

"That is the introduction," said Godfather, "like the playbill in front of the theater. It is the entrance to the story I am going to tell. It could have been written as a play and called: *Oil and Gas, or the Life and Career of a City: Copenhagen.* That would not have been a bad title either.

"At the bottom of the page there's a little picture that really shouldn't have been there at all; it belongs at the end of the book. It is a hell-horse: a demon, who always reads books from the back to the front, and is always dissatisfied with them because he thinks he could have written them better himself. During the day he is tethered to a newspaper, where he runs up and down the columns. At night the hell-horse is let loose and gallops straight to a poet's house, and in front of it he whinnies his message that the poor writer inside is dead. He isn't, of course: that is, if there's any life in him at all. The hell-horse is usually a poor confused fellow who can hardly earn his daily bread, which he needs in order to keep on whinnying. I am sure he will not like this picture book; but that doesn't mean that it isn't worth the paper that it's written on.

"Well, that was the first page of the book: the playbill!

"It was the last night that the oil lamps were lighted; the new gaslights were burning as well, and they shone so brightly that the oil lamps didn't seem to be giving any light at all. I saw it myself," explained Godfather. "I had gone out for a stroll that evening. There were lots of people in the streets; twice as many legs as there were heads. We had all come for the same reason: to say good-by to the old lamps and have a look at the new ones. The night watchmen stood around looking very depressed. They were not sure that they weren't going to be fired just as the old lamps had been.

"The oil lamps were thinking of the past, for which you could not blame them; they did not dare think of the future. They had a long memory and remembered much from the long dark winter nights and the still summer evenings. I was leaning against a lamppost. The wick sputtered. I heard what it said and now I shall tell it to you:

"'We have done all we could do,' began the old oil lamp. 'We have served our time. We have lighted the steps of those who were happy

and those who were sad. Many strange sights have we seen. We have
been the eyes of the city at night. Let the new lamps take over our
office. How long they will keep it and on what they will shine, only
time can tell. They shine a little more brightly than we do, but that is
easily explained. They are metal candelabra and they have connec-
tions! They have tubes that run all over town and even beyond it.
They gain strength from each other. We oil lamps gave what light we
had within ourselves, we didn't ask for help from the family. We—
and the generations of oil lamps before us—have lighted the streets of
Copenhagen since ancient times. We have been demoted, we must
stand behind you, our brighter brothers; but we shall not spend our
last night here in envy. On the contrary, we greet you—the new
sentries—good-naturedly and happily. We are the old. You have
come to relieve us of our guard duty: your uniform is brighter and
more beautiful than ours. We should like to spend the time we have
together in telling you what has happened to us and to our great-
grandparents. It will be the history of a city, Copenhagen. May you
and your children—until the last gaslight is extinguished—experience as much as we have, and may you be able to tell of it when at
last you, too, are dismissed. That time will come for you as well.
Human beings will discover something brighter than gas with which
to light the streets. I have heard a student say that eventually they will
be able to burn sea water.' At these words, the oil lamp sputtered as
if it had got water in its wick."

Godfather had listened carefully and had pondered over what he
had heard; and he thought it was admirable of the old oil lamps, on
such a night of transition, to tell the story of Copenhagen.

"When you are given a good idea you shouldn't let it go," said Godfather. "I went straight home and made this picture book for you; and
it goes even further back in time than the oil lamps could remember.

"Now here is the book: *The Biography of the City of Copenhagen*.
It begins in darkness and that is why the first page is painted black.
Now we shall turn the leaf and look at the next one.

"On this page there is only the wild ocean and the ferocious northwest wind. The wind is driving before it great floes of ice; and on
some of them there are great granite boulders that have come from
the mountains of Norway. The ice is being blown south, for the
northeast wind wants to show the mountains of Germany how huge
the granite blocks of the north can be. That fleet of ice passed

through the Sound, along whose coast Copenhagen now lies; then there were only some sandbanks, and the ice floes, carrying the big boulders from Norway, stranded on the sand.

"The northwest wind blew, but he couldn't free his fleet. He got as angry as the northeast wind can get; and then he cursed the sandbank. He called it the 'Robber Reef' and predicted that if it ever rose above the water, it would be inhabited by thieves and a gallows would be the only structure on it.

"But while he shouted and cursed, the sun came out, and its rays and beams—those sweet and pure spirits, those children of light— danced. They danced across the ice floes and melted them, and the great granite boulders sank down into the sand.

"'Rabble that follow the sun!' shouted the wind. 'Is that friendship, is that the comradeship of nature, to destroy my fleet? I shall remember this and revenge myself. I curse this place!'

"'And we bless it,' said the children of the sun. 'The sandbank shall rise above the water, and we shall protect it. The good, the true, and the beautiful shall flourish there!'

"'Chitchat and nonsense,' returned the wind.

"All of this the oil lamps could not have known about," explained Godfather. "But I know it, and it is of great importance to the history of the city."

"Now we shall turn another page. Centuries have gone by. The sandbank has risen and the great boulders that were carried from Norway by the ice floes are now sticking up above the water. A sea gull is sitting on one of them. You can see it in the picture I have drawn. More centuries pass and the sandbank itself is above water. The sea has thrown dead fish upon the beach and lyme grass has begun to appear in the sand. The tough lyme grass withers, rots, and fertilizes the sand. Slowly it changes to become a light loam. Other grasses and even herbs begin to grow.

"The Vikings landed on the island. It provided safe anchorage near the great island of Zealand. It was an ideal place to fight in single combat, and here the Vikings settled those disputes between two men, which were so grave that they fought to the death.

"The first oil lamp was lighted about that time, and it was probably used for frying fish. Fish were plentiful. There were such great shoals of herring in the Sound that boats could have difficulty passing through them. The scales of the herring glistened and reflected the sunlight, so that it appeared as though the northern lights were imprisoned in the sea. The fish brought prosperity to the shores of Zealand. Small communities grew up along the coastline. The people built their houses of oak with bark roofs, for there was wood in abundance.

"Ships seek new and better harbors; they have oil lamps hanging in their rigging. The northeast wind blew across the island and sang, 'Away. . . . Be gone! Away!' And if there was a light on that little island, then it was a thieves' light, for only smugglers and thieves landed on 'Thieves' Island.'

"'See how it grows: all the evil that I willed!' sang the northeast wind. 'Soon the tree will grow, whose fruits I shall shake.'

"And here is the tree: the gallows tree on 'Thieves' Island,'" said Godfather, pointing to the picture. "They used to hang robbers and murderers in iron chains. The wind would play with the corpses and make their limbs dance, and the moon would shine as happily upon them as it did upon those who dance in the forest. The sun rays would shine on the hanged men, too, till their bones fell from the gallows and finally became dust in the dust.

"'We know. . . . We know,' sang the sun rays. 'But in time to come it shall be beautiful here. The true and the good shall flourish.'

"'Chicken talk!' screeched the northeast wind.

"That's enough of that page. Now let's turn to another," said Godfather.

"The bells were ringing in the town of Roskilde. There lived Bishop Absalon, who could not only read the Bible but swing a sword as well. Some bold fishermen had settled with their families on the island. There was a tiny village with a market place, and Bishop Absalon had decided to protect it from pirates and foreign fleets; and he had the power to turn his will into deeds. 'Thieves' Island' was consecrated with holy water and now was a place where Christians could settle. Masons and carpenters were put to work; at the bidding of the bishop a brick building was constructed. The sun rays kissed the red walls as they were being built.

"That was Absalon's Castle, and the village around it was simply called 'the harbor,' or *havn* as it is in Danish. But the merchants who came to buy fish also built warehouses, and soon it had another word added to its name, and it was called—as it still is today—'Merchants' Harbor,' which in Danish is *København*. Foreigners have found that too difficult to pronounce and have called it Copenhagen, as the first Germans who came there did.

"The town grew and the northeast wind blew through its streets and alleys, and sometimes he carried a thatched roof away with him. 'If I cannot get inside, I shall blow around them and above them, both the houses and the castle,' he said. 'And this promise I make: the castle shall be called Absalon's stake.'

"And that happened too. I have drawn a picture of it for you," said Godfather. "See, there is a castle with a stockade erected around it, and on every post the head of a pirate has been impaled.

"Let me tell you the story, it's worth knowing and trying to understand. Bishop Absalon was in his bathhouse on the beach, and through the thin walls he heard a pirate ship in the Sound. Quickly he dressed, buckled on his sword, and blew on the ram's horn to call his men. The pirates tried to flee. They rowed with all their might, but the arrows of Bishop Absalon and his men pierced their backs and their hands. They were overtaken, and every one of them was captured. Their heads were chopped off and put on the stakes that surrounded the castle. That night when the northeast wind blew, his cheeks were large and round: 'He carried ugly weather in his mouth,' as the seamen say.

"'I'll stretch myself and rest now,' said the wind, 'and just watch what's going on.' He rested for hours and blew for days; and the years passed."

"There is a guard standing in the tower. He looks toward the east, toward the south, west, and the north. You can see him here in the picture I have drawn; and now I am going to tell you what he is looking at. He can see the shores of Zealand and across the wide bay to Køge. In the distance he can see villages. And below him the town is large and it keeps on growing. There are half-timbered houses with gables. Each of the crafts has a whole street: shoemakers, tanners, brewers. There are a market place and a guildhall. So near the sea that its spires and towers can be mirrored in the clear water, stands the Church of St. Nicholas. Not far from it is the Church of Our Lady. There they are saying mass; the air is heavy with incense, and wax candles are burning. The town of Copenhagen is in the diocese of Roskilde and the Bishop of Roskilde rules over it.

"Bishop Erlandsen is in Absalon's Castle. The cooks are busy in the kitchen. The servants are pouring wine and beer for the bishop and his men; there is the sound of lute and drums. In the great hall, wax candles and oil lamps are burning. The castle is illuminated as though it were a beacon for the whole country. The northeast wind blows above the towers and around the walls, but they are solid. The wind strikes against the west wall of the city; it is only of wood, but it holds.

"King Christopher I of Denmark is at the city gate. He has been defeated by rebels in a battle at Skelskør, and now he seeks refuge inside the walls of Copenhagen. But Bishop Erlandsen is no friend of the king and the drawbridge is not lowered.

"The wind sings the same song as the bishop: 'Stay away! The door is locked!'"

"It is a time of unrest: hard times when each man trusts only himself. From the tower flies the banner of Holstein. The country is wracked by war and war's brother, the Black Plague. It is a night of sorrow and fear that seems endless. But then there is a new king. His name is Valdemar and he is called by the people 'Atterdag'—for during his reign it became 'again day' in Denmark.

"Copenhagen is no longer a bishop's town, it is under the Crown. More houses have been built, more narrow streets have been laid, and these are guarded at night by watchmen. There is a town hall, and near the western gate has been erected a gallows made of bricks. In order to be hanged there and enjoy the view of the wide bay, you have to have been born in Copenhagen; strangers are not given such a privilege.

"'It is a beautiful gallows,' sighs the northeast wind. 'The sun rays were right: how the beautiful does flourish!'

"And from Germany there came trouble and want. It was the Hanseatic League," explained Godfather, "rich merchants from Rostock, Lübeck, and Bremen. King Valdemar had put a golden goose on the tower of his castle at Vordingborg to make fun of them. But soon these 'geese' ruled more of Denmark than did the king.

"A fleet was sailing toward Copenhagen. King Erik, the grandson of Valdemar, did not have the courage or the will to fight against his German relatives. The enemy were so well armed and there were so many of them. Taking his men with him, the king fled to Sorø: the town by the gentle lake, near the quiet forest, where he spent his days amusing himself and his court to the sound of love songs and the clinking of glasses.

"But one member of the court had remained in the city, a person with a royal heart and a regal soul. Look at the picture of her. She was delicate, almost fragile, with eyes as blue as the ocean and yellow hair. She was Queen Philippa of Denmark, who had once been an English princess. She had stayed behind in the fear-ridden city, with its narrow streets and lanes, its earthen-walled huts and stalls. The people did not know whether it was wiser to leave or to remain within the city. The queen called the peasants, the merchants, and the tradesmen together. She quieted their fears and gave them courage. Boats were manned and armed; the defenses of the city were restored. A battle was fought and God gave the people of Copenhagen victory. The sun shone again over their city. Blessed be Philippa! She went everywhere—into the huts, the hovels, the houses. She ordered that the wounded be brought to her own castle, where she herself helped nurse them. I have cut out a picture of a laurel wreath and pasted it above her," said Godfather. "God bless you, Queen Philippa!"

"Now we leap forward in time," explained Godfather. "Christian I has returned from Rome, where he has been blessed by the Pope. A great brick building is being erected. Here learning will have its seat, and here not Danish but Latin will be spoken. The poor men's sons can study here too. They leave the plow and the workshop behind, to make their way begging. In long black capes they stand before the rich merchant's house singing and waiting for alms.

"Nearby, in a humbler building, Danish is spoken and Danish customs are observed. Beer porridge when you arise and dinner at ten in the morning. The sun shines in through the tiny windows and dances on the shelves of the larder and the shelves of the bookcase, where true treasures stand: Mikkel's *The Rosary of Our Lady* and his *Divine Comedy;* Henrik Harpenstreng's *Book of Healing;* and the verse chronicles, which tell the history of Denmark, that were written down by a monk in Sorø, Brother Niels.

" 'Any Dane who can read should read these books,' says the master of the house. He is the man who makes that possible: a Dutchman named Gotfred van Gehmen. He is the first one to practice in Denmark that black, that blessed art of book printing.

"Now books are to be found not only in the royal castles but in the houses of ordinary citizens as well. Proverbs and folk songs have been given eternal life. What men have not dared utter—whether in sorrow or in joy—the folk song, saying it covertly and yet clearly, has expressed. It is a bird whose wings never have been clipped. It flies freely in the one small room of the peasant's hovel and through the halls of the mighty. As a falcon it sits on the noble lady's hand, as a sparrow it chirps in the hut of the serf.

" 'It is idle talk! It is prattle!' cries the northeast wind.

" 'It is spring,' say the sun rays. 'Can't you see that everything is in bloom?' "

"We turn the page of our picture book," said Godfather. "See how beautiful Copenhagen looks! Tournaments are being held, and contests and games. There is a procession: noble knights in armor and their ladies dressed in silk, embroidered with gold. King Hans is marrying his daughter Elisabeth to the Duke of Brandenburg. Look how young and happy she is as she stands on the velvet carpet. She is thinking of her future. Near her stands her brother, Prince Christian. In his eyes there is melancholy. He has a passionate nature. He is the friend of merchants and tradesmen, and he knows of their troubles and of the misery of the poor.

"Only God can give us happiness!"

"On the next page of our picture book," Godfather says, "the wind is blowing hard and it is sharp; it sounds like a sword that is being swung. It is a time of strife, of civil war.

"It is an ice-cold day in April. There is a crowd of people in front of the king's castle. There are also people gathering at the old customs house, near which the royal ship is lying at anchor. There are people in the windows and on the roofs, but no one is smiling. They stare sadly and intently at the castle. There is no dancing, no feasting inside; it looks as if it were empty, abandoned. No one is to be seen in the bow window where King Christian II used to stand, to look across the drawbridge and up Kings Row to the little house where his 'dove' lived. Who knows whether the young Dutch girl whom he loved so dearly was poisoned by Thorben Oxe, who has been beheaded for the crime?

"Now the great portal of the castle opens. The drawbridge is lowered. There is King Christian II. His wife, Queen Elisabeth, stands beside him. She will not desert her royal husband now that he has been deserted by everyone else.

"He is a man who behaves rashly and thinks rashly. He wants to break time-honored laws. He wishes to free the peasant and protect the artisan. He has tried to clip the wing of the 'greedy falcon'—as the nobility were called in the folk songs. But they are stronger than he is and that is why he is leaving Denmark now: to seek aid abroad. There are tears in the eyes of the citizens of Copenhagen, for they must part with their king.

"There are other voices that want to tell of the times. Some speak for and others speak against him. There are three parts in the chorus. Listen to the words of the nobility; they were written down and printed:

"'Woe to you, King Christian, who ordered the blood bath of Stockholm in which our noble cousins of Sweden were slaughtered. Cursed be your name!'

"The monks shout in agreement: 'God condemns you and we condemn you! You have brought the heresy of Martin Luther into the churches of Denmark. You have let the Devil's tongue speak from the pulpit. Cursed be your name!'

"But the commoners—the merchants, the peasants, the artisans— weep bitterly. 'Christian is the friend of the people. He made laws that the peasants could not be treated like cattle, that a man could not be traded for a hunting dog. These laws will witness of your virtue.' But the words of the poor are like chaff.

"The ship sails past the castle, and the people have climbed up on the walls of the city to get a last glimpse of their king."

"Hard times pass slowly. Do not trust your kith and even less your kin. King Christian's uncle, Frederik of Holstein, would rather be king than help his nephew. The realm falls into his hands; only Copenhagen still remains loyal to King Christian II. Duke Frederik lays siege to the city. 'Loyal Copenhagen,' the long months of its suffering have been described in song and in story.

"You want to know what happened to King Christian—'the lonely eagle' as the folk songs called him?" asks Godfather. "Birds fly far and wide over land and sea. The stork came from the south one spring and told of what he had seen:

" 'I saw King Christian in flight across the great heath in northern Germany. There he met a woman in a cart pulled by an old nag; that woman was his sister, who had been the Duchess of Brandenburg. Her husband had driven her from his home because she had remained true to the teachings of Martin Luther. On the dark heath met the two children of King Hans of Denmark, who in those times of unrest could trust neither their kith nor their kin.'

"The swallow came from Sønderborg Castle and sang its lament. 'King Christian has been betrayed. He is in a dungeon as deep as a well; there he is imprisoned. He walks round and round in his cell. His feet are wearing a furrow in the stone floor as his thumb makes a groove in the marble table.'

"The fish hawk flies over the open sea. There he has seen the ship of the brave Søren Nordby, who fights for King Christian II. So far luck has been with him, but luck is like the wind and the weather, subject to change.

"In Jutland and on the island of Fyn the ravens and the crows call: 'All goes well. War is good!' There are corpses of both horses and men for them to feed upon.

"No one feels safe; the peasant keeps a bludgeon and the townsman a sharp knife, and both of them agree, 'Kill the wolves and let none of their cubs survive.' Clouds of smoke drift across the land from burning towns. There is civil war!

"Duke Frederik took the title of king but did not live long enough to enjoy it. Now his son Christian carries on the fight. The old King Christian II is still a prisoner in Sønderborg Castle. He will never be set free, never again see his loyal city of Copenhagen.

"The young King Christian III stands where his father stood, at the gates of Copenhagen. Despair reigns within the hunger-ridden city. Leaning against the wall of the Church of Our Lady is a woman. . . . No, it is the body of a woman, and two living, starving children are sucking blood from her dead breasts.

" 'Loyal Copenhagen!' Its resistance is dying, its courage is gone."

"Listen to the trumpets and the drums, they are playing a fanfare. Dressed splendidly in silk and velvet, on horses with gilded reins, the noblemen are riding through the streets of Copenhagen on their way to the market place. The tradesmen and the merchants and the peasants are dressed in their best clothes and are walking in the same direction. Is there to be a fair? Or a tournament as there used to be in earlier times? What else could be about to happen? Is there to be a bonfire, a burning of popish books? Or is the executioner there, waiting to bind a heretic to the stake, as he has Bishop Slaghoek?

"Christian III, the ruler of Denmark, is a Protestant, a Lutheran. This is to be made known, proclaimed throughout the land.

"Noble ladies, with high white collars and little caps with pearls embroidered on them, watch the spectacle from their windows. Under a canopy stand the king's council; they are wearing the clothes that tradition demands of their office. In the center on the throne sits King Christian III, but he is silent. The chief of the council reads the decrees; they have been written in Danish, not in Latin. They are hard words, words composed in anger, words of judgment against the people for their opposition to the nobility.

"The merchants and the tradesmen lose their rights, the peasants become slaves. Then the churchmen—the monks, the priests, the bishops—are stripped of their wealth and power. The property of the Church of Rome is divided between the king and the nobility.

"Hate and arrogance are having their day. Pride rules and it is a pitiful sight.

> "The poor bird comes hobbling and limping,
> Hobbling and limping.
> The rich bird comes soaring and flying,
> Soaring and flying.

"In times of change, dark clouds obscure the heavens, but even then, the sunlight does sometimes break through. Hans Tausen and Petrus Palladius, which is only the Latin for the Danish Peter Plade, are both sons of poor blacksmiths. Hans, who is from the island of Fyn, becomes known as Denmark's Martin Luther. Petrus Palladius, once a poor lad from Jutland, is Bishop of Roskilde. Also among the nobility there is a name worth remembering: Hans Friis, Lord Chancellor of Denmark, who did his best to lighten the lot of the students. King Christian III did much for the university. Yes, there were sun rays even in those dark, dismal times."

"A new page and a new era. Near the coast of Samsø, a mermaid with sea-green hair, rises out of the water and sings to a peasant a song about a prince who will soon be born and who will be a great King.

"A legend tells that this prince was born in the open fields, beneath a hawthorn tree. There are many songs and legends about King Christian IV, for of all the kings of Denmark, he was the most loved. Remembered he will be, for all the most beautiful buildings in Copenhagen were built in his time and planned by the king himself. Who does not know them? Rosenborg, "the castle of the roses," as beautiful as the flower that gave it its name; the Stock Exchange with its great spire of three intertwined dragons' tails; the dormitories near the university where the students could live; the Round Tower, like a pillar of Urania, pointing upwards toward the sky.

"From there you can see the island of Hveen, where once stood the Castle of Urania, with its cupolas glittering in the moonlight. Within that castle lived the great astronomer Tycho Brahe. He was of noble blood and mermaids sang of him, too. Their songs told of the kings and the others—those whom the spirit of knowledge had ennobled— who had come to the island to visit this great man. He lifted Denmark's name so high that he inscribed it in the heavens; yet Denmark was not grateful and he lived in exile. In his sorrow, to dull his pain, he wrote: 'Isn't heaven above me everywhere, what more need I ask?'

"His poems and songs have the spirit of the folk song within them, the same spirit that the mermaid's song of Christian IV has."

"Now this page of the book I want you to look at very carefully," said Godfather. "There are many pictures on it, as there are many verses in the old sagas. It is a story that starts very happily and ends very sadly.

"Here is the first picture. You see a little princess dancing in a king's castle. Now she sits down on her father's lap. King Christian IV loves his daughter Eleanora. As she grows older her feminine charm and steadfast character become more apparent. Already as a child she has been engaged to young Corfits Ulfeldt, the most noble of all the noblemen. Her governess is strict, and the girl complains to her future husband that she uses the rod too much; and he defends her. She is so clever, so learned. She knows Greek and Latin. She accompanies herself on the lute while she sings in Italian. She can discuss religion, talk about Martin Luther and the Pope.

"King Christian IV rests in his grave chamber in the cathedral at Roskilde. Now Eleanora's brother is king. His court is known for its elegance and its pomp; the beautiful Sophie Amalie of Lüneburg—now Queen of Denmark—sets the style. Amid the courtly splendor, is there anyone more enchanting than the queen? Does anyone ride a horse more daringly than Her Majesty? Can anyone speak more spiritedly and with more knowledge than Denmark's queen?

" 'Eleanora Christine Ulfeldt!' answered the French ambassador, and then adds, 'In beauty and intelligence, she is superior to everyone.'

"On the polished dance floors of the castle, the thorns of envy take root; they enter the skin, they hurt; they cannot be removed and around the insult vengeance grows. 'She is a whore child. She may not drive across the drawbridge in her carriage; where a queen rides, she may only walk.' Slander, gossip, accusations, and lies fly like snowflakes in a snowstorm.

"One still night, Corfits Ulfeldt takes his wife by the hand and leads her to the city gate, of which he has the key. Outside horses are waiting. They ride along the beach. A ship awaits them and they sail for Sweden."

"Now we turn the page," said Godfather, "just as fortune turned against these two.

"It is autumn. The days are short and the nights are long. It is wet and gray. On the ramparts around the city stand full-grown trees. The wind plays with the withered leaves that still cling to the branches. Leaves fall into the yard behind Peder Oxe's great house; it stands empty. The wind plays around the home of Kai Lykke, near the harbor; it has been converted into a jail, its master lives in exile. His coat of arms has been broken in two and his portrait hanged on the gallows.

"You are wondering why all this has happened," remarked Godfather, and raised his eyes from the picture book. "I'll tell you. It is because one cannot speak disrespectfully of the Queen of Denmark and go unpunished.

"Where is Corfits Ulfeldt, once Lord Chancellor of Denmark? The wind howls like a pack of wolves. It blows across a flat field where once his castle stood. Stone by stone, it was taken down until there was only one large piece of granite left standing. The wind laughs. 'That is one of the boulders that I loaded on an ice floe in Norway and blew south. It stranded on the sandbank that became "Thieves'

Island." I cursed it. Later it was used in the building of Ulfeldt's Castle, inside whose walls his wife sang to the lute and read Greek and Latin. She strutted about proudly; now only the stone struts, it is so proud of its inscription:

> "Erected in memory of the traitor,
> Corfits Ulfeldt, to his everlasting
> shame, disgrace, and dishonor.

" 'But where is his wife: the princess, the highborn lady?'

" 'Wooooh. . . . Waaaaah . . .' pipes the wind in a high-pitched voice. 'She is in the Blue Tower, at the back of the king's castle. The waves of the ocean reach the slimy walls. She has been imprisoned there now for many years, in a chamber where the fireplace gives more smoke than heat, and there is only one window, high above, to let in the gray light. How far she has fallen: King Christian IV's beloved, spoiled daughter, the elegant lady, the favorite at court. But memory can reconstruct the glory that was and change the foul walls of the prison, cover them with the splendor of her childhood and youth. She recalls her father's mild, lovable traits, her magnificent wedding, and her years of exile in Holland, England, and on the Danish island of Bornholm.

" 'No suffering is so heavy that true love cannot lighten it.'

" 'But then she was with her husband, they had each other. Now she is alone. She does not even know where he is buried, for that no one knows.

" 'Loyalty to her husband was her crime.'

"She was imprisoned for twenty-two years," said Godfather slowly. "Outside, life went on, only inside her tower had time stood still. Life always goes on, even tragedy cannot stop it; but we will pause for a moment and think of Eleanora Christine, and the words of the song about her:

> "My oath to my husband I kept,
> And alone tears of sorrow I wept.

"Do you see this picture?" asked Godfather. "It is winter. King Frost has made so strong a bridge between the islands of Laaland and Fyn that even an army dare cross it. Charles X of Sweden takes advantage of it. Murder and plunder follow in his footsteps; want and fear are rampant throughout Denmark.

"The Swedes have laid siege to Copenhagen; their army is outside the walls. It is bitterly cold and snow is falling. True to their king and true to themselves, the men and women of Copenhagen are ready to fight for their city and for their lives. Every artisan and his apprentices, every student at the university and his teachers are helping to man the defenses. Under the worst attack they show no fear. King Frederik III has taken an oath that he will not leave the city 'but die in his nest.' He rides on top of the city walls with his queen at his side. He is courageous, steadfast, and loves his country. Let the Swedes cover their uniforms with white shirts so that they cannot be seen in the snow; those white shirts will be their winding sheets.

"The Swedish army attacks, they attempt to storm the walls of the city. Logs and stones are thrown over the ramparts. Women come, bearing caldrons of pitch and tar, which are poured on the advancing enemy. During that night king and commoner are as one man protecting his city. Copenhagen is saved! In the morning the bells of the city peal for victory and prayers of thanks are offered. Truly, during that night the commoners won their patent of nobility."

"What was the result?" asked Godfather, nodding. "Just look at the next picture. There is the wife of Bishop Svane driving in a closed carriage; but that is a privilege reserved for the ladies of the nobility. Some young, proud aristocrats stop the carriage and destroy it. The bishop's wife must walk to church.

"Is that the whole story? . . . No, it is only the beginning, and much more than a carriage will be broken—the power of the haughty nobility.

"The mayor of Copenhagen, Hans Nansen, and Bishop Svane meet, shake hands, and agree that something must be done. They speak wisely and honestly; in the churches and in their homes, the people hear of the solemn accord between the bishop and the mayor. Their words become action. The harbor is closed, the gates of the city are locked. All power is given to the king who stayed in the city in the time of peril, who said that he would 'die in his nest.' The great bells of the church are ringing. The era of the divine right of kings has begun.

"We turn the page and by the same act we travel forward in time.

"'Tallyho! Tallyho! The heather is blooming and spreading over fields where the peasant used to plow.

"'Tallyho!' Listen to the hunters' horns and the barking dogs.

There they are," said Godfather, and pointed to the picture of a hunting scene that he had pasted on the page. "King Christian V is there among them. He is young and merry. Everywhere there is gaiety, in the castles and in the burghers' houses.

"In the halls wax candles are burning, in the courtyards, torches; and Copenhagen has got its first street lamps. Everything is so new and shiny. There is a new nobility, imported from Germany. They are called barons and counts, and their privileges and their wealth increase. At court more German than Danish is heard. Yet there is one who speaks Danish purely: Kingo, a poor weaver's son who has risen to be bishop and who writes the most beautiful psalms.

"Another son of a commoner—his father was only a wine tapster— is codifying the law. The name of Christian V is engraved in gold on the cover of these lawbooks that will stand for generations to come. Griffenfeld, the commoner's son, became the mightiest man in the kingdom and was rewarded with a title and enemies. The latter proved to be the stronger. His crest of nobility was broken in two; and only at the very last minute, when the executioner's sword had already been lifted, came the reprieve: life imprisonment. He was sent to an island off the coast of Norway: Munkholm, Denmark's St. Helena.

"In the king's castle the festivities continued, the grandeur and the pomp. Here danced the courtiers and their ladies."

"Now we have come to the reign of Frederik IV, the period of the great Scandinavian Wars. See those proud ships in the harbor, see the rolling waves of the sea. Yes, they can tell stories of courage and honor, of Danish victory. We remember the names Sehested and Gyldenløve! And Hvidtfeldt, who saved the Danish fleet by staying on his burning ship until the flames reached the powder kegs and blew him and his men to heaven. We recall the times, the conflicts that raged, and the heroes. The greatest of them all was Peter Tordenskjold. *Torden . . . skjold . . .* shield of thunder, a child from the mountains of Norway who guarded the Danish coast.

"From Greenland a milder wind blows; it carries the scent of Bethlehem. Hans Egede is preaching God's word in those icy regions.

"You will notice," said Godfather, "that half this page is covered with gold; the other half has the gray color of ashes, and its edges are charred, as if they had caught on fire.

"In Copenhagen the plague is raging. The streets are empty, the doors of the houses closed. On some of them a cross has been drawn with chalk; this means that the pest is within. On others there is a black cross, for everyone within is dead.

"During the night the dead are buried. The bells do not toll. The dead—and often the dying along with them—are carried out of the houses, piled on carts that rumble through the streets with their loads of corpses.

"From the taverns come boisterous singing and rowdy screams. The survivors are trying to forget their grief and fear; they would like to escape time until this terrible time ends. Yes, all things must come to an end, no matter how horrible they are. But when one misfortune ends, another may begin. This is the end of the page but not the end of Copenhagen's misery."

"King Frederik IV is still alive. His hair is gray. From a window in his castle he looks out over his city. It is late in the year and looks as if a storm might be on its way.

"In a small house by the western gate a little boy is playing with a ball. He throws it up, it lands in the attic. The boy takes a candle and climbs up to look for it. He sets fire to the house and within minutes the whole street is ablaze. It becomes as light as day and the flames are reflected in the clouds. The fire spreads. There is so much for it to feed upon: straw, hay, firewood piled high for use during the winter, barrels filled with tar. Everything is burning and there is chaos. Weeping and screaming mixes with the crashing sound of falling beams.

"In the midst of it all is the old king. He is on horseback giving orders to try to stem the panic. Some of the houses are blown up, in the hope that their destruction will make empty places over which the flames cannot leap, but it is in vain. There is fire in the northern district of the city now. The churches are burning: St. Petri and the Church of Our Lady. Listen, the bells of one of them is playing a psalm. 'Turn Your anger away from us, Lord of Hosts!'

"The Round Tower and the king's castle are untouched by flames; they stand alone, surrounded by charred and smoking ruins. King Frederik IV does his best to alleviate the suffering of the people; he is the friend of the homeless. May God bless his name."

"Now for the next page. Here comes a golden carriage. In front of and behind it are an armed escort. An iron chain crosses the square

in front of the king's castle. It is to keep the people at a distance.
When a commoner enters the square he must remove his hat and
proceed bareheaded. People avoid walking there. But there comes one
man, his hat in hand, his head bowed, and his gaze directed toward
the cobblestones. It is the greatest man of his time, Ludvig Holberg,
the witty and clever playwright. The Royal Theater has been closed
and called a 'den of iniquity.' Laughter, song, dancing, music—
everything that is gay is now called immoral. A somber, dark Christianity rules the land."

"King Frederik V is crowned. His mother called him *der Dänen-
prinz*, for she neither could nor would speak Danish. The iron chain
is removed from the square in front of the castle. Old times make way
for new. The sun has come out. The birds are singing. The Royal
Theater is open. Danish is spoken in court again. Laughter and music
are heard. After the period of fasting come days of joy. The peasants
are dancing around the maypole once more. The arts are thriving.
Everything is in flower and the harvest will be good. The new queen,
Princess Louise of England, loves her new people. She is gentle and
kind. The sun rays are singing of three great queens of Denmark:
Philippa, Elisabeth, and Louise.

"Our bodies are more perishable than either our souls or our names.
Again from England comes a princess, so young and yet so soon to be
abandoned. Future poets will write about Queen Matilda, finding inspiration in the suffering of one so kind and lovely. The power of
poetry over man and time is great. When the Castle of Copenhagen
burned, an attempt was made to save the most valuable treasures
within it. Two seamen had been carrying hampers filled with silverware and other valuables, when through the smoke they caught a
glimpse of a bronze bust of Christian IV. They decided that it must
be saved at all cost, and left the silver and gold. King Christian they
knew from the poet Ewald's songs set to Harmann's beautiful music.
Yes, there is power in poetry and music; and one day Queen Matilda, too, may be loved when a poet has told us of her tragic life."

"Again we turn a page. The stone with the inscription to Corfits
Ulfeldt still stands, telling of his shame and dishonor. In what other
country in the world can you find such a monument? Now by the
western gate another monument is being raised. Look at it. How many
others will you find like it?

"Rays of the sun kiss the stone that is the foundation of the obelisk of freedom. The church bells are ringing, and everywhere flags are flying. The people cheer Crown Prince Frederik. Bernstorff, Reventlow, Colbjørnson: their names are on the lips of the young and the old. Gratefully, with happy hearts and shining eyes, they read the inscription:

" 'The king decrees the end of serfdom; henceforth, the aim of the laws of the land shall be to help the peasant so that he may be enlightened, industrious, honest, happy: an honorable citizen of the country.'

"The children of light sing: 'The good, the true, and the beautiful are flourishing. Soon Ulfeldt's stone of shame will disappear, but the obelisk of freedom will stand forever, trebly blessed: by God, by the king, and by the people.' "

"There is an old road that ends
where the world ends.

"The high seas are open to both friend and enemy; and the enemy came. Sailing up the Sound was the mighty English fleet. A great power had come to make war on a small one:

"Every man with great courage fought,
Counting the embrace of death as naught.

"To this day flags are flown on the second of April, in memory of Nelson's attack on the Danish fleet."

"A few years later," Godfather said, and his face became stern. "Again a fleet of English frigates is sighted in the Sound. Is it sailing for Russia or for Denmark? No one knows, not even the officers and men aboard the ships, for they are sailing with sealed orders.

"There is a legend, a folk tale, about an English captain who was present that fateful morning, when the seal was broken and the order read aloud: the command that the Danish fleet was to be attacked. According to the legend, he stepped forward and declared, 'I have taken an oath to fight for the English flag; and I would fight to my death in an honorable struggle. But I will not come sneaking like a thief in the night.' And having said these words, he threw himself overboard. His body was found a few days later by Swedish fishermen.

"Without declaring war, the English troops landed and laid siege to Copenhagen. The city was in flames, surrender was inevitable, and Denmark lost its fleet. But we did not lose our courage or our faith in God. As God could humble us, so could He raise us again. Wounds that are not fatal eventually heal. Soon the sun shone on the city. New houses were built on the ruins of the old.

"Copenhagen's history is filled with consolations: Hans Christian Oersted's discoveries were building a bridge to the future. A great building was being constructed to house the sculpture of Thorvaldsen. All the people of Copenhagen, rich and poor alike, had given money to make it possible.

"You remember the great granite blocks that came sailing down on ice floes from Norway, the ones I talked about in the beginning of the book, those on which Copenhagen was first built. Some of them were used to make the museum, where you can see the beauty that Thorvaldsen's hand has hewn in marble.

"Try to remember what I have told you. How the sandbank rose to form a harbor, on which a bishop built his castle; and later a king built a larger castle; and now a temple to beauty stands on 'Thieves' Island.' The northeast wind's curse is forgotten, and the words of the children of light have come true.

"Many storms have raged and new ones may come; but even the worst storm must end and be forgotten. Only the true, the good, and the beautiful are remembered forever.

"This is the end of the book, but not of the history of Copenhagen. Who knows what you, my child, may live to see? Often things look bad; a storm can rage, but it cannot blow the sun away. And stronger than the sun is God. He is master of more than the fate of Copenhagen."

With these words Godfather gave me the book. He looked kindly down at me. His eyes were shining; he was so sure that everything he said was true. And I took the book from his hands as carefully and as proudly as I had taken my baby sister in my arms the first time my mother allowed me to carry her.

"You may show it to your friends," he added. "And you may tell them that I was the one who cut out the pictures that are pasted in the book, and that I drew the others myself; the work is all mine.

But you mustn't forget to explain that I got the idea from the oil lamps, whom I heard talking on the last night they were lit, telling all that had happened in Copenhagen from their first night until the night the gaslights came.

"As I said, you may show the book to anyone you wish, as long as the expression in their eyes is friendly and kind, but should a hell-horse try to look at it, then close *Godfather's Picture Book.*"

## 133

## The Rags

Outside the paper mill was a whole mountain of rags. Each one had its own history and pleaded its own cause, but we do not have time to listen to them all. The rags had been collected from far and wide: some were natives, others were from foreign countries. Now it happened that a Danish rag lay close to a Norwegian one. Both of them were patriots: the Dane was as Danish as gooseberry porridge, the Norwegian as Norwegian as brown goat cheese; and as any sensible Dane or Norwegian would agree, this was what was amusing about them.

Each spoke his own language and yet they were able to understand each other, though the Norwegian claimed that there was as much difference between Norwegian and Danish as there was between French and Hebrew. "You have to go to Norway to hear the original language, raw and strong as the mountains. Danish is sugar-sweet. It's like a pacifier that has been dipped in syrup: flat and insipid."

That was the way the Norwegian rag talked, for rags are rags in any country, and are of no account except among their equals.

"I am a Norwegian," he continued, "and when I have said that I have said everything. I am tightly woven and as solid as the Archean rock of old Norway, that country which, like the land of liberty, America, has a constitution. It tickles my threads to think who I am and to let my thoughts ring out in granite words."

"But we have a literature," whispered the Danish rag. "Do you understand what that word means?"

"Understand!" The Norwegian rag repeated the word very loudly.

"I ought to take you who have never seen anything but a dull and flat country and deposit you on one of our mountaintops, so that the northern lights could shine through you—rag that you are. In the spring when the Norwegian sun melts the ice in the fjords, old Danish tubs sail up to Norway with butter and cheese which are quite eatable, but as ballast they carry Danish literature. We don't need it. Why drink flat beer when there are clear springs of pure water all around you? In Norway the wells aren't artificially drilled and then filled with European swagger, newspaper notoriety, and authors doing each other favors or telling about their precious experiences in foreign lands. I speak freely, directly from the lungs, and you, Danes, will have to get used to the language of free men. If you want to be Scandinavians, it is the proud, primeval mountains of Norway you will have to cling to."

"A Danish rag would never think of speaking in such a manner," began the Danish rag. "It would be against our nature. I know myself and, as I am, all other Danish rags are. We are good-natured and modest; we undervalue ourselves. Naturally, there's nothing to be gained by it, but I like being that way, it is so utterly charming. Just because I don't talk about it doesn't mean that I don't know how valuable I am: I do! But no one shall accuse me of bragging. I am soft and flexible and can endure anything. I envy no one and speak well of everyone, though hardly anyone deserves it—but that's their problem, not mine. I like to poke fun at everything, even myself, which proves my superior intelligence."

"Don't talk to me in that insipid, guttural, gluelike dialect from that pancake that you call a country. It makes me sick to my stomach." And with these words the Norwegian rag allowed the wind to carry it to another place in the rag pile.

Both rags were made into paper. By chance, the Norwegian rag became a piece of stationery on which a young Norwegian wrote a love letter to a Danish girl. And the Danish rag fared just as strangely. It became a sheet of paper on which a Danish poet composed an ode in praise of the loveliness and strength of Norway.

This shows that something good can come out of rags, as long as they end up in the rag pile and are made into paper, on which truth and beauty are written. Anything that helps our understanding is a blessing.

That was the story of the rags, and only rags need be offended by it.

## 134

## The Two Islands

Off the coast of Zealand, near the Castle of Holstein, there once lay two islands: Vaeno and Glaeno. There were forests, farms, and fields on both; and each had a village with a church. They lay close together and close to the coast of Zealand. Now there is only one island.

One night a horrible storm swept over the country. The waters rose so high that no one could remember ever having seen anything like it. It was weather fit for the end of the world. It sounded as if the earth were cracking; and the church bells started ringing, though no one pulled the ropes.

That night Vaeno disappeared into the sea. The following morning there was nothing on the surface of the water to prove that it had ever existed. But on a still summer night many a fisherman claimed that he had seen the island's white church tower down below, in the water, and that he had heard the bells ring. But the fishermen must have been wrong. What they probably heard were the many swans that often swim nearby; their calling and groaning can sound, in the distance, like church bells.

"Vaeno is lying at the bottom of the sea, waiting for Glaeno!" is what the legend says.

There was a time when some of the old people on Glaeno still remembered that frightful night of the storm. When they were children they had driven across in wagons at low tide to Vaeno, just as we today drive, from a point near the Castle Holstein, over to Glaeno—the water never reaches more than halfway up the wheels.

When there is a storm, many of the children of Glaeno listen terrified for the sound of rushing water. "Is it tonight that Vaeno will come and take our island?" They are so afraid that they say their evening prayers once more before they fall asleep. And the next morning Glaeno is still there with its forests and fields of grain, its picturesque little houses with gardens filled with hops. The birds are still singing, the deer jumping in the thicket, and the mole does not taste salt water no matter where he digs.

Yet Glaeno is doomed. How long it will still be there I cannot say, but one day it will be gone.

Maybe you have seen it yourself, only yesterday stood on the beach and watched the swans swimming in the narrow Sound or a sailboat gliding by. You may even have driven across to the island, the horses splashing in the water, and the cart almost sailing behind.

Now if you leave for a while to see a little of the great wide world and return in a decade or so, then you will find the forest surrounded by meadows, and your nostrils will be filled with the sweet smell of hay. There may even be some new houses you have never seen before, and you will ask yourself where you are. Holstein Castle with its gold spire will still be there as showy as ever, but it will seem as if the castle has moved a mile inland. You will walk through the forest and across the fields, and then you are at the sea, but where is the island? In front of you is the open sea. "Did Vaeno finally come to get Glaeno?" you will ask yourself. "Was there really a terrible storm one night that shook the earth and moved Holstein Castle a mile inland?"

No, no storm will have come. This will have been work done by the light of day. Human beings will have built a dam across to Glaeno and have drained the Sound. The skill of man will bind Glaeno to Zealand and make rich meadows where once there was water. Glaeno will attach itself to Zealand, and all its old farms will still be where they have always been. It will not be Vaeno that has come to take Glaeno, but Zealand, with two dikes as arms, that will grab it.

As the legend foretold, Glaeno will disappear; but Zealand will become many acres larger. Go there in a few years and you will see it for yourself: Glaeno will be no more visible than Vaeno.

## 135

## Who Was the Happiest?

"What beautiful roses," said the sunshine. "And all the little buds will soon become as beautiful as they are. They are all my children, I gave them life by kissing them."

"They are my children," said the dew. "Didn't I suckle them with my tears?"

"I should think they are mine," interrupted the rosebush. "You may call yourself godparents. As for your presents, I consider them christening gifts, for which I say thank you."

"My sweet little rose-child!" they all three said at the same time, and wished each rose the greatest happiness in the world. But that was not really possible. Only one rose could be the happiest, as one would also have to be the least happy of all the roses on the bush. But what we want to know is, which would be the happiest?

"I will find that out for you," said the wind. "I travel a great deal and am thin enough to get through the narrowest crack. I know everything inside and out."

Each rose had heard what had been said and every swelling bud sensed it.

Just at that moment a woman dressed in the black clothes of sorrow came walking through the garden. She looked at the roses and then picked one that was not completely unfolded. Just because it was not fully in bloom, she considered it the most beautiful of them all. She carried the flower to the still silent room where only a few days ago her young daughter had played and laughed happily. Now she lay in a black coffin and looked like a marble sculpture of a sleeping figure. The poor mother kissed the dead child and then kissed the rose, before she placed it on the young girl's chest, as if she hoped that the freshness of a rose and a mother's kiss could make the girl's heart beat again.

The petals of the rose shook with happiness. It was as if the whole rose swelled and grew. "I have become more than a rose, for, like a child, I have received a mother's kiss. I have been blessed and will travel into the unknown realm, dreaming on the dead girl's breast. Truly, I am the happiest of us all."

In the garden where the rosebush grew, there worked an old woman; she did the weeding. She had also been admiring the rosebush, but she had especially been observing the only fully unfolded rose among the flowers. One more day of sunshine, one more drop of the pearly dew of night, and its life would be over. Now that it had bloomed for beauty, it might as well end its days being useful, thought the woman. She picked it and put it in an old newspaper with some other flowers she had collected that had, as she said, bloomed their time. When she got home she would mix the rose petals with lavender, sprinkle a little salt over them, and put them in a jar; that was call "making a potpourri."

"I am being embalmed," thought the rose. "That is something that only happens to kings and roses. I have been the most honored. Certainly I am the happiest."

Two young men were out walking in the garden. One of them was an artist, the other a poet. Each of them picked a rose—the one he thought was the most beautiful.

The artist painted a picture of the rose that was so true to life that the rose almost mistook the canvas for a mirror.

"In this way," said the artist, "the rose will live through many, many years, while millions and millions of other roses will have bloomed and died."

The rose heard it and thought, "I am the most highly favored, the happiest."

The poet contemplated his flower and the rose inspired him. It was as if he could read a story on each petal. It was a work of love, a piece of immortal poetry.

"I am immortal!" sighed the rose. "Oh, surely, I am the happiest."

Amid all this array of perfect roses there was one little flower that had a defect. It sat by chance—or maybe good luck—hidden behind the others. The petals on one side were not exactly like the petals on the opposite side, and in the middle of the flower a little green leaf grew. This sort of thing can happen among roses.

"Poor child," said the wind, and kissed the little rose on her cheek. The flower thought it was done in homage. She knew that she was a little different from the others and that she had a green leaf growing in the middle of her flower, but she had never considered it a flaw. On the contrary, she had always thought it a sign of distinction.

A butterfly landed on the rose and kissed each of her petals; it was proposing, but the rose let it fly away without an answer. A grasshopper came; true, he landed on another flower, but it was one quite nearby. He rubbed his legs together and that is a sure sign of love among grasshoppers. The rose that the grasshopper had sat on didn't understand this; but the little rose who had been singled out for special merit, she understood it very well. The grasshopper had looked at her and especially at her little green leaf and in his eyes had been written, "I love you so much that I could eat you up." Greater love no one can show, because that means that truly the two become one. But the little rose did not want to be joined quite so firmly to the grasshopper.

The nightingale sang in the star-filled night. "She sings for me, only for me," whispered the rose with the defect or the badge of merit—all as you look at it. "Why is it always I who am singled out for recognition, and not my sisters? Why was I created so exceptional that I had to become happiest of all roses?"

At that moment two gentlemen smoking cigars came walking past the rosebush. They had been discussing roses and tobacco. They had been told that the smoke from a cigar would turn a rose green, and now the experiment had to be tried. They did not want to take one of the more beautiful roses and that is why they decided on the little rose.

"Again I am the chosen one," she cried. "Oh, I am overwhelmed by the honor, I am the happiest!" The little rose turned quite green, both from the smoke and from being so very extraordinary.

One rose was perhaps the loveliest of them all; she was still a bud when the gardener picked her. She was given the place of honor in the bouquet he made of all the most beautiful flowers in the garden. The bouquet was brought to the young gentleman who owned the house and the garden, and he took it along that evening in his carriage. The flower was the symbol of beauty amid beauty, for the young man took the bouquet along to the theater. The audience were dressed in their very best, thousands of lamps burned, and music played.

When the ballet was almost finished and the ballerina, who was the most admired dancer at the theater, came out for her last great dance, bouquets fell down on the stage like a rain of flowers. Among them was the bouquet with the rose in it, and the flower felt an indescribable joy as it flew through the air. As it touched the wooden floor, the bouquet seemed to be dancing too. It jumped and then slid along the stage. But in its final fall the rose broke her stem. The ballerina for whom, as homage, it had been picked was never to hold the rose in her hand. A stagehand picked it up, for it had fallen behind the sets. He smelled it and acknowledged its beauty, but it had no stem so he could not put it in his buttonhole. He did not throw the rose away but slid it into his pocket. Later that night, when he returned home, he filled a little liqueur glass with water and put the flower in it.

In the morning it was placed on the little table that stood beside his grandmother's chair. The old woman, too weak to get outside in the sunshine, looked at the beautiful rose and smelled its fragrance.

"Poor rose, you were meant for the rich and famous young girl and instead you have come to a poor old woman. But to her you would only have been one more flower, to me you are as lovely as a whole rosebush," the old woman said, and gazed at the flower with eyes as happy as a child's. Maybe the freshness of the rose brought back to her memories of her own youth, long ago past.

"The windowpane was broken, so it was easy for me to get in," said the wind. "I noticed the old woman's eyes and it is true they were like a child's: expectant. I saw the rose too, in the liqueur glass on the table beside her. Who was the happiest of all the roses? I know, I could tell you!"

Every rose on the bush had her own story and each of them believed herself to be the happiest; and such faith is a blessing in itself. The last rose left on the bush was certain that it was far happier than any of her sisters could have been.

"I have survived them all. I am the last one, the only one left. I am my mother's most beloved, her favorite child."

"I was their mother," said the rosebush.

"No, I was," said the sunshine.

"No, it was I who was their mother," said the dew.

"You all had part in them, and now I shall share the last rose among you." And the wind blew and scattered the petals of the flower over the branches where the dewdrops hung in the morning and where the sun would shine during the day. "I had my part in it, for I collected the stories of the roses and I will tell them to the world. Which one of them was the happiest, can you tell? I won't, I have said enough."

With those words the wind lay down behind the rosebush and the day was still.

## 136

# The Wood Nymph

We are going to Paris to see the great exhibition.

Now we are there. The journey did not take long, and there was no witchcraft involved; we went by steam, across both the sea and the land. Our age is the age in which fairy tales come true.

Now we are in the middle of Paris in a grand hotel. There are even potted plants along the staircases, and soft carpeting covers every step.

Our room is comfortable. The doors to the balcony are open, and from it you can look down on the square. There spring came that day in the form of a young chestnut tree with new and tender leaves. The other trees on the square still have barren branches, and one of them no longer belongs to the living. It has gone out, and there it lies, out-stretched on the ground, dug up by the roots. The young chestnut tree that is to take its place is still standing in the wagon which brought it this morning from the country.

It is several decades old, which is young for a chestnut tree. It grew up close to an old oak tree, under which there was a bench. Here during the summer an old priest liked to sit and tell stories to the children of the village. The young chestnut tree listened too—or rather, the wood nymph or dryad, as they are called, liked to listen. Every tree, as you know, has a nymph within it. This dryad was still a child. She could remember the time when she had been younger and the chestnut tree was so small that it had hardly reached above the tallest grass, and had been shorter than the ferns. The grass and the ferns had been full grown, but the tree hadn't. It had drunk of the air and sunshine, the rain and the dew; and each year it had grown. The wind had shaken it, but that had been necessary and only good for the tree: it was part of being brought up.

The dryad had been happy, satisfied with her lot. She loved the sunshine and the songs of the birds, but best of all she liked to listen to a human voice. She understood human language as well as she understood the animals.

Dragonflies, butterflies, even houseflies would come visiting—everything that had wings. Gossip they all did. They told about the village, the vineyards, the school, and the old castle with its park, where there were canals and a lake. Down in the water there lived animals that flew under water. They were very intelligent and knew so much that they never said anything.

The swallow had told the dryad about the beautiful goldfish, the fat tench, and the old algae-covered carp. The swallow was good at describing them, but—as she admitted herself—it wasn't the same as seeing the fish with one's own eyes. But how was the dryad ever to be able to do that? She was imprisoned in her tree and had to be satisfied with seeing the landscape from where she stood and trying to imagine all the human activity.

Guests were welcome but, of all of them, she liked best the old priest who came to sit beneath the oak tree and told stories to the children about the history of France: tales about great deeds done in bygone days, about the men and women whose names are still mentioned with reverence. The dryad heard about Joan of Arc, Charlotte Corday, Henry IV, and Napoleon. She heard the stories of the lives of all those dead whose names still echo in living hearts. France is a great country. Here freedom was born, and skill and talent are nourished.

The children listened with great attention to the old priest, and the dryad listened too. She was a schoolgirl like the others. She would look up at the sky. That was her picture book, and the ever changing shapes of the clouds were the illustrations for the stories she heard.

She was happy living in the beautiful French countryside, yet she could not help feeling that the birds, and every other animal that could fly, were more fortunate than she was. Even the fly could travel and see much more than she could.

France was so large and beautiful, as the dryad knew, and she could see only so small a part of it. The country was as wide as a world, with vineyards, forests, and great towns. The greatest of them all was Paris. The birds had been there; but she—the wood nymph—would never see it.

Among the children of the village was a little girl who was terribly poor; her clothes were only rags, but she was beautiful. She sang, laughed, and danced, and braided bright red flowers in her jet-black hair.

"You must never go to Paris," said the old priest. "Poor child, if you ever go there, it will be your ruin."

She went to Paris anyway, and the dryad often thought about her, for the wood nymph had the same longing as the girl had had for the great city.

A few years went by. The dryad's tree blossomed for the first time and the birds sang about it. A fine carriage drove by; the horses were beautiful. An elegant lady held the reins herself, while the groom sat behind. The dryad recognized her, and so did the old priest. He shook his head sadly and said: "You went to Paris and it became your ruin, poor Marie."

"She, poor!" thought the dryad. "Why, she is so different. She is dressed like a duchess, and the change was made by Paris; it must be a magic town. Oh, if only I could go there myself and see its glory, its splendors. Even the clouds are illuminated at night. I have seen it when I look in the direction of the city."

Every night the dryad looked toward Paris and saw the golden fog on the horizon. On clear, moonlit nights, it could not be seen and she missed the great sailing clouds that told her stories of Paris. A child looks at her picture book, the dryad at the world of clouds, for it is her book of thoughts, from it she draws her inspiration.

It was summer and the cloudless sky was like an empty page. For days it had been like that. Every animal, every plant dozed from the heat, and so did the human beings. Then suddenly a great bank of clouds rose in the direction where Paris lay. The clouds grew and became a gigantic mountain landscape. Then they spread until they covered the horizon as far as the wood nymph could see. Like layer upon layer of great blue-black stone cliffs, the clouds rose higher and higher in the air. Then lightning burst from them.—"They, too, are the servants of God," the old priest had said.—Suddenly a bolt of lightning, blue-white and as bright as the sun, emerged from the cliff of clouds. It struck the great oak tree and split it down to its roots; the trunk was cloven in two, as if it had wanted to embrace the messenger of light.

No brass cannon sounding at the birth of a prince has ever let forth such noise as the peal of thunder that rang out on the death of the old oak tree. The rain streamed down; then a mild wind blew: the storm was over. It was like a Sunday. The people of the village ran out to look at the old oak tree. The priest gave a little speech, and a painter made a drawing of the tree itself, so they would always be able to remember it.

"Everything passes," said the dryad. "Passes as the clouds pass by in the sky: pass and never return."

The old priest never came back. The "roof" of his schoolhouse was gone and so was the bench. The children, too, stayed away. But fall came, and winter was followed by spring and summer; and during all the changing seasons the wood nymph looked longingly at that spot on the horizon where the lights of Paris shone like a golden fog.

Trains rushed out of the city, great black locomotives running along the iron rails, both night and day. From all corners of the world people came to look at the new wonder of Paris. What was this new wonder?

"It is the flower of art and industry that now is blooming on the barren sandy soil of the Field of Mars. A gigantic sunflower on whose leaves one can read lessons in geography and statistics and become as clever as a schoolteacher. Knowledge, lifted up into the realm of poetry, to be the power and pride of nations." That was one explanation.

Here is another: "A fairy-tale flower, a lotus spreading its green leaves over the sandy ground, like a velvet carpet; it shot forth in spring and will be full grown in its magnificence come summer; but by fall it will be gone, it is a plant without roots."

Outside the military school is an area that in times of peace is called the Field of Mars. It is a large sandy expanse without a blade of grass, as though it had been cut out of the Sahara Desert, there where the mirage exists, building castles and planting gardens in the air. Now on the Field of Mars such castles were built, such gardens grew, and they were real. It was the Paris World's Fair of 1867.

"The palace of Aladdin is being constructed day by day; hour by hour, it grows more beautiful," people say. The endless halls have been decorated with colorful marble. Master Bloodless has a round pavilion of his own, to exhibit his steel and iron limbs. Works of art in stone, metal, and weaving show the diversity of mind and spirit of the people of the world. Halls of painting, of flowers, of everything that human skill and intelligence have produced, from ancient times up to our own, have been collected here.

This enormous market place—this gaudy sight—has to be transformed into miniature, into toy size, before one can understand it in its entirety. The Field of Mars has become a gigantic Christmas table, decked with everything—knickknacks from everywhere, the bric-a-brac of greatness, each nation exhibiting what is peculiarly its own.

There is a royal Egyptian castle attended and guarded by Bedouins on camels from the land of the burning sun. Russian stables, with the horses from the great steppes, are there; and even a little thatched cottage, flying the Danish flag, which is next to Gustav Vasa's house, carved in wood by the artisans from Dalarna. An American log cabin, English cottages, and French pavilions stand beside kiosks or theaters or churches in a strange and wonderful chaos. Before all these buildings there are green lawns, flowering bushes, rare trees, and little running streams of clear water. In great greenhouses tropical forests grow and magnificent roses brought from Damascus bloom. What fragrance! What color!

Artificial caves with stalactites have been placed around great pools of water—both fresh and salt—where almost all the fishes of the world can be observed. It is as if the spectator found himself on the bottom of the sea, among polyps and fishes. All of this can be seen on the Field of Mars. And upon this table decked for a feast, a swarm of ants—of human beings—perpetually moves, some walking and some drawn in little carts, for human legs soon get tired.

From morning to late in the evening, steamships filled with passengers sail up and down the Seine; every day brings more and more carriages, more coaches; and they are full. People come on horseback and on foot, and all of this stream of humanity has only one goal, the Paris Exposition.

The entrance is decorated with the flags of France, and from each of the buildings in this gigantic bazaar flies the flag of the exhibitor; the flags of all nations can be seen.

From the Hall of Technique, the machines clang, grind, and drone. From the towers, bells ring, and in the churches organs play. The sounds blend with the strange, monotonous songs coming from the oriental cafés. This is the Kingdom of Babel, where all the languages of Babel are spoken: a wonder of the world!

This is what was told about the Field of Mars, and the news spread far and wide. Who has not heard of it? It is the new wonder of the city of cities.

"Fly, little bird, and come back and tell me of it," the wood nymph prayed.

Her desire swelled and became her lifelong dream, her only purpose in living. The full moon rose in the still silent night. Suddenly a spark flew from the luminous disk. The dryad saw it, it fell toward the earth like a falling star. The branches of the tree shook as if a storm were raging. In front of it stood a gigantic, radiant shape. It spoke softly and yet as penetratingly as the trumpet that will sound on Judgment Day.

"You shall enter the magic city. Your roots shall be buried in its soil and you shall sense the whirlwind and the air and the sun of Paris. But your life will be shortened by it. The many years you might have lived out here in nature will shrink to but a fraction. Poor dryad, it will be your ruin. For your longing will not be satisfied. Instead it will grow, until your tree will seem to you a prison. Then if you leave, abandoning your tree, your life will be but half that of the mayfly: one single night. The leaves of your tree will fade and wither and never become green again."

So spoke the specter and the light disappeared. But the longing of the dryad only increased. The tree rustled its leaves in wild, feverish expectancy.

"I will come to Paris, to the town of towns," the dryad said jubilantly. "Life is beginning, it grows like the clouds; and no one knows where they are sailing."

One morning, when the moon paled and the clouds in the horizon grew red, the moment came, the promise was fulfilled.

Workmen with spades and shovels began digging around the tree and deep down underneath it. With iron bars it was forced out of the earth. Mats woven of rushes were tied around its roots and the soil that clung to them. Then it was lifted up into a horse-drawn wagon and tied securely to its sides. Its journey to Paris, to the capital of France, had begun.

As the wagon lurched forward the branches of the chestnut tree shook with the passionate pleasure of expectancy. "Let's go . . .

let's go," the dryad's pulse seemed to throb. "Gone . . . gone . . ." were the words whispered by the wind.

The dryad forgot to say good-by to the place where she had grown up: to the swaying grass, to the innocent daisies that lived beneath her shade and adored her as though she had been a princess playing at being a shepherdess.

The chestnut tree in the wagon waved its branches. Was it saying "Let's go" or "Farewell"? The dryad didn't notice. She was dreaming of all the new things she would see, that she already knew so well. No child's heart, in innocent joy, was ever more expectant, and no sensuous mind more passionate in its longing, than the dryad's were, as she started on her journey to Paris. That is why "Farewell" had become "Let's go."

The wagon wheels turned; the distant became the near and then disappeared. The landscape changed like the clouds in the sky: new vineyards, forests, villages, houses, and gardens came forward and were gone again, left behind. The locomotives passed, telling in the puffs of smoke from their stacks of the wonder that was Paris.

The chestnut tree traveled and the wood nymph journeyed inside it. She thought that everyone along the way knew where she was going. She thought that the trees along the road reached out their limbs and begged: "Take me with you! Take me with you!" Maybe they did, for in each of them lived a dryad.

The scene changed constantly. To the wood nymph, it seemed as though the houses sprouted up out of the ground. There were more and more of them, closer and closer together. On their roofs there were chimneys that looked like flowerpots set in a row. On the gables and the walls of the houses big letters—some of them several feet high—were painted; some places there were also figures.

"Where does Paris begin? When will I be there?" the dryad asked herself. The traffic increased, there seemed to be people everywhere: driving in carriages, walking, riding on horseback. More and more shops appeared. Music could be heard, song and the din of people talking, broken by loud shouts and curses from the carriage drivers. Finally the dryad, inside her tree, was in the very center of Paris.

The heavy wagon stopped at a little square. Trees were growing there, but it was surrounded by houses that were several stories high; every window was a door that opened onto a balcony, on which people stood and looked down upon the fresh, young tree that had

been brought from the country into the city, where it was destined
to replace the dead tree now lying on the ground.

As they walked across the square, people stopped to look at it, and
they smiled happily at the spring-green tree. The older trees were
still only in bud; they greeted the young tree by shaking their limbs:
"Welcome! Welcome!" The fountain that shot its stream of water
high into the air, only to let it fall and splash into its broad basin,
let the wind carry a little of the water to the new tree as a toast of
welcome.

The dryad felt her tree being lifted off the wagon and carefully
planted. Its roots were again covered with soil, and fresh turf was
placed on the scars in the lawn that the removal of the dead tree
had caused. Fresh bushes and flowers were planted near the young
tree. It was almost a little garden in the middle of the square.

The dead tree, which had been strangled by the foul, polluted air
of the city, was loaded on the wagon and driven away. People were
looking on. Young and old were sitting on benches together and admiring the new tree's green leaves. The person who is telling the tale
stood on one of the balconies and looked down into the square. I
saw the messenger of spring that had come from the country where
the air is sweet and fresh, and I said, as the old priest would have,
"Poor dryad. . . . Poor little wood nymph!"

"Oh, this is bliss! This is truly happiness!" said the dryad. "Yet I
cannot quite understand . . . cannot quite explain . . . why everything is as I imagined it, but not as I expected it would be."

The houses were so tall and so very near. There was only one wall
on which the sun really shone, and that was covered with signs and
posters. There was always a great crowd of people there. The traffic
was terrible: carriages and overcrowded coaches drove by the square
all day. No one made way for anyone else, and everyone rushed as if
only his business were of importance.

"I wish those tall houses would move a little, change shape like
drifting clouds, and allow me to see Notre Dame or the pillars of
Vendôme, and that great wonder that has attracted so many foreigners here, and that I am sure all those people who are rushing by
are going to look at."

But the buildings never moved. A little before nightfall, the lamps
were lighted. From the shopwindows rays of gaslight shone upon the
branches of the chestnut tree, almost as brightly as the sun. The stars

came out, and they were the same ones that she knew in the country. The dryad recognized them and thought that a breath of fresh air came from them: a mild sweet breeze. She felt a new strength, as if she could see the world around her with the tips of her leaves and experience it with her tiny, fine roots. She felt a part of the living, human world, which she believed was kind. All about her were motion and sound, light and color.

From the streets that led into the square, music could be heard—horns and barrel organs—and the instruments seemed to call: "Dance . . . Dance . . . Enjoy! Enjoy!"

It was a music so gay that human beings, horses, carts, houses, and trees had to dance; that is, if they could. The dryad felt an intoxicating happiness fill her heart.

"How glorious! How lovely it is!" she shouted in joy. "I am in Paris!"

The next day and night and the day that followed were alike: the same traffic, the same people went by. Life on the square was ever changing and yet always the same.

"Now I know every tree, every flower around me, every house, every balcony, every store in this little dead corner that hides from me the great city. Where is the Arch of Triumph? Where are the boulevards? Where is that great wonder that has brought people from all over the world to the city? I see none of it. I am imprisoned here among the tall houses. I know them by heart; I have looked through their windows and read all the posters on their walls. They are candy and I have had enough of it. Where is all that I heard about and which I longed for? What have I gained, won, or found by coming here? My longing, my desires, are as overpowering now as they were before. There is a life, I can sense it; and that I must grasp. I must be alive among the living, be part of the human world, and fly like the birds. I would give up the years of boredom—the everyday life that wears you away slowly, till you disappear like a fog on the meadow—for one night of being alive. I want to shine like a cloud in the sunlight, see everything as the clouds do, float in every direction, and then disappear, who knows where."

That was the sigh of the dryad and it was transformed into a prayer: "Take my life, my years, and give me instead half of a mayfly's life. Free me from my jail, give me a human shape and human happiness, if only for one night. Then punish me if you wish, for my courage, my spirit, the passionate longing that has filled my life, by destroying me. Let the young tree that was my body—my jail—die, wither and be cut down, used as firewood so that the wind can spread the ashes."

A tremor went through the tree. Every leaf quivered and the tree felt as though fire had passed through it. Then a great gust of wind hit it; its boughs bent and the figure of a woman emerged: the dryad herself. She floated down upon the grass and sat underneath the gas-lit leaves of the tree. She was as young and beautiful as Marie, of whom it had been said: "The great town will be her undoing."

The dryad was leaning against the trunk of the tree, the door of her house; but she had locked it and thrown the key away. She was so young and so beautiful. The stars saw her and winked. The gas lamps saw her and seemed to wave and shine more brightly. Her body was slender and firm. She was both a child and a maiden. Her dress was as fine as silk, and as green as the tender leaves of the tree. In her nut-brown hair was a chestnut flower that had just begun to bloom. She looked like the Goddess of Spring.

Only for a moment did she rest beneath the tree, then she was up and gone. Like a gazelle, she ran around the corner, away from the square. She darted as the light of the sun skips across a mirror—here, there. And what could be seen of her, when one got a moment's glimpse, was lovely. Wherever she tarried, her clothes changed to suit the place she was visiting and the light cast upon her.

She came to one of the grand boulevards. The gas lamps of the café and stores formed a sea of light. Here stood a row of trees, young and slender. Each of them hid its wood nymph from the arti-ficial light. The seemingly never ending broad sidewalks were like one grand festival hall. Here tables were decked with all kinds of refreshments: coffee, chartreuse, champagne. Here were exhibitions of paintings, sculpture, flowers, and colorful fabrics.

From the crowd in front of the tall buildings the dryad looked at the terrifying stream of traffic: a river of carriages, coaches, horse-drawn buses, droshkies, horseback riders, and marching regiments of soldiers. Indeed, one had to be brave to cross to the opposite shore. A bengal light was lit and from somewhere a rocket rose high into the air and disappeared. Truly, the boulevard was the great high-way of this city called Paris.

From somewhere the soft music of Italy could be heard, from somewhere else the music of Spain with the rhythmic beat of castanets. But loudest of all was the current ephemeral music-box melody: the cancan, which neither Orpheus nor the beautiful Helen had ever heard. If a wheelbarrow could have danced that melody would have made it do so. The dryad did dance; she floated and flew, and changed her color as a hummingbird does in the sun. Every house and the world within it reflected itself in her dress.

As a lotus flower, freed from its roots, drifts with the current, so the dryad drifted through the city, and everywhere she stopped she changed shape, and therefore no one could follow her, or recognize and observe her.

To the wood nymph, the world moved by like cloud pictures. Faces blended with faces. Not one of them did she recognize, none had she ever seen before. Two bright eyes came into her mind. She thought of Marie, the poor child dressed in rags, with red flowers braided in her black hair. She lived in the great city and was happy and rich. The dryad remembered her in her carriage as she had driven past the oak tree beneath which the priest had sat. "Poor Marie," he had said.

Somewhere in this chaos, in this noise, she could be found. Maybe right at this moment she was stepping out of her elegant carriage.

The dryad had come to a place where, indeed, one elegant carriage after another drew up. Servants in gold-embroidered livery opened the doors. The passengers were all women: richly dressed ladies. They walked through an open gate and up tall broad stairs that led to a building with white marble columns. Was that the "wonder of the world"? Surely Marie would be in there.

"Santa Maria," sang the choir. Clouds of incense hung in the still air under the great gilded arches where dusk reigned eternally. The dryad had entered the Church of Mary Magdalene.

Clothed in costly black dresses sewn according to the latest fashion, refined, wealthy ladies strode across the marble floor of the church. Their prayer books had coats of arms depicted in silver or gold on their velvet bindings. On their perfumed handkerchiefs, fringed with Brussels lace, the same emblems of vanity were embroidered. Some of the ladies were kneeling in silent prayer in front of the altars, others were in the confession boxes.

The dryad felt a strange agitation, a fear that she had entered a place where she was not allowed to be. This was the home of silence, the grand palace of secrets. Here no one talked, but all whispered; almost soundlessly they confided what could not be said aloud.

The dryad saw herself disguised in black silk, wearing a veil. She looked like any of the noblewomen around her: were they, too, children of longing? Someone sighed, so deeply, so painfully. Did it come from a dark confession box or from the breast of the poor wood nymph? Here she breathed not fresh air but incense. This was not the place where her yearning could find rest.

Away! Away! In constant flight, for the mayfly cannot rest; to that poor insect, flight is life.

Once again the dryad was out on the boulevard, underneath the gas candelabra. Near her was a beautiful fountain. Someone in the crowd said, "Not all the water in the fountain can wash this place clean of the innocent blood that once was shed here." They were foreigners—visitors. They spoke loudly, for they meant to be heard; they were not like the people in the palace of secrets that the dryad had just come from.

A large slab of stone was lifted and turned like a door. The dryad looked into a dark passage leading down into the earth. She did not know what it was or where it led to. The strangers decended into the dark, away from the starlit night and the bright gaslight, away from life itself.

"I'm afraid to go down," one of them said. It was a woman. "Please stay up here with me. What's the point of seeing that?"

"You want to go home without having seen this? Why, people call it the wonder of our time, and it was created by one man's genius," replied her husband.

"I don't care, I am not going down," said the woman.

"The wonder of our time!"

The words were repeated and the dryad understood them. This must be the wonder that she had wanted to see, the goal of her longing. This was the entrance; but that this "wonder" would lie deep underneath the city of Paris, she had never thought possible. Still, that was what they said, and when she saw the strangers descend she followed them.

The iron stairs that led down like a spiral were broad and comfortable. A lamp lighted the shaft; deep down she could see another lamp.

They were in a labyrinth of vaulted corridors and halls. All the streets of Paris were here reproduced, like a reflection in a dirty mirror. The names of the streets could be read on large signs and every house had a number down here too. These were the roots of the houses. Along the canals of mire ran narrow macadamized sidewalks. Above the canals were pipes of fresh water, and under the vaulted ceiling a mass of telegraph wires and gas pipes could be seen. A few widely separated lamps lighted the scene. Every once in a while one could hear the rumble from above, as a heavy cart drove across one of the stone entrances.

Where was the dryad? You have heard of the catacombs of Rome. Well, they are nothing compared to this new subterranean world of our times, the wonder of the world, the sewage system of Paris. It was here the dryad had come, instead of to the Field of Mars where the World's Fair was located. Around her, her fellow spectators spoke enthusiastically about what they were looking at.

"From this place grows the health of the city. Good sewers will add years of life to the citizens who live above them. Our age is the age of progress, and progress is a blessing."

That was the opinion of a human being spoken in human language. But it was not the opinion of the citizens of the sewers themselves, those who had been born and bred there. The dryad could hear them whimper and whine behind the walls. An old male rat, who had had half of its tail bitten off, squeaked, heart-rendingly, his feeling in the matter—which was the only correct one, as his whole family agreed.

"It makes me sick to my stomach, all this meow, this human meow: 'Isn't it beautiful here, with gas and porcelain!' That is the voice of abysmal ignorance speaking. Who eats gas and porcelain? I don't! The sewers have gotten so light and clean that it makes you feel ashamed; and the worst of it is that you do not even know why you feel ashamed. I wish I lived in the age of the tallow candle. It is not so long ago. That was the romantic period, as the human beings call it."

"I didn't hear everything you said, and I don't quite understand you. Won't you explain it to me again?" asked the dryad.

"He was talking about the old times," squeaked the other rats in a chorus. "The wonderful old times of our great-grandfathers and great-grandmothers. It was very elevating for a rat to be allowed to live down here then. It was the greatest rats' nest in all of Paris. Old Mother Plague lived down here. She killed human beings but never rats. Robbers and smugglers could breathe freely here; this was the refuge of the most interesting personalities. Today you can only meet such people in the melodramas at the theaters. The times of romance are over even in our rats' nest. Fresh air and petroleum have killed it." This was the manner in which the rats squeaked against the modern times and in favor of the old: of the time of Mother Plague.

In the largest of the tunnels, the sidewalks were so broad that a little cart could be driven there. The company stepped on board and the two little horses drew them briskly along underneath the great Boulevard Sebastopol; just above them milled the crowds of Paris. The cart disappeared in the darkness. The dryad was not among the passengers. She had returned up through the entrance shaft to the world of light above. She felt sure that the wonder she was seeking could not be found in the silent, vaulted passages below the earth. No, the wonder of the world that she sought in this short life of hers, of only one night, must shine even brighter than all the gas flames of the city; yes, even brighter than the moon, which was just rising.

There it must be! The wood nymph saw an entrance brightly lighted by a hundred lamps, and she thought that they were beckoning to her.

Through the radiant portal she entered. The garden was filled with light and music. Gaslights illuminated little lakes in which artificial lotus flowers floated. In the center of these tin flowers—which had been cut out, shaped, and painted most charmingly—a jet of water rose. Weeping willow trees lined the shores; their long, fresh, green branches hung like a veil down into the water. A fire was burning and its red light shone upon the small, silent bowers within the garden. Music tickled the ear, charmed and captivated the listener, making his blood rush more quickly.

There were young girls everywhere. They were beautiful and dressed as though they were at a ball. On their lips were innocent smiles; they were lighthearted, ready to laugh: "young Maries" with roses in their hair, but without carriages or grooms. How wildly they danced; they were dancing the tarantella. They were ecstatic. They twisted and twirled as if the music bit them. They laughed and seemed so happy to be alive that they could have embraced the whole world.

The wood nymph felt herself being carried away by the music and the dance. On her little feet were fine silk boots made for dancing. They were chestnut brown, the same color as the ribbons that hung from her hair down over her bare shoulders. Her green silk dress moved in waves as she danced, and did not hide her pretty legs or her little feet that made magic circles in the air to enchant any young man who saw them.

Where was she? Was she in the magic garden of Armida? What was the name of this place?

It could be read outside above the gate in colored gaslight; it was called:

MABILE

The clapping to the rhythm of the music, the splashing sound of the water from the fountains, and the loud thump when champagne bottles were uncorked, blended together. A rocket rose, the dance grew as wild as a bacchanal, while high above in the sky the moon sailed a little crookedly. The air was fresh and the sky was cloudless. It was as if one could see right up into heaven from Mabile. The dryad felt herself being devoured by her own lust for life, as though she were in an opium dream.

Her eyes spoke and her lips spoke, but her words could not be heard above the music of the violins and the flutes.

Her partner whispered something in her ear, as their bodies swayed to the rhythm of the cancan. She did not understand his words—we do not understand them. Her partner stretched out his arms, intending to embrace her, but he encircled only the gaslit air.

A current of air had carried the dryad upward as the wind carries the petal of a rose. From up there she saw a flame, a blinking light from a tall tower. It was the beacon from the Field of Mars, the vision that was the goal of her dreams. She was borne by the spring wind to the great red lighthouse. She encircled it and then descended to the ground. Some workmen who had watched her thought they had seen a butterfly that was gliding to earth to die, because it had come too soon.

The moon shone, and gaslights and lanterns illuminated the great exhibition halls and the pavilions representing all the countries of the world. The light shone on the paths and the grass and the high cliffs that had been built so a waterfall could cascade down over them. Master Bloodless, the machine, pumped it back up so it could repeat its journey. Inside the mountain were caves, where there were great aquariums in which all the fishes of the world could be seen. One felt as if one were visiting the very depths of the ocean in a great glass diving bell. The water pressed against the thick glass walls. A great slimy, cunning octopus with its long tentacles descended slowly to the bottom; a big lazy flounder lay comfortably in the sand; a crab crawled like a giant spider, while the shrimps swam swiftly by—they are the butterflies or moths of the ocean.

In the fresh-water basins water lilies grew, amid reeds; and the goldfishes stood in rows like little cows tethered in a field. All had turned their heads in the same direction and their mouths were open; that was because of the current. Big fat carp glared with their stupid eyes through the glass wall. They knew where they were, they had journeyed for days in barrels filled with fresh water to get there. The railway trip had made them landsick and they had been as uncomfortable as some human beings are on board a boat. They had come to see the Paris World's Fair, too, and they saw it from their own particular fresh-water box. The fishes saw the mass of human beings who passed during the day and evening in front of the glass walls, and they thought that all the men and women of the world had been gathered here and put on exhibition so that they could look at them, examine them, and discuss them.

"They have scales just as we do, but they can change theirs. They do it two or three times a day," said a little muddy roach. "And they can make noises with their mouths—talk, they call it. We don't change our scales; it is indecent. And when we want to express ourselves we do it with the corner of our mouths and our eyes. We are far more advanced than man."

"They have learned to swim," said another little fresh-water fish. "My home is a very large lake and I have often seen human beings swim in it. But first they take off their scales and then they swim. I think the frogs have taught them: they kick with their hind legs and row with their front ones. They can't do it for very long though. They want to be like us, but they won't achieve it, poor things!"

The fishes stared. They thought the teeming multitude of human beings that they had seen during the daytime were still there. They were sure they still saw the very figures that had first made an impression on their senses.

A little perch with tiger-striped skin and a beautifully rounded back told everyone that the "human mud" was still there, she could see it.

"I can see them, too, very distinctly," said a tench, with yellow skin as if she were suffering from jaundice. "I see very clearly a lovely-shaped human being: a legged lady. I think she is female. She has our eyes, made for staring, and a big mouth that slants down in the prettiest manner. She is well fed and that shows both in front and in back; but she has seaweed around her neck and loose scales on her body. She ought to get rid of all that and do as we do. If she would let herself be as the Creator made her, then she would make quite a decent tench."

"What happened to the one in the chair? The one they pushed?"

"The one who had paper and ink and wrote everything down? The others called him a writer!"

"He is still out there," answered an old algae-covered carp. She was an old maid whom the world had treated cruelly. She had swallowed a hook when young and still carried it in her throat, which made her hoarse, poor thing.

"A writer," she said, "is a kind of octopus among human beings."

This was the way the fishes talked in their artificially made lakes. The exhibitions were closed for the night, but still the sound of hammer and saws could be heard inside the caves, for the work wasn't altogether finished. In the daytime there were visitors, so the night had to be used for work. Some of the workmen sang, and their song became part of the dryad's "Midsummer Night's Dream," which would soon be over.

"There are the goldfishes!" The dryad nodded to them. "I know you, the swallow told me about you, and now I have seen you. How beautiful you are, all shiny. I could kiss every one of you! I recognize the rest of you, too. There is the tench, and the perch and the fat old algae-covered carp. I know you, but you do not know me."

The fish stared. They did not understand a word she said.

She was gone. She had left the cave to go out into the fresh air, into the great gardens, where plants from all the countries of the world blossomed: the lands where black bread is eaten, the ones where the codfish is dried, where eau de cologne is made, where camphor is produced—all different and strange to one another.

When we drive home in the early morning, after having attended a ball, all the melodies we have heard still echo in our ears, and we can hum every one of them. They say, too, that in the pupils of a dead man's eyes are photographed the last things he has seen, and the picture fades slowly. For the dryad, the hours of the night still seemed to contain the noise and bustle of the day before, and because she could still sense it all, she thought: "Tomorrow it will all be repeated, and again the river of life will roar and rush through this river bed."

The dryad stood among the roses and thought she recognized them. They were the roses from the castle park and the priest's garden of the village she came from. There was a pomegranate flower like the one that Marie had worn in her black hair. Memories from home, from the country, invaded her mind, filled her thoughts. But still her eyes craved to see more, and a restless fever racked her body. She hurried on through the great halls filled with wonders.

She felt more and more tired. She wanted to rest, to lie down on the thick colorful carpets from India, or sit under the weeping willow tree near the clear pool of water. But the mayfly cannot rest; in minutes her life would be over.

Her body shook, her mind trembled. She fell in the grass by the running water.

"You who spring from the depth of the earth and have everlasting life," she whispered, "let me drink from you. Refresh me, eternal one."

"I do not spring from our eternal mother," answered the water. "My water rushes because a machine wills it."

"Let me borrow freshness from you, green grass and flowering plants, please!" pleaded the dryad.

"If we are torn from the soil where we grow, then we die," answered the grass and the flowers.

"Then kiss me, wind. Kiss me once more, you giver of life!"

"Soon the sun will kiss the clouds until they blush," answered the wind. "Then you will be among the dead. Gone, as all this will be gone before the year is over. Then the Field of Mars will again be my playing field, and I shall blow its dust into little clouds, for all is dust, only dust."

The dryad felt the fear and terror of a woman who has committed suicide in her bath by cutting the veins of her wrists and sees the blood leaving her body, while she still wants to live. She rose, took a few steps, and then fell again, this time in front of a little church. The doors were open, candles burned, and from the inside of the church music from the organ could be heard.

What strange music. The dryad had never heard such melodies before, and yet it was as if it spoke with a voice well known to her. The voice was her own, it came from the very depth of her soul, from the heart of all things created. She heard the wind play in the old oak tree, and the voice of the old priest telling his stories of great men and the gifts they had given to future generations: the gifts they had had to offer in order to give life to their names.

The tones of the organ grew louder and seemed to speak: "Your longing, your desire, tore you from the place that God had given you; that was your tragedy, poor dryad!" The music changed, grew softer. Now it sounded like a lament, then slowly it ceased. In the heavens toward the east, the clouds were red, the wind sang its monotonous song.

"Be gone, all you who are dead, now the sun is rising."

The first of its rays fell on the dryad. Her body shone in all the colors of the rainbow, like a soap bubble before it bursts and becomes a drop of water: a tear that falls to the earth and disappears. Poor dryad, a dewdrop was all that was left, a pearl of water, and then she was gone.

The sun shone on the fata morgana on the Field of Mars; it shone on the great city of Paris, on the square with the fountain and the tall houses. The chestnut tree stood with sagging branches and dead leaves. Only yesterday it had seemed as green as spring itself. Now it was dead; the dryad had left it, as people said. She was gone like the clouds, no one knew where.

On the ground lay a withered chestnut flower. Holy water from the church could not bring it back to life. Soon the feet of passers-by would tread it down into the dust.

This all happened, I saw it myself, during the great World's Fair of Paris, in the year 1867, in our own wonderful times, the age when fairy tales come true.

## 137

# The Family of Hen-Grethe

Hen-Grethe was the only human being who lived in the fine new house that had been built on the manor for the hens and the ducks. It stood on the site of the old castle, which had had a tower, corbie gables, a moat, and a drawbridge; but nothing was left of that now. There had been a garden that stretched as far as a lake, but that was now a swamp, and a wilderness of trees and bushes led down to it. Crows, jackdaws, and rooks flew among the old trees and filled the air with their hoarse screams. There were so many of them that, even though the squire did shoot them, there never seemed to be any fewer; indeed, they always seemed to be increasing. You could hear them inside the henhouse where Hen-Grethe sat with the ducklings running all about her—they even stepped on her clogs. She knew every hen and duck from the moment it hatched. She was proud of them and proud of the good house that had been built for them. Her own room was clean and neat; the lady of the manor demanded that. It was she who had ordered that the henhouse be built, and she often brought her guests to see "the barracks of the ducks and hens," as she called it.

In Hen-Grethe's room there were a wardrobe, an easy chair, and even a chest of drawers on top of which rested a polished brass plate with the word "Grubbe" engraved in it. That was the name of the very noble family who had once owned the old castle. The brass plate had been found when the foundations of the henhouse were dug; and the local schoolteacher had declared that it had no value except a historical one. The schoolteacher, who was also a deacon, knew a great deal about the castle and its history. He had his knowledge from books. The drawer of his table was filled with notes that he had made. He knew a lot about olden times but maybe the oldest crow in the trees knew as much as, if not more than, he did. But the crow spoke crow language, and however learned the deacon was, he did not understand it.

On summer days when the weather was warm, a fog would lie over the swamp where the rooks, jackdaws, and crows sat in the trees, and then it would again look like the lake it once had been when the castle was there with its red brick walls and the most noble knight, Grubbe, living in it. Then a fierce watchdog had dragged its chain in front of the gate. Let us enter through the door in the tower and walk along the stone-paved corridors that led to the rooms.

The windows were narrow and the windowpanes small even in the hall, where the dances were held. During the time of the last Grubbe there had not been any dancing. Still in a corner of the hall stood an old kettledrum; it had served its time. Here, too, was an old, intricately carved chest in which Mistress Grubbe kept rare flower bulbs, for she was interested in gardening; she planted trees and grew herbs. Her husband was more interested in hunting wolves and wild boars, and his daughter Marie rode beside him on these wild hunting trips. Ever since she was five years old, little Marie had sat proudly on a horse, her black eyes staring without fear at everything about her. She liked to let the dogs feel her whip, but her father would have preferred that she used it to lash out at the peasant boys who came to watch their master and the young mistress.

There lived in a hut near the castle a peasant who had a son named Soren; he was the same age as the young noble lady. He was good at climbing trees and little Marie often ordered him up in the highest ones to fetch birds' nests for her. Once a mother bird attacked him and pecked him above one of his eyes. It bled a great deal; and at first they thought that he had lost his eye, but it had not been harmed. Marie called him "my Soren" and that was a great honor, which once benefited his father, poor Jon. He had done something wrong and was condemned to ride the wooden horse. That "animal" stood firmly with its four legs made of beams on the cobblestones of the courtyard. Its back was one narrow plank; this poor Jon had to straddle. In order that he should not sit too lightly, heavy stones were tied to his feet. Jon's face was drawn in pain, and little Soren cried and begged Marie to help his father. She ordered that Jon's father be set free at once, and when no one paid any attention to her, she pulled on her father's sleeve until she ripped it. She stamped her little feet. She wanted to be obeyed and she was. Soren's father was released. Mistress Grubbe came, and her hand stroked her daughter's hair lightly. She looked at her with warm approval but little Marie did not understand why.

She wanted to be with the hunting dogs, not with her mother in the garden. She watched her mother walking down toward the lake where water lilies bloomed and bulrushes stood among the reeds. She did not see any beauty in all this luxuriant and yet fresh greenness. "How ordinary, how common it is," she remarked.

In the middle of the garden stood a copper beech. Marie's mother had planted it herself; in those days it was a very rare tree. Its leaves were dark brown; it was a Moor among all the green trees. The copper beech needs plenty of sunlight; if it stands in the shade, its leaves will stay green, and then it will look like any other tree. There were also some tall chestnut trees; in them and in the bushes there were birds' nests. It was as if the birds knew that the garden was the safest place to build; here no one dared to shoot them.

Little Marie Grubbe went down to the garden one day with Soren, who, as we know, was good at climbing trees. That day many eggs and downy little chicks were gathered. Birds flew up in fury and fear. All tried to fly, both the big and the small—the plover from the field; and the rooks, crows, and jackdaws from the tall trees in the garden, shrieked and cried as shrilly as they do today.

The noble Mistress Grubbe came running from the castle. "What are you doing? . . . It is ungodly!"

Soren looked down at his feet. Maria, too, looked away, but she said glumly: "I have my father's permission to do it."

"Away! Away!" screamed the large black birds, and flew; but they came back the next day, for the garden was their home. The noble mistress of the castle, however, did not stay. God called her and she went; and maybe His house was a more fitting home for her than the castle had ever been. The bells tolled when her corpse was driven to the churchyard. Many a poor man had tears in his eyes, for she had been kind and good.

When she was gone, no one any longer took care of the garden and it became a wilderness.

Squire Grubbe was a hard man, so the peasants said. But his young daughter could handle him. She made him laugh and he always let her have her way. She was only twelve but strong and well built. She rode a horse like a man, handled a gun like a hunter, and looked boldly at everyone with her black eyes.

The most distinguished men in Denmark—the young king and his friend and half brother, Master Ulrik Frederik Gyldenløve—had come to hunt wild boars in the district, and they stayed the night at Squire Grubbe's castle.

At dinner Master Gyldenløve sat down next to Marie. He gave her a kiss, as if they were related. Marie slapped his face and told him that she hated him. Everybody laughed as though this were the funniest of jokes. And maybe it was a good joke, for five years later, when Maria was seventeen, a letter came from Master Gyldenløve asking for her hand—that was something!

"He is the noblest and most gallant man in the kingdom," said Squire Grubbe. "A proposal like that is not easy to reject."

"I do not care much for him," Marie Grubbe said thoughtfully, but she did not refuse Master Gyldenløve, the nobleman who was always at the king's side.

Silverware, linen, and most of her clothes were packed and sent by ship to Copenhagen. Marie traveled by land; it took ten days. The ship ran into bad winds or no wind, and it was four months before her goods arrived, and by that time Mistress Gyldenløve was gone.

"I would rather sleep on straw than in his silken bed, and I would rather walk on bare feet than ride in his coach," she had said.

Late one November evening, two women came riding into the town of Aarhus from Vejle, where they had been brought by ship from Copenhagen. One of them was the wife of the half brother of the king, Mistress Gyldenløve, and the other was her maid. They walked up to the locked entrance of Squire Grubbe's town house. He was not pleased to see his visitors. He spoke harshly to his daughter, although he allowed her and her servant to stay in his home. The following morning, with her porridge, Marie was served more words of reproach, and they were not easy to swallow. Her father showed his hardness and ill temper, and that Marie was not used to. But she herself was not meek, and she answered as rudely as she was questioned.

Of her husband she spoke with bitterness and hatred, and said that she would never go back to him, for she had too much self-respect.

A year went by, and it was not a happy year. Cruel words passed between father and daughter, and cruel words bear evil fruit. How was it all going to end?

"We two cannot live under the same roof!" her father finally said. "Go. . . . Move to the old castle but, mind you, it would be better for you to bite off your tongue than to start spreading lies."

So father and daughter parted. Marie and her maid journeyed to the old castle where she had been born and brought up, and where her mother—the silent, noble, pious lady—rested in her grave chamber. An old cowherd was the only person still living there. He and the maid became Marie's only servants. The rooms were filled with spider webs that were black with dust. Bindweed and wild hop vines made nets between the bushes and the trees in the garden. Hemlock and nettles flourished. The copper beech's leaves were now green as though it were an ordinary tree, for it stood completely in the shade; its time of glory had passed.

Rooks, crows, and jackdaws in great flocks flew above the tall chestnut trees. They screamed and cried as though they had some important news. "She has come again," they said. But where was the other egg thief? The boy had become a seaman. Now he climbed a leafless tree to sit high up in the mast, and got a taste of the cat-o'-nine-tails when he didn't behave.

All this the schoolteacher told us. He had collected the information from old books and letters, and they lay, together with his notes and other printed matter, in his table drawer.

"Up and down, that is the way of the world," said the schoolteacher. "But it is a very strange story you are about to hear."

Although we want to hear more of Marie Grubbe, we must not forget Hen-Grethe. She sits in her nice henhouse in our own times, as Marie Grubbe sat in her castle then; but Marie didn't have old Grethe's kind disposition.

Winter passed, spring and summer passed, and again it was autumn. The fog swept in from the sea, wet and cold. Life in the castle was boring and lonely.

Marie Grubbe took down her gun and went hunting on the heath, shot foxes and hares and whatever birds came within range. Out there among the heather-covered hills she met another hunter with his gun and his dogs, the noble Palle Dyre from Norrebaek. He was big and strong and loved to boast. In imitation of the late Squire Brockenhouse of Egeskov, whose strength was legendary, he had suspended an iron chain from the top of the entrance gate of his estate; to the chain was attached a hunting horn, which he would blow, on arriving home, by grabbing hold of the chain while he pressed his legs around the horse, lifting both himself and the animal off the ground.

"Come and see me do it for yourself, Mistress Marie," he invited. "At Norrebaek, the winds blow freshly!"

Exactly when she went to his manor to live we do not know, but on one of the candlesticks in the church is engraved that it was a gift from Palle Dyre and Marie Grubbe of Norrebaek.

Palle Dyre was big-bodied and strong. He drank like a fish. He was a bottomless barrel that never could be filled. He snored like a whole pigpen; his face was red and his skin spongy.

"He is as sly as an old boar and as mischievous," said his wife, who was soon tired of that sort of life, but being tired of it did not change it.

One day when the table was set for dinner, no one came. The master was fox hunting and the servants could not find their mistress. Palle Dyre came home near midnight, but his wife did not, nor did she come the next morning. She had saddled a horse and ridden away. She had turned her back on Norrebaek without even a word of farewell.

The weather was gray and wet, a cold wind blew. Some crows flew screaming above her; the birds were not as homeless as she. She rode south all the way to the German border. There she sold her golden rings with their precious stones and her horse. She walked east, turned and went west, for her wandering had no goal. She was angry at everyone, even God; and her spirit was wretched and broken. Soon her body was as weak as her soul. She felt that she could not walk any farther. The lapwing flew from its nest and cried as it always cries: "Thief, thief!" Marie Grubbe smiled. She had never stolen her neighbors' goods, but birds' eggs and chicks she had ordered to be brought to her when she was a girl; she remembered it when she heard the cry of the bird.

Finally she fell. From where she lay she could see the sand dunes; on the beach fishermen lived, but she was too sick, too weak, to go that far. The big white gulls flew over her and screamed as the rooks, crows, and jackdaws had screamed in the garden at home. The gulls came nearer, and suddenly it seemed to her that they were not white but black; and then she remembered no more.

When she opened her eyes again, she was being carried by a man. She looked into his bearded face. He had a scar over one eye that split his eyebrow in two. He carried her, sick as she was, down to a boat. The captain did not praise him for the deed, but he was allowed to take her on board.

The next day the ship sailed. Marie Grubbe had not been returned to land. What happened to her? Where did the ship carry her?

To these questions also the schoolteacher knew the answers. But this was not a story he himself had pieced together; he had read it in a book. The Danish author, Ludvig Holberg, who wrote so many books worth reading and so many comedies worth seeing, that bring to life his times, described in his letters how and where he met Marie Grubbe, and that tale is worth hearing. We shan't forget Hen-Grethe because of that, she is still sitting in her henhouse, happy and contented.

Marie Grubbe sailed away on board the ship; that's where we left off. Now we will start again but many years later.

It is 1711. The plague is raging in Copenhagen. The queen had departed for her native Germany, the king, too, had thought it better to leave, and those of the citizens of the capital who could, followed the royal examples. The students, even those who had free room and board, sought refuge in the country. One of the last of the students to leave—he lived at Borchs Collegium near the Round Tower—departed from the stricken town early one morning. It was two o'clock; on his back he carried a knapsack, which had more books in it than clothes.

A damp fog hung over the city. The streets were empty. On some of the doors crosses had been painted; which meant that the pest was within or that all the inhabitants were dead. Even on the main thoroughfare, from the Round Tower down to the king's castle, not a person was to be seen.

A large public hearse rumbled by. The driver swung his whip, the horses galloped. It was filled with corpses. The young student took a sponge soaked in ammonia out of a little brass box and held it up to his nostrils. From a tavern in one of the narrow streets the noise of hysterical laughter and drunken singing could be heard. It was frightful: people were drinking to forget their fear, to forget that the pest stood outside the door, beckoning them to take their places on the hearse among the dead. The student had reached the pier near the castle. A couple of small ships were moored there. One of them was getting ready to sail away from the plague-infested town.

"If God wills and the wind will blow, we are sailing to Grønsund near Falster," the captain said, and asked the young man, who wanted passage, what his name was.

"Ludvig Holberg," answered the student, and that name sounded then as common as any other name, for he was not yet the most famous of all Danish writers; he was just another student.

The sun had not risen yet. The ship passed the castle silently, and soon they were out on the open sea. A light breeze blew and the sails filled out. The young man sat down, leaned up against the mast and, breathing the fresh air, soon fell asleep, although this was hardly advisable.

Only three days later, the ship lay off the shore of the island of Falster. "Do you know anyone around here who might put me up and not charge too much?" the student asked the captain.

"I think you might do best with the ferryman's wife at Borrehuset," he said, and then added with a grin, "If you want to speak politely, then she is called Mother Soren Sorensen Miller, but be careful and don't speak too refined, for she has no use for that. Her goodman is in jail for some misdeed or another, so she rows the ferry herself. She has hands fit for it."

The student took his knapsack and walked to the ferryman's house. The door was not locked and he entered. The main room had a cobblestone floor. A bench covered with skins, which could be used as a bed at night, was the most imposing piece of furniture in it. A white hen who had chicks was tied to the leg of the bench. She had upset her trough and the water was running all over the floor. In a small room next to the large one, there was a cradle with a baby in it; otherwise the place was empty. The young man walked outside again. The ferryboat was coming. There was only one person in it, the one who was rowing. It was hard to see whether it was a man or a woman, for the rower wore a greatcoat and a hat that looked like an oversized bonnet and hid the face. Finally the boat reached the little wooden pier.

A woman entered the room. She carried herself well. Straightening her shoulders, with proud dark eyes, she looked at the young man. She was Mother Soren, the ferryman's wife. The crows, rooks, and jackdaws would have screamed a different name, and that one we would have recognized.

She was sullen and did not like to talk, but enough of a conversation took place so that they agreed upon the price of room and board, and that the young student might stay as long as was necessary to avoid the plague in Copenhagen.

From the nearby town respectable citizens came to the ferryman's house to drink a glass of beer. Frands Knife-maker and Sivert "Bag Peeper"—that was the nickname for the local customs official—liked to sit and talk to the student, for they thought him a bright young lad who knew about all the things he was supposed to. He could read both Latin and Greek, and had studied other scholarly matters.

"The less you know, the happier you are," said Mother Soren.

"You have had a hard life," said Holberg one morning while he stood watching Mother Soren washing clothes. Earlier the same morning he had seen her chopping wood like a man.

"That is my business, not yours," she answered, but her tone did not discourage him from asking if she had always had to work so hard, even when she was a child.

"Maybe you can read it in my hands," she replied, and held out two small hands, with bitten nails, that in spite of their size appeared strong. "You have learned to read, haven't you?"

At Christmas the weather turned very cold, and it began to snow. The wind was so sharp that it felt like acid when it whipped your face. But it did not seem to bother Mother Soren. She put on her greatcoat and her strange hat and rowed her customers across the Sound.

There were only a few hours of daylight, and by early afternoon it was dark in the house. Mother Soren put peat and wood in the fireplace and sat down beside it to darn stockings. That evening she spoke more than was her habit, and told Holberg something about her husband.

"He killed a man by accident, a captain from Dragor. Now he is in

irons and must serve a term of three years on Holmen. He was
only an ordinary seaman, so the law took its course."

"The law is the same for everyone," replied the student.

"Do you really believe that?" Mother Soren said, staring at the fire
for a long time. Then she continued: "Have you ever heard of Kai
Lykke? He tore down one of the churches on his estate, and when
the local minister, Herr Mads, rumbled about it from the pulpit,
Squire Lykke had him put in irons and ordered a court convened
with himself as judge. It was said that Herr Mads's throat had offended him, and so it was cut in two. . . . That was not an accident,
and yet Kai Lykke remained a free man and was respected."

"In his time, he had the right to do what he did," argued Holberg.
"Times have changed; today he could not act like that."

"Save your theories for fools who can be convinced by them."
Mother Soren rose and went into the little room. She took the baby—
that "brat" as she called it—in her arms and then put it back into the
cradle. She made up the student's bed on the bench and gave him
the skin covering, since he suffered more from the cold than she, in
spite of his having been born in Norway.

New Year's morning the sky was cloudless and the sun shone. The
frost had been severe the night before, and the snow had such a
strong crust that one could walk on it without sinking down into it.
The bells of the church rang in the nearby town, and Ludvig Holberg
put on his woolen cloak and went to services.

Above the house flew so many screaming rooks, crows, and jackdaws that one could hardly hear the church bells. Mother Soren had
come outside with her copper kettle, to fill it with snow, which she
would melt for drinking water. She stopped to look up pensively at
the swarm of birds.

Both entering and leaving the town, Holberg passed the cottage at
the gate of the "Bag Peeper," and on his way home he was invited
in to have a cup of warm beer with molasses and ginger in it. The
conversation turned to Mother Soren. The customs official knew
little about her and doubted that anyone else knew more: she was not
from Falster, of that he was certain. She had had a bit of money,
but that was gone long ago. Her husband was an ordinary seaman
with a bad temper and he had killed a captain from Dragor in a fight.
"He beats his old woman too, but she defends him," he added.

"I wouldn't stand for that!" said Sivert's wife, and glared at her husband. "But then I come from a better class; my father was a royal stocking knitter."

"And that is why you are married to a royal official," said the student, and bowed toward her and the "Bag Peeper." Sivert's work was to examine the carts and wagons of the peasants as they entered the town and collect taxes on the wares to be sold in the market.

On Twelfth Night, Mother Soren made the "Holy Kings' Light"; that is, she placed three candles that she had dipped herself next to each other and lit them.

"One candle for each man," said Holberg, smiling.

"What do you mean?" Mother Soren demanded sternly.

"One for each of the wise men who came from the east," Holberg explained, surprised at her anger.

"Oh, them." Mother Soren looked thoughtfully at the candles and again was silent. Yes, that evening Ludvig Holberg learned more about her than he had during all his stay.

"You love the man you live with and yet people tell me that he does not treat you well," he said.

"That is my own business," she replied. "Those beatings I get now would have done me good when I was a child. I suppose they come now because of my sins. How my husband beats me everybody knows, but the good that man has done me only I know. When I lay sick on the heath, and no one cared what happened to me, except maybe the jackdaws and the crows that would have liked to pick my eyes out, he found me. He carried me in his arms to his ship, and he received nothing but hard words from the captain and rest of the crew for the deed. I was not created for sickness, so I got well. Each of us has his own peculiarities and Soren has his; one should not judge a horse by the harness it wears. I have lived better with him than with the 'noblest man in the kingdom,' as Gyldenløve was called. For I have been married to the Governor of Norway, the king's half brother, and later to Palle Dyre. One was as bad as the other, and I probably am no better than they. That was a long talk, now you know my story." Mother Soren rose and walked into the other room.

She was Marie Grubbe, and that was the story of her strange tumble through life—for journey it could hardly be called. She did not live to see many more Twelfth Nights. Holberg wrote in his diary that she died in June 1716. But he did not add—for he did not know it—that when Mother Soren lay dead in Borrehuset a great flock of birds gathered above the house. They did not scream as rooks, jackdaws, and crows usually do but flew about silently, as if they knew that stillness was the proper behavior during a funeral.

As soon as she was laid in her grave the birds disappeared. They had flown to Jutland to the old castle. There an ungodly amount of crows, jackdaws, and rooks were seen. They screamed at each other as though they had great news to tell. Maybe they told how the peasant's son who had stolen eggs and little downy chicks now wore iron fetters, by order of the king; and that the noblewoman who had been mistress of the castle had become wife of a ferryman at Grønsund and now was dead. "Caw! Caw!"

Their children—new rooks, crows, and jackdaws—screeched when the old castle was torn down: "Caw! Caw!"

"And now, although there is nothing left to scream about, they still open their mouths to make their hoarse cry," said the schoolteacher. "No one today bears the name Grubbe. The castle is gone, and where it stood, Hen-Grethe's henhouse now stands. She is happy with her house. If she had not become mistress of the hens and ducks she would have had to live in the poorhouse."

The doves cooed above Hen-Grethe, the turkeys gobbled around her, and the ducks said: "Quack!"

"Nobody knows where she came from," a duck remarked. "She has no family. It is a blessing for her that she is allowed to live among us. She doesn't know which drake is her father or which duck is her mother."

But parents she did have, even though she did not know who they were. The schoolteacher, in spite of all the notes he had in the table drawer, didn't know who Hen-Grethe's parents were either. But one of the old crows knew, and she told. She had heard about Hen-Grethe's mother and grandmother from her own mother and grandmother. We know Hen-Grethe's grandmother, too: from the time she was a small child riding proudly across the drawbridge, as though all the world and all its birds' nests belonged to her. We saw her on the heath, and near the sand dunes, and finally at Borrehuset.

Her grandchild, the last of the noble family, had come home to the spot where the ancestral castle once stood. The wild birds cried above her, but she sat inside among the tame fowl, whom she knew and who knew her. Hen-Grethe had nothing more to wish for; she was old enough for death and she was happy to die.

"Grave! Grave!" screamed the crows.

Hen-Grethe was properly buried, although none knows where her grave is, except the old crow, if she is still alive.

Now we know the story of the old castle, the noble family, and the ancestors of Hen-Grethe.

## 138

## The Adventures of a Thistle

Around the manor house was a lovely garden with very rare and beautiful plants and trees. Guests always expressed their delight and wonder when they saw it. On Sundays, people from the district, and even from the towns, asked for permission to look at the garden, and sometimes classes of school children came with their teachers.

Outside the garden, right up next to the fence, grew a thistle. It was so big, spreading its branches out in all directions, that it could be called a bush. No one noticed it except the donkey who drew the milk wagon. He would stretch his neck toward the thistle and say, "You are so beautiful that I could eat you up." But he couldn't, for the rope with which he was tethered wasn't long enough for him to reach it.

The manor house was filled with guests: members of the most distinguished families in Copenhagen were there. Many of the young girls were beautiful, and among them was an heiress from Scotland. In her homeland she belonged to the very best society, and she was wealthy. "A bride worth winning," whispered many of the young men and their mothers, too.

The young people were meandering on the lawns. Some of them were playing croquet. They walked among the flower beds, and one of the girls picked a flower and gave it to a young man to wear in his buttonhole. And all the other girls did the same. But the Scottish girl went about for a very long time without being able to decide which flower to choose. None seemed to satisfy her. Then she noticed the thistle bush with its bright reddish-blue flowers, growing on the other side of the fence. She smiled and asked her host's son if he would pluck one of them for her. "It is the national flower of Scotland," she explained. "It is portrayed in our coat of arms. Get one of them for me, please."

The young man climbed over the fence and plucked the most beautiful of the thistle's flowers; and was pricked as properly as though he had picked a rose.

The girl put the flower in his buttonhole, and the young man felt deeply honored. The other young men envied him, and every one of them would gladly have exchanged his lovely garden flower for the thistle given by the Scottish girl. But if the son of the owner of the manor was pleased, how do you think the thistle felt? It was as if dew had fallen upon it in the middle of the day.

"I am more than I thought I was," she mumbled to herself. "I undoubtedly belong on the other side of the fence: inside the garden, not outside it. It is strange, the world we live in, and not everything gets the position it deserves. Now, at least, one of my flowers is on the other side of the fence, and that in a buttonhole."

Every new bud that came and unfolded itself into a flower was told the story, for there is no reason to keep good news a secret. Soon the thistle bush heard—not from the chatter of birds or the voices of human beings, but from the air, which knows all secrets and can penetrate locked doors—that the young man who had been given the thistle flower had also gained the hand of the young Scottish girl. It was a good match.

"I have joined them together," the thistle bush said. She was thinking of the flower that she had supplied for the buttonhole. Now there was still another story to tell her offspring. "I shall probably be planted inside the garden," she thought. "Maybe I'll be put in a flowerpot; you get squeezed a little, but it is glorious." And the thistle bush imagined it all so vividly that soon she was convinced that this was her future. "I know it, I shall be planted in a flowerpot!"

She promised every new flower that it would be potted, or be put in a buttonhole, which was an even greater honor. But none of them ever was placed in either. The thistle drank the air and the sunshine during the day and licked the dew at night. She was visited by bees in search of honey for their dowries, and they took the honey from the flowers and left the flowers themselves behind. "Robbers!"

screamed the thistle bush. "I wish I could prick every one of you." But it couldn't.

Old flowers hung their heads, withered, and died; but new ones came, and every one was greeted with the same joy and expectation by the bush. "You have come just at the right moment," she would say to each one. "Any minute now we are moving into the garden."

There were a couple of innocent daisies and a plantain who admired the thistle bush greatly; they heard every word she had said and believed them all.

The old donkey who pulled the milk wagon was standing in the ditch. He glanced at the flowering thistle, but his rope was too short, he could not reach it.

The thistle bush gave so much thought to the thistle from Scotland, whom she felt she must be related to, that at last she believed that she, too, had come from that country; and that her parents were probably the thistles that had grown in the Scottish coat of arms. This was a daring assumption, but a great thistle is capable of great thoughts.

"Sometimes one is descended from so great a family that one hardly dares to think about it," said a nettle that grew nearby. She had once heard that, in olden times, cloth had been woven from nettles, and she had never forgotten it.

Summer passed and fall passed, the leaves fell from the trees, and the few flowers that were left had even brighter colors, but less fragrance. The gardener's apprentice sang while he worked in the garden:

> "Uphill and downhill,
> All is God's will."

The young spruce trees down in the forest began to get "Christmas-yearning," although it was only the end of October and there was long to wait.

"Here I stand. No one thinks about me, and yet I was the match-maker," said the thistle. "First they got engaged and then they were married a week ago. And I am going nowhere because I can't move."

A few weeks went by. The thistle now had only one last flower. It grew on the stem near the root and was particularly large and beautiful. The cold winds blew on it and its color and loveliness faded; finally its pod stood naked: it looked like a silver sunflower.

The young couple were out walking in the garden. They took the path along the fence, and the young woman was looking beyond it.

"The thistle is still there!" she exclaimed. "But now it has no more flowers."

"Yes, it does," her husband laughed. "There is the ghost of one." And he pointed at the silver-colored pod, which had become as beautiful as a flower.

"How lovely it is!" she said. "It should be carved in the frame around our portrait."

Again the young man had to climb the fence and pick a flower from the thistle bush. It pricked him—that was revenge for calling its last flower a ghost. The silver pod was brought into the garden, and from there into the hall of the manor house, where it was placed beside the painting of the young couple. In the bridegroom's buttonhole a thistle flower had been painted. Everyone talked about the flower in the buttonhole and the silver pod whose image was to be carved into the frame. And the air carried the conversation far and wide.

"What adventures I have had!" cried the thistle bush. "My first-born was put in a buttonhole and my last is going to be in a frame. I wonder what is going to happen to me?"

The donkey who was tethered nearby brayed. "Come over here to me, my sweetheart, and I will show you what could happen to you, if my rope were long enough."

But the thistle bush didn't answer. She grew more and more thoughtful. She thought and thought, and at Christmas her thinking bore a flower: "When your children are inside the fence, then a mother doesn't mind being outside herself."

"What a kind thought," said the sun ray. "You, too, will go far."

"Will I be put in a pot or a frame?" asked the thistle bush.

"You will be put in a fairy tale," answered the sun ray.

And here it is!

## 139

## A Question of Imagination

There was once a young man who was studying to be an author, and he wanted to become one before Easter; then he would marry and live by his pen. It would be easy, if only he could find something to write about, but no ideas ever came to him. He had been born too late; everything had been thought about and written down before he came into the world.

"How fortunate the people were who were born a thousand years ago," he said. "Even those born a hundred years ago were luckier than I am, for then there was still something left to write about. Everything in the world has been written up; no wonder I can't find anything to write down."

He studied and thought so long and so hard that he made himself ill. No doctor could help him, but maybe the old wise woman could. She lived in a little house where the road entered the pastures. She was the gatekeeper; she lifted the latch for carriages and those on horseback. But she knew a great deal more than how to open a gate. Some say that she knew even more than the doctor, even though he drove in his own carriage and had to pay "rank tax," which only the nobility and the very rich must pay.

"I'll visit her," declared the young man.

Though her house was small, it was nice, if a bit ordinary. There wasn't a tree or a flower anywhere near it. Next to the door there was a beehive—very useful! There was a little potato patch—very useful!

There was a hedge of blackthorn bushes; they had already flowered but their berries would be bitter until after the first frost.

"The very picture of our prosaic times," thought the young man, and that, after all, was a thought: a pearl found in front of the old wise woman's house.

"Write it down," she said. "Crumbs are also bread. I know why you've come, you want to be an author by Easter and you cannot find anything to write about. You have no ideas."

"Everything is already written. Our times are not like the old."

"No," she agreed, "they are not. In the old times they used to burn old wise women like me at the stake, and the poets had empty stomachs as well as empty pockets. These times are not only just right: they are the best! It is you who have poor eyes. You cannot see and I doubt if you can hear either. Have you been saying your prayers before you go to bed? . . . There is enough to write about if you can write. You will find, peeping out of the earth with the first flowers, stories enough for your pen. In the running water of the brook or the still waters of the lake there are poems to be caught like fish. All you have to do is to learn to understand, learn to catch a sun ray and keep it in your hand. Now you can try my glasses and my ear trumpet. Pray to God, and stop thinking about yourself."

The last thing was the most difficult, and really more than the old wise woman could demand.

The young man put on the glasses and stuck the ear trumpet in his ear. They were standing in the middle of the potato patch, and the old wise woman picked up a potato and gave it to him. It spoke, told its story: the history of the potato, an everyday tale in ten lines.

What did it tell? It talked about itself and its family: how it had come to Europe as an immigrant and had at first been persecuted and condemned because of misunderstanding and ignorance, until finally its true value, which was greater than gold's, was recognized. "By royal messenger, we were distributed to all the town halls in the country, and our importance was proclaimed. But the people didn't believe it, and they did not know how to plant us. One man dug a hole and dumped a whole bushel of us into it. Another planted us here and there in the garden; he expected that we would grow up like trees and that he would be able to shake down the fruit. We grew, flowered, and set fruit, and then we withered and no one thought that below us in the earth lay that blessed wealth, the potato. Yes, we have

suffered; that is, our forefathers have. But if you have any family feeling, then you can feel the suffering yourself. We have a most interesting history."

"That's enough," said the old wise woman, and threw the potato
back on the ground. "Now take a look at the blackthorn bush."

"We have family abroad, in the home of the potato," said the blackthorn bushes, "but farther north than they grow. The Norsemen came,
steering a westerly course, through storms and fogs to an unknown
land, and there—beyond the ice and snowbound coast—they found
herbs, green grass, and bushes with deep blue berries the color of
grapes. Sloeberries are turned into fruit as sweet as grapes by the first
frost. The same will happen to our berries. They called that country
Vineland, Greenland, Sloenland!"

"That was a very romantic story," said the young man.

"Yes, but come along." The old wise woman had heard the blackthorn bush's story before. She led the young man to the beehive.

He could see right through it. What a busy place it was! In all the
corridors stood bees fluttering their wings in order to keep the air
fresh in the great factory: that was their job. Bees came streaming in
from the outside. They had been born with little baskets on their legs,
which they filled with pollen. The baskets were emptied, and the
pollen was sorted and made into honey and wax. The bees flew away
again. The queen bee wanted to fly too, but wherever she flew, all the
other bees would have to follow; and it wasn't the season for changing hives. Still she wanted to fly, so the wings were bitten off Her
Majesty by the other bees, and then she had to stay where she was.

"Come along," the old wise woman said, and tapped the young man
on the shoulder. "Let's go out into the road and look at the travelers."

"What a mass of people!" exclaimed the young man. "And each one
of them has a story. It's too much for me, we'd better go back."

"No, go straight ahead, right into the midst of the multitude. Look
at them, listen to them, and try to understand them with your heart.
Then you will find that you have lots of ideas and plenty to write
about. But before you go, give me back my glasses and my ear trumpet." And she took both of them away from the young man.

"I cannot see anything!" he complained. "I can't hear a thing."

"Then you can't become an author by Easter." The old wise woman
shook her head.

"What shall I do then?" wailed the young man.

"Neither by Easter nor by Whitsun. Imagination can't be taught."

"But what am I to do? I would love to earn a living by serving the muses."

"That's not difficult, that can be arranged in time for the Mardi Gras. Buy some masks and make faces at the poets. Even when you understand them, don't be impressed, just make a grimace, and you'll get paid well enough to feed a family."

"Isn't that amazing," said the young man, and followed her advice. He became an expert at looking down his nose at poets because he couldn't become one himself.

The old wise woman told me his story, and she has so much imagination that she would give it away, if only one could.

## 140

## Luck Can be Found in a Stick

I want to tell you a story about luck. We all know what it means to be lucky or have good fortune. To some it is a daily experience, to others something that may happen once a year, and a few may be lucky only once in their lifetime. But we all have good fortune at least once.

Now I don't have to tell what everyone knows: that is that God brings little children and lays them in their mothers' laps. Some He brings to a castle and some are born on the open fields where the cold wind plays. But what everyone does not know—and it is just as true— is that God also gives to each child a piece of good fortune. This gift He does not place beside the child where everyone can see it. No, He hides it where you would least think of searching for it, and yet you will find it. The good fortune can lie in an apple; that happened to a learned man named Newton: the apple fell and he caught his good fortune. If you don't know the story ask someone who does to tell it to you. I want to tell you another story, and it is a story about a pear. Once upon a time there was a poor man. He had been born poor and grown up in poverty; and on that fortune, he had married. By profession he was a turner; he made wooden handles for umbrellas, but he earned so little by it that he and his family lived from hand to mouth.

"I never have any luck," he would say. This story is really true. I could give both the man's name and his address, though it wouldn't change the story—but I won't.

Rowan trees, with their pretty but sour red berries, grew around his house. In the middle of the lawn stood a pear tree that had never borne any fruit, and yet the gift of good fortune was locked in that very tree, in its invisible pears.

One night there was such a terrible storm that the stagecoach was lifted off the road and thrown into the ditch, "as if the heavy wagon were a rag"—so it had been described in the newspapers. The storm broke a great branch off the pear tree. This was taken into the workroom and cut up. The turner put a piece of pearwood on his lathe and made a pear. He did it for fun, and he made a whole family of pears, the smallest was bigger than the nail on your little finger.

"Now at last the pear tree has borne pears," he said, and gave them to his children to play with.

An umbrella is a necessity in a wet country. The turner had only one for his whole family to use. Sometimes the wind turned it inside out and broke it, but the turner fixed it every time. The most irritating thing that happened—and it happened often—was that the little button that held the umbrella together when it was closed would break off.

One day when the button got lost, the turner looked all over the floor for it. He didn't find it, but he did find the smallest of the wooden pears he had made.

"I can't find the button," he said. "Well then, this will do just as well." He drilled a hole in the little wooden pear, sewed it on, slipped it through the little ring, and it worked even better than the button. Why, it was the best closing mechanism the umbrella had ever had!

When next he sent some umbrella handles to the factory that made the finished umbrellas, he sent along a few of his little wooden pears and asked them to try them instead of buttons. They did, and some of them were sent to America. Over there they soon found out that the little pears closed the umbrellas much more securely than the buttons did. From then on, the Americans demanded that all the umbrellas they bought be closed with little wooden pears.

Now there was work to do, wooden pears by the thousands, one on each umbrella. The turner worked hard at his lathe; the whole pear tree was soon made into pears. And silver and gold took its place.

"That pear tree was my good fortune," said the turner. Now he had several men working for him, and apprentices as well. He was always in splendid humor and as content as he ought to be. "Luck can be found in a stick," he would say.

I, who am telling his story, say the same. You know that people say that one can become invisible if one puts a white stick in one's mouth. It is true, but it has to be the right stick: the one God has given you as good fortune. I have found mine and, just like the turner, I can make it change into gold: the most lustrous, the most valuable gold of all: the one that shines from a child's eye, the one whose value can be tested by a child's laughter. When father or mother reads aloud, I am there standing in the room, but I have my white stick in my mouth and am invisible; and if I feel that one of my stories has made them happier, then I join the turner in saying, "Luck can be found in a stick."

## 141

## The Comet

The comet came! It flashed with its fiery tail across the heavens and brought omens of the future. Everybody looked at it: the rich from their balconies, the poor from the streets, and the lonely traveler wandering across the pathless heath. Each one had his own thoughts at the sight.

"Come! Look, it is a sign from heaven. Hurry outside, it is beautiful!" And everybody did hurry and almost everyone saw it.

Inside a little room sat a mother and her child. On the table a candle burned. The wick had curled like a wood shaving.

"That is a bad sign," thought the mother. "It is an omen that the boy won't live." That was an old superstition and she was filled with them.

The boy was, in fact, to have a long life here on earth; he was to live to see the comet when it returned sixty years later.

The little boy had not noticed the wick or thought about the comet —this first time during his life that it appeared in the sky. He gave all his attention to a little cracked bowl filled with soapsuds in front of him. He dipped the head of a little clay pipe into it, gently lifted it up, and blew soap bubbles. The bubbles floated through the air. There were big ones and small ones. They had the most beautiful colors. They changed from yellow to red, to purple and blue, and then became as green as a leaf in the forest when the sun shines through it.

"May God give you as many years of life on earth as you can blow soap bubbles," said his mother.

"So many, so many," laughed the little one. "Why, I have so much soapsuds that I will never be able to finish." And then he dipped the clay pipe again and blew some more.

"There flies a year, and there another, look how they fly!" he exclaimed every time a bubble loosened itself from the pipe and glided away. Some of them burst as they hit his face. The soapy water made his eyes smart and brought forth a tear. In each bubble he saw his future brilliantly reflected.

"Come, now you can see the comet clearly," called the neighbors. "Do come, don't stay inside!"

The mother took her son's hand in hers. He had to leave his pipe and bowl of soapy water to see the comet. He saw the fiery ball with its long tail of sparks. Some said it was nine feet long; others, nine hundred. People see so differently.

"Our children and our grandchildren will be dead before it comes again," the people said.

And that was true. Most of the people who saw the comet then were dead when it again appeared. But the little boy for whom the wick had curled like a wood shaving, and whose mother had thought he soon would die, was still alive. He was old and his hair was white. There is an old saying: "A white hair is the flower of age." And of these the old schoolteacher had many.

His pupils said he was wise; he knew so much about geography, history, and all the stars in the sky.

"Everything repeats itself," he would say. "Notice that when something happens in one country it soon happens again in another, just 'dressed' a little differently."

The schoolteacher told them about William Tell, who had had to shoot an apple off his son's head, and how he had hid another arrow inside his cloak, to shoot into the heart of evil Gessler. It was in Switzerland that this happened, but the same events had taken place many years earlier in Denmark, when Palnatoke had been forced to shoot an apple off the head of his son; and he also had kept an extra arrow for revenge. More than a thousand years earlier still, in Egypt, the same story had been written down. These stories are like the comets: they disappear, are forgotten, and then reappear.

He talked about the comet that was to appear, the one he had seen as a young boy. The old schoolmaster knew a lot about astronomy, but that did not mean that he had forgotten history or geography. He had arranged his garden so that it was a map of all of Denmark; in each flower bed, which was shaped like the island it represented, grew the plants native to that district.

"Get the peas," he would say to one of his pupils, and the child would find them in Laaland.

"Get the buckwheat," he would order, and one of the children would walk over to Langeland.

Sweet gale and blue gentian flowers were planted on the very tip of northern Jutland, and holly near Silkeborg. The towns were marked by little statues. St. Knud stood in Odense, Absalon with his bishop's staff at Sorø. Oh yes, in the schoolteacher's garden you could learn the geography of Denmark; but first he had to explain everything about it, and that was the best part.

Now when the comet was expected he told the children what the people had said when last it was seen. "The comet year is supposed to be a good wine year," he said, "and the wine merchants can add water to the wine without their customers finding out. Wine merchants should be very fond of comets."

The weather had been cloudy, both day and night, for fourteen days. The comet could not be seen, but it was there.

The old schoolmaster sat in his study, near the schoolroom. The old grandfather clock that he had inherited from his parents stood in the corner. Its heavy lead weights did not move, the pendulum was still, and the little cuckoo sat soundlessly behind a closed door. The room was silent. It had been years since the clock stopped. But the piano—that, too, he had from his parents—could still be played on, and even though it sounded a little out of tune, it still contained a whole lifetime of melodies. When the old man played, memories came to him, both of moments of happiness and of times of sorrow— all that had happened during the long years that had passed since he first saw the comet. Now he recalled what his mother had said about the curly wick of the candle. He remembered the lovely soap bubbles he had blown, each of which was to be a year of his life. How they had glistened and sparkled. Then they had seemed to him to contain all happiness and beauty. The whole wide world had been mirrored in them and, with the lightheartedness of childhood and the desire of youth, he had wanted to go out into it. They had been bubbles of the future and had held nothing but sunshine. Now, as the old man played, the music was the bubbles of memory, melodies from a time

past. Lines and phrases occurred to him, the song his grandmother
sang when knitting:

> "No Amazon ever
> A stocking did knit."

And a verse from a sweet song that an old maid, who had taken
care of him when he was small, had sung:

> "So many a rock and reef
> Has the sea so wild.
> So many tears and grief
> Await the innocent child."

He played a tune to which he had danced at his first ball: a minuet. The soft, sad melody brought tears to his eyes. He played a
march, then a psalm, and again a gay little song. Bubble after bubble,
just like the ones he had blown from the soapsuds when he was a little
boy.

His glance was turned toward the window. The clouds parted, and
in the clear sky he saw the comet: its brilliant center and its long
shining foggy tail. It was as if it were only yesterday he had seen it. It
had not changed and yet a whole long life had passed. Then he had
read the future in the bubbles, as now the past was mirrored in
them. He stopped playing. His hands were resting on the keys. It
sounded as if a string had broken in the piano.

"Come out! Come and see the comet!" his neighbors called. "The
sky is clear, come and see it!"

The old schoolmaster did not answer; his soul had left and followed
now its own course, through an even greater space than the other
comet traveled.

The comet was seen by the rich from their balconies, the poor
from the streets, and by the lonely traveler wandering across the pathless heath. The schoolmaster's soul was only seen by God and by those
among the dead he had loved and longed for.

## 142

## *The Days of the Week*

The days of the week wanted to have some time off so they could hold a party. They were so busy the whole year round, and they were never free, all at the same time; but every fourth year is leap year, when an extra day is added to February, to keep accounts straight.

On this day they would have their party, and since it was in February, when Mardi Gras is, they decided to have a masquerade. They were to dress themselves according to whim and taste. They would eat well, drink well, and in a spirit of comradeship give speeches in which they told each other the truth, both pleasant and unpleasant. The old Vikings used to throw at each other bones that they had gnawed on; the days of the week would throw jests and jokes in an innocent carnival mood.

The twenty-ninth of February arrived and so did the days of the week.

Sunday, who is chairman of the week, came dressed in a black suit with a silk cape. Pious human beings believed he was dressed for church, but the worldly ones knew that he was dressed as a domino and ready for a masquerade. The red carnation he wore in his button-hole was the red lamp that sometimes is lit outside the theater and shouts: "Everything sold out. Have fun, have fun!"

Monday was a young man, closely related to Sunday, and fond of diversions. He always left his work if there was a parade in the street. "I must hear the music of Offenbach," he exclaimed. "It does not affect my brain or my heart, it goes directly into my legs and then I must dance. I had a little too much to drink last night, and my right eye is swollen from a fight, but after a night's sleep I will be ready to work. Remember that I am young!"

Tuesday is strong, the day of the bull, of work. "Yes, I am strong!" Tuesday agreed. "I am used to work. It is I who ties the wings of Mercury to the merchant's boots. I look into the factories to make sure that the wheels are oiled and the machines are working. I watch the tailor at his table and the joiner at his lathe. I keep an eye on everyone, that is why I am dressed in a policeman's uniform. You might call me Policeday." That was meant as a joke, but then policemen are seldom very good at joking.

"Here am I!" said Wednesday. "I am in the middle of the week, the Germans call me Herr Mittwoch. I am the salesman in the store, the flower standing in the middle of all the other honorable days. If we marched in a row, I would have three days in front and three behind me; the others would be my guard of honor. I am sure I am the most important day in the week."

Thursday came dressed as a coppersmith, with a kettle in one hand and a hammer in the other; they were the symbols of his nobility. "I am of the most noble descent," he claimed, "from the heathen gods. In the northern countries I am named after the god Thor, and in the south after Jupiter. Both of them were masters of lightning and thunder, and I am their heir." And then he hit the copper kettle with the hammer.

Friday was a girl. She called herself Freya, or sometimes Venus, depending upon the country she was in. She was quiet and gentle, according to herself. But this particular day she was dressed in her best and looking very gay, for it is the day when women are free. They can even propose, if they want to, such is the tradition on that day, they don't have to sit and wait for a suitor.

Saturday was dressed as an old housekeeper; she had a broom in one hand and a bucket in the other. Her favorite dish was gruel. She didn't demand that the others eat it, just that it be served for herself, and it was.

All the days of the week sat down at the table. I have made a drawing of it. It could be used as an idea for a pantomime, and how amusing it will be depends upon how well you perform it. I have only written it as a February jest, for the only month that sometimes receives an extra day.

## 143

## The Sunshine's Story

"Now I want to talk," said the wind.

"No, permit me," interrupted the rain. "It must be my turn now, you have been standing whistling at the street corner long enough."

"That is the thanks one gets," grumbled the wind, "for breaking all the umbrellas I could, and all for your sake. No wonder people don't want to have anything to do with you."

"I will tell a story," said the sunshine. "Be quiet, both of you."

And that was said in such a firm majestic tone that the wind dropped to the ground. The rain shook it, but the wind lay perfectly still even though the rain whispered in its ear, "Why should we stand for it? She is always interrupting, that Madame Sunshine. Let us not listen to her, it is not worth our while."

This is the story that the sunshine told:

"A swan flew over the ocean. Its plumage shone like the purest gold. One of its feathers fell down on a great merchant ship that was sailing by, with its tall mast and its white sails unfurled. It landed in the curly hair of a young man who was in charge of the wares on board—'supercargo' the other seamen called him. The feather from the bird of luck touched his forehead and became a pen. He soon was a wealthy merchant who could change gold into a shield of nobility," said the sunshine. "I have reflected myself in that shield.

"The swan flew over the green meadows, where a little boy, seven years old, was herding sheep. He lay down to rest in the shade of an old tree. The swan kissed one of the leaves of the tree, and that leaf fell down beside the sleeping boy. The one leaf became ten and then a book, in which the boy read and studied about the wonders of nature and our language, of the difference between faith and knowledge. At night he kept the book under his pillow, in order not to forget what he had read. That book led him to school, to the seat of learning. I have read his name among the great scholars," said the sunshine.

"The swan flew over the lonely forests—where the wild apple trees bend their branches toward the earth and the wood pigeon and the cuckoo live. There the bird rested on one of the deep lakes in which water lilies bloom.

"A poor woman was out collecting wood for her stove. She carried a great bundle of branches on her back; in her arms she had her little child. She was on her way home when she saw the golden swan—the bird of fortune—fly up from its resting place among the reeds, and she heard the heavy wings' beat. She saw something shiny. What was it? A golden egg! She picked it up and put it in her bodice. Was there something alive within it? She was not sure; maybe it was only her own heartbeat she felt.

"When she arrived at her hovel she took out the egg. 'Tick . . . tick . . .' it said, as if it were a golden watch. But it was an egg with a living creature inside it. The egg broke and a little swan—a golden cygnet—stuck out its head. Its feathers shone like the purest gold, and around its neck it carried four rings. The woman had four children, four boys; eagerly she took the rings, for she understood that they were meant for her sons. The little golden bird spread its wings and flew away.

"She kissed all the rings and ordered each of her sons to kiss his ring as she put it on his finger. . . . It is all true, and I know what became of them," said the sunshine.

"One of the boys ran to the clay pits and, taking the damp clay in his hand, he formed it into a statue of Jason with the golden fleece. Another ran to the meadows, where the flowers grew that had all the colors that Nature knows. He picked them and held them so tightly that he crushed them in his hands. Their juices wet the ring and sprayed in his eyes. A thousand pictures were in his mind and his hands. Years later they talked in the capital of this great painter.

"The third boy stuck the ring into his mouth and from it came music: echoes from the heart's sounding board that could fly like swans. Singing, they dipped into the deep lake that is the source of thought. He became a great master of music, and now every country claims him as her own.

"The fourth and youngest was the scapegoat. He was the one who had been in the lonely forest with his mother when she found the golden egg. People sometimes ran after him shouting: 'You have the *pip,* and ought to be treated with pepper and butter just as sick chickens are!' And it wasn't meant kindly; and pepper and butter he got. But from me," the sunshine said, "he received sun kisses: ten for every one that I gave everyone else. He was a poet, and therefore he was both kissed and beaten. Still he possessed the ring of good fortune given him by the bird of luck, the golden swan. His thoughts flew like golden butterflies, and the butterfly is the symbol of immortality."

"That was a very long story," said the wind.

"And a boring one," said the rain. Then he turned to the wind. "Blow on me, please; I feel faint."

And the wind began to blow but the sunshine kept on telling its story! "The golden swan flew over the great bay where the fishermen had cast their nets. The poorest of them was dreaming of marrying, and though he couldn't afford it, he married. To him the swan brought a piece of amber, for amber attracts happiness to a house. Amber is the most beautiful incense; from it comes the smell of God's great church: Nature. It brings contentment to the home and a whole life of sunshine."

"You must shut up!" said the wind. "Now you have talked a long time, and I have been bored every minute of it."

"Me too," said the rain.

What should the rest of us say: we who have listened to the stories? We say: "That was all. . . . The end."

## 144

## *Great-Grandfather*

Great-grandfather was such a kind and intelligent old man, we all admired him. As far back as I could remember he had always been called Grandfather, but then my older brother Frederik had a son, and Grandfather was promoted to Great-grandfather. It was the highest position he would ever reach. He loved us all, but not the age. He would say, "Life was more leisurely and you knew what to expect. Now everything has to move so fast—at a gallop—and values have been turned upside down. The young act as if they were masters and even speak to the king as if they were his equal. Anyone can dip a rag in the gutter of the street and wring it over the head of a decent citizen."

When Great-grandfather spoke like that, his face would grow red with anger, but a moment later he would smile again and say kindly, "Maybe I am mistaken. I stand in an earlier age and cannot get a foothold in the new. May God lead and direct it."

When Great-grandfather told about olden times, I felt as if I were almost there. In my imagination I drove in a golden carriage with footmen. I saw the guilds' parades with banners and music, when the guild signs were moved to a new hall; and I attended the pre-Christmas celebrations, and played forfeits and acted in pantomimes. In those times also many terrible things took place. Not only could a man have his head cut off but that head was put on a stake for all to see. Yet the horror of a bygone age has an attraction, and it did inspire some people to do beautiful deeds. Great-grandfather told me how the noblemen gave the peasants their freedom and a Danish crown prince put a stop to the slave trade.

It was wonderful to hear Great-grandfather tell about all this and about his youth, but the age just before he was born had been even better. Then there had been men of character and strength.

"It was a brutal age. Thank God that it is past," said my brother Frederik to Great-grandfather. It wasn't nice to say that right to Great-grandfather's face, yet I had a great deal of respect for Frederik. He was the oldest of my brothers and old enough to be my father, as he always remarked himself. He had graduated from high school with the highest grades in his class and was already so respected by my father that he talked about taking him into the business. No one was closer to Great-grandfather than Frederik was, even though the two of them always argued. They will never understand each other, the rest of the family said; but I knew—although I was still a child—that they could hardly get along without each other.

Great-grandfather loved to listen to Frederik when he told about the latest scientific advancement; those discoveries of the secrets of nature, which are the strange and wonderful part of our times.

"Human beings are getting cleverer, but not better," Great-grandfather said. "They are using their knowledge to invent the most horrible ways of destroying one another."

"Then the wars are over all the more quickly," Frederik retorted, and shrugged his shoulders. "One does not have to wait seven years for peace. The world is overpopulated, a little bloodletting is good for it."

One day Frederik told him about something that had really taken place in one small town. The great clock in the tower of the town hall had kept time for the whole town. That the clock didn't keep perfect time mattered little as long as everyone agreed that it did. But along came the railroad, and that passed through other towns and connected this particular town with the great countries of Europe. Now one had to know the exact time, for the train had to be on schedule, so the railroad station got its own clock, which kept accurate time. Soon all the citizens set their watches according to the railroad clock and not the one in the tower of the town hall.

I laughed and thought it a good story, but Great-grandfather did not laugh, he looked very serious.

"There is a moral in what you have told and I have not grown so old that I do not understand it," he said. "And I know why you told it to me. But your little story has made me remember the old grandfather clock that stood in my parents' home when I was a child. With its simple lead weights, it was the measurer of our time. It was not very exact, but it worked. We looked at the hands and accepted their message as true; the machinery inside we did not give much thought to. So it was with the great clock of state: with confidence we looked at its hands and believed they told the true time. Now the machinery of the state has become a clock made of glass. We can look into it and see whether the many little wheels are turning, and we begin to fear that this wheel or that one may suddenly stop and then how shall we know the time? We have lost the faith we had in our childhood; that is the weakness of the new age!"

As Great-grandfather talked, he grew angrier. He and Frederik would never agree, and yet they couldn't be separated, just as the past and the present cannot be. This they realized—as did the rest of the family—when Frederik had to travel. He was going far away: to America. It was a business trip that he had to make. It was a sad parting for Great-grandfather; America is on the other side of the world.

"You shall have a letter from me every fortnight," Frederik said to console the old man. "And even quicker than that you can hear from me over the wires of the telegraph, for that changes days to hours and hours to minutes."

And from Frederik a telegram came, a greeting before he went on board the ship in England. It came faster than a letter would have even if the drifting clouds had been the mailman. When he arrived in America, we at home knew about it only hours later.

"That was a divine thought that God granted us," Great-grandfather said. "That is a real blessing for humanity."

"It was here in Denmark that a man first recognized nature's power and told the world about it. Frederik told me so himself."

Great-grandfather laughed and kissed me. "Yes, that was true," he said. "I have met the man who first saw and understood magnetism and electricity. He had the kindest expression in his eyes. They were the eyes of a child, like yours. I shook hands with him." And then Great-grandfather gave me another kiss.

Several months went by, and then Frederik wrote that he had become engaged to a young girl of whom he was sure the whole family would approve. Her photograph was in the letter. It was studied by all of us, both with the naked eye and with a magnifying glass. And that is the most marvelous thing about a photograph: it can bear being looked at closely. Yes, you might even say that likeness is more striking then, and that is more than can be said for a painting, even by the greatest artist.

"If one only had had that invention in the old times, then we could meet face to face all the great and good men who lived before us," said Great-grandfather. "What a sweet face the girl has. I shall recognize her as soon as she steps into the room."

But that almost didn't happen; luckily we did not hear about the danger until it was over. The young newlyweds reached England safely. There they embarked on a steamer for Copenhagen. They were within sight of the coast of Jutland when a storm blew up. The ship went aground. The sea was high; the raging waves would have torn a lifeboat to pieces. From the white sand dunes, people watched the stranded ship that the sea threatened with its fury.

Night fell and the passengers began to give up hope, when through the darkness was seen a rocket. It had been sent up from the shore and a rope was attached to it. It landed on the far side of the vessel, and eager hands grabbed it. Now the ship was connected to the shore, and a cable strong enough to carry a breeches buoy was soon rigged. A beautiful young girl was carried above the heavy, rolling waves to the beach. And how inexpressibly happy she was a few minutes later when her husband stood once more beside her. Everyone on board was saved, and that before daybreak.

We slept undisturbed in Copenhagen, and thought neither of danger nor sorrow. In the morning at breakfast we heard a rumor—someone had received a telegram—that an English ship had been stranded on the west coast of Jutland. We all grew frightened. But within an hour, a telegram came from the young couple that they had been saved and soon would be with us.

Everybody cried; I cried too, and so did Great-grandfather. He folded his hands and I am sure he blessed the new times. That day Great-grandfather gave two hundred marks to the committee that was collecting money for a monument in honor of Hans Christian Oersted.

When Frederik heard about it, after he and his wife had come home, he said to Great-grandfather: "Good for you! And now I'll read to you what Oersted said about earlier ages and our own."

"He agreed with you, I suppose," said the old man.

"You know that," Frederik said, and smiled. "And so do you, or you wouldn't have given money to erect a monument to him!"

## 145

## The Candles

There once was a big wax candle that knew who it was. "I am made of wax and have been cast, not dipped," it said. "My light is clearer and I burn longer than other candles. I belong in a chandelier or a silver candlestick."

"That must be lovely," said a tallow candle. "I am only made from tallow, but I have been dipped eight times and have a decent-sized waistline; some tallow candles are only dipped twice. I am satisfied! Though I admit it is better to be born in wax than in tallow; but you cannot decide yourself how and where to be born. Wax candles are put in the living room and I have to stay in the kitchen, but that is a good place too, all the food for the whole house is made there."

"There is something more important than food," said the wax candle, "and that is social life. To shine while others shine. There is going to be a ball tonight, any moment they will come for me and my whole family."

Hardly had this been said when the lady of the house came to get the wax candles, but she took the little tallow candle too. She brought it out into the kitchen. There stood a little boy with a basket on his arm; it was filled with potatoes, and a few apples had been put in it, too. All this the kind mistress had given to the poor boy. "Here, my little friend," she said, and she put the tallow candle into his basket. "I know that your mother often works so late into the night." Her little daughter, who was standing nearby, smiled when she heard her mother say "so late into the night."

"We are going to have a party, a ball, and my dress has red bows on it, and I will be allowed to be up, so late into the night," she said joyfully. Her eyes sparkled with expectation, she was so happy. No wax candles can shine like the eyes of a child.

"That was a blessed sight," thought the tallow candle. "I shall never forget it, nor am I likely ever to see such happiness again."

The boy went on his way and the tallow candle went with him.

"I wonder where I am going," it thought. "Probably to people so poor that they don't even have a brass candlestick; while the wax candle sits in silver and is in the finest company. Well, it was my lot to be tallow and not wax."

And the tallow candle was brought to a poor home where a widow lived with her three children. From their rooms, with their low ceilings and narrow windows, one could look across the street into the great house.

"God bless her who gave you this," said the boy's mother when she saw the candle. "It will burn late into the night."

And the candle was lit. "Phew!" it said. "Those sulphur matches smell awful. I am sure they don't dare light the wax candle with such things."

In the rich house also the candles were lit. From the windows their light fell out into the street. Coaches rumbled along the cobblestones as they arrived, bringing the elegantly dressed guests, and soon music could be heard.

"Now the ball is starting," thought the tallow candle, and recalled the little rich girl and how her eyes had sparkled even brighter than wax candles. "I shall never see eyes like those again."

The youngest of the poor woman's children was a girl too. She put her arms around her brother and sister and whispered to them, "We are going to have hot potatoes for dinner." Her eyes looked bright and happy too, just as happy as the little girl's across the street had looked when she said, "We are going to have a ball tonight, and my dress has red bows on it."

"I wonder," thought the tallow candle, "whether to get hot potatoes for dinner is as good. The two little ones seem equally pleased." The tallow candle sneezed; that is to say, it sputtered, for a tallow candle can't do much to express itself.

The table was set. The potatoes were eaten. How good they tasted!

And then there were apples for dessert. The youngest child recited a little verse:

> "Dear God, thanks to Your will,
> I once more my stomach did fill.
> Amen.

"Did I say it nicely?" the girl asked her mother.

The mother smiled and shook her head. "That you mustn't ask or think about. What is important is to be thankful to God for what He does for us."

The children were put to bed and each given a kiss, and they fell right to sleep. The mother stayed up and sewed late into the night. She had to earn a living for herself and her children. Over in the house of the rich the candles were still burning and the music played. Above in the sky the stars shone, and they shone as brightly on the poor home as on the rich one.

"That was a nice evening," thought the tallow candle. "I wonder if the wax candle has had a better time in the silver candlesticks? That is a question I would like to have answered before I am burned out." Then it thought of the two equally happy faces: one shining in the light of a wax candle and the other in the light of a tallow one.

Well, that is really the end of the story, there is no more, just as there is no more left of either the wax or the tallow candle.

## 146

## The Most Incredible

The one who could accomplish the most incredible was to marry the king's daughter and have half the kingdom.

Everybody tried, not only the young but the old as well. They all exhausted their brains, their sinews, and their muscles trying to do something incredible. Two men ate themselves to death, and a third did the same with drink. That was doing the most unbelievable according to their taste, but it was hardly the right way to go about it. The street urchins practiced spitting on their own backs; that, they thought, was doing the most incredible.

A day had been set when everyone could come forward and show what he considered his most incredible accomplishment. Judges had been appointed. The youngest was three years old, and the oldest over ninety. There was a great exhibition of the strangest things, but all the judges and the people, too, soon agreed that the most incredible was a great clock. It was most cunningly and artfully constructed both inside and out. Every time the clock struck the hour, little figures enacted a story to tell what the time was: twelve performances in all.

"It is quite incredible!" everyone said.

When the clock struck one, Moses came out and wrote down the first commandment: "There is only one God."

When it struck two, you saw the garden of Eden, with both Adam and Eve as happy as kings, and that without owning so much as a wardrobe, or having need of it.

When the clock struck three, the holy three kings appeared with all their costly gifts. One of them was black.

At four, the seasons of the year came out. Spring carried a cuckoo and a beech branch that had just come into leaf; summer a grasshopper on a straw of wheat ready for harvest; fall held an empty stork's nest—the bird had flown; winter had an old crow who could tell stories in the long cold nights: old memories.

When the clock struck five, the senses came. Sight was an optometrist; hearing, a coppersmith; smell, an old woman selling violets; taste was a cook; and feeling was dressed as an undertaker with black crepe right down to his heels.

At the stroke of six, a gamester came out; he rolled his dice and they showed six!

Then came the seven days of the week or the seven deadly sins, no one was quite sure which they were. But they belong together and you cannot tell them apart.

At eight a choir of monks sang vespers.

At nine the muses came. One had steady employment at an observatory, another worked in the historical archives, the rest were engaged in the theater.

When the clock struck ten, Moses appeared again with the tablets of the law; God's commandments are ten.

Again the clock struck and this time children came out. They played and sang and there were exactly eleven of them.

Now there was only the last performance left, twelve o'clock. The night watchman came, carrying the spiked mace of his office; he sang his midnight song:

> "It was near the middle of the night
> That our Saviour, Jesus Christ, was born."

As he sang roses grew, changed, and became the heads of angels with wings that were all the colors of the rainbow.

It was beautiful to look at and lovely to listen to. It was a unique work of art. It was the most incredible; about that everyone agreed. The artist was a young man: goodhearted, as happy as a child, friendly and helpful to everyone, and kind to his poor old parents. He certainly deserved a princess and half a kingdom.

The day for announcing the winner of the competition had come.

The whole town had been decorated. The princess sat on the throne of state. It had been restuffed with horsehair, but that hadn't made it any more comfortable to sit on. The judges all glanced slyly at the young man and tittered among themselves. He looked happy and had reason to be; after all, he had created "the most incredible."

"No! I will do the most incredible," shouted a tall, gangly, strong man who had just entered the hall. "I am just the man for it." Then he swung the ax he had brought with him and smashed the clock. Crash! There it lay, wheels and springs and figures all broken into tiny bits, completely spoiled!

"Only I could do that!" he said, turning toward the judges. "He could create it, but I could and dared destroy it, that is the most incredible of all!"

"To break such a work of art," the judges all agreed, "that was the most unbelievable deed of all." The people said the same. Now he must have the princess and half the kingdom. The law is the law, even when it is incredible!

The heralds blew their trumpets; the marriage was announced. The princess was most unhappy. Still she looked beautiful, dressed in her costly robes. All the candles in the church were lit. It was to be an evening wedding; that is the most fashionable. Young noblewomen escorted the princess, and young noblemen the groom. They sang as they walked up to the altar.

The groom looked about arrogantly. He walked as straight as if his back could never bend.

The singing ceased. The church was so quiet that you could have heard a pin drop. Then the stillness was broken by the great doors of the church being thrown open.

"Boom, boom!" The great clock that the young man had made came marching up the aisle. It stepped between the bride and bridegroom. That the dead do not rise to haunt the living we all know; but a work of art can. The body had been hurt, but the spirit of a work of art no ax can break.

The clock looked exactly as it had before it was destroyed. It began to strike the hours, one after the other, and all the figures came out. First came Moses; he threw the heavy stone tablets of the law at the feet of the bridegroom. He looked so angry that it appeared as if flames were darting from his eyes. "I cannot pick them up again, for you have broken my arms," he said, and the bridegroom felt that he could not move, his feet were held by the stone tablets.

Adam and Eve, the holy three kings, and the four seasons now appeared; and all of them told him the truth about himself and cried: "Shame!"

But the bridegroom did not feel any shame.

As the figures appeared, they grew in size until they seemed so large that they filled the church. When the twelve strokes of midnight sounded, the night watchman came forth and everyone stepped aside. He walked straight to the bridegroom and dealt him such a resounding blow with his spiked mace that he fell to the floor.

"Stay there!" the watchman shouted. "And never rise again. We are revenged and so is our master. Now we will be gone."

And the clock disappeared and was never seen again. But the candles in the church formed great flowers of light, and the golden star in the ceiling sparkled as if it were on fire, and the organ began to play by itself. Everybody who was there declared that this was the most incredible thing they had ever seen.

"Now," said the princess, "let me marry the right one. He who created the clock is the one I want as a husband and master."

He was there in the church and the people became his attendants. Everyone was happy, everyone blessed him, and not one person envied him, and that is incredible!

## 147

## What the Whole Family Said

What did the family say? Let us hear first what little Maria said. It was her birthday and Maria thought that it was the most wonderful day of the year. All her little friends came to visit her and she had her best dress on, the one her grandmother had sewn. The table in her room was filled with presents. There were a beautiful little kitchen with pots and pans, and a dolly that could cry when you pressed its stomach. There was also a book with pictures in it and the loveliest stories to read, when one had learned the words by heart—little Maria couldn't read yet. But better than even the best of fairy tales was a birthday, and preferably, many of them.

"It is lovely to live," said little Maria, and her godfather added that life was the best of all fairy tales.

Her brothers were in the next room. They were older: one was nine, the other eleven. They also thought that life was pleasant, but it had to be lived as theirs was, not the way the little children managed it. A friendly fight with another schoolboy, a good report card, skating in the wintertime, and bicycling in the summer: that was the life. As for reading, books about knights and castles with dungeons in them, or an explorer who went to Africa—they were things worth learning the alphabet for. One of the boys had a secret fear; he was worried that everything would be discovered by the time he grew up and was ready for adventure.

"Yes," said Godfather, "life is the best fairy tale, for one is in it oneself."

These children lived on the ground floor of the house. Above them lived another branch of the family. They had children too, but they were grown up and had flown from the nest. The youngest of them was seventeen, the second twenty, and the third—they were boys, all three of them—he was terribly old, according to little Maria: he was twenty-five and engaged. They were fortunate children; they had kind parents, good clothes, were clever, and they knew what they wanted.

"Advance! Tear down all the old walls so that one can get a view of the world! The world is good, Godfather is right, life is the best of all fairy tales!"

Their father and mother were older people; naturally, they had to be older than their children, they had once said, and smiled. "How terribly young the young ones are. Everything won't work out just as they want it to, but it is true that life is the most amazing fairy tale of all."

Above that family, a little nearer to heaven, as one might say, lived Godfather. He was old and yet his spirit was young and he could tell stories; he knew so many, even long ones. He had traveled far and wide in the world, and his room was filled with things he had brought back from foreign countries. His walls were covered with paintings, and the glass in his windows was colored red and yellow. The room seemed to be always bathed in sunshine, even on the grayest days. He had an aquarium with goldfish in it, and they looked at one as if they knew a whole lot of things that they weren't going to tell anyone about. Even in the wintertime the room was filled with the fragrance of flowers, and he would keep a fire burning in the fireplace. It was so nice to sit in front of it and look into the flames and listen to the fire crackle. "It is telling me stories from times past, old memories," said Godfather. And little Maria thought that she understood what he meant, for she could see pictures in the flames.

His bookshelf was filled with books, and one of them, which he called the book of books, he read often. It was the Bible, and in that was the whole history of the world and humanity: the creation, the flood, the kings, and the King of Kings.

"Everything that has happened or will happen is written about in that book," claimed Godfather. "So much in one book, that is worth thinking about! Everything that is worth praying for is laid down in the Lord's Prayer, that is a pearl of comfort which God has given us. It is put inside the cradle, near the child's heart. Don't lose it when you grow up, for then you will never be alone on the changing roads that you will walk. It will glow inside you and you will never be lost."

Godfather looked so happy as he spoke, and his eyes sparkled. Once long ago those eyes had shed their tears. "That was good too," he said. "It was during my days of trial; and then I wept out the tears that were within me. The older you get the clearer you see that God is with you—both in adversity and when fortune shines upon you— and that life is the very best fairy tale, and it is He who has given it to us for all eternity."

"It is lovely to live," said little Maria.

To this everyone agreed: her brothers, her parents, the grownup boys, and most of all Godfather, who said: "Life is the best fairy tale of all."

## 148

## *"Dance, Dance, Dolly Mine!"*

"That song must be for very tiny children," said Aunt Malle. "I think it all nonsense, that 'Dance, Dance, Dolly Mine.'"

Little Amalie didn't feel the same way about it, but then she was only three years old and played with dolls. She was bringing them up to be just as clever as Aunt Malle.

There was a student who came to the house every day to help Amalie's brothers with their homework, and he often spoke to the little girl and to her dolls. His manner of talking was entirely different from the other grownups, and Amalie thought him wonderfully funny. Aunt Malle claimed that the young man had no idea of how to treat children; she said that their little heads would burst from all the words he used. But Amalie's head didn't; it was he who had taught her to sing "Dance, Dance, Dolly Mine!" She knew it by heart and sang it for her dolls. She had three of them; two of them were new: a boy and a girl. The third was an old doll named Lise. She was mentioned in the song.

> Dance, dance, dolly mine!
> Oh, you look so very fine,
> And your beau, too, is dressed,
> Wears his flannels newly pressed.
> His shoes are of patent leather
> Made for summer weather.
> He is fine and you are fine.
> Dance, dance, dollies mine!

Lise is a dolly dear.
She is old, from last year.
Wears her hair in a braid,
And is timid and afraid.
Lise, come and join the dance,
Don't look so askance.
Come, come and join the ball.
It is no fun to sit by the wall.

Dance, dance, dollies mine!
Light your steps, that is fine.
Turn about at the door,
Promenade across the floor.
There they dance, hand in hand,
Around and around as fast as they can.
Oh, how sweet, you will agree,
Are my dollies, all three.

The dolls understood the song, little Amalie understood it, and the student understood it; but then he ought to, for he had composed it himself. And he declared that it was an excellent song. Only Aunt Malle didn't understand or appreciate it, but then she had long since climbed over the fence that divides the child's world from the adult's. Amalie hadn't and she kept singing the song and taught it to me.

## 149

## "It Is You the Fable Is About"

The wise man in ancient times had a way of telling people the truth without being rude. They held up in front of them a mirror, in which animals and the strangest things appeared. It was both amusing and edifying to look at. They called it a fable, and whatever foolish or wise deeds the animals did were meant as lessons to the men who saw it. They would realize this and say to themselves, "It is I the fable is about." But no one had said this to them, and therefore there was no reason for anyone to become angry. Let me, as an example, tell you one.

There were two high mountains, and on top of each of them there was a castle. Down in the valley a dog ran sniffing about as if it were trying to find the scent of a mouse or a partridge to still its hunger. Suddenly, from one of the castles, the trumpet blew, which was a signal that dinner was served. The dog immediately ran up the mountain, hoping to get a few scraps too, but when it had come halfway up that trumpet call ceased. Then the trumpet from the other castle was being blown. Now the dog thought, "Here they will have finished eating by the time I get there; but in the other castle they are just sitting down to the table." So it ran down again and started up the other mountain. But before it had gone halfway up, the first trumpet was sounded again, whereas the second one could be heard no more. The dog ran down and up again, and so kept changing mountains until both trumpets were silent and the meal was over in both of the castles before the dog arrived at either one.

Guess what the ancient wise men wanted to tell with this fable, and who is the fool that keeps running back and forth until he is tired, without ever gaining anything!

## 150

## The Great Sea Serpent

There once was a little fish. He was of good family; his name I have forgotten—if you want to know it, you must ask someone learned in these matters. He had one thousand and eight hundred brothers and sisters, all born at the same time. They did not know their parents and had to take care of themselves. They swam around happily in the sea. They had enough water to drink—all the great oceans of the world. They did not speculate upon where their food would come from, that would come by itself. Each wanted to follow his own inclinations and live his own life; not that they gave much thought to that either.

The sun shone down into the sea and illuminated the water. It was a strange world, filled with the most fantastic creatures; some of them were so big and had such huge jaws that they could have swallowed all eighteen hundred of the little fish at once. But this, too, they did not worry about, for none of them had been eaten yet.

The little fishes swam close together, as herring or mackerel do. They were thinking about nothing except swimming. Suddenly they heard a terrible noise, and from the surface of the sea a great thing was cast among them. There was more and more of it; it was endless and had neither head nor tail. It was heavy and every one of the small fishes that it hit was either stunned and thrown aside or had its back broken.

The fishes—big and small, the ones who lived up near the waves and those who dwelled in the depths—all fled, while this monstrous serpent grew longer and longer as it sank deeper and deeper, until at last it was hundreds of miles long, and lay at the bottom of the sea, crossing the whole ocean.

All the fishes—yes, even the snails and all the other animals that live in the sea—saw or heard about the strange, gigantic, unknown eel that had descended into the sea from the air above.

What was it? We know that it was the telegraph cable, thousands of miles long, that human beings had laid to connect America and Europe.

All the inhabitants of the sea were frightened of this new huge animal that had come to live among them. The flying fishes leaped up from the sea and into the air; and the gurnard since it knew how, shot up out of the water like a bullet. Others went down into the depths of the ocean so fast that they were there before the telegraph cable. They frightened both the cod and the flounder, who were swimming around peacefully, hunting and eating their fellow creatures.

A couple of sea cucumbers were so petrified that they spat out their own stomachs in fright; but they survived, for they knew how to swallow them again. Lots of lobsters and crabs left their shells in the confusion. During all this, the eighteen hundred little fishes were separated; most of them never saw one another again, nor would they have recognized one another if they had. Only a dozen of them stayed in the same spot, and after they had lain still a couple of hours their worst fright was over and curiosity became stronger than fear.

They looked about, both above and below themselves, and there at the bottom of the sea they thought they saw the monster that had frightened them all. It looked thin, but who knew how big it could make itself or how strong it was. It lay very still, but it might be up to something.

The more timid of the small fish said, "Let it lie where it is, it is no concern of ours." But the tiniest of them were determined to find out what it was. Since the monster had come from above, it was better to seek information about it up there. They swam up to the surface of the ocean. The wind was still and the sea was like a mirror.

They met a dolphin. He is a fellow who likes to jump and to turn somersaults in the sea. The dolphin has eyes to see with and ought to have seen what happened, and therefore the little fishes approached it. But a dolphin only thinks about himself and his somersaults; he didn't know what to say, so he didn't say anything, but looked very proud.

A seal came swimming by just at that moment, and even though it eats small fishes, it was more polite than the dolphin. Luckily it happened to be full, and it knew more than the jumping fish. "Many a night have I lain on a wet stone—miles and miles away from here— and looked toward land, where live those treacherous creatures who call themselves, in their own language, men. They are always hunting me and my kind, though usually we manage to escape. That is exactly what happened to the great sea serpent that you are asking about—it got away from them. They had had it in their power for ever so long, and kept it up on land. Now men wanted to transport it to another country, across the sea.—Why? you may ask, but I can't answer.—They had a lot of trouble getting it on board the ship. But they finally succeeded; after all, it was weakened from its stay on land. They rolled it up, round and round into a coil. It wiggled and writhed, and what a lot of noise it made! I heard it. When the ship got out to sea, the great eel slipped overboard. They tried to stop it. I saw them, there were dozens of hands holding onto its body. But they couldn't. Now it is lying down at the bottom of the sea, and I guess it will stay there for a while."

"It looks awfully thin," said the tiny fishes.

"They have starved it," explained the seal. "But it will soon get its old figure and strength back. I am sure it is the great sea serpent: the one men are so afraid of that they talk about it all the time. I had not believed it existed, but now I do. And that was it." With a flip of its tail, the seal dived and was gone.

"How much he knew and how well he talked," said one of the little fishes admiringly. "I have never known so much as I do now—I just hope it wasn't all lies."

"We could swim down and look," suggested the tiniest of the tiny fishes. "And on the way down we could hear what the other fishes think."

"We wouldn't move a fin to know anything more," said all the other tiny fishes, turned, and swam away.

"But I will," shouted the tiniest one, and swam down into the depths. But he was far away from where the great sea serpent had sunk. The little fish searched in every direction. Never had he realized that the world was so big. Great shoals of herring glided by like silver boats, and behind them came schools of mackerel that were even more splendid and brilliant. There were fishes of all shapes, with all kinds of markings and colors. Jellyfish, looking like transparent plants, floated by, carried by the currents. Down at the bottom of the sea the strangest things grew: tall grasses and palm-shaped trees whose every leaf was covered with crustaceans.

At last the tiny fish spied a long dark line far below it and swam down to it. It was not the giant serpent but the railing of a sunken ship, whose upper and lower decks had been torn in two by the pressure of the sea. The little fish entered the great cabin, where the terrified passengers had gathered as the ship went down; they had all drowned and the currents of the sea had carried their bodies away, except for two of them: a young woman who lay on a bench with her babe in her arms. The sea rocked them gently; they looked as though they were sleeping. The little fish grew frightened as he looked at them. What if they were to wake? The cabin was so quiet and so lonely that the tiny fish hurried away again, out into the light, where there were other fishes. It had not swum very far when it met a young whale; it was awfully big.

"Please don't swallow me," pleaded the little fish. "I am so little you could hardly taste me, and I find it such a great pleasure to live."

"What are you doing down here?" grunted the whale. "It is much too deep for your kind." Then the tiny fish told the whale about the great eel—or whatever it could be—that had come from the air and descended into the sea, frightening even the most courageous fishes.

"Ha, ha, ha!" laughed the whale, and swallowed so much water that it had to surface in order to breathe and spout the water out. "Ho-ho . . . ha-ha. That must have been the thing that tickled my back when I was turning over. I thought it was the mast of a ship and was just about to use it as a back scratcher; but it must have been that. It lies farther out. I think I will go and have a look at it; I haven't anything else to do."

The whale swam away and the tiny fish followed it, but not too closely for the great animal left a turbulent wake behind it.

They met a shark and an old sawfish. They, too, had heard about the strange great eel that was so thin and yet longer than any other fish. They hadn't seen it but wanted to.

A catfish joined them. "If that sea serpent is not thicker than an anchor cable, then I will cut it in two, in one bite," he said, and opened his monstrous jaws to show his six rows of teeth. "If I can make a mark in an anchor I guess I can bite a stem like that in two."

"There it is," cried the whale. "Look how it moves, twisting and turning." The whale thought he had better eyesight than the others. As a matter of fact he hadn't; what he had seen was merely an old conger eel, several yards long, that was swimming toward them.

"That fellow has never caused any commotion in the sea before, or frightened any other big fish," said the catfish with disgust. "I have met him often."

They told the conger about the new sea serpent and asked him if he wanted to go with them to discover what it was.

"I wonder if it is longer than I am," said the conger eel, and stretched himself. "If it is, then it will be sorry."

"It certainly will," said the rest of the company. "There are enough of us so we don't have to tolerate it if we don't want to!" they exclaimed, and hurried on.

They saw something that looked like a floating island that was having trouble keeping itself from sinking. It was an old whale. His head was overgrown with seaweed, and on his back were so many mussels and oysters that its black skin looked as if it had white spots.

"Come on, old man," the young whale said. "There is a new fish in the ocean and we won't tolerate it!"

"Oh, let me stay where I am!" grumbled the old whale. "Peace is all I ask, to be left in peace. Ow! Ow! . . . I am very sick, it will be the death of me. My only comfort is to let my back emerge above the water, then the sea gulls scratch it: the sweet birds. That helps a lot as long as they don't dig too deep with their bills and get into the blubber. There's the skeleton of one still sitting on my back. It got stuck and couldn't get loose when I had to submerge. The little fishes picked his bones clean. You can see it. . . . Look at him, and look at me. . . . Oh, I am very sick."

"You are just imagining all that," said the young whale. "I am not sick, no one that lives in the sea is ever sick."

"I am sorry!" said the old whale. "The eels have skin diseases, the carp have smallpox, and we all suffer from worms."

"Nonsense!" shouted the shark, who didn't like to listen to that kind of talk. Neither did the others, so they all swam on.

At last they came to the place where part of the telegraph cable lies, that stretches from Europe to America across sand shoals and high mountains, through endless forests of seaweed and coral. The currents move as the winds do in the heavens above, and through them swim schools of fishes, more numerous than the flocks of migratory birds that fly through the air. There was a noise, a sound, a humming, the ghost of which you hear in the great conch shell when you hold it up to your ear.

"There is the serpent!" shouted the bigger fish and the little fishes too. They had caught sight of some of the telegraph cable but neither the beginning nor the end of it, for they were both lost in the far distance. Sponges, polyps, and gorgonia swayed above it and leaned against it, sometimes hiding it from view. Sea urchins and snails climbed over it; and great crabs, like giant spiders, walked tight-rope along it. Deep blue sea cucumbers—or whatever those creatures are called who eat with their whole body—lay next to it; one would think that they were trying to smell it. Flounders and cod kept turning from side to side, in order to be able to listen to what everyone was saying. The starfishes had dug themselves down in the mire; only two of their points were sticking up, but they had eyes on them and were staring at the black snake, hoping to see something come out of it.

The telegraph cable lay perfectly still, as if it were lifeless; but inside, it was filled with life: with thoughts, human thoughts.

"That thing is treacherous," said the whale. "It might hit me in the stomach, and that is my weak point."

"Let's feel our way forward," said one of the polyps. "I have long arms and flexible fingers. I've already touched it, but now I'll take a firmer grasp."

And it stuck out its arms and encircled the cable. "I have felt both its stomach and its back. It is not scaly. I don't think it has any skin either. I don't believe it lays eggs and I don't think it gives birth to live children."

The conger eel lay down beside the cable and stretched itself as far as it could. "It is longer than I am," it admitted. "But length isn't everything. One has to have skin, a good stomach and, above all, suppleness."

The whale—the young strong whale!—bowed more deeply than it ever had before. "Are you a fish or a plant?" he asked. "Or are you a surface creation, one of those who can't live down here?"

The telegraph didn't answer, though it was filled with words. Thoughts traveled through it so fast that they took only seconds to move from one end to the other: hundreds of miles away.

"Will you answer or be bitten in two?" asked the ill-mannered shark.

All the other fishes repeated the question: "Answer or be bitten in two?"

The telegraph cable didn't move; it had its own ideas, which isn't surprising for someone so full of thoughts. "Let them bite me in two," it thought. "Then I will be pulled up and repaired. It has happened to lots of my relations, that are not half as long as I am." But it didn't speak, it telegraphed; besides, it found the question impertinent; after all, it was lying there on official business.

Dusk had come. The sun was setting, as men say. It was a fiery red, and the clouds were as brilliant as fire—one more beautiful than the other.

"Now comes the red illumination," said the polyp. "Maybe the thing will be easier to see in that light, though I hardly think it worth looking at."

"Attack it! Attack it!" screamed the catfish, and showed all his teeth.

"Attack it! Attack it!" shouted the whale, the shark, the swordfish, and the conger eel.

They pushed forward. The catfish was first; but just as it was going to bite the cable the swordfish, who was a little too eager, stuck its sword into the behind of the catfish. It was a mistake, but it kept the catfish from using the full strength of its jaw muscles.

There was a great muddle in the mud. The sea cucumbers, the big fishes, and the small ones swam around in circles; they pushed and shoved and squashed and ate each other up. The crabs and the lobsters fought, and the snails pulled their heads into their houses. The telegraph cable just minded its own business, which is the proper thing for a telegraph cable to do.

Night came to the sky above, but down in the ocean millions and millions of little animals illuminated the water. Crayfish no larger than the head of a pin gave off light. It is incredible and wonderful; and quite true.

All the animals of the sea looked at the telegraph cable. "If only we knew what it was—or at least what it wasn't," said one of the fishes. And that was a very important question.

An old sea cow—human beings call them mermen and mermaids—came gliding by. This one was a mermaid. She had a tail and short arms for splashing, hanging breasts, and seaweed and parasites on her head—and of these she was very proud. "If you want learning and knowledge," she said, "then I think I am the best equipped to give it to you. But I want free passage on the bottom of the sea for myself and my family. I am a fish like you, and a reptile by training. I am the most intelligent citizen of the ocean. I know about everything under the water and everything above it. The thing that you are worrying about comes from up there; and everything from above is dead and powerless, once it comes down here. So let it lie, it is only a human invention and of no importance."

"I think it may be more than that," said the tiny fish.

"Shut up, mackerel!" said the sea cow.

"Shrimp!" shouted the others, and they meant it as an insult.

The sea cow explained to them that the sea serpent who had frightened them—the cable itself, by the way, didn't make a sound—was not dangerous. It was only an invention of those animals up on dry land called human beings. When she finished talking about the sea serpent, she gave a little lesson in the craftiness and wickedness of men: "They are always trying to catch us. That is the only reason for their existence. They throw down nets, traps, and long fishing lines that have hooks, with bait attached to them, to try and fool us. This is probably another—bigger—fishing line. They are so stupid that they expect us to bite on it. But we aren't as dumb as that. Don't touch that piece of junk. It will unravel, fall apart, and become mud and mire—the whole thing. Let it lie there and rot. Anything that comes from above is worthless; it breaks or creaks; it is no good!"

"No good!" said all the creatures of the sea, accepting the mermaid's opinion in order to have one.

The little tiny fish didn't agree, but it had learned to keep its thoughts to itself. "That enormously long snake may be the most marvelous fish in the sea. I have a feeling that it is."

"Marvelous!" we human beings agree; and we can prove that it is true.

The great sea serpent of the fable has become a fact. It was constructed by human skill, conceived by human intelligence. It stretches from the Eastern Hemisphere to the Western, carrying messages from country to country faster than light travels from the sun down to the earth. Each year the great serpent grows. Soon it will stretch across all the great oceans, under the storm-whipped waves and the glasslike water, through which the skipper can look down as if he were sailing through the air and see the multitude of fish and the fireworks of color.

At the very depths is a *Midgards-worm,* biting its own tail as it circumscribes the world. Fish and reptiles hit their heads against it: it is impossible to understand what it is by looking at it. Human thoughts expressed in all the languages of the world, and yet silent: the snake of knowledge of good and evil. The most wonderful of the wonders of the sea: our time's great sea serpent!

## 151

## The Gardener and His Master

A few miles from Copenhagen stood an old castle with thick walls, towers, and corbie gables. Here lived, in the summertime, a noble family. This castle was the handsomest of all the castles and farms they owned. It was in such good repair that it looked as if it had been newly built. Inside it was both cozy and comfortable. Over the entrance portal had been cut in stone the coat of arms of the family. Rose vines grew up the wall and made a frame around the shield and the windows. A big lawn that was smooth as a carpet stretched in front of the castle; hawthorn bushes, both red and white, grew in the garden, besides beautiful and rare flowers seldom seen outside the hothouse.

The noble family had an excellent gardener. It was a pleasure to look not only at the flower garden but at the vegetable garden and the fruit orchard as well. Near the orchard a small part of the original garden was still to be seen. It was filled with bushes cut in the shapes of pyramids and crowns. Among these stood two big ancient trees. They had but few leaves on them, even in summer; and if one did not know better, one could have believed that all the branches that had been cut off the bushes had been carried by the wind into the trees. But all the little bunches of twigs had been flown up there: they were birds' nests.

From ancient times, rooks and crows had nested there. The two old trees were a city of birds, and the birds were the proprietors. They were the oldest family in the castle, and they felt that they were the masters. They tolerated the two-legged ones that could not fly but had to stay forever on the ground. But human beings did not interest them, even when they came with their guns and frightened them, so they flew out of their trees, screaming with hoarse voices: "Caw! Caw!"

The gardener had often asked his master for permission to have the old trees cut down; they were half dead as it was, and ugly. If they were gone, the birds would be gone too, and one would be spared listening to their screaming. But the master wanted to get rid of neither trees nor birds. He said they had been there from ancient times, and they belonged to the castle.

"Those trees are the birds' inheritance; let them keep it, my good Larsen," he would say. The gardener's name was Larsen—but that is neither here nor there, as far as my story is concerned. "Haven't you enough land, little Larsen? Why do you need to take the birds'? If the park isn't big enough, you have a kitchen garden, the orchard, and the hothouse."

And what the master said was true, the gardener had a large domain that he took great pains to keep. His master and mistress acknowledged it, but at times they could not help informing him that they had seen flowers or eaten fruits at the table of friends that were superior to what he could produce. This made the gardener quite sad, for he always did his very best. He had a simple, loving heart and took great pride in his work.

One day his master called him to the castle and told him, in a most courteous but patronizing way, that while dining with some noble friends the day before they had been served some pears and apples so succulent that they and all the other guests had never before tasted their like. The fruits were not native, of that he felt sure, but they ought to be imported; that is, if they could be made to grow here. They had been bought in the biggest greengrocery in the city, and the master wanted the gardener to ride in immediately and inquire what the names of the fruit were and if shoots for grafting could be sent for.

The gardener knew the greengrocer well, for it was to him that he sold, with his master's permission, the surplus fruit and vegetables from the gardens. He saddled a horse and rode to town and asked the greengrocer where the much-praised apples and pears had come from.

"They are from your own orchard," said the greengrocer, and showed the gardener some of the fruit, which he recognized at once. He hurried back and told his master the good news that the apples and pears he had found so delicious had come from his own garden.

Both the master and mistress refused to believe it. "I don't think it possible, Larsen," said the master. "You will have to get it in writing from the greengrocer before I will believe it."

The gardener rode to town once more, and this time he returned with a testimonial from the greengrocer.

"It is strange, but I guess it must be true," said the master. From then on great bowls filled with pears and apples from their garden stood on the table, and they were proud of them. Crates were sent to all their friends in town, in the country, and even to some in foreign lands. It really was quite exciting, quite an honor; but it had to be remembered that that particular year had been a good year for fruit everywhere.

Some months later the master and the mistress were invited to the king's table. The day after, the gardener was called into the drawing room again. For dessert His Majesty had served some melons, from the royal hothouses, that had been most succulent and tasty.

"You must go to the royal gardener, Larsen, and get some melon seeds so we can grow them ourselves."

"But the royal gardener got his seeds from us," answered the gardener, very pleased.

"In that case, the royal gardener has understood how to grow them. Every one of them was superb," said the master, looking more annoyed than pleased.

"I guess I can be proud of them," said the gardener, "for it will please you to know that the royal gardener had no luck with his melons this year; when he saw ours he asked for three of them for the royal table."

"Larsen! Don't tell me that it was our own melons we ate."

"I am sure they were," said the gardener. "But I will go and ask."

And he did and it was their own melons they had eaten and he got it in writing from the royal gardener.

His master and mistress were both pleased and surprised, and told everyone the story and even showed the testimonial from the royal gardener. Melon seeds were dispatched to their friends, as apples and pears and shoots for grafting had been sent before.

Seeds from the new type of melon were exported. They were named after the castle, so now its name could be read in French, German, and English. It was all quite unexpected.

"I hope the gardener won't begin thinking too much of himself," said the master to the mistress.

He didn't; but the fame was a spur, he wanted to be one of the best gardeners in the country. Every year he tried to improve some of the vegetables and fruits, and often he was successful. It was not always appreciated. He would be told that the pears and apples were good but not as good as the ones last year. The melons were excellent but not quite up to the standard of the first ones he had grown.

As for the strawberries, they were fine, but berries as big and juicy were served at other tables. The year the worms ate the radishes, no one seemed to be interested in talking about anything else, even though so many other things had grown well that year. It was as if his master felt relieved at being able to point to a failure.

"The radishes didn't work out this year, little Larsen," they would say, and repeat it. "The radishes didn't work out."

Twice a week the gardener took fresh flowers up to the castle. He arranged them marvelously so each color complemented the others; his bouquets were a delight.

"You have taste, Larsen," his mistress would say. "But remember, taste is a gift from God, not of your own making."

One day he arranged in a crystal bowl a water-lily leaf and a strange blue flower as big as a sunflower.

"It is the lotus flower from Hindustan!" exclaimed the mistress. She had never seen anything so beautiful before. The bowl was put where the sun could shine on it in the daytime, and at night it was illuminated with candles. Everyone who saw it found it lovely and rare, and said they had never seen a flower like it before. The young princess, who was both good and kind, was so delighted with it that she was given the flower to take home with her to her castle.

The next day the master and mistress went down into the garden. They wanted to pick one of the marvelous flowers themselves. They looked everywhere, but they couldn't find it. At last they called the gardener and asked him where the blue lotus flower grew.

"We have looked everywhere," they said, "both in the flower garden and in the hothouse."

"You won't find it either place," answered the gardener. "It is only a humble flower from the kitchen garden. But beautiful it is, like a blue cactus, though it is only an artichoke."

"I wish you had told us that." The master sounded annoyed. "We thought it was a rare foreign flower. How could we have thought anything else? It is most embarrassing. The young princess was so enamored of it that we gave it to her. Although she is very well versed in botany, she did not recognize it; but then I am sure botany has little to do with vegetables. My good Larsen, how could you bring such a flower up into the rooms of the castle? You have made us appear ridiculous."

The beautiful blue flower from the kitchen garden was banished from the elegant rooms of the old castle. It didn't belong there! The master and mistress excused themselves to the princess and explained that the beautiful blue lotus flower was only a common vegetable. Their gardener was the culprit who had been so impertinent; they had reprimanded him severely.

"Oh, what a pity! How unjust!" exclaimed the princess. "He has opened our eyes, showed us a beautiful flower, where we would never have thought of looking for it. I will order the royal gardener to bring me an artichoke flower every day as long as they are in bloom."

And the royal gardener did; and the master and the mistress told Larsen that he, too, could bring a freshly cut artichoke flower to their rooms every day.

"It is really quite a fascinating flower," they said, and complimented the gardener. "Larsen loves praise, he is like a spoiled child," the mistress said, and the master nodded in agreement.

That autumn there was a terrible storm. During the night it grew worse and on the outskirts of the forest great trees fell; their roots were pulled right out of the earth. The two great old trees that housed the colony of birds did not fare better. Down they came, nests and all. Inside the castle one could hear the angry screams of the birds, and some of the servants said that the birds knocked on the windowpanes with their wings. The master said it was an affliction. The gardener said nothing; he was happy to see the old trees gone.

"Now you are contented, Larsen." The master looked at the fallen trees. "The storm has cut them down for you; the birds have departed for the forest, a part of the old times has gone. Soon there will be nothing left to remind us of it. You, this has delighted; me, it has grieved."

The gardener had a plan—it was an old one he had thought of long ago—as to what he would do with the area where the trees had stood. It was a sunny spot and he meant to make it the most beautiful part of the park.

The trees had smashed the bushes in their fall, and they could not be saved. In the cleared plot of land he now planted all the typical common plants of Denmark, gathered from forests and fields. Bushes, trees, and flowers that no other gardener had ever dreamed of introducing into the park of a castle he planted there. Each got the soil, the sun or shade it desired; he nursed them with devotion and the plants grew and flourished.

The juniper from the heath of Jutland thrived. It rose like a miniature Italian cypress. Near it grew the holly, green in winter and summer. And in front of them were ferns of all different types, like dwarf palm trees. The great thistle, the most despised of all weeds, bloomed with flowers so beautiful that they would have enhanced any bouquet. Not far from them, where the soil was a little more moist, the common dock was allowed to flourish, with its big picturesque leaves. From the fields had been brought great mulleins that looked like giant candelabra. Woodruff, primrose, lily of the valley, the calla, and the three-leafed wood sorrel: all were there; none had been forgotten. It was a marvel to look at.

In the direction of the fields the garden was fenced by a row of dwarf pear trees. They had been imported from France but, having been given plenty of sun and careful nursing, they soon bore fruits as big and succulent as in their own country.

Where the two old trees had stood a flagpole was erected and from its top the white and red flag of Denmark flew. Near the flagpole another smaller pole stood, around which the vines of the hops twisted themselves; in the late summer the sweet scent of their flowers could be smelled far away. In the winter a sheaf of oats hung from the pole; it is an old custom to provide a meal in this way for the birds at Christmas.

"Larsen is getting sentimental in his old age," said the master.

"But he is loyal and true," added the mistress.

At New Year's, one of the illustrated papers from Copenhagen carried a picture of the old castle. One could see the flagpole and the sheaf of oats for the birds. It was particularly mentioned how pleasing it was to see that such an old tradition was kept alive.

"It does not matter what Larsen does," the master remarked. "The whole world will beat the drums for it. There is a happy man. We must be almost proud of having him."

But they weren't really proud of it. They felt that they were the owners and that they could dismiss Larsen if they wanted to. They didn't, for they were decent people, and there are lots of their kind, which is fortunate for the Larsens.

That was the story of the gardener and his master. I have told it, now why don't you think about it.

## 152

## The Professor and the Flea

There once was a balloonist—that is, a captain of a balloon—who came to a bad end: his balloon ripped and he fell straight to the ground and was smashed. His son, who had been along on the trip, had parachuted down two minutes before the tragedy. That was the young man's good luck. He landed safe and sound, with invaluable experience in ballooning and a great desire to make use of it; but he didn't have a balloon or any money to buy one with.

He had to make a living, so he taught himself how to talk with his stomach; that is called being a ventriloquist. He was young and handsome, and when he had bought new clothes and grown a mustache he had such a noble look that he might have been mistaken for the younger son of a count. All the ladies found him handsome; and one of them so much so that she ran away from home to follow him. They traveled to distant towns and foreign lands, and there he called himself professor, no less would do.

His greatest desire was still to get a balloon and then ascend into the sky with his wife, but balloons are expensive.

"Our day will come," he declared.

"I hope it will be soon," said his wife.

"We can wait; we are young. Now I am a professor. Crumbs are not slices, but they are bread," he said, quoting an old proverb.

His wife helped him. She sat at the door and sold tickets, which was no fun in the winter when it was cold. She also took part in the act. She climbed into a chest and then vanished. The chest had a double bottom; it was a matter of agility, and was called an optical illusion.

One evening after the performance, when he opened the false bottom, she wasn't there. He looked everywhere but she was gone. Too much dexterity. She never came back. She had been sorry and now he was sorry. He lost his spirit, couldn't laugh or clown, and then he lost his audience. His earnings went from bad to worse and so did his clothes. At last the only thing he owned was a big flea. He had inherited the animal from his wife and therefore was fond of it. He trained the flea, taught it the art of dexterity: how to present arms and to shoot off a cannon; the latter was very small.

The professor was proud of the flea and the flea was proud of himself. After all, he had human blood in his stomach, if not in his veins. He had visited the grand capitals of Europe and performed before kings and queens, at least that was what was printed in the playbill and the newspapers. He knew he was famous and could support a professor—or a whole family if he had had one.

The flea was proud and famous; and yet, when he and the professor traveled, they always went fourth class—it gets you to your destination just as quickly as first. They had a silent agreement that they would never part; the flea would remain a bachelor and the professor a widower, which amounts to the same thing.

"A place where one has had a great success one should never revisit," said the professor. He knew human nature and that is not the poorest sort of knowledge.

At last they had traveled in all the civilized parts of the world; only the lands of the savages were left. The professor knew that there were cannibals who ate Christian human beings. But he was not a real Christian and the flea not a human being, so he thought that there was no reason not to go there, and he expected it to be a profitable trip.

They traveled by steamer and sailing ship. The flea performed and that paid for their passage.

At last they came to the land of the savages. Here a little princess reigned. She had overthrown her own parents, for though she was only eight years old she had a will of her own and was marvelously charming and naughty.

As soon as she had seen the flea present arms and shoot off his little cannon, she fell wildly in love with him. As love can make a civilized man into a savage, imagine what it can do to one who is already a savage. She screamed, stamped her feet, and said, "It is him or no one!"

"My sweet little sensible girl, we shall have to make him into a human first," said her father.

"You leave that to me, old man," she answered, and that was not a very nice way to speak to her own father, but she was a savage.

The professor put the flea in her little hand.

"Now you are a human being," declared the princess. "You shall reign together with me, but you will have to obey or I shall kill you and eat the professor."

The professor got a room for himself. The walls were made of sugar cane; if he had had a sweet tooth, he could have licked them; but he didn't. He got a hammock for a bed, and lying in that was almost like being in the balloon he still dreamed about.

The flea stayed with the princess, sat on her hand and on her sweet neck. She pulled a long hair out of her head and made the professor tie one end around the leg of the flea; the other end was fastened to her coral earring.

The princess was happy, and she thought that if she was happy, then the flea ought to be happy too. But the one who was not happy was the professor. He was used to traveling, sleeping one night in one town and the next in another. He loved reading in the newspaper about himself, how clever he was at teaching a flea human accomplishments; but there were no newspapers among the savages. Day after day he lay in his hammock, lazy and idle. He was well fed. He was given fresh birds' eggs, stewed elephants' eyes, and roasted leg of giraffe, for the cannibals did not eat human flesh every day, it was a delicacy. "A child's shoulder in a spicy gravy with peppers is the most delicious dish there is," claimed the princess.

The professor was bored. He wanted to leave the land of the savages but he had to take the flea along; it was his protégé and the supplier of his daily bread.

He strained his power of thought as much as he could, and then he jumped out of the hammock and exclaimed, "I've got it!"

He went to the princess' father and said, "Please allow me to work. I want to introduce your people to what we, in the great world, call culture."

"And what can you teach me?" asked the father of the princess.

"My greatest accomplishment," answered the professor, "is a can-

non which when fired makes such a bang that the earth trembles and
all the birds in the air fall down roasted and ready to eat."

"Bring on that cannon," said the king.

But the only cannon in the whole country was the little one the flea
could fire, and that was much too small.

"I will make a bigger one," said the professor. "I need lots of silk
material, ropes, strings, needles, and thread. Besides some oil of
camphor, which is good against airsickness."

All that he asked for, he got. Not until he was finished and the
balloon was ready to be filled with hot air and sent up did he call
the people together to see his cannon.

The flea was sitting on the princess' hand, watching the balloon
being blown up. And the balloon stretched itself and grew fatter and
swelled. It was so wild it was difficult to hold.

"I have to take the cannon up in the air to cool it off. Alone, I cannot manage it, I have to have someone who knows something about
cannons along to help me, and here only the flea will do."

"I hate giving him permission to go," said the princess as she held
out the flea to the professor, who took it on his hand.

"Let go of the ropes, up goes the balloon!" he cried.

The savages thought he said "up goes the cannon," and the balloon
rose up into the air above the clouds and flew away from the land of
the savages.

The little princess, her father and her mother, and all their people
stood and waited. They are waiting still and if you don't believe me
you can travel to the land of the savages. Every child there will tell you
the story of the flea and the professor. They are expecting him back
as soon as the "cannon" has cooled off. But he will never return, he is
back home. When he travels on the railroad he always goes first class,
not fourth. He has done well for himself, with the help of the balloon,
and nobody asks him where or how he got it. The flea and the professor are wealthy and respectable, and that kind of people are
never asked embarrassing questions.

## 153

## The Story Old Johanna Told

The wind is blowing through the branches of the old willow. Listen, it sounds like a song; the wind is singing it, the tree is telling it. If you cannot understand the words, then ask old Johanna, who lives in the poorhouse. She was born in the village and has lived here all her life.

Many, many years ago, when the old King's Highway was still in use, the willow tree was already full grown. It stood where it stands now, near the tailor's whitewashed half-timbered cottage, close to the pond where the cows were watered and on warm summer days naked little peasant boys bathed. Next to the tree was a milestone, but it has fallen down and is covered by brambles now.

When the new King's Highway, which passes on the far side of the rich farmer's fields, was constructed, the old one became a path, then only a track, and now all sign of it is gone. The pond is overgrown with duckweed. When a frog jumps into it, the green surface parts and you can see the black water beneath. Reeds, cattails, and yellow irises grow along the shore.

The tailor's house became crooked with age. On the thatched roof moss grew. The pigeon coop was so dilapidated that the starlings took it over to build their home in. In the gables of the house, swallows' nests stood in a row, as if this were the most ideal place to live.

Once the house had been filled with life, but now it was silent and lonely. But it was still inhabited. Inside lived "poor Rasmus," as he was called. He had been born in the house, played there as a child, splashed in the pond, and climbed in the willow tree.

Then the tree lifted its great branches toward the sky as it does now, but a storm split and twisted its trunk. In the crevice the wind deposited dirt, then grass grew there, and finally a rowan tree planted itself.

In the spring when the swallows returned, they flew about busily repairing their old nests. "Poor Rasmus" had let his nest go to ruin; its walls were never repaired or whitewashed. "What is the use?" he would say. That was his proverb, as it had been his father's. Every autumn the birds flew away, but Rasmus stayed at home. And the birds returned faithfully, once winter was over. The starlings whistled their songs. Once Rasmus had been able to whistle as loudly as they, but he neither whistled nor sang any more.

The wind blew through the branches of the old willow—and it blows through them still. It sounds as though the wind were singing a song. If you cannot understand the words, then go and ask old Johanna, who lives in the poorhouse. She is wise and knows what happened long ago; she is like an old story book: the keeper of memory.

Once, when it was new, it had been a good house. That was when the village tailor, Ivar Olse, had moved into it with his wife Maren. Hard-working and honest folk they were.

Old Johanna had been only a child then. She was the daughter of the clogmaker, who was one of the poorest men in the village. Many a good sandwich did Maren give little Johanna, for although Ivar and Maren were poor they always had enough to eat, because Maren was on friendly terms with the noblewoman who was the mistress of the castle nearby.

Maren was happy. She sang and talked all day long and always was cheerful, although she was never idle. She sewed almost as well as her husband, and kept both the house and her children neat and clean. She had almost a dozen of them: eleven to be exact, the twelfth never arrived.

"The poor have too many chicks in their nests," grumbled the noble owner of the castle. "If they could drown some of them, as one does with kittens, and only keep one or two of the strongest, they would be better off."

"God preserve us!" said Maren. "Why, children are a blessing sent by God. Every child is one more prayer rising to heaven. For each little new mouth to be fed, one works a little harder, tries a little more. God will not desert one if one does not desert Him."

The noble lady agreed with Maren, not with her husband. She nodded to Maren and held her hand. That she had done many times and kissed her as well, for Maren had been her nurse when she was small and that bound them together.

Every year at Christmas from the castle would come to the tailor's house a cart with winter supplies: a barrel of flour, a pig, two geese, butter, cheese, and apples. It almost filled the larder. Ivar the tailor would smile for a moment, and there was reason to rejoice, but that did not keep him from repeating his old slogan, "What's the use?"

The house was neat, the windows had curtains, and on the window sills were flowerpots with carnations and sweet peas. A framed sampler that Maren had embroidered herself hung on the wall. Next to it—and also framed—was a handwritten verse that Maren had composed when she became engaged. It rhymed at all the proper places. She had even found a rhyme for Olse; her married name was pronounced like the Danish word for sausage: polse. "It is always nice to possess something no one else has," she would say about her husband's odd name, and laugh. She never said, "What's the use?" Her motto was "Trust in God and yourself." And Maren did. It was she who held the family together. The children grew and flew from the nest. They traveled far and wide and did well.

Rasmus was the youngest. He was such a beautiful child that one of the painters from Copenhagen hired him as a model. Rasmus was painted with the same amount of clothes on that he had had when he was born. The painting hangs in the castle of the king; the noblewoman whom Maren had nursed saw it there and recognized Rasmus, even though he was naked.

As the years passed, their conditions grew worse. The tailor's hands grew stiff from rheumatism and he could no longer sew. No doctor could help him, nor could the old "wise woman," Stine, who was known to be so good at "doctoring."

"There is no point in crying," said Maren. "That has never helped anyone. If Father's hands cannot work, then mine will have to make up for it. Little Rasmus is so clever, he can learn to sew too."

Little Rasmus sat on the table, cross-legged, with a needle in his hand. He whistled and sang. He was a happy little lad. His mother would not keep him there all day. He, too, was sent outside to play like other children.

The daughter of the clogmaker, little Johanna, was his best friend. Her home was even poorer than Rasmus' was. Beautiful she was not. She was always barelegged, even in winter. She had never owned a pair of warm stockings. Her clothes hung in tatters. There was no one to fix them at home, but she was happy as a bird in the sunshine.

By the milestone, under the willow tree, the two of them played. Rasmus' dreams flew high. He wanted to be a master tailor, like the ones in the capital who have ten journeymen working for them. He had heard about them from his father, and as soon as he was old enough he would apprentice himself to one of them. Then, in due time, he himself would become a master tailor, and then Johanna could come and visit him. She could make the food for all of them, and she would have a room for herself.

Johanna did not dare believe that all this would happen, but Rasmus felt certain that it would. The wind played in the branches and leaves of the tree. It was as though the wind sang a song and the tree told a story.

Autumn came, and every leaf fell from the tree. The rain dripped from its naked branches.

"It will soon be green again," said Maren.

"What's the use?" replied her husband. "Another year will only bring more unhappiness."

"The larder is filled, thanks to the kindness of others. I am still well and can work. It is a sin to complain."

The noblewoman and her husband celebrated Christmas in their castle; then they were to move to Copenhagen for the winter. There they would go to dances and parties. They were even invited to the king's table. The lady had sent for two dresses from France. They were of such fine material, of such elegant design, and so beautifully made that Maren had never seen anything like them before, so she asked the gracious lady if her husband, Ivar, might see them, too, for it was rare that a village tailor ever saw such fine work.

Ivar was invited to examine the two fashionable Parisian dresses, but he didn't comment at all: neither up in the castle nor on the way home. Finally, when he again sat in his chair by the stove, he said his usual "What's the use?" This time, events proved his words to be correct.

No sooner had the family arrived in Copenhagen and the season, with its balls and dinners, begun, than the master fell sick and died. Her ladyship never did get to wear her fancy dresses from France. Instead she was dressed in mourning from her black hat to her little black shoes. Not so much as a bit of white embroidery was to be seen. All the servants, too, were dressed in black, even the family coach was upholstered in black. That had never been seen in the district before.

Everybody talked about all the "mourning finery" the whole winter through. It had been a really noble funeral. "It shows that if you are born well you are buried well," was the comment most often repeated.

"What's the use?" said Ivar. "Now he has neither his wealth nor his life. We, at least, have one of them."

"You mustn't say that!" said Maren, very disturbed. "He has an eternal life in paradise."

"And who told you that, Maren?" asked her husband. "Dead men are good fertilizer. But this one is too fine for that, he lies in a stone tomb."

"Don't talk like that; one would think you weren't a Christian." Maren's face grew red with anger. "I tell you he has an eternal life."

"And who told you that?" the tailor repeated.

Maren threw her apron over Rasmus' head. She didn't want him to hear talk like that. Then she carried the child out to the woodshed, where she burst into tears.

"That was not your father speaking," she explained to the frightened boy. "That was the Devil who walked through the room, and he pretended to have your father's voice. Say the Lord's Prayer. Come, we shall say it together." And both mother and child folded their hands and prayed.

"Now I am happy again," Maren said, and dried her eyes. "Trust in God and yourself."

The year of mourning was over. The widow now wore "half" mourning, but her heart was all happiness. Some said that she had a suitor and was thinking about getting married again. Maren knew a little about it; the minister knew more.

On Palm Sunday, after the sermon, the banns were read for the widow and her suitor. He was a wood carver or a stone carver. Few of the people in the congregation had ever heard of a sculptor. He wasn't of the nobility, but he carried himself well. He was a "something"—though no one knew exactly what. He "carved pictures," they said, and did it well; besides, he was young and handsome.

"What's the use?" was all the good tailor said. He had been in church with his family on Palm Sunday. Maren and Ivar had taken holy communion after the sermon, while Rasmus waited in the pew; he wasn't confirmed yet.

For a long time the clothes of the family had been in very bad condition. There was hardly a place for any more patches. But that day they all three had new clothes on. They were dressed in black as if they were now in mourning. Ivar's new pants and jacket, Maren's high-necked dress, and even little Rasmus' clothes, which were a little too big, so that he would be able to use them for his confirmation, had all been made from the cloth that had covered the nobleman's carriage at the funeral. No one need have known where the material came from, but everyone did. Stine—the "wise woman"— and a few other women who thought themselves wise, though they were not wise enough to earn a living by it, prophesied that the new wardrobe would bring sickness and death to the house of the tailor. "If one dresses in the curtains of a hearse, one is bound for the grave," Stine said.

Johanna cried when she heard it, for she feared for little Rasmus. But it was Ivar, his father, who got sick. And the old women nodded their heads. The tailor grew weaker and weaker.

On the first Sunday after Trinity, he died. Now Maren was alone; she had to take care of everything, and she needed both her faith in God and herself.

The next year Rasmus was confirmed and apprenticed to a tailor in the city, not so great a one that he employed ten journeymen, but he kept one and a half. Rasmus was the half.

Rasmus was satisfied and he looked happy. Little Johanna wept. She cared for him even more than she knew herself. His mother stayed in the little house by the pond and carried on as before.

It was about that time that the new King's Highway was opened. The old one, which went past the tailor's house and the old willow tree, became just a field track. No cows came to drink from the pond and duckweed covered it. The milestone fell; there was no reason for it to stand any more. Only the willow tree remained as before and the wind sang through its leaves and its branches.

The swallows and the starlings flew away, but they came back in the spring. When they returned for the fourth time, Rasmus also came home. He had served his apprenticeship and was now a journeyman tailor. He was a handsome but delicately built lad; now he wanted to travel and see foreign lands. But Maren, his mother, kept him home. He was the last of her children; all the others were far away. He would inherit the house. As a journeyman tailor, there was enough work for him in the district. He could go from farm to farm, working a week or so at each; that, after all, was a kind of traveling, too. Rasmus followed his mother's advice and stayed. Again he slept in the bed he had slept in as a child and sat under the willow tree and listened to the wind.

He was handsome and he could whistle like a bird, and sing the latest songs from the city. He was welcome wherever he went, but especially at Klaus Hansen's. He was the second richest farmer in the district. His daughter Else was like a beautiful flower: gay, always laughing. Evil tongues said that she laughed just to show off her beautiful teeth. She was full of fun and ready to play tricks on anyone. She fell in love with Rasmus and he with her, but neither of them spoke of love to the other.

Rasmus grew melancholy, for he had more of his father's disposition than he had of his mother's. Only when he was together with Else did he laugh.

Although he had many opportunities to talk to her of his love, he never did. He would think, "What's the use? Her parents will want her to marry well, and I am poor. It would have been better if I had never come to the farm."

But he could not keep away, it was as if Else held him on a string. He was a tame bird that had to sing and whistle to please his mistress when she demanded it.

Johanna, the clogmaker's daughter, was a servant on the farm; she did the most menial work. She drove the milk cart out to the field when it was milking time; she sometimes even had to cart manure when that was needed. Into the parlor of the farmhouse, where Rasmus and Else sat, she never came. She heard from the other servants that the two of them were almost engaged.

"Then Rasmus will be rich," she said. "That makes me happy." But her eyes got all glassy with tears as she spoke, though there was nothing to cry about.

There was a fair on market day in the nearby town. Klaus Hansen was taking his family to it, and he invited Rasmus to join them. Both on the way to town and on the way home, he and Else sat close together. Never had Rasmus been so much in love, but he did not speak of it.

"He ought to say something to me. He must declare his feelings first," said the girl to a friend; and in that she was right. "If he doesn't do it soon, then I'll scare him into it." And she laid her plans.

Soon it was rumored that the richest farmer in the district had proposed marriage to Else; and this was true, but no one knew what her answer had been. Poor Rasmus felt quite confused and did not know what to do.

One evening Else had a gold ring on her finger. She asked the young man if he knew what that meant.

"It means you are engaged!" Rasmus grew pale.

"And can you guess to whom?" Else asked.

"To the rich farmer," answered Rasmus.

"You guessed it," Else lied, and ran away.

But Rasmus ran away too, straight home to his mother's house. There he packed his knapsack. He was leaving and it did not matter how much his mother cried.

He cut a walking cane from a branch of the willow tree, and he whistled while he did it, as though he were happy to be going out into the world.

"For me this is a sorrowful moment," said his mother. "But maybe it is best for you to leave; and then, I will have to bear it. If you trust in God and yourself, I am sure you will come home again safe, sound, and happy."

He walked down to the new King's Highway. There he saw Johanna come driving with a load of dung. She had not seen him and he did not want to see her, so he hid behind the hedge and Johanna drove by.

Out into the wide, wide world he went; no one knew where he had gone. His mother thought that he would be home before the year was over. It would be good for him to see something new and different; it would give him something else to think about. But she was worried that there were "creases" in his soul that no amount of pressing could iron smooth. "There is too much of his father in him, poor boy!" she thought. "He should have been more like me. But he will come back; he won't forget his home or his mother."

His mother would wait patiently for years, but Else had not waited a month before she went secretly to the "wise woman," Stine Mads-daughter, who was not only good at "doctoring" but could read the future in coffee grounds and cards and knew other prayers besides the Lord's. She knew, too, where Rasmus was; she read it in the coffee grounds. He was in a foreign city, she couldn't quite make out the name. There were a lot of soldiers in the town and young girls; he was thinking about becoming a soldier and wondering which girl to choose for himself. Else covered her ears with her hands; she didn't want to hear any more. If Rasmus had become a soldier, she would buy him free with her own savings, but no one was to know about it.

Old Stine promised that she would bring Rasmus back. She knew a remedy that was powerful, but it was also so dangerous that it was never used except as a last resort. She would put a caldron over the fire and cook him home. Wherever he was in the world, he would have to return. It might take a month, but he would come home to the boiling pot and the girl who loved him. He would not be able to rest, either night or day, and it would not matter whether the weather was fair or foul, he would continue on his way homeward and not stop, however tired he was, until he arrived.

The moon was in its first quarter, and that was just right, Stine declared. The wind blew a storm from the northeast and whipped the boughs of the old willow tree. Stine cut a twig from it and tied it into a knot, and put it in a caldron with some moss and thatch from the roof of his mother's house. They needed a leaf from a hymnbook. Else had torn the last page out; it was the one that listed the printer's errors, but Stine said that it didn't matter, for all the pages had equal power. Stine's own rooster lost its red comb. Else's gold ring went into the vessel too—the old woman told the girl that she would never get it back. She was very wise, Stine. Many other things were dumped in that caldron, and there it stood over the fire, or over the glowing embers, or over the white-hot ash, but it did not stop boiling.

The moon was full and then again new. Each time Else went to Stine and asked, "When is he coming, do you see him?"

"Much do I know," answered Stine, looking very wise. "And much do I see. But how far away he is I cannot make out. He has traveled over the mountains and sailed across some stormy seas, but he has

still to go through a great forest. He is tired and feverish and his feet
are filled with blisters."

"No! No!" exclaimed Else. "I feel so sorry for him."

"We can't let him stop now," said Stine. "If we do, he will drop
dead upon the road."

A year and a day went by, and then one night, when the moon was
full and the wind played in the old willow tree, a rainbow appeared
in the night sky. "It is a sign, an affirmation!" cried Stine. "Now he is
coming."

But Rasmus did not come.

"Time passes slowly when you are waiting for someone," Stine
explained.

"Yes," said Else. And she visited Stine less and less, and she
brought her no more gifts.

Her soul grew gay again and soon everyone in the district knew
that Else had become engaged to the rich farmer. She had visited
him and looked at his fields and cows. Everything was in the best of
order, there was no reason to wait with the wedding.

Three days they celebrated, and danced to the music of two violins
and a clarinet. It was a grand party and no one in the county was forgotten. Maren was invited too. When, finally, the festivities were
over and the trumpet had blown a last fanfare, she went home with a
basket of leftovers on her arm.

She had latched the door when she left; now it was open. Inside
sat Rasmus. He had come home that day, poor man. He was as thin
as a scarecrow, his skin yellow and pale.

"Rasmus!" said the mother. "Is it you? How wretched you look!
But I am glad that you have come home." And she fed him with the
food she had taken home from the feast. There was even a piece of
wedding cake.

He told her that lately he had dreamed about her, the house, and
the willow tree. It was strange how often in his sleep he had seen
that tree and Johanna, with her bare feet.

Else he did not mention. He was sick and had to go to bed. We do
not believe that it was the caldron that had called him home; only
old Stine and Else believed that, but they told no one about it.

Rasmus' fever was high, and his illness was contagious; therefore,
no one came to the tailor's cottage except Johanna. She cried when

she saw how weak Rasmus was. The doctor prescribed medicine but the patient wouldn't take it. "What's the use?" he would say.

"I will make you well." His mother sat by his bed. "You must trust in God and yourself. If only I could see you well again, whistling and singing, then I would gladly give my own life."

Rasmus did get well, but his mother caught the fever; it was she, not he, whom God called.

It was lonely in the house, and soon poverty and hopelessness sat at the table. "He is finished," they all agreed. "There's no hope for Rasmus," they said.

It was the wild life he had led on his journey that had drained his will power and strength, and not the caldron that had boiled them away. His hair became thin and gray. He would not work. "What's the use?" he would say. His legs carried him oftener to the inn than to the church.

One evening he was stumbling home from the inn. It was late autumn; the swallows and starlings had long since departed, and his mother had been dead for years. But Johanna, the clogmaker's daughter, was still there. It was raining and the wind was blowing. Johanna caught up with him.

"You should pull yourself together, Rasmus," she began.

Rasmus answered as he always did: "What's the use?"

Johanna shook her head. "That's a harmful saying! It would be better to remember your mother's words: 'Trust in God and yourself.' That's what you should do and you never do it! Stop saying, 'What's the use?' For then there's no reason for doing anything. You pull up the roots of all the deeds you could ever do."

She walked with him to his house and then she left. He did not go inside but staggered over to the willow tree and sat down on the old milestone.

The wind blew through the branches of the willow; it sounded as if someone were singing a song and telling a story. Rasmus listened and answered. He talked loudly, although no one heard him but the tree and the wind.

"I feel so cold, I must go in and go to bed," he thought. But he walked not toward the house but toward the pond. Near it he fell. It was raining hard now and the wind was cold. He didn't feel it, he slept; but when the sun rose and the crows flew over the reeds he woke half dead. Had his head rested where his feet were, then he would never have risen again and the duckweed would have been his winding sheet.

At noon Johanna came to his house. She helped him. She called the doctor, and Rasmus was taken to the hospital.

"We have known each other since we were tiny tots. Many a meal has your mother given me when I was hungry and that I cannot repay her now. You will get well," Johanna said, "God wants you to live."

Rasmus came home from the hospital, but both his health and his mind had their ups and downs. The starlings and the swallows came faithfully, and flew away again. Rasmus became old beyond his years.

He lived alone in a house that more and more became a ruin. Now he was poorer than Johanna.

"You have no faith," she would say when she visited him. "If we did not have God, how would it fare with us? You should go to communion, I am sure you haven't been there since you were confirmed."

"What's the use? How can that help?" he would answer. And she would look away.

"If you feel that way, don't go. An unwilling guest is not welcome at God's table. Think of your mother and your youth, you were such a good boy. May I read a psalm for you?"

"And what's the use of that?" Rasmus said with a crooked smile.

"It always comforts me." Johanna glanced at her hands.

"Have you become one of the pious ones?" Rasmus looked at Johanna; his eyes were dull and tired.

She read a psalm; that is, she did not read it, for she owned no hymnbook; she knew it by heart.

"They were lovely words," Rasmus said slowly, "but I did not understand them. My head is so heavy. It feels as though there were a stone inside it."

Rasmus had become an old man, but Else was not young either any more. We will mention her, but Rasmus never did. She was already a grandmother; her granddaughter was a sweet, talkative little girl. She was playing with the other children in the village. Rasmus came by, leaning on his stick; he stood watching them. She smiled to him. Memories of his childhood came to his mind. Else's granddaughter pointed her finger at him and screamed, "Poor Rasmus!" as loudly as she could. The other children took up the cry and chased the old man all the way home.

Gray, dark days came, and more followed; but after gray, dark days, the sun comes out. Finally, on Whitsunday, when the church was decorated with birch branches with tender green leaves, the sun shone through the great windows and the smell of the forest permeated the room. Communion was served. Johanna was among the guests. Rasmus was not. That very morning, God in His grace and mercy had called him to Him.

Many years have gone by. The tailor's house still stands, though no one lives in it. It will fall during the first winter storm. The pond is overgrown with reeds and duckweed. The wind is blowing through the branches of the old willow; it is as if one were listening to a song: the wind is singing it, the tree is telling it. If you do not understand the words, then ask old Johanna, who lives in the poorhouse.

She is still alive. She still sings the old hymn that she sang for Rasmus. She thinks about him and prays for him. She is faithful. She can tell you about times past: the memories that the wind sings about in the old tree.

## 154

## The Front Door Key

Every key has its history; and there are many of them: the key for winding up the clock, the key to the city, St. Peter's keys. We could tell about them all, but this story is only about the key that opened the main entrance of the home of a highly respected gentleman. He was a city councilor.

The key had been made by a locksmith, but if one judged by its size and weight, it could have been the work of a blacksmith. It was too big for the councilor's trousers pocket and could only just be forced into his coat pocket. There it lay in the darkness, but the rest of the time it had its own special place, where it always hung on a nail, beside the framed silhouette of the councilor as a child, in which he looked like a muffin with a frilly shirt on.

It is said that everyone's character is influenced by the astrological sign he is born under: the Scorpion, the Twins, the Ram as they are called in the almanac. The councilor's wife did not mention any of these when she referred to her husband. She said that he had been born under the sign of the wheelbarrow; he had to be pushed.

His father had pushed him into an office and his mother into matrimony; and then his wife had pushed him into becoming a councilor. This she never told anyone, for she was a clever woman who knew when to be silent, when to talk, and when to push.

He was not young any longer and had grown stout, which he himself called "well proportioned." He was well read, good-natured, and "key-wise." What the latter is will be explained in the story. He was full of good will toward everyone and would converse with anyone. This meant that when he went for a walk one never knew when he was coming home, unless his wife went along, for then she would push him home. He would talk to every one of his acquaintances and he had many of them, which meant that dinner often got cold.

His wife would watch from a window. "I see him!" she would call to the maid. "Put the pot on the fire. . . . No! he has met someone, take the pot off or the food will be spoiled. . . . Now put it on again, he is coming."

But he didn't come. Just as he was about to enter his home he spied a friend coming up the street, and he had to wait to say just a few friendly words to him. While he was thus engaged, another acquaintance came along, and so he had to stay for just a few minutes longer, to tell him about the weather.

It was a trial for his wife. At last she would open the window and call him, saying to herself at the same time, "He was born under the sign of the wheelbarrow; if he isn't pushed, he won't move."

He loved to browse in a bookstore and look through the magazines. He even paid his own bookseller a small amount in order to be able to read all the new books without buying them. He was, himself, a living newspaper and knew all about engagements, marriages, funerals, literary gossip, and town gossip. Sometimes he would make mysterious allusions, and if anyone asked where he knew this or that from, he would say that he had it "directly from the key to his front door."

The councilor and his wife had lived in the same house since they were married and had had the same front door key all the time; but at first they did not know of its strange power.

It was the time of King Frederik VI. Copenhagen still only had the old oil lamps; there were no streetcars or railroads, no Tivoli or Casino Theater. Sources of amusement were limited; it wasn't as it is now. An excursion to the great churchyard outside the gates, where—after you had read the inscriptions on the tombstones—you could lie in the grass and eat your lunch, or a trip to Frederiksberg and the royal gardens was considered a treat. On Sunday, a regimental band played in front of Frederiksberg Castle, and after that you could watch the royal family sailing on the canals. Old King

Frederik steered the boat himself and nodded to everyone, regardless of their station. Lots of the wealthier families would gather there in the summer for afternoon tea. Hot water could be bought at a little farmhouse just outside the park, but the teapot you had to bring yourself.

To partake of all this gaiety, the councilor, his wife, and the maid— she carried a basket containing sandwiches and the teapot—departed on foot from Copenhagen one Sunday afternoon.

"Remember to take the key to the front door," said the councilor's wife. "The door is locked at sunset and the bell rope broke this morning. We will be late coming home. On the way—after we have been to Frederiksberg—I want to see the pantomime at the Casortis Theater. It is called *Harlequin Gives a Beating*. In the last act they all descend from a cloud, it costs two marks per person!"

They walked to the royal gardens, where they heard the military band and saw the king and the white swans that swam behind the royal boat, as if they were guarding it. Then they drank their tea and hurried to get to the theater, but they arrived too late.

The tightrope walker and the jugglers had already done their acts and the pantomime had started. They always arrived too late and that was the councilor's fault; he just had to stop and pass the time of day with everyone he knew. Also the theater was full of his acquaintances, and when the performance was over the councilor and his wife went home with a friend who lived outside the city gate, for a glass of punch. They were only going to stay for ten minutes, but they stayed for an hour. How they talked! Especially a Swedish baron—or was he German? the councilor could not recall where this gentleman came from—had been most entertaining. Although he could not recall the gentleman's nationality, he would remember all his life the trick the baron had taught him with the key. It was most interesting! The baron could make the key answer all questions, even those most secret and personal.

The key to the councilor's front door was particularly well suited for the game because it was heavy. The baron let the key hang by the loop from the index finger of his right hand, so loosely that the pulse in the finger could make it move. If by chance that did not happen, then the baron knew how to make it happen anyway. Every turning of the key was a different letter, from A to Z. As soon as the first letter was "stated," the key turned to the opposite side and began the second letter; and this went on until it had spelled out the answer to a question.

"It is a lot of nonsense but most entertaining," thought the councilor at first. But he changed his mind when the key showed how much it could unlock.

"Husband, husband!" exclaimed his wife. "It is late, the western gate to the city will be closed in fifteen minutes, we shall never make it."

They had to hurry and they were not the only ones who had tarried too long. When the clock struck twelve they had just passed the first of the guardhouses. The gate closed and they were left outside. There they stood among the other latecomers: the councilor, his wife, and the maid, carrying the basket with the teapot in it. Each reacted to the calamity according to his own nature; a few were frightened, some angry, and many merely annoyed. But what was to be done?

A new civic order had just gone into effect: the northern gate of the city was to remain open all night for pedestrians. It was a good walk but the night was pleasant, the stars were out, and the frogs gave a free concert from every pond and ditch. The unfortunate all walked on together. Soon someone started singing and the rest joined in. The councilor did not sing, neither did he admire the stars, nor did he even look where he was going, for he fell in the ditch. One might have thought that he was drunk from too much punch. It wasn't the punch but the key that had gone to his head; he could not think of anything else.

Finally they reached the northern gate, crossed the bridge, and through the "small" door entered the city.

"Now I am happy again, at last we are home," said the councilor's wife. "Here we are in front of our own door."

"But where is the key?" The councilor's voice sounded a little disturbed. "It is not in my coat pocket and it is not in my back pocket!"

"For mercy's sake!" screamed his wife. "Don't you have the key? You know that the bell rope broke this morning and the night watchman doesn't have the key to our front door. You must have lost it playing that silly game with the baron. Oh, what a desperate situation!"

The maid started to cry. The councilor was the only one who kept his head. In the cellar of the house there was a small general store.

"We can break a window in the basement and get Petersen to open up for us," declared the master of the family.

First he broke one window and, when that did not help, he broke another. "Petersen!" he called. Then he pushed his umbrella through the broken window and waved it, which so frightened the storekeeper's daughter, who had just got up, that she screamed.

Petersen opened his door and shouted for the night watchman; then he recognized the councilor and his wife and let them in.

The night watchman was blowing his whistle and other watchmen were answering it. Windows opened and heads peered out. "Where is the fire?" several people shouted.

By that time the councilor was up in his own apartment, taking off his coat. He found the key! It had slipped through a hole in his pocket—that shouldn't have been there—down into the lining.

From that evening on the key took on increasing importance. It was not only of use when the family left the house, it was the center of attention when they stayed at home. The councilor would ask questions of the key and then he would manipulate its answers; that is to say, he thought of the most reasonable answers and let the key say them. But as time went by he actually began to believe in its powers.

The apothecary didn't. He was a young relative of the councilor's wife, and a skeptic. He was known to be a clever and very critical person. When he was still a schoolboy he had produced reviews of books and plays for a newspaper—anonymously, because that is safer. He was spirited, but he didn't believe in spirits—at least, not in key spirits.

"I believe it, I believe it," he declared one evening to everyone's surprise. "My good Councilor, I am not only sure that your front door key has a spirit, I think all keys have one. It is a new science that is just becoming known. Table-tilting it is called. Have you heard of it? Every piece of furniture has a spirit, both the new and the old. I was doubtful. You know how much of a skeptic I am, but I have been convinced by an article in a foreign newspaper. It is a monstrous story, but I will tell you exactly what I read:

"There were two sweet and clever children who had watched their parents arouse the spirit of a large dining-room table. The next evening, when they were home alone, they decided to awaken the spirit of a chest of drawers. They succeeded, the spirit woke, but it would not take orders from children. It got angry, its drawers jumped out; and with the help of its little legs, it put each child in a drawer. Then it ran out of the house. Down to the nearby canal it went and jumped in, which resulted, of course, in the poor children getting drowned. The corpses of the victims were given Christian burial, but the chest of drawers was taken to the courthouse, where the city councilors declared that it was a murderer, and it was publicly burned.

"I read it all in a foreign newspaper. It's not just something I have made up. I will swear to that by the Keys of the Kingdom; and that oath is binding!"

The councilor found the story too coarse even for a joke. He refused to discuss keys with the apothecary, for he was convinced that they would never agree: he himself was key-wise and the apothecary "key-stupid." The councilor's study of keyology progressed. It was his favorite amusement and occupation.

One evening when the councilor was just about to retire—indeed, he was half undressed—there was a knock at the door. It was the grocer, Mr. Petersen. He was sorry to disturb the councilor so late at night, but he himself had been just about to go to bed when he had got an idea that he couldn't wait until morning to tell the councilor.

"You know my daughter Lotte-Lene, I must talk to you about her. She is both a good and a good-looking girl. She has been confirmed and now I should like to see her well taken care of."

"Well, I am sure it does you credit," said the councilor, "but I am not a widower and I have no son that I can offer her."

"Oh, please! You must try to understand me!" the grocer begged. "The girl can play the piano and sing; you must have heard her. But that is not the half of it, she can imitate anyone, even walk as they do. I thought to myself: 'She is made for the stage.' It is a good living for a girl of decent family; and many an actress has married into the nobility. Not that my Lotte-Lene has any such thoughts. She can play the piano and she can sing; so not long ago I went up to the music school with her. She sang for them, but unfortunately she couldn't screech like a canary, and that seems to be necessary today. 'Well,' I thought, 'if she can't be a singer, then she can be an actress, for that she only needs to be able to speak.' Today I talked to one of the producers, as they are called, and he asked if she had done any readings! I answered, not that I knew of, and then he said that to have done some reading was a necessity for an artist of the stage.

"Well, I thought it not too late to start—there is a lending library down the street—but then it occurred to me that there was no reason to throw away money renting books if one could borrow them. And I thought, 'The councilor has lots of books, I will ask him if she can read them.' Books are books and those she can read for free."

"Lotte-Lene is a sweet girl," replied the councilor. "A good-looking girl. She shall have all the books that she desires. But tell me, has she got spirit, talent, and genius? Has she got something that is even more important: luck?"

"She has won twice in a lottery," her father said proudly. "Once she got a clothes closet; and another time, two pairs of sheets. If that isn't luck, then I don't know what luck is."

"We'd better ask the key," said the councilor, and the key was brought forth and hung on his index finger. It turned first one way, then the other and spelled out: "Victory and Happiness."

That decided Lotte-Lene's future. The councilor immediately gave her two books to read; one of them was *Dyveke,* the other Knigge's *Associating with Human Beings.*

From that day on the councilor's apartment was frequented by Lotte-Lene. She almost became one of the family. The councilor thought her very clever; she had faith in both him and the key. The councilor's wife loved the naïve way the young girl showed her ignorance; she was almost like a child. They liked her and she liked them.

"It smells so lovely up there," said Lotte-Lene. The councilor's wife had a whole barrel of apples standing in the hall, and there were dried lavender and rose leaves in all the drawers.

"They are so refined," thought Lotte-Lene, and she loved to look at the many beautiful flowers the councilor's wife had, even in the winter. Lilac and cherry branches were brought into the warm rooms and put in water; soon they blossomed as if it were already spring.

The councilor's wife said to the girl, "Out in nature the branches look dead, as if all life had gone from them. But look at them now; it is a resurrection."

"I never thought of it that way before." Lotte-Lene was impressed. "Nature is beautiful."

The councilor let her see his "key-book," in which he had written down all the questions he had asked the key and the strange and curious answers it had given. Here everything was recorded, even the time that half an apple pie had been missing, on the very day when the maid's young man had come visiting. The councilor had asked the key to tell him who had eaten the pie: the cat or the young man.

"The young man," answered the key. That was what the councilor had suspected, and the maid had confessed at once. For what could a poor servant girl do against magic?

"Yes, isn't it strange!" sighed the councilor. "That key, that key. And about you it has said: 'Victory and Happiness.' I am sure it will come true."

"That will be lovely," said Lotte-Lene.

The councilor's wife did not have the same faith in the key, but this she never let her husband know. Once, in the deepest confidence, she told Lotte-Lene that when the councilor was a young man he had been completely addicted to the theater. If anybody had pushed him, he would have become an actor; but the family, wisely enough, had pushed the other way. Well, if he couldn't become an actor, he thought he could become a playwright; and the councilor had written a comedy.

"It is a great secret that I am telling you, little Lotte-Lene. The comedy was good. It was performed at the Royal Theater but it was booed. Now it is quite forgotten, and for that I am not sorry. I am his wife and I know him. Now you want to try your luck in theater. I wish you well, but I don't believe you will succeed. I do not trust the key."

But Lotte-Lene did, she trusted and believed in it; and in their faith in the key's wisdom, the hearts of the councilor and the girl met.

The girl had other virtues which the councilor's wife appreciated: Lotte-Lene knew how to make starch from potato flower, new silk gloves out of old silk stockings, and could replace the silk on dancing shoes—not that the girl needed to do any of these things, for she had, according to her father, money in the drawer of her night table and bonds in the safe.

"She would make a good wife for the apothecary," thought the councilor's wife. But she didn't say it out loud, nor did she let the key say it. The apothecary was soon to set up shop in one of the larger country towns.

Lotte-Lene was still reading *Dyveke* and Knigge's *Associating with Human Beings*. She had kept the books for two years, but by now she knew one of them by heart: *Dyveke;* and she could play all the parts, but the only one she wanted to play was the female lead. She

did not want to have her debut in Copenhagen; it was so filled with
envy and she couldn't find a theater director who would engage her.
No, she would take her first step on the "artistic path," as the councilor called it, in the provinces.

Now it happened, by chance, that the town where she was to have
her debut was the same one in which the apothecary had just settled,
and where he was the youngest if not the only apothecary.

The great and longed-for evening finally came. Lotte-Lene was to
appear before an audience for the first time. She was to be "Victorious
and Happy," as the key had predicted. The councilor could not attend her opening night; he was sick. His wife stayed home, too, because she had to prepare camomile tea and hot compresses for her
husband: the compresses for the outside of his stomach, and the tea
for the inside. They did not see the performance of *Dyveke*.

But the apothecary did, and sent a letter to his relative, the councilor's wife. "It was too marvelous," he wrote. "If I had had the
councilor's key in my pocket, I would have taken it out and whistled
through it. She deserved it; and the key, too, for having lied to the
poor girl. 'Victory and Happiness,' indeed!"

The councilor read the letter and declared that it was inspired by
"key-hatred" and that it was mean to poke fun at Lotte-Lene. As
soon as he was out of bed he wrote a "poisonous" note to the young
apothecary, who did not notice the poison, perhaps because he was
used to being in contact with it.

He replied in the best of humors. He began by saying that he was
always happy to receive the latest news about keyology, and held this
modern science in high esteem. Then he confessed that he was writing what we Danes call a "keyhole" novel. But instead of revealing
family secrets it would be about keys. Whatever time the apothecary
had to spare from his profession was devoted to this book. All the
characters would be keys. The key to the front door would, naturally,
be the main character. He said that he had been inspired by the councilor's front door key, for its ability to look into the future was awe-
inspiring. It was the greatest of all keys, and to it all other keys would
have to pay homage: even the key of the chamberlain that knows its
way around the court; the watch key that was so elegant, slim-
waisted, and tiny; the key to the family pew that thought itself a cleric,
because it had spent a single night in church, once when its owner
had forgotten it, and there had seen a ghost; larder keys; cellar keys

—both to the coal and the wine closet—all would have to be humble. The whole novel was to be one eulogy to the key of the front door. The sun was to shine on it and make it appear as if it were made of silver, and all the spirits of the world, like gusts of wind, were to whistle through it. It was to be proclaimed the key of all keys, and it was the councilor's key to his front door, but it was to become the key to heaven, as infallible as the key of the Pope.

"It is wicked," declared the councilor when he read it. "A pyramid of malice." He saw the apothecary only once after that; at the funeral of his wife, for she died first.

Sorrow invaded the house, even the newly cut cherry branches refused to bloom. The other flowers hung their heads; they were used to careful nursing and their mistress had died. The apothecary and the councilor walked side by side behind the hearse. It was not the moment for quarrels.

Lotte-Lene tied the black crepe around the councilor's hat. She was back, without the "Victory and Happiness" on the stage that the key had predicted. But it could still happen, Lotte-Lene had a future; both the key and the councilor had foreseen it.

She often visited the councilor; they talked about his late wife, and Lotte-Lene, who had a sensitive soul, cried. They talked about the theater and Lotte-Lene tempered her heart. "The theater is sinful," she declared. "It is filled with envy. I shall go my own way. First life, then art." She now realized that what Knigge had said in his chapter about actors had been perfectly correct. That the key had lied was something she never discussed with the councilor, for she was fond of him.

During the year of mourning the key was the good councilor's only comfort and consolation. He asked it questions and it answered.

After the year was over, he and Lotte-Lene were sitting alone one lovely evening when he asked the key, "Shall I ever marry again? And if so whom?"

No one pushed him; but he pushed the key, and it answered, "Lotte-Lene." The words were said. He had proposed; Lotte-Lene accepted and became a city councilor's wife. The front door key had predicted it long ago: "Victory and Happiness."

## 155

## The Cripple

Once upon a time there was a big farm with a manor house. The master and mistress were rich, young, and happy. Fortune had smiled on them and they smiled back; they wanted everyone to be as happy as they were.

On Christmas Eve a large, beautifully decorated Christmas tree stood in the grand hall. A log fire burned in the fireplace and all the old paintings had their frames decorated with spruce branches. Here there were to be dancing and gaiety on the happiest night of the year, for the wealthy couple and their friends.

In the big dining room where the farm hands ate, Christmas was already being celebrated. Here, too, stood a Christmas tree, with red and white candles, tinsel, little Danish flags, and hearts woven from glossy paper which were filled with sweets. All the poor children in the countryside had been invited; they had come with their mothers. The grownups did not look long at the tree, they were more interested in the table where the presents were laid out. There were linen and woolen cloth, from which little girls' dresses and boys' pants could be sewn. Only the little children stretched out their hands toward the candles, flags, and tinsel.

They had come early in the afternoon and had been served the traditional Christmas dinner, which began with rice porridge and whose main course was roast goose and red cabbage. Afterward the candles on the tree were lit, and when the children had emptied the little paper baskets of their sweets, the presents were distributed. Finally everyone was given a glass of punch and apple fritters. Then it was time for the guests to go back to their own poor cottages; there the gifts were evaluated once more and the dinner discussed.

"Garden-Kirsten" and "Garden-Ole"—they were called by these names because they did the hoeing and the weeding in the park— were a married couple who had five children. Every year they received their share of gifts.

"Both the master and mistress are generous," they would say. "But they can afford to be; and besides, they enjoy it."

"There are clothes enough for the four children, but haven't they given anything to the cripple? They don't usually forget him even though he can't come to the party."

By the "cripple" Garden-Ole meant his oldest son; his name was Hans. He was a clever boy and once had been very active, but then his legs had suddenly "grown wobbly," as his mother said. For the last five years he had been bedridden.

"Well, I did get something," said his mother. "But it wasn't anything much, only a book he could read."

"He won't get fat from that!" his father remarked.

But the gift made Hans happy. He was a very alert child and loved to read. Not that he didn't work, for even though he was confined to bed he had lots to do: he knitted socks and even bedspreads. The young mistress had praised his work and bought two of the bedspreads. The book was a collection of fairy tales. It was thick; there was a lot to read and think about.

"It is useless!" said his parents. "But let him read; it helps him pass the time, and he can't always be knitting."

Spring came. The cherries bloomed and flowers came up from the ground; weeds did too, which meant that there was plenty of work in the park, not only for the gardener and his apprentices but for Garden-Ole and Garden-Kirsten as well.

"It is drudgery!" they both complained. "As soon as we have raked the garden paths, the guests come walking on them and spoil our work. The master must be rich to be able to afford to have so many strangers here."

"Yes, the blessings of the world are strangely distributed," said Ole.

"The minister said that we are all God's children, but then why do some get everything and so many almost nothing?"

"It is all because of man's fall from grace," replied his wife.

That evening, when they returned to their cottage, they had the same discussion. Hans was lying in his bed reading his book of fairy tales.

Life had not dealt easily with them. Hard work had made not only their hands hard but also their opinions and judgments. Their situation was beyond their own power to change it; they had not been able to get along; life was too difficult. As they talked they grew angrier and more bitter.

"Some people have wealth and happiness and others only poverty. Why should we suffer for Adam's and Eve's disobedience? Had we been in their place we wouldn't have behaved as they did."

"But we would have," exclaimed Cripple-Hans. "It is all written down here in this book."

"What is written down in the book?" asked his father.

Hans read aloud for them the old fairy tale about the woodcutter and his wife. They, too, had been complaining about Adam's and Eve's curiosity being the cause of their misery, and claiming that, had they been in their stead, then the apple would have stayed on the tree. The king, who had been riding past, heard what they said. "Come with me to the palace," he offered, "and you shall live as well as I do. You will be served seven courses at every meal plus dessert; but the tureen that stands in the middle of the table you must never touch, for then your life of leisure will be over."

They followed the king to the castle and the very first day the wife said, "I wonder what is in that tureen."

"That is no concern of ours," replied her husband.

"Oh, I am only curious," exclaimed his wife. "I would just like to know what is inside. . . . If only I dared lift the lid a bit. I am sure it is a great delicacy."

"It may have a mechanical attachment, like a pistol, so that it goes off the moment you touch it, and then everybody in the whole place can hear it," said the woodcutter thoughtfully.

"Ugh!" cried the wife, and she didn't touch the tureen. But she dreamed about it that night. In her dream the lid of the tureen lifted itself and she smelled the loveliest punch, the kind one gets at weddings and funerals. Next to the tureen lay a silver coin and on it was inscribed: "Drink, and you will become the richest person in the world, and all others will become paupers." When she awoke, she told her husband about her dream.

"You shouldn't think so much about the tureen," was his comment.

"We could just lift the lid a little, ever so gently," pleaded the wife.

"Very, very gently," agreed her husband.

And the wife lifted the lid the tiniest bit, and out jumped two little mice and ran away, down into a mousehole.

"That was it!" said the king, who had been watching them. "Now you can go back where you came from, and don't be bitter about Adam and Eve. You have been just as curious and ungrateful as they were."

"I wonder how such a story has become known and printed," said Garden-Ole. "It might have been us! Such a tale is worth thinking about."

The next day they went to work. The sun scorched them and the rain soaked them; and they grumbled. All the disgruntled thoughts they had during the day they chewed on in the evening.

It was still light when they had finished supper and Ole asked his son to read the story of the woodcutter once more.

"But there are many other stories in the book," Hans replied. "Stories you don't know."

"Those I don't care about," said Garden-Ole. "I want to hear the one I know."

And Hans read the story again, and that was not the only evening he had to read it, or that it was discussed.

"It still does not explain everything," Ole said one evening. "Human beings are like milk. Some are churned into sweet butter and some become whey. Why should some always be lucky, be born to a high station, and never experience sorrow or want?"

Cripple-Hans was listening to what his father said and, though his legs were wobbly, his mind wasn't. He read another story from his book of fairy tales, the story of the man who had never known sorrow or want:

The king lay dying and could only be cured by being given the shirt of a man of whom it could truthfully be said that he had never known sorrow or want.

Messengers were sent to all the corners of the world, to all kings and noblemen, who one might suppose were happy; but every one of them had experienced, at some time or other, sorrow and want.

"But I haven't!" said the swineherd who was sitting in the ditch. "I have been happy all my life." And as if to prove it he both laughed and sang.

"Then give me your shirt," ordered the messenger. "You shall have half the kingdom for it."

But the swineherd did not own a shirt, even though he called himself the happiest person in the world.

"That was a fellow," shouted Ole; and he and his wife laughed as they hadn't for years.

"What are you all so happy about?" asked the schoolteacher, who had just entered the cottage. "Laughter is new with you. Have you won in the lottery?"

"No, nothing like that," explained Ole. "Hans has been reading to us the story of the man who had never known sorrow or want. That fellow was so poor he didn't even have a shirt on his back. When you hear a story like that it is hard not to laugh. Imagine, it is printed in a book of fairy tales. Well, everyone has their load to bear, and hearing about others makes your own lighter."

"Where have you got the book from?" asked the schoolteacher, and smiled.

"Hans got it at Christmastime over a year ago. The mistress gave it to him because he is a cripple and has a liking for reading. Then we would have preferred a new shirt; but the book is strange, it can give answers to the questions you've been thinking about."

The schoolteacher picked up the book and started to leaf through it.

"Let's listen to the same story all over again!" exclaimed Garden-Ole. "And when you've finished that one, we can hear about the woodcutter and his wife." Those two stories remained enough for Ole. They were like two sun rays in the low-ceilinged rooms of the cottage, in the warped, cowed soul of the man.

Hans had read the whole book, not only once, but countless times. The fairy tales carried him where his legs refused to go—out into the world beyond the cottage walls. From that day on the schoolmaster came often during the afternoons, when the cripple lay alone in the house. Such visits were a feast to the boy. The old man told him about the size of the earth and its strange lands; how the sun was almost half a million times as big as the earth, and so far away that it would take a cannon ball twenty-five years to reach it: a journey that the rays of the sun could make in eight minutes. These were things that any school child knew, but to Hans it was all new and even more wonderful than the stories in the book of fairy tales.

Once or twice a year the schoolteacher dined at the manor house, and here he told what a blessing the gift of the fairy-tale book had been, not only to the boy but to the whole family. As the schoolteacher was leaving, the mistress gave him a silver mark to give to Hans when next he visited him.

"That my parents can have," said Hans when the schoolmaster gave him the money.

And they were most happy to receive it. "Cripple-Hans can be both a blessing and of use," they commented. It sounded harsh but wasn't meant so.

A few days after the schoolteacher's visit to the manor house, the carriage of the young mistress stopped in front of the cottage. The sweet, tender-hearted woman had come to pay a visit to the boy, because she was so pleased that her Christmas gift had brought so much happiness to both the child and his family. She had a basket with her that contained a fine wheat bread, fruits, and a bottle of black currant juice. But for Hans she had something really amusing: a wire cage, painted gold, in which sat a little black bird that whistled ever so prettily. The cage was put on a chest at a distance from the boy's bed.

Hans could lie in bed and look at it and listen to it. The bird sang so loudly that even the passers-by could hear it.

Garden-Ole and Garden-Kirsten did not get home until long after the lady of the manor had departed. They saw how happy Hans was, but they were not happy; the gift seemed to them nothing but trouble.

"The rich never think about things like that, having servants at their beck and call," they said. "Cripple-Hans can't take care of it, so we'll have to. In the end the cat will get it."

One week went by and then another. The cat had been in the room many times without scaring the bird or harming it. Then one afternoon, while Hans was reading his book of fairy tales, it happened. The boy was reading the story of the fisherman's wife who wished that she was king and then became it; then she desired to be Pope and also that wish was granted; but when she wished that she was God Himself, she was put right back into the muddy ditch where she had come from. From this story no moral can be drawn about the cat and the bird, it just happened by chance to be the one Hans was reading.

The cage stood on the chest; the cat sat on the floor and looked with its yellow-green eyes up at the bird. The animal's expression said, "You are so beautiful, I would love to eat you." Hans guessed its intentions; he read it on the face of the cat and screamed.

"Go away, cat! Go outside!" The cat tightened its muscles, ready to jump. Hans could not reach it and he had nothing to throw at the animal but his treasure, the book of fairy tales.

He threw it! But the binding was loose. Half of it went one way and half another, and neither hit the cat.

The cat turned and looked at the boy as if to say: "Don't mix in my affairs, little Hans, I can run and leap and you can do neither."

Hans kept staring at the cat. The bird was beginning to be frightened now. There was no one whom Hans could call; he was alone in the house. It was as if the cat knew it. Again it got ready to leap. Hans waved his bedcover and finally threw that at the cat, but the cat didn't mind, it jumped up on a chair and then onto the window sill. Now it was nearer the chest and the cage.

Hans could feel the pulsing of his heart, though he did not give it thought; all his attention was on his bird and the cat. He could not get out of bed, he could not walk, for his legs could not carry him.

It felt as if a hand were squeezing his heart when the cat leaped from the window sill to the chest, pushing over the cage so it fell on the floor. The bird screeched and flapped its wings against the wires of the cage. With a scream Hans jumped out of bed and ran over to pick up the cage and chase the cat away. He was not aware of what he was doing until he stood with the cage in his hand; then he ran out of the house to the road. Tears streamed down his face and he kept repeating as loudly as he could: "I can walk! I can walk!"

He was no longer a cripple; such things can happen and it did happen to Hans. The schoolmaster lived not far away. Hans entered his

room, barefoot, wearing his nightshirt and still carrying the cage with
the bird in it. "I can walk!" he sobbed to the old man. "Oh, my God!
I can walk!"

That was a happy day in the little cottage. Both Garden-Ole and
Garden-Kirsten agreed that it was the happiest day of their lives.
Hans was asked to come to the manor, along the path he had not
walked for many a year.

It seemed to the boy that the hazelnut bushes and the trees nodded
to him and said, "Good day, Hans, welcome out here." The sun
shone in his face and his heart.

The young squire and his wife looked so happy that one would
have thought that Hans was a member of the family. The young
woman was the happier of the two, for she had given the child both
the book of fairy tales and the little bird that had been the cause of his
recovery.

The bird had died of fright, but the book the boy would keep and
read, no matter how old he became. Now he would be able to learn
a trade; perhaps he could become a bookbinder. "Then I would be
able to read all the latest books."

Later that day, his parents were called to the manor house. The
young mistress explained to them that she and her husband thought
that Hans was a very good and clever boy, who could read well, and
understood what he read. "God always blesses a good cause," she
added.

That evening Garden-Ole and his wife were really happy, especially
Garden-Kirsten. But not a week had passed before their eyes were
filled with tears. Hans was a good boy, and he had new clothes, but
now he was leaving, traveling across the water to the capital, to go to
school, where he would learn such things as Latin. It would be several
years before they would see him again.

The book of fairy tales Hans was not allowed to take with him.
His parents wanted to keep it, and Ole often read from it, but only the
same two stories that he knew.

Letters came from Hans, one happier than the next. The family he
lived with were well to do and ever so nice, but the best of all was
the school. There was so much to learn that he wished he could live to
be a hundred and become a schoolmaster himself.

"It is so strange that it should happen to us," said his parents, and held each other's hands and looked as solemn as when they went to communion.

"That it should happen to Hans," said Ole, "shows that God also remembers the poor man's child; and his being a cripple makes it sound like one of the stories from Hans's book of fairy tales."

## 156

## Auntie Toothache

Where did we get this story from?

Would you like to know?

We got it from the grocer's paper barrel. Many good and even rare books have ended up in the paper barrel. When they are taken out again, it is not to be read but to be used as wrapping for coffee, sugar, cheese, butter, and pickled herrings—the latter gets a double portion—which proves that written matter has a practical value.

Often things go into the paper barrel that shouldn't.

I have a friend who knows all about it, because he is not only the son of a greengrocer, who has a store in the basement; but he is apprenticed to a grocer. The young man had advanced himself from the cellar to the street floor. He is very well read in barrel literature: both the handwritten and the printed. He has a whole library of it, but he has two stores to choose from. It is an interesting collection. There are several love letters; official government communications that were thrown in a wastepaper basket by an absent-minded bureaucrat; and some long, gossipy letters filled with scandal that must never be told to a soul. My young friend is a rescuer of literature and has saved, if not books, then many pages of books that deserved to be read more than once.

He has shown me his collection, both of printed and handwritten documents. A few sheets of large folio paper caught my attention because of the beautiful handwriting.

"That belonged to the student," my friend explained. "The one who lived across from us. He died last month. He suffered terribly from toothaches. It is amusing to read about. There are only a few pages left. There was a whole book, if not more, when my father bought it from his landlady. He paid half a pound of green soap for it. This is all I managed to save; the rest had already been used for wrapping."

I borrowed it, I read it, and now I will let you read it. Its title was:

### AUNTIE TOOTHACHE

When I was a little boy, Auntie always fed me sweets. My teeth survived it. Now when I am older and have become a student she still spoils me with sweets; she calls me a poet.

I have something of a poet in me, but not enough. Sometimes as I walk through the streets of the city it seems to me to be a giant library. All the houses are bookcases, each floor a shelf with books. Here is an everyday story, written realistically; there an old-fashioned comedy; and beside it, where the gauze curtains hang, a scientific treatise. Pornography and literature of real value are on the same shelf. I can daydream and philosophize while I walk through my "library."

Yes, there is something of a poet in me, but not enough. I think many people have as much of a poet in them as I do, without calling themselves one. They are lucky and I am lucky too, for to have an imagination is a blessing, even when it is so small that it cannot be shared. It is like a sun ray that fills your soul and your mind. It comes as a sudden smell of flowers, a melody that one knows and remembers, but cannot recall where from.

The other evening as I sat in my room I had no book to read and was in need of one, when a leaf fell from the linden tree outside. The wind carried it through the open window into my room. I picked it up and looked at its green surface with its many veins. A little bug was studying it too; at least, it plodded across the leaf as if that were what it was doing. Suddenly it struck me that such was human wisdom. Don't we study merely the leaf, and yet lecture about the whole tree: root, crown, and trunk—God, death, and immortality? And all we know anything about is the leaf.

Just at that moment Aunt Mille came to visit me. I told her my thoughts and showed her the leaf, upon which the insect was still crawling.

She clapped her hands. "You are a poet!" she exclaimed. "Maybe the greatest we have. If only I live to see you fulfill your destiny, then I shall die contented. Ever since the funeral of Brewer Rasmussen I have been amazed by your imagination!"

This is what Auntie said, word for word; and then she kissed me. But who was Auntie Mille and who was Brewer Rasmussen?

II

My mother's aunt was called by us children simply Auntie, we had no other name for her.

She gave us jam and sugar sandwiches, though she knew it was bad for our teeth. As she said herself, she could not help indulging such sweet children. It seemed to her cruel to deny them something they so adored, and therefore we all loved Auntie.

She was an old maid. As long as I can remember, she had been old. It was as if her age had reached a certain point and then stood still. She used to suffer from toothaches, and talked about it a good deal; therefore her friend Brewer Rasmussen nicknamed her "Auntie Toothache."

The brewer, who had sold his brewery and now lived on his savings, often visited Auntie. He was a little older than she, and he did not have a whole tooth in his mouth, only black stubs. He said that this was because he had eaten too much sugar as a child, and we children should be careful or the same thing would happen to us.

Auntie had obviously not eaten any sugar as a child, because she had the most beautiful white teeth.

"She takes such good care of her teeth that she won't even sleep with them at night," explained Brewer Rasmussen.

We knew that this was not a nice thing to say, but Auntie smiled and explained that he didn't know what he was talking about.

Another time, when both she and Brewer Rasmussen were having lunch with us, Auntie mentioned that she had had a nightmare, in which she dreamed that one of her teeth fell out. "That means that I shall lose a true friend."

"But if it was a false tooth," said the brewer, and laughed, "then it must be a false friend."

"You are a very rude old man!" Auntie replied. She was angrier than I have ever seen her, either before or since.

Later she said that it was only nonsense; her old friend, who was one of the noblest persons she had ever known, had only been teasing her. When he died he would become one of God's little angels up in heaven.

I thought a great deal about this transformation and wondered if I would be able to recognize Brewer Rasmussen in this new shape.

When Auntie was young, the brewer had proposed to her, but it had taken her too long to make up her mind. She had kept putting it off until she became an old maid, but they had remained faithful friends.

Brewer Rasmussen died. He was driven to his grave in a hearse with four black horses and followed by a great many mourners, among them several in uniform, wearing decorations.

Auntie stood at her window dressed in black, together with all her nieces and nephews, except for my little brother whom the stork had brought only three weeks before. When the hearse and the mourners had passed and the street was empty again, Auntie wanted to leave. But I didn't, I was waiting for the little angel Brewer Rasmussen was supposed to become. I was sure that he would show up.

"Auntie," I began, "don't you think he's coming now? Or maybe, when the stork brings us another little brother, it will be Angel Rasmussen?"

Auntie was so impressed by my great imagination that she said, "That child will become a great poet." This she repeated all through my childhood, even after I was confirmed and right up to now, when I am a student.

She was and is my most compassionate friend, both when I suffer from poetry "pains" and when I suffer from toothaches. I have attacks of both.

"Write down all your thoughts," she would say. "Put them in a drawer, that is what Jean Paul did, and he became a great author. Though I am not fond of him; he is too narrow-minded. You must be broad. You will broaden yourself!"

That night I lay sleepless and in agony because of my longing and desire to become the great poet that Auntie saw in me; that's what I call "poet pain." But there is a suffering that is more ferocious, and that is a toothache, for it pokes and squeezes you until you are no longer a man but a squirming worm, chewing on a spice bag.

"Oh, that pain I know," said Auntie. Her lips smiled sorrowfully; her teeth were pure white.

But now I must begin the third section of the story of myself and Auntie.

III

I had moved to new lodgings and had lived there about a month and was telling Auntie about it.

"The family that I have rented my room from care so little what happens to me, I can ring the bell three times without anyone answering it. It just occurred to me that it could be because no one hears it, for the house is a circus of noises, from wind and weather and human beings. I live just above the entrance. Every cart or carriage that passes below makes the pictures on my walls dance. When the janitor finally shuts the gate at night, it sounds and feels like an earthquake. The whole house shakes. If I am already in bed, the jolt goes through every limb of my body, but they say that that is good for the nerves. If the wind blows—and when does it not blow in this country?—then the big iron hasps that hold the windows, when they are open, bang against the walls; and the bell above the neighbor's portal tolls with every gust of wind.

"The other lodgers come home in bunches, at every hour of the night. The fellow who has rented the room above mine gives trombone lessons during the day; at night before he goes to bed, which is never before midnight, he always takes a brisk walk around his room, wearing his iron-shod alpine boots.

"There are no storm windows, but there is a broken window, the landlady has glued paper over it. When the winds blow it makes a noise like a bumblebee. That is good bedtime music. When I finally do fall asleep, I am awakened early by the cock crowing in a henyard that is in the back of the house. The hen and the rooster wish to let me know that it will soon be morning. My landlord has two small horses but no stables. He keeps the animals in a small room to the right of the gateway, underneath my room. The poor beasts have so little space that, in order to get exercise, they kick at the walls and the door.

"As soon as the sun is up the janitor, whose domicile is in the garret, puts on his wooden shoes and runs down the stairs. He opens the gate with a bang and the whole house shakes. When that is over the lodger above me starts his morning exercises; this physical-training act is accomplished with great iron balls. He holds one in each hand, but they are too heavy for him, and time and again they fall to the floor—which is my ceiling.

"Then it is time for children to go to school. They run through the house screaming and shouting as if they were being tortured. I open my window to get some fresh air for my health. But I am reminded that across the yard there is a tannery. All in all, it is a very nice house, and I live with a quiet family."

This was about the way I described my lodgings to Auntie; possibly the spoken words were a little livelier than the written, I often find that that is so.

"You are a poet!" screamed Auntie. "Write it down, it is as good as Dickens. I think it is better; at least, I find it more interesting. You draw as you talk. I can see the house in front of me. I shudder! . . . You must begin to write. Just put some living creatures in that picture: human beings—lovely people, but preferably unhappy ones; they are the most interesting."

Well, I wrote it down. I have described the house exactly as it is, with all its sounds and noises, but without any plot or characters except myself. They will come later!

IV

It was winter and late in the evening. It was terrible weather. There was a snowstorm and the wind was blowing so hard that I could hardly hold myself upright.

Auntie had been at the theater, and I had come to escort her home. I had trouble trying to keep myself from falling and I couldn't get a cab, because they were all taken.

Auntie lived far from the theater, but my room was nearby. Had it been otherwise, we should have had to seek shelter in a sentry box.

We tramped through the deep snow with the snowflakes whirling about us. Auntie held onto my arm. I supported her like a buttress against the wind. Some places I even had to carry her. We only fell twice, and then we fell softly.

When we came to the entrance of the house where I lived we shook the snow off our clothes—or at least we tried to, but when we stood in the vestibule we noticed that we had covered the floor with snow. We took off our coats, hats, and shoes; we were wet to the skin. My landlady loaned Auntie stockings and a dressing gown. That was necessary, she said, or Auntie would catch a cold. Then she added that Auntie would not be able to get home that night, which was quite apparent. She offered Auntie the couch in their living room to sleep on. It stood next to the closed and locked door between that room and mine. Auntie agreed to stay.

The fire was burning in the stove. The samovar was on the table. My room appeared quite cozy, although not as cozy as Auntie's, which in the winter has heavy curtains in front of all doors and windows and double carpets on the floor, with three layers of newspapers underneath. At Auntie's one feels as if one were inside a properly corked bottle filled with hot air. But, as I said, even my poor room grew cozy, while the wind blew outside.

Auntie talked about her youth. She recounted her early years and Brewer Rasmussen's; they were old memories.

She could remember when I had got my first tooth, and the family's joy at this amazing achievement. The first tooth. The tooth of innocence, shining as white as milk: a milk tooth! If one arrived, then there would soon be a rank and file. But the beautiful baby teeth are only the avant-garde; later come the company that should last you all your life. The last to arrive are the wisdom teeth: one on every flank. They are born with great difficulty and in pain. Every tooth leaves you again, and that out of turn, before the need for its service is over. That day the last tooth leaves is no day of rejoicing; on the contrary, it is a day of mourning. Then one is old, even though one's spirit may be young.

Such things are not a pleasure to talk about, and yet that's what Auntie and I happened to discuss. We talked and talked, and it was past midnight before Auntie went to bed in the room next door.

"Good night, my boy," she called through the locked door. "Here I am as comfortable as in my own bed at home."

She slept peacefully, though there was no peace in the house:

neither inside nor out. The storm shook the windows, rattled the iron hasps, and rang the neighbor's bell. The lodger upstairs had come home and was taking his constitutional around the room; finally he took off his boots, threw them across the floor, and went to bed. He slept well. I could hear his snoring through the ceiling.

There was no peace for me. I was restless. The storm didn't rest either; it was most rudely alert. The wind kept blowing, singing through every crack it could find. It was very lively. So were my teeth. They whistled and sang in their own fashion, a toothache was brewing.

There was a draft from the window. The moonlight shone in and spilled its light upon the floor. It grew sharper and then disappeared, as the wind whipped the clouds across the sky. There was a commotion of light and shadow, and finally the shadow on the floor seemed to grow into a shape. At the same time I felt a gust of ice-cold air thrust itself against my face.

On the floor sat a figure. It looked like a person drawn by a child with chalk on a blackboard: something that is supposed to look like a man. The body is but one thin line, the legs and arms are a line each, and the head is only a circle. As the figure became more visible, I realized that it had a thin and very fine gown on, which showed that it was a female.

There was a humming noise. Where did it come from? Was it the wind that was playing with the broken window? Or was it the shadow on the floor that was talking?

It was she! Madame Toothache herself! In all her horrible, monstrous splendor. *Satania infernalis!* May God free us and save us from her visit!

"This is a nice place to be," she hummed. "I think the house is built on a filled-in swamp. Here the poisonous mosquitoes have buzzed. They are gone, but I have their sting, and I sharpen it on human teeth. Look how nice and white they shine in the mouth of the fellow in the bed. They have tasted sour and sweet, hot and cold, nutshells and plum pits! I will rock them loose, fertilize them with an icy wind; they will feel a draft around their roots."

What a horrible harangue! What a horrible hag!

"So you are a poet!" she squeaked. "I shall help you to compose an 'Ode to Pain.' You will be so versed in shooting and sharp pain, I shall make your jaded nerves jingle!"

It felt as if a hot iron awl had been driven through my cheekbone.

"You have a good set of teeth!" she continued. "It is an organ to play upon—a mouth organ! We'll have a concert with drums, flutes, trumpets. The wisdom teeth can play the bassoons. For a great poet, great music!"

Hideously did she play, and hideous did she look, although all I saw was her hand. It was ice-cold and she held it in front of my face: her shadowy gray hand. She had long awl-like fingers. The thumb and the index finger were pinchers; the middle finger was a pointed needle; the ring finger, a drill; and the little finger stung.

"I shall teach you to write verses," she screamed. "For a great poet a great toothache, to a little poet a little toothache."

"Oh, let me be a little poet," I begged. "Oh, let me just be! I am no poet! I only have attacks of poetry, as I have attacks of toothaches. Let me be! Leave me alone!"

"Do you admit that I am greater than poetry, mathematics, philosophy, and all the rest of the music?" she asked. "Do you confess that I am stronger and more penetrating than all other feeling that has been painted on canvas or carved in marble? I am older than all the others. I was born right outside the gates of paradise, where the wet winds blow and the toadstools grow. I made Eve put an extra fig leaf on; and Adam—oh, believe me, that was some toothache, the first one in the world!"

"I agree to anything, to everything!" I moaned. "Just leave!"

"Will you agree to give up trying to become a poet? Never again to write a verse down on a piece of paper or a blackboard or anything else? If you promise, I shall let you go, but if you break your promise I shall come back!"

"I swear I won't!" I screamed. "Let me never sense your presence again!"

"Feel me you won't, but see me you shall. In a more substantial form than I have now. In the shape that is more pleasing to you than the one I now possess. You shall see me as Aunt Mille and I shall say to you: 'You are a dear boy and a great poet, the greatest we have!' But if you believe that and start writing verses, then I shall compose music to them and play them on your mouth organ. You sweet child! Remember me when you look at Auntie."

Then she disappeared, giving me a sharp jab with the awl before she left. The pain disappeared and I felt as though I were gliding through still waters, where the white lotus flower bloomed with its great green leaves. I sank beneath the water, into the great stillness where peace reigns.

"Die, melt like the snow," the waters sang around me. "Sail like the cloud and disappear." Through the waters I saw the victorious banners on which the names of the immortal were inscribed; the banners were made of mayfly wings.

I slept deeply and my sleep was dreamless. I did not hear the singing wind, or the banging of the gates, or the lodger above me doing his morning exercises. Oh, bliss!

A gust of wind shook the house, and the door next to Auntie's bed rattled. She woke, got dressed, and came into my room. I was sleeping like "one of God's little angels," she declared, and she could not bear to wake me.

A little later I opened my eyes. I had forgotten that Auntie had spent the night there. When I saw her I remembered my toothache: dream and reality walked hand in hand.

"Did you write anything last night after I left?" asked Auntie. "I wish you had! You are my poet, and a great poet you will become."

It seemed to me that she smiled curiously while she spoke. I did not know whether it was sweet old Aunt Mille who sat on the chair across from me or the horror of my dream, to whom I had made a promise.

"Have you written something, a verse, my sweet boy?"

"No! No!" I screamed. "Are you Aunt Mille?"

"Who else should I be?" she answered; and she was Aunt Mille. She kissed me, got into a cab, and drove home. I wrote down what is written here, but it is not in verse, and it will never be published.

Here the manuscript ended. It had been longer but my friend, the grocer's apprentice, could not find the missing pages. They had disappeared out in the world, not as literature, but as wrapping for pickled herring, butter, and green soap. The paper had done its duty.

The brewer is dead. Auntie is dead. The student is dead—the spark of whose brain ended in the paper barrel. The story is over: the story of Auntie Toothache.

## Translator's Note

*In an age more economical than our own, paperbacks were published first; and then, if they were successful, a bound volume appeared. Throughout Andersen's life his fairy tales and stories were printed in almost leaflet-sized booklets, without binding or illustrations—containing anywhere from one to more than a dozen tales—before they were collected and printed in book form. It is to these booklets that Andersen refers in his notes.*

*The notes were written for the Danish editions of Andersen's works. Many of his stories appeared in Germany, some in England, and a few in the United States, before they were published in his native land. Although he always wrote his tales in Danish, he was able to supervise the German translations personally.*

*The present translation follows the text and order of the Danish edition of 1874, which Andersen himself edited; except for two insignificant changes: an ABC Book and a poem titled* Ask Mother Amager—*a joke, the humor of which depends on the reader knowing Amager, which is a district of Copenhagen—for obvious reasons, have been replaced by two brief sketches.* The Talisman *and* It Is You the Fable Is About, *which Andersen wrote for a Danish newspaper; thus the magic number of 156 fairy tales and stories has been kept.*

## Preface, 1837: for the Older Readers

Nothing that I have written has been evaluated so differently as *Fairy Tales, told for children.* A few people, whose judgment I prize, have said that these fairy tales are the most valuable of all my work; while others have remarked that they are of no importance whatever and advised me not to write any more of them. This diversity of opinion, and the silence with which the professional critics greeted these tales, weakened my desire to write again in this literary form. Thus a year has passed before the third booklet follows the second and the first.

While I was engaged in writing something larger and completely different, the idea and the plot of THE LITTLE MERMAID intruded and would not go away, so I had to write this fairy tale.

I feared that if I published it alone it would seem a little too presumptuous, so I decided to place it among a group of tales that I had already begun. The others in this booklet are more children's stories than this one, whose deeper meaning only an adult can understand; but I believe that a child will enjoy it for the story's sake alone: that the plot, in itself, is exciting enough to absorb a child's attention.

The shorter tale, THE EMPEROR'S NEW CLOTHES, is a Spanish story. For the whole amusing idea we must thank Prince Don Juan Manuel, who was born in 1277 and died in 1347.

While talking about these two tales, I will take the opportunity of saying a few words about my earlier stories.

In my childhood I loved to listen to fairy tales and stories. Many of them are still very alive in my memory. Certain of them seem to me to be Danish in origin for I have never heard them anywhere else. These I have told in my own way: where I thought it fitting, I have changed them and let imagination freshen the colors in the picture that had begun to fade. There are four such stories in this volume: THE TINDER-BOX, LITTLE CLAUS AND BIG CLAUS, THE PRINCESS AND THE PEA; and THE TRAVELING COMPANION. In Anacreon's poem, as most people know, the fable THE NAUGHTY BOY is to be found.

Three of the stories are entirely my own: LITTLE IDA'S FLOWERS, INCHELINA, THE LITTLE MERMAID.

With the third booklet, the tales become a little volume; whether this will be the only one depends upon the impression this collection makes on the public.

In a little land like ours, the poet is always poor; honor, therefore, is the golden bird he tries to grasp. Time will tell whether I can catch it by telling fairy tales.

Copenhagen, March 1837                    H. C. Andersen

# Notes for My
# Fairy Tales and Stories

It has been said to me that a few remarks as to how my fairy tales came into being, and what happened to them once they did, might be of interest to some of my readers; therefore I am writing these notes.

At Christmastime 1829, I had printed a small volume of poetry, in which was included a fairy tale: THE SPECTER. This story, which I had heard as a child, I retold in a style resembling that of Musäus. It was not a success and I rewrote it several years later, in a different manner, and called it THE TRAVELING COMPANION.

In 1831, during a journey to Hartzen, the true spirit of the fairy tale came to me for the first time; I found it in the story about the old king who believed that he had never heard a lie and therefore offered his daughter and half his kingdom to anyone who could tell him one.

My first booklet, *Fairy Tales, told for children*, was published in 1835. It was 61 pages long and contained:

THE TINDERBOX

LITTLE CLAUS AND BIG CLAUS

THE PRINCESS AND THE PEA

LITTLE IDA'S FLOWERS

I wanted the style to be such that the reader felt the presence of the storyteller; therefore the spoken language had to be used. I wrote the stories for children, but older people ought to find them worth listening to. The first three of the tales I had heard as a child, either in the spinning room or during the harvesting of the hops.

LITTLE IDA'S FLOWERS came to me during a visit to the poet Thiele, while I was telling his little daughter Ida about the flowers in the botanical gardens; and some of the child's remarks are recorded in the story.

The second booklet appeared in 1836 and contained:

INCHELINA

THE NAUGHTY BOY

THE TRAVELING COMPANION

The year after followed a third which included:

THE LITTLE MERMAID

THE EMPEROR'S NEW CLOTHES

The three booklets were made into a volume and published in book form, with a title page and a table of contents; and I wrote a little introduction for it, in which I complained that my tales had met with indifference, which was true. Of the nine stories, only LITTLE IDA'S FLOWERS, INCHELINA, and THE LITTLE MERMAID are original fairy tales, not folk tales which I have retold. THE LITTLE MERMAID did receive some applause, which encouraged me to try to write more tales of my own invention.

THE MAGIC GALOSHES was published in 1838; the poet Hostrup borrowed my galoshes in his marvelous student comedy, *The Neighbors*.

The same year at Chistmastime appeared a booklet containing:

THE DAISY

THE STEADFAST TIN SOLDIER

These are both original, whereas the third fairy tale, THE WILD SWANS, is a Danish folk tale retold.

The second booklet included:

THE GARDEN OF EDEN

THE FLYING TRUNK

THE STORKS

The first of these is an old tale that I had heard as a child and that had pleased me very much. I wanted, however, to make it longer; I felt the winds must have more to tell; and the garden should be more fully described, and this I attempted to do.

The theme for THE FLYING TRUNK is from *The Arabian Nights*. THE STORKS is based on the common superstitions about that bird and on those nursery rhymes that children know about storks.

In the years 1840 and '41, after a journey to Greece and

Constantinople, I published a book called *A Poet's Bazaar*. In the German edition of my collected *Fairy Tales*, three stories from this book were included: THE BRONZE PIG, THE PACT OF FRIENDSHIP, and A ROSE FROM HOMER'S GRAVE. I have now included them in the Danish collection, in the order that they appeared in the German.

The third booklet with the title *Fairy Tales, told for children* was published in 1842; it contained:

THE SANDMAN

THE ROSE ELF

THE SWINEHERD

THE BUCKWHEAT

In THE SANDMAN, only the name and the idea of there being a creature who appears and makes children sleepy have been borrowed. The plot of THE ROSE ELF comes from an Italian folk song. THE SWINEHERD has certain traits in common with an old Danish folk tale, but the version I heard, as a child, would be quite unprintable. This fairy tale has been dramatized in Germany. It was called *Die Prinzessin von Marzipan und der Schweinehirt von Zuckerland* and was performed in Berlin.

THE BUCKWHEAT stems from the common superstition that lightning will scorch it black.

This was the final booklet in the second volume of fairy tales and was dedicated to Johanne Louise Heiberg: "It was said that fairies only exist in the fairy tale; but then you came, and everyone believes what he can see, that one exists also in reality."

This book was dedicated to Mrs. Heiberg not only because she was a great artist and actress but also because she was one of the few persons who had liked and appreciated my fairy tales when they first appeared. Her kind words and H. C. Oersted's often repeated fondness for the humorous aspects of my fairy tales were my first real encouragement.

In the year 1842 the fairy tale MOTHER ELDERBERRY was published in a magazine. The "seed" for that story comes from a legend, retold by Thiele: "In the elderberry tree lives a creature called the 'elderberry woman' or 'Mother Elderberry.' She will revenge any harm done to the tree, and it has been told that a man who cut down an elderberry tree which grew in one of the little gardens of 'the new cottages' had died shortly after he did the deed." In my fairy tale,

Mother Elderberry has become a Danish dryad: memory herself. Later the story was dramatized.

That same year, in Gerson's and Kaalund's monthly magazine, the fairy tale THE BELL was published. This, like nearly all of my later fairy tales and stories, was wholly original. They lay in my mind like seeds and only needed a gentle touch—the kiss of a sunbeam or drop of malice—to flower.

How much could be accomplished through the fairy tale became clearer and clearer to me as I learned through the years of my own power and its limitation.

My fairy tales won me readers not alone among the children but among grownups as well. When in 1845 a new booklet was published, it was given the shorter title of *New Fairy Tales*. This little booklet contained:

THE ANGEL

THE NIGHTINGALE

THE SWEETHEARTS

THE UGLY DUCKLING

This was dedicated to the poet Carl Bagger "as a humble thank you for all those inspiring thoughts and wealth of feeling which his poetry has given me."

The first half of THE UGLY DUCKLING was written at Gisselfeldt but it was not completed until six months later. The other three works were written one after another, as if from the same inspiration. With the publication of this booklet, my fairy tales began to receive widespread recognition.

In the summer of 1846, I stayed at Nysø Castle while Thorvaldsen was there. He had been very amused by THE SWEETHEARTS and THE UGLY DUCKLING, and said to me: "Now write us a new and funny fairy tale! Why, you can write about anything, even a darning needle." I went straight up to my room and wrote THE DARNING NEEDLE.

The second booklet contained:

THE PINE TREE

THE SNOW QUEEN

These were dedicated to the poet Professor Frederik Hoegh-Guldberg. The story of the pine tree came to me in the Royal Theater during a performance of Mozart's *Don Juan,* and I wrote it down the same night. The first chapter of THE SNOW QUEEN was written in Maxen near Dresden in Germany, the rest of the fairy tale was written in Denmark.

The third booklet was published as a spring greeting to the poet Henrik Hertz, "in gratitude for all that his works, his deeply poetic soul, and rich wit have given us." It contained:

THE HILL OF THE ELVES

THE RED SHOES

THE JUMPING COMPETITION

THE SHEPHERDESS AND THE CHIMNEY SWEEP

HOLGER THE DANE

In *The Fairy Tale of My Life,* I have told how I received for my confirmation my first pair of boots; and how they squeaked as I walked up the aisle of the church; this pleased me no end, for I felt that now the whole congregation must know that my boots were new. But at the same time my conscience bothered me terribly, for I was aware that I was thinking as much about my new boots as I was about Our Lord. It was this recollection that inspired the fairy tale THE RED SHOES. This story has been particularly popular in the United States and in Holland.

THE JUMPING COMPETITION was told on the spur of the moment to some children who demanded a story.

HOLGER THE DANE is based on a Danish legend; it is very similar to a legend told about Frederick Barbarossa, who is supposed to be sitting inside the Kyffhäuser Mountain.

The first booklet that was included in the second volume of my fairy tales was published in 1847 and dedicated to J. L. Heiberg's mother, "the witty, brilliant and intelligent Mrs. Gyllembourg." It included:

THE OLD STREET LAMP

THE NEIGHBORS

THE DARNING NEEDLE

LITTLE TUCK

THE SHADOW

LITTLE TUCK was thought out during a visit to Oldenburg; it contains some reminiscences from my childhood.

THE SHADOW was composed during a visit to Naples but not written down before my return to Copenhagen.

The year after, a second booklet was published; it contained:
THE OLD HOUSE
A DROP OF WATER
THE LITTLE MATCH GIRL
THE STORY OF A MOTHER
THE COLLAR

In many of my fairy tales are recorded incidents that have happened to me. In *The Fairy Tale of My Life,* I have mentioned two that are to be found in THE OLD HOUSE. The writer Mosen's little son gave me, when I left Oldenburg, one of his tin soldiers, so that I should not be so terribly alone. It was the composer Hartmann's little daughter Maria who as a two-year-old always had to dance whenever she heard music. Once she entered the room while her older sisters and brothers were singing a hymn. She started to dance, and her musicality was such that it did not permit her to change the rhythm, so she danced by standing first on one leg and then on the other as long as the measure of the hymn demanded.

A DROP OF WATER was written for H. C. Oersted.

THE LITTLE MATCH GIRL was written during a stay at Graasten Castle, on my way south to foreign lands. There I received a letter from Mr. Flinch, containing three pictures. He wanted me to write a story about one of them for his almanac. I chose the picture of the poor little girl selling matches.

In the gardens of Glorup Castle on Fyn, where I used to spend several weeks in the summer, there was an area completely overgrown with giant dock weeds. These had been planted in bygone times as food for the white snails, which had been considered a delicacy. The dock plants and the snails were the inspiration for THE HAPPY FAMILY, which I wrote during a visit to London.

THE STORY OF A MOTHER came to me without any apparent reason while I was walking along the street, complete and ready to be written down. I have been told that this story is very popular with the Hindus.

THE FLAX was written in 1849 and first printed in the magazine *Native Land.*

After a journey in the north in 1851, I published a book entitled

*In Sweden.* From this book were taken for the German edition of my tales, illustrated by Lieutenant Pedersen, the following stories:

THE BIRD PHOENIX

GRANDMOTHER

A STORY

THE SILENT ALBUM

Many of my early fairy tales published in Germany had been illustrated, some by Hosemann, others by Count Pocci, Ludvig Richter, and Otto Speckter. The latter's very brilliantly conceived and splendid pictures had been used in the English edition that was published under the title *The Shoes of Fortune and other tales.* Now my German publisher, Lorck, in Leipzig, decided to publish my collected fairy tales and asked me to find a Danish artist to illustrate them. I chose the naval officer, V. Pedersen. Later my Danish publisher, Reitzel, bought the rights to his work from Mr. Lorck; and in 1849 a Danish edition with 125 illustrations by Lieutenant Pedersen was published.

In this beautiful volume all of my fairy tales were collected and it was referred to as the complete edition. But I did not feel that I was finished with this art form. A new title had to be found for the next collection. I decided to call it *Stories.* It seemed to me that our language has no better name for my tales, it encompasses their nature in its broadest sense. Nursery tales, legends, folk tales, fables, and narratives are all given the same title by children, peasants, and ordinary workingmen: they are called stories.

The first little booklet printed in 1852 contained:

THE YEAR'S STORY

THE WORLD'S MOST BEAUTIFUL ROSE

FROM THE RAMPARTS OF THE CITADEL

ON THE LAST DAY

IT IS PERFECTLY TRUE!

THE SWANS' NEST

A HAPPY DISPOSITION

In 1853 came the next booklet, containing:

GRIEF

EVERYTHING IN ITS RIGHT PLACE

THE PIXY AND THE GROCER

THE MILLENNIUM

UNDER THE WILLOW TREE

"Write," said the poet Thiele, "a fairy tale about a whistle that can blow everything into its right place." In these words lay the plot of the story and from that the fairy tale sprang.

UNDER THE WILLOW TREE contains some pages from the story of my own life.

The first edition of my stories was already out of print; and therefore it was decided by my Danish publisher, C. A. Reitzel, and my German publisher, Lorck, in Leipzig, to make an enlarged edition illustrated with drawings by V. Pedersen, as my book of fairy tales had been. This appeared in 1855 and the volume included, besides the stories already mentioned, those that had been published in the *The People's Calendar* and a few new ones:

THERE IS A DIFFERENCE

FIVE PEAS FROM THE SAME POD

A LEAF FROM HEAVEN

THE OLD GRAVESTONE

CLOD HANS

FROM A WINDOW IN VARTOV

IB AND LITTLE CHRISTINA

THE LAST PEARL

SHE WAS NO GOOD

THE UTTERMOST PARTS OF THE SEA

THE PIGGY BANK

The fairy tale, THERE IS A DIFFERENCE, was written at Christinelund, near the town of Praesto. There stood in a ditch a flowering apple tree, a picture of spring itself. The tree kept blooming so fragrantly in my mind that I could not get rid of it until I had planted it in a fairy tale.

FIVE PEAS FROM THE SAME POD stems from childhood memories of the little wooden box with chives and a single pea growing in it, which was then my garden.

THE OLD GRAVESTONE is a mosaic of memories. In my mind I place the story in the town of Svendborg, for it was there that I first thought of it. The gravestone itself was one that formed a step in the stone staircase that led up to Collin's house on Broad Street in Copenhagen; that, too, had a half-destroyed inscription. The picture of old Preben, sitting in the room next to the one in which his dead wife is lying, and becoming so absorbed in telling us about her in her youth, when they first became engaged, that he himself appears young and happy is a portrait of the composer Hartmann's old father, talking to us about his wife while she lay dead in a room nearby. All these memories of mine I have used in that story. It was first printed in Germany for an almanac in Bavaria, which I had been asked to write something for.

CLOD HANS is a Danish folk tale, very freely retold. It is quite singular among my later stories, practically all of which are of my own invention.

The kernel of SHE WAS NO GOOD lay in a couple of words my mother said when I was a little boy. One day, on the street in Odense, I saw another boy on his way to the stream where his mother, who was a washerwoman, stood in the water rinsing linen. A widow, well known for her sharp tongue and severely puritanical beliefs, screamed at the child from the window of her house: "Are you taking schnapps down to your mother again? It is disgusting! For shame! Let me never see you grow up to be like her, for she is no good!"

When I came home I told about the incident and everybody in the room agreed, "Yes, she drinks too much; she is no good!"

Only my mother was of a different opinion; she said, "Do not judge so harshly. The poor woman works so hard, she often spends the whole day standing in the cold water; and it is not every day that she gets a hot meal. She has to have something to fortify herself with. What she takes isn't right, that is true; but she does not know of anything better. She is an honest woman and she keeps her little boy neat and clean." I had been as willing as the others in the room to judge the washerwoman harshly; and therefore the mild and understanding words of my mother made a deep impression on me. Many years later when another incident made me reflect upon how often man judges harshly and severely, where charity might have seen the case from a different angle, this memory from my childhood came back to me so vividly that I wrote it down as the story, SHE WAS NO GOOD.

The German edition was soon out of print and a new one was to be published. This was augmented by the stories which I have already mentioned from *A Poet's Bazaar* and *In Sweden*. Also included were three stories from *The People's Calendar:* THE THORNY PATH, THE SERVANT, which is a retelling of a Hungarian tale, and THE

BOTTLE, all illustrated by V. Pedersen. The last story in the volume, THE PHILOSOPHER'S STONE, was also the last one that Lieutenant Pedersen illustrated; shortly afterward he died.

June 1862                                                    H. C. Andersen

# Notes for My
## Fairy Tales and Stories

After the death of V. Pedersen we had the difficult problem of finding someone with talent and ability similar to his, to illustrate my future stories and fairy tales. Among the many artists here in Denmark who—for their own amusement—had made sketches for my stories was Mr. Lorenz Frolich. He had already illustrated a couple of French children's books, which had been read with delight by both young people and grownups, and was justly well known for his accomplishments as an artist. He was now requested to illustrate my stories when they appeared in book form.

As in the past, the stories and fairy tales in the next three volumes followed the order, more or less, in which they were written and originally printed.

Each new group of stories was first published without illustrations. The first booklet—or collection, as they have also been called—appeared at Christmastime, 1857, and was reprinted four times. It was dedicated to Mrs. Serre in Maxen and included:

HOW TO COOK SOUP UPON A SAUSAGE PIN
THE BOTTLE
THE PEPPERMAN'S NIGHTCAP
"SOMETHING"
THE OLD OAK TREE'S LAST DREAM

In the proverbs and other phrases that we use to help us to express ourselves often lies hidden the seed of a story. HOW TO COOK SOUP

UPON A SAUSAGE PIN was a conscious attempt to write such a fairy tale.

One day my friend Councilman Thiele said to me in a teasing tone, "You must write for us the history of a bottle; from the moment it was created till the time when only the neck of it remains whole and it is used as a bird bath." And that's how THE BOTTLE came into existence.

THE PEPPERMAN'S NIGHTCAP has two sources: the origin of the word "pepperman"; and the myth about St. Elisabeth.

In "SOMETHING" I made use of a story that I had heard while visiting the west coast of Schleswig. There I was told about an old woman who had set fire to her house to save the many people who were out on the ice as the spring tide was coming in.

THE OLD OAK TREE'S LAST DREAM came in a moment's inspiration.

The second collection was printed in the spring of 1858 and was dedicated to Mrs. Laessoe, nee Abrahamson, and included:

THE BOG KING'S DAUGHTER

THE WINNERS

THE BELL DEEP

The first of these is one of those fairy tales on which I have spent the most time and hard work. It may be of interest to some to see how it sprouted, unfolded, and developed, as if they were watching it through a microscope. The basic story—as has been the case with all my fairy tales—occurred to me in a single moment, in the same way as a well-known melody or song can sometimes come into one's mind. I told the whole story at once to one of my friends and then wrote it down. Afterward I rewrote it; but even after the third version lay before me, I had to admit that there were still whole sections of it that were neither as clear nor as colorful as I thought they could or should be. I read some Icelandic sagas and these transported me backward in time. Inspired by them, I came a little closer to the truth. Then I read some modern travel writers' descriptions of Africa, until I began to feel the glowing tropical heat, and a strange new world around me; then I was able to write about it more honestly. Some scientific reports about the migrations of birds were also very helpful. They gave me new ideas; and to them I owe the descriptions of the typical traits of the birds, as they move about in my fairy tale. In a short time this story was rewritten six or seven times, until finally I was convinced that I could not improve upon it.

THE BELL DEEP is based on a story told by the people of Odense concerning the stream that runs through the city and the legend about the church bell from the tower of Albani Church.

THE EVIL KING is an old legend and is one of the first stories I wrote. It was first printed in Siesbye's *The Salon* and was later included in the German and English editions of my collected fairy tales and stories; so I think it should not be excluded in the Danish one.

The third collection of stories was published in the spring of 1859 and was dedicated to the composer J. P. E. Hartmann; it included:

WHAT THE WIND TOLD ABOUT VALDEMAR DAAE AND HIS DAUGHTERS
THE GIRL WHO STEPPED ON BREAD
THE WATCHMAN OF THE TOWER
ANNE LISBETH
CHILDREN'S PRATTLE
A STRING OF PEARLS

Among the folk legends of Denmark, as well as among the historical records of Borreby Castle near Skelskor, Valdemar Daae and his daughters are mentioned. It is one of the stories that I have revised most for the sake of style, so that the language would have the tone of the blistering, whistling wind, who tells the story.

I had long known the story of THE GIRL WHO STEPPED ON BREAD: of how the bread had turned to stone and dragged her down with it into the bog, where she disappeared. I set myself the task of lifting her out of the swamp psychologically, so that she could be redeemed; and from it the story developed.

In ANNE LISBETH, I wanted to show that all virtues lie in every human breast; and, like seeds, they must sprout, though sometimes it is in a roundabout way. This is the story of mother love and how it is given life and strength by experiencing fear and terror.

CHILDREN'S PRATTLE is based on personal experience.

A STRING OF PEARLS tells of the period of transition that I have lived through. In my childhood a trip from Odense to Copenhagen took about five days. Now it takes as many hours.

The fourth collection came out at Christmas, 1859, and included:

THE PEN AND THE INKWELL
THE DEAD CHILD
THE COCK AND THE WEATHERCOCK
"LOVELY"
A STORY FROM THE DUNES

Everyone who has heard Ernst or Leonard play the violin will be reminded of that wonderful experience while reading THE PEN AND THE INKWELL.

Of all my stories, I am happiest to have written THE DEAD CHILD and THE STORY OF A MOTHER, for they have given many grief-stricken mothers consolation and courage.

A STORY FROM THE DUNES came into existence after a trip to the west coast of Jutland and Skagen. Here I found the people and the natural surroundings that could provide a setting for thoughts that I had long wanted to weave into a story; these ideas grew out of a conversation with Oehlenschläger. His words had made a very deep impression upon me. When I first heard them I thought only about the words themselves and did not try—as seems natural to me now— to find out why he had said them.

We all know that mood in which we are tempted to express as a doubt, a truth which we have long since ceased to doubt, in order to hear our own arguments on someone else's tongue. Perhaps that was the situation in this case, or was Oehlenschläger testing my faith?

We were talking about eternal life when he asked: "Are you really convinced that there is a life after death?"

I insisted that I was and used as my basic argument my belief that God was just; but in my eagerness I spoke without thinking. "Man has a right to an afterlife!" I exclaimed.

"Isn't it vanity on your part to think you have a right to an eternal life?" he argued. "Hasn't God given you more than enough in this world? I know," he continued, "how very much I have enjoyed this life, so when Death closes my eyes I shall bless him and be grateful; if an eternal life awaits me, then I shall call it something new that God in His infinite mercy has given."

"*You* can talk like that," I replied. "God has given you so much here on earth—I, too, can say the same. But how many people in this world live quite differently? What about those who have a sick body or a stunted soul; those who are born into poverty and misery? Why have they suffered? Why are the blessings of life so unequally distributed? There is injustice; and this God would not have allowed, unless He intended to make up for it. He gives His word; and He keeps it as we cannot always do."

What I said that day is the material which the little tale, A STORY FROM THE DUNES, is made of. When it was printed a critic said that

I had never heard anyone express this doubt nor had I ever had it myself, and that was why the story did not ring true. If I remember correctly, it was the same critic—or another as well versed as he—who claimed that any reader would certainly be disappointed if—after reading my description of Skagen—he took a trip up there, expecting to find the poetic landscape I had written about. Since then I have had the pleasure of a visit from Brink Seidelin, a man who is really qualified to judge in this matter, since it is he who has written that excellent description of Skagen for the official geographical report of the district; and he congratulated me for having described so faithfully the scenery of northern Jutland. I received a letter from the minister of the church at Skagen, in which he complimented me for the description of the landscape because it was so true to life; and he added: "We also believe the other things you have told us; and from now on, when we show the old church to strangers, we shall say: 'That is where Jurgen is buried.'"

A young man of the district had been so kind as to take me for a drive up to the end of "the branch" and out to Old Skagen. Along the way we caught a glimpse of the church on the distant hill. Only the tower, which was now a seamark, could be seen above the sand. It would be a difficult climb for his horses and my host preferred not to drive up there; so I got out of the carriage and went alone up to the buried church. The impressions that I gathered on the walk can be found in A STORY FROM THE DUNES. Not long after the tale was published, this otherwise honest young man reported that I had never been at the church but only seen it at a distance; this he knew, for it was he who had driven me out there. It amused many to think that I had described something which I had, in fact, never seen; but I was not amused.

One day I met the young man in Copenhagen and asked him if he remembered our trip. "Oh yes!" he replied. "We drove along the road below the church out to Old Skagen."

"Yes," I agreed, "that was the way you drove. But don't you remember that I got out of the carriage and walked up to the church alone?" And then I told him about some of the things I had seen up there.

"You are right," he confessed. "You must have been up there, and I must have forgotten it."

I reminded him of the ridge of sand where I caught up with the carriage.

"I remembered that I had not been up to look at the tower, so I assumed that you hadn't either," the young man said.

I have recorded this incident for the sake of truth; otherwise, someone who has heard it from my guide's "own mouth" may, after my death, again tell how I described something that I had not seen with my own eyes.

The peasants and fishermen told me about many things that characterize life in that district, and some of their explanations I quoted in my story. Oddly enough, one critic gave me the "friendly advice" that when I talked about local customs I ought to ask the local people about them, which was exactly what I had done.

A STORY FROM THE DUNES brought me into contact with the poet Paludan-Müller. His appreciation of my tale has meant so much to me that I record it here.

THE TWO BROTHERS is an imaginary vignette about the life of the Oersted brothers.

THE OLD CHURCH BELL I was asked to write as a contribution to the *Schiller Album*. I wanted it to have something Danish in it; and how I managed that you will see when you read the story.

In the spring of 1861 the second volume of *New Fairy Tales and Stories* appeared. It contained:

THE TWELVE PASSENGERS
THE DUNG BEETLE
WHAT FATHER DOES IS ALWAYS RIGHT
THE PHILOSOPHER'S STONE
THE SNOWMAN
IN THE DUCKYARD
THE MUSE OF THE TWENTIETH CENTURY

It was dedicated to D. G. Murad, who was at the time Minister of Culture.

For the first number of *Household Words,* Charles Dickens had collected some Arabian proverbs; among them he found one particularly interesting: *"When the emperor's horse was given golden shoes, the dung beetle stuck forth his legs."*

"We suggest," Dickens commented, "that Hans Christian Andersen write a fairy tale about this." I wanted to very much, but no fairy tale came. Nine years later, when I was visiting the Danish castle Basnaes, where by chance I read Dickens' remark again, the fairy tale THE DUNG BEETLE suddenly stood before me.

WHAT FATHER DOES IS ALWAYS RIGHT is a Danish folk tale that I heard as a child and have retold in my own way.

Through the years I have tried to walk every radius, so to speak, in the circle of the fairy tale; therefore, quite often, if an idea or a subject has occurred to me that would bring me back to a form I have already tried, I have either let it go or attempted to give it a different form; that is why THE PHILOSOPHER'S STONE has an oriental style and is reminiscent of an allegory.

I have been reproached for having written, during my later years, philosophical stories, which, according to my critics, lie beyond my scope. These remarks were especially meant for THE MUSE OF THE TWENTIETH CENTURY. But this story is a natural outgrowth of the fairy tale.

It has been both said and written that this collection was the poorest I have yet produced, and yet among its pages are to be found two of my best fairy tales: WHAT FATHER DOES IS ALWAYS RIGHT and THE SNOWMAN. The latter was written at Christmastime at beautiful Basnaes Castle; and it is read aloud very often in preference to many other stories. Mantzius, the actor from the Royal Theater, includes it in his repertoire and his audiences seem to appreciate it greatly.

In later years a few people have said that only my very early fairy tales are of any importance, and all these that followed were inferior to them. This is hardly the case, but I believe that I can explain why the claim is made. Those people who read my stories when they were children have grown older and lost the fresh spirit with which they once approached and absorbed literature. There is also the possibility that some people feel that, since the fairy tales have been so widely known and acclaimed throughout the world, their author has been made happier than any living man ought to be. My earlier fairy tales have stood the test of time, so they must be left in peace, while the newer ones are attacked—for one must find fault with something.

Sometimes people comment without explaining exactly what they mean. How many times have I heard someone say, "I like your real fairy tales best, the first stories you wrote." And if I am so bold as to ask which fairy tale he or she may prefer, I am very often told: IT IS PERFECTLY TRUE!, THE BUTTERFLY, or THE SNOWMAN: all of which are of recent date.

If my previous booklet was my weakest collection—which I do not believe—the one that followed was one of the best. It came out at Christmas, 1861, and included:

THE ICE MAIDEN
THE BUTTERFLY
PSYCHE
THE SNAIL AND THE ROSEBUSH

It was dedicated to Björnstjerne Björnson: "You who are the tree of Norway: its budding, its flowering, and its fruit. From you have I learned of your native land. In Rome, which is filled with monuments to greatness, I glanced into your poetic heart. I care for you, therefore I bring you what maturity has placed in my lyre."

THE ICE MAIDEN was written during a longer stay in Switzerland, which I have visited so often. This time I was on my way home from Italy. The story about the eagle's nest was an experience of the Bavarian poet Koppel; and he told me about it.

THE BUTTERFLY was also written in Switzerland, during a trip from Montreux to Chillon.

PSYCHE had been written a few months before while I was still in Rome. Something that had happened during my first stay in the city, in 1833, came into my mind and became the seed of a story: while digging a grave for a young nun who had just died, a beautiful statue of Bacchus had been unearthed.

THE SNAIL AND THE ROSEBUSH belongs to that group of stories that I experienced myself.

After that booklet was published began the bitter, long years: the years of war. Denmark lost Als and Schleswig. Who could think of anything else? Days and years passed without any stories being written. Finally, at Christmas, 1865, a booklet dedicated to the ballet master August Bournonville was published. It included:

"THE WILL-O'-THE-WISPS ARE IN TOWN," SAID THE BOG WITCH
THE WINDMILL
THE SILVER SHILLING
THE BISHOP OF BOERGLUM CLOISTER AND HIS KINSMEN
IN THE CHILDREN'S ROOM
THE GOLDEN TREASURE
HOW THE STORM CHANGED THE SIGNS

The story about the will-o'-the-wisps leaped out of those long, sad years of the war.

Along the road between Sorø and Holsteinborg is a windmill. I passed it often; it always seemed on the verge of telling me a story, and finally it did, enclosed in a confession of faith. That's all I have to say about THE WINDMILL.

THE SILVER SHILLING was written in Leghorn. I arrived there from Civitavecchia on a steamboat. While on board I had exchanged a *scudo* for some smaller coins, and among them was a false two-franc piece. No one would accept it, and it irritated me that I had been fooled. But then came the idea for a story, and I got my money back.

THE BISHOP OF BOERGLUM CLOISTER was written after a visit to Boerglum Cloister. A well-known historical legend from the cruel Dark Ages, which so many people still talk of as having been lovely and desirable to live in, is told in contrast to our own lighter, happier age.

THE GOLDEN TREASURE was written at Frijsensborg. The lonely, lovely forest, the beautiful flower gardens, and the cozy rooms of the castle are, in my memory, inseparable from the story, which bloomed there like a flower on a lovely day.

HOW THE STORM CHANGED THE SIGNS and THE SONGBIRD OF THE PEOPLE were written in Copenhagen just before Christmas. The wonderful parade is a description of one that I saw in Odense when I was a child.

THE TEAPOT was written in Toledo.

THE LITTLE GREEN ONES and PEITER, PETER, AND PEER were written at Rolighed, near the limekiln, and were inspired by the contentment and good humor of a happy home.

THE PIXY AND THE GARDENER'S WIFE has its roots in an old folk tale about a pixy who teased a chained dog.

The next booklet with new stories and fairy tales appeared at Christmas, 1866, and was dedicated to the painter Carl Bloch. It contained:

HIDDEN BUT NOT FORGOTTEN

THE JANITOR'S SON

MOVING DAY

THE SNOWDROP

AUNTIE

THE TOAD

In HIDDEN BUT NOT FORGOTTEN there are three pictures. The first was from Thiele's folk tale that tells of a young noblewoman whom thieves chained before the doghouse, at the entrance to her own castle. How and why she was freed I added to the original story. The second story takes place in modern times and I saw it happen at Holsteinborg. The third, about the poor sorrowful young girl, also belongs to personal experiences. I heard the story from the girl's own lips and wrote it down in her own words.

Many of the incidents from THE JANITOR'S SON were taken from life.

AUNTIE I have known as several people, all of whom are now dead.

THE SNOWDROP was written on request. My friend Councilman Drewsen, who cares so much for Danish customs and language, complained to me about how many good Danish names are being changed. In the newspapers one reads about the *winter fool* that we, in our childhood, much more reasonably called a *summer fool,* since it fools us into thinking that summer is near. He asked me to write a fairy tale in which I referred to the flower by its original name, *summer fool;* and so I did.

THE TOAD was written during my stay in Setúbal in the summer of 1866. There water is drawn out of the deep well by means of ceramic pots, which are attached to a great black wheel and tip their contents into a ditch that has branches throughout the whole garden. In one of these pots I saw a large ugly toad being brought to the surface. As I looked at it closely, I noticed how intelligent the expression in its eyes was, and soon a whole fairy tale was mine. Later, when I returned to Denmark, I rewrote it, making it more homely by placing it in a Danish setting.

GODFATHER'S PICTURE BOOK has its own little story. One day on the street I met our eminent archaeologist Thomsen. He had just returned from Paris and told me that there he had seen, in a little theater, a light comedy about the history of Paris. It had been very prosaic and poorly plotted; nonetheless, it had been of interest to him to see the series of tableaus depicting the different periods in Parisian history. He thought that I might make use of the idea to write a more inspired comedy for the Casino Theater, about the history of Copenhagen. I thought it over; and on the evening when Copenhagen's first gas street lights were lighted, while the oil lamps—for that one night only—burned at the same time, I found I had a frame in which to place my historical pictures. As the element of beauty—the spiritual thread that would run through the whole story—I decided to have a great rock that in prehistoric times had been carried here on an ice floe and been stranded on a sandbank, where Absalon's castle, which was the first building in Copenhagen, later stood; and where, in modern times, Thorvaldsen's Museum stands. I worked for a very long time on the play; it grew and grew until it would have been impossible to perform on the small stage at the Casino, with the actors available there—that is, if I ever finished it. Finally, it had become too big for me and I gave it up; but later I used the idea for a picture book. On bound white pages I pasted pictures, which I had collected here and there, and wrote under each a few words, to relate them to each other; and the result was a story: COPENHAGEN'S LIFE AND CAREER SEEN BY GASLIGHT AND OIL LAMPS. Much later—naturally, without pictures—the story was shortened and printed in the *Danish Illustrated Times*. It was published among *Travel Sketches and Pen Drawings*. But critics complained that it belonged to *Stories and Fairy Tales,* where I have now included it; and Frolich has supplied it with illustrations.

THE RAGS was written long before GODFATHER'S PICTURE BOOK. Then Norwegian literature had not yet shown that freshness and vitality in so many fields that it now has. Munch had only just begun to write. Björnson, Ibsen, Jonas Lie, Magdalene Thoresen, etc., were unknown; but there was the habitual nagging of the Danish authors, even Oehlenschläger. This annoyed me and I wanted to say a word or two about it: to hit back in some clever, short tale. One summer, while I was in Silkeborg, at the home of Michael Drewsen, who owned a paper mill, I noticed the huge piles of rags that appeared every day in front of the building. They had been collected from everywhere, so I was told; and this gave me the idea for THE RAGS. People said it was amusing; but personally, I found in it more of the bee's sting than the flower's honey and therefore put it aside. Many years later, when the satire—if there ever had been any—no longer fitted the situation, the tale was brought out again. The opposing rags were treated with equal good nature and seen in a humorous light. Both Norwegian and Danish friends encouraged me to publish it, and it was printed in *The Danish Calendar* of 1869.

THE TWO ISLANDS was improvised for a dinner party at Holsteinborg because the engineer who was to build the dike that would connect Glaeno with Zealand was a dinner guest.

In 1868 a little booklet with only one tale, THE WOOD NYMPH was printed. In 1867 I had been in Paris to see the Paris Universal Exposition; never before or since have I been so delighted or so overwhelmed as I was on that occasion. The exhibition had already been officially opened when I came, although the marvelous and amazing wonders were not yet all completely built. In France and throughout the world, newspapers wrote of this splendor. One Danish report claimed that no author except Charles Dickens had the ability to describe it. It occurred to me that I, too, might have the necessary talent; and how pleased I would be if I were able to do it so well that both my countrymen and others would have to acknowledge it. I was filled with these thoughts as I stood on the balcony of my hotel room one day. Down in the square I noticed a tree that had died and been uprooted. Nearby in a cart was a fresh, young tree which had been brought that morning from the country to take its place. The idea for a story about the Paris Exposition was hidden in the young tree. The wood nymph waved to me. Every day during my stay in Paris, and long after, when I had returned to Denmark, there grew and sang through my mind the life story of the dryad and it was interwoven with the Paris Exposition. But I had not seen the entire exhibition, and if my story were to be a true and complete picture of the exhibition I would have to return to Paris, which I did in September. In Copenhagen, after I came home again, the tale was finally finished and dedicated to the poet J. M. Thiele.

In 1870 a little booklet of the same size as THE WOOD NYMPH was published. It contained three new fairy tales and stories:

THE FAMILY OF HEN-GRETHE

THE ADVENTURES OF A THISTLE

A QUESTION OF IMAGINATION

It was dedicated to my good friend, E. Collin, who has been loyal to me through happy days and bitter ones.

One day in the Students' Union, I happened to read a newspaper from Laaland-Falster which had an article in it about a young noblewoman, Marie Grubbe. She had been married three times: first, to the half brother of Christian V, Ulrich Frederik Gyldenløve; then to a nobleman from Jutland; and finally to a poor seaman. While her third husband was in prison, she herself had rowed the ferry. This report referred to the letters of Holberg. In these, Holberg, who was then a young student fleeing from the plague that raged in Copenhagen, tells of his stay on Falster where he lived with the poverty-stricken ferrywoman, Mother Sorensen Miller, the once noble Marie Grubbe.

Here was material for a poet. From the Danish *Atlas* and Thiele's *Folk Legends* I learned more details, and I wrote THE FAMILY OF HEN-GRETHE.

THE ADVENTURES OF A THISTLE came to me as I was walking on a field near Basnaes and saw a most beautiful thistle. I felt that I must describe it in words.

A QUESTION OF IMAGINATION comes from my own experiences.

At Christmas, 1871, *New Fairy Tales and Stories* appeared. It was dedicated to my publishers, Theodor and Carl Reitzel. In that booklet, in the usual format, with the traditional picture on the cover, there were twelve stories:

LUCK CAN BE FOUND IN A STICK
THE COMET
THE DAYS OF THE WEEK
THE SUNSHINE'S STORY
GREAT-GRANDFATHER
WHO WAS THE HAPPIEST?
THE CANDLES
THE MOST INCREDIBLE
WHAT THE WHOLE FAMILY SAID
"DANCE, DANCE, DOLLY MINE!"
THE GREAT SEA SERPENT
THE GARDENER AND HIS MASTER

All had been written during that year, and eleven of them had already been printed.

LUCK CAN BE FOUND IN A STICK was written in the Jura Mountains. Here I was told about a very poor carpenter who had made a little wooden pear to hold his umbrella together. This proved to be more effective than the button that ordinarily was used; it really did keep the umbrella from springing open all the time. For his neighbors he made a few pears as well; and soon people in both the city and the country began to order from him small pears for their umbrellas;

and within a few years he was a wealthy man. This was the source of LUCK CAN BE FOUND IN A STICK.

As an older man, I saw once more the comet that I had seen as a child. It seemed as if I had seen it first only the night before, yet years and so many memories separated the two events; and I wrote THE COMET.

THE DAYS OF THE WEEK was written at someone's request and had to be done in haste. Later it was published in *Thorkildsen's Calendar*.

In the distribution of the gifts in THE SUNSHINE'S STORY, I had in mind a particular important countryman of mine.

GREAT-GRANDFATHER was based on my memory of a conversation with H. C. Oersted about olden and modern times, concerning which he had written an article in *The Almanac of Copenhagen*.

THE CANDLES is a little story taken from real life. THE MOST INCREDIBLE and WHAT THE WHOLE FAMILY SAID also belong, at least in part, to the stories that come from personal experience.

THE GREAT SEA SERPENT, like THE WOOD NYMPH, is a modern tale. Modern science, and the changes it brings about, offer rich material for poetry; for opening my eyes to this fact, I am indebted to H. C. Oersted.

THE GARDENER AND HIS MASTER was neither known nor published before it appeared in this collection. It is a story of our time, and that, I believe, accounts for its success. It has been read aloud and dramatized and on all occasions has met with immediate approval. In my youth it was usual for one of the numbers at a concert to be a recitation—almost always a poem. The excellent actress Miss Jorgensen from the Royal Theater was the first person who attempted to read aloud one of my fairy tales as part of such a program. Since then many of my stories have been read in concert halls, especially CLOD HANS, THE EMPEROR'S NEW CLOTHES, THE COLLAR, and IT IS PERFECTLY TRUE!

At Christmas, 1872, came the second booklet, which later was part of the third volume of *New Fairy Tales and Stories,* with a poetic dedication to "Rolighed."

Outside of Copenhagen near the limekiln is the estate, Rolighed (Quietude). In the older parts of the building there lived, many years ago, the wife of General Hegermann-Lindencrone. This woman had written a play about Eleanora Ulfeldt and some short stories. Later

H. C. Oersted lived here. The present owner is a businessman, Moritz Melchior; and he has rebuilt the old house so that it now resembles the little royal castle, Rosenborg. Here I have been given a summer home, and here many of my later stories and fairy tales have been written. All of the four in the present little booklet were written at Rolighed:

THE STORY OLD JOHANNA TOLD

THE FRONT DOOR KEY

THE CRIPPLE

AUNTIE TOOTHACHE

I can make a few remarks and give some explanations concerning these too. In my childhood I saw in Odense a man who looked like a skeleton; his complexion was sallow and he was only skin and bone. An old woman, who often told me fairy tales and ghost stories, explained to me why he looked so dreadful: "The pot was put on to boil for him while he was in a foreign country." When a young man was traveling abroad, even though he was far away, his sweetheart—when she could bear his absence no longer—would go to a wise woman and persuade her to put "the pot over the fire for him." In this there was a witch's brew, and it boiled day and night. No matter where in the world the young man was, he would have to get up and go, as fast as he could, back to the sweetheart who was longing for him. When he finally arrived home he would be only skin and bone; and sometimes he would remain so for the rest of his life. That was what had happened to the man I had seen. The story made a very deep impression upon me, and it is the basis for THE STORY OLD JOHANNA TOLD.

In THE FRONT DOOR KEY, I have also used superstition's knowledge. Not so many years ago, also in Copenhagen, the "dancing table" played a role. Many people tried it, even folk of intelligence and intellectual standing; and some actually believed that there were spirits in tables and other furniture. In Germany, on a large estate owned by enlightened, intelligent people, I was made acquainted with the spirits of keys. Keys could tell about everything, and many people believed what they said. I have in the story THE FRONT DOOR KEY explained the way this worked and its importance, although I have set the story some years before my own initiation into "key knowledge." The visit, which the grocer who lives in the cellar makes in the middle of the night to the councilman, in order to discuss his daughter's "education for the theater," is an incident I experienced.

THE CRIPPLE is one of the last stories that I have written—and perhaps ever will write; and I believe that it is one of my best stories. As a kind of homage to the fairy tale as a literary form, it might have been a fitting close to the whole collection, but AUNTIE TOOTHACHE was the last to be conceived and written down.

My *Complete Fairy Tales and Stories* have been translated into almost all the languages of Europe. Both in my native land and far out in the world, they have been read by young and old alike. No greater blessing could be given any man than to have experienced such happiness in his own life. I have now lived to be an old man—the Bible's "three score and ten"—so the happy performance must be nearing its end. At this Christmas, I bring together what remains of my wealth: 156 fairy tales and stories. Let my last words be the violinist's remark in THE PEN AND THE INKWELL: if what I have accomplished has any value, "The honor is God's alone!"

Rolighed, 1874                                                    H. C. Andersen

# Index